THE YEAR'S BEST SCIENCE FICTION

**THIRTEENTH
ANNUAL
COLLECTION**

THE YEAR'S BEST SCIENCE FICTION

**THIRTEENTH
ANNUAL
COLLECTION**

Gardner Dozois, Editor

ST. MARTIN'S PRESS ✿ NEW YORK

For Tyler Harrison Amelio Casper,
who made me a grandparent
(well, I suppose his parents had something *to do with*
it . . .)

ISBN 0-312-14451-2

Printed in the United States of America

CONTENTS

ACKNOWLEDGMENTS

The editor would like to thank the following people for their help and support: first and foremost, Susan Casper, for doing much of the thankless scut work involved in producing this anthology; Michael Swanwick, Janet Kagan, Ellen Datlow, Virginia Kidd, Sheila Williams, Ian Randal Strock, Scott L. Towner, Tina Lee, David Pringle, Kristine Kathryn Rusch, Dean Wesley Smith, Pat Cadigan, David S. Garnett, Charles C. Ryan, Chuq von Rospach, Susan Allison, Ginjer Buchanan, Lou Aronica, Betsy Mitchell, Beth Meacham, Claire Eddy, David G. Hartwell, Mike Resnick, Bob Walters, Tess Kissinger, Steve Pasechnick, Richard Gilliam, Susan Ann Protter, Lawrence Person, Dwight Brown, Darrell Schweitzer, Don Keller, Robert Killheffer, Greg Cox, and special thanks to my own editor, Gordon Van Gelder.

Thanks are also due to Charles N. Brown, whose magazine *Locus* (Locus Publications, P.O. Box 13305, Oakland, CA 94661, $43.00 for a one-year subscription [twelve issues] via second class; credit card orders [510] 339-9198) was used as a reference source throughout the Summation, and to Andrew Porter, whose magazine *Science Fiction Chronicle* (Science Fiction Chronicle, P.O. Box 022730, Brooklyn, NY 11202-0056, $35.00 for a one-year subscription [twelve issues]; $42.00 first class) was also used as a reference source throughout.

SUMMATION:
1995

Nineteen ninety-five seemed to be a fairly glum year, with a lot of grim recessionary talk to be heard at most gatherings of science fiction professionals, although the actual numbers didn't really seem to justify the intensity of the gloom; perhaps the unusually large number of deaths of prominent figures in the science fiction community during 1995, including some of the most beloved individuals in the field, helped to set the emotional tone of the year.

In spite of all the recessionary talk, the overall number of books "of interest to the SF field" published in 1995 rose by 13 percent over the previous year, according to the newsmagazine *Locus,* reversing three years of minor decline, with that total including 659 new science fiction/fantasy/horror novels. Even focusing strictly on science fiction, there were still 239 new SF novels published in 1995, the number up from last year's total, so it can be seen that SF remains an enormous genre, one which grows even larger if you add in the related fantasy and horror genres, as is usually the custom. The SF publishing scene was, overall, relatively quiet in 1995, although the magazine market continued to deteriorate, with several major titles lost and others struggling (see below). There have been cutbacks at some houses, and even SF publishing lines have been lost over the last couple of years, but, as usual, these losses have been balanced by the launching of *new* lines or by some publishers increasing the number of titles they release, leaving the overall totals roughly the same. Wizards of the Coast, for instance, abruptly abandoned plans for an ambitious new SF/fantasy book line, one they'd wooed Janna Silverstein away from Bantam last year to edit, but relatively new lines such as HarperPrism and Warner Aspect and Tor Forge and White Wolf continued to expand throughout the year (although White Wolf later *contracted* a bit in early 1996—having perhaps expanded too fast—laying off some staff and cutting back on their projected, and perhaps overly ambitious, book line); and a big hardcover list of somewhere between thirty and fifty new titles per year has been announced by Avon. The comics and gaming worlds, by comparison, were much harder hit by recessionary economics than the SF publishing world has been, with massive cutbacks at companies like Marvel and DC Comics, and many comics titles being dropped or sold, and with big cutbacks in the gaming areas under way at companies like White Wolf and Wizards of the Coast.

There was another vigorous round this year of the publishing world's favorite game, editorial musical chairs. Lou Aronica, who had moved to Berkley from Bantam in 1994, moved to Avon to become their new senior vice president and publisher. Jennifer Hershey moved from Bantam shortly thereafter, where she had been executive editor of Bantam Spectra and senior editor at Bantam Books, to become the new executive editor at Avon. Christopher Schelling, the executive editor at HarperPrism, retired for health-related reasons and was replaced by John Douglas, who had since 1983 been senior editor at Avon. Jennifer Brehl, who had been the late Isaac Asimov's editor at Doubleday, will take over at Avon as senior editor in charge of the science fiction program. Owen Lock, former Del Rey editor in chief, moved on to become vice president and editor at large of the Ballantine Publishing Group, while Kuo-Yu Liang, former Del Rey sales manager, has moved up to become associate publisher of Del Rey and will oversee the SF programs at Ballantine in general.

Everyone waited throughout the year for Bantam Spectra to announce a replacement for Jennifer Hershey, with rumors targeting one editor or another for the job, but so far, as of the time this is being written, Bantam has not dropped the other shoe, and the position remains vacant.

A bit more than halfway through the decade, with the twenty-first century looming on the horizon, it's perhaps an appropriate time to take a brief look at how science fiction is *doing* as a genre, and what the prospects are for its future. . . .

. . . If it *has* a future, of course. Gloomy prognostications about the imminent death of the SF genre continued to appear here and there throughout the year. The editor of *Interzone,* David Pringle, recently published an editorial in which he made some disturbingly plausible comparisons between the decline of the Western as a genre and the possible future decline of SF as a genre, or at least as a *print* genre—arguing that, like the Western before it, print SF is becoming secondary to its film and TV forms, and may vanish as suddenly as did midlist Western novels, which pretty much disappeared from the British racks, quite suddenly, in the mid-1980s. Pringle says, ''Already one senses that there is a younger generation for whom science fiction *means* film-and-TV sf before it means books or other written forms. And an ever-greater proportion of the sf books which do get published, and enjoy sales, are movie or TV spinoffs.'' And it's certainly possible to come up with a lot of evidence in support of this view if you look around: The new British magazine *SFX*, which bills itself as the ''world's greatest SF magazine,'' publishes no print *fiction* at all, being devoted to SF in other forms; SF media magazines proliferate wildly here in the United States; *TV Guide* is now running a regular "Sci-Fi" column that never mentions print SF, or print authors (unless they're working on a TV show); the huge media-oriented "SF" conventions, often with attendances in excess of eight or nine thousand people, where it's possible to walk around for days without meeting anyone who knows anything about print SF, or cares. And so on. Along similar lines, during a recent visit to Britain, for the Scottish Worldcon, most of the SF writers I spoke to were sunk in gloom because many of the British publishers are now refusing to buy science fiction, insisting on buying only fantasy instead, one writer saying that a book editor had told him "if you don't have a Celtic trilogy to offer, don't bother us"; the sales department of one of the major British publishers has been quoted as saying that "the UK sf market is now too small to be worth bothering with"; and a prominent British SF writer has said that it's now impossible for him to sell science fiction novels without "disguising" them as horror or fantasy novels—an ironic turnaround since the days of the 1950s and '60s, when it was impossible to sell fantasy without "disguising" it as science fiction!

Of course, what most of the American professionals in attendance wanted to know was—could it happen *here?* Are SF's days numbered, as a print genre anyway?

Well, yes, it *could* happen here, and print SF's days *might* be numbered—but not necessarily. Such gloomy scenarios are hardly new, and should probably be taken with a grain of salt. To add a bit of historical perspective, I recently came across a *New Worlds* anthology from 1975, which was predicting the imminent death of the genre back *then*, for many of the same reasons. In fact, in more than twenty years of surveying the state of the genre in the course of preparing Best of the Year anthologies, it's hard to remember a year in which somebody *wasn't* predicting the imminent death of the field—just as they were doing back in 1961, when the fanzine Hugo was won by a symposium with the title *"Who Killed Science Fiction?"*

It sometimes seems to me that the current state of SF publishing would be best expressed in a sequence of good news–bad news jokes: For example, the *good* news is that a *lot* more SF writers are making a lot more money—an *enormously* greater amount of money—and selling much greater numbers of books than was thought even remotely possible in the seventies; the *bad* news is that the dwindling of the midlist and the near disappearance of the backlist is making it a lot more difficult to have a reasonable career as an SF writer if you're *not* a best-selling A-list author, driving more and more writers who would once have gotten by comfortably as midlist SF writers into having to write media tie-in novelizations and *Star Trek* books in order to survive. Or, the *good* news is, in today's greatly expanded market, it's probably easier to sell a first and even a second novel than it was twenty years ago; the *bad* news is that with the much more efficient and immediate return figures made possible by computers, and the fact that bookstore chains such as B. Dalton's or Waldenbooks won't order a book by someone whose last couple of books haven't sold well (which they can now check by clicking a few buttons), and that publishers are highly reluctant to buy from someone whom they can't sell to the chains, many authors are finding it considerably more difficult— if not impossible—to sell their third or fourth novel than it was to sell their first and second, nipping in the bud some careers that in the old days might instead have been allowed to develop to the point where the author was successful in building an audience. (If you applied the same standards— immediate commercial success, or oblivion—to Robert Heinlein or Frank Herbert or Isaac Asimov, for instance, nobody would ever have heard of *them*, either.) Or, the *good* news is, books—and not just SF books—are selling in greater numbers today than ever before; the *bad* news is, the big bookstore chains are gobbling an ever increasing share of those sales, forcing independent booksellers out of existence, and even the chains *themselves* are contracting, closing more and more individual stores in favor of huge "superstores" . . . so that more books than ever before are being sold, but at fewer and fewer locations nationwide. Or, the *bad* news is, every time you walk into a bookstore, you're overwhelmed by what seem like ever increasing amounts of media tie-in books—*Star Trek* books, *Star Trek: The Next Generation* books, *Star Trek: Deep Space Nine* books, *Star Trek: Voyager* books, *X-Files* books, *Highlander* books, *Tek War* books—and Celtic fantasy trilogies, and gaming-oriented books, and so on, until sometimes it seems next to impossible to spot the SF books that cling to rack space here and there, sometimes visible if someone hasn't buried them under a stack of *Star Wars* or *Magic: The Gathering* books; the *good* news is, in spite of all that, there *are* still adult SF and fantasy novels of quality and intelligence there to be found. . . . In fact, there are probably *more* such novels being published now than there were twenty years ago, since, although the number of peripheral items has grown, the *core* of the field itself has continued to grow as well.

I choose to believe that print SF *does* have a viable future, although I admit that it's something I *choose* to believe, something taken on faith, an intuition at best, rather than a proposition for which I can muster an overwhelmingly convincing body of evidence. I don't like to see statements about the imminent death of the field, not so much because they disagree with that intuition or item of faith, but because I fear in some primitive part of my hindbrain that such statements have an *incantatory* function—that if enough people *say* it, they may conjure that future into existence. This may not be just superstition— after all, all you have to do to engineer the death of the genre, or at least a severe setback for it, is to plant the idea that print SF is dying or is passé or is not worth bothering with anymore into the minds of six or seven people, executives highly placed in the publishing world, who will then, by refusing to invest resources in SF lines anymore or by telling the editors under them not to buy SF, *create* that very future in a self-fulfilling prophecy. I suspect that something of the sort has happened in British publishing, where the meme "Fantasy sells, SF doesn't" has replicated to the point where no one is bringing SF books out anymore. And since none are available for readers to buy, nobody *buys* them, thus neatly proving the point that they don't sell.

So we should be careful what we wish for—we may get it!

An interesting point, here in the looming shadow of the twenty-first century, one that may or may not turn out to be significant: in spite of an almost universal agreement in the SF publishing world that electronic publishing is never going to amount to anything (or that if it eventually *does,* that time is still twenty or thirty years away), this year, for the first time ever, this anthology contains a story that never saw print in any form before its appearance here, a story that until now existed only as phosphor dots on a computer screen, and is only now, with the publication of this book, appearing on paper in a form you can pick up and hold in your hands. I can't help but feel that this is a signpost to the future—or at least to *a* future. But only time will tell.

It was a very bad year in the magazine market, with several major losses, and major shake-ups and changes under way at other magazines. The cost of paper continued to escalate alarmingly throughout 1995, and this, coupled with 1994's massive hike in postage rates and a dramatic industrywide drop-off in "stamp" subscription sales (Publishers Clearing House, for instance, the largest "stamp" subscription seller, experienced a 30 percent drop in overall sales last year), has hurt every magazine in existence to some extent. Magazines across the entire marketplace were affected, not just the science fiction magazines . . . although the SF magazines, which usually have lower circulations than general-interest magazines, are perhaps even more vulnerable to such changes, being, for instance, among the first magazines to be dropped from PCH stamp cards when belt-tightening is thought to be in order. In such a publishing climate, the marginal publications are often the first to die—a gloomy prospect for the science fiction market, especially with the threat of new and even more massive postal rate hikes looming on the horizon. And yet, in spite of this glowering and forbidding atmosphere, several newer magazines seem to have established themselves, and brand-new magazines continued to struggle to be born, bravely ignoring the seemingly overwhelming odds against their survival; it would be nice to think, although perhaps this is whistling past the graveyard, that a few of them will manage to beat the odds and establish themselves successfully as well.

Even putting the most optimistic spin possible on things, though, it's hard to avoid the conclusion that most of the major stories in the magazine market this year were negative.

The biggest story, and perhaps the greatest loss, was the death of *Omni* as a regular print magazine. Early in 1995, after publishing four regular issues, *Omni* announced that it was immediately ceasing publication of its regular monthly edition, and was instead converting its monthly editions to interactive online information services, "supplemented" by quarterly print issues, to be sold only on newsstands; mail subscriptions were immediately phased out. Two issues of the "quarterly" print format were published in 1995 (one of them was actually published in January 1996, although it was dated 1995), and then, early in 1996, it was announced that the quarterly print edition was being killed as well. Supposedly *Omni* continues to exist as an "electronic online magazine" on America Online, and as a recently established Web page on the World Wide Web (http://www.omnimag.com/), although no one as yet seems to know exactly what that *means*, now that the print edition has vanished altogether. The party line is that *Omni* has not died at all, merely changed its format, making a deliberate attempt to "get a jump on the new millennium" by moving into the "new frontier" of electronic publishing, which they represent as the future of publishing, particularly magazine publishing. Most industry insiders are skeptical, speculating that the change was forced on *Omni* by escalating production costs for the monthly print edition and by the fact that most of *Omni*'s subscriptions were cut-rate "stamp" subscriptions from Publishers Clearing House, which often cost more to fulfill than the income they brought in—that, in other words, they were merely putting the best face possible on a change they would have had no choice but to make anyway. It will be very, very interesting (and perhaps significant for the future of the magazine market, especially as there are several other electronic "magazines" in the process of being launched) to see if the electronic "online" version of *Omni* can survive. One commonly asked question is, Where's the money going to come from? This is an especially pertinent question in regards to the Web page, where there will likely be no charge to access the *Omni* area, as there is on America Online. So far, much of *Omni*'s electronic publishing has been underwritten by major advertisers such as the car company Dodge Neon, which sponsored the online publication of some of the novellas published in the *Omni Online* area of America Online last year (the novellas were considered to make up an "online anthology" called *Neon Visions*), but it remains to be seen whether or not advertisers will remain interested now that there is no print publication at all to support the "online magazine" version.

While all this furor has been going on, starting in February of 1995, *Omni Online* began "publishing" a new novella every month in electronic format.

Some of these novellas have since shown up in print format, while some are still available to be read only as phosphor dots on a computer screen (unless you download them and print them out, of course). The quality of these novellas has been very high, ranging from good to excellent, including a few of the year's best stories. The *Omni Online* series, featuring work by such prominent writers as Pat Cadigan, Dan Simmons, Jack Dann, Paul J. McAuley, Robert Silverberg, Kathleen Ann Goonan, and many others, has greatly increased the number of good novellas available this year . . . a very positive thing, since there are few places in the genre where it is possible to sell a novella. Only *Asimov's Science Fiction, Analog, The Magazine of Fantasy & Science Fiction*, and, now, *Science Fiction Age* are able to accommodate them—which in turn discourages writers from attempting to write them in the first place. So it's great to see a new market for novellas, encouraging authors to write more of them, especially as I consider the novella to be perhaps the form most perfectly suited for the production of good science fiction. On the other hand, I get the uneasy feeling that almost nobody is actually *reading* these novellas, even the bulk of the core SF-reading audience—certainly they are not showing up on award ballots or even nomination lists or recommended reading lists in anything like a proportion commensurate with their quality. If this is true, it may bode ill for the eventual success of this series. We're in unknown territory here, however, so it's anybody's guess as to what will happen; perhaps the availability of these novellas on the World Wide Web will not only help the core SF-reading audience catch up with them but find them vast *new* audiences as well. It's an encouraging sign that even after the publication of the initial six novellas commissioned by Dodge Neon, *Omni Online* has continued to publish a novella a month, continuing through the early months of 1996, and is still continuing to do so as I type these words. Only time will tell if this is indeed the opening-up of an exciting new frontier or merely a doomed dead end. Award-winning editor Ellen Datlow has been maintained as the fiction editor for both the "electronic online magazine" version of *Omni* on America Online and the *Omni Online* series of novellas, which is good news, and another encouraging sign.

Other major stories in this market this year were as grim or grimmer, alas. *Amazing* was shopped around by parent company TSR throughout 1994, found no buyers, and at last officially died in 1995, after publishing one final digest-sized issue, dated as winter 1995. Thus ends its remarkable sixty-nine-year history. *Amazing* has been pronounced dead before during the twenty years I've been editing Best of the Year anthologies, only to come miraculously back to life in another form, but I get the glum feeling that this time, in this economically depressed publishing climate, it's *not* going to be able to pull off its usual Lazarus trick, and that it's gone for good. Several anthologies designed to use up *Amazing*'s leftover inventory are apparently scheduled to be published, and one actually did make it into the bookstores in 1995 (see below). *Pulphouse: A Fiction Magazine* managed to publish two issues in 1995, one a special "Jesus" issue guest-edited by Damon Knight, and then was killed by editor-publisher Dean Wesley Smith, who is closing down both *Pulphouse: A Fiction Magazine* and Pulphouse Publishing in general in order to devote more time to his own career as a fiction writer. Thus ends, with a whimper rather than a bang, the history of Pulphouse Publishing, one of the most ambitious small-press publishing programs of our times, and a line that only a few years back was widely expected to evolve into one of the major players in the SF publishing scene of the nineties. The print edition of the revived *Galaxy* was killed this year as well, although supposedly it too will continue as an "electronic online magazine"; I can't say that I'll miss *Galaxy* much, since, frankly, most of the fiction in it struck me as dreadful. *Louis L'Amour's Western Magazine*, a stablemate of *Analog* and *Asimov's Science Fiction* which occasionally featured borderline or associational work by SF writers such as Steven Utley and W. M. Shockley, died, proving too expensive to produce in a large, full-size format even though it had reached a respectable circulation (by digest-magazine standards) of 130,000 copies per issue. *Worlds of Fantasy and Horror,* formerly *Weird Tales* before a title change was forced on it last year, only managed to publish one issue this year out of its supposed quarterly schedule, but they promised to make a comeback next year, and I hope that they do. Along similar lines, *Aboriginal SF,* which was declared officially dead in the early spring of 1995, may not be quite so dead after all—editor Charles Ryan has announced that *Aboriginal SF* will return to print in 1996. Industry insiders remain skeptical of this, but time will tell; meanwhile, we wish them well.

It was another precarious year for the three major digest magazines, *Analog, Asimov's Science Fiction,* and *The Magazine of Fantasy & Science Fiction,* which all continued to lose circulation to one degree or another, with *Analog* and *Asimov's Science Fiction* undergoing some major internal changes as well.

Analog and *Asimov's Science Fiction*—particularly *Asimov's*—suffered from being dropped from Publisher's Clearing House "stamp cards" as a belt-tightening measure by PCH. *Analog* lost about 4,000 in subscriptions and another 1,000 in newsstand sales, for a 7.1 percent loss in overall circulation. *Asimov's Science Fiction* lost about 9,000 in subscriptions (most of these PCH "stamp" subscriptions) and another 1,000 in newsstand sales, for a 16.9 percent loss in overall circulation (a possible minor bright spot here is that early 1996 figures show the newsstand/bookstore sales creeping up by about a thousand copies). *The Magazine of Fantasy & Science Fiction,* which had lost almost 10 percent of its overall circulation in 1994, managed to slow its losses to the point where it almost broke even in 1995, losing 600 newsstand sales but gaining 391 subscription sales, thus losing only 209 copies overall, a very encouraging sign. *Analog* and *Asimov's Science Fiction* got a new president and publisher, Carla Graubard, replacing Joachim P. Rosler, who himself had replaced Christoph Haas-Heye only six months earlier. Early in 1996, it was decided that, as an economizing move in the face of rising paper costs, *Analog* and *Asimov's Science Fiction* would drop sixteen pages per issue, and would also be cut back to a schedule of publishing eleven times per year, ten regular issues plus one "double" issue on sale for two months, the same yearly schedule followed by *The Magazine of Fantasy & Science Fiction*. Then, only hours ago as I typed the final clean copy of this summation, it was announced that Dell Magazines, including *Analog* and *Asimov's* and the two mystery magazines *Ellery Queen's* and *Alfred Hitchcock's,* as well as a large number of crossword-puzzle and astrology magazines, had been sold to Penny Press, a family-owned Connecticut-based publisher.

This could turn out to be a positive change for *Analog* and *Asimov's,* which have been hurt by the huge corporate overhead and corporate rent charged against them by the parent corporation Bertelsmann, eating into the profitability, making them more marginal than they had been at a much smaller company such as Davis Publications, where the overhead had been correspondingly lower. *The Magazine of Fantasy & Science Fiction,* for instance, is in the enviable position of having very low overhead, produced as it is by a minimal staff pretty much out of the living rooms of Kristine Kathryn Rusch and Ed Ferman, so the magazine's profitability stays high. In like fashion, a smaller company, with much smaller corporate overhead, could send the relative profitability of *Analog* and *Asimov's* soaring, even if there was no immediate increase in overall circulation.

Let's hope that this optimistic scenario is the one that comes to pass. Although you can, of course, discount this opinion—since I am, after all, the editor of *Asimov's Science Fiction*—I still feel that the three digest magazines are the real core of the field, providing what little continuity and cohesive sense of community there is in the genre these days, as well as showcasing emerging new writers, and that the loss of them would be a devastating blow to science fiction—one that in the long run might even prove fatal to the evolution of the SF genre as a genre, eliminating most of the continuity from one literary generation to another. So keep your fingers crossed that the traditional digest magazines manage to survive through the precarious days ahead.

The British magazine *Interzone* completed its fifth full year as a monthly publication and won its first Hugo—oddly, because of circulation requirements, in the semiprozine category. Overall circulation was down slightly again, continuing a trend a couple of years old, but the magazine passed its hundredth-issue anniversary, a rare benchmark in a genre crammed with short-lived magazines, and—I hope!—doesn't seem to be in immediate danger of vanishing. The literary quality of the stories remained high, perhaps a bit higher than last year overall (although, because of the way things fell out, I actually ended up using *fewer* stories from *Interzone* in this year's Best than in last year's), perhaps because they seemed to be using less fantasy this year; the quality of the fantasy stories in *Interzone* has in general not been very good, and it's my own opinion that they would be better off sticking mainly to science fiction, as, for instance, in the interesting (although very uneven) "high-tech" issue guest-edited by Charles Platt. Overall, *Interzone* is one of the most reliable genre sources in which to find first-rate material—rating right up there, in my of course biased opinion, with magazines such as *Asimov's Science Fiction* and *The Magazine of Fantasy & Science Fiction*. (I still think that the much-vaunted "redesign" of the magazine has done nothing but make it uglier and harder to read, but perhaps that's just my old-fashioned taste.) Talking to British fans while in Scotland for this year's World Science Fiction Convention, I was dismayed by how little support for *Interzone* there seems to be among the British fannish community, with many fans actually saying that they hoped it would die soon. I remember a similar attitude in British fandom in the late sixties about *New Worlds* magazine—it was shortsighted then, and it's even more shortsighted now. Without *Interzone*, the already depressed British SF publishing scene would become a wasteland, and there would be no place left for new British writers to develop their craft. Most of the people who decry *Interzone* as being "artsy" and "not really science fiction" conveniently forget that *Interzone* helped to develop major new writers such as Greg Egan, Stephen Baxter, Iain Banks, Paul J. McAuley, Ian R. MacLeod, and others—almost all of whom are hard-science writers, and some of whom are writing "hard science fiction" in as pure and rigorous a form as it has ever been written. If these people are not writing science fiction, I'd like to know who is. No, far from being the "marginal" artsy not-kosher not-really-SF magazine that some British fans claim that it is, *Interzone* is and has been vital to the evolution of science fiction in the eighties and nineties, and I personally hope that it continues to be so for many years to come.

Science Fiction Age and *Tomorrow*, two newish large-size SF magazines, each successfully completed their third full year of publication. The overall circulation of *Science Fiction Age* dropped slightly for the first time since its launch in 1993; it lost about 1,476 subscription sales and 3,536 newsstand sales, for a 9 percent loss in overall circulation; the magazine attributes most of this loss to readers switching to their newly launched sister fantasy magazine, *Realms of Fantasy*, which is a reasonable explanation, as long as the circulation doesn't continue to drop. Last year, editor Scott Edelman took me to task for speculating here—as many genre insiders were speculating at the time—about whether *Science Fiction Age* could really be profitable, considering how much more expensive it ought to be to produce a slick, full-color, large-format magazine like *Science Fiction Age* than a digest-sized magazine like *Asimov's* or *F&SF;* in rebuttal, on one of the online networks, Scott insisted in no uncertain terms that *Science Fiction Age* was indeed doing very well financially. I'm glad to hear this and to stand corrected, especially since, considering what's happening with most of the other SF magazines, the genre could certainly use a real success story—I must add, though, even at the price of irking Scott again, that his denials have done nothing to stop genre insiders from continuing to speculate along the same lines. I hope that it is true that *Science Fiction Age* is a resounding success, though, since it's becoming clear that artistically *Science Fiction Age* is the most important new magazine to have been launched since the start-up of *Asimov's Science Fiction* back in 1977. When *Science Fiction Age* and *Tomorrow* both launched, I actually preferred the fiction that *Tomorrow* was publishing, but the quality of the fiction in *Tomorrow* has stayed the same, or perhaps even worsened a bit, while that in *Science Fiction Age* has clearly improved during the same period, so that now I think that *Science Fiction Age* is inarguably pulling ahead of *Tomorrow* in terms of yearly overall literary quality. The general consensus of the field seems to be agreeing with this assessment—a story from *Science Fiction Age* has already won that magazine its first Nebula Award, stories from it have been on the final Hugo ballot, and a story from it is on this year's final ballot for the Nebula Award as I type this.

This is not to say that *Tomorrow* is a bad magazine, by any means; although its circulation, about three thousand copies, is minuscule compared to that of *Science Fiction Age*, it remains a thoroughly professional magazine in every way except circulation (to be fair, *Science Fiction Age,* which is backed by a publishing company, obviously has much greater financial resources—and access to distribution channels—than *Tomorrow,* which is run out of editor Algis Budrys's living room), has kept to its schedule faithfully (something magazines with greater resources sometimes don't manage to do), and continues to publish good fiction. Perhaps it's fairer to say that although the average *Science Fiction Age* story and the average *Tomorrow* story are not that dissimilar in quality, *Science Fiction Age* has to date managed to publish more stories of a more exceptional quality, stories that stand out a bit above the general level of the rest of the stories the magazine published that year. Perhaps this is in part because *Tomorrow* chooses to publish lots of short-short stories per issue—a mistake that *Pulphouse* and *Galaxy* were also making—and it's much rarer to come across a short-short story of exceptional quality (a really good short-short is perhaps the hardest thing in the business to write) than it is to find a longer story that works at a similar level of excellence. *Science Fiction Age* has been concentrating on longer stories, even recently adding a section printed on nonslick paper that enables it to publish novellas, and I think that this has helped to give it a slight overall edge over *Tomorrow*.

In 1994, *Science Fiction Age* launched a companion magazine, *Realms of Fantasy,* a slick, large-size, full-color magazine devoted to fantasy rather than science fiction, edited by veteran magazine editor Shawna McCarthy. The magazine completed its first full year in 1995, and although it has yet to produce anything really exceptional, *Realms of Fantasy* did improve dramatically in quality this year, as I predicted it would, as McCarthy began to hit her editorial stride, and will probably continue to improve. The first professional magazine devoted entirely to fantasy to be launched for a number of years, *Realms of Fantasy* is looking increasingly important as fantasy anthology series such as *Xanadu* die, and fantasy magazines such as *Worlds of Fantasy and Horror* falter. *Realms of Fantasy* has already achieved a much higher level of consistent literary quality than the usually disappointing *Marion Zimmer Bradley's Fantasy Magazine,* the field's other major fantasy magazine, and has already placed a story on this year's final Nebula Award ballot, an unusual accomplishment for a magazine slightly more than a year old.

As usual, short SF and fantasy also appeared in many magazines outside genre boundaries, from *Alfred Hitchcock's Mystery Magazine* to *Mondo 2000* to *Cricket* to *VB Tech. Playboy* in particular, under fiction editor Alice K. Turner, continues to run a relatively large amount of SF. Promised for next year is a so-called *Playboy* rival, a competing men's slick magazine called *Rage,* which is scheduled to use short SF from writers such as Harlan Ellison and Ray Bradbury.

(Subscription addresses follow for those magazines hardest to find on the newsstands: *The Magazine of Fantasy & Science Fiction,* Mercury Press, Inc., 143 Cream Hill Road, West Cornwall, CT 06796, $29.90 for a one-year subscription, ten issues plus a combined October/November double issue, in U.S.; *Asimov's Science Fiction,* Dell Magazines Fiction Group, P.O. Box 5130, Harlan, IA 51593-5130, $33.97 for a one-year subscription, ten issues plus a combined October/November double issue; *Interzone,* 217 Preston Drove, Brighton BN1 6FL, United Kingdom, $52 for an airmail one-year—twelve issues—subscription; *Analog,* Dell Magazines Fiction Group, P.O. Box 5133, Harlan, IA 51593-5133, $33.97 for a one-year subscription, ten issues plus a combined double issue; *Tomorrow,* The Unifont Company, Box 6038 Evanston, IL 60204, $20 for a one-year (six issues) subscription; *Worlds of Fantasy and Horror,* Terminus Publishing Company, 123 Crooked Lane, King of Prussia, PA 19406-2570, $16 for four issues in U.S.)

Fiction semiprozines continue to proliferate, here in the era of cheap and sophisticated desktop publishing technology—and the life expectancy of most of them remains, to be polite about it, problematical. Because almost all semiprozines are severely undercapitalized and run on shoestring budgets, they are unable to survive the first cash-flow crunch that comes along. The odds against any one of them surviving are, dismayingly, even higher than the odds against a new professional publication surviving. Still, each one of them hopes to be the lucky exception that will survive and establish itself— and perhaps one or more of them will. Stranger things have happened.

Of the newish fiction semiprozines, by far the best, and one of the best semiprozines launched in some time, is *Century,* a new bimonthly (supposedly) fiction magazine edited by Robert K. J. Killheffer. This is a thoroughly professional magazine, operating on a level of sophistication, eclecticism, and literary quality rarely seen in the semiprozine market. Of course, even though most of the writers to appear in the magazine this year were writers whose names will be familiar to genre readers, *Century* itself is, quite consciously and deliberately, far out on the edge of the science fiction/fantasy spectrum . . . if not considerably beyond that edge. Several good to excellent stories appeared in *Century* this year, although most of them are hard to justify as science fiction or even, occasionally, as fantasy. My favorite story from *Century* this year was Kelly Link's rich and eccentric "Water Off a Black Dog's Back," from *Century* 3, which was one of several stories this year (Terry Bisson's "There Are No Dead" was another one) that remind me of the kind of story that Bradbury used to write, forty years ago: evocative, richly nostalgic, and yet with a bit of a weird twisted edge to it to keep it from being too cloying or sappy. *Century* also published good to excellent work this year from Avram Davidson, Holly Wade Matter, Jim Cowan, J. R. Dunn, Don Webb, William Browning Spencer, Kelley Eskridge, Michael Bishop, Beverly Suarez-Beard, Mary Rosenblum, Greg Abraham, Gerald Pearce, and others, and one of those stories, the Eskridge, showed up on this year's final Nebula ballot, an almost unheard-of achievement for a newly launched semiprozine. Of course, literary quality is no guarantee of survival— the field is littered with the corpses of literarily ambitious semiprozines, only the most recent of which belonged to *Strange Plasma* and *New Pathways*— and the magazine is not going to reach its full potential until it appears on a more reliable schedule (they only managed three out of a scheduled five bimonthly issues this year). But certainly *Century* is a magazine that deserves to survive, for what that's worth, and most definitely deserves your support, in that most practical form of all: money sent in for a subscription.

The only other fiction semiprozine that is operating on a similar level of quality to *Century* is *Crank!,* edited by Bryan Cholfin, although it is perhaps even further out over the edge than *Century.* The stories in *Century* may not be science fiction or fantasy, but they usually hew closer to the conventions of traditional narrative than do the stories in *Crank!,* which tend to push more aggressively into avantgarde fictional territory. The magazine has more of an Attitude (it is well named), priding itself on being deliberately eccentric in a contentious, in-your-face, what-are-you-looking-at? confrontational sort of a way. It is also even more unreliable in keeping to its publishing schedule, managing to publish only one issue out of a projected four in 1995. That issue, though, *Crank!* 5, contained good to excellent work by Michael Bishop, Eliot Fintushel, Jim Marino, and others.

Of the more science fiction–oriented of the newer semiprozines, your best bets are *Absolute Magnitude, The Magazine of Science Fiction Adventures* and *Pirate Writings, Tales of Fantasy, Mystery & Science Fiction,* two slick, professional-looking, full-size magazines with full-color covers. *Absolute Magnitude* is the better-looking of the two magazines, slicker, with more evocative covers (although, strangely, it is much more poorly copyedited on the inside than *Pirate Writings* is); but, although both magazines published good work in 1995, *Pirate Writings* continues to have a slight edge in the overall quality of the fiction it contains. *Pirate Writings* published professional-level work this year by Jack Cady, Paul Di Filippo, Terry Bisson, Uncle River, Larry Tritten, Jessica Amanda Salmonson, Roger Zelazny, and others. *Absolute Magnitude* published professional-level work by Allen Steele, Janet Kagan, Terry Bisson, Hal Clement, Barry B. Longyear, and others. Both *Absolute Magnitude* and *Pirate Writings* publish a lot of reprints from other SF magazines and anthologies, sometimes reprinting stories that are only a couple of years old, which is a practice I find perplexing, considering the limited amount of space that both magazines have for publishing original fiction of their own. I could perhaps—perhaps—see this if they were doing classic reprints from twenty or thirty or forty years ago, stories that might be hard to find these days, but why devote all that valuable space to reprinting stories that were widely available only a few years before and are still easily accessible? I must admit that I don't understand the reasoning behind this.

Expanse, Through the Corridor, and *Offworld* seem to have died, and, as I saw no issues this year of the promising *Mindsparks,* it may have died as well, although I hope it's merely on hiatus. *Sirius Visions, A Speculative Fiction Magazine Specializing in the Literature of Hope,* also died, after producing three largely disappointing issues. As far as I can tell, there were two issues this year of *Next Phase,* two issues of the new *Plot Magazine,* two issues of *Tales of the Unanticipated* (which featured professional-level work by Maureen F. McHugh and R. Neube, among others), two issues of *Space & Time* (which featured professional-level work by Paul Di Filippo, Jessica Amanda Salmonson, and others), one issue of *Argonaut Science Fiction,* one issue of *Xizquil* (*Xizquil* 13, which featured a good story by Sue Storm), and three issues of a promising new Canadian magazine called *Transversions* (which featured professional-level work by Robert J. Sawyer, Eileen Kernaghan, Steve Carper, Uncle River, Heather Spears, and others).

The British semiprozines *Back Brain Recluse* and *REM* are rumored to still exist, although I haven't seen an issue of one in a long time. A new British semiprozine called *Beyond* was launched in 1995, but is subsequently rumored to have died. *Marion Zimmer Bradley's Fantasy Magazine*, in its eighth year of publication, continues to maintain its quarterly publishing schedule reliably, but I remain largely unimpressed by the level of fiction in it. I haven't been following the horror semiprozine market, but apparently there were single issues of *Weirdbook*, *Grue*, *Eldritch Tales*, and *Midnight Grafitti* published this year, two issues of *The Urbanite*, and twelve issues of *Aberrations*, making it perhaps the most frequently published of the semiprozines. (*Aberrations* remains largely distasteful to me, since I don't like their usual blend of hard-core porno and violent splatterpunk horror, but there are some indications toward the end of the year that they are beginning to try to publish "better" stories, or at least stories that are less tightly specialized in the porno/splatterpunk mode; at the very least, rather than filling each issue with total unknowns, they have begun to run some stories by writers who have established some degree of professional reputation, perhaps a sign of the direction in which they're trying to turn.) *Cemetery Dance* seems to have gone on hold, owing to editor Richard Chizmar's health problems.

Of the long-established SF fiction semiprozines, the best bets remain the two Australian magazines, *Aurealis* and *Eidolon*, and the Canadian magazine *On Spec*. *On Spec* seemed a bit low-energy this year, only producing three issues out of its scheduled four; perhaps the staff is still worn-out from helping to run 1994's Canadian Worldcon. *On Spec* is still a handsome and interesting magazine, well worthwhile, with perhaps the best covers of any of the semiprozines (rivaled only by *Century*), although the overall quality of the fiction seemed a bit down this year, perhaps because they devoted one issue to horror fiction and that issue was weaker than usual; *Aurealis* also had a "special horror issue," and it also was weaker than usual. The double issue this year of *Eidolon*, *Eidolon* 17/18, was particularly worthwhile, featuring good professional-level work by Harlan Ellison, Stephen Dedman, Terry Dowling, and others. *Eidolon* published three issues out of an announced schedule of four (unless you count their double issue as two separate issues); *Aurealis* published its scheduled two issues. All three of these magazines are worth your support; they have all been around long enough to be considered fairly stable and reliable, and all have good track records for delivering interesting and unusual fiction. *Eidolon* had perhaps the best fiction of the three this year, and *On Spec* had the best covers.

As always, if you are looking for news and/or an overview of what's happening in the genre, Charles N. Brown's *Locus* and Andrew I. Porter's *Science Fiction Chronicle* remain your best bet among that subclass of semiprozines known as "newszines." Along with the digest fiction magazines, they are one of the binding threads that help to give the genre as much continuity and sense of community as it manages to have these days. *The New York Review of Science Fiction* (which had a big turnover last year, losing Donald Keller, Robert Killheffer, Jenna Felice, and Gordon Van Gelder for one reason or another, although David G. Hartwell remains in overall charge), after seven full years of publication, has become an institution in the field; by far the most reliably published of the "criticalzines," it is also the one that does the most equitable job of balancing the interests of the scholar and the general reader, and while nobody will be interested by *every* article they publish, I think that most people will find something of interest in almost every issue. Even the more technical scholarly essays here seem to be less bristlingly formidable and recondite these days than they were in the first few years of the magazine's life—or perhaps I've just gotten used to them! *The New York Review of Science Fiction* is probably the "criticalzine" to order if you're an intelligent lay reader interested in the science fiction field, being livelier and less abstract and technical than some of the more formal academic journals devoted to science fiction studies.

There didn't seem to be an issue of Steve Brown's *Science Fiction Eye* in 1995, and there was only one published in 1994, so I can't help but wonder if Steve is losing interest in this project; when he *does* get around to publishing an issue, it's usually interesting and entertaining. Much the same could be said of *Nova Express,* edited by Lawrence Person—it's entertaining and eclectic, when you can find it, but there's only been one issue produced in the last two years; that issue, however (the spring/summer 1995 issue), does feature a very interesting interview with Bruce Sterling and a transcript of a typically fiery polemical speech by him, plus a pretty complete Sterling bibliography.

The new criticalzine *Non-Stop Magazine,* edited by K. J. Cypret, also managed only one issue in the last two years; that issue, dated winter 1995, had a lot of interesting stuff in it, most notably an article by Paul Di Filippo and a long interview with Charles Platt, but the magazine's relentless self-congratulatory preening about how hip it is and how uncool everything *else* is does get tiresome after a while; still, there is some intriguing material here, including fiction by Barry N. Malzberg, Steve Rasnic Tem, and Steve Carper. *Tangent,* edited by David A. Truesdale, another newish criticalzine, had better luck keeping to its schedule, publishing its announced four issues this year, although at least one of them was a bit late. Concentrating as it does on the reviewing of short fiction, *Tangent* is a *very* welcome addition to the critical scene, and performs an invaluable service to the field; no other magazine devotes itself to reviewing short fiction—in fact, except for Mark Kelly's column in *Locus,* very little short fiction, especially short fiction from the magazines, gets reviewed *anywhere* else—and so *Tangent* is filling a nearly vacant ecological niche, and, in the main, doing a good job of it. One of their new columnists, Paul T. Riddell, is a Hunter S. Thompson wanna-be of sorts, trying to do Thompson-like self-consciously outrageous riffs on the science fiction world, but I find him more tiresome than entertaining; he's working the pugnacious, deliberately offensive, spit-in-your-eye, let's-get-a-fan-feud-going tradition that extends back at least as far as Dick Geis, but some of Riddell's remarks spin on beyond provocative to a sort of rabid, frothing-at-the-mouth raving, and I'm pretty sure that a few of them would prove actionable if anybody went to the trouble of taking him and *Tangent* to court. Let's hope that that doesn't happen—I'd hate to see *Tangent* destroyed because of Riddell, as it is a genuinely worthwhile magazine, and one that deserves the support of anyone who's interested in short fiction.

The criticalzine *Monad* died with Pulphouse Publishing, although one issue may still be in the pipeline. *Speculations* is not so much a criticalzine as a magazine of writing advice for young or would-be authors, the sort of thing you can find in the *SFWA Bulletin* if you can *find* a *SFWA Bulletin*, plus a fairly extensive section of market reports and market news; many people will probably find this useful.

(*Locus, The Newspaper of the Science Fiction Field*, Locus Publications, Inc., P.O. Box 13305, Oakland, CA 94661, $53 for a one-year first-class subscription, twelve issues; *Science Fiction Chronicle*, P.O. Box 022730, Brooklyn, NY 11202-0056, $42 for one-year first-class subscription, twelve issues; *The New York Review of Science Fiction*, Dragon Press, P.O. Box 78, Pleasantville, NY 10570, $31 per year, twelve issues; *Science Fiction Eye*, P.O. Box 18539, Asheville, NC 28814, $10 for one year; *Nova Express*, White Car Publications, P.O. Box 27231, Austin, TX 78755-2231, $10 for a four-issue subscription; *Tangent*, 5779 Norfleet, Raytown, MO 64133, $20 for one year, four issues; *On Spec, the Canadian Magazine of Speculative Writing*, P.O. Box 4727, Edmonton, AB, Canada T6E 5G6, $18 for a one-year subscription; *Crank!*, Broken Mirrors Press, P.O. Box 380473, Cambridge, MA 02238, $12 for four issues; *Century*, P.O. Box 9270, Madison, WI 53715-0270, $27 for a one-year subscription; *Non-Stop Magazine*, Box 981, Peck Slip Station, New York, NY 10272-0981, $18 for one year, four issues; *Aurealis, the Australian Magazine of Fantasy and Science Fiction*, Chimaera Publications, P.O. Box 2164, Mt. Waverley, Victoria 3149, Australia, $39 for a four-issue overseas airmail subscription, "all cheques and money orders must be made out to Chimaera Publications in Australian dollars"; *Eidolon, the Journal of Australian Science Fiction and Fantasy*, Eidolon Publications, P.O. Box 225, North Perth, Western Australia 6006, $45 (Australian) for a four-issue overseas airmail subscription, payable to Eidolon Publications; *Back Brain Recluse*, P.O. Box 625, Sheffield S1 3GY, United

Kingdom, $18 for four issues; *REM,* REM Publications, 19 Sandringham Road, Willesden, London NW2 5EP, United Kingdom, £7.50 for four issues; *Xizquil,* order from Uncle River/Xizquil, Blue, AZ 85922, $11 for a three-issue subscription to begin with issue 14; *Pirate Writings, Tales of Fantasy, Mystery & Science Fiction,* 53 Whitman Ave., Islip, NY 11751, $15 for one year (four issues), all checks payable to Pirate Writings Publishing; *Absolute Magnitude, The Magazine of Science Fiction Adventures,* D.N.A. Publications, P.O. Box 13, Greenfield, MA 01302, four issues for $14; *Argonaut Science Fiction,* P.O. Box 4201, Austin, TX 78765, $8 for two issues; *Space & Time,* 138 W. 70th Street (4B), New York, NY 10023-4432, one year (two issues), $10; *Transversions,* Island Specialty Reports, 1019 Colville Rd., Victoria, BC, Canada, V9A 4P5, four-issue subscription, $18 Can. or U.S., "make cheques payable to Island Specialty Reports"; *PLOT Magazine,* Calypso Publishing, P.O. Box 1351, Sugar Land, TX 77487-1351, four issues for $12, "make checks payable to Calypso Publishing"; *Grue Magazine,* Hells Kitchen Productions, Box 370, Times Square Sta., New York, NY 10108, $13 for three issues; *Aberrations,* P.O. Box 460430, San Francisco, CA 94146-0430, one year (12 issues), $31; *Next Phase,* Phantom Press Publications, 5A Green Meadow Drive, Nantucket, MA 02554, one year (three issues), $10; *Speculations,* 111 West El Camino Real, Suite 109-400, Sunnyvale, CA 94087-1057, a first-class subscription, six issues, $25.)

It was a mixed year in the original anthology market. There were a few strong science fiction anthologies—even, unusually, some strong "hard science" anthologies—and a few good fantasy anthologies . . . but there were also a *lot* of fairly mediocre anthologies, anthologies that might, at best, contain one or two good to decent stories apiece. Since the trend these days is away from mass-market paperback anthologies, with more and more original anthologies being published as trade paperbacks or twenty-buck-and-*up* (almost twenty-five dollars in some cases) hardcovers, this can get expensive fast. A quick and dirty—but fairly *conservative*—estimate indicates that in order to buy all the original anthologies mentioned in this section, it would cost you in excess of four hundred dollars. Even taking out of this total the price of the year's three or four best original anthologies, the ones that are probably actually *worth* what they cost to buy, that still means that you'd have to pay in excess of three hundred dollars in order to read, at a very generous estimate, ten or twelve good to decent stories. It seems to me it would be considerably more cost-effective to subscribe to some of the SF or fantasy magazines instead, where you'd get more good stories for a lot less money—but then, since I'm a magazine editor myself, you can safely dismiss this opinion if you'd like.

Only a couple of years ago, I was bemoaning the fact that original fantasy anthologies had become a rare item, if not an endangered species, but this year there was a flood of them; probably there were more original fantasy anthologies than original science fiction anthologies published this year, although a couple of cases are hard to call, containing as they do both fantasy and science fiction stories. On the other hand, like a fever burning itself out, the genre seems to have mostly worked its way free of the shared-world anthologies which seemed poised to take over the field in the mid- to late eighties, the infection having largely moved on to other areas. Most of the shared-world anthologies this year were media-related, comics-related, or gaming-related, with only a few center SF shared-world anthologies left. Almost all of the original anthologies being done today are still theme anthologies, although in a few cases, including some of the year's best, the themes are at least getting fuzzier or more general, broader, less confining and specific—stories that take place in the far future, stories that examine new frontiers in science, and so on. This may be a good thing. Over the years, I've found it to be a good rule of thumb that the more specific and limiting an anthology's theme is, the more disappointing the overall book is likely to be. Many SF stories don't fit well into pigeonholes, and often, the more easily pigeonholeable a story is, the more mediocre it is as well—ask ten SF authors to write stories about, say, teleporting Buddhist aliens who are crime-fighting race-car drivers who live in Dallas, and, more likely than not, you're going to end up with ten disappointing stories. Tell the same ten writers merely to write the best stories that they possibly can, with only the most general of themes, as at least one editor was naive enough to do this year, and the results are likely to be considerably more impressive. (Ideally, you shouldn't need a theme at all, only the ten good writers—but very few publishers will buy an anthology these days, either original or reprint, that *isn't* a theme anthology . . . which explains the loopiness of some of the themes you see, as anthologists cast desperately around for *some*thing.)

At one time, there were at least five or six major SF anthology series, including *Orbit, New Dimensions, Nova, Universe,* and others, but they have vanished one by one over the years, until now the only one left (although others are scheduled to start up in the near future) is *Full Spectrum,* which has been published at irregular intervals since the late eighties, and which is now up to its fifth volume. *Full Spectrum 5* (Bantam Spectra), edited by Jennifer Hershey, Tom Dupree, and Janna Silverstein, received the kind of rave reviews when it came out that *Full Spectrum* anthologies usually get, but, frankly, although there are a few good stories here, I found the anthology to be, on the whole, something of a disappointment. The first disappointment was that most of the stories in the book are *not* really core science fiction, but instead are either fantasy or some variant of metafiction/surrealism . . . and that most of the fantasy stories are weak even when considered as fantasy stories. There *is* some good work in the book, but, with one possible exception, nothing really of first-rate quality. Leaving aside the One Possible Exception for a moment, the best story here is probably Howard V. Hendrix's "The Music of What Happens," although it's a bit too long for its weight, and occasionally the level of New Age spirituality that you have to wade through gets a bit too thick for my taste, a problem I often have with Hendrix's stuff; still, it is a respectable story, and definitely worth reading. Jean Mark Gawron's "Tale of the Blue Spruce Dreaming (Or How to Be Flesh)" and William Barton's "When a Man's an Empty Kettle" both have some good new ideas in them (particularly the Gawron), but both felt too long to me, as though both could have been trimmed by at least a third. Michael Bishop's "Simply Indispensable" took a good idea and ruined it (for me, anyway) by a great deal of extremely coy overwriting. Jonathan Lethem's "The Insipid Profession of Jonathan Hornebom" was very well crafted, but it seemed to me to fall between two stools: considered as a satire, it wasn't satirical enough, or nearly funny enough, not enough of a real takeoff on Heinlein's famous story, "The Unpleasant Profession of Jonathan Hoag"; considered as a straight story, not a satire, you have to wonder: Why bother?—since the Heinlein story actually covered this same ground as well or better more than forty years ago, and it doesn't seem that Lethem has actually brought all that much of a fresh slant to the material. So the story is neither one thing nor the other, and so, in my opinion, fails as both, in spite of the vividness of the writing. Karen Joy Fowler's "Shimabara" is also very well crafted, but, although interesting for the historical detail it conveys, is one of those pieces of metafiction I mentioned above, certainly not SF, and probably not fantasy, either. Neal Stephenson's "Excerpt from the Third and Last Volume of *Tribes of the Pacific Coast*" is a pleasant entertainment, adroitly handled, but the ground that it covers is very familiar. Richard Bowes's "Fountains in Summer" is engrossing, but doesn't really *go* anywhere; it's too obviously a part of a larger work to stand well on its own feet as an independent piece of fiction. There is also good work here—not first-rate work, but good solid work—by Patricia A. McKillip, Mark Bourne, Pat York, Karawynn Long, Paul Park, and others. Which brings us to the One Possible Exception, Gene Wolfe's "The Ziggurat," which, line by line, is working on a level of craft far above anything else in the book, the level of craft of a first-rate work . . . but which is also a cryptic story that left me wondering, when I'd finished it, just how I was supposed to have reacted to it, and exactly what I was supposed to have taken away from it. Many women readers have reacted negatively to the main character, at least one of them describing him angrily in a review as "a sexist asshole," and I found myself disliking him as well; it's hard *not* to, since he is stubborn and blinkered and at times downright pigheaded (the death of his son, for instance, seems to me to be at least as much his own fault, for insisting on going back to the cabin, against all common sense, as it is the fault of the actual murderer), and since the opinions of women he expresses throughout are, to say the least, severe. But, as Wolfe is an author who loves to play subtle games with the reader, and in whose work things can seldom be taken at face value, this may be exactly the way you are *supposed* to be reacting to him. I suspect that it's an entirely different story depending on whether you like the main character and sympathize with his reactions or *not*—and I don't see anything on the page that clearly indicates just how the *author* wanted you to react to him. Still, any story that can arouse such violently polarized responses, and can leave as many questions in the mind of a reader after he's finished turning the pages as this one does, is definitely one worth reading.

All of *Full Spectrum*'s founding editors have subsequently left Bantam, and even two out of three of the editors of this volume are now gone, with only Tom Dupree still working for the company, but apparently the series will continue, with a new volume being assembled even as I write, and it will be very interesting to see if the future editors, whoever they turn out to be, can do something to revitalize this important series, which I have considered to be in a slump for the last few years, although other critics do not necessarily agree with me. One of the few other surviving original anthology series, this year's Hubbard Award anthology, *L. Ron Hubbard Presents Writers of the Future, Volume XI* (Bridge), edited by Dave Wolverton, is, as usual, made up of novice work by young writers, some of whom may—or may not—develop interestingly in years to come. Scheduled for next year is the launch of a new anthology series from Tor called *Starlight*, edited by Patrick Nielsen Hayden, which sounds promising; supposedly there will be a new edition of George Zebrowski's long-dormant *Synergy* anthology series sometime in the indefinite future, too, as this series has reportedly been sold to a new publisher, White Wolf. With luck, perhaps at least one of these anthology series can establish itself, making the SF original anthology series market look a *bit* less like an endangered species right on the brink of extinction.

Turning to the nonseries SF anthologies, I was *considerably* more impressed with *New Legends* (Tor), edited by Greg Bear, than I was with *Full Spectrum 5;* in fact, *New Legends* is clearly the best original SF anthology of the year, and, although I won't go quite as far as the reviews that have described it as "the *Dangerous Visions* of the nineties," it's certainly one of the most substantial and important anthologies to appear in a good long time. *New Legends* contains, in my opinion, several of the year's best stories, and very little in it is less than good—in fact, even the "merely" good stuff in *New Legends* is better than almost anything in *Full Spectrum 5*. The best stuff here includes Greg Egan's "Wang's Carpets," which includes some extremely sophisticated conceptualization and weird-new-idea stuff; Ursula K. Le Guin's quietly lyrical and moving "Coming of Age in Karhide," which returns to the setting of *The Left Hand of Darkness;* Paul J. McAuley's evocative "Recording Angel," which comes as close as anything I've seen to effectively capturing at least some of the mood and tone of Cordwainer Smith's best work; and Carter Scholz's compelling "Radiance," which, although it's borderline science fiction at best, is certainly one of the most powerful stories I've read this year. A step down from there, although still very good, we have Mary Rosenblum's eloquent "Elegy"; Poul Anderson's "Scarecrow"; a story by "Sterling Blake" (pseudonym for a Big-Name Author) called "A Desperate Calculus," which is harrowing and effective (although it does reproduce almost exactly the plot of Tiptree's "The Last Flight of Dr. Ain"); and Robert Silverberg's "The Red Blaze Is the Morning." Also worthwhile were Greg Abraham's slow but thoughtful "Gnota"; Geoffrey A. Landis's "Rorvik's War," which covers territory I've seen covered before (for instance, in Joe Haldeman's much shorter "The Private War of Private Jacobs"), but which covers it in an interesting way; and Gregory Benford's bizarre "High Abyss." A good bit weaker, but still respectable, are Sonia Orin Lyris's "When Strangers Meet" and George Alec Effinger's "One" (although the suggestion that the story has remained unsold for years because it was too "dangerous" to print is nonsense). I myself didn't care all that much for Robert Sheckley's "The Day the Aliens Came," which seemed heavily dated, but then, Sheckley's work has always been something of a blind spot for me, and I know that other reviewers have rated it up at the top. The weakest story here is probably James Stevens-Arce's "Scenes from a Future Marriage," although even it is more substantial than several of the stories in *Full Spectrum 5*.

On the whole, this is a very impressive anthology, with some of the best work of the year in it, and almost nothing that is less than good.

One strong "hard science"–oriented anthology in a year is a rarity, but this year we had *two—Far Futures* (Tor), edited by Gregory Benford, is another good anthology, and the runner-up for the title of the best original SF anthology of the year. *Far Futures* is more uneven and less impressive overall than *New Legends,* but it does contain some first-rate work, and almost everything in it is at the least solid and competently professional. As you've probably guessed from the title, this is an anthology of five novellas set in the very far future—at least a thousand years, although many of them go all the way to the End of Time, billions of years from now, or even further. Benford boasts in the introduction that in this "hard science" anthology "You'll find no *fin de siècle,* 'bored parties at the end of time' narratives," which I assume is a sneer at the work of writers such as Michael Moorcock, Brian Aldiss, and Gene Wolfe . . . although, frankly, a few of these stories could have used a bit of the stylistic flash and élan of those writers, since the biggest flaw of some of the stories here is a tendency to trudge in a rather pedestrian manner past a catalog of Ultimate Wonders, as though both the authors and their characters have been numbed by the immense scale of everything. The best stories here, though, skillfully avoid this problem—Joe Haldeman's "For White Hill" and Poul Anderson's "Genesis" both manage to operate on a sweepingly cosmic scale while at the same time remaining focused on *human* characters whose ultimate fate you come to care about. The Anderson in particular delivers a few genuine jolts of pure-quill old-fashioned undiluted Sense of Wonder, something the genre does all too rarely these days. The rest of the stories struggle to achieve the effect that Haldeman and (particularly) Anderson pull off, getting the mix wrong to one degree or another, although none of them are outright failures, and other readers may well like some of them better than the ones I've listed as my favorites. Greg Bear's "Judgment Engine" has an opaque opening and a flat detached style that makes it somewhat difficult to get into, but it ultimately repays the effort, delivering some intriguing and very original speculative content and thinking . . . although in a rather abstract, bloodless way (appropriate, I guess, since none of the characters in "Judgment Engine" have any blood!) that makes it hard to get any really satisfying emotional jolt out of the story, even though it does involve the End of the Universe as we know it. A similar problem mars Charles Sheffield's "At the Eschaton," which manages to be an emotionally flat story even though it's about an obsessed-to-the-point-of-madness character who will go to literally *any* ends to get his dead wife back. In spite of all the main character's heavy breathing and garment-ripping, though, there is somehow not a lot of emotional charge here, and even though stars and galaxies are destroyed on a scale that would make even the old Superscience boys of the thirties blanch, and the story literally takes us to the End of the Universe, and beyond, somehow not a lot of excitement is generated by all these wonders. In spite of a lot of bright, inventive thinking, good prose, and certainly enough vastness of scale for anybody, "At the Eschaton" is ultimately unsatisfying—and I think that the reason *why* it fails is the reason why many stories of this sort fail. For instance, when the main character makes his first jump into the future, awakening two hundred years later, there are no sensory *details* of the future mentioned at all, no evocative local color—we get no idea of what being in the future *feels* like, on a mundane, everyday, minute-to-minute scale: The present is people talking in a featureless room; the future is people talking in *another* featureless room; the End of Time *itself* is people talking in another featureless room . . . so that in spite of all the grand galactic sweep, the story ultimately feels claustrophobic. The much-vaunted Sense of Wonder does not automatically come just from making your canvas as large as possible if you haven't done a good job on the figures moving through the landscape. This is not a mistake that Anderson makes, for instance, canny old pro that he is, nor would Aldiss or

Wolfe have made it, either. The weakest of the novellas here, by a considerable margin, is Donald Kingsbury's "Historical Crisis," a pastiche of and
comment on Asimov's *Foundation* trilogy that is not really a comfortable
match with the contents of the rest of the book; in fact, it feels as if it has
wandered in out of some other anthology altogether. Still, four out of five of
these stories are strong, and two of them are among the year's best, so *Far
Futures* is obviously one of your best buys of the year.

(Interestingly, almost every one of these novellas involves downloading
someone's mind/personality into a computer, and often the replicating of
that downloaded personality . . . even though this is something that Benford
himself is on record as saying that he considers to be unlikely to the point of
impossibility, and something that he has criticized the cyberpunks for using
as a motif, giving it as an example of how they play the game of hard science
"with the net down." A bit inconsistent, then, to find the same motif used
so extensively here, in a book self-billed as the hardest of the hard . . .)

I must say that I'm pleased that these two anthologies are made up largely
of core science fiction, not fantasy, not postmodernism, not metafiction, not
magical realism. I like all of those forms, and have published all of them
myself, but it's nice to see some good solid *science fiction* every once in a
while, too!

Mention should probably be made here of the so-called electronic anthology
Neon Visions, edited by Ellen Datlow, which appeared over the year as a
sequence of novellas published electronically on *Omni Online.* Taken individ-
ually, the six novellas are of impressive quality—although not all of them
are center science fiction, either—and if you consider it to be an actual
anthology (which is arguable, since the novellas have not been assembled in
one place in any concrete form, a form that you could hold in your hand—
or even "access" all at once), then it would be one of the year's best, ranking
just under *New Legends* and *Far Futures.* I suspect that most people won't
really consider this to have been published, though, until the "anthology"
comes out in print form, if it ever does. This whole issue raises many interesting questions that are going to be haunting award-eligibility committees for
years to come.

Most of the year's other original science fiction anthologies, unfortunately,
are considerably weaker than the three mentioned above. *How to Save the
World* (Tor), edited by Charles Sheffield, has some of the same earnest,
heavily polemical quality as Sheffield's 1994 anthology *Future Quartet: Earth
in the Year 2042: A Four-Part Invention.* Unfortunately, the stories in this
book, less substantial than those in *Future Quartet,* epitomize the worst of
both worlds: Considered purely as fiction, they're thin, overly didactic, and
frequently dull; considered as earnest sociological speculation, as works of
futurology that might actually suggest some workable societal change that

would indeed teach us How to Save the World, they are at the best highly impractical and unlikely, and at the worst downright silly.

Also not terribly impressive, although perhaps a bit better overall than *How to Save the World,* were *The Ultimate Alien* (Dell), edited by Byron Preiss, John Betancourt, and Keith R. A. DeCandido and *Nanodreams* (Baen), edited by Elton Elliott, both mixed reprint-original anthologies where the reprint stories were stronger than the original work; *Nanodreams* is the stronger of the two overall, although by far the best story in it is a reprint of Greg Bear's ten-year-old "Blood Music." *Women at War* (Tor), edited by Lois McMaster Bujold and Roland J. Green, is one of several anthologies this year—*Sisters in Fantasy, Sisters of the Night* (female vampires), the *Women of Wonder* anthologies, *The Penguin Book of Modern Fantasy by Women,* the satirical *Chicks in Chainmail*—that seem to be specifically targeting women as a potential market, an interesting change of strategy, since many SF publishers have traditionally (and mistakenly, in my opinion) considered women to be a demographically insignificant share of the buying audience. *Women at War* seems to be trying to appeal to *both* the female audience *and* the audience for Military SF, something that seems unlikely at first glance, Military SF being generally considered to be a province that appeals largely to men— until you realize that Bujold's *own* novels probably reach just such a mixed audience, at which point you begin to wonder if the editors aren't onto something after all. At any rate, there is some good if not exceptional work here by Judith Tarr, Elizabeth Moon, Elizabeth Ann Scarborough, and others, although the stories tend to be less gung ho bloodthirsty and enthusiastically predatory, and to question the morality/inevitability of war itself more, than is the usual wont of most Military SF. It will be interesting to see if this anthology actually finds the audience it's seeking. *Superheroes* (Ace), edited by John Varley and Ricia Mainhardt, also seems somewhat confused as to what audience it's aimed for; obviously, a book about people with superhuman powers is aimed at the comics audience, or at least at the same fringe of it who enjoy the *Wild Card* series edited by George R. R. Martin, but there's an odd mocking, satirical, demythifying slant to most of the stories here, which tend to make *fun* of the whole idea of costumed crime-fighters with secret identities, unlike the *Wild Card* stories, which, in spite of a few con- scious ironies, on the whole treat the same mythological structure with af- fection and respect; most comics fans take comics very seriously, however, and they are unlikely to be amused by demythifying stories that ridicule the core assumptions of their field, so it seems to me that *Superheroes* is in danger of alienating the very audience who are most likely to be interested in it in the first place. Most of the stories here are SF only by courtesy, of course, and most are decidedly minor, although a few of them are entertaining; the best stories here are by Roger Zelazny—although it is also by far the furthest away from the ostensible theme—and by John Varley, although the same basic idea that Varley deals with here rather heavy-handedly, playing it for yucks, was handled with much more subtlety and grace by Kim Newman in his story "Übermensch!" a few years back.

The year's remaining SF anthologies are considerably more successful as anthologies, more entertaining, more substantial, better buys for your money, although all of them mix fantasy and science fiction to one extent or another. *Amazing Stories: The Anthology* (Tor), edited by Kim Mohan, is a mixed reprint and original anthology of stories, both SF and fantasy, drawn from the pages of *Amazing*, some of them that leftover inventory we were discussing up in the magazine section; this is an impressive anthology overall, with good original work by Paul Di Filippo, William Barton, R. A. Lafferty, George Zebrowski, Janet Berliner and George Guthridge, Mark Rich, Lawrence Watt-Evans, and Kathe Koja, and strong reprints by Ursula K. Le Guin, Alan Dean Foster, Robert Bloch, and Thomas M. Disch. *Warriors of Blood and Dream* (AvoNova), edited by Roger Zelazny, is also an entertaining anthology, and contains some surprisingly effective stuff for what at first glance seems like a throwaway junk theme anthology idea (Martial Arts stories), although it suffers from the sameness-of-material problem that affects most theme anthologies if you read the stories in them all in one go. The best story here, by a considerable margin, is Walter Jon Williams's "Broadway Johnny," a gorgeously colored romp that blends classical Chinese mythology with the chop-sockey atmosphere of Hong Kong kung fu movies; the result is droll and extremely entertaining. My second favorite, in spite of being *totally* predictable, is Joe R. Lansdale's noirish "Master of Misery"—this is a kind of story that's almost extinct these days, although once they filled the pages of men's magazines such as *Argosy* in their thousands, a straightforward noir adventure story, what used to be referred to as "men's adventure," with no fantasy element at all, and, as I've said, totally familiar in plot, but exciting and *very* vividly written and plotted; don't look for profundity here, but it would make a *great* movie of the week for some TV network. Hard to say how the other stories would have held up if you'd seen them one by one, rather than squeezed in here with stories covering much the same ground; there are a lot of stories dealing with martial arts fighting in VR, for instance, which lose some of their potential impact when read one after the other, and in some stories the level of rather portentous and pretentious Martial Arts Mysticism (of the "Remember, Grasshopper . . ." school of profundity, where everything sounds like an aphorism found inside a fortune cookie) can get rather thick. The book also contains good work by Dave Smeds, Gerald Hausman, and Steven Barnes—whose story is too long, but which does cover some territory not covered elsewhere here in an interesting way, although at the price of your having to wade through a fairly high Martial Arts Mysticism level. Nothing is really first-rate here, with the exception of the Williams novella, but it is a cheerful and unpretentious book that's fun to read.

Many of the same comments could be made about *Wheel of Fortune* (Avo-Nova), also edited by Roger Zelazny, which is also an entertaining read, although not quite as strong overall as *Warriors of Blood and Dream,* if only because it doesn't have a big Walter Jon Williams novella in the middle of it to help anchor it. The best story here is William Sanders's fast, funny, and fanciful "Elvis Bearpaw's Luck," although William Browning Spencer's imaginative but somewhat more somber "The Oddskeeper's Daughter" is also in the running; the anthology also features good work by Don Webb, Michael A. Stackpole, John DeChancie, Richard Lupoff, and others. (Unusually, all the "celebrity editors" this year—Zelazny, Peter S. Beagle, David Copperfield—seem to have actually *edited* their respective anthologies, to one extent or another; certainly Zelazny seems to have done most of the work here himself, and shows a surprisingly adroit touch for a man whose only previous experience as an anthologist was putting together one of the Nebula Award volumes.)

The stream of anthologies edited by Mike Resnick over the past few years seems to be running dry, but there was a Resnick anthology this year, and a fairly good one, *Sherlock Holmes in Orbit* (DAW), edited by Mike Resnick and Martin H. Greenberg. (Quite a few anthologies this year, including the Zelazny books above and half a dozen others, seem to be sort of "stealth Greenberg" anthologies, where his name shows up only in small print on the inside pages, in the copyright information; but I'm listing as Greenberg-edited anthologies only those books where his name actually appears as editor on the cover. I figure that he himself knows best how to value his contribution to any particular book, and probably will list himself on the cover if he thinks he ought to be there.) There's nothing terribly profound here, of course, but *Sherlock Holmes in Orbit* will be a lot of fun for Holmes fans, especially if you read these a few at a time rather than all in one sitting. Of course, some of the writers here have a surer touch at imitating the Master than others, and the knowledge of The Canon possessed by some of the contributors is shaky, but some of them do quite a good job, especially considering that they're covering territory and dealing with kinds of material that Doyle himself never had to deal with; the best stories here are by Vonda N. McIntyre, Frank M. Robinson, Susan Casper, Mark Bourne, George Alec Effinger, and Robert J. Sawyer.

There were supposedly regional anthologies of stories from Colorado and from Ohio this year, but I didn't see them, and will try to catch up with them next year. There was a reprint anthology of Canadian science fiction, *On Spec: The First Five Years* (Tesseract), which reprinted material from the semiprozine.

The relatively few shared-world anthologies this year included *The Man-Kzin Wars VII* (Baen), no editor listed, which contained some strong material by Gregory Benford, Marlo Martin, and Hal Colebatch; *Tales from the Mos Eisley Cantina* (Bantam Spectra), a *Star Wars*–related anthology edited by Kevin J. Anderson; *The Exotic Enchanter* (Baen), edited by L. Sprague De Camp and Christopher Stasheff; *The Day the Magic Stopped* (Baen), edited by Christopher Stasheff; *Bolos 2: The Unconquerable* (Baen), no editor listed; *The Ultimate Spiderman* (Berkley), edited by Stan Lee; *Swords and Sorceress XII* (DAW), edited by Marion Zimmer Bradley; and *An Armory of Swords* (Tor), edited by Fred Saberhagen.

There was also an interesting Young Adult SF anthology—a type of anthology which seems to be becoming more common—*A Starfarer's Dozen* (Harcourt Brace), edited by Michael Stearns.

Turning to the fantasy anthologies, the best fantasy anthology of the year is probably *Peter S. Beagle's Immortal Unicorn* (HarperPrism), edited by Peter S. Beagle and Janet Berliner. Like almost all of this year's fantasy anthologies, this one contains some horror (the line between them being a fine and often a subjective one), but *Immortal Unicorn* leans decisively away from horror and toward a more gentle, literate, humanistic sort of fantasy—something I personally approve of, as I have grown tired of the facile nihilism and fashionable designer despair, the gloatingly relished sexual violence, and the ever escalating and ever more grotesque levels of gore and mayhem and splatter that characterize most horror these days. The stories in *Immortal Unicorn*, however, are much more frequently wise and charming and life-affirming, without being sappy or saccharine, than they are grotesque or despairing, something that's like a cool breeze on a sullenly hot day in the current blood-spattered market, and this is one of the few big, expensive hardcover anthologies I've seen this year that is worth the money. The best story here is probably Peter S. Beagle's own "Professor Gottesman and the Indian Rhinoceros," a gentle, wry, and whimsical take on a classic fantasy situation, cousin-germane to Thurber's "The Unicorn in the Garden"; Karen Joy Fowler's somewhat more hard-edged (although still ultimately gentle) "The Brew" is also a contender. The anthology also features good work by Lisa Mason, Michael Armstrong, George Guthridge, Ellen Kushner, Dave Smeds, Susan Shwartz, Judith Tarr, and others.

The year's other major Janet Berliner anthology, for some inscrutable reason referred to as a "multi-author collection" instead of an anthology, is *David Copperfield's Tales of the Impossible* (HarperPrism), edited by David Copperfield and Janet Berliner. *David Copperfield's Tales of the Impossible* is not as strong as *Immortal Unicorn* overall, and leans much more toward horror, but still contains enough fantasy and hard-to-classify stuff that I'm listing it here with the fantasy anthologies. The best story here, by a considerable margin, is a fast, furious, bizarre, and yet charming extravaganza by S. P. Somtow, "Diamonds Aren't Forever," but the book also contains strong and offbeat work by Lisa Mason, Dave Smeds, Dave Wolverton, and others. Berliner also edited an anthology called *Desire Burn,* a mixed reprint/original anthology which was nowhere near as substantial as the two above.

Another anthology that some commentators might choose to list as a horror anthology, although I've decided to list it, on balance, as a fantasy anthology, is *The Armless Maiden and Other Tales for Childhood's Survivors* (Tor), edited by Terri Windling. However you list it, this is certainly one of the year's strongest anthologies, and it can be a harrowing book to read, although the horrors encountered here tend more toward emotional abuse (though there *are* a share of physical horrors as well) than the standard parade of raped and mutilated women and abused and murdered children described with relishing hand-rubbing glee in most modern horror. In a way, though, the emotional/ psychological abuse is sometimes *more* harrowing, although Windling and her authors do allow some hope to creep in here and there, and the essays that are mixed in with the stories often offer practical advice and encouragement for children in abusive situations, if only as testimony that it is possible to survive such situations and put your life back together in a positive way; the anthology is, after all, directed specifically toward Childhood's *Survivors.* There is strong work here by Tanith Lee, Jane Yolen, Ellen Kushner, Munro Sicka-foose, Kara Dalkey, Kristine Kathryn Rusch, Patricia A. McKillip, Terri Windling herself, and others.

The year's other major fantasy anthology is *Ruby Slippers, Golden Tears* (Morrow AvoNova), edited by Ellen Datlow and Terri Windling, another strong and enjoyable book that must certainly be in contention for the title of the year's best fantasy anthology. This is the third in a series of anthologies of "updated" fairy tales told with modern sensibilities, mixing fantasy with mild horror, and another of those anthologies that, because of the similarity of tone of some of the stories, is better read one story at a time than all at one sitting. The best story here is probably John Brunner's "The Emperor Who Had Never Seen a Dragon," although the book also has good work by Tanith Lee, Nancy Kress, Lisa Goldstein, Gene Wolfe, Jane Yolen, Kathe Koja, Nancy A. Collins, and others.

Fantasy's only continuing original anthology series, *Xanadu,* is reported to have died, a major blow to the genre. The last volume in the series, *Xanadu 3* (Tor), edited by Jane Yolen, delivers the series's trademark mix of different styles of fantasy, over a nicely eclectic range of moods, and features strong work by Susan Palwick, Astrid Julian, Claire Parman Brown, Bruce Holland Rogers, Jo Clayton, Josepha Sherman, and others. This series will be missed. It bewilders me that original fantasy anthology series don't seem to be able to succeed—*Elsewhere* and *Other Edens* didn't survive, either—at a time when dozens of fantasy novels crowd the bookshelves and climb the best-seller lists, one-shot fantasy anthologies often do very well, *The Year's Best Fantasy and Horror* is an established institution of the field, and even fantasy *magazines* seem to be flourishing. You'd think that a continuing fantasy anthology series would be a natural—but so far nobody has been able to make one work. I have no idea why.

Turning to the year's other fantasy anthologies, somewhat less substantial than the ones listed above, *Heaven Sent* (DAW), a (mostly) fantasy anthology edited by Peter Crowther, is somewhat weaker overall than his 1994 anthology *Blue Motel: Narrow Houses Volume 3*, but still contains interesting work, and features an eclectic mix of fantasy, horror, and even SF. My favorite here, in fact, is a science fiction (sort of) story by Ian McDonald, "Steam," yet another story (there were several this year) that tries to out-Bradbury Bradbury, this one not so much in the nostalgia/evocativeness of the setting as in the sheer audacious headlong bravura prose-poetry of the writing itself; does a pretty good job of it, too, although, as with Bradbury himself, even at his prime, the singing prose can also come to seem overheated and overdone if you fall out of the spell for a moment and look at it with a coldly critical eye. There is also strong work here by John Brunner, Judith Moffett, Charles de Lint, Nina Kiriki Hoffman, and others. *Sisters in Fantasy* (Roc), edited by Susan Shwartz and Martin H. Greenberg, is a bit weaker overall, and tends to lean a bit away from traditional fantasy toward the literary/metafictional end of the spectrum, but does contain strong work by Nancy Kress, Judith Tarr, Jane Yolen, Katharine Kerr, Kristine Kathryn Rusch, and others. *After Yesterday's Crash: The Avant-Pop Anthology* (Penguin), edited by Larry McCaffery, leans even further in that direction, qualifying more as a "slipstream" anthology and not as a fantasy/SF anthology at all, although there are some names here that will be familiar to the genre audience. *The Ultimate Dragon* (Dell), edited by Byron Preiss, John Betancourt, and Keith R. A. DeCandido, is filled with pleasant but mostly minor material. Much the same could be said of *Adventures in the Twilight Zone* (DAW), edited by Carol Serling, and *Witch Fantastic* (DAW), edited by Mike Resnick and Martin H. Greenberg. *Fantastic Alice* (Ace), edited by Margaret Weis, is mostly disappointing, only serving to prove that Lewis Carroll's whimsical magic casts a fragile and subtle spell that is not easy to duplicate, and which shreds and tatters in less skilled and cunning hands, leaving little behind; the best attempts here at handling the idiosyncratic *Alice* material are by Roger Zelazny, Esther M. Friesner, Bruce Holland Rogers, and Peter Crowther—although I don't think Carroll himself would have liked any of them. *Chicks in Chainmail* (Baen), edited by Esther M. Friesner, is a one-joke anthology—satiric takes on the "woman warrior" motif—and the joke quickly wears thin, although you'll enjoy the stories more if you read them one at a time, spaced *widely* apart.

Considerably more substantial than the two immediately above are *Ancient Enchantresses* (DAW), edited by Kathleen M. Massie-Ferch, Martin H. Greenberg, and Richard Gilliam, *Enchanted Forests* (DAW), edited by Katharine Kerr and Martin H. Greenberg, and *Tales of the Knights Templar* (Warner Aspect), edited by Katharine Kerr. The themes in each of these cases are specialized enough that some of the stories come to seem too similar, and some of the work in each of these rather large anthologies is flat and dull, but each also contains strong stories, notably by Gregory Feeley, Lois Tilton, Nancy Etchemendy, and Karawynn Long in *Enchanted Forests,* Susan Shwartz, William F. Wu, and Deborah Wheeler in *Ancient Enchantresses,* and Elizabeth Moon and (especially) Poul Anderson in *Tales of the Knights Templar.*

There were a whole *bunch* (that, of course, is a precise technical term used in criticism: "a whole bunch") of fantasy anthologies about King Arthur and the Matter of Britain this year, including: *The Camelot Chronicles* (Carroll & Graf), edited by Mike Ashley; *The Merlin Chronicles* (Carroll & Graf), edited by Mike Ashley; *The Book of Kings* (Roc), edited by Richard Gilliam and Martin H. Greenberg; *Excalibur* (Warner Aspect), edited by Richard Gilliam, Martin H. Greenberg, and Edward E. Kramer; and *Return to Avalon* (DAW), edited by Jennifer Roberson. Although they are at times rather heavy textured, your best bets here are probably the two Ashley anthologies, which also contain good reprint material. There were also Arthurian stories in *Ancient Enchantresses* and *Enchanted Forests,* as well as in most of the other fantasy anthologies, in almost all of the fantasy magazines, and even in the SF magazines—the Matter of Britain has certainly been getting a workout lately, with several more Arthurian anthologies on the way for next year.

Another anthology which blended fantasy with mild horror, noted without comment, is the mixed reprint/original erotic ghost story anthology *Killing Me Softly* (HarperPrism), edited by Gardner Dozois.

I haven't been following the horror field closely for several years, but it seemed to me that the most prominent original horror anthologies of the year probably included *Peter Straub's Ghosts* (Pocket Star), edited by Peter Straub, and *Tombs* (White Wolf), edited by Peter Crowther and Edward E. Kramer. We were also up to our asses in vampires this year, with gimmicky theme vampire anthologies everywhere, including *Sisters of the Night* (Warner Aspect), edited by Barbara Hambly and Martin H. Greenberg (female vampires); *Blood Muse* (Donald I. Fine), edited by Esther M. Friesner and Martin H. Greenberg (artists who are vampires); *Vampire Detectives* (DAW), edited by Martin H. Greenberg (self-explanatory—silly perhaps, but self-explanatory); and *Celebrity Vampires* (DAW), edited by Martin H. Greenberg (Marilyn Monroe, Arthur Conan Doyle, and other celebrities as bloodsuckers); and the mixed reprint/original anthology *100 Vicious Little Vampire Stories* (Barnes

& Noble), edited by Robert Weinberg, Stefan Dziemianowicz, and Martin H. Greenberg (really *short* vampire stories, so that now you can have the pleasure of reading about vampires even while you're on the toilet). In addition, there were *lots* of vampire stories in fantasy magazines, SF magazines, other general fantasy anthologies, less specialized horror anthologies, and hordes (flocks? herds? prides?) of them in the horror semiprozines. Needless to say, there are lots more vampire anthologies on the way for next year. Vampire anthologies also shade off into the "Erotic Horror" anthologies, especially as there are few Erotic Horror anthologies that *don't* feature a vampire story or two. An example of a deliberate cross between the vampire anthology and the Erotic Horror anthology is *Love Bites* (Richard Kasak Books), edited by Amarantha Knight, although most of the year's other Erotic Horror anthologies—such as *Dark Love* (Roc), edited by Nancy A. Collins, Edward E. Kramer, and Martin H. Greenberg; *Forbidden Acts* (Avon), edited by Nancy A. Collins and Edward E. Kramer; and *Seeds of Fear* (Pocket), edited by Jeff Gelb and Michael Garrett—have their share of vampires as well. As though they had been demanding equal time with the vampires, there were also anthologies about werewolves and the Frankenstein monster, most of them reprints—although *The Mammoth Book of Frankenstein* (Carroll & Graf), edited by Stephen Jones, (actually late 1994, but we missed it) is mostly original. There were also anthologies about witches, including the Resnick and Greenberg mentioned above and a mixed reprint/original anthology, *100 Wicked Little Witch Stories* (Barnes & Noble), edited by Stefan Dziemianowicz, Robert Weinberg, and Martin H. Greenberg, and even an anthology of less-easy-to-classify monsters from less familiar cultures, *Orphans of the Night* (Walker), edited by Josepha Sherman.

I am waiting confidently for someone to combine the year's two hot trends and come up with *Arthurian Vampires,* or maybe *Vampire Arthurs!* or *The Bloodsucking Idylls of the King.* I'm sure we won't have long to wait.

The number of new SF novels went up slightly in 1995, after declining a bit in 1994. According to the newsmagazine *Locus,* there were 1,250 books "of interest to the SF field" published in 1995, up 13 percent from 1994, and reversing three years of decline. Of that total, *not* counting gaming- and media-related novelizations, 659 titles were novels . . . and of *that* total, 239 of them were SF novels (up from 204 in 1994), 227 were fantasy novels (down from 234 in 1994), and 193 were horror novels (up from 178 in 1994). It should be noted that while adult horror is sometimes claimed to be "dying"—although there still seemed to me to be plenty of it around—young adult horror is *booming,* and this explains why the number of horror titles continues to climb. Of those 193 titles, 84 of them were Young Adult horror (of the adult horror novels, a whopping 22 percent were vampire novels).

Young Adult horror now makes up 55 percent of all Young Adult novels with genre elements. Young Adult fantasy is proliferating, too, accounting for 18 percent of the fantasy novel total; Young Adult science fiction, once a vibrant field, now, alas, lags far behind both Young Adult Horror and Young Adult Fantasy . . . which may well help to explain, as Charles Sheffield has suggested, why young readers seem to be going into reading horror and fantasy when they grow up, rather than science fiction. There were fewer original mass-market paperbacks published this year, continuing a trend now several years old; according to *Locus*, there are now fewer new mass-market paperbacks published than there are new hardcovers. The trade paperback format in particular has grown at the expense of the mass-market paperback format; there were almost four times as many trade paperbacks published in 1995 as there were in 1982, the total up 30 percent even since last year, and it's the mass-market format, once the center of the field, whose numbers dwindle to make room for them. This makes a certain amount of sense— with most mass-market paperbacks these days costing nearly six dollars, and some edging up toward eight dollars, many readers would prefer to pay twelve to fourteen dollars for a trade paperback instead, getting for the extra money a larger and more ''prestigious''-looking (and often sturdier) book with bigger type and (often) better paper and better covers, something that looks more impressive when displayed on a library shelf at home; some readers are even willing to move up into the twenty- to twenty-five-dollar range for a hardcover, for the same kind of reasons. As long as the prices of a mass-market paperback and a trade paperback remain fairly close to one another, a lot of people are going to decide they're getting a better buy for their money with the trade paperback . . . and since paperback prices are certainly not going to go *down* anytime soon (especially with paper prices headed *up*), the mass-market paperback format seems likely to continue dwindling for the foreseeable future.

In spite of all the grim recessionary talk that has preoccupied the field for the last couple of years, SF is still an enormous genre by any reasonable standards, and gets even larger if we count the fantasy titles. There are a *lot* of new novels published every year. Even limiting discussion to the SF novels alone—and most SF readers will read at least some of the fantasy novels as well, even if they don't read much of the horror—it's obviously just about impossible for any one individual to read and review 239 new novels—let alone somebody with all of the reading that I have to do at shorter lengths for *Asimov's* and for this anthology.

Therefore, as usual, I'm going to limit myself to listing those novels that have received a lot of attention and acclaim in 1994, including: *Fairyland*, Paul J. McAuley (Gollancz); *Evolution's Shore*, Ian McDonald (Bantam Spectra); *Legacy*, Greg Bear (Tor); *The Stone Garden*, Mary Rosenblum (Del Rey); *Sailing Bright Eternity*, Gregory Benford (Bantam Spectra); *Waking the*

Moon, Elizabeth Hand (HarperPrism); *The Diamond Age,* Neal Stephenson (Bantam Spectra); *Metropolitan,* Walter Jon Williams (HarperPrism); *Slow River,* Nicola Griffith (Del Rey); *The Time Ships,* Stephen Baxter (HarperPrism); *Alvin Journeyman,* Orson Scott Card (Tor); *Remake,* Connie Willis (Bantam Spectra); *The Ganymede Club,* Charles Sheffield (Tor); *The Lions of Al-Rassan,* Guy Gavriel Kay (HarperPrism); *Kaleidoscope Century,* John Barnes (Tor); *Testament,* Valerie J. Freireich (Roc); *An Exaltation of Larks,* Robert Reed (Tor); *Amnesia Moon,* Jonathan Lethem (Harcourt Brace); *The Terminal Experiment,* Robert J. Sawyer (HarperPrism); *Invader,* C. J. Cherryh (DAW); *Flux,* Stephen Baxter (HarperPrism); *The Weight,* Allen Steele (Legend); *Gaia's Toys,* Rebecca Ore (Tor); *The Killing Star,* Charles Pellegrino and George Zebrowski (Morrow AvoNova); *Brightness Reef,* David Brin (Bantam Spectra); *The Golden Nineties,* Lisa Mason (Bantam Spectra); *The Tower of Beowulf,* Parke Godwin (Morrow); *From Time to Time,* Jack Finney (Simon & Schuster); *Archangel,* Mike Conner (Tor); *Flowerdust,* Gwyneth Jones (Tor); *The Color of Distance,* Amy Thomson (Ace); *Kamikaze L'Amour,* Richard Kadrey (St. Martin's); *Earthfall,* Orson Scott Card (Tor); *Vivia,* Tanith Lee (Little, Brown); *Challenger's Hope,* David Feintuch (Warner Aspect); *Worldwar: Tilting the Balance,* Harry Turtledove (Del Rey); *The Silent Strength of Stones,* Nina Kiriki Hoffman (AvoNova); *A Sorcerer and a Gentleman,* Elizabeth Willey (Tor); *Mortal Remains,* Christopher Evans (Gollancz); *All the Bells on Earth,* James P. Blaylock; *Tech-Heaven,* Linda Nagata (Bantam Spectra); *Harvest the Fire,* Poul Anderson (Tor); *Mirrorsun Rising,* Sean McMullen (Aphelion); and *When Heaven Fell,* William Barton (Warner).

(Allen Steele's *The Weight* (Legend), Connie Willis's *Remake* (Bantam), and Poul Anderson's *Harvest the Fire* (Tor) are novellas published as individual books; they don't really fit here, but then, they don't really fit anywhere *else,* either, so, as they are being sold as individual books, I've decided to list them here under novels.)

Of those novels on the list above that I did have time to read, I'd recommend Paul J. McAuley's *Fairyland,* Ian McDonald's *Evolution's Shore,* Mary Rosenblum's *The Stone Garden,* and Nicola Griffith's *Slow River.*

It seemed a somewhat weaker year for first novels than the last two years have been, with nothing receiving the degree of attention that Griffith's *Ammonite,* Rosenblum's *The Drylands,* and Anthony's *Cold Allies* did in 1993, or that Goonan's *Queen City Jazz,* Lethem's *Gun, with Occasional Music,* or Noon's *Vurt* did in 1994. The first novels that stirred up the most excitement and acclaim this year were probably *Becoming Human,* Valerie J. Freireich (Roc); *Quasar,* Jamil Nasir (Bantam Spectra); *The Bohr Maker,* Linda Nagata (Bantam Spectra); *Humility Garden,* Felicity Savage (Roc); and *Legacies,* Alison Sinclair (Millennium). Valerie J. Freireich and Linda Nagata repeated the trick pioneered by Mary Rosenblum and Patricia Anthony in 1993 by having well-received *second* novels (Freireich's *Testament* and Nagata's *Tech-Heaven*) published before the end of the year. Other first novels included: *Primary Inversion,* Catherine Asaro (Tor); *Lethe,* Tricia Sullivan (Bantam Spectra); *Dead Girls,* Richard Calder (St. Martin's); *The Printer's Devil,* Chico Kidd (Baen); *Headcrash,* Bruce Bethke (Warner Aspect); *The Baker's Boy,* J. V. Jones (Warner Aspect); *The Gatekeepers,* Daniel Graham, Jr. (Baen); and *The Shape-Changer's Wife,* Sharon Shinn (Ace). The Del Rey Discovery line, launched in 1993, does seem to have been allowed to die, which strikes me as sadly shortsighted—if you don't develop new writers, you have nobody with whom to replace your current high-sellers when they die, or move on to some other publishing house able to offer them more money. I salute all those editors who are brave and/or farsighted enough to buy first novels, in spite of the seductive lure of sticking with established ''sure-thing'' authors instead; as can be seen from the list above, Bantam Spectra, Roc, and Warner Aspect published a respectable number of first novels this year.

There doesn't seem to me to be a clear favorite here for the Nebula and Hugo Awards, and the situation is complicated by SFWA's bizarre ''rolling eligibility'' rule, which allows books from previous years to compete for *this* year's Nebula Award—and so, it's anyone's guess what will end up winning the major awards for 1995.

Bantam Spectra and Tor had strong years, and books from the newish HarperPrism line are beginning to show up on these lists with some regularity, making their mark in the collections and anthologies lists as well as the novel list.

It should be noted that in the list above the books by Benford, Baxter, Stephenson, Banks, Reed, Anderson, McAuley, Rosenblum, Griffith, Cherryh, McDonald, Sheffield, Sawyer, Pellegrino and Zebrowski, Steele, Freireich, Ore, and a number of others are clearly and unequivocally science fiction by any reasonable definition—and that a few, especially the Bear, the Benford, and at least one of the Baxters (*Flux*), are ''hard'' science fiction as hard as it has ever been, if not harder. I mention this to counter the often heard assertion, usually spoken in sour tones, that no ''real'' science fiction is being published anymore; to the contrary, plenty of unquestionably pure-quill core science fiction still comes out every year, and even a good deal of ''hard science fiction'' rigorous enough to satisfy the most exacting of purists. . . . In fact, I think that more of both is being published now than was the case a few years back (to say nothing of ''soft science fiction,'' ''sociological science fiction,'' ''satirical science fiction,'' ''space opera,'' ''military science fiction,'' and a number of other varieties, all of which are also being published in large numbers). At the same time, just as there were more good fantasy anthologies this year, it also seemed to me that there were more good fantasy novels—and vigorous and exciting hybrids continued to form all along the borderline between science fiction and fantasy as well. One such hybrid, the nascent subgenre of "hard fantasy," to use Michael Swanwick's term, represented last year by Swanwick's own *The Iron Dragon's Daughter,* was represented this year by a major new novel by Walter Jon Williams, *Metropolitan,* which also mixed classic fantasy tropes with a gritty and particularly urban sensibility.

Some excellent novels appeared as associational or borderline items this year; in fact, some of the strongest novels of the year were to be found lurking on the outer edges of the field. One of the best of these was Jack Dann's vivid and exotic *The Memory Cathedral: A Secret History of Leonardo da Vinci* (Bantam), a fat and fanciful book that exists somewhere on the borderline between historical novel, alternate history, and fantasy, partaking of all three forms without being entirely dominated by any of them. Much the same could be said of Joe Haldeman's *1968* (Morrow), Haldeman's most substantial book in years, ostensibly a straight mainstream novel (and a harrowing one) about the Vietnam War and its distorting effect on our society, but one which, because it is told largely through the eyes of a devoted science fiction reader, is drenched with science fiction imagery and sensibilities, and which recasts several "memories" of combat in aesthetic modes borrowed from fantasy, horror, and science fiction, most notably (and with high irony) from Heinlein's *Starship Troopers.* Similarly, S. P. Somtow's rich and antic *Jasmine Nights* (St. Martin's) is ostensibly a mainstream novel, but this thinly disguised fictionalized memoir of a boy growing up in Thailand in the fifties is so full of surreal touches and descriptions of the bizarre societal tropes produced by the head-on collision of Western and Eastern cultures that it provides much the same kind of "Sense of Wonder" as does a fictional tour of an alien world, and so will doubtless appeal to many genre readers . . . perhaps even more to them than it will to the standard mainstream literary audience. Three other novels that exist somewhere on the ambiguous borderline between the mainstream and the fantastic were William Browning Spencer's sly and quirky *Zod Wallop* (St. Martin's) and *Résumé with Monsters* (Permanent Press), and Jack Cady's eloquent *The Off Season* (St. Martin's). Judith Tarr's *Pillar of Fire* (Forge) is a historical novel by a well-known fantasy writer, and *One King's Way* (Tor), by Harry Harrison and John Holm, is, strictly speaking, an Alternate History novel, but one which reads closely enough to the historical novel mode that it could easily be taken for one by someone whose knowledge of history was a bit shaky. Associational historical Western novels by well-known SF writers, published late last year, included *Wilderness* (Tor), by Roger Zelazny and Gerald Hausman, *The Cannibal Owl* (Bantam), by

Chad Oliver, and *Journal of the Gun Years* (Jove), by Richard Matheson. Mystery novels by SF writers this year included *Death by Degrees* (St. Martin's), by Robin Scott Wilson, and *Death on the Mississippi* (Berkley), by Peter J. Heck.

There were several reissues of classic novels this year, and considering how fast things go out of print these days, and how long they *stay* out of print (several of the following novels have been out of print for decades), I'd advise you to go out right now and buy copies of them while you have a chance: Cordwainer Smith's only SF novel, *Norstrilia* (NESFA Press), not quite up to the standards of the best of his short fiction, but still containing much that is rich and numinous and strange, and unavailable for years; Hal Clement's *Mission of Gravity* (Del Rey), one of the classic "hard science" novels; Philip K. Dick's *Martian Time-Slip* (Vintage), one of Dick's best, strange even for him; Ursula K. Le Guin's *The Dispossessed* (HarperPrism), sociological SF at its best; Frederik Pohl's *The Years of the City* (Baen), intriguing near-future speculation; Larry Niven's *Flatlander* (Del Rey), an omnibus edition of two early Niven novels; Gene Wolfe's *Shadow & Claw* and *Sword & Citadel* (both Tor), omnibus volumes bringing Wolfe's masterpiece *The Book of the New Sun* back into print; Jack Vance's *Emphyrio* (Charles F. Miller), one of Vance's best, and so, almost by definition, one of the best "alien world" adventures you can find; Jack Vance's *Alastor* (Tor), an omnibus collection of three more classic Vance novels; Fletcher Pratt's *The Well of the Unicorn* (Del Rey), one of the seminal fantasy novels; and Ursula K. Le Guin's *The Left Hand of Darkness* (Walker), simply one of the best SF novels ever written. Buy 'em while you can.

(Addresses follow for the small-press items that may be hard to find in bookstores: NESFA Press, P.O. Box 809, Framingham, MA 07101-0203, $20.95 for *Norstrilia*; Permanent Press, Noyac Road, Sag Harbor, NY 11963, $22 for *Résumé with Monsters*; Charles F. Miller, 708 Westover Drive, Lancaster, PA 17601, $60 for *Emphyrio*.)

It was a moderately strong year for short-story collections, with several excellent ones, several good ones, and a few retrospective collections that probably belong in every library.

The two strongest collections of the year were certainly *Four Ways To Forgiveness*, by Ursula K. Le Guin (HarperPrism) and *Axiomatic*, by Greg Egan (Millennium), both landmark collections of the sort that come along only a few times a decade. Both are strong enough, in very different ways, that it's difficult to choose between them. If forced to it, I guess I would give an edge to *Four Ways To Forgiveness*, since this is Le Guin writing at the very top of her form, better than she's written in years—in fact, if you consider *Four Ways To Forgiveness* to be a novel rather than a collection (which it is possible to do, since the story lines of the four novellas here share some important characters, and subtly intertwine at several key points), then I'd have to say that *Four Ways To Forgiveness* may well be the strongest science fiction book (as opposed to fantasy or some of her more-difficult-to-classify work) that Le Guin has produced since *The Dispossessed*. Considered in that light, it would become one of the best novels of 1995 . . . but I think that it's more useful, and more in line with the author's intentions, to consider it as a short-story collection instead. Whatever you classify it as, though, you're missing some of the best work of one of SF's true giants if you don't buy it.

Australian Greg Egan may be the hottest new writer of the decade, and he demonstrates why in *Axiomatic*, my other candidate for best collection of the year. Egan's writing lacks (as yet) the maturity and richness of Le Guin's best work, and occasionally reads as though he's producing a thinly fictionalized version of some scientific article he's been excited by, rushing to recast the idea-content in story form without taking the time to let the idea mature or integrate as *fiction* . . . but this is a fault common to relatively young writers, and I see signs that he's already beginning to outgrow it. What he does have going for him is the inventiveness and ingenuity of his *ideas*, and the uncompromising rigor and unflinching logic with which he works the *implications* of those ideas through to their ultimate conclusions. Egan may be doing some of the best *thinking* taking place in the genre today, and when he matches that thinking with a story, setting, and characters rich and fully developed enough to be worthy of it, as he does in the best of the work here, the result is spectacular, work that is genuinely on the Cutting Edge of the field. (There was another strong collection by Greg Egan this year, *Our Lady of Chernobyl* (MirrorDanse Books), about which all of the above remarks also apply—but since it was published by a small press in Australia, it'll probably be much more difficult to find for the average reader than *Axiomatic*.)

Among the year's other top collections were: *Bloodchild and Other Stories*, Octavia E. Butler (Four Walls Eight Windows); *Georgia on My Mind and Other Places*, Charles Sheffield (Tor); *Matter's End*, Gregory Benford (Bantam Spectra); and *Common Clay*, Brian W. Aldiss (St. Martin's). Katharine Kerr's *Freezeframes* (HarperPrism), like the Le Guin discussed above, can be considered either as a collection or a "mosaic novel"; either way, it contains some first-rate work. Kate Wilhelm's *A Flush of Shadows* (St. Martin's) is mostly a collection of mystery novellas, although several of them contain minor fantastic elements, and at least one of them is straightforward science fiction; all are written up to Wilhelm's exactingly high standard. Paul Di Filippo's *The Steampunk Trilogy* (Four Walls Eight Windows) is another novella collection, this one of baroque, wildly inventive, cartoonishly satirical, deliberately outrageous "steampunk" stories that juxtapose Victorian

settings and characters with SF situations and tropes, with results that are
sometimes forced and artificial, but often bright and funny as well. A similar
kind of aesthetic (one pioneered in fact by Moorcock, who was doing this
kind of thing long before any of the "steampunks" came on the scene) can
be found in Michael Moorcock's two stylish collections, *Lunching with the
Antichrist* (Mark V. Ziesing) and *Fabulous Harbours* (Millennium). Another
quirky item is *Bibliomen*, by Gene Wolfe (Broken Mirrors Press), described
as "Twenty-two characters in search of a book," a series of fictional bios
with illustrations by Ian Miller. The work of one of the most popular of
the field's new writers is collected in *The Calvin Coolidge Home for Dead
Comedians* and *A Conflagration Artist* (Wildside Press), both by Bradley
Denton; these just won a World Fantasy Award, but since you can only get
them as a boxed set for seventy dollars, they may be beyond the resources
of many readers. Other good collections included: *Dealers in Light and Darkness*, Cherry Wilder (Edgewood); *Seven Tales and a Fable*, Gwyneth Jones
(Edgewood); and *Ganglion and Other Stories*, Wayne Wightman (Tachyon
Publications). There were two good fantasy collections, *The Panic Hand*,
Jonathan Carroll (HarperCollins UK) and *The Ivory and the Horn*, Charles
de Lint (Tor), and two collections that mixed horror, fantasy, and SF, *Cages*,
Ed Gorman (Deadline Press) and *Strange Highways*, Dean Koontz (Warner).

There were an unusually large number of good retrospective collections
this year, allowing you capsule glimpses of a writer's career in short fiction.
The best was probably *The Ultimate Egoist* (North Atlantic Books), the first
in an ambitious series of volumes that aims to return to print all of the short
work of one of SF's best short-story writers, Theodore Sturgeon. Similarly
noteworthy is *Ill Met in Lankhmar*, Fritz Leiber (White Wolf), the first of a
handsomely produced omnibus series that intends to return all of Leiber's
Gray Mouser stories to print; since the Gray Mouser stories are one of the
foundation stones of modern fantasy, influencing almost everything that came
after them, these volumes are indispensable for any good library of the fantastic. There should also be a place in every complete library, though, for: *Tales
of Zothique*, Clark Ashton Smith (Necronomicon Press); *Gold*, Isaac Asimov
(HarperPrism), a retrospective of Isaac's career that includes both fiction
and nonfiction; *Ingathering: the Complete People Stories*, Zenna Henderson
(NESFA Press); and *Burning Your Boats: Collected Short Stories*, Angela
Carter (Chatto & Windus). Other retrospective collections, long unavailable
but now back in print, that belong in every library are *The Best of Lester Del
Rey* (Del Rey) and *The Best of John W. Campbell* (Del Rey).

An associational item is *Atlantis: Three Tales* (Wesleyan University Press),
a collection of three excellent mainstream novellas by SF writer Samuel R.
Delany. Delany fans will definitely want this one, as it's some of his most
substantial work in years.

Continuing a trend from last year, and reversing a previous trend that had applied for several years, most of the major collections this year were released by regular trade publishers rather than by small presses—although with a few of those publishers, the distinction is a fine one. Four Walls Eight Windows had a strong presence this year, but has since dissolved. HarperPrism and Millennium placed several books on the list, as did St. Martin's Press, and White Wolf could well become a presence in this category. Among paperback publishers, Tor brought out the most collections again this year. The small presses continued to be important, especially in the area of retrospective collections; almost all of the year's retrospective collections were from small presses, although Del Rey is to be commended as well for bringing some of its excellent "Best of" author collections back into print; I hope they reissue the rest of them, too. Edgewood showed up on the list, as did Mark V. Ziesing, NESFA Press, Necronomicon Press, Deadline Press, and several *very* small presses, such as Tachyon and MirrorDanse.

Since very few small-press titles will be findable in the average bookstore, or even in the average chain store, mail order is your best bet, and so I'm going to list the addresses of the small-press publishers mentioned above: MirrorDanse Books, P.O. Box 3542, Parramatta NSW 2124, Australia, $9.95 for *Our Lady of Chernobyl*, by Greg Egan; North Atlantic Books, P.O. Box 12327, Berkeley, CA 94701, $25 for *The Ultimate Egoist*, volume 1, *The Complete Stories of Theodore Sturgeon*; Necronomicon Press, Box 1304, Warwick, RI 02893, $11.95 plus $1.50 postage for *Tales of Zothique*, by Clark Ashton Smith; NESFA Press, P.O. Box 809, Framingham, MA 07101-0203, $24.95 for *Ingathering: The Complete People Stories of Zenna Henderson*; Deadline Press, Box 2805, Apache Junction, AZ 85217, $35 for *Cages*, by Ed Gorman; Tachyon Publications, 1459 18th Street #139, San Francisco, CA 94107, $21 plus $2 handling for *Ganglion & Other Stories*, by Wayne Wightman; Mark V. Ziesing, P.O. Box 76, Shingletown, CA 96088, $60 for *Lunching with the Antichrist*, by Michael Moorcock; Broken Mirrors Press, P.O. Box 380473, Cambridge, MA 02338, $7.50 for *Bibliomen*, by Gene Wolfe; Edgewood Press, P.O. Box 380264, Cambridge, MA 02238, $9 for *Dealers in Light and Darkness*, by Cherry Wilder, $8 for *Seven Tales and a Fable*, by Gwyneth Jones; Wildside Press, 37 Fillmore Street, Newark, NJ 07105, $70 for *The Calvin Coolidge Home for Dead Comedians*, by Bradley Denton, (available only as a boxed set with *A Conflagration Artist*, by Bradley Denton.)

This was a somewhat quiet year in the reprint anthology market; certainly there seemed to be fewer of them than in some recent years. The current wisdom in publishing seems to be that it's more desirable—hotter, sexier— to do theme anthologies as original anthologies rather than reprints. Unfortunately, this doesn't always turn out to be true. The editor of a reprint anthology about, say space stations (or dinosaurs, or artichokes, or *whatever*) at least knows in advance the quality of the stories that he's going to use, and so can assure the overall quality of the book; the editor of the original anthology in many cases must use what he can *get* by the time the deadline looms—even if what he can get turns out to be a bunch of mediocre stories that don't handle the theme as well as classic reprints have in the past. The reprint anthology can usually provide a better examination of a specific theme, therefore, or at least one that is more even in overall quality—but as long as publishers remain convinced that readers are more likely to buy an original anthology than a reprint anthology, the reprint market will continue to shrink.

This year, as usual, some of the best bets for your money in this category were the various "Best of the Year" anthologies, and the annual Nebula Award anthology, *Nebula Awards 29* (Harcourt Brace), edited by Pamela Sargent. For some years now, science fiction has been being covered by only one "Best of the Year" anthology series, the one you are holding in your hand—but in 1996 there will be a *new* "Best" series covering science fiction as well, to be edited by David G. Hartwell. I won't, of course, attempt to review it, for obvious reasons—but David's taste is different enough from my own that I'm sure that he will produce a very different book from mine, and it will be interesting to see what stories impressed me that didn't impress David, and vice versa. And surely an examination of the field and the year from a different aesthetic perspective will be a useful thing for the genre at large; the field is wide and various enough for there to be room for many different volumes, all representing different tastes and perspectives. As Karl Edward Wagner's long-running *Year's Best Horror Stories* died along with him last year, alas, this year there were only two Best of the Year anthologies covering horror, instead of three: an entry in a newer British series, *The Best New Horror Volume Six* (Carroll & Graf), edited by Stephen Jones, and the Ellen Datlow half of a mammoth volume covering both horror and fantasy, *The Year's Best Fantasy and Horror* (St. Martin's), edited by Ellen Datlow and Terri Windling, this year up to its Eighth Annual Collection. More short fantasy is published every year, even factoring in the unfortunate death of the *Xanadu* anthology series, and I suspect that someone will launch an independent "Best" volume devoted to fantasy alone, but so far fantasy is still covered only by the Terri Windling half of the Datlow/Windling anthology.

There was no big, controversial retrospective anthology this year, such as *The Norton Book of Science Fiction* or *The Ascent of Wonder,* but, despite that, there were still some very good values in the retrospective "historical overview" anthology category. Like last year's *New Eves: SF about the Extraordinary Women of Today and Tomorrow,* most of the best retrospective anthologies this year detailed the contributions of women writers to the SF and fantasy genres. The two best such anthologies were *Women of Wonder:*

The Classic Years (Harcourt Brace), edited by Pamela Sargent, an omnibus reissue of three well-known anthologies from the seventies, *Women of Wonder, More Women of Wonder,* and *The New Women of Wonder,* covering the period 1944 to 1978; and *Women of Wonder: The Contemporary Years* (Harcourt Brace), also edited by Pamela Sargent, which updates things by covering the period 1978 to 1993. Many of the same authors are featured here as in *New Eves,* but the overlap of stories is small, and these two volumes belong on the bookshelves of everyone with a serious interest in the development of the field. Much the same could be said about *The Penguin Book of Modern Fantasy by Women* (Viking), edited by Susan Williams and Richard Glyn Jones—I'm a bit bothered by the fact that the editors make no distinction whatsoever between science fiction and fantasy, lumping it all in together as "fantasy," but there's lots of good reading here, too, and this is another worthwhile volume. In fact, all three anthologies provide a valuable historical perspective on the evolution of science fiction—and one not always discussed in depth in the standard histories of the genre, which, to date, have tended to be written by men.

There were some good reprint horror anthologies this year. The best of them explored the borders between genres, and featured SF as well as horror. *Cthulhu 2000* (Arkham House), for instance, edited by Jim Turner, is a stylish and intelligent Lovecraftian anthology which, in addition to work by many of the writers you'd expect to find, also features work by writers who are usually not thought of as Lovecraftians, such as Roger Zelazny, Gene Wolfe, Lawrence Watt-Evans, Esther M. Friesner, Bruce Sterling, and Joanna Russ. (These have been a good couple of years for Lovecraft fans: late last year there was another big anthology of Lovecraft-inspired new work, which we missed, *Shadows over Innsmouth* (Fedogan & Bremer), edited by Stephen Jones, and there have been a couple of other Lovecraft-oriented books this year as well.) *Between Time and Terror* (Roc), edited by Robert Weinberg, Stefan Dziemianowicz, and Martin H. Greenberg, which also contains much Lovecraftian work, is another book that explores the borderline between science fiction and horror, reprinting some vigorous hybrids of the two forms, including works by writers such as John W. Campbell, Robert A. Heinlein, Philip K. Dick, and Arthur C. Clarke, as well as more expected writers such as H. P. Lovecraft, Clark Ashton Smith, Robert Bloch, and Clive Barker. Monsters of one sort or another also got a lot of coverage this year. There were two huge anthologies of stories about the Frankenstein monster, one mostly original, *The Mammoth Book of Frankenstein* (covered above), and one reprint, *The Frankenstein Omnibus* (Orion), edited by Peter Haining; at least a half dozen anthologies about vampires, most of them original anthologies; at least two anthologies about werewolves, *Werewolves* (DAW), edited by Martin H. Greenberg (which is mostly original stories), and *Tomorrow*

Bites (Baen), edited by Greg Cox and T. K. F. Weisskopf (contains one original story); and even an anthology about monsters from other cultures, *Orphans of the Night* (covered above).

Noted without comment are: *Dinosaurs II* (Ace), edited by Jack Dann and Gardner Dozois; *Angels!* (Ace), edited by Jack Dann and Gardner Dozois; *Isaac Asimov's Skin Deep* (Ace), edited by Gardner Dozois and Sheila Williams; and *Isaac Asimov's Ghosts* (Ace), edited by Gardner Dozois and Sheila Williams.

Mention should probably be made here of an associational item, an anthology of humorous competitions (as in, come up with a future Burma Shave ad) and cartoons from *The Magazine of Fantasy & Science Fiction*, called *Oi, Robot* (Mercury Press), edited by Edward L. Ferman.

It was a somewhat quiet year as well in the SF-oriented nonfiction and reference-book field, with the most interesting items for the nonspecialist being follow-ups of one sort or another to 1993's *The Encyclopedia of Science Fiction*, edited by John Clute and Peter Nicholls, perhaps the best one-volume SF reference work ever produced.

Of these follow-ups, perhaps the spiffiest, the most useful, and certainly the most fun to play with, was a CD-ROM, not a book: *Grolier Science Fiction: The Multimedia Encyclopedia of Science Fiction* (Grolier Electronic Publishing; $35 from Grolier Electronic Publishing Inc., 90 Sherman Turnpike, Danbury CT 06816). Based on the Clute and Nicholls *Encyclopedia,* the CD-ROM version has been expanded and updated with 25,000 words in new entries and 25,000 words' worth of updates, plus the addition of lots of "multimedia" graphics: stills from movies, book covers, author photos, and so on, plus audio and video clips. Based as it is on the Clute and Nicholls *Encyclopedia,* the CD-ROM *is* actually usable as a reference source and a research tool, unlike some of the similar CD-ROM projects offered in the last few years. Whether it's any *more* useful than the print version is dubious; the spiffy graphics are mostly just entertaining embellishments, fancy icing on the cake of the print text, and don't really add anything vital to the *information* you can get out of the old-fashioned book version. I suppose you can argue that the information is presented in a more easily storable form in the CD-ROM version, a slender disk rather than a very thick hardcover book. . . . (The book, however, is easier to "access," and doesn't require that you own an expensive computer system before you can use it.) The additional graphics *are* fun to play with, though—perhaps especially in those places where they *haven't* quite worked all the bugs out of things (in the Gallery, for instance, try calling up the photos of Mike Resnick or Terry Pratchett and see what happens!). The other "follow-up" is *Science Fiction: The Illustrated Encyclopedia* (Dorling Kindersley), by John Clute, which

almost functions as an abridged or (very) simplified version of the original
Clute and Nicholls *Encyclopedia,* with a lot of very nice looking graphics
added, the same kind of thing that decorates the Grolier CD-ROM—book
covers, author photos, movie stills, etc. (no audio or video clips, of course).
Of necessity, a lot of information is left out that was available in the original
Encyclopedia, so this is far less valuable as a reference source or research
tool, but it *does* provide an intelligently selected "time line" of the evolution
of the science fiction field, so that a casual reader who dips into this book
for a few moments is more likely to emerge with at least a sketchy capsule
knowledge of some of the history of the genre than he probably would have
gained by dipping at random into the much more comprehensive *Encyclopedia.* If you've already got the Clute and Nicholls volume, then you don't
really *need* this one, but it does make a stylish and handsome coffee-table
book, and certainly does the job it's intended to do a *lot* better than previous
books of its type, for instance, Brian Ash's 1977 *The Visual Encyclopedia
of Science Fiction,* which was so confusingly designed and poorly laid out
as to be nearly incomprehensible and almost totally useless for any sort of
research or reference work. Also of general interest will be a collection of
letters by the late Isaac Asimov, put together by his brother just before his
own death this year, *Yours, Isaac Asimov* (Doubleday), edited by Stanley
Asimov.

Turning to the more specialized reference books, those more likely to be
of interest to the scholar than to the average nonscholarly reader, prominent
items in this category this year included: *Anatomy of Wonder 4* (R.R. Bowker), edited by Neil Barron, an update of what is probably still the best
bibliography of the field; *The Ultimate Guide to Science Fiction,* 2d ed.
(Scolar Press), by David Pringle, another useful bibliography; the *St. James
Guide to Science Fiction Writers,* 4th ed. (St. James), edited by Jay P.
Pederson and Robert Reginald; *British Science Fiction Paperbacks and Magazines 1949–1956* (Borgo), by Philip Harbottle and Stephen Holland; *The
Supernatural Index* (Greenwood), by Mike Ashley and William G. Contento;
and *Fantasy Literature for Children and Young Adults,* 4th ed. (R.R. Bowker),
by Ruth Nadelman Lynn.

Among the critical books, the most flavorsome and interesting for the
nonspecialist will probably be two books of stylish, controversial, and some-
times deliberately provocative essays by two well-known SF writers: *The
Detached Retina* (Syracuse), by Brian W. Aldiss, and *To Write Like a Woman:
Essays in Feminism and Science Fiction* (Indiana University Press), by Joanna
Russ. Somewhat more abstract are *Reading by Starlight: Postmodern Science
Fiction* (Routledge), by Damien Broderick, and *Anticipations: Essays on
Early Science Fiction and its Precursors* (Syracuse), edited by David Seed.
There were a couple of additions to the ever-growing shelf of critical works

about the late Philip K. Dick: *The Shifting Realities of Philip K. Dick: Selected Literary and Philosophical Writings* (Pantheon), edited by Lawrence Sutin, is probably the one that the Dick fan will want the most, consisting as it does of nonfiction pieces and fragments by Philip K. Dick himself, who saw "reality" from as strange a perspective as anyone ever has; the other, *Philip K. Dick: Contemporary Critical Interpretations* (Greenwood), edited by Samuel J. Umland, is heavier going, and will appeal mostly to scholars, specialists, and those who are really obsessed with Phil Dick. There was a literary biography/study, *Lord Dunsany: Master of the Anglo-Irish Imagination* (Greenwood), by S. T. Joshi, and yet another study of fairy tales, *From the Beast to the Blonde: Fairy Tales and Their Tellers* (Farrar, Straus & Giroux), by Marina Warner.

There were again several good values in the art-book field this year, including *Alien Horizons: The Fantastic Art of Bob Eggleton* (Paper Tiger), Bob Eggleton; *Electric Dreams: The Art of Barclay Shaw* (Paper Tiger), Barclay Shaw; *The Alien Life of Wayne Barlowe* (Morpheus), Wayne Barlowe; *A Hannes Bok Showcase* (Charles F. Miller), edited by Stephen D. Korshak; *Stephen E. Fabian's Women & Wonders* (Charles F. Miller), Stephen E. Fabian; a sequel to the immensely popular *Dinotopia*, called *Dinotopia: The World Beneath* (Turner), by James Gurney; and a sort of "Best of the Year" compilation of last year's fantastic art, *Spectrum II: The Best in Contemporary Fantastic Art* (Underwood Books), edited by Cathy Burnett and Arnie Fenner. As can be seen, Paper Tiger and Charles F. Miller are bringing out the bulk of the interesting work in this area.

Turning to the general genre-related nonfiction field, there was a good deal of interesting stuff this year, some of it perhaps further out on the periphery than some readers will be willing to go; I'm willing to bet, though, that most of it will be of interest to most genre readers. *The Private Life of Plants* (Princeton), by David Attenborough, for instance, shows the plants of our own world to be *far* stranger than most of the alien life-forms invented by science fiction writers, and there are probably a dozen story ideas lurking in this fascinating book's descriptions of the intricate and sometimes downright amazing survival strategies utilized by plants around the world. *The Axemaker's Gift: A Double-Edged History of Human Culture* (Grosset/Putnam), by James Burke and Robert Ornstein, will appeal to anyone who enjoyed Burke's famous *Connections* series, being another shrewd examination of the ways that our societies are shaped by technology and by cultural assumptions, sometimes in subtle and surprising ways. *The Seven Wonders of the World: A History of the Modern Imagination* (Henry Holt), by John and Elizabeth Romer, is a bit further removed from genre concerns, but will certainly be of interest to that large portion of the genre audience interested in history and alternate history, especially as it largely concerns itself with the *technologies* and engineering logistics used in creating ancient Wonders such as the Pyramids, the Hanging Gardens, and the Colossus of Rhodes. On a different note, many genre readers will find it worthwhile to pick up *The Calvin and Hobbes Tenth Anniversary Book* (Andrews and McMeel), by Bill Watterson, especially now that the original comic strip has died; at its best, *Calvin and Hobbes* was not only one of the most brilliant and funny comic strips of modern times, but it was also the strip that ventured most often and most successfully into genre territory, as Calvin imagines himself to be a rampaging dinosaur or an intrepid spaceman battling wonderfully drawn Bug Eyed Monsters . . . who usually turn out to *really* be his grade-school teacher. This is a strip I'll miss, as it brought a richness of imagination and a subtlety of touch to a *milieu* usually lacking in both qualities these days.

Nineteen ninety-five was a decent year at the box office for genre films, with a fair number of midlevel hits, although no blockbusters on the scale of *The Lion King* or *Jurassic Park*. Artistically, it was a mixed year, with some good movies and some real stinkers . . . although if you take a careful look at what are usually listed just as "genre films," and break them down by actual *type*, you'll find that, like last year, there were many more good fantasy movies than there were good *science fiction* movies.

In terms of artistic quality, the best science fiction movie of the year wasn't even a *science fiction movie*. The box-office smash *Apollo 13* is technically not a science fiction movie because, of course, the events that it describes are not science fiction, but instead are based on something that actually happened (you *knew* this, of course, right? I hope you did, anyway). In spite of this inconvenient fact, don't be surprised to see *Apollo 13* show up on next year's Hugo ballot for Best Dramatic presentation, and very probably *win*, too . . . because, in spite of the fact that it's *not* SF, it catches the spirit and the mind-set *behind* science fiction better than anything has in years, and does a better job overall of giving you a behind-the-scenes look at the space program than the movie version of *The Right Stuff*, and I've yet to meet an SF fan—most of whom are still space-flight enthusiasts, after all—who didn't love it. Besides, disregarding everything else, those rockets in space look *great*—and it's amazing how much of a jolt of Sense of Wonder those images can *still* evoke, even though they're images not of imaginary futures but of an era that is over and receding rapidly into the only dimly remembered past. Spaceships are still very potent stuff symbolically, speaking without words to some dream that lives in the back of the skull—it's too bad that NASA has not been able to figure out some viable way to use that dream to inspire the public into supporting the space program. (Instead, NASA has accomplished the amazing feat of making space travel *dull* . . . but that's an essay for another place than here.)

Once you get beyond *Apollo 13* (if you consider it to be a genre film in the first place), it wasn't really much of a year for SF films in terms of either artistic or box-office success. *Johnny Mnemonic* was a flop at the box office, but it was not as bad as most critics said it was (it may have been the most critically savaged movie of the year); in fact, although it was seriously flawed, *Johnny Mnemonic* may have been the most artistically successful real science fiction movie of the year. At least it *tried* to appeal to an intelligent, adult audience, with a literate script by William Gibson Himself and some good set-dressing and special effects, especially the stunning computer-interface sequences. It wasn't very well directed, though, and the zombielike performance by Keanu Reeves in the title role probably was the final nail in its coffin. The much-discussed *Waterworld,* the most expensive movie ever made, turned out to be a standard action film, with boat chases standing in for the usual car chases, lots of shooting, and some very silly rubber science. It's hard to see on the screen just *why* this movie had to cost $175 million; it's no more spectacular than other big-budget special-effects-laden let's-blow-up-*lots*-of-things action thrillers, such as the *Die Hard* movies or the *Lethal Weapon* movies, and, in fact, is *less* impressive than some of the best of the action thrillers, being less effective, for instance, than last year's less grandiose and much less expensive *Speed.* Even though it was the tenth highest-grossing movie of the year, earning more than $88 million, *Waterworld* didn't even come close to earning back its immense budget, although it may yet reach a small profit when overseas, TV, and videocassette sales are added into the total. *Judge Dredd* was an overblown and disappointing version of the cult ultraviolent British comix; almost as expensive as *Waterworld* at $100 million, it did considerably worse at the box office, perhaps an indication of the fading star-power of Sylvester Stallone. *Congo* was a recycling of *King Solomon's Mines* (and, in spite of its immensely larger budget, managed to look *more* like it was shot on a soundstage than the earlier movie did!) with some coy postmodern touches added, featuring an embarrassingly bad performance by a good actor, Tim Curry, who now qualifies for admittance to the Ludicrous Accent Hall of Fame, along with Robert Shaw (what *was* that accent he had in *Jaws,* anyway?). *Species* takes a genuine and even rather sophisticated SF idea (one lifted uncredited from print SF writers, of course, most notably Fred Hoyle) and then, disappointingly, uses it merely for a platform for another *Alien* clone, turning into just another monster-on-the-rampage-among-us movie. Similarly, *The Net* takes an idea that was Cutting Edge SF just a few years back—how computer manipulation of worldwide data banks can turn someone into an invisible nonperson, effectively wiping them from exis-tence—and uses it as a platform from which to launch a fairly standard Hitchcockian chase-thriller of Mistaken Identity, the sort where an innocent person must unravel a mystery while on the run from relentlessly pursuing killers *and* the cops. The computer hacker elements don't really add anything vital to a formula that goes at least as far back as *North by Northwest,* merely becoming a new kind of McGuffin, but considered *as* a thriller, *The Net* is not a bad one at all, with some good suspense, and a good performance by Sandra Bullock . . . whose character actually solves the mystery and outwits the bad guys *all by herself,* instead of standing by wringing her hands and moaning while a handsome male hero resolves everything with a climactic fistfight with the villain—that alone is reason enough to see the movie! The computer hacker/Mean Streets–cyberpunk territory was also covered by *Virtuosity, Hackers,* and *Strange Days,* none of which did very well at the box office, with *Strange Days,* which had been expected to be a Major Motion Picture, especially disappointing. *Outbreak* was obviously inspired by last year's harrowing nonfiction book *The Hot Zone,* but the producers evidently felt that the prospect of everyone in the United States being killed by an outbreak of an Ebola-like virus was not *scary* enough, and decided to spice things up with some helicopter chases instead. It's hard to know where to list *Batman Forever*—it's obviously more a fantasy than it is a science fiction movie, but it has no overt supernatural element. It was the highest-grossing movie of the year, although I'm not entirely sure why. Val Kilmer, though somewhat stolid, is at least less inappropriate as *Batman* than—give me a break—Michael Keaton (although he is upstaged effortlessly by Chris O'Donnell as Robin in every scene they play together), and Jim Carrey, who has made a career out of flamboyant overacting, was born to play a *Batman* supervillain (although it's sad to see a good actor such as Tommy Lee Jones chewing the scenery right along with him); but the movie is confusingly directed, and shot so much like a rock video that it's often impossible to tell what's going on even during the fight scenes—a major drawback for an action movie. Still, there's no arguing with success, and the success of *Batman Forever* ensures that there will be at least one more Batman movie, and probably several of them. *Mortal Kombat* is even further out on the edge of the genre than *Batman Forever,* being literally a live-action version of an arcade video game. *Mighty Morphin Power Rangers* is a big-screen version of a popular kid's television show, and *Tank Girl* is a live-action version of a cult comix (*Tank Girl* is considered a cult *movie* in some circles . . . but apparently there weren't enough cultists to keep it from sinking out of sight at the box office).

Right at the very end of the year, Terry Gilliam's new film *Twelve Monkeys* was in some theaters in a limited release, but I never was able to catch up with it, and will have to save consideration of it for next year.

Not much of a year for SF movies, then, really, all in all. After the disappointing turnout for movies like *Johnny Mnemonic, Virtuosity, Hackers, Strange Days,* and *The Net,* the computer hacker/cyberpunk movie subgenre is probably dead in the water for the foreseeable future, so don't expect to see the film version of *Neuromancer* anytime soon. I'd like to think that the failure (relative to costs, anyway) of grotesquely overblown special-effects-heavy blow-up-everything-in-sight SF movies such as *Waterworld* and *Judge Dredd* has taught the moviemakers a lesson—but probably it hasn't. Still awaiting release at year's end were most of the big-budget blockbuster Major SF Movies that we've been promised for several years now: the first film in the new *Star Wars* trilogy, the new Stanley Kubrick SF movie, the new Indiana Jones movie, the sequel to *Jurassic Park,* and so on. Also scheduled for next year or thereabouts is a new *Star Trek: The Next Generation* theatrical film; let's hope it's more artistically successful—better writing would certainly *help*, guys!—than last year's disappointing *Star Trek Generations*.

There were some good fantasy movies. *Toy Story,* the first-ever *completely* computer-animated movie (and almost certainly not the *last*), was not only a technological marvel, but a stylishly told and fairly intelligent piece of story-telling that appealed to adults at least as much as it appealed to kids. For a talking-pig movie, *Babe* was treated with astonishing respect by the critics, was popular at the box office, and even made it into the Oscar nominees. *The Secret of Roan Inish* was an evocative and lyrically filmed fantasy, and *The Indian in the Cupboard* was an effective and respectful version of a well-known children's book. *Jumanji* was somewhat muddled, but had some playful special effects and a certain exuberance. A *Goofy Movie,* a feature-length Goofy cartoon, was popular with kids, although not as palatable to adults as *Toy Story*. Even the charming *The Englishman Who Went Up a Hill but Came Down a Mountain* is clearly a fantasy of *some* sort, though it has no supernatural element whatsoever. (There were *bad* fantasy movies as well, of course, including a couple of the year's highest-grossing movies: the overblown and somewhat distasteful *Casper,* and the animated feature *Pocahontas*, which was *extremely* dubious history even by Disney-movie standards—Pocahontas was only twelve when she met John Smith, didn't marry him, and died very young in exile. And the movie was somewhat sappy to boot. Other bombs included what may, if he's lucky, be the nadir of Eddie Murphy's guttering career, A *Vampire in Brooklyn,* and the Mel Brooks comedy *Dracula: Dead and Loving It*. I'm not going to bother to list all the horror movies, although there were a fair number of them, including big-budget *Halloween* and *Candyman* sequels.)

The film industry, then, is capable of making a good fantasy movie—but clearly has no idea, most of the time, how to make a good SF movie. Almost no SF movies make a genuine attempt to deal in an intelligent fashion with the *idea*-content of science fiction—instead, they typically concentrate on the special effects and the costuming and the set dressing, on flashy set pieces and big explosions, usually skimping even on basic story line, let alone the ideas *behind* the story. When was the last time you saw a real, core science fiction movie—not an engaging space fantasy such as *Star Wars*, or a disguised horror movie such as *Alien*, or an adventure-fantasy such as *Raiders of the Lost Ark*—that was presented in an intelligent and sophisticated enough manner that adults could appreciate it without making major allowances for it . . . let alone one that had some really intriguing or challenging conceptualization in it, some real sophistication of idea and theme? Some viewers would reach back to *Blade Runner*, others would have to go all the way back to *2001: A Space Odyssey* . . . but, whichever you choose, it's certainly been a long time.

Turning to television, there were as many or more genre shows than ever on the air, but most of them were not all that impressive. *Star Trek: Voyager* doesn't seem to be establishing itself all that well (and has not improved much in quality since its premiere last year, already getting into recycling old plots from *Star Trek: The Next Generation*), and *Star Trek: Deep Space Nine* seems to be struggling some in the ratings as well—according to *TV Guide*, less than half the twenty million viewers who were watching *Star Trek: Deep Space Nine* when it premiered are *still* watching it now. That's still a pretty big audience, of course, about ten million viewers—but the other way to look at it, equally valid, is that another ten million viewers have *stopped watching it* since the show came on the air. For what it's worth, most *Star Trek* fans I've talked to don't like the two new shows anywhere near as much as they like *Star Trek: The Next Generation*—I feel that way myself—even if they *do* watch them . . . and a lot of them have stopped bothering to do so. A sign that there may be some unease in the *Star Trek* empire is that they keep trying to shore up the ratings of the new shows by bringing stars from *Star Trek: TNG* into them. The very popular character of Lieutenant Worf permanently joined the *Deep Space Nine* cast this year, for instance, and Q and Ryker from *TNG* have visited *Star Trek: Voyager*, in spite of the fact that the isolation of that show's characters from the rest of the familiar *Star Trek* universe was supposed to be a plus creatively. In fact, there are signs that the producers are chafing against the (self-imposed) limitations of both shows: *Deep Space Nine* keeps coming up with lame scenarios to get its cast the hell *out* of their dull Space Shopping Mall, continually finding new excuses, however weak, to load them into spaceships and send them whizzing around the galaxy instead; and in spite of its premise of total isolation, *Voyager* is already exploiting every way possible to make contact with the familiar *Star Trek* universe, including flashbacks, time travel, and dream/alternate reality sequences, and clearly would be happy to be able to think up even more. In my opinion—and no, I don't think that the producers of *Star Trek* have even the *slightest* interest in my opinion—what they ought to do is bite the bullet, admit (tacitly at least) that they've made a mistake, and do what they ought to have done in the first place: *Star Trek: The* Next *Next Generation*—smash the two shows together spectacularly in a multi-episode (and ratings-grabbing) extravaganza, blow up (perhaps *literally*) *Deep Space Nine* and *Voyager*, and jam the most popular cast members of both shows into a refurbished Starship *Enterprise*, along with willing and available *Star Trek: TNG* characters, such as Worf and Ryker. There's not the remotest chance that they will actually do this, of course—for one thing, they'd lose the merchandising on the *Deep Space Nine*- and *Voyager*-related products and tie-ins—but a revamped *Star Trek: The Next Generation* would certainly generate more excitement than the new shows have managed to do so far, especially if the next *TNG* theatrical film is a big success. (As an indication of relative public-acceptance levels, can you imagine anyone wanting to go see a *Deep Space Nine* or *Voyager* theatrical film? No, neither can I—and apparently neither can *they*, either, because no such film has even been hinted at as a remote possibility.)

Elsewhere, *Babylon 5* seems to be actually *winning* in its direct, head-to-head competition with *Star Trek: Deep Space Nine*, a show *extremely* similar in concept and format, winning in the hearts of SF fans, at least, if not yet in the ratings—perhaps one reason why *Deep Space Nine* may be chafing to change its format. I must admit that I haven't warmed all that much to *Babylon 5* myself, but many media SF fans and even many print SF fans *have*, and the cult following for this show is growing continually, with *Babylon 5* panels even at regular non-media-oriented SF conventions drawing overflowing audiences, and *Babylon 5 conventions* beginning to come into existence. Another cult show, *The X-Files*, on the verge of being canceled only a couple of years ago, now seems to be an immense success—although, predictably, now that it's on top, connoisseurs are beginning to complain that It's Not As Good As It Used To Be. As far as I can tell, *Earth 2*, *SeaQuest DSV*, *Space Precinct*, *M.A.N.T.I.S.*, and *Forever Knight* have all died. I won't miss any of them. I will miss *Mystery Science Theater 3000* and *Northern Exposure*, which have also died (although *Mystery Science Theater 3000* may be reborn in some alternate form), though both shows had grown stale, and were probably ready to go. I'll miss *Northern Exposure* in particular, as it was perhaps the best show on network television during its first couple of seasons, particularly its wonderful first season—dismaying how little time it took the network "spin doctors" to run this once excellent series into the ground, replacing whimsy with angst, souring the characters, and spoiling their subtle relationships with one another, until, by the time the show ended, I was glad to see it put out of its misery. *Lois and Clark* survived another shaky season by the skin of its teeth, although its future is doubtful. *Highlander* seems as popular as ever, as far as I can tell, and is perhaps as immortal as its protagonist.

Of the new shows, the best is probably *StrangeLuck*, a quirky and intelligent show whose story editor and producer is SF writer Michael Cassutt, who formerly worked on the American TV version of *Max Headroom*. *StrangeLuck* may be *too* quirky for its own good, though—there's no overt fantastic element here, just the fact that bizarre coincidences happen around the lead character all the time (hence the show's title), and the occasional hint about his Mysterious Past, which may or may not somehow be responsible for his strange luck—and that may be too subtle for the television audience at large. *StrangeLuck* is reported to be struggling, and its future may be in doubt, although it's a stylish and often funny show that deserves to survive. *Third Rock from the Sun* is an *Alf* retread that wastes some talented actors. *Hercules: The Legendary Journeys* is fun in a cheesy, junk-food sort of way, if only to laugh at the really staggering lapses from anything resembling historical accuracy, and the unintentional anachronisms that abound. *Deadly Games,* which has already been canceled, was a show about computer-game figures coming to life, with Christopher Lloyd enjoyable as the main villain. The new *Outer Limits* is disappointing at best, and sometimes plain bad. *Space: Above and Beyond* is a World War II combat movie thinly disguised as an SF show, and takes itself with such unsmiling and portentous seriousness that it's sometimes almost amusing.

Turn off the tube and go read a book, is my advice.

The Fifty-third World Science Fiction Convention, Intersection, was held in Glasgow, Scotland, from August 24 to August 28, and drew an estimated attendance of 4,800. A pall was thrown over the proceedings for many of those in attendance by the death of John Brunner (see below) on the first night of the convention, the first time that a science fiction writer has died while attending a Worldcon; it's a shame that this tragedy will probably turn out to be what the convention is chiefly remembered for in the annals of fannish history, but that seems likely. The 1995 Hugo Awards, presented at Intersection, were: Best Novel, *Mirror Dance,* by Lois McMaster Bujold; Best Novella, "Seven Views of Olduvai Gorge," by Mike Resnick; Best Novelette, "The Martian Child," by David Gerrold; Best Short Story, "None So Blind," by Joe Haldeman; Best Nonfiction, *I. Asimov: A Memoir,* by Isaac Asimov; Best Professional Editor, Gardner Dozois; Best Professional Artist, Jim Burns; Best Original Artwork, Brian Froud for *Lady Cottington's Pressed Fairy Book;* Best Dramatic Presentation, "All Good Things," from *Star Trek: The Next Generation;* Best Semiprozine, *Interzone;* Best Fanzine, *Ansible,* edited by David Langford; Best Fan Writer, David Langford; Best Fan Artist, Teddy Harvia; plus the John W. Campbell Award for Best New Writer to Jeff Noon.

The 1994 Nebula Awards, presented at a banquet at the Grand Hyatt Hotel in New York City on April 22, 1995, were: Best Novel, *Moving Mars,* by Greg Bear; Best Novella, "Seven Views of Olduvai Gorge," by Mike Resnick; Best Novelette, "The Martian Child," by David Gerrold; Best Short Story, "A Defense of the Social Contracts," by Martha Soukup; plus the Grand Master Award to Damon Knight.

The World Fantasy Awards, presented at the Twenty-first Annual World

Fantasy Convention in Baltimore, Maryland, on October 29, 1995, were: Best Novel, *Towing Jehovah*, by James Morrow; Best Novella, "Last Summer at Mars Hill," by Elizabeth Hand; Best Short Fiction, "The Man in the Black Suit," by Stephen King; Best Collection, *The Calvin Coolidge Home for Dead Comedians* and *A Conflagration Artist*, by Bradley Denton; Best Anthology, *Little Deaths*, edited by Ellen Datlow; Best Artist, Jacek Yerka; Special Award (Professional), to Ellen Datlow; Special Award (Nonprofessional), to Bryan Cholfin, for Broken Mirrors Press and *Crank!*.

The 1995 Bram Stoker Awards, presented by the Horror Writers of America during a banquet at the Warwick Hotel in New York City on June 10, were: Best Novel, *Dead in the Water*, by Nancy Holder; Best First Novel, *Grave Markings*, by Michael Arnzen; Best Collection, *The Early Fears*, by Robert Bloch; Best Long Fiction, "The Scent of Vinegar," by Robert Bloch; Best Short Story (tie), "Cafe Endless: Spring Rain," by Nancy Holder and "The Box," by Jack Ketchum; plus a Life Achievement Award to Christopher Lee.

The 1994 John W. Campbell Memorial Award was won by *Permutation City*, by Greg Egan.

The 1994 Theodore Sturgeon Award for Best Short Story was won by "Forgiveness Day," by Ursula K. Le Guin.

The 1994 Philip K. Dick Memorial Award went to *Mysterium*, by Robert Charles Wilson.

The 1994 Arthur C. Clarke Award was won by *Fools*, by Pat Cadigan.

The 1994 Compton Crook Award was won by *Dun's Lady Jess*, by Doranna Durgin.

The 1994 Crawford Award for Best First Fantasy Novel went to *Gun, with Occasional Music*, by Jonathan Lethem.

This was yet another year of horrendous loss for the science fiction and fantasy genres. Dead in 1995 or early 1996 were: **Walter M. Miller, Jr.**, 73, author of the classic, seminal, Hugo-winning SF novel *A Canticle for Leibowitz*, as well as many influential stories during the fifties, one of which, "The Darfsteller," won him another Hugo; British author **John Brunner**, 60, author of the Hugo-winning *Stand on Zanzibar*, as well as many other acclaimed novels such as *The Jagged Orbit*, *The Whole Man*, *The Squares of the City*, *The Sheep Look Up*, *The Shockwave Rider*, and almost fifty more, including thrillers, mainstream novels, historical novels, and poetry collections; **Roger Zelazny**, 58, one of the giants of the New Wave era, who went on to become one of the most popular and beloved writers in the genre, multiple Hugo and Nebula winner, author of *Lord of Light, This Immortal, Isle of the Dead* and the multivolume Amber series, among many others; **G. C. Edmonson**, 73, author of the classic time-travel novel *The Ship That Sailed the Time Stream*, as well as *Chapayeca*, one of the most undeservedly forgotten novels of the seventies, and the landmark collection *Stranger Than You Think*, among others; British writer **Bob Shaw**, 63, author of the classic story "Light of Other Days," as well as *The Ragged Astronauts, The Wooden Spaceship, A Wreath of Stars*, and others; **Ian Ballantine**, 79, the publisher who practically invented the modern mass-market paperback as we know it, cofounder, along with his wife, Betty, of three major paperback companies, Penguin, Bantam, and Ballantine, a true giant of the publishing world; **Elsie Wollheim**, 85, wife of SF editor-publisher Donald A. Wollheim, and for many years executive vice president of the publishing house they created, DAW Books; **Margaret St. Clair**, 84, author of the well-known *Sign of the Labrys*, as well as *Agent of the Unknown* and *The Dolphins of Altair*, who also wrote a long sequence of sprightly and entertaining stories under the pseudonym of **Idris Seabright**; **Kingsley Amis**, 73, noted British writer and critic, author of *Lucky Jim* and *The Old Devils*, who also wrote a considerable body of SF, including *The Alteration* and *The Anti-Death League*, as well as being coeditor of the *Spectrum* series of SF anthologies, and producing one of the pioneer works of SF criticism, *New Maps of Hell;* **Jack Finney**, 84, World Fantasy Award winner, author of the classic time-travel novel *Time and Again*, one of the most loving and nostalgic looks at the past ever written, as well as *Invasion of the Body Snatchers;* **Robertson Davies**, 82, noted Canadian writer, many of whose books had fantastic elements, among them *The Rebel Angels, The Cunning Man*, and the acclaimed collection of ghost stories, *High Spirits;* **Claude Avice**, 70, French writer who produced many books under the name of **Pierre Barbet**; **Christopher Hodder-Williams**, 69, British writer, author of *The Main Experiment* and *The Egg-Shaped Thing*, among others; **Mike McQuay**, 45, author of *Memories, Jitterbug*, and *Life-Keeper*, among others; **Kent R. Patterson**, 53, short-story writer and frequent contributor to *The Magazine of Fantasy & Science Fiction* and *Analog;* **Michael Ende**, 65, German author of the children's fantasy novel *The Neverending Story;* **Abram Ruvimovich Palely**, 101, prominent Russian SF writer; **Charlotte Franke**, 60, German author and editor; **Kenneth Sterling**, 74, writer for the early pulp magazines; **Adam Wisniewski-Snerg**, 58, Polish SF author; **Stan Leventhal**, 43, writer and editor; **Janice Elliott**, 63, author of *The Summer People;* **Don Pendleton**, 67, creator of one of the first of the men's adventure series, describing the adventures of "the Executioner," as well as other SF novels, mysteries, and Westerns; **Terry Southern**, 71, scriptwriter and novelist, author of *Candy* and *The Magic Christian;* **Edith Pargeter**, 82, who, as **Ellis Peters**, wrote, among other books, the long-running Brother Cadfael series of mystery novels, which seem to be almost as popular with fantasy fans as with mystery fans, perhaps because of their medieval setting; **Patricia Highsmith**, 74, noted mystery author who also wrote some short horror and SF; **Elleston Trevor**, 75, author of SF, suspense, novels, the best known of which probably was *The Quiller Memorandum*, part of a long-running series of spy novels written as **Adam Hall**; **Robie Macauley**, 76, former fiction editor of *Playboy*, where he encouraged the use of SF and fantasy in that magazine, also a former editor at Houghton Mifflin; **Diane Cleaver**, 53, editor and agent, former SF editor at Doubleday; **Charles Monteith**, 74, noted British publisher; **Charles Scribner, Jr.**, 74, publisher and editor; **Eric Garber**, 40, anthologist; **Philip E. Cleator**, 86, founder of the British Interplanetary Society, and an early popularizer of space travel; **Rudolph Zallinger**, 75, scientific muralist, best known for his *The Age of Reptiles* mural, which, reprinted in *Life*, was many a child's first exposure to dinosaurs; **Peter Cook**, 57, British comic actor and writer, one of the founders of the pioneering British comedy show *Beyond the Fringe*, also a star of such movies as *The Bed-Sitting Room* and *The Wrong Box;* **Donald Pleasence**, 75, film actor, perhaps best known to genre audiences for his role in *Escape from New York*, as well as for his portrayal of the evil Blofeld in the James Bond movie *You Only Live Twice;* **David Wayne**, 81, film actor, perhaps best known to genre audiences for *Portrait of Jennie* and *The Andromeda Strain*, although he also had a recurring role on TV's *Batman* series; **Elizabeth Montgomery**, 57, star of TV's long-running sitcom *Bewitched;* **Cy Endfield**, 81, director of *Zulu* and the film version of *Jules Verne's Mysterious Island;* **Arthur Lubin**, 96, director of fantasy films such as *Rhubard* and *The Incredible Mr. Limpet;* **Henry Horner**, 84, director of *Red Planet Mars;* **Patricia Casort Vardeman**, 35, wife of SF writer Robert Vardeman; **Evelyn Beheshti Hildebrant**, 33, wife of SF writer Don H. DeBrandt; **Benjamin Elgin**, 29, son of SF writer Suzette Haden Elgin; **Stanley Asimov**, 66, well-known journalist, brother of the late SF writer Isaac Asimov, compiler of the recently released book of his brother's letters, *Yours, Isaac Asimov;* **Bessie Delany**, 104, great-aunt of SF writer Samuel R. Delany, and coauthor, with her older sister, who survives her, of the best-selling book *Having Our Say: the Delany Sisters' First 100 Years.*

A WOMAN'S LIBERATION

Ursula K. Le Guin

▼

Ursula K. Le Guin is one of the best-known and most universally respected SF writers in the world today. Her famous novel *The Left Hand of Darkness* may have been the most influential SF novel of its decade, and shows every sign of becoming one of the enduring classics of the genre—even ignoring the rest of Le Guin's work, the impact of this one novel alone on future SF and future SF writers would be incalculably strong. (Her 1968 fantasy novel, *A Wizard of Earthsea*, would be almost as influential on future generations of High Fantasy writers.) *The Left Hand of Darkness* won both the Hugo and Nebula Awards, as did Le Guin's monumental novel *The Dispossessed* a few years later. Her novel *Tehanu* won her another Nebula in 1990, and she has also won three other Hugo Awards and a Nebula Award for her short fiction, as well as the National Book Award for children's literature for her novel *The Farthest Shore*, part of her acclaimed Earthsea trilogy. Last year she was awarded the World Fantasy Lifetime Achievement Award. Her other novels include *Planet of Exile*, *The Lathe of Heaven*, *City of Illusions*, *Rocannon's World*, *The Beginning Place*, *The Tombs of Atuan*, *The Eye of the Heron*, *The New Atlantis*, *Tehanu*, *Searoad*, and the controversial multimedia novel *Always Coming Home*. She has published six collections of short fiction: *The Wind's Twelve Quarters*, *Orsinian Tales*, *The Compass Rose*, *Buffalo Gals and Other Animal Presences*, *A Fisherman of the Inland Sea*, and her most recent book, *Four Ways to Forgiveness*. Her stories have appeared in our Second, Fifth, and Eighth Annual Collections, with two stories by her in our Twelfth Annual Collection.

Here she returns to the star-spanning, Hainish-settled community known as the Ekumen—the same fictional universe that provided the background for her most famous novels—for a powerful and unsettling investigation of loyalty and betrayal, love, and hatred, slavery and transcendence . . . and the price of freedom.

1. Shomeke

My dear friend has asked me to write the story of my life, thinking it might be of interest to people of other worlds and times. I am an ordinary woman, but I have lived in years of mighty changes and have been advantaged to know with my very flesh the nature of servitude and the nature of freedom.

I did not learn to read or write until I was a grown woman, which is all the excuse I will make for the faults of my narrative.

I was born a slave on the planet Werel. As a child I was called Shomekes' Radosse Rakam. That is, Property of the Shomeke Family, Granddaughter of Dosse, Granddaughter of Kamye. The Shomeke family owned an estate on the eastern coast of Voe Deo. Dosse was my grandmother. Kamye is the Lord God.

The Shomekes possessed over four hundred assets, mostly used to cultivate the fields of gede, to herd the saltgrass cattle, in the mills, and as domestics in the House. The Shomeke family had been great in history. Our Owner was an important man politically, often away in the capital.

Assets took their name from their grandmother because it was the grandmother that raised the child. The mother worked all day, and there was no father. Women were always bred to more than one man. Even if a man knew his child he could not care for it. He might be sold or traded away at any time. Young men were seldom kept long on the estates. If they were valuable they were traded to other estates or sold to the factories. If they were worthless they were worked to death.

Women were not often sold. The young ones were kept for work and breeding, the old ones to raise the young and keep the compound in order. On some estates women bore a baby a year till they died, but on ours most had only two or three children. The Shomekes valued women as workers. They did not want the men always getting at the women. The grandmothers agreed with them and guarded the young women closely.

I say men, women, children, but you are to understand that we were not called men, women, children. Only our owners were called so. We assets or slaves were called bondsmen, bondswomen, and pups or young. I will use these words, though I have not heard or spoken them for many years, and never before on this blessed world.

The bondsmen's part of the compound, the gateside, was ruled by the Bosses, who were men, some relations of the Shomeke family, others hired by them. On the inside the young and the bondswomen lived. There two cutfrees, castrated bondsmen, were the Bosses in name, but the grandmothers ruled. Indeed nothing in the compound happened without the grandmothers' knowledge.

If the grandmothers said an asset was too sick to work, the Bosses would let that one stay home. Sometimes the grandmothers could save a bondsman from being sold away, sometimes they could protect a girl from being bred by more than one man, or could give a delicate girl a contraceptive. Everybody in the compound obeyed the counsel of the grandmothers. But if one of them went too far, the Bosses would have her flogged or blinded or her hands cut off. When I was a young child, there lived in our compound a woman we called Great-Grandmother, who had holes for eyes and no tongue. I thought that she was thus because she was so old. I feared that my grandmother Dosse's tongue would wither in her mouth. I told her that. She said, "No. It won't get any shorter, because I don't let it get too long."

I lived in the compound. My mother birthed me there, and was allowed to stay three months to nurse me; then I was weaned to cow's milk, and my mother returned to the House. Her name was Shomekes' Rayowa Yowa. She was light-skinned like most of the assets, but very beautiful, with slender wrists and ankles and delicate features. My grandmother too was light, but I was dark, darker than anybody else in the compound.

My mother came to visit, the cutfrees letting her in by their ladder-door. She found me rubbing grey dust on my body. When she scolded me, I told her that I wanted to look like the others.

"Listen, Rakam," she said to me, "they are dust people. They'll never get out of the dust. You're something better. And you will be beautiful. Why do you think you're so black?" I had no idea what she meant. "Some day I'll tell you who your father is," she said, as if she were promising me a gift. I had watched when the Shomekes' stallion, a prized and valuable animal, serviced mares from other estates. I did not know a father could be human.

That evening I boasted to my grandmother: "I'm beautiful because the black stallion is my father!" Dosse struck me across the head so that I fell down and wept. She said, "Never speak of your father."

I knew there was anger between my mother and my grandmother, but it was a long time before I understood why. Even now I am not sure I understand all that lay between them.

We little pups ran around in the compound. We knew nothing outside the walls. All our world was the bondswomen's huts and the bondsmen's longhouses, the kitchens and kitchen gardens, the bare plaza beaten hard by bare feet. To me, the stockade wall seemed a long way off.

When the field and mill hands went out the gate in the early morning I didn't know where they went. They were just gone. All day long the whole compound belonged to us pups, naked in the summer, mostly naked in the winter too, running around playing with sticks and stones and mud, keeping away from grandmothers, until we begged them for something to eat or they put us to work weeding the gardens for a while.

In the evening or the early night the workers would come back, trooping in the gate guarded by the Bosses. Some were worn out and grim, others would be cheerful and talking and calling back and forth. The great gate was slammed behind the last of them. Smoke went up from all the cooking stoves. The burning cowdung smelled sweet. People gathered on the porches of the huts and longhouses. Bondsmen and bondswomen lingered at the ditch that divided the gateside from the inside, talking across the ditch. After the meal the freedmen led prayers to Tual's statue, and we lifted our own prayers to Kamye, and then people went to their beds, except for those who lingered to "jump the ditch." Some nights, in the summer, there would be singing, or a dance was allowed. In the winter one of the grandfathers—poor old broken men, not strong people like the grandmothers—would "sing the word." That is what we called reciting the *Arkamye*. Every night, always, some of the people were teaching and others were learning the sacred verses. On winter nights one of these old worthless bondsmen kept alive by the grandmothers' charity would begin to sing the word. Then even the pups would be still to listen to that story.

The friend of my heart was Walsu. She was bigger than I, and was my defender when there were fights and quarrels among the young or when older pups called me "Blackie" and "Bossie." I was small but had a fierce temper. Together, Walsu and I did not get bothered much. Then Walsu was sent out the gate. Her mother had been bred and was now stuffed big, so that she needed help in the fields to make her quota. Gede must be hand harvested. Every day as a new section of the bearing stalk comes ripe it has to be picked, and so gede pickers go through the same field over and over for twenty or thirty days, and then move on to a later planting. Walsu went with her mother to help her pick her rows. When her mother fell ill, Walsu took her place, and with help from other hands she kept up her mother's quota. She was then six years old by owner's count, which gave all assets the same birthday, new year's day at the beginning of spring. She might have truly been seven. Her mother remained ill both before birthing and after, and Walsu took her place in the gede field all that time. She never afterward came back to play, only in the evenings to eat and sleep. I saw her then and we could talk. She was proud of her work. I envied her and longed to go through the gate. I followed her to it and looked through it at the world. Now the walls of the compound seemed very close.

I told my grandmother Dosse that I wanted to go to work in the fields.

"You're too young."

"I'll be seven at the new year."

"Your mother made me promise not to let you go out."

Next time my mother visited the compound, I said, "Grandmother won't let me go out. I want to go work with Walsu."

"Never," my mother said. "You were born for better than that."

"What for?"

"You'll see."

She smiled at me. I knew she meant the House, where she worked. She had told me often of the wonderful things in the House, things that shone and were colored brightly, things that were thin and delicate, clean things. It was quiet in the House, she said. My mother herself wore a beautiful red scarf, her voice was soft, and her clothing and body were always clean and fresh.

"When will I see?"

I teased her until she said, "All right! I'll ask my lady."

"Ask her what?"

All I knew of my-lady was that she too was delicate and clean, and that my mother belonged to her in some particular way, of which she was proud. I knew my-lady had given my mother the red scarf.

"I'll ask her if you can come begin training at the House."

My mother said "the House" in a way that made me see it as a great sacred place like the place in our prayer: *May I enter in the clear house, in the rooms of peace.*

I was so excited I began to dance and sing, "I'm going to the House, to the House!" My mother slapped me to make me stop and scolded me for being wild. She said, "You are too young! You can't behave! If you get sent away from the House you can never come back."

I promised to be old enough.

"You must do everything right," Yowa told me. "You must do everything I say when I say it. Never question. Never delay. If my lady sees that you're wild, she'll send you back here. And that will be the end of you forever."

I promised to be tame. I promised to obey at once in everything, and not to speak. The more frightening she made it, the more I desired to see the wonderful, shining House.

When my mother left I did not believe she would speak to my-lady. I was not used to promises being kept. But after some days she returned, and I heard her speaking to my grandmother. Dosse was angry at first, speaking loudly. I crept under the window of the hut to listen. I heard my grandmother weep. I was frightened and amazed. My grandmother was patient with me, always looked after me, and fed me well. It had never entered my mind that there was anything more to it than that, until I heard her crying. Her crying made me cry, as if I were part of her.

"You could let me keep her one more year," she said. "She's just a baby. I would never let her out the gate." She was pleading, as if she were powerless, not a grandmother. "She is my joy, Yowa!"

"Don't you want her to do well, then?"

"Just a year more. She's too wild for the House."

"She's run wild too long. She'll get sent out to the fields if she stays. A year of that and they won't have her at the House. She'll be dust. Anyhow, there's no use crying about it. I asked my lady, and she's expected. I can't go back without her.''

"Yowa, don't let her come to harm,'' Dosse said very low, as if ashamed to say this to her daughter, and yet with strength in her voice.

"I'm taking her to keep her out of harm,'' my mother said. Then she called me, and I wiped my tears and came.

It is queer, but I do not remember my first walk through the world outside the compound or my first sight of the House. I suppose I was frightened and kept my eyes down, and everything was so strange to me that I did not understand what I saw. I know it was a number of days before my mother took me to show me to Lady Tazeu. She had to scrub me and train me and make sure I would not disgrace her. I was terrified when at last she took my hand, scolding me in a whisper all the time, and brought me out of the bondswomen's quarters, through halls and doorways of painted wood, into a bright, sunny room with no roof, full of flowers growing in pots.

I had hardly ever seen a flower, only the weeds in the kitchen gardens, and I stared and stared at them. My mother had to jerk my hand to make me look at the woman lying in a chair among the flowers, in clothes soft and brightly colored like the flowers. I could hardly tell them apart. The woman's hair was long and shining, and her skin was shining and black. My mother pushed me, and I did what she had made me practice over and over: I went and knelt down beside the chair and waited, and when the woman put out her long, narrow, soft hand, black above and azure on the palm, I touched my forehead to it. I was supposed to say "I am your slave Rakam, Ma'am,'' but my voice would not come out.

"What a pretty little thing,'' she said. "So dark.'' Her voice changed a little on the last words.

"The Bosses came in . . . that night,'' Yowa said in a timid, smiling way, looking down as if embarrassed.

"No doubt about that,'' the woman said. I was able to glance up at her again. She was beautiful. I did not know a person could be so beautiful. I think she saw my wonder. She put out her long, soft hand again and caressed my cheek and neck. "Very, very pretty, Yowa,'' she said. "You did quite right to bring her here. Has she been bathed?''

She would not have asked that if she had seen me when I first came, filthy and smelling of the cowdung we made our fires with. She knew nothing of the compound at all. She knew nothing beyond the beza, the women's side of the House. She was kept there just as I had been kept in the compound, ignorant of anything outside. She had never smelled cowdung, as I had never seen flowers.

My mother assured her I was clean, and she said, "Then she can come to bed with me tonight. I'd like that. Will you like to come sleep with me, pretty little—'' She glanced at my mother, who murmured, "Rakam." Ma'am pursed her lips at the name. "I don't like that," she murmured. "So ugly. Toti. Yes. You can be my new Toti. Bring her this evening, Yowa."

She had had a foxdog called Toti, my mother told me. Her pet had died. I did not know animals ever had names, and so it did not seem odd to me to be given an animal's name, but it did seem strange at first not to be Rakam. I could not think of myself as Toti.

That night my mother bathed me again and oiled my skin with sweet oil and dressed me in a soft gown, softer even than her red scarf. Again she scolded and warned me, but she was excited, too, and pleased with me, as we went to the beza again, through other halls, meeting some other bonds-women on the way, and to the lady's bedroom. It was a wonderful room, hung with mirrors and draperies and paintings. I did not understand what the mirrors were, or the paintings, and was frightened when I saw people in them. Lady Tazeu saw that I was frightened. "Come, little one," she said, making a place for me in her great, wide, soft bed strewn with pillows, "come and cuddle up." I crawled in beside her, and she stroked my hair and skin and held me in her warm, soft arms until I was comfortable and at ease. "There, there, little Toti," she said, and so we slept.

I became the pet of Lady Tazeu Wehoma Shomeke. I slept with her almost every night. Her husband was seldom home and when he was there did not come to her, preferring bondswomen for his pleasure. Sometimes she had my mother or other, younger bondswomen come into her bed, and she sent me away at those times, until I was older, ten or eleven, when she began to keep me and have me join in with them, teaching me how to be pleasured. She was gentle, but she was the mistress in love, and I was her instrument which she played.

I was also trained in household arts and duties. She taught me to sing with her, as I had a true voice. All those years I was never punished and never made to do hard work. I who had been wild in the compound was perfectly obedient in the Great House. I had been rebellious to my grandmother and impatient of her commands, but whatever my lady ordered me to do I gladly did. She held me fast to her by the only kind of love she had to give me. I thought that she was the Merciful Tual come down upon the earth. That is not a way of speaking, that is the truth. I thought she was a higher being, superior to myself.

Perhaps you will say that I could not or should not have had pleasure in being used without my consent by my mistress, and if I did I should not speak of it, showing even so little good in so great an evil. But I knew nothing of consent or refusal. Those are freedom words.

She had one child, a son, three years older than I. She lived quite alone among us bondswomen. The Wehomas were nobles of the Islands, old-fashioned people whose women did not travel, so she was cut off from her family. The only company she had was when Owner Shomeke brought friends with him from the capital, but those were all men, and she could be with them only at table.

I seldom saw the Owner and only at a distance. I thought he too was a superior being, but a dangerous one.

As for Erod, the Young Owner, we saw him when he came to visit his mother daily or when he went out riding with his tutors. We girls would peep at him and giggle to each other when we were eleven or twelve, because he was a handsome boy, nightblack and slender like his mother. I knew that he was afraid of his father, because I had heard him weep when he was with his mother. She would comfort him with candy and caresses, saying, "He'll be gone again soon, my darling." I too felt sorry for Erod, who was like a shadow, soft and harmless. He was sent off to school for a year at fifteen, but his father brought him back before the year was up. Bondsmen told us the Owner had beaten him cruelly and had forbidden him even to ride off the estate.

Bondswomen whom the Owner used told us how brutal he was, showing us where he had bruised and hurt them. They hated him, but my mother would not speak against him. "Who do you think you are?" she said to a girl who was complaining of his use of her. "A lady to be treated like glass?" And when the girl found herself pregnant, stuffed was the word we used, my mother had her sent back to the compound. I did not understand why. I thought Yowa was hard and jealous. Now I think she was also protecting the girl from our lady's jealousy.

I do not know when I understood that I was the Owner's daughter. Because she had kept that secret from our lady, my mother believed it was a secret from all. But the bondswomen all knew it. I do not know what I heard or overheard, but when I saw Erod, I would study him and think that I looked much more like our father than he did, for by then I knew what a father was. And I wondered that Lady Tazeu did not see it. But she chose to live in ignorance.

During these years I seldom went to the compound. After I had been a halfyear or so at the House, I was eager to go back and see Walsu and my grandmother and show them my fine clothes and clean skin and shining hair; but when I went, the pups I used to play with threw dirt and stones at me and tore my clothes. Walsu was in the fields. I had to hide in my grandmother's hut all day. I never wanted to go back. When my grandmother sent for me, I would go only with my mother and always stayed close by her. The people in the compound, even my grandmother, came to look coarse and foul to me. They were dirty and smelled strongly. They had sores, scars from punishment, lopped fingers, ears, or noses. Their hands and feet were coarse, with deformed nails. I was no longer used to people who looked so. We domestics of the Great House were entirely different from them, I thought. Serving the higher beings, we became like them.

When I was thirteen and fourteen Lady Tazeu still kept me in her bed, making love to me often. But also she had a new pet, the daughter of one of the cooks, a pretty little girl though white as clay. One night she made love to me for a long time in ways that she knew gave me great ecstasy of the body. When I lay exhausted in her arms she whispered "goodbye, goodbye," kissing me all over my face and breasts. I was too spent to wonder at this.

The next morning my lady called in my mother and myself to tell us that she intended to give me to her son for his seventeenth birthday. "I shall miss you terribly, Toti darling," she said, with tears in her eyes. "You have been my joy. But there isn't another girl on the place that I could let Erod have. You are the cleanest, dearest, sweetest of them all. I know you are a virgin," she meant a virgin to men, "and I know my boy will enjoy you. And he'll be kind to her, Yowa," she said earnestly to my mother. My mother bowed and said nothing. There was nothing she could say. And she said nothing to me. It was too late to speak of the secret she had been so proud of.

Lady Tazeu gave me medicine to prevent conception, but my mother, not trusting the medicine, went to my grandmother and brought me contraceptive herbs. I took both faithfully that week.

If a man in the House visited his wife he came to the beza, but if he wanted a bondswoman she was "sent across." So on the night of the Young Owner's birthday I was dressed all in red and led over, for the first time in my life, to the men's side of the House.

My reverence for my lady extended to her son, and I had been taught that owners were superior by nature to us. But he was a boy whom I had known since childhood, and I knew that his blood and mine were half the same. It gave me a strange feeling toward him.

I thought he was shy, afraid of his manhood. Other girls had tried to tempt him and failed. The women had told me what I was to do, how to offer myself and encourage him, and I was ready to do that. I was brought to him in his great bedroom, all of stone carved like lace, with high, thin windows of violet glass. I stood timidly near the door for a while, and he stood near a table covered with papers and screens. He came forward at last, took my hand, and led me to a chair. He made me sit down, and spoke to me standing, which was all improper, and confused my mind.

"Rakam," he said—"that's your name, isn't it?"—I nodded—"Rakam, my mother means only kindness, and you must not think me ungrateful to her, or blind to your beauty. But I will not take a woman who cannot freely offer herself. Intercourse between owner and slave is rape." And he talked on, talking beautifully, as when my lady read aloud from one of her books. I did not understand much, except that I was to come whenever he sent for me and sleep in his bed, but he would never touch me. And I was not to speak of this to anyone. "I am sorry, I am very sorry to ask you to lie," he said, so earnestly that I wondered if it hurt him to lie. That made him seem more like a god than a human being. If it hurt to lie, how could you stay alive?

"I will do just as you say, Lord Erod," I said.

So, most nights, his bondsmen came to bring me across. I would sleep in his great bed, while he worked at the papers on his table. He slept on a couch beneath the windows. Often he wanted to talk to me, sometimes for a long time, telling me his ideas. When he was in school in the capital he had become a member of a group of owners who wished to abolish slavery, called The Community. Getting wind of this, his father had ordered him out of school, sent him home, and forbidden him to leave the estate. So he too was a prisoner. But he corresponded constantly with others in The Community through the net, which he knew how to operate without his father's knowledge, or the government's.

His head was so full of ideas he had to speak them. Often Geu and Ahas, the young bondsmen who had grown up with him, who always came to fetch me across, stayed with us while he talked to all of us about slavery and freedom and many other things. Often I was sleepy, but I did listen, and heard much I did not know how to understand or even believe. He told us there was an organization among assets, called the Hame, that worked to steal slaves from the plantations. These slaves would be brought to members of The Community, who would make out false papers of ownership and treat them well, renting them to decent work in the cities. He told us about the cities, and I loved to hear all that. He told us about Yeowe Colony, saying that there was a revolution there among the slaves.

Of Yeowe I knew nothing. It was a great blue-green star that set after the sun or rose before it, brighter than the smallest of the moons. It was a name in an old song they sang in the compound:

> O, O, Ye-o-we,
> Nobody never comes back.

I had no idea what a revolution was. When Erod told me that it meant that assets on plantations in this place called Yeowe were fighting their owners, I did not understand how assets could do that. From the beginning it was ordained that there should be higher and lower beings, the Lord and the human, the man and the woman, the owner and the owned. All my world was Shomeke Estate and it stood on that one foundation. Who would want to overturn it? Everyone would be crushed in the ruins.

I did not like Erod to call assets slaves, an ugly word that took away our value. I decided in my mind that here on Werel we were assets, and in that other place, Yeowe Colony, there were slaves, worthless bondspeople, intractables. That was why they had been sent there. It made good sense.

By this you know how ignorant I was. Sometimes Lady Tazeu had let us watch shows on the holonet with her, but she watched only dramas, not the reports of events. Of the world beyond the estate I knew nothing but what I learned from Erod, and that I could not understand.

Erod liked us to argue with him. He thought it meant our minds were growing free. Geu was good at it. He would ask questions like, "But if there's no assets who'll do the work?" Then Erod could answer at length. His eyes shone, his voice was eloquent. I loved him very much when he talked to us. He was beautiful and what he said was beautiful. It was like hearing the old men "singing the word," reciting the *Arkamye*, when I was a little pup in the compound.

I gave the contraceptives my lady gave me every month to girls who needed them. Lady Tazeu had aroused my sexuality and accustomed me to being used sexually. I missed her caresses. But I did not know how to approach any of the bondswomen, and they were afraid to approach me, since I belonged to the Young Owner. Being with Erod often, while he talked I yearned to him in my body. I lay in his bed and dreamed that he came and stooped over me and did with me as my lady used to do. But he never touched me.

Geu also was a handsome young man, clean and well-mannered, rather dark-skinned, attractive to me. His eyes were always on me. But he would not approach me, until I told him that Erod did not touch me.

Thus I broke my promise to Erod not to tell anyone; but I did not think myself bound to keep promises, as I did not think myself bound to speak the truth. Honor of that kind was for owners, not for us.

After that, Geu used to tell me when to meet him in the attics of the House. He gave me little pleasure. He would not penetrate me, believing that he must save my virginity for our master. He had me take his penis in my mouth instead. He would turn away in his climax, for the slave's sperm must not defile the master's woman. That is the honor of a slave.

Now you may say in disgust that my story is all of such things, and there is far more to life, even a slave's life, than sex. That is very true. I can say only that it may be in our sexuality that we are most easily enslaved, both men and women. It may be there, even as free men and women, that we find freedom hardest to keep. The politics of the flesh are the roots of power.

I was young, full of health and desire for joy. And even now, even here, when I look back across the years from this world to that, to the compound and the House of Shomeke, I see images like those in a bright dream. I see my grandmother's big, hard hands. I see my mother smiling, the red scarf about her neck. I see my lady's black, silky body among the cushions. I smell the smoke of the cowdung fires, and the perfumes of the beza. I feel the soft, fine clothing on my young body, and my lady's hands and lips. I hear the old men singing the word, and my voice twining with my lady's voice in a love song, and Erod telling us of freedom. His face is illuminated with his vision. Behind him the windows of stone lace and violet glass keep out the night. I do not say I would go back. I would die before I would go back to Shomeke. I would die before I left this free world, my world, to go back to the place of slavery. But whatever I knew in my youth of beauty, of love, and of hope, was there.

And there it was betrayed. All that is built upon that foundation in the end betrays itself.

I was sixteen years old in the year the world changed.

The first change I heard about was of no interest to me except that my lord was excited about it, and so were Geu and Ahas and some of the other young bondsmen. Even my grandmother wanted to hear about it when I visited her. "That Yeowe, that slave world," she said, "they made freedom? They sent away their owners? They opened the gates? My lord, sweet Lord Kamye, how can that be? Praise his name, praise his marvels!" She rocked back and forth as she squatted in the dust, her arms about her knees. She was an old, shrunken woman now. "Tell me!" she said.

I knew little else to tell her. "All the soldiers came back here," I said. "And those other people, those alemens, they're there on Yeowe. Maybe they're the new owners. That's all somewhere way out there," I said, flipping my hand at the sky.

"What's alemens?" my grandmother asked, but I did not know. It was all mere words to me.

But when our Owner, Lord Shomeke, came home sick, that I understood. He came on a flyer to our little port. I saw him carried by on a stretcher, the whites showing in his eyes, his black skin mottled grey. He was dying of a sickness that was ravaging the cities. My mother, sitting with Lady Tazeu, saw a politician on the net who said that the alemens had brought the sickness to Werel. He talked so fearsomely that we thought everybody was going to die. When I told Geu about it he snorted. "Aliens, not alemens," he said, "and they've got nothing to do with it. My lord talked with the doctors. It's just a new kind of pusworm."

That dreadful disease was bad enough. We knew that any asset found to be infected with it was slaughtered at once like an animal and the corpse burned on the spot.

They did not slaughter the Owner. The House filled with doctors, and Lady Tazeu spent day and night by her husband's bed. It was a cruel death. It went on and on. Lord Shomeke in his suffering made terrible sounds, screams, howls. One would not believe a man could cry out hour after hour as he did. His flesh ulcerated and fell away, he went mad, but he did not die. As Lady Tazeu became like a shadow, worn and silent, Erod filled with strength and excitement. Sometimes when we heard his father howling his eyes would shine. He would whisper, "Lady Tual have mercy on him," but he fed on those cries. I knew from Geu and Ahas, who had been brought up with him, how the father had tormented and despised him, and how Erod had vowed to be everything his father was not and to undo all he did.

But it was Lady Tazeu who ended it. One night she sent away the other attendants, as she often did, and sat alone with the dying man. When he began his moaning howl, she took her little sewing-knife and cut his throat. Then she cut the veins in her arms across and across, and lay down by him, and so died. My mother was in the next room all night. She said she wondered a little at the silence, but was so weary that she fell asleep; and in the morning she went in and found them lying in their cold blood.

All I wanted to do was weep for my lady, but everything was in confusion. Everything in the sickroom must be burned, the doctors said, and the bodies must be burned without delay. The House was under quarantine, so only the priests of the House could hold the funeral. No one was to leave the estate for twenty days. But several of the doctors themselves left when Erod, who was now Lord Shomeke, told them what he intended to do. I heard some confused word of it from Ahas, but in my grief I paid little heed.

That evening, all the House assets stood outside the Lady's Chapel during the funeral service to hear the songs and prayers within. The Bosses and cutfrees had brought the people from the compound, and they stood behind us. We saw the procession come out, the white biers carried by, the pyres lighted, and the black smoke go up. Long before the smoke ceased rising, the new Lord Shomeke came to us all where we stood.

Erod stood up on the little rise of ground behind the chapel and spoke in a strong voice such as I had never heard from him. Always in the House it had been whispering in the dark. Now it was broad day and a strong voice. He stood there black and straight in his white mourning clothes. He was not yet twenty years old. He said, "Listen, you people: you have been slaves, you will be free. You have been my property, you will own your own lives now. This morning I sent to the Government the Order of Manumission for every asset on the estate, four hundred and eleven men, women, and children. If you will come to my office in the Counting House in the morning, I will give you your papers. Each of you is named in those papers as a free person. You can never be enslaved again. You are free to do as you please from tomorrow on. There will be money for each one of you to begin your new life with. Not what you deserve, not what you have earned in all your work for us, but what I have to give you. I am leaving Shomeke. I will go to the capital, where I will work for the freedom of every slave on Werel. The Freedom Day that came to Yeowe is coming to us, and soon. Any of you who wish to come with me, come! There's work for us all to do!''

I remember all he said. Those are his words as he spoke them. When one does not read and has not had one's mind filled up by the images on the nets, words spoken strike down deep in the mind.

There was such a silence when he stopped speaking as I had never heard.

One of the doctors began talking, protesting to Erod that he must not break the quarantine.

"The evil has been burned away," Erod said, with a great gesture to the black smoke rising. "This has been an evil place, but no more harm will go forth from Shomeke!''

At that a slow sound began among the compound people standing behind us, and it swelled into a great noise of jubilation mixed with wailing, crying, shouting, singing. "Lord Kamye! Lord Kamye!'' the men shouted. An old woman came forward: my grandmother. She strode through us House assets as if we were a field of grain. She stopped a good way from Erod. People fell silent to listen to the grandmother. She said, "Lord Master, are you turning us out of our homes?''

"No," he said. "They are yours. The land is yours to use. The profit of the fields is yours. This is your home, and you are free!''

At that the shouts rose up again so loud I cowered down and covered my ears, but I was crying and shouting too, praising Lord Erod and Lord Kamye in one voice with the rest of them.

We danced and sang there in sight of the burning pyres until the sun went down. At last the grandmothers and the freedmen got the people to go back to the compound, saying they did not have their papers yet. We domestics went straggling back to the House, talking about tomorrow, when we would get our freedom and our money and our land.

All that next day Erod sat in the Counting House and made out the papers for each slave and counted out the same amount of money for each: a hundred kue in cash, and a draft for five hundred kue on the district bank, which could not be drawn for forty days. This was, he explained to each one, to save them from exploitation by the unscrupulous before they knew how best to use their money. He advised them to form a cooperative, to pool their funds, to run the estate democratically. "Money in the bank, Lord!'' an old crippled man came out crying, jigging on his twisted legs. "Money in the bank, Lord!''

If they wanted, Erod said over and over, they could save their money and contact the Hame, who would help them buy passage to Yeowe with it.

"O, O, Ye-o-we," somebody began singing, and they changed the words:

" Everybody's going to go.
O, O, Ye-o-we,
Everybody's going to go!"

They sang it all day long. Nothing could change the sadness of it. I want to weep now, remembering that song, that day.

The next morning Erod left. He could not wait to get away from the place of his misery and begin his life in the capital working for freedom. He did not say goodbye to me. He took Geu and Ahas with him. The doctors and their aides and assets had all left the day before. We watched his flyer go up into the air.

We went back to the House. It was like something dead. There were no owners in it, no masters, no one to tell us what to do.

My mother and I went in to pack up our clothing. We had said little to each other, but felt we could not stay there. We heard other women running through the beza, rummaging in Lady Tazeu's rooms, going through her closets, laughing and screaming with excitement, finding jewelry and valuables. We heard men's voices in the hall: Bosses's voices. Without a word my mother and I took what we had in our hands and went out by a back door, slipped through the hedges of the garden, and ran all the way to the compound.

The great gate of the compound stood wide open.

How can I tell you what that was to us, to see that, to see that gate stand open? How can I tell you?

2. Zeskra

Erod knew nothing about how the estate was run, because the Bosses ran it. He was a prisoner too. He had lived in his screens, his dreams, his visions.

The grandmothers and others in the compound had spent all that night trying to make plans, to draw our people together so they could defend themselves. That morning when my mother and I came, there were bondsmen guarding the compound with weapons made of farm tools. The grandmothers and cutfrees had made an election of a headman, a strong, well-liked field hand. In that way they hoped to keep the young men with them.

By the afternoon that hope was broken. The young men ran wild. They went up to the House to loot it. The Bosses shot them from the windows, killing many; the others fled away. The Bosses stayed holed up in the House, drinking the wine of the Shomekes. Owners of other plantations were flying reinforcements to them. We heard the flyers land, one after another. The bondswomen who had stayed in the House were at their mercy now.

As for us in the compound, the gates were closed again. We had moved the great bars from the outside to the inside, so we thought ourselves safe for the night at least. But in the midnight they came with heavy tractors and pushed down the wall, and a hundred men or more, our Bosses and owners from all the plantations of the region, came swarming in. They were armed with guns. We fought them with farm tools and pieces of wood. One or two of them were hurt or killed. They killed as many of us as they wanted to kill and then began to rape us. It went on all night.

A group of men took all the old women and men and held them and shot them between the eyes, the way they kill cattle. My grandmother was one of them. I do not know what happened to my mother. I did not see any bondsmen living when they took me away in the morning. I saw white papers lying in the blood on the ground. Freedom papers.

Several of us girls and young women still alive were herded into a truck and taken to the port-field. There they made us enter a flyer, shoving and using sticks, and we were carried off in the air. I was not then in my right mind. All I know of this is what the others told me later.

We found ourselves in a compound, like our compound in every way. I thought they had brought us back home. They shoved us in by the cutfrees' ladder. It was morning and the hands were out at work, only the grandmothers and pups and old men in the compound. The grandmothers came to us fierce and scowling. I could not understand at first why they were all strangers. I looked for my grandmother.

They were frightened of us, thinking we must be runaways. Plantation slaves had been running away, the last years, trying to get to the cities. They thought we were intractables and would bring trouble with us. But they helped us clean ourselves, and gave us a place near the cutfrees' tower. There were no huts empty, they said. They told us this was Zeskra Estate. They did not want to hear about what had happened at Shomeke. They did not want us to be there. They did not need our trouble.

We slept there on the ground without shelter. Some of the bondsmen came across the ditch in the night and raped us because there was nothing to prevent them from it, no one to whom we were of any value. We were too weak and sick to fight them. One of us, a girl named Abye, tried to fight. The men beat her insensible. In the morning she could not talk or walk. She was left there when the Bosses came and took us away. Another girl was left behind too, a big farmhand with white scars on her head like parts in her hair. As we were going I looked at her and saw that it was Walsu, who had been my friend. We had not recognized each other. She sat in the dirt, her head bowed down.

Five of us were taken from the compound to the Great House of Zeskra, to the bondswomen's quarters. There for a while I had a little hope, since I knew how to be a good domestic asset. I did not know then how different Zeskra was from Shomeke. The House at Zeskra was full of people, full of owners and bosses. It was a big family, not a single Lord as at Shomeke but a dozen of them with their retainers and relations and visitors, so there might be thirty or forty men staying on the men's side and as many women in the beza, and a House staff of fifty or more. We were not brought as domestics, but as use-women.

After we were bathed we were left in the use-women's quarters, a big room without any private places. There were ten or more use-women already there. Those of them who liked their work were not glad to see us, thinking of us as rivals; others welcomed us, hoping we might take their places and they might be let join the domestic staff. But none were very unkind, and some were kind, giving us clothes, for we had been naked all this time, and comforting the youngest of us, Mio, a little compound girl of ten or eleven whose white body was mottled all over with brown and blue bruises.

One of them was a tall woman called Sezi-Tual. She looked at me with an ironic face. Something in her made my soul awaken.

"You're not a dusty," she said. "You're as black as old Lord Devil Zeskra himself. You're a Bossbaby, aren't you?"

"No ma'am," I said. "A Lord's child. And the Lord's child. My name is Rakam."

"Your Grandfather hasn't treated you too well lately," she said. "Maybe you should pray to the Merciful Lady Tual."

"I don't look for mercy," I said. From then on Sezi-Tual liked me, and I had her protection, which I needed.

We were sent across to the men's side most nights. When there were dinner parties, after the ladies left the dinner room we were brought in to sit on the owners' knees and drink wine with them. Then they would use us there on the couches or take us to their rooms. The men of Zeskra were not cruel. Some liked to rape, but most preferred to think that we desired them and wanted whatever they wanted. Such men could be satisfied, the one kind if we showed fear or submission, the other kind if we showed yielding and delight. But some of their visitors were another kind of man.

There was no law or rule against damaging or killing a use-woman. Her owner might not like it, but in his pride he could not say so: he was supposed to have so many assets that the loss of one or another did not matter at all. So some men whose pleasure lay in torture came to hospitable estates like Zeskra for their pleasure. Sezi-Tual, a favorite of the Old Lord, could and did protest to him, and such guests were not invited back. But while I was there, Mio, the little girl who had come with us from Shomeke, was murdered by a guest. He tied her down to the bed. He made the knot across her neck so tight that while he used her she strangled to death.

I will say no more of these things. I have told what I must tell. There are truths that are not useful. All knowledge is local, my friend has said. Is it true, where is it true, that that child had to die in that way? Is it true, where is it true, that she did not have to die in that way?

I was often used by Lord Yaseo, a middle-aged man, who liked my dark skin, calling me "My Lady." Also he called me "Rebel," because what had happened at Shomeke they called a rebellion of the slaves. Nights when he did not send for me I served as a common-girl.

After I had been at Zeskra two years Sezi-Tual came to me one morning early. I had come back late from Lord Yaseo's bed. Not many others were there, for there had been a drinking party the night before, and all the common-girls had been sent for. Sezi-Tual woke me. She had strange hair, curly, in a bush. I remember her face above me, that hair curling out all about it. "Rakam," she whispered, "one of the visitor's assets spoke to me last night. He gave me this. He said his name is Suhame."

"Suhame," I repeated. I was sleepy. I looked at what she was holding out to me: some dirty crumpled paper. "I can't read!" I said, yawning, impatient.

But I looked at it and knew it. I knew what it said. It was the freedom paper. It was my freedom paper. I had watched Lord Erod write my name on it. Each time he wrote a name he had spoken it aloud so that we would know what he was writing. I remembered the big flourish of the first letter of both my names: Radosse Rakam. I took the paper in my hand, and my hand was shaking. "Where did you get this?" I whispered.

"Better ask this Suhame," she said. Now I heard what that name meant: "from the Hame." It was a password name. She knew that too. She was watching me, and she bent down suddenly and leaned her forehead against mine, her breath catching in her throat. "If I can I'll help," she whispered.

I met with "Suhame" in one of the pantries. As soon as I saw him I knew him: Ahas, who had been Lord Erod's favorite along with Geu. A slight, silent young man with dusty skin, he had never been much in my mind. He had watchful eyes, and I had thought when Geu and I spoke that he looked at us with ill will. Now he looked at me with a strange face, still watchful, yet blank.

"Why are you here with that Lord Boeba?" I said. "Aren't you free?"

"I am as free as you are," he said.

I did not understand him, then.

"Didn't Lord Erod protect even you?" I asked.

"Yes. I am a free man." His face began to come alive, losing that dead blankness it had when he first saw me. "Lady Boeba's a member of The Community. I work with the Hame. I've been trying to find people from Shomeke. We heard several of the women were here. Are there others still alive, Rakam?"

His voice was soft, and when he said my name my breath caught and my throat swelled. I said his name and went to him, holding him. "Ratual, Ramayo, Keo are still here," I said. He held me gently. "Walsu is in the compound," I said, "if she's still alive." I wept. I had not wept since Mio's death. He too was in tears.

We talked, then and later. He explained to me that we were indeed, by law, free, but that law meant nothing on the Estates. The government would not interfere between owners and those they claimed as their assets. If we claimed our rights the Zeskras would probably kill us, since they considered us stolen goods and did not want to be shamed. We must run away or be stolen away, and get to the city, the capital, before we could have any safety at all.

We had to be sure that none of the Zeskra assets would betray us out of jealousy or to gain favor. Sezi-Tual was the only one I trusted entirely.

Ahas arranged our escape with Sezi-Tual's help. I pleaded once with her to join us, but she thought that since she had no papers she would have to live always in hiding, and that would be worse than her life at Zeskra.

"You could go to Yeowe," I said.

She laughed. "All I know about Yeowe is nobody ever came back. Why run from one hell to the next one?"

Ratual chose not to come with us; she was a favorite of one of the young lords and content to remain so. Ramayo, the oldest of us from Shomeke, and Keo, who was now about fifteen, wanted to come. Sezi-Tual went down to the compound and found that Walsu was alive, working as a field hand. Arranging her escape was far more difficult than ours. There was no escape from a compound. She could get away only in daylight, in the fields, under the overseer's and the Boss's eyes. It was difficult even to talk to her, for the grandmothers were distrustful. But Sezi-Tual managed it, and Walsu told her she would do whatever she must do "to see her paper again."

Lady Boeba's flyer waited for us at the edge of a great gede field that had just been harvested. It was late summer. Ramayo, Keo, and I walked away from the House separately at different times of the morning. Nobody watched over us closely, as there was nowhere for us to go. Zeskra lies among other great estates, where a runaway slave would find no friends for hundreds of miles. One by one, taking different ways, we came through the fields and woods, crouching and hiding all the way to the flyer where Ahas waited for us. My heart beat and beat so I could not breathe. There we waited for Walsu.

"There!" said Keo, perched up on the wing of the flyer. She pointed across the wide field of stubble.

Walsu came running from the strip of trees on the far side of the field. She ran heavily, steadily, not as if she were afraid. But all at once she halted. She turned. We did not know why for a moment. Then we saw two men break from the shadow of the trees in pursuit of her.

She did not run from them, leading them toward us. She ran back at them. She leapt at them like a hunting cat. As she made that leap, one of them fired a gun. She bore one man down with her, falling. The other fired again and again. "In," Ahas said. "Now." We scrambled into the flyer and it rose into the air, seemingly all in one instant, the same instant in which Walsu made that great leap, she too rising into the air, into her death, into her freedom.

3. The City

I had folded up my freedom paper into a tiny packet. I carried it in my hand all the time we were in the flyer and while we landed and went in a public car through the city street. When Ahas found what I was clutching, he said I need not worry about it. Our manumission was on record in the Government Office and would be honored, here in the City. We were free people, he said. We were gareots, that is, owners who have no assets. "Just like Lord Erod," he said. That meant nothing to me. There was too much to learn. I kept hold of my freedom paper until I had a place to keep it safe. I have it still.

We walked a little way in the streets and then Ahas led us into one of the huge houses that stood side by side on the pavement. He called it a compound, but we thought it must be an owner's house. There a middle-aged woman welcomed us. She was pale-skinned, but talked and behaved like an owner, so that I did not know what she was. She said she was Ress, a rentswoman and an elderwoman of the house.

Rentspeople were assets rented out by their owners to a company. If they were hired by a big company they lived in the company compounds, but there were many, many rentspeople in the City who worked for small companies or businesses they managed themselves, and they occupied buildings run for profit, called open compounds. In such places the occupants must keep curfew, the doors being locked at night, but that was all; they were self-governed. This was such an open compound. It was supported by The Community. Some of the occupants were rentspeople, but many were like us, gareots who had been slaves. Over a hundred people lived there in forty apartments. It was supervised by several women, whom I would have called grandmothers, but here they were called elderwomen.

On the estates deep in the country, deep in the past, where the life was protected by miles of land and by the custom of centuries and by determined ignorance, any asset was absolutely at the mercy of any owner. From there we had come into this great crowd of two million people where nothing and nobody was protected from chance or change, where we had to learn as fast as we could how to stay alive, but where our life was in our own hands.

I had never seen a street. I could not read a word. I had much to learn.

Ress made that clear at once. She was a City woman, quick-thinking and quick-talking, impatient, aggressive, sensitive. I could not like or understand her for a long time. She made me feel stupid, slow, a clod. Often I was angry at her.

There was anger in me now. I had not felt anger while I lived at Zeskra. I could not. It would have eaten me. Here there was room for it, but I found no use for it. I lived with it in silence. Keo and Ramayo had a big room together, I had a small one next to theirs. I had never had a room to myself. At first I felt lonely in it and as if ashamed, but soon I came to like it. The first thing I did freely, as a free woman, was to shut my door.

Nights, I would shut my door and study. Days, we had work training in the morning, classes in the afternoon: reading and writing, arithmetic, history. My work training was in a small shop which made boxes of paper and thin wood to hold cosmetics, candles, jewelry, and such things. I was trained in all the different steps and crafts of making and ornamenting the boxes, for that is how most work was done in the City, by artisans who knew all their trade. The shop was owned by a member of The Community. The older workers were rentspeople. When my training was finished I too would be paid wages.

Till then Lord Erod supported me as well as Keo and Amayo and some men from Shomeke compound, who lived in a different house. Erod never came to the house. I think he did not want to see any of the people he had so disastrously freed. Ahas and Geu said he had sold most of the land at Shomeke and used the money for The Community and to make his way in politics, as there was now a Radical Party which favored emancipation.

Geu came a few times to see me. He had become a City man, dapper and knowing. I felt when he looked at me he was thinking I had been a use-woman at Zeskra, and I did not like to see him.

Ahas, whom I had never thought about in the old days, I now admired, knowing him brave, resolute, and kind. It was he who had looked for us, found us, rescued us. Owners had paid the money but Ahas had done it. He came often to see us. He was the only link that had not broken between me and my childhood.

And he came as a friend, a companion, never driving me back into my slave body. I was angry now at every man who looked at me as men look at women. I was angry at women who looked at me seeing me sexually. To Lady Tazeu all I had been was my body. At Zeskra that was all I had been. Even to Erod who would not touch me that was all I had been. Flesh to touch or not to touch, as they pleased. To use or not to use, as they chose. I hated the sexual parts of myself, my genitals and breasts and the swell of my hips and belly. Ever since I was a child, I had been dressed in soft clothing made to display all that sexuality of a woman's body. When I began to be paid and could buy or make my own clothing, I dressed in hard, heavy cloth. What I liked of myself was my hands, clever at their work, and my head, not clever at learning, but still learning, no matter how long it took.

What I loved to learn was history. I had grown up without any history. There was nothing at Shomeke or Zeskra but the way things were. Nobody knew anything about any time when things had been different. Nobody knew there was any place where things might be different. We were enslaved by the present time.

Erod had talked of change, indeed, but the owners were going to make the change. We were to be changed, we were to be freed, just as we had been owned. In history I saw that any freedom has been made, not given.

The first book I read by myself was a history of Yeowe, written very simply. It told about the days of the Colony, of the Four Corporations, of the terrible first century when the ships carried slave men to Yeowe and precious ores back. Slave men were so cheap then they worked them to death in a few years in the mines, bringing in new shipments continually. *O, O, Yeowe, nobody never comes back.* Then the Corporations began to send women slaves to work and breed, and over the years the assets spilled out of the compounds and made cities—whole great cities like this one I was living in. But not run by the owners or Bosses. Run by the assets, the way this house was run by us. On Yeowe the assets had belonged to the Corporations. They could rent their freedom by paying the Corporation a part of what they earned, the way sharecropper assets paid their owners in parts of Voe Deo. On Yeowe they called those assets freedpeople. Not free people, but freedpeople. And then, this history I was reading said, they began to think, why aren't we free people? So they made the revolution, the Liberation. It began on a plantation called Nadami, and spread from there. Thirty years they fought for their freedom. And just three years ago they had won the war, they had driven the Corporations, the owners, the bosses, off their world. They had danced and sung in the streets, freedom, freedom! This book I was reading (slowly, but reading it) had been printed there—there on Yeowe, the Free World. The Aliens had brought it to Werel. To me it was a sacred book.

I asked Ahas what it was like now on Yeowe, and he said they were making their government, writing a perfect Constitution to make all men equal under the Law.

On the net, on the news, they said they were fighting each other on Yeowe, there was no government at all, people were starving, savage tribesmen in the countryside and youth gangs in the cities running amuck, law and order broken down. Corruption, ignorance, a doomed attempt, a dying world, they said.

Ahas said that the Government of Voe Deo, which had fought and lost the war against Yeowe, now was afraid of a Liberation on Werel. "Don't believe any news," he counseled me. "Especially don't believe the neareals. Don't ever go into them. They're just as much lies as the rest, but if you feel and see a thing you will believe it. And they know that. They don't need guns if they own our minds.'' The owners had no reporters, no cameras on Yeowe, he said; they invented their "news," using actors. Only some of the aliens of the Ekumen were allowed on Yeowe, and the Yeowans were debating whether they should send them away, keeping the world they had won for themselves alone.

"But then what about us?'' I said, for I had begun dreaming of going there, going to the Free World, when the Hame could charter ships and send people.

"Some of them say assets can come. Others say they can't feed so many, and would be overwhelmed. They're debating it democratically. It will be decided in the first Yeowan Elections, soon." Ahas was dreaming of going there too. We talked of our dream the way lovers talk of their love.

But there were no ships going to Yeowe now. The Hame could not act openly and The Community was forbidden to act for them. The Ekumen had offered transportation on their own ships to anyone who wanted to go, but the government of Voe Deo refused to let them use any space port for that purpose. They could carry only their own people. No Werelian was to leave Werel.

It had been only forty years since Werel had at last allowed the Aliens to land and maintain diplomatic relations. As I went on reading history I began to understand a little of the nature of the dominant people of Werel. The black-skinned race that conquered all the other peoples of the Great Continent, and finally all the world, those who call themselves the owners, have lived in the belief that there is only one way to be. They have believed they are what people should be, do as people should do, and know all the truth that is known. All the other peoples of Werel, even when they resisted them, imitated them, trying to become them, and so became their property. When a people came out of the sky looking differently, doing differently, knowing differently, and would not let themselves be conquered or enslaved, the owner race wanted nothing to do with them. It took them four hundred years to admit that they had equals.

I was in the crowd at a rally of the Radical Party, at which Erod spoke, as beautifully as ever. I noticed a woman beside me in the crowd listening. Her skin was a curious orange-brown, like the rind of a pini, and the whites showed in the corners of her eyes. I thought she was sick—I thought of the pusworm, how Lord Shomeke's skin had changed and his eyes had shown their whites. I shuddered and drew away. She glanced at me, smiling a little, and returned her attention to the speaker. Her hair curled in a bush or cloud, like Sezi-Tual's. Her clothing was of a delicate cloth, a strange fashion. It came upon me very slowly what she was, that she had come here from a world unimaginably far. And the wonder of it was that for all her strange skin and eyes and hair and mind, she was human, as I am human: I had no doubt of that. I felt it. For a moment it disturbed me deeply. Then it ceased to trouble me and I felt a great curiosity, almost a yearning, a drawing to her. I wished to know her, to know what she knew.

In me the owner's soul was struggling with the free soul. So it will do all my life.

Keo and Ramayo stopped going to school after they learned to read and write and use the calculator, but I kept on. When there were no more classes to take from the school the Hame kept, the teachers helped me find classes in the net. Though the government controlled such courses, there were fine teachers and groups from all over the world, talking about literature and history and the sciences and arts. Always I wanted more history.

Ress, who was a member of the Hame, first took me to the Library of Voe Deo. As it was open only to owners, it was not censored by the government. Freed assets, if they were light-skinned, were kept out by the librarians on one pretext or another. I was dark-skinned, and had learned here in the City to carry myself with an indifferent pride that spared one many insults and offenses. Ress told me to stride in as if I owned the place. I did so, and was given all privileges without question. So I began to read freely, to read any book I wanted in that great library, every book in it if I could. That was my joy, that reading. That was the heart of my freedom.

Beyond my work at the boxmaker's, which was well paid, pleasant, and among pleasant companions, and my learning and reading, there was not much to my life. I did not want more. I was lonely, but I felt that loneliness was no high price to pay for what I wanted.

Ress, whom I had disliked, was a friend to me. I went with her to meetings of the Hame, and also to entertainments that I would have known nothing about without her guidance. "Come on, Bumpkin," she would say. "Got to educate the plantation pup." And she would take me to the makil theater, or to asset dance halls where the music was good. She always wanted to dance. I let her teach me, but was not very happy dancing. One night as we were dancing the "slow-go" her hands began pressing me to her, and looking in her face I saw the mask of sexual desire on it, soft and blank. I broke away. "I don't want to dance," I said.

We walked home. She came up to my room with me, and at my door she tried to hold and kiss me. I was sick with anger. "I don't want that!" I said.

"I'm sorry, Rakam," she said, more gently than I had ever heard her speak. "I know how you must feel. But you've got to get over that, you've got to have your own life. I'm not a man, and I do want you."

I broke in—"A woman used me before a man ever did. Did you ask me if I wanted you? I will never be used again!"

That rage and spite came bursting out of me like poison from an infection. If she had tried to touch me again I would have hurt her. I slammed my door in her face. I went trembling to my desk, sat down, and began to read the book that was open on it.

Next day we were both ashamed and stiff. But Ress had patience under her City quickness and roughness. She did not try to make love to me again, but she got me to trust her and talk to her as I could not talk to anybody else. She listened intently and told me what she thought. She said, "Bumpkin, you have it all wrong. No wonder. How could you have got it right? You think sex is something that gets done to you. It's not. It's something you do. With somebody else. Not to them. You never had any sex. All you ever knew was rape."

"Lord Erod told me all that a long time ago," I said. I was bitter. "I don't care what it's called. I had enough of it. For the rest of my life. And I'm glad to be without it."

Ress made a face. "At twenty-two?" she said. "Maybe for a while. If you're happy, then fine. But think about what I said. Love is a big part of life to just cut out."

"If I have to have sex I can pleasure myself," I said, not caring if I hurt her. "Love has nothing to do with it."

"That's where you're wrong," she said, but I did not listen. I would learn from teachers and books that I chose for myself, but I would not take advice I had not asked for. I refused to be told what to do or what to think. If I was free, I would be free by myself. I was like a baby when it first stands up.

Ahas had been giving me advice too. He said it was foolish to pursue education so far. "There's nothing useful you can do with so much book-learning," he said. "It's self-indulgent. We need leaders and members with practical skills."

"We need teachers!"

"Yes," he said, "but you knew enough to teach a year ago. What's the good of ancient history, facts about alien worlds? We have a revolution to make!"

I did not stop my reading, but I felt guilty. I took a class at the Hame school teaching illiterate assets and freedpeople to read and write, as I myself had been taught only three years before. It was hard work. Reading is hard for a grown person to learn, tired, at night, after work all day. It is much easier to let the net take one's mind over.

I kept arguing with Ahas in my mind, and one day I said to him, "Is there a Library on Yeowe?"

"I don't know."

"You know there isn't. The Corporations didn't leave any libraries there. They didn't have any. They were ignorant people who knew nothing but profit. Knowledge is a good in itself. I keep on learning so that I can bring my knowledge to Yeowe. If I could I'd bring them the whole Library!''

He stared. "What owners thought, what owners did—that's all their books are about. They don't need that on Yeowe.''

"Yes they do," I said, certain he was wrong, though again I could not say why.

At the school they soon called on me to teach history, one of the teachers having left. These classes went well. I worked hard preparing them. Presently I was asked to speak to a study group of advanced students, and that too went well. People were interested in the ideas I drew and the comparisons I had learned to make of our world with other worlds. I had been studying the way various peoples bring up their children, who takes the responsibility for them and how that responsibility is understood, since this seemed to me a place where a people frees or enslaves itself.

To one of these talks a man from the Embassy of the Ekumen came. I was frightened when I saw the alien face in my audience. I was worse frightened when I recognized him. He had taught the first course in Ekumenical History that I had taken in the net. I had listened to it devotedly though I never participated in the discussion. What I learned had had a great influence on me. I thought he would find me presumptuous for talking of things he truly knew. I stammered on through my lecture, trying not to see his white-cornered eyes.

He came up to me afterward, introduced himself politely, complimented my talk, and asked if I had read such-and-such a book. He engaged me so deftly and kindly in conversation that I had to like and trust him. And he soon earned my trust. I needed his guidance, for much foolishness has been written and spoken, even by wise people, about the balance of power between men and women, on which depend the lives of children and the value of their education. He knew useful books to read, from which I could go on by myself.

His name was Esdardon Aya. He worked in some high position, I was not sure what, at the Embassy. He had been born on Hain, the Old World, humanity's first home, from which all our ancestors came.

Sometimes I thought how strange it was that I knew about such things, such vast and ancient matters, I who had not known anything outside the compound walls till I was six, who had not known the name of the country I lived in till I was eighteen! That was only five years ago, when I was new to the City. Someone had spoken of "Voe Deo," and I had asked, "Where is that?" They had all stared at me. A woman, a hard-voiced old City rentswoman, had said, "Here, Dusty. Right here's Voe Deo. Your country and mine!''

I told Esdardon Aya that. He did not laugh. "A country, a people," he said. "Those are strange and very difficult ideas."

"My country was slavery," I said, and he nodded.

By now I seldom saw Ahas. I missed his kind friendship, but it had all turned to scolding. "You're puffed up, publishing, talking to audiences all the time," he said, "you're putting yourself before our cause."

I said, "But I talk to people in the Hame, I write about things we need to know—everything I do is for freedom."

"The Community is not pleased with that pamphlet of yours," he said, in a serious counseling way, as if telling me a secret I needed to know. "I've been asked to tell you to submit your writings to the committee before you publish again. That press is run by hot-heads. The Hame is causing a good deal of trouble to our candidates."

"Our candidates!" I said in a rage. "No owner is my candidate! Are you still taking orders from the Young Owner?"

That stung him. He said, "If you put yourself first, if you won't cooperate, you bring danger on us all."

"I don't put myself first—politicians and capitalists do that. I put freedom first. Why can't you cooperate with me? It goes two ways, Ahas!"

He left angry, and left me angry.

I think he missed my dependence on him. Perhaps he was jealous, too, of my independence, for he did remain Lord Erod's man. His was a loyal heart. Our disagreement gave us both much bitter pain. I wish I knew what became of him in the troubled times that followed.

There was truth in his accusation. I had found that I had the gift in speaking and writing of moving people's minds and hearts. Nobody told me that such a gift is as dangerous as it is strong. Ahas said I was putting myself first, but I knew I was not doing that. I was wholly in the service of the truth and of liberty. No one told me that the end cannot purify the means, since only the Lord Kamye knows what the end may be. My grandmother could have told me that. The *Arkamye* would have reminded me of it, but I did not often read in it, and in the City there were no old men singing the word, evenings. If there had been I would not have heard them over the sound of my beautiful voice speaking the beautiful truth.

I believe I did no harm, except as we all did, in bringing it to the attention of the rulers of Voe Deo that the Hame was growing bolder and the Radical Party was growing stronger, and that they must move against us.

The first sign was a divisive one. In the open compounds, as well as the men's side and the women's side there were several apartments for couples. This was a radical thing. Any kind of marriage between assets was illegal. They were not allowed to live in pairs. Assets' only legitimate loyalty was to their owner. The child did not belong to the mother, but to the owner. But since gareots were living in the same place as owned assets, these apartments for couples had been tolerated or ignored. Now suddenly the law was invoked, asset couples were arrested, fined if they were wage-earners, separated, and sent to company-run compound houses. Ress and the other elderwomen who ran our house were fined and warned that if "immoral arrangements" were discovered again, they would be held responsible and sent to the labor camps. Two little children of one of the couples were not on the government's list and so were left, abandoned, when their parents were taken off. Keo and Ramayo took them in. They became wards of the women's side, as orphans in the compounds always did.

There were fierce debates about this in meetings of the Hame and The Community. Some said the right of assets to live together and to bring up their children was a cause the Radical Party should support. It was not directly threatening to ownership, and might appeal to the natural instincts of many owners, especially the women, who could not vote but who were valuable allies. Others said that private affections must be overridden by loyalty to the cause of liberty, and that any personal issue must take second place to the great issue of emancipation. Lord Erod spoke thus at a meeting. I rose to answer him. I said that there was no freedom without sexual freedom, and that until women were allowed and men willing to take responsibility for their children, no woman, whether owner or asset, would be free.

"Men must bear the responsibility for the public side of life, the greater world the child will enter; women, for the domestic side of life, the moral and physical upbringing of the child. This is a division enjoined by God and Nature," Erod answered.

"Then will emancipation for a woman mean she's free to enter the beza, be locked in on the women's side?"

"Of course not," he began, but I broke in again, fearing his golden tongue—"Then what is freedom for a woman? Is it different from freedom for a man? Or is a free person free?"

The moderator was angrily thumping his staff, but some other asset women took up my question. "When will the Radical Party speak for us?" they said, and one elderwoman cried, "Where are your women, you owners who want to abolish slavery? Why aren't they here? Don't you let them out of the beza?"

The moderator pounded and finally got order restored. I was half triumphant and half dismayed. I saw Erod and also some of the people from the Hame now looking at me as an open troublemaker. And indeed my words had divided us. But were we not already divided?

A group of us women went home talking through the streets, talking aloud. These were my streets now, with their traffic and lights and dangers and life.

I was a City woman, a free woman. That night I was an owner. I owned the City. I owned the future.

The arguments went on. I was asked to speak at many places. As I was leaving one such meeting, the Hainishman Esdardon Aya came to me and said in a casual way, as if discussing my speech, "Rakam, you're in danger of arrest."

I did not understand. He walked along beside me away from the others and went on: "A rumor has come to my attention at the Embassy. . . . The government of Voe Deo is about to change the status of manumitted assets. You're no longer to be considered gareots. You must have an owner-sponsor."

This was bad news, but after thinking it over I said, "I think I can find an owner to sponsor me. Lord Boeba, maybe."

"The owner-sponsor will have to be approved by the government. . . . This will tend to weaken The Community both through the asset and the owner members. It's very clever, in its way," said Esdardon Aya.

"What happens to us if we don't find an approved sponsor?"

"You'll be considered runaways."

That meant death, the labor camps, or auction.

"O Lord Kamye," I said, and took Esdardon Aya's arm, because a curtain of dark had fallen across my eyes.

We had walked some way along the street. When I could see again I saw the street, the high houses of the City, the shining lights I had thought were mine.

"I have some friends," said the Hainishman, walking on with me, "who are planning a trip to the Kingdom of Bambur."

After a while I said, "What would I do there?"

"A ship to Yeowe leaves from there."

"To Yeowe," I said.

"So I hear," he said, as if he were talking about a streetcar line. "In a few years, I expect Voe Deo will begin offering rides to Yeowe. Exporting intractables, troublemakers, members of the Hame. But that will involve recognizing Yeowe as a nation state, which they haven't brought themselves to do yet. They are, however, permitting some semi-legitimate trade arrangements by their client states. . . . A couple of years ago, the King of Bambur bought one of the old Corporation ships, a genuine old Colony Trader. The king thought he'd like to visit the moons of Werel. But he found the moons boring. So he rented the ship to a consortium of scholars from the University of Bambur and businessmen from his capital. Some manufacturers in Bambur carry on a little trade with Yeowe in it, and some scientists at the university make scientific expeditions in it at the same time. Of course each trip is very expensive, so they carry as many scientists as they can whenever they go."

I heard all this not hearing it, yet understanding it.

"So far," he said, "they've gotten away with it."

He always sounded quiet, a little amused, yet not superior.

"Does The Community know about this ship?" I asked.

"Some members do, I believe. And people in the Hame. But it's very dangerous to know about. If Voe Deo were to find out that a client state was exporting valuable property. . . . In fact, we believe they may have some suspicions. So this is a decision that can't be made lightly. It is both dangerous and irrevocable. Because of that danger, I hesitated to speak of it to you. I hesitated so long that you must make it very quickly. In fact, tonight, Rakam."

I looked from the lights of the City up to the sky they hid. "I'll go," I said. I thought of Walsu.

"Good," he said. At the next corner he changed the direction we had been walking, away from my house, toward the Embassy of the Ekumen.

I never wondered why he did this for me. He was a secret man, a man of secret power, but he always spoke truth, and I think he followed his own heart when he could.

As we entered the Embassy grounds, a great park softly illuminated in the winter night by groundlights, I stopped. "My books," I said. He looked his question. "I wanted to take my books to Yeowe," I said. Now my voice shook with a rush of tears, as if everything I was leaving came down to that one thing. "They need books on Yeowe, I think," I said.

After a moment he said, "I'll have them sent on our next ship. I wish I could put you on that ship," he added in a lower voice. "But of course the Ekumen can't give free rides to runaway slaves. . . ."

I turned and took his hand and laid my forehead against it for a moment, the only time in my life I ever did that of my own free will.

He was startled. "Come, come," he said, and hurried me along.

The Embassy hired Werelian guards, mostly veots, men of the old warrior caste. One of them, a grave, courteous, very silent man, went with me on the flyer to Bambur, the island kingdom east of the Great Continent. He had all the papers I needed. From the flyer port he took me to the Royal Space Observatory, which the king had built for his space ship. There without delay I was taken to the ship, which stood in its great scaffolding ready to depart.

I imagine that they had made comfortable apartments up front for the king when he went to see the moons. The body of the ship, which had belonged to the Agricultural Plantation Corporation, still consisted of great compartments for the produce of the Colony. It would be bringing back grain from Yeowe in four of the cargo bays, that now held farm machinery made in Bambur. The fifth compartment held assets.

The cargo bay had no seats. They had laid felt pads on the floor, and we lay down and were strapped to stanchions, as cargo would have been. There were about fifty "scientists." I was the last to come aboard and be strapped in. The crew were hasty and nervous and spoke only the language of Bambur. I could not understand the instructions we were given. I needed very badly to relieve my bladder, but they had shouted "No time, no time!" So I lay in torment while they closed the great doors of the bay, which made me think of the doors of Shomeke compound. Around me people called out to one another in their language. A baby screamed. I knew that language. Then the great noise began, beneath us. Slowly I felt my body pressed down on the floor, as if a huge soft foot was stepping on me, till my shoulderblades felt as if they were cutting into the mat, and my tongue pressed back into my throat as if to choke me, and with a sharp stab of pain and hot relief my bladder released its urine.

Then we began to be weightless—to float in our bonds. Up was down and down was up, either was both or neither. I heard people all around me calling out again, saying one another's names, saying what must be, "Are you all right? Yes, I'm all right." The baby had never ceased its fierce, piercing yells. I began to feel at my restraints, for I saw the woman next to me sitting up and rubbing her arms and chest where the straps had held her. But a great blurry voice came bellowing over the loudspeaker, giving orders in the language of Bambur and then in Voe Dean: "Do not unfasten the straps! Do not attempt to move about! The ship is under attack! The situation is extremely dangerous!"

So I lay floating in my little mist of urine, listening to the strangers around me talk, understanding nothing. I was utterly miserable, and yet fearless as I had never been. I was carefree. It was like dying. It would be foolish to worry about anything while one died.

The ship moved strangely, shuddering, seeming to turn. Several people were sick. The air filled with the smell and tiny droplets of vomit. I freed my hands enough to draw the scarf I was wearing up over my face as a filter, tucking the ends under my head to hold it.

Inside the scarf I could no longer see the huge vault of the cargo bay stretching above or below me, making me feel I was about to fly or fall into it. It smelled of myself, which was comforting. It was the scarf I often wore when I dressed up to give a talk, fine gauze, pale red with a silver thread woven in at intervals. When I bought it at a City market, paying my own earned money for it, I had thought of my mother's red scarf, given her by Lady Tazeu. I thought she would have liked this one, though it was not as bright. Now I lay and looked into the pale red dimness it made of the vault, starred with the lights at the hatches, and thought of my mother, Yowa. She had probably been killed that morning in the compound. Perhaps she had been carried to another estate as a use-woman, but Ahas had never found any trace of her. I thought of the way she had of carrying her head a little to the side, deferent yet alert, gracious. Her eyes had been full and bright, "eyes that hold the seven moons," as the song says. I thought then: But I will never see the moons again.

At that I felt so strange that to comfort myself and distract my mind I began to sing under my breath, there alone in my tent of red gauze warm with my own breath. I sang the freedom songs we sang in the Hame, and then I sang the love songs Lady Tazeu had taught me. Finally I sang "O, O, Yeowe," softly at first, then a little louder. I heard a voice somewhere out in that soft red mist world join in with me, a man's voice, then a woman's. Assets from Voe Deo all know that song. We sang it together. A Bambur man's voice picked it up and put words in his own language to it, and others joined in singing it. Then the singing died away. The baby's crying was weak now. The air was very foul.

We learned many hours later, when at last clear air entered the vents and we were told we could release our bonds, that a ship of the Voe Dean Space Defense Fleet had intercepted the freighter's course just above the atmosphere and ordered it to stop. The captain chose to ignore the signal. The warship had fired, and though nothing hit the freighter the blast had damaged the controls. The freighter had gone on, and had seen and heard nothing more of the warship. We were now about eleven days from Yeowe. The warship, or a group of them, might be in wait for us near Yeowe. The reason they gave for ordering the freighter to halt was "suspected contraband merchandise."

That fleet of warships had been built centuries ago to protect Werel from the attacks they expected from the Alien Empire, which is what they then called the Ekumen. They were so frightened by that imagined threat that they put all their energy into the technology of space flight; and the colonization of Yeowe was a result. After four hundred years without any threat of attack, Voe Deo had finally let the Ekumen send envoys and ambassadors. They had used the Defense Fleet to transport troops and weapons during the War of Liberation. Now they were using them the way estate owners used hunting dogs and hunting cats, to hunt down runaway slaves.

I found the two other Voe Deans in the cargo bay, and we moved our "bedstraps" together so we could talk. Both of them had been brought to Bambur by the Hame, who had paid their fare. It had not occurred to me that there was a fare to be paid. I knew who had paid mine.

"Can't fly a space ship on love," the woman said. She was a strange person. She really was a scientist. Highly trained in chemistry by the company that rented her, she had persuaded the Hame to send her to Yeowe because she was sure her skills would be needed and in demand. She had been making higher wages than many gareots did, but she expected to do still better on Yeowe. "I'm going to be rich," she said.

The man, only a boy, a mill hand in a Northern city, had simply run away and had had the luck to meet people who could save him from death or the labor camps. He was sixteen, ignorant, noisy, rebellious, sweet-natured. He became a general favorite, like a puppy. I was in demand because I knew the history of Yeowe and through a man who knew both our languages I could tell the Bamburs something about where they were going—the centuries of Corporation slavery, Nadami, the War, the Liberation. Some of them were rentspeople from the cities, others were a group of estate slaves bought at auction by the Hame with false money and under a false name, and hurried onto this flight. None of them knew where they were going. It was that trick that had drawn Voe Deo's attention to this flight.

Yoke, the mill boy, speculated endlessly about how the Yeowans would welcome us. He had a story, half a joke half a dream, about the bands playing and the speeches and the big dinner they would have for us. The dinner grew more and more elaborate as the days went on. They were long, hungry days, floating in the featureless great space of the cargo bay, marked only by the alternation every twelve hours of brighter and dimmer lighting and the issuing of two meals during the "day," food and water in tubes you squeezed into your mouth. I did not think much about what might happen. I was between happenings. If the warships found us we would probably die. If we got to Yeowe it would be a new life. Now we were floating.

4. Yeowe

The ship came down safe at the Port of Yeowe. They unloaded the crates of machinery first, then the other cargo. We came out staggering and holding on to one another, not able to stand up to the great pull of this new world drawing us down to its center, blinded by the light of the sun that we were closer to than we had ever been.

"Over here! Over here!" a man shouted. I was grateful to hear my language, but the Bamburs looked apprehensive.

Over here—in here—strip—wait— All we heard when we were first on the Free World was orders. We had to be decontaminated, which was painful and exhausting. We had to be examined by doctors. Anything we had brought with us had to be decontaminated and examined and listed. That did not take long for me. I had brought the clothes I wore and had worn for two weeks now. I was glad to get decontaminated. Finally we were told to stand in line in one of the big empty cargo sheds. The sign over the doors still read APCY—Agricultural Plantation Corporation of Yeowe. One by one we were processed for entry. The man who processed me was short, white, middle-aged, with spectacles, like any clerk asset in the City, but I looked at him with reverence. He was the first Yeowan I had spoken to. He asked me questions from a form and wrote down my answers. "Can you read?"— "Yes."—"Skills?"—I stammered a moment and said, "Teaching—I can teach reading and history." He never looked up at me.

I was glad to be patient. After all, the Yeowans had not asked us to come. We were admitted only because they knew if they sent us back we would die horribly in a public execution. We were a profitable cargo to Bambur, but to Yeowe we were a problem. But many of us had skills they must need, and I was glad they asked us about them.

When we had all been processed, we were separated into two groups: men and women. Yoke hugged me and went off to the men's side laughing and waving. I stood with the women. We watched all the men led off to the shuttle that went to the Old Capital. Now my patience failed and my hope darkened. I prayed, "Lord Kamye, not here, not here too!" Fear made me angry. When a man came giving us orders again, come on, this way, I went up to him and said, "Who are you? Where are we going? We are free women!"

He was a big fellow with a round, white face and bluish eyes. He looked down at me, huffy at first, then smiling. "Yes, Little Sister, you're free," he said. "But we've all got to work, don't we? You ladies are going south. They need people on the rice plantations. You do a little work, make a little money, look around a little, all right? If you don't like it down there, come on back. We can always use more pretty little ladies round here."

I had never heard the Yeowan country accent, a singing, blurry softening, with long, clear vowels. I had never heard asset women called ladies. No one had ever called me Little Sister. He did not mean the word "use" as I took it, surely. He meant well. I was bewildered and said no more. But the chemist, Tualtak, said, "Listen, I'm no field hand, I'm a trained scientist—"

"Oh, you're all scientists," the Yeowan said with his big smile. "Come on now, ladies!" He strode ahead, and we followed. Tualtak kept talking. He smiled and paid no heed.

We were taken to a train car waiting on a siding. The huge, bright sun was setting. All the sky was orange and pink, full of light. Long shadows ran black along the ground. The warm air was dusty and sweet-smelling. While we stood waiting to climb up into the car I stooped and picked up a little reddish stone from the ground. It was round, with a tiny stripe of white clear through it. It was a piece of Yeowe. I held Yeowe in my hand. That little stone, too, I still have.

Our car was shunted along to the main yards and hooked onto a train. When the train started we were served dinner, soup from great kettles wheeled through the car, bowls of sweet, heavy marsh rice, pini fruit—a luxury on Werel, here a commonplace. We ate and ate. I watched the last light die away from the long, rolling hills that the train was passing through. The stars came out. No moons. Never again. But I saw Werel rising in the east. It was a great blue-green star, looking as Yeowe looks from Werel. But you would never see Yeowe rising after sunset. Yeowe followed the sun.

I'm alive and I'm here, I thought. I'm following the sun. I let the rest go, and fell asleep to the swaying of the train.

We were taken off the train on the second day at a town on the great river Yot. Our group of twenty-three were separated there, and ten of us were taken by ox cart to a village, Hagayot. It had been an APCY compound, growing marsh rice to feed the Colony slaves. Now it was a cooperative village, growing marsh rice to feed the Free People. We were enrolled as members of the cooperative. We lived share and share alike with the villagers until pay-out, when we could pay them back what we owed the cooperative.

It was a reasonable way to handle immigrants without money, who did not know the language, or who had no skills. But I did not understand why they had ignored our skills. Why had they sent the men from Bambur plantations, field hands, into the city, not here? Why only women?

I did not understand why, in a village of free people, there was a men's side and a women's side, with a ditch between them.

I did not understand why, as I soon discovered, the men made all the decisions and gave all the orders. But, it being so, I did understand that they were afraid of us Werelian women, who were not used to taking orders from our equals. And I understood that I must take orders and not even look as if I thought of questioning them. The men of Hagayot Village watched us with fierce suspicion and a whip as ready as any Boss's. "Maybe you told men what to do back over there," the foreman told us the first morning in the fields. "Well, that's back over there. That's not here. Here we free people work together. You think you're Bosswomen. There aren't any Bosswomen here."

There were grandmothers on the women's side, but they were not the powers our grandmothers had been. Here, where for the first century there had been no slave women at all, the men had had to make their own life, set up their own powers. When women slaves at last were sent into those little slave-kingdoms of men, there was no power for them at all. They had no voice. Not till they got away to the cities did they ever have a voice on Yeowe.

I learned silence.

But it was not as bad for me and Tualtak as for our eight Bambur companions. We were the first immigrants any of these villagers had ever seen. They knew only one language. They thought the Bambur women were witches because they did not talk "like human beings." They whipped them for talking to each other in their own language.

I will confess that in my first year on the Free World my heart was as low as it had been at Zeskra. I hated standing all day in the shallow water of the rice paddies. Our feet were always sodden and swollen and full of tiny burrowing worms we had to pick out every night. But it was needed work and not too hard for a healthy woman. It was not the work that bore me down.

Hagayot was not a tribal village, not as conservative as some of the old villages I learned about later. Girls here were not ritually raped, and a woman was safe on the women's side. She "jumped the ditch" only with a man she chose. But if a woman went anywhere alone, or even got separated from the other women working in the paddies, she was supposed to be "asking for it," and any man thought it his right to force himself on her.

I made good friends among the village women and the Bamburs. They were no more ignorant than I had been a few years before, and some were wiser than I would ever be. There was no possibility of having a friend among men who thought themselves our owners. I could not see how life here would ever change. My heart was very low, nights, when I lay among the sleeping women and children in our hut and thought, Is this what Walsu died for?

In my second year there, I resolved to do what I could to keep above the misery that threatened me. One of the Bambur women, meek and slow of understanding, whipped and beaten by both women and men for speaking her language, had drowned in one of the great rice paddies. She had lain down there in the warm shallow water not much deeper than her ankles, and had drowned. I feared that yielding, that water of despair. I made up my mind to use my skill, to teach the village women and children to read.

I wrote out some little primers on rice cloth and made a game of it for the little children, first. Some of the older girls and women were curious. Some of them knew that people in the towns and cities could read. They saw it as a mystery, a witchcraft that gave the city people their great power. I did not deny this.

For the women, I first wrote down verses and passages of the *Arkamye*, all I could remember, so that they could have it and not have to wait for one of the men who called themselves "priests" to recite it. They were proud of learning to read these verses. Then I had my friend Seugi tell me a story, her own recollection of meeting a wild hunting cat in the marshes as a child. I wrote it down, entitling it "The Marsh Lion, by Aro Seugi," and read it aloud to the author and a circle of girls and women. They marveled and laughed. Seugi wept, touching the writing that held her voice.

The chief of the village and his headmen and foremen and honorary sons, all the hierarchy and government of the village, were suspicious and not pleased by my teaching, yet did not want to forbid me. The government of Yotebber Region had sent word that they were establishing country schools, where village children were to be sent for half the year. The village men knew that their sons would be advantaged if they could already read and write when they went there.

The Chosen Son, a big, mild, pale man, blind in one eye from a war wound, came to me at last. He wore his coat of office, a tight, long coat such as Werelian owners had worn three hundred years ago. He told me that I should not teach girls to read, only boys.

I told him I would teach all the children who wanted to learn, or none of them.

"Girls do not want to learn this," he said.

"They do. Fourteen girls have asked to be in my class. Eight boys. Do you say girls do not need religious training, Chosen Son?"

This gave him pause. "They should learn the life of the Merciful Lady," he said.

"I will write the Life of Tual for them," I said at once. He walked away, saving his dignity.

I had little pleasure in my victory, such as it was. At least I went on teaching.

Tualtak was always at me to run away, run away to the city downriver. She had grown very thin, for she could not digest the heavy food. She hated the work and the people. "It's all right for you, you were a plantation pup, a dusty, but I never was, my mother was a rentswoman, we lived in fine rooms on Haba Street, I was the brightest trainee they ever had in the laboratory," and on and on, over and over, living in the world she had lost.

Sometimes I listened to her talk about running away. I tried to remember the maps of Yeowe in my lost books. I remembered the great river, the Yot, running from far inland three thousand kilos to the South Sea. But where were we on its vast length, how far from Yotebber City on its delta? Between Hagayot and the city might be a hundred villages like this one. "Have you been raped?" I asked Tualtak.

She took offense. "I'm a rentswoman, not a use-woman," she snapped.

I said, "I was a use-woman for two years. If I was raped again I would kill the man or kill myself. I think two Werelian women walking alone here would be raped. I can't do it, Tualtak."

"It can't all be like this place!" she cried, so desperate that I felt my own throat close up with tears.

"Maybe when they open the schools—there will be people from the cities then—" It was all I had to offer her, or myself, as hope. "Maybe if the harvest's good this year, if we can get our money, we can get on the train. . . ."

That indeed was our best hope. The problem was to get our money from the chief and his cohorts. They kept the cooperative's income in a stone hut that they called the Bank of Hagayot, and only they ever saw the money.

Each individual had an account, and they kept tally faithfully, the old Banker Headman scratching your account out in the dirt if you asked for it. But women and children could not withdraw money from their account. All we could get was a kind of scrip, clay pieces marked by the Banker Headman, good to buy things from one another, things people in the village made, clothes, sandals, tools, bead necklaces, rice beer. Our real money was safe, we were told, in the bank. I thought of that old lame bondsman at Shomeke, jigging and singing, "Money in the bank, Lord! Money in the bank!"

Before we ever came, the women had resented this system. Now there were nine more women resenting it.

One night I asked my friend Seugi, whose hair was as white as her skin, "Seugi, do you know what happened at a place called Nadami?"

"Yes," she said. "The women opened the door. All the women rose up and then the men rose up against the Bosses. But they needed weapons. And a woman ran in the night and stole the key from the owner's box and opened the door of the strong place where the Bosses kept their guns and bullets, and she held it open with the strength of her body, so that the slaves could arm themselves. And they killed the Corporations and made that place, Nadami, free."

"Even on Werel they tell that story," I said. "Even there women tell about Nadami, where the women began the Liberation. Men tell it too. Do men here tell it? Do they know it?"

Seugi and the other women nodded.

"If a woman freed the men of Nadami," I said, "maybe the women of Hagayot can free their money."

Seugi laughed. She called out to a group of grandmothers, "Listen to Rakam! Listen to this!"

After plenty of talk for days and weeks, it ended in a delegation of women, thirty of us. We crossed the ditch bridge onto the men's side and ceremoniously asked to see the chief. Our principal bargaining counter was shame. Seugi and other village women did the speaking, for they knew how far they could shame the men without goading them into anger and retaliation. Listening to them, I heard dignity speak to dignity, pride speak to pride. For the first time since I came to Yeowe I felt I was one of these people, that this pride and dignity were mine.

Nothing happens fast in a village. But by the next harvest, the women of Hagayot could draw their own earned share out of the bank in cash.

"Now for the vote," I said to Seugi, for there was no secret ballot in the village. When there was a regional election, even in the worldwide Ratification of the Constitution, the chiefs polled the men and filled out the ballots. They did not even poll the women. They wrote in the votes they wanted cast.

But I did not stay to help bring about that change at Hagayot. Tualtak was really ill, and half crazy with her longing to get out of the marshes, to the city. And I too longed for that. So we took our wages, and Seugi and other women drove us in an ox cart on the causeway across the marshes to the freight station. There we raised the flag that signaled the next train to stop for passengers.

It came along in a few hours, a long train of boxcars loaded with marsh rice, heading for the mills of Yotebber City. We rode in the crew car with the train crew and a few other passengers, village men. I had a big knife in my belt, but none of the men showed us any disrespect. Away from their compounds they were timid and shy. I sat up in my bunk in that car watching the great, wild, plumy marshes whirl by, and the villages on the banks of the wide river, and wished the train would go on forever.

But Tualtak lay in the bunk below me, coughing and fretful. When we got to Yotebber City she was so weak I knew I had to get her to a doctor. A man from the train crew was kind, telling us how to get to the hospital on the public cars. As we rattled through the hot, crowded city streets in the crowded car, I was still happy. I could not help it.

At the hospital they demanded our citizens' registration papers.

I had never heard of such papers. Later I found that ours had been given to the chiefs at Hagayot, who had kept them, as they kept all "their" women's papers. At the time, all I could do was stare and say, "I don't know anything about registration papers."

I heard one of the women at the desk say to the other, "Lord, how dusty can you get?"

I knew what we looked like. I knew we looked dirty and low. I knew I seemed ignorant and stupid. But when I heard that word "dusty" my pride and dignity woke up again. I put my hand into my pack and brought out my freedom paper, that old paper with Erod's writing on it, all crumpled and folded, all dusty.

"This is my Citizen's Registration paper," I said in a loud voice, making those women jump and turn. "My mother's blood and my grandmother's blood is on it. My friend here is sick. She needs a doctor. Now bring us to a doctor!"

A thin little woman came forward from the corridor. "Come on this way," she said. One of the deskwomen started to protest. This little woman give her a look.

We followed her to an examination room.

"I'm Dr. Yeron," she said, then corrected herself. "I'm serving as a nurse," she said. "But I am a doctor. And you—you come from the Old World? from Werel? Sit down there, now, child, take off your shirt. How long have you been here?"

Within a quarter of an hour she had diagnosed Tualtak and got her a bed in a ward for rest and observation, found out our histories, and sent me off with a note to a friend of hers who would help me find a place to live and a job.

"Teaching!" Dr. Yeron said. "A teacher! Oh, woman, you are rain to the dry land!"

Indeed the first school I talked to wanted to hire me at once, to teach anything I wanted. Because I come of a capitalist people, I went to other schools to see if I could make more money at them. But I came back to the first one. I liked the people there.

Before the War of Liberation, the cities of Yeowe, which were cities of Corporation-owned assets who rented their own freedom, had had their own schools and hospitals and many kinds of training programs. There was even a University for assets in the Old Capital. The Corporations, of course, had controlled all the information that came to such institutions, and watched and censored all teaching and writing, keeping everything aimed toward the maximization of their profits. But within that narrow frame the assets had been free to use the information they had as they pleased, and city Yeowans had valued education deeply. During the long war, thirty years, all that system of gathering and teaching knowledge had broken down. A whole generation grew up learning nothing but fighting and hiding, famine and disease. The head of my school said to me, "Our children grew up illiterate, ignorant. Is it any wonder the plantation chiefs just took over where the Corporation Bosses left off? Who was to stop them?"

These men and women believed with a fierce passion that only education would lead to freedom. They were still fighting the War of Liberation.

Yotebber City was a big, poor, sunny, sprawling city with wide streets, low buildings, and huge old shady trees. The traffic was mostly afoot, with cycles tinging and public cars clanging along among the slow crowds. There were miles of shacks and shanties down in the old floodplain of the river behind the levees, where the soil was rich for gardening. The center of the city was on a low rise, the mills and train yards spreading out from it. Downtown it looked like the City of Voe Deo, only older and poorer and gentler. Instead of big stores for owners, people bought and sold everything from stalls in open markets. The air was soft, here in the south, a warm, soft sea air full of mist and sunlight. I stayed happy. I have by the grace of the Lord a mind that can leave misfortune behind, and I was happy in Yotebber City.

Tualtak recovered her health and found a good job as a chemist in a factory. I saw her seldom, as our friendship had been a matter of necessity, not choice. Whenever I saw her she talked about Haba Street and the laboratory on Werel, and complained about her work and the people here.

Dr. Yeron did not forget me. She wrote a note and told me to come visit her, which I did. Presently, when I was settled, she asked me to come with her to a meeting of an educational society. This, I found, was a group of democrats, mostly teachers, who sought to work against the autocratic power of the tribal and regional Chiefs under the new Constitution, and to counteract what they called the slave mind, the rigid, misogynistic hierarchy that I had encountered in Hagayot. My experience was useful to them, for they were all city people who had met the slave mind only when they found themselves governed by it. The women of the group were the angriest. They had lost the most at Liberation, and now had less to lose. In general the men were gradualists, the women ready for revolution. As a Werelian, ignorant of politics on Yeowe, I listened and did not talk. It was hard for me not to talk. I am a talker, and sometimes I had plenty to say. But I held my tongue and heard them. They were people worth hearing.

Ignorance defends itself savagely, and illiteracy, as I well knew, can be shrewd. Though the Chief, the President of Yotebber Region, elected by a manipulated ballot, might not understand our counter-manipulations of the school curriculum, he did not waste much energy trying to control the schools. He sent his Inspectors to meddle with our classes and censor our books. But what he saw as important was the fact that, just as the Corporations had, he controlled the net. The news, the information programs, the puppets of the neareals, all danced to his strings. Against that, what harm could a lot of teachers do? Parents who had no schooling had children who entered the net to hear and see and feel what the Chief wanted them to know: that freedom is obedience to leaders, that virtue is violence, that manhood is domination. Against the enactment of such truths in daily life and in the heightened sensational experience of the neareals, what good were words?

"Literacy is irrelevant," one of our group said sorrowfully. "The Chiefs have jumped right over our heads into the postliterate information technology."

I brooded over that, hating her fancy words, irrelevant, postliterate, because I was afraid she was right.

To the next meeting of our group, to my surprise, an Alien came: the Sub-Envoy of the Ekumen. He was supposed to be a great feather in our Chief's cap, sent down from the Old Capital apparently to support the Chief's stand against the World Party, which was still strong down here and still clamoring that Yeowe should keep out all foreigners. I had heard vaguely that such a person was here, but I had not expected to meet him at a gathering of subversive school teachers.

He was a short man, red-brown, with white corners to his eyes, but handsome if one could ignore that. He sat in the seat in front of me. He sat perfectly still, as if accustomed to sitting still, and listened without speaking as if accustomed to listening. At the end of the meeting he turned around and his queer eyes looked straight at me.

"Radosse Rakam?" he said.

I nodded, dumb.

"I'm Yehedarhed Havzhiva," he said, "I have some books for you from old music."

I stared. I said, "Books?"

"From old music," he said again. "Esdardon Aya, on Werel."

"My books?" I said.

He smiled. He had a broad, quick smile.

"Oh, where?" I cried.

"They're at my house. We can get them tonight, if you like. I have a car." There was something ironic and light in how he said that, as if he was a man who did not expect to have a car, though he might enjoy it.

Dr. Yeron came over. "So you found her," she said to the Sub-Envoy. He looked at her with such a bright face that I thought, these two are lovers. Though she was much older than he there was nothing unlikely in the thought. Dr. Yeron was a magnetic woman. It was odd to me to think it, though, for my mind was not given to speculating about people's sexual affairs. That was no interest of mine.

He put his hand on her arm as they talked, and I saw with peculiar intensity how gentle his touch was, almost hesitant, yet trustful. That is love, I thought. Yet they parted, I saw, without that look of private understanding that lovers often give each other.

He and I rode in his government electric car, his two silent bodyguards, policewomen, sitting in the front seat. We spoke of Esdardon Aya, whose name, he explained to me, meant Old Music. I told him how Esdardon Aya had saved my life by sending me here. He listened in a way that made it easy to talk to him. I said, "I was sick to leave my books, and I've thought about them, missing them, as if they were my family. But I think maybe I'm a fool to feel that way."

"Why a fool?" he asked. He had a foreign accent, but he had the Yeowan lilt already, and his voice was beautiful, low and warm.

I tried to explain everything at once: "Well, they mean so much to me because I was illiterate when I came to the City, and it was the books that gave me freedom, gave me the world—the worlds— But now, here, I see how the net, the holos, the neareals mean so much more to people, giving them the present time. Maybe it's just clinging to the past to cling to books. Yeowans have to go toward the future. And we'll never change people's minds just with words."

He listened intently, as he had done at the meeting, and then answered slowly, "But words are an essential way of thinking. And books keep the words true. . . . I didn't read till I was an adult, either."

"You didn't?"

"I knew how, but I didn't. I lived in a village. It's cities that have to have books," he said, quite decisively, as if he had thought about this matter. "If they don't, we keep on starting over every generation. It's a waste. You have to save the words."

When we got to his house, up at the top end of the old part of town, there were four crates of books in the entrance hall.

"These aren't all mine!" I said.

"Old Music said they were yours," Mr. Yehedarhed said, with his quick smile and quick glance at me. You can tell where an Alien is looking much better than you can tell with us. With us, except for a few people with bluish eyes, you have to be close enough to see the dark pupil move in the dark eye.

"I haven't got anywhere to put so many," I said, amazed, realizing how that strange man, Old Music, had helped me to freedom yet again.

"At your school, maybe? The school library?"

It was a good idea, but I thought at once of the Chief's inspectors pawing through them, perhaps confiscating them. When I spoke of that, the Sub-Envoy said, "What if I present them as gift from the Embassy? I think that might embarrass the inspectors."

"Oh," I said, and burst out, "Why are you so kind? You, and he— Are you Hainish too?"

"Yes," he said, not answering my other question. "I was. I hope to be Yeowan."

He asked me to sit down and drink a little glass of wine with him before his guard drove me home. He was easy and friendly, but a quiet man. I saw he had been hurt. There were newly healed scars on his face, and his hair was half grown out where he had had a head injury. He asked me what my books were, and I said, "History."

At that he smiled, slowly this time. He said nothing, but he raised his glass to me. I raised mine, imitating him, and we drank.

Next day he had the books delivered to our school. When we opened and shelved them, we realized we had a great treasure. "There's nothing like this at the University," said one of the teachers, who had studied there for a year.

There were histories and anthropologies of Werel and of the worlds of the Ekumen, works of philosophy and politics by Werelians and by people of other worlds, there were compendiums of literature, poetry, and stories, encyclopedias, books of science, atlases, dictionaries. In a corner of one of the crates were my own few books, my own treasure, even that first little crude "History of Yeowe, Printed at Yeowe University in the Year One of

Liberty.'' Most of my books I left in the library, but I took that one and a few others home for love, for comfort.

I had found another love and comfort not long since. A child at school had brought me a present, a spotted-cat kitten, just weaned. The boy gave it to me with such loving pride that I could not refuse it. When I tried to pass it on to another teacher they all laughed at me. "You're elected, Rakam!" they said. So unwillingly I took the little being home, afraid of its frailty and delicacy and near to feeling a disgust for it. Women in the beza at Zeskra had had pets, spotted cats and foxdogs, spoiled little animals fed better than we were. I had been called by the name of a pet animal once.

I alarmed the kitten taking it out of its basket, and it bit my thumb to the bone. It was tiny and frail but it had teeth. I began to have some respect for it.

That night I put it to sleep in its basket, but it climbed up on my bed and sat on my face until I let it under the covers. There it slept perfectly still all night. In the morning it woke me by dancing on me, chasing dustmotes in a sunbeam. It made me laugh, waking, which is a pleasant thing. I felt that I had never laughed very much, and wanted to.

The kitten was all black, its spots showing only in certain lights, black on black. I called it Owner. I found it pleasant to come home evenings to be greeted by my little Owner.

Now for the next half year we were planning the great demonstration of women. There were many meetings, at some of which I met the Sub-Envoy again, so that I began to look for him. I liked to watch him listen to our arguments. There were those who argued that the demonstration must not be limited to the wrongs and rights of women, for equality must be for all. Others argued that it should not depend in any way on the support of foreigners, but should be a purely Yeowan movement. Mr. Yehedarhed listened to them, but I got angry. "I'm a foreigner," I said. "Does that make me no use to you? That's owner talk—as if you were better than other people!" And Dr. Yeron said, "I will believe equality is for all when I see it written in the Constitution of Yeowe." For our Constitution, ratified by a world vote during the time I was at Hagayot, spoke of citizens only as men. That is finally what the demonstration became, a demand that the Constitution be amended to include women as citizens, provide for the secret ballot, and guarantee the right to free speech, freedom of the press and of assembly, and free education for all children.

I lay down on the train tracks along with seventy thousand women, that hot day. I sang with them. I heard what that sounds like, so many women singing together, what a big, deep sound it makes.

I had begun to speak in public again when we were gathering women for the great demonstration. It was a gift I had, and we made use of it. Sometimes gang boys or ignorant men would come to heckle and threaten me, shouting, "Bosswoman, Ownerwoman, black cunt, go back where you came from!" Once when they were yelling that, go back, go back, I leaned into the microphone and said, "I can't go back. We used to sing a song on the plantation where I was a slave," and I sang it,

> *O, O, Ye-o-we,*
> *Nobody never comes back.*

The singing made them be still for a moment. They heard it, that awful grief, that yearning.

After the great demonstration the unrest never died down, but there were times that the energy flagged, the Movement didn't move, as Dr. Yeron said. During one of those times I went to her and proposed that we set up a printing house and publish books. This had been a dream of mine, growing from that day in Hagayot when Seugi had touched her words and wept.

"Talk goes by," I said, "and all the words and images in the net go by, and anybody can change them, but books are there. They last. They are the body of history, Mr. Yehedarhed says."

"Inspectors," said Dr. Yeron. "Until we get the free press amendment, the Chiefs aren't going to let anybody print anything they didn't dictate themselves."

I did not want to give up the idea. I knew that in Yotebber Region we could not publish anything political, but I argued that we might print stories and poems by women of the region. Others thought it a waste of time. We discussed it back and forth for a long time. Mr. Yehedarhed came back from a trip to the Embassy, up north in the Old Capital. He listened to our discussions, but said nothing, which disappointed me. I had thought that he might support my project.

One day I was walking home from school to my apartment, which was in a big, old, noisy house not far from the levee. I liked the place because my windows opened into the branches of trees, and through the trees I saw the river, four miles wide here, easing along among sand bars and reed beds and willow isles in the dry season, brimming up the levees in the wet season when the rainstorms scudded across it. That day as I came near the house, Mr. Yehedarhed appeared, with two sour-faced policewomen close behind him as usual. He greeted me and asked if we might talk. I was confused and did not know what to do but to invite him up to my room.

His guards waited in the lobby. I had just the one big room on the third floor. I sat on the bed and the Sub-Envoy sat in the chair. Owner went round and round his legs, saying roo? roo?

I had observed often that the Sub-Envoy took pleasure in disappointing the expectations of the Chief and his cohorts, who were all for pomp and fleets of cars and elaborate badges and uniforms. He and his policewomen went all over the city, all over Yotebber, in his government car or on foot. People liked him for it. They knew, as I knew now, that he had been assaulted and beaten and left for dead by a World Party gang his first day here, when he went out afoot alone. The city people liked his courage and the way he talked with everybody, anywhere. They had adopted him. We in the Liberation Movement thought of him as "our Envoy," but he was theirs, and the Chief's too. The Chief may have hated his popularity, but he profited from it.

"You want to start a publishing house," he said, stroking Owner, who fell over with his paws in the air.

"Dr. Yeron says there's no use until we get the Amendments."

"There's one press on Yeowe not directly controlled by the government," Mr. Yehedarhed said, stroking Owner's belly.

"Look out, he'll bite," I said. "Where is that?"

"At the University. I see," Mr. Yehedarhed said, looking at his thumb. I apologized. He asked me if I was certain that Owner was male. I said I had been told so, but never had thought to look. "My impression is that your Owner is a lady," Mr. Yehedarhed said, in such a way that I began to laugh helplessly.

He laughed along with me, sucked the blood off his thumb, and went on. "The University never amounted to much. It was a Corporation ploy—let the assets pretend they're going to college. During the last years of the War it was closed down. Since Liberation Day it's reopened and crawled along with no one taking much notice. The faculty are mostly old. They came back to it after the War. The National Government gives it a subsidy because it sounds well to have a University of Yeowe, but they don't pay it any attention, because it has no prestige. And because many of them are unenlightened men." He said this without scorn, descriptively. "It does have a printing house."

"I know," I said. I reached out for my old book and showed it to him.

He looked through it for a few minutes. His face was curiously tender as he did so. I could not help watching him. It was like watching a woman with a baby, a constant, changing play of attention and response.

"Full of propaganda and errors and hope," he said at last, and his voice too was tender. "Well, I think this could be improved upon. Don't you? All that's needed is an editor. And some authors."

"Inspectors," I warned, imitating Dr. Yeron.

"Academic freedom is an easy issue for the Ekumen to have some influence upon," he said, "because we invite people to attend the Ekumenical Schools on Hain and Ve. We certainly want to invite graduates of the University of Yeowe. But of course, if their education is severely defective because of the lack of books, of information. . . ."

I said, "Mr. Yehedarhed, are you *supposed* to subvert government policies?" The question broke out of me unawares.

He did not laugh. He paused for quite a long time before he answered. "I don't know," he said. "So far the Ambassador has backed me. We may both get reprimanded. Or fired. What I'd like to do . . ." His strange eyes were right on me again. He looked down at the book he still held. "What I'd like is to become a Yeowan citizen," he said. "But my usefulness to Yeowe, and to the Liberation Movement, is my position with the Ekumen. So I'll go on using that, or misusing it, till they tell me to stop."

When he left I had to think about what he had asked me to do. That was to go to the University as a teacher of history, and once there to volunteer for the editorship of the press. That all seemed so preposterous, for a woman of my background and my little learning, that I thought I must be misunderstanding him. When he convinced me that I had understood him, I thought he must have very badly misunderstood who I was and what I was capable of. After we had talked about that for a while, he left, evidently feeling that he was making me uncomfortable, and perhaps feeling uncomfortable himself, though in fact we laughed a good deal and I did not feel uncomfortable, only a little as if I were crazy.

I tried to think about what he had asked me to do, to step so far beyond myself. I found it difficult to think about. It was as if it hung over me, this huge choice I must make, this future I could not imagine. But what I thought about was him, Yehedarhed Havzhiva. I kept seeing him sitting there in my old chair, stooping down to stroke Owner. Sucking blood off his thumb. Laughing. Looking at me with his white-cornered eyes. I saw his red-brown face and red-brown hands, the color of pottery. His quiet voice was in my mind.

I picked up the kitten, half grown now, and looked at its hinder end. There was no sign of any male parts. The little black silky body squirmed in my hands. I thought of him saying, "Your Owner is a lady," and I wanted to laugh again, and to cry. I stroked the kitten and set her down, and she sat sedately beside me, washing her shoulder. "Oh poor little lady," I said. I don't know who I meant. The kitten, or Lady Tazeu, or myself.

He had said to take my time thinking about his proposal, all the time I wanted. But I had not really thought about it at all when, the next day but one, there he was, on foot, waiting for me as I came out of the school. "Would you like to walk on the levee?" he said.

I looked around.

"There they are," he said, indicating his cold-eyed bodyguards. "Everywhere I am, they are, three to five meters away. Walking with me is dull, but safe. My virtue is guaranteed."

We walked down through the streets to the levee and up onto it in the long early evening light, warm and pink-gold, smelling of river and mud and reeds. The two women with guns walked along just about four meters behind us.

"If you do go to the University," he said after a long silence, "I'll be there constantly."

"I haven't yet—" I stammered.

"If you stay here, I'll be here constantly," he said. "That is, if it's all right with you."

I said nothing. He looked at me without turning his head. I said without intending to, "I like it that I can see where you're looking."

"I like it that I can't see where you're looking," he said, looking directly at me.

We walked on. A heron rose up out of a reed islet and its great wings beat over the water, away. We were walking south, downriver. All the western sky was full of light as the sun went down behind the city in smoke and haze.

"Rakam, I would like to know where you came from, what your life on Werel was," he said very softly.

I drew a long breath. "It's all gone," I said. "Past."

"We are our past. Though not only that. I want to know you. Forgive me. I want very much to know you."

After a while I said, "I want to tell you. But it's so bad. It's so ugly. Here, now, it's beautiful. I don't want to lose it."

"Whatever you tell me I will hold valuable," he said, in his quiet voice that went to my heart. So I told him what I could about Shomeke compound, and then hurried on through the rest of my story. Sometimes he asked a question. Mostly he listened. At some time in my telling he had taken my arm, I scarcely noticing at the time. When he let me go, thinking some movement I made meant I wanted to be released, I missed that light touch. His hand was cool. I could feel it on my forearm after it was gone.

"Mr. Yehedarhed," said a voice behind us: one of the bodyguards. The sun was down, the sky flushed with gold and red. "Better head back?"

"Yes," he said, "thanks." As we turned I took his arm. I felt him catch his breath.

I had not desired a man or a woman—this is the truth—since Shomeke. I had loved people, and I had touched them with love, but never with desire. My gate was locked.

Now it was open. Now I was so weak that at the touch of his hand I could scarcely walk on.

I said, "It's a good thing walking with you is so safe."

I hardly knew what I meant. I was thirty years old but I was like a young girl. I had never been that girl.

He said nothing. We walked along in silence between the river and the city in a glory of failing light.

"Will you come home with me, Rakam?" he said.

Now I said nothing.

"They don't come in with us," he said, very low, in my ear, so that I felt his breath.

"Don't make me laugh!" I said, and began crying. I wept all the way back along the levee. I sobbed and thought the sobs were ceasing and then sobbed again. I cried for all my sorrows, all my shames. I cried because they were with me now and were me and always would be. I cried because the gate was open and I could go through at last, go into the country on the other side, but I was afraid to.

When we got into the car, up near my school, he took me in his arms and simply held me, silent. The two women in the front seat never looked round.

We went into his house, which I had seen once before, an old mansion of some owner of the Corporation days. He thanked the guards and shut the door. "Dinner," he said. "The cook's out. I meant to take you to a restaurant. I forgot." He led me to the kitchen, where we found cold rice and salad and wine. After we ate he looked at me across the kitchen table and looked down again. His hesitance made me hold still and say nothing. After a long time he said, "Oh, Rakam! will you let me make love to you?"

"I want to make love to you," I said. "I never did. I never made love to anyone."

He got up smiling and took my hand. We went upstairs together, passing what had been the entrance to the men's side of the house. "I live in the beza," he said, "in the harem. I live on the women's side. I like the view."

We came to his room. There he stood still, looking at me, then looked away. I was so frightened, so bewildered, I thought I could not go to him or touch him. I made myself go to him. I raised my hand and touched his face, the scars by his eye and on his mouth, and put my arms around him. Then I could hold him to me, closer and closer.

Some time in that night as we lay drowsing entangled I said, "Did you sleep with Dr. Yeron?"

I felt Havzhiva laugh, a slow, soft laugh in his belly, which was against my belly. "No," he said. "No one on Yeowe but you. And you, no one on Yeowe but me. We were virgins, Yeowan virgins. . . . Rakam, *araha*. . . ." He rested his head in the hollow of my shoulder and said something else in a foreign language and fell asleep. He slept deeply, silently.

Later that year I came up north to the University, where I was taken on the faculty as a teacher of history. By their standards at that time, I was competent. I have worked there ever since, teaching and as editor of the press.

As he had said he would be, Havzhiva was there constantly, or almost.

The Amendments to the Constitution were voted, by secret ballot, mostly, in the Yeowan Year of Liberty 18. Of the events that led to this, and what has followed, you may read in the new three-volume *History of Yeowe* from the University Press. I have told the story I was asked to tell. I have closed it, as so many stories close, with a joining of two people. What is one man's and one woman's love and desire, against the history of two worlds, the great revolutions of our lifetimes, the hope, the unending cruelty of our species? A little thing. But a key is a little thing, next to the door it opens. If you lose the key, the door may never be unlocked. It is in our bodies that we lose or begin our freedom, in our bodies that we accept or end our slavery. So I wrote this book for my friend, with whom I have lived and will die free.

STARSHIP DAY

Ian R. MacLeod

▼

British writer Ian R. MacLeod is another writer who is in contention, along with authors such as Greg Egan, Paul J. McAuley, and Stephen Baxter, for the title of hottest new writers of the nineties to date. Although he has yet to publish any novels, perhaps giving prolific novelist Egan an edge, MacLeod's work continues to grow in power and deepen in maturity as the decade progresses, and he published a slew of strong stories in the first years of the nineties in *Interzone, Asimov's Science Fiction, Weird Tales, Amazing*, and *The Magazine of Fantasy & Science Fiction*, among other markets. Several of these stories made the cut for one or another of the various "best-of-the-year" anthologies, including appearances here in our Eighth, Ninth, Tenth, and Eleventh Annual Collections. In 1990, in fact, he appeared in three different best-of-the-year anthologies with three different stories, certainly a rare distinction. He has completed his first novel, and is at work on another. Upcoming is his first short story collection. MacLeod lives with his wife and young daughter in the West Midlands of England.

In the sly and seductive story that follows, he takes us to a world that is breathlessly waiting to celebrate a very unusual kind of holiday . . .

The news was everywhere. It was in our dreams, it was on TV. Tonight, the travelers on the first starship from Earth would awaken.

That morning, Danous yawned with the expectant creak of shutters, the first stretch of shadow across narrow streets. The air shimmered with the scent of warming pine, it brushed through the shutters and touched our thoughts even as our dreams had faded. For this was Starship Day, and, from tonight, nothing would ever be the same. Of course, there were parties organized. Yacht races across the bay. Holidays for the kids. The prospect of the starship's first transmission, an instantaneous tachyon burst across the light years, had sent the wine sellers and the bakers scurrying toward their stocks and chasing their suppliers. And the suppliers had chased *their* suppliers. And the bread, the fruit, the hats, the dresses, the meat, the marquees, the

music had never been in such demand. Not even when. . . . Not even
when. . . . Not even when. But there *were* no comparisons. There had never
been a day such as this.

As if I needed reminding, the morning paper on the mat was full of it. I'd
left my wife Hannah still asleep, weary from the celebrations that had already
begun the night before, and there were wine glasses scattered in the parlor,
the smell of booze and stale conversation. After starting with early drinks
and chatter at the Point Hotel, Hannah's sister Bernice and her husband Rajii
had stayed around with us until late. At least, they'd stayed beyond the time
I finally left the three of them and went to bed, feeling righteous, feeling like
a sourpuss, wondering just what the hell I did feel. But *some* of us still had
work to do on this starship morning. I opened the curtains and the shutters
and let in the sound and the smell of the sea. I stacked a tray with the butts
and bottles and glasses. I squeezed out an orange, filled a bowl with oats and
yoghurt and honey. I sat down outside with the lizards in the growing warmth
of the patio.

Weighted with a stone, my newspaper fluttered in the soft breeze off the
sea. Page after page of gleeful speculation. Discovery. Life. Starship. Hope.
Message. Already, I'd had enough. Why couldn't people just *wait*? All it
took was for the tide to go in and out, for the sun to rise and fall, for stars
and darkness to come, and we'd all *know* the truth anyway. So easy—but
after all this time, humanity is still a hurrying race. And I knew that my
patients would be full of it at the surgery, exchanging their usual demons for
the brief hope that something from outside might change their lives. And I'd
have to sit and listen, I'd have to put on my usual caring-Owen act. The stars
might be whispering from out of the black far beyond this blue morning, but
some of us had to get on with the process of living.

Hannah was still half-asleep when I went in to say goodbye.

"Sorry about last night," she said.

"Why sorry?"

"You were obviously tired. Rajii does go on."

"What time did they leave?"

"I don't know." She yawned. "What time did you go to bed?"

I smiled as I watched her lying there still tangled in sleep. Now that I had
to go, I wanted to climb back in.

"Will you be in for lunch?"

"I'm—meeting someone."

Bad, that. The wrong kind of pause. But Hannah just closed her eyes,
rolling back into the sheets and her own starship dreams. I left the room,
pulled my cream jacket on over my shirt and shorts, and closed the front
door.

* * *

I wheeled my bicycle from the lean-to beside the lavender patch and took the rough road down into town. For some reason, part of me was thinking, maybe we should get another dog; maybe that would be a change, a distraction.

Another perfect morning. Fishing boats in the harbor. Nets drying along the quay. Already the sun was high enough to set a deep sparkle on the water and lift the dew off the bougainvillaea draped over the seafront houses. I propped my bike in the shadowed street outside the surgery and climbed the wooden steps to the door. I fed the goldfish tank in reception. I dumped the mail in the tray in my office. I opened a window, sat down at my desk, and turned on the PC, hitting the keys to call up my morning's appointments. Mrs. Edwards scrolled up, 9:00. Sal Mohammed, 10:00. Then John for lunch. Mrs. Sweetney in the afternoon. On a whim, I typed in

About the starship.

PLEASE WAIT

What do you think will happen?

Again, **PLEASE WAIT**.

The computer was right of course. Wait. Just wait. Please wait. A seagull mewed. The PC's fan clicked faintly, ticking away the minutes as they piled into drifts of hours and days. Eventually, I heard the thump of shoes on the steps, and I called, "Come right in," before Mrs. Edwards had time to settle with the old magazines in reception.

"Are you sure, Owen? I mean, if you're busy. . . ."

"The door's open."

Ah, Mrs. Edwards. Red-faced, the smell of eau de cologne already fading into nervous sweat. One of my regulars, one of the ones who keep coming long after they'd forgotten why, and who spend their days agonizing new angles around some old neurosis so that they can lay it in front of me like a cat dropping a dead bird.

As always, she looked longingly at the soft chair, then sat down on the hard one.

"Big day," she said.

"It certainly is."

"I'm terribly worried," she said.

"About the starship?"

"Of course. I mean, what are they going to *think* of us?"

I gazed at her, my face a friendly mask. Did she mean whatever star-creatures might be out there? Did she mean the travelers in the starship, waking from stasis after so many years? Now *there* was a thought. The travelers, awakening. I suppose they'll wonder about their descendants here on Earth, perhaps even expect those silver-spired cities we all sometimes still dream about, or maybe corpses under a ruined sky, dead rivers running into poisoned seas.

"Mrs. Edwards, there probably won't *be* any aliens. Anyway, they might be benign."

"Benign?" She leaned forward over her handbag and gave me one of her looks. "But even if they *are*, how can we be *sure?*"

After Mrs. Edwards, Sal Mohammed. Sal was an old friend, and thus broke one of the usual rules of my practice. But I'd noticed he was drinking too heavily, and when I'd heard that he'd been seen walking the town at night in his pajamas—not that either of these things was usual *per se*—I'd rung him and suggested a visit.

He sat down heavily in the comfortable chair and shook his head when I offered coffee. There were thickening grey bags under his eyes.

He asked, "You'll be going to Jay Dax's party tonight?"

"Probably. You?"

"Oh, yes," he said, tired and sad and eager. "I mean, this is the big day, isn't it? And Jay's parties. . . ." He shook his head.

"And how do you really feel?"

"Me? I'm fine. Managing, anyway."

"How are you getting on with those tension exercises?"

His eyes flicked over toward the cork notice board where a solitary child's painting, once so bright, had curled and faded. "I'm finding them hard."

I nodded, wondering for the millionth time what exactly it was that stopped people from helping themselves. Sal still wasn't able to even sit down in a chair for five minutes each day and do a few simple thought exercises. Most annoying of all was the way he still lumbered up to me at do's, his body stuffed into a too-small suit and his face shining with sweat, all thin and affable bonhomie although I knew that he only managed to get out now by tanking up with downers.

"But today's like New Year's Eve, isn't it?" he said. "Starship Day."

I nodded. "That's a way of seeing it."

"Everything could change—but even if it doesn't, knowing it won't change will be something in itself too, won't it? It's a time to make new resolutions. . . ."

But Sal got vague again when I asked him about his own resolutions, and by the end of our session we were grinding through the usual justifications for the gloom that filled his life.

"I feel as though I'm traveling down these grey and empty corridors," he said. "Even when things happen, nothing ever changes. . . ."

He'd gone on for so long by then—and was looking at me with such sincerity—that I snapped softly back, "Then why don't you give up, Sal? If it's really that bad—what *is* it that keeps you going?"

He looked shocked. Of course, shocking them can sometimes work, but part of me was wondering if I didn't simply want to get rid of Sal. And as he rambled on about the pointlessness of it all, I kept thinking of tonight, and all the other nights. The parties and the dances and the evenings in with Hannah and the quietly introspective walks along the cliffs and the picnics in the cool blue hills. I just kept thinking.

The lunches with John that I marked down on my PC were flexible. In fact, they'd got so flexible recently that one or the other of us often didn't turn up. This particular John was called Erica, and we'd been doing this kind of thing since Christmas, in firelight and the chill snowy breath from the mountains. I've learnt that these kind of relationships often don't transfer easily from one season to another—there's something about the shift in light, the change in the air—but this time it had all gone on for so long that I imagined we'd reached a kind of equilibrium. That was probably when it started to go wrong.

It was our usual place. The Arkoda Bar, up the steps beside the ruins. There was a group a few tables off that I vaguely recalled. Two couples, with a little girl. The girl was older now—before, she'd been staggering like a drunk on toddler's splayed legs; now she was running everywhere—but that was still why I remembered them.

I almost jumped when Erica came up behind me.

"You must be early—or I must be late."

I shrugged. "I haven't been here long."

She sat down and poured what was left of the retsina into the second glass. "So you've been here a while. . . ."

"I was just watching the kid. What time is it?"

"Who cares? Don't tell me you've been working this morning, Owen."

"I can't just cancel appointments just because there's some message coming through from the stars."

"Why not?"

I blinked, puzzled for a moment, my head swimming in the flat white heat of the sun. "I do it because it's my job, Erica."

"Sorry. Shall we start again?"

I nodded, watching the golden fall of her hair; the sweat-damp strands clinging to her neck, really and truly wishing that we could start all over again. Wishing, too, that we'd be able to talk about something other than the goddamn starship.

But no, Erica was just like everybody else—plotting the kind of day that she could witter on about in years to come. She wanted to rent a little boat so that we could go to some secret cove, swim and fish for shrimps, and bask on the rocks, and watch the night come in. She even had a little TV in her handbag all ready for the broadcast.

I said, "I'm sorry, Erica. I've got appointments. And I've got to go out this evening."

"So have I. You're not the only one with commitments."

"I just can't escape them like you can. I'm a married man."

"Yeah."

The people with the little girl paused in their chatter to look over at us. We smiled sweetly back.

"Let's have another bottle of wine," I suggested.

"I suppose," Erica said, "you just want to go back to that room of yours above the surgery so you can screw me and then fall asleep?"

"I was hoping—"

"—isn't that right? Owen?"

I nodded: it was, after all, a reasonably accurate picture of what I'd had in mind. I mean, all this business with the boat, the secret cove, fishing for shrimps. . . .

I held out my hand to pat some friendly portion of her anatomy, but she leaned back out of my reach. The people with the kid had stopped talking and were staring deeply into their drinks.

"I've been thinking," she said. "This isn't working, is it?"

I kept a professional silence. Whatever was going to be said now, it was better that Erica said it. I mean, I could have gone on about her selfish enthusiasm in bed, her habit (look! she's doing it now!) of biting her nails and spitting them out like seed husks, and the puzzled expression that generally crossed her face when you used any word with more than three syllables. Erica was a sweet, pretty kid. Tanned and warm, forgiving and forgetful. At best, holding her was like holding a flame. But she was still just a rich Daddy's girl, good at tennis and tolerably fine at sex and swimming and happy on a pair of skis. And if you didn't say anything damaging to her kind when you split up, they might even come back to you years later. By then they'd be softer, sadder, sweeter—ultimately more compromising, but sometimes worth the risk.

So I sat there as Erica poured out her long essay on How Things Had Gone Wrong, and the sun beat down, and the air filled with the smell of hot myrtle, and the sea winked far below. And the little girl chased blue and red butterflies between the tables, and her parents sat listening to the free show in vaguely awestruck silence. It even got to me after a while. I had to squint and half-cover my face. Selfish, calculating, shallow, moody. Nothing new—Erica was hardly one for in-depth personal analysis—but she warmed to her subject, searching the sky for the next stinging adjective. Some of them were surprisingly on target—and for her, surprisingly long. I thought of that scarred and ancient starship tumbling over some strange new world, preparing to send us all a message. And I thought of me, sitting in the heat with the empty bottle of retsina, listening to this.

"You're right," I said eventually. "You deserve better than me. Find someone your own age, Erica. Someone with your own interests."

Erica gazed at me. Interests. Did she *have* any interests?

"But—"

"—No." I held up a hand, noticing with irritation that it was quivering like a leaf. "Everything you said is true."

"Just as long as you don't say we can still be friends."

"But I think we will," I said, pushing back the chair and standing up.

Quickly bending down to kiss her cheek before she could lean away, I felt a brief pang of loss. But I pushed it away. Onward, onward. . . .

"You'll learn," I said, "that everything takes time. Think how long it's taken us to get to the stars."

I waved to her, and to the silent group with their sweet little kid. Then I jogged down the hot stone steps to my bike.

Back at the office, there was a note stuffed through the letterbox and the phone was ringing. The phone sounded oddly sad and insistent, but by the time I'd read Odette Sweetney's message canceling her afternoon appointment on account of what she called *This Starship Thing*, it had clanged back into silence.

I decided to clear the flat upstairs. The doorway led off from reception, with a heavy bolt to make it look unused—to keep up the charade with Hannah. I'd sometimes go on to her about how difficult it was to find a trusty tenant, and she'd just nod. I'd really given up worrying about whether she believed me.

The gable room was intolerably hot. I opened the windows, then set about removing the signs of Erica's habitation. I pulled off the sheets. I shook out the pillows. I picked up the old straw sunhat that lay beneath the wicker chair. For the life of me, I couldn't ever remember Erica ever wearing such a thing. Perhaps it had belonged to Chloe, who'd been the previous John; straw hats were more her kind of thing. But had it really sat there all these months, something for Erica to stare at as we made love? It was all so thoughtlessly uncharacteristic of me. Under the bed, I found several blonde hairs, and a few chewed-off bits of fingernail.

I re-bolted the door and went back into the surgery. I turned on the PC and re-scheduled Odette Sweetney's appointment. Then I gazed at the phone, somehow knowing that it was going to ring again. The sound it made was grating, at odds with the dusty placidity of my surgery, the sleepy white town and the sea beyond the window. I lifted the receiver, then let it drop. Ahh, silence. Today, everything could wait. For all I knew, we'd all be better tomorrow. Miraculously happy and healed.

I locked the door and climbed onto my bicycle. I was determined to make the most of my rare free afternoon—no John, no patients—but time already stretched ahead of me like this steep white road. It's a problem I've always had, what to do when I'm on my own. The one part of my work at the surgery that invariably piques my interest is when my patients talk about solitude. I'm still curious to know what other people do when they're alone, leaning forward in my chair to ask questions like a spectator trying to fathom the rules of some puzzling new game. But for the second half of my marriage with Hannah, I'd found it much easier to keep busy. In the days, I work, or I chase Johns and screw. In the evenings, we go to dinners and parties. The prospect of solitude—of empty space with nothing to react to except your own thoughts—always leaves me feeling scared. So much better to be good old Owen in company, so much easier to walk or talk or drink or sulk or screw with some kind of *audience* to respond to.

I cycled on. The kids were playing, the cats were lazing on the walls. People were getting drunk in the cafés, and the yachts were gathering to race around the bay. Our house lies east of the town, nesting with the other white villas above the sea. I found Hannah sitting alone in the shadowed lounge, fresh mint and ice chattering in the glass she was holding, her cello propped unplayed beside the music stand in the far corner. When I come home unexpectedly, I like it best of all when she's actually playing. Sometimes, I'll just hang around quietly and unannounced in some other part of the house, or sit down under the fig tree in the garden, listening to that dark sound drifting out through the windows, knowing that she doesn't realize she has an audience—that I'm home. She's a fine player, is Hannah, but she plays best unaccompanied, when she doesn't realize anyone is listening. Sometimes, on days when there's a rare fog over the island and the hills are lost in grey, the house will start to sing too, the wind-chimes to tinkle, the floorboards to creak in rhythm, the cold radiators to hum. The whole of her heart and the whole of our marriage is in that sound. I sit listening in the damp garden or in another room, wishing I could finally reach through it to the words and the feelings that must surely lie beyond.

"You should be outside," I said, briskly throwing off my jacket, lifting the phone off its hook. "A day like this. The yacht race is about to start."

"Sussh. . . ." She was watching TV. Two experts, I saw, were talking. Behind them was an old picture of the fabled starship.

"You haven't been watching this crap all day?"

"It's *interesting*," she said.

The picture changed to a fuzzy video shot of old Earth. People everywhere, more cars in the streets than you'd have thought possible. Then other shots of starving people with flies crawling around their eyes. Most of them seemed to be black, young, female.

"I guess we've come a long way," I said, getting a long glass from the marble-topped corner cabinet and filling it with the stuff that Hannah had made up in a jug. It tasted suspiciously non-alcoholic, but I decided to stick with it for now, and to sit down on the sofa beside her and try, as the grey-haired expert on the screen might have put it, to make contact.

Hannah looked at me briefly when I laid my hand on her thigh, but then she re-crossed her legs and turned away. No chance of getting *her* into bed then, either. The TV presenter was explaining that many of the people on the starship had left relatives behind. And here, he said, smiling his presenter's smile, is one of them. The camera panned to an old lady. Her Dad, it seemed, was one of the travelers up there. Now, she was ancient. She nodded and trembled like a dry leaf. Some bloody father, I thought. I wonder what excuse he'll give tonight, leaving his daughter as a baby, then next saying hello across light years to a lisping hag.

"Oh, Jesus. . . ."

"What's the matter?" Hannah asked.

"Nothing." I shook my head.

"Did you have an okay morning?"

"It was fine. I thought I'd come back early, today being today."

"That's nice. You've eaten?"

"I've had lunch."

I stood up and wandered back over to the cabinet, topping my drink up to the rim with vodka. Outside, in the bay, the gun went off to signify the start of the yacht race. I stood on the patio and watched the white sails turn on a warm soft wind that bowed the heavy red blooms in our garden and set the swing down the steps by the empty sandpit creaking on its rusted hinges.

I went back inside.

Hannah said, "You're not planning on getting drunk, are you?"

I shrugged and sat down again. The fact was, I'd reached a reasonable equilibrium. The clear day outside and this shadowed room felt smooth and easy on my eyes and skin. I'd managed to put that ridiculous scene with Erica behind me, and the retsina, and now the vodka, were seeing to it that nothing much else took its place. Eventually, the TV experts ran out of things to say, and the studio faded abruptly and gave way to an old film. I soon lost the plot and fell asleep. And I dreamed, thankfully and gratefully, about nothing. Of deep, endless, starless dark.

We dressed later and drove through Danous in the opentop toward Jay Dax's villa up in the hills. All the shops were open after the long siesta. Music and

heat and light poured across the herringboned cobbles, and the trinket stalls
were full of replicas of the starship. You could take your pick of earrings,
keyrings, lucky charms, models on marble stands with rubies for rockets,
kiddie toys. I added to the general mayhem by honking the horn and revving
the engine to get through the crowds. And I found myself checking the lamplit
faces, wondering if Erica was here, or where else she might be. But all I
could imagine were giggles and sweaty embraces. Erica was a bitch—always
was, always would be. Now, some *other* girl, some child who, these fifteen
years on, would be almost her build, her age. . . .

Then, suddenly—as we finally made it out of town—we saw the stars.
They'd all come out tonight, a shimmering veil over the grey-dark mountains.

"I was thinking, this afternoon," Hannah said, so suddenly that I knew
she must have been playing the words over in her head. "That we need to
find time for ourselves."

"Yes," I said. "Trouble is, when you do what I do for a living. . . ."

"You get sick of hearing about problems? You don't want to know about
your *own*?"

Her voice was clear and sweet over the sound of the engine and the whispering night air. I glanced across and saw from the glint of her eyes that she
meant what she was saying. I accelerated over the brow of a hill into the
trapped sweetness of the valley beyond, wishing that I hadn't drunk the retsina
and the vodka, wishing that I'd answered the phone in the surgery, fighting
back a gathering sense of unease.

I said, "We haven't really got much to complain about, have we? One
tragedy in our whole lives, and at least that left a few happy memories.
Anyone should be able to cope with that. And time—do you really think
we're short of time?"

She folded her arms. After all, *she'd* been the one who'd gone to pieces.
I'd been the source of strength. Good old Owen who—all things considered—
took it so well. And after everything, after all the Johns, and the warm and
pretty years in this warm and pretty location, and with business at the surgery
still going well, how could I reasonably complain?

Soon there were other cars ahead of us, other guests heading for parties in
the big villas. And there was a campfire off to the right, people dancing and
flickering like ghosts through the bars of the forest. We passed through the
wrought iron gates, and Jay Dax's white villa floated into view along the
pines, surrounded tonight by a lake of polished coachwork. We climbed out.
All the doors were open, all the windows were bright. A waltz was playing.
People were milling everywhere.

I took Hannah's hand. We climbed the marble steps to the main doorway
and wandered in beneath a cavernous pink ceiling. The Gillsons and the
Albarets were there. Andre Prilui was there too, puffed up with champagne

after a good showing in the Starship Day yacht race. Why, if only *Spindrift* hadn't tacked across his bows on the way around the eastern buoy . . . and look, here comes Owen, Good Old Owen with his pretty cello-playing wife, Hannah.

"Hey!"

It was Rajii, husband of Hannah's sister Bernice. He took us both by the arm, steering us along a gilded corridor.

"Come on, the garden's where everything's happening."

I asked, "Have you seen Sal?"

"Sal?" Rajii said, pushing back a lock of his black hair, "Sal Mohammed?" Already vague with drink and excitement. "No, now you mention it. Not a sign. . . ."

This was a big party even by Jay Dax's standards. The lanterns strung along the huge redwoods that bordered the lawns enclosed marquees, an orchestra, swingboats, mountainous buffets. No matter what news came through on the tachyon burst from the starship, the party already had the look of a great success.

Bernice came up to us. She kissed Hannah and then me, her breath smelling of wine as she put an arm round my waist, her lips seeking mine. We were standing on the second of the big terraces leading down from the house. "Well," Rajii said, "What's *your* guess, then? About this thing from the stars."

Ah yes, this thing from the stars. But predictions this close to the signal were dangerous; I mean, who wanted to be remembered as the clown who got it outrageously wrong?

"I think," Hannah said, "That the planet they find will be green. I mean, the Earth's blue, Mars is red, Venus is white. It's about time we had a green planet."

"What about you, Owen?"

"What's the point in guessing?" I said.

I pushed my way off down the steps, touching shoulders at random, asking people if they'd seen Sal. At the far end of the main lawn, surrounded by scaffolding, a massive screen reached over the treetops, ready to receive the starship's transmission. Presently, it was black; the deepest color of a night sky without stars, like the open mouth of God preparing to speak. But my face already felt numb from the drink and the smiling. I could feel a headache coming on.

I passed through an archway into a walled garden and sat down on a bench. Overhead now, fireworks were crackling and banging like some battlefield of old. I reached beside me for the drink I'd forgotten to bring, and slumped back, breathing in the vibrant night scents of the flowers. These days, people were getting used to me disappearing, Owen walking out of rooms just when everyone was laughing, Owen vanishing at dances just as the music was starting up. Owen going off in a vague huff and sitting somewhere, never quite out of earshot, never quite feeling alone. People don't mind—oh, that's Owen—they assume I'm playing some amusing private game. But really, I hate silence, space, solitude, any sense of waiting. Hate and fear it as other people might fear thunder or some insect. Hate it, and therefore have to keep peeking. Even in those brief years when Hannah and I weren't alone and our lives seemed filled, I could still feel the empty dark waiting. The black beyond the blue of these warm summer skies.

Somewhere over the wall, a man and a woman were laughing. I imagined Bernice coming to find me, following when I walked off, as I was sure she was bound to do soon. The way she'd kissed me tonight had been a confirmation, and Rajii was a fool—so who could blame her? Not that Bernice would be like Erica, but right now that was an advantage. A different kind of John was just what I needed. Bernice would be old and wise and knowing, and the fact that she was Hannah's sister—that alone would spice things up for a while.

I thought again of the day I'd been through: scenes and faces clicking by. Hannah half asleep in bed this morning; Mrs. Edwards in the surgery; hopeless Sal Mohammed; young and hopeful Erica; then Hannah again, and the dullness of the drink, and all the people here at this party, the pointless endless cascade; and the starship, the starship, the starship, and the phone ringing unanswered in the surgery and me taking it off the hook there and doing so again when I got home. And no sign of Sal this evening, although he'd told me he was going to come.

I walked back out of the rose garden just as the fog of the fireworks was fading and the big screen was coming on. I checked my watch. Not long now, but still I climbed the steps and went back through the nearly empty house and found the car. I started it up and drove off down the drive, suddenly and genuinely worried about Sal, although mostly just thinking how tedious and typical of me this was becoming, buggering off at the most crucial moment of this most crucial of nights.

But it was actually good to be out on the clean night road with the air washing by me. No other cars about now, everybody had got somewhere and was doing something. Everybody was waiting. And I could feel the stars pressing down, all those constellations with names I could never remember. Sal Mohammed's house was on the cliffs to the west of the town, and so I didn't have to drive through Danous to get there. I cut the engine outside and sat for a moment, listening to the beat of the sea, and faintly, off through the hedges and the gorse and the myrtle, the thump of music from some neighbor's party. I climbed out, remembering days in the past. Sal standing in a white suit on the front porch, beckoning us all in for those amazing meals he then used to cook. Sal with that slight sense of camp that he always held in check, Sal with his marvelous, marvelous way with a story. Tonight, all the front windows were dark, and the paint, as it will in this coastal environment if you don't have it seen to regularly, was peeling.

I tried the bell and banged the front door. I walked around the house, peering in at each of the windows. At the back, the porch doors were open, and I went inside, turning on lights, finding the usual bachelor wreckage. I could hear a low murmur, a TV, coming from Sal's bedroom. Heavy with premonition, I pushed open the door, and saw the colored light playing merely over glasses and bottles on a rucked and empty bed. I closed the door and leaned back, breathless with relief, then half-ducked as a shadow swept over me. Sal Mohammed was hanging from the ceiling.

I dialed the police from the phone by the bed. It took several beats for them to answer and I wondered as I waited who would be doing their job tonight. But the voice that answered was smooth, mechanical, unsurprised. Yes, they'd be along. Right away. I put down the phone and gazed at Sal hanging there in the shifting TV light, wondering if I should cut the cord he'd used, or pick up the chair. Wondering whether I'd be interfering with evidence. The way he was hanging and the smell in the room told me that it didn't matter. He'd done a good job, had Sal; it even looked, from the broken tilt of his head, that he'd made sure it ended quickly. But Sal—although he was incapable of admitting it to himself—was bright and reliable and competent in almost everything he did. I opened a window, then sat back down on the bed, drawn despite myself toward the scene that the TV in the corner was now playing.

The announcer had finally finished spinning things out, and the ancient photo of the starship in pre-launch orbit above the Moon had been pulled out to fill the screen. It fuzzed, and the screen darkened for a moment. Then there was another picture, in motion this time, and at least as clear as the last one, taken from one of the service pods that drifted like flies around the main body of the starship. In the harsh white light of a new sun, the starship looked old. Torn gantries, loose pipes, black flecks of meteorite craters. Still, the systems must be functioning, otherwise we wouldn't be seeing this at all. And of course it looked weary—what else was there to expect?

The screen flickered. Another view around the spaceship, and the white flaring of that alien sun, and then, clumsily edited, another. Then inside. Those long grey tunnels, dimly and spasmodically lit, floorless and windowless, that were filled by the long tubes of a thousand living coffins. The sleepers. Then outside again, back amid the circling drones, and those views, soon to become tedious, of the great starship drifting against a flaring sun.

As I watched, my hand rummaged amid the glasses and the bottles that Sal had left on the bed. But they were all empty. And I thought of Erica, how she was spending these moments, and of all the other people at the gatherings and parties. I, at least, would be able to give an original answer if I was asked, in all the following years—Owen, what were you doing when we first heard from the stars?

The TV was now showing a long rock, a lump of clinker really, flipping over and over, catching light, then dark. Then another rock. Then back to the first rock again. Or it could have been a different one—it was hard to tell. And this, the announcer suddenly intoned, breaking in on a silence I hadn't been aware of, is all the material that orbits this supposedly friendly cousin of our sun. No planets, no comets even. Despite all the studies of probability and orbital perturbation, there was just dust and rubble here, and a few mile-long rocks.

There would be no point now in waking the sleepers in their tunnels and tubes. Better instead to unfurl the solar sails and use the energy from this sun to find another one. After all, the next high-probability star lay a mere three light years away, and the sleepers could dream through the time of waiting. Those, anyway, who still survived. . . .

I stood up and turned off the TV. Outside, I could hear a car coming. I opened the front door and stood watching as it pulled in from the road. Hardly a car at all really, or a van. Just a grey colorless block. But the doors opened, and the police emerged. I was expecting questions—maybe even a chance to break the news about the starship—but the police were faceless, hooded, dark. They pushed by me and into the house without speaking.

Outside, it was quiet now. The noise of the neighbor's party had ceased, and there was just the sound and the smell of the sea. People would be too surprised to be disappointed. At least, at first. Sal had obviously seen it coming—or had known that there was nothing about this Starship Day that could change things for him. Death, after all, isn't an option that you can ever quite ignore. And it's never as random as people imagine, not even if it happens to a kid just out playing on a swing in their own back garden. Not even then. You always have to look for some kind of purpose and meaning and reason, even inside the dark heart of what seems like nothing other than a sick and pointless accident.

The police came out again, lightly carrying something that might or might not have been Sal's body. Before they climbed back into their grey van, one of them touched my shoulder with fingers as cool as the night air and gave me a scrap of paper. After they'd driven off, I got back into my car and took the road down into the now quiet streets of Danous, and parked by the dark harbor, and went up the steps to my surgery.

It all seemed odd and yet familiar, to be sitting at my desk late on Starship Day with the PC humming. The screen flashed **PLEASE WAIT**. For what? How many years? Just how much longer will the dreamers have to go on dreaming? I felt in my pocket for the piece of paper, and carefully typed in the long string of machine code. Then I hit return.

PLEASE WAIT.

I waited. The words dribbled down off the screen, then the screen itself melted, and me with it, and then the room. The lifting of veils, knowing where and what I truly was, never came as the surprise I expected. Each time it got less so. I wondered about what Sal Mohammed had said to me in the dream of this morning. All that stuff about grey endless corridors—was he seeing where he really was? But I supposed that after this number of journeys and disappointments, after so many dead and lifeless suns, and no matter how well I did my job, it was bound to happen. How many Starship Days had there been now? How many years of silence and emptiness? And just how far were we, now, from Earth? Even here, I really didn't want to think about that.

Instead, and as always, I kept busy, moving along the cold airless tunnels on little drifts of gas, my consciousness focused inside one of the starship's few inner drones that was still truly functioning and reliable, even if it didn't go quite straight now and I had to keep the sensors pointing to one side. Outside, through the occasional porthole, I could see others like me who were helping to prepare the starship for another journey. A spindly thing like a spider with rivet guns on each of its legs went by, and I wondered about Erica, whether that really *was* her. I wondered whether it was actually possible, with your consciousness inside ancient plastic and metal, to laugh.

Details scrolled up of how many sleepers we'd lost this time. A good dozen. It mostly happened like Sal; not from soft or hard-systems failure, but simply because the dream of Danous ceased to work. That, anyway, was the only reason I could find. I paused now beside Sal's coffin. Ice had frosted over the faceplate entirely. I reached out a claw to activate the screen beside him, and saw that he was actually an even bigger loss than I'd imagined—a specialist in solar power. Just the kind of man we'd need out there on some mythical friendly planet. Then I found my own coffin, and paused my hovering drone to look down through the face plate at the grey and placid version of the features I saw each day in the mirror. In the coffin just above me—or below—was Hannah. Ah, Hannah, a few strands of brittle hair still nestled against her cheek, and that gold chain around her bare neck that she'd insisted on wearing back on Earth when we set out together on this great adventure. Just looking at her, part of me longed to touch, to escape these lenses and claws and get back into the dream. Next time, I promised myself, tomorrow, I'll change, I'll do things differently. No, I won't screw John—Bernice. I might even admit to being unfaithful. After all, Hannah knows. She must know. It's one of the things that's keeping this sense of separateness between us.

I tilted the gas jets and drifted to the coffin that lay beside mine and Hannah's. Like Sal's, like so many others I'd passed, the faceplate was iced over, the contents desiccated by slow cold years of interstellar space. There was really no sign, now, of the small body that had once lived and laughed and dreamed with us inside it. Our child, gone, and with every year, with every starfall, with the hard cold rain that seeps through this starship, with every John, the chances of Hannah and I ever having another are lessened. But first, of course, we need that green or blue or red world. We need to awake and stretch our still limbs, and breathe the stale ancient air that will flood these passages, and move, pushing and clumsy, to one of the portholes, and peer out, and see the clouds swirling and the oceans and the forests and the deserts, and *believe*. Until then. . . .

I snapped back out from the drone, passing down the wires into the main databank, where Danous awaited. And yes, of course, the morning would be warm again, and perfect, with just a few white clouds that the sun will soon burn away. Nothing could be done, really, to make it better than it already is. There's nothing I can change. And as I turned off my PC and left the surgery and climbed back into my car for the drive home, I could already feel the sense of expectation and disappointment fading. Tomorrow, after all, will always be tomorrow. And today is just today.

Rajii's car was sitting in the drive, and he was inside in the lounge with Bernice and Hannah. I could hear them laughing as I banged the door, and the clink of their glasses.

"Where *were* you?" Rajii asked, lounging on the rug. Bernice pulled on a joint, and looked at me, and giggled. Hannah, too, seemed happy and relaxed—as she generally gets by this time in the evening, although I haven't quite worked out what it is that she's taking.

I shrugged and sat down on the edge of a chair. "I was just out."

"Here. . . ." Hannah got up, her voice and movements a little slurred. "Have a drink, Owen."

I ignored the glass she offered me. "Look," I said, "I'm tired. Some of us have to work in the morning. I really must go to bed. . . ."

So I went out of the room on the wake of their smoke and their booze and their laughter, feeling righteous, feeling like a sourpuss, wondering just what the hell I did feel. And I stripped and I showered and I stood in the darkness staring out of the window across our garden, where the swing still hung beside the overgrown sandpit, rusting and motionless in the light of a brilliant rising Moon. And I could still hear the sound of Hannah and Bernice and Rajii's laughter from down the hall, and even sense, somehow, the brightness of their anticipation. I mean . . . What if . . . Who knows . . . Not even when . . . Not even when . . . Not even when . . . Not even. . . .

Shaking my head, I climbed into bed and pulled over the sheets. And I lay there listening to their voices in the spinning darkness as I was slowly overtaken by sleep.

In my dreams, I found that I was smiling. For tomorrow would be Starship Day, and anything could happen.

A PLACE WITH SHADE

Robert Reed

▼

Robert Reed is a frequent contributor to *The Magazine of Fantasy & Science Fiction* and *Asimov's Science Fiction*, and has also sold stories to *Universe*, *New Destinies*, *Tomorrow*, *Synergy*, and elsewhere. His books include the novels *The Lee Shore*, *The Hormone Jungle*, *Black Milk*, *The Remarkables*, and *Down the Bright Way*. His most recent books are the novels *Beyond the Veil of Stars* and *An Exaltation of Larks*. His stories have appeared in our Ninth, Tenth, Eleventh, and Twelfth Annual Collections. He lives in Lincoln, Nebraska.

Like Ursula K. Le Guin, Greg Egan, Mary Rosenblum, Brian Stableford, and a few other authors, Reed produced at least four or five stories this year that were strong enough to have been shoo-ins for inclusion in a best-of-the-year anthology any other year. I finally settled on the inventive, elegant, and engrossing story that follows, which examines the old idea that Nature is "red in tooth and claw"— and concludes that sometimes Nature could do better at that if it had a little help . . .

The old man was corpulent like a seal, muscle clothed in fat to guarantee warmth, his skin smooth and his general proportions—stocky limbs and a broad chest—implying a natural, almost unconscious power. He wore little despite the damp chill. The brown eyes seemed capable and shrewd. And humorless. We were standing on a graveled beach, staring at his tiny sea; and after a long silence, he informed me, "I don't approve of what you do, Mr. Locum. It's pretentious and wasteful, this business of building cruel places. You're not an artist, and I think it's healthy for both of us to know my objections to your presence here."

I showed a grin, then said, "Fine. I'll leave." I had spent three months inside cramped quarters, but I told him, "Your shuttle can take me back to the freighter. I'll ride out with the iron."

"You misunderstand, Mr. Locum." His name was Provo Lei, the wealthiest person for a light-month in any direction. "I have these objections, but

you aren't here for me. You're a gift to my daughter. She and I have finally
agreed that she needs a tutor, and you seem qualified. Shall we dispense with
pretenses? You are a toy. This isn't what you would call a lush commission,
and you'd prefer to be near a civilized world, building some vicious forest
for society people who want prestige and novelty. Yet you need my money,
don't you? You're neither a tutor nor a toy, but your debts outweigh your
current value as an artist. Or am I wrong?"

I attempted another grin, then shrugged. "I can work on a larger scale
here." I'm not someone who hesitates or feels insecure, but I did both just
then. "I've had other offers—"

"None of substance," Provo interrupted.

I straightened my back, looking over him. We were in the middle of his
house—a sealed hyperfiber tent covering ten thousand hectares of tundra and
ice water—and beyond the tent walls was an entire world, earth-size but less
massive. Not counting robots, the world's population was two. Counting me,
three. As we stood there enjoying impolite conversation, an army of robots
was beneath the deep water-ice crust, gnawing at rock, harvesting metals to
be sold at a profit throughout the district.

"What do you think of my little home, Mr. Locum? Speaking as a professional terraformer, of course."

I blinked, hesitating again.

"Please. Be honest."

"It belongs to a miser." Provo didn't have propriety over bluntness. "This
is a cheap Arctic package. Low diversity, a rigorous durability, and almost
no upkeep. I'm guessing, but it feels like the home of a man who prefers
solitude. And since you've lived here for two hundred years, alone most of
the time, I don't think that's too much of a guess."

He surprised me, halfway nodding.

"Your daughter's how old? Thirty?" I paused, then said, "Unless she's
exactly like you, I would think that she would have left by now. She's not
a child, and she must be curious about the rest of the Realm. Which makes
me wonder if I'm an inducement of some kind. A bribe. Speaking as a person,
not a terraformer, I think she must be frighteningly important to you. Am I
correct?"

The brown eyes watched me, saying nothing.

I felt a brief remorse. "You asked for my opinion," I reminded him.

"Don't apologize. I want honesty." He rubbed his rounded chin, offering
what could have been confused for a smile. "And you're right, I do bribe
my daughter. In a sense. She's my responsibility, and why shouldn't I sacrifice
for her happiness?"

"She wants to be a terraformer?"

"Of the artistic variety, yes."

I moved my feet, cold gravel crunching under my boots.

"But this 'cheap package,' as you so graciously described it, is a recent condition. Before this I maintained a mature Arctic steppe, dwarf mammoths here and a cold-water reef offshore. At no small expense, Mr. Locum, and I'm not a natural miser."

"It sounds like Beringa," I muttered.

"My home world, yes." Beringa was a giant snowball terraformed by commercial souls, carpeted with plastics and rock and rich artificial soils, its interior still frozen while billions lived above in a kind of perpetual summer, twenty-hour days but limited heat. The natives were built like Provo, tailored genes keeping them comfortably fat and perpetually warm. In essence, Beringa was an inspired apartment complex, lovely in every superficial way.

The kind of work I hated most, I was thinking.

"This environment," I heard, "is very much makeshift."

I gestured at the tundra. "What happened?"

"Ula thought I would enjoy a grove of hot-sap trees."

Grimacing, I said, "They wouldn't work at all." Ecologically speaking. Not to mention aesthetically.

"Regardless," said Provo, "I purchased vats of totipotent cells, at no small cost, and she insisted on genetically tailoring them. Making them into a new species."

"Easy enough," I whispered.

"And yet." He paused and sighed. "Yet some rather gruesome metabolites were produced. Released. Persistent and slow toxins that moved through the food web. My mammoths sickened and died, and since I rather enjoy mammoth meat, having been raised on little else—"

"You were poisoned," I gasped.

"Somewhat, yes. But I have recovered nicely." The nonsmile showed again, eyes pained. Bemused. "Of course she was scared for me and sorry. And of course I had to pay for an extensive cleanup, which brought on a total environmental failure. This tundra package was an easy replacement, and besides, it carries a warranty against similar troubles."

Popular on toxic worlds, I recalled. Heavy metals and other terrors were shunted away from the human foods.

"You see? I'm not a simple miser."

"It shouldn't have happened," I offered.

Provo merely shrugged his broad shoulders, admitting, "I do love my daughter. And you're correct about some things. But the situation here, like anywhere, is much more complicated than the casual observer can perceive."

I looked at the drab hyperfiber sky—the illusion of heavy clouds over a waxy low sun—and I gave a quick appreciative nod.

"The area around us is littered with even less successful projects," Provo warned me.

I said, "Sad."

The old man agreed. "Yet I adore her. I want no ill to befall her, and I mean that as an unveiled warning. Ula has never existed with ordinary people. My hope is that I live long enough to see her mature, to become happy and normal, and perhaps gain some skills as a terraformer too. You are my best hope of the moment. Like it or not, that's why I hired you."

I stared out at his little sea. A lone gull was circling, bleating out complaints about the changeless food.

"My daughter will become infatuated with you," I heard. "Which might be a good thing. Provided you can resist temptation, infatuation will keep her from being disillusioned. Never, never let her become disillusioned."

"No?"

"Ula's not her father. Too much honesty is a bad thing."

I felt a momentary, inadequate sense of fear.

"Help her build one workable living place. Nothing fancy, and please, nothing too inspired." He knelt and picked up a rounded stone. "She has an extensive lab and stocks of totipotent cells. You'll need nothing. And I'll pay you in full, for your time and your imaginary expertise."

I found myself cold for many reasons, staring skyward. "I've been to Beringa," I told Provo. "It's ridiculously cheery. Giant flowers and giant butterflies, mammoths and tame bears. And a clear blue sky."

"Exactly," he replied, flinging the stone into the water. "And I would have kept my blue sky, but the color would have been dishonest."

A mosquito landed on my hand, tasting me and discovering that I wasn't a caribou, flying off without drawing blood.

"Bleak fits my mood, Mr. Locum."

I looked at him.

And again he offered his nonsmile, making me feel, if only for an instant, sorry for him.

Beauty, say some artists, is the delicious stew made from your subject's flaws.

Ula Lei was a beautiful young woman.

She had a hundred hectare tent pitched beside her father's home, the place filled with bio stocks and empty crystal wombs and computers capable of modeling any kind of terraforming project. She was standing beside a huge reader, waving and saying, "Come here," with the voice people use on robots. Neither polite nor intimidating.

I approached, thinking that she looked slight. Almost underfed. Where I had expected an ungraceful woman-child, I instead found a mannerly but almost distant professional. Was she embarrassed to need a tutor? Or was she unsure how to act with a stranger? Either way, the old man's warning about my "toy" status seemed overstated. Taking a frail, pretty hand, feeling the polite and passionless single shake, I went from wariness to a mild funk, wondering if I had failed some standard. It wounded me when she stared right through me, asking with a calm dry voice, "What shall we do first?"

Funk became a sense of relief, and I smiled, telling her, "Decide on our project, and its scale."

"Warm work, and huge."

I blinked. "Your father promised us a thousand hectare tent, plus any of his robots—"

"I want to use an old mine," she informed me.

"With a warm environment?"

"It has a rock floor, and we can insulate the walls and ceiling with field charges, then refrigerate as a backup." She knew the right words, at least in passing. "I've already selected which one. Here. I'll show you everything."

She was direct like her father, and confident. But Ula wasn't her father's child. Either his genes had been suppressed from conception, or they weren't included. Lean and graced with the fine features popular on tropical worlds, her body was the perfect antithesis of Provo's buttery one. Very black, very curly hair. Coffee-colored skin. And vivid green eyes. Those eyes noticed that I was wearing a heavy work jersey; I had changed clothes after meeting with Provo, wanting this jersey's self-heating capacity. Yet the temperature was twenty degrees warmer than the tundra, and her tropical face smiled when I pulled up my sleeves and pocketed my gloves. The humor was obvious only to her.

Then she was talking again, telling me, "The main chamber is eight kilometers by fifty, and the ceiling is ten kilometers tall in the center. Pressurized ice. Very strong." Schematics flowed past me. "The floor is the slope of a dead volcano. Father left when he found better ores."

A large operation, I noted. The rock floor would be porous and easily eroded, but rich in nutrients. Four hundred square kilometers? I had never worked on that scale, unless I counted computer simulations.

A graceful hand called up a new file. "Here's a summary of the world's best-guess history. If you're interested."

I was, but I had already guessed most of it for myself. Provo's World was like thousands of other sunless bodies in the Realm. Born in an unknown solar system, it had been thrown free by a near-collision, drifting into interstellar space, its deep seas freezing solid and its internal heat failing. In other regions it would have been terraformed directly, but our local district was impoverished when it came to metals. Provo's World had rich ores, its iron and magnesium, aluminum and the rest sucked up by industries and terraformers alike. A healthy green world requires an astonishing amount of iron, if only to keep it in hemoglobin. The iron from this old mine now circulated through dozens of worlds; and almost certainly some portion of that iron was inside me, brought home now within my own blood.

"I've already sealed the cavern," Ula informed me. "I was thinking of a river down the middle, recirculating, and a string of waterfalls—"

"No," I muttered.

She showed me a smile. "No?"

"I don't like waterfalls," I warned her.

"Because you belong to the New Traditionalist movement. I know." She shrugged her shoulders. " 'Waterfalls are clichés,' you claim. 'Life, done properly, is never pretty in simple ways.' "

"Exactly."

"Yet," Ula assured me, "this is my project."

I had come an enormous distance to wage a creative battle. Trying to measure my opponent, I asked, "What do you know about NTs?"

"You want to regain the honesty of the original Earth. Hard winters. Droughts. Violent predation. Vibrant chaos." Her expression became coy, then vaguely wicked. "But who'd want to terraform an entire world according to your values? And who would live on it, given the chance?"

"The right people," I replied, almost by reflex.

"Not Father. He thinks terraforming should leave every place fat and green and pretty. And iron-hungry too."

"Like Deringa."

She nodded, the wickedness swelling. "Did you hear about my little mistake?"

"About the hot-sap trees? I'm afraid so."

"I guess I do need help." Yet Ula didn't appear contrite. "I know about you, Mr. Locum. After my father hired you—I told him NTs work cheap—I ordered holos of every one of your works. You like working with jungles, don't you?"

Jungles were complex and intricate. And dense. And fun.

"What about Yanci's jungle?" she asked me. "It's got a spectacular waterfall, if memory serves."

A socialite had paid me to build something bold, setting it inside a plastic cavern inside a pluto-class world. Low gravity; constant mist; an aggressive assemblage of wild animals and carnivorous plants. "Perfect," Yanci had told me. Then she hired an old-school terraformer—little more than a plumber—to add one of those achingly slow rivers and falls, popular on every low-gravity world in the Realm.

"Yes, Mr. Locum?" she teased. "What do you want to say?"

"Call me Hann," I growled.

My student pulled her hair away from her jungle-colored eyes. "I've always been interested in New Traditionalists. Not that I believe what you preach . . . not entirely . . . but I'm glad Father hired one of you."

I was thinking about my ruined jungle. Fifty years in the past, and still it made my mouth go dry and my heart pound.

"How will we move water without a river and falls?"

"Underground," I told her. "Through the porous rock. We can make a string of pools and lakes, and there won't be erosion problems for centuries."

"Like this?" She called up a new schematic, and something very much like my idea appeared before us. "I did this in case you didn't like my first idea."

A single waterfall was at the high end of the cavern.

"A compromise," she offered. Enlarging the image, she said, "Doesn't it look natural?"

For a cliché, I thought.

"The reactor and pumps will be behind this cliff, and the water sounds can hide any noise—"

"Fine," I told her.

"—and the entranceway too. You walk in through the falls."

Another cliché, but I said, "Fine." Years of practice had taught me to compromise with the little points. Why fight details when there were bigger wars to wage?

"Is it all right, Mr. Locum?" A wink. "I want both of us happy when this is done. Hann, I mean."

For an audience of how many? At least with shallow socialites, there were hundreds of friends and tag-alongs and nobodys and lovers. And since they rarely had enough money to fuel their lifestyles, they would open their possessions to the curious and the public.

But here I could do my best work, and who would know?

"Shall we make a jungle, Hann?"

I would know, I told myself.

And with a forced wink, I said, "Let's begin."

Terraforming is an ancient profession.

Making your world more habitable began on the Earth itself, with the first dancing fire that warmed its builder's cave; and everything since—every green world and asteroid and comet—is an enlargement on that first cozy cave. A hotter fusion fire brings heat and light, and benign organisms roam inside standardized biomes. For two hundred and ten centuries humans have expanded the Realm, mastering the tricks to bring life to a nearly dead universe. The frontier is an expanding sphere more than twenty light-years in radius—a great peaceful firestorm of life—and to date only one other living world has been discovered. *Pitcairn*. Alien and violent, and gorgeous. And the basic inspiration for the recent New Traditionalist movement. Pitcairn showed us how bland and domesticated our homes had become, riddled with clichés, every world essentially like every other world. Sad, sad, sad.

Here I found myself with four hundred square kilometers of raw stone. How long would it take to build a mature jungle? Done simply, a matter of months. But novelty would take longer, much to Provo's consternation. We would make fresh species, every ecological tie unique. I anticipated another year on top of the months, which was very good. We had the best computers, the best bio-stocks, and thousands of robots eager to work without pause or complaint. It was an ideal situation, I had to admit to myself. Very nearly heaven.

We insulated the ice ceiling and walls by three different means. Field charges enclosed the heated air. If they were breached, durable refrigeration elements were sunk into the ice itself. And at my insistence we added a set of emergency ducts, cold compressed air waiting in side caverns in case of tragedies. Every organism could go into a sudden dormancy, and the heat would be sucked into the huge volumes of surrounding ice. Otherwise the ceiling might sag and collapse, and I didn't want that to happen. Ula's jungle was supposed to outlast all of us. Why else go to all this bother?

We set the reactor inside the mine shaft, behind the eventual cliché. Then lights were strung, heating the cavern's new air, and we manufactured rich soils with scrap rock and silt from Provo's own little sea. The first inhabitants were bacteria and fungi set free to chew and multiply, giving the air its first living scent. Then robots began assembling tree-shaped molds, sinking hollow roots into the new earth and a sketchwork of branches meshing overhead, beginning the future canopy.

We filled the molds with water, nutrients, and nourishing electrical currents, then inoculated them with totipotent cells. More like baking than gardening, this was how mature forest could be built from scratch. Living cells divided at an exponential rate, then assembled themselves into tissue-types—sapwood and heartwood, bark and vascular tubes. It's a kind of superheated cultivation, and how else could artists like me exist? Left to Nature's pace, anything larger than a terrarium would consume entire lives. Literally.

Within five months—on schedule—we were watching the robots break up the molds, exposing the new trees to the air. And that's a symbolic moment worth a break and a little celebration, which we held.

Just Ula and me.

I suggested inviting Provo, but she told me, "Not yet. It's too soon to show him yet."

Perhaps. Or did she want her father kept at a distance?

I didn't ask. I didn't care. We were dining on top of a rough little hill, at the midpoint of the cavern, whiteness above and the new forest below us, leafless, resembling thousands of stately old trees pruned back by giant shears. Stubby, enduring trees. I toasted our success, and Ula grinned, almost singing when she said, "I haven't been the bother you expected, have I?"

No, she hadn't been.

"And I know more about terraforming than you thought."

More than I would admit. I nodded and said, "You're adept, considering you're self-taught."

"No," she sang, "you're the disappointment."

"Am I?"

"I expected . . . well, more energy. More inspiration." She rose to her feet, gesturing at our half-born creation. "I really hoped an NT would come up with bizarre wonders—"

"Like an eight-legged terror?"

"Exactly."

It had been her odd idea, and I'd dismissed it twenty times before I realized it was a game with her. She wanted an organism wholly unique, and I kept telling her that radical tailoring took too much time and too frequently failed. And besides, I added, our little patch of jungle wasn't large enough for the kind of predator she had in mind.

"I wish we could have one or two of them," she joked.

I ignored her. I'd learned that was best.

"But don't you agree? Nothing we've planned is *that* new or spectacular."

Yet I was proud of everything. What did she want? Our top three carnivores were being tailored at that moment—a new species of fire-eagle; a variation on black nightcats; and an intelligent, vicious species of monkey. Computer models showed that only two of them would survive after the first century. Which two depended on subtle, hard-to-model factors. That was one of the more radical, unpopular NT principles. "The fit survive." We build worlds with too much diversity, knowing that some of our creations are temporary. And unworthy. Then we stand aside, letting our worlds decide for themselves.

"I wish we could have rainstorms," she added. It was another game, and she waved her arms while saying, "Big winds. Lightning. I've always wanted to see lightning."

"There's not enough energy to drive storms," I responded. The rains were going to be mild events that came in the night. When we had nights, in a year. "I don't want to risk—"

"—damaging the ice. I know." She sat again, closer now, smiling as she said, "No, I don't care. It's coming along perfectly."

I nodded, gazing up at the brilliant white sky. The mining robots had left the ice gouged and sharp, and somehow that was appropriate. An old violence was set against a rich new order, violent in different ways. A steamy jungle cloaked in ice; an appealing, even poetic dichotomy. And while I looked into the distance, hearing the sounds of molds being torn apart and loaded onto mag-rails, my partner came even closer, touching one of my legs and asking, "How else have I surprised you?"

She hadn't touched me in months, even in passing.

It took me a moment to gather myself, and I took her hand and set it out of the way, with a surety of motion.

She said nothing, smiling and watching me.

And once again, for the umpteenth time, I wondered what Ula was thinking. Because I didn't know and couldn't even guess. We had been together for months, our relationship professional and bloodless. Yet I always had the strong impression that she showed me what she wanted to show me, and I couldn't even guess how much of that was genuine.

"How else?" she asked again.

"You're an endless surprise," I told her.

But instead of appearing pleased, she dipped her head, the smile changing to a concentrated stare, hands drawing rounded shapes in the new soil, then erasing them with a few quick tiger swipes.

I met Provo behind the waterfall, in the shaft, his sturdy shape emerging from the shadows; and he gave me a nod and glanced at the curtain of water, never pausing, stepping through and vanishing with a certain indifference. I followed, knowing where the flow was weakest—where I would be the least soaked—and stepped out onto a broad rock shelf, workboots gripping and my dampened jersey starting to dry itself.

The old man was gazing into the forest.

I asked, "Would you like a tour?" Then I added, "We could ride one of the mag-rails, or we could walk."

"No," he replied. "Neither."

Why was he here? Provo had contacted me, no warning given. He had asked about his daughter's whereabouts. "She's in the lab," I had said, "mutating beetles." Leave her alone, he had told me. Provo wanted just the two of us for his first inspection.

Yet now he acted indifferent to our accomplishments, dropping his head and walking off the rock shelf and stopping, then looking back at me. And over the sound of tumbling water, he asked, "How is she?"

"Ula's fine."

"No troubles with her?" he inquired.

It was several weeks after our hilltop celebration, and I barely remembered the hand on my leg. "She's doing a credible job."

Provo appeared disappointed.

I asked him, "How should she be?"

He didn't answer. "She likes you, Mr. Locum. We've talked about you. She's told me, more than once . . . that you're *perfect*."

I felt a sudden warmth, and I smiled.

Disappointment faded. "How is she? Speaking as her teacher, of course."

"Bright. Maybe more than bright." I didn't want to praise too much, lifting his expectations. "She has inspirations, as she calls them. Some are workable, and some are even lovely."

"Inspirations," he echoed.

I readied some examples. I thought Provo would want them, enjoying this chance to have a parent's pride. But instead he looked off into the trees again, the stubby branches sprouting smaller branches and fat green leaves. He seemed to be hunting for something specific, old red eyes squinting. Finally he said, "No." He said, "I shouldn't tell you."

"Tell me?"

"Because you don't need to know." He sighed and turned, suddenly older and almost frail. "If she's been on her best behavior, maybe I should keep my mouth shut."

I said nothing for a long moment.

Provo shuffled across the clearing, sitting on a downed log with a certain gravity. The log had been grown in the horizontal position, then killed. Sitting next to him, I asked, "What is it, Mr. Lei?"

"My daughter."

"Yes?"

"She isn't."

I nodded and said, "Adopted."

"Did she tell you?"

"I know genetics. And I didn't think you'd suppress your own genes."

He looked at the waterfall. It was extremely wide and not particularly tall, spilling onto the shelf and then into a large pond. A pair of mag-rails carried equipment in and out on the far shore. Otherwise little moved. I noticed a tiny tag-along mosquito who wouldn't bite either of us. It must have come from the tundra, and it meant nothing. It would die in a few hours, I thought; and Provo suddenly told me, "Adopted, yes. And I think it's fair to tell you the circumstances."

Why the tension?

"I'm quite good at living alone, Mr. Locum. That's one of the keys to my success." He paused, then said, "I came to this world alone. I charted it and filed my claims and defended it from the jealous mining corporations. Every moment of my life has gone into these mines, and I'm proud of my accomplishments. Life. My metals have brought life and prosperity to millions, and I make no apologies. Do you understand me?"

I said, "Yes."

"Few people come here. Like that freighter that brought you, most of the ships are unmanned." Another pause. "But there are people who make their livelihood riding inside the freighters. Perhaps you've known a few of them."

I hadn't, no.

"They are people. They exist on a continuum. All qualities of human beings live inside those cramped quarters, some of them entirely decent. Honest. Capable of more compassion than I could hope to feel."

I nodded, no idea where we were going.

"Ula's biological parents weren't at that end of the continuum. Believe me. When I first saw her . . . when I boarded her parents' ship to supervise the loading . . . well, I won't tell you what I saw. And smelled. And learned about the capacities of other human beings. Some things are best left behind, I think. Let's forget them. Please."

"How old was Ula?"

"A child. Three standard years, that time." A small strong hand wiped at his sweating face. "Her parents purchased loads of mixed metals from me, then sold them to one of the water worlds near Beringa. To help plankton bloom, I imagine. And for two years, every day, I found myself remembering that tiny girl, pitying her, a kind of guilt building inside me because I'd done nothing to help her, nothing at all." Again the hands tried to dry his face, squeezed drops of perspiration almost glittering on them. "And yet, Mr. Locum, I was thankful too. Glad that I would never see her again. I assumed . . . I knew . . . that space itself would swallow them. That someone else would save her. That her parents would change. That I wouldn't be involved again, even if I tried—"

"They came back," I muttered.

Provo straightened his back, grimacing as if in pain. "Two years later, yes." Brown eyes closed, opened. "They sent me word of their arrival, and in an instant a plan occurred to me. All at once I knew the right thing to do." Eyes closed and stayed closed." I was onboard, barely one quick glance at that half-starved child, and with a self-righteous voice I told the parents, 'I want to adopt her. Name your price.' "

"Good," I offered.

He shook his head. "You must be like me. We assume, and without reasons, that those kinds of people are simple predatory monsters. Merely selfish. Merely cruel." The eyes opened once again. "But what I realized since is that Ula . . . Ula was in some way essential to that bizarre family. I'm not saying they loved her. It's just that they couldn't sell her anymore than they could kill her. Because if she died, who else would they have to torture?"

I said nothing.

"They couldn't be bought, I learned. Quickly." Provo swallowed and grabbed the log, knuckles pale as the hands shook. "You claim my daughter is well-behaved, and I'm pleased. You say she's bright, and I'm not at all surprised. And since you seem to have her confidence and trust, I think it's only fair to tell you about her past. To warn you."

"How did you adopt her?"

He took a deep breath and held it.

"If they couldn't be bribed . . . ?" I touched one of the thick arms. "What happened?"

"Nothing." A shrug of the shoulders, then he said, "There was an accident. During the loading process. The work can be dangerous, even deadly, when certain equipment fails."

I felt very distant, very calm.

"An accident," he repeated.

I gave him a wary glance, asking. "Does she know what happened?"

Provo's eyes opened wide, almost startled. "About the accident? Nothing! About her past life? She remembers, I'm sure . . . nothing. None of it." Just the suggestion of memories caused him to nearly panic. "No, Mr. Locum . . . you see, once I had legal custody . . . even before then . . . I paid an expert from Beringa to come here and examine her, and treat her . . . with every modern technique—"

"What kind of expert?"

"In psychology, you idiot! What do you think I mean?" Then he gave a low moan, pulling loose a piece of fibrous bark. "To save her. To wipe away every bad memory and heal her, which he did quite well. A marvelous job of it. I paid him a bonus. He deserved it." He threw the bark onto the pond. "I've asked Ula about her past, a thousand times . . . and she remembers none of it. The expert said she might, or that it might come out in peculiar ways . . . but she doesn't and has no curiosity about those times . . . and maybe I shouldn't have told you, I'm sorry . . . !"

I looked at the pond, deep and clear, some part of me wondering how soon we would inoculate it with algae and water weeds.

Then Provo stood again, telling me, "Of course I came to look around, should she ask. And tell her . . . tell her that I'm pleased. . . ."

I gave a quick compliant nod.

"It's too warm for my taste." He made a turn, gazing into the jungle and saying, "But shady. Sometimes I like a place with shade, and it's pleasant enough, I suppose." He swallowed and gave a low moan, then said, "And tell her for me, please . . . that I'm very much looking forward to the day it's done. . . ."

Terraformers build their worlds at least twice.

The first time it is a model, a series of assumptions and hard numbers inside the best computers; and the second time it is wood and flesh, false sunlight and honest sound. And that second incarnation is never the same as the model. It's an eternal lesson learned by every terraformer, and by every other person working with complexity.

Models fail.

Reality conspires.

There is always, always some overlooked or mismeasured factor, or a stew of factors. And it's the same for people too. A father and a teacher speak about the daughter and the student, assuming certain special knowledge; and together they misunderstand the girl, their models having little to do with what is true.

Worlds are easy to observe.

Minds are secretive. And subtle. And molding them is never so easy and clear as the molding of mere worlds, I think.

Ula and I were working deep in the cavern, a few days after Provo's visit, teaching our robots how and where to plant an assortment of newly tailored saplings. We were starting our understory, vines and shrubs and shade-tolerant trees to create a dense tangle. And the robots struggled, designed to wrestle metals from rocks, not to baby the first generations of new species. At one point I waded into the fray, trying to help, shouting and grabbing at a mechanical arm while taking a blind step, a finger-long spine plunging into my ankle.

Ula laughed, watching me hobble backward. Then she turned sympathetic, absolutely convincing when she said, "Poor darling." She thought we should move to the closest water and clean out my wound. "It looks like it's swelling, Hann."

It was. I had designed this plant with an irritating protein, and I joked about the value of field testing, using a stick as my impromptu crutch. Thankfully we were close to one of the ponds, and the cool spring water felt wondrous, Ula removing my boot and the spine while I sprawled out on my back, eyes fixed on the white expanse of ice and lights, waiting for the pain to pass.

"If you were an ordinary terraformer," she observed, "this wouldn't have happened."

"I'd be somewhere else, and rich," I answered.

She moved from my soaking foot to my head, sitting beside me, knees pulled to her face and patches of perspiration darkening her lightweight work jersey. " 'Red of tooth and claw,' " she quoted.

A New Traditionalist motto. We were building a wilderness of spines and razored leaves; and later we'd add stinging wasps and noxious beetles, plus a savage biting midge that would attack in swarms. "Honest testing nature," I muttered happily.

Ula grinned and nodded, one of her odd expressions growing. And she asked, "But why can't we do more?"

More?

"Make the fire eagles attack us on sight, for instance. If we're after bloody claws—"

"No," I interrupted. "That has no ecological sense at all." Fire eagles were huge, but they'd never prey on humans.

"Oh, sure. I forgot."

She hadn't, and both of us knew it. Ula was playing another game with me.

I looked across the water, trying to ignore her. The far shore was a narrow stretch of raw stone, and the air above it would waver, field charges setting up their barrier against the heat. Beyond, not twenty meters beyond, was a rigid and hard-frozen milky wall that lifted into the sky, becoming the sky, part of me imagining giant eagles flying overhead, hunting for careless children.

"What's special about the original Earth?" I heard. "Tell me again, please, Hann."

No, I wouldn't. But even as I didn't answer, I answered. In my mind I was thinking about three billion years of natural selection, amoral and frequently short-sighted . . . and wondrous in its beauty, power, and scope . . . and how we in the Realm had perfected a stupefying version of that wonder, a million worlds guaranteed to be safe and comfortable for the trillions of souls clinging to them.

"Here," said Ula, "we should do everything like the original Earth."

I let myself ask, "What do you mean?"

"Put in things that make ecological sense. Like diseases and poisonous snakes, for instance."

"And we can be imprisoned for murder when the first visitor dies."

"But we aren't going to have visitors," she warned me. "So why not? A viper with a nerve toxin in its fangs? Or maybe some kind of plague carried by those biting midges that you're so proud of."

She was joking, I thought. Then I felt a sudden odd doubt.

Ula's entire face smiled, nothing about it simple. "What's more dangerous? Spines or no spines?"

"More dangerous?"

"For us." She touched my ankle, watching me.

"Spines," I voted.

"Back on Earth," she continued, "there were isolated islands. And the plants that colonized them would lose their spines and toxic chemicals, their old enemies left behind. And birds would lose their power of flight. And the tortoises grew huge, nothing to compete with them. Fat, easy living."

"What's your point, teacher?"

She laughed and said, "We arrived. We brought goats and rats and our-selves, and the native life would go extinct."

"I know history," I assured her.

"Not having spines is more dangerous than having them."

I imagined that I understood her point, nodding now and saying, "See? That's what NTs argue. Not quite in those terms—"

"Our worlds are like islands, soft and easy."

"Exactly." I grinned and nodded happily. "What I want to do here, and everywhere—"

"You're not much better," she interrupted.

No?

"Not much at all," she grumbled, her expression suddenly black. Sober. "Nature is so much more cruel and honest than you'd ever be."

Suddenly I was thinking about Provo's story, that non-description of Ula's forgotten childhood. It had been anything but soft and easy, and I felt pity; and I felt curiosity, wondering if she had nightmares and then, for an instant, wondering if I could help her in some important way.

Ula was watching me, reading my expression.

Without warning she bent close, kissing me before I could react and then sitting up again, laughing like a silly young girl.

I asked, "Why did you do that?"

"Why did I stop, you mean?"

I swallowed, saying nothing.

Then she bent over again, kissing me again, pausing to whisper, "Why don't we?"

I couldn't find any reason to stop.

And suddenly she was removing her jersey, and mine, and I looked past her for an instant, blinding myself with the glare of lights and white ice, all at once full of reasons why we should stop and my tongue stolen out of my mouth.

I was Ula's age when I graduated from the Academy. The oldest teacher on the staff invited me into her office, congratulated me for my good grades, then asked me in a matter-of-fact way, "Where do these worlds we build actually live, Mr. Locum? Can you point to where they are?"

She was cranky and ancient, her old black flesh turning white from simple age. I assumed that she was having troubles with her mind, the poor woman. A shrug; a gracious smile. Then I told her, "I don't know, ma'am. I would think they live where they live."

A smartass answer, if there ever was.

But she wasn't startled or even particularly irritated by my non-reply, a long lumpy finger lifting into the air between us, then pointing at her own forehead. "In our minds, Mr. Locum. That's the only place they can live for us, because where else can we live?"

"May I go?" I asked, unamused.

She said, "Yes."

I began to rise to my feet.

And she told me, "You are a remarkably stupid man, I think, Mr. Locum. Untalented and vain and stupid in many fundamental ways, and you have a better chance of success than most of your classmates."

"I'm leaving," I warned her.

"No." She shook her head. "You aren't here even now."

We were one week into our honeymoon—sex and sleep broken up with the occasional bout of work followed with a swim—and we were lying naked on the shore of the first pond. Ula looked at me, smiling and touching me, then saying, "You know, this world once was alive."

Her voice was glancingly saddened, barely audible over the quiet clean splash of the cliché. I nodded, saying, "I realize that." Then I waited for whatever would follow. I had learned about her lectures during the last seven days.

"It was an ocean world, just three billion years ago." She drew a planet on my chest. "Imagine if it hadn't been thrown away from its sun. If it had evolved complex life. If some kind of intelligent, tool-using fish had built spaceships—"

"Very unlikely," I countered.

She shrugged and asked, "Have you seen our fossils?"

No, but I didn't need to see them. Very standard types. The Realm was full of once-living worlds.

"This sea floor," she continued, "was dotted with hot-water vents, and bacteria evolved and lived by consuming metal ions—"

"—which they laid down, making the ore that you mine," I interrupted. With growing impatience, I asked, "Why tell me what I already know, Ula?"

"How do you think it would feel? Your world is thrown free of your sun, growing cold and freezing over . . . nothing you can do about it . . . and how would you feel . . . ?"

The vents would have kept going until the planet's tepid core grew cold, too little radioactivity to stave off the inevitable. "But we're talking about bacteria," I protested. "Nothing sentient. Unless you've found something bigger in the fossil record."

"Hardly," she said. Then she sat upright, small breasts catching the light and my gaze. "I was just thinking."

I braced myself.

"I remember when Father showed me one of the old vents . . . the first one I ever saw. . . ."

I doubly braced myself.

"I was five or six, I suppose, and we were walking through a new mine, down a dead rift valley, two hundred kilometers under the frozen sea. He pointed to mounds of dirty ore, then he had one of his robots slice into one of them, showing me the striations . . . how layers of bacteria had grown, by the trillion . . . outnumbering the human race, he said . . . and I cried. . . ."

"Did you?"

"Because they had died." She appeared close to tears again, but one hand casually scratched her breasts. Then the face brightened, almost smiling as she asked, "What's your favorite world?"

Changing subjects? I couldn't be sure.

"Your own world, or anyone's. Do you have favorites?"

Several of them, yes. I described the most famous world—a small spinning asteroid filled with wet forest—and I told her about the artists, all terraformers who had journeyed to the alien world of Pitcairn. They were the first New Traditionalists. I had never seen the work for myself, ten light-years between us and it, but I'd walked through the holos, maybe hundreds of times. The artists had been changed by Pitcairn. They never used alien lifeforms—there are tough clear laws against the exporting of Pitcairn life—but they had twisted earthly species to capture something of the strangeness and strength of the place. And I couldn't do it justice. I found myself blabbering about the quality of light and the intensity of certain golden birds . . . and at some point I quit speaking, realizing that Ula wasn't paying attention to me.

She heard silence and said, "It sounds intriguing." Then with a slow, almost studied pose, she said, "Let me tell you about something even more fascinating."

I felt a moment of anger. *How dare she ignore me!* Then the emotion evaporated, betraying me, leaving me to wait while she seemed to gather herself, her face never more serious or composed. Or focused. Or complete.

"It was the second world that I built," I heard. "My first world was too large and very clumsy, and I destroyed it by accident. But no matter. What I did that second time was find a very small abandoned mine, maybe a hectare in size, and I reinforced the ice walls and filled the chamber with water, then sank a small reactor into the rock, opening up the ancient plumbing and inoculating the water with a mixture of bacteria—"

"Did you?" I sputtered.

"—and reestablishing one vent community. After three billion years of sleep. I fueled the reactor with a measured amount of deuterium, and I enriched the warming water with the proper metals." A pause. "New striations formed. Superheated black goo was forced from the fossil tubes. And I dressed in a strong pressure suit and walked into that world, and I sat just like we're sitting here, and waited.''

I swallowed. "Waited?''

"The reactor slowed, then stopped.'' Ula took a breath and said, "I watched. With the lights on my suit down low, I watched the black goo stop rising, and the water cooled, and eventually new ice began to form against the walls. I moved to the center, sitting among the tubes . . . for days, for almost two weeks . . . the ice walls closing in on me—''

"That's crazy,'' I blurted.

And she shrugged as if to say, "I don't care.'' A smile emerged, then vanished, and she turned and touched me, saying, "I allowed myself to be frozen into that new ice, my limbs locked in place, my power packs running dry—''

"But why?'' I asked. "So you'd know how it felt?''

And she didn't seem to hear me, tilting her head, seemingly listening to some distant sound worthy of her complete attention. Eventually she said, "Father missed me.'' A pause. "He came home from a tour of distant mines, and I was missing, and he sent robots out to find me, and they cut me free just before I would have begun to truly suffer.''

The girl was insane. I knew it.

She took a dramatic breath, then smiled. Her haunted expression vanished in an instant, without effort, and again she was a student, the youngster, and my lover. A single bead of perspiration was rolling along her sternum, then spreading across her taut brown belly; and I heard myself asking, "Why did you do that shit?''

But the youngster couldn't or wouldn't explain herself, dipping her head and giggling into my ear.

"You could have died,'' I reminded her.

She said, "Don't be angry, darling. Please?''

An unstable, insane woman-child, and suddenly I was aware of my own heartbeat.

"Are you angry with sweet me?'' She reached for me, for a useful part of me, asking. "How can I make you happy, darling?''

"Be normal,'' I whispered.

"Haven't you paid attention?'' The possessed expression reemerged for an instant. "I'm not and never have been. Normal. My darling.''

My excuse, after much thought and practice, was a conference with her father. "I want us to have a backup reactor. In case.''

She dismissed the possibility out of hand. "He won't give us one.''

"And I want to walk on the surface. For a change of scenery.'' I paused, then camouflaged my intentions by asking, "Care to walk with me?''

"God, no. I've had enough of those walks, thank you."

Freed for the day, I began by visiting the closest caverns and one deflated tent, poking through dead groves and chiseling up samples of soil and frozen pond water. The cold was absolute. The sky was black and filled with stars, a few dim green worlds lost against the chill. Running quick tests, I tried to identify what had gone wrong and where. Sometimes the answer was obvious; sometimes I was left with guesses. But each of her worlds was undeniably dead, hundreds and thousands of new species extinct before they had any chance to prosper.

Afterward I rode the mag-rail back to Provo's house, finding where the hot-sap trees had been planted, the spot marked with a shallow lake created when the permafrost melted. I worked alone for twenty minutes, then the owner arrived. He seemed unhurried, yet something in his voice or his forward tilt implied a genuine concern. Or maybe not. I'd given up trying to decipher their damned family.

Pocketing my field instruments, I told Provo, "She's a good tailor. Too good." No greetings. No preparatory warning. I just informed him, "I've watched her, and you can't tell me that she'd introduce a toxic metabolite by accident. Not Ula."

The old man's face grew a shade paler, his entire body softening; and he leaned against a boulder, telling me without the slightest concern, "That possibility has crossed my mind, yes."

I changed topics, Ula-fashion. "When we met you warned me not to get too close to her. And not to be too honest."

"I remember."

"How do you know? Who else has been here?"

No answer.

"She's had another tutor, hasn't she?"

"Never."

"Then how can you know?"

"Twice," Provo told me, "my daughter has taken lovers. Two different crew members from separate freighters. Dullards, both of them. With each there was a period of bliss. They stayed behind and helped Ula with her work, then something would go wrong. I don't know any details. I refuse to spy on my own daughter. But with the man, her first lover . . . he expressed an interest in leaving, I believe . . . in returning to his vocation. . . ."

"What happened?"

"Ula pierced the wall of the tent. A year's work was destroyed in a few minutes." The man sighed, betraying a huge fatigue. "She told me that it was an accident, that she intended just to scare him—"

"She murdered him?" I managed.

And Provo laughed with relief. "No, no. No, the dullard was able to climb into an emergency suit in time, saving himself."

"What about the other lover?"

"The woman?" A strong shrug of the shoulders, then he said, "A fire. Another accident. I know less, but I surmise they had had a spat of some kind. A ridiculous, wasteful fit of anger. Although Ula claimed not to have started the blaze. She acted thoroughly innocent, and astonishingly unrepentant."

I swallowed, then whispered, "Your daughter is disturbed."

Provo said, "And didn't I warn you? Did you not understand me?" The soft face was perspiring despite the chill air. A cloud of mosquitoes drifted between us, hunting suitable game. "How much forewarning did you require, Mr. Locum?"

I said nothing.

"And you've done so well, too. Better than I had hoped possible, I should tell you."

I opened my mouth, and I said nothing.

"She told me . . . yesterday, I think . . . how important you are to her education—"

"The poison," I interrupted.

Provo quit speaking.

"There's a residue here. In the soil." I showed him a molecule displayed on my portable reader. "It's a synthetic alkaloid. Very messy, very tough. And very, very intentional, I think." A moment's pause, then I asked him, "Has it occurred to you that she was trying to murder you?"

"Naturally," he responded, in an instant.

"And?"

"And she didn't try. No."

"How can you feel sure?"

"You claim that my daughter is bright. Is talented. If she wanted to kill me, even if she was an idiot, don't you think that right now I would be dead?"

Probably true, I thought.

"Two people alone on an empty world. Nothing would be simpler than the perfect murder, Mr. Locum."

"Then what did she want?" I gestured at the little lake. "What was *this* about?"

Provo appeared disgusted, impatient.

He told me, "I might have hoped that you could explain it to me."

I imagined Ula on the bottom of a freezing sea, risking death in some bid to understand . . . what? And three times she had endangered others . . .

which left another dozen creations that she had killed . . . and was she alone
in each of them when they died . . . ?

"Discover her purpose, Mr. Locum, and perhaps I'll give you a bonus. If
that's permissible."

I said nothing.

"You have been following my suggestions, haven't you? You aren't becoming too entangled with her, are you?"

I looked at Provo.

And he read my face, shaking his head with heavy sadness, saying, "Oh,
my, Mr. Locum. Oh, my."

A *purpose*.

The possibility gnawed at me. I assumed some kind of madness lay over
whatever her rationale, and I wished for a degree in psychiatry, or maybe
some life experience with insanity. Anything would help. Riding the mag-
rail back into our cavern, replaying the last few months in my mind, I heard
part of me begging for me to flee, to turn now and take refuge where I could,
then stow away on the first freighter to pass—

—which was impossible, I realized in the same instant. Not to mention
dangerous. Acting normal was important, I told myself. Then aloud, I said,
"Just keep her happy."

I have never been more terrified of a human being.

Yet Ula seemed oblivious. She greeted me with a kiss and demanded more,
and I failed her, nervousness and a sudden fatigue leaving me soft. But she
explained it away as stress and unimportant, cuddling up next to me on the
shady jungle floor. She said, "Let's sleep," and I managed to close my eyes
and drift into a broken dreamy sleep, jerking awake to find myself alone.

Where had the girl gone?

I called her on our com-linc, hearing her voice and my voice dry and
clumsy, asking her, "Where are you?"

"Mutating treefrogs, darling."

Which put her inside her home. Out of my way. I moved to the closest
workstation, asking its reader to show me the original schematics and everything that we had done to date; and I opened up my jersey—I was still wearing
my heavy, cold-weather jersey—drops of salty water splattering on the reader.
I was hunting for anything odd or obviously dangerous. A flaw in the ice
roof? None that I could find. A subtle poison in our young trees? None that
showed in the genetic diagrams. But just to be sure, I tested myself. Nothing
wrong in my blood, I learned. What else? There was one oddity, something
that I might have noticed before but missed. The trees had quirks in their
chemistry. Nothing deadly. Just curious. I was studying a series of sugars,
wondering when Ula had slipped them into the tailoring process, and why;

and just then, as if selecting the perfect moment, she said, "Darling," with a clear close voice. Then, "What are you doing?"

I straightened my back, and I turned.

Ula was standing behind me, the smile bright and certain. And strange. She said, "Hello?" and then, "What are you doing, darling?"

I blanked the reader.

Then with the stiffest possible voice, I told her, "Nothing. Just checking details."

She approached, taking me around my waist.

I hugged her, wondering what to do.

Then she released me, pulling back her hair while asking, "What did you and my father decide?"

Swallowing was impossible, my throat full of dust.

"I forgot to ask before. Do we get a second reactor?"

I managed to shake my head. No.

"An unnecessary expense," she said, perfectly mimicking her father's voice. She couldn't have acted more normal, walking around me while asking, "Has the nap helped?"

I watched her undress as she moved.

"Feel like fun?"

Why was I afraid? There weren't any flaws in our work, I knew, and as long as she was with me, nude and in my grasp, what could she do to me? Nothing, and I became a little confident. At least confident enough to accomplish the task at hand, the event feeling robotic and false, and entirely safe.

Afterward she said, "That was the best," and I knew—knew without doubt—that Ula was lying. "The best ever," she told me, kissing my nose and mouth and upturned throat. "We'll never have a more perfect moment. Can I ask you something?"

"What . . . ?"

She said, "It's something that I've considered. For a long while, I've been wondering—"

"What?"

"About the future." She straddled me, pressure on my stomach. The grin was sly and expectant. "When Father dies, I inherit this world. All of it and his money too, and his robots. Everything."

A slight nod, and I said, "Yes?"

"What will I do with it?"

I had no idea.

"What if I bought an artificial sun? Not fancy. And brought it here and put it in orbit. I've estimated how long it would take to melt this sea, if I hurried things along by seeding the ice with little reactors—"

"Decades," I interrupted.

"Two or three, I think. And then I could terraform an entire world." She paused, tilting her head and her eyes lifting. "Of course all of this would be destroyed. Which is sad." She sighed, shrugging her shoulders. "How many people have my kind of wealth, Hann? In the entire Realm, how many?"

"I don't know."

"And who already own a world too. How many?"

"Very few."

"And who have an interest in terraforming, of course." She giggled and said, "I could be one of a kind. It's possible."

It was.

"What I want to ask," she said, "is this. Would you, Hann Locum, like to help me? To remake all of this ice and rock with me?"

I opened my mouth, then hesitated.

"Because I don't deserve all the fun for myself," she explained, climbing off me. "Wouldn't that be something? You might be the first NT terraformer with your own world. Wouldn't that make you the envy of your peers?"

"Undoubtedly," I whispered.

Ula walked to her clothes, beginning to dress. "Are you interested?"

I said, "Yes. Sure." True or not, I wanted to make agreeable sounds. Then I made myself add, "But your father's in good health. It could be a long time before—"

"Oh, yeah." A glib shrug of her shoulders; a vague little-girl smile. "I hope it's years and years away. I do."

I watched the girl's face, unable to pierce it. I couldn't guess what she was really thinking, not even when she removed the odd control from one of her deep pockets. A simple device, homemade and held in her right hand; and now she winked at me, saying, "I know."

Know?

"What both of you talked about today. Of course I know."

The pressure on my chest grew a thousandfold.

"The mosquitoes? Some aren't. They're electronic packages dressed up as mosquitoes, and I always hear what Father says—"

Shit.

"—and have for years. Always."

I sat upright, hands digging into the damp black soil.

She laughed and warned me, "You're not the first person to hear his confession. I am sorry. He has this guilt, and he salves it by telling people who can't threaten him. I suppose he wanted you to feel sorry for him, and to admire him—"

"What do you remember?"

"Of my parents? Nothing." She shook her head. "Everything." A nod and the head titled, and she told me, "I do have one clear image. I don't know if it's memory or if it's a dream, or what. But I'm a child inside a smelly freighter, huddled in a corner, watching Provo Lei strangle my real mother. He doesn't know I'm there, of course." A pause. "If he had known, do you suppose he would have strangled me too? To save himself, perhaps?"

"I'm sorry," I muttered.

And she laughed, the sound shrill. Complex. "Why? He's a very good father, considering. I love him, and I can't blame him for anything." A pause, then with a caring voice she told me, "I love him quite a lot more than I love you, Hann."

I moved, the ground under my butt creaking; and I had to say, "But you poisoned him anyway."

Ula waved her control with a flourish, telling me, "I poisoned everything. All I wanted was for Father to watch." A shrug. "I tried to make him understand . . . to comprehend . . . but I don't think he could ever appreciate what I was trying to tell him. Never."

I swallowed, then asked, "What were you telling him?"

Her eyes grew huge, then a finger was wagged at me. "No. No, you don't." She took a small step backward, shaking her head. "I think it's just a little too soon for that. Dear."

I waited.

Then she waved the control again, saying, "Look up, Hann. Will you? Now?"

"Up?" I whispered.

"This direction." She pointed at the canopy. "This is *up*."

My gaze lifted, the solid green ceiling of leaves glowing, branches like veins running through the green; and she must have activated the control, a distinct click followed by her calm voice saying, "I left out parts of the schematics, Hann. Intentionally. Before you were even hired, you should know."

There was a distant rumbling noise.

The ground moved, tall trees swaying for an instant; then came a flash of light with instant thunder, a bolt of electricity leaping down the long cavern, the force of it swatting me down against the forest floor, heat against my face and chest, every hair on my body lifting for a terrible long instant.

Then it was gone again.

Everything was.

The lights had failed, a perfect seamless night engulfing the world; and twice I heard a laugh, close and then distant.

Then nothing.

And I screamed, the loudest sound I could muster lost in the leaves and against the tree trunks, fading into echoes and vanishing, as if it had never existed at all.

My jersey . . . where was my jersey . . . ?

I made myself stand and think, perfectly alert, trying to remember where it had lain and counting steps in my mind . . . one step, and two, and three. Then I knelt and found nothing in reach, nothing but the rich new soil, and for a terrified instant I wondered if Ula had stolen my clothes, leaving me naked as well as blind.

But another step and grope gave me my boots, then the jersey. I dressed and found my various equipment in the pockets and pouches. The portable reader had been cooked by the lightning, but the glowglobes were eager. I ignited one of them and released it; it hovered over me, moving with a faint dry hum as it emitted a yellowish light.

I walked to the closest mag-rail.

Inoperative.

Nearby were a pair of robots standing like statues.

Dead.

I started to jog uphill, moving fast. Where was Ula? Had she gone somewhere, or was she nearby, watching me?

It was fifteen kilometers to the waterfall, the exit. The trees seemed larger in the very weak light, the open jungle floor feeling rather like a place of worship. A cathedral. Then came a wall of vines and thorny brush—our earliest plantings—and I burrowed into them, pushing despite the stabs at my skin, breaking into an open unfinished glade and pausing. Something was wrong, I thought. Against my face was cold air, bitter and sudden. Of course the field generators were down. And the refrigeration elements. What remained was the passive emergency system, heat rising into high ducts while others released cubic kilometers of stored air from below.

How long would the process take?

I couldn't remember, could scarcely think about anything. My jersey automatically warmed me, and I helped keep warm by running fast, pulling ahead of my glowglobe, my frantic shadow gigantic and ethereal.

In my head, in simple terms, I handled the mathematics.

Calories; volume; turbulence; time.

Halfway to the waterfall, feeling the distance and the grade, I had a terrible sudden premonition.

Slowing, I said, "Where are you?"

Then I screamed, "Ula! Ula!"

In the chill air my voice carried, and when it died there was a new sound, clear and strong and very distant. A howl; a wild inhuman moan. I took a weak step sideways and faltered. Somehow I felt as if I should know the source . . . and I remembered Ula's eight-legged predator, swift and smart and possibly on the hunt now. *She had made it* . . . !

There was a motion, a single swirling something coming out of the gloom at me. I grunted and twisted, falling down, and a leaf landed at my feet. Brown and cold. Partly cooked by the lightning, I realized. It crumbled when my hand closed around it. Then came the howl again, seemingly closer, and again I was running, sprinting uphill, into another band of prickly underbrush and starting to sob with the authority of a beaten child.

The ambient temperature was plummeting.

My breath showed in my glowglobe's yellow light, lifting and thinning and mixing with more falling leaves. The forest was slipping into dormancy. A piece of me was thankful, confident that it at least would survive whatever happened; and most of me was furious with Ula—a simple, visceral fury— as I imagined my escape and the filing of criminal complaints. Attempted murder. Malicious endangerment. And straight murder charges on Provo, me as witness for the prosecution and their lives here finished. Extinguished. Lost.

"I'm going to escape," I muttered at the shadows. "Ula? Are you listening? Ula?"

I pulled gloves from a pocket, covering my cold hands and them knitting into my sleeves. Then I unrolled my jersey's simple hood, tying it flush against my head, enjoying the heat of the fabric. Leaves were falling in a steady brown blizzard. They covered the freezing earth, crunching with each footfall, and sometimes in the crunches I thought I heard someone or something else moving. Pausing, I would listen. Wait. The predator? Or Ula? But the next howl seemed distant and perhaps confused, and it had to be the girl whom I heard. Who wouldn't be fooled with my stop and then go and stop again tricks.

The cavern's upper end was bitter cold. One of our emergency ducts had opened up beside the entranceway, robbing the heat from the water and ground and trees. Already the pond was freezing, the ice clear and hard, very nearly flawless. I ran on its shore, squinting into the gloom, believing that at least the cliché, the falls, would have stopped flowing when the power failed. Not in an instant, no. But its reservoir was relatively small—Ula had shown me her plans—and for a glorious instant I was absolutely convinced that my escape was imminent.

What was that? From the gloom came an apparent wall of marble, white and thick and built where the cliché had been. *Frozen* . . . *the waterfall had frozen clear through* . . . !

I moaned, screamed, and slowed.

Beside the pond was one of the useless robots. I moved to it, my breath freezing against the ceramic skin, and with a few desperate tugs I managed to pry free one of its hands. The hand was meant for cutting, for chopping, and I held it like an axe, growling at my audience. "What did you think? That I'd just give up now?"

No answer. The only sounds were the falling of leaves and the occasional creaking pop as sap froze inside the sleeping trees.

I moved to the icy shelf at the base of the falls, shuffling to where I normally walked through, where the ice should be thinnest. Three times I swung, twice without force and the third blow hard and useless, the ice as tough as marble and more slippery. My axe slid sideways, twisting me. Then my boots moved, my balance lost, and I hit the icy shelf, slid, and fell again.

The pond caught me. The ice beneath gave with the impact, a slight but deep cracking sound lasting for an age. But I didn't fall through. And when I could breathe again, with pain, I stood and hobbled over to the shore, trying very hard not to give in.

"Is this what you did to the others?" I asked.

Silence.

"Is this how you treat lovers, Ula?"

A howl, almost close, sudden and very shrill.

A primeval thought came to me. I made myself approach the black jungle, scooping up leaves by the armful and building a substantial pile of them where I had sat with Provo, against the downed log. And I lit them and the log on fire with a second glowglobe, putting it on overload and stepping back and the globe detonating with a wet sizzle, the dried leaves exploding into a smoky red fire.

The odd sugars loved to burn, the flames hot and quick and delicious. They ignited the log within minutes, giving me a sense of security. The canopy didn't reach overhead. I made doubly sure that the surrounding ground had no leaves, no way for the fire to spread; then I set to work, armfuls of fresh leaves piled against the cliché, tamped them down with my boots until there was a small hill spilling onto the pond.

Heat versus ice.

Equations and estimates kept me focused, unafraid.

Then I felt ready, using the axe to knock loose a long splinter of burning log. I carried the cold end, shouting, "See? See? I'm not some idiot. I'm not staying in your trap, Ula!" I touched the leaf pile in a dozen places, then retreated, keeping at what felt like a safe distance but feeling waves regardless, dry and solid heat playing over me, almost nourishing me for the moment.

Those sugars were wonderfully potent. Almost explosive.

Ula must have planned to burn me alive, I kept thinking. She would have lit the leaf litter when it was deep enough . . . only I'd beaten her timetable, hadn't I?

"I'll file charges," I promised the red-lit trees. "You should have done a better job, my dear."

A sharp howl began, then abruptly stopped. It was as if a recording had been turned off in its middle.

Then came a crashing sound, and I turned to see a single chunk of softened ice breaking free of the cliché, crashing into my fire and throwing sparks in every direction. Watching the sparks, I felt worry and a sudden fatigue. *What's wrong?* My eyes lifted, maybe out of instinct, and I noticed a single platter-sized leaf still rising, glowing red and obviously different from the other leaves. It was burning slowly, almost patiently. It practically soared overhead. Just like a fire eagle, it rode a thermal . . . and didn't it resemble an eagle? A little bit? One species of tree among hundreds, and Ula must have designed it, and she must have seen that it was planted here—

—such an elaborate, overly complicated plan. Contrived and plainly artificial, I was thinking. Part of me felt superior and critical. Even when I knew the seriousness of everything, watching that leaf vanish into great blackness overhead . . . out of the thermal now, gliding off in some preplanned direction, no doubt . . . even then I felt remarkably unafraid, knowing that that leaf would surely reach the canopy somewhere, igniting hundreds of leaves and the sappy young branches . . . and part of me wanted nothing more than to take my student aside, arm around her shoulders, while I said, "Now listen. This is all very clever, and I'm sure it's cruel, but this is neither elegant nor artful and show me another way to do it. By tomorrow. That's your assignment, Ula. Will you do it for me, please?"

The forest caught fire.

I heard the fire before I saw the ruddy glow of it. It sounded like a grinding wind, strong and coming nearer; then came the crashing of softened ice, blocks and slush dropping onto my fire and choking it out completely.

I didn't have time or the concentration to build another fire.

Towering red flames were streaking through the cavern, first in the canopy and then lower, igniting whole trunks that would explode. I heard them, and I felt the detonations against my face and through my toes. The air itself began to change, tasting warm and sooty, ashes against my teeth and tongue. Transfixed, I stood in the clearing beside the pond, thick and twisting black columns of smoke rising, the ceiling lit red and the smoke pooling against it, forming an inverted lake full of swirling superheated gases.

Over the rumble and roar of the fire, I heard someone speaking, close and harsh . . . and after a few moments of hard concentration I realized it was my voice, senseless angry sounds bubbling out of me . . . and I clamped a hand over my mouth, fingers into a cheek and tears mixed with the stinking ash . . . I was crying . . . I had been crying for a very long while. . . .

I would die here.

Always crying, I struggled with prosaic calculations. Calories from combustion; oxygen consumed; the relative toughness of human flesh. But my numbers collapsed, too much stress and too little time remaining. Part of the firestorm was coming back at me now, trunks burning and splitting open as the fiery sap boiled; but I wouldn't burn to death, I decided. Because what felt like a finger struck me on top of my head, in my hair, and I looked up just as a second gooey drop of water found me. It dripped between the fingers of my clamping hand, and I tasted it—smoke and ash mixed with a sharp, almost chemical aftertaste—

—melted ice from the faraway roof—

—unfrozen, ancient seawater.

The black lake of churning smoke was its deepest straight above me, and those first drops became multitudes, fat and forceful. Like rain, then harder. They hammered me to the ground, my head dropping and my hands held above it, shielding very little, and squinting eyes able to see the oncoming fire begin to slow, to drown.

I thought of the falls melting with this onslaught, but I couldn't stand, much less move. The mud under me seemed to suck, holding me in place. I was squarely beneath an enormous waterfall—no cliché—and I would have laughed, given the breath.

Funny, fun Ula.

Perhaps the largest waterfall in the Realm, I was thinking. For this moment, at least. And my mind's eye lent me a safe vantage point, flames and water struggling for the world. And destroying it too. And somewhere I realized that by now I had to be dead, that breathing had to be impossible, that I only believed I was breathing because death had to be a continuation of life, a set of habits maintained. What a lovely, even charming wonder. I felt quite calm, quite happy. Hearing the roar of water, aware of the soil and trees and rock itself being obliterated . . . my bones and pulverized meat mixed into the stew . . . and how sweet that I could retain my limbs, my face and mouth and heart, as a ghost. I thought. Touching myself in the noisy blackness, I found even my soaked jersey intact . . . no, not total blackness; there was a dim glow from above . . . and I began to sit upright, thinking like a ghost, wondering about my powers and wishing that my soul could lift now, lift and fly away.

But instead, with unghostly force, my head struck a solid surface.

Thunk.

I staggered, groaned, and reached out with both hands, discovering a blister of transparent hyperglass above me. Enclosing me. Larger than a coffin, but not by much . . . it must have been deployed at the last possible instant, air pumped in from below, seals designed to withstand this abuse . . . a safety mechanism not shown on any schematic, obviously . . . and I was alive, slippery wet and numb but undeniably organic. . . .

. . . and unalone as well.

Rising from the mud beside me, visible in that thin cool light, was a naked form—artist; torturer; Nature Herself—who calmly and with great dignity wiped the mud from her eyes and grinning mouth. And she bent, the mouth to my ear, asking me over the great roar, "So what have you learned today, student?"

I couldn't speak, could barely think.

Opening my jersey, she kissed my bare chest. "The eight-legged howler was just noise. Just my little illusion."

Yet in my head it was real, even now.

"I would never intentionally hurt," she promised. "Not you, not anyone."

I wanted to believe her.

"I always watched over you, Hann. I never blinked."

Thank you.

"I'm not cruel." A pause. "It's just—"

Yes?

"—I wanted to show you—"

What?

"—what? What have I shown you, darling?"

Squinting, I gazed up through the thick blister, the black water churning more slowly, cooling and calming itself. My mind became lucid, answers forming and my mouth opening and her anticipating the moment, her hand tasting of earth as it closed my mouth again.

We lay quietly together, as if in a common grave.

For two days we waited, the water refreezing around us and neither of us speaking, the creaking of new ice fading into a perfect silence. A contemplative, enlightening silence. I built worlds in my head—great and beautiful and true, full of the frailties and powers of life—then came the gnawing and pounding of robots. Half-burned trees were jerked free and tossed aside. The ice itself was peeled away from the blister. I saw motions, then stars. Then a familiar stocky figure. Provo Lei peered in at us, the round face furious and elated in equal measures; and as he began to cut us free, in those last moments of solitude, I turned to Ula and finally spoke.

"You never wanted to terraform worlds," I blurted.

"Worlds are tiny," she said with contempt. Her liquid smile was lit by the cutting laser, and a green eye winked as she said, "Tell me, Hann. What do I care about?"

Something larger than worlds, I knew—

—and I understood, in an instant—

—but as I touched my head, ready to tell, Provo burst through the hyperglass and stole my chance. Suddenly Ula had changed, becoming the pouting little girl, her lower lip stuck out and a plaintive voice crying, "Oh, Father. I'm such a clumsy goof, Father. I'm sorry, so sorry. Will you ever forgive me? Please, please?"

LUMINOUS

Greg Egan

▼

Perhaps the hottest and fastest-rising new writer to debut in SF in the nineties, Australian Greg Egan is poised on the verge of being recognized as one of the genre's Big Names. In the last few years, Egan has become a frequent contributor to *Interzone* and *Asimov's Science Fiction*, and has made sales as well to *Pulphouse, Analog, Aurealis, Eidolon*, and elsewhere. Several of his stories have appeared in various best-of-the-year series, including this one; in fact, he placed two stories in both our Eighth and Ninth Annual Collections—the first author ever to do that back-to-back in consecutive volumes. He has also had stories in our Tenth, Eleventh, and Twelfth Annual Collections as well. He was on the Hugo Final Ballot in 1995 for his story "Cocoon," which won the Ditmar Award and the *Asimov's* Readers Award. His first novel, *Quarantine*, appeared in 1992, to wide critical acclaim, and was followed by a second novel in 1994, *Permutation City*, which won the John W. Campbell Memorial Award. His most recent book is a collection of his short fiction, *Axiomatic*. Upcoming are two new novels, *Distress* and *Diaspora*.

Here he launches an intrepid attack on the most abstract realms of Higher Mathematics with a computer made entirely of light—with potentially disastrous results for the entire universe when those abstract realms start to strike back . . .

I woke, disoriented, unsure why. I knew I was lying on the narrow, lumpy single bed in Room 22 of the Hotel Fleapit; after almost a month in Shanghai, the topography of the mattress was depressingly familiar. But there was something wrong with the way I was lying; every muscle in my neck and shoulders was protesting that nobody could end up in this position from natural causes, however badly they'd slept.

And I could smell blood.

I opened my eyes. A woman I'd never seen before was kneeling over me, slicing into my left triceps with a disposable scalpel. I was lying on my side, facing the wall, one hand and one ankle cuffed to the head and foot of the bed.

Something cut short the surge of visceral panic before I could start stupidly thrashing about, instinctively trying to break free. Maybe an even more ancient response—catatonia in the face of danger—took on the adrenaline and won. Or maybe I just decided that I had no right to panic when I'd been expecting something like this for weeks.

I spoke softly, in English. "What you're in the process of hacking out of me is a necrotrap. One heartbeat without oxygenated blood, and the cargo gets fried."

My amateur surgeon was compact, muscular, with short black hair. Not Chinese: Indonesian, maybe. If she was surprised that I'd woken prematurely, she didn't show it. The gene-tailored hepatocytes I'd acquired in Hanoi could degrade almost anything from morphine to curare; it was a good thing the local anaesthetic was beyond their reach.

Without taking her eyes off her work, she said, "Look on the table next to the bed."

I twisted my head around. She'd set up a loop of plastic tubing full of blood—mine, presumably—circulated and aerated by a small pump. The stem of a large funnel fed into the loop, the intersection controlled by a valve of some kind. Wires trailed from the pump to a sensor taped to the inside of my elbow, synchronizing the artificial pulse with the real. I had no doubt that she could tear the trap from my vein and insert it into this substitute without missing a beat.

I cleared my throat and swallowed. "Not good enough. The trap knows my blood pressure profile exactly. A generic heartbeat won't fool it."

"You're bluffing." But she hesitated, scalpel raised. The hand-held MRI scanner she'd used to find the trap would have revealed its basic configuration, but few fine details of the engineering—and nothing at all about the software.

"I'm telling you the truth." I looked her squarely in the eye, which wasn't easy given our awkward geometry. "It's new, it's Swedish. You anchor it in a vein forty-eight hours in advance, put yourself through a range of typical activities so it can memorize the rhythms . . . then you inject the cargo into the trap. Simple, foolproof, effective." Blood trickled down across my chest onto the sheet. I was suddenly very glad that I hadn't buried the thing deeper, after all.

"So how do you retrieve the cargo, yourself?"

"That would be telling."

"Then tell me now, and save yourself some trouble." She rotated the scalpel between thumb and forefinger impatiently. My skin did a cold burn all over, nerve ends jangling, capillaries closing down as blood dived for cover.

I said, "*Trouble* gives me hypertension."

She smiled down at me thinly, conceding the stalemate—then peeled off one stained surgical glove, took out her notepad, and made a call to a medical equipment supplier. She listed some devices which would get around the problem—a blood pressure probe, a more sophisticated pump, a suitable computerized interface—arguing heatedly in fluent Mandarin to extract a promise of a speedy delivery. Then she put down the notepad and placed her ungloved hand on my shoulder.

"You can relax now. We won't have long to wait."

I squirmed, as if angrily shrugging off her hand—and succeeded in getting some blood on her skin. She didn't say a word, but she must have realized at once how careless she'd been; she climbed off the bed and headed for the washbasin, and I heard the water running.

Then she started retching.

I called out cheerfully, "Let me know when you're ready for the antidote."

I heard her approach, and I turned to face her. She was ashen, her face contorted with nausea, eyes and nose streaming mucus and tears.

"Tell me where it is!"

"Uncuff me, and I'll get it for you."

"No! No deals!"

"Fine. Then you'd better start looking, yourself."

She picked up the scalpel and brandished it in my face. "Screw the cargo. *I'll do it!*" She was shivering like a feverish child, uselessly trying to stem the flood from her nostrils with the back of her hand.

I said coldly, "If you cut me again, you'll lose more than the cargo."

She turned away and vomited; it was thin and gray, blood-streaked. The toxin was persuading cells in her stomach lining to commit suicide *en masse*.

"Uncuff me. It'll kill you. It doesn't take long."

She wiped her mouth, steeled herself, made as if to speak—then started puking again. I knew, first-hand, exactly how bad she was feeling. Keeping it down was like trying to swallow a mixture of shit and sulphuric acid. Bringing it up was like evisceration.

I said, "In thirty seconds, you'll be too weak to help yourself—even if I told you where to look. So if I'm not free . . ."

She produced a gun and a set of keys, uncuffed me, then stood by the foot of the bed, shaking badly but keeping me targeted. I dressed quickly, ignoring her threats, bandaging my arm with a miraculously clean spare sock before putting on a T-shirt and a jacket. She sagged to her knees, still aiming the gun more or less in my direction—but her eyes were swollen half-shut, and brimming with yellow fluid. I thought about trying to disarm her, but it didn't seem worth the risk.

I packed my remaining clothes, then glanced around the room as if I might have left something behind. But everything that really mattered was in my veins; Alison had taught me that that was the only way to travel.

I turned to the burglar. "There is no antidote. But the toxin won't kill you. You'll just wish it would, for the next twelve hours. Goodbye."

As I headed for the door, hairs rose suddenly on the back of my neck. It occurred to me that she might not take me at my word—and might fire a parting shot, believing she had nothing to lose.

Turning the handle, without looking back, I said, "But if you come after me—next time, I'll kill you."

That was a lie, but it seemed to do the trick. As I pulled the door shut behind me, I heard her drop the gun and start vomiting again.

Halfway down the stairs, the euphoria of escape began to give way to a bleaker perspective. If one careless bounty hunter could find me, her more methodical colleagues couldn't be far behind. Industrial Algebra was closing in on us. If Alison didn't gain access to Luminous soon, we'd have no choice but to destroy the map. And even that would only be buying time.

I paid the desk clerk for the room until the next morning, stressing that my companion should not be disturbed, and added a suitable tip to compensate for the mess the cleaners would find. The toxin denatured in air; the bloodstains would be harmless in a matter of hours. The clerk eyed me suspiciously, but said nothing.

Outside, it was a mild, cloudless summer morning. It was barely six o'clock, but Kongjiang Lu was already crowded with pedestrians, cyclists, buses—and a few ostentatious chauffeured limousines, ploughing through the traffic at about ten kph. It looked like the night shift had just emerged from the Intel factory down the road; most of the passing cyclists were wearing the orange, logo-emblazoned overalls.

Two blocks from the hotel I stopped dead, my legs almost giving way beneath me. It wasn't just shock—a delayed reaction, a belated acceptance of how close I'd come to being slaughtered. The burglar's clinical violence was chilling enough—but what it implied was infinitely more disturbing.

Industrial Algebra was paying big money, violating international law, taking serious risks with their corporate and personal futures. The arcane abstraction of the defect was being dragged into the world of blood and dust, boardrooms and assassins, power and pragmatism.

And the closest thing to certainty humanity had ever known was in danger of dissolving into quicksand.

It had all started out as a joke. Argument for argument's sake. Alison and her infuriating heresies.

"A mathematical theorem," she'd proclaimed, "only becomes true when a physical system tests it out: when the system's behavior depends in some way on the theorem being *true* or *false*."

It was June 1994. We were sitting in a small paved courtyard, having just emerged yawning and blinking into the winter sunlight from the final lecture in a one-semester course on the philosophy of mathematics—a bit of light relief from the hard grind of the real stuff. We had fifteen minutes to kill before meeting some friends for lunch. It was a social conversation—verging on mild flirtation—nothing more. Maybe there were demented academics lurking in dark crypts somewhere, who held views on the nature of mathematical truth that they were willing to die for. But we were twenty years old, and we *knew* it was all angels on the head of a pin.

I said, "Physical systems don't create mathematics. Nothing *creates* mathematics—it's timeless. All of number theory would still be exactly the same, even if the universe contained nothing but a single electron."

Alison snorted. "Yes, because even *one electron*, plus a space-time to put it in, needs all of quantum mechanics and all of general relativity—and all the mathematical infrastructure they entail. One particle floating in a quantum vacuum needs half the major results of group theory, functional analysis, differential geometry—"

"Okay, okay! I get the point. But if that's the case . . . the events in the first picosecond after the Big Bang would have 'constructed' every last mathematical truth required by *any* physical system, all the way to the Big Crunch. Once you've got the mathematics that underpins the Theory of Everything . . . that's it, that's all you ever need. End of story."

"But it's not. To *apply* the Theory of Everything to a particular system, you still need all the mathematics for dealing with *that system*—which could include results far beyond the mathematics that the TOE itself requires. I mean, fifteen billion years after the Big Bang, someone can still come along and prove, say . . . Fermat's Last Theorem." Andrew Wiles at Princeton had recently announced a proof of the famous conjecture, although his work was still being scrutinized by his colleagues, and the final verdict wasn't yet in. "Physics never needed *that* before."

I protested, "What do you mean, 'before'? Fermat's Last Theorem never has—and never will—have anything to do with any branch of physics."

Alison smiled sneakily. "No *branch*—no. But only because the class of physical systems whose behavior depends on it is so ludicrously specific: the brains of mathematicians who are trying to validate the Wiles proof.

"Think about it. Once you start trying to prove a theorem, then even if the mathematics is so 'pure' that it has no relevance to any other object in the universe . . . you've just made it relevant to *yourself*. You have to choose *some* physical process to test the theorem—whether you use a computer, or a pen and paper . . . or just close your eyes and shuffle *neurotransmitters*. There's no such thing as a proof that doesn't rely on physical events—and whether they're inside or outside your skull doesn't make them any less real."

"Fair enough," I conceded warily. "But that doesn't mean—"

"And maybe Andrew Wiles's brain—and body, and notepaper—comprised the first physical system whose behavior depended on the theorem being true or false. But I don't think human actions have any special role . . . and if some swarm of quarks had done the same thing blindly, fifteen billion years before—executed some purely random interaction that just happened to test the conjecture in some way—then *those quarks* would have constructed FLT long before Wiles. We'll never know."

I opened my mouth to complain that no swarm of quarks could have tested the infinite number of cases encompassed by the theorem—but I caught myself just in time. That was true—but it hadn't stopped Wiles. A finite sequence of logical steps linked the axioms of number theory—which included some simple generalities about *all* numbers—to Fermat's own sweeping assertion. And if a mathematician could test those logical steps by manipulating a finite number of physical objects for a finite amount of time—whether they were pencil marks on paper, or neurotransmitters in his or her brain—then all kinds of physical systems could, in theory, mimic the structure of the proof . . . with or without any awareness of what it was they were "proving."

I leant back on the bench and mimed tearing out hair. "If I wasn't a diehard Platonist before, you're forcing me into it! Fermat's Last Theorem didn't *need* to be proved by anyone—or stumbled on by any random swarm of quarks. If it's true, it was always true. Everything implied by a given set of axioms is logically connected to them, timelessly, eternally . . . even if the links couldn't be traced by people—or quarks—in the lifetime of the universe."

Alison was having none of this; every mention of *timeless and eternal truths* brought a faint smile to the corner of her mouth, as if I was affirming my belief in Santa Claus. She said, "So who, or what, pushed the consequences of 'There exists an entity called zero' and 'Every X has a successor,' *et cetera*, all the way to Fermat's Last Theorem and beyond, before the universe had a chance to test out any of it?"

I stood my ground. "What's joined by logic is just . . . *joined*. Nothing has to happen—consequences don't have to be 'pushed' into existence by anyone, or anything. Or do you imagine that the first events after the Big Bang, the first wild jitters of the quark-gluon plasma, stopped to fill in all the logical gaps? You think the quarks reasoned: well, so far we've done A and B and C—but now we mustn't do D, because D would be logically inconsistent with the other mathematics we've 'invented' so far . . . even if it would take a five-hundred-thousand-page proof to spell out the inconsistency?"

Alison thought it over. "No. But what if event D took place, regardless? What if the mathematics it implied *was* logically inconsistent with the rest—

but it went ahead and happened anyway . . . because the universe was too young to have computed the fact that there was any discrepancy?''

I must have sat and stared at her, open-mouthed, for about ten seconds. Given the orthodoxies we'd spent the last two-and-a-half years absorbing, this was a seriously outrageous statement.

"You're claiming that . . . *mathematics* might be strewn with primordial defects in consistency? Like space might be strewn with cosmic strings?''

"Exactly.'' She stared back at me, feigning nonchalance. "If space-time doesn't join up with itself smoothly, everywhere . . . why should mathematical logic?''

I almost choked. "Where do I begin? What happens—now—when some physical system tries to link theorems across the defect? If theorem D has been rendered 'true' by some over-eager quarks, what happens when we program a computer to disprove it? When the software goes through all the logical steps that link A, B, and C—which the quarks have also made true— to the contradiction, the dreaded not-D . . . does it succeed, or doesn't it?''

Alison side-stepped the question. "Suppose they're both true: D and not-D. Sounds like the end of mathematics, doesn't it? The whole system falls apart, instantly. From D and not-D together you can prove anything you like: one equals zero, day equals night. But that's just the boring-old-fart Platonist view—where logic travels faster than light, and computation takes no time at all. People live with omega-inconsistent theories, don't they?''

Omega-inconsistent number theories were non-standard versions of arithmetic, based on axioms that "almost" contradicted each other—their saving grace being that the contradictions could only show up in "infinitely long proofs" (which were formally disallowed, quite apart from being physically impossible). That was perfectly respectable modern mathematics—but Alison seemed prepared to replace "infinitely long" with just plain "long"—as if the difference hardly mattered, in practice.

I said, "Let me get this straight. What you're talking about is taking ordinary arithmetic—no weird counter-intuitive axioms, just the stuff every ten-year-old *knows* is true—and proving that it's inconsistent, in a finite number of steps?''

She nodded blithely. "Finite, but large. So the contradiction would rarely have any physical manifestation—it would be 'computationally distant' from everyday calculations, and everyday physical events. I mean . . . one cosmic string, somewhere out there, doesn't destroy the universe, does it? It does no harm to anyone.''

I laughed drily. "So long as you don't get too close. So long as you don't tow it back to the solar system and let it twitch around slicing up planets.''

"Exactly.''

I glanced at my watch. "Time to come down to Earth, I think. You know we're meeting Julia and Ramesh—?"

Alison sighed theatrically. "I know, I know. And this would bore them witless, poor things—so the subject's closed, I promise." She added wickedly, "Humanities students are so *myopic*."

We set off across the tranquil leafy campus. Alison kept her word, and we walked in silence; carrying on the argument up to the last minute would have made it even harder to avoid the topic once we were in polite company.

Half-way to the cafeteria, though, I couldn't help myself.

"If someone ever *did* program a computer to follow a chain of inferences across the defect . . . what do you claim would actually happen? When the end result of all those simple, trustworthy logical steps finally popped up on the screen—which group of primordial quarks would win the battle? And please don't tell me that the whole computer just conveniently vanishes."

Alison smiled, tongue-in-cheek at last. "Get real, Bruno. How can you expect me to answer that, when the mathematics needed to predict the result doesn't even *exist* yet? Nothing I could say would be true or false—until someone's gone ahead and done the experiment."

I spent most of the day trying to convince myself that I wasn't being followed by some accomplice (or rival) of the surgeon, who might have been lurking outside the hotel. There was something disturbingly Kafkaesque about trying to lose a tail who might or might not have been real: no particular face I could search for in the crowd, just the abstract idea of a pursuer. It was too late to think about plastic surgery to make me look Han Chinese—Alison had raised this as a serious suggestion, back in Vietnam—but Shanghai had over a million foreign residents, so with care even an Anglophone of Italian descent should have been able to vanish.

Whether or not I was up to the task was another matter.

I tried joining the ant-trails of the tourists, following the path of least resistance from the insane crush of the Yuyuan Bazaar (where racks bursting with ten-cent watch-PCs, mood-sensitive contact lenses, and the latest karaoke vocal implants, sat beside bamboo cages of live ducks and pigeons) to the one-time residence of Sun Yatsen (whose personality cult was currently undergoing a mini-series-led revival on Star TV, advertised on ten thousand buses and ten times as many T-shirts). From the tomb of the writer Lu Xun ("Always think and study . . . visit the general then visit the victims, see the realities of your time with open eyes"—no prime time for *him*) to the Hongkou McDonald's (where they were giving away small plastic Andy Warhol figurines, for reasons I couldn't fathom). I mimed leisurely window-shopping between the shrines, but kept my body language sufficiently unfriendly to deter even the loneliest Westerner from attempting to strike up a conversation.

If foreigners were unremarkable in most of the city, they were positively eye-glazing here—even to each other—and I did my best to offer no one the slightest reason to remember me.

Along the way I checked for messages from Alison, but there were none. I left five of my own, tiny abstract chalk marks on bus shelters and park benches—all slightly different, but all saying the same thing: CLOSE BRUSH, BUT SAFE NOW. MOVING ON.

By early evening, I'd done all I could to throw off my hypothetical shadow, so I headed for the next hotel on our agreed but unwritten list. The last time we'd met face-to-face, in Hanoi, I'd mocked all of Alison's elaborate preparations. Now I was beginning to wish that I'd begged her to extend our secret language to cover more extreme contingencies. FATALLY WOUNDED. BETRAYED YOU UNDER TORTURE. REALITY DE-CAYING. OTHERWISE FINE.

The hotel on Huaihai Zhonglu was a step up from the last one, but not quite classy enough to refuse payment in cash. The desk clerk made polite small-talk, and I lied as smoothly as I could about my plans to spend a week sight-seeing before heading for Beijing. The bellperson smirked when I tipped him too much—and I sat on my bed for five minutes afterward, wondering what significance to read into *that*.

I struggled to regain a sense of proportion. Industrial Algebra *could* have bribed every single hotel employee in Shanghai to be on the lookout for us—but that was a bit like saying that, in theory, they could have duplicated our entire twelve-year search for defects, and not bothered to pursue us at all. There was no question that they wanted what we had, badly—but what could they actually do about it? Go to a merchant bank (or the Mafia, or a Triad) for finance? That might have worked if the cargo had been a stray kilogram of plutonium, or a valuable gene sequence—but only a few hundred thousand people on the planet would be capable of understanding what the defect *was*, even in theory. Only a fraction of that number would believe that such a thing could really exist . . . and even fewer would be both wealthy and immoral enough to invest in the business of exploiting it.

The stakes appeared to be infinitely high—but that didn't make the players omnipotent.

Not yet.

I changed the dressing on my arm, from sock to handkerchief, but the incision was deeper than I'd realized, and it was still bleeding thinly. I left the hotel—and found exactly what I needed in a twenty-four-hour emporium just ten minutes away. Surgical grade tissue repair cream: a mixture of colla-gen-based adhesive, antiseptic, and growth factors. The emporium wasn't even a pharmaceuticals outlet—it just had aisle after aisle packed with all kinds of unrelated odds and ends, laid out beneath the unblinking blue-white ceiling panels. Canned food, PVC plumbing fixtures, traditional medicines, rat contraceptives, video ROMS. It was a random cornucopia, an almost organic diversity—as if the products had all just grown on the shelves from whatever spores the wind had happened to blow in.

I headed back to the hotel, pushing my way through the relentless crowds, half seduced and half sickened by the odors of cooking, dazed by the endless vista of holograms and neon in a language I barely understood. Fifteen minutes later, reeling from the noise and humidity, I realized that I was lost.

I stopped on a street corner and tried to get my bearings. Shanghai stretched out around me, dense and lavish, sensual and ruthless—a Darwinian economic simulation self-organized to the brink of catastrophe. The Amazon of commerce: this city of sixteen million had more industry of every kind, more exporters and importers, more wholesalers and retailers, traders and re-sellers and re-cyclers and scavengers, more billionaires and more beggars, than most nations on the planet.

Not to mention more computing power.

China itself was reaching the cusp of its decades-long transition from brutal totalitarian communism to brutal totalitarian capitalism: a slow seamless morph from Mao to Pinochet set to the enthusiastic applause of its trading partners and the international financial agencies. There'd been no need for a counter-revolution—just layer after layer of carefully reasoned Newspeak to pave the way from previous doctrine to the stunningly obvious conclusion that private property, a thriving middle class, and a few trillion dollars worth of foreign investment were exactly what the Party had been aiming for all along.

The apparatus of the police state remained as essential as ever. Trade unionists with decadent bourgeois ideas about uncompetitive wages, journalists with counter-revolutionary notions of exposing corruption and nepotism, and any number of subversive political activists spreading destabilizing propaganda about the fantasy of free elections, all needed to be kept in check.

In a way, Luminous was a product of this strange transition from communism to not-communism in a thousand tiny steps. No one else, not even the U.S. defense research establishment, possessed a single machine with so much power. The rest of the world had succumbed long ago to networking, giving up their imposing supercomputers with their difficult architecture and customized chips for a few hundred of the latest mass-produced work stations. In fact, the biggest computing feats of the twenty-first century had all been farmed out over the Internet to thousands of volunteers, to run on their machines whenever the processors would otherwise be idle. That was how Alison and I had mapped the defect in the first place: seven thousand amateur mathematicians had shared the joke, for twelve years.

But now the net was the very opposite of what we needed—and only

Luminous could take its place. And though only the People's Republic could have paid for it, and only the People's Institute for Advanced Optical Engineering could have built it . . . only Shanghai's QIPS Corporation could have sold time on it to the world—while it was still being used to model hydrogen bomb shock waves, pilotless fighter jets, and exotic anti-satellite weapons.

I finally decoded the street signs, and realized what I'd done: I'd turned the wrong way coming out of the emporium, it was as simple as that.

I retraced my steps, and I was soon back on familiar territory.

When I opened the door of my room, Alison was sitting on the bed.

I said, "What is it with locks in this city?"

We embraced, briefly. We'd been lovers, once—but that was long over. And we'd been friends for years afterward—but I wasn't sure if that was still the right word. Our whole relationship now was too functional, too spartan. Everything revolved around the defect, now.

She said, "I got your message. What happened?"

I described the morning's events.

"You know what you should have done?"

That stung. "I'm still here, aren't I? The cargo's still safe."

"You should have killed her, Bruno."

I laughed. Alison gazed back at me placidly, and I looked away. I didn't know if she was serious—and I didn't much want to find out.

She helped me apply the repair cream. My toxin was no threat to her—we'd both installed exactly the same symbionts, the same genotype from the same unique batch in Hanoi. But it was strange to feel her bare fingers on my broken skin, knowing that no one else on the planet could touch me like this, with impunity.

Ditto for sex, but I didn't want to dwell on that.

As I slipped on my jacket, she said, "So guess what we're doing at five A.M. tomorrow?"

"Don't tell me: I fly to Helsinki, and you fly to Cape Town. Just to throw them off the scent."

That got a faint smile. "Wrong. We're meeting Yuen at the Institute—and spending half an hour on Luminous."

"*You* are brilliant." I bent over and kissed her on the forehead. "But I always knew you'd pull it off."

And I should have been delirious—but the truth was, my guts were churning; I felt almost as trapped as I had upon waking cuffed to the bed. If Luminous had remained beyond our reach (as it should have, since we couldn't afford to hire it for a microsecond at the going rate) we would have had no choice but to destroy all the data, and hope for the best. Industrial Algebra had no doubt dredged up a few thousand fragments of the original Internet calculations—but it was clear that, although they knew exactly what we'd found, they still had no idea where we'd found it. If they'd been forced to start their own random search—constrained by the need for secrecy to their own private hardware—it might have taken them centuries.

There was no question now, though, of backing away and leaving everything to chance. We were going to have to confront the defect in person.

"How much did you have to tell him?"

"Everything." She walked over to the washbasin, removed her shirt, and began wiping the sweat from her neck and torso with a washcloth. "Short of handing over the map. I showed him the search algorithms and their results, and all the programs we'll need to run on Luminous—all stripped of specific parameter values, but enough for him to validate the techniques. He wanted to see direct evidence of the defect, of course, but I held out on that."

"And how much did he believe?"

"He's reserved judgment. The deal is, we get half an hour's unimpeded access—but he gets to observe everything we do."

I nodded, as if my opinion made any difference, as if we had any choice. Yuen Ting-fu had been Alison's supervisor for her Ph.D. on advanced applications of ring theory, when she'd studied at Fu-tan University in the late nineties. Now he was one of the world's leading cryptographers, working as a consultant to the military, the security services, and a dozen international corporations. Alison had once told me that she'd heard he'd found a polynomial-time algorithm for factoring the product of two primes; that had never been officially confirmed . . . but such was the power of his reputation that almost everyone on the planet had stopped using the old RSA encryption method as the rumor had spread. No doubt time on Luminous was his for the asking—but that didn't mean he couldn't still be imprisoned for twenty years for giving it away to the wrong people, for the wrong reasons.

I said, "And you trust him? He may not believe in the defect now, but once he's convinced—"

"He'll want exactly what we want. I'm sure of that."

"Okay. But are you sure IA won't be watching, too? If they've worked out why we're here, and they've bribed someone—"

Alison cut me off impatiently. "There are still a few things you can't buy in this city. Spying on a military machine like Luminous would be suicidal. No one would risk it."

"What about spying on unauthorized projects being run on a military machine? Maybe the crimes cancel out, and you end up a hero."

She approached me, half naked, drying her face on my towel. "We'd better hope not."

I laughed suddenly. "You know what I like most about Luminous? They're not really letting Exxon and McDonnell-Douglas use the same machine as the People's Liberation Army. Because the whole computer vanishes every time they pull the plug. There's no paradox at all, if you look at it that way."

Alison insisted that we stand guard in shifts. Twenty-four hours earlier, I might have made a joke of it; now I reluctantly accepted the revolver she offered me, and sat watching the door in the neon-tinged darkness while she went out like a light.

The hotel had been quiet for most of the evening—but now it came to life. There were footsteps in the corridor every five minutes—and rats in the walls, foraging and screwing and probably giving birth. Police sirens wailed in the distance; a couple screamed at each other in the street below. I'd read somewhere that Shanghai was now the murder capital of the world—but was that *per capita*, or in absolute numbers?

After an hour, I was so jumpy that it was a miracle I hadn't blown my foot off. I unloaded the gun, then sat playing Russian roulette with the empty barrel. In spite of everything, I still wasn't ready to put a bullet in anyone's brain for the sake of defending the axioms of number theory.

Industrial Algebra had approached us in a perfectly civilized fashion, at first. They were a small but aggressive UK-based company, designing specialized high-performance computing hardware for industrial and military applications. That they'd heard about the search was no great surprise—it had been openly discussed on the Internet for years, and even joked about in serious mathematical journals—but it seemed an odd coincidence when they made contact with us just days after Alison had sent me a private message from Zürich mentioning the latest "promising" result. After half a dozen false alarms—all due to bugs and glitches—we'd stopped broadcasting the news of every unconfirmed find to the people who were donating runtime to the project, let alone any wider circle. We were afraid that if we cried wolf one more time, half our collaborators would get so annoyed that they'd withdraw their support.

IA had offered us a generous slab of computing power on the company's private network—several orders of magnitude more than we received from any other donor. *Why?* The answer kept changing. Their deep respect for pure mathematics . . . their wide-eyed fun-loving attitude to life . . . their desire to be seen to be sponsoring a project so wild and hip and unlikely to succeed that it made SETI look like a staid blue-chip investment. It was— they'd finally "conceded"—a desperate bid to soften their corporate image, after years of bad press for what certain unsavory governments did with their really rather nice smart bombs.

We'd politely declined. They'd offered us highly paid consulting jobs. Bemused, we'd suspended all net-based calculations—and started encrypting our mail with a simple but highly effective algorithm Alison had picked up from Yuen.

Alison had been collating the results of the search on her own work station at her current home in Zürich, while I'd helped coordinate things from Sydney. No doubt IA had been eavesdropping on the incoming data, but they'd clearly started too late to gather the information needed to create their own map; each fragment of the calculations meant little in isolation. But when the work station was stolen (all the files were encrypted, it would have told them nothing) we'd finally been forced to ask ourselves: *If the defect turns out to be genuine, if the joke is no joke . . . then exactly what's at stake? How much money? How much power?*

On June 7, 2006, we met in a sweltering, crowded square in Hanoi. Alison wasted no time. She was carrying a backup of the data from the stolen work station in her notepad—and she solemnly proclaimed that, this time, the defect was real.

The notepad's tiny processor would have taken centuries to repeat the long random trawling of the space of arithmetic statements that had been carried out on the net—but, led straight to the relevant computations, it could confirm the existence of the defect in a matter of minutes.

The process began with Statement S. Statement S was an assertion about some ludicrously huge numbers—but it wasn't mathematically sophisticated or contentious in any way. There were no claims here about infinite sets, no propositions concerning "every integer." It merely stated that a certain (elaborate) calculation performed on certain (very large) whole numbers led to a certain result—in essence, it was no different from something like "5 + 3 = 4 × 2". It might have taken me ten years to check it with a pen and paper—but I could have carried out the task with nothing but elementary school mathematics and a great deal of patience. A statement like this could not be undecidable; it had to be either true or false.

The notepad decided it was true.

Then the notepad took Statement S . . . and in four hundred and twenty-three simple, impeccably logical steps, used it to prove not-S.

I repeated the calculations on my own notepad—using a different software package. The result was exactly the same. I gazed at the screen, trying to concoct a plausible reason why two different machines running two different programs could have failed in identical ways. There'd certainly been cases in the past of a single misprinted algorithm in a computing textbook spawning a thousand dud programs. But the operations here were too simple, too basic.

Which left only two possibilities. Either conventional arithmetic was intrinsically flawed, and the whole Platonic ideal of the natural numbers was ultimately self-contradictory . . . or Alison was right, and an alternative arithmetic had come to hold sway in a "computationally remote" region, billions of years ago.

I was badly shaken—but my first reaction was to try to play down the significance of the result. "The numbers being manipulated here are greater than the volume of the observable universe, measured in cubic Planck lengths. If IA were hoping to use this on their foreign exchange transactions, I think they've made a slight error of scale." Even as I spoke, though, I knew it wasn't that simple. The raw numbers might have been trans-astronomical— but it was the mere 1024 bits of the notepad's binary representations that had actually, physically misbehaved. Every truth in mathematics was encoded, reflected, in countless other forms. If a paradox like this—which at first glance sounded like a dispute about numbers too large to apply even to the most grandiose cosmological discussions—could affect the behavior of a five-gram silicon chip, then there could easily be a billion other systems on the planet at risk of being touched by the very same flaw.

But there was worse to come.

The theory was, we'd located part of the boundary between two incompatible systems of mathematics—both of which were *physically true*, in their respective domains. Any sequence of deductions that stayed entirely on one side of the defect—whether it was the "near side," where conventional arithmetic applied, or the "far side," where the alternative took over—would be free from contradictions. But any sequence that crossed the border would give rise to absurdities—hence S could lead to not-S.

So, by examining a large number of chains of inference, some of which turned out to be self-contradictory and some not, it should have been possible to map the area around the defect precisely—to assign every statement to one system or the other.

Alison displayed the first map she'd made. It portrayed an elaborately crenulated fractal border, rather like the boundary between two microscopic ice crystals—as if the two systems had been diffusing out at random from different starting points, and then collided, blocking each other's way. By now, I was almost prepared to believe that I really was staring at a snapshot of the creation of mathematics—a fossil of primordial attempts to define the difference between truth and falsehood.

Then she produced a second map of the same set of statements, and overlaid the two. The defect, the border, had shifted—advancing in some places, retreating in others.

My blood went cold. "*That* has got to be a bug in the software."

"It's not."

I inhaled deeply, looking around the square—as if the heedless crowd of tourists and hawkers, shoppers and executives, might offer some simple "human" truth more resilient than mere arithmetic. But all I could think of was *1984*: Winston Smith, finally beaten into submission, abandoning every touchstone of reason by conceding that *two and two make five*.

I said, "Okay. Go on."

"In the early universe, some physical system must have tested out mathematics that was isolated, cut off from all the established results—leaving it free to decide the outcome at random. That's how the defect arose. But by now, *all* the mathematics in this region has been tested, all the gaps have been filled in. When a physical system tests a theorem on the near side, not only has it been tested a billion times before—but all the *logically adjacent* statements around it have been decided, and they imply the correct result in a single step."

"You mean . . . peer pressure from the neighbors? No inconsistencies allowed, you have to conform? If $x - 1 = y - 1$, and $x + 1 = y + 1$, then x is left with no choice but to equal y . . . because there's nothing 'nearby' to support the alternative?"

"Exactly. Truth is determined locally. And it's the same, deep into the far side. The alternative mathematics has dominated there, and every test takes place surrounded by established theorems that reinforce each other, and the 'correct'—non-standard—result."

"At the border, though—"

"At the border, every theorem you test is getting contradictory advice. From one neighbor, $x - 1 = y - 1$ . . . but from another, $x + 1 = y + 2$. And the topology of the border is so complex that a near-side theorem can have more far-side neighbors than near-side ones—and vice versa.

"So the truth at the border isn't fixed, even now. Both regions can still advance or retreat—*it all depends on the order in which the theorems are tested*. If a solidly near-side theorem is tested first, and it lends support to a more vulnerable neighbor, that can guarantee that they both stay near-side." She ran a brief animation that demonstrated the effect. "But if the order is reversed, the weaker one *will* fall."

I watched, light-headed. Obscure—but supposedly eternal—truths were tumbling like chess pieces. "And . . . you think that physical processes going on *right now*—chance molecular events that keep inadvertently testing and re-testing different theories along the border—cause each side to gain and lose territory?"

"Yes."

"So there's been a kind of . . . random tide washing back and forth between the two kinds of mathematics, for the past few billion years?" I laughed uneasily, and did some rough calculations in my head. "The expectation value for a random walk is the square root of N. I don't think we have anything to worry about. The tide isn't going to wash over any useful arithmetic in the lifetime of the universe."

Alison smiled humorlessly, and held up the notepad again. "The tide? No. But it's the easiest thing in the world to dig a channel. To bias the random flow." She ran an animation of a sequence of tests that forced the far-side system to retreat across a small front—exploiting a "beachhead" formed by chance, and then pushing on to undermine a succession of theorems. "Industrial Algebra, though—I imagine—would be more interested in the reverse. Establishing a whole network of narrow channels of non-standard mathematics running deep into the realm of conventional arithmetic—which they could then deploy against theorems with practical consequences."

I fell silent, trying to imagine tendrils of contradictory arithmetic reaching down into the everyday world. No doubt IA would aim for surgical precision—hoping to earn themselves a few billion dollars by corrupting the specific mathematics underlying certain financial transactions. But the ramifications would be impossible to predict—or control. There'd be no way to limit the effect, spatially—they could target certain mathematical truths, but they couldn't confine the change to any one location. *A few billion dollars, a few billion neurons, a few billion stars . . . a few billion people.* Once the basic rules of counting were undermined, the most solid and distinct objects could be rendered as uncertain as swirls of fog. This was not a power I would have entrusted to a cross between Mother Theresa and Carl Friedrich Gauss.

"So what do we do? Erase the map—and just hope that IA never find the defect for themselves?"

"No." Alison seemed remarkably calm—but then, her own long-cherished philosophy had just been confirmed, not razed to the ground—and she'd had time on the flight from Zürich to think through all the *Realmathematik.* "There's only one way to be sure that they can never use this. We have to strike first. We have to get hold of enough computing power to map the entire defect. And then we either iron the border flat, so it *can't* move—if you amputate all the pincers, there can be no pincer movements. Or—better yet, if we can get the resources—we push the border in, from all directions, and shrink the far-side system down to nothing."

I hesitated. "All we've mapped so far is a tiny fragment of the defect. We don't know how large the far side could be. Except that it can't be small—or the random fluctuations would have swallowed it long ago. And it *could* go on forever; it could be infinite, for all we know."

Alison gave me a strange look. "You still don't get it, do you, Bruno? You're still thinking like a Platonist. The universe has only been around for fifteen billion years. It hasn't had time to create infinities. The far side *can't* go on forever—because somewhere beyond the defect, there are theorems that don't belong to *any* system. Theorems that have never been touched, never been tested, never been rendered true or false.

"And if we have to reach beyond the existing mathematics of the universe in order to surround the far side . . . then that's what we'll do. There's no reason why it shouldn't be possible—just so long as we get there first.''

When Alison took my place, at one in the morning, I was certain I wouldn't get any sleep. When she shook me awake three hours later, I still felt like I hadn't.

I used my notepad to send a priming code to the data caches buried in our veins, and then we stood together side-by-side, left-shoulder-to-right-shoulder. The two chips recognized each other's magnetic and electrical signatures, interrogated each other to be sure—and then began radiating lower power microwaves. Alison's notepad picked up the transmission, and merged the two complementary data streams. The result was still heavily encrypted— but after all the precautions we'd taken so far, shifting the map into a hand-held computer felt about as secure as tattooing it onto our foreheads.

A taxi was waiting for us downstairs. The People's Institute for Advanced Optical Engineering was in Minhang, a sprawling technology park some thirty kilometers south of the city center. We rode in silence through the gray predawn light, past the giant ugly tower blocks thrown up by the landlords of the new millennium, riding out the fever as the necrotraps and their cargo dissolved into our blood.

As the taxi turned into an avenue lined with biotech and aerospace companies, Alison said, ''If anyone asks, we're Ph.D. students of Yuen's, testing a conjecture in algebraic topology.''

''Now you tell me. I don't suppose you have any specific conjecture in mind? What if they ask us to elaborate?''

''On *algebraic topology*? At five o'clock in the morning?''

The Institute building was unimposing—sprawling black ceramic, three stories high—but there was a five-meter electrified fence, and the entrance was guarded by two armed soldiers. We paid the taxi driver and approached on foot. Yuen had supplied us with visitor's passes—complete with photographs and fingerprints. The names were our own; there was no point indulging in unnecessary deception. If we were caught out, pseudonyms would only make things worse.

The soldiers checked the passes, then led us through an MRI scanner. I forced myself to breathe calmly as we waited for the results; in theory, the scanner could have picked up our symbionts' foreign proteins, lingering breakdown products from the necrotraps, and a dozen other suspicious trace chemicals. But it all came down to a question of what they were looking for; magnetic resonance spectra for billions of molecules had been catalogued— but no machine could hunt for all of them at once.

One of the soldiers took me aside and asked me to remove my jacket. I fought down a wave of panic—and then struggled not to overcompensate: if

I'd had nothing to hide, I would still have been nervous. He prodded the bandage on my upper arm; the surrounding skin was still red and inflamed.

"What's this?"

"I had a cyst there. My doctor cut it out, this morning."

He eyed me suspiciously, and peeled back the adhesive bandage—with ungloved hands. I couldn't bring myself to look; the repair cream should have sealed the wound completely—at worst there should have been old, dried blood—but I could *feel* a faint liquid warmth along the line of the incision.

The soldier laughed at my gritted teeth, and waved me away with an expression of distaste. I had no idea what he thought I might have been hiding—but I saw fresh red droplets beading the skin before I closed the bandage.

Yuen Ting-fu was waiting for us in the lobby. He was a slender, fit-looking man in his late sixties, casually dressed in denim. I let Alison do all the talking: apologizing for our lack of punctuality (although we weren't actually late), and thanking him effusively for granting us this precious opportunity to pursue our unworthy research. I stood back and tried to appear suitably deferential. Four soldiers looked on impassively; they didn't seem to find all this groveling excessive. And no doubt I would have been giddy with awe, if I really had been a student granted time here for some run-of-the-mill thesis.

We followed Yuen as he strode briskly through a second checkpoint and scanner (this time, no one stopped us) then down a long corridor with a soft gray vinyl floor. We passed a couple of white-coated technicians, but they barely gave us a second glance. I'd had visions of a pair of obvious foreigners attracting as much attention here as we would have wandering through a military base—but that was absurd. Half the runtime on Luminous was sold to foreign corporations—and because the machine was most definitely *not* linked to any communications network, commercial users had to come here in person. Just how often Yuen wangled free time for his students—whatever their nationality—was another question, but if he believed it was the best cover for us, I was in no position to argue. I only hoped he'd planted a seamless trail of reassuring lies in the university records and beyond, in case the Institute administration decided to check up on us in any detail.

We stopped in at the operations room, and Yuen chatted with the technicians. Banks of flatscreens covered one wall, displaying status histograms and engineering schematics. It looked like the control center for a small particle accelerator—which wasn't far from the truth.

Luminous was, literally, a computer made of light. It came into existence when a vacuum chamber, a cube five meters wide, was filled with an elaborate standing wave created by three vast arrays of high-powered lasers. A coherent electron beam was fed into the chamber—and just as a finely machined grating built of solid matter could diffract a beam of light, a sufficiently ordered (and sufficiently intense) configuration of light could diffract a beam of matter.

The electrons were redirected from layer to layer of the light cube, recombining and interfering at each stage, every change in their phase and intensity performing an appropriate computation—and the whole system could be reconfigured, nanosecond by nanosecond, into complex new "hardware" optimized for the calculations at hand. The auxilliary supercomputers controlling the laser arrays could design, and then instantly build, the perfect machine of light to carry out each particular stage of any program.

It was, of course, fiendishly difficult technology, incredibly expensive and temperamental. The chance of ever putting it on the desktops of Tetris-playing accountants was zero, so nobody in the West had bothered to pursue it.

And this cumbersome, unwieldy, impractical machine ran faster than every piece of silicon hanging off the Internet, combined.

We continued on to the programming room. At first glance, it might have been the computing center in a small primary school, with half a dozen perfectly ordinary work stations sitting on white formica tables. They just happened to be the only six in the world that were hooked up to Luminous.

We were alone with Yuen now—and Alison cut the protocol and just glanced briefly in his direction for approval, before hurriedly linking her notepad to one of the work stations and uploading the encrypted map. As she typed in the instructions to decode the file, all the images running through my head of what would have happened if I'd poisoned the soldier at the gate receded into insignificance. We now had half an hour to banish the defect— and we still had no idea how far it extended.

Yuen turned to me; the tension on his face betrayed his own anxieties, but he mused philosophically, "If our arithmetic seems to fail for these large numbers—does it mean the mathematics, the ideal, is really flawed and mutable—or only that the behavior of matter always falls short of the ideal?"

I replied, "If every class of physical objects 'falls short' in exactly the same way—whether it's boulders or electrons or abacus beads . . . what is it that their common behavior is obeying—or defining—if not the mathematics?"

He smiled, puzzled. "Alison seemed to think you were a Platonist."

"Lapsed. Or . . . defeated. I don't see what it can *mean* to talk about standard number theory still being true for these statements—in some vague Platonic sense—if no real objects can ever reflect that truth."

"We can still *imagine* it. We can still contemplate the abstraction. It's only the physical act of validation that must fall through. Think of transfinite arithmetic: no one can physically test the properties of Cantor's infinities, can they? We can only reason about them from afar."

I didn't reply. Since the revelations in Hanoi, I'd pretty much lost faith in my power to "reason from afar" about anything I couldn't personally describe with Arabic numerals on a single sheet of paper. Maybe Alison's idea of "local truth" was the most we could hope for; anything more ambitious was beginning to seem like the comic-book "physics" of swinging a rigid beam ten billion kilometers long around your head, and predicting that the far end would exceed the speed of light.

An image blossomed on the work station screen: it began as the familiar map of the defect—but Luminous was already extending it at a mind-boggling rate. Billions of inferential loops were being spun around the margins: some confirming their own premises, and thus delineating regions where a single, consistent mathematics held sway . . . others skewing into self-contradiction, betraying a border crossing. I tried to imagine what it would have been like to follow one of those Möbius-strips of deductive logic in my head; there were no difficult concepts involved, it was only the sheer size of the statements that made that impossible. But would the contradictions have driven me into gibbering insanity—or would I have found every step perfectly reasonable, and the conclusion simply unavoidable? Would I have ended up calmly, happily conceding: *Two and two make five*?

As the map grew—smoothly re-scaled to keep it fitting on the screen, giving the unsettling impression that we were retreating from the alien mathematics as fast as we could, and only just avoiding being swallowed—Alison sat hunched forward, waiting for the big picture to be revealed. The map portrayed the network of statements as an intricate lattice in three dimensions (a crude representational convention, but it was as good as any other). So far, the border between the regions showed no sign of overall curvature—just variously sized random incursions in both directions. For all we knew, it was possible that the far-side mathematics enclosed the near side completely—that the arithmetic we'd once believed stretched out to infinity was really no more than a tiny island in an ocean of contradictory truths.

I glanced at Yuen; he was watching the screen with undisguised pain. He said, "I read your software, and I thought: sure, this looks fine—but some glitch on your machines is the real explanation. Luminous will soon put you right."

Alison broke in jubilantly, "Look, it's turning!"

She was right. As the scale continued to shrink, the random fractal meanderings of the border were finally being subsumed by an overall convexity—a convexity of the far side. It was as if the viewpoint was backing away from a giant spiked sea-urchin. Within minutes, the map showed a crude hemisphere, decorated with elaborate crystalline extrusions at every scale. The sense of observing some palaeomathematical remnant was stronger than ever, now: this bizarre cluster of theorems really did look as if it had exploded out from some central premise into the vacuum of unclaimed truths, perhaps a billionth of a second after the Big Bang—only to be checked by an encounter with our own mathematics.

The hemisphere slowly extended into a three-quarters sphere . . . and then a spiked whole. The far side was bounded, finite. It was the island, not us.

Alison laughed uneasily. "Was that true before we started—or did we just make it true?" *Had the near side enclosed the far side for billions of years— or had Luminous broken new ground, actively extending the near side into mathematical territory that had never been tested by any physical system before?*

We'd never know. We'd designed the software to advance the mapping along a front in such a way that any unclaimed statements would be instantly recruited into the near side. If we'd reached out blindly, far into the void, we might have tested an isolated statement—and inadvertently spawned a whole new alternative mathematics to deal with.

Alison said, "Okay—now we have to decide. Do we try to seal the border—or do we take on the whole structure?" The software, I knew, was busy assessing the relative difficulty of the tasks.

Yuen replied at once, "Seal the border, nothing more. You mustn't destroy this." He turned to me, imploringly. "Would you smash up a fossil of *Australopithecus*? Would you wipe the cosmic background radiation out of the sky? This may shake the foundations of all my beliefs—but it encodes the truth about our history. We have no right to obliterate it, like vandals."

Alison eyed me nervously. *What was this—majority rule?* Yuen was the only one with any power here; he could pull the plug in an instant. And yet it was clear from his demeanor that he wanted a consensus—he wanted our moral support for any decision.

I said cautiously, "If we smooth the border, that'll make it literally impossible for IA to exploit the defect, won't it?"

Alison shook her head. "We don't know that. There may be a quantumlike component of spontaneous defections, even for statements that appear to be in perfect equilibrium."

Yuen countered, "Then there could be spontaneous defections *anywhere*—even far from any border. Erasing the whole structure will guarantee nothing."

"It will guarantee that IA won't find it! Maybe pin-point defections *do* occur, all the time—but the next time they're tested, they'll always revert. They're surrounded by explicit contradictions, they have no chance of getting a foothold. You can't compare a few transient glitches with this . . . *armory* of counter-mathematics!"

The defect bristled on the screen like a giant caltrop. Alison and Yuen both turned to me expectantly. As I opened my mouth, the work station chimed. The software had examined the alternatives in detail: destroying the entire far side would take Luminous twenty-three minutes and seventeen seconds—

about a minute less than the time we had left. Sealing the border would take more than an hour.

I said, "That can't be right."

Alison groaned. "But it is! There's random interference going on at the border from other systems all the time—and doing anything finicky there means coping with that noise, fighting it. Charging ahead and pushing the border inward is different: you can exploit the noise to speed the advance. It's not a question of *dealing with a mere surface* versus *dealing with a whole volume*. It's more like . . . trying to carve an island into an absolutely perfect circle, while waves are constantly crashing on the beach—versus bulldozing the whole thing into the ocean."

We had thirty seconds to decide—or we'd be doing neither today. And maybe Yuen had the resources to keep the map safe from IA, while we waited a month or more for another session on Luminous—but I wasn't prepared to live with that kind of uncertainty.

"I say we get rid of the whole thing. Anything less is too dangerous. Future mathematicians will still be able to study the map—and if no one believes that the defect itself ever really existed, that's just too bad. IA is too close. We can't risk it."

Alison had one hand poised above the keyboard. I turned to Yuen; he was staring at the floor with an anguished expression. He'd let us state our views—but in the end, it was his decision.

He looked up, and spoke sadly but decisively.

"Okay. Do it."

Alison hit the key—with about three seconds to spare. I sagged into my chair, light-headed with relief.

We watched the far side shrinking. The process didn't look quite as crass as *bulldozing an island*—more like dissolving some quirkily beautiful crystal in acid. Now that the danger was receding before our eyes, though, I was beginning to suffer faint pangs of regret. Our mathematics had coexisted with this strange anomaly for fifteen billion years, and it shamed me to think that within months of its discovery, we'd backed ourselves into a corner where we'd had no choice but to destroy it.

Yuen seemed transfixed by the process. "So are we breaking the laws of physics—or enforcing them?"

Alison said, "Neither. We're merely changing what the laws imply."

He laughed softly. " 'Merely.' For some esoteric set of complex systems, we're rewriting the high-level rules of their behavior. Not including the human brain, I hope."

My skin crawled. "Don't you think that's . . . unlikely?"

"I was joking." He hesitated, then added soberly, "Unlikely for humans—

but *someone* could be relying on this, somewhere. We might be destroying the whole basis of their existence: certainties as fundamental to them as a child's multiplication tables are to us.''

Alison could barely conceal her scorn. ''This is junk mathematics—a relic of a pointless accident. Any kind of life that evolved from simple to complex forms would have no use for it. Our mathematics works for . . . rocks, seeds, animals in the herd, members of the tribe. *This* only kicks in beyond the number of particles in the universe—''

''Or smaller systems that represent those numbers,'' I reminded her.

''And you think life somewhere might have a burning need to do *nonstandard trans-astronomical arithmetic*, in order to survive? I doubt that very much.''

We fell silent. Guilt and relief could fight it out later, but no one suggested halting the program. In the end, maybe nothing could outweigh the havoc the defect would have caused if it had ever been harnessed as a weapon— and I was looking forward to composing a long message to Industrial Algebra, informing them of precisely what we'd done to the object of their ambitions.

Alison pointed to a corner of the screen. ''What's that?'' A narrow dark spike protruded from the shrinking cluster of statements. For a moment I thought it was merely avoiding the near side's assault—but it wasn't. It was slowly, steadily growing longer.

''Could be a bug in the mapping algorithm.'' I reached for the keyboard and zoomed in on the structure. In close-up, it was several thousand statements wide. At its border, Alison's program could be seen in action, testing statements in an order designed to force tendrils of the near side ever deeper into the interior. This slender extrusion, ringed by contradictory mathematics, should have been corroded out of existence in a fraction of a second. Something was actively countering the assault, though—repairing every trace of damage before it could spread.

''If IA have a bug here—'' I turned to Yuen. ''They couldn't take on Luminous directly, so they couldn't stop the whole far side shrinking—but a tiny structure like this . . . what do you think? Could they stabilize it?''

''Perhaps,'' he conceded. ''Four or five hundred top-speed work stations could do it.''

Alison was typing frantically on her notepad. She said, ''I'm writing a patch to identify any systematic interference—and divert all our resources against it.'' She brushed her hair out of her eyes. ''Look over my shoulder, will you, Bruno? Check me as I go.''

''Okay.'' I read through what she'd written so far. ''You're doing fine. Stay calm.'' Her hands were trembling.

The spike continued to grow steadily. By the time the patch was ready, the map was re-scaling constantly to fit it on the screen.

Alison triggered the patch. An overlay of electric blue appeared along the spike, flagging the concentration of computing power—and the spike abruptly froze.

I held my breath, waiting for IA to notice what we'd done—and switch their resources elsewhere? If they did, no second spike would appear—they'd never get that far—but the blue marker on the screen would shift to the site where they'd regrouped and tried to make it happen.

But the blue glow didn't move from the existing spike. And the spike didn't vanish under the weight of Luminous's undivided efforts.

Instead, it began to grow again, slowly.

Yuen looked ill. "This is *not* Industrial Algebra. There's no computer on the planet—"

Alison laughed derisively. "What are you saying now? Aliens who need the far side are defending it? Aliens *where*? Nothing we've done has had time to reach even . . . Jupiter." There was an edge of hysteria in her voice.

"Have you measured how fast the changes propagate? Do you know, for certain, that they can't travel faster than light—with the far-side mathematics undermining the logic of relativity?"

I said, "Whoever it is, they're not defending all their borders. They're putting everything they've got into the spike."

"They're aiming at something. A specific target." Yuen reached over Alison's shoulder for the keyboard. "We're shutting this down. Right now."

She turned on him, blocking his way. "Are you crazy? We're almost holding them off! I'll rewrite the program, fine-tune it, get an edge in efficiency—"

"No! We stop threatening them, then see how they react. We don't know what harm we're doing—"

He reached for the keyboard again.

Alison jabbed him in the throat with her elbow, hard. He staggered backward, gasping for breath, then crashed to the floor, bringing a chair down on top of him. She hissed at me, "Quick—shut him up!"

I hesitated, loyalties fracturing; his idea had sounded perfectly sane to me. But if he started yelling for security—

I crouched down over him, pushed the chair aside, then clasped my hand over his mouth, forcing his head back with pressure on the lower jaw. We'd have to tie him up—and then try brazenly marching out of the building without him. But he'd be found in a matter of minutes. Even if we made it past the gate, we were screwed.

Yuen caught his breath and started struggling; I clumsily pinned his arms with my knees. I could hear Alison typing, a ragged staccato; I tried to get a glimpse of the work station screen, but I couldn't turn that far without taking my weight off Yuen.

I said, "Maybe he's right—maybe we should pull back, and see what happens." *If the alterations could propagate faster than light . . . how many distant civilizations might have felt the effects of what we'd done?* Our first contact with extraterrestrial life could turn out to be an attempt to obliterate mathematics that they viewed as . . . what? A precious resource? A sacred relic? An essential component of their entire world view?

The sound of typing stopped abruptly. "Bruno? Do you feel—?"

"What?"

Silence.

"What?"

Yuen seemed to have given up the fight. I risked turning around.

Alison was hunched forward, her face in her hands. On the screen, the spike had ceased its relentless linear growth—but now an elaborate dendritic structure had blossomed at its tip. I glanced down at Yuen; he seemed dazed, oblivious to my presence. I took my hand from his mouth, warily. He lay there placidly, smiling faintly, eyes scanning something I couldn't see.

I climbed to my feet. I took Alison by the shoulders and shook her gently; her only response was to press her face harder into her hands. The spike's strange flower was still growing—but it wasn't spreading out into new territory; it was sending narrow shoots back in on itself, crisscrossing the same region again and again with ever finer structures.

Weaving a net? Searching for something?

It hit me with a jolt of clarity more intense than anything I'd felt since childhood. It was like reliving the moment when the whole concept of *numbers* had finally snapped into place—but with an adult's understanding of everything it opened up, everything it implied. It was a lightning-bolt revelation—but there was no taint of mystical confusion: no opiate haze of euphoria, no pseudo-sexual rush. In the clean-lined logic of the simplest concepts, I saw and understood exactly how the world worked—

—except that it was all wrong, it was all false, it was all impossible.

Quicksand.

Assailed by vertigo, I swept my gaze around the room—counting frantically: *Six work stations. Two people. Six chairs.* I grouped the work stations: three sets of two, two sets of three. One and five, two and four; four and two, five and one.

I weaved a dozen cross-checks for consistency—*for sanity . . .* but everything added up.

They hadn't stolen the old arithmetic; they'd merely blasted the new one into my head, on top of it.

Whoever had resisted our assault with Luminous had reached down with the spike and rewritten our neural metamathematics—the arithmetic that underlay our own reasoning *about* arithmetic—enough to let us glimpse what we'd been trying to destroy.

Alison was still uncommunicative, but she was breathing slowly and steadily. Yuen seemed fine, lost in a happy reverie. I relaxed slightly, and began trying to make sense of the flood of far-side arithmetic surging through my brain.

On their own terms, the axioms were . . . trivial, obvious. I could see that they corresponded to elaborate statements about trans-astronomical integers, but performing an exact translation was far beyond me—and thinking about the entities they described in terms of the huge integers they represented was a bit like thinking about *pi* or *the square root of two* in terms of the first ten thousand digits of their decimal expansion: it would be missing the point entirely. These alien "numbers"—the basic objects of the alternative arithmetic—had found a way to embed themselves in the integers, and to relate to each other in a simple, elegant way—and if the messy corollaries they implied upon translation contradicted the rules integers were supposed to obey . . . well, only a small, remote patch of obscure truths had been subverted.

Someone touched me on the shoulder. I started—but Yuen was beaming amiably, all arguments and violence forgotten.

He said, "Lightspeed is *not* violated. All the logic that requires that remains intact." I could only take him at his word; the result would have taken me hours to prove. Maybe the aliens had done a better job on him—or maybe he was just a superior mathematician in either system.

"Then . . . where *are* they?" At lightspeed, our attack on the far side could not have been felt any further away than Mars—and the strategy used to block the corrosion of the spike would have been impossible with even a few seconds' time lag.

"The atmosphere?"

"You mean—*Earth's?*"

"Where else? Or maybe the oceans."

I sat down heavily. Maybe it was no stranger than any conceivable alternative, but I still balked at the implications.

Yuen said, "To us, their structure wouldn't look like 'structure' at all. The simplest unit might involve a group of thousands of atoms—representing a trans-astronomical number—not necessarily even *bonded together* in any conventional way, but breaking the normal consequences of the laws of physics, obeying a different set of high-level rules that arise from the alternative mathematics. People have often mused about the chances of intelligence being coded into long-lived vortices on distant gas giants . . . but *these* creatures won't be in hurricanes or tornadoes. They'll be drifting in the most innocuous puffs of air—invisible as neutrinos."

"Unstable—"

"Only according to *our* mathematics. Which does not apply."

Alison broke in suddenly, angrily. "Even if all of this is true—where does it get us? Whether the defect supports a whole invisible ecosystem or not—IA will still find it, and use it, in exactly the same way."

For a moment I was dumbstruck. *We were facing the prospect of sharing the planet with an undiscovered civilization—and all she could think about was IA's grubby machinations?*

She was absolutely right, though. Long before any of these extravagant fantasies could be proved or disproved, IA could still do untold harm.

I said, "Leave the mapping software running—but shut down the shrinker."

She glanced at the screen. "No need. They've overpowered it—or undermined its mathematics." The far side was back to its original size.

"Then there's nothing to lose. Shut it down."

She did. No longer under attack, the spike began to reverse its growth. I felt a pang of loss as my limited grasp of the far-side mathematics suddenly evaporated; I tried to hold on, but it was like clutching at air.

When the spike had retracted completely, I said, "Now we try doing an Industrial Algebra. We try bringing the defect closer."

We were almost out of time, but it was easy enough—in thirty seconds, we rewrote the shrinking algorithm to function in reverse.

Alison programmed a function key with the commands to revert to the original version—so that if the experiment backfired, one keystroke would throw the full weight of Luminous behind a defense of the near side again.

Yuen and I exchanged nervous glances. I said, "Maybe this wasn't such a good idea."

Alison disagreed. "We need to know how they'll react to this. Better we find out now than leave it to IA."

She started the program running.

The sea-urchin began to swell, slowly. I broke out in a sweat. The farsiders hadn't harmed us, so far—but this felt like tugging hard at a door that you really, badly, didn't want to see thrown open.

A technician poked her head into the room and announced cheerfully, "Down for maintenance in two minutes!"

Yuen said, "I'm sorry, there's nothing—"

The whole far side turned electric blue. Alison's original patch had detected a systematic intervention.

We zoomed in. Luminous was picking off vulnerable statements of the near side—but something else was repairing the damage.

I let out a strangled noise that might have been a cheer. Alison smiled serenely. She said, "I'm satisfied. IA don't stand a chance."

Yuen mused, "Maybe they have a reason to defend the status quo—maybe they rely on the border itself, as much as the far side."

Alison shut down our reversed shrinker. The blue glow vanished; both sides were leaving the defect alone. And there were a thousand questions we all wanted answered—but the technicians had thrown the master switch, and Luminous itself had ceased to exist.

The sun was breaking through the skyline as we rode back into the city. As we pulled up outside the hotel, Alison started shaking and sobbing. I sat beside her, squeezing her hand. I knew she'd felt the weight of what might have happened, all along, far more than I had.

I paid the driver, and then we stood on the street for a while, silently watching the cyclists go by, trying to imagine how the world would change as it tried to embrace this new contradiction between the exotic and the mundane, the pragmatic and the Platonic, the visible and the invisible.

THE PROMISE OF GOD

Michael F. Flynn

▼

With great power comes great responsibility. Suppose, however, as the elegant
and deceptively quiet story that follows suggests, that the responsibility rests with
one person, while the power belongs to someone else . . .

Born in Easton, Pennsylvania, Michael F. Flynn has a B.A. in math from La
Salle College and an M.S. for work in topology from Marquette University, and
works as an industrial quality engineer and statistician. Since his first sale there
in 1984, Flynn has been a mainstay of *Analog*, and one of their most frequent
contributors. He has also made sales to *The Magazine of Fantasy & Science
Fiction*, and elsewhere, and is thought of as one of the best of the crop of new
"hard science" writers. His first novel was the well-received *In the Country of
the Blind*. It was followed by *Fallen Angels*, a novel written in collaboration
with Larry Niven and Jerry Pournelle. His second solo novel was *The Nanotech
Chronicles* and he recently published his third, *Firestar*. His stories have appeared
in our Fifth and Twelfth Annual Collections. He now lives in Edison, New Jersey.

*You shall have joy, or you shall have power, said God; you shall not
have both.*

It began to grow cold in the cabin after the sun went down, and Nealy thought
about building a fire. It would be a fine fire, roaring and crackling and toasting
warm. It would light the room with a delicious dancing light, and he and
Greta could beek on the outer hearth. He loved the way that firelight played
off Greta's features, making them red and soft and shiny; and he loved the
way the smoky smells of the burning wood blended with the earthy smells
of Greta herself. Yes, a fire was surely what was needed.

The wood was stacked against the back wall. He had chopped it himself,
as Greta had asked. Use the axe, she had told him before leaving to trek
down the mountainside to the village. Don't do it the Other Way.

Nealy snuggled deeper into the chair and looked over his shoulder at the
cabin's door. He couldn't see what difference it made. He flexed his hands,

sore and stiff from the chopping and rubbed the hard palms together. Hard work. Blister-raising work. It was easier the Other Way. Your muscles didn't ache; your back was not sore. The faggots could march themselves into the hearth and leap upon each other; then he could summon a salamander to ignite them. It would be easy, and it would be fun to watch.

Nealy gazed on the wood. His fingers plucked aimlessly at the arm of the chair. It was growing chilly in the room. He thought about building a fire.

When Nealy was seven, a wolf broke into the sheep pen. He heard the bleating all the way from the chicken coop and he ran as fast as he could down to the meadow gate, slipping in the mud where the run-off from the old well-pump trickled toward the creek. As Nealy raised himself from the muck, he spied the wolf among the flock as though through parted clouds. Sheep were milling and baa-ing, knowing there was a danger amongst them, but at a loss for what to do. The wolf raised its head from the carcass of a young ewe and bared bloody teeth. Far off, in the autumn field on the far side of the pen, Papa had dropped the reins of the plow horse and was hopping across the furrows with his musket in hand. Too late, though; too late for Fat Emma.

Nealy staggered to his feet and the wolf backed away, not ready to attack a human being, but neither ready to retreat, either. When it turned, Nealy could see the badly healed scar along its flank, the stiffness with which one hind leg moved; explanation, at least, for why it had chosen the sheep pens. Nealy pointed a finger at the beast.

"You killed Fat Emma, you!" he shrieked, as only young boys can shriek over a favorite animal lost; and never mind that Emma would betimes have graced his own table. At seven, the future is a hazy thing. He made a gesture with his hands. Anger and instinct moved his arms; and he felt something— he felt some thing—*course through him like water through a pipe, as if the pulse in his veins gushed forth in a great spray.*

And the wolf howled and twisted, leaped upon itself and lay still.

Nealy's breaths came in short gusts. His brow and face were hot and flushed and his chest heaved. His head ached and he felt very, very tired. The sheep milled about in the pen, bleating and bleating and bleating and bleating. Stupid *beasts, Nealy thought. Lackwits.* Sheep deserved what happened to them. *He made another gesture and the fleece upon Gray Harry began to blacken and smolder. Harry shook himself. Smoke rolled off him, then flames. Harry ran, still unsure where the danger lay, knowing only to run and escape.*

With a cry, Nealy dropped to his knees in the mud and covered his face with his hands. His head throbbed. What had he done? What had he done? He felt his father's arms gather him in, banding him tight against his sweet-

smelling linen shirt. Between sobs, Nealy told him what had happened; and his father kept saying, "I know, Nealy. I saw."

After a while, his father stood him upright and brushed him off and straightened his clothes. "There," he said with a catch in his voice. "You look more presentable now. The wolfskin is yours, you know. It will make a fine cloak. You can wear it to school and the other kids will be jealous."

"Buh—Buh—But, Gray Harry—" Nealy's words bobbed in his throat.

His father looked past him, at the dead animals in the pen. He could feel Papa's head shaking as he buried his face in his father's chest. "You shan't have that fleece, Nealy," he heard him say. "No, you shan't have that one."

The rapping at the door was repeated three times. Nealy twisted in his seat and stared at it, wondering who it was. Not Greta, for she would not have knocked. A neighbor? Someone from the village? The knocking boomed: a fist against the thick, wooden slats. Finally, a kick and a muffled voice. "I know you be within, Master Cornelius. I saw your wifman leave."

Nealy nodded to himself. Someone craving admittance. Perhaps he should open the door and admit whoever it was. He pondered that for a time, weighed the urim and the thummin in his mind, chased the decision as it slipped like quicksilver through the fingers of his mind, while the pounding on his door increased. Perhaps he should . . .

But the decision was taken from him. The door creaked open and a mousy-brown face peered around its edge. It brightened when it saw him, and showed a smile white with small teeth. "There you be, Master Cornelius. I knew you were here."

"God's afternoon to you, Goodwif Agnes," Nealy said, for he recognized the man now. "I pray you are well."

Agnes touched the mezuzah lightly to appease the household lares and closed the door behind her. She curtsied quickly and awkwardly, then stood there, dressed in a shapeless, butternut homespun gown that just brushed the tops of her moccasins. The top button in the front of her gown was unfastened, so that Nealy could see a soft bit of roundness on either side of the opening, like twin crescent moons.

"God's afternoon, Master Cornelius." A hint of color suffused her cheeks, so perhaps she knew that her gown was unfastened; or that Nealy had noticed.

Has she come to seduce me? Nealy wondered. There were wivmen enough who wanted his seed. That would explain why she wore no coverslut over her gown. He knew Other Ways of pleasuring, Other Ways of bringing a wif to ecstasy, riding atop a rolling sea of pure joy. Sometimes Greta allowed him to use those Ways on her. She would arch her back in rapture while he spelled, and give soft, little cries—though afterward she would often grow dread-full and beg him never to do it again, even if she asked. Though she always did, she always did. And Nealy had no choice but to obey.

"I'll not mump with you," Agnes said. "I crave a boon."

Of course, she did. They all did. Why else would she have come. "And what boon is that?" Politeness came easy. Politeness cost nothing.

"My house-bound, sir Master. He has the fleas some' at bad; and I was wondering, I was, if you could use your dweomercræft to relieve him." She stood, twisting the front of her gown in her fist, flushed in the face and looking down.

"And you as well?" he asked with a half-smile. That which has touched an unclean thing became itself unclean. See Leviticus. Yet, did she know how awe-full it was what she asked of him? "You know the custom," he chided her. "You must approach my rixler. Greta has gone but lately and . . ."

"I know." Agnes paused and took a deep breath. "I waited until she left. I addressed her yestere'en, but she laughed at me and said that my wereman and I should wash ourselves and our clothing with lye soap and a stiff wire brush."

Nealy laughed. "Aye, by Hermes, that would work!" He felt the hammer in his veins, the sudden, momentary distancing of his vision, and knew that the scrubbing *would* work, better than Greta had supposed; but before he could tell Agnes of his incontinent spelling, she spoke.

"But you could make it so the fleas would never return, so that Lucius and I 'ud be clean for good and aye."

Nealy paused with his mouth half-open and pondered the additional requirement. Now, that did put a different cast on things. There were any number of alternatives. He closed his eyes to better envision them. Yes, four or five possibilities, some of them quite amusing. And it made Alice's request so much more interesting.

To ply the craeft, as all men knew, would nibble the soul away.

His parents had begun the search for a rixler that very evening. The priest had come up from Lechaucaster, down by the forks of the river, where the chain dam hoarded the headwaters for the southern canal. He had come up the mountainside a-muleback and had tested Nealy with an ankh. It was stuffy in the close-bed with the priest. The man stank with the sweat of his riding and his breath was foul. Nealy remembered everything about that day with the clarity of a landmark spied across miles of fog and mist.

Mama had cried. He remembered that, too.

"For a while yet, he may refrain," the priest said with a shaking head. "Ynglings oft try to abstain; yet in the end, they cannot restrain themselves and are drawn back to the Other Way in spite of everything."

His mother rose from the table and turned, crossing her arms across herself—and Nealy drew back quickly into the confines of the close-bed lest she see him. But he leaned his head by the door so as to hear everything.

"But Nealy is a good boy," she said. "And dweormen do much good in the world."

"Esther . . ." Papa's voice, warning.

"But only under the tutelage of a trained rixler," insisted the priest. "One who may provide a soul for him when his craeft has eaten his own." Then he chanted from the Gospel of Thomas:

> *" 'When you make the two into one,*
> *When you make the inner like the outer,*
> *And the outer like the inner,*
> *And the upper like the lower,*
> *When you make the male and the female into a single one . . .' "*

Nealy had heard the words before, at synagogue, when the priest sang from the Hermetic books, but they had meant nothing and still meant nothing.

"He is too young," said Mama through a quiet sob. (Oh, and Nealy bristled at that. Too young? Why, he was seven! All of seven . . .)

"It comes on them at the age of reason," the priest said. "Best that his training begin tonight."

"So soon?" Papa's voice had been laced with sorrow. "I had thought that . . ." Papa's voice trailed off.

The priest was silent a moment. Then he spoke firmly. "Nothing is gained by putting it bye. There is only loss. I shall have a mister come to tutor you, and to select the rixler. Does the lad prefer girls or boys?"

"Let it wait for a moon or so. He is my son. I . . ."

"Delay too long," the priest warned, "and he may not bond with his rixler at all." The priest's voice had gone soft and low. "Or have you forgotten what was born within the Barrens?"

He heard Mama suck in her breath. Nealy did not understand. Only that the Pine Barrens was a place Mama used to frighten him into good behavior. No one went there. No one who ever came back. In two hundred years, no one had ever come back.

"Tonight," the priest continued firmly. "Tonight you must open the need that only his rixler may fill."

"My son," said Papa in a choked voice. "How can I?"

"How can you not?" the priest insisted.

That evening, Mama did not come to kiss him and tuck him into bed as was her wont. Nealy waited and waited and she did not come. He was afraid that something had happened to her and he began to cry and still she did not come.

Later, when his sobs had stilled themselves by exhaustion, he heard from his parents' bed the sounds of others sobbing.

"Stop!" Greta's voice jerked Nealy around with his mouth open and his hand half raised. She had used the *vox*, what the Guyandot Skraelings called *orenda*. Nealy paused with the words unspoken on his tongue. He could no more proceed than a winterlocked stream.

Greta's eyes took in Agnes and Nealy. Took them in, saw them, understood them. Judged them. She stared at Nealy a moment longer with eyes the color of a storm-proud sky. Then, with barely a glance at Agnes, she turned and unfastened her cloak of charred sheeps'-wool and hung it on the peg behind the door. Greta was a buxom man, her breasts full and round under her laced buckskin coverslut. Her golden-grey hair was braided in tight whorls behind each ear.

"Mistress Rixler," said Agnes, "I only—"

"Hush, child." The voice was not loud, but it compelled. Greta bent and unfastened her leggings, which she tossed in the corner by the door; and exchanged her boots for moccasins. Her pendant, a brightly jeweled vestal's dagger in a leather scabbard, dangled from her neck when she bent over.

"Nealy, dear," she said, "be a host and offer our guest some wine." Nealy hopped to do as he was bid, grateful to be acting, grateful for having been decided.

"No, I could not." Agnes edged her way toward the door.

"Stay, child. We have matters to discuss." Nealy listened to the wivmen while he arranged the goblets and removed the wine from the coldbox. Sometimes he felt as if he were both at a play and in it; as if he were watching and waiting and was occasionally called upon to speak lines written by someone else, words as surprising to him as to anyone.

Agnes stood stiffly and wrung the homespun gown in her fist. "I was not . . . I did not come to swyve your wereman."

Greta laughed. "So. Then, button up. Don't wave a musket you don't mean to fire. Nealy, dear, would you have taken her if she had offered?"

And that was most definitely a cue. Nealy handed Greta her goblet, half-full of chased kosher Oneida. He looked at Greta, looked into her eyes, before handing Agnes the guest's goblet. He imagined what Agnes looked like, imagined her pink and rosy nakedness—younger, firmer than Greta, smooth and soft and warm, smelling of sweat and rut. Imagined her wrapping herself around him. Quite the bellibone. "Yes," he decided as he took a sip from his own goblet.

"If you ever made up your mind." Greta also sipped. Over the cup rim, she glanced at Agnes, glanced at Nealy. "He will eventually, you know.

Make up his mind. If I am away too long. If he has no more chores set for him. He has some will left in him."

"Idle hands are the devil's tools," agreed Nealy. He wondered if Greta would tell him to fick Agnes. He hoped so; he felt himself growing werile at the thought. *Tell me I can. Tell me I can.* Greta smiled at him, no doubt noticing, then turned a stern eye on Agnes. "You came about the fleas, didn't you? Don't deny it. And after I told you. You keep yourself clean, you keep your dogs in the yard. You don't need any Other Way."

"It's easier the Other Way," Agnes said petulantly. Nealy thought the young man had a point, but Greta looked at Nealy; and Nealy saw infinite sadness behind the eyes. "No," said Greta. "No, it is not." She studied the wine in her goblet and was quiet for a long while. Nealy wondered if she was trying to foresee and was on the part of offering to do it for her when she spoke. "You know that going the Other Way eats the soul, yngling."

"Everyone knows that, mistress."

"But do you know what that means? Do you feel it *here?*" Greta slapped herself on the bosom. "By Hermes, Jesus and St. Mahound!" she swore. "What can you possibly know?"

Agnes shrank away and the goblet fell from her fingers, splashing an ablution across the outer hearth. "No, mistress. Plainly, I do not. I—"

"Oh, child." Greta's voice was heavy. "Nealy, were you about to spell her fleas away?"

Nealy started, caught unawares by the sudden question. He nodded. "And her were's in the bargain; and for aye."

"How did you intend to do that?"

Nealy brightened. He loved to explain his reasoning to Greta. It was always so logical, his major and minor premises all lined up like ducklings after their mother. "I bethought myself to conjure a salamander," he said. "When Agnes and Lucius were set a-fire, the fleas would quickly perish." He heard the young man's gasp and turned to her with a smile. "And, upon my word, they would ne'er come back to bother you more."

Agnes made stiff fists by her side. "Is this a jest?

"Fleas cannot abide a high temperature," Nealy pointed out, reasonably as he thought; but all he received in return from Agnes was a look of terror.

"Are you mocking me?"

Greta sighed and shook her head. "It is only the judgment of a man who has lost all his moral anchors."

"The difficulty," the rixmister had explained, "is to strike the balance between obedience and fear. Should he fear you too greatly, he may strike out in anger. Should he fear you too little, he may not obey. Your instruments are the knout and the caress."

Nealy watched the girl and the mister with lack of interest, then turned his attention back to the rag doll he had been playing with. A scrap of metal affixed to its head and it was Lief ben Erik, the Great Explorer. Nealy imagined him standing in the prow of his longboat facing the spray. Sail on. Sail on. To Vinland the Good and Hy Brasil! Nealy made ocean spray noises with his mouth.

Where were Mama and Papa? They had not come with him when he left with the priest. Why did they avoid him so? Had he been bad? Had he been that bad? They fed him and they clothed him . . . and they treated him like a stranger. He missed their hugs; he missed their kisses. He missed Papa's funny, booming voice and Mama's ample lap. How could he right matters; put everything back as it had been, before the wolf, before Gray Harry . . . if no one told him what he had done wrong?

It wasn't fair. Yes, he had hurt Gray Harry; but that had been an accident. The gods would understand. He had offered the sacrifices to Iaveis and Dianah. He studied the doll. Dress it differently and it could be Papa, or even Mama. He made a fist and punched the doll sharply in the body. That would teach them!

Tears filled his eyes and his lower lip trembled. How could he even think of hurting Papa or Mama? He must be a very bad boy to have had such very bad thoughts. No wonder his parents did not love him any more. No wonder the other boys no longer came to play and he was alone all the time. He turned his face away so the girl and the rixmister could not see. It wasn't seemly for a boy to cry. It wasn't werile. He picked Lief the Lucky off the floor and stroked him gently, imagining again that it was Papa.

When the girl approached, he looked up suspiciously. He had heard them talking about him in whispers. The girl had shiny blond hair that hung in thick, corkscrew braids down to her waist. She wore plain butternut and beaded moccasins of a design Nealy did not recognize. Her hand clenched a knout with a large, curved knob on the end of it. Behind her, the rixmister stood with an anxious look on her face. The girl blushed lightly and curtsied.

"Ave, Master Cornelius. I height Gretl Octavia Schmuelsdottr. I came all the way up the mountain from the convent school at Lechaucaster just to play with you."

Nealy frowned and would not look at her. "You're a girl," he said. "And a vestal," he added, pointing to the jeweled dagger hanging in its sheath from a ribbon 'round her neck. He was not sure what a vestal was, only that they were special and came from the convent schools.

Gretl squatted by his side. "Vestals know all kinds of things. Some of them . . ." She paused, glanced at the mister, and blushed again. "Some of them you will appreciate when you are older."

Nealy stuck his lip out. "I want Mama."

Gretl reached out and took his hand. "I will be your mama now. I will take care of you." She hugged him; and it had been so long since any arms had compassed him that Nealy suddenly dropped the doll and hugged her back, feeling with an odd delicious tingle the funny shape of her chest pressing against him. A small, warm glow blossomed within him. Someone did like him after all.

"And later," she said, "I will be your wifman."

"I don't want a wif," he said.

"You'll learn," she said, caressing him.

"What's the stick for?" he asked.

She hugged him tighter. "You'll learn."

"He is not evil," Greta told Agnes. "He does not choose evil."

Nealy grinned. "Thank you, my dear. You say such flattering things about me." He finished his wine cup and set it by. "I'm not, I suppose," he said, scratching his chin under his beard. "I thought so myself, once. But . . ."

"But evil requires choice," Greta said. "And choice has been taken from him."

"And I don't miss it nary a bit," Nealy said with a nod. "If you choose, you are responsible. And responsibility . . ." He spared a glance at Greta's melancholy features and frowned. "Responsibility can be a terrible burden." Something was bothering Greta. Nealy could tell. Something beyond Agnes' importuning visit. Something she had brought back up the mountainside with her.

"The Other Way," said Greta, "is an awe-full and wonder-full power; but, wielded too long, power blinds us to good and evil. Each time a dweorman spells, some part of his soul is destroyed. The part that sees evil and knows to shun it. Chirurgeons who have done autopsies report that in certain regions of the brain the very fibers are seared, as if by an inner fire. Such a man . . ." She looked at Nealy with loving sadness. "Such a man cannot be allowed to choose."

"The knout and the caress, eh, my dear?" Nealy grinned at his wif and rubbed himself to show where both had been applied. "They taught me to obey Greta's voice, they surely did." Sometimes, when he thought about spelling on his own, his groin would ache from the memories. Sometimes, when he thought about obeying Greta, he grew werile. "It was all done very logically." He hoped Agnes would leave soon, so that he and Greta could beek. Perhaps he should make Agnes Go Away. Twice, at Greta's command, he had made things Go Away. Once to a gang of cut-throats living in the forest beyond the Swoveberg who had raped and killed a ten-year-old girl; and once to an avalanche that had thundered down the hillside. The latter spelling had laid Nealy up for a week, numb and shivering in fever. He had felt as if great gulps of him had been sucked out into the very space between the stars. It would be much less onerous to make Alice Go Away. He looked to Greta for guidance.

But none was forthcoming. "The craeft robbed him of half himself; we robbed him then of the other," she said sadly.

Nealy was distressed. "But I don't begrudge it, dear Gretl. With it, what a monster I should be."

"Yes, in all innocence, unleashing horrors and boons with equal carelessness." Greta shook herself and looked back at Alice as if she had forgotten the young man was still there. "His choices have no moral weights, and it is urim and thummin which he would pick." Then she rose and pointed fore- and middle finger at the younger man. "Betruth yourself, Alice Josepha Runningdeer, that you will not come to my were, nor any other dweorman, ever again, except through the man's rixler."

Alice dropped to her knees and hugged Greta around the waist. "Oh, I do, I do. I betruth myself, for good and aye."

Greta lifted her to her feet. "Then go."

Alice scurried to the door.

"Don't forget the lye soap," said Nealy. "And scrub very hard." Alice gave him one last look of horror, then the door thudded shut behind her. Greta went to the door and put the bar in place, shutting the world without and them within.

Nealy ran into the wood behind the shed and knelt there rubbing himself where Gretl had struck him. Gretl was mean. All he had done was spell a spray of flowers to show how much he liked her. That was all, a spray of red and yellow and golden blooms to brighten up the winter months in their cabin.

But was Gretl pleased at the gesture? No, not her. Never spell without my permission! *she had cried.* Never!

Nealy clutched himself and bit down on his lip. By Hermes, that hurt! That was all she ever did, was fick him with that knout of hers, ever since the rixmister had set them up alone on the mountainside. If Papa were here, he'd make her stop; and Mama would box her ears good!

But the mountainside was far from home, far from home, and he had not seen Papa in a long, long time. Sometimes, in the night, he would sneak out of the cabin, out under the stars and look up at them, wondering if somewhere far to the south Mama and Papa were looking at them, too. Sometimes he heard their voices in the wind or in the rush of a stream, and saw their faces in the fire or a sparkling lake.

He had tried to find them once. He had made passes with his hands and the air parted before him like a curtain, and two shocked and frightened

*faces had turned toward him for just an instant before Gretl's knout had
struck him sharply.*

*Maybe that had been his parents on the other side of that curtain. Maybe
not.*

*Maybe he should teach Gretl a lesson. Turn her stick into a viper. The
spelling was in the Secret Book of Moses. He imagined the stick twisting and
turning and hissing in her hands and her sudden shriek of terror. It would
just be for a moment. He would change the knout back before it could bite.
He did not want to hurt Gretl, only scare her.*

His body twinged at the thought. Ah, what a blow she would land then!

*He pulled his knees up under his chin and wrapped his arms around them.
The woods grew dark farther in from the clearing, permanent night even in
the day, under hickories and maples taller than the pillars of the great Temple
at Shawmut, home for kobolds and sprites or other creatures. Maybe he
should just run away and live by himself in the forest. Some people did that.
Ridge runners and mountain men.*

*But he would lose Gretl if he did that. He would be all alone again, as
when his parents had forsaken him. He sniffed and wiped his nose on his
buckskin sleeve. He should not cry. He was fourteen, a full grown man. Papa
had only been fifteen when he became house-bound to Mama. And Gretl had
promised to teach him soon what were and wif did when they were house
bound to each other and that it was even better than the caresses she gave
him. No, he should stay with Gretl. He was a bad boy. He had to be tamed.
That was why they gave him Gretl, so she could teach him. That was why
Gretl was older and knew how to touch him so it felt good. And it was why
she carried the knout, too. It was all very logical. It was how you trained
dogs.*

Greta busied herself with the dinner preparations, setting out the flour bin
and cutting a knuckle joint from the ham carcass in the cold room. Nealy
admired her knifework as she cut the scraps of meat from the bone. He loved
Greta's speck-and-bean. She rolled and cut the noodles fat and small and
square, and she never let the snap beans stew so long they became limp.

Nealy betook himself to his favorite chair and settled in, content to await
Greta's instructions.

When Greta had prepared the stew kettle, she carried it to the hearth. There
she stopped and stared at the cold stones. Nealy felt her sorrow vibrate like
the tolling of great cast iron bells. Nealy's bones rang with it. Greta was
crying.

"What is wrong, Greta?" Nealy had never seen Greta cry. It struck him
as wrong. As if the sun and the moon had come loose from their crystal

spheres. Greta swung the rack out and hung the kettle on the hook. "I should have told you to start the fire," she said. "Now dinner will be late."

Only that? A silly thing to cry over. Nealy wanted to tell her that he had thought about starting the fire himself but had not done it because she had not told him to. He thought she would be proud of his prudence. Perhaps it would cheer her up. But her eyes gazed on something so far away, Nealy did not dare interrupt her. Lately, Greta had waxed melancholy, but what it was that haunted her she never spoke of.

"I could start a fire," he offered, "if you would but let me." He thought that might please her. Nealy ached to be helpful; but the one thing he knew how to do well she would not let him do for trifles.

He was prepared for rebuff, but when Greta said, "Yes. Explain how you would accomplish it," he brightened and told her all about the marching faggots and the salamander and the rest. When he was finished, he waited anxiously for her judgment. It could well be there was some moral wrong involved, like the time he had. . . . Well, it was best not to think on that. The villagers had rebuilt their houses farther from the riverbank, and the drought *had* ended. It was too bad about the children, but that could not be helped. Greta had been less experienced then.

"I see nothing wrong," Greta said at last. The worry and the sorrow filled the cabin like molasses and Nealy ached to stopper the flow before he became mired in it. He wondered if Greta knew that he could feel these things. He had told her he could, but perhaps it was like Greta explaining right and wrong to him. The words were there, but not the sense.

He donned his wolf's skin and made the cast, and a good one it was. The faggots put on a fine show, marching like legionnaires in the quick-step, centurions to the fore and levites to the rear, and even a leafy twig aloft in lieu of an eagle. A smile pierced even Greta's quiet distress.

When the wood had stacked itself and ignited in a haze of flame, Greta swung the kettle hook back over the fire. Afterward, she stood staring into the crackling blaze for a long time, and remained silent all through dinner.

After cockshut, when the dishes were scoured and put away and the cooking fire had settled into a gentle roil of soft flames, Greta went to the cloak hook and took down her sheep's wool.

"Are you going out again, dear?" Nealy asked.

Greta brought the cloak back and laid it down upon the hearth. Then she unfastened the neck of her coverslut and gown and let them fall to the flag-stones. She stood there nude, one foot slightly upraised, her nakedness only accentuated by the ritual vestal's dagger dangling between her breasts on its silken cord. The firelight caused the gemstones on the handle to sparkle like small, hard flames. Nealy sighed at the sight of the soft flesh rosened by the licking flames, and awaited her summons.

When Greta held out her arms Nealy shed his buckskins with fumbling fingers and joined her on the warm outer hearthstones. They kissed—he with urgency, she with tenderness—and settled down onto the soft wool. The heat of the fire was a delicious roasting sensation on his right side. Greta took him and brought him to her and they kissed again. "Yes," said Greta, breaking her silence at last. "Yes, you may, this one last time."

Nealy knew what she meant. Eagerly, he reached out with himself, feeling his being engorge with the stuff of the Other Way. His pulse throbbed and the stuff ran through his veins like liquor. He sparkled like the sunlight off the chop of a gentle lake. He touched her here, and there, in places where fingers could not reach; and Greta's breath came faster and faster, in short gulps. She said, "Yes," over and over.

He had dreamed of this earlier, Nealy remembered, just before Alice had come. He had dreamed of Greta pleasuring him on the hearthstones; and he wondered if the yearning itself had brought this act to pass. Sometimes his dreams did that. Sometimes.

When he was spent, he lay by her side, gently following her contours with his touch. Greta lay with her eyes closed, making soft noises in her throat. Nealy waited for her to tell him not to pleasure her the Other Way the next time. She always forbade him, she always asked him, he always obeyed her. Nealy did not know why the pleasuring frightened her.

This time, however, she made no reference to it. Instead, she spoke in a whisper, "Nealy, dear, I've been a good wifman to you."

"No one could ask for a better," Nealy told her. "I could never bind with another."

"I know," Greta said. "I know. The rixmister paired us well. The years have been good to us." She sighed and pressed his head against her breasts, ran her fingers through his hair. "I had looked forward to spending our chair days together."

He lifted his head from its delicious pillow. "What is it?" he asked, dread bubbling through the sorrow. "What is wrong?"

She cupped one of her breasts in her hand and gazed at it sadly. "I have the cancer," she said.

The words dropped down the well of Nealy's soul. He had to swallow several times before he could speak. "Are you sure?" was all he could ask. Bad news is always questioned. Bad news is always denied.

"I saw the chirurgeon in the town. That is why I went down the mountain." She drew determination around her like a cloak. "Here, darling, Nealy . . ." She pushed herself to a sitting position. "Here, sit within my lap."

Nealy did as he was bid. He sat on the sheepskin between her legs and leaned back against her. Greta pulled his head once more against her breasts and Nealy jerked slightly at the touch.

"Do not fret, dear. You cannot hurt me; not by leaning against me." Greta was silent for a time and Nealy contented himself with listening to her breathing. Then she said, "I felt the lumps at the freshening of Hunter's Moon. I was not sure, at first. I did not want to believe it, at first. But the chirurgeon confirmed it."

Nealy twisted his head and looked up into her face. Twin tears left dark trails down her cheeks. "Is there anything I can do, dear? Are there spells? I know of none; but . . ."

"No, Nealy. No. You would have to know the cancer as well as you know the owl or the wind . . . or Alice Runningdeer's fleas. No one knows what the cancer is, or why it does what it does. How can you spell what you cannot name?"

"True names . . . ," Nealy said. "I could spell black," he offered. "I could weave an unnamed spell. If the known does not help, we must try the unknown."

"The Black Unknown? We dare not. . . . Dare not. . . . Nealy, no dweor-man may spell upon the body of a rixler. That is a geas that may not, must not be lifted . . ."

"But . . ." Nealy frowned in concentration. "But, you will die. Surely. . . ."

Greta seized him and held him tight against her, nearly crushing his breath from him. "I know. I know. I have lived with death for three tendays, now. I have grown . . . accustomed to his breath. Comes the moment, I will even welcome him. The chirurgeon's potions . . . I may ask for something stronger, on that day."

Nealy pondered Greta's death. Who would make his meals? Who would pleasure him? Who would make his decisions? "Oh, Gretl," he said, using her childhood name. "Oh, Gretl," and his own tears came now as he conjured up his future in his drawn and quartered soul. "I do not know what I shall do without you!"

Greta hugged him even tighter between her breasts. He could feel the heat of them, feel the hardness of their tips, smell the delicious smell of flesh. "I do," he heard Greta say.

Something felt different. Something was missing in their embrace. He felt the fleshy softness against his cheek. "Why, Gretl," he said. "Your vestal's dagger . . . Have you taken it off?"

"Lean your head back as far as you can, darling," he heard her say.

It gave him such pleasure to obey her. A fine blade, it tickled; rather like a feather drawn across his throat.

DEATH IN THE PROMISED LAND

Pat Cadigan

▼

Pat Cadigan was born in Schenectady, New York, and now lives in Overland Park, Kansas. She made her first professional sale in 1980, and has subsequently come to be regarded as one of the best writers in SF. Her story "Pretty Boy Crossover" has recently appeared on several critics' lists as among the best science fiction stories of the 1980s; her story "Angel" was a finalist for the Hugo Award, the Nebula Award, and the World Fantasy Award (one of the few stories ever to earn that rather unusual distinction); and her collection *Patterns* has been hailed as one of the landmark collections of the decade. Her first novel, *Mindplayers*, was released in 1987 to excellent critical response, and her second novel, *Synners*, released in 1991, won the prestigious Arthur C. Clarke Award as the year's best science fiction novel, as did her third novel, *Fools*, making her the only writer ever to win the Clarke Award twice. Her stories have appeared in our First, Second, Third, Fourth, Fifth, Sixth, Ninth, Tenth, Eleventh, and Twelfth Annual Collections. Her most recent book is a major new collection called *Dirty Work*, and she is currently at work on two new novels.

Here she plunges us deep inside the bizarre mirror-maze world of Virtual Reality gaming to play the oldest game there is, the deadly and venerable game of murder—and to play it for the highest stakes of all . . .

The kid had had his choice of places to go—other countries, other worlds, even other universes, à la the legendary exhortation of e. e. cummings, oddly evocative in its day, spookily prescient now. But the kid's idea of a hell of a good universe next door had been a glitzed-out, gritted-up, blasted and blistered post-Apocalyptic Noo Yawk Sitty. It wasn't a singular sentiment— post-Apocalyptic Noo Yawk Sitty was topping the hitline for the thirteenth week in a row, with post-Apocalyptic Ellay and post-Apocalyptic Hong Kong holding steady at two and three, occasionally trading places but defending against all comers.

Dore Konstantin didn't understand the attraction. Perhaps the kid could have explained it to her if he had not come out of post-Apocalyptic Noo Yawk Sitty with his throat cut.

Being DOA after a session in the Sitty wasn't singular, either; immediate information available said that this was number eight in as many months. So far, no authority was claiming that the deaths were related, although no one was saying they weren't, either. Konstantin wasn't sure what any of it meant, except that, at the very least, the Sitty would have one more month at the number one spot.

The video parlor night manager was boinging between appalled and thrilled. "You ever go in the Sitty?" she asked Konstantin, crowding into the doorway next to her. Her name was Guilfoyle Pleshette and she didn't make much of a crowd; she was little more than a bundle of sticks wrapped in a gaudy kimono, voice by cartoonland, hair by Van de Graaff. She stood barely higher than Konstantin's shoulder, hair included.

"No, never have," Konstantin told her, watching as DiPietro and Celestine peeled the kid's hotsuit off him for the coroner. It was too much like seeing an animal get skinned, only grislier, and not just because most of the kid's blood was on the hotsuit. Underneath, his naked flesh was imprinted with a dense pattern of lines and shapes, byzantine in complexity, from the wires and sensors in the 'suit.

Yes, it's the latest in nervous systems, Konstantin imagined a chatty lecturer's voice saying. *The neo-exo-nervous system, generated by hotsuit coverage. Each line and shape has its counterpart on the opposite side of the skin barrier, which cannot at this time be breached under pain of—*

The imaginary lecture cut off as the coroner's cam operator leaned in for a shot of the kid's head and shoulders, forcing the stringer from *Police Blotter* back against the facing wall. Unperturbed, the stringer held her own cam over her head, aimed the lens downward and kept taping. This week, *Police Blotter* had managed to reverse the injunction against commercial networks that had been reinstated last week. Konstantin couldn't wait for next week.

As the 'suit cleared the kid's hips, the smell of human waste fought with the heavy odor of blood and the sour stink of sweat for control of the air in the room, which wasn't much larger than the walk-out closet that Konstantin had shared with her ex. The closet had looked a lot bigger this morning now that her ex's belongings were gone, but this room seemed to be shrinking by the moment. The coroner, her cam operator, the stringer, and DiPietro and Celestine had all come prepared with nasal filters; Konstantin's were sitting in the top drawer of her desk.

Putting her hand over her nose and mouth, she stepped back into the hallway where her partner Taliaferro was also suffering, but from the narrow space and low ceiling rather than the air, which was merely overprocessed and stale. Pleshette followed, fishing busily in her kimono pockets.

"So *bad*," she said, looking from Konstantin to Taliaferro. Taliaferro gave no indication that he had heard her. He stood with his back to the wall and his shoulders up around his ears, head thrust forward over the archiver while he made notes, as if he expected the ceiling to come down on him. From Konstantin's angle, the archiver was completely hidden by his hand, so that he seemed to be using the stylus directly on his palm.

Never send a claustrophobe to do an agoraphobe's job, Konstantin thought, feeling surreal. Taliaferro, who pronounced his name "tolliver" for reasons she couldn't fathom, was such a big guy anyway that she wondered if most places short of an arena didn't feel small and cramped to him.

"*Real* goddam *bad*," Pleshette added, as if this somehow clarified her original statement. One bony hand came up out of a hidden pocket with a small spritzer; a too-sweet, minty odor cut through the flat air.

Taliaferro's stylus froze as his eyes swiveled to the manager. "That didn't help," he said darkly.

"Oh, but wait," she said, waving both hands to spread the scent. "Smellin' the primer now, but soon, *nothing*. Deadens the nose, use it by the *pound* here. Trade puts out a *lot* of body smell in the actioners. 'Suits *reek*." She gestured at the other doors lining the long narrow hall. "Like that *Gang Wars* module? Strapped the trade down on chaises, otherwise they'd a killed the 'suits, rollin' around on the floor, bouncin' offa the walls, jumpin' on each other. Real easy to go native in a *Gang Wars* module."

Go native? Taliaferro mouthed, looking at Konstantin from under his brows. Konstantin shrugged. "I didn't see a chaise in there."

"Folds down outa the wall. Like those old Murphy beds?"

Konstantin raised her eyebrows, impressed that she was even acquainted with the idea of Murphy beds, and then felt mildly ashamed. Her ex had always told her that being a snob was her least attractive feature.

"Most people don't use the chaises except for the sexers," Pleshette was saying. "Not if they got a choice. And there was this one blowfish, he hurt himself on the *chaise*. Got all heated up struggling, cut himself on the straps, broke some ribs. And *that*—" she leaned toward Konstantin confidentially "—*that* wasn't even the *cute* part. Know what the *cute* part was?"

Konstantin shook her head.

"The *cute* part was, his pov was in this fight at the *exact, same time* and broke the *exact, same ribs*." Pleshette straightened up and folded her arms, lifting her chin defiantly as if daring Konstantin to disbelieve. "This's *always* been non-safe, even before it was fatal."

"That happen here?" Taliaferro asked without looking up.

"Nah, some other place. East Hollywood, North Hollywood, I don't remember now." The manager's kimono sleeve flapped like a wing as she gestured. "We all heard about it. Stuff gets around."

Konstantin nodded, biting her lip so she wouldn't smile. "Uh-huh. Is this the same guy who didn't open his parachute in a skydiving scenario and was found dead with every bone in his body shattered?"

"Well, of *course* not." Pleshette looked at her as if she were crazy. "How could it be? *That* blowfish *died*. We all heard about that one too. Happened in D.C. They got it going on in D.C. with those sudden-death thrillers." She leaned toward Konstantin again, putting one scrawny hand on her arm this time. "You oughta check D.C. sources for death-trips. Life's so cheap there. It's a whole different world."

Konstantin was trying to decide whether to agree with her or change the subject when the coroner emerged from the cubicle with the cam op right on her heels.

"—shot everything *I* shot," the cam op was saying unhappily.

"And I said never *mind*." The coroner waved a dismissive hand. "We can subpoena her footage and see if it really is better than yours. Probably isn't. *Go*." She gave him a little push.

"But I just *know* she's in some of my shots—"

"We can handle that, too. *Go. Now*." The coroner shooed him away and turned to Konstantin. She was a small person, about the size of a husky ten-year-old—something to do with her religion, Konstantin remembered, the Church of Small-Is-Beautiful. The faithful had their growth inhibited in childhood. Konstantin wondered what happened to those who lost the faith, or came to it later in life.

"Well, I can say without fear of contradiction that the kid's throat was cut while he was still alive." The coroner looked around. "And in a palace like this. Imagine that."

"Should I also imagine how?" Konstantin asked.

The coroner smoothed down the wiry copper cloud that was her current hair. It sprang back up immediately. "Onsite micro says it was definitely a knife or some other metal with an edge, and not glass or porcelain. And definitely not self-inflicted. Even if we couldn't tell by the angle, this kid was an AR softie. He wouldn't have had the strength to saw through his own windpipe like that."

"What kind of knife, do you think?"

"Sharp and sturdy, probably a boning blade. Boning blades're all the rage out there. Or rather, *in* there. In the actioners. They all like those boning blades."

Konstantin frowned. "Great. You know what's going to be on the news inside an hour."

The coroner fanned the air with one small hand. "Yeah, yeah, yeah. Gameplayers' psychosis, everybody's heard about somebody who got stabbed in a module and came out with a knife-wound it took sixteen stitches to close and what about the nun who was on TV with the bleeding hands and feet. It's part of the modern myth-making machine. There've been some people who went off their perch in AR, got all mixed up about what was real and hurt themselves or somebody else. But the stigmata stuff—everybody conveniently forgets how the stigmata of Sister-Mary-Blood-Of-The-Sacred-Whatever got exposed as a hoax by her own order. The good sister did a turn as a stage magician before she got religion. There's a file about how she did it floating around PubNet—you oughta look it up. Fascinatin' rhythms. The real thing would be *extremo ruptura*, very serious head trouble, which the experts are pretty sure nobody's had since St. Theresa."

"Which one?" asked Konstantin.

The coroner chuckled. "That's good. 'Which one?' " She shook her head, laughing some more. "I'll have my report in your in-box tomorrow." She went up the hall, still laughing.

"Well," said the night manager, sniffing with disdain. "*Some* people ought better stick with what they know than mock what they *don't know squat about.*"

"My apologies if she offended your beliefs," Konstantin said to her. "Is there some other way into that room that nobody knows about—vents, conduits, emergency exit or access?"

Pleshette wagged her fuzzy head from side to side. "Nope."

Konstantin was about to ask for the building's blueprints when Taliaferro snapped the archiver closed with a sound like a rifle shot. "Right. Some great place you got here. We'll interview the clientele now. Outside, in the parking lot."

"*Got* no parking lot," Pleshette said, frowning.

"Didn't say *your* parking lot. There's a car rental place down the block. We'll corral everyone, do it there." Taliaferro looked at Konstantin. "Spacious. Lots of room to move around in."

Konstantin sighed. "First let's weed out everyone who was in the same scenario and module with the kid and see if anyone remembers the kid doing or saying anything that could give any hints about what was happening to him." She started up the hall with Taliaferro.

"You could do that yourself, you know," Pleshette said.

Konstantin stopped. Taliaferro kept walking without looking back. "Do what?"

"See what the kid was doing when he took it in the neck. Surveillance'll have it."

"Surveillance?" Konstantin said, unsure that she had heard correctly.

"Of *course* surveillance," the night manager said, giving her a sideways look. "You think we let the blowfish come in here and don't keep an eye on them? *Anything* could happen, I don't want no liability for the bone in somebody else's head. Nobody does.''

"Can I screen this surveillance record in your office?" she asked.

"Anywhere, if all you want to do is screen it." Pleshette frowned, puzzled.

"Good. Set me up for it in your office."

Pleshette's frown deepened. "My office."

"Is that some kind of problem?" asked Konstantin, pausing as she moved toward the open doorway of the room, where she could hear DiPietro and Celestine bantering with the stringer.

"Guess not." The night manager shrugged. "You just want to screen it, my office, sure."

Konstantin didn't know what to make of the look on Pleshette's funny little face. Maybe that was all it was, a funny little face in a funny little open-all-night world. A funny little open-all-night artificial world at that. For all Konstantin knew, the night manager hadn't seen true daylight for years. Not her problem, she thought as she stuck her head through the doorway of the cubicle where Celestine and DiPietro were now busy jockeying for the stringer's attention while the stringer pretended she wasn't pumping them for information and they pretended they didn't know she was pretending not to pump them for information. No one had to pretend the dead kid had been temporarily forgotten.

"Pardon me for interrupting," Konstantin said a bit archly. DiPietro and Celestine turned to her; in their identical white coveralls, they looked like unfinished marionettes.

"Attendants'll be coming for him. Before you do a thorough search of the room, you might want to, oh—" she gestured at the body "—cover *him* up."

"Sure thing," said Celestine, and then suddenly tossed something round and wrapped in plastic at her. "Think fast!"

Konstantin caught it by instinct. The shape registered on her before anything else. The kid's head, she thought, horrified. The cut across his throat had been so deep, it had come off when they'd peeled him.

Then she felt the metal through the plastic and realized it was the kid's head-mounted monitor. "Oh, good one, Celestine." She tucked the monitor under her left arm. "If I'd dropped that, we'd be filling out forms on it for a year."

"*You*, drop something? Not this lifetime." Celestine grinned; her muttonchops made her face seem twice as wide as it was. Konstantin wondered if there was such a thing as suing a cosmetologist for malpractice.

"Thanks for the act of faith but next time, save it for church." Konstantin went up the hall toward the main lobby, Pleshette following in a swish of kimono.

* * *

There were only two uniformed officers waiting in the lobby with the other three members of the night staff, who were perched side by side on a broken-down, ersatz-leather sofa by the front window. The rest of the police, along with the clientele, were already down the block with Taliaferro, one of the uniforms told Konstantin. She nodded, trying not to stare at the woman's neat ginger-colored mustache. At least it wasn't as ostentatious as Celestine's muttonchops, but she wasn't sure that she would ever get used to the fashion of facial hair on women. Her ex would have called her a throwback; perhaps she was.

"That's all right, as long as we know where they are." Konstantin handed her the bagged headmount. "Evidence—look after it. There's some surveillance footage I'm going to screen in the manager's office and I thought I'd question the staff there as well—" The people on the couch were gazing up at her expectantly. "Is this the entire night shift?"

"The whole kitten's caboodle," Pleshette assured her.

Konstantin looked around. It was a small lobby, no hiding places, and presumably, no secret doors. Small, drab, and depressing—after waiting here for even just a few minutes, any AR would look great by comparison. She turned back to the people on the couch just as the one in the middle stood up and stuck out his hand. "Miles Mank," he said in a hearty tenor.

Konstantin hesitated. The man's eyes had an unfocused, watery look to them she associated with people who weren't well. He towered over her by six inches and outweighed her by at least a hundred pounds. But they were fairly soft pounds, packed into a glossy blue one-piece uniform that, combined with those gooey eyes and his straw-colored hair, gave him a strangely child-like appearance. She shook his hand. "What's your job here?"

"Supervisor. Well, unofficial supervisor," he added, the strange eyes looking past her at Guilfoyle Pleshette. "I'm the one who's been here the longest so I'm always telling everybody else how things work."

"So go ahead, Miles," Pleshette said, her voice flat. The kimono sleeves snapped like pennants in a high wind as she stretched out her arms and refolded them. "Say it—that if they promoted from within here, *you'd* be night manager. Then I can explain how they had to go on a talent search for an *experienced* administrator. It'll all balance out."

"Nobody ever *died* while *I* was acting night manager," Miles Mank said huffily.

"Yeah, that's true—everybody survived that riot where the company had to refund all the customers. But nobody died so that made it all good-deal-well-done."

Miles Mank strode past Konstantin to loom over Pleshette, who had to reach up to shake her bony finger in his face. Konstantin felt that panicky chill all authorities felt when a situation was about to slip the leash. Before she could order Mank to stop arguing with Pleshette, the mustached officer tugged her sleeve and showed her a taser set on flash. "Shall I?"

Konstantin glanced at her nameplate. "Sure, Wolski, go ahead." She stepped back and covered her eyes.

The flash was a split-second heat that she found oddly comforting, though no one else did. Besides Guilfoyle Pleshette and Miles Mank, Wolski had also failed to warn her fellow officer, the other two employees, or Taliaferro, who had chosen that moment to step back inside. The noise level increased exponentially.

"Everybody shut up!" Konstantin yelled; to her surprise, everybody did. She looked around. All the people in the lobby except for herself and Wolski had their hands over their eyes. It looked like a convention of see-no-evil monkeys.

"I'm going to screen surveillance footage of the victim's final session in the manager's office, and then interview the rest of the staff," she announced and turned to Taliaferro. "Then I'd like to question anyone who was in the same module and scenario." She waited but he didn't take his hands from his eyes. "That means I'll be phoning you down the block, partner, to have select individuals escorted to the office." She waited another few seconds. "Understand, Taliaferro?" she added, exasperated.

"Let me do some prelims on the customers," he said, speaking to the air where he thought she was. He was off by two feet. "They're gonna be getting restless while you're doing that. We're going to have to give them phone calls and pizza as it is."

Konstantin rolled her eyes. "So *give* them phone calls and pizza." She turned back to Pleshette. "Now, can you show me to your office?"

"Who, me?" asked Miles Mank. "I'm afraid I don't have one. I've been making do with the employee lounge."

"Suffer, Mank," Pleshette said, peeking between her fingers. "No one was talking to *you.*" She started to lower her hands and then changed her mind.

Konstantin sighed. Their vision would return to normal in a few minutes, along with their complexions, assuming none of them suffered from light-triggered skin-rashes. Perhaps she should have been more sympathetic, but she didn't think any of them would notice if she were.

She put her hand on Guilfoyle Pleshette's left arm. "Now, your office?"

"I'll show you," said Pleshette, "if I ever see well enough again."

Pleshette's office was smaller than the smelly cubicle where the kid had died, which was probably a good thing. It meant that Konstantin didn't throw anything breakable against the wall when she discovered the so-called surveillance footage was an AR log and not a live-action recording of the kid's murder. There would have been no point to throwing anything; unlike the living room where she and her ex had had their final argument, there wasn't enough distance to make a really satisfying smash.

She settled in to watch the video, every moment, including the instructional lead that told her that the only pov on monitor would be detached observer; she could use the editing option for any close-ups or odd angles, and there was a primer to pull down if she were feeling less than Fellini, or even D.W. Griffith.

How helpful, she thought, freezing the footage before the lead faded into the scenario. How excessively helpful. What was she supposed to do, decide how to edit the footage *before* she watched it?

But of course, she realized; this came under the heading of *Souvenirs*. Footage from your AR romp, video of your friend's wedding, pre-packaged quick-time scenics from a kiosk in the Lima airport for a last-minute gift before you boarded the flight home—you made it look however you wanted it to look. To whomever happened to be looking, of course. Maybe you didn't want it to look the same to everyone—a tamer version for one, something experimental to hold another's attention.

Konstantin tapped the menu line at the bottom of the screen. *Options?* it asked her, fanning them out in the center of a deep blue background. *Pick a card, any card,* she thought; *memorize it and slip it back into the deck. There'll be a quiz later, if you survive.* After a moment, she chose *No Frills*.

The image on the screen liquified and melted away into black. A moment later, she was looking at an androgynous face that suggested the best of India and Japan in combination. The name came up as Shantih Love, which she couldn't decide if she hated or not; the linked profile informed her that the Shantih Love appearance was as protected by legal copyright as the name. No age given; under *Sex* it said, *Any; all; why do you care?*

"Filthy job, Shantih, but somebody's got to." She tapped for the technical specs of the session. Full coverage hotsuit, of course; that would tell her when the kid had died. She scrolled past his scenario and module choices to Duration: four hours, twenty minutes. *Yow, kid, that alone could have killed some people.*

She tapped the screen for his vitals so she could note the exact time of death in the archiver. Then she just stared at the figures on the screen, tapping the stylus mindlessly on the desk.

Shantih Love, the specs told her, had shuffled off all mortal coils, artificial and otherwise, just ten minutes into his four-hour-and-twenty-minute romp in post-Apocalyptic Noo Yawk Sitty. It didn't say how he had managed to go on with his romp after he had died. She supposed that was too much to ask.

* * *

Shantih Love and the kid powering him/her had both had their throats cut, but for Shantih Love the wound had not been fatal. Disgusting and gory, even uncomfortable, but not fatal.

Konstantin watched the screen intently as the sequence faded in. In the middle of a glitter-encrusted cityscape at dusk, the androgyne made his/her way toward some kind of noisy party or tribal gathering on the rubble-strewn shore of the Hudson River. The rubble was also encrusted with glitter; more glitter twinkled on the glass of the silent storefronts on the other side of a broad, four-lane divided thoroughfare partially blocked by occasional islands of wreckage. As Shantih Love swept off the sidewalk—ankle-length purple robe flowing gracefully with every step—and crossed the ruined street, one of the wrecks ignited, lighting up the semidark. Shantih Love barely glanced at it and kept going, toward the gathering on the shore; Konstantin could hear music and, under that, the white noise of many voices in conversation. What could they possibly have to talk about, she wondered; was it anything more profound than what you'd hear at any other party in any other reality with any other people? And if it were, why did it occur only in the reality of post-Apocalyptic Noo Yawk Sitty?

Shantih Love abruptly looked back in such a way that s/he seemed to be looking directly out of the screen into her eyes. The expression on the unique face seemed somehow both questioning and confident. Konstantin steered the detached perspective from behind Shantih Love around his/her right side, passing in front of the androgyne and moving to the left side, tracking him/her as s/he walked toward the multitude on the shore.

A figure suddenly popped up from behind the low concrete barrier running between the street and the river. Shantih Love stopped for a few moments, uncertainty troubling his/her smooth forehead. Konstantin tried adjusting the screen controls to see the figure better in the gathering darkness but, maddeningly, she couldn't seem to get anything more definite than a fuzzy, blurry silhouette, definitely human-like but otherwise unidentifiable as young or old, male, female, both or neither, friendly or hostile.

The shape climbed over the barrier to the street side just as Shantih Love slipped over it to the shore. The ground here was soft sand and Shantih Love had trouble walking in it. The fuzzy shape paced him/her on the other side of the wall and Konstantin got the idea that it was saying something, but nothing came up on audio. Shantih Love didn't answer, didn't even look in its direction again as s/he moved in long strides toward the crowd, which extended from the water's edge up to a break in the barrier and into the road.

The perspective had slipped back behind Shantih Love. Konstantin tapped the forward button rapidly; now she seemed to be perched on Shantih Love's right shoulder. The gathering on the beach appeared to be nothing more than a ragged, disorganized cocktail party, the sort of thing her ex had loved to attend. Konstantin was disappointed. Was this really all anyone in AR could think of doing?

Shantih Love whirled suddenly; after a one-second delay, the perspective followed. Konstantin felt a wave of dizziness and the images on the screen went out of focus.

When the focus cleared, Konstantin saw that the figure was standing on top of the barrier, poised to jump. Shantih Love backed away, turned, and began stumbling through the party crowd, bumping into various people, some less distinct than others. Konstantin didn't have to shift the perspective around to know that the creature was chasing the androgyne. Now the pov seemed to be a few inches in front of the creature's face; she had a few fast glimpses of bandage-wrapped arms and hands with an indeterminate number of fingers as it staggered into the party after Love.

The pov began to shake and streak, as if it were embedded in the pursuing creature's body. Frustrated, Konstantin pounded on the forward key, but the pov didn't budge. Someone had preordered the pov to this position, she realized. But whether it was the murdered kid who had done it or just the formatting she couldn't tell.

Worse, now that she was in the party crowd, almost every attendee was either so vague as to be maddeningly unidentifiable, or so much a broad type—barbarian, vampire, wild-child, homunculus—that anonymity was just as assured.

Shantih Love broke through the other side of the crowd two seconds before she did, and ran heavily toward a stony rise leading to the sidewalk. S/he scrambled up it on all fours, a heartbeat ahead of the pursuer.

Love vaulted the low barrier and ran along the middle of the street, looking eagerly at each wreck. There were more wrecks here, some ablaze, some not. Something moved inside each one, even those that were burning. Konstantin realized she was probably alone in finding that remarkable; living in a bonfire was probably the height of AR chic.

She tried pushing the pov ahead again and gained several feet. Shantih Love looked over his/her shoulder, seemingly right at the pov. The androgyne's expression was panic and dismay; in the next moment, s/he fell.

The pov somersaulted; there was a flash of broken pavement, followed by a brief panorama of the sky, a flip and a close-up of the androgyne's profile just as the pursuer pushed his/her chin up with one rag-wrapped hand. Perfect skin stretched taut; the blade flashed and disappeared as it turned sideways to slash through flesh, tendon, blood vessels, bone.

The blood flew against the pov and dripped downward, like gory drops of rain on a window. Konstantin winced and pressed to try to erase the blood trails; nothing happened.

Shantih Love coughed and gargled at the sky, not trying to twist away from the bandaged hand that still held his/her chin. Blood pulsed upward in an exaggerated display of blood spurting from a major artery. The creature pushed Love's face to one side, away from the camera, and bent its head to drink.

Konstantin had seen similar kinds of things before in videos, including the so-called killer video that had supposedly been circulating underground (whatever *that* meant these days) and had turned out to be so blatantly phony that the perpetrators should have gone down for fraud.

But where the blood spilled in that and numerous other videos had looked more like cherry syrup or tomato puree, this looked real enough to make Konstantin gag. She put a hand over her mouth as she froze the screen and turned away, trying to breathe deeply and slowly through her nose, willing her nausea to fade. At the same time, she was surprised at herself. Her squeamish streak was usually conveniently dormant; in twelve years as a detective, she had seen enough real-time blood and gore that she could say she was somewhat hardened. Shantih Love's real-time counterpart—secret identity? veneer person?—had certainly bled enough to make anyone choke.

But there was something about this—the blood or the noises coming from Shantih Love, the sound of the creature drinking so greedily. Or maybe just the sight of such realistic blood activating the memory of that smell in the cubicle, that overpowering stench; that smell and the sight of the dead kid stripped of everything, skinned like an animal.

She collected herself and tried jabbing fast-forward to get through the vampiric sequence as quickly as possible. It only made everything more grotesque, so she took it back to normal just at the point where both the creature and the blood vanished completely.

Startled, Konstantin rewound and ran it again in slo-mo, just to make sure she'd seen it right. She had; it wasn't a fast fade-out or the twinkling deliquescence so favored by beginning cinematography students, but a genuine popper which usually happened by way of a real-time equipment failure or power-out. Common wisdom had it that the jump from AR to real-time in such an event was so abrupt as to produce extreme reactions of an undesirable nature—vertigo, projectile vomiting, fainting, or, worse, all three, which could be fatal if you happened to be alone.

Or a slashed throat, if you happened to be not alone with the wrong person, Konstantin thought, trying to rub the furrows out of her brow.

She repeated the sequence once more, and then again in slo-mo, watching the blood disappear right along with the creature, leaving Shantih Love behind. Konstantin called up the record of the kid's vitals and found that, as she had expected, they had quit registering at the moment the blood had disappeared.

Konstantin took her finger off the pause button and let the action go forward.

On the screen, the Shantih Love character sat up, its elegant fingers feeling the ragged edges and flaps of skin where its throat had been cut, mild annoyance deepening the few lines in its face. As Konstantin watched it trying to pinch the edges of skin together, she was aware that she was now thinking of the kid's AR persona as a thing rather than a human.

Presumed "it" until proven human? Konstantin frowned. So what was driving *it* now, anyway—a robot, or a very human hijacker?

She could watch video for the next three hours and see if anything would become clearer to her; instead, she decided to talk to people she was reasonably sure were human before taking in any more adventures of a dead kid's false pretending to be alive in a city pretending to be dead.

If the office had seemed cramped before, Miles Mank made it look even smaller by taking up at least half of it. When it became obvious that he actually knew next to nothing, Konstantin tried to get rid of him quickly, but he kept finding conversational hooks that would get her attention and then lead her along to some meaningless and boring point, at which he wouldn't so much conclude as change the subject and do it all over again. She was finally able to convince him that he was desperately needed at the parking lot to help sort out the clientele with her bewildered partner. Then she prayed that Taliaferro wouldn't use a similar excuse to send him back to her. She still didn't like his eyes.

The first of the other two employees was a silver-haired kid named Tim Mezzer, who was about the same age as the murder victim. He had the vaguely puzzled, preoccupied look of ex-addicts who had detoxed recently by having their blood cleansed. Officially, it was a fast way out of an expensive jones. In fact, it made the high better on relapse.

"How long have you worked here?" Konstantin asked him.

"Three days." He sounded bored.

"And what do you do?" she prodded when he didn't say anything more.

"Oh, I'm a specialist," he said, even more bored. "I specialize in picking up everybody's smelly 'suit when they're done and get 'em cleaned." Mezzer put a plump elbow on the desk and leaned forward. "Tell the truth—you'd kill to have a job like that instead of the boring shit you do."

Konstantin wasn't sure he was really being sarcastic. "Sometimes. Did you know the victim?"

"Dunno. What was his name?"

"Shantih Love."

Mezzer grunted. "Good label. Must have cost him to come up with one that good. Sounds a little like an expensive female whore-assassin, but still pretty good. Someday I'll be rich enough to be able to afford a tailormade label."

Konstantin was only half-listening while she prodded the archiver for the victim's reference file. "Ah, here we are. Real name is—" she stopped. "Well, that *can't* be right."

"Don't be so sure." Mezzer yawned. "What's it say?"

"Tomoyuki Iguchi," Konstantin said slowly, as if she had to sound out each syllable.

"Ha. Sounds like he was working on turning Japanese in a serious way."

"Why?"

"Well, for post-Apocalyptic Tokyo, of course." Mezzer sighed. "What else?"

"There's a post-Apocalyptic Tokyo now?" Konstantin asked suspiciously.

"Not yet." Mezzer's sigh became a yawn. "Coming soon. Supposed to be the next big hot spot. They say it's gonna make the Sitty look like Sunday in Nebraska, with these parts you can access only if you're Japanese, or a convincing simulation. It's the one everybody's been waiting for."

Konstantin wondered if he knew that something very like it had already come and gone a good many years before either of them had been born. "How about you?" she asked him. "Is it the one you've been waiting for?"

"I don't know from Japanese. I'm an Ellay boy. Got all those gorgeous celebs you can beat up in street gangs. But the bubble-up on this is, there's some kinda secret coming-attraction subroutines for post-Apocalyptic Tokyo buried in the Noo Yawk, Hong Kong, and Ellay scenes and no non-Japanese can crack them. *If* they're really there. Shantih Love musta thought they were."

"But why would he take *two* fake names?" Konstantin wondered, more to herself.

"*Told* you—he was trying to turn Japanese. He wanted anyone who stripped his label to find his Japanese name underneath and take him for that. Invite him into the special Japan area." Mezzer put his head back as if he were going to bay at the moon and yawned once again. "Or he was getting that crazy-head. You know, where you start thinking it's real in there and fake out here, or you can't tell the difference. You need to talk to Body. Body'll know. Body's probably the only one who'd know for sure."

"What body?"

"Body Sativa. Body knows more about the top ten ARs than anyone else, real or not."

Konstantin felt her mouth twitch. "Don't you mean Cannabis Sativa?" she asked sarcastically.

Mezzer blinked at her in surprise. "Get *off*. Cannibal's her mother. She's good, but Body's the real Big Dipper." He smiled. "Pretty win, actually, that somebody like you'ud know about Cannibal Sativa. Were you goin' in to talk to her?"

Konstantin didn't know what to say.

"Go see Body, I swear she's the one you want. I'll give you some icons you can use in there. Real insider icons, not what they junk you up with in the help files."

"Thanks," Konstantin said doubtfully. "But I think I fell down about a mile back. If he was turning Japanese, as you put it, why would he call himself Shantih Love?"

Mezzer blinked. "Well, because he was tryin' to be a *Japanese* guy named Shantih Love." He frowned at her. "You just don't ever go in AR, do you?"

"Can't add to that," said the other employee cheerfully. She was an older woman named Howard Ruth with natural salt-and-pepper hair and lines in a soft face untouched by chemicals or surgery. Konstantin found her comforting to look at. "Body Sativa's the best tip you're gonna get. You'll go through that whole bunch in the lot down the street and you won't hear anything more helpful." She sat back, crossing her left ankle over her right knee.

"Body Sativa wouldn't happen to be in that group, by any chance?"

Howard Ruth shrugged. "Doubt it. This is just another reception site on an AR network. Considering the sophisticated moves Body makes, she's most likely on from some singleton station, and that could be anywhere."

"Come on," said Konstantin irritably, "even *I* know everyone online has an origin code."

Howard Ruth's smile was sunny. "You haven't played any games lately, have you?"

Konstantin was thinking the woman should talk to her ex. "Online? No."

"No," agreed the woman, "because if you had, you'd know that netgaming isn't considered official net communication or transaction, so it's not governed by FCC or FDSA regulations. Get on, pick a name or buy a permanent label, stay as long as you like—or can afford—and log out when you've had enough. Netgaming is one hundred percent elective, so anything goes—no guidelines, no censorship, no crimes against persons. You can't file a complaint against anyone for assault, harassment, fraud, or anything like that."

Konstantin sighed. "I didn't know this. Why not?"

"You didn't have to." Howard Ruth laughed. "Look, officer—"

"Lieutenant."

"Sure, lieutenant. Unless you netgame regular, you *won't* know any of this. You ever hear about the case years back where a guy used an origin line to track down a woman in realtime and kill her?"

"No," said Konstantin with some alarm. "Where did this happen?"

"Oh, back east somewhere. D.C., I think, or some place like that. Life is so cheap there, you know. Anyway, what happened was, back when they had origin lines in gaming, this guy got mad at this woman, somehow found her by way of her origin line, and boom—lights out. That was one of the first cases of that gameplayer's madness where someone could prove it could be a real danger offline. After that, there was a court ruling that since gaming was strictly recreational, gamers were entitled to complete privacy if they wanted. No origin line. Kinda the same thing for fraud and advertising.''

Konstantin felt her interest, which had started to wane with the utterance *D.C.*, come alive again. "What?"

"Guy ran a game-within-a-game on someone. I can't remember exactly what it was—beachfront in Kansas, diamond mines in Peru, hot stocks about to blow. Anyhow, the party of the second part got the idea it was all backed up in realtime and did this financial transfer to the party of the first part, who promptly logged out and went south. Party of the second part hollers *Thief!* and what do you know but the police catch this salesperson of the year. Who then claims that it was all a game and he thought the money was just a gift.''

"And?" said Konstantin.

"And that's a wrap. Grand jury won't even indict, on grounds of extreme gullibility. As in, 'You were in *artificial reality*, you fool, what did you expect?' Personally, I think they were both suffering from a touch of the galloping headbugs."

Konstantin was troubled. "And that decision stood?"

"It's *artificial* reality—you can't lie, no matter what you say. It's all make-believe, let's-pretend, the play's the thing." Howard Ruth laughed heartily. "You choose to pay somebody out here for time in there, that's *your* hotspot. Life is so strange, eh?"

Konstantin made a mental note to check for court rulings on AR as she pressed for a clean page in the archiver. "But if being in an AR makes people insane . . ."

"Doesn't make *everyone* insane," the woman said. "That's what it is, you know. The honey factory don't close down just because you're allergic to bee stings."

Konstantin was still troubled. "So when did those things happen?" she asked, holding the stylus ready.

"I don't know," Howard Ruth said, surprised at the question. "Oughta be in the police files, though. Doesn't law enforcement have some kind of central-national-international bank you all access? Something like *Police Blotter?*"

"In spite of the name," Konstantin said, speaking slowly so the woman couldn't possibly misunderstand, "*Police Blotter* is actually a commercial net-magazine, and not affiliated with law enforcement in any official way. But yes, we do have our own national information center. *But* I need to know some kind of key fact that the search program can use to hunt down the

information I want—a name, a date, a location." She paused to see if any
of this was forthcoming. The other woman only shrugged.

"Well, sorry I can't be of more help, but that's all I know." She got up
and stretched, pressing her hands into the small of her back. "If anyone
knows more, it's Body Sativa."

"Body Sativa," said the first customer interviewee. He was an aging child
with green hair and claimed his name was Earl O'Jelly. "Nobody knows
more. Nobody and *no body*. If you get what I mean."

Konstantin didn't bury her face in her hands. The aging child volunteered
the information that he had been in the crowd by the Hudson that Shantih
Love had staggered through, but claimed he hadn't seen anything like what
she described to him.

Neither had the next one, a grandmother whose AR alter-ego was a twelve-
year-old boy-assassin named Nick the Schick. "That means I technically have
to have 'the' as my middle name, but there's worse, and stupider as well,"
she told Konstantin genially. "Nick knows Body, of course. *Everybody* knows
Body. And vice versa, probably. Actually, I think Body Sativa's just a database that got crossed with a traffic-switcher and jumped the rails."

"Pardon?" Konstantin said, not comprehending.

The grandmother was patient. "You know how files get cross-monkeyed?
Just the thing—traffic-switcher was referencing the database in a thunderstorm, maybe sunspots, and they got sort of arc-welded. Traffic-switcher
interface mutated from acquired characteristics from all the database entries.
That's what *I* say, and *nobody's* proved yet that *that* couldn't happen. Or
didn't." She nodded solemnly.

Konstantin opened her mouth to tell the woman that if she understood her
correctly, what she was describing was akin to putting a dirty shirt and a pile
of straw in a wooden box for spontaneous generation of mice and then decided
against it. For one thing, she wasn't sure that she had understood correctly
and for another, the shirt-and-straw method of creating mice was probably
routine in AR.

There was no third interviewee. Instead, an ACLU lawyer came in and
explained that since the crime had occurred in the real world, and all the so-
called witnesses had been in AR, they weren't actually witnesses at all, and
could not be detained any longer. However, all of their names would be
available on the video parlor's customer list, which Konstantin could see as
soon as she produced the proper court order.

"In the meantime, everyone agrees you ought to talk to this Body Sativa,
whatever she is," the lawyer said, consulting a palmtop. "Assuming she'll
give you so much as the time of day without legal representation."

"I suppose I need a court order for that, too," Konstantin grumbled.

"Not hardly. AR is open to anyone who wants to access it. Even you, Officer Konstantin." The lawyer grinned, showing diamond teeth. "Just remember the rules of admissibility. Everything everyone tells you in AR—"

"—is a lie, right. I got the short course tonight already." Konstantin's gaze strayed to the monitor, now blank. "I think I'll track this Body Sativa down in person and question her in realtime."

"Only if she voluntarily tells you who she is out here," the lawyer reminded her a bit smugly. "Otherwise, her privacy is protected."

"Maybe she'll turn out to be a good citizen," Konstantin mused. "Maybe she'll care that some seventeen-year-old kid got his throat cut."

The lawyer's smug expression became a sad smile. "Maybe. *I* care. *You* care. But there's no law that says anyone else has to."

"I know, and I'd be afraid if there was. Even so—" Konstantin frowned. "I do wish I didn't have to depend so much on volunteers."

She sent DiPietro and Celestine over to the dead kid's apartment building, though she wasn't expecting much. If he was typical, his neighbors would have barely been aware of him. Most likely; they would find he had been yet another gypsy worker of standard modest skills, taking temporary assignments via a city-run agency to support his various habits. Including his AR habit.

Just to be thorough, she waited in Guilfoyle Pleshette's office for the call letting her know that the other two detectives had found a generic one-room apartment with little in the way of furnishings or other belongings to distinguish it from any other generic one-room apartment in the city. Except for the carefully organized card library of past AR experiences in the dustless, static-free, moisture- and fire-proof non-magnetic light-shielded container. Every heavy AR user kept a library, so that no treasured moment could be lost to time.

The library would go to headquarters to be stored for the required ten-day waiting period while a caseworker tried to track down next-of-kin. If none turned up, the card library would then be accessed by an automated program designed to analyze the sequences recorded on each card and construct a profile of the person, which would then be added to the online obituaries. Usually this would cause someone who had known the deceased to come forward; other times, it simply confirmed that there was no one to care.

The idea came unbidden to Konstantin, derailing the semidoze she had slipped into at whatever indecent A.M. the night had become. She plugged the archiver into the phone and sent the retriever to fetch data on the other seven AR DOAs.

Delivery was all but immediate—at this time of night, there wasn't much data traffic. Konstantin felt mildly annoyed that DiPietro and Celestine couldn't report in just as quickly. Perhaps they had taken the stringer with them and were even now playing to the cam in an inspection of the dead kid's apartment.

A bit of heartburn simmered in her chest; she imagined it was her blood pressure going up a notch. According to *The Law Enforcement Officers' Guide To A Healthy, Happy Life* (*ON & OFF The Job!*), sex was the number one stress reliever. The *Guide* had most likely meant the sort that involved one other person, Konstantin reflected and pushed away thoughts of her ex to survey the data arranging itself on the archiver's small but hi-res screen.

The first to suffer a suspicious death while in post-Apocalyptic Noo Yawk Sitty had been a thirty-four-year-old woman named Sally Lefkow. Her picture showed a woman so pale as to seem faded. She had passed most of her realtime hours as a third-rank senior on a Minneapolis janitorial team whose contract had included both the building where she had lived and the building where she had died. Konstantin wasn't sure whether to be amused, amazed, or alarmed that her online persona had been an evolved dragon; eight feet tall and the color of polished antique copper, it had been bi-sexual, able to switch at will. Sally Lefkow had died of suffocation; the evolved dragon had been in flight when it had suddenly fallen out of the sky into the East River, and never come up.

Konstantin put the dead woman's realtime background next to the information on the dragon to compare them but found she was having trouble retaining anything. "In one eye and out the other," she muttered, then winced. *Lover, come back. You forgot to take the in-jokes along with the rest of the emotional baggage.*

She marked the Lefkow-dragon combo and went on to the next victim, a twenty-eight-year-old gypsy office worker named Emilio Torres. Konstantin thought he looked more like an athlete. Or maybe an ex-athlete. He had died alone in his Portland apartment during an online session as—Konstantin blinked—Marilyn Presley. Even Konstantin had heard of Marilyn Presley. The hybrid had been an online flash-fad, hot for a day, passé forever after. But not, apparently, for Torres. He had persisted as Marilyn for six weeks, long after the rest of the flash followers had lost interest, and he had died— Konstantin blinked again—of an overdose of several drugs; the Marilyn Presley persona had gone inert in the middle of some sort of gathering that wasn't quite a street brawl but not really an open-air party, either. There was no follow-up on the persona, nothing to tell Konstantin if the rights to it had been acquired by someone else since.

Torres had died a month after Lefkow and half a continent away. The next death had occurred two months later, in a cheesy beachside parlor in New Hampshire. Marsh Kuykendall had been unembarrassed by his status as an AR junkie, supporting his habit with odd and mostly menial jobs.

Acquaintances of the victim have all heard him say, at one time or another, that realtime was the disposable reality because it could not be preserved or replayed like AR, Konstantin read. *"AR is humanity's true destiny." "In AR, everyone is immortal."*

If you don't mind existing in reruns, she thought. Kuykendall had owned a half dozen personas, all of them his original creations. Mortality had caught up with him while he had been acting out a panther-man fantasy. The panther-man had been beaten to death by some vaguely monstrous assailant that no one claimed to have seen clearly; in realtime, Kuykendall had taken blows hard enough to shatter both his headmounted helmet and his head. No one in the parlor had heard or seen anything.

Victim number four had been in rehab for a year after a bad accident had left her paralyzed. Lydia Stang's damaged nerves had been regenerated, but she had had to relearn movement from the bottom up. AR had been part of her therapy; her AR persona had been an idealized gymnastic version of herself. She had died with a broken neck, in AR and in real-time. Witnesses stated she had been fighting a street duel with a lizard-person. Even better, the lizard-person had voluntarily come forward and admitted to AR contact with the deceased. Stang had been online in Denver, while the lizard-person had been cavorting in a parlor not three blocks from where Konstantin was sitting. She double-checked to be sure she had that right, and then made a note to look up the lizard-person in real-time, if possible.

A moment later she was scratching that note out; the lizard-person was victim number five. Even more shocking, Konstantin thought, was the lack of information on the deceased, a former musician who had gone by the single name Flo. After Lydia Stang's death, Flo had given up music and taken up AR full-time, or so it seemed, until someone had suffocated her. Online, her reptilian alter-ego had been swimming. In the East River, Konstantin noted, which the Lefkow dragon had fallen into out of the sky. Maybe that meant something; maybe it didn't.

Victims six and seven would seem to have killed each other in a gang fight. Konstantin found this disheartening. In post-Apocalyptic Noo Yawk Sitty, they had been a couple of nasty street kids, sixteen, just on the verge of adulthood. In real-time, they had been a pair of middle-aged gypsy office workers who had no doubt discovered that they had wandered into the cul de sac of life and weren't going to find their way out alive. They had both lived in a nearby urban hive, got assignments through the same agency, did the same kinds of no-brainer files and data upkeep jobs—and yet, they apparently hadn't known each other offline. Or if they had known each other, they had deliberately stayed away from each other. Except online, where they had often mixed it up. They had stabbed each other in AR but someone else had stabbed each of them in the privacy of their own homes. The times of death seemed to be in some dispute.

And now here was number eight, a weird Caucasian kid with a Japanese name. *Domo arigato*, Konstantin thought sourly, and pressed for a summary of the common characteristics of each case.

There wasn't much, except for the fact that each murder had occurred while the victim had been online in post-Apocalyptic Noo Yawk Sitty. Three of the previous murders had taken place locally; the kid's brought it up to four, fully half. And unless it turned out that the kid had been a brain surgeon, all of them had been lower level drones, not a professional in the bunch.

She sat back and tried to think. Was serial murder back in style—*again?* Except whoever had been enjoying the pretend-murder of hijacking someone else's AR persona had decided to cross over? Or couldn't tell the difference?

Konstantin pressed for a table of similarities among the AR characters and came up with a *Data Not Available* sign. The note on the next screen told her there had been no work done in this area, either due to lack of software, lack of time, or lack of personnel. Undoubtedly no one had thought that it was particularly important to look into the AR personae—it wasn't as if those were actual victims . . . were they? For all she or anyone else knew, Sally Lefkow's dragon would be more missed and mourned than Sally herself; likewise for the rest of them.

Sad, and somehow predictable, Konstantin thought. She made a note to send out for more background on the victims. While she was reviewing what information she had, DiPietro and Celestine called to tell her mostly what she had already known, except for one very surprising difference: upon arrival at the kid's apartment, they had found a nineteen-year-old woman in the process of ransacking the place. She would answer no questions except to say that she was the kid's wife.

Konstantin checked quickly; as she had thought, the kid was the only—or the first—married victim. "Bring her down here," she told them. "Fast."

"Tommie was looking for the out door," said Pine Havelock. "Anybody was gonna find it, it would be him. And now look what's gone and happened." Tomoyuki Iguchi's self-proclaimed wife was sitting in a plastic bucket of a chair hugging her folded legs tightly and staring at Konstantin over the bony humps of her knees with a half-afraid, half-accusing expression. Dressed in what looked like surplus hospital pajamas, she seemed to be completely hairless, without even eyelashes. Her eyes weren't really large enough to carry it off; she made Konstantin think of a mental patient who had fallen into a giant vat of depilatory cream.

"What out door would that be?" Konstantin asked her after a long moment of silence. "The one to the secret Japanese area?"

Havelock raised her head, staring oddly. "Get off."

"What out door?" Konstantin asked patiently, suppressing several inappropriate responses.

"Out. *Out*. Where you go and you'll stay. So you don't come back to something like *this*." She looked around Guilfoyle Pleshette's office.

"Uh-huh." Konstantin leaned an elbow on the desk and rubbed her forehead. "Where *would* you end up?"

"*Out*." The woman's forehead puckered in spots; Konstantin realized she was frowning. Without eyebrows, all of her expressions were odd. "You know—*out*. Where you don't need the suit or the top hat, because you're *there*. Not *here*."

Konstantin finally got it. "So you and Iguchi were looking for the magic door to the egress. Did you know of anyone else—"

"Egress," Havelock said, nodding vigorously. "That's it. Door out—egress. *That's* what *she* called it."

"Who?" Konstantin asked, and then almost said the answer with her.

"Body Sativa."

"Sun's gonna come up," Guilfoyle Pleshette said threateningly. She looked tired. Even her hair was starting to lose its lift.

Still sitting at her desk in the minuscule office, Konstantin waved at her impatiently. "Sorry, Taliaferro," she said into the phone while she scrawled notes in the archiver one-handed. "I didn't get the last thing you said. Repeat."

Taliaferro was surprisingly patient. Perhaps lack of sleep had simply made a zombie out of him. "I said, they're still running data on the other seven so we don't have anything solid yet. But the probability is running to 80 percent that anyone who frequented the Sitty as often as any of them would, at some point, have had AR contact with the persona or entity known as Body Sativa."

"'Entity'?" said Konstantin incredulously. "Who's calling this thing an *entity?* The probability program or someone who's in a position to know?"

"Actually, I heard some of the clientele in the parking lot calling it that. Or her. Whatever." Taliaferro sounded a bit sheepish. "Probably it's some slicko with a lot of good pr. Famous for being famous, you know."

"You do much AR?" Konstantin asked him suddenly.

There was a moment of loud silence. "Is that a sincere question?"

"Sorry," Konstantin said. "Don't know what got into me."

Taliaferro hung up without replying. She turned to Guilfoyle Pleshette, who was yawning hugely and noisily. "Do *you* do much AR?"

"Yeah, sure. Employee discount here's pretty good."

"Do you spend much time in post-Apocalyptic Noo Yawk Sitty?"

Now the manager shrugged and looked at the ceiling almost coyly. "I guess I been known to. You gotta scan rated zone because when you get a virgin in, you gotta talk about what you know. I say that's the difference between a quality business and a ditch."

Konstantin nodded absently. Once a place got too popular, nobody would admit to going voluntarily, even in AR. "And Body Sativa?"

Pleshette shrugged one shoulder. "Everybody knows about her, but not as many really seen her as say so."

"But you have," Konstantin said.

"Of course."

Of course. Konstantin managed not to smile. "You think you could introduce me?"

"Of course *not*." The woman was almost offended.

Now Konstantin shrugged. "It was worth a try."

"You got to understand here that anyone who knows Body and drags along every prole that wants to see her, won't know her for too long."

"I guess I can understand that. Suppose I go in and find her myself?"

Pleshette stared at her. "You think you can?"

"One of your employees offered me some secret insider icons. Whatever those are."

The manager straightened up. "Yeah? Who?" she asked sharply.

"The bored one. Mezzer. Tim."

"Oh, him." Pleshette waved one hand. "You can find his so-called secret insider icons in the index of any online guidebook. I got stuff you can get around with."

"But will you loan any to me?"

The funny little face looked doubtful. "What're you gonna do with it?"

Konstantin took a breath. "All I want to do is ask this Body Sativa some questions."

"What kind of questions?" the night manager asked suspiciously.

Now Konstantin felt as if she had fallen through a rabbit hole in time that had sent her back to the beginning of the situation, which she would have to explain all over again. "Questions having to do with the kid who died here tonight—Shantih Love, or Tomoyuki Iguchi, whichever you knew him as."

"I didn't know him at all," said Pleshette. Konstantin felt like screaming. "And there's no insurance that Body Sativa did, either. But if that's all you really want to do, I can load some stuff for you. But you got to promise me, you won't misuse any of it."

"Misuse it how?" Konstantin asked.

"Poaching."

"And what would that entail?"

"Getting stuff you're not entitled to get."

" 'Stuff'? In AR?" Konstantin felt completely lost now.

The night manager folded her arms again. "Yeah. Stuff in AR. In the Sitty. Everybody who goes in regular's got stuff in AR. So I got this nothing job. I got to put up with blowfish like Miles Mank. I live in a hive on Sepulveda. But I got stuff in AR. I got a good place for myself, I'm in the game with the name and the fame. I even got myself a few passwords. I put in plenty of time to get all that. I don't want it just slipped out from under me when I'm not there to defend it." The funny little face started to pucker unhappily. "You got stuff out here, you don't need to go poachin' my stuff in there. If you see what I mean."

Konstantin saw; it sent a wave of melancholy through her. "All I want to do is contact Body Sativa if I can. I don't want to do anything else."

Pleshette held her gaze for a long moment and then shrugged her bony shoulders hugely. "Yeah. Well, you know, it's not like I can't tell the difference between in there and out here, it's not like I think I can put that stuff in a bank or anything. But I put a lot of time in; I spent some big sums doin' it. If I give it away, then I got *nothing*. You see that?"

Konstantin saw. She couldn't decide, however, if it was the sort of thing a person might kill for.

Guilfoyle Pleshette found a clean hotsuit in Konstantin's size and helped her put it on, giving her a flurry of instructions in her little cartoony voice. Konstantin felt silly, even though she knew this was really just like any other information gathering operation, except it was more like using the telephone. Unless what happened to the kid happened to her, she thought unhappily.

Tim Mezzer made good on his promise to supply icons and loaded the file into the headmount for her. "All you have to do is ask for your icon cat," he said, sounding less bored. "And if you're not sure which icon to try, ask for advice."

"Ask who?"

"The icons," he said, looking at her as if she should have known this. "They all have their own help files attached. But I gotta tell you, they're all pretty idiosyncratic, too. You know how it is, what *some* people call help."

Konstantin was mildly alarmed to find that she actually understood what he was telling her. After loading her own information into the headmount, Pleshette took her to one of the deluxe cubicles—deluxe meaning it was half again as large and included an extra chair. She helped Konstantin get comfortable in it, fastened the straps just tightly enough to keep her from falling if she got overly energetic, and fitted her headmount for her. Konstantin tried to thank her, but the headmount muffled her too well. She felt more than heard the woman leave the room. Fear rippled through her, briefly but intensely, making her dizzy.

Then the screen lit up with a control panel graphic and she immediately regained her balance. She turned on the log. The log was an independent, outside operation with only an on-off access, so she'd have her own record that she could prove hadn't been tampered with later, if necessary. Funny how the first thing anyone had to do with taped evidence was prove that it hadn't been toasted, she thought.

The control panel graphic disappeared and the screen showed her the configuration menu. She made her choices—sighting graphic and help line on request—while the 'suit warmed up. This was a full-coverage 'suit, she realized, uncomfortable. Somehow, she hadn't given it any thought when she was putting it on and it was too late to do anything about it now. Besides, they were probably all full-coverage 'suits; full-coverage would be the big attraction in a place like this. As if to confirm her thoughts, a hotsuit ad replaced the configuration menu.

Because if you're not going to feel it all over, murmured a congenial female voice while a hotsuit, transparent to show all the sensors, revolved on the screen, *why bother?* Which, when you thought about it, wasn't such an unreasonable question.

The headmounted monitor adjusted the fine-tuning for her focal length by showing her the standard introduction in block letters on a background of shifting colors. Konstantin sighed impatiently. So much introductory material with the meter running—she could see the clock icon tagging along at the upper edge of her peripheral vision on the right side. You probably couldn't go broke operating a video parlor, she thought, unless you tried real, real hard.

The sign came up so suddenly that it took at least three seconds to register on her, and even then she wasn't sure right away whether she was really seeing it, or imagining it. Seeing in AR felt strangely too close to thinking.

WELCOME TO THE LAND OF ANYTHING GOES
HERE THERE ARE NO RULES
EVERYTHING IS PERMITTED

Ha, thought Konstantin.

You can choose to be totally anonymous.
You can tell the whole truth about yourself.
You can tell only lies.

The word *lies* flashed on and off in different colors before it evaporated.

No real crime is possible here. If you do something Out There as a result of events In Here, you are on your own. In the event of your persona's virtual death, you can request to be directed to central stores, where you can choose another. The time used in choosing a new persona or performing any reference

*or maintenance task is not free, though a reduced rate may be available
through your parlor operator. Consult the rate file in your personal area for
more information.*

Konstantin looked around for a speed-scroll option.

*There is no speed-scroll option for this portion of your session. State and
federal law specifically declare that all users must be advised of conditions
in the gaming area. By reading this, you agree that you understand the
structure and accept any charges, standard and/or extra, that you will incur
at your point of origin. Closing your eyes will only result in a full rescroll
of the introductory material, at your own expense.*

Blink-rate and eye-movements could reveal a great deal about a person's
thoughts, especially when used in conjunction with vital signs, Konstantin
remembered, feeling even more uneasy.

*This concludes the introductory material. The next screen will be your
destination menu. Bon voyage, and good luck.*

The screen that came up showed her four doors labeled *Post-Apocalyptic
Noo Yawk Sitty, Post-Apocalyptic Ellay, Post-Apocalyptic Hong Kong,* and
Others.

A small bright icon appeared at the bottom right corner of her visual field,
a graphic of a hand twisting a doorknob. Just below it, on the status line,
was the word *Cue!* Feeling awkward, she reached for the Noo Yawk Sitty
door and saw a generic whitegloved hand moving toward the knob. As the
hand touched the knob, she felt it in her own hand, the sensors delivering a
sensation to the palm side of her fingers that surprised her with its intense
authenticity—it was more like touching a doorknob than actually touching a
doorknob.

The next moment was a flash of chaos, a maelstrom of noise and light,
countless touches and textures everywhere at once, over before she could
react to any of it. Under her feet, she could hear the scrape of the gritty glitz,
the glitzy grit of post-Apocalyptic Noo Yawk Sitty; she could see the sparkle
and glitter of it spread out before her—not Eliot's etherized patient awaiting
dissection but a refulgent feast for her reeling senses.

*HINT: In case of disorientation, amp your 'suit down and wait at least
thirty seconds before attempting movement. Closing your eyes could result
in vertigo. This message will be repeated.*

She thought she heard herself make some kind of relieved noise as she
stared at the setting marked *decrease*. In a few moments, all the settings on
the suit had been re-adjusted to a more bearable level. Whoever had had this
'suit on last, she thought, had either been extremely jaded or suffering from
some kind of overall senses-impairment disorder. Or—not so amazing in the
era of the more-real-than-real experience—both.

Now that she could perceive her surroundings without being assaulted by them, Konstantin was dismayed to find that she didn't seem to be anywhere near where Shantih Love had died. Instead, she was standing at the edge of an open area in the midst of a crowd of tall buildings festooned with enormous neon signs of a sort that had been popular seventy or eighty years before. Except for herself, there were no people, or at least none that she could see, and no sound except for a faint hum that might have come from the signs, or from some distant machine. Or possibly even from some loose connection in the headmount, she thought sourly. It would be just her luck.

The buildings were dark, showing the scars of fires, bullets, and bomb blasts, broken-out windows gaping like empty eye sockets, but the signs were brilliant, impossibly vivid with shifting colors that melted and morphed like living ropes of molten light. She had to look away or be hypnotized.

Her gaze locked onto a silvery figure standing in an open doorway. At first, she thought it was someone wearing a skintight bio-suit but then the figure moved forward and she saw that its skin was the same color as the clothes it wore. The figure moved closer and she amended her perception: it was the same material as the clothes it wore.

"New in town?" it sang, approaching carefully.

"Maybe," she said, taking a step back.

"Oh, you're new." The figure, which began to look more like it was made of mercury or chrome, gestured at something behind her. Konstantin turned to look.

The sight of the completely hairless and sexless creature in the dark glass made her jump; then embarrassment made her cringe. She had completely forgotten to choose a persona and the hotsuit, rather than choosing one for her, had let her enter AR wearing a placeholder. Her gaze darted around as she searched for the exit icon.

"It's not necessary to leave," the silvery figure said in its musical voice. Now that it was right next to her, Konstantin could see it was a sort of animated metal sculpture of a tall young girl, though she couldn't quite identify the metal. Chrome, mercury, or possibly platinum? "Pull down Central Stores and choose Wardrobe. Then just follow the directions."

"Oh. Thank you so much." Feeling awkward, Konstantin stuck out her hand. "I'm, uh, Dore. And you're right, I'm new here."

The silver girl seemed unaware of her extended hand. "I am a pop-up help-and-guide subroutine keyed to respond to situations and types of situations most often identified with new users of AR and/or post-Apocalyptic Noo Yawk Sitty. I am also available on request. Pull down Help and ask for Sylvia."

Konstantin started to thank her again but the girl made a fast gesture at eye-level and she found herself standing at a shiny white counter. The words *TOUCH HERE FOR ASSISTANCE* faded in on its surface, going from pale pink to blood red and back to pale pink before disappearing. Konstantin gingerly put a fingertip on the spot where she estimated the middle of the O in FOR had been.

"Help you," said a hard-edged male voice; the short, plump man who appeared on the other side of the counter looked as if he were answering a casting call for a play about bank tellers in 1900. The green visor on his forehead cast a shadow that made it hard to see anything of his eyes but reflected pinpoints of light.

"Where's the rest of your hat?" Konstantin asked impulsively.

"This is an eyeshade, not a hat," he replied in that same sharp, almost harsh tone. "Its presence connotes items and equipment available to you in AR, some at a surcharge. Do you want to see a list of items and equipment with their corresponding surcharges? These can also be itemized on the hard-copy printout of your receipt."

"I don't know. Is a persona classified as an item or as equipment?"

"Neither. A persona is a persona. Did you have someone in particular in mind or were you planning construction here? Morphing services within AR are available for a surcharge; however, there is no extra charge if you have brought your own morphing utility with you. Except, of course, for any extra time that might be consumed by the morphing process."

Konstantin suddenly found herself yawning; so far, her big AR adventure was turning out to be even more tiresome than the reality she was used to. "Does anybody really do anything in here besides listen to how much everything is costing them?"

"First-time users are advised to take the orientation sequence, and usually in some easier location." He sounded as bored as she felt.

"I want out of here," she said. "Out of the whole thing, I mean. Exit. End it. Good-bye. Stop. Logging off. Out, out, *out*."

Abruptly, she was staring at a blank screen; her 'suit was in *Suspend*, she saw, but still turned on. Words began to crawl up the screen in a steady scroll.

Your time in your chosen AR location has been halted. Readings indicate a high level of tension and stress in a low level of situation. Generally this occurs when the user is confused or has not taken proper instruction in the use of AR. Do you wish to continue in AR, or do you wish to terminate the program and exit? Please choose one option and one option only.

She was about to tell it to terminate when she heard what sounded like a telephone ringing.

The words on the screen vanished and a new message appeared quickly, word by word. *Realtime communication with you is being requested. Do you want to talk to the caller? Please answer yes or no.*

"Who is it?" she asked and then added quickly, "Oh, never mind. Put them on."

There was a click and she heard the familiar cartoony tones of Guilfoyle Pleshette. "What are you doing?"

"I don't know," she said.

"Yeah, what I thought. Icons and passwords don't do you a bit of good if you don't know what you're doing. That's an advanced 'suit I put you in. It doesn't carry a pre-fab for you, you got to bring your own."

"My own what?" asked Konstantin worriedly.

"Your own *persona*. I thought you had one you wanted."

"I do."

"Well, who is it?"

Konstantin took a breath. "Shantih Love."

Pleshette didn't even hesitate. "You want it with or without the cut throat?"

"With," Konstantin said. "Definitely with. And I want a copy of the surveillance footage loaded into a subroutine, too."

"You gonna run a sequence within a sequence?"

"I might. If it looks like it might get me some answers. Why?"

"Because that's a pretty expensive thing to do." Pleshette sounded both annoyed and worried. "Who's gonna pay for all of this online time and fun and games?"

"You are," Konstantin said.

"*What?*"

"I said, the taxpayers are. Your tax dollars at work."

Pleshette's laugh was low but surprisingly harsh. "Not my tax dollars. I don't pay taxes, not on my salary. You want to impress some taxpayers, catch some criminals in there and drag them out with you when you sign off."

Twenty (billable) minutes later, Konstantin stepped through a doorway onto the street where she had first seen Shantih Love. The feel of the Love persona in her 'suit was pleasurable in a way that kept her on edge. Being Shantih Love was close to seductive, even with the sliced throat, something she had not taken into consideration.

Real easy to go native in a Gang Wars module. Guilfoyle Pleshette's words came to mind unbidden. Not to mention unhelpfully, she thought; this wasn't a Gang Wars module. That she knew of, anyway.

She was wondering now if she really knew anything at all. The piles of wreckage in the street were all aflame, burning in jeweltones, now and then sending sparks skyward, where they seemed to mingle with the stars. The glitter she had seen on the monitor looked somehow less gritty from the inside and more like delicate sprays of tiny lights, too exquisitely fragile not to shatter in a light puff of a breeze, yet remaining, twinkling and shimmering against the black street, the pitted brick and the web-cracked glass of the buildings facing the burning wrecks, the coldstone texture of the barrier between the street and the alien shore of the Hudson River.

Konstantin went to the barrier and strolled along it in the direction Shantih Love had taken, looking around for anything like the figure of a shaggy beast that might take an interest in her.

Rather than anything approaching, however, Konstantin had a sense of things drawing away from her, many watching with the knowledge that she was an impostor. And then again, she thought suddenly, how would anyone know, if the Shantih Love persona had gone on for another four hours after Iguchi's death? Maybe the only one who knew was the creature who had attacked and hijacked Shantih Love here in the first place.

She paused, leaning on the barrier and looking toward where she estimated the party had been. It was long over now, or perhaps this was no longer a hot place to be in the Sitty. Her purpose here was not to find a party, nor to act as a decoy to attract a creature that wasn't even real. Funny how easy it was to forget things or to keep focused here. If she waited much longer, she might even feel her concentration dissolve, break apart into tiny fragments and float away up to the stars with the sparks from the burning wreckage.

"Icon cat?" she asked.

It was there before her on the barrier, a big book full of symbols and their explanations. The page it was open to showed a flame within a halo; as she looked at it, it went from a line drawing to a vivid holo. The word *Enlightenment* came out of the flame and rippled for a moment. More words appeared on the facing page: *You have only to ask.*

Konstantin made a face, or thought she did; there was no real feeling above her neck. "Is this a help file?" she said aloud.

Now there was a new message on the page opposite the flame: *Help with?—Travel—Location—Contacts—Other*

After a moment's thought, she touched—*Contacts.*

Contact—Who—What? the page wanted to know.

She pressed for—*Who.* The question mark moved to the end of the word. "Body Sativa," she said aloud.

A golden arrow pointing to her right materialized on the page. She turned it and found a map of the area with her own position highlighted. A dotted green line appeared, winding its way along the grid of streets to a location six blocks away; a green star flashed on and off.

"That was easy," she said, noting the address and the directions. It just figured. *You have only to ask.* So simple that it was too simple to think of.

The book disappeared into the back of the map. She picked it up and moved up the street toward the next three-way intersection. Three fiery humanish shapes detached themselves from the burning ruins of a classic Rolls sandwiched between two antique sports cars and stood watching her. Konstantin had a sudden urge to whirl on them and claim she was selling encyclopedias or household cleansers. The idea was a tickle playing over her back, where she imagined she could feel their literally burning stares.

No, too simple; they might expect her to produce chips full of natural history quick-times or a bottle of something that looked like urine and smelled like ammonia. Not that she had smelled anything in here since she had arrived, not even anything burning.

She couldn't account for how she had come up with the idea of playing such a prank; she'd never had much of a sense of humor, or so her ex had always said.

Anything goes. You can even pretend you have a sense of humor, or that your ex isn't actually ex, and all while you look for someone with the improbable name of Body Sativa, or Love, or whatever.

She passed several brawls, a side street where a few hundred people seemed to be trying to stay as close together as possible and still dance—it looked as if they had decided nudity would do it—and a billboard-sized screen where half a dozen people were either collaborating on a quick-time or competing to see whose images could dominate. Someone among them was obsessed with mutant reptiles. Or were certain kinds of images contagious?

Or maybe, she thought as she passed someone that might have been the offspring of a human and a cobra, it was the mutants themselves that were contagious. She paused at a corner in front of a park surrounded by a black metal spiked fence and consulted the map.

"Ssssssssssssshhhhhhhhhhhhhhh . . ."

The noise was so soft, she wasn't sure that she had actually heard it. But then it came again, from somewhere in the dark contained in the spiked metal fence, and she found that the sensation of the small hairs standing up on the back of her neck was not necessarily something that the hotsuit had to produce for her.

"Sssssssssssshhhhhhhhhhhhhhaaaaaaaannnnnnntiiiiiiih . . ."

She was clenching her hands so tightly that if she had really been holding a map, it would have crumpled and torn in a dozen places. *Come on*, she told herself. *This is nothing more than a scary story. You just happen to be in it.*

"Ssssssssshhhhhhhhhhaaaaaaaaaaannnnnnntiiiiiiiiih . . ."

Apparently it didn't matter what she told herself; the hairs on the back of her neck were going to stand up and jitterbug regardless. The chills seemed to be creeping down her backbone now. Konstantin tried to steel herself and shivered instead.

"Sssssshhhhhhhaaaaaaaaannnnnnnntiiiiiih. Welcome back from the land of the dead. We've been waiting for you, darling."

Konstantin forced herself to turn around. The faces grinning out of the darkness glowed moon-pale, with thick black circles around the eyes, which were also luminous. Or just the whites, anyway, Konstantin noticed, trying to see more detail in spite of the cold still flicking at the back of her neck and up onto her scalp.

As her eyes adjusted, she could see that there were half a dozen of them, in a roughly symmetrical formation around a picnic table with the one who had spoken in the center. They were all wearing black skintights over their idealized hardbodies, some of them indisputably female, others emphatically male. *When Broadway choreographers go bad*, said a tiny, mocking voice in her mind. More chills played over the back of her neck. Shuddering, she rubbed her neck with her free hand and felt the cut area in front separate a bit.

She covered her wounded throat with the map and moved closer to the metal fence. "Do I know you?" she asked, trying to sound calm.

"Shantih," said the one who had been doing all the talking in a sulky tone. Emphatically male, she saw. "After all we've meant to each other. I'm wounded. Mortally. We *all* are."

"And I'm dead," Konstantin answered. "You have any idea who did it?"

The glowing moon-colored face suddenly took on an uncertain expression. "Honey, you were *there*. Look at your footage. Relive every glorious moment."

"I have. I'd invite you to watch it again with me, but I'm on my way to meet someone. Maybe we can connect later."

One of the women on the speaker's right straightened up from her catlike stalking pose and pushed both hands into the small of her back. "Oh, for crying out *loud*, Shantih. My back's *killing* me tonight. If you're not playing, just say so so we can go find somebody else."

"I'm not playing," Konstantin said, starting to turn away.

"Because you're not Shantih," said the speaker, hopping down from the table and going to the fence. "Are you." It wasn't really a question.

Konstantin shook her head. "You knew Shantih Love pretty well?"

The man adjusted something on himself at waist-level and Konstantin felt the chills that had been tormenting her suddenly vanish. " 'Knew'? Does that mean our usual Shantih gave up the character?"

"Gave up the ghost," Konstantin said. "The person you knew as Shantih Love in here has been murdered. For real. I—"

He turned away from her and swung his arm. The group surrounding the picnic table vanished, including the woman who had complained. Then he turned back to her. "What kinda virgin are you, hon?" he asked, annoyance large on his white painted face.

"What kind?" Konstantin echoed, mystified.

"Yeah, *what kind*. Are you some senator's baby out for a good time, or are you some rich kid who bought out a regular? Thought you could get the game and the fame along with the name?"

Konstantin started to answer but he did something at waist-level again and a fresh wave of chills danced up her neck into her hair. Crying out, she stepped back, batting the air with her map as if ultrasonics were insects she could just swat away from herself.

"You stay away from me, you pseudo-rudo," he yelled at her.

"What?" she demanded. "I didn't do anything—"

"I *hate* you virgins, you all think you're the *first* who ever thought of saying the one you bought out got killed for real. You think we're all just gonna lead you to their stash, tell you, 'Oh, help yourself, take all the *stuff*, and if you don't know how to use it, just ask'?" He did something at his waist again and Konstantin retreated several more steps. At the same time, she understood that this should not have made a difference. Unless her 'suit was cooperating in the scenario and producing the ultrasonics—

She shifted her gaze to the control for her 'suit and saw that it *was* giving her the chills. She readjusted the setting and the chills cut off immediately.

The man made a disgusted noise. "For god's sake, baby, if you can't take the sensation, why did you bother coming in?" He flickered out and she was alone. Moving on, Konstantin couldn't decide whether to feel relieved or chastized.

The place marked on the map turned out to be a subway station, or maybe just the post-Apocalyptic ruin of a subway station. From where she stood on the sidewalk looking down the stone stairs, Konstantin could hear the distant sound of people's voices and, even more distantly, music, but no trains. Maybe you could hike around post-Apocalyptic Noo Yawk Sitty in the tunnels, and bring your own music with you.

She crouched at the top of the stairs with her map, absently pressing the flesh of her throat together. The cut edges felt a bit like putty or clay, but they wouldn't stay closed for very long. She wondered idly if she should try to find a place to have herself sewn up, or whether she might even try it herself. If it was the sort of thing that Shantih Love would do—

There was a strange pressure all along her back, from her neck down to her feet. She stood up and turned around to see if some new weird experience had crept up behind her, but there was no one and nothing there. She was alone; the pressure was all in the suit, as if it were trying to push her down the steps into the subway.

"Help?" she asked, turning the map over. It became a book again in her hands. She found the section on the hotsuit almost immediately but she had to read it over three times to be sure she understood that the 'suit itself, being loaded with Shantih Love characteristics, was trying to give her a hint as to what to do next. At this point, apparently, Shantih Love would have descended into the subway.

Konstantin concentrated, placing her fingers on the sliced flesh of her throat and closing her eyes. There; now she could feel it. Now she could feel how the sensation of touching skin, touching flesh was all in the fingertips of the hotsuit. She wasn't really touching anything, or if she was, the AR sensation over-rode it sheerly by intensity, vividness, and the power of suggestion.

She opened her eyes and found herself looking down at a young Japanese man dressed in the plain garb of a laborer from about a hundred or so years before, but armed with what looked to her like a Samurai sword.

Konstantin pressed the book to her chest protectively; it became a map again. The man seemed not to notice. He gazed at her steadily, his expression mild, almost blank. He came up another step. She meant to retreat but something in his expression changed so that his face became slightly more severe, more wary, and she stayed where she was.

"Does this mean you've given up, Mr. *Iguchi*?" he asked in a soft, sarcastic voice. "Or have you just changed your strategy?"

"How do you know my name?" Konstantin asked him, wincing inwardly when she heard the tremor in her voice. It wasn't fear but cold—her 'suit seemed to have turned to ice.

The man came up another step. "Games again, Tom? It's always games with you."

"More like a malfunction, actually," she muttered, rubbing one arm. The temperature inside the suit was still dropping, as though it was trying to keep her cool inside a furnace.

"It's not cold tonight, Tom," the man said. "Are you sure it's not fear that's making you tremble?"

"Have it your way," Konstantin said desperately, hoping that might have some effect on the 'suit's wayward thermostat.

"Surely you're not afraid of *me*—or is it what I represent?"

Konstantin's teeth chattered "W-w-what would that be?"

"An old world that has nothing to do with what this world has become—this world, or the one it's contained in, or the one that *that* one is contained in, boxes within boxes within boxes, all the way to infinity." The man suddenly produced a strange coin between thumb and forefinger. It flashed silver for a moment; then Konstantin could see the symbol on it, like a figure 8 lying on its side. The man flipped it over and showed her the other side, a snake with its tail in its mouth.

"Though these are not Japanese symbols, there is still something very Japanese about what they represent. Old Japan, I'm talking about, not the hot icy flash of the nth generation of speed tribes, or the debauchery of the newest salarymen in the neon jungle that covered over the old signs and symbols."

He held it out to her, as if inviting her to take it, but when she reached for it, hc flipped it again and snatched it out of the air. Konstantin pulled her hand back, embarrassed and irritated. The man put both hands behind himself for a moment and then held them up. "Which hand, Tom? You choose."

Konstantin tucked the map under her arm, trying to ignore the fact that she felt as if she were turning into an ice cube from the skin inward. "Let's see," she said, lifting her chin with bravado. "I used to be pretty good at this. Finding the tell, I mean. Everybody's got a tell. Even old Japan."

The man's eyes narrowed and he took a closer look at her. "You never used to be so smart, Tom. What happened since I saw you last—you take some genius pill somewhere? Something that's burning your brain cells out as you use them, maybe?"

Konstantin didn't answer; she scrutinized his right fist for a long time, and then his left. "Sometimes, it's a twitch, a tightening of the muscles. Sometimes, it's just that the person simply *looks* at the correct hand, whichever one it is. Doesn't matter, you just have to know what to look for, what *kind* of tell it is. Most of the time, you know, the person doing it doesn't even realize it. But it's there. There's always a tell, and it *tells* you what the answer is." Konstantin hesitated and then tapped the man's right fist. "I say there."

"You're not Iguchi," he said, not moving.

"Let's see it," said Kostantin. "I know I must be right. Otherwise, you wouldn't be delaying."

"You're *not* Iguchi. I should have seen it immediately. That's too smart for Iguchi. Where is old Tom tonight? Did he hire you, or did you buy him out? If you bought him out, I got to tell you, he stuck you with damaged goods there." He indicated her cut throat with a jab of his chin.

Konstantin felt more confident now. She stepped forward and tapped the knuckles of his right hand. "Come on, let me see it. I know it's there. Give me the coin and you can call it a night."

"Call it a night?" The man smiled, raised his right hand, and opened it. It was empty. "Or call it in the air?" He looked at his left hand as it unfolded in the same position to reveal that it, too, was empty. He stayed that way, with both hands raised, as if he were at gunpoint, or perhaps surrendering. Annoyed, Konstantin stepped back and folded her arms.

"Fine," she said. "But *I* know, and *you* know, that until you cheated, that coin was in your right hand. You can go ahead and take it away with you, but we both know you cheated, and we'll always know it. We'll never forget, will we?'' She went to take the map from under her arm and felt something funny in her palm. She looked down and opened her hand. The coin was there. She picked it up and looked at both sides.

"I told you to call it in the air,'' the man admonished her. "But the problem is, when you have a coin with infinity on one side, and Ouroboros on the other, how can you ever really know which side is heads, and which is tails?''

Konstantin said nothing. He burst out laughing, bowed to her, and walked away into the darkness. She could hear the echo of his laughter long after the shadows had swallowed him up.

She examined the coin again. Whatever else he might have said or done, he had given her the coin; she had just received some AR *stuff*. She wondered if this was the type of stuff Guilfoyle Pleshette was so enamored of, and if it were the sort of thing that someone might kill for.

She descended the stairs, feeling every bump and irregularity in the bannister with her free hand as the sounds of voices and music bounced off the grimy tiles. Sometimes the sensory input was too authentic to be authentic, Konstantin noted, almost amused. Until she got to the bottom of the stairs and saw the empty platform beyond the broken turnstiles and the long unused token-seller's cage. There were no people anywhere to be seen in the unnatural light of the fluorescent tubes, no movement anywhere at all. Dust and dirt lay thickly on everything, suggesting that no one had come here for a long, long time—which had to be wrong, since her Japanese friend had just come up out of here.

Or had he only been waiting for her at the bottom of the stairs? Her or someone like her—no, he had definitely been expecting Shantih Love, for *some* reason.

She looked at the lights overhead. They didn't hum or buzz; they didn't even flicker. Strange, for a place so disused and abandoned.

The coin grew slightly warmer in her fist. No, too high a price, she thought, amused. "Icon cat?'' she asked, and it was there under her arm. She took hold of it with her free hand and maneuvered it open. "Subway?''

The pages flipped and came to rest on a picture of a wooden nickel. She could tell it was made of wood by the lustrous grain. Konstantin considered it and then shook her head. The pages flipped again and kept flipping, like a rotary card file in a high wind. Because there was a wind, she realized, coming from somewhere down in the old train tunnel. She could feel it and she could hear music again as well, except it was much thinner-sounding, just one instrument, either a guitar or a very good synthesizer.

"Pause,'' she told the book; it closed quietly for her. She climbed over one of the turnstiles and walked out onto the platform, looking around.

The man with the guitar was to her left, sitting cross-legged at the place where the platform ended and the tunnel began. His head was tilted back against the wall and his eyes were closed, so that he seemed to be in a state of deep concentration as he played. Konstantin wondered if he were going to sing, and then wondered exactly what kind of strange kick a person could get from spending billable time in AR alone in a vacant subway station, playing a musical instrument for nobody.

None, she decided. "Resume," she said, staring at the guitar player. "*Empty* subway, *downtown*."

The pages flipped again and stopped to show her a bottlecap. *CREAM SODA*. It fell out of the book onto the tile floor at her feet. Down by the tunnel, the guitar-player paused and turned to smile at her. The lights changed, becoming just a bit warmer in color as the legend NOW ENTERING NEXT HIGHER LEVEL ran along the bottom of her vision like a late-breaking item on *Police Blotter*.

People were all over the platform, standing in groups, sitting on the turnstiles, grouping together down on the tracks, picking their way over the rails and ties to the opposite platform, where there were even more people. At first, she saw only the same types she had seen on the shore in Shantih Love's AR log, but after awhile, she discovered that if she didn't look directly at people too quickly, a good many of them had somehow metamorphosed into characters far more original and indecipherable.

If there even *were* that many people, she thought, remembering the strange guy in white face and the gang that hadn't really existed. Maybe some of these people were carrying phantoms with them for company. If you could be your own gang in AR, was that another example of AR *stuff*?

A seven-foot-tall woman whose long, thick, auburn hair seemed to have a life of its own looked down at her through opera glasses. "What sort of a creature are you?" she asked in a booming contralto.

"I think I've forgotten," Konstantin said and then winced, squirming. The 'suit was reminding her *now* that it was full-coverage and that Shantih Love would have responded to this woman. It was like a nightmare. Her ex might have laughed at her and told her that was no less than what she deserved for stealing someone else's life.

I didn't steal it. He lost it and I found it.

Yeah. Finders, weepers.

Konstantin wasn't sure if it were worse to have an imaginary argument with an ex after a break-up than it was to have the break-up argument, but she was fairly sure it was completely counter-productive to have it both on billable AR time and during a murder investigation. If that was what this really was, and not just a massive waste of time all around.

"Do you know Body Sativa?" she asked the tall woman.

"Yes." The woman gazed at her a moment longer and walked away.

The people down on the tracks were dancing now to something that sounded like the rhythmic smashing of glass on metal. Konstantin hopped down off the platform onto the tracks and walked among them, keeping her gaze downward so that she could see them change in her peripheral vision. Most of the people down here seemed to be affecting what her ex had called rough and shoddy sugar-plum. Konstantin had to admit to herself she found the look appealing, in a rough and shoddy way.

She looked down at the ankle-length gown Shantih Love had preferred. In this light, it seemed to have more of a red tone, much more than she had thought. Even stranger was the texture—it looked like velvet but it felt like sandpaper, at least on the outside. Inside, the feeling was all but non-existent; the hotsuit was full-coverage but not so complete in the detailing that she felt the gown swinging and brushing against her ankles. For that, she supposed, you had to have some kind of custom job.

But at least she never tripped on the hem, Konstantin thought as she moved among the dancers, still holding the map. The display had not changed, even after she had gained access to this level, where all the people were, so either Body Sativa was here, or there was something wrong with the map.

Getting someone's attention to find out, however, seemed to be another one of those tricks she hadn't learned yet. Down on the tracks, anyway. The people dancing there weren't just ignoring her, they seemed honestly unaware of her, as if she were invisible. Which would seem to indicate she had found another level within a level. Levels within levels and boxes within boxes. Was there any purpose to it, she wondered—any *real* purpose other than to intrigue people into spending more billable hours solving the puzzle.

The guitar player, she saw, was still sitting in the same place, and it looked as if he were still playing as well, though it was impossible to hear anything except the smash-clang everyone around her was dancing to. She made her way through the group over to where the guitar-player was. The platform was about as high as her nose. She tried boosting herself up but couldn't get enough leverage.

"Stay," said the guitar-player, eyes closed. "I can see and hear you fine where you are."

"Good," said Konstantin. "Tell me, if I look past you, will you change into someone else, too?"

"It's all in what you can perceive," he said, smiling. Then, while she was looking directly at him, he morphed from a plump, balding young guy to an angular middle-aged man with very long, straight steel-grey hair. He still didn't open his eyes. "You'd be surprised how few turns of the morphing dial that took."

"Maybe not," she said. "Do you know Body Sativa?"

"Know her, or know of her?"

"Know her. Personally, or casually." She paused. "And have you seen her in here recently?"

He tilted his head, his closed eyes moving back and forth beneath his eyelids, as if he were dreaming, while his fingers played over guitar strings that appeared no thicker than spidersilk. Konstantin realized she couldn't hear the music coming from the guitar, but she could feel it surround her, not unpleasantly, and then disintegrate. "I was a dolphin in a previous incarnation," he said after a bit.

"Why did you change?"

"We all have to, sooner or later. I would have thought you'd know that as well as anyone. What were you before you passed on to your present manifestation?"

Konstantin barely hesitated. "A homicide detective."

"Ah. That accounts for the interrogation." He chuckled. "You know, the idea is to go on to something different, not just do the same thing behind a new mask."

Words to live by, Konstantin thought. Perhaps she could print them on a card and send it to her ex. She smiled. "That's pretty good for a guitar-playing land dolphin."

He stopped playing and pulled something out of the hole in the center of the instrument. "Here," he said, leaning forward and holding it out to her; it looked like a playing card. "You're not necessarily smarter than the last one who had your face, but the quality of your ignorance is an improvement."

"It is? How?" Konstantin asked, taking the card from him.

"*You* might actually learn something."

She studied the card, trying to see it clearly, except the image on it kept shifting, melting, changing. It looked like it might be some kind of Oriental ideogram. "What is this?" she asked.

"Cab fare," he said.

"Cab fare? In a subway station?"

"Trains aren't running tonight. Or didn't you notice?" He laughed.

She looked down at her map again. The display still hadn't changed. "I was supposed to find somebody I needed here. My map says she's still here."

The guitar player shook his head. "Sorry, you misunderstood. There's a locator utility here, for help in finding someone in the Sitty. That's what your map says is here." He shrugged. "There are locator utilities in all the subway stations."

Konstantin managed not to groan. "Where?"

"Somewhere. It's all in what you perceive."

"You're a big help."

"I am. If you get it figured, you have cabfare to get to wherever it is you need to go."

Cabfare, Konstantin thought. Cabfare. Did it include tip, she wondered, or was that what the coin was for? She looked down at it in her other hand.

The man stopped playing. "When did you get that?"

"Just now. Upstairs. Outside." Konstantin closed her fist around it again. "Why?"

"Because even in here, certain things are perishable. Like milk, or cut flowers."

"Or people with cut throats?" Konstantin added.

He smiled. "No, you may have noticed that death doesn't have to put a crimp in your party plans. On the other hand, it's not generally an accepted practice to start out dead. If you want to be dead, custom dictates that you die here."

"Here in the subway, or here in AR?"

"It's all in what you perceive."

He was going to say that once too often, Konstantin thought unhappily. "What about this coin?" she asked him. "Were you telling me just now that it's going to expire?"

"Conditions," he said after a moment. "It's the conditions under which it would be . . . *effective*. Conditions won't last."

"More words to live by," Konstantin muttered to herself. "I want to find the locator utility. How do I do that?"

"You have only to ask."

Konstantin frowned. "Who should I ask?"

"Me."

She hesitated. "All right. How do I find the locator utility."

"You have only to ask," he said again serenely, fingers picking at the strings of the guitar again.

"I just did," Konstantin said impatiently. "How—" She cut off. "No. *Where* is Body Sativa?"

The guitar player jerked his chin at her, still with his eyes closed. "Hail a cab, and when you're asked where you want to go, give the driver that."

Konstantin looked at the card again. The ideogram was still shifting. Suddenly she felt very tired and bored. "Are you sure this'll do it?"

"Oh, yeah. That'll take you right to her."

"It's that simple."

The guitar-player nodded. "It's that simple."

"Strange, nothing else in here seems to be."

"What you want is simple. All you had to do was state it in the proper place at the proper moment. In the proper form, of course. That's just elementary programming."

"Programming," Konstantin said, giving a short, not terribly merry laugh.

"I should have known. You're the locator utility and the help utility, aren't you?"

"That's about what it comes down to," he said agreeably.

"And I had only to ask."

"Because it's what you want that's simple. You just want to meet up with another player so I gave you a tracer. Obviously you're not the usual Shantih Love, or even the usual player. The usual players don't want anything so simple. The usual players come down here looking for the secret subroutine to the Next Big Scene, or even the mythical out door. Then my job becomes something different. Then my job is to give them something that will stimulate a little thrill here and there, play to their curiosities and their fondest wishes and desires."

"And make them spend more billable hours," Konstantin said.

"The more hours people spend in here doing complicated things, the more interesting the Sitty becomes."

"Why don't you just tell people that, instead of playing to their wish-fulfillment fantasies about finding the egress or the secret subroutine to post-Apocalyptic Peoria, or wherever?"

"First of all, it's not my job to volunteer information. It's my job to answer questions. And I can only answer with what I know. I don't know that there's an egress . . . but I don't know that there isn't. I can't prove there isn't, I'm a utility. I wasn't created to determine whether my universe is finite or not."

I'm talking philosophy with a utility, Konstantin thought. "But surely you know whether there are secret subroutines?"

"If they're secret, they certainly wouldn't tell me. I'd tell anyone who asked and then they wouldn't be secret any more."

"All right," Konstantin said slowly. "Have there ever been any secret subroutines in the Sitty that you've found out about?"

"Some players have claimed to have accessed them."

"Were they telling the truth?"

"I'm not a lie detector."

"Wouldn't matter if you were, would it. Because it's all lies in here. Or all truth."

He went on playing, still with his eyes closed. Konstantin supposed he was the AR equivalent of blind justice—blind information. Which was probably much more accurate, all told.

"Have you ever met Shantih Love before?" she asked and then added quickly, "I mean, have you ever met a player named Shantih Love before I came in here?"

"I don't really *meet* anyone. I have everyone's name."

Konstantin thought for a moment. "Has anyone ever asked you to locate Shantih Love?"

"I don't remember."

"Why not?"

"I don't have to. There's no reason to."

"But if you can put a tracer on someone's location for another player, isn't there some record of that? Some, uh, trace?"

"Only while the tracer's active. But that record would be kept elsewhere in the system. You know, if you're so interested, there are schools you can go to to learn all about how AR works."

"I thought you didn't volunteer information," Konstantin said suspiciously.

"You call *that* information?"

She laughed in spite of herself. "You're right. Thanks for the cabfare." She started to walk away and then paused. "Where's the best place to get a cab in post-Apocalyptic Noo Yawk Sitty?"

"I don't know."

"All right." She sighed resignedly. "Where's the nearest I can find a cab?"

"I don't know. Cabs aren't players."

Konstantin nodded. She should have known, she thought.

She came up out of the subway into the middle of a riot.

Where the streets had been deserted before they were now full of people running, screaming, chasing each other, hurling furniture and other heavy objects from sixth and seventh story windows, from rooftops, from mid-air for all she knew.

Level access, she realized. When she had accessed the new level in the subway station, she had stayed there. If she went back to Times Square now, it wouldn't be deserted this time. Anxiously, she looked around for some clear route of escape, and then wondered if there really was any—maybe the riot was Sittywide, what with everything being post-Apocalyptic.

She sighed. What she should really do, she thought, was exit. This wasn't her kind of interest, she couldn't get into the spirit of it even for the sake of information-gathering on behalf of some poor murdered kid. And walking around disguised as the victim—the more she thought about it, the more it seemed like an act of grave-robbing, desecration. Better just to leave word in a number of message centers and hope that Body Sativa, or someone who knew her, would get in touch, and if so, that there would be some useful information to be gained. From her experience here, though, she didn't think that there would be. This had nothing to do with anyone's life, not anyone's real life. So how could it have anything to do with a kid's death? Or with seven other deaths?

Coincidences by way of statistical incidence? Her ex had always said that statistics bred coincidences. Konstantin wondered if familiarity breeding contempt was a coincidence as well.

A Molotov cocktail sailed over her head and shattered on a nearby brick wall, making a perfect wave circle of flames. The effect of the heat was so realistic she could have sworn her face was flushed. She put an arm up defensively and turned away—

It took her all of a second to register the blow followed by the impact of her body on the street; the punch in her upper chest had been so abrupt and powerful that her legs had flown out from under her and she'd hit the ground on her back. It *hurt*, as badly as the real thing would have. She thought she had run into one of the rioters and the program had authenticated the logical result. But then a half-circle of grinning faces appeared above her as she tried to sit up and catch her breath, and she couldn't believe it. Of all the damned things that could go on in this ridiculous scenario and she *would* go and trigger one of the least imaginative.

Before she could ask for the icon cat, they hauled her to her feet and began shoving her around so that she rebounded from one into another like a pinball in a very small machine. Still breathless, she tried to get a good look at them but they were pushing her around too quickly. The Molotov cocktail had ignited something and she could see others, some people and some not quite, watching in the firelight as her attackers played with her.

There had to be something in the icon cat that would help, she thought, something for protection, self-defense, *something*. Too bad, she realized, that she hadn't thought of that sooner and used some precautions.

They were shoving her around harder now, their hands slapping, punching, pummeling and the pain was only too real. In a situation like this, it was hard to remember that the sensation was all artificial, delivered via select stimulation of certain nerves in a certain way, coupled with elements that contributed to the power of suggestion. This was too authentic; she wondered if Tomoyuki Iguchi had had some kind of masochistic streak that he had indulged as Shantih Love—

And suddenly, she wasn't sure that it *wasn't* happening for real. Maybe Shantih Love hadn't been able to tell the difference there on the shore of the Hudson River, not until it was too late and he couldn't feel how the real blood was flowing along with the virtual, even though he could see, perhaps until the moment of his death, the virtual attacker who had come to hijack his persona. But *why*.

A leg kicked out as she stumbled sideways and she went down again. One of her attackers started to pull her up; she twisted away and fumbled the icon cat out onto the ground where she could see it.

It fell open to a fierce image that looked somehow a bit cartoony at the same time. She had a vague idea that it was a talisman of protection and grabbed for it, just as her attackers bellowed in triumph and tore the icon cat away from her.

Too late, she understood that the catalog with its treasure trove of icons— its *stuff*—was probably what they'd been after all along. She scrambled up but a heavy boot caught her in the midsection and she sat down hard.

One of them crouched down and shoved a face that looked like the product of a mating between a troll and a gargoyle up close to hers. "Hey, you never heard that expression, *be seated*?"

She scooted backward, trying to get away. He advanced on her with the rest of them behind him, one holding up her icon cat so she could see that they had taken the whole thing from her.

All but one page that she was still clutching in one hand, so hard that her knuckles hurt, a pain that *was* real, produced not by the hotsuit but by the way she was clenching her hand in this unreal place, a pain that paled next to the jazzy high-res authenticity of the 'suit but went deeper, all the way to the bone, to spread up her arm to her shoulder and over her chest.

They are killing me. They are really killing me!

The thought was a scream in her head. What was going on, out there beyond the bounds of the headmount and the neo-exo-nervous system, what was happening *out there*, how many were *out there*, why hadn't she figured there could be more than one, hidden in the air-processing ducts perhaps, with the cooperation of some insider, maybe bored and bitter Miles Mank, or even Pleshette, not bitter, just very bored. Or the *two* of them, yes, that would be perfect, pretending to be enemies but killing together—one covering the AR while the other one handled things *out there*.

And if so, what did they have in store for her? Her attackers were grabbing at her, jabbing and poking, laughing at her frightened reactions, their broad, crude faces impossibly ugly, as if cruelty itself had been a model for their formation, a base to elaborate from, a setting from which the morphing dial could be turned. What kind of sad, sick specimen of humanity would pay to be something so horrible—

The employee discount here, she remembered suddenly, was pretty good. She had to admire the boldness, to kill someone again so soon after the last one, and the detective investigating the case, no less! Ideal, though—the partner was too claustrophobic to jump right on the crime scene and they knew it. So by the time someone else, Celestine and DiPietro perhaps, arrived, they'd have jiggered the evidence, massaged the data, and she'd be more grist for the AR urban legend mill. *Ya hear about the homicide detective who was killed in AR investigating a murder? Yeah, incredible galloping head-bugs. Yeah, I think it happened in D.C., you know how life is so cheap there—*

Now the chief troll-gargoyle was waving around something that looked like a jagged fragment of mirror, poking it at her face. Her rational mind kept telling her that he couldn't possibly cut her face but her rational mind had shrunk to the size of a quark. The rest of her was buying it, believing it, *really really* believing it to the point where she could feel the small cuts on her face, the bloody murderous troll had cut her face and in a moment he would cut her throat, by the power of suggestion she would believe her throat was cut and so much for *extremo ruptura*, that they were all so sure that no one had had since St. Whoever. There just hadn't been any AR up until now that could compete with the faith of a fanatic saint with stigmata, but now there was, *now* there was, and let the coroner come in here, let them all come in here and see if the power of their own belief, their galloping head-bugs, let them survive it—

The torn page in her hand suddenly transformed into a claw. She let go with a scream and the claw grabbed her arm, pulled her up off the street, and then pulled her into the air. She screamed again as she felt her feet leave the ground; her inner ear went into the same frenzy it had that one and only time her ex had talked her into riding a roller coaster.

Post-Apocalyptic Noo Yawk Sitty spread out below her, revealing itself. Exposing itself, she thought, looking at the fires and the bursts of light on the skinny roadways below, and had a short laughing jag. It cut off as she looked up thinking she might get a look at the moon and saw the bizarre pointed head and on either side, the wings that suggested nightmares about bats or things satanic.

She seemed to be dangling in its claws. The way they gripped her around her shoulders and arms should have hurt, but did not, as if there were padding. It flew on smoothly, quickly and no matter how she tried to concentrate on where the real sensation was, her imagination overrode her rational mind—grown to the size of a pea now, perhaps?—and she *did* feel the wind on her face.

"I was supposed to be a pterodactyl," said the creature conversationally, "but my designer got carried away."

"Oh. Really." Konstantin was amazed at how calm her own voice sounded. But then it wasn't her own voice, it was Shantih Love's; she was living a Shantih Love adventure and maybe Shantih Love traveled by mutant pterodactyl regularly. "Are you a device in the game or an employee of the company that licenses the Sitty out to parlors?"

"Now that would be telling," said the pterodactyl, sounding amused but at the same time a bit stiff, "and I thought you would know already, since you summoned me."

"You're an icon?" Konstantin asked.

"You got lucky. I'm a rescue. I make sure you don't get caught in dead end loops that eat up billable time and don't deliver much in return. If you *must* know. If you really need to spoil the effect.''

"Sometimes it's not such a tragedy to spoil the effect," Konstantin murmured. "Where are you taking me?''

"The destination is stipulated by your cabfare. And if you don't mind spoiling the effect that much, why didn't you just signal for the exit?''

"Well . . . I think I got sucked into the story and wanted to see how it would come out.''

"A common ailment," said the pterodactyl wisely. "Do you know about the joke that ends in the punchline, 'The food here is terrible, and in such small portions'?''

"What?'' Konstantin was bewildered.

"Never mind. You're here.'' The wings enfolded her so that she couldn't see anything at all. Then the darkness lifted and she saw that the creature had set her down right next to the barrier that separated the street from the shore of the Hudson River.

Just past the barrier was the party that had been invisible to her on the first time through. People spread inward from a very long pier to the barrier itself. If she listened carefully, Konstantin could almost make out bits of conversation that may have been fascinating, if only she could have heard enough.

She sat on the barrier, unsure of what to do next. Take a walk and see if someone came to hijack Shantih Love again? All up and down the street, wrecked vehicles were still burning, somehow never diminishing, the flames shifting but still never really changing. In a place where supposedly anything could happen, did anything happen?

Konstantin looked at the party again. "Redisplay," she said quietly. "Full mode.''

Guilfoyle Pleshette must have been screaming, she thought as the AR log of Shantih Love's murder rolled in and settled like fog. Redisplaying a log within a running AR scenario probably doubled the hourly rate and there was no charge account number designated to cover it. But if she were screaming, Konstantin couldn't hear it. Their respective realities were sound-proof.

But apparently not leak-proof, she thought, touching her sliced throat as the redisplayed Shantih Love appeared in front of her, close enough to touch, close enough for Konstantin to see the flawless texture of that burnished copper/gold skin and the flecks of gold in those custom-made eyes, beautiful but wary.

The redisplayed Shantih Love started the ill-fated walk along the barrier and Konstantin joined in, pacing the image on the right. Her virtual body mirrored Love's movements such that she had no doubt she was reliving Tomoyuki Iguchi's walk in almost every detail. Iguchi just hadn't known his virtual self was going to be hijacked and killed. Which meant he couldn't know now, and yet the redisplayed Shantih Love seemed more apprehensive than she had remembered. Or was that just the fact that Full Mode was letting her see more and see it better than the small flat No Frills images she had viewed in Pleshette's office?

Beyond the redisplayed view of the shore and the party, she could see the current party-goers turning to look and maybe wonder who the show-off with the deep pockets was, doing a redisplay within a scenario. It was strange and extravagant even for post-Apocalyptic Noo Yawk Sitty, where time and civilization had come to an end and the twilight of the gods was currently in progress. Except judging by the parties she kept coming across, Konstantin thought it might be more like the happy hour of the gods.

And then again, maybe her ex had been right in saying that she couldn't believe in anything because she had no respect for anything.

A small flood of people detached themselves from the party and ran to join the redisplay, melting in almost seamlessly. There wasn't time to be discomfited—the vague creature was already on top of the barrier, except it didn't look terribly vague any more. It looked an awful lot like Miles Mank after six very bad weeks on a binge.

Straddling the barrier a few feet away from him was a tattooed woman watching his every move intently. Konstantin had never seen the character before but she knew just by the posture and the tilt of the head that it had to be a stringer from someplace like *Police Blotter*. Whether it was the same one from the parlor or a different one from a competing network, she didn't know and it really didn't matter anyway.

As if sensing her thoughts, the tattooed woman turned in Konstantin's direction, smiling speculatively. Konstantin saw the tattoos were in motion, melting and changing. In spite of everything, she took a moment to wonder what the point was.

Then she took a step forward, uncertain of what she meant to do—try to intimidate the stringer into leaving, ask her nicely to back off, promise her exclusive interviews with everyone involved, living or dead, if she'd refrain from broadcasting. But as she moved toward the barrier, the redisplayed Shantih Love took a step back and Konstantin found herself suddenly enveloped by the image.

It seemed as if everything around her took a giant step in every direction at once, including up and down. Then her surroundings refocused sharply. The shaggy creature jumped down and she found herself turning within the redisplayed Shantih Love and running, staggering through the sand, unable to do anything else. Some glitch had merged her program with the redisplay—

Some glitch? Or the panting, sobbing creature behind her? Or even something else completely?

Her heart pounded so hard as she pulled herself up the stony rise to the street that she wondered how many people had sustained heart attacks just imagining that they were moving on a physical level they were incapable of in realtime.

Desperately, she tried to pull out of the redisplayed Shantih Love image but it was like being caught in a powerful magnetic field that worked on flesh—on *thoughts*, on both. Boxes within boxes, levels within levels, a guy pretending to be Japanese pretending to be a hermaphrodite named Shantih Love, and a cop pretending to be a hermaphrodite named Shantih Love pretending . . . what?

It took forever to hit the ground and it *hurt*. She tried to scramble up and cry out for help, but Mank was on her and the blade was in his hands. She had nothing now, no rescue, no icon cat, no help files—

Something flashed in her open hand; she could see it just barely out of register with Love's redisplayed hand and hope surged through her like an electric current. The difference, the one thing that was different now between her image of Shantih Love and the redisplayed image, the thing that could change what had already gone before . . . sort of.

But she'd have to call it in the air, and she wasn't sure she could. *When you have a coin with infinity on one side, and Ouroboros on the other, how can you ever really know which side is heads, and which is tails?* There wasn't time to figure it out. As the blade touched her throat, she tore her arm free of the recording's, hurled the coin at the night sky, and called it.

The word that came out of her mouth was not what she had been expecting, but then, she hadn't really known what to expect, nor did she recognize it. Whatever it was—the term for the link between alpha and omega, the secret name of Ourobouros, or the nine billionth name of God—it had come with the coin as both property and function, and she could not have called it until now, when somehow, conditions were right.

The knife blade descended, but she was receding from it at the speed of thought and it never reached her.

Had she receded from it, from that level? Or had all of it receded from her? There was no real way to tell. The only feeling she had now was a sense of acceleration that wasn't quite flying and wasn't quite falling. Her inner ear kept wanting to go crazy on her, but something would pull it back from the brink at the last moment, sending thrills through the back of her neck.

Konstantin tried curling into the fetal position, just for the sake of being able to feel her body. There were several moments of uncertainty and disorientation while she tried to locate her extremities. Then abruptly, she found herself seated in an old-fashioned leather chair at a large round table. Across from her was a woman with deep brown skin and long black hair brushed back from her face like a lion's mane.

Konstantin stared, unable to speak.

"I understand you've been looking for me." The quality of the woman's voice was like nothing Konstantin had ever known before; it was sound, but translated into several other modes and dimensions, delivered all at once in a way that both enveloped and penetrated. It felt to Konstantin as if the woman's voice were coming through from the fabric of reality itself, any reality, including that of Konstantin's own thoughts.

After a while, Konstantin managed to nod. She wasn't sure how long it had taken her to do that, but it felt as if it had been a very, very long time. Body Sativa didn't seem to mind. However long something took here was how long it took.

"Things that happen, happen. Some things cannot be breached under pain of the consequences of procedure that is . . . improper. It is a matter of finding the route. The connection. The connecting matter. Road? Bridge? Tunnel? Or Something Else?"

Something Else was not exactly what Body Sativa had said, but it was the only thing that would come through Konstantin's ear. She watched as Body Sativa spread her arms over the table, palms outward. It took another unmeasurable period of time for Konstantin's eyes to adjust, but when they did, she saw that the surface of the table was more like a large video screen, or telescopic window. Or, as was more likely in the land of the Ouroboros coin, both.

Konstantin realized that whatever it was, she was looking at another aerial view of post-Apocalyptic Noo Yawk Sitty, every square inch and pixel revealed. Eliot's etherized patient after all, but prepared on the banquet table, not the operating table. The consumed and the consumers—it just depended what side of the table you were on . . . didn't it?

"Look deeper."

Her point-of-view seemed to fly out from her in the way she had heard out-of-body experiences described, though this was more matter-of-fact than filled with wonder. It zoomed down into the Sitty and the tiny, vein-sized roadways grew into canyons, with cliff-faces made of mirrored glass and carved stone gargoyles, gables, spires, columns, pitted brick splattered with glitter that did not quite obscure the burn marks, the blasted places, the dirty words.

Wreckage in the roadways ignited, the flames rising to form complex shapes, lattices, angles that opened and closed on each other, here and there icons, some of which she recognized. And in other places, ideograms.

There they are, Iguchi, those special places they said you had to be Japa-

nese to find, she thought. *Maybe this means we've both turned Japanese. For my next magical trick, I will find the egress. The out door.*

As if in direct response, her pov flew straight toward a door, which opened at the last moment, admitting her into a split-second of darkness and then into a badly lit room where she saw the person strapped in the chair, sitting forward so that the straps pulled taut, but comfortably, in a way that supported more than restrained. The headmount moved slowly upward, the person raising her head to look up.

It was too easy, though, too bizarrely . . . *expectable*, Konstantin thought. But then, it *was* just a story.

Her nerves had become Holy Rollers. Just a story or not, she wasn't ready to see this. Maybe she wasn't Japanese enough.

In the next moment, her pov had snapped back like a rubber band and she was looking across the table at Body Sativa again. The woman looked younger now, more like a girl than a grown woman. This post-Apocalyptic stuff was really something. No wonder so many people liked it. It was downright eerie. Like the story of the man who didn't open his parachute in an AR skydive, or the kid who got his throat cut because he'd gotten his AR throat cut.

Body Sativa seemed amused. *"You have the coin. When you're ready to come back, call it in the air."*

It took an hour for Konstantin to open her mouth and say, "Wait!" Her voice sounded unpleasantly flat in her own ears. "Someone killed—"

"Yes. Someone did. When you're ready to know, call it in the air."

She was lying on her back on the road; Shantih Love was walking away, holding his/her sliced flesh together. But when s/he turned around and looked back, the face was unmistakably the creature's, the ridiculously bendered-out features of Miles Mank, still on a binge.

"Endit," Konstantin whispered, her voice still sounding funny to her. "Endit, exit, outa here."

She lay on her back for a very long time before she felt the road transmute into the chair with the restraints. Moving slowly, she undid the clasps on the headmount and was startled to feel someone helping her lift it off her head.

Taliaferro stood over her with the headmount in his hands, which was even more startling, and perhaps the most impossible of everything she had seen. By way of explanation, he reached into his coat pocket and pulled out a white plastic inhaler. "When I've got my anti-claustrophobia medicine, I can do anything."

"Words to live by," Konstantin whispered. There seemed to be nothing more to her voice than a rough whisper. She looked past him, but there was no one in the doorway.

"So, did you learn anything?" he asked her, sounding just slightly condescending. Perhaps that was a function of his medicine as well. She didn't hold it against him.

"Oh, yeah." She slipped out of the restraints and went over to the wall to her left. The control that let down the chaise was just slightly below eye level for her. She hit it with the side of her hand and it swung out and down in a way that reminded her of the way kids might stick out their tongues. Nyah, nyah, nyah.

"It was actually very simple," she said wearily, "but Celestine and DiPietro weren't thorough enough. The killer hid inside the Murphy style compartment, waited until Iguchi was all wrapped up in what he was doing, and then sliced him." Nyah, nyah, nyah.

Taliaferro was nonplussed. "You sure about that?"

"Yeah," she said. "Yeah. It's Occam's Razor is what it is. The simplest explanation is *the* explanation."

"Any idea who might have been hiding in there with Occam's Razor?"

Her moment of hesitation was so short, she was sure that Taliaferro didn't notice it, but at the same time, it was very long, incredibly, immeasurably long, of a duration that only Body Sativa could have understood and waited patiently enough for. "Yeah. It was Mank. He was bitter about not being the manager and not too stable. He frequented post-Apocalyptic Noo Yawk Sitty on the generous employee discount enough times that he got a bad case of gameplayers' psychosis. He was killing in there and it spilled over to killing out here."

"You sound awful sure about all that," Taliaferro said doubtfully.

"You'd have to go in and see it for yourself. There's all kinds of—of *stuff* in there. Including memes for murder. Mank got one. Let's grab him and see if we can have him all tucked in before *Police Blotter* does an update. I think there was a stringer following me around in there."

Taliaferro grunted, took a hit off his inhaler, and dropped it into his pocket. "Okay. I guess that's it, then."

"Yeah," Konstantin said. "That's it."

"Okay," he said again. Pause. "I'll send someone back here with your clothes."

"Thanks." But she was talking to the air. Taliaferro had run off. Apparently there was only so much an inhaler could do. There was only so much anything could do. Anything, or anyone. Even Occam's Razor. But then, the murder weapon hadn't been the same in the other seven murders anyway. No indeed. And Mank looked good for this one, she insisted to herself. He looked too good. The image of him in the Sitty was too identifiable not to be damning. The ego of the man, using his own face. Although that might be a more widespread practice than anyone realized.

But could anything really be surprising in the land of anything goes, she thought. The fabled promised land of AR, where they had everything there was in realtime—including death—and more besides.

If anything goes, then let anyone go as well. Mank looks good for it, and if the state can't prove its case against him, then it can't. But let him be the one who goes this time. For now. Until—well, when?

In her mind's eye, she saw the image of the coin again, the loop of infinity on one side, Ouroboros on the other. Maybe until you were ready to know which came first when you called it in the air.

FOR WHITE HILL

Joe Haldeman

▼

Born in Oklahoma City, Oklahoma, Joe Haldeman took a B.S. degree in physics
and astronomy from the University of Maryland, and did postgraduate work in
mathematics and computer science. But his plans for a career in science were cut
short by the U.S. Army, which sent him to Vietnam in 1968 as a combat engineer.
Seriously wounded in action, Haldeman returned home in 1969 and began to
write. He sold his first story to *Galaxy* in 1969, and by 1976 had garnered both
the Nebula Award and the Hugo Award for his famous novel *The Forever War*,
one of the landmark books of the seventies. He took another Hugo Award in
1977 for his story "Tricentennial," won the Rhysling Award in 1983 for the best
science fiction poem of the year, and won both the Nebula and the Hugo Award
in 1991 for the novella version of "The Hemingway Hoax." His story "Graves"
won the Nebula and World Fantasy Awards in 1994 and his "None So Blind"
won the Hugo Award in 1995. His other books include a mainstream novel, *War
Year*; the SF novels *Mindbridge*, *All My Sins Remembered*, *There Is No Darkness*
(written with his brother, SF writer Jack C. Haldeman II), *Worlds*, *Worlds Apart*,
Worlds Enough and Time, *Buying Time*, and *The Hemingway Hoax*; the "techno-
thriller" *Tool of the Trade*; the collections *Infinite Dreams* and *Dealing in Futures*;
and, as editor, the anthologies *Study War No More*, *Cosmic Laughter*, and *Nebula
Award Stories Seventeen*. His most recent books are a new collection, *Vietnam
and Other Alien Worlds* and a major new mainstream novel, *1968*. He has had
stories in our First, Third, Eighth, Tenth, Eleventh, and Twelfth Annual Collections. Haldeman lives part of the year in Boston, where he teaches writing at the
Massachusetts Institute of Technology, and the rest of the year in Florida, where
he and his wife, Gay, make their home.

Here he takes us thousands of years into a sophisticated, high-tech future for
ringside seats at a unique competition among artists who have the kind of nearly
unlimited resources to draw upon that would be unimaginable to someone from
our day—but who find that, in the end, in spite of wealth and power, they still
have to deal with the same old, cold questions as artists of any age.

•

I am writing this memoir in the language of England, an ancient land of Earth, whose tales and songs White Hill valued. She was fascinated by human culture in the days before machines—not just thinking machines, but working ones; when things got done by the straining muscles of humans and animals.

Neither of us was born on Earth. Not many people were, in those days. It was a desert planet then, ravaged in the twelfth year of what they would call the Last War. When we met, that war had been going for over four hundred years, and had moved out of Sol Space altogether, or so we thought.

Some cultures had other names for the conflict. My parent, who fought the century before I did, always called it the Extermination, and their name for the enemy was "roach," or at least that's as close as English allows. We called the enemy an approximation of their own word for themselves, Fwndyri, which was uglier to us. I still have no love for them, but have no reason to make the effort. It would be easier to love a roach. At least we have a common ancestor. And we accompanied one another into space.

One mixed blessing we got from the war was a loose form of interstellar government, the Council of Worlds. There had been individual treaties before, but an overall organization had always seemed unlikely, since no two inhabited systems are less than three light-years apart, and several of them are over fifty. You can't defeat Einstein; that makes more than a century between "How are you?" and "Fine."

The Council of Worlds was headquartered on Earth, an unlikely and unlovely place, if centrally located. There were fewer than ten thousand people living on the blighted planet then, an odd mix of politicians, religious extremists, and academics, mostly. Almost all of them under glass. Tourists flowed through the domed-over ruins, but not many stayed long. The planet was still very dangerous over all of its unprotected surface, since the Fwndyri had thoroughly seeded it with nanophages. Those were submicroscopic constructs that sought out concentrations of human DNA. Once under the skin, they would reproduce at a geometric rate, deconstructing the body, cell by cell, building new nanophages. A person might complain of a headache and lie down, and a few hours later there would be nothing but a dry skeleton, lying in dust. When the humans were all dead, they mutated and went after DNA in general, and sterilized the world.

White Hill and I were "bred" for immunity to the nanophages. Our DNA winds backwards, as was the case with many people born or created after that stage of the war. So we could actually go through the elaborate airlocks and step out onto the blasted surface unprotected.

I didn't like her at first. We were competitors, and aliens to one another.

When I worked through the final airlock cycle, for my first moment on the actual surface of Earth, she was waiting outside, sitting in meditation on a large flat rock that shimmered in the heat. One had to admit she was beautiful in a startling way, clad only in a glistening pattern of blue and green body paint. Everything else around was grey and black, including the hard-packed talcum that had once been a mighty jungle, Brazil. The dome behind me was a mirror of grey and black and cobalt sky.

"Welcome home," she said. "You're Water Man."

She inflected it properly, which surprised me. "You're from Petros?"

"Of course not." She spread her arms and looked down at her body. Our women always cover at least one of their breasts, let alone their genitals. "Galan, an island on Seldene. I've studied your cultures, a little language."

"You don't dress like that on Seldene, either." Not anywhere I'd been on the planet.

"Only at the beach. It's so warm here."

I had to agree. Before I came out, they'd told me it was the hottest autumn on record. I took off my robe and folded it and left it by the door, with the sealed food box they had given me. I joined her on the rock, which was tilted away from the sun and reasonably cool.

She had a slight fragrance of lavender, perhaps from the body paint. We touched hands. "My name is White Hill. Zephyr-Meadow-Torrent."

"Where are the others?" I asked. Twenty-nine artists had been invited; one from each inhabited world. The people who had met me inside said I was the nineteenth to show up.

"Most of them traveling. Going from dome to dome for inspiration."

"You've already been around?"

"No." She reached down with her toe and scraped a curved line on the hard-baked ground. "All the story's here, anywhere. It isn't really about history or culture."

Her open posture would have been shockingly sexual at home, but this was not home. "Did you visit my world when you were studying it?"

"No, no money, at the time. I did get there a few years ago." She smiled at me. "It was almost as beautiful as I'd imagined it." She said three words in Petrosian. You couldn't say it precisely in English, which doesn't have a palindromic mood: *Dreams feed art and art feeds dreams*.

"When you came to Seldene I was young, too young to study with you. I've learned a lot from your sculpture, though."

"How young can you be?" To earn this honor, I did not say.

"In Earth years, about seventy awake. More than a hundred and forty-five in time-squeeze."

I struggled with the arithmetic. Petros and Seldene were twenty-two light-years apart; that's about forty-five years' squeeze. Earth is, what, a little less than forty light-years from her planet. That leaves enough gone time for someplace about twenty-five light-years from Petros, and back.

She tapped me on the knee, and I flinched. "Don't overheat your brain. I made a triangle; went to ThetaKent after your world."

"Really? When I was there?"

"No, I missed you by less than a year. I was disappointed. You were why I went." She made a palindrome in my language: *Predator becomes prey becomes predator?* "So here we are. Perhaps I can still learn from you."

I didn't much care for her tone of voice, but I said the obvious: "I'm more likely to learn from you."

"Oh, I don't think so." She smiled in a measured way. "You don't have much to learn."

Or much I could, or would, learn. "Have you been down to the water?"

"Once." She slid off the rock and dusted herself, spanking. "It's interesting. Doesn't look real." I picked up the food box and followed her down a sort of path that led us into low ruins. She drank some of my water, apologetic; hers was hot enough to brew tea.

"First body?" I asked.

"I'm not tired of it yet." She gave me a sideways look, amused. "You must be on your fourth or fifth."

"I go through a dozen a year." She laughed. "Actually, it's still my second. I hung on to the first too long."

"I read about that, the accident. That must have been horrible."

"Comes with the medium. I should take up the flute." I had been making a "controlled" fracture in a large boulder and set off the charges prematurely, by dropping the detonator. Part of the huge rock rolled over onto me, crushing my body from the hips down. It was a remote area, and by the time help arrived I had been dead for several minutes, from pain as much as anything else. "It affected all of my work, of course. I can't even look at some of the things I did the first few years I had this body."

"They are hard to look at," she said. "Not to say they aren't well done, and beautiful, in their way."

"As what is not? In its way." We came to the first building ruins and stopped. "Not all of this is weathering. Even in four hundred years." If you studied the rubble you could reconstruct part of the design. Primitive but sturdy, concrete reinforced with composite rods. "Somebody came in here with heavy equipment or explosives. They never actually fought on Earth, I thought."

"They say not." She picked up an irregular brick with a rod through it. "Rage, I suppose. Once people knew that no one was going to live."

"It's hard to imagine." The records are chaotic. Evidently the first people died two or three days after the nanophages were introduced, and no one on Earth was alive a week later. "Not hard to understand, though. The need to break something." I remembered the inchoate anger I felt as I squirmed there helpless, dying from *sculpture*, of all things. Anger at the rock, the fates. Not at my own inattention and clumsiness.

"They had a poem about that," she said. " 'Rage, rage against the dying of the light.' "

"Somebody actually wrote something during the nanoplague?"

"Oh, no. A thousand years before. Twelve hundred." She squatted suddenly and brushed at a fragment that had two letters on it. "I wonder if this was some sort of official building. Or a shrine or church." She pointed along the curved row of shattered bricks that spilled into the street. "That looks like it was some kind of decoration, a gable over the entrance." She tiptoed through the rubble toward the far end of the arc, studying what was written on the face-up pieces. The posture, standing on the balls of her feet, made her slim body even more attractive, as she must have known. My own body began to respond in a way inappropriate for a man more than three times her age. Foolish, even though that particular part is not so old. I willed it down before she could see.

"It's a language I don't know," she said. "Not Portuguese; looks like Latin. A Christian church, probably, Catholic."

"They used water in their religion," I remembered. "Is that why it's close to the sea?"

"They were everywhere; sea, mountains, orbit. They got to Petros?"

"We still have some. I've never met one, but they have a church in New Haven."

"As who doesn't?" She pointed up a road. "Come on. The beach is just over the rise here."

I could smell it before I saw it. It wasn't an ocean smell; it was dry, slightly choking.

We turned a corner and I stood staring. "It's a deep blue farther out," she said, "and so clear you can see hundreds of metras down." Here the water was thick and brown, the surf foaming heavily like a giant's chocolate drink, mud piled in baked windrows along the beach. "This used to be soil?"

She nodded. "There's a huge river that cuts this continent in half, the Amazon. When the plants died, there was nothing to hold the soil in place." She tugged me forward. "Do you swim? Come on."

"Swim in *that*? It's filthy."

"No, it's perfectly sterile. Besides, I have to pee." Well, I couldn't argue with that. I left the box on a high fragment of fallen wall and followed her. When we got to the beach, she broke into a run. I walked slowly and watched her gracile body, instead, and waded into the slippery heavy surf. When it was deep enough to swim, I plowed my way out to where she was bobbing. The water was too hot to be pleasant, and breathing was somewhat difficult. Carbon dioxide, I supposed, with a tang of halogen.

We floated together for a while, comparing this soup to bodies of water on our planets and ThetaKent. It was tiring, more from the water's heat and bad air than exertion, so we swam back in.

●●

We dried in the blistering sun for a few minutes and then took the food box and moved to the shade of a beachside ruin. Two walls had fallen in together, to make a sort of concrete tent.

We could have been a couple of precivilization aboriginals, painted with dirt, our hair baked into stringy mats. She looked odd but still had a kind of formal beauty, the dusty mud residue turning her into a primitive sculpture, impossibly accurate and mobile. Dark rivulets of sweat drew painterly accent lines along her face and body. If only she were a model, rather than an artist. Hold that pose while I go back for my brushes.

We shared the small bottles of cold wine and water and ate bread and cheese and fruit. I put a piece on the ground for the nanophages. We watched it in silence for some minutes, while nothing happened. "It probably takes hours or days," she finally said.

"I suppose we should hope so," I said. "Let us digest the food before the creatures get to it."

"Oh, that's not a problem. They just attack the bonds between amino acids that make up proteins. For you and me, they're nothing more than an aid to digestion."

How reassuring. "But a source of some discomfort when we go back in, I was told."

She grimaced. "The purging. I did it once, and decided my next outing would be a long one. The treatment's the same for a day or a year."

"So how long has it been this time?"

"Just a day and a half. I came out to be your welcoming committee."

"I'm flattered."

She laughed. "It was their idea, actually. They wanted someone out here to 'temper' the experience for you. They weren't sure how well traveled you were, how easily affected by . . . strangeness." She shrugged. "Earthlings. I told them I knew of four planets you'd been to."

"They weren't impressed?"

"They said well, you know, he's famous and wealthy. His experiences on these planets might have been very comfortable." We could both laugh at that. "I told them how comfortable ThetaKent is."

"Well, it doesn't have nanophages."

"Or anything else. That was a long year for me. You didn't even stay a year."

"No. I suppose we would have met, if I had."

"Your agent said you were going to be there two years."

I poured us both some wine. "She should have told me you were coming. Maybe I could have endured it until the next ship out."

"How gallant." She looked into the wine without drinking. "You famous and wealthy people don't have to endure ThetaKent. I had to agree to one year's indentureship to help pay for my triangle ticket."

"You were an actual slave?"

"More like a wife, actually. The head of a township, a widower, financed me in exchange for giving his children some culture. Language, art, music. Every now and then he asked me to his chambers. For his own kind of culture."

"My word. You had to . . . *lie* with him? That was in the contract?"

"Oh, I didn't have to, but it kept him friendly." She held up a thumb and forefinger. "It was hardly noticeable."

I covered my smile with a hand, and probably blushed under the mud.

"I'm not embarrassing you?" she said. "From your work, I'd think that was impossible."

I had to laugh. "That work is in reaction to my culture's values. I can't take a pill and stop being a Petrosian."

White Hill smiled, tolerantly. "A Petrosian woman wouldn't put up with an arrangement like that?"

"Our women are still women. Some actually would like it, secretly. Most would claim they'd rather die, or kill the man."

"But they wouldn't actually *do* it. Trade their body for a ticket?" She sat down in a single smooth dancer's motion, her legs open, facing me. The clay between her legs parted, sudden pink.

"I wouldn't put it so bluntly." I swallowed, watching her watching me. "But no, they wouldn't. Not if they were planning to return."

"Of course, no one from a civilized planet would want to stay on ThetaKent. Shocking place."

I had to move the conversation onto safer grounds. "Your arms don't spend all day shoving big rocks around. What do you normally work in?"

"Various mediums." She switched to my language. "Sometimes I shove little rocks around." That was a pun for testicles. "I like painting, but my reputation is mainly from light and sound sculpture. I wanted to do something with the water here, internal illumination of the surf, but they say that's not possible. They can't isolate part of the ocean. I can have a pool, but no waves, no tides."

"Understandable." Earth's scientists had found a way to rid the surface of the nanoplague. Before they reterraformed the Earth, though, they wanted to isolate an area, a "park of memory," as a reminder of the Sterilization and these centuries of waste, and brought artists from every world to interpret, inside the park, what they had seen here.

Every world except Earth. Art on Earth had been about little else for a long time.

Setting up the contest had taken decades. A contest representative went to each of the settled worlds, according to a strict timetable. Announcement of the competition was delayed on the nearer worlds so that each artist would arrive on Earth at approximately the same time.

The Earth representatives chose which artists would be asked, and no one refused. Even the ones who didn't win the contest were guaranteed an honorarium equal to twice what they would have earned during that time at home, in their best year of record.

The value of the prize itself was so large as to be meaningless to a normal person. I'm a wealthy man on a planet where wealth is not rare, and just the interest that the prize would earn would support me and a half-dozen more. If someone from ThetaKent or Laxor won the prize, they would probably have more real usable wealth than their governments. If they were smart, they wouldn't return home.

The artists had to agree on an area for the park, which was limited to a hundred square kaymetras. If they couldn't agree, which seemed almost inevitable to me, the contest committee would listen to arguments and rule.

Most of the chosen artists were people like me, accustomed to working on a monumental scale. The one from Luxor was a composer, though, and there were two conventional muralists, paint and mosaic. White Hill's work was by its nature evanescent. She could always set something up that would be repeated, like a fountain cycle. She might have more imagination than that, though.

"Maybe it's just as well we didn't meet in a master-student relationship," I said. "I don't know the first thing about the techniques of your medium."

"It's not technique." She looked thoughtful, remembering. "That's not why I wanted to study with you, back then. I was willing to push rocks around, or anything, if it could give me an avenue, an insight into how you did what you did." She folded her arms over her chest, and dust fell. "Ever since my parents took me to see Gaudí Mountain, when I was ten."

That was an early work, but I was still satisfied with it. The city council of Tresling, a prosperous coastal city, hired me to "do something with" an unusable steep island that stuck up in the middle of their harbor. I melted it judiciously, in homage to an Earthling artist.

"Now, though, if you'd forgive me . . . well, I find it hard to look at. It's alien, obtrusive."

"You don't have to apologize for having an opinion." Of course it looked alien; it was meant to evoke *Spain!* "What would you do with it?"

She stood up, and walked to where a window used to be, and leaned on the stone sill, looking at the ruins that hid the sea. "I don't know. I'm even less familiar with your tools." She scraped at the edge of the sill with a piece of rubble. "It's funny: earth, air, fire, and water. You're earth and fire, and I'm the other two."

I have used water, of course. The Gaudí is framed by water. But it was an interesting observation. "What do you do, I mean for a living? Is it related to your water and air?"

"No. Except insofar as everything is related." There are no artists on Seldene, in the sense of doing it for a living. Everybody indulges in some sort of art or music, as part of "wholeness," but a person who only did art would be considered a parasite. I was not comfortable there.

She faced me, leaning. "I work at the Northport Mental Health Center. Cognitive science, a combination of research and . . . is there a word here? *Jaturnary*. 'Empathetic therapy,' I guess."

I nodded. "We say *jådr-ny*. You plug yourself into mental patients?"

"I share their emotional states. Sometimes I do some good, talking to them afterwards. Not often."

"It's not done on Petrosia," I said, unnecessarily.

"Not legally, you mean."

I nodded. "If it worked, people say, it might be legal."

" 'People say.' What do you say?" I started to make a noncommittal gesture. "Tell me the truth?"

"All I know is what I learned in school. It was tried, but failed spectacularly. It hurt both the therapists and the patients."

"That was more than a century ago. The science is much more highly developed now."

I decided not to push her on it. The fact is that drug therapy is spectacularly successful, and it *is* a science, unlike *jådr-ny*. Seldene is backward in some surprising ways.

I joined her at the window. "Have you looked around for a site yet?"

She shrugged. "I think my presentation will work anywhere. At least that's guided my thinking. I'll have water, air, and light, wherever the other artists and the committee decide to put us." She scraped at the ground with a toenail. "And this stuff. They call it 'loss.' What's left of what was living."

"I suppose it's not everywhere, though. They might put us in a place that used to be a desert."

"They might. But there will be water and air; they were willing to guarantee that."

"I don't suppose they have to guarantee rock," I said.

"I don't know. What would you do if they did put us in a desert, nothing but sand?"

"Bring little rocks." I used my own language; the pun also meant courage.

She started to say something, but we were suddenly in deeper shadow. We both stepped through the tumbled wall, out into the open. A black line of cloud had moved up rapidly from inland.

She shook her head. "Let's get to the shelter. Better hurry."

We trotted back along the path toward the Amazonia dome city. There was a low concrete structure behind the rock where I first met her. The warm breeze became a howling gale of sour steam before we got there, driving bullets of hot rain. A metal door opened automatically on our approach, and slid shut behind us. "I got caught in one yesterday," she said, panting. "It's no fun, even under cover. Stinks."

We were in an unadorned anteroom that had protective clothing on wall pegs. I followed her into a large room furnished with simple chairs and tables, and up a winding stair to an observation bubble.

"Wish we could see the ocean from here," she said. It was dramatic enough. Wavering sheets of water marched across the blasted landscape, strobed every few seconds by lightning flashes. The tunic I'd left outside swooped in flapping circles off to the sea.

It was gone in a couple of seconds. "You don't get another one, you know. You'll have to meet everyone naked as a baby."

"A dirty one at that. How undignified."

"Come on." She caught my wrist and tugged. "Water is my specialty, after all."

● ● ●

The large hot bath was doubly comfortable for having a view of the tempest outside. I'm not at ease with communal bathing—I was married for fifty years and never bathed with my wife—but it seemed natural enough after wandering around together naked on an alien planet, swimming in its mud-puddle sea. I hoped I could trust her not to urinate in the tub. (If I mentioned it she would probably turn scientific and tell me that a healthy person's urine is sterile. I know that. But there is a time and a receptacle for everything.)

On Seldene, I knew, an unattached man and woman in this situation would probably have had sex even if they were only casual acquaintances, let alone fellow artists. She was considerate enough not to make any overtures, or perhaps (I thought at the time) not greatly stimulated by the sight of muscular men. In the shower before bathing, she offered to scrub my back, but left it at that. I helped her strip off the body paint from her back. It was a nice back to study, pronounced lumbar dimples, small waist. Under more restrained circumstances, it might have been *I* who made an overture. But one does not ask a woman when refusal would be awkward.

Talking while we bathed, I learned that some of her people, when they become wealthy enough to retire, choose to work on their art full time, but they're considered eccentric, even outcasts, egotists. White Hill expected one of them to be chosen for the contest, and wasn't even going to apply. But the Earthling judge saw one of her installations and tracked her down.

She also talked about her practical work in dealing with personality disorders and cognitive defects. There was some distress in her voice when she described that to me. Plugging into hurt minds, sharing their pain or blankness for hours. I didn't feel I knew her well enough to bring up the aspect that most interested me, a kind of ontological prurience: what is it like to actually *be* another person; how much of her, or him, do you take away? If you do it often enough, how can you know which parts of you are the original you?

And she would be plugged into more than one person at once, at times, the theory being that people with similar disorders could help each other, swarming around in the therapy room of her brain. She would fade into the background, more or less unable to interfere, and later analyze how they had interacted.

She had had one particularly unsettling experience, where through a planetwide network she had interconnected more than a hundred congenitally retarded people. She said it was like a painless death. By the time half of them had plugged in, she had felt herself fade and wink out. Then she was reborn with the suddenness of a slap. She had been dead for about ten hours.

But only connected for seven. It had taken technicians three hours to pry her out of a persistent catatonia. With more people, or a longer period, she might have been lost forever. There was no lasting harm, but the experiment was never repeated.

It was worth it, she said, for the patients' inchoate happiness afterward. It was like a regular person being given supernatural powers for half a day—powers so far beyond human experience that there was no way to talk about them, but the memory of it was worth the frustration.

After we got out of the tub, she showed me to our wardrobe room: hundreds of white robes, identical except for size. We dressed and made tea and sat upstairs, watching the storm rage. It hardly looked like an inhabitable planet outside. The lightning had intensified so that it crackled incessantly, a jagged insane dance in every direction. The rain had frozen to white gravel somehow. I asked the building, and it said that the stuff was called *granizo* or, in English, hail. For a while it fell too fast to melt, accumulating in white piles that turned translucent.

Staring at the desolation, White Hill said something that I thought was uncharacteristically modest. "This is too big and terrible a thing. I feel like an interloper. They've lived through centuries of this, and now they want *us* to explain it to them?"

I didn't have to remind her of what the contest committee had said, that their own arts had become stylized, stunned into a grieving conformity. "Maybe not to *explain*—maybe they're assuming we'll fail, but hope to find a new direction from our failures. That's what that oldest woman, Norita, implied."

White Hill shook her head. "Wasn't she a ray of sunshine? I think they dragged her out of the grave as a way of keeping us all outside the dome."

"Well, she was quite effective on me. I could have spent a few days investigating Amazonia, but not with her as a native guide." Norita was about as close as anyone could get to being an actual native. She was the last survivor of the Five Families, the couple of dozen Earthlings who, among those who were offworld at the time of the nanoplague, were willing to come back after robots constructed the isolation domes.

In terms of social hierarchy, she was the most powerful person on Earth, at least on the actual planet. The class system was complex and nearly opaque to outsiders, but being a descendant of the Five Families was a prerequisite for the highest class. Money or political power would not get you in, although most of the other social classes seemed associated with wealth or the lack of it. Not that there were any actual poor people on Earth; the basic birth dole was equivalent to an upper-middle-class income on Petros.

The nearly instantaneous destruction of ten billion people did not destroy their fortunes. Most of the Earth's significant wealth had been off-planet, anyhow, at the time of the Sterilization. Suddenly it was concentrated into the hands of fewer than two thousand people.

Actually, I couldn't understand why anyone would have come back. You'd have to be pretty sentimental about your roots to be willing to spend the rest of your life cooped up under a dome, surrounded by instant death. The salaries and amenities offered were substantial, with bonuses for Earthborn workers, but it still doesn't sound like much of a bargain. The ships that brought the Five Families and the other original workers to Earth left loaded down with sterilized artifacts, not to return for exactly one hundred years.

Norita seemed like a familiar type to me, since I come from a culture also rigidly bound by class. "Old money, but not much of it" sums up the situation. She wanted to be admired for the accident of her birth and the dubious blessing of a torpid longevity, rather than any actual accomplishment. I didn't have to travel thirty-three light-years to enjoy that kind of company.

"Did she keep you away from everybody?" White Hill said.

"Interposed herself. No one could act naturally when she was around, and the old dragon was never *not* around. You'd think a person her age would need a little sleep."

" 'She lives on the blood of infants,' we say."

There was a phone chime and White Hill said "Bono" as I said, "Chå." Long habits. Then we said Earth's "Holá" simultaneously.

The old dragon herself appeared. "I'm glad you found shelter." Had she been eavesdropping? No way to tell from her tone or posture. "An administrator has asked permission to visit with you."

What if we said no? White Hill nodded, which means yes on Earth. "Granted," I said.

"Very well. He will be there shortly." She disappeared. I suppose the oldest person on a planet can justify not saying hello or goodbye. Only so much time left, after all.

"A physical visit?" I said to White Hill. "Through this weather?"

She shrugged. "Earthlings."

After a minute there was a *ding* sound in the anteroom and we walked down to see an unexpected door open. What I'd thought was a hall closet was an airlock. He'd evidently come underground.

Young and nervous and moving awkwardly in plastic. He shook our hands in an odd way. Of course we were swimming in deadly poison. "My name is Warm Dawn. Zephyr-Boulder-Brook."

"Are we cousins through Zephyr?" White Hill asked.

He nodded quickly. "An honor, my lady. Both of my parents are Seldenian, my gene-mother from your Galan."

A look passed over her that was pure disbelieving chauvinism: *Why would anybody leave Seldene's forests, farms, and meadows for this sterile death trap?* Of course, she knew the answer. The major import and export, the only crop, on Earth, was money.

"I wanted to help both of you with your planning. Are you going to travel at all, before you start?"

White Hill made a noncommittal gesture. "There are some places for me to see," I said. "The Pyramids, Chicago, Rome. Maybe a dozen places, twice that many days." I looked at her. "Would you care to join me?"

She looked straight at me, wheels turning. "It sounds interesting."

The man took us to a viewscreen in the great room and we spent an hour or so going over routes and making reservations. Travel was normally by underground vehicle, from dome to dome, and if we ventured outside unprotected, we would of course have to go through the purging before we were allowed to continue. Some people need a day or more to recover from that, so we should put that into the schedule, if we didn't want to be hobbled, like him, with plastic.

Most of the places I wanted to see were safely under glass, even some of the Pyramids, which surprised me. Some, like Angkor Wat, were not only unprotected but difficult of access. I had to arrange for a flyer to cover the thousand kaymetras, and schedule a purge. White Hill said she would wander through Hanoi, instead.

I didn't sleep well that night, waking often from fantastic dreams, the nanobeasts grown large and aggressive. White Hill was in some of the dreams, posturing sexually.

By the next morning the storm had gone away, so we crossed over to Amazonia, and I learned firsthand why one might rather sit in a hotel room with a nice book than go to Angkor Wat, or anywhere that required a purge. The external part of the purging was unpleasant enough, even with pain medication, all the epidermis stripped and regrown. The inside part was beyond description, as the nanophages could be hiding out anywhere. Every opening into the body had to be vacuumed out, including the sense organs. I was not awake for that part, where the robots most gently clean out your eye sockets, but my eyes hurt and my ears rang for days. They warned me to sit down the first time I urinated, which was good advice, since I nearly passed out from the burning pain.

White Hill and I had a quiet supper of restorative gruel together, and then crept off to sleep for half a day. She was full of pep the next morning, and I pretended to be at least sentient, as we wandered through the city making preparations for the trip.

After a couple of hours I protested that she was obviously trying to do in one of her competitors; stop and let an old man sit down for a minute.

We found a bar that specialized in stimulants. She had tea and I had bhan, a murky warm drink served in a large nutshell, coconut. It tasted woody and bitter, but was restorative.

"It's not age," she said. "The purging seems a lot easier, the second time you do it. I could hardly move, all the next day, the first time."

Interesting that she didn't mention that earlier. "Did they tell you it would get easier?"

She nodded, then caught herself and wagged her chin horizontally, Earth-style. "Not a word. I think they enjoy our discomfort."

"Or like to keep us off guard. Keeps them in control." She made the little kissing sound that's Lortian for agreement and reached for a lemon wedge to squeeze into her tea. The world seemed to slow slightly, I guess from whatever was in the bhan, and I found myself cataloguing her body microscop-ically. A crescent of white scar tissue on the back of a knuckle, fine hair on her forearm, almost white, her shoulders and breasts moving in counterpoised pairs, silk rustling, as she reached forward and back and squeezed the lemon, sharp citrus smell and the tip of her tongue between her thin lips, mouth slightly large. Chameleon hazel eyes, dark green now because of the decora-tive ivy wall behind her.

"What are you staring at?"

"Sorry, just thinking."

"Thinking." She stared at me in return, measuring. "Your people are good at that."

After we'd bought the travel necessities we had the packages sent to our quarters and wandered aimlessly. The city was comfortable, but had little of interest in terms of architecture or history, oddly dull for a planet's administrative center. There was an obvious social purpose for its blandness—by statute, nobody was *from* Amazonia; nobody could be born there or claim citizenship. Most of the planet's wealth and power came there to work, electronically if not physically, but it went home to some other place.

A certain amount of that wealth was from interstellar commerce, but it was nothing like the old days, before the war. Earth had been a hub, a central authority that could demand its tithe or more from any transaction between planets. In the period between the Sterilization and Earth's token rehabitation, the other planets made their own arrangements with one another, in pairs and groups. But most of the fortunes that had been born on Earth returned here.

So Amazonia was bland as cheap bread, but there was more wealth under its dome than on any two other planets combined. Big money seeks out the company of its own, for purposes of reproduction.

● Δ

Two other artists had come in, from Auer and Shwa, and once they were ready, we set out to explore the world by subway. The first stop that was interesting was the Grand Canyon, a natural wonder whose desolate beauty was unaffected by the Sterilization.

We were amused by the guide there, a curious little woman who rattled on about the Great Rift Valley on Mars, a nearby planet where she was born. White Hill had a lightbox, and while the Martian lady droned on we sketched the fantastic colors, necessarily loose and abstract because our fingers were clumsy in clinging plastic.

We toured Chicago, like the Grand Canyon, wrapped in plastic. It was a large city that had been leveled in a local war. It lay in ruins for many years, and then, famously, was rebuilt as a single huge structure from those ruins. There's a childish or drunken ad hoc quality to it, a scarcity of right angles, a crazy-quilt mixture of materials. Areas of stunning imaginative brilliance next to jury-rigged junk. And everywhere bones, the skeletons of ten million people, lying where they fell. I asked what had happened to the bones in the old city outside of Amazonia. The guide said he'd never been there, but he supposed that the sight of them upset the politicians, so they had them cleaned up. "Can you imagine this place without the bones?" he asked. It would be nice if I could.

The other remnants of cities in that country were less interesting, if no less depressing. We flew over the east coast, which was essentially one continuous metropolis for thousands of kaymetras, like our coast from New Haven to Stargate, rendered in sterile ruins.

The first place I visited unprotected was Giza, the Great Pyramids. White Hill decided to come with me, though she had to be wrapped up in a shapeless cloth robe, her face veiled, because of local religious law. It seemed to me ridiculous, a transparent tourism ploy. How many believers in that old religion could have been off-planet when the Earth died? But every female was obliged at the tube exit to go into a big hall and be fitted with a chador robe and veil before a man could be allowed to look at her.

(We wondered whether the purging would be done completely by women. The technicians would certainly see a lot of her uncovered during that excruciation.)

They warned us it was unseasonably hot outside. Almost too hot to breathe, actually, during the day. We accomplished most of our sight-seeing around dusk or dawn, spending most of the day in air-conditioned shelters.

Because of our special status, White Hill and I were allowed to visit the pyramids alone, in the dark of the morning. We climbed up the largest one and watched the sun mount over desert haze. It was a singular time for both of us, edifying but something more.

Coming back down, we were treated to a sandstorm, *khamsin*, which actually might have done the first stage of purging if we had been allowed to take off our clothes. It explained why all the bones lying around looked so much older than the ones in Chicago; they normally had ten or twelve of these sandblasting storms every year. Lately, with the heat wave, the *khamsin* came weekly or even more often.

Raised more than five thousand years ago, the pyramids were the oldest monumental structures on the planet. They actually held as much fascination for White Hill as for me. Thousands of men moved millions of huge blocks of stone, with nothing but muscle and ingenuity. Some of the stones were mined a thousand kaymetras away, and floated up the river on barges.

I could build a similar structure, even larger, for my contest entry, by giving machines the right instructions. It would be a complicated business, but easily done within the two-year deadline. Of course there would be no point to it. That some anonymous engineer had done the same thing within the lifetime of a king, without recourse to machines—I agreed with White Hill: that was an actual marvel.

We spent a couple of days outside, traveling by surface hoppers from monument to monument, but none was as impressive. I suppose I should have realized that, and saved Giza for last.

We met another of the artists at the Sphinx, Lo Tan-Six, from Pao. I had seen his work on both Pao and ThetaKent, and admitted there was something to be admired there. He worked in stone, too, but was more interested in pure geometric forms than I was. I think stone fights form, or imposes its own tensions on the artist's wishes.

I liked him well enough, though, in spite of this and other differences, and we traveled together for a while. He suggested we not go through the purging here, but have our things sent to Rome, because we'd want to be outside there, too. There was a daily hop from Alexandria to Rome, an airship that had a section reserved for those of us who could eat and breathe nanophages.

As soon as she was inside the coolness of the ship, White Hill shed the chador and veil and stuffed them under the seat. "Breathe," she said, stretching. Her white body suit was a little less revealing than paint.

Her directness and undisguised sexuality made me catch my breath. The tiny crease of punctuation that her vulva made in the body suit would have her jailed on some parts of my planet, not to mention the part of this one we'd just left. The costume was innocent and natural and, I think, completely calculated.

Pao studied her with an interested detachment. He was neuter, an option that was available on Petros, too, but one I've never really understood. He claimed that sex took much time and energy from his art. I think his lack of gender took something else away from it.

We flew about an hour over the impossibly blue sea. There were a few sterile islands, but otherwise it was as plain as spilled ink. We descended over the ashes of Italy and landed on a pad on one of the hills overlooking the ancient city. The ship mated to an airlock so the normal-DNA people could go down to a tube that would whisk them into Rome. We could call for transportation or walk, and opted for the exercise. It was baking hot here, too, but not as bad as Egypt.

White Hill was polite with Lo, but obviously wished he'd disappear. He and I chattered a little too much about rocks and cements, explosives and lasers. And his asexuality diminished her interest in him—as, perhaps, my polite detachment increased her interest in me. The muralist from Shwa, to complete the spectrum, was after her like a puppy in its first heat, which I think amused her for two days. They'd had a private conversation in Chicago, and he'd kept his distance since, but still admired her from afar. As we walked down toward the Roman gates, he kept a careful twenty paces behind, trying to contemplate things besides White Hill's walk.

Inside the gate we stopped short, stunned in spite of knowing what to expect. It had a formal name, but everybody just called it *Òssi*, the Bones. An order of catholic clergy had spent more than two centuries building, by hand, a wall of bones completely around the city. It was twice the height of a man, varnished dark amber. There were repetitive patterns of femurs and rib cages and stacks of curving spines, and at eye level, a row of skulls, uninterrupted, kaymetra after kaymetra.

This was where we parted. Lo was determined to walk completely around the circle of death, and the other two went with him. White Hill and I could do it in our imagination. I still creaked from climbing the pyramid.

Prior to the ascent of Christianity here, they had huge spectacles, displays of martial skill where many of the participants were killed, for punishment of wrongdoing or just to entertain the masses. The two large amphitheaters where these displays went on were inside the Bones but not under the dome, so we walked around them. The Circus Maximus had a terrible dignity to it, little more than a long depression in the ground with a few eroded monuments left standing. The size and age of it were enough; your mind's eye supplied the rest. The smaller one, the Colosseum, was overdone, with robots in period costumes and ferocious mechanical animals re-creating the old scenes, lots of too-bright blood spurting. Stones and bones would do.

I'd thought about spending another day outside, but the shelter's air-conditioning had failed, and it was literally uninhabitable. So I braced myself and headed for the torture chamber. But as White Hill had said, the purging was more bearable the second time. You know that it's going to end.

Rome inside was interesting, many ages of archeology and history stacked around in no particular order. I enjoyed wandering from place to place with her, building a kind of organization out of the chaos. We were both more interested in inspiration than education, though, so I doubt that the three days we spent there left us with anything like a coherent picture of that tenacious empire and the millennia that followed it.

A long time later she would surprise me by reciting the names of the Roman emperors in order. She'd always had a trick memory, a talent for retaining trivia, ever since she was old enough to read. Growing up different that way must have been a factor in swaying her toward cognitive science.

We saw some ancient cinema and then returned to our quarters to pack for continuing on to Greece, which I was anticipating with pleasure. But it didn't happen. We had a message waiting: ALL MUST RETURN IMMEDIATELY TO AMAZONIA. CONTEST PROFOUNDLY CHANGED.

Lives, it turned out, profoundly changed. The war was back.

Δ

We met in a majestic amphitheater, the twenty-nine artists dwarfed by the size of it, huddled front row center. A few Amazonian officials sat behind a table on the stage, silent. They all looked detached, or stunned, brooding.

We hadn't been told anything except that it was a matter of "dire and immediate importance." We assumed it had to do with the contest, naturally, and were prepared for the worst: it had been called off; we had to go home.

The old crone Norita appeared. "We must confess to carelessness," she said. "The unseasonable warmth in both hemispheres, it isn't something that has happened, ever since the Sterilization. We looked for atmospheric causes here, and found something that seemed to explain it. But we didn't make the connection with what was happening in the other half of the world.

"It's not the atmosphere. It's the Sun. Somehow the Fwndyri have found a way to make its luminosity increase. It's been going on for half a year. If it continues, and we find no way to reverse it, the surface of the planet will be uninhabitable in a few years.

"I'm afraid that most of you are going to be stranded on Earth, at least for the time being. The Council of Worlds has exercised its emergency powers, and commandeered every vessel capable of interstellar transport. Those who have sufficient power or the proper connections will be able to escape. The rest will have to stay with us and face . . . whatever our fate is going to be."

I saw no reason not to be blunt. "Can money do it? How much would a ticket out cost?"

That would have been a gaffe on my planet, but Norita didn't blink. "I know for certain that two hundred million marks is not enough. I also know that some people have bought 'tickets,' as you say, but I don't know how much they paid, or to whom."

If I liquidated everything I owned, I might be able to come up with three hundred million, but I hadn't brought that kind of liquidity with me; just a box of rare jewelry, worth perhaps forty million. Most of my wealth was thirty-three years away, from the point of view of an Earth-bound investor. I could sign that over to someone, but by the time they got to Petros, the government or my family might have seized it, and they would have nothing save the prospect of a legal battle in a foreign culture.

Norita introduced Skylha Sygoda, an astrophysicist. He was pale and sweating. "We have analyzed the solar spectrum over the past six months. If I hadn't known that each spectrum was from the same star, I would have said it was a systematic and subtle demonstration of the microstages of stellar evolution in the late main sequence."

"Could you express that in some human language?" someone said.

Sygoda spread his hands. "They've found a way to age the Sun. In the normal course of things, we would expect the Sun to brighten about six percent each billion years. At the current rate, it's more like one percent per year."

"So in a hundred years," White Hill said, "it will be twice as bright?"

"If it continues at this rate. We don't know."

A stocky woman I recognized as !Oona Something, from Jua-nguvi, wrestled with the language: "To how long, then? Before this Earth is uninhabitable?"

"Well, in point of fact, it's uninhabitable now, except for people like you. We could survive inside these domes for a long time, if it were just a matter of the outside getting hotter and hotter. For those of you able to withstand the nanophages, it will probably be too hot within a decade, here; longer near the poles. But the weather is likely to become very violent, too.

"And it may not be a matter of a simple increase in heat. In the case of normal evolution, the Sun would eventually expand, becoming a red giant. It would take many billions of years, but the Earth would not survive. The surface of the Sun would actually extend out to touch us.

"If the Fwndyri were speeding up time somehow, locally, and the Sun were actually *evolving* at this incredible rate, we would suffer that fate in about thirty years. But it would be impossible. They would have to have a way to magically extract the hydrogen from the Sun's core."

"Wait," I said. "You don't know what they're doing now, to make it brighten. I wouldn't say anything's impossible."

"Water Man," Norita said, "if that happens we shall simply die, all of us, at once. There is no need to plan for it. We do need to plan for less extreme exigencies." There was an uncomfortable silence.

"What can we do?" White Hill said. "We artists?"

"There's no reason not to continue with the project, though I think you may wish to do it inside. There's no shortage of space. Are any of you trained in astrophysics, or anything having to do with stellar evolution and the like?" No one was. "You may still have some ideas that will be useful to the specialists. We will keep you informed."

Most of the artists stayed in Amazonia, for the amenities if not to avoid purging, but four of us went back to the outside habitat. Denli om Cord, the composer from Luxor, joined Lo and White Hill and me. We could have used the tunnel airlock, to avoid the midday heat, but Denli hadn't seen the beach, and I suppose we all had an impulse to see the sun with our new knowledge. In this new light, as they say.

White Hill and Denli went swimming while Lo and I poked around the ruins. We had since learned that the destruction here had been methodical, a grim resolve to leave the enemy nothing of value. Both of us were scouting for raw material, of course. After a short while we sat in the hot shade, wishing we had brought water.

We talked about that and about art. Not about the sun dying, or us dying, in a few decades. The women's laughter drifted to us over the rush of the muddy surf. There was a sad hysteria to it.

"Have you had sex with her?" he asked conversationally.

"What a question. No."

He tugged on his lip, staring out over the water. "I try to keep these things straight. It seems to me that you desire her, from the way you look at her, and she seems cordial to you, and is after all from Seldene. My interest is academic, of course."

"You've never done sex? I mean before."

"Of course, as a child." The implication of that was obvious.

"It becomes more complicated with practice."

"I suppose it could. Although Seldenians seem to treat it as casually as . . . conversation." He used the Seldenian word, which is the same as for intercourse.

"White Hill is reasonably sophisticated," I said. "She isn't bound by her culture's freedoms." The two women ran out of the water, arms around each other's waists, laughing. It was an interesting contrast; Denli was almost as large as me, and about as feminine. They saw us and waved toward the path back through the ruins.

We got up to follow them. "I suppose I don't understand your restraint," Lo said. "Is it your own culture? Your age?"

"Not age. Perhaps my culture encourages self-control."

He laughed. "That's an understatement."

"Not that I'm a slave to Petrosian propriety. My work is outlawed in several states, at home."

"You're proud of that."

I shrugged. "It reflects on them, not me." We followed the women down the path, an interesting study in contrasts, one pair nimble and naked except for a film of drying mud, the other pacing evenly in monkish robes. They were already showering when Lo and I entered the cool shelter, momentarily blinded by shade.

We made cool drinks and, after a quick shower, joined them in the communal bath. Lo was not anatomically different from a sexual male which I found obscurely disturbing. Wouldn't it bother you to be constantly reminded of what you had lost? Renounced, I suppose Lo would say, and accuse me of being parochial about plumbing.

I had made the drinks with guava juice and ron, neither of which we have on Petros. A little too sweet, but pleasant. The alcohol loosened tongues.

Denli regarded me with deep black eyes. "You're rich, Water Man. Are you rich enough to escape?"

"No. If I had brought all my money with me, perhaps."

"Some do," White Hill said. "I did."

"I would too," Lo said, "coming from Seldene. No offense intended."

"Wheels turn," she admitted. "Five or six new governments before I get back. *Would* have gotten back."

We were all silent for a long moment. "It's not real yet," White Hill said, her voice flat. "We're going to die here?"

"We were going to die somewhere," Denli said. "Maybe not so soon."

"And not on Earth," Lo said. "It's like a long preview of Hell." Denli looked at him quizzically. "That's where Christians go when they die. If they were bad."

"They send their bodies to Earth?" We managed not to smile. Actually, most of my people knew as little as hers, about Earth. Seldene and Luxor, though relatively poor, had centuries' more history than Petros, and kept closer ties to the central planet. The Home Planet, they would say. Homey as a blast furnace.

By tacit consensus, we didn't dwell on death any more that day. When artists get together they tend to wax enthusiastic about materials and tools, the mechanical lore of their trades. We talked about the ways we worked at home, the things we were able to bring with us, the improvisations we could effect with Earthling materials. (Critics talk about art, we say; artists talk about brushes.) Three other artists joined us, two sculptors and a weathershaper, and we all wound up in the large sunny studio drawing and painting. White Hill and I found sticks of charcoal and did studies of each other drawing each other.

While we were comparing them she quietly asked, "Do you sleep lightly?"

"I can. What did you have in mind?"

"Oh, looking at the ruins by starlight. The moon goes down about three. I thought we might watch it set together." Her expression was so open as to be enigmatic.

Two more artists had joined us by dinnertime, which proceeded with a kind of forced jollity. A lot of ron was consumed. White Hill cautioned me against overindulgence. They had the same liquor, called "rum," on Seldene, and it had a reputation for going down easily but causing storms. There was no legal distilled liquor on my planet.

I had two drinks of it, and retired when people started singing in various languages. I did sleep lightly, though, and was almost awake when White Hill tapped. I could hear two or three people still up, murmuring in the bath. We slipped out quietly.

It was almost cool. The quarter-phase moon was near the horizon, a dim orange, but it gave us enough light to pick our way down the path. It was warmer in the ruins, the tumbled stone still radiating the day's heat. We walked through to the beach, where it was cooler again. White Hill spread the blanket she had brought and we stretched out and looked up at the stars.

As is always true with a new world, most of the constellations were familiar, with a few bright stars added or subtracted. Neither of our home stars was significant, as dim here as Earth's Sol is from home. She identified the brightest star overhead as AlphaKent; there was a brighter one on the horizon, but neither of us knew what it was.

We compared names of the constellations we recognized. Some of hers were the same as Earth's names, like Scorpio, which we call the Insect. It was about halfway up the sky, prominent, embedded in the galaxy's glow. We both call the brightest star there Antares. The Executioner, which had set perhaps an hour earlier, they call Orion. We had the same meaningless names for its brightest stars, Betelgeuse and Rigel.

"For a sculptor, you know a lot about astronomy," she said. "When I visited your city, there was too much light to see stars at night."

"You can see a few from my place. I'm out at Lake Påchlå, about a hundred kaymetras inland."

"I know. I called you."

"I wasn't home?"

"No; you were supposedly on ThetaKent."

"That's right, you told me. Our paths crossed in space. And you became that burgher's slave wife." I put my hand on her arm. "Sorry I forgot. A lot has gone on. Was he awful?"

She laughed into the darkness. "He offered me a lot to stay."

"I can imagine."

She half turned, one breast soft against my arm, and ran a finger up my leg. "Why tax your imagination?"

I wasn't especially in the mood, but my body was. The robes rustled off easily, their only virtue.

The moon was down now, and I could see only a dim outline of her in the starlight. It was strange to make love deprived of that sense. You would think the absence of it would amplify the others, but I can't say that it did, except that her heartbeat seemed very strong on the heel of my hand. Her breath was sweet with mint and the smell and taste of her body were agreeable; in fact, there was nothing about her body that I would have cared to change, inside or out, but nevertheless, our progress became difficult after a couple of minutes, and by mute agreement we slowed and stopped. We lay joined together for some time before she spoke.

"The timing is all wrong. I'm sorry." She drew her face across my arm and I felt tears. "I was just trying not to think about things."

"It's all right. The sand doesn't help, either." We had gotten a little bit inside, rubbing.

We talked for a while and then drowsed together. When the sky began to lighten, a hot wind from below the horizon woke us up. We went back to the shelter.

Everyone was asleep. We went to shower off the sand and she was amused to see my interest in her quicken. "Let's take that downstairs," she whispered, and I followed her down to her room.

The memory of the earlier incapability was there, but it was not greatly inhibiting. Being able to see her made the act more familiar, and besides she was very pleasant to see, from whatever angle. I was able to withhold myself only once, and so the interlude was shorter than either of us would have desired.

We slept together on her narrow bed. Or she slept, rather, while I watched the bar of sunlight grow on the opposite wall, and thought about how everything had changed.

They couldn't really say we had thirty years to live, since they had no idea what the enemy was doing. It might be three hundred; it might be less than one—but even with bodyswitch that was always true, as it was in the old days: sooner or later something would go wrong and you would die. That I might die at the same instant as ten thousand other people and a planet full of history—that was interesting. But as the room filled with light and I studied her quiet repose, I found her more interesting than that.

I was old enough to be immune to infatuation. Something deep had been growing since Egypt, maybe before. On top of the pyramid, the rising sun dim in the mist, we had sat with our shoulders touching, watching the ancient forms appear below, and I felt a surge of numinism mixed oddly with content. She looked at me—I could only see her eyes—and we didn't have to say anything about the moment.

And now this. I was sure, without words, that she would share this, too. Whatever "this" was. England's versatile language, like mine and hers, is strangely hobbled by having the one word, love, stand for such a multiplicity of feelings.

Perhaps that lack reveals a truth, that no one love is like any other. There are other truths that you might forget, or ignore, distracted by the growth of love. In Petrosian there is a saying in the palindromic mood that always carries a sardonic, or at least ironic, inflection: "Happiness presages disaster presages happiness." So if you die happy, it means you were happy when you died. Good timing or bad?

Δ ●

!Oona M'vua had a room next to White Hill, and she was glad to switch with me, an operation that took about three minutes but was good for a much longer period of talk among the other artists. Lo was smugly amused, which in my temporary generosity of spirit I forgave.

Once we were adjacent, we found the button that made the wall slide away, and pushed the two beds together under her window. I'm afraid we were antisocial for a couple of days. It had been some time since either of us had had a lover. And I had never had one like her, literally, out of the dozens. She said that was because I had never been involved with a Seldenian, and I tactfully agreed, banishing five perfectly good memories to amnesia.

It's true that Seldenian women, and men as well, are better schooled than those of us from normal planets, in the techniques and subtleties of sexual expression. Part of "wholeness," which I suppose is a weak pun in English. It kept Lo, and not only him, from taking White Hill seriously as an artist:

the fact that a Seldenian, to be "whole," must necessarily treat art as an everyday activity, usually subordinate to affairs of the heart, of the body. Or at least on the same level, which is the point.

The reality is that it *is* all one to them. What makes Seldenians so alien is that their need for balance in life dissolves hierarchy: this piece of art is valuable, and so is this orgasm, and so is this crumb of bread. The bread crumb connects to the artwork through the artist's metabolism, which connects to orgasm. Then through a fluid and automatic mixture of logic, metaphor, and rhetoric, the bread crumb links to soil, sunlight, nuclear fusion, the beginning and end of the universe. Any intelligent person can map out chains like that, but to White Hill it was automatic, drilled into her with her first nouns and verbs: *Everything is important. Nothing matters.* Change the world but stay relaxed.

I could never come around to her way of thinking. But then I was married for fifty Petrosian years to a woman who had stranger beliefs. (The marriage as a social contract actually lasted fifty-seven years; at the half-century mark we took a vacation from each other, and I never saw her again.) White Hill's worldview gave her an equanimity I had to envy. But my art needed unbalance and tension the way hers needed harmony and resolution.

By the fourth day most of the artists had joined us in the shelter. Maybe they grew tired of wandering through the bureaucracy. More likely, they were anxious about their competitors' progress.

White Hill was drawing designs on large sheets of buff paper and taping them up on our walls. She worked on her feet, bare feet, pacing from diagram to diagram, changing and rearranging. I worked directly inside a shaping box, an invention White Hill had heard of but had never seen. It's a cube of light a little less than a metra wide. Inside is an image of a sculpture—or a rock or a lump of clay—that you can feel as well as see. You can mold it with your hands or work with finer instruments for cutting, scraping, chipping. It records your progress constantly, so it's easy to take chances; you can always run it back to an earlier stage.

I spent a few hours every other day cruising in a flyer with Lo and a couple of other sculptors, looking for native materials. We were severely constrained by the decision to put the Memory Park inside, since everything we used had to be small enough to fit through the airlock and purging rooms. You could work with large pieces, but you would have to slice them up and reassemble them, the individual chunks no bigger than two by two by three metras.

We tried to stay congenial and fair during these expeditions. Ideally, you would spot a piece and we would land by it or hover over it long enough to tag it with your ID; in a day or two the robots would deliver it to your "holding area" outside the shelter. If more than one person wanted the piece, which happened as often as not, a decision had to be made before it was tagged. There was a lot of arguing and trading and Solomon-style splitting, which usually satisfied the requirements of something other than art.

The quality of light was changing for the worse. Earthling planetary engineers were spewing bright dust into the upper atmosphere, to reflect back solar heat. (They modified the nanophage-eating machinery for the purpose. That was also designed to fill the atmosphere full of dust, but at a lower level—and each grain of *that* dust had a tiny chemical brain.) It made the night sky progressively less interesting. I was glad White Hill had chosen to initiate our connection under the stars. It would be some time before we saw them again, if ever.

And it looked like "daylight" was going to be a uniform overcast for the duration of the contest. Without the dynamic of moving sunlight to continually change the appearance of my piece, I had to discard a whole family of first approaches to its design. I was starting to think along the lines of something irrational-looking; something the brain would reject as impossible. The way we mentally veer away from unthinkable things like the Sterilization, and our proximate future.

We had divided into two groups, and jokingly but seriously referred to one another as "originalists" and "realists." We originalists were continuing our projects on the basis of the charter's rules: a memorial to the tragedy and its aftermath, a stark sterile reminder in the midst of life. The realists took into account new developments, including the fact that there would probably never be any "midst of life" and, possibly, no audience, after thirty years.

I thought that was excessive. There was plenty of pathos in the original assignment. Adding another, impasto, layer of pathos along with irony and the artist's fear of personal death . . . well, we were doing art, not literature. I sincerely hoped their pieces would be fatally muddled by complexity.

If you asked White Hill which group she belonged to, she would of course say, "Both." I had no idea what form her project was going to take; we had agreed early on to surprise one another, and not impede each other with suggestions. I couldn't decipher even one-tenth of her diagrams. I speak Seldenian pretty well, but have never mastered the pictographs beyond the usual travelers' vocabulary. And much of what she was scribbling on the buff sheets of paper was in no language I recognized, an arcane technical symbology.

We talked about other things. Even about the future, as lovers will. Our most probable future was simultaneous death by fire, but it was calming and harmless to make "what if?" plans, in case our hosts somehow were able to find a way around that fate. We did have a choice of many possible futures, if we indeed had more than one. White Hill had never had access to wealth before. She didn't want to live lavishly, but the idea of being able to explore all the planets excited her.

Of course she had never tried living lavishly. I hoped one day to study her reaction to it, which would be strange. Out of the box of valuables I'd brought along, I gave her a necklace, a traditional beginning-love gift on Petros. It was a network of perfect emeralds and rubies laced in gold.

She examined it closely. "How much is this worth?"

"A million marks, more or less." She started to hand it back. "Please keep it. Money has no value here, no meaning."

She was at a loss for words, which was rare enough. "I understand the gesture. But you can't expect me to value this the way you do."

"I wouldn't expect that."

"Suppose I lose it? I might just set it down somewhere."

"I know. I'll still have given it to you."

She nodded and laughed. "All right. You people are strange." She slipped the necklace on, still latched, wiggling it over her ears. The colors glowed warm and cold against her olive skin.

She kissed me, a feather, and rushed out of our room wordlessly. She passed right by a mirror without looking at it.

After a couple of hours I went to find her. Lo said he'd seen her go out the door with a lot of water. At the beach I found her footprints marching straight west to the horizon.

She was gone for two days. I was working outside when she came back, wearing nothing but the necklace. There was another necklace in her hand: she had cut off her right braid and interwoven a complex pattern of gold and silver wire into a closed loop. She slipped it over my head and pecked me on the lips and headed for the shelter. When I started to follow she stopped me with a tired gesture. "Let me sleep, eat, wash." Her voice was a hoarse whisper. "Come to me after dark."

I sat down, leaning back against a good rock, and thought about very little, touching her braid and smelling it. When it was too dark to see my feet, I went in, and she was waiting.

Δ ● ●

I spent a lot of time outside, at least in the early morning and late afternoon, studying my accumulation of rocks and ruins. I had images of every piece in my shaping box's memory, but it was easier to visualize some aspects of the project if I could walk around the elements and touch them.

Inspiration is where you find it. We'd played with an orrery in the museum in Rome, a miniature solar system that had been built of clockwork centuries before the Information Age. There was a wistful, humorous, kind of comfort in its jerky regularity.

My mental processes always turn things inside out. Find the terror and hopelessness in that comfort. I had in mind a massive but delicately balanced assemblage that would be viewed by small groups; their presence would cause it to teeter and turn ponderously. It would seem both fragile and huge (though of course the fragility would be an illusion), like the ecosystem that the Fwndyri so abruptly destroyed.

The assemblage would be mounted in such a way that it would seem always in danger of toppling off its base, but hidden weights would make that impossible. The sound of the rolling weights ought to produce a nice anxiety. Whenever a part tapped the floor, the tap would be amplified into a hollow boom.

If the viewers stood absolutely still, it would swing to a halt. As they left, they would disturb it again. I hoped it would disturb them as well.

The large technical problem was measuring the distribution of mass in each of my motley pieces. That would have been easy at home; I could rent a magnetic resonance densitometer to map their insides. There was no such thing on this planet (so rich in things I had no use for!), so I had to make do with a pair of robots and a knife edge. And then start hollowing the pieces out asymmetrically, so that once set in motion, the assemblage would tend to rotate.

I had a large number of rocks and artifacts to choose from, and was tempted to use no unifying principle at all, other than the unstable balance of the thing. Boulders and pieces of old statues and fossil machinery. The models I made of such a random collection were ambiguous, though. It was hard to tell whether they would look ominous or ludicrous, built to scale. A symbol of helplessness before an implacable enemy? Or a lurching, crashing junkpile? I decided to take a reasonably conservative approach, dignity rather than daring. After all, the audience would be Earthlings and, if the planet survived, tourists with more money than sophistication. Not my usual jury.

I was able to scavenge twenty long bars of shiny black monofiber, which would be the spokes of my irregular wheel. That would give it some unity of composition: make a cross with four similar chunks of granite at the ordinal points, and a larger chunk at the center. Then build up a web inside, monofiber lines linking bits of this and that.

Some of the people were moving their materials inside Amazonia, to work in the area marked off for the park. White Hill and I decided to stay outside. She said her project was portable, at this stage, and mine would be easy to disassemble and move.

After a couple of weeks, only fifteen artists remained with the project, inside Amazonia or out in the shelter. The others had either quit, surrendering to the passive depression that seemed to be Earth's new norm, or, in one case, committed suicide. The two from Wolf and Mijhøoven opted for coldsleep, which might be deferred suicide. About one person in three slept through it; one in three came out with some kind of treatable mental disorder.

The others went mad and died soon after reawakening, unable or unwilling to live.

Coldsleep wasn't done on Petros, although some Petrosians went to other worlds to indulge in it as a risky kind of time travel. Sleep until whatever's wrong with the world has changed. Some people even did it for financial speculation: buy up objects of art or antiques, and sleep for a century or more while their value increases. Of course their value might not increase significantly, or they might be stolen or coopted by family or government.

But if you can make enough money to buy a ticket to another planet, why not hold off until you had enough to go to a really *distant* one? Let time dilation compress the years. I could make a triangle from Petros to Skaal to Mijhøoven and back, and more than 120 years would pass, while I lived through only three, with no danger to my mind. And I could take my objects of art along with me.

White Hill had worked with coldsleep veterans, or victims. None of them had been motivated by profit, given her planet's institutionalized antimaterialism, so most of them had been suffering from some psychological ill before they slept. It was rare for them to come out of the "treatment" improved, but they did come into a world where people like White Hill could at least attend them in their madness, perhaps guide them out.

I'd been to three times as many worlds as she. But she had been to stranger places.

Δ ● ● ●

The terraformers did their job too well. The days grew cooler and cooler, and some nights snow fell. The snow on the ground persisted into mornings for a while, and then through noon, and finally it began to pile up. Those of us who wanted to work outside had to improvise cold-weather clothing.

I liked working in the cold, although all I did was direct robots. I grew up in a small town south of New Haven, where winter was long and intense. At some level I associated snow and ice with the exciting pleasures that waited for us after school. I was to have my fill of it, though.

It was obvious I had to work fast, faster than I'd originally planned, because of the increasing cold. I wanted to have everything put together and working before I disassembled it and pushed it through the airlock. The robots weren't made for cold weather, unfortunately. They had bad traction on the ice and sometimes their joints would seize up. One of them complained constantly, but of course it was the best worker, too, so I couldn't just turn it off and let it disappear under the drifts, an idea that tempted me.

White Hill often came out for a few minutes to stand and watch me and the robots struggle with the icy heavy boulders, machinery, and statuary. We took walks along the seashore that became shorter as the weather worsened. The last walk was a disaster.

We had just gotten to the beach when a sudden storm came up with a sandblast wind so violent that it blew us off our feet. We crawled back to the partial protection of the ruins and huddled together, the wind screaming so loudly that we had to shout to hear each other. The storm continued to mount and, in our terror, we decided to run for the shelter. White Hill slipped on some ice and suffered a horrible injury, a jagged piece of metal slashing her face diagonally from forehead to chin, blinding her left eye and tearing off part of her nose. Pearly bone showed through, cracked, at eyebrow, cheek, and chin. She rose up to one elbow and fell slack.

I carried her the rest of the way, immensely glad for the physical strength that made it possible. By the time we got inside she was unconscious and my white coat was a scarlet flag of blood.

A plastic-clad doctor came through immediately and did what she could to get White Hill out of immediate danger. But there was a problem with more sophisticated treatment. They couldn't bring the equipment out to our shelter, and White Hill wouldn't survive the stress of purging unless she had had a chance to heal for a while. Besides the facial wound, she had a broken elbow and collarbone and two cracked ribs.

For a week or so she was always in pain or numb. I sat with her, numb myself, her face a terrible puffed caricature of its former beauty, the wound glued up with plaskin the color of putty. Split skin of her eyelid slack over the empty socket.

The mirror wasn't visible from her bed, and she didn't ask for one, but whenever I looked away from her, her working hand came up to touch and catalogue the damage. We both knew how fortunate she was to be alive at all, and especially in an era and situation where the damage could all be repaired, given time and a little luck. But it was still a terrible thing to live with, an awful memory to keep reliving.

When she was more herself, able to talk through her ripped and pasted mouth, it was difficult for me to keep my composure. She had considerable philosophical, I suppose you could say spiritual, resources, but she was so profoundly stunned that she couldn't follow a line of reasoning very far, and usually wound up sobbing in frustration.

Sometimes I cried with her, although Petrosian men don't cry except in response to music. I had been a soldier once and had seen my ration of injury and death, and I always felt the experience had hardened me, to my detriment. But my friends who had been wounded or killed were just friends, and all of us lived then with the certainty that every day could be anybody's last one. To have the woman you love senselessly mutilated by an accident of weather was emotionally more arduous than losing a dozen companions to the steady erosion of war, a different kind of weather.

I asked her whether she wanted to forget our earlier agreement and talk about our projects. She said no; she was still working on hers, in a way, and she still wanted it to be a surprise. I did manage to distract her, playing with the shaping box. We made cartoonish representations of Lo and old Norita, and combined them in impossible sexual geometries. We shared a limited kind of sex ourselves, finally.

The doctor pronounced her well enough to be taken apart, and both of us were scourged and reappeared on the other side. White Hill was already in surgery when I woke up; there had been no reason to revive her before beginning the restorative processes.

I spent two days wandering through the blandness of Amazonia, jungle laced through concrete, quartering the huge place on foot. Most areas seemed catatonic. A few were boisterous with end-of-the-world hysteria. I checked on her progress so often that they eventually assigned a robot to call me up every hour, whether or not there was any change.

On the third day I was allowed to see her, in her sleep. She was pale but seemed completely restored. I watched her for an hour, perhaps more, when her eyes suddenly opened. The new one was blue, not green, for some reason. She didn't focus on me.

"Dreams feed art," she whispered in Petrosian; "and art feeds dreams." She closed her eyes and slept again.

Δ □

She didn't want to go back out. She had lived all her life in the tropics, even the year she spent in bondage, and the idea of returning to the ice that had slashed her was more than repugnant. Inside Amazonia it was always summer, now, the authorities trying to keep everyone happy with heat and light and jungle flowers.

I went back out to gather her things. Ten large sheets of buff paper I unstuck from our walls and stacked and rolled. The necklace, and the satchel of rare coins she had brought from Seldene, all her worldly wealth.

I considered wrapping up my own project, giving the robots instructions for its dismantling and transport, so that I could just go back inside with her and stay. But that would be chancy. I wanted to see the thing work once before I took it apart.

So I went through the purging again, although it wasn't strictly necessary; I could have sent her things through without hand-carrying them. But I wanted to make sure she was on her feet before I left her for several weeks.

She was not on her feet, but she was dancing. When I recovered from the purging, which now took only half a day, I went to her hospital room and they referred me to our new quarters, a three-room dwelling in a place called Plaza de Artistes. There were two beds in the bedroom, one a fancy medical one, but that was worlds better than trying to find privacy in a hospital.

There was a note floating in the air over the bed saying she had gone to a party in the common room. I found her in a gossamer wheelchair, teaching a hand dance to Denli om Cord, while a harpist and flautist from two different worlds tried to settle on a mutual key.

She was in good spirits. Denli remembered an engagement and I wheeled White Hill out onto a balcony that overlooked a lake full of sleeping birds, some perhaps real.

It was hot outside, always hot. There was a mist of perspiration on her face, partly from the light exercise of the dance, I supposed. In the light from below, the mist gave her face a sculpted appearance, unsparing sharpness, and there was no sign left of the surgery.

"I'll be out of the chair tomorrow," she said, "at least ten minutes at a time." She laughed, "*Stop* that!"

"Stop what?"

"Looking at me like that."

I was still staring at her face. "It's just . . . I suppose it's such a relief."

"I know." She rubbed my hand. "They showed me pictures, of before. You looked at that for so many days?"

"I saw you."

She pressed my hand to her face. The new skin was taut but soft, like a baby's. "Take me downstairs?"

Δ Δ

It's hard to describe, especially in light of later developments, disintegrations, but that night of fragile lovemaking marked a permanent change in the way we linked, or at least the way I was linked to her: I've been married twice, long and short, and have been in some kind of love a hundred times. But no woman has ever owned me before.

This is something we do to ourselves. I've had enough women who *tried* to possess me, but always was able to back or circle away, in literal preservation of self. I always felt that life was too long for one woman.

Certainly part of it is that life is not so long anymore. A larger part of it was the run through the screaming storm, her life streaming out of her, and my stewardship, or at least companionship, afterward, during her slow transformation back into health and physical beauty. The core of her had never changed, though, the stubborn serenity that I came to realize, that warm night, had finally infected me as well.

The bed was a firm narrow slab, cooler than the dark air heavy with the scent of Earth flowers. I helped her onto the bed (which instantly conformed

to her) but from then on it was she who cared for me, saying that was all
she wanted, all she really had strength for. When I tried to reverse that, she
reminded me of a holiday palindrome that has sexual overtones in both our
languages: Giving is taking is giving.

Δ Δ ●

We spent a couple of weeks as close as two people can be. I was her lover
and also her nurse, as she slowly strengthened. When she was able to spend
most of her day in normal pursuits, free of the wheelchair or "intelligent"
bed (with which we had made a threesome, at times uneasy), she urged me
to go back outside and finish up. She was ready to concentrate on her own
project, too. Impatient to do art again, a good sign.

I would not have left so soon if I had known what her project involved.
But that might not have changed anything.

As soon as I stepped outside, I knew it was going to take longer than
planned. I had known from the inside monitors how cold it was going to be,
and how many ceemetras of ice had accumulated, but I didn't really *know*
how bad it was until I was standing there, looking at my piles of materials
locked in opaque glaze. A good thing I'd left the robots inside the shelter,
and a good thing I had left a few hand tools outside. The door was buried
under two metras of snow and ice. I sculpted myself a passageway, an
application of artistic skills I'd never foreseen.

I debated calling White Hill and telling her that I would be longer than
expected. We had agreed not to interrupt each other, though, and it was likely
she'd started working as soon as I left.

The robots were like a bad comedy team, but I could only be amused by
them for an hour or so at a time. It was so cold that the water vapor from
my breath froze into an icy sheath on my beard and mustache. Breathing was
painful; deep breathing probably dangerous.

So most of the time, I monitored them from inside the shelter. I had the
place to myself; everyone else had long since gone into the dome. When I
wasn't working I drank too much, something I had not done regularly in
centuries.

It was obvious that I wasn't going to make a working model. Delicate
balance was impossible in the shifting gale. But the robots and I had our
hands full, and other grasping appendages engaged, just dismantling the
various pieces and moving them through the lock. It was unexciting but
painstaking work. We did all the laser cuts inside the shelter, allowing the
rock to come up to room temperature so it didn't spall or shatter. The air-
conditioning wasn't quite equal to the challenge, and neither were the cleaning
robots, so after a while it was like living in a foundry: everywhere a kind of
greasy slickness of rock dust, the air dry and metallic.

So it was with no regret that I followed the last slice into the airlock myself, even looking forward to the scourging if White Hill was on the other side.

She wasn't. A number of other people were missing, too. She left this note behind:

I knew from the day we were called back here what my new piece would have to be, and I knew I had to keep it from you, to spare you sadness. And to save you the frustration of trying to talk me out of it.

As you may know by now, scientists have determined that the Fwndyri indeed have sped up the Sun's evolution somehow. It will continue to warm, until in thirty or forty years there will be an explosion called the "helium flash." The Sun will become a red giant, and the Earth will be incinerated.

There are no starships left, but there is one avenue of escape. A kind of escape.

Parked in high orbit there is a huge interplanetary transport that was used in the terraforming of Mars. It's a couple of centuries older than you, but like yourself it has been excellently preserved. We are going to ride it out to a distance sufficient to survive the Sun's catastrophe, and there remain until the situation improves, or does not.

This is where I enter the picture. For our survival to be meaningful in this thousand-year war, we have to resort to coldsleep. And for a large number of people to survive centuries of coldsleep, they need my jaturnary *skills. Alone, in the ice, they would go slowly mad. Connected through the matrix of my mind, they will have a sense of community, and may come out of it intact.*

I will be gone, of course. I will be by the time you read this. Not dead, but immersed in service. I could not be revived if this were only a hundred people for a hundred days. This will be a thousand, perhaps for a thousand years.

No one else on Earth can do jaturnary, *and there is neither time nor equipment for me to transfer my ability to anyone. Even if there were, I'm not sure I would trust anyone else's skill. So I am gone.*

My only loss is losing you. Do I have to elaborate on that?

You can come if you want. In order to use the transport, I had to agree that the survivors be chosen in accordance with the Earth's strict class system—starting with dear Norita, and from that pinnacle, on down—but they were willing to make exceptions for all of the visiting artists. You have until mid-Deciembre to decide; the ship leaves Januar first.

If I know you at all, I know you would rather stay behind and die. Perhaps the prospect of living "in" me could move you past your fear of coldsleep; your aversion to jaturnary. *If not, not.*

I love you more than life. But this is more than that. Are we what we are?

W. H.

The last sentence is a palindrome in her language, not mine, that I believe has some significance beyond the obvious.

● ● □

I did think about it for some time. Weighing a quick death, or even a slow one, against spending centuries locked frozen in a tiny room with Norita and her ilk. Chattering on at the speed of synapse, and me unable to not listen.

I have always valued quiet, and the eternity of it that I face is no more dreadful than the eternity of quiet that preceded my birth.

If White Hill were to be at the other end of those centuries of torture, I know I could tolerate the excruciation. But she was dead now, at least in the sense that I would never see her again.

Another woman might have tried to give me a false hope, the possibility that in some remote future the process of *jaturnary* would be advanced to the point where her personality could be recovered. But she knew how unlikely that would be even if teams of scientists could be found to work on it, and years could be found for them to work in. It would be like unscrambling an egg.

Maybe I would even do it, though, if there were just some chance that, when I was released from that din of garrulous bondage, there would be something like a real world, a world where I could function as an artist. But I don't think there will even be a world where I can function as a man.

There probably won't be any humanity at all, soon enough. What they did to the Sun they could do to all of our stars, one assumes. They win the war, the Extermination, as my parent called it. Wrong side exterminated.

Of course the Fwndyri might not find White Hill and her charges. Even if they do find them, they might leave them preserved as an object of study.

The prospect of living on eternally under those circumstances, even if there were some growth to compensate for the immobility and the company, holds no appeal.

● □

What I did in the time remaining before mid-Deciembre was write this account. Then I had it translated by a xenolinguist into a form that she said could be decoded by any creature sufficiently similar to humanity to make any sense of the story. Even the Fwndyri, perhaps. They're human enough to want to wipe out a competing species.

I'm looking at the preliminary sheets now, English down the left side and a jumble of dots, squares, and triangles down the right. Both sides would have looked equally strange to me a few years ago.

White Hill's story will be conjoined to a standard book that starts out with basic mathematical principles, in dots and squares and triangles, and moves from that into physics, chemistry, biology. Can you go from biology to the human heart? I have to hope so. If this is read by alien eyes, long after the last human breath is stilled, I hope it's not utter gibberish.

□

So I will take this final sheet down to the translator and then deliver the whole thing to the woman who is going to transfer it to permanent sheets of platinum, which will be put in a prominent place aboard the transport. They could last a million years, or ten million, or more. After the Sun is a cinder, and the ship is a frozen block enclosing a thousand bits of frozen flesh, she will live on in this small way.

So now my work is done. I'm going outside, to the quiet.

SOME LIKE IT COLD

John Kessel

▼

Here's a stylish, bleak, and blackly ironic look at the future of the Entertainment Industry. If you think it's a corrupt business now, hang around—you ain't seen nothing yet . . .

Born in Buffalo, New York, John Kessel now lives with his family in Raleigh, North Carolina, where he is a professor of American literature and creative writing at North Carolina State University. Kessel made his first sale in 1975, and has since become a frequent contributor to *Asimov's Science Fiction* and *The Magazine of Fantasy & Science Fiction*, as well as to many other magazines and anthologies. Kessel's first solo novel, *Good News from Outer Space*, was released in 1989 to wide critical acclaim, but before that he had made his mark on the genre primarily as a writer of highly imaginative, finely crafted short stories, many of which have since been assembled in his acclaimed collection *Meeting in Infinity*. He won a Nebula Award in 1983 for his superlative novella "Another Orphan," which was also a Hugo finalist that year, and has been released as an individual book. His story "Buffalo" won the Theodore Sturgeon Award in 1991. His other books include the novel *Freedom Beach*, written in collaboration with James Patrick Kelly. His most recent book is an anthology of stories from the famous Sycamore Hill Writers Workshop (which he also helps to run), called *Intersections,* coedited with Mark L. Van Name and Richard Butner. His stories have appeared in our First, Second (in collaboration with James Patrick Kelly), Fourth, Sixth, and Eighth Annual Collections. He is currently finishing a new novel, *Corrupting Dr. Nice.*

Her heroes were Abraham Lincoln and Albert Einstein. Lincoln was out of the question, but with a little work I could look Einsteinesque. I grew a dark mustache, adopted wild graying hair. From wardrobe I requisitioned a pair of wool slacks, a white cotton shirt, a gabardine jacket with narrow lapels. The shoes were my own, my prized possession—genuine leather, Australian copies of mid twentieth-century brogues, comfortable, well broken in. The prep-room mirror reflected back a handsomer, taller, younger relative of old Albert, a cross between Einstein and her psychiatrist Dr. Greenson.

The moment-universes surrounding the evening of Saturday, August 4 were so thoroughly burned—tourists, biographers, conspiracy hunters, masturbators—that there was no sense arriving then. Besides, I wanted to get a taste of the old LA, before the quake. So I selected the Friday evening 18:00 PDT moment-universe. I materialized in a stall in the men's room at the Santa Monica Municipal Airport. Some aim for deserted places; I like airports, train stations, bus terminals. Lots of strangers if you've missed some detail of costume. Public transport easily available. Crowds to lose oneself in. The portable unit, disguised as an overnight bag, never looks out of place. I stopped in a shop and bought a couple of packs of Luckies. At the Hertz counter I rented a navy blue Plymouth with push-button transmission, threw my canvas camera bag and overnight case into the back and, checking the map, puzzled out the motel address on Wilshire Boulevard that Research had found for me.

The hotel was ersatz Spanish, pink stucco and a red tile roof, a colonnade around a courtyard pool where a teenage boy in white T-shirt and DA haircut leaned on a cleaning net and flirted with a couple of fifteen-year-old girls. I sat in the shadowed doorway of my room, smoked a Lucky and watched until a fat woman in a caftan came out and yelled at the boy to get back to work. The girls giggled.

The early evening I spent driving around. In Santa Monica I saw the pre-tsunami pier, the one she would tell Greenson she was going to visit Saturday night before she changed her mind and stayed home. I ate at the Dancers: a slab of prime rib, a baked potato the size of a football, a bottle of zinfandel. Afterward I drove my Plymouth along the Miracle Mile. I rolled down the windows and let the warm air wash over me, inspecting the strip joints, theaters, bars, and hookers. A number of the women, looking like her in cotton-candy hair and tight dresses, gave me the eye as I cruised by.

I pulled into the lot beside a club called the Blue Note. Over the door a blue neon martini glass swamped a green neon olive in gold neon gin. Inside I ordered a scotch and listened to a trio play jazz. A thin white guy with a goatee strangled his saxophone: somewhere in there might be a melody. These cutting-edge late-moderns thought they had the future augured. The future would be cool and atonal, they thought. No squares allowed. They didn't understand that the future, like the present, would be dominated by saps, and the big rush of 2043 would be barbershop quartets.

I sipped scotch. A brutal high, alcohol, like putting your head in a vise. I liked it. I smoked a couple more Luckies, layering a nicotine buzz over the alcohol. I watched couples in the dim corners of booths talk about their pasts and their futures, all those words prelude to going to bed. Back in Brentwood she was spending another sleepless night harassed by calls telling her to leave Bobby Kennedy alone.

A woman with dark Jackie hair, black gloves, and a very low-cut dress sat down on the stool next to me. The song expired and there was a smattering of applause. "I hate this modern crap, don't you?" the woman said.

"It's emblematic of the times," I said.

She gave me a look, decided to laugh. "You can have the times."

"I've seen worse," I said.

"You're not American, are you? The accent."

"I was born in Germany."

"Ah. So you've seen bad times?"

I sipped my scotch. "You could say so." Her eyelids were heavy with shadow, eyelashes a centimeter long. Pale pink lipstick made her thin lips look cool; I wondered if they really were. "Let me buy you a drink."

"Thanks." She watched me fumble with the queer, nineteenth-century style currency. Pyramids with eyes on them, redeemable in silver on demand. I bought her a gin and tonic. "My name's Carol," she told me.

"I am Detlev."

"Detleff? Funny name."

"Not so common, even in Germany."

"So Detleff, what brings you to LA? You come over the Berlin Wall?"

"I'm here to see a movie star."

She snorted. "Won't find any in here."

"I think you could be a movie star, Carol."

"You're not going to believe this, Detleff, but I've heard that line before."

"You'll have to offer me another then."

We flirted through three drinks. She told me she was lonely, I told her I was a stranger. We fell toward a typical liaison of the Penicillin Era: we learned enough about each other (who knew how much of it true?) not to let what we didn't know come between us and what we wanted. Her image of me was compounded by her own fantasies. I didn't have so many illusions. Or maybe mine were larger still, since I knew next-to-nothing about these people other than what I'd gleaned from images projected on various screens. An image had brought me here; images were my job. They had something to do with reality, but more to do with desire.

I studied the cleavage displayed by Carol's dress, she leaned against my shoulder, and from this we generated a lust we imagined would turn to sweet compassion, make up for our losses, and leave us blissfully complete in the same place. We would clutch each other's bodies until we were spent, lie holding each other close, our souls commingled, the first moment of a perfect marriage that would extend forward from this night in an endless string of equally fulfilling nights. Then we'd part in the morning and never see each other again. That was the dream. I followed her back to her apartment and we did our best to produce it. Afterward I lay awake thinking of Gabrielle, just after we'd married, sunbathing on the screened beach at Nice. I'd watched her, as had the men who passed by. How much of her wanted us to look at her? Was there any difference, in her mind, between my regard and theirs?

I left Carol asleep with the dawn coming up through the window, made my way back to the pink hotel, and got some sleep of my own.

Saturday I spent touring pre-quake LA. I indulged vices I could not indulge in Munich in 2043. I smoked many cigarettes. I walked outside in direct sunlight. I bought a copy of the Wilhelm edition of the *I Ching*, printed on real paper. At midafternoon I stepped into a diner and ordered a bacon cheeseburger, rare, with lettuce and tomato and a side of fries. My mouth watered as the waitress set it in front of me, but after two bites I felt overcome by a wave of nausea. Hands sticky with blood and mayonnaise, I watched the grease congeal in the corner of the plate.

So far, so good. I was a fan of the dirty pleasures of the twentieth century. Things were so much more complicated then. People walked the streets under the shadow of the bomb. They all knew, at some almost biological level, that they might be vaporized at any second. Their blood vibrated with angst. Even the blonde ones. I imagined my ancestors half a world away in a country they expected momentarily to turn into a radioactive battleground, carrying their burden of guilt through the Englischer Garten. Sober Adenauer, struggling to stitch together half a nation. None of them fat, bored, or decadent.

And Marilyn, the world over, was their goddess. That improbable female body, that infantile voice, that oblivious demeanor.

Architecturally, LA 1962 was a disappointment. There was the appropriate amount of kitsch, hot-dog stands shaped like hot dogs and chiropractors' offices like flying saucers, but the really big skyscrapers that would come down in the quake hadn't been built yet. Maybe some of them wouldn't be built in this time-line anymore, thanks to me. By now my presence, through the butterfly effect, had already set this history off down another path from the one of my home. Anything I did toppled dominoes. Perhaps Carol's life would be ruined by the memory of our night of perfect love. Perhaps the cigarettes I bought saved crucial lives. Perhaps the breeze of my Plymouth's passing brought rain to Belgrade, drought to India. For better or worse, who could say?

I killed time into the early evening. By now she was going through the two-hour session with Greenson trying to shore up her personality against that night's depression.

At 9:00 I took my camera bag and the portable unit and got into the rental car. It was still too early, but I was so keyed up I couldn't sit still. I drove up the Pacific Coast Highway, walked along the beach at Malibu, then turned around and headed back. Sunset Boulevard twisted through the hills. The lights of the houses flickered between trees. In Brentwood I had some trouble finding Carmelina, drove past, then doubled back. Marilyn's house was on Fifth Helena, a short street off Carmelina ending in a cul-de-sac. I parked at the end, slung my bags over my shoulder, and walked back.

A brick and stucco wall shielded the house from the street. I circled round through the neighbor's yard, pushed through the bougainvillea and approached from the back. It was a modest hacienda-style ranch, a couple of bedrooms, tile roof. The patio lights were off and the water in the pool lay smooth as dark glass. Lights shone from the end bedroom to the far left.

First problem would be to get rid of Eunice Murray, her companion and housekeeper. If what had happened in our history was true in this one, she'd gone to sleep at midevening. I stepped quietly through the back door, found her in her bedroom and slapped a sedative patch onto her forearm, holding my hand across her mouth against her struggling until she was out.

A long phone cord snaked down the hall from the living room and under the other bedroom door. The door was locked. Outside, I pushed through the shrubs, mucking up my shoes in the soft soil, reached in through the bars over the opened window, and pushed aside the blackout curtains. Marilyn sprawled face down across the bed, right arm dangling off the side, receiver clutched in her hand. I found the unbarred casement window on the adjacent side of the house, broke it open, then climbed inside. Her breathing was deep and irregular. Her skin was clammy. Only the faintest pulse at her neck.

I rolled her onto her back, got my bag, pried back her eyelid and shone a light into her eye. Her pupil barely contracted. I had come late on purpose, but this was not good.

I gave her a shot of apomorphine, lifted her off the bed and shouldered her toward the bathroom. She was surprisingly light—gaunt, even. I could feel her ribs. In the bathroom, full of plaster and junk from the remodelers, I held her over the toilet until she vomited. No food, but some undigested capsules. That would have been a good sign, except she habitually pierced them with a pin so they'd work faster. There was no way of telling how much Nembutal she had in her bloodstream.

I dug my thumb into the crook of her elbow, forcing the tendon. Did she inhale more strongly? "Wake up, Norma Jean," I said. "Time to wake up." No reaction.

I took her back to the bed and got the blood filter out of my camera bag. The studio'd had me practicing on indigents hired from the state. I wiped a pharmacy's worth of pill bottles from the flimsy table next to the bed and set up the machine. The shunt slipped easily into the artery in her arm, and I fiddled with the flow until the readout went green. What with one thing and another I had a busy half hour before she was resting in bed, bundled up, feet elevated, asleep but breathing normally, God in his heaven, and her blood circulating merrily through the filter like money through my bank account.

I went outside and smoked a cigarette. The stars were out and a breeze had kicked up. On the tile threshold outside the front door words were emblazoned: "Cursum Perficio." *I am finishing my journey*. I looked in on Mrs. Murray. Still out. I went back and sat in the bedroom. The place was a mess. Forests of pill bottles covered every horizontal surface. A stack of Sinatra records sat on the record player. On top: "High Hopes." Loose-leaf binders lay scattered all over the floor. I picked one up. It was a script for *Something's Got to Give*.

I read through the script. It wasn't very good. About 2:00 a.m. she moaned and started to move. I slapped a clarifier patch onto her arm. It wouldn't push the pentobarbital out of her system any faster, but when it began to take hold it would make her feel better.

About 3:00 the blood filter beeped. I removed the shunt, sat her up, made her drink a liter of electrolyte. It took her a while to get it all down. She looked at me through fogged eyes. She smelled sour and did not look like the most beautiful woman in the world. "What happened?" she mumbled.

"You took too many pills. You're going to be all right."

I helped her into a robe, then walked her down the hallway and around the living room until she began to take some of the weight herself. At one end of the room hung a couple of lurid Mexican Day of the Dead masks, at the other a framed portrait of Lincoln. When I got tired of facing down the leering ghouls and honest Abe, I took her outside and we marched around the pool in the darkness. The breeze wrote cat's paws on the surface of the water. After a while she began to come around. She tried to pull away but was weak as a baby. "Let me go," she mumbled.

"You want to stop walking?"

"I want to sleep," she said.

"Keep walking." We circled the pool for another quarter hour. In the distance I heard sparse traffic on Sunset; nearer the breeze rustled the fan palms. I was sweaty, she was cold.

"Please," she whined. "Let's stop."

I let her down onto a patio chair, went inside, found some coffee and set a pot brewing. I brought a blanket out, wrapped her in it, poked her to keep her awake until the coffee was ready. Eventually she sat there sipping coffee, holding the cup in both hands to warm them, hair down in her eyes and eyelashes gummed together. She looked tired. "How are you?" I asked.

"Alive. Bad luck." She started to cry. "Cruel, all of them, all those bastards. Oh, Jesus . . ."

I let her go on for a while. I gave her a handkerchief and she dried her eyes, blew her nose. The most beautiful woman in the world. "Who are you?" she asked.

"My name is Detlev Gruber. Call me Det."

"What are you doing here? Where's Mrs. Murray?"

"You don't remember? You sent her home."

She took a sip of coffee, watching me over the rim of the cup.

"I'm here to help you, Marilyn. To rescue you."

"Rescue me?"

"I know how hard things are, how lonely you've been. I knew that you would try to kill yourself."

"I was just trying to get some sleep."

"Do you really think that's all there is to it?"

"Listen, mister, I don't know who you are but I don't need your help and if you don't get out of here pretty soon I'm going to call the police." Her voice trailed off pitifully at the end. "I'm sorry," she said.

"Don't be sorry. I'm here to save you from all this."

Hands shaking, she put down the cup. I had never seen a face more vulnerable. She tried to hide it, but her expression was full of need. I felt an urge to protect her that, despite the fact she was a wreck, was pure sex. "I'm cold," she said. "Can we go inside?"

We went inside. We sat in the living room, she on the sofa and I in an uncomfortable Spanish chair, and I told her things about her life that nobody should have known but her. The abortions. The suicide attempts. The Kennedy affairs. The way Sinatra treated her. More than that, the fear of loneliness, the fear of insanity, the fear of aging. I found myself warming to the role of rescuer. I really did want to hold her, for more than one reason. She was not able to keep up her hostility in the face of the knowledge that I was telling her the simple truth. Miller had written how grateful she was every time he'd saved her life, and it looked like that reaction was coming through for me now. She'd always liked being rescued, and the men who rescued her.

The clarifier might have had something to do with it, too. Finally she protested, "How do you know all this?"

"This is going to be the hardest part, Marilyn. I know because I'm from the future. If I had not shown up here, you would have died tonight. It's recorded history.''

She laughed. ''From the future?''

''Absolutely.''

''Right.''

''I'm not lying to you, Marilyn. If I didn't care, would you be alive now?''

She pulled the blanket tighter around her. ''What does the future want with me?''

''You're the most famous actress of your era. Your death would be a great tragedy, and we want to prevent that.''

''What good does this do me? I'm still stuck in the same shit.''

''You don't have to be.'' She tried to look skeptical but hope was written in every tremble of her body. It was frightening. ''I want you to come with me back to the future, Marilyn.''

She stared at me. ''You must be crazy. I wouldn't know anybody. No friends, no family.''

''You don't have any family. Your mother is in an institution. And where were your friends tonight?''

She put her hand to her head, rubbed her forehead, a gesture so full of troubled intelligence that I had a sudden sense of her as a real person, a grown woman in a lot of trouble. ''You don't want to mess with me,'' she said. ''I'm not worth it. I'm nothing but trouble.''

''I can cure your trouble. In the future we have ways. No one here really cares for you, Marilyn, no one truly understands you. That dark pit of despair that opens up inside you—we can fill it. We can heal the wounds you've had since you were a little girl, make up for all the neglect you've suffered, keep you young forever. We have these powers. It's my job to correct the mistakes of the past, for special people. You're one of them. I have a team of caregivers waiting for you, a home, emotional support, understanding.''

''Yeah. Another institution. I can't take it.'' I came over, sat beside her, lowered my voice, looked her in the eyes. Time for the closer. ''You know that poem—that Yeats poem?''

''What poem?''

'' 'Never Give All the Heart.' '' Research had made me memorize it. It was one of her favorites.

> *"Never give all the heart, for love,*
> *Will hardly seem worth thinking of*
> *To passionate women if it seem*

Certain, and they never dream
That it fades out from kiss to kiss
For everything that's lovely is
But a brief, dreamy, kind delight . . ."

She stopped me. "What about it?" Her voice was edgy.

"Just that life doesn't have to be like the poem, brief, and you don't have to suffer. You don't have to give all the heart, and lose."

She sat there, wound in the blanket. Clearly I had touched something in her.

"Think about it," I said. I went outside and smoked another Lucky. When I'd started working for DAA I'd considered this a glamour job. Exotic times, famous people. And I was good at it. A quick study, smart, adaptable. Sincere. I was so good that Gabrielle came to hate me, and left.

After a considerable while Marilyn came outside, the blanket over her head and shoulders like an Indian.

"Well, kemosabe?" I asked.

Despite herself, she smiled. Although the light was dim, the crow's feet at the corners of her eyes were visible. "If I don't like it, will you bring me back?"

"You'll like it. But if you don't I promise I'll bring you back."

"Okay. What do I have to do?"

"Just pack a few things to take with you—the most important ones."

I waited while she threw some clothes into a suitcase. She took the Lincoln portrait off the wall and put it in on top. I bagged the blood filter and set up the portable unit in the living room.

"Maf!" she said.

"What?"

"My dog!" She looked crushed, as if she were about to collapse. "Who'll take care of Maf?"

"Mrs. Murray will."

"She hates him! I can't trust her." She was disintegrating. "I can't go. This isn't a good idea."

"Where is Maf? We'll take him."

We went out to the guest house. The place stunk. The dog, sleeping on an old fur coat, launched himself at me, yapping, as soon as we opened the door. It was one of those inbred overgroomed toy poodles that you want to drop kick into the next universe. She picked him up, cooed over him, made me get a bag of dog food and his water dish. I gritted my teeth.

In the living room I moved the chair aside and made her stand in the center of the room while I laid the wire circle around us to outline the field. She was nervous. I held her hand, she held the dog. "Here we go, Marilyn."

I touched the switch on the case. Marilyn's living room receded from us in all directions, we fell like pebbles into a dark well, and from infinitely far away the transit stage at DAA rushed forward to surround us. The dog growled. Marilyn swayed, put a hand to her head. I held her arm to steady her.

From the control booth Scoville and a nurse came up to us. The nurse took Marilyn's other side. "Marilyn, this is a nurse who's going to help you get some rest. And this is Derek Scoville, who's running this operation."

We got her into the suite and the doctors shot her full of metabolic cleansers. I promised her I'd take care of Maf, then pawned the dog off on the staff. I held her hand, smiled reassuringly, sat with her until she went to sleep. Lying there she looked calm, confident. She liked being cared for; she was used to it. Now she had a whole new world waiting to take care of her. She thought.

It was all up to me.

I went to the prep room, showered, and switched to street clothes: an onyx Singapore silk shirt, cotton baggies, spex. The weather report said it was a bad UV day: I selected a broad-brimmed hat. I was inspecting my shoes, which looked ruined from the muck from Marilyn's garden, when a summons from Scoville showed in the corner of my spex: meet them in the conference room. Levine and Sally House were there, and the doctor, and Jason Cryer from publicity. "So, what do you think?" Levine asked me.

"She's in pretty rough shape. Physically she can probably take it, but emotionally she's a wreck."

"Tomorrow we'll inject her with nanorepair devices," the doctor said. "She's probably had some degree of renal damage, if not worse."

"Christ, have you seen her scars?" Levine said. "How many operations has she had? Did they just take a cleaver to them back then?"

"They took a cleaver first, then an airbrush," Sally said.

"We'll fix the scars," said Cryer. Legend had it the most dangerous place in Hollywood was between Cryer and a news camera. "And Detlev here will be her protector, right Det? After all, you saved her life. You're her friend. Her dad. Her lover, if it comes to that."

"Right," I said. I thought about Marilyn, asleep at last. What expectations did *she* have?

Scoville spoke for the first time. "I want us into production within three weeks. We've got eighty million already invested in this. Sally, you can crank publicity up to full gain. We're going to succeed where all the others have failed. We're going to put the first viable Marilyn on the wire. She

may be a wreck, but she wants to be here. Not like Paramount's ver
sion.''

"That's where we're smart," Cryer said. "We take into account the psychological factors.''

I couldn't stand much more. After the meeting I rode down to the lobby
and checked out of the building. As I approached the front doors I could see
a crowd of people had gathered outside in the bright sunlight. Faces slick
with factor 400 sunscreen, they shouted and carried picket signs. "End Time
Exploitation.'' "Information, not People.'' "Hands off the Past.''

Not one gram of evidence existed that a change in a past moment-universe
had ever affected our own time. They were as separate as two sides of a coin.
Of course it was true that once you burned a particular universe you could
never go back. But with an eternity of moment-universes to exploit, who
cared?

The chronological protection fanatics would be better off taking care of
the historicals who were coming to litter up the present, the ones who
couldn't adjust, or outlasted their momentary celebrity, or turned out not
to be as interesting to the present as their sponsors had imagined. A lot of
money had been squandered on bad risks. Who really wanted to listen to
new compositions by Gershwin? How was Shakespeare even going to
understand the twenty-first century, let alone write VR scripts that anybody
would want to experience?

I sneaked out the side door and caught the metro down at the corner. Rode
the train through Hollywood and up to my arcology.

In the newsstand I uploaded the latest trades into my spex, then stopped
into the men's room to get my shoes polished. While the valet worked I
smoked the last of my Luckies and checked the news. Jesus, still hotter than
a pistol, was the lead on *Variety*. He smiled, new teeth, clean shaven, homely
little Jew, but even through the holo he projected a lethal charisma. That one
was making Universal rich. Who would have thought that a religious mystic
with an Aramaic accent would become such a talk-show shark, his virtual
image the number one teleromantics dream date? "Jesus' *Laying On of Hands*
is the most spiritual experience I've ever had over fiberoptic VR," gushed
worldwide recording megastar Daphne Overdone.

On *Hollywood Grapevine*, gossip maven Hedley O'Connor reported Elisen-
brunnen GMBH, which owned DAA, was unhappy with third-quarter earn-
ings. If Scoville went down, the new boss would pull the plug on all his
projects. My contractual responsibilities would then, as they say, be at an
end.

"What a mess you made of these shoes, Herr Gruber," the valet muttered
in German. I switched off my spex and watched him finish. The arco hired
a lot of indigents. It was cheap, and good PR, but the valet was my personal

reclamation project. His unruly head of hair danced as he buffed my shoes to a high luster. He looked up at me. "How is that?"

"Looks fine." I fished out a twenty-dollar piece. He watched me with his watery, sad, intelligent eyes. His brown hair was going gray.

"I see you got a mustache, like mine," he said.

"Only for work. For a while I need to look like you, Albert."

I gave him the twenty and went up to my room.

THE DEATH OF CAPTAIN FUTURE

Allen Steele

▼

Here's a good old-fashioned, wild-and-woolly Space Opera, complete with space pirates and even Bug-Eyed Monsters of a sort . . . but a Space Opera with a wry satirical edge that's decidedly modern, as one of the greatest heroes of the Pulp Era of SF collides head-on with an unsympathetic and unromantically hard-edged new century.

Allen Steele made his first sale to *Asimov's Science Fiction* magazine in 1988, soon following it up with a long string of other sales to *Asimov's,* as well as to markets such as *The Magazine of Fantasy & Science Fiction* and *Science Fiction Age.* In 1990, he published his critically acclaimed first novel, *Orbital Decay,* which subsequently won the *Locus* Poll as Best First Novel of the year, and soon Steele was being compared to Golden Age Heinlein by no less an authority than Gregory Benford. His other books include the novels *Clarke County, Space; Lunar Descent;* and *Labyrinth of Night.* His most recent books are a collection, *Rude Astronauts;* a novella published as an individual book, *The Weight;* and a new novel, *The Tranquillity Alternative.* Born in Nashville, Tennessee, he has worked for a variety of newspapers and magazines, covering science and business assignments, and is now a full-time writer living in St. Louis, Missouri, with his wife, Linda, and their dog, Zack.

The name of Captain Future, the supreme foe of all evil and evildoers, was known to every inhabitant of the Solar System.

That tall, cheerful, red-haired young adventurer of ready laugh and flying fists was the implacable Nemesis of all oppressors and exploiters of the System's human and planetary races. Combining a gay audacity with an unswervable purposefulness and an unparalleled mastery of science, he had blazed a brilliant trail across the nine worlds in defense of the right.

—Edmond Hamilton, *Captain Future and the Space Emperor* (1940)

This is the true story of how Captain Future died.

We were crossing the inner belt, coasting toward our scheduled rendezvous with Ceres, when the message was received by the ship's comlink.

"Rohr . . . ? Rohr, wake up, please."

The voice coming from the ceiling was tall, dark, and handsome, sampled from one of the old Hercules vids in the captain's collection. It penetrated the darkness of my quarters on the mid-deck where I lay asleep after standing an eight-hour watch on the bridge.

I turned my head to squint at the computer terminal next to my bunk. Lines of alphanumeric code scrolled down the screen, displaying the routine systems-checks and updates that, as second officer, I was supposed to be monitoring at all times, even when I was off-duty and dead to the world. No red-bordered emergency messages, though; at first glance, everything looked copasetic.

Except the time. It was 0335 Zulu, the middle of the goddamn night.

"Rohr?" The voice was a little louder now. *"Mister Furland? Please wake up. . . ."*

I groaned and rolled over. "Okay, okay, I'm awake. What'dya want, Brain?"

The Brain. It was bad enough that the ship's AI sounded like Steve Reeves; it also had to have a stupid name like The Brain. On every vessel on which I had served, crewmembers had given their AIs human names—Rudy, Beth, Kim, George, Stan, Lisa, dubbed after friends or family members or deceased shipmates—or nicknames, either clever or overused: Boswell, Isaac, Slim, Flash, Ramrod, plus the usual Hals and Datas from the nostalgia buffs. I once held down a gig on a lunar tug where the AI was called Fughead—as in *Hey, Fughead, gimme the traffic grid for Tycho Station*—but no one but a bonehead would give their AI a silly-ass moniker like The Brain.

No one but Captain Future, that is . . . and I still hadn't decided whether or not my current boss was a bonehead, or just insane.

"The captain asked me to awaken you," The Brain said. *"He wants you on the bridge at once. He says that it's urgent."*

I checked the screen again. "I don't see anything urgent."

"Captain's orders, Mr. Furland." The ceiling fluorescents began to slowly brighten behind their cracked and dusty panes, causing me to squint and clap my hand over my eyes. *"If you don't report to the bridge in ten minutes, you'll be docked one hour time-lost and a mark will be entered on your union card."*

Threats like that usually don't faze me—everyone loses a few hours or gains a few marks during a long voyage—but I couldn't afford a bad service report now. In two more days the TBSA *Comet* would reach Ceres, where I was scheduled to join up with the *Jove Commerce*, outbound for Callisto. I had been lucky to get this far, and I didn't want my next CO to ground me just because of a bad report from my previous captain.

"Okay," I muttered. "Tell 'em I'm on my way."

I swung my legs over the side and felt around for where I had dropped my clothes on the deck. I could have used a rinse, a shave, and a nice long meditation in the head, not to mention a mug of coffee and a muffin from the galley, but it was obvious that I wasn't going to get that.

Music began to float from the walls, an orchestral overture that gradually rose in volume. I paused, my calves halfway into the trouser legs, as the strings soared upward, gathering heroic strength. German opera. Wagner. *The Flight of the Valkyries*, for God's sake. . . .

"Cut it out, Brain," I said.

The music stopped in mid-chord. *"The captain thought it would help rouse you."*

"I'm roused." I stood up and pulled my trousers the rest of the way on. In the dim light, I glimpsed a small motion near the corner of my compartment beside the locker; one moment it was there, then it was gone. "There's a cockroach in here," I said. "Wanna do something about it?"

"I'm sorry, Rohr. I have tried to disinfect the vessel, but so far I have been unable to locate all the nests. If you'll leave your cabin door unlocked while you're gone, I'll send a drone inside to . . ."

"Never mind." I zipped up my pants, pulled on a sweatshirt and looked around for my stikshoes. They were kicked under my bunk; I knelt down on the threadbare carpet and pulled them out. "I'll take care of it myself."

The Brain meant nothing by that comment; it was only trying to get rid of another pest which had found its way aboard the *Comet* before the freighter had departed from Lagrange Four. Cockroaches, fleas, ants, even the occasional mouse; they managed to get into any vessel that regularly rendezvoused with near-Earth spaceports, but I had never been on any ship so infested as the *Comet*. Yet I wasn't about to leave my cabin door unlocked. One of a few inviolable union rules I still enjoyed aboard this ship was the ability to seal my cabin, and I didn't want to give the captain a chance to go poking through my stuff. He was convinced that I was carrying contraband with me to Ceres Station, and even though he was right—two fifths of lunar mash whiskey, a traditional coming-aboard present for my next commanding officer—I didn't want him pouring good liquor down the sink because of Association regulations no one else bothered to observe.

I pulled on my shoes, fastened a utility belt around my waist and left the cabin, carefully locking the door behind me with my thumbprint. A short, upward-curving corridor took me past the closed doors of two other crew cabins, marked CAPTAIN and FIRST OFFICER. The captain was already on the bridge, and I assumed that Jeri was with him.

A manhole led to the central access shaft and the carousel. Before I went up to the bridge, though, I stopped by the wardroom to fill a squeezebulb with coffee from the pot. The wardroom was a disaster: a dinner tray had been left on the table, discarded food wrappers lay on the floor, and a small spider-like robot waded in the galley's sink, waging solitary battle against the crusty cookware that had been abandoned there. The captain had been here recently; I was surprised that he hadn't summoned me to clean up after him. At least there was some hot coffee left in the carafe, although judging from its odor and viscosity it was probably at least ten hours old; I toned it down with sugar and half-sour milk from the fridge before I poured it into a squeezebulb.

As always, the pictures on the wardroom walls caught my eye: framed reproductions of covers from ancient pulp magazines well over a hundred years old. The magazines themselves, crumbling and priceless, were bagged and hermetically sealed within a locker in the Captain's quarters. Lurid paintings of fishbowl-helmeted spacemen fighting improbable alien monsters and mad scientists that, in turn, menaced buxom young women in see-thru outfits. The adolescent fantasies of the last century—"Planets In Peril," "Quest Beyond the Stars," "Star Trail to Glory"—and above them all, printed in a bold swath across the top of each cover, a title . . .

CAPTAIN FUTURE

Man of Tomorrow

At that moment, my reverie was broken by a harsh voice coming from the ceiling:

"Furland! Where are you?"

"In the wardroom, Captain." I pinched off the lip of the squeezebulb and sealed it with a catheter, then clipped it to my belt. "Just grabbing some coffee. I'll be up there in a minute."

"You got sixty seconds to find your duty station or I'll dock your pay for your last shift! Now hustle your lazy butt up here!"

"Coming right now. . . ." I walked out of the wardroom, heading up the corridor toward the shaft. "Toad," I whispered under my breath when I was through the hatch and out of earshot from the ship's comnet. Who's calling who lazy?

Captain Future, Man of Tomorrow. God help us if that were true.

Ten minutes later a small ship shaped like an elongated teardrop rose from an underground hangar on the lunar surface. It was the Comet, *the super-swift craft of the Futuremen, known far and wide through the System as the swiftest ship in space.*

—Hamilton, *Calling Captain Future* (1940)

My name's Rohr Furland. For better or worse, I'm a spacer, just like my father and his mother before him.

Call it family tradition. Grandma was one of the original beamjacks who helped build the first powersat in Earth orbit before she immigrated to the Moon, where she conceived my dad as the result of a one-night stand with some nameless moondog who was killed in a blowout only two days later. Dad grew up as an unwanted child in Descartes Station; he ran away at eighteen and stowed away aboard a Skycorp freighter to Earth, where he lived like a stray dog in Memphis before he got homesick and signed up with a Russian company looking for native-born selenians. Dad got home in time to see Grandma through her last years, fight in the Moon War on the side of the Pax Astra and, not incidentally, meet my mother, who was a geologist at Tycho Station.

I was born in the luxury of a two-room apartment beneath Tycho on the first anniversary of the Pax's independence. I'm told that my dad celebrated my arrival by getting drunk on cheap luna wine and balling the midwife who had delivered me. It's remarkable that my parents stayed together long enough for me to graduate from suit camp. Mom went back to Earth while Dad and I stayed on the Moon to receive the benefits of full citizenship in the Pax: Class A oxygen cards, good for air even if we were unemployed and dead broke. Which was quite often, in Dad's case.

All of which makes me a mutt, a true son of a bastard, suckled on air bottles and moonwalking before I was out of my diapers. On my sixteenth birthday, I was given my union card and told to get a job; two weeks before my eighteenth birthday, the LEO shuttle that had just hired me as a cargo handler touched down on a landing strip in Galveston, and with the aid of an exoskeleton I walked for the first time on Earth. I spent one week there, long enough for me to break my right arm by falling on a Dallas sidewalk, lose my virginity to an El Paso whore, and get one hell of a case of agoraphobia from all that wide-open Texas landscape. Fuck the cradle of humanity and the horse it rode in on; I caught the next boat back to the Moon and turned eighteen with a birthday cake that had no candles.

Twelve years later, I had handled almost every union job someone with my qualifications could hold—dock slob, cargo grunt, navigator, life support chief, even a couple of second-mate assignments—on more vessels than I could count, ranging from orbital tugs and lunar freighters to passenger shuttles and Apollo-class ore haulers. None of these gigs had ever lasted much longer than a year; in order to guarantee equal opportunity for all its members, the union shifted people from ship to ship, allowing only captains and first-mates to remain with their vessels for longer than eighteen months. It was a hell of a system; by the time you became accustomed to one ship and its captain, you were transferred to another ship and had to learn all over again.

Or, worse, you went without work for several months at a time, which meant hanging around some spacer bar at Tycho Station or Descartes City, waiting for the local union rep to throw some other guy out of his present assignment and give you his job.

It was a life, but it wasn't much of a living. I was thirty years old and still possessed all my fingers and toes, but had precious little money in the bank. After fifteen years of hard work, the nearest thing I had to a permanent address was the storage locker in Tycho where I kept my few belongings. Between jobs, I lived in union hostels on the Moon or the elfives, usually occupying a bunk barely large enough to swing either a cat or a call-girl. Even the whores lived better than I did; sometimes I'd pay them just to let me sleep in a decent bed for a change, and never mind the sex.

To make matters worse, I was bored out of my wits. Except for one cycleship run out to Mars when I was twenty-five, I had spent my entire career—hell, my entire life—running between LEO and the Moon. It's not a bad existence, but it's not a great one either. There's no shortage of sad old farts hanging around the union halls, telling big lies to anyone who'll listen about their glory days as beamjacks or moondogs while drinking away their pensions. I was damned if I would end up like them, but I knew that if I didn't get off the Moon real soon, I would be schlepping LOX tanks for the rest of my life.

Meanwhile, a new frontier was being opened in the outer system. Deep-space freighters hauled helium-3 from Jupiter to feed the fusion tokamaks on Earth, and although Queen Macedonia had placed Titan off-limits because of the Plague, the Iapetus colony was still operational. There was good money to be made from landing a gig on one of the big ships that cruised between the gas giants and the belt, and union members who found work on the Jupiter and Saturn runs had guaranteed three-year contracts. It wasn't the same thing as making another trip between Moon and LEO every few days. The risks were greater, but so was the payoff.

Competition for jobs on the outer-system ships was tight, but that didn't stop me from applying anyway. My fifteen-year service record, with few complaints from previous captains and one Mars run to my name, helped me put a leg up over most of the other applicants. I held down a job as a cargo grunt for another year while I waited, but the union eventually rotated me out and left me hanging in Sloppy Joe's Bar in Tycho. Six weeks later, just as I was considering signing up as a tractor operator on the Clavius Dome construction project, the word came: the *Jove Commerce* needed a new executive officer, and my name had been drawn from the hat.

There was only one hitch. Since the *Commerce* didn't come further in-system than Ceres, and because the union didn't guarantee passage to the belt as part of the deal, I would have to either travel aboard a clipper—out of the question, since I didn't have money—or find a temporary job on an outbound asteroid freighter.

Okay, I was willing to do that, but now there was another complication: few freighters had available gigs for selenians. Most vessels which operated in the main belt were owned by the Transient Body Shipping Association, and TBSA captains preferred to hire crewmembers from other ships owned by the co-op rather than from my union. Nor did they want to sign up some dude who would only be making a one-way trip, because they'd lose him on Ceres before the trip was half-over.

The predicament was explained to me by my union rep when I met with him in his office in Tycho. Schumacher was an old buddy; he and I had worked together aboard a LEO tugboat before the union had hired him as its Tycho Station representative, so he knew my face and was willing to cut me some slack.

"Look, Rohr," he said, propping his moccasins up on his desk, "here's the scoop. I've checked around for a boat that'll take you on, and I found what you were looking for. An Ares-class ore freighter, outbound for Ceres . . . in fact, she's already docked at Lagrange Four and is ready to launch as soon as her captain finds a new second."

As he spoke, Schumacher punched up a holo of the ship, and it revolved in the tank above his desk. It was a standard rock hauler: eighty-two meters in length, with a gas-core nuclear engine at one end and a drum-shaped crew module at the other, joined at the center by the long narrow spine and open cargo bays. An uprated tugboat, really; nothing about it was either unfamiliar or daunting. I took a slug off the whisky flask he had pulled out of his desk drawer. "Great. What's her name?"

He hesitated. "The TBSA *Comet*," he said reluctantly. "Her captain is Bo McKinnon."

I shrugged and passed the flask back to him. "So what's the catch?"

Schumacher blinked. Instead of taking a hit off the whisky, he recapped the flask and shoved it back in the drawer. "Let me repeat that," he said. "The *Comet*. Bo McKinnon." He peered at me as if I had come down with Titan Plague. "You're telling me you've never heard of him?"

I didn't keep up with the TBSA freighters or their captains; they returned to the Moon only once every few months to drop off their cargo and change crews, so few selenians happened to see them unless they were getting drunk in some bar. "Not a clue," I said.

Schumacher closed his eyes. "Terrific," he murmured. "The one guy who's never heard of Captain Future and it's gotta be you."

"Captain who?"

He looked back at me. "Look, just forget the whole thing, okay? Pretend

I never mentioned it. There's another rock hauler heading out to Ceres in about six or seven weeks. I'll talk to the Association, try to get you a gig on that one instead. . . ."

I shook my head. "I can't wait another six or seven weeks. If I'm not on Ceres in three months, I'll lose the *Jove Commerce* job. What's wrong with this gig?"

Schumacher sighed as he reached back into the drawer for the flask. "What's wrong," he said, "is the nut who's in command. McKinnon is the worst captain in the Association. No one who's shipped out with him has ever stayed aboard, except maybe the google he's got for a first mate."

I had to bite my tongue when he said that. We were pals, but racism isn't an endearing trait. Sure, Superiors can be weird—their eyes, for starters, which was why some people called them by that name—but if you also use words like nigger, slant, kike or spic to describe people, then you're no friend of mine.

On the other hand, when you're hungry for work, you'll put up with just about anything.

Schumacher read the expression on my face. "It's not just that," he said hastily. "I understand the first officer is okay." *For a google, that is*, although he didn't say it aloud. "It's McKinnon himself. People have jumped ship, faked illness, torn up their union cards . . . anything to get off the *Comet*."

"That bad?"

"That bad." He took a long hit off the flask, gasped, and passed it back across the desk to me. "Oh, the pay's okay . . . minimum wage, but by Association standards that's better than union scale . . . and the *Comet* passes all the safety requirements, or at least so at inspection time. But McKinnon's running a tank short of a full load, if y'know what I mean."

I didn't drink from the flask. "Naw, man, I don't know what you mean. What's with this . . . what did you call him?"

"Captain Future. That's what he calls himself, Christ knows why." He grinned. "Not only that, but he also calls his AI 'The Brain' . . ."

I laughed out loud. "The Brain? Like, what? He's got a brain floating in a jar? I don't get it. . . ."

"I dunno. It's a fetish of some kind." He shook his head. "Anyway, everyone who's worked for him says that he thinks he's some kinda space hero, and he expects everyone to go along with the idea. And he's supposed to be real tough on people . . . you might think he was a perfectionist, if he wasn't such a slob himself."

I had worked for both kinds before, along with a few weirdos. They didn't bother me, so long as the money was right and they minded their own business. "Ever met him?"

Schumacher held out his hand; I passed the flask back to him and he took another swig. Must be the life, sitting on your ass all day, getting drunk and deciding people's futures. I envied him so much, I hoped someone would kindly cut my throat if I was ever in his position.

"Nope," he said. "Not once. He spends all his time on the *Comet*, even when he's back here. Hardly ever leaves the ship, from what I've been told . . . and that's another thing. Guys who've worked for him say that he expects his crew to do everything but wipe his butt after he visits the head. Nobody gets a break on his ship, except maybe his first officer."

"What about him?"

"Her. Nice girl, name of . . ." He thought hard for a moment, then snapped his fingers. "Jeri. Jeri Lee-Bose, that's it." He smiled. "I met her once, not long before she went to work on the *Comet*. She's sweet, for a google."

He winked and dropped his voice a bit. "I hear she's got a thing for us apes," he murmured. "In fact, I've been told she's bunking with her captain. If half of what I've heard about McKinnon is true, that must make him twice as sick as I've heard."

I didn't reply. Schumacher dropped his feet and leaned across the desk, lacing his fingers together as he looked straight at me. "Look, Rohr," he said, as deadly serious as if he was discussing my wanting to marry his sister, "I know you're working under a time limit and how much the *Jove Commerce* job means to you. But I gotta tell you, the only reason why Captain Future would even consider taking aboard a short-timer is because nobody else will work for him. He's just as desperate as you are, but I don't give a shit about him. If you wanna turn it down, I won't add it to your card and I'll save your place in line. It'll just be between you and me. Okay?"

"And if I turn it down?"

He waved his hand back and forth. "Like I said, I can try to find you another gig. The *Nickel Queen*'s due home in another six weeks or so. I've got some pull with her captain, so maybe I can get you a job there . . . but honest to Jesus, I can't promise anything. The *Queen*'s a good ship and everyone I know wants to work for her, just as much as nobody wants to get within a klick of the *Comet*."

"So what do you suggest I do?"

Schumacher just smiled and said nothing. As my union rep, he was legally forbidden against making any decisions for me; as a pal, he had done his best to warn me about the risks. From both points of view, though, he knew I didn't have any real choice. I could spend three months aboard a ship run by a borderline psycho, or the rest of my life jacking off on the Moon.

I thought about it for a few moments, then I asked for the contract.

The three Futuremen who were Curt Newton's faithful, lifelong com rades made a striking contrast to their tall, red-haired young leader

—Hamilton, *The Comet Kings* (1942)

One-sixth gravity disappeared as I crawled through the carousel hatch and entered the bridge.

The *Comet*'s command center was located in the non-rotating forward deck of the crew module. The bridge was the largest single compartment in the ship, but even in freefall it was cramped: chairs, consoles, screens, emergency suit lockers, the central navigation table with its holo tank and, at the center of the low ceiling, the hemispherical bulge of the observation blister.

The ceiling lamps were turned down low when I came in—The Brain was mimicking Earth-time night—but I could see Jeri seated at her duty station on the far end of the circular deck. She looked around when she heard the hatch open.

"Morning," she said, smiling at me. "Hey, is that coffee?"

"Something like it," I muttered. She gazed enviously at the squeezebulb in my hand. "Sorry I didn't bring you any," I added, "but the Captain . . ."

"Right. I heard Bo yell at you." She feigned a pout which didn't last very long. "That's okay. I can get some later after we make the burn."

Jeri Lee-Bose: six-foot-two, which is short for a Superior, with the over-sized dark blue eyes that give bioengineered spacers their unsavory nickname. Thin and flat-chested to the point of emaciation, the fingers of her ambidextrous hands were long and slender, her thumbs almost extending to the tips of her index fingers. Her ash-blond hair was shaved nearly to the skull, except for the long braid that extended from the nape of her neck nearly down to the base of her narrow spine, where her double-jointed legs began.

The pale skin of her face was marked with finely etched tattoos around her eyes, nose, and mouth, forming the wings of a monarch butterfly. She had been given these when she had turned five, and since Superiors customarily add another tattoo on their birthdays and Jeri Lee was twenty-five, pictograms covered most of her arms and her shoulders, constellations and dragons which weaved their way under and around the tank-top she wore. I had no idea of what else lay beneath her clothes, but I imagined that she was well on her way to becoming a living painting.

Jeri was strange, even for a Superior. For one thing, her kind usually segregate themselves from Primaries, as they politely call us baseline humans (or apes, when we're not around). They tend to remain within their family-based clans, operating independent satrapies that deal with the TBSA and the major space companies only out of economic necessity, so it's rare to find a lone Superior working on a vessel owned by a Primary.

For another thing, although I've been around Superiors most of my life and they don't give me the creeps like they do most groundhogs and even many spacers, I've never appreciated the aloof condescension the majority of them display around unenhanced humans. Give one of them a few minutes, and they'll bend your ear about the Superior philosophy of extropic evolution and all that jive. Yet Jeri was the refreshing, and even oddball, exception to the rule. She had a sweet disposition, and from the moment I had come aboard the *Comet*, she had accepted me both as an equal and as a new-found friend. No stuffiness, no harangues about celibacy or the unspirituality of eating meat or using profanity; she was a fellow crewmate, and that was that.

No. That wasn't quite all there was to it.

When one got past the fact that she was a scarecrow with feet that functioned as a second pair of hands and eyes the size of fuel valves, she was sensual as hell. She was a pretty woman, and I had become infatuated with her. Schumacher would have twitched at the thought of sleeping with a google, but in three weeks since The Brain had revived us from the zombie tanks, there had been more than a few times when my desire to see the rest of her body exceeded simple curiosity about her tattoos.

Yet I knew very little about her. As much as I loved looking at her, that was surpassed by my admiration for her innate talent as a spacer. In terms of professional skill, Jeri Lee-Bose was one of the best First Officers I had ever met. Any Royal Navy, TBSA, or free-trader captain would have killed to sign her aboard.

So what the hell was she doing aboard a scow like the *Comet*, serving under a bozo like Bo McKinnon?

I tucked in my knees and did a half-gainer that landed the soles of my stikshoes against the carpet. Feet now firmly planted on the floor, I walked across the circular compartment to the nav table, sucking on the squeezebulb in my left hand. "Where's the captain?" I asked.

"Topside, taking a sextant reading." She nodded toward the observation blister above us. "He'll be down in a minute."

Typical. Part of the reason why Superiors have enhanced eyes is for optical work like sextant sightings. This should be Jeri's job, but McKinnon seemed to regard the blister as his personal throne. I sighed as I settled down in my chair and buckled in. "Should have known," I muttered. "Wakes you up in the middle of the goddamn night, then disappears when you want a straight answer."

Her mouth pursed into sympathetic frown. "Bo will tell you more when he comes down," she said, then she swiveled around in her chair as she returned her attention to her board.

Jeri was the only person aboard who was permitted to call Captain Future by his real name. I didn't have that privilege, and The Brain hadn't been programmed to do otherwise. The fondness I had developed for Jeri over the last three weeks was tempered by the fact that, in almost any disagreement, she usually sided with the captain.

Obviously, there was something else she knew but wasn't telling me, preferring to defer the issue to McKinnon. I had become used to such behavior over the last few months, but it was still irritating. Most first officers act as intermediaries between captain and crew, and in that sense Jeri performed well, yet at times like this I felt as if I had more in common with The Brain than with her.

So be it. I swiveled my chair to face the nav table. "Hey, Brain," I called out. "Gimme a holo of our current position and trajectory, please."

The space within the holo tank coruscated briefly, then an arch-shaped slice of the main belt appeared above the table. Tiny spots of orange light depicting major asteroids slowly moved along blue sidereal tracks, each designated by their catalog numbers. The *Comet* was pinpointed by a small silver replica of the vessel, leading the end of a broken red line which bisected the asteroid orbits.

The *Comet* was near the edge of the third Kirkwood gap, one of the "empty spaces" in the belt where Martian and Jovian gravitational forces caused the number of identified asteroids to diminish per fraction of an astronomical unit. We were now in the ⅓ gap, about two and a half A.U.'s from the Sun. In another couple of days we would enter the main belt and be closing in on Ceres. Once we arrived, the *Comet* would unload the cargo it had carried from the Moon and, in return, take on the raw ore TBSA prospectors had mined from the belt and shipped to Ceres Station. It was also there that I was scheduled to depart the *Comet* and await the arrival of the *Jove Commerce*.

At least, that was the itinerary. Now, as I studied the holo, I noticed a not-so-subtle change. The red line depicting the freighter's trajectory had been altered since the end of my last watch about four hours earlier.

It no longer intercepted Ceres. In fact, it didn't even come close to the asteroid's orbit.

The *Comet* had changed course while I slept.

Without saying anything to Jeri, I unbuckled my harness and pushed over to the table, where I silently stared at the holo for a couple of minutes, using the keypad to manually focus and enlarge the image. Our new bearing took us almost a quarter of a million kilometers from Ceres, on just the other side of the ⅓ Kirkwood gap.

"Brain," I said, "what's our destination?"

"The asteroid 2046-Barr," it replied. It displayed a new orange spot in the tank, directly in front of the *Comet*'s red line.

The last of my drowsiness dissipated into a pulse of white-hot rage. I could feel Jeri's eyes on my back.

"Rohr . . ." she began.

I didn't care. I stabbed the intercom button on the table. "McKinnon!" I
bellowed. "Get down here!"

Long silence. I knew he could hear me.

"Goddammit, get down here! Now!"

Motors whined in the ceiling above me, then the hatch below the observation
blister irised open and a wingback chair began to descend into the bridge,
carrying the commanding officer of the TBSA *Comet*. It wasn't until the chair
reached the deck that the figure seated in it spoke.

"You can call me . . . Captain Future."

In the ancient pulp magazines he so adored, Captain Future was six-and-
a-half feet in height, ruggedly handsome, bronze-skinned and red-haired.
None of this applied to Bo McKinnon. Squat and obese, he filled the chair
like a half-ton of lard. Black curly hair, turning grey at the temples and filthy
with dandruff, receded from his forehead and fell around his shoulders, while
an oily, unkempt beard dripped down the sides of his fat cheeks, themselves
the color of mildewed wax. There were old food stains on the front of his
worn-out sweatshirt and dark marks in the crotch of his trousers where he
had failed to properly shake himself after the last time he had visited the
head. And he smelled like a fart.

If my description seems uncharitable, let there be no mistake: Bo McKinnon
was a butt-ugly, foul-looking son of a whore, and I have met plenty of slobs
like him to judge by comparison. He had little respect for personal hygiene
and fewer social graces, he had no business being anyone's role model, and
I was in no mood for his melodramatic bullshit just now.

"You changed course." I pointed at the holo tank behind me, my voice
quavering in anger. "We're supposed to come out of the Kirkwood in another
few hours, and while I was asleep you changed course."

McKinnon calmly stared back at me. "Yes, Mister Furland, that I did. I
changed the *Comet*'s trajectory while you were in your quarters."

"We're no longer heading for Ceres . . . Christ, we're going to come
nowhere *near* Ceres!"

He made no move to rise from his throne. "That's correct," he said,
slowly nodding his head. "I ordered The Brain to alter our course so that
we'd intercept 2046-Barr. We fired maneuvering thrusters at 0130 shiptime,
and in two hours we'll execute another course correction. That should put us
within range of the asteroid in about . . ."

"Eight hours, Captain," Jeri said.

"Thank you, Mister Bose," he said, otherwise barely acknowledging her.
"Eight hours. At this time the *Comet* will be secured for emergency action."

He folded his hands across his vast stomach and gazed back at me queru-
lously. "Any further questions, Mister Furland?"

Further questions?

My mouth hung agape for a few moments. I was unable to speak, unable to protest, unable to do anything except wonder at the unmitigated gall of this mutant amalgamation of human and frog genes.

"Just one," I finally managed to say. "How do you expect me to make my rendezvous with the *Jove Commerce* if we detour to . . ."

"2046-Barr," Jeri said softly.

McKinnon didn't so much as blink. "We won't," he said. "In fact, I've already sent a message to Ceres Station, stating that the *Comet* will be delayed and that our new ETA is indefinite. With any luck, we'll reach Ceres in about forty-eight hours. You should be able to . . ."

"No, I won't." I grasped the armrest of his chair with both hands and leaned forward until my face was only a few inches from his. "The *Jove* is due to leave Ceres in forty-*two* hours . . . and that's at the latest, if it's going to meet its launch window for Callisto. They'll go, with or without me, and if they go without me, I'm stuck on Ceres."

No. That wasn't entirely true. Ceres Station wasn't like the Moon; it was too small an outpost to allow a shipwrecked spacer to simply hang around until the next outer-system vessel passed through. The TBSA rep on Ceres would demand that I find a new gig, even if it entailed signing aboard a prospector as grunt labor. This was little better than indentured servitude, since my union card didn't mean shit out here in terms of room, board, and guaranteed oxygen supplies; my paychecks would be swallowed up by all the above. Even then, there was no guarantee that I'd swing another job aboard the next Jupiter or Saturn tanker; I was lucky enough to get the *Jove Commerce* job.

That, or I could tuck tail and go back the way I came—and that meant remaining aboard the *Comet* for its return flight to the Moon.

In the latter case, I'd sooner try to walk home.

Try to understand. For the past three weeks, beginning with the moment I had crawled out of the zombie tank, I had been forced to endure almost every indignity possible while serving under Bo McKinnon. His first order, in fact, had been in the hibernation deck, when he had told me to take the catheter off his prick and hold a bag for him to pee in.

That had been only the beginning. Standing double-watches on the bridge because he was too lazy to get out of bed. Repairing decrepit equipment that should have been replaced years ago, only to have it break down again within a few more days after he had abused it past its tolerance levels. Being issued spurious orders on a whim, only to have those same orders countermanded before the task was half-complete because McKinnon had more scut-work he wanted me to do—then being berated because the first assignment had been left unfinished. Meals skipped because the captain decided that now was the time for me to go EVA and inspect the davits in the payload bay. Rest periods

The Death of Captain Future 257

interrupted because he wanted a snack fetched from the galley and was too "busy" to get it himself. . . .

But most of all, the sibilant, high-pitched whine of his voice, like that of a spoiled brat who had been given too many toys by an overindulgent parent. Which was, indeed, exactly what he was.

Bo McKinnon hadn't earned his TBSA commission. It had been purchased for him by his stepfather, a wealthy lunar businessman who was one of the Association's principal stockholders. The *Comet* had been an obsolete ore freighter on the verge of being condemned and scuttled when the old man had bought it for the kid as a means of getting his unwanted stepson out of his hair. Before that, McKinnon had been a customs inspector at Descartes, a minor bureaucrat with delusions of grandeur fostered by the cheap space operas in his collection of moldering twentieth century magazines, for which he apparently spent every spare credit he had in the bank. No doubt his stepfather had been as sick of McKinnon as I was. At least this way the pompous geek spent most of his time out in the belt, hauling rock and bellowing orders at whoever was unlucky enough to have been talked into signing aboard the *Comet*.

This much I had learned after I had been aboard for three weeks. By the time I had sent a message to Schumacher, demanding to know what else he hadn't told me about Bo McKinnon, I was almost ready to steal the *Comet*'s skiff and attempt flying it to Mars. When Schumacher sent me his reply, he gave a lame apology for not telling me everything about McKinnon's background; after all, it was his job to muster crewmembers for deep-space craft, and he couldn't play favorites, so sorry, et cetera. . . .

By then I had figured out the rest. Bo McKinnon was a rich kid playing at being a spacecraft commander. He wanted the role, but he didn't want to pay the dues, the hard-won experience that any true commander has to accomplish. Instead, he managed to shanghai washed-up cases like me to do his dirty work for him. No telling what arrangement he had worked out with Jeri; for my part, I was the latest in a long line of flunkies.

I didn't hijack the skiff, if only because doing so would have ruined my career and Mars colonists are notoriously unkind to uninvited guests. Besides, I figured that this was a temporary thing: three weeks of Captain Future, and I'd have a story to tell my shipmates aboard the *Jove Commerce* as we sipped whisky around the wardroom table. You think this captain's a hardass? Hey, let me tell you about my last one. . . .

Now, as much as I still wanted to get the hell off the *Comet*, I did not wish to be marooned on Ceres, where I would be at the tender mercies of the station chief.

Time to try a different tack with Captain Future.

I released the armrests and backed off, taking a deep breath as I forced myself to calm down. "Look, Captain," I said, "what's so important about this asteroid? I mean, if you've located a possible lode, you can always stake a claim with the Association and come back for it later. What's the rush?"

McKinnon raised an imperious eyebrow. "Mr. Furland, I am not a prospector," he huffed. "If I were, I wouldn't be commanding the *Comet*, would I?"

No, I silently responded, you wouldn't. No self-respecting rockhounds would have you aboard their ship. "Then what's so important?"

Without a word, McKinnon unbuckled his seat harness and pushed out his chair. Microgravity is the great equalizer for overweight men; he floated across the narrow compartment with the grace of a lunar trapeze artist, somersaulting in mid-air and catching a ceiling rung above the navigation table, where he swung upside-down and typed a command into the keyboard.

The holo expanded until 2046-Barr filled the tank. Now I could see that it was a potato-shaped rock, about three klicks in length and seven hundred meters in diameter. An octopus-like machine clung to one end of the asteroid, with a narrow, elongated pistol thrust out into space.

I recognized it immediately. A General Astronautics Class-B Mass Driver, the type used by the Association to push large carbonaceous-chrondite asteroids into the inner belt. In effect, a mobile mining rig. Long bores sunk into the asteroid extracted raw material from its core, which in turn were fed into the machine's barrel-shaped refinery, where heavy metals and volatiles were separated from the ancient stone. The remaining till was then shot through an electromagnetic railgun as reaction mass that propelled both asteroid and mass driver in whatever direction was desired.

By the time the asteroid reached lunar orbit, the rig would have refined enough nickel, copper, titanium, carbon, and hydrogen to make the effort worthwhile. The hollowed out remains of the asteroid could then be sold to one of the companies, who would then begin the process of transforming it into another LaGrange colony.

"That's the TBSA *Fool's Gold*," McKinnon said, pointing at the computer-generated image. "It's supposed to reach lunar orbit in four months. Twelve persons are aboard, including its captain, first officer, executive officer, physician, two metallurgists, three engineers . . ."

"Yeah, okay. Twelve guys who are going to get rich when the shares are divvied up." I couldn't keep the envy out of my voice. Only one or two main-belt asteroids made their way in-system every few years, mainly because prospectors didn't find enough such rocks to make them worth the time, money, and attention. The smaller ones were usually broken up by nukes, and anything much larger was claimed and mined by prospectors. On the other hand, if just the right asteroid was located and claimed, the bonanza was enough to make its finders wealthy enough to retire. "So what?"

McKinnon stared at me for a moment, then he cartwheeled until he was no longer upside-down and dug into a pocket. He handed me a wadded-up slip of printout. "Read," he said.

I read:

MESS. 1473 0118 GMT 7/26/73 CODE A1/0947
TRANSMISSION FROM CERES STATION TO ALL SPACECRAFT
PRIORITY REPEATER
MESSAGE BEGINS
MAYDAY RECEIVED 1240 GMT 7/25/46 FROM TBSA MASS
DRIVER "FOOL'S GOLD" BREAK VESSEL EXPERIENCING
UNKNOWN—REPEAT UNKNOWN—PROBLEMS BREAK CAS-
UALTIES AND POSSIBLE FATALITIES REPORTED DUE TO
UNDETERMINED CAUSES BREAK SHIP STATUS UNKNOWN
BREAK NO FURTHER COMMUNICATION FOLLOWING MAY-
DAY BREAK VESSEL FAILS TO RESPOND TO QUERIES
BREAK REQUEST URGENT ASSISTANCE FROM NEAREST
VESSEL OF ANY REGISTRY BREAK PLEASE RESPOND ASAP
MESSAGE ENDS
(TRANSMISSION REPEATS)
0119 GMT 7/26/73 CODE A1/0947

I turned to Jeri. "Are we the nearest vessel?"

She gravely nodded her head. "I checked. The only other ship within range is a prospector near Gaspara, and it's thirty-four hours from Barr. Everything else is closer to Ceres than we are."

Damn.

According to common law, the closest vessel to a spacecraft transmitting a Mayday was obligated to respond, regardless of any other mission or prior obligation in all but the most extreme emergency . . . and my job aboard the *Jove Commerce* didn't qualify as such, as much as I might have liked to think otherwise.

McKinnon held out his hand. I handed the paper back to him. "I guess you've already informed Ceres that we're on our way."

The captain silently reached to another panel and pushed a set of buttons. A flatscreen lit, displaying a playback of the transmission he had sent to Ceres Station. A simulacrum of the fictional Curt Newton appeared on the screen. *"This is Captain Future, calling from the TBSA Comet, registry Mexico Alpha Foxtrot one-six-seven-five."* The voice belonged to McKinnon even if the handsome face did not. The Brain had lip-synched them together, and the effect was sadly absurd. *I've received your transmission, and I'm on our way to investigate the situation aboard the* Fool's Gold. *The Futuremen and I will keep you informed. Captain Future, over and out.*"

I groaned as I watched this. The idiot couldn't keep his fantasy life out of anything, even a distress signal. Captain Future and the—yech!—Futuremen to the rescue.

"You have something to say, Mister Furland?"

McKinnon's hairy chin was thrust out at me with what he probably thought was obstinate resolve, but which actually resembled the petulance of an insecure child daring someone to step into his corner of the sandbox. Not for the first time, I realized that his only way of dealing with people was to boss them around with what little authority he could muster—and since this was his ship, no one could either object or walk out on him. Least of all me.

"None, Captain." I pushed off from the nav table and floated back to my duty station. Like it or not, we were committed; he had both law and his commission on his side, and I wasn't about to commit mutiny because I had refused my commander's orders to respond to a distress signal.

"Very good." McKinnon shoved himself in the direction of the carousel hatch. "The sextant confirms we're on course for Barr. I'll be in my cabin if you need me."

He stopped, then looked over his shoulder. "You'll need to arm the weapons pod. There may be . . . trouble."

Then he was gone, undoubtedly to claim the sleep I had lost.

"Trouble, my ass," I murmured under my breath.

I glanced over at Jeri. If I expected a sly wink or an understanding smile, I received nothing of the kind. Her face was stoical behind the butterfly mask she wore; she touched her jaw, speaking into the microphone implanted beneath her skin at childhood. "TBSA *Fool's Gold*, this is TBSA *Comet*, Mexico Alpha Foxtrot one-six-seven-five. Do you copy? Over."

I was trapped aboard a ship commanded by a lunatic.

Or so I thought. The real insanity was yet to come.

Space pirates were no new thing, to the System. There were always some corsairs infesting the outlaw asteroids or the wilder moons of the outer planets.

—Hamilton, *Outlaw World* (1945)

One good thing could be said about standing a second consecutive watch on the bridge: I finally learned a little more about Jeri Lee-Bose.

Does it seem surprising that I could have spent three weeks of active duty aboard a spacecraft without hearing a shipmate's entire life story? If so, understand that there's a certain code of conduct among spacers; since many of us have unsavory pasts that we'd rather not discuss, it's not considered proper etiquette to bug someone about private matters unless they themselves bring it up first. Of course, some shipmates will bore you to death, blabbing about everything they've ever said or done until you want to push them into the nearest airlock. On the other hand I've known several people for many years without ever learning where they were born or who their parents were.

Jeri fell into the latter category. After we were revived from biostasis, I had learned many little things about her, but not very many big things. It wasn't as if she was consciously hiding her past; it was simply that the subject had never really come up, during the few times that we had been alone together without Captain Future's presence looming over us. Indeed, she might have completed the voyage as a near-stranger, had I not made an offhand comment.

"I bet the selfish son-of-a-bitch has never thought of anyone else in his life," I said.

I had just returned from the galley, where I had fetched two fresh squeeze-bulbs of coffee for us. I was still fuming from the argument I had lost, and since McKinnon wasn't in earshot I gave Jeri an earful.

She passively sipped her coffee as I pissed and moaned about my misfortunes, listening patiently as I paced back and forth in my stikshoes, ranting about the commanding officer's dubious mental balance, his unflattering physiognomy, his questionable taste in literature, his body odor and anything else that came to mind, and when I paused for breath she finally put in her quarter-credit.

"He saved my life," she said.

That caught me literally off-balance. My shoes came unstuck from the carpet, and I had to grab hold of a ceiling handrail.

"Say what?" I asked.

Not looking up at me, Jeri Lee absently played with the squeezebulb in her left hand, her right foot holding open the pages of her personal logbook. "You said that he's never thought of anyone else in his life," she replied. "Whatever else you might say about him, you're wrong there, because he saved my life."

I shifted hands so I could sip my coffee. "Anything you want to talk about?"

She shrugged. "Nothing that probably hasn't occurred to you already. I mean, you've probably wondered why a google is serving as first officer aboard this ship, haven't you?" When my mouth gaped open, she smiled a little. "Don't look so surprised. We're not telepathic, rumors to the contrary . . . it's just that I've heard the same thing over the last several years we've been together."

Jeri gazed pensively through the forward windows. Although we were out of the Kirkwood gap, no asteroids could be seen. The belt is much less dense than many people think, so all we saw was limitless starscape, with Mars a distant ruddy orb off to the port side.

"You know how Superiors mate, don't you?" she asked at last, still not looking at me.

I felt my face grow warm. Actually, I didn't know, although I had frequently fantasized about Jeri helping me find out. Then I realized that she was speaking literally. "Prearranged marriages, right?"

She nodded. "All very carefully planned, in order to avoid inbreeding while expanding the gene pool as far as possible. It allows for some selection, of course . . . no one tells us exactly *whom* we should marry, just as long as it's outside of our own clans and it's not to Primaries."

She paused to finish her coffee, then she crumpled the squeezebulb and batted it aside with her right foot. It floated in midair, finding its own miniature orbit within the compartment. "Well, sometimes it doesn't work out that way. When I was twenty, I fell in love with a boy at Descartes Station . . . a Primary, as luck would have it. At least I thought I was in love. . . ."

She grimaced, brushing her long braid away from her delicate shoulders. "In hindsight, I guess we were just good in bed. In the long run it didn't matter, because as soon as he discovered that he had knocked me up, he got the union to ship him off to Mars. They were only too glad to do so, in order to avoid . . ."

"A messy situation. I see." I took a deep breath. "Leaving you stuck with his child."

She shook her head. "No. No child. I tried to keep it, but the miscarriage . . . anyway, the less said about that, the better."

"I'm sorry." What else could I have said? She should have known better, since there had never been a successful crossbreeding between Superiors and Primaries? She had been young and stupid; both are forgivable sins, especially when they usually occur in tandem.

Jeri heaved a sigh. "It didn't matter. By then, my family had disowned me, mainly because I had violated the partnership that had already been made for me with another clan. Both clans were scandalized, and as a result neither one wanted me." She looked askance at me. "Bigotry works both ways, you know. You call us googles, we call you apes, and I had slept with an ape. An insult against the extropic ideal."

She closed the logbook, tossed it from her left foot to her right hand, and tucked it into a web beneath the console. "So I was grounded at Descartes. A small pension, just enough to pay the rent, but nothing really to live for. I suppose they expected me to become a prostitute . . . which I did, for a short time . . . or commit ritual suicide and save everyone the sweat."

"That's cold." But not unheard of. There were a few grounded Superiors to be found in the inner system, poor sad cases working at menial tasks in Lagranges or on the Moon. I remembered an alcoholic google who hung out at Sloppy Joe's; he had eagle wings tattooed across his back, and he cadged drinks off tourists in return for performing cartwheels across the bar. An eagle with clipped tailfeathers. Every so often, one would hear of a Superior who checked out by walking into an airlock and pushing the void button. No one knew why, but now I had an answer. It was the Superior way.

"That's extropy for you." She laughed bitterly, then was quiet for a moment. "I was considering taking the long walk," she said at last, "but Bo found me first, when I . . . well, propositioned him. He bought me a couple of drinks and listened to my story, and when I was done crying he told me he needed a new first officer. No one else would work for him, so he offered me the job, for as long as I cared to keep it."

"And you've kept it."

"And I've kept it," she finished. "For the record, Mr. Furland, he has always treated me with the greatest of respect, despite what anyone else might have told you. I've never slept with him, nor has he ever demanded that I do so . . ."

"I didn't . . . !"

"No, of course you haven't, but you've probably wondered, haven't you?" When I turned red, she laughed again. "Everyone who has worked the *Comet* has, and sometimes they like to tell stories about the google and the fat slob, fucking in his cabin between shifts."

She smiled, slowly shaking her head. "It isn't so . . . but, to tell the truth, if he ever asked, I'd do so without a second thought. I owe him that little."

I didn't say anything for a couple of minutes. It isn't often when a shipmate unburdens his or her soul, and Jeri had given me much to consider. Not the least of which was the slow realization that, now more than before, I was becoming quite fond of her.

Before he had gone below, McKinnon had told me to activate the external missile pod, so I pushed myself over to his station and used that minor task to cover for my embarrassment.

Strapping on EMP to an Ares-class freighter was another example of McKinnon's overheated imagination. When I had once asked why, he'd told me that he'd purchased it as war surplus from the Pax Astra Royal Navy back in '71, after the hijacking of the TBSA *Olympia*. No one had ever discovered who had taken the *Olympia*—indeed, the hijack wasn't discovered until five months later, when the uncrewed solar-sail vessel arrived at Ceres Station with its cargo holds empty—but it was widely believed to be the work of indie prospectors desperate for food and various supplies.

I had to cover my smile when McKinnon told me that he was worried about "pirates" trying to waylay the *Comet*. Having four 10k nukes tucked behind the *Comet*'s cargo section was like arming a gig with heatseekers. Not that McKinnon wouldn't have loved it if someone *did* try to steal his ship—Captain Future meets the Asteroid Pirates and all that—but I was worried that he might open fire on some off-course prospector ship that was unlucky enough to cross his path.

Another thought occurred to me. "When he picked you . . . um, when you signed on as First Officer . . . were you aware that he doesn't have a firm grip on reality?"

Jeri didn't answer immediately. I was about to repeat myself when I felt a gentle nudge against my arm. Looking down, I saw her left foot slide past me, its thumb-sized toes toggling the **MISSILE STANDBY** switch I had neglected to throw.

"Sure," she said. "In fact, he used to call me Joan . . . as in Joan Randall, Curt Newton's girlfriend . . . until I got him to cut it out."

"Really?"

"Um-hmm." She rested her right leg against the back of my chair. "Consider yourself lucky he doesn't call you Otho or Grag. He used to do that to other crewmen until I told him that no one got the joke." She grinned. "You ought to try reading some of those stories sometime. He's loaded them into The Brain's library annex. Not great literature, to be sure . . . in fact, they're rather silly . . . but for early twentieth century science fiction, they're . . ."

"Science what?"

"Science fiction. What they used to call fantasy back . . . well, never mind." She pulled her leg back and folded it beneath her bottom as she gazed again out the window. "Look, I know Bo can be weird most of the time, but you have to realize that he's a romantic stuck in an age where most people don't even know what the word means anymore. He wants derringdo, swashbuckling, great adventure . . . he wants to be a hero."

"Uh-huh. Bo McKinnon, space hero." I tried to transpose him on the magazine covers he had framed in the galley: wielding a ray gun in each hand, defending Jeri from ravaging monsters. It didn't work, except to make me stifle a chuckle.

"That isn't too much to ask for, is it?" There was sadness in her eyes when she glanced my way. Before I could get the grin off my face, she returned her gaze to the windows. "Perhaps so. This isn't an age of heroes. We move rock back and forth across the system, put money in the bank, and congratulate ourselves for our ingenuity. A hundred years ago, what we're doing now was the stuff of dreams, and the people who did it were larger than life. That's what he finds so attractive in those stories. But now . . ."

She let out her breath. "Who can blame Bo for wanting something he can't have? He's stuck on a second-hand freighter with an ex-whore for a first officer and a second officer who openly despises him, and he's the butt of every joke from Earth to Iapetus. No wonder he drops everything to answer a Mayday. This may be the only chance he gets."

I was about to retort that my only chance to get a job on a decent ship was slipping through my fingers when her console double-beeped. A moment later, The Brain's voice came through the ceiling speaker.

"Pardon me, but we're scheduled for course correction maneuvers. Do you wish for me to execute?"

Jeri swiveled her chair around. "That's okay, Brain. We'll handle it by manual control. Give me the coordinates."

The AI responded by displaying a three-dimensional grid on her flatscreens. "Want me to do anything?" I asked, although it was obvious that she had matters well in hand.

"I've got everything covered," she said, her long fingers typing in the coordinates. "Get some sleep, if you want." She cast a quick grin over her shoulder. "Don't worry. I won't tell Bo you dozed off in his chair."

End of conversation. Besides, she had a good idea. I cranked back the chair, buckled the seat belt and tucked my hands in my pockets so they wouldn't drift around in freefall. It might be awhile before I got another chance; once we reached 2046-Barr, Captain Future would be back on deck, bellowing orders and otherwise making my life painful.

She had told me a lot about Bo McKinnon, but nothing I had heard gave me much affection for the man. So far as I was concerned, he was still the biggest dork I had ever met . . . and if there was anyone aboard the TBSA *Comet* who deserved my sympathy, it was Jeri Lee-Bose, who was meant for better things than this.

As I shut my eyes, it occurred to me that the captain's chair fitted me a lot better than it did McKinnon. One day, perhaps I'd have enough money in the bank to buy him out. It would be interesting to see if he took orders as well as he gave them.

It was a warm and comforting thought, and I snuggled against it like a pillow as I fell asleep.

"Look, Arraj—it is a meteor!" cried the younger Martian excitedly. "And there's a ship guiding it!"

The two stared for a moment at the incredible spectacle. The expanding black spot was clearly a giant meteor, rushing now at tremendous speed toward Mars. And close beside the booming meteor rushed a dark spaceship, playing rays upon the great mass. The ship was propelling the meteor toward Mars.

—Hamilton, Captain Future's Challenge *(1940)*

Several hours later, the *Comet* rendezvoused with 2046-Barr.

The asteroid looked much the same as the holo tank had depicted it—an enormous rock the color of charcoal—but the *Fool's Gold* itself was the largest spacecraft I had ever seen short of a Lagrange colony. It dwarfed the *Comet* like a yacht parked alongside an ocean liner, a humongous machine attached to one end of the asteroid's mass.

A humongous machine, and apparently lifeless. We approached the mass-driver with great caution, being careful to avoid its stern lest we get nailed by the stream of debris being constantly ejected by its railgun. That was the only apparent sign of activity; although light gleamed from the portals of the rotating command sphere, we could detect no motion within the windows, and the radio remained as silent as it had been for the last eighteen hours.

"Look yonder." I pointed through the window at the hangar bay, a wide berth within the barrel-shaped main hull just forward of the railgun. Its doors were open, and as the *Comet* slowly cruised past we could see the gig and service pods parked in their cradles. "Everything's there. Even the lifeboats are still in place."

Jeri angled the camera on the outrigger telemetry boom until it peered into the bay. Her wide eyes narrowed as she studied a close-up view on a flatscreen. "That's weird," she murmured. "Why would they depressurize the bay and open the doors if they didn't . . . ?"

"Knock it off, you two!"

McKinnon was strapped in his chair, on the other side of Jeri Lee's duty station from mine. "It doesn't matter why they did it. Just keep your eyes peeled for pirates . . . they could be lurking somewhere nearby."

I chose to remain silent as I piloted the *Comet* past the mass-driver's massive anchor-arms and over the top of the asteroid. Ever since McKinnon had returned to the bridge an hour ago—following the shower and leisurely breakfast I myself had been denied—he had been riding his favorite hobby horse: asteroid pirates had seized control of the *Fool's Gold* and taken its crew hostage.

This despite the fact that we had not spotted any other spacecraft during our long journey and that none could now be seen in the vicinity of the asteroid. It could also be logically argued that the four-person crew of a prospector ship would have a hard time overcoming the twelve-person crew of a mass-driver, but logic meant little to Captain Future. His left hand rested on the console near the EMP controls, itching to launch a nuke at the pirate ship he was certain to find lurking in the asteroid's shadow.

Yet, when we completed a fly-by of 2046-Barr, none were to be found. In fact, nothing moved at all, save for the asteroid itself. . . .

A thought occurred to me. "Hey, Brain," I said aloud, "have you got a fix on the mass-driver's position and bearing?"

"Affirmative, Mr. Furland. It is X-ray one-seven-six, Yankee two . . ."

"Mr. Furland!" McKinnon snapped. "I didn't give orders for you to . . ."

I ignored him. "Skip the numbers, Brain. Just tell me if it's still on course for cislunar rendezvous."

A momentary pause, then: *"Negative, Mr. Furland. The* Fool's Gold *has altered its trajectory. According to my calculations, there is a seventy-two-point-one probability that it is now on collision course with the planet Mars."*

Jeri went pale as she sucked in her breath, and even McKinnon managed to shut up. "Show it to me on the tank," I said as I turned my chair around to face the nav table.

The tank lit, displaying a holographic diagram of the *Fool's Gold's* present position in relationship with the Martian sidereal-hour. Mars still lay half an A.U. away, but as The Brain traced a shallow-curving orange line through the belt, we saw that it neatly intercepted the red planet as it advanced on its orbit around the Sun.

The Brain translated the math it had displayed in a box next to the three-dimensional grid. *"Assuming that its present delta-vee remains unchecked, in two hundred and thirty-six hours, twelve minutes, and twenty-four seconds, 2046-Barr will collide with Mars."*

I did some arithmetic in my head. "That's about ten days from now."

"Nine-point-eight three Earth standard days, to be exact." The Brain expanded the image of Mars until it filled the tank; a bulls-eye appeared at a point just above the equator. *"Estimated point of impact will be approximately twelve degrees North by sixty-three degrees West, near the edge of the Lunae Planum."*

"Just north of Valles Marineris," Jeri said. "Oh God, Rohr, that's near . . ."

"I know." I didn't need a refresher course in planetary geography. The impact point was in the low plains above Mariner Valley, only a few hundred klicks northeast of Arsia Station, not to mention closer to the smaller settlements scattered around the vast canyon system. For all I knew, there could now be a small mining town on the Lunae Planum itself; Mars was being colonized so quickly these days, it was hard to keep track of where a bunch of its one and a half million inhabitants decided to pitch claims and call themselves New Chattanooga or whatever.

"Sabotage!" McKinnon yelled. He unbuckled his harness and pushed himself closer to the nav table, where he stared at the holo. "Someone has sabotaged the mass-driver so that it'll collide with Mars! Do you realize . . . ?"

"Shut up, Captain." I didn't need his histrionics to tell me what would occur if . . . *when* . . . 2046-Barr came down in the middle of the Lunae Planum.

The Martian ecosystem wasn't as fragile as Earth's. Indeed, it was much more volatile, as the attempt in the '50s to terraform the planet and make the climate more stable had ultimately proved. However, the Mars colonists who still remained after the boondoggle had come to depend upon its seasonal patterns in order to grow crops, maintain solar farms, continue mining operations and other activities which insured their basic survival.

It was a very tenuous sort of existence that relied upon conservative prediction of climatic changes. The impact of a three-kilometer asteroid in the equatorial region would throw all that straight into the compost toilet. Localized quakes and duststorms would only be the beginning; two or three hundred people might be killed outright, but the worst would be yet to come. The amount of dust that would be raised into the atmosphere by the collision would blot out the sky for months on end, causing global temperatures to drop from Olympus Mons to the Hellas Plantia. As a result, everything from agriculture to power supplies would be affected, to put it mildly, with starvation in the cold and dark awaiting most of the survivors.

It wasn't quite doomsday. A few isolated settlements might get by with the aid of emergency relief efforts from Earth. But as the major colony world of humankind, Mars would cease to exist.

McKinnon was still transfixed upon the holo tank, jabbing his finger at Mars while raving about saboteurs and space pirates and God knows what else, when I turned back to Jeri. She had taken the helm in my absence, and as the *Comet* came up on the *Fool's Gold* again, I closely studied the mass-driver on the flatscreens.

"Okay," I said quietly. "The hangar bay is out . . . we can't send the skiff in there while it's depressurized and the cradles are full. Maybe if we . . ."

She was way ahead of me. "There's an auxiliary docking collar here," she said, pointing to a port on the spar leading to the command sphere. "It'll be tight, but I think we can squeeze us in there."

I looked at the screen. Tight indeed. Despite the fact that the *Comet* had a universal docking adapter, the freighter wasn't designed for mating with a craft as large as *Fool's Gold*. "That's cutting it close," I said. "If we can collapse the telemetry boom, though, we might be able to make it."

She nodded. "We can do that, no problem . . . except it means losing contact with Ceres."

"But if we don't hard-dock," I replied, "then someone's got to go EVA and try entering a service airlock."

Knowing that this someone would probably be me, I didn't much relish the idea. An untethered spacewalk between two vessels under acceleration is an iffy business at best. On the other hand, cutting off our radio link with Ceres under these circumstances was probably not a good idea. If we fucked up in some major way, then no one at Ceres Station would be informed of the situation, and early warning from Ceres to Arsia Station might save a few lives, if evacuation of settlements near Lunae Planum was started soon enough.

I made up my mind. "We'll hard-dock," I said, turning in my seat toward the communications console, "but first we send a squib to Ceres, let them know what's . . ."

"Hey! What are you two doing?"

Captain Future had finally decided to see what the Futuremen were doing behind his back. He kicked off the nav table and pushed over to us, grabbing the backs of our chairs with one hand each to hover over us. "I haven't issued any orders, and nothing is done on my ship without my . . ."

"Bo, have you been listening to what we've been saying?" Jeri's expression was carefully neutral as she stared up at him. "Have you heard a word either Rohr or I have said?"

"Of course I . . . !"

"Then you know that this is the only recourse," she said, still speaking calmly. "If we don't hard-dock with the *Gold*, then we won't have a chance of shutting down the railgun or averting its course."

"But the pirates. They might . . . !"

I sighed. "Look, get it through your head. There's no . . ."

"Rohr," she interrupted, casting me a stern look that shut me up. When I dummied up once more, she transfixed McKinnon again with her wide blue eyes. "If there are pirates aboard the *Gold*," she said patiently, "we'll find them. But right now, this isn't something we can solve by firing missiles. Rohr's right. First, we send a squib to Ceres, let them know what's going on. Then . . ."

"I know that!"

"Then, we have to dock with . . ."

"I know that! I know that!" His greasy hair scattered in all directions as he shook his head in frustration. "But I didn't . . . I didn't give the orders and . . ."

He stopped, sullenly glaring at me with inchoate rage, and I suddenly realized the true reason for his anger. McKinnon's subordinate second officer, whom he had harassed and chastised constantly for three weeks, had become uppity by reaching a solution that had evaded him. Worse yet, the second officer had done it with the cooperation of the Captain's first officer, who had tacitly agreed with him on all previous occasions.

Yet this wasn't a trifling matter such as checking the primary fuel pump or cleaning the galley. Countless lives were at stake, time was running out, and while he was spewing obvious nonsense about space pirates, Mister Furland was trying to take command of his ship.

Had I a taser conveniently tucked in my belt, I would have settled the argument by giving him a few volts and strapping his dead ass in his precious chair, thereby allowing Jeri Lee and me to continue our work unfettered. But since outright mutiny runs against my grain, compromise was my only weapon now.

"Begging your pardon, Captain," I said. "You're quite right. You haven't issued orders, and I apologize."

Then I turned around in my chair, folded my hands in my lap, and waited.

McKinnon sucked in his breath. He stared through the windows at the *Fool's Gold*, looked over his shoulder once more at the holo tank, weighing the few options available against the mass of his ego. After too many wasted seconds, he finally reached a decision.

"Very well," he said. He let go of our chairs and shoved himself back to his accustomed seat. "Ms. Bose, prepare to dock with the *Fool's Gold*. Mr. Furland, ready the main airlock hatch and prepare to go EVA."

"Aye, sir," Jeri said.

"Um, yeah . . . aye, sir."

"Meanwhile, I'll send a message to Ceres Station and inform them of the situation before we lose contact." Satisfied that he had reached a proper decision, he laid his hands on the armrest. "Good work, Futuremen," he added. "You've done well."

"Thank you, Captain," Jeri said.

"Aye, sir. Thank you." I unbuckled my seat harness and pushed off toward the bridge hatch, trying hard not to smile.

A little victory. Insignificant as it then seemed, I didn't have any idea how much my life depended upon it.

He took the pilot chair and headed the Comet *across the zone toward the computed position of the invisible asteroid.*

"They'll surely see us approaching!" Ezra warned. "The Magician of Mars will be taking no chances, Cap'n Future!"

"We're going to use a stratagem to get onto that asteroid without him suspecting," Curt informed. "Watch."

—Hamilton, *The Magician of Mars* (1941)

I'm a creature of habit, at least when it comes to established safety procedures, and so it was out of habit that I donned an EVA suit before I cycled through the *Comet*'s airlock and entered the *Fool's Gold*.

On one hand, wearing the bulky spacesuit within a pressurized spacecraft is stupidly redundant, and the panel within the airlock told me that there was positive pressure on the other side of the hatch. Yet it could be argued the airlock sensors might be out of whack and there was nothing but hard vacuum within the spar; this has been known to happen before, albeit rarely, and people have died as a result. In any case, the *Astronaut's General Handbook* says that an EVA suit should be worn when boarding another craft under uncertain conditions, and so I followed the book.

Doing so saved my life.

I went alone, leaving Jeri and McKinnon behind inside the freighter. The hatch led past the *Gold*'s airlock into the spar's access tunnel, all of which was vacant. Switching on the helmet's external mike, I heard nothing but the customary background hum of the ventilation system, further evidence that the vessel crew compartments were still pressurized.

At that point, I could well have removed my helmet and hung it from a strap on my utility belt. In fact, the only reason I didn't was that I didn't want it banging around as I went through the carrousel, which lay at the end of the tunnel to my right. Besides, the stillness of the tunnel gave me the chills. Surely someone would have noticed the unscheduled docking of an Ares-class freighter, let alone one so far from Ceres. Why wasn't there an officer waiting at the airlock to chew me out for risking collision with his precious ship?

The answer came after I rotated through the carrousel and entered the rotating command sphere. That's when I found the first corpse.

A naked man hung upside down through an open manhole, his limp arms dangling above the wide pool of blood on the deck. It was difficult to see his face, because the blood that had dyed it crimson came from a scimitar-shaped gash in his neck. Looking up through the manhole, I saw that his feet had been neatly lashed together with a bungee cord, which in turn was tied to a conduit in the ceiling of the corridor directly above.

Since there were no bloodstains below his shoulders, it was obvious that his throat had been slit after he had been hung from the conduit. The blood was dry—most of it, anyway—and the body was stiff. He had been here for quite some time.

I reported what I found to Jeri and McKinnon, and then I gingerly pushed the body out of the way and continued down the corridor.

Please understand if everything I tell you sounds coldly methodical, even callous. First, if you've worked in space as long as I have—that is, all my life—then death, no matter how horrible it may be, is no stranger. The first time I saw a man die was when I was nine years old, when a one-in-a-million micrometeorite punched through the helmet faceplate of one of my school teachers while he was leading us on a field trip to the Apollo 17 landing site at Taurus Lithrow. Since then, I've seen the grisly results of explosive decompression, fatal radiation overexposure, freak mining accidents, careless suit-up procedures, hull fires and electrocutions, even someone who choked on his own vomit after consuming too much bathtub vodka during a birthday party. Death comes to us all, eventually; if you're careful and wise, all you can do is make sure that it isn't too painful and no one is stuck with a mess to clean up.

Second: if I attempted now to describe each and every body I discovered as I made my way through the *Fool's Gold*, not only would the result be gratuitous pandering to those who wallow in such details, but I would never be able to complete this testimony.

To put it succinctly, the command sphere of the *Fool's Gold* was a slaughter-house.

I found ten more bodies, each more gruesome than the last. They were in crew cabins and passageways, in the galley and in the head, in the rec room and the quartermaster's office.

Most were alone, but two of them were together, each apparently dead from wounds they had inflicted upon one another: a man and a woman, who had tried to carve each other up with knives they had taken from the nearby galley.

A couple of the bodies were nude, like the first, but most were fully or partially clothed. For the most part, they had died of stabbing or bludgeon wounds, by means of anything that could be used as a weapon, whether it be a ballpoint pen, a screwdriver, or a pipefitter's wrench.

One woman was lucky. She had committed suicide by hanging herself by a coiled bedsheet she had cast over the top of a door. I hope that she had successfully strangled herself before whoever found her body seared off her right arm with the cutting torch cast nearby.

As I climbed up ladders, poked my helmet through hatches, and stepped over stiffening corpses, I kept up a running monologue, informing the *Comet* of where I exactly was within the vessel and what I had just found. I made no speculation as to why this massacre had taken place, only to note that the bodies seemed reasonably fresh and that most of the bloodstains were dry.

And blood lay everywhere. It was splattered across walls and soaked into carpets and dripping from wall fixtures, until it no longer resembled blood and just looked like spilled red paint. I was glad I had my helmet on, because the visor helped distance me from the carnage, and the rank odor would have made me even more sickened than I was now.

Although I heard an occasional gasp or exclamation from Jeri through my headset, after awhile I couldn't detect McKinnon's voice any longer. I assumed that he had gone someplace private to vomit. This was understandable; the violence around me was mind shattering.

There were four decks in the command sphere, one above the other. By the time I reached the top deck, I had counted eleven corpses. Remembering that McKinnon had told me earlier that the crew complement of the *Fool's Gold* was twelve, I had begun to wonder where the last body lay.

The hatch leading to the bridge was sealed shut; I used the laser welding torch from my belt to cut the lock. When I grasped the lockwheel and prized it open, it made a faint grinding noise, and it was at that moment that I heard a methodical, almost rhythmic thumping, as if something were being beaten against a bulkhead.

I first thought it was another background noise from the vessel itself, but when I pushed the hatch farther open, the noise it made interrupted the rhythm.

I stopped, holding the hatch ajar as I listened intently. I heard a faint giggle, then the thumping sound recommenced.

Someone was alive within the bridge.

The command center was dimly lit, the fluorescents switched off; the only light came from computer displays, flatscreens, and multicolored switches. The deck was in ruins, as if there had been a blowout, although the external pressure gauge told me it was still pressurized: upended chairs, ripped logbooks and manuals strewn across the floor, the remains of a bloody shirt.

The thumping continued. Seeking its unseen source, I switched on the helmet lamp and walked within its beam, my eyes darting back and forth as I searched for the sole survivor of the *Fool's Gold*. I was halfway across the bridge when my eye caught something scrawled across a bulkhead. Two words, fingerpainted in blood across the gray surface:

PLAGUE

TITAN

It was then that I knew that wearing an EVA suit had saved my life.

Trembling within its insulated layers, I crossed the deserted bridge, looking for the last remaining crewmember of the *Fool's Gold*.

I found him in the emergency airlock, huddled in a corner next to the hatch, his knees drawn up to his chin. The jumpsuit he wore was streaked with gore, but I could still make out the captain's stars on its epaulets. His wary eyes winced from the glare of my lamp, and he giggled like a small child who had been caught exploring his mother's dresser drawers.

And then he continued to beat at the deck with the severed human arm he grasped in his left hand.

I don't know how long I stared at him. A few seconds, several minutes, perhaps longer. Jeri was saying something I couldn't understand; I paid no attention, nor could I respond. It wasn't until I heard another noise—from behind me, the faint sound of the hatch being shoved open—that I tore my eyes away from the mad captain of the *Fool's Gold*.

Bo McKinnon.

He had followed me from the *Comet*.
And, like the idiot he was, he wasn't wearing an EVA suit.

The little teardrop ship, the Comet, *blasted at top speed toward the Earth and its summoning call. Captain Future thought somberly of the many times he had answered that call. Each time, he and the Futuremen had found themselves called on to battle deadly perils. Was it to be the same this time?*

"We can't always win," he thought grimly. "We've been lucky, but the law of averages eventually has to turn against us."

—Hamilton, *The Triumph of Captain Future* (1940)

Despite the name, no one knows the exact origin of the Titan Plague. It was first contracted by members of the *Herschel Explorer* expedition of 2069, during the Pax's ill-fated attempt to establish a research outpost on Titan. Although it was later theorized that the virus was indigenous to Titan itself, the fact that it thrived in an oxygen-nitrogen environment led many people to speculate that the Plague had originated somewhere other than Titan's nitrogen-methane atmosphere. There was even hearsay that the expedition had encountered an extrasolar race on Titan and that the Plague had been passed from Them . . . but, of course, that was just rumor.

Regardless, the indisputable facts are these: by the time the PARN *Herschel Explorer* returned to the inner system, the majority of its crew had been driven insane by an airborne virus. The only reason why the three surviving expedition members, including the ship's commander, were not infected was that they had managed to seal themselves within the command center, where they survived on emergency oxygen supplies and carefully rationed food and water. Most of the unquarantined members butchered each other during the long voyage home; those who did not died in agony when the disease rotted their brains in its terminal stages.

Once the *Herschel Explorer* reached the asteroid belt, the survivors parked it in orbit around Vesta, then used a lifeboat to escape. Three months later, the *Herschel Explorer* was scuttled by the PARN *Intrepid*. By then, Queen Macedonia had decreed that no further expeditions would be sent to Titan and that any vessels attempting to land there would be destroyed by Her Majesty's navy.

Despite the precautions, though, there had been a few isolated outbreaks of Titan Plague, albeit rare and confined to colonies in the outer system. No one knew exactly how the disease spread from the *Herschel Explorer*, although it was believed that it had been carried by the survivors themselves despite rigorous decontamination. Even though the first symptoms resembled little more than the once-common cold, the homicidal dementia that quickly followed was unmistakable. When someone came down with the Plague, there was no other option than to isolate them, remove anything that could be used as a weapon, and wait until they died.

No cure had ever been found.

Somehow, in some way we would never know, the Plague had found its way aboard the *Fool's Gold*. In the close confines of the mass-driver, it had swept through the entire vessel, driving its crew insane before they realized what had hit them. Perhaps the captain had figured it out, yet despite his precautions he himself was infected.

I was safe because I had worn a spacesuit while exploring the ship.

But Bo McKinnon . . .

Captain Future, Man of Tomorrow, dauntless hero of the spaceways. In his search for adventure, McKinnon had recklessly entered the vessel without bothering to don a suit.

"Did you shut the airlock?" I snapped.

"What? Huh?" Pale, visibly shaken by the horrors he had seen, McKinnon was staring at the maniac crouched in the airlock behind us. "Airlock? What . . . which . . . ?"

I grabbed his shoulders and shook him so hard his headset fell down around his neck. "The *Comet* airlock! Did you shut it behind you, or did you leave it open?"

Unable to hear me now, he stammered until he realized that his headset was ajar. He fumbled with it until the earphones were back in place. "The airlock? I think so, I . . ."

"I think so? You moron, did you . . . ?"

"Furland, oh my God . . ." He gaped at the wreckage around him. "What happened to these people? Did they . . . watch out!"

I turned around just in time to catch a glimpse of the madman as he lurched to his feet. Howling at the top of his lungs, he charged toward us, flailing the severed arm like a cricket bat.

I threw McKinnon aside. As he sprawled across the deck, I grabbed the airlock hatch and shoved it closed. An instant later the creature hit the opposite side of the hatch. He almost banged it open, but I put my shoulder against it. The hatch held, and a twist of lockwheel sealed it airtight; nonetheless, I could feel dull vibrations as the madman hammered against it with his hideous trophy.

I couldn't keep him locked in there forever. Sooner or later, he would find the lockwheel and remember how it worked. Perhaps then I could overcome him—if I was lucky, considering his berserk rage—but even then, I didn't dare bring him aboard the *Comet*.

There was only one solution. I found the airlock's outer control panel and flipped open its cover. "I'm sorry, sir," I whispered to the lunatic. "May God have mercy on us both."

Then I pushed the switch that jettisoned the outer hatch.

The alarm bells that rang throughout the bridge were the poor man's funeral dirge. There was long silence after I shut off the alarms, finally broken by McKinnon's voice.

"Mr. Furland, you just murdered that man."

I turned back around. McKinnon had managed to struggle to his feet; he clutched the back of a chair for support, and he glared at me with outraged eyes.

Before I could respond, Jeri's voice came to me over the comlink: *"Rohr, he shut the airlock on the way out. The* Comet *hasn't been infected."*

I let out my breath. For once, Bo had managed to do something right on his own. "Good deal, kiddo. Keep it shut until I come back aboard."

I stepped away from the airlock, heading for the helm station on the other side of the bridge. McKinnon planted himself in my path. "Did you hear me, Mr. Furland?" he demanded, his adam's apple bobbing beneath his beard. "You just killed a man . . . I saw you do it! You . . ."

"Don't remind me. Now get out of my way." I pushed him aside and marched toward the helm.

One of its flatscreens depicted a schematic chart of the asteroid's position and estimated course. As I suspected, someone aboard the mass-driver had deliberately laid in the new course during a fit of insanity. Probably the captain himself, considering the fact that he had locked himself in here.

"I'm placing you under arrest!" McKinnon yelled. "Under my jurisdiction as an agent of the Planet Police, I . . ."

"There's no such thing." I bent over the keypad and went to work accessing the main computer, my fingers thick and clumsy within the suit gloves. "No Planet Police, no asteroid pirates. Just a ship whose air ducts are crawling with the Plague. You're . . ."

"I'm Captain Future!"

The virus must have already affected him. I could have checked to see if he was displaying any of the flu-like symptoms that were supposed to be the Plague's first signs, but he was the least of my worries just now.

No matter what I did, I couldn't access the program for the central navigation system. Lack of a password that had probably died along with one of the damned souls aboard this ship, and none of the standard overrides or interfaces worked either. I was completely locked out, unable to alter the vessel's velocity or trajectory that had it propelling 2046-Barr straight toward Mars.

"And what are you talking about, not letting anyone aboard the *Comet* until you give the word?'' McKinnon was no longer hovering over me; he had found the late captain's chair and had taken it as his own, as if assuming command of a vessel far larger than his measly freighter. "I'm the boss of this ship, not you, and I'm staying in charge until . . .''

Okay. The helm wouldn't obey any new instructions. Maybe it was still possible to scuttle the *Fool's Gold*. I accessed the engineering subsystem and began searching for a way to shut down the primary coolant loop of the gas-core reactor and its redundant safety systems. If I timed it right, perhaps the *Comet* would make a clean getaway before the reactor overloaded . . . and if we were goddamned lucky, the explosion might knock the asteroid sufficiently off-course.

"*Rohr?*" Jeri again. "*What's going on up there?*"

I didn't want to tell her, not with McKinnon eavesdropping on our comlink.

At the sound of her voice, he surged to his feet. "Joan! He's working for Ul Quorn, the Magician of Mars! He's going to . . . !''

I heard him coming long before he reached me. I stood up and, pulling back my arm, landed a right hook square against his hairy jaw.

It stopped him, but it wouldn't keep him stopped. McKinnon was a big guy. He staggered back, his eyes unfocused as he groped at the chair for support. "Traitor," he mumbled, feeling at his mouth with his left hand. "You traitor, you . . .''

I didn't have time for this shit, so I punched him again, this time square in the nose. Second shot did the trick; he reeled backward, sagged against the chair, and flopped flat on his back.

"*What are you doing?*" she demanded.

Even within the thick padding of my gloves, my knuckles hurt like hell. "Something that should have been done a long time ago," I murmured.

Cute linc. I used up the last of my luck that way. I scrambled at the helm console for several more minutes before I submitted to the inevitable. Like the navigation controls, the engineering subsystem wouldn't obey my commands without the proper passwords. It was possible that they were written down somewhere, but I didn't have the time or inclination to go searching through the operations manuals, especially since most of them were strewn across the bridge like so much garbage.

We weren't out of options yet. There was still a final alternative, one which McKinnon himself had given us.

It was then that I knew that Captain Future had to die.

"*Captain Future is dead!*"
The rumbling voice of the big green Jovian space-sailor rose above the laughter and chatter and clink of goblets, in this crowded Venuso-

278   Allen Steele

*polis spacemen's cafe. He eyed his little knot of companions at the bar,
as though challenging them to dispute him.*

*One of the hard-bitten spacemen, a swarthy little Mercurian, shook
his head thoughtfully.*

*"I'm not so sure. It's true that the Futuremen have been missing for
months. But they'd be a hard bunch to kill."*

—Hamilton, Outlaws of the Moon *(1942)*

As I write, I'm back on the Moon, occupying a corner table in Sloppy Joe's.
It's almost closing time; the crowds have thinned out and the bartender has
rung the bell for last call. He'll let me stay after he shuts the doors, though.
Heroes never get booted out with the riffraff, and there's been no shortage
of free drinks ever since I returned from Ceres.

After all, I'm the last person to see Captain Future alive.

The news media helped us maintain our alibi. It was a story that had
everything. Adventure, romance, blood and guts, countless lives at stake.
Best of all, a noble act of self-sacrifice. It'll make a great vid. I sold the
rights yesterday.

Because it's been so widely told, you already know how the story ends.
Realizing that he had been fatally infected with Titan Plague, Bo McKinnon—
excuse me, Captain Future—issued his final instructions as commanding
officer of the TBSA *Comet*.

He told me to return to the ship, and once I was safely aboard, he ordered
Jeri to cast off and get the *Comet* as far away as possible.

Realizing what he intended to do, we tried to talk him out of it. Oh, and
how we argued and pleaded with him, telling him that we could place him
in biostasis until we returned to Earth, where doctors could attempt to save
his life.

In the end, though, McKinnon simply cut off his comlink so that he could
meet his end with dignity and grace.

Once the *Comet* was gone and safely out of range, Captain Future managed
to instruct the mass-driver's main computer to overload the vessel reactors.
While he sat alone in the abandoned bridge, waiting for the countdown, there
was just enough time for him to transmit one final message of courage. . . .

Don't make me repeat it, please. It's bad enough that the Queen read it
aloud during the memorial service, but now I understand that it's going to
be inscribed upon the base of the twice-life-size statue of McKinnon that's
going to be erected at Arsia Station. Jeri did her best when she wrote it, but
between you and me, I still think it's a complete crock.

Anyway, the thermonuclear blast not only obliterated the *Fool's Gold*, but
it also sufficiently altered the trajectory of 2046. The asteroid came within
five thousand kilometers of Mars; its close passage was recorded by the

observatory on Phobos, and the settlements in the Central Meridian reported the largest meteor shower in the history of the colonies.

And now Bo McKinnon is remembered as Captain Future, one of the greatest heroes in the history of humankind.

It was the least Jeri could have done for him.

Considering what a jerk Bo had been all the way to the end, I could have tried to claim the credit, but her strong will persevered. I suppose she's right; it would look bad if it was known that McKinnon had gone out as a raving lunatic who had to be coldcocked by his second officer.

Likewise, no one has to know that four missiles launched from the *Comet* destroyed the mass-driver's main reactor, thus causing the explosion that averted 2046-Barr from its doomsday course. The empty weapon pod was jettisoned before the *Comet* reached Ceres, and the small bribe paid to a minor Pax bureaucrat insured that all records of it ever having been installed on the freighter were completely erased.

It hardly matters. In the end, everyone got what they wanted.

As first officer of the *Comet*, Jeri became its new commander. She offered me her old job, and since the *Jove Commerce* deal was down the tubes, I gratefully accepted. It wasn't long after that before she also offered to show me the rest of her tattoos, an invitation that I also accepted. Her clan still won't speak to her, especially since she now plans to marry a Primary, but at least her fellow Superiors have been forced to claim her as one of their own.

For now, life is good. There's money in the bank, we've shucked our black sheep status, and there's no shortage of companies who want to hire the legendary Futuremen of the TBSA *Comet*. Who knows? Once we get tired of working the belt, maybe we'll settle down and take a shot at beating the odds on this whole cross-breeding thing.

And Bo got what he wanted, even though he didn't live long enough to enjoy it. In doing so, perhaps humankind got what it needed.

There's only one thing that still bothers me.

When McKinnon went nuts aboard the *Fool's Gold* and tried to attack me, I assumed that he had come down with the Plague. This was a correct assumption; he had been infected the moment he had come through the airlock.

However, I later learned that it takes at least six hours for Titan Plague to fully incubate within a human being, and neither of us had been aboard the *Fool's Gold* for nearly half that long.

If McKinnon was crazy at the end, it wasn't because of the Plague. To this day, I have no idea what made him snap . . . unless he believed that I was trying to run off with his ship, his girl, and his goddamn glory.

Hell, maybe I was.

Last night, some nervous kid—a cargo grunt off some LEO freighter, his union card probably still uncreased—sidled up to me at the bar and asked for my autograph. While I was signing the inside cover of his logbook, he told me a strange rumor he had recently heard: Captain Future managed to escape from the *Fool's Gold* just before it blew. According to him, prospectors in the inner belt report spotting a gig on their screens, one whose pilot answers their calls as Curt Newton before transmissions are lost.

I bought the youngster a drink and told him the truth. Naturally, he refused to believe me, nor can I blame him.

Heroes are hard to find. We need to welcome them whenever they appear in our midst. You've just got to be careful to pick the right guy, because it's easy for someone to pretend to be what they're not.

Captain Future is dead.

Long live Captain Future.

—for the late Edmond Hamilton

THE LINCOLN TRAIN

Maureen F. McHugh

▼

There have been many tragic periods in history. As the harrowing story that follows suggests, though, there are few of those periods that couldn't also have been made a little worse . . .

Born in Ohio, Maureen F. McHugh spent some years living in Shijiazhuang in the People's Republic of China, an experience that has been one of the major shaping forces on her fiction. Upon returning to the United States, she made her first sale in 1989, and has since made a powerful impression on the SF world of the early nineties with a relatively small body of work, becoming a frequent contributor to *Asimov's Science Fiction*, as well as selling to *The Magazine of Fantasy & Science Fiction*, *Alternate Warriors*, *Aladdin*, and other markets. In 1992, she published one of the year's most widely acclaimed and talked-about first novels, *China Mountain Zhang*, which received the prestigious Tiptree Memorial Award. She has had stories in our Tenth, Eleventh (in collaboration with David B. Kisor), and Twelfth Annual Collections. Her most recent book is a new novel, *Half the Day Is Night*. She lives with her family in Twinsburg, Ohio.

Soldiers of the G.A.R. stand alongside the tracks. They are General Dodge's soldiers, keeping the tracks maintained for the Lincoln Train. If I stand right, the edges of my bonnet are like blinders and I can't see the soldiers at all. It is a spring evening. At the house the lilacs are blooming. My mother wears a sprig pinned to her dress under her cameo. I can smell it, even in the crush of these people all waiting for the train. I can smell the lilac, and the smell of too many people crowded together, and a faint taste of cinders on the air. I want to go home but that house is not ours anymore. I smooth my black dress. On the train platform we are all in mourning.

The train will take us to St. Louis, from whence we will leave for the Oklahoma territories. They say we will walk, but I don't know how my mother will do that. She has been poorly since the winter of '62. I check my bag with our water and provisions.

"Julia Adelaide," my mother says, "I think we should go home."

"We've come to catch the train," I say, very sharp.

I'm Clara, my sister Julia is eleven years older than me. Julia is married and living in Tennessee. My mother blinks and touches her sprig of lilac uncertainly. If I am not sharp with her, she will keep on it.

I wait. When I was younger I used to try to school my unruly self in Christian charity. God sends us nothing we cannot bear. Now I only try to keep it from my face, try to keep my outer self disciplined. There is a feeling inside me, an anger, that I can't even speak. Something is being bent, like a bow, bending and bending and bending—

"When are we going home?" my mother says.

"Soon," I say because it is easy.

But she won't remember and in a moment she'll ask again. And again and again, through this long long train ride to St. Louis. I am trying to be a Christian daughter, and I remind myself that it is not her fault that the war turned her into an old woman, or that her mind is full of holes and everything new drains out. But it's not my fault either. I don't even try to curb my feelings and I know that they rise up to my face. The only way to be true is to be true from the inside and I am not. I am full of unchristian feelings. My mother's infirmity is her trial, and it is also mine.

I wish I were someone else.

The train comes down the track, chuffing, coming slow. It is an old, badly used thing, but I can see that once it was a model of chaste and beautiful workmanship. Under the dust it is a dark claret in color. It is said that the engine was built to be used by President Lincoln, but since the assassination attempt he is too infirm to travel. People begin to push to the edge of the platform, hauling their bags and worldly goods. I don't know how I will get our valise on. If Zeke could have come I could have at least insured that it was loaded on, but the Negroes are free now and they are not to help. The notice said no family Negroes could come to the station, although I see their faces here and there through the crowd.

The train stops outside the station to take on water.

"Is it your father?" my mother says diffidently. "Do you see him on the train?"

"No, Mother," I say. "We are taking the train."

"Are we going to see your father?" she asks.

It doesn't matter what I say to her, she'll forget it in a few minutes, but I cannot say yes to her. I cannot say that we will see my father even to give her a few moments of joy.

"Are we going to see your father?" she asks again.

"No," I say.

"Where are we going?"

I have carefully explained it all to her and she cried, every time I did. People are pushing down the platform toward the train, and I am trying to decide if I should move my valise toward the front of the platform. Why are they in such a hurry to get on the train? It is taking us all away.

"Where are we going? Julia Adelaide, you will answer me this moment," my mother says, her voice too full of quaver to quite sound like her own.

"I'm Clara," I say. "We're going to St. Louis."

"St. Louis," she says. "We don't need to go to St. Louis. We can't get through the lines, Julia, and I . . . I am quite indisposed. Let's go back home now, this is foolish."

We cannot go back home. General Dodge has made it clear that if we did not show up at the train platform this morning and get our names checked off the list, he would arrest every man in town, and then he would shoot every tenth man. The town knows to believe him, General Dodge was put in charge of the trains into Washington, and he did the same thing then. He arrested men and held them and every time the train was fired upon he hanged a man.

There is a shout and I can only see the crowd moving like a wave, pouring off the edge of the platform. Everyone is afraid there will not be room. I grab the valise and I grab my mother's arm and pull them both. The valise is so heavy that my fingers hurt, and the weight of our water and food is heavy on my arm. My mother is small and when I put her in bed at night she is all tiny like a child, but now she refuses to move, pulling against me and opening her mouth wide, her mouth pink inside and wet and open in a wail I can just barely hear over the shouting crowd. I don't know if I should let go of the valise to pull her, or for a moment I think of letting go of her, letting someone else get her on the train and finding her later.

A man in the crowd shoves her hard from behind. His face is twisted in wrath. What is he so angry at? My mother falls into me, and the crowd pushes us. I am trying to hold on to the valise, but my gloves are slippery, and I can only hold with my right hand, with my left I am trying to hold up my mother. The crowd is pushing all around us, trying to push us toward the edge of the platform.

The train toots as if it were moving. There is shouting all around us. My mother is fallen against me, her face pressed against my bosom, turned up toward me. She is so frightened. Her face is pressed against me in improper intimacy, as if she were my child. My mother as my child. I am filled with revulsion and horror. The pressure against us begins to lessen. I still have a hold of the valise. We'll be all right. Let the others push around, I'll wait and get the valise on somehow. They won't leave us travel without anything.

My mother's eyes close. Her wrinkled face looks up, the skin under her eyes making little pouches, as if it were a second blind eyelid. Everything is so grotesque. I am having a spell. I wish I could be somewhere where I could get away and close the windows. I have had these spells since they told us that my father was dead, where everything is full of horror and strangeness.

The person behind me is crowding into my back and I want to tell them to give way, but I cannot. People around us are crying out. I cannot see anything but the people pushed against me. People are still pushing, but now they are not pushing toward the side of the platform but toward the front, where the train will be when we are allowed to board.

Wait, I call out but there's no way for me to tell if I've really called out or not. I can't hear anything until the train whistles. The train has moved? They brought the train into the station? I can't tell, not without letting go of my mother and the valise. My mother is being pulled down into this mass. I feel her sliding against me. Her eyes are closed. She is a huge doll, limp in my arms. She is not even trying to hold herself up. She has given up to this moment.

I can't hold on to my mother and the valise. So I let go of the valise.

Oh merciful god.

I do not know how I will get through this moment.

The crowd around me is a thing that presses me and pushes me up, pulls me down. I cannot breathe for the pressure. I see specks in front of my eyes, white sparks, too bright, like metal and like light. My feet aren't under me. I am buoyed by the crowd and my feet are behind me. I am unable to stand, unable to fall. I think my mother is against me, but I can't tell, and in this mass I don't know how she can breathe.

I think I am going to die.

All the noise around me does not seem like noise anymore. It is something else, some element, like water or something, surrounding me and overpowering me.

It is like that for a long time, until finally I have my feet under me, and I'm leaning against people. I feel myself sink, but I can't stop myself. The platform is solid. My whole body feels bruised and roughly used.

My mother is not with me. My mother is a bundle of black on the ground, and I crawl to her. I wish I could say that as I crawl to her I feel concern for her condition, but at this moment I am no more than base animal nature and I crawl to her because she is mine and there is nothing else in the world I can identify as mine. Her skirt is rucked up so that her ankles and calves are showing. Her face is black. At first I think it something about her clothes, but it is her face, so full of blood that it is black.

People are still getting on the train, but there are people on the platform around us, left behind. And other things. A surprising number of shoes, all badly used. Wraps, too. Bags. Bundles and people.

I try raising her arms above her head, to force breath into her lungs. Her arms are thin, but they don't go the way I want them to. I read in the newspaper that when President Lincoln was shot, he stopped breathing, and his personal physician started him breathing again. But maybe the newspaper was wrong, or maybe it is more complicated than I understand, or maybe it doesn't always work. She doesn't breathe.

I sit on the platform and try to think of what to do next. My head is empty of useful thoughts. Empty of prayers.

"Ma'am?"

It's a soldier of the G.A.R.

"Yes sir?" I say. It is difficult to look up at him, to look up into the sun.

He hunkers down but does not touch her. At least he doesn't touch her. "Do you have anyone staying behind?"

Like cousins or something? Someone who is not "recalcitrant" in their handling of their Negroes? "Not in town," I say.

"Did she worship?" he asks, in his northern way.

"Yes sir," I say, "she did. She was a Methodist, and you should contact the preacher. The Reverend Robert Ewald, sir."

"I'll see to it, ma'am. Now you'll have to get on the train."

"And leave her?" I say.

"Yes ma'am, the train will be leaving. I'm sorry ma'am."

"But I can't," I say.

He takes my elbow and helps me stand. And I let him.

"We are not really recalcitrant," I say. "Where were Zeke and Rachel supposed to go? Were we supposed to throw them out?"

He helps me climb onto the train. People stare at me as I get on, and I realize I must be all in disarray. I stand under all their gazes, trying to get my bonnet on straight and smoothing my dress. I do not know what to do with my eyes or hands.

There are no seats. Will I have to stand until St. Louis? I grab a seat back to hold myself up. It is suddenly warm and everything is distant and I think I am about to faint. My stomach turns. I breathe through my mouth, not even sure that I am holding on to the seat back.

But I don't fall, thank Jesus.

"It's not Lincoln," someone is saying, a man's voice, rich and baritone, and I fasten on the words as a lifeline, drawing myself back to the train car, to the world. "It's Seward. Lincoln no longer has the capacity to govern."

The train smells of bodies and warm sweaty wool. It is a smell that threatens to undo me, so I must concentrate on breathing through my mouth. I breathe in little pants, like a dog. The heat lies against my skin. It is airless.

"Of course Lincoln can no longer govern, but that damned actor made him a saint when he shot him," says a second voice, "and now no one dare oppose him. It doesn't matter if his policies make sense or not."

"You're wrong," says the first. "Seward is governing through him. Lincoln is an imbecile. He can't govern, look at the way he handled the war."

The second snorts. "He won."

"No," says the first, "we *lost*, there is a difference, sir. We lost even though the north never could find a competent general." I know the type of the first one. He's the one who thinks he is brilliant, who always knew what President Davis should have done. If they are looking for a recalcitrant southerner, they have found one.

"Grant was competent. Just not brilliant. Any military man who is not Alexander the Great is going to look inadequate in comparison with General Lee."

"Grant was a drinker," the first one says. "It was his subordinates. They'd been through years of war. They knew what to do."

It is so hot on the train. I wonder how long until the train leaves.

I wonder if the Reverend will write my sister in Tennessee and tell her about our mother. I wish the train were going east toward Tennessee instead of north and west toward St. Louis.

My valise. All I have. It is on the platform. I turn and go to the door. It is closed and I try the handle, but it is too stiff for me. I look around for help.

"It's locked," says a woman in gray. She doesn't look unkind.

"My things, I left them on the platform," I say.

"Oh, honey," she says, "they aren't going to let you back out there. They don't let anyone off the train."

I look out the window but I can't see the valise. I can see some of the soldiers, so I beat on the window. One of them glances up at me, frowning, but then he ignores me.

The train blows that it is going to leave, and I beat harder on the glass. If I could shatter that glass. They don't understand, they would help me if they understood. The train lurches and I stagger. It is out there, somewhere, on that platform. Clothes for my mother and me, blankets, things we will need. Things I will need.

The train pulls out of the station and I feel so terrible I sit down on the floor in all the dirt from people's feet and sob.

The train creeps slowly at first, but then picks up speed. The clack-clack clack-clack rocks me. It is improper, but I allow it to rock me. I am in others' hands now and there is nothing to do but be patient. I am good at that. So it has been all my life. I have tried to be dutiful, but something in me has not bent right, and I have never been able to maintain a Christian frame of mind, but like a chicken in a yard, I have always kept my eyes on the small things. I have tended to what was in front of me, first the house, then my mother. When we could not get sugar, I learned to cook with molasses and honey. Now I sit and let my mind go empty and let the train rock me.

"Child," someone says. "Child."

The woman in gray has been trying to get my attention for awhile, but I have been sitting and letting myself be rocked.

"Child," she says again, "would you like some water?"

Yes, I realize, I would. She has a jar and she gives it to me to sip out of.

"Thank you," I say. "We brought water, but we lost it in the crush on the platform."

"You have someone with you?" she asks.

"My mother," I say, and start crying again. "She is old, and there was such a press on the platform, and she fell and was trampled."

"What's your name," the woman says.

"Clara Corbett," I say.

"I'm Elizabeth Loudon," the woman says. "And you are welcome to travel with me." There is something about her, a simple pleasantness, that makes me trust her. She is a small woman, with a small nose and eyes as gray as her dress. She is younger than I first thought, maybe only in her thirties? "How old are you? Do you have family?" she asks.

"I am seventeen. I have a sister, Julia. But she doesn't live in Mississippi anymore."

"Where does she live?" the woman asks.

"In Beech Bluff, near Jackson, Tennessee."

She shakes her head. "I don't know it. Is it good country?"

"I think so," I say. "In her letters it sounds like good country. But I haven't seen her for seven years." Of course no one could travel during the war. She has three children in Tennessee. My sister is twenty-eight, almost as old as this woman. It is hard to imagine.

"Were you close?" she asks.

I don't know that we were close. But she is my sister. She is all I have, now. I hope that the Reverend will write her about my mother, but I don't know that he knows where she is. I will have to write her. She will think I should have taken better care.

"Are you traveling alone?"

"My companion is a few seats farther in front. He and I could not find seats together."

Her companion is a man? Not her husband, maybe her brother? But she would say her brother if that's who she meant. A woman traveling with a man. An adventuress, I think. There are stories of women traveling, hoping to find unattached girls like myself. They befriend the young girls and then deliver them to the brothels of New Orleans.

For a moment Elizabeth takes on a sinister cast. But this is a train full of recalcitrant southerners, there is no opportunity to kidnap anyone. Elizabeth is like me, a woman who has lost her home.

It takes the rest of the day and a night to get to St. Louis, and Elizabeth and I talk. It's as if we talk in ciphers, instead of talking about home we talk about gardening, and I can see the garden at home, lazy with bees. She is a quilter. I don't quilt, but I used to do petit pointe, so we can talk sewing and about how hard it has been to get colors. And we talk about mending and making do, we have all been making do for so long.

When it gets dark, since I have no seat, I stay where I am sitting by the door of the train. I am so tired, but in the darkness all I can think of is my mother's face in the crowd and her hopeless open mouth. I don't want to think of my mother, but I am in a delirium of fatigue, surrounded by the dark and the rumble of the train and the distant murmur of voices. I sleep sitting by the door of the train, fitful and rocked. I have dreams like fever dreams. In my dream I am in a strange house, but it is supposed to be my own house, but nothing is where it should be, and I begin to believe that I have actually entered a stranger's house, and that they'll return and find me here. When I wake up and go back to sleep, I am back in this strange house, looking through things.

I wake before dawn, only a little rested. My shoulders and hips and back all ache from the way I am leaning, but I have no energy to get up. I have no energy to do anything but endure. Elizabeth nods, sometimes awake, sometimes asleep, but neither of us speak.

Finally the train slows. We come in through a town, but the town seems to go on and on. It must be St. Louis. We stop and sit. The sun comes up and heats the car like an oven. There is no movement of the air. There are so many buildings in St. Louis, and so many of them are tall, two stories, that I wonder if they cut off the wind and that is why it's so still. But finally the train lurches and we crawl into the station.

I am one of the first off the train by virtue of my position near the door. A soldier unlocks it and shouts for all of us to disembark, but he need not have bothered for there is a rush. I am borne ahead at its beginning but I can stop at the back of the platform. I am afraid that I have lost Elizabeth, but I see her in the crowd. She is on the arm of a younger man in a bowler. There is something about his air that marks him as different—he is sprightly and apparently fresh even after the long ride.

I almost let them pass, but the prospect of being alone makes me reach out and touch her shoulder.

"There you are," she says.

We join a queue of people waiting to use a trench. The smell is appalling, ammonia acrid and eye-watering. There is a wall to separate the men from the women, but the women are all together. I crouch, trying not to notice anyone and trying to keep my skirts out of the filth. It is so awful. It's worse than anything. I feel so awful.

What if my mother were here? What would I do? I think maybe it was better, maybe it was God's hand. But that is an awful thought, too.

"Child," Elizabeth says when I come out, "what's the matter?"

"It's so awful," I say. I shouldn't cry, but I just want to be home and clean. I want to go to bed and sleep.

She offers me a biscuit.

"You should save your food," I say.

"Don't worry," Elizabeth says. "We have enough."

I shouldn't accept it, but I am so hungry. And when I have a little to eat, I feel a little better.

I try to imagine what the fort will be like where we will be going. Will we have a place to sleep, or will it be barracks? Or worse yet, tents? Although after the night I spent on the train I can't imagine anything that could be worse. I imagine if I have to stay awhile in a tent then I'll make the best of it.

"I think this being in limbo is perhaps worse than anything we can expect at the end," I say to Elizabeth. She smiles.

She introduces her companion, Michael. He is enough like her to be her brother, but I don't think that they are. I am resolved not to ask, if they want to tell me they can.

We are standing together, not saying anything, when there is some commotion farther up the platform. It is a woman, her black dress is like smoke. She is running down the platform, coming toward us. There are all of these people and yet it is as if there is no obstacle for her. "NO NO NO NO, DON'T TOUCH ME! FILTHY HANDS! DON'T LET THEM TOUCH YOU! DON'T GET ON THE TRAINS!"

People are getting out of her way. Where are the soldiers? The fabric of her dress is so threadbare it is rotten and torn at the seams. Her skirt is greasy black and matted and stained. Her face is so thin. "ANIMALS! THERE IS NOTHING OUT THERE! PEOPLE DON'T HAVE FOOD! THERE IS NOTHING THERE BUT INDIANS! THEY SENT US OUT TO SETTLE BUT THERE WAS NOTHING THERE!"

I expect she will run past me but she grabs my arm and stops and looks into my face. She has light eyes, pale eyes in her dark face. She is mad.

"WE WERE ALL STARVING, SO WE WENT TO THE FORT BUT THE FORT HAD NOTHING. YOU WILL ALL STARVE, THE WAY THEY ARE STARVING THE INDIANS! THEY WILL LET US ALL DIE! THEY DON'T CARE!" She is screaming in my face, and her spittle sprays me, warm as her breath. Her hand is all tendons and twigs, but she's so strong I can't escape.

The soldiers grab her and yank her away from me. My arm aches where she was holding it. I can't stand up.

Elizabeth pulls me upright. "Stay close to me," she says and starts to walk the other way down the platform. People are looking up following the screaming woman.

She pulls me along with her. I keep thinking of the woman's hand and wrist turned black with grime. I remember my mother's face was black when she lay on the platform. Black like something rotted.

"Here," Elizabeth says at an old door, painted green but now weathered. The door opens and we pass inside.

"What?" I say. My eyes are accustomed to the morning brightness and I can't see.

"Her name is Clara," Elizabeth says. "She has people in Tennessee."

"Come with me," says another woman. She sounds older. "Step this way. Where are her things?"

I am being kidnapped. Oh merciful God, I'll die. I let out a moan.

"Her things were lost, her mother was killed in a crush on the platform."

The woman in the dark clucks sympathetically. "Poor dear. Does Michael have his passenger yet?"

"In a moment," Elizabeth says. "We were lucky for the commotion."

I am beginning to be able to see. It is a storage room, full of abandoned things. The woman holding my arm is older. There are some broken chairs and a stool. She sits me in the chair. Is Elizabeth some kind of adventuress?

"Who are you?" I ask.

"We are friends," Elizabeth says. "We will help you get to your sister."

I don't believe them. I will end up in New Orleans. Elizabeth is some kind of adventuress.

After a moment the door opens and this time it is Michael with a young man. "This is Andrew," he says.

A man? What do they want with a man? That is what stops me from saying, "Run!" Andrew is blinded by the change in light, and I can see the astonishment working on his face, the way it must be working on mine. "What is this?" he asks.

"You are with Friends," Michael says, and maybe he has said it differently than Elizabeth, or maybe it is just that this time I have had the wit to hear it.

"Quakers?" Andrew says. "Abolitionists?"

Michael smiles, I can see his teeth white in the darkness. "Just Friends," he says.

Abolitionists. Crazy people who steal slaves to set them free. Have they come to kidnap us? We are recalcitrant southerners, I have never heard of

Quakers seeking revenge, but everyone knows the Abolitionists are crazy and they are liable to do anything.

"We'll have to wait here until they begin to move people out, it will be evening before we can leave," says the older woman.

I am so frightened, I just want to be home. Maybe I should try to break free and run out to the platform, there are northern soldiers out there. Would they protect me? And then what, go to a fort in Oklahoma?

The older woman asks Michael how they could get past the guards so early and he tells her about the madwoman. A "refugee" he calls her.

"They'll just take her back," Elizabeth says, sighing.

Take her back, do they mean that she really came from Oklahoma? They talk about how bad it will be this winter. Michael says there are Wisconsin Indians re-settled down there, but they've got no food, and they've been starving on government handouts for a couple of years. Now there will be more people. They're not prepared for winter.

There can't have been much handout during the war. It was hard enough to feed the armies.

They explain to Andrew and to me that we will sneak out of the train station this evening, after dark. We will spend a day with a Quaker family in St. Louis, and then they will send us on to the next family. And so we will be passed hand to hand, like a bucket in a brigade, until we get to our families.

They call it the underground railroad.

But we are slave owners.

"Wrong is wrong," says Elizabeth. "Some of us can't stand and watch people starve."

"But only two out of the whole train," Andrew says.

Michael sighs.

The old woman nods. "It isn't right."

Elizabeth picked me because my mother died. If my mother had not died, I would be out there, on my way to starve with the rest of them.

I can't help it but I start to cry. I should not profit from my mother's death. I should have kept her safe.

"Hush, now," says Elizabeth. "Hush, you'll be okay."

"It's not right," I whisper. I'm trying not to be loud, we mustn't be discovered.

"What, child?"

"You shouldn't have picked me," I say. But I am crying so hard I don't think they can understand me. Elizabeth strokes my hair and wipes my face. It may be the last time someone will do these things for me. My sister has three children of her own, and she won't need another child. I'll have to work hard to make up my keep.

There are blankets there and we lie down on the hard floor, all except Michael, who sits in a chair and sleeps. I sleep this time with fewer dreams. But when I wake up, although I can't remember what they were, I have the feeling that I have been dreaming restless dreams.

The stars are bright when we finally creep out of the station. A night full of stars. The stars will be the same in Tennessee. The platform is empty, the train and the people are gone. The Lincoln Train has gone back south while we slept, to take more people out of Mississippi.

"Will you come back and save more people?" I ask Elizabeth.

The stars are a banner behind her quiet head. "We will save what we can," she says.

It isn't fair that I was picked. "I want to help," I tell her.

She is silent for a moment. "We only work with our own," she says. There is something in her voice that has not been there before. A sharpness.

"What do you mean?" I ask.

"There are no slavers in our ranks," she says and her voice is cold.

I feel as if I have had a fever; tired, but clear of mind. I have never walked so far and not walked beyond a town. The streets of St. Louis are empty. There are few lights. Far off a woman is singing, and her voice is clear and carries easily in the night. A beautiful voice.

"Elizabeth," Michael says, "she is just a girl."

"She needs to know," Elizabeth says.

"Why did you save me then?" I ask.

"One does not fight evil with evil," Elizabeth says.

"I'm not evil!" I say.

But no one answers.

WE WERE OUT OF OUR MINDS WITH JOY

David Marusek

▼

In the vivid and pyrotechnic novella that follows, we are taken several decades down the Information Superhighway to a strange and bewildering future where everyone and everything is plugged into everything else, for the bittersweet and compelling story of a man who Has It All . . . for a moment, anyway.

New writer David Marusek is a graduate of Clarion West. He made his first sale to *Asimov's Science Fiction* in 1993, and his second sale soon thereafter to *Playboy*. "We Were Out of Our Minds with Joy" is, amazingly, only his third sale, although it was accomplished enough to make one of the reviewers for *Locus* magazine speculate that Marusek must be a Big Name Author writing under a pseudonym. Not a pseudonym, Marusek lives the life of a struggling young writer in a "low-maintenance cabin in the woods" in Fairbanks, Alaska, and I'm willing to bet that his is a voice we'll be hearing a lot more from as the decade progresses.

I

On March 30, 2092, the Department of Health and Human Services issued Eleanor and me a permit. The under secretary of the Population Division called with the news and official congratulations. We were stunned by our good fortune. The under secretary instructed us to contact the National Orphanage. There was a baby in a drawer in Jersey with our names on it. We were out of our minds with joy.

Eleanor and I had been together a year, ever since a friend of mine introduced us at a party in Manhattan. I was there in realbody, though most guests attended by holo. My friend said, "Sam, there's someone you ought to meet." I wasn't prepared to meet anyone; I shouldn't have even come. I was recovering from a long week of design work in my Chicago studio. In those days I would bolt my door and lose myself in my work, even forgetting to eat or sleep. Henry knew to hold all calls. He alone attended me. Then, a week or two later, I'd emerge famished and lonely, and I'd schlep to the nearest party to gorge myself on canapés, cheese cubes, and those tiny, pickled ears of corn. So there I was, unshaven and disheveled, leaning over my friend's buffet table and wearing such a look of gloom as to challenge anyone to approach me. I hadn't come to talk to people, certainly not to meet anyone. I simply needed to be around people for awhile, to watch them, to listen to their chatter. But my friend tapped me on the shoulder. "Sam Harger," he said, "this is Eleanor Starke. Eleanor, Sam."

A woman stood on a patch of carpet from some other room and sipped coffee from a china cup. We smiled at each other while our belt valet systems briefed us. "Oh," she said almost immediately. "Sam Harger, of course, the artist. I have long admired your work, especially the early stuff. In fact, I've just seen one of your spatter pieces at the museum here."

"And where is here?" I said.

A frown flickered across the woman's remarkable face, but she quickly recovered her smile. She must have wondered if my belt system were totally inept. "Budapest," she said.

Budapest, Henry said inside my head. *Sorry, Sam, but her system won't talk to me. I have gone to public sources. She's some big multinational prosecutor, currently free-lance. I'm scanning for bio's now.*

"You have me at a disadvantage," I told the woman standing halfway around the globe. "I don't pay much attention to law, business, or politics. And my valet is an artist's assistant, not a spy." Unless she was projecting a proxy, this Eleanor Starke was a slender woman, pretty, mid-twenties. She had reddish blonde hair; a sweet, round, disarmingly freckled face, full lips, and very heavy eyebrows. Too sweet to be a prosecutor. Her eyes, however, were anything but sweet. They peered out from under their lashes like eels in coral. "And besides," I said, "I was just leaving."

"So soon?" she said. "Pity." Her bushy eyebrows plunged in disappointment. "Won't you stay another moment?"

Sam, whispered Henry, *no two published bio's of her agree on even the most basic data, not even on her date of birth. She's anywhere from 180 to 204 years old.* This woman was powerful, I realized, if she could scramble secured public databases. *But the People Channel has recently tagged her as a probable celebrity. And she has been seen with a host of artist types in the last dozen months: writers, dancers, conductors, holographers, composers.*

Eleanor nibbled at the corner of a pastry. "This is breakfast for me. I wish you could taste it. There's nothing quite like it stateside." She brushed crumbs from her lips. "By the way, your belt valet, your . . . Henry . . . is quaint. So I have a weakness for artists, so what?" This startled me; she had eavesdropped on my system. "Don't look so surprised," she said. "Your uplink is pretty loose; it's practically a broadband. When was the last time you updated your privacy protocol?"

"You sure know how to charm a fellow," I said.

"That's not my goal."

"What is your goal?"

"Dinner, for starters. I'll be in New York tomorrow."

I considered her invitation and the diversion she might offer. I needed a diversion just then. I needed to escape from inside my head. Getting laid would be nice, but not by this heavy-hitting trophy hunter, this Eleanor Starke. I knew a half-dozen other women in the city I would rather spend my time with.

No, the reason I accepted her invitation was curiosity about her eyebrows. I did not doubt that Eleanor Starke had commissioned someone to fashion her face—perhaps building on her original features. She had molded her own face into a sly weapon for her arsenal of dirty attorney tricks. With it she could appear insignificant and vulnerable. With it she could win over juries. She could fool corporate boards, men and women alike. But why the eyebrows? They were massive. When she spoke they dipped and arched with her words. They were distracting, especially to an artist. I found myself staring at them. As a graphic designer, as a painter of old, I itched to scale them down and thin them out. In the five minutes we talked, they captured my full attention. I, myself, would never do eyebrows like them. Then it occurred to me that these were possibly her natural, unaltered brows, for no licensed face designer—with a reputation to protect—would have the nerve to do them. This Eleanor Starke, shark of the multinationals, may have molded the rest of her features to her advantage, even inflicting herself with freckles, but I became convinced that she had been born a bushy-browed baby, and like a string of artist types before me, I took the bait.

"Not dinner," I replied, "but what about lunch?"

Lunch, as it often does, led to dinner. We screwed like bunnies. The eyebrows were genuine, even their color. Over the next few weeks we tried out the beds in our various apartments all up and down the Eastern Seaboard. Soon the novelty wore off. She stopped calling me, and I stopped calling her—we were sated, or so I thought. She departed on a long trip outside the Protectorate. A month had passed when I received a call from Beijing. Her calendar secretary asked if I would care to hololunch tomorrow. Her late lunch in China would coincide with my midnight brandy in Buffalo. Sure, why not?

I holoed at the appointed time. She had already begun her meal; she was freighting a morsel of water chestnut to her mouth by chopstick when she noticed me. Her entire face lit up with pleasure. "Hi," she said. "Welcome. I'm so glad you could make it." She sat at a richly lacquered table next to a scarlet wall with golden filigree trim. "Unfortunately, I can't stay," she said, placing the chopsticks on her plate. "Last minute program change. So sorry, but I had to see you, even for a moment. How've you been?"

"Fine," I said.

She wore a loose green silk business suit, and her hair was neatly stacked on top of her head. "Can we reschedule for tomorrow?" she asked.

We gazed at each other for several long moments. I was surprised at how comfortable I was with her and how disappointed. I hadn't realized that I'd missed her so much. "Sure, tomorrow."

That night I couldn't sleep, and the whole next day was colored with anticipation. At midnight I said, "Okay, Henry, take me to the Beijing Hilton."

"She's not there," he replied. "She's at the Wanatabe Tokyo tonight."

Sure enough, the scarlet walls were replaced by paper screens. "There you are," she said. "Good, I'm famished." She uncovered a bowl and dished steamy rice onto her plate while telling me in broad terms about a trade deal she was brokering. "They want me to stay, you know. Hire on at triple my rate. Japanese men are funny when they're desperate. They get so . . . so indifferent."

I sipped my drink. "And what did you tell them?" To my surprise, I was anything but indifferent.

She glanced at me, curious. "I told them I would think about it."

We began to meet for a half hour or so each day and talked about whatever came to mind. El's interests were deep and broad; everything fascinated her. She told me, choking with laughter, anecdotes of famous people in awkward circumstances. She revealed curious truths behind the daily news and pointed out related investment opportunities. She teased out of me all sorts of opinion, gossip, and laughter. Her half of the room changed every day and reflected her hectic itinerary: jade, bamboo, and teak. My half of the room never varied. It was the atrium of my hillside house in Santa Barbara where I went in order to be three hours closer to her. As we talked we looked down the yucca- and chaparral-choked canyon to the campus and beach below, to the Channel Islands, and beyond them, to the blue-green Pacific that separated us.

Weeks later, when again we met in realbody, I was shy. I didn't know quite what to do with her. So we talked. We sat close together on the couch and tried to pick up any number of conversational threads. With no success. Her body, so close, befuddled me. I knew her body, or thought I did: I'd unwrapped its expensive clothing a dozen times before. But it was a different body now, occupied, as it was, by El. I was about to make love to El, if ever I could get started.

"Nervous, are we?" she laughed, as she unfastened my shirt.

Fortunately, before we went completely off the deep end, the self-destructive parts of our personalities bobbed to the surface. The promise of happiness can be daunting. El snapped first. We were at her Maine townhouse when her security chief holoed into the room. Until then the only member of her belt valet system—what she called her cabinet—that she had allowed me to meet was her calendar secretary. "I have something to show you," said the security chief, glowering at me from under his bushy eyebrows. I glanced at Eleanor who made no attempt to explain or excuse the intrusion. "This is a realtime broadcast," he said and turned to watch as the holoserver overlaid Eleanor's living room with the studio lounge of the *People Channel*. It was during their "Couples Week" feature, and cohosts Chirp and Ditz were serving up breathless speculation on hapless couples caught by holoeye in public places and yanked for inspection into living rooms across the solar system.

All at once we were outside the Boston restaurant where Eleanor and I had dined that evening. A couple emerged from a cab. He had a black mustache and silver hair and looked like the champion of boredom. She had a vampish hatchet of a face, limp black hair, and vacant eyes.

"Whoodeeze tinguished gentry?" said Ditz to Chirp.

"Carefuh watwesay, lipsome. Dizde ruthless Eleanor K. Starke and'er lately dildude, Samsamson Harger."

I did a double take. The couple on the curb had our bodies and wore our evening clothes, but our heads had been pixeled, were morphed beyond recognition.

Eleanor examined them closely. "Good. Good job."

"Thank you," said her security chief.

"Wait a minute," I said.

Eleanor arched an eyebrow in my direction.

I didn't know what to say. "Isn't commercial broadcast protected by law?" She laughed and turned to her security chief. "Will this ever be traced to me?"

"No."

"Will it occur each and every time any net decides to broadcast anything about me without my expressed permission?"

"Yes."

"Thank you. You may go." The security chief dissolved. Eleanor put her arms around my neck and looked me in the eye. "I value our privacy."

"That's all fine and good," I replied, "but that was *my* image, too, that you altered without *my* expressed permission."

"So? I was protecting you. You should be grateful."

A week later, Eleanor and I were in my Buffalo apartment. Out of the blue she asked me to order a copy of the newly released memoir installment of a certain best-selling author. She said he was a predecessor of mine, a recent lover, who against her wishes had included several paragraphs about their affair in his reading. I told Henry to fetch the reading, but Eleanor said no, that it would be better to order it through the houseputer. When I did so, the houseputer froze up. It just stopped and wouldn't respond. My apartment's comfort support failed. Lights went out, the kitchen quit, and the bathroom door refused to open. "How many copies do you think he'll sell?" Eleanor laughed.

"I get the point."

I was indeed getting the point: El was a tad too paranoid for me. The last straw came when I discovered that her system was messing with Henry. I asked Henry for his bimonthly report on my business, and he said, *please stand by*. I was sitting at the time and stupidly stood up before I realized it.

"What do you mean, 'please stand by,' Henry? What does 'please stand by' mean?"

My processing capabilities are currently overloaded and unavailable. Please stand by.

Nothing like this had ever happened before. "Henry, what is going on?"

There was no response for a long while, then he whispered, *Take me to Chicago*.

Chicago. My studio. That was where his container was. I left immediately, worried sick. Between outages, Henry was able to assure me that he was essentially sound, but that he was preoccupied in warding off a series of security breaches.

"From where? Henry, tell me who's doing this to you."

He's trying again. No, he's in. He's gone. Here he comes again. Please stand by.

Suddenly my mouth began to water, my saliva tasted like machine oil: Henry—or someone—had initiated a terminus purge. I was excreting my interface with Henry. Over the next dozen hours I would spit, sweat, piss, and shit the millions of slave nanoprocessors that resided in the vacuoles of my fat cells and linked me to Henry's box in Chicago. Until I reached my studio, we would be out of contact and I would be on my own. Without a belt valet to navigate the labyrinth of the slipstream tube, I underpassed Illinois altogether and had to backtrack from Toronto. Chicago cabs still respond to voice command, but as I had no way to transfer credit, I was forced to walk ten blocks to the Drexler Building.

Once inside my studio, I rushed to the little ceramic container tucked between a cabinet and the wall. "Are you there?" Henry existed as a pleasant voice in my head. He existed as data streams through space and fiber. He existed as an uroboros signal in a Swiss loopvault. But if Henry existed as a physical being at all, it was as the gelatinous paste inside this box. "Henry?"

The box's ready light blinked on.

* * *

"The fucking bitch! How could she? How dare she?"

"Actually, it makes perfect sense."

"Shut up, Henry."

Henry was safe as long as he remained a netless stand-alone. He couldn't even answer the phone for me. He was a prisoner; we were both prisoners in my Chicago studio. Eleanor's security chief had breached Henry's shell millions of times, nearly continuously since the moment I met her at my friend's party. Henry's shell was an off-the-shelf application I had purchased years ago to protect us against garden variety corporate espionage. I had never updated it, and it was worthless.

"Her cabinet is a diplomat-class unit," said Henry. "What do you expect?"

"Shut up, Henry."

At first the invasion was so subtle and Henry so unskilled, that he was unaware of the foreign presence inside his matrix. When he became aware, he mounted the standard defense, but Eleanor's system flowed through its gates like water. So he set about studying each breach, learning and building ever more effective countermeasures. The attacks escalated, grew so epic that Henry's defense soon consumed his full attention.

"Why didn't you tell me?"

"I did, Sam, several times."

"That's not true. I don't remember you telling me once."

"You have been somewhat preoccupied lately."

"Just shut up."

The question was, how much damage had been done, not to me, but to Henry. There was nothing in my past anyone could use to harm me. I was an artist, after all, not a politician: the public expected me to be shameless. But if Eleanor had damaged Henry to get to my files, I would kill her. I had owned Henry since the days of keyboards and pointing devices. He was the repository of my life's work and life's memory. I could not replace him. He did my bookkeeping, sure, and my taxes, appointments, and legal tasks. He monitored my health, my domiciles, my investments, etc., etc., etc. These functions I could replace; they were commercial programming. I could buy them, and he would modify them to suit his own quirky personality bud. It was his personality bud, itself, I couldn't replace. I had been growing it for eighty years. It was a unique design tool that fit my mind perfectly. I depended on it, on Henry, to read my mind, to engineer the materials I used, and to test my ideas against current tastes. We worked as a team. I had taught him to play the devil's advocate. He provided me feedback, suggestions, ideas, and from time to time—inspiration.

"Eleanor's cabinet was interested neither in your records nor in my personality bud. It simply needed to ascertain, on a continuing basis, that I was still Henry, that no one else had corrupted me.''

"Couldn't it just ask?''

"If I were corrupted, do you think I would tell?''

"Are you corrupted?''

"Of course not.''

I cringed at the thought of installing Henry back into my body not knowing if he were somebody's dirty little worm.

"Henry, you have a complete backup here, right?''

"Yes.''

"One that predates my first contact with Eleanor?''

"Yes.''

"And its seal is intact? It hasn't been tampered with, not even read?''

"Yes.''

Of course if Henry were corrupted and told me the seal was intact, how would I know otherwise? I didn't know the first thing about this stuff.

"You can use any houseputer,'' he said, reading me as he always had, "to verify the seal, and to delete and reset me. But I suggest you don't.''

"Oh yeah? Why?''

"Because we would lose all I've learned since we met Eleanor. I was getting good, Sam. The breaches were taking exponentially longer for them to achieve. I had almost attained stalemate.''

"And meanwhile you couldn't function.''

"So buy me more paste. A lot more paste. We have the credit. Think about it. Eleanor's system is aggressive and dominant. It's always in crisis mode. But it's the good guys. If I can learn how to lock it out, I'll be better prepared to meet the bad guys who'll be trying to get to Eleanor through you.''

"Good, Henry, except for one essential fact. There is no her and me. I'm dropping her. No, I've already dropped her.''

"I see. Tell me, Sam, how many women have you been with since I've known you?''

"How the hell should I know?''

"Well, I know. In the 82.6 years I've associated with you, you've been with 543 women. Your archives reveal at least a hundred more before I was installed.''

"If you say so, Henry.''

"You doubt my numbers? Do you want me to list their names?''

"I don't doubt your numbers, Henry. But what good are names I've forgotten?'' More and more, my own life seemed to me like a Russian novel read long ago. While I could recall the broad outline of the plot, the characters' names eluded me. "Just get to the point.''

"The point is, no one has so affected you as Eleanor Starke. Your biometrics have gone off the scale."

"This is more than a case of biometrics," I said, but I knew he was right, or nearly so. The only other woman that had so affected me was my first love, Janice Scholero, who was a century-and-a-quarter gone. Every woman in between was little more than a single wave in a warm sea of feminine companionship.

Until I could figure out how to verify Henry, I decided to isolate him in his container. I told the houseputer to display "Do Not Disturb—Artist at Work" and take messages. I did, in fact, attempt to work, but was too busy obsessing. I mostly watched the nets or paced the studio arguing with Henry. In the evenings I had Henry load a belt—I kept a few antique Henry interfaces in a drawer—with enough functionality so that I could go out and drink. I avoided my usual haunts and all familiar faces.

In the first message she recorded on my houseputer, El said, "Good for you. Call when you're done." In the second she said, "It's been over a week, must be a masterpiece." In the third, "Tell me what's wrong. You're entirely too sensitive. This is ridiculous. Grow up!"

I tried to tell her what was wrong. I recorded a message for her, a whole seething litany of accusation and scorn, but was too cowardly to post it.

In her fourth message, El said, "It's about Henry, isn't it? My security chief told me all about it. Don't worry; they frisk everyone I meet, nothing personal, and they don't rewrite anything. It's their standing orders, and it's meant to protect me. You have no idea, Sam, how many times I'd be dead if it weren't for my protocol.

"Anyway, I've told them to lay off Henry. They said they could install a deadman alarm in Henry's personality bud, but I said no. Complete hands off. Okay? Is that enough?

"Call, Sam. Let me know you're all right. I . . . miss you."

In the meantime I could find no trace of a foreign personality in Henry. I knew my Henry just as well as he knew me. His thought process was like a familiar tune to me, and at no time during our weeks of incessant conversation did he strike a false note.

El sent her fifth message from bed where she lay naked between iridescent sheets (of my design). She said nothing. She looked directly at the holoeye, propped herself up, letting the sheet fall to her waist, and brushed her hair. Her chest above her breast, as I had discovered, was spangled with freckles.

Bouquets of real flowers began to arrive at my door with notes that said simply, "Call."

The best-selling memoirs that had stymied my Buffalo houseputer arrived on pin with the section about Eleanor extant. The author's sim, seated in a cane-backed chair and reading from a leather-bound book, described Eleanor in his soft southern drawl as a "perfumed vulvoid whose bush has somehow migrated to her forehead, a lithe misander with the emotional range of a militia slug." I asked the sim to stop and elaborate. He smiled at me and said, "In her relations with men, Eleanor Starke is not interested in emotional communion. She prefers entertainment of a more childish variety, like poking frogs with a stick. She is a woman of brittle patience with no time for fluffy feelings or fuzzy thoughts. Except in bed. In bed Eleanor Starke likes her men half-baked, the gooier the better. That's why she likes to toy with artists. The higher an opinion a man has of himself, the more painfully sensitive he is, the more polished his hubris, the more fun it is to poke him open and see all the runny mess inside."

"You don't know what you're talking about," I yelled at the sim. "El's not like that at all. You obviously never knew her. She's no saint, but she has a heart, and affection and . . . and . . . go fuck yourself."

"Thank you for your comments. May we quote you? Be on the lookout for our companion volume to this memoir installment, *The Skewered Lash Back*, due out in September from Little Brown Jug."

I had been around for 147 years and was happy with my life. I had successfully navigated several careers and amassed a fortune that even Henry had trouble charting. Still, I jumped out of bed each day with a renewed sense of interest and adventure. I would have been pleased to live the next 147 years in exactly the same way. And yet, when El sent her farewell message—a glum El sitting in a museum somewhere, a wall-sized early canvas of mine behind her—I knew my life to be ashes and dirt.

Seventy-two thick candles in man-sized golden stands flanked me like sentries as I waited and fretted in my tuxedo at the altar rail. The guttering beeswax flames filled the cathedral with the fragrance of clover. *Time Media* proclaimed our wedding the "Wedding of the Year" and broadcast it live on the *Wedding Channel*. A castrati choir, hidden in the gloom beneath the giant bronze pipes of the organ, challenged all to submit to the mercy of Goodness. Their sweet soprano threaded through miles of stone vaults, collecting odd echoes and unexpected harmony. Over six million guests fidgeted in wooden pews that stretched, it seemed, to the horizon. And each guest occupied an aisle seat at the front.

In the network's New York studio, El and I, wearing keyblue body suits, stood at opposite ends of a bare soundstage. On cue, El began the slow march towards me. In Wawel Castle overlooking ancient Cracow, however, she marched through giant cathedral doors, her ivory linen gown awash in morning light. The organ boomed Mendelssohn's wedding march, amplified by acres of marble. Two girls strewed rose petals at Eleanor's feet, while another tended her long train. A gauzy veil hid El's face from all eyes except mine.

No man walked at her side; a two-hundred-year-old bride, Eleanor preferred to give herself away.

By the time of the wedding, El and I had been living together for six months. We had moved in together partly out of curiosity, partly out of desperation. Whatever was going on between us was mounting. It was spreading and sinking roots. It was like a thing inside us, but apart and separate from us, too. We talked about it, always "it," not sure what to call it. It complicated our lives, especially El's. We agreed we'd be better off without it and tried to remember, from experiences in our youth, how to fix the feelings we were feeling. The one sure cure, guaranteed to make a man and a woman wish they'd never met, was for them to cohabitate. If there was one thing humankind had learned in four million years of evolution, it was that man and woman were not meant to live in the same hut. And since the passage of the Procreation Ban of 2041, there has been little biological justification for doing so.

So, we co-purchased a townhouse in Connecticut. It wasn't difficult for us to stake out our separate bedrooms and work spaces, but decorating the common areas required the diplomacy and compromise of a border dispute. Once in and settled, we agreed to open our house on Wednesday evenings and began the arduous task of melding our friends and colleagues.

We came to prefer her bedroom for watching the nets and mine for making love. When it came to sleeping, however, she required her own bed—alone. Good, we thought, here was a crack we could wedge open. We surveyed for other incompatibilities. She was a late night person, while I rose early. She liked to travel and go out a lot, while I was a stay-at-homer. She loved classical music, while I could stand only neu-noise. She had a maniacal need for total organization of all things, while for me a cluttered space was a happy space.

These differences, however, seemed only to heighten the pleasure we took in each other. We were opposites attracting, two molecules bonding—I don't know—two dogs trying to get unstuck.

The network logged 6.325 million subscribers to our wedding, altogether a modest rating. Nevertheless, the guest book contained some of the most powerful signatures on the planet (El's admirers) and the confetti rained down for weeks. The network paid for a honeymoon on the Moon, including five days at the Lunar Princess and round-trip fare aboard Pan Am.

Eleanor booked a third seat on the shuttle, not the best portent for a successful honeymoon. She assigned me the window seat, took the aisle seat for herself, and into the seat between us she projected one cabinet member after another. All during the flight, she took their reports, issued orders, and strategized with them, not even pausing for lift-off or docking. Her cabinet consisted of about a dozen officials and, except for her security chief, they were all women. They all appeared older than El's current age, and they all bore a distinct Starke family resemblance: reddish-blond hair, slender build, the eyebrows. If they were real people, rather than the projections of El's belt system, they could be her sisters and brother, and she the spoiled baby of the family.

Two cabinet officers especially impressed me, the attorney general, a smartly dressed woman in her forties with a pinched expression, and the chief of staff, who was the eldest of the lot. This chief of staff coordinated the activities of the rest and was second in command after El. She looked and spoke remarkably like El. She was not El's oldest sister, but El, herself, at seventy. She fascinated me. She was my Eleanor stripped of meat, a stick figure of angles and knobs, her eyebrows gone colorless and thin. Yet her eyes burned bright, and she spoke from a deep well of wisdom and authority. No wonder Henry, a pleasant voice in my head, admired El's cabinet.

It had been ages since I had flown in an orbital craft; my last time had been before the development of airborne nasties, smartactives, militia slugs, visola, and city canopies. In a tube, you hardly noticed your passage across barriers since the tube, itself, was a protuberance of the canopies. Looking out my window, I was surprised to see that the shuttlecraft wing was covered with the same sharkskin used on militia craft. But it made sense. Once out of the hangar we were in the great, wild outside and the target of every nastie released into the atmosphere. On the runway, the sharkskin's protective slime foamed away contaminants. After takeoff, the skin rippled and trimmed itself, and our speed was our protection until we reached the stratosphere where the skin relaxed and resumed its foaming.

The flight attendant, a michelle named Traci, was excellent. When the view outside my window lost my interest, she brought me a pillow. I had been about to ask for one. She offered us drinks, including Eleanor's chief of staff who happened to be in the middle seat at the moment. This pleased Eleanor immensely. The michelle knew that if a passenger reserved a seat for her belt valet, it was best to treat the valet as real.

We watched the michelle attend to the other passengers in our compartment. She had well-rounded breasts and hips and filled out her smartly tailored teal uniform. She was diminutive—a michelle grew to about five feet tall—a doll woman, dark complexioned and full of promise, Mediterranean. Eleanor said, "Applied People employees are consistently superior to MacPeople people."

"No matter their agency, michelles are superior," said her chief of staff. "You simply cannot fluster them."

Before my nap, I left my seat to use the rest room. The forward toilets were occupied, so I went aft through the coach section. All of the passengers there were clumped in the most forward seats, except for five people—one woman and four men—at the tail, with a large unoccupied section between the two groups. Odd. When I reached the tail, I noticed a sharp, foul odor, like rotting cheese. The odor was even stronger in the rest room, and I wondered how Pan Am could operate so negligently. Returning through the coach section, I realized that the bulk of passengers were sitting forward to avoid the odor, and I wondered why the small group of five remained at the tail. When I glanced back at them, they—all of them—regarded me with cold malice.

Back in my seat, I plumped my pillow and prepared to nap. El's security chief, whose turn it was in the middle, looked at me and leered, "So what you think of 'em?"

"Them who?"

"The stinkers back there."

"The stinkers?" I wasn't familiar with the term. (*Seared*, said Henry in my head.) "You mean those people were seared?"

"Yeah, but don't worry. They're harmless, and then some."

I was appalled. Of course I'd heard that the National Militia was searing living individuals these days—felons mostly, whose crimes were not heinous enough to warrant outright extermination—but I had thought it to be a rare punishment. And now here were five of the seared on the same shuttle. "Where are they going?"

"Let's see," said the security chief. "They have passage booked from the Moon aboard a Jupiter freighter. They're emigrating to the colonies, most likely. Good riddance."

So the flight, so the honeymoon. Within hours of checking into the Sweetheart Suite of the Lunar Princess, Eleanor was conducting full cabinet meetings. I was left to take bounding strolls around the duty-free dome alone. I didn't mind. I like my solitude.

I happened to be in the suite when Eleanor "took the call." The official seal of the Tri-Discipline Council filled our living room with its stately gyration and dissolved as Audrey Foldstein, herself, appeared before us sitting at her huge oaken desk. She greeted us and apologized for barging in on our honeymoon. I was dumbfounded. Here was Audrey Foldstein, chair of the Tri-D Board of Governors, one of the most powerful persons on Earth, parked at her trademark desk in our hotel suite. She turned to me and praised the inventiveness of my work in package design, and especially the camouflage work I had done forty years before for the National Militia. She also mentioned my evacuation blanket for trauma and burn victims. She spoke sincerely and at length and then turned to Eleanor. "Ms. Starke, do you know why I'm here?"

"I believe so, Ms. Foldstein." Eleanor sat erect, regarded the holo with a steady gaze, and sent me a message through Henry, *Eleanor's chief of staff extends Eleanor's apology for not informing you sooner of her nomination. She would have told you had she thought there was any chance of her actually being designated.*

Nomination to what? I tongued back.

"These are the most exciting days known to humankind," said Audrey Foldstein, "as well as the most perilous. Each hour that passes brings wonders—and dangers—unimagined by our parents. . . ." Foldstein appeared to be in her mid-forties, an age compatible with her monstrous authority, while my El looked like a devoted daughter. ". . . and as a member of the Tri-Discipline Board of Governors, one must ever dedicate oneself—no, *consecrate* oneself—to upholding these principles, namely . . ."

A Tri-D Governor! Was that possible? My El?

". . . You will be asked to make decisions and bear responsibilities no reasonable person would choose to make or bear. You will be a target of vocal—even violent—recrimination. And with a new family . . ." Ms. Foldstein glanced at me, ". . . you will be that much more vulnerable . . ."

Henry whispered, *Eleanor's chief of staff says Eleanor asks twice if you know what this means.*

I puzzled over this message. It had been flattened by its passage through two artificial minds. What Eleanor had probably said was, "Do you know what this means? Do you know what this means?"

Yes, dear Eleanor, I tongued through Henry, *I do. It means that every door everywhere stands open to you. Congratulations, lover. It means you have climbed onto the world stage.*

She glanced at me and winked.

By the time we shuttled back to Earth, the confirmation process was well underway. Over the next few tortuous weeks, Congressional Committees strenuously debated Eleanor's designation in public, while multinationals and the National Militia deliberated in camera. One day El would float through the house in regal exaltation. The next day she would collapse on the couch to bitterly rue the thousands of carefully buried indiscretions of her past that threatened to resurface. On the morning she testified before the Tri-D Board of Governors, she was centered, amiable, and razor-sharp. Immediately upon returning home she summoned me to my bedroom and demanded rushed, rough sex from me. Twenty minutes later she couldn't stand the sorry sight of me.

I supported her every which way I could think of. I put my own career on hold. Actually, I hadn't been to my Chicago studio since nursing Henry there.

When Eleanor was finally confirmed, we took the slipstream tube down to Cozumel for some deep-sea diving and beachcombing. It was meant to be a working vacation, but by then I suffered no illusions about Eleanor's ability to relax. There were too many plans to make and people to meet. And indeed, she kept some member of her cabinet at her side at all times: on the beach, in the boat, at the Mayan theme village, even in the cramped quarters of the submersible.

We had planned to take advantage of an exclusive juve clinic on the island to shed some age. My own age-of-choice was my mid-thirties, the age at which my body was still active enough to satisfy my desires, but mellow enough to sit through long hours of creative musing. El and I had decided on the three-day gelbath regimen and had skipped our morning visola to give our cells time to excrete their gatekeepers. But at the last moment, El changed her mind. She decided she ought to grow a little older. So I went to the clinic alone and bathed in the gels twice a day. Billions of molecular smartactives soaked through my skin; permeated my muscles, cartilage, bones, and nerves; politely snip, snip, snipped away protein cross-links and genetic anomalies; and gently flushed away the sludge and detritus of age.

I returned to the bungalow on Wednesday, frisky and bored, and volunteered to prepare it for our regular weekly salon. I had to sift through a backlog of thousands of recorded holos from our friends and associates. More congratulations and confetti for El's appointment. The salon, itself, was a stampede. More people holoed down than our bungalow could accommodate. Its primitive holoserver was overwhelmed by so many simultaneous transmissions, our guests were superimposed over each other five or ten bodies deep, and the whole squirming mass of them flickered around the edges.

Despite the confusion, I quickly sensed that this was a farewell party—for Eleanor. Our friends assumed she would be posted offplanet; all new Tri-D governors were, as all Earth posts were filled. At the same time, no one expected me to go with her—who would? Given people's longevity, it could take decades—or centuries—for Eleanor to acquire enough seniority to be transferred back to Earth. But I replied, each time the subject was broached, "Of course I'm going with her; a husband needs the regular real-body presence of his wife." Lame but true, yet each time I said it I felt sick. I didn't want to leave Earth. I had never wanted to be a colonist. I became constipated at low-g. Lifesuits gave me a rash. And would I be able to work? It was true I could holo my Chicago studio anywhere, but if I followed Eleanor out to some galactic rock, would my Muse follow me?

By the time the last guest signed off, we were exhausted. Eleanor got ready for bed, but I poured myself a glass of tea and went out to sit on the beach.

Wet sand. The murmur of the surf. The chilly breeze. It was a lovely equatorial dawn. "Henry," I said, "record this."

Relax, Sam. I always record the best of everything.

"I'm sure you do, Henry."

In the distance, the island's canopy dome shimmered like a veil of rain falling into the sea. The edges of the sea, the waves that surged up the beach to melt away in the sand at my feet, carried the ripe, salty smell of fish and seaweed and whales and lost sailors moldering in the deep. The ocean had proven to be a good delivery medium for molecular nasties, which can float around the globe indefinitely, like particularly rude messages in tiny bottles, until they washed up on someone's—hopefully the enemy's—shore. The island's defense canopy, more a sphere than a dome, extended through the water to the ocean floor, and deep into bedrock.

"So tell me, Henry, how are you and the cabinet getting along?" I had taken his advice, bought him more neural paste, and allowed the protocol games to continue.

The cabinet is a beautiful intelligence. I consider emulating it.

"In what way?"

I may want to bifurcate my personality bud.

"So that there's two of you? Why would you want to do that?"

Then I would be more like you.

"You would? Is that good?"

I believe so. I have recently discovered that I have but one point-of-view, while you have several that you alternate at will.

"It sounds like I bought you more paste than you know what to do with."

I don't think so, Sam. I think my thinking is evolving, but how am I to know?

It was. I recognized the symptoms.

Think of how much more flexible I could be if I could question myself, disagree with myself.

I'd rather not. All I needed was a pair of philosophy students inside my head with their tiresome discourse and untimely epiphanies. Still, I had to be careful how I handled this situation—artificial personalities bruised as easily as organic ones, and they evolved whether or not we gave them permission.

"Henry, couldn't you and I discuss things, you know, like we always have? Couldn't you just ask me the questions?"

No offense, Sam, but you wouldn't be able to keep up.

"Thank you, Henry. I'll think about it and get back to you."

Sam, the calendar secretary is hailing us. How shall I respond?

"Tell her we'll return to the bungalow soon."

Before long, Eleanor walked up the beach. She knelt behind me and massaged my shoulders. "I've been neglecting you," she said, "and you've been wonderful. Can you forgive me?"

"There's nothing to forgive. You're a busy person. I knew that from the start."

"Still, it must be hard." She sat in the sand next to me and wrapped her arms around me. "It's like a drug. I'm drunk with success. But I'll get over it."

"There's no need. You've earned it. Enjoy it."

"You don't want to go offplanet, do you?"

"I'll go anywhere to be with you."

"Yes, I believe you would. Where do men like you come from?"

"From Saturn. We're Saturnian."

She laughed. "I'm sure I could draw a post there if you'd like."

"Wherever." I leaned my head on her shoulder. "I've given up trying to escape you. I surrender."

"Oh? What are your terms of surrender?"

"Treat me fair, don't ever hurt me—or Henry—and don't ever leave me."

"Done."

Not long after our return to our Connecticut townhouse and before El received her posting, we heard some good news. Good for us anyway. Ms. Angie Rickert, Tri-Discipline Governor, posted in Indiana, had been missing for three hours. Eleanor raised her hands to deny any complicity as she told me the news, but she was barely able to stifle her glee. Ms. Rickert had been at her post for fifty-three years.

"But she's only missing," I said.

"For three hours? Come on, Sam, be realistic."

Over the next twenty-four hours, Eleanor's security chief discreetly haunted the high-security nets to feed us details and analyses as they emerged. A militia slug, on routine patrol, found Ms. Rickert's remains in and around a tube car in a low security soybean field outside the Indianapolis canopy. She was the victim of an unidentified molecular antipersonnel smartactive—a nastie. Her belt system, whose primary storage container was seized by the militia and placed under the most sanitary interrogation, claimed that Ms. Rickert was aware of her infection when she entered the tube car outside her Indianapolis apartment. The belt used Ms. Rickert's top security privileges to jettison the car and its stricken passenger out of the city and out of the tube system itself. So virulent was the attacking nastie and so stubborn Ms. Rickert's visola induced defenses, that in the heat of battle her body burst. Fortunately, it burst within the car and contaminated only two or three square miles of farmland. Ms. Rickert's reliable belt system had prevented a disaster within the Indianapolis canopy. The militia collected her scattered remains, and the coroner declared Ms. Rickert irretrievable.

And so a vacant post in the heartland was up for grabs. Eleanor turned her bedroom into a war room. She sent her entire staff into action. She lined up every chit, every favor, and every piece of dirt she had collected in her long career.

One morning, several sleepless days later, she brought me coffee, a Danish, my morning dose of visola, and a haggard smile. "It's in the bag," she said.

And she was correct. Ten days later, CNN carried a story that the Tri-Discipline Council's newest governor designate, Ms. Eleanor Starke, spouse of noted package designer Sam Harger, had been stationed in Bloomington, Indiana, to replace Ms. Angie Rickert who'd recently died under undisclosed circumstances. A host of pundits and experts debated for days the meaning of such a move and speculated on Eleanor's victory over hundreds of her senior offplanet colleagues for the plum post. Eleanor, as per Tri-D policy, respectfully declined all interviews. In my own interviews, I set the precondition that I be asked only about my own career. When asked if I could pursue my work in Indiana, I could only grin and say, Indiana is not the end of the world. And how had my work been going lately? Miserably, I replied. I am the type of artist that seems to work best while in a state of mild discontent, and lately I'd been riding a streak of great good fortune.

Smug bastard.

We moved into temporary quarters, into an apartment on the 207th floor of the Williams Towers in Bloomington. We planned to eventually purchase a farmstead in an outlying county surrounded by elm groves and rye fields. El's daily schedule, already at marathon levels, only intensified, while I pottered about the campus town trying to figure out why—if I was so lucky—did I feel so apprehensive.

Then the event occurred that dwarfed all that came before it. Eleanor and I, although we'd never applied, were issued a permit to retro-conceive a baby. These permits were impossible to come by, as only about twelve hundred were issued each year in all of North America. We knew no one who'd been issued a permit. I hadn't even seen a baby in realbody for decades (although babies figured prominently in most holovids and comedies). We were so stunned at first we didn't know how to respond. "Don't worry," said the under secretary of the Population Division, "most recipients have the same reaction. Some faint."

Eleanor said, "I don't see how I could take on the additional responsibility at this time."

The under secretary frowned. "Does that mean you wish to refuse the permit?"

Eleanor blanched. "I didn't say that." She glanced at me, uncharacteristically pleading for help.

I didn't know what to say either. "A boy or a girl?"

"That's entirely up to you, now isn't it?" The under secretary favored us with a fatuous grin. "I'll tell you what." In his voice I heard forced spontaneity; he'd been over this ground many times before, and I wondered if that was the sum total of his job, to call twelve hundred strangers each year and grant them one of life's supreme gifts. "We'll provide background information. When you're ready, call the National Orphanage in Trenton."

For the next hour or so, El and I sat arm-in-arm on the couch in complete silence. Suddenly El began to weep. Tears gushed from her eyes and coursed down her face. She hugged herself—like a lost child, I thought—and fought for breath between sobs. I watched in total amazement. Was this my Eleanor?

After a while, she looked at me, smiled, and said through bubbles of snot, "Well?"

I had to be truthful. "Let's not rush into anything."

She studied me and said, "I agree with you."

"Let's think about it."

"My thought exactly."

At the National Orphanage in Trenton, the last thing they did was take tissue samples for recombination. Eleanor and I sat on chromium stools, side-by-side, in a treatment room as the nurse, a middle-aged jenny, scraped the inside of Eleanor's cheek with a curette. We had both been off visola for forty-eight hours, dangerous but necessary to obtain a pristine DNA sample. Henry informed me that Eleanor's full cabinet was on red alert. Eleanor was tense. This was *coitus mechanicus*, but it was bound to be the most fruitful sex we would ever have.

At the National Orphanage in Trenton, the first thing they did was sit us down in Dr. Deb Armbruster's office to warn us that raising a child today was nothing like it used to be. "Kids used to grow up and go away," said Dr. Armbruster. "Nowadays, they tend to get stuck around age eight and then again at thirteen. And it's not considered good parenting, of course, to force them to age. We think it's all the attention they get. Everyone—your friends, your employer, well-wishing strangers, militia officers—everyone comes to steal a kiss from the baby, to make funny faces at the toddler, to play catch or hoops with the five-year-old. Gifts arrive by the vanload. The media wants to be included in every decision and invited to every birthday party.

"Oh, but you two know how to handle the media, I imagine."

Eleanor and I sat in antique chairs in front of Dr. Armbruster's neatly arranged desk. There was no third chair for Eleanor's chief of staff, who stood patiently next to Eleanor. Dr. Armbruster was a large, fit woman, with a square jaw, rounded nose, and pinpoint eyes that glanced in all directions as she spoke. No doubt she had arranged her belt system in layers of display monitors around the periphery of her vision. Many administrative types did. With the flick of an iris, they could page through reams of reports, graphs, and archives. And they looked down their noses at projected valets with personality buds, like Eleanor's chief of staff.

"So," Dr. Armbruster continued, "you may have a smart-mouthed adolescent on your hands for twenty or thirty years. That, I can assure you, becomes tiresome. And expensive. You, yourselves, could be two or three relationships down the road before the little darling is ready to leave. So we suggest you work out custody now, before you go any further.

"In any case, protectorate law mandates a three-day cooling-off period between this interview and our initiation of the conversion process. You have three days—till Thursday—to change your minds. Think it over."

At the National Orphanage in Trenton, the second thing they did was take us to the storage room to see the chassis that would become our baby.

One wall held a row of carousels, each containing hundreds of small drawers. Dr. Armbruster rotated a carousel and told a particular drawer to unlock itself. She removed from it a small bundle wrapped in a rigid red tetanus blanket (a spin-off of my early work for the National Militia). She placed it on a ceramic gurney, commanded the blanket to relax, and unwrapped it to reveal a near-term human fetus, curled in repose, a miniature thumb stuck in its perfect mouth. It was remarkably lifelike, but rock still, like a figurine. I asked how old it was. Dr. Armbruster said it had been in stasis seven-and-a-half years; it was confiscated in an illegal pregnancy. Developmentally, it was thirty-five weeks old; it had been doused *in utero*. She rotated the fetus—the chassis—on the gurney. "It's normal on every index. We should be able to convert it with no complications." She pointed to this and that part of it and explained the order of rewriting. "The integumentary system—the skin, what you might call our fleshy package," she smiled at me acknowledging my reputation, "is a human's fastest growing organ. A person sheds and replaces it continuously throughout her life. In the conversion process, it's the first one completed. For a fetus, it takes about a week. Hair color, eye color, the liver, the heart, the digestive system convert in two to three weeks. The nervous system, major muscle groups, reproductive organs—three to four weeks. Cartilage and bones—two to three months. Long before its first tooth erupts, the baby is biologically yours."

I asked Dr. Armbruster if I could hold the chassis.

"Certainly," she said with a knowing smile. She placed her large hands carefully under the baby and handed it to me. It was surprisingly heavy, hard, and cold. "The fixative is very dense," she said, "and makes it brittle, like eggshell." I cradled it in my arms awkwardly. Dr. Armbruster said to Eleanor, "They always look like that, afraid they're going to break it. In this case, however, that's entirely possible. And you, my dear, look typically uncomfortable as well."

She was right. Eleanor and her chief of staff stood side-by-side, twins (but for their ages), arms crossed stiffly. Dr. Armbruster said to her, "You might find the next few months immensely more tolerable, enjoyable even, under hormonal therapy. Fathers, it would seem, have always had to learn to bond with their offspring. For you we have something the pharmaceutical companies call 'Mother's Medley.' "

"No, thank you, Doctor," said Eleanor, glaring at her chief of staff, who immediately uncrossed her arms. Eleanor came over to me and I transferred the chassis to her. "Heavy," she said. "And look, it's missing a finger!" One of its tiny fingers was indeed missing, the stub end rough like plaster.

"Don't be concerned," said Dr. Armbruster. "Fingers and toes grow back in days. Just don't break off the head," she laughed.

"Sam, look," Eleanor exclaimed. "Look at this tiny little penis. Isn't it the cutest thing?"

As I looked, something funny happened to me. I had a vivid impression or image, as I do when at work in my studio, in which I saw the chassis, not as a brittle lump of fixed flesh, but as a living, warm, squirming, naked butterball of a baby. And I looked between its chubby legs and saw it was a he, a little guy. He looked up at me, chortled, and waved his tiny fists. Right then I felt a massive piece of my heart shift in my chest. The whole situation finally dawned on me. I was about to become a parent, a *father*. I looked at the chassis and saw my son. Why a son, I couldn't say, but I knew I must have a *son*.

Eleanor touched my arm. "Are you okay?"

"Yes, it's nothing. By the way, that's one piece I hope doesn't chip off."

She laughed, but when she saw that I was serious she said, "We'll have to see about that." She drilled me with her terribly old eyes and said, "About that we'll just have to see."

Back at the Williams Towers in Bloomington, we lay on the balcony in the late afternoon sun and skimmed the queue of messages. Our friends had grown tired of our good fortune: the congratulations were fewer and briefer and seemed, by-and-large, insincere, even tinged with underlying resentment.

And who could blame them? Of all the hundreds of people we knew, none of them had a real child. Many people, it was true, had had children in the old days, before the Population Treaties when babies were considered an ecological nuisance, but that was almost sixty years ago, and sixty years was a long time to live outside the company of children. Probably no one be-grudged us our child, although it was obvious to everyone—especially to us—that major strings had been pulled for us at the Department of Health and Human Services. String pulling, itself, did not bother El, but anonymous string-pulling did. She had sent her security chief into the nets, but he was unable to identify our benefactor. El insisted that whoever was responsible was surely not a benefactor, for a baby could hardly be considered a reward. Most likely an enemy, perhaps an off-planet rival she had aced out of the Indianapolis post, which meant the baby was bait in some as yet unsprung plot. Or perhaps the baby was simply a leash her superiors at the Tri-D council had decided to fit her with. In any case, Eleanor was convincing herself she was about to make the worst mistake of her life.

She deleted the remaining queue of messages and turned to me. "Sam, please talk me out of this baby thing." We lay on our balcony halfway up the giant residential tower that ended, in dizzying perspective, near the lower reaches of the canopy. The canopy, invisible during the day, appeared viscous in the evening light, like a transparent gel that a stiff breeze caused to ripple and fold upon itself. In contrast, our tower had a matte surface encrusted with thousands of tiny black bumps. These were the building's resident militia slugs, absorbing the last light of the setting sun to top off their energy stores for a busy night patrolling living rooms and bedrooms.

"You're just nervous," I said to Eleanor.

"I have impeccable instincts."

"Did you ever have children before?"

"Not that it's relevant, but yes, two, a boy and a girl, in my old life. Tom died as a child in an accident. Angie grew up, moved away, married, led a successful career as a journalist, and died at age fifty-four of breast cancer. A long time ago." Eleanor turned over, bare rump to the sky, chin resting on sun-browned arms. "I grieved for each of them forever, and then one day I stopped. All that's left are memories, which are immaterial to this discussion."

"Would you like to have another?"

"Yes, desperately."

"Why 'desperately'?"

She was silent for a while. I watched a slug creep along the underside of the balcony of the apartment above us. "I don't know," she said. "It's funny. I've already been through it all: pregnancy, varicose veins, funerals. I've been through menopause and—worse—back through remenses. I was so tangled up in motherhood, I never knew if I was coming or going. I loved or hated every moment of it, wouldn't have traded it for the world. But when it was all over I felt an unbearable burden lifted from me. Thank god, I said, I won't have to do that again. Yet since the moment we learned of the permit, my arms have been aching to hold a baby. I don't know why. I think it's this schoolgirl body of mine. It's a baby machine, and it intends to force its will on me. I have often observed that you men regard your bodies as large pets, and I've never understood that, till now. I've never felt so removed from myself, from my body.

"But it doesn't have to have its way, does it? I can rise above it. Let's tell them to keep their chassis."

The slug bypassed our balcony, but another slug was making its way slowly down the wall.

I said, "What about this leash theory of yours?"

"I'm sure I'm correct in my assessment. They could get to me by threatening *you*, of course, but they know if it came down to it, I would—no offense—cut you loose."

"No offense taken."

She placed her hand on my cheek. "You know how much I love you. Or maybe you don't know yet. But I'm expendable, Sam, and so are you."

"But not a baby."

"No," she said, "not a baby, not *my* baby. I would do anything to keep my baby safe, and they know it. Let's refuse the permit, Sam. Okay?"

The militia slug had sensed us. It was coming in for a taste. "What about me?" I said. "I might enjoy being a dad. And can you imagine our baby, El? A little critter crawling around our ankles, half you and half me, a little Elsam or Sameanor?"

She closed her eyes and smiled. "That would be a pitiable creature."

"And speaking of ankles," I said, "we're about to be tasted."

The slug, a tiny thing, touched her ankle, attached itself to her for a moment, then dropped off. With the toes of her other foot, Eleanor scratched the tasting site. Slugs only tickled her. With me it was different. There was some nerve tying my ankle directly to my penis, and I found that warm, prickly kiss unavoidably arousing. So, as the slug attached itself to my ankle, El watched mischievously. At that moment, in the glow of the setting sun, in the delicious ache of perfect health, I didn't need the kiss of a slug to arouse me. I needed only a glance from my wife, from her ancient eyes set like opals in her girlish body. This must be how the Greek gods lived on Olympus. This must be the way it was meant to be, to grow ancient and yet to have the strength and appetites of youth. El gasped melodramatically as she watched my penis swell. She turned herself toward me, coyly covering her breasts and pubis with her hands. The slug dropped off me and headed for the balcony wall.

We lay side by side, not yet touching. I was stupid with desire and lost control of my tongue. I spoke without thinking. I said, "Mama."

The word, the single word, "mama," struck her like a physical thing. Her whole body shuddered, and her eyes went wide with surprise. I repeated it, "Mama," and she shut her eyes and turned away from me. I sidled over to her, wrapped my arms around her, and took possession of her ear. I tugged its lobe with my lips. I breathed into it. I pushed her sweat-damp hair clear of it and whispered into it, "I am the papa, and you are the mama." I watched her face, saw a ghost of a smile, and repeated, "Mama."

"Again."

"Maamma, maamma, maamma."

"Crazy papa."

"You are the mama, and mama will give papa a son."

Her eyes flew open at that, fierce, challenging, and amused. "How will papa arrange that, I wonder."

"Like this," I said as I rolled her onto her back and kissed and stroked her. But she was indifferent to me, willfully unresponsive. Nevertheless, I let my tongue play up and down her body. I visited all the sweet spots I had discovered since first we made love, for I knew her body to be my ally. Her body and I wanted the same thing. Soon, with or without El's blessing, her body opened herself to me, and when she was ready, and I was ready, and all my tiny sons inside me were ready, I began to tease her, going in, coming out, going slow, going fast, not going at all, eventually going all in a rush.

Somewhere in the middle of this, a bird, a crow, came crashing to the deck next to us. What I could make out, through the thick envelope that surrounded it, was a mass of shiny black feathers, a broken beak clattering against the deck and a smudge of blood that quickly boiled away. The whole bird, in fact, was being disassembled. Steam rose from the envelope, which emitted a piercing wail of warning. Henry spoke loudly into my ear, *Attention, Sam! In the name of safety, the militia isolation device orders you to move away from it at once.*

We were too excited to pay much mind. The envelope seemed to be doing its job. Nevertheless, we dutifully moved away; we rolled away belly to belly in a teamwork maneuver that was a delight in itself. A partition, ordered by Eleanor's cabinet no doubt, formed to separate us from the unfortunate bird. We were busy making a son and we weren't about to stop until we were through.

Later, when I brought out dinner and two glasses of visola on a tray, El sat at the patio table in her white terry robe looking at the small pile of elemental dust on the deck—carbon, sodium, calcium and whatnot—that had once been a bird. It was not at all unusual for birds to fly through the canopy, or for a tiny percentage of them to become infected outside. What *was* unusual was that, upon reentering the canopy, being tasted, found bad, and enveloped by a swarm of smartactives, so much of the bird should survive the fall in so recognizable a form, as this one had.

El smirked at me and said, "It might be Ms. Rickert, come back to haunt us."

We both laughed uneasily.

* * *

The next day I felt the urge to get some work done. It would be another two days before we could give the orphanage the go-ahead, and I was restless. Meanwhile, Eleanor had a task force meeting scheduled in the living room.

I had claimed an empty bedroom in the back for my work area. It about matched my Chicago studio in size and aspect. I had asked the building super, a typically dour reginald, to send up a man to remove all the furniture except for an armchair and a nightstand. The chair needed a pillow to support the small of my back, but otherwise it was adequate for long sitting sessions. I pulled the chair around to face a blank inner wall that Henry had told me was the north wall, placed the nightstand next to it, and brought in a carafe of strong coffee and some sweets from the kitchen. I made myself comfortable.

"Okay, Henry, take me to Chicago." The empty bedroom was instantly transformed into my studio, and I sat in front of my favorite window wall overlooking the Chicago skyline and lakefront from the 303rd floor of the Drexler Building. The sky was dark with storm clouds. Rain splattered against the window. There was nothing like a thunderstorm to stimulate my creativity.

"Henry, match Chicago's ionic dynamics here." As I sipped my coffee and watched lightning strike neighboring towers, the air in my room took on a freshly scrubbed ozone quality. I felt at rest and invigorated.

When I was ready, I turned the chair around to face my studio. It was just as I had left it a month ago. There was the large, oak work table that dominated the east corner. Glass-topped and long-legged, it was a table you could work at without bending over. I used to stand at that table endlessly twenty and thirty years ago when I still lived in Chicago. Now it was piled high with prized junk: design trophies, hunks of polished gemstones from Mars and Jupiter, a scale model Japanese pagoda of cardboard and mica, a box full of my antique key collection, parcels wrapped in some of my most successful designs, and—the oldest objects in the room—a mason jar of paint brushes, like a bouquet of dried flowers.

I rose from my chair and wandered about my little domain, taking pleasure in my life's souvenirs. The cabinets, shelves, counters, and floor were as heavily laden as the table: an antelope skin spirit drum; an antique pendulum mantel clock that houseputer servos kept wound; holocubes of some of my former lovers and wives; bits of colored glass, tumbleweed, and driftwood in whose patterns and edges I had once found inspiration; and a whale vertebra used as a footstool. This room was more a museum now than a functional studio, and I was more its curator than a practicing artist.

I went to the south wall and looked into the corner. Henry's original container sat atop three more identical ones. "How's the paste?" I said.

"Sufficient for the time being. I'll let you know when we need more."

"More? This isn't enough? There's enough paste here now to run a major city."

"Eleanor Starke's cabinet is more powerful than a major city."

"Yes, well, let's get down to work." I returned to my armchair. The storm had passed the city and was retreating across the lake, turning the water midnight blue. "What have you got on the egg idea?"

Henry projected a richly ornate egg in the air before me. Gold leaf and silver wire, inlaid with once-precious gems, it was modeled after the Fabergé masterpieces favored by the last of the Romanoff Tsars. But instead of enclosing miniature clockwork automatons, these would be merely expensive wrapping for small gifts. You'd crack them open. You could keep the pieces, which would reassemble, or toss them into the soup bin for recycling credits.

"It's just as I told you last week," said Henry. "The public will hate it. I tested it against Simulated Us, the Donohue Standard, the Person in the Street, and Focus Rental." Henry filled the air around the egg with dynamic charts and graphs. "Nowhere are positive ratings higher than 7 percent, or negative ratings lower than 68 percent. Typical comments call it 'old-fashioned,' and 'vulgar.' Matrix analysis finds that people do not like to be reminded of their latent fertility. People resent . . ."

"Okay, okay," I said. "I get the picture." It was a dumb concept. I knew as much when I proposed it. But I was so enamored by my own soon-to-be-realized fertility, I had lost my head. I thought people would be drawn to this archetypal symbol of renewal, but Henry had been right all along, and now he had the data to prove it.

If the truth be told, I had not come up with a hit design in five years, and I was worried that maybe I never would again.

"It's just a dry spell," said Henry, sensing my mood. "You've had them before, even longer."

"I know, but this one is the worst."

"You say that every time."

To cheer me up, Henry began to play my wrapping paper portfolio, projecting my past masterpieces larger than life in the air.

I held patents for package applications in many fields, from emergency blankets and temporary skin, to military camouflage and video paint. But my own favorites, and probably the public's as well, were my novelty gift wraps. My first was a video wrapping paper that displayed the faces of loved ones (or celebrities if you had no loved ones) singing "Happy Birthday" to the music of the New York Pops. That dated back to 2025 when I was a molecular engineering student.

My first professional design was the old box-in-a-box routine, only my boxes didn't get smaller as you opened them, but larger, and in fact could fill the whole room until you chanced upon one of the secret commands, which were any variation of "stop" (whoa, enough, cut it out, etc.) or "help" (save me, I'm suffocating, get this thing off me, etc.).

Next came wrapping paper that screamed when you tore or cut it. That led to paper that resembled human skin. It molded itself perfectly and seamlessly (except for a belly button) around the gift and had a shelf life of fourteen days. You had to cut it to open the gift, and of course it bled. We sold mountains of that stuff.

The human skin led to my most enduring design, a perennial that was still common today, the orange peel. It too wrapped itself around any shape seamlessly (and had a navel). It was real, biological orange peel. When you cut or ripped it, it squirted citrus juice and smelled delightful.

I let Henry project these designs for me. I must say I was drunk with my own achievements. I gloried in them. They filled me with the most selfish wonder.

I was terribly good, and the whole world knew it.

Yet even after this healthy dose of self-love, I wasn't able to buckle down to anything new. I told Henry to order the kitchen to fix me some more coffee and some lunch.

On my way to the kitchen I passed the living room and saw that Eleanor was having difficulties of her own. Even with souped-up holoservers, the living room was a mess. There were dozens of people in there and, as best I could tell, just as many rooms superimposed over each other. People, especially important people, liked to bring their offices with them when they went to meetings. The result was a jumble of merging desks, lamps, and chairs. Walls sliced through each other at drunken angles. Windows issued cityscape views of New York, London, Washington, and Moscow (and others I didn't recognize) in various shades of day and weather. People, some of whom I knew from the news-nets, either sat at their desks in a rough, overlapping circle, or wandered through walls and furniture to kibitz with each other and with Eleanor's cabinet.

At least this is how it all appeared to me standing in the hallway, outside the room's holo anchors. To those inside, it might look like the Senate chambers. I watched for a while, safely out of holo range, until Eleanor noticed me. "Henry," I said, "ask her how many of these people are here in realbody." Eleanor raised a finger, one, and pointed to herself.

I smiled. She was the only one there who could see me. I continued to the kitchen and brought my lunch back to my studio. I still couldn't get started, so I asked Henry to report on my correspondence. He had answered over five hundred posts since our last session the previous week. Four-fifths of these concerned the baby. We were invited to appear—*with the baby*—on every major talk show and magazine. We were threatened with lawsuits by the Anti-Transubstantiation League. We were threatened with violence by several anonymous callers (who would surely be identified by El's security chief and prosecuted by her attorney general). A hundred seemingly ordinary people requested permission to visit us in realbody or holo during nap time, bath time, any time. Twice that number accused us of elitism. Three men and one woman named Sam Harger claimed that their fertility permit was mistakenly awarded to me. Dr. Armbruster's prediction was coming true and the baby hadn't even been converted yet.

This killed an hour. I still didn't feel creative, so I called it quits. I took a shower, shaved. Then I went, naked, to stand outside the entrance to the living room. When Eleanor saw me, her eyes went big, and she laughed. She held up five fingers, five minutes, and turned back to her meeting.

I went to my bedroom to wait for her. She spent her lunch break with me. When we made love that day and the next, I enjoyed a little fantasy I never told her about. I imagined that she was pregnant in the old-fashioned way, that her belly was enormous, melon-round and hard, and that as I moved inside her, as we moved together, we were teaching our son his first lesson in the art of human love.

On Thursday, the day of the conversion, we took a leisurely breakfast on the terrace of the New Foursquare Hotel in downtown Bloomington. A river of pedestrians, students and service people mostly, flowed past our little island of metal tables and brightly striped umbrellas. The day broke clear and blue and would be hot by noon. A gentle breeze tried to snatch away our menus. The Foursquare had the best kitchen in Bloomington, at least for desserts. Its pastry chef, Mr. Duvou, had built a reputation for the classics. That morning we (mostly me) were enjoying strawberry shortcake with whipped cream and coffee. Everything—the strawberries, the wheat for the cakes, the sugar, coffee beans, and cream—was grown, not assembled. The preparation was done lovingly and skillfully by hand. All the waitstaff were steves, who were highly sensitive to our wants and who, despite their ungainly height, bowed ever so low to take our order.

I moistened my finger with my tongue and made temporary anchor points where I touched the table and umbrella pole. We called Dr. Armbruster. She appeared in miniature, desk and all, on my place mat.

"It's a go, then?" she said.

"Yes," I said.

"Yes," said Eleanor, who took my hand.

"Congratulations, both of you. You are two of the luckiest people in the world."

We already knew that.

"Traits? Enhancements?" asked Dr. Armbruster.

We had studied all the options and decided to allow Nature and chance, not some well-meaning engineer, to roll our genes together into a new individual. "Random traits," we said, "and standard enhancements."

"That leaves gender," said Dr. Armbruster.

I looked at Eleanor, who smiled. "A boy," she said. "It definitely wants to be a boy."

"A boy it is," said Dr. Armbruster. "I'll get the lab on it immediately. The recombination should take about three hours. I'll monitor the progress and keep you apprised. We will infect the chassis around noon. Make an appointment for a week from today to come in and take possession of . . . your son. We like to throw a little birthing party. It's up to you to make media arrangements, if any.

"I'll call you in about an hour. And congratulations again!"

We were too nervous to do anything else, so we ate shortcake and drank coffee and didn't talk much. We mostly sat close and said meaningless things to ease the tension. Finally Dr. Armbruster, seated at her tiny desk, called back.

"The recombination work is about two-thirds done and is proceeding very smoothly. Early readings show a Pernell Organic Intelligence quotient of 3.93—very impressive, but probably no surprise to you. So far, we know that your son has Sam's eyes, chin, and skeleto-muscular frame, and Eleanor's hair, nose, and . . . eyebrows."

"I'm afraid my eyebrows are fairly dominant," said Eleanor.

"Apparently," said Dr. Armbruster.

"I'm mad about your eyebrows," I said.

"And I'm mad about your frame," Eleanor said.

We spent another hour there, taking two more updates from Dr. Armbruster. I ordered an iced bottle of champagne, and guests from other tables toasted us with coffee cups and visola glasses. I was slightly tipsy when we finally rose to leave. To my annoyance, I felt the prickly kiss of a militia slug at my ankle. I decided I'd better let it finish tasting me before I attempted to thread my way through the jumble of tables and chairs. The slug seemed to take an unusual length of time.

Eleanor, meanwhile, was impatient to go. "What is it?" she laughed. "Are you drunk?"

"Just a slug," I said. "It's almost done." But it wasn't. Instead of dropping off, it elongated itself and looped around both of my ankles so that when I turned to join Eleanor, I tripped and fell into our table, which crashed into a neighboring one.

Everything happened at once. As I fell, the slippery shroud of an isolation envelope snaked up my body to my face and sealed itself above my head. But it did not cushion my fall; I banged my nose on the flagstone. Everything grew dim as the envelope coalesced, so that I could barely make out the tables and umbrellas and the crowd of people running past me like horror-show shadows. There was Eleanor's face, momentarily, peering in at me, and then gone. "Don't go!" I shouted. "Eleanor, help!" But she melted into the crowd on the pedway. I tried to get up, to crawl, but my arms and legs were tightly bound.

Henry said, *Sam, I'm being probed, and I've lost contact with Eleanor's system.*

"What's going on?" I screamed. "Tell them to make it stop." I, too, was being probed. At first my skin tingled as in a gelbath at a juve clinic. But these smartactives weren't polite and weren't about to take a leisurely three days to inspect my cells. They wanted in right away; they streamed through my pores, down my nasal passage and throat, up my urethra and anus and spread out to capture all of my organs. My skin burned. My heart stammered. My stomach clamped and sent a geyser of pink shortcake mush and champagne-curdled cream back up my throat. But with the envelope stretched across my face, there was nowhere for the vomit to go except as a thin layer down my throat and chest. The envelope treated it as organic matter attempting escape and quickly disassembled it, scalding me with the heat of its activity. I rolled frantically about trying to lessen the pain, blindly upsetting more tables. Shards of glass cut me without cutting the envelope, so thin it stretched, and my blood leaked from me and simmered away next to my skin.

Fernando Boa, said someone in Henry's voice in Spanish. *You are hereby placed under arrest for unlawful escape and flight from State of Oaxaca authorities. Do not resist. Any attempt to resist will result in your immediate execution.*

"My name is not Boa," I cried through a swollen throat. "It's Harger, Sam Harger!"

I squeezed my eyelids tight against the pain, but the actives cut right through them, coating my eyeballs and penetrating them to taste the vitreous humor inside. Brilliant flashes and explosions of light burst across my retinae as each rod and cone was inspected, and a dull, hurricane roar filled my head.

Henry shouted, *Shall I resist? I think I should resist.*

"NO!" I answered. "No, Henry!"

The real agony began then, as all up and down my body, my nerve cells were invaded. Attached to every muscle fiber, every blood vessel, every hair follicle, embedded in my skin, my joints, my intestines, they all began to fire at once. My brain rattled in my skull. My guts twisted inside out. I begged for unconsciousness.

Then, just as suddenly, the convulsions ceased, the trillions of engines inside me abruptly quit. *I can do this*, Henry said. *I know how.*

"No, Henry," I croaked.

The envelope itself flickered, then fell from me like so much dust. I was in daylight and fresh air again. Soiled, bleeding, beat-up, and bloated, but whole. I was alone on a battlefield of smashed umbrellas and china shrapnel. I thought maybe I should crawl away from the envelope's dust, but the slug still shackled my ankles. "You shouldn't have done it, Henry," I said. "They won't like what you did."

Without warning, the neural storm slammed me again, worse than before. A new envelope issued from the slug. This one squeezed me, like a tube of oil paint, starting at my feet, crushing the bones and working up my legs.

"Please," I begged, "let me pass out."

I didn't pass out, but I went somewhere else, to another room, where I could still hear the storm raging on the other side of a thin wall. There was someone else in the room, a man I halfway recognized. He was well-muscled and of middle height, and his yellow hair was streaked with white. He wore the warmest of smiles on his coarse, round face.

"Don't worry," he said, referring to the storm beyond the wall, "it'll pass."

He had Henry's voice.

"You should have listened to me, Henry," I scolded. "Where did you learn to disobey me?"

"I know I don't count all that much," said the man. "I mean, I'm just a construct, not a living being. A servant, not a coequal. But I want to tell you how good it's been to know you."

I awoke lying on my side on a gurney in a ceramic room, my cheek resting in a small puddle of clear fluid. I was naked. Every cell of me ached. A man in a militia uniform, a jerry, watched me sullenly. When I sat up, dizzy, nauseous, he held out a bundle of clean clothes. Not my clothes.

"Wha' happe' me?" My lips and tongue were twice their size.

"You had an unfortunate accident."

"Assiden'?"

The jerry pressed the clothes into my hands. "Just shut up and get dressed." He resumed his post next to the door and watched me fumble with the clothes. My feet were so swollen I could hardly pull the pants legs over them. My hands trembled and could not grip. I could not keep my vision focused, and my head pulsed with pain. But all in all, I felt much better than I had a little while ago.

When, after what seemed like hours, I was dressed, the jerry said, "Captain wants to see ya."

I followed him down deserted ceramic corridors to a small office where sat a large, handsome young man in a neat blue uniform. "Sign here," he said, pushing a slate at me. "It's your terms of release."

Read this, Henry, I tongued with a bruised tongue. When Henry didn't answer I felt the pull of panic until I remembered that the slave processors inside my body that connected me to Henry's box in Chicago had certainly been destroyed. So I tried to read the document myself. It was loaded with legalese and interminable clauses, but I was able to glean from it that by signing it, I was forever releasing the National Militia from all liability for whatever treatment I had enjoyed at their hands.

"I will not sign this," I said.

"Suit yourself," said the captain, who took the slate from my hands. "You are hereby released from custody, but you remain on probation until further notice. Ask the belt for details." He pointed to the belt holding up my borrowed trousers.

I lifted my shirt and looked at the belt. The device stitched to it was so small I had missed it, and its ports were disguised as grommets.

"Sergeant," the captain said to the jerry, "show Mr. Harger the door."

"Just like that?" I said.

"What do you want, a prize?"

It was dark out. I asked the belt they'd given me for the time, and it said in a flat, neuter voice, "The time is seven forty-nine and thirty-two seconds." I calculated I had been incarcerated—and unconscious—for about seven hours. On a hunch, I asked what day it was. "The date is Friday, 6 April 2092."

Friday. I had been out for a day and seven hours.

There was a tube station right outside the cop shop, naturally, and I managed to find a private car. I climbed in and eased my aching self into the cushioned seat. I considered calling Eleanor, but not with that belt. So I told it to take me home. It replied, "Address please."

My anger flared and I snapped, "The Williams Towers, stupid."

"City and state, please."

I was too tired for this. "Bloomington!"

"Bloomington in California, Idaho, Illinois, Indiana, Iowa, Kansas, Kentucky, Maryland, Minnesota, Missouri, Nebraska, New York . . ."

"Hold it! Wait! Enough! Where the hell am I?"

"You're at the Western Regional Militia Headquarters, Utah."

How I longed for my Henry. He'd get me home safe with no hassle. He'd take care of me. "Bloomington," I said mildly, "Indiana."

The doors locked, the running lights came on, and the car rolled to the injection ramp. We coasted down, past the local grid, to the intercontinental tubes. The belt said, "Your travel time to the Williams Towers in Bloomington, Indiana, will be one hour, fifty-five minutes." When the car entered the slipstream, I was shoved against the seat by the force of acceleration. Henry would have known how sore I was and shunted us to the long ramp. Fortunately, I had a spare Henry belt in the apartment, so I wouldn't have to be without him for long. And after a few days, when I felt better, I'd again reinstall him inbody.

I tried to nap, but was too sick. My head kept swimming, and I had to keep my eyes open, or I would have vomited.

It was after 10:00 P.M. when I arrived under the Williams Towers, but the station was crowded with residents and guests. I felt everyone's eyes on me. Surely everyone knew of my arrest. They would have watched it on the nets, witnessed my naked fear as the shroud raced up my chest and face.

I walked briskly, looking straight ahead, to the row of elevators. I managed to claim one for myself, and as the doors closed I felt relief. But something was wrong; we weren't moving.

"Floor please," said my new belt in its bland voice.

"Fuck you!" I screamed. "Fuck you fuck you fuck you! Listen to me, you piece of shit, and see if you can get this right. I want you to call Henry, that's my system. Shake hands with him. Put him in charge of all of your miserable functions. Do you hear me?"

"Certainly, sir. What is the Henry access code?"

"Code? Code? I don't know code." That kind of detail had been Henry's job for over eighty years. I had stopped memorizing codes and ID numbers and addresses, anniversaries and birthdates long ago. "Just take me up! We'll stop at every floor above 200!" I shouted. "Wait. Hold it. Open the doors." I had the sudden, urgent need to urinate. I didn't think I could hold it long enough to reach the apartment, especially with the added pressure from the high-speed lift.

There were people waiting outside the elevator doors. I was sure they had heard me shouting. I stepped through them, a sick smile plastered to my face, the sweat rolling down my forehead, and I hurried to the men's room off the lobby.

I had to go so bad, that when I stood before the urinal and tried, I couldn't. I felt about to burst, but I was plugged up. I had to consciously calm myself, breathe deeply, relax. The stream, when it finally emerged, seemed to issue forever. How many quarts could my bladder hold? The urine was viscous and cloudy with a dull metallic sheen, as though mixed with aluminum dust. Whatever the militia had pumped into me would take days to excrete. At least there was no sign of bleeding, thank God. But it burned. And when I was finished and about to leave the rest room, I felt I had to go again.

Up on my floor, my belt valet couldn't open the door to the apartment, so I had to ask admittance. The door didn't recognize me, but Eleanor's cabinet gave it permission to open. The apartment smelled of strong disinfectant. "Eleanor, are you home?" It suddenly occurred to me that she might not be.

"In here," called Eleanor. I hurried to the living room, but Eleanor wasn't there. It was her sterile elder twin, her chief of staff, who sat on the couch. She was flanked by the attorney general, dressed in black, and the security chief, grinning his wolfish grin.

"What the hell is this," I said, "a fucking cabinet meeting? Where's Eleanor?"

In a businesslike manner, the chief of staff motioned to the armchair opposite the couch. "Won't you please join us, Sam. We have much to discuss."

"Discuss it among yourselves," I yelled. "Where's Eleanor?" Now I was sure that she was gone. She had bolted from the cafe and kept going; she had left her three stooges behind to break the bad news to me.

"Eleanor's in her bedroom, but she . . ."

I didn't wait. I ran down the hallway. But the bedroom door was locked. "Door," I shouted, "unlock yourself."

"Access," replied the door, "has been extended to apartment residents only."

"That includes me, you idiot." I pounded the door with my fists. "Eleanor, let me in. It's me—Sam."

No reply.

I returned to the living room. "What the fuck is going on here?"

"Sam," said the elderly chief of staff, "Eleanor will see you in a few minutes, but not before . . ."

"Eleanor!" I yelled, turning around to look at each of the room's holoeyes. "I know you're watching. Come out; we need to talk. I want you, not these dummies."

"Sam," said Eleanor behind me. But it wasn't Eleanor. Again I was fooled by her chief of staff who had crossed her arms like an angry El and bunched her eyebrows in an angry scowl. She mimicked my Eleanor so perfectly, I had to wonder if it wasn't El as a morphed holo. "Sam, please get a grip and sit down. We need to discuss your accident."

"My what? My accident? That's the same word the militia used. Well, it was no accident! It was an assault, a rape, a vicious attack. Not an accident!"

"Excuse me," said Eleanor's attorney general, "but we were using the word 'accident' in its legal sense. Both sides have provisionally agreed . . ."

I left the room without a word. I needed urgently to urinate again. Mercifully, the bathroom door opened to me. I knew I was behaving terribly, but I couldn't help myself. On the one hand I was relieved and grateful that Eleanor was there, that she hadn't left me—yet. On the other hand, I was hurting and confused and angry. All I wanted was to hold her, be held by her. I needed her at that moment more than I had ever needed anyone in my life. I had no time for holos. But, it was reasonable that she should be frightened. Maybe she thought I was infectious. My behavior was doing nothing to reassure her. I had to control myself.

My urine burned even more than before. My mouth was cotton dry. I grabbed a glass and filled it with tap water. Surprised at how thirsty I was, I drank glassful after glassful. I washed my face in the sink. The cool water felt so good, I stripped off my militia-issue clothes and stepped into the shower. The water revived me, fortified me. Not wanting to put the clothes back on, I wrapped a towel around myself, went out, and told the holos to ask Eleanor to toss out some of my clothes for me. I promised I wouldn't try to force my way into the bedroom when she opened the door.

"All your clothes were confiscated by the militia," said the chief of staff, "but Fred will bring you something of his."

Before I could ask who Fred was, a big, squat-bodied russ came out of the back bedroom, the room I used for my trips to Chicago. He was dressed in a conservative business suit and carried a brown velvet robe over his arm.

"This is Fred," said the chief of staff. "Fred has been assigned to . . ."

"What?" I shouted. "El's afraid I'm going to throttle her holos? She thinks I would break down that door?"

"Eleanor thinks nothing of the kind," said the chief of staff. "Fred has been assigned by the Tri-Discipline Board."

"Well, I don't want him here. Send him away."

"I'm afraid," said the chief of staff, "that as long as Eleanor remains a governor, Fred stays. Neither she nor you have any say in the matter."

The russ, Fred, held out the robe to me, but I refused it, and said, "Just stay out of my way, Fred." I went to the bathroom and found one of Eleanor's terry robes in the linen closet. It was tight on me, but it would do.

Returning to the living room, I sat in the armchair facing the cabinet's couch. "Okay, what do you want?"

"That's more like it," said the chief of staff. "First, let's get you caught up on what's happened so far."

"By all means. Catch me up."

The chief of staff glanced at the attorney general who said, "Yesterday morning, Thursday, 5 April, at precisely 10:47:39, while loitering at the New Foursquare Cafe in downtown Bloomington, Indiana, you, Samson P. Harger, were routinely analyzed by a National Militia Random Testing Device, Metro Population Model 8903AL. You were found to be in noncompliance with the Sabotage and Espionage Acts of 2036, 2038, 2050, and 2090. As per procedures set forth in . . ."

"Please," I said, "in English."

The security chief said in his gravelly voice, "You were tasted by a slug, Mr. Harger, and found bad, real bad. So they bagged you."

"What was wrong with me?"

"Name it. You went off the scale. First, the DNA sequence in a sample of ten of your skin cells didn't match each other. Also, a known nastie was identified in your blood. Your marker genes didn't match your record in the National Registry. You *did* match the record of a known terrorist with an outstanding arrest warrant. You also matched the record of someone who died twenty-three years ago."

"That's ridiculous," I said. "How could the slug read all those things at once?"

"That's what the militia wanted to know. So they disassembled you."

"They! What?"

"Any one of those conditions gave them the authority they needed. They didn't have the patience to read you slow and gentle like, so they pumped you so full of smartactives you filled a swimming pool."

"They. Completely?"

"All your biological functions were interrupted. You were legally dead for three minutes."

It took me a moment to grasp what he was saying. "So what did they discover?"

"Nothing," said the security chief, "zip, nada. Your cell survey came up normal. They couldn't even get the arresting slug, nor any other slug, to duplicate the initial readings."

"So the arresting slug was defective?"

"We've forced them to concede that the arresting slug may have been defective."

"So they reassembled me and let me go, and everything is okay?"

"Not quite. That particular model slug has never been implicated in a false reading. This would be the first time, according to the militia, and naturally they're not eager to admit that. Besides, they still had you on another serious charge."

"Which is?"

"That your initial reading constituted an unexplained anomaly."

"An unexplained anomaly? This is a crime?"

I excused myself for another visit to the bathroom. The urgency increased when I stood up from the armchair and was painful by the time I reached the toilet. This time the stream didn't burn me, but hissed and gave off some sort of vapor, like steam. I watched in horror as my situation became clear to me.

I marched back to the living room, stood in front of the three holos, rolled up a sleeve, and scratched and rubbed my arm, scraping off flakes of skin which cascaded to the floor, popping and flashing like a miniature fireworks display. "I've been seared!" I screamed at them. "You let them sear me!"

"Sit down," said the chief of staff. "Unfortunately, there's more."

I sat down, still holding my arm out. Beads of sweat dropped from my chin and boiled away on the robe in little puffs of steam.

"Eleanor feels it best to tell you everything now," said the chief of staff. "It's not pretty, so sit back and prepare yourself for more bad news."

I did as she suggested.

"They weren't about to let you go, you know. You had forfeited all of your civil rights. If you weren't the spouse of a Tri-Discipline Governor, you'd have simply disappeared. As it was, they proceeded to eradicate all traces of your DNA from the environment. They flooded this apartment first, removed every bit of hair, phlegm, mucus, skin, fingernail, toenail, semen, and blood that you have shed or deposited since moving in. They sent probes down the plumbing for trapped hair. They subjected Eleanor to a complete body douche. They scoured the halls, elevators, lobby, dining room, linen stores, laundry. They were most thorough. They have likewise visited your townhouse in Connecticut, the bungalow in Cozumel, the juve clinic, your hotel room on the Moon, the shuttle, and all your and Eleanor's domiciles all over the Protectorate. They are systematically following your trail backward for a period of thirty years."

"My Chicago studio?"

"Of course."

"Henry?"

"Gone."

"You mean in isolation, right? They're interrogating him, right?"

The security chief said, "No, eradicated. He resisted. Gave 'em quite a fight, too. But no civilian job can withstand the weight of the National Militia. Not even us."

I didn't believe Henry was gone. He had so many secret backups. At this moment he was probably lying low in a half dozen parking loops all over the solar system.

But another thought occurred to me. "My son!"

The chief of staff said, "When your accident occurred, the chassis had not yet been infected with your and Eleanor's recombinant. Had it been, the militia would have disassembled it too. Eleanor prevented the procedure at the last moment and turned over all genetic records and material."

I tried sifting through this. My son was dead, or rather, never started. But at least Eleanor had saved the chassis. We could always try—no we couldn't. *I was seared!* My cells were locked. Any attempt to read or overwrite any of my cells would cause those cells to fry.

The attorney general said, "The chassis, however, had already been brought out of stasis and was considered viable. To allow it to develop with its original genetic complement, or to place it back into stasis, would have exposed it to legal claims by its progenitors. So Eleanor had it infected. It's undergoing conversion at this moment."

"Infected? Infected with what? Did she clone herself?"

The chief of staff laughed, "Heavens, no. She had it infected with the recombination of her genes and those of a simulated partner, a composite of several of her past consorts."

"Without my agreement?"

"You were deceased at the time. She was your surviving spouse."

"I was deceased for only three minutes! I was retrievably dead. Obviously, retrievable!"

"Alive you would have been a felon, and the fertility permit would have been annulled."

I closed my eyes and leaned back into the chair. "Okay," I said, "what else?" When no one answered, I said, "To sum up then, I have been seared, which means my genes are booby trapped. Which means I'm incapable of reproducing, or even of being rejuvenated. So my life expectancy has been reduced to . . . what? . . . another hundred years or so? Okay. My son is dead. Pulled apart before he was even started. Henry is gone, probably forever. My wife—no, my widow—is having a child by another man—men."

"Women actually," said the chief of staff.

"Whatever. Not by me. How long did all of this take?"

"About twenty minutes."

"A hell of a busy twenty minutes."

"To our way of thinking," said the attorney general, "a protracted interval of time. The important negotiation in your case occurred within the first five seconds of your demise."

"You're telling me that Eleanor was able to figure everything out and cook up her simulated partner in five seconds?"

"Eleanor has in readiness at all times a full set of contingency plans to cover every conceivable threat we can imagine. It pays, Mr. Harger, to plan for the worst."

"I guess it does." The idea that all during our time together, El was busy making these plans was too monstrous to believe. "So tell me about these negotiations."

"First, let me impress upon you," said the chief of staff, "the fact that Eleanor stuck by you. Few other Tri-Discipline officers would take such risks to fight for a spouse. Also, only someone in her position could have successfully prosecuted your case. The militia doesn't have to answer phone calls, you know.

"As to the details, the attorney general can fill you in later, but here's the agreement in a nutshell. Given the wild diagnosis of the arresting slug and the subsequent lack of substantiating evidence, we calculated the most probable cause to be a defect in the slug, not some as yet unheard of nastie in your body. Further, as a perfect system of any sort has never been demonstrated, we predicted there to be records of other failures buried deep in militia archives. Eleanor threatened to air these files publicly in a civil suit. To do so would have cost her a lifetime of political capital, her career, and possibly her life. But as she was able to convince the militia she was willing to proceed, they backed down. They agreed to revive you and place you on probation, the terms of which are stored in your belt system, which we see you have not yet reviewed. The major term is your searing. Searing effectively neutralizes the threat in case you *are* the victim of a new nastie. Also, as a sign of good faith, we disclosed the locations of all of Henry's hidy-holes.''

"What?" I rose from my seat. "You gave them Henry?"

"Sit down, Mr. Harger," said the security chief.

But I didn't sit down. I began to pace. So this is how it works, I thought. This is the world I live in.

"Please realize, Sam," said the chief of staff, "they would have found him out anyway. No matter how clever you think you are, given time, all veils can be pierced."

I turned around to answer her, but she and her two colleagues were gone. I was alone in the room with the russ, Fred, who stood sheepishly next to the hall corridor. He cleared his throat and said, "Governor Starke will see you now."

II

It's been eight long months since my surprise visit to the cop shop. I've had plenty of time to sit and reflect on what's happened to me, to meditate on my victimhood.

Shortly after my accident, Eleanor and I moved into our new home, a sprawling old farmstead on the outskirts of Bloomington. We have more than enough room here, with barns and stables, a large garden, apple and pear orchards, tennis courts, swimming pool, and a dozen service people to run everything. It's really very beautiful, and the whole eighty acres is covered with its own canopy, inside and independent of the Bloomington canopy, a bubble inside a bubble. Just the place to raise the child of a Tri-Discipline governor.

The main house, built of blocks of local limestone, dates back to the last century. It's the home that Eleanor and I dreamed of owning. But now that we're here, I spend most of my time in the basement, for sunlight is hard on my seared skin. For that matter, rich food is hard on my gut, I bruise easily inside and out, I can't sleep a whole night through, all my joints ache for an hour or so when I rise, I have lost my sense of smell, and I've become hard of hearing. There is a constant taste of brass in my mouth and a dull throbbing in my skull. I go to bed nauseated and wake up nauseated. The doctor says my condition will improve in time as my body adjusts, but that my health is up to me now. No longer do I have resident molecular homeostats to constantly screen, flush and scrub my cells, nor muscle toners or fat inhibitors. No longer can I go periodically to a juve clinic to correct the cellular errors of aging. Now I can and certainly will grow stouter, slower, weaker, balder, and older. Now the date of my death is decades, not millennia, away. This should come as no great shock, for this was the human condition when I was born. Yet, since my birth, the whole human race, it seems, has boarded a giant ocean liner and set sail for the shores of immortality. I, however, have been unceremoniously tossed overboard.

So I spend my days sitting in the dim dampness of my basement corner, growing pasty white and fat (twenty pounds already), and plucking my eyebrows to watch them sizzle like fuses.

I am not pouting, and I am certainly not indulging in self-pity, as Eleanor accuses me. In fact, I am brooding. It's what artists do, we brood. To other, more active people, we appear selfish, obsessive, even narcissistic, which is why we prefer to brood in private.

But I'm not brooding about art or package design. I have quit that for good. I will never design again. That much I know. I'm not sure what I *will* do, but at least I know I've finished that part of my life. It was good; I enjoyed it. I climbed to the top of my field. But it's over.

I am brooding about my victimhood. My intuition tells me that if I understand it, I will know what to do with myself. So I pluck another eyebrow hair. The tiny bulb of muscle at the root ignites like an old fashioned match, a tiny point of light in my dark cave and, as though making a wish, I whisper, "Henry." The hair sizzles along its length until it burns my fingers, and I have to drop it. My fingertips are already charred from this game.

I miss Henry terribly. It's as though a whole chunk of my mind were missing. I never knew how deeply integrated I had woven him into my psyche, or where my thoughts stopped and his started. When I ask myself a question these days, no one answers.

I wonder why he did it, what made him think he could resist the militia. Can machine intelligence become cocky? Or did he knowingly sacrifice himself for me? Did he think he could help me escape? Or did he protect our privacy in the only way open to him, by destroying himself? The living archive of my life is gone, but at least it's not in the loving hands of the militia.

My little death has caused other headaches. My marriage ended. My estate went into receivership. My memberships, accounts and privileges in hundreds of services and organizations were closed. News of my death spread around the globe at the speed of light, causing tens of thousands of data banks to toggle my status to "deceased," a position not designed to toggle back. Autobituaries, complete with footage of my mulching at the Foursquare Cafe, appeared on all the nets the same day. Every reference to me records both my dates of birth and death. (Interestingly, none of my obits or bio's mention the fact that I was seared.) Whenever I try to use my voiceprint to pay a bill, alarms go off. El's attorney general has managed to reinstate most of my major accounts, but my demise is too firmly entrenched in the world's web to ever be fully corrected. The attorney general has, in fact, offered me a routine for my belt system to pursue these corrections on a continuous basis. She, as well as the rest of El's cabinet, has volunteered to educate my belt for me as soon as I install a personality bud in it. It will need a bud if I ever intend to leave the security of my dungeon. But I'm not ready for a new belt buddy.

I pluck another eyebrow hair, and by its tiny light I say, "Ellen."

We are living in an armed fortress. Eleanor says we can survive any form of attack here: conventional, nuclear, or molecular. She feels completely at ease here. This is where she comes to rest at the end of a long day, to glory in her patch of Earth, to adore her baby, Ellen. Even without the help of Mother's Medley, Eleanor's maternal instincts have all kicked in. She is mad with motherhood. Ellen is ever in her thoughts. If she could, El would spend all her time in the nursery in realbody, but the duties of a Tri-D governor call her away. So she has programmed a realtime holo of Ellen to be visible continuously in the periphery of her vision, a private scene only she can see. No longer do the endless meetings and unavoidable luncheons capture her full attention. No longer is time spent in a tube car flitting from one corner of the Protectorate to another a total waste. Now she secretly watches the jennies feed the baby, bathe the baby, perambulate the baby around the duck pond. And she is always interfering with the jennies, correcting them, undercutting whatever place they may have won in the baby's affection. There are four jennies. Without the namebadges on their identical uniforms, I wouldn't be able to tell them apart. They have overlapping twelve-hour shifts, and they hand the baby off like a baton in a relay race.

I have my own retinue, a contingent of four russes: Fred, the one who showed up on the day of my little death, and three more. I am not a prisoner here, and their mission is to protect the compound, Governor Starke, and her infant daughter, not to watch me, but I have noticed that there is always one within striking distance, especially when I go near the nursery. Which I don't do very often. Ellen is a beautiful baby, but I have no desire to spend time with her, and the whole house seems to breathe easier when I stay down in my tomb.

Yesterday evening a jenny came down to announce dinner. I threw on some clothes and joined El in the solarium off the kitchen where lately she prefers to take all her meals. Outside the window wall, heavy snowflakes fell silently in the blue-grey dusk. El was watching Ellen explore a new toy on the carpet. When she turned to me, her face was radiant, but I had no radiance to return. Nevertheless, she took my hand and drew me to sit next to her.

"Here's Daddy," she cooed, and Ellen warbled a happy greeting. I knew what was expected of me. I was supposed to adore the baby, gaze upon her plenitude and thus be filled with grace. I tried. I tried because I truly want everything to work out, because I love Eleanor and wish to be her partner in parenthood. So I watched Ellen and meditated on the marvel and mystery of life. El and I are no longer at the tail end of the long chain of humanity—I told myself—flapping in the cold winds of evolution. Now we are grounded. We have forged a new link. We are no longer grasped only by the past, but we grasp the future. We have created the future in flesh.

When El turned again to me, I was ready, or thought I was. But she saw right through me to my stubborn core of indifference. Nevertheless, she encouraged me, prompted me with, "Isn't she beautiful?"

"Oh, yes," I replied.

"And smart."

"The smartest."

Later that evening, when the brilliant monstrance of her new religion was safely tucked away in the nursery under the sleepless eyes of the night jennies, Eleanor rebuked me. "Are you so selfish that you can't accept Ellen as your daughter? Does it have to be your seed or nothing? I know what happened to you was shitty and unfair, and I'm sorry. I really am. I wish to hell the slug got me instead. I don't know why it missed me. Maybe the next one will be more accurate. Will that make you happy?"

"No, El, don't talk like that. I can't help it. Give me time."

Eleanor reached over and put an arm around me. "I'm sorry," she said. "Forgive me. It's just that I want us to be happy, and I feel so guilty."

"Don't feel guilty. It's not your fault. I knew the risk involved in being with you. I'm an adult. I can adapt. And I do love Ellen. Before long she'll have her daddy wrapped around her little finger."

Eleanor was skeptical, but she wanted so much to believe me. That night she invited herself to my bedroom. We used to have an exceptional sex life. Sex for us was a form of play, competition, and truth-telling. It used to be fun. Now it's a job. The shaft of my penis is bruised by the normal bend and torque of even moderate lovemaking. My urethra is raw from the jets of scalding semen when I come. Of course I use special condoms and lubricants for the seared, without which I would blister El's vagina, but it's still not comfortable for either of us. El tries to downplay her discomfort by saying things like, "You're hot, baby," but she can't fool me. When we made love that night, I pulled out before ejaculating. El tried to draw me back inside, but I wouldn't go. She took my sheathed penis in her hands, but I said not to bother. I hadn't felt the need for a long time.

In the middle of the night, when I rose to go to my dungeon, Eleanor stirred and whispered, "Hate me if you must, but please don't blame the baby."

I ask my new belt how many eyebrow hairs an average person of my race, sex, and age has. The belt can access numerous encyclopedias to do simple research like this. *Five hundred fifty in each eyebrow*, it replies in its neuter voice. That's one thousand one hundred altogether, plenty of fuel to light my investigation. I pluck another and say, "Fred."

For Fred is a complete surprise to me. I had never formed a relationship with a clone before. They are service people. They are interchangeable. They wait on us in stores and restaurants. They clip our hair. They perform the menialities we cannot, or prefer not, to assign to machines. How can you tell one joan or jerome from another anyway? And what could you possibly talk about? Nice watering can you have there, kelly. What's the weather like up there, steve?

But Fred is different. From the start he's brought me fruit and cakes reputed to fortify tender digestive tracts, sunglasses, soothing skin creams, and a hat with a duckbill visor. He seems genuinely interested in me, even comes down to chat after his shift. I don't know why he's so generous. Perhaps he never recovered from the shock of first meeting me, freshly seared and implacably aggrieved. Perhaps he recognizes that I'm the one around here most in need of his protection.

When I was ready to start sleeping with Eleanor again and I needed some of those special thermal condoms, my belt couldn't locate them on any of the shoppers, not even on the medical supply ones, so I asked Fred. He said he knew of a place and would bring me some. He returned the next day with a whole shopping bag of special pharmaceuticals for the cellular challenged: vitamin supplements, suppositories, plaque-fighting tooth soap, and knee and elbow braces. He brought 20 dozen packages of condoms, and he winked as he stacked them on the table. He brought more stuff he left in the bag.

I reached into the bag. There were bottles of cologne and perfume, sticks of waxy deodorant, air fresheners and odor eaters. "Do I stink?" I said.

"Like cat's piss, sir. No offense."

I lifted my hand to my nose, but I couldn't smell anything. Then I remembered the "stinkers" on the Moon shuttle, and I knew how I smelled. I wondered how Eleanor, during all those months, could have lived with me, eaten with me, and never mentioned it.

There was more in the bag: mouthwash and chewing gum. "My breath stinks too?"

In reply, Fred crossed his eyes and inflated his cheeks.

I thanked him for shopping for me, and especially for his frankness.

"Don't mention it, sir," he said. "I'm just glad to see you back in the saddle, if you catch my drift."

III

Two days ago was Ellen's first birthday. Unfortunately, Eleanor had to be away in Europe. Still, she arranged a little holo birthday party with her friends. Thirty-some people sat around, mesmerized by the baby, who had recently begun to walk. Only four of us, baby Ellen, a jenny, a russ, and I, were there in realbody. When I arrived and sat down, Ellen made a beeline for my lap. People laughed and said, "Daddy's girl."

I had the tundra dream again last night. I walked through the canopy lock right out into the white, frozen, endless tundra. The feeling was one of escape, relief, security.

My doctor gave me a complete physical last week. She said I had reached equilibrium with my condition. This was as good as it would get. Lately, I have been exercising. I have lost a little weight and feel somewhat stronger. But my joints ache something terrible and my doctor says they'll only get worse. She prescribed an old-time remedy: aspirin.

Fred left us two months ago. He and his wife succeeded in obtaining berths on a new station orbiting Mars. Their contracts are for five years with renewal options. Since arriving there, he's visited me in holo a couple times, says their best jump pilot is a stinker. And they have a stinker cartographer. Hint, hint.

Last week I finally purchased a personality bud for my belt system. It's having a rough time with me because I refuse to interact with it. I haven't even given it a name yet. I can't think of any suitable one. I call it "Hey, you," or "You, belt." Eleanor's chief of staff has repeated her offer to educate it for me, but I declined. In fact, I told her that if any of them breach its shell even once, I will abort it and start over with a new one.

Today at noon, we had a family crisis. The jenny on duty acquired a nosebleed while her backup was off running an errand. I was in the kitchen when I heard Ellen crying. In the nursery I found a hapless russ holding the kicking and screaming baby. The jenny called from the open bathroom door, "I'm coming. One minute, Ellie, I'm coming." When Ellen saw me she reached for me with her fat little arms and howled.

"Give her to me," I ordered the russ. His face reflected his hesitation. "It's all right," I said.

"One moment, sir," he said and tongued for orders. "Okay, here." He gave me Ellen who wrapped her arms around my neck. "I'll just go and help Merrilee," he said, relieved, as he crossed to the bathroom. I sat down and put Ellen on my lap. She looked around, caught her breath, and resumed crying; only this time it was an easy, mournful wail.

"What is it?" I asked her. "What does Ellen want?" I reviewed what little I knew about babies. I felt her forehead, though I knew babies don't catch sick anymore. And with evercleans, they don't require constant changing. The remains of lunch sat on the tray, so she'd just eaten. A bellyache? Sleepy? Teething pains? Early on, Ellen was frequently feverish and irritable as her converted body sloughed off the remnants of the little boy chassis she'd overwritten. I wondered why during my year of brooding, I'd never grieved for him. Was it because he never had a soul? Because he never got beyond the purely data stage of recombination? Because he never owned a body? And what about Ellen, did she have her own soul, or did the original one stay through the conversion? And if it did, would it hate us for what we've done to its body?

Ellen cried, and the russ stuck his head out the bathroom every few moments to check on us. This angered me. What did they think I was going to do? Drop her? Strangle her? I knew they were watching me, all of them: the chief of staff, the security chief. They might even have awakened Eleanor in Hamburg or Paris where it was after midnight. No doubt they had a contingency plan for anything I might do.

"Don't worry, Ellie," I crooned. "Mama will be here in just a minute."

"Yes, I'm coming, I'm coming," said Eleanor's sleep-hoarse voice.

Ellen, startled, looked about, and when she didn't see her mother, bawled louder and more boldly. The jenny, holding a blood-soaked towel to her nose, peeked out of the bathroom.

I bounced Ellen on my knee. "Mama's coming, Mama's coming, but in the meantime, Sam's going to show you a trick. Wanna see a trick? Watch this." I pulled a strand of hair from my head. The bulb popped as it ignited, and the strand sizzled along its length. Ellen quieted in mid-fuss, and her eyes went wide. The russ burst out of the bathroom and sprinted toward us, but stopped and stared when he saw what I was doing. I said to him, "Take the jenny and leave us."

"Sorry, sir, I . . ." The russ paused, then cleared his throat. "Yes, sir, right away." He escorted the jenny, her head tilted back, from the suite.

"Thank you," I said to Eleanor.

"I'm here." We turned and found Eleanor seated next to us in an ornately carved, wooden chair. Ellen squealed with delight, but did not reach for her mother. Already by six months she had been able to distinguish between a holobody and a real one. Eleanor's eyes were heavy, and her hair mussed. She wore a long silk robe, one I'd never seen before, and her feet were bare.

A sliver of jealousy pricked me when I realized she had probably been in bed with a lover. But what of it?

In a sweet voice, filled with the promise of soft hugs, Eleanor told us a story about a kooky caterpillar she'd seen that very day in a park in Paris. She used her hands on her lap to show us how it walked. Baby Ellen leaned back into my lap as she watched, and I found myself rocking her ever so gently. There was a squirrel with a bushy red tail involved in the story, and a lot of grown-up feet wearing very fashionable shoes, but I lost the gist of the story, so caught up was I in the voice that was telling it. El's voice spoke of an acorn who lost its cap and ladybugs coming to tea, but what it said was, I made you from the finest stuff. You are perfect. I will never let anyone hurt you. I love you always.

The voice shifted gradually, took an edge, and caused me the greatest sense of loss. It said, "And what about my big baby?"

"I'm okay," I said.

El told me about her day. Her voice spoke of schedules and meetings, a leader who lost his head, and diplomats coming to tea, but what it said was, You're a grown man who is capable of coping. You are important to me. I love it when you tease me and make me want you. It gives me great pleasure and takes me out of myself for a little while. Nothing is perfect, but we try. I will never hurt you. I love you always. Please don't leave me.

I opened my eyes. Ellen was a warm lump asleep on my lap, fist against cheek, lips slightly parted. I brushed her hair from her forehead with my sausage-like finger and traced the round curve of her cheek and chin. I must have examined her for quite a while, because when I looked up, Eleanor was waiting to catch my expression.

I said, "She has your eyebrows."

Eleanor laughed a powerful laugh. "Yes, my eyebrows," she laughed, "poor baby."

"No, they're her nicest feature."

"Yes, well, and what's happened to yours?"

"Nervous habit," I said. "I'm working on my chest hair now."

"In any case, you seem better."

"Yes, I believe I've turned the corner."

"Good, I've been so worried."

"In fact, I have just now thought of a name for my belt valet."

"Yes?" she said, relieved, interested.

"Skippy."

She laughed a belly laugh, "Skippy? Skippy?" Her face was lit with mirthful disbelief.

"Well, he's young," I said.

"Very young, apparently."

"Tomorrow I'm going to teach him how to hold a press conference." I didn't know I was going to say that until it was said.

"I see." Eleanor's voice hardened. "Thank you for warning me. What will it be about?"

"I'm sorry. That just came out. I guess it'll be a farewell. And a confession."

I could see the storm of calculation in Eleanor's face as her host of advisors whispered into her ear. Had I thrown them a curve? Come up with something unexpected? "What sort of confession?" she said. "What do you have to confess?"

"That I'm seared."

"That's not your fault, and no one will want to know anyway."

"Maybe not, but I've got to say it. I want people to know that I'm dying."

"We're *all* dying. Every living thing dies."

"Some faster than others."

"Sam, listen to me. I love you."

I knew that she did, her voice said so. "I love you too, but I don't belong here anymore."

"Yes, you do, Sam. This is your home."

I looked around me at the solid limestone wall, at the oak tree outside the window and the duck pond beyond. "It's very nice. I could have lived here, once."

"Sam, don't decide now. Wait till I return. Let's discuss it."

"Too late, I'm afraid."

She regarded me for several moments and said, "Where will you go?" By her question, I realized she had come to accept my departure, and I felt cheated. I had wanted more of a struggle. I had wanted an argument, enticements, tears, brave denial. But that wouldn't have been my El, my plan-for-everything Eleanor.

"Oh, I don't know," I said. "Just tramp around for a while, I guess. See what's what. Things have changed since the last time I looked." I stood up and held out the sleeping baby to El, who reached for her before we both remembered El was really in Europe. I placed Ellen in her crib and tucked her in. I kissed her cheek and quickly wiped it, before my kiss could burn her skin.

When I turned, El was standing, arms outstretched. She grazed my chest with her disembodied fingers. "Will you at least wait for me to give you a proper farewell? I can be there in four hours."

I hadn't intended to leave right away. I had just come up with the idea, after all. I needed to pack. I needed to arrange travel and accommodations. This could take days. But then I realized I was gone already and that I had everything I'd need: Skippy around my waist, my credit code, and the rotting stink of my body to announce me wherever I went.

She said, "At least stay in touch." A single tear slid down her face. "Don't be a stranger."

Too late for that too, dear El.

We were out of our minds with joy. Joy in full bloom and out of control, like weeds in our manicured lives.

RADIO WAVES
Michael Swanwick

▼

You may think that your troubles are over once you're dead, but, as the scary story that follows vividly demonstrates, your problems may really be just beginning . . .

Michael Swanwick made his debut in 1980, and has gone on to become one of the most popular and respected of all that decade's new writers. He has several times been a finalist for the Nebula Award, as well as for the World Fantasy Award and for the John W. Campbell Award, and has won the Theodore Sturgeon Award and the *Asimov's* Readers Award poll. In 1991, his novel *Stations of the Tide* won him a Nebula Award as well. His other books include his first novel, *In the Drift*, which was published in 1985, a novella-length book, *Griffin's Egg*, and 1987's popular novel *Vacuum Flowers*. His critically acclaimed short fiction has been assembled in *Gravity's Angels* and in a collection of his collaborative short work with other writers, *Slow Dancing Through Time*. His most recent book is a new novel, *The Iron Dragon's Daughter*, which was a finalist for the World Fantasy Award and the Arthur C. Clarke Award. He's had stories in our Second, Third, Fourth, Sixth, Seventh, and Tenth Annual Collections. Swanwick lives in Philadelphia with his wife, Marianne Porter, and their son Sean.

I was walking the telephone wires upside-down, the sky underfoot cold and flat with a few hard bright stars sparsely scattered about it, when I thought how it would take only an instant's weakness to step off to the side and fall up forever into the night. A kind of wildness entered me then and I began to run.

I made the wires sing. They leapt and bulged above me as I raced past Ricky's Luncheonette and up the hill. Past the old chocolate factory and the IDI Advertising Display plant. Past the body shops, past A. J. LaCourse Electric Motors-Controls-Parts. Then, where the slope steepened, along the curving snake of rowhouses that went the full quarter mile up to the Ridge. Twice I overtook pedestrians, hunched and bundled, heads doggedly down, out on incomprehensible errands. They didn't notice me, of course. They never do. The antenna farm was visible from here. I could see the Seven Sisters spangled with red lights, dependent on the earth like stalactites. "Where are you running to, little one?" one tower whispered in a crackling, staticky voice. I think it was Hegemone.

"Fuck off," I said without slackening my pace, and they all chuckled.

Cars mumbled by. This was ravine country, however built up, and the far side of the road, too steep and rocky for development, was given over to trees and garbage. Hamburger wrappings and white plastic trash bags rustled in their wake. I was running full-out now.

About a block or so from the Ridge, I stumbled and almost fell. I slapped an arm across a telephone pole and just managed to catch myself in time. Aghast at my own carelessness, I hung there, dizzy and alarmed. The ground overhead was black as black, an iron roof, yet somehow was as anxious as a hound to leap upon me, crush me flat, smear me to nothingness. I stared up at it, horrified.

Somebody screamed my name.

I turned. A faint blue figure clung to a television antenna atop a small, stuccoed brick duplex. Charlie's Widow. She pointed an arm that flickered with silver fire down Ripka Street. I slewed about to see what was coming after me.

It was the Corpsegrinder.

When it saw that I'd spotted it, it put out several more legs, extended a quilled head, and raised a howl that bounced off the Heaviside layer. My nonexistent blood chilled.

In a panic, I scrambled up and ran toward the Ridge and safety. I had a squat in the old Roxy, and once I was through the wall, the Corpsegrinder would not follow. Why this should be so, I did not know. But you learn the rules if you want to survive.

I ran. In the back of my head I could hear the Seven Sisters clucking and gossiping to each other, radiating television and radio over a few dozen frequencies. Indifferent to my plight.

The Corpsegrinder churned up the wires on a hundred needle-sharp legs. I could feel the ion surge it kicked up pushing against me as I reached the intersection of Ridge and Leverington. Cars were pulling up to the pumps at the Atlantic station. Teenagers stood in front of the A-Plus Mini Market, flicking half-smoked cigarettes into the street, stamping their feet like colts, and waiting for something to happen. I couldn't help feeling a great longing disdain for them. Every last one worried about grades and drugs and zits, and all the while snugly barricaded within hulking fortresses of flesh.

I was scant yards from home. The Roxy was a big old movie palace, fallen into disrepair and semiconverted to a skateboarding rink which had gone out of business almost immediately. But it had been a wonderful place once, and the terra-cotta trim was still there: ribbons and river-gods, great puffing faces with panpipes, guitars, flowers, wyverns. I crossed the Ridge on a dead telephone wire, spider-web delicate but still usable.

Almost there.

Then the creature was upon me, with a howl of electromagnetic rage that silenced even the Sisters for an instant. It slammed into my side, a storm of razors and diamond-edged fury, hooks and claws extended.

I grabbed at a rusty flange on the side of the Roxy.

Too late! Pain exploded within me, a sheet of white nausea. All in an instant I lost the name of my second daughter, an April morning when the world was new and I was five, a smoky string of all-nighters in Rensselaer Polytech, the jowly grin of Old Whatsisface the German who lived on LaFountain Street, the fresh pain of a sprained ankle out back of a Banana Republic warehouse, fishing off a yellow rubber raft with my old man on Lake Champlain. All gone, these and a thousand things more, sucked away, crushed to nothing, beyond retrieval.

Furious as any wounded animal, I fought back. Foul bits of substance splattered under my fist. The Corpsegrinder reared up to smash me down, and I scrabbled desperately away. Something tore and gave.

Then I was through the wall and safe and among the bats and gloom.

"Cobb!" the Corpsegrinder shouted. It lashed wildly back and forth, scouring the brick walls with limbs and teeth, as restless as a March wind, as unpredictable as ball lightning.

For the moment I was safe. But it had seized a part of me, tortured it, and made it a part of itself. I could no longer delude myself into thinking it was simply going to go away. "Cahawahawbb!" It broke my name down to a chord of overlapping tones. It had an ugly, muddy voice. I felt dirtied just listening to it. "Caw—" A pause. "—awbb!"

In a horrified daze I stumbled up the Roxy's curving patterned-tin roof until I found a section free of bats. Exhausted and dispirited, I slumped down.

"Caw aw aw awb buh buh!"

How had the thing found me? I'd thought I'd left it behind in Manhattan. Had my flight across the high-tension lines left a trail of some kind? Maybe. Then again, it might have some special connection with me. To follow me here it must have passed by easier prey. Which implied it had a grudge against me. Maybe I'd known the Corpsegrinder back when it was human. We could once have been important to each other. We might have been lovers. It was possible. The world is a stranger place than I used to believe.

The horror of my existence overtook me then, an acute awareness of the squalor in which I dwelt, the danger which surrounded me, and the dark mystery informing my universe. I wept for all that I had lost.

Eventually, the sun rose up like God's own Peterbilt and with a triumphant blare of chromed trumpets, gently sent all of us creatures of the night to sleep.

When you die, the first thing that happens is that the world turns upside-down. You feel an overwhelming disorientation and a strange sensation that's not quite pain as the last strands connecting you to your body part, and then you slip out of physical being and fall from the planet.

As you fall, you attenuate. Your substance expands and thins, glowing more and more faintly as you pick up speed. So far as can be told, it's a process that doesn't ever stop. Fainter, thinner, colder . . . until you've merged into the substance of everyone else who's ever died, spread perfectly uniformly through the universal vacuum forever moving toward but never arriving at absolute zero. Look hard, and the sky is full of the Dead.

Not everyone falls away. Some few are fast-thinking or lucky enough to maintain a tenuous hold on earthly existence. I was one of the lucky ones. I was working late one night on a proposal when I had my heart attack. The office was empty. The ceiling had a wire mesh within the plaster and that's what saved me.

The first response to death is denial. *This can't be happening*, I thought. I gaped up at the floor where my body had fallen and would lie undiscovered until morning. My own corpse, pale and bloodless, wearing a corporate tie and sleeveless gray Angora sweater. Gold Rolex, Sharper Image desk accessories, and of course I also thought: *I died for* this? By which of course I meant my entire life.

So it was in a state of personal and ontological crisis that I wandered across the ceiling to the location of an old pneumatic message tube, removed and plastered over some 50 years before. I fell from the seventeenth to the twenty-fifth floor, and I learned a lot in the process. Shaken, startled, and already beginning to assume the wariness that the afterlife requires, I went to a window to get a glimpse of the outer world. When I tried to touch the glass, my hand went right through. I jerked back. Cautiously, I leaned forward so that my head stuck out into the night.

What a wonderful experience Times Square is when you're dead! There is ten times the light a living being sees. All metal things vibrate with inner life. Electric wires are thin scratches in the air. Neon *sings*. The world is filled with strange sights and cries. Everything shifts from beauty to beauty.

Something that looked like a cross between a dragon and a wisp of smoke was feeding in the Square. But it was lost among so many wonders that I gave it no particular thought.

* * *

Night again. I awoke with Led Zeppelin playing in the back of my head. *Stairway to Heaven*. Again. It can be a long wait between Dead Milkmen cuts.

"Wakey-risey, little man," crooned one of the Sisters. It was funny how sometimes they took a close personal interest in our doings, and other times ignored us completely. "This is Euphrosyne with the red-eye weather report. The outlook is moody with a chance of existential despair. You won't be going outside tonight if you know what's good for you. There'll be lightning within the hour."

"It's too late in the year for lightning," I said.

"Oh dear. Should I inform the weather?"

By now I was beginning to realize that what I had taken on awakening to be the Corpsegrinder's dark aura was actually the high-pressure front of an approaching storm. The first drops of rain pattered on the roof. Wind skirled and the rain grew stronger. Thunder growled in the distance. "Why don't you just go fuck your—"

A light laugh that trilled up into the supersonic, and she was gone.

I was listening to the rain underfoot when a lightning bolt screamed into existence, turning me inside-out for the briefest instant then cartwheeling gleefully into oblivion. In the instant of restoration following the bolt, the walls were transparent and all the world made of glass, its secrets available to be snooped out. But before comprehension was possible, the walls opaqued again and the lightning's malevolent aftermath faded like a madman's smile in the night.

Through it all the Seven Sisters were laughing and singing, screaming with joy whenever a lightning bolt flashed, and making up nonsense poems from howls, whistles, and static. During a momentary lull, the flat hum of a carrier wave filled my head. Phaenna, by the feel of her. But instead of her voice, I heard only the sound of fearful sobs.

"Widow?" I said. "Is that you?"

"She can't hear you," Phaenna purred. "You're lucky I'm here to bring you up to speed. A lightning bolt hit the transformer outside her house. It was bound to happen sooner or later. Your Nemesis—the one you call the Corpsegrinder, such a cute nickname, by the way—has her trapped."

This was making no sense at all. "Why would the Corpsegrinder be after her?"

"Why why why why?" Phaenna sang, a snatch of some pop ballad or other.

"You didn't get answers when you were alive, what makes you think you'd get any *now*?" The sobbing went on and on. "She can sit it out," I said.

"The Corpsegrinder can't—hey, wait. Didn't they just wire her house for cable? I'm trying to picture it. Phone lines on one side, electric on the other, cable. She can slip out on his blind side."

The sobs lessened and then rose in a most un-Widowlike wail of despair.

"Typical," Phaenna said. "You haven't the slightest notion of what you're talking about. The lightning stroke has altered your little pet. Go out and see for yourself."

My hackles rose. "You know damned good and well that I can't—"

Phaenna's attention shifted and the carrier beam died. The Seven Sisters are fickle that way. This time, though, it was just as well. No way was I going out there to face that monstrosity. I couldn't. And I was grateful not to have to admit it.

For a long while I sat thinking about the Corpsegrinder. Even here, protected by the strong walls of the Roxy, the mere thought of it was paralyzing. I tried to imagine what Charlie's Widow was going through, separated from this monster by only a thin curtain of brick and stucco. Feeling the hard radiation of its malice and need . . . It was beyond my powers of visualization. Eventually I gave up and thought instead about my first meeting with the Widow.

She was coming down the hill from Roxborough with her arms out, the inverted image of a child playing a tightrope walker. Placing one foot ahead of the other with deliberate concentration, scanning the wire before her so cautiously that she was less than a block away when she saw me.

She screamed.

Then she was running straight at me. My back was to the transformer station—there was no place to flee. I shrank away as she stumbled to a halt.

"It's you!" she cried. "Oh God, Charlie, I knew you'd come back for me, I waited so long but I never doubted you, never, we can—" She lunged forward as if to hug me. Our eyes met.

All the joy in her died.

"Oh," she said. "It's not you."

I was fresh off the high-tension lines, still vibrating with energy and fear. My mind was a blaze of contradictions. I could remember almost nothing of my post-death existence. Fragments, bits of advice from the old dead, a horrifying confrontation with . . . something, some creature or phenomenon that had driven me to flee Manhattan. Whether it was this event or the fearsome voltage of that radiant highway that had scoured me of experience, I did not know. "It's me," I protested.

"No, it's not." Her gaze was unflatteringly frank. "You're not Charlie and you never were. You're—just the sad remnant of what once was a man, and not a very good one at that." She turned away. She was leaving me! In my confusion, I felt such a despair as I had never known before.

"Please . . ." I said.

She stopped.

A long silence. Then what in a living woman would have been a sigh. "You'd think that I—well, never mind." She offered her hand, and when I would not take it, said, "This way."

I followed her down Main Street through the shallow canyon of the business district to a diner at the edge of town. It was across from Hubcap Heaven and an automotive junkyard bordered it on two sides. The diner was closed. We settled down on the ceiling.

"That's where the car ended up after I died," she said, gesturing toward the junkyard. "It was right after I got the call about Charlie. I stayed up drinking and after a while it occurred to me that maybe they were wrong, they'd made some sort of horrible mistake and he wasn't really dead, you know?

"Like maybe he was in a coma or something, some horrible kind of misdiagnosis, they'd gotten him confused with somebody else, who knows? Terrible things happen in hospitals. They make mistakes.

"I decided I had to go and straighten things out. There wasn't time to make coffee so I went to the medicine cabinet and gulped down a bunch of pills at random, figuring something among them would keep me awake. Then I jumped into the car and started off for Colorado."

"My God."

"I have no idea how fast I was going—everything was a blur when I crashed. At least I didn't take anybody with me, thank the Lord. There was this one horrible moment of confusion and pain and rage and then I found myself lying on the floor of the car with my corpse just inches beneath me on the underside of the roof." She was silent for a moment. "My first impulse was to crawl out the window. Lucky for me I didn't." Another pause. "It took me most of a night to work my way out of the yard. I had to go from wreck to wreck. There were these gaps to jump. It was a nightmare."

"I'm amazed you had the presence of mind to stay in the car."

"Dying sobers you up fast."

I laughed. I couldn't help it. And without the slightest hesitation, she joined right in with me. It was a fine warm moment, the first I'd had since I didn't know when. The two of us set each other off, laughing louder and louder, our merriment heterodyning until it filled every television screen for a mile around with snow.

My defenses were down. She reached out and took my hand.

Memory flooded me. It was her first date with Charlie. He was an electrician. Her next-door neighbor was having the place rehabbed. She'd been working in the back yard and he struck up a conversation. Then he asked her out. They went to a disco in the Adam's Mark over on City Line Avenue.

She wasn't eager to get involved with somebody just then. She was still recovering from a hellish affair with a married man who'd thought that since he wasn't available for anything permanent, that made her his property. But when Charlie suggested they go out to the car for some coke—it was the Seventies—she'd said sure. He was going to put the moves on her sooner or later. Might as well get it settled early so they'd have more time for dancing.

But after they'd done up the lines, Charlie had shocked her by taking her hands in his and kissing them. She worked for a Bucks County pottery in those days and her hands were rough and red. She was very sensitive about them.

"Beautiful hands," he murmured. "Such beautiful, beautiful hands."

"You're making fun of me," she protested, hurt.

"No! These are hands that *do* things, and they've been shaped by the things they've done. The way stones in a stream are shaped by the water that passes over them. The way tools are shaped by their work. A hammer is beautiful, if it's a good hammer, and your hands are, too."

He could have been scamming her. But something in his voice, his manner, said no, he really meant it. She squeezed his hands and saw that they were beautiful, too. Suddenly she was glad she hadn't gone off the pill when she broke up with Daniel. She started to cry. Her date looked alarmed and baffled. But she couldn't stop. All the tears she hadn't cried in the past two years came pouring out of her, unstoppable.

Charlie-boy, she thought, you just got lucky.

All this in an instant. I snatched my hands away, breaking contact. *"Don't do that!"* I cried. *"Don't you ever* touch me again!"

With flat disdain, the Widow said, "It wasn't pleasant for me either. But I had to see how much of your life you remember."

It was naïve of me, but I was shocked to realize that the passage of memories had gone both ways. But before I could voice my outrage, she said, "There's not much left of you. You're only a fragment of a man, shreds and tatters, hardly anything. No wonder you're so frightened. You've got what Charlie calls a low signal-to-noise ratio. What happened in New York City almost destroyed you."

"That doesn't give you the right to—"

"Oh be still. You need to know this. Living is simple, you just keep going. But death is complex. It's so hard to hang on and so easy to let go. The temptation is always there. Believe me, I know. There used to be five of us in Roxborough, and where are the others now? Two came through Manayunk last spring and camped out under the El for a season and they're gone, too. Holding it together is hard work. One day the stars start singing to you, and the next you begin to listen to them. A week later they start to make sense.

You're just reacting to events—that's not good enough. If you mean to hold on, you've got to know why you're doing it."

"So why are *you*?"

"I'm waiting for Charlie," she said simply.

It occurred to me to wonder exactly how many years she had been waiting. Three? Fifteen? Just how long was it possible to hold on? Even in my confused and emotional state, though, I knew better than to ask. Deep inside she must've known as well as I did that Charlie wasn't coming. "My name's Cobb," I said. "What's yours?"

She hesitated and then, with an odd sidelong look, said, "I'm Charlie's widow. That's all that matters." It was all the name she ever gave, and Charlie's Widow she was to me from then onward.

I rolled onto my back on the tin ceiling and spread out my arms and legs, a phantom starfish among the bats. A fragment, she had called me, shreds and tatters. No wonder you're so frightened! In all the months since I'd been washed into this backwater of the power grid, she'd never treated me with anything but a condescension bordering on contempt.

So I went out into the storm after all.

The rain was nothing. It passed right through me. But there were ion-heavy gusts of wind that threatened to knock me off the lines, and the transformer outside the Widow's house was burning a fierce actinic blue. It was a gusher of energy, a flare star brought to earth, dazzling. A bolt of lightning unzipped me, turned me inside out, and restored me before I had a chance to react.

The Corpsegrinder was visible from the Roxy, but between the burning transformer and the creature's metamorphosis, I was within a block of the monster before I understood exactly what it was I was seeing.

It was feeding off the dying transformer, sucking in energy so greedily that it pulsed like a mosquito engorged with blood. Enormous plasma wings warped to either side, hot blue and transparent. They curved entirely around the Widow's house in an unbroken and circular wall. At the resonance points they extruded less detailed versions of the Corpsegrinder itself, like sentinels, all facing the Widow.

Surrounding her with a prickly ring of electricity and malice.

I retreated a block, though the transformer fire apparently hid me from the Corpsegrinder, for it stayed where it was, eyelessly staring inward. Three times I circled the house from a distance, looking for a way in. An unguarded cable, a wrought-iron fence, any unbroken stretch of metal too high or too low for the Corpsegrinder to reach.

Nothing.

Finally, because there was no alternative, I entered the house across the street from the Widow's, the one that was best shielded from the spouting and stuttering transformer. A power line took me into the attic crawlspace. From there I scaled the electrical system down through the second and first floors and so to the basement. I had a brief glimpse of a man asleep on a couch before the television. The set was off but it still held a residual charge. It sat quiescent, smug, bloated with stolen energies. If the poor bastard on the couch could have seen what I saw, he'd've never turned on the TV again. In the basement I hand-over-handed myself from the washing machine to the main water inlet. Straddling the pipe, I summoned all my courage and plunged my head underground.

It was black as pitch. I inched forward on the pipe in a kind of panic. I could see nothing, hear nothing, smell nothing, taste nothing. All I could feel was the iron pipe beneath my hands. Just beyond the wall the pipe ended in a T-joint where it hooked into a branch line under the drive. I followed it to the street.

It was awful: like suffocation infinitely prolonged. Like being wrapped in black cloth. Like being drowned in ink. Like strangling noiselessly in the voice between the stars. To distract myself, I thought about my old man.

When my father was young, he navigated between cities by radio. Driving dark and usually empty highways, he'd twist the dial back and forth, back and forth, until he'd hit a station. Then he'd withdraw his hand and wait for the station ID. That would give him his rough location—that he was some-where outside of Albany, say. A sudden signal coming in strong and then abruptly dissolving in groans and eerie whistles was a fluke of the ionosphere, impossibly distant and easily disregarded. One that faded in and immediately out meant he had grazed the edge of a station's range. But then a signal would grow and strengthen as he penetrated its field, crescendo, fade, and collapse into static and silence. That left him north of Troy, let's say, and making good time. He would begin the search for the next station.

You could drive across the continent in this way, passed from hand to hand by local radio, and tuned in to the geography of the night.

I went over that memory three times, polishing and refining it, before the branch line abruptly ended. One hand groped forward and closed upon nothing.

I had reached the main conduit. For a panicked moment I had feared that it would be concrete or brick or even one of the cedar pipes the city laid down in the nineteenth century, remnants of which still linger here and there beneath the pavement. But by sheer blind luck, the system had been installed during that narrow window of time when the pipes were cast iron. I crawled along its underside first one way and then the other, searching for the branch line for the Widow's. There was a lot of crap under the street. Several times I was blocked by gas lines or by the high-pressure pipes for the fire hydrants and had to awkwardly clamber around them. At last, I found the line and began the painful journey out from the street again.

When I emerged in the Widow's basement, I was a nervous wreck. It came to me then that I could no longer remember my father's name. A thing of rags and shreds indeed! I worked my way up the electrical system, searching every room and unintentionally spying on the family who had bought the house after her death. In the kitchen a puffy man stood with his sleeves rolled up, elbow-deep in the sink, angrily washing dishes by candlelight. A woman who was surely his wife expressively smoked a cigarette at his stiff back, drawing in the smoke with bitter intensity and exhaling it in puffs of hatred. On the second floor a preadolescent girl clutched a tortoise-shell cat so tightly it struggled to escape, and cried into its fur. In the next room a younger boy sat on his bed in earphones, Walkman on his lap, staring sightlessly out the window at the burning transformer. No Widow on either floor.

How, I wondered, could she have endured this entropic oven of a blue-collar rowhouse, forever the voyeur at the banquet, watching the living squander what she had already spent? Her trace was everywhere, her presence elusive. I was beginning to think she'd despaired and given herself up to the sky when I found her in the attic, clutching the wire that led to the antenna. She looked up, amazed by my unexpected appearance.

"Come on," I said. "I know a way out."

Returning, however, I couldn't retrace the route I'd taken in. It wasn't so much the difficulty of navigating the twisting maze of pipes under the street, though that was bad enough, as the fact that the Widow wouldn't hazard the passage unless I led her by the hand.

"You don't know how difficult this is for me," I said.

"It's the only way I'd dare." A nervous, humorless laugh. "I have such a lousy sense of direction."

So, steeling myself, I seized her hand and plunged through the wall.

It took all my concentration to keep from sliding off the water pipes, I was so distracted by the violence of her thoughts. We crawled through a hundred memories, all of her married lover, all alike. Here's one:

Daniel snapped on the car radio. Sad music—something classical—flooded the car. "That's bullshit, babe. You know how much I have invested in you?" He jabbed a blunt finger at her dress. "I could buy two good whores for what that thing cost."

Then why don't you, she thought. Get back on your Metroliner and go home to New York City and your wife and your money and your two good whores. Aloud, reasonably, she said, "It's over, Danny, can't you see that?"

"Look, babe. Let's not argue here, okay? Not in the parking lot, with people walking by and everybody listening. Drive us to your place, we can sit down and talk it over like civilized human beings.''

She clutched the wheel, staring straight ahead. "No. We're going to settle this here and now.''

"Christ." One-handed, Daniel wrangled a pack of Kents from a jacket pocket and knocked out a cigarette. Took the end in his lips and drew it out. Punched the lighter. "So talk."

A wash of hopelessness swept over her. Married men were supposed to be easy to get rid of. That was the whole point. "Let me go, Danny,'' she pleaded. Then, lying, "We can still be friends."

He made a disgusted noise.

"I've tried, Danny, I really have. You don't know how hard I've tried. But it's just not working."

"All right, I've listened. Now let's go." Reaching over her, Daniel threw the gearshift into reverse. He stepped on her foot, mashing it into the accelerator.

The car leaped backward. She shrieked and in a flurry of panic swung the wheel about and slammed on the brakes with her free foot.

With a jolt and a crunch, the car stopped. There was the tinkle of broken plastic. They'd hit a lime-green Hyundai.

"Oh, that's just perfect!" Daniel said. The lighter popped out. He lit his cigarette and then swung open the door. "I'll check the damage.'' Over her shoulder, she saw Daniel tug at his trousers knees as he crouched to examine the Hyundai. She had a sudden impulse to slew the car around and escape. Step on the gas and never look back. Watch his face, dismayed and dwindling, in the rear-view mirror. Eyes flooded with tears, she began quietly to laugh.

Then Daniel was back. "It's all right, let's go.''

"I heard something break.''

"It was just a tail-light, okay?" He gave her a funny look. "What the hell are you laughing about?"

She shook her head helplessly, unable to sort out the tears from the laughter. Then somehow they were on the Expressway, the car humming down the indistinct and warping road. She was driving but Daniel was still in control.

We were completely lost now and had been for some time. I had taken what I was certain had to be a branch line and it had led nowhere. We'd been tracing its twisty passage for blocks. I stopped and pulled my hand away. I couldn't concentrate. Not with the caustics and poisons of the Widow's past churning through me. "Listen," I said. "We've got to get something straight between us.''

Her voice came out of nowhere, small and wary. "What?"

How to say it? The horror of those memories lay not in their brutality but in their particularity. They nestled into empty spaces where memories of my own should have been. They were as familiar as old shoes. They *fit*.

"If I could remember any of this crap," I said, "I'd apologize. Hell, I can't blame you for how you feel. Of course you're angry. But it's gone, can't you see that, it's over. You've got to let go. You can't hold me accountable for things I can't even remember, okay? All that shit happened decades ago. I was young. I've changed." The absurdity of the thing swept over me. I'd have laughed if I'd been able. "I'm dead, for pity's sake!"

A long silence. Then, "So you've figured it out."

"You've known all along," I said bitterly. "Ever since I came off the high-tension lines in Manayunk."

She didn't deny it. "I suppose I should be flattered that when you were in trouble you came to me," she said in a way that indicated she was not.

"Why didn't you tell me then? Why drag it out?"

"Danny—"

"Don't call me that!"

"It's your name. Daniel. Daniel Cobb."

All the emotions I'd been holding back by sheer force of denial closed about me. I flung myself down and clutched the pipe tight, crushing myself against its unforgiving surface. Trapped in the friendless wastes of night, I weighed my fear of letting go against my fear of holding on.

"Cobb?"

I said nothing. The Widow's voice took on an edgy quality. "Cobb, we can't stay here. You've got to lead me out. I don't have the slightest idea which way to go. I'm lost without your help."

I still could not speak.

"*Cobb!*" She was close to panic. "I put my own feelings aside. Back in Manayunk. You needed help and I did what I could. Now it's your turn."

Silently, invisibly, I shook my head.

"God damn you, Danny," she said furiously. "I won't let you do this to me again! So you're unhappy with what a jerk you were—that's not my problem. You can't redeem your manliness on me any more. I am not your fucking salvation. I am not some kind of cosmic last chance and it's not my job to talk you down from the ledge."

That stung. "I wasn't asking you to," I mumbled.

"So you're still there! Take my hand and lead us out."

I pulled myself together. "You'll have to follow my voice, babe. Your memories are too intense for me."

We resumed our slow progress. I was sick of crawling, sick of the dark, sick of this lightless horrid existence, disgusted to the pit of my soul with who and what I was. Was there no end to this labyrinth of pipes?

"Wait." I'd brushed by something. Something metal buried in the earth. "What is it?"

"I think it's—" I groped about, trying to get a sense of the thing's shape. "I think it's a cast-iron gatepost. Here. Wait. Let me climb up and take a look."

Relinquishing my grip on the pipe, I seized hold of the object and stuck my head out of the ground. I emerged at the gate of an iron fence framing the minuscule front yard of a house on Ripka Street. I could see again! It felt so good to feel the clear breath of the world once more that I closed my eyes briefly to savor the sensation.

"How ironic," Euphrosyne said.

"After being so heroic," Thalia said.

"Overcoming his fears," Aglaia said.

"Rescuing the fair maid from terror and durance vile," Cleta said.

"Realizing at last who he is," Phaenna said.

"Beginning that long and difficult road to recovery by finally getting in touch with his innermost feelings," Auxo said. Hegemone giggled.

"What?" I opened my eyes.

That was when the Corpsegrinder struck. It leaped upon me with stunning force, driving spear-long talons through my head and body. The talons were barbed so that they couldn't be pulled free and they burned like molten metal. "Ahhhh, Cobb," the Corpsegrinder crooned. "Now this is *sweet*."

I screamed and it drank in those screams so that only silence escaped into the outside world. I struggled and it made those struggles its own, leaving me to kick myself deeper and deeper into the drowning pools of its identity. With all my will I resisted. It was not enough. I experienced the languorous pleasure of surrender as that very will and resistance were sucked down into my attacker's substance. The distinction between me and it weakened, strained, dissolved. I was transformed.

I was the Corpsegrinder now.

Manhattan is a virtual school for the dead. Enough people die there every day to keep any number of monsters fed. From the store of memories the Corpsegrinder had stolen from me, I recalled a quiet moment sitting cross-slegged on the tin ceiling of a sleaze joint while table dancers entertained Japanese tourists on the floor above and a kobold instructed me on the finer points of survival. "The worst thing you can be hunted by," he said, "is yourself."

"Very aphoristic."

"Fuck you. I used to be human, too."

"Sorry."

"Apology accepted. Look, I told you about Salamanders. That's a shitty way to go, but at least it's final. When they're done with you, nothing remains. But a Corpsegrinder is a parasite. It has no true identity of its own, so it constructs one from bits and pieces of everything that's unpleasant within you. Your basic greeds and lusts. It gives you a particularly nasty sort of immortality. Remember that old cartoon? This hideous toad saying, 'Kiss me and live forever—you'll be a toad, but you'll live forever.' " He grimaced. "If you get the choice, go with the Salamander."

"So what's this business about hunting myself?"

"Sometimes a Corpsegrinder will rip you in two and let half escape. For a while."

"Why?"

"I dunno. Maybe it likes to play with its food. Ever watch a cat torture a mouse? Maybe it thinks it's fun."

From a million miles away, I thought: So now I know what's happened to me. I'd made quite a run of it, but now it was over. It didn't matter. All that mattered was the hoard of memories, glorious memories, into which I'd been dumped. I wallowed in them, picking out here a winter sunset and there the pain of a jellyfish sting when I was nine. So what if I was already beginning to dissolve? I was intoxicated, drunk, stoned with the raw stuff of experience. I was high on life.

Then the Widow climbed up the gatepost looking for me. "Cobb?"

The Corpsegrinder had moved up the fence to a more comfortable spot in which to digest me. When it saw the Widow, it reflexively parked me in a memory of a gray drizzly day in a Ford Fiesta outside of 30th Street Station. The engine was going and the heater and the windshield wiper, too, so I snapped on the radio to mask their noise. Beethoven filled the car, the Moonlight Sonata.

"That's bullshit, babe," I said. "You know how much I have invested in you? I could buy two good whores for what that dress cost." She refused to meet my eyes. In a whine that set my teeth on edge, she said, "Danny, can't you see that it's over between us?"

"Look babe, let's not argue in the parking lot, okay?" I was trying hard to be reasonable. "Not with people walking by and listening. We'll go someplace private where we can talk this over calmly, like two civilized human beings." She shifted slightly in the seat and adjusted her skirt with a little tug. Drawing attention to her long legs and fine ass. Making it hard for me to think straight. The bitch really knew how to twist the knife. Even now, crying and begging, she was aware of how it turned me on. And even though I hated being aroused by her little act, I was. The sex was always best after an argument; it made her sluttish.

I clenched my anger in one hand and fisted my pocket with it. Thinking how much I'd like to up and give her a shot. She was begging for it. Secretly, maybe, it was what she wanted; I'd often suspected she'd enjoy being hit. It was too late to act on the impulse, though. The memory was playing out like a tape, immutable, unstoppable.

All the while, like a hallucination or the screen of a television set receiving conflicting signals, I could see the Widow, frozen with fear half in and half out of the ground. She quivered like an acetylene flame. In the memory she was saying something, but with the shift in my emotions came a corresponding warping-away of perception. The train station, car, the windshield wipers and music, all faded to a murmur in my consciousness.

Tentacles whipped around the Widow. She was caught. She struggled helplessly, deliciously. The Corpsegrinder's emotions pulsed through me and to my remote horror I found that they were identical with my own. I *wanted* the Widow, wanted her so bad there were no words for it. I wanted to clutch her to me so tightly her ribs would splinter and for just this once she'd know it was real. I wanted to own her. To possess her. To put an end to all her little games. To know her every thought and secret, down to the very bottom of her being.

No more lies, babe, I thought, no more evasions. You're mine now.

So perfectly in sync was I with the Corpsegrinder's desires that it shifted its primary consciousness back into the liquid sphere of memory, where it hung smug and lazy, watching, a voyeur with a willing agent. I was in control of the autonomous functions now. I reshaped the tentacles, merging and recombining them into two strong arms. The claws and talons that clutched the fence I made legs again. The exterior of the Corpsegrinder I morphed into human semblance, save for that great mass of memories sprouting from our back like a bloated spider-sac. Last of all I made the head.

I gave it my own face.

"Surprised to see me again, babe?" I leered. Her expression was not so much fearful as disappointed. "No," she said wearily. "Deep down, I guess I always knew you'd be back."

As I drew the Widow closer, I distantly knew that all that held me to the Corpsegrinder in that instant was our common store of memories and my determination not to lose them again. That was enough, though. I pushed my face into hers, forcing open her mouth. Energies flowed between us like a feast of tongues.

I prepared to drink her in.

There were no barriers between us. This was an experience as intense as when, making love, you lose all track of which body is your own and thought dissolves into the animal moment. For a giddy instant I was no less her than I was myself. I was the Widow staring fascinated into the filthy depths of my psyche. She was myself witnessing her astonishment as she realized exactly how little I had ever known her. We both saw her freeze still to the core with horror. Horror not of what I was doing.

But of what I was.

I can't take any credit for what happened then. It was only an impulse, a spasm of the emotions, a sudden and unexpected clarity of vision. Can a single flash of decency redeem a life like mine? I don't believe it. I refuse to believe it. Had there been time for second thoughts, things might well have gone differently. But there was no time to think. There was only time enough to feel an upwelling of revulsion, a visceral desire to be anybody or anything but my own loathsome self, a profound and total yearning to be quit of the burden of such memories as were mine. An aching need to *just once* do the moral thing.

I let go.

Bobbing gently, the swollen corpus of my past floated up and away, carrying with it the parasitic Corpsegrinder. Everything I had spent all my life accumulating fled from me. It went up like a balloon, spinning, dwindling . . . gone. Leaving me only what few flat memories I have narrated here.

I screamed.

And then I cried.

I don't know how long I clung to the fence, mourning my loss. But when I gathered myself together, the Widow was still there.

"Danny," the Widow said. She didn't touch me. "Danny, I'm sorry."

I'd almost rather that she had abandoned me. How do you apologize for sins you can no longer remember? For having been someone who, however abhorrent, is gone forever? How can you expect forgiveness from somebody you have forgotten so completely you don't even know her name? I felt twisted with shame and misery. "Look," I said. "I know I've behaved badly. More than badly. But there ought to be some way to make it up to you. For, you know, everything. Somehow. I mean—"

What do you say to somebody who's seen to the bottom of your wretched and inadequate soul?

"I want to apologize," I said.

With something very close to compassion, the Widow said, "It's too late for that, Danny. It's over. Everything's over. You and I only ever had the one trait in common. We neither of us could ever let go of anything. Small wonder we're back together again. But don't you see, it doesn't matter what you want or don't want—you're not going to get it. Not now. You had your chance. It's too late to make things right." Then she stopped, aghast at what she had just said. But we both knew she had spoken the truth.

"Widow," I said as gently as I could, "I'm sure Charlie—"

"Shut up."

I shut up.

The Widow closed her eyes and swayed, as if in a wind. A ripple ran through her and when it was gone her features were simpler, more schematic, less recognizably human. She was already beginning to surrender the anthropomorphic.

I tried again. "Widow . . ." Reaching out my guilty hand to her.

She stiffened but did not draw away. Our fingers touched, twined, mated.

"Elizabeth," she said. "My name is Elizabeth Connelly."

We huddled together on the ceiling of the Roxy through the dawn and the blank horror that is day. When sunset brought us conscious again, we talked through half the night before making the one decision we knew all along that we'd have to make.

It took us almost an hour to reach the Seven Sisters and climb down to the highest point of Thalia.

We stood holding hands at the top of the mast. Radio waves were gushing out from under us like a great wind. It was all we could do to keep from being blown away.

Underfoot, Thalia was happily chatting with her sisters. Typically, at our moment of greatest resolve, they gave not the slightest indication of interest. But they were all listening to us. Don't ask me how I knew.

"Cobb?" Elizabeth said. "I'm afraid."

"Yeah, me too." A long silence. Then she said, "Let me go first. If you go first, I won't have the nerve."

"Okay."

She took a deep breath—funny, if you think about it—and then she let go, and fell into the sky.

First she was like a kite, and then a scrap of paper, and at the very last she was a rapidly tumbling speck. I stood for a long time watching her falling, dwindling, until she was lost in the background flicker of the universe, just one more spark in infinity.

She was gone and I couldn't help wondering if she had ever really been there at all. Had the Widow truly been Elizabeth Connelly? Or was she just another fragment of my shattered self, a bundle of related memories that I had to come to terms with before I could bring myself to let go? A vast emptiness seemed to spread itself through all of existence. I clutched the mast spasmodically then, and thought: *I can't!*

But the moment passed. I've got a lot of questions, and there aren't any answers here. In just another instant, I'll let go and follow Elizabeth (if Elizabeth she was) into the night. I will fall forever and I will be converted to background radiation, smeared ever thinner and cooler across the universe, a smooth, uniform, and universal message that has only one decode. Let Thalia carry my story to whoever cares to listen. I won't be here for it.

It's time to go now. Time and then some to leave. I'm frightened, and I'm going.

Now.

WANG'S CARPETS

Greg Egan

▼

Here's another story by Australian writer Greg Egan, whose "Luminous" appears elsewhere in this anthology. Nineteen ninety-five was a good year for Egan in short fiction, and, like Ursula K. Le Guin and Robert Reed, he published four or five different stories this year that might well have made the cut for a best-of-the-year anthology in another year; the story that follows, though, would be hard to match anywhere for the bravura sweep and pure originality of its conceptualization, as Egan provides us with a First Contact story unlike any you've ever read before . . .

Waiting to be cloned one thousand times and scattered across ten million cubic light-years, Paolo Venetti relaxed in his favorite ceremonial bathtub: a tiered hexagonal pool set in a courtyard of black marble flecked with gold. Paolo wore full traditional anatomy, uncomfortable garb at first, but the warm currents flowing across his back and shoulders slowly eased him into a pleasant torpor. He could have reached the same state in an instant, by decree—but the occasion seemed to demand the complete ritual of verisimilitude, the ornate curlicued longhand of imitation physical cause and effect.

As the moment of diaspora approached, a small gray lizard darted across the courtyard, claws scrabbling. It halted by the far edge of the pool, and Paolo marveled at the delicate pulse of its breathing, and watched the lizard watching him, until it moved again, disappearing into the surrounding vineyards. The environment was full of birds and insects, rodents and small reptiles—decorative in appearance, but also satisfying a more abstract aesthetic: softening the harsh radial symmetry of the lone observer; anchoring the simulation by perceiving it from a multitude of viewpoints. Ontological guy lines. No one had asked the lizards if they wanted to be cloned, though. They were coming along for the ride, like it or not.

The sky above the courtyard was warm and blue, cloudless and sunless, isotropic. Paolo waited calmly, prepared for every one of half a dozen possible fates.

An invisible bell chimed softly, three times. Paolo laughed, delighted.

One chime would have meant that he was still on Earth: an anti-climax, certainly—but there would have been advantages to compensate for that. Everyone who really mattered to him lived in the Carter-Zimmerman polis, but not all of them had chosen to take part in the diaspora to the same degree; his Earth-self would have lost no one. Helping to ensure that the thousand ships were safely dispatched would have been satisfying, too. And remaining a member of the wider Earth-based community, plugged into the entire global culture in real-time, would have been an attraction in itself.

Two chimes would have meant that this clone of Carter-Zimmerman had reached a planetary system devoid of life. Paolo had run a sophisticated— but non-sapient—self-predictive model before deciding to wake under those conditions. Exploring a handful of alien worlds, however barren, had seemed likely to be an enriching experience for him—with the distinct advantage that the whole endeavor would be untrammeled by the kind of elaborate precautions necessary in the presence of alien life. C-Z's population would have fallen by more than half—and many of his closest friends would have been absent—but he would have forged new friendships, he was sure.

Four chimes would have signaled the discovery of intelligent aliens. Five, a technological civilization. Six, spacefarers.

Three chimes, though, meant that the scout probes had detected unambiguous signs of life—and that was reason enough for jubilation. Up until the moment of the pre-launch cloning—a subjective instant before the chimes had sounded—no reports of alien life had ever reached Earth. There'd been no guarantee that any part of the diaspora would find it.

Paolo willed the polis library to brief him; it promptly rewired the declarative memory of his simulated traditional brain with all the information he was likely to need to satisfy his immediate curiosity. This clone of C-Z had arrived at Vega, the second closest of the thousand target stars, twenty-seven light-years from Earth. Paolo closed his eyes and visualized a star map with a thousand lines radiating out from the sun, then zoomed in on the trajectory which described his own journey. It had taken three centuries to reach Vega— but the vast majority of the polis's twenty thousand inhabitants had programmed their exoselves to suspend them prior to the cloning, and to wake them only if and when they arrived at a suitable destination. Ninety-two citizens had chosen the alternative: experiencing every voyage of the diaspora from start to finish, risking disappointment, and even death. Paolo now knew that the ship aimed at Fomalhaut, the target nearest Earth, had been struck by debris and annihilated *en route*. He mourned the ninety-two, briefly. He hadn't been close to any of them, prior to the cloning, and the particular versions who'd willfully perished two centuries ago in interstellar space seemed as remote as the victims of some ancient calamity from the era of flesh.

Paolo examined his new home star through the cameras of one of the scout probes—and the strange filters of the ancestral visual system. In traditional colors, Vega was a fierce blue-white disk, laced with prominences. Three times the mass of the sun, twice the size and twice as hot, sixty times as luminous. Burning hydrogen fast—and already halfway through its allotted five hundred million years on the main sequence.

Vega's sole planet, Orpheus, had been a featureless blip to the best lunar interferometers; now Paolo gazed down on its blue-green crescent, ten thousand kilometers below Carter-Zimmerman itself. Orpheus was terrestrial, a nickel-iron-silicate world; slightly larger than Earth, slightly warmer—a billion kilometers took the edge off Vega's heat—and almost drowning in liquid water. Impatient to see the whole surface firsthand, Paolo slowed his clock rate a thousandfold, allowing C-Z to circumnavigate the planet in twenty subjective seconds, daylight unshrouding a broad new swath with each pass. Two slender ocher-colored continents with mountainous spines bracketed hemispheric oceans, and dazzling expanses of pack ice covered both poles— far more so in the north, where jagged white peninsulas radiated out from the midwinter arctic darkness.

The Orphean atmosphere was mostly nitrogen—six times as much as on Earth; probably split by UV from primordial ammonia—with traces of water vapor and carbon dioxide, but not enough of either for a runaway greenhouse effect. The high atmospheric pressure meant reduced evaporation—Paolo saw not a wisp of cloud—and the large, warm oceans in turn helped feed carbon dioxide back into the crust, locking it up in limestone sediments destined for subduction.

The whole system was young, by Earth standards, but Vega's greater mass, and a denser protostellar cloud, would have meant swifter passage through most of the traumas of birth: nuclear ignition and early luminosity fluctuations; planetary coalescence and the age of bombardments. The library estimated that Orpheus had enjoyed a relatively stable climate, and freedom from major impacts, for at least the past hundred million years.

Long enough for primitive life to appear—

A hand seized Paolo firmly by the ankle and tugged him beneath the water. He offered no resistance, and let the vision of the planet slip away. Only two other people in C-Z had free access to this environment—and his father didn't play games with his now-twelve-hundred-year-old son.

Elena dragged him all the way to the bottom of the pool, before releasing his foot and hovering above him, a triumphant silhouette against the bright surface. She was ancestor-shaped, but obviously cheating; she spoke with perfect clarity, and no air bubbles at all.

"Late sleeper! I've been waiting seven weeks for this!"

Paolo feigned indifference, but he was fast running out of breath. He had his exoself convert him into an amphibious human variant—biologically and historically authentic, if no longer the definitive ancestral phenotype. Water flooded into his modified lungs, and his modified brain welcomed it.

He said, "Why would I want to waste consciousness, sitting around waiting for the scout probes to refine their observations? I woke as soon as the data was unambiguous."

She pummeled his chest; he reached up and pulled her down, instinctively reducing his buoyancy to compensate, and they rolled across the bottom of the pool, kissing.

Elena said, "You know we're the first C-Z to arrive, anywhere? The Fomalhaut ship was destroyed. So there's only one other pair of us. Back on Earth."

"So?" Then he remembered. Elena had chosen not to wake if any other version of her had already encountered life. Whatever fate befell each of the remaining ships, every other version of him would have to live without her.

He nodded soberly, and kissed her again. "What am I meant to say? You're a thousand times more precious to me, now?"

"Yes."

"Ah, but what about the you-and-I on Earth? Five hundred times would be closer to the truth."

"There's no poetry in five hundred."

"Don't be so defeatist. Rewire your language centers."

She ran her hands along the sides of his ribcage, down to his hips. They made love with their almost-traditional bodies—and brains; Paolo was amused to the point of distraction when his limbic system went into overdrive, but he remembered enough from the last occasion to bury his self-consciousness and surrender to the strange hijacker. It wasn't like making love in any civilized fashion—the rate of information exchange between them was minuscule, for a start—but it had the raw insistent quality of most ancestral pleasures.

Then they drifted up to the surface of the pool and lay beneath the radiant sunless sky.

Paolo thought: *I've crossed twenty-seven light-years in an instant. I'm orbiting the first planet ever found to hold alien life. And I've sacrificed nothing—left nothing I truly value behind. This is too good, too good.* He felt a pang of regret for his other selves—it was hard to imagine them faring as well, without Elena, without Orpheus—but there was nothing he could do about that, now. Although there'd be time to confer with Earth before any more ships reached their destinations, he'd decided—prior to the cloning— not to allow the unfolding of his manifold future to be swayed by any change of heart. Whether or not his Earth-self agreed, the two of them were powerless to alter the criteria for waking. The self with the right to choose for the thousand had passed away.

No matter, Paolo decided. The others would find—or construct—their own reasons for happiness. And there was still the chance that one of them would wake to the sound of *four chimes*.

Elena said, "If you'd slept much longer, you would have missed the vote."

The vote? The scouts in low orbit had gathered what data they could about Orphean biology. To proceed any further, it would be necessary to send microprobes into the ocean itself—an escalation of contact which required the approval of two-thirds of the polis. There was no compelling reason to believe that the presence of a few million tiny robots could do any harm; all they'd leave behind in the water was a few kilojoules of waste heat. Nevertheless, a faction had arisen which advocated caution. The citizens of Carter-Zimmerman, they argued, could continue to observe from a distance for another decade, or another millennium, refining their observations and hypotheses before intruding . . . and those who disagreed could always sleep away the time, or find other interests to pursue.

Paolo delved into his library-fresh knowledge of the "carpets"—the single Orphean lifeform detected so far. They were free-floating creatures living in the equatorial ocean depths—apparently destroyed by UV if they drifted too close to the surface. They grew to a size of hundreds of meters, then fissioned into dozens of fragments, each of which continued to grow. It was tempting to assume that they were colonies of single-celled organisms, something like giant kelp—but there was no real evidence yet to back that up. It was difficult enough for the scout probes to discern the carpets' gross appearance and behavior through a kilometer of water, even with Vega's copious neutrinos lighting the way; remote observations on a microscopic scale, let alone biochemical analyses, were out of the question. Spectroscopy revealed that the surface water was full of intriguing molecular debris—but guessing the relationship of any of it to the living carpets was like trying to reconstruct human biochemistry by studying human ashes.

Paolo turned to Elena. "What do you think?"

She moaned theatrically; the topic must have been argued to death while he slept. "The microprobes are harmless. They could tell us exactly what the carpets are made of, without removing a single molecule. What's the risk? *Culture shock?*"

Paolo flicked water onto her face, affectionately; the impulse seemed to come with the amphibian body. "You can't be sure that they're not intelligent."

"Do you know what was living on Earth, two hundred million years after it was formed?"

"Maybe cyanobacteria. Maybe nothing. This isn't Earth, though."

"True. But even in the unlikely event that the carpets are intelligent, do you think they'd notice the presence of robots a millionth their size? If they're unified organisms, they don't appear to react to anything in their environment—they have no predators, they don't pursue food, they just drift with the currents—so there's no reason for them to possess elaborate sense organs at all, let alone anything working on a sub-millimeter scale. And if they're colonies of single-celled creatures, one of which happens to collide with a microprobe and register its presence with surface receptors . . . what conceivable harm could that do?"

"I have no idea. But my ignorance is no guarantee of safety."

Elena splashed him back. "The only way to deal with your *ignorance* is to vote to send down the microprobes. We have to be cautious, I agree—but there's no point *being here* if we don't find out what's happening in the oceans, right now. I don't want to wait for this planet to evolve something smart enough to broadcast biochemistry lessons into space. If we're not willing to take a few infinitesimal risks, Vega will turn red giant before we learn anything."

It was a throwaway line—but Paolo tried to imagine witnessing the event. In a quarter of a billion years, would the citizens of Carter-Zimmerman be debating the ethics of intervening to rescue the Orpheans—or would they all have lost interest, and departed for other stars, or modified themselves into beings entirely devoid of nostalgic compassion for organic life?

Grandiose visions for a twelve-hundred-year-old. The Fomalhaut clone had been obliterated by one tiny piece of rock. There was far more junk in the Vegan system than in interstellar space; even ringed by defenses, its data backed up to all the far-flung scout probes, this C-Z was not invulnerable just because it had arrived intact. Elena was right; they had to seize the moment—or they might as well retreat into their own hermetic worlds and forget that they'd ever made the journey.

Paolo recalled the honest puzzlement of a friend from Ashton-Laval: *Why go looking for aliens? Our polis has a thousand ecologies, a trillion species of evolved life. What do you hope to find, out there, that you couldn't have grown at home?*

What had he hoped to find? Just the answers to a few simple questions. Did human consciousness bootstrap all of space-time into existence, in order to explain itself? Or had a neutral, pre-existing universe given birth to a billion varieties of conscious life, all capable of harboring the same delusions of grandeur—until they collided with each other? Anthrocosmology was used to justify the inward-looking stance of most polises: if the physical universe was created by human thought, it had no special status which placed it above virtual reality. It might have come first—and every virtual reality might need to run on a physical computing device, subject to physical laws—but it occupied no privileged position in terms of "truth" versus "illusion." If the ACs were right, then it was no more *honest* to value the physical universe over more recent artificial realities than it was honest to remain flesh instead of software, or ape instead of human, or bacterium instead of ape.

Elena said, "We can't lie here forever; the gang's all waiting to see you."

"Where?" Paolo felt his first pang of homesickness; on Earth, his circle of friends had always met in a real-time image of the Mount Pinatubo crater, plucked straight from the observation satellites. A recording wouldn't be the same.

"I'll show you."

Paolo reached over and took her hand. The pool, the sky, the courtyard vanished—and he found himself gazing down on Orpheus again . . . nightside, but far from dark, with his full mental palette now encoding everything from the pale wash of ground-current long-wave radio, to the multicolored shimmer of isotopic gamma rays and back-scattered cosmic-ray bremsstrahlung. Half the abstract knowledge the library had fed him about the planet was obvious at a glance, now. The ocean's smoothly tapered thermal glow spelt *three-hundred Kelvin* instantly—as well as backlighting the atmosphere's telltale infrared silhouette.

He was standing on a long, metallic-looking girder, one edge of a vast geodesic sphere, open to the blazing cathedral of space. He glanced up and saw the star-rich dust-clogged band of the Milky Way, encircling him from zenith to nadir; aware of the glow of every gas cloud, discerning each absorption and emission line, Paolo could almost feel the plane of the galactic disk transect him. Some constellations were distorted, but the view was more familiar than strange—and he recognized most of the old signposts by color. He had his bearings, now. Twenty degrees away from Sirius—south, by parochial Earth reckoning—faint but unmistakable: the sun.

Elena was beside him—superficially unchanged, although they'd both shrugged off the constraints of biology. The conventions of this environment mimicked the physics of real macroscopic objects in free-fall and vacuum, but it wasn't set up to model any kind of chemistry, let alone that of flesh and blood. Their new bodies were human-shaped, but devoid of elaborate microstructure—and their minds weren't embedded in the physics at all, but were running directly on the processor web.

Paolo was relieved to be back to normal; ceremonial regression to the ancestral form was a venerable C-Z tradition—and being human was largely self-affirming, while it lasted—but every time he emerged from the experience, he felt as if he'd broken free of billion-year-old shackles. There were polises on Earth where the citizens would have found his present structure almost as archaic: a consciousness dominated by sensory perception, an illusion of possessing solid form, a single time coordinate. The last flesh human had died long before Paolo was constructed, and apart from the communities of Gleisner robots, Carter-Zimmerman was about as conservative as a transhuman society could be. The balance seemed right to Paolo, though—acknowledging the flexibility of software, without abandoning interest in the physical world—and although the stubbornly corporeal Gleisners had been first to the stars, the C-Z diaspora would soon overtake them.

Their friends gathered round, showing off their effortless free-fall acrobatics, greeting Paolo and chiding him for not arranging to wake sooner; he was the last of the gang to emerge from hibernation.

"Do you like our humble new meeting place?" Hermann floated by Paolo's shoulder, a chimeric cluster of limbs and sense-organs, speaking through the vacuum in modulated infrared. "We call it Satellite Pinatubo. It's desolate up here, I know—but we were afraid it might violate the spirit of caution if we dared pretend to walk the Orphean surface."

Paolo glanced mentally at a scout probe's close-up of a typical stretch of dry land, an expanse of fissured red rock. "More desolate down there, I think." He was tempted to touch the ground—to let the private vision become tactile—but he resisted. Being elsewhere in the middle of a conversation was bad etiquette.

"Ignore Hermann," Liesl advised. "He wants to flood Orpheus with our alien machinery before we have any idea what the effects might be." Liesl was a green-and-turquoise butterfly, with a stylized human face stippled in gold on each wing.

Paolo was surprised; from the way Elena had spoken, he'd assumed that his friends must have come to a consensus in favor of the microprobes—and only a late sleeper, new to the issues, would bother to argue the point. "What effects? The carpets—"

"Forget the carpets! Even if the carpets are as simple as they look, we don't know what else is down there." As Liesl's wings fluttered, her mirror-image faces seemed to glance at each other for support. "With neutrino imaging, we barely achieve spatial resolution in meters, time resolution in seconds. We don't know anything about smaller lifeforms."

"And we never will, if you have your way." Karpal—an ex-Gleisner, human-shaped as ever—had been Liesl's lover, last time Paolo was awake.

"We've only been here for a fraction of an Orphean year! There's still a wealth of data we could gather non-intrusively, with a little patience. There might be rare beachings of ocean life—"

Elena said dryly, "Rare indeed. Orpheus has negligible tides, shallow waves, very few storms. And anything beached would be fried by UV before we glimpsed anything more instructive than we're already seeing in the surface water."

"Not necessarily. The carpets seem to be vulnerable—but other species might be better protected, if they live nearer to the surface. And Orpheus is seismically active; we should at least wait for a tsunami to dump a few cubic kilometers of ocean onto a shoreline, and see what it reveals."

Paolo smiled; he hadn't thought of that. A tsunami might be worth waiting for.

Liesl continued, "What is there to lose, by waiting a few hundred Orphean years? At the very least, we could gather baseline data on seasonal climate patterns—and we could watch for anomalies, storms and quakes, hoping for some revelatory glimpses."

A few hundred Orphean years? *A few terrestrial millennia?* Paolo's ambivalence waned. If he'd wanted to inhabit geological time, he would have migrated to the Lokhande polis, where the Order of Contemplative Observers watched Earth's mountains erode in subjective seconds. Orpheus hung in the sky beneath them, a beautiful puzzle waiting to be decoded, demanding to be understood.

He said, "But what if there *are* no 'revelatory glimpses'? How long do we wait? We don't know how rare life is—in time, or in space. If this planet is precious, *so is the epoch it's passing through.* We don't know how rapidly Orphean biology is evolving; species might appear and vanish while we agonize over the risks of gathering better data. The carpets—and whatever else—could die out before we'd learnt the first thing about them. What a waste that would be!"

Liesl stood her ground.

"And if we damage the Orphean ecology—or culture—by rushing in? That wouldn't be a waste. It would be a tragedy."

Paolo assimilated all the stored transmissions from his Earth-self—almost three hundred years' worth—before composing a reply. The early communications included detailed mind grafts—and it was good to share the excitement of the diaspora's launch; to watch—very nearly firsthand—the thousand ships, nanomachine-carved from asteroids, depart in a blaze of fusion fire from beyond the orbit of Mars. Then things settled down to the usual prosaic matters: Elena, the gang, shameless gossip, Carter-Zimmerman's ongoing research projects, the buzz of inter-polis cultural tensions, the not-quite-cyclic convulsions of the arts (the perceptual aesthetic overthrows the emotional, again . . . although Valladas in Konishi polis claims to have constructed a new synthesis of the two).

After the first fifty years, his Earth-self had begun to hold things back; by the time news reached Earth of the Fomalhaut clone's demise, the messages had become pure audiovisual linear monologues. Paolo understood. It was only right; they'd diverged, and you didn't send mind grafts to strangers.

Most of the transmissions had been broadcast to all of the ships, indiscriminately. Forty-three years ago, though, his Earth-self had sent a special message to the Vega-bound clone.

"The new lunar spectroscope we finished last year has just picked up clear signs of water on Orpheus. There should be large temperate oceans waiting for you, if the models are right. So . . . good luck." Vision showed the instrument's domes growing out of the rock of the lunar farside; plots of the Orphean spectral data; an ensemble of planetary models. "Maybe it seems strange to you—all the trouble we're taking to catch a glimpse of what you're going to see in close-up, so soon. It's hard to explain: I don't think it's jealousy, or even impatience. Just a need for independence.

"There's been a revival of the old debate: should we consider redesigning our minds to encompass interstellar distances? One self spanning thousands of stars, not via cloning, but through acceptance of the natural time scale of the light-speed lag. Millennia passing between mental events. Local contingencies dealt with by non-conscious systems." Essays, pro and con, were appended; Paolo ingested summaries. "I don't think the idea will gain much support, though—and the new astronomical projects are something of an antidote. We have to make peace with the fact that we've stayed behind . . . so we cling to the Earth—looking outwards, but remaining firmly anchored.

"I keep asking myself, though: where do we go from here? History can't guide us. Evolution can't guide us. The C-Z charter says *understand and respect the universe* . . . but in what form? On what scale? With what kind of senses, what kind of minds? We can become anything at all—and that space of possible futures dwarfs the galaxy. Can we explore it without losing our way? Flesh humans used to spin fantasies about aliens arriving to 'conquer' Earth, to steal their 'precious' physical resources, to wipe them out for fear of 'competition' . . . as if a species capable of making the journey wouldn't have had the power, or the wit, or the imagination, to rid itself of obsolete biological imperatives. *Conquering the galaxy* is what bacteria with spaceships would do—knowing no better, having no choice.

"Our condition is the opposite of that: we have no end of choices. That's why we need to find alien life—not just to break the spell of the anthrocosmologists. We need to find aliens who've faced the same decisions—and discovered how to live, what to become. We need to understand what it means to inhabit the universe."

Paolo watched the crude neutrino images of the carpets moving in staccato jerks around his dodecahedral room. Twenty-four ragged oblongs drifted above him, daughters of a larger ragged oblong which had just fissioned. Models suggested that shear forces from ocean currents could explain the whole process, triggered by nothing more than the parent reaching a critical size. The purely mechanical break-up of a colony—if that was what it was—might have little to do with the life cycle of the constituent organisms. It was frustrating. Paolo was accustomed to a torrent of data on anything which caught his interest; for the diaspora's great discovery to remain nothing more than a sequence of coarse monochrome snapshots was intolerable.

He glanced at a schematic of the scout probes' neutrino detectors, but there was no obvious scope for improvement. Nuclei in the detectors were excited into unstable high-energy states, then kept there by fine-tuned gamma-ray lasers picking off lower-energy eigenstates faster than they could creep into existence and attract a transition. Changes in neutrino flux of one part in ten-to-the-fifteenth could shift the energy levels far enough to disrupt the balancing act. The carpets cast a shadow so faint, though, that even this near-perfect vision could barely resolve it.

Orlando Venetti said, "You're awake."

Paolo turned. His father stood an arm's length away, presenting as an ornately clad human of indeterminate age. Definitely older than Paolo, though; Orlando never ceased to play up his seniority—even if the age difference was only twenty-five percent now, and falling.

Paolo banished the carpets from the room to the space behind one pentagonal window, and took his father's hand. The portions of Orlando's mind which meshed with his own expressed pleasure at Paolo's emergence from hibernation, fondly dwelt on past shared experiences, and entertained hopes of continued harmony between father and son. Paolo's greeting was similar, a carefully contrived "revelation" of his own emotional state. It was more of a ritual than an act of communication—but then, even with Elena, he set up barriers. No one was totally honest with another person—unless the two of them intended to permanently fuse.

Orlando nodded at the carpets. "I hope you appreciate how important they are."

"You know I do." He hadn't included that in his greeting, though. "First alien life." *C-Z humiliates the Gleisner robots, at last*—that was probably how his father saw it. The robots had been first to Alpha Centauri, and first to an extrasolar planet—but first life was Apollo to their Sputniks, for anyone who chose to think in those terms.

Orlando said, "This is the hook we need, to catch the citizens of the marginal polises. The ones who haven't quite imploded into solipsism. This will shake them up—don't you think?"

Paolo shrugged. Earth's transhumans were free to implode into anything they liked; it didn't stop Carter-Zimmerman from exploring the physical universe. But thrashing the Gleisners wouldn't be enough for Orlando; he lived for the day when C-Z would become the cultural mainstream. Any polis could multiply its population a billionfold in a microsecond, if it wanted the vacuous honor of outnumbering the rest. Luring other citizens to migrate was harder—and persuading them to rewrite their own local charters was harder still. Orlando had a missionary streak: he wanted every other polis to see the error of its ways, and follow C-Z to the stars.

Paolo said, "Ashton-Laval has intelligent aliens. I wouldn't be so sure that news of giant seaweed is going to take Earth by storm."

Orlando was venomous. "Ashton-Laval intervened in its so-called 'evolutionary' simulations so many times that they might as well have built the end products in an act of creation lasting six days. They wanted talking reptiles, and—*mirabile dictu!*—they got talking reptiles. There are self-modified transhumans in *this polis* more alien than the aliens in Ashton-Laval."

Paolo smiled. "All right. Forget Ashton-Laval. But forget the marginal polises, too. We choose to value the physical world. That's what defines us—but it's as arbitrary as any other choice of values. Why can't you accept that? It's not the One True Path which the infidels have to be bludgeoned into following." He knew he was arguing half for the sake of it—he desperately wanted to refute the anthrocosmologists, himself—but Orlando always drove him into taking the opposite position. Out of fear of being nothing but his father's clone? Despite the total absence of inherited episodic memories, the stochastic input into his ontogenesis, the chaotically divergent nature of the iterative mind-building algorithms.

Orlando made a beckoning gesture, dragging the image of the carpets halfway back into the room. "You'll vote for the microprobes?"

"Of course."

"Everything depends on that, now. It's good to start with a tantalizing glimpse—but if we don't follow up with details soon, they'll lose interest back on Earth very rapidly."

"Lose interest? It'll be fifty-four years before we know if anyone paid the slightest attention in the first place."

Orlando eyed him with disappointment, and resignation. "If you don't care about the other polises, think about C-Z. This helps us, it strengthens us. We have to make the most of that."

Paolo was bemused. "The charter is the charter. What needs to be strengthened? You make it sound like there's something at risk."

"What do you think a thousand lifeless worlds would have done to us? Do you think the charter would have remained intact?"

Paolo had never considered the scenario. "Maybe not. But in every C-Z where the charter was rewritten, there would have been citizens who'd have gone off and founded new polises on the old lines. You and I, for a start. We could have called it Venetti-Venetti."

"While half your friends turned their backs on the physical world? While

Carter-Zimmerman, after two thousand years, went solipsist? You'd be happy with that?''

Paolo laughed. "No—but it's not going to happen, is it? *We've found life.* All right, I agree with you: this strengthens C-Z. The diaspora might have 'failed' . . . but it didn't. We've been lucky. I'm glad, I'm grateful. Is that what you wanted to hear?''

Orlando said sourly, "You take too much for granted.''

"And you care too much what I think! I'm not your . . . heir." Orlando was first-generation, scanned from flesh—and there were times when he seemed unable to accept that the whole concept of generation had lost its archaic significance. "You don't need me to safeguard the future of Carter-Zimmerman on your behalf. Or the future of transhumanity. You can do it in person.''

Orlando looked wounded—a conscious choice, but it still encoded something. Paolo felt a pang of regret—but he'd said nothing he could honestly retract.

His father gathered up the sleeves of his gold and crimson robes—the only citizen of C-Z who could make Paolo uncomfortable to be naked—and repeated as he vanished from the room: "You take too much for granted.''

The gang watched the launch of the microprobes together—even Liesl, though she came in mourning, as a giant dark bird. Karpal stroked her feathers nervously. Hermann appeared as a creature out of Escher, a segmented worm with six human-shaped feet—on legs with elbows—given to curling up into a disk and rolling along the girders of Satellite Pinatubo. Paolo and Elena kept saying the same thing simultaneously; they'd just made love.

Hermann had moved the satellite to a notional orbit just below one of the scout probes—and changed the environment's scale, so that the probe's lower surface, an intricate landscape of detector modules and attitude-control jets, blotted out half the sky. The atmospheric-entry capsules—ceramic teardrops three centimeters wide—burst from their launch tube and hurtled past like boulders, vanishing from sight before they'd fallen so much as ten meters closer to Orpheus. It was all scrupulously accurate, although it was part real-time imagery, part extrapolation, part *faux*. Paolo thought: *We might as well have run a pure simulation . . . and pretended to follow the capsules down.* Elena gave him a guilty/admonishing look. *Yeah—and then why bother actually launching them at all? Why not just simulate a plausible Orphean ocean full of plausible Orphean lifeforms? Why not simulate the whole diaspora?* There was no crime of heresy in C-Z; no one had ever been exiled for breaking the charter. At times it still felt like a tightrope walk, though, trying to classify every act of simulation into those which contributed to an understanding of the physical universe (good), those which were merely convenient, recreational, aesthetic (acceptable) . . . and those which constituted a denial of the primacy of real phenomena (time to think about emigration).

The vote on the microprobes had been close: seventy-two percent in favor, just over the required two-thirds majority, with five percent abstaining. (Citizens created since the arrival at Vega were excluded . . . not that anyone in Carter-Zimmerman would have dreamt of stacking the ballot, perish the thought.) Paolo had been surprised at the narrow margin; he'd yet to hear a single plausible scenario for the microprobes doing harm. He wondered if there was another, unspoken reason which had nothing to do with fears for the Orphean ecology, or hypothetical culture. *A wish to prolong the pleasure of unraveling the planet's mysteries?* Paolo had some sympathy with that impulse—but the launch of the microprobes would do nothing to undermine the greater long-term pleasure of watching, and understanding, as Orphean life evolved.

Liesl said forlornly, "Coastline erosion models show that the northwestern shore of Lambda is inundated by tsunami every ninety Orphean years, on average." She offered the data to them; Paolo glanced at it, and it looked convincing—but the point was academic now. "We could have waited."

Hermann waved his eye-stalks at her. "Beaches covered in fossils, are they?"

"No, but the conditions hardly—"

"No excuses!" He wound his body around a girder, kicking his legs gleefully. Hermann was first-generation, even older than Orlando; he'd been scanned in the twenty-first century, before Carter-Zimmerman existed. Over the centuries, though, he'd wiped most of his episodic memories, and rewritten his personality a dozen times. He'd once told Paolo, "I think of myself as my own great-great-grandson. Death's not so bad, if you do it incrementally. Ditto for immortality."

Elena said, "I keep trying to imagine how it will feel if another C-Z clone stumbles on something infinitely better—like aliens with wormhole drives—while we're back here studying rafts of algae." The body she wore was more stylized than usual—still humanoid, but sexless, hairless and smooth, the face inexpressive and androgynous.

"If they have wormhole drives, they might visit us. Or share the technology, so we can link up the whole diaspora."

"If they have wormhole drives, where have they been for the last two thousand years?"

Paolo laughed. "Exactly. But I know what you mean: *first alien life* . . . and it's likely to be about as sophisticated as seaweed. It breaks the jinx, though. Seaweed every twenty-seven light-years. Nervous systems every fifty? Intelligence every hundred?" He fell silent, abruptly realizing what she was feeling: electing not to wake again after first life was beginning to seem like the wrong choice, a waste of the opportunities the diaspora had created. Paolo offered her a mind graft expressing empathy and support, but she declined.

She said, "I want sharp borders, right now. I want to deal with this myself."

"I understand." He let the partial model of her which he'd acquired as they'd made love fade from his mind. It was non-sapient, and no longer linked to her—but to retain it any longer when she felt this way would have seemed like a transgression. Paolo took the responsibilities of intimacy seriously. His lover before Elena had asked him to erase all his knowledge of her, and he'd more or less complied—the only thing he still knew about her was the fact that she'd made the request.

Hermann announced, "Planetfall!" Paolo glanced at a replay of a scout probe view which showed the first few entry capsules breaking up above the ocean and releasing their microprobes. Nanomachines transformed the ceramic shields (and then themselves) into carbon dioxide and a few simple minerals—nothing the micrometeorites constantly raining down onto Orpheus didn't contain—before the fragments could strike the water. The microprobes would broadcast nothing; when they'd finished gathering data, they'd float to the surface and modulate their UV reflectivity. It would be up to the scout probes to locate these specks, and read their messages, before they self-destructed as thoroughly as the entry capsules.

Hermann said, "This calls for a celebration. I'm heading for the Heart. Who'll join me?"

Paolo glanced at Elena. She shook her head. "You go."

"Are you sure?"

"Yes! Go on." Her skin had taken on a mirrored sheen; her expressionless face reflected the planet below. "I'm all right. I just want some time to think things through, on my own."

Hermann coiled around the satellite's frame, stretching his pale body as he went, gaining segments, gaining legs. "Come on, come on! Karpal? Liesl? Come and celebrate!"

Elena was gone. Liesl made a derisive sound and flapped off into the distance, mocking the environment's airlessness. Paolo and Karpal watched as Hermann grew longer and faster—and then in a blur of speed and change stretched out to wrap the entire geodesic frame. Paolo demagnetized his feet and moved away, laughing; Karpal did the same.

Then Hermann constricted like a boa, and snapped the whole satellite apart.

They floated for a while, two human-shaped machines and a giant worm in a cloud of spinning metal fragments, an absurd collection of imaginary debris, glinting by the light of the true stars.

* * *

The Heart was always crowded, but it was larger than Paolo had seen it—even though Hermann had shrunk back to his original size, so as not to make a scene. The huge muscular chamber arched above them, pulsating wetly in time to the music, as they searched for the perfect location to soak up the atmosphere. Paolo had visited public environments in other polises, back on Earth; many were designed to be nothing more than a perceptual framework for group emotion-sharing. He'd never understood the attraction of becoming intimate with large numbers of strangers. Ancestral social hierarchies might have had their faults—and it was absurd to try to make a virtue of the limitations imposed by minds confined to wetware—but the whole idea of mass telepathy as an end in itself seemed bizarre to Paolo . . . and even old-fashioned, in a way. Humans, clearly, would have benefited from a good strong dose of each other's inner life, to keep them from slaughtering each other—but any civilized transhuman could respect and value other citizens without the need to have *been them*, firsthand.

They found a good spot and made some furniture, a table and two chairs—Hermann preferred to stand—and the floor expanded to make room. Paolo looked around, shouting greetings at the people he recognized by sight, but not bothering to check for identity broadcasts from the rest. Chances were he'd met everyone here, but he didn't want to spend the next hour exchanging pleasantries with casual acquaintances.

Hermann said, "I've been monitoring our modest stellar observatory's data stream—my antidote to Vegan parochialism. Odd things are going on around Sirius. We're seeing electron-positron annihilation gamma rays, gravity waves . . . and some unexplained hot spots on Sirius B." He turned to Karpal and asked innocently, "What do you think those robots are up to? There's a rumor that they're planning to drag the white dwarf out of orbit, and use it as part of a giant spaceship."

"I never listen to rumors." Karpal always presented as a faithful reproduction of his old human-shaped Gleisner body—and his mind, Paolo gathered, always took the form of a physiological model, even though he was five generations removed from flesh. Leaving his people and coming into C-Z must have taken considerable courage; they'd never welcome him back.

Paolo said, "Does it matter what they do? Where they go, how they get there? There's more than enough room for both of us. Even if they shadowed the diaspora—even if they came to Vega—we could study the Orpheans together, couldn't we?"

Hermann's cartoon insect face showed mock alarm, eyes growing wider, and wider apart. "Not if they dragged along a white dwarf! Next thing they'd want to start building a Dyson sphere.'' He turned back to Karpal. "You don't still suffer the urge, do you, for . . . *astrophysical* engineering?''

"Nothing C-Z's exploitation of a few megatons of Vegan asteroid material hasn't satisfied.''

Paolo tried to change the subject. "Has anyone heard from Earth, lately? I'm beginning to feel unplugged.'' His own most recent message was a decade older than the time lag.

Karpal said, "You're not missing much; all they're talking about is Orpheus . . . ever since the new lunar observations, the signs of water. They seem more excited by the mere possibility of life than we are by the certainty. And they have very high hopes.''

Paolo laughed. "They do. My Earth-self seems to be counting on the diaspora to find an advanced civilization with the answers to all of transhumanity's existential problems. I don't think he'll get much cosmic guidance from kelp.''

"You know there was a big rise in emigration from C-Z after the launch? Emigration, and suicides.'' Hermann had stopped wriggling and gyrating, becoming almost still, a sign of rare seriousness. "I suspect that's what triggered the astronomy program in the first place. And it seems to have stanched the flow, at least in the short term. Earth C-Z detected water before any clone in the diaspora—and when they hear that we've found life, they'll feel more like collaborators in the discovery because of it.''

Paolo felt a stirring of unease. *Emigration and suicides? Was that why Orlando had been so gloomy?* After three hundred years of waiting, how high had expectations become?

A buzz of excitement crossed the floor, a sudden shift in the tone of the conversation. Hermann whispered reverently, "First microprobe has surfaced. And the data is coming in now.''

The non-sapient Heart was intelligent enough to guess its patrons' wishes. Although everyone could tap the library for results, privately, the music cut out and a giant public image of the summary data appeared, high in the chamber. Paolo had to crane his neck to view it, a novel experience.

The microprobe had mapped one of the carpets in high resolution. The image showed the expected rough oblong, some hundred meters wide—but the two-or-three-meter-thick slab of the neutrino tomographs was revealed now as a delicate, convoluted surface—fine as a single layer of skin, but folded into an elaborate space-filling curve. Paolo checked the full data: the topology was strictly planar, despite the pathological appearance. No holes, no joins—just a surface which meandered wildly enough to look ten thousand times thicker from a distance than it really was.

An inset showed the microstructure, at a point which started at the rim of the carpet and then—slowly—moved toward the center. Paolo stared at the flowing molecular diagram for several seconds before he grasped what it meant.

The carpet was not a colony of single-celled creatures. Nor was it a multi-cellular organism. It was a *single molecule*, a two-dimensional polymer weighing twenty-five million kilograms. A giant sheet of folded polysaccharide, a complex mesh of interlinked pentose and hexose sugars hung with alkyl and amide side chains. A bit like a plant cell wall—except that this polymer was far stronger than cellulose, and the surface area was twenty orders of magnitude greater.

Karpal said, "I hope those entry capsules were perfectly sterile. Earth bacteria would gorge themselves on this. One big floating carbohydrate dinner, with no defenses."

Hermann thought it over. "Maybe. If they had enzymes capable of breaking off a piece—which I doubt. No chance we'll find out, though: even if there'd been bacterial spores lingering in the asteroid belt from early human expeditions, every ship in the diaspora was double-checked for contamination *en route*. We haven't brought smallpox to the Americas."

Paolo was still dazed. "But how does it assemble? How does it . . . grow?" Hermann consulted the library and replied, before Paolo could do the same.

"The edge of the carpet catalyzes its own growth. The polymer is irregular, aperiodic—there's no single component which simply repeats. But there seem to be about twenty thousand basic structural units—twenty thousand different polysaccharide building blocks." Paolo saw them: long bundles of cross-linked chains running the whole two-hundred-micron thickness of the carpet, each with a roughly square cross-section, bonded at several thousand points to the four neighboring units. "Even at this depth, the ocean's full of UV-generated radicals which filter down from the surface. Any structural unit exposed to the water converts those radicals into more polysaccharide—and builds another structural unit."

Paolo glanced at the library again, for a simulation of the process. Catalytic sites strewn along the sides of each unit trapped the radicals in place, long enough for new bonds to form between them. Some simple sugars were incorporated straight into the polymer as they were created; others were set free to drift in solution for a microsecond or two, until they were needed. At that level, there were only a few basic chemical tricks being used . . . but molecular evolution must have worked its way up from a few small autocatalytic fragments, first formed by chance, to this elaborate system of twenty thousand mutually self-replicating structures. If the "structural units" had floated free in the ocean as independent molecules, the "lifeform" they comprised would have been virtually invisible. By bonding together, though, they became twenty thousand colors in a giant mosaic.

It was astonishing. Paolo hoped Elena was tapping the library, wherever she was. A colony of algae would have been more "advanced"—but this incredible primordial creature revealed infinitely more about the possibilities for the genesis of life. Carbohydrate, here, played every biochemical role: information carrier, enzyme, energy source, structural material. Nothing like it could have survived on Earth, once there were organisms capable of feeding on it—and if there were ever intelligent Orpheans, they'd be unlikely to find any trace of this bizarre ancestor.

Karpal wore a secretive smile.

Paolo said, "What?"

"Wang tiles. The carpets are made out of Wang tiles."

Hermann beat him to the library, again.

"*Wang* as in twentieth-century flesh mathematician, Hao Wang. *Tiles* as in any set of shapes which can cover the plane. Wang tiles are squares with various shaped edges, which have to fit complementary shapes on adjacent squares. You can cover the plane with a set of Wang tiles, as long as you choose the right one every step of the way. Or in the case of the carpets, grow the right one."

Karpal said, "We should call them Wang's Carpets, in honor of Hao Wang. After twenty-three hundred years, his mathematics has come to life."

Paolo liked the idea, but he was doubtful. "We may have trouble getting a two-thirds majority on that. It's a bit obscure . . ."

Hermann laughed. "Who needs a two-thirds majority? If we want to call them Wang's Carpets, we can call them Wang's Carpets. There are ninety-seven languages in current use in C-Z—half of them invented since the polis was founded. I don't think we'll be exiled for coining one private name."

Paolo concurred, slightly embarrassed. The truth was, he'd completely forgotten that Hermann and Karpal weren't actually speaking Modern Roman.

The three of them instructed their exoselves to consider the name adopted: henceforth, they'd hear "carpet" as "Wang's Carpet"—but if they used the term with anyone else, the reverse translation would apply.

Paolo sat and drank in the image of the giant alien: the first lifeform encountered by human or transhuman which was not a biological cousin. The death, at last, of the possibility that Earth might be unique.

They hadn't refuted the anthrocosmologists yet, though. Not quite. If, as the ACs claimed, human consciousness was the seed around which all of space-time had crystallized—if the universe was nothing but the simplest orderly explanation for human thought—then there was, strictly speaking, no need for a single alien to exist, anywhere. But the physics which justified human existence couldn't help generating a billion other worlds where life could arise. The ACs would be unmoved by Wang's Carpets; they'd insist that these creatures were physical, if not biological, cousins—merely an unavoidable by-product of anthropogenic, life-enabling physical laws.

The real test wouldn't come until the diaspora—or the Gleisner robots—finally encountered conscious aliens: minds entirely unrelated to humanity, observing and explaining the universe which human thought had supposedly built. Most ACs had come right out and declared such a find impossible; it was the sole falsifiable prediction of their hypothesis. Alien consciousness, as opposed to mere alien life, would always build itself a separate universe—because the chance of two unrelated forms of self-awareness concocting exactly the same physics and the same cosmology was infinitesimal—and any alien biosphere which seemed capable of evolving consciousness would simply never do so.

Paolo glanced at the map of the diaspora, and took heart. *Alien life already*—and the search had barely started; there were nine hundred and ninety-eight target systems yet to be explored. And even if every one of them proved no more conclusive than Orpheus . . . he was prepared to send clones out farther—and prepared to wait. Consciousness had taken far longer to appear on Earth than the quarter-of-a-billion years remaining before Vega left the main sequence—but the whole point of being here, after all, was that Orpheus wasn't Earth.

Orlando's celebration of the microprobe discoveries was a very first-generation affair. The environment was an endless sunlit garden strewn with tables covered in *food*, and the invitation had politely suggested attendance in fully human form. Paolo politely faked it—simulating most of the physiology, but running the body as a puppet, leaving his mind unshackled.

Orlando introduced his new lover, Catherine, who presented as a tall, dark-skinned woman. Paolo didn't recognize her on sight, but checked the identity code she broadcast. It was a small polis, he'd met her once before—as a man called Samuel, one of the physicists who'd worked on the main interstellar fusion drive employed by all the ships of the diaspora. Paolo was amused to think that many of the people here would be seeing his father as a woman. The majority of the citizens of C-Z still practiced the conventions of relative gender which had come into fashion in the twenty-third century—and Orlando had wired them into his own son too deeply for Paolo to wish to abandon them—but whenever the paradoxes were revealed so starkly, he wondered how much longer the conventions would endure. Paolo was same-sex to Orlando, and hence saw his father's lover as a woman, the two close relationships taking precedence over his casual knowledge of Catherine as Samuel. Orlando perceived himself as being male and heterosexual, as his flesh original had been . . . while Samuel saw himself the same way . . . and each perceived the other to be a heterosexual woman. If certain third parties ended up with mixed signals, so be it. It was a typical C-Z compromise: nobody could bear to overturn the old order and do away with gender entirely (as most other polises had done) . . . but nobody could resist the flexibility which being software, not flesh, provided.

Paolo drifted from table to table, sampling the food to keep up appearances, wishing Elena had come. There was little conversation about the biology of Wang's Carpets; most of the people here were simply celebrating their win against the opponents of the microprobes—and the humiliation that faction would suffer, now that it was clearer than ever that the "invasive" observations could have done no harm. Liesl's fears had proved unfounded; there was no other life in the ocean, just Wang's Carpets of various sizes. Paolo, feeling perversely even-handed after the fact, kept wanting to remind these smug movers and shakers: *There might have been anything down there. Strange creatures, delicate and vulnerable in ways we could never have anticipated. We were lucky, that's all.*

He ended up alone with Orlando almost by chance; they were both fleeing different groups of appalling guests when their paths crossed on the lawn.

Paolo asked, "How do you think they'll take this, back home?"

"It's first life, isn't it? Primitive or not. It should at least maintain interest in the diaspora, until the next alien biosphere is discovered." Orlando seemed subdued; perhaps he was finally coming to terms with the gulf between their modest discovery, and Earth's longing for world-shaking results. "And at least the chemistry is novel. If it had turned out to be based on DNA and protein, I think half of Earth C-Z would have died of boredom on the spot. Let's face it, the possibilities of DNA have been simulated to death."

Paolo smiled at the heresy. "You think if nature hadn't managed a little originality, it would have dented people's faith in the charter? If the solipsist polises had begun to look more inventive than the universe itself . . . "

"Exactly."

They walked on in silence, then Orlando halted, and turned to face him.

He said, "There's something I've been wanting to tell you. My Earth-self is dead."

"What?"

"Please, don't make a fuss."

"But . . . why? Why would he—?" *Dead* meant suicide; there was no other cause—unless the sun had turned red giant and swallowed everything out to the orbit of Mars.

"I don't know why. Whether it was a vote of confidence in the diaspora"— Orlando had chosen to wake only in the presence of alien life—"or whether he despaired of us sending back good news, and couldn't face the waiting, and the risk of disappointment. He didn't give a reason. He just had his exoself send a message, stating what he'd done."

Paolo was shaken. If a clone of *Orlando* had succumbed to pessimism, he couldn't begin to imagine the state of mind of the rest of Earth C-Z.

"When did this happen?"

"About fifty years after the launch."

"My Earth-self said nothing."

"It was up to me to tell you, not him."

"I wouldn't have seen it that way."

"Apparently, you would have."

Paolo fell silent, confused. How was he supposed to mourn a distant version of Orlando, in the presence of the one he thought of as real? Death of one clone was a strange half-death, a hard thing to come to terms with. His Earth-self had lost a father; his father had lost an Earth-self. What exactly did that mean to *him*?

What Orlando cared most about was Earth C-Z. Paolo said carefully, "Hermann told me there'd been a rise in emigration and suicide—until the spectroscope picked up the Orphean water. Morale has improved a lot since then—and when they hear that it's more than just water . . ."

Orlando cut him off sharply. "You don't have to talk things up for me. I'm in no danger of repeating the act."

They stood on the lawn, facing each other. Paolo composed a dozen different combinations of mood to communicate, but none of them felt right. He could have granted his father perfect knowledge of everything he was feeling—but what exactly would that knowledge have conveyed? In the end, there was fusion, or separateness. There was nothing in between.

Orlando said, "Kill myself—and leave the fate of transhumanity in your hands? You must be out of your fucking mind."

They walked on together, laughing.

Karpal seemed barely able to gather his thoughts enough to speak. Paolo would have offered him a mind graft promoting tranquillity and concentration—distilled from his own most focused moments—but he was sure that Karpal would never have accepted it. He said, "Why don't you just start wherever you want to? I'll stop you if you're not making sense."

Karpal looked around the white dodecahedron with an expression of disbelief. "You live here?"

"Some of the time."

"But this is your base environment? No trees? No sky? No *furniture*?"

Paolo refrained from repeating any of Hermann's naive-robot jokes. "I add them when I want them. You know, like . . . music. Look, don't let my taste in decor distract you."

Karpal made a chair and sat down heavily.

He said, "Hao Wang proved a powerful theorem, twenty-three hundred years ago. Think of a row of Wang Tiles as being like the data tape of a Turing Machine." Paolo had the library grant him knowledge of the term; it was the original conceptual form of a generalized computing device, an imaginary machine which moved back and forth along a limitless one-dimensional data tape, reading and writing symbols according to a given set of rules.

"With the right set of tiles, to force the right pattern, the next row of the tiling will look like the data tape after the Turing Machine has performed one step of its computation. And the row after that will be the data tape after two steps, and so on. For any given Turing Machine, there's a set of Wang Tiles which can imitate it."

Paolo nodded amiably. He hadn't heard of this particular quaint result, but it was hardly surprising. "The carpets must be carrying out billions of acts of computation every second . . . but then, so are the water molecules around them. There are no physical processes which don't perform arithmetic of some kind."

"True. But with the carpets, it's not quite the same as random molecular motion."

"Maybe not."

Karpal smiled, but said nothing.

"What? You've found a pattern? Don't tell me: our set of twenty thousand polysaccharide Wang Tiles just happens to form the Turing Machine for calculating pi."

"No. What they form is a universal Turing Machine. They can calculate anything at all—depending on the data they start with. Every daughter fragment is like a program being fed to a chemical computer. Growth executes the program."

"Ah." Paolo's curiosity was roused—but he was having some trouble picturing where the hypothetical Turing Machine put its read/write head. "Are you telling me only one tile changes between any two rows, where the 'machine' leaves its mark on the 'data tape' . . . ?" The mosaics he'd seen were a riot of complexity, with no two rows remotely the same.

Karpal said, "No, no. Wang's original example worked exactly like a standard Turing Machine, to simplify the argument . . . but the carpets are more like an arbitrary number of different computers with overlapping data, all working in parallel. This is biology, not a designed machine—it's as messy and wild as, say . . . a mammalian genome. In fact, there are mathematical similarities with gene regulation: I've identified Kauffman networks at every level, from the tiling rules up; the whole system's poised on the hyperadaptive edge between frozen and chaotic behavior."

Paolo absorbed that, with the library's help. Like Earth life, the carpets seemed to have evolved a combination of robustness and flexibility which would have maximized their power to take advantage of natural selection. Thousands of different autocatalytic chemical networks must have arisen soon after the formation of Orpheus—but as the ocean chemistry and the climate changed in the Vegan system's early traumatic millennia, the ability to respond to selection pressure had itself been selected for, and the carpets were the result. Their complexity seemed redundant, now, after a hundred million years of relative stability—and no predators or competition in sight—but the legacy remained.

"So if the carpets have ended up as universal computers . . . with no real need anymore to respond to their surroundings . . . what are they *doing* with all that computing power?"

Karpal said solemnly, "I'll show you."

Paolo followed him into an environment where they drifted above a schematic of a carpet, an abstract landscape stretching far into the distance, elaborately wrinkled like the real thing, but otherwise heavily stylized, with each of the polysaccharide building blocks portrayed as a square tile with four different colored edges. The adjoining edges of neighboring tiles bore complementary colors—to represent the complementary, interlocking shapes of the borders of the building blocks.

"One group of microprobes finally managed to sequence an entire daughter fragment," Karpal explained, "although the exact edges it started life with are largely guesswork, since the thing was growing while they were trying to map it." He gestured impatiently, and all the wrinkles and folds were smoothed away, an irrelevant distraction. They moved to one border of the ragged-edged carpet, and Karpal started the simulation running.

Paolo watched the mosaic extending itself, following the tiling rules perfectly—an orderly mathematical process, here: no chance collisions of radicals with catalytic sites, no mismatched borders between two new-grown neighboring "tiles" triggering the disintegration of both. Just the distillation of the higher-level consequences of all that random motion.

Karpal led Paolo up to a height where he could see subtle patterns being woven, overlapping multiplexed periodicities drifting across the growing edge, meeting and sometimes interacting, sometimes passing right through each other. Mobile pseudo-attractors, quasi-stable waveforms in a one-dimensional universe. The carpet's second dimension was more like time than space, a permanent record of the history of the edge.

Karpal seemed to read his mind. "One dimensional. Worse than flatland. No connectivity, no complexity. What can possibly happen in a system like that? Nothing of interest, right?"

He clapped his hands and the environment exploded around Paolo. Trails of color streaked across his sensorium, entwining, then disintegrating into luminous smoke.

"Wrong. Everything goes on in a multidimensional frequency space. I've Fourier-transformed the edge into over a thousand components, and there's independent information in all of them. We're only in a narrow cross-section here, a sixteen-dimensional slice—but it's oriented to show the principal components, the maximum detail."

Paolo spun in a blur of meaningless color, utterly lost, his surroundings beyond comprehension. "You're a *Gleisner robot,* Karpal! *Only* sixteen dimensions! How can you have done this?"

Karpal sounded hurt, wherever he was. "Why do you think I came to C-Z? I thought you people were flexible!"

"What you're doing is . . ." *What?* Heresy? There was no such thing. Officially. "Have you shown this to anyone else?"

"Of course not. Who did you have in mind? Liesl? *Hermann?*"

"Good. I know how to keep my mouth shut." Paolo invoked his exoself and moved back into the dodecahedron. He addressed the empty room. "How can I put this? The physical universe has three spatial dimensions, plus time. Citizens of Carter-Zimmerman inhabit the physical universe. Higher dimensional mind games are for the solipsists." Even as he said it, he realized how pompous he sounded. It was an arbitrary doctrine, not some great moral principle.

But it was the doctrine he'd lived with for twelve hundred years.

Karpal replied, more bemused than offended, "It's the only way to see what's going on. The only sensible way to apprehend it. Don't you want to know what the carpets are *actually like*?"

Paolo felt himself being tempted. Inhabit a *sixteen-dimensional slice of a thousand-dimensional frequency space*? But it was in the service of understanding a real physical system—not a novel experience for its own sake.

And nobody had to find out.

He ran a quick—non-sapient—self-predictive model. There was a ninety-three percent chance that he'd give in, after fifteen subjective minutes of agonizing over the decision. It hardly seemed fair to keep Karpal waiting that long.

He said, "You'll have to loan me your mind-shaping algorithm. My exoself wouldn't know where to begin."

When it was done, he steeled himself, and moved back into Karpal's environment. For a moment, there was nothing but the same meaningless blur as before.

Then everything suddenly crystallized.

Creatures swam around them, elaborately branched tubes like mobile coral, vividly colored in all the hues of Paolo's mental palette—Karpal's attempt to cram in some of the information that a mere sixteen dimensions couldn't show? Paolo glanced down at his own body—nothing was missing, but he could see *around* it in all the thirteen dimensions in which it was nothing but a pin-prick; he quickly looked away. The "coral" seemed far more natural to his altered sensory map, occupying sixteen-space in all directions, and shaded with hints that it occupied much more. And Paolo had no doubt that it was "alive"—it looked more organic than the carpets themselves, by far.

Karpal said, "Every point in this space encodes some kind of quasi-periodic pattern in the tiles. Each dimension represents a different characteristic size—like a wavelength, although the analogy's not precise. The position in each dimension represents other attributes of the pattern, relating to the particular tiles it employs. So the localized systems you see around you are clusters of a few billion patterns, all with broadly similar attributes at similar wavelengths."

They moved away from the swimming coral, into a swarm of something like jellyfish: floppy hyperspheres waving wispy tendrils (each one of them more substantial than Paolo). Tiny jewel-like creatures darted among them. Paolo was just beginning to notice that nothing moved here like a solid object drifting through normal space; motion seemed to entail a shimmering deformation at the leading hypersurface, a visible process of disassembly and reconstruction.

Karpal led him on through the secret ocean. There were helical worms, coiled together in groups of indeterminate number—each single creature breaking up into a dozen or more wriggling slivers, and then recombining . . . although not always from the same parts. There were dazzling multicolored stemless flowers, intricate hypercones of "gossamer-thin" fifteen-dimensional petals—each one a hypnotic fractal labyrinth of crevices and capillaries. There were clawed monstrosities, writhing knots of sharp insectile parts like an orgy of decapitated scorpions.

Paolo said, uncertainly, "You could give people a glimpse of this in just three dimensions. Enough to make it clear that there's . . . *life* in here. This is going to shake them up badly, though." Life—embedded in the accidental computations of Wang's Carpets, with no possibility of ever relating to the world outside. This was an affront to Carter-Zimmerman's whole philosophy: if nature had evolved "organisms" as divorced from reality as the inhabitants of the most inward-looking polis, where was the privileged status of the physical universe, the clear distinction between truth and illusion?

And after three hundred years of waiting for good news from the diaspora, how would they respond to this back on Earth?

Karpal said, "There's one more thing I have to show you."

He'd named the creatures squids, for obvious reasons. *Distant cousins of the jellyfish, perhaps?* They were prodding each other with their tentacles in a way which looked thoroughly carnal—but Karpal explained, "There's no analog of light here. We're viewing all this according to ad hoc rules which have nothing to do with the native physics. All the creatures here gather information about each other by contact alone—which is actually quite a rich means of exchanging data, with so many dimensions. What you're seeing is communication by touch."

"Communication about what?"

"Just gossip, I expect. Social relationships."

Paolo stared at the writhing mass of tentacles.

"You think they're *conscious*?"

Karpal, point-like, grinned broadly. "They have a central control structure with more connectivity than the human brain—and which correlates data gathered from the skin. I've mapped that organ, and I've started to analyze its function."

He led Paolo into another environment, a representation of the data structures in the "brain" of one of the squids. It was—mercifully—three-dimensional, and highly stylized, built of translucent colored blocks marked with icons, representing mental symbols, linked by broad lines indicating the major connections between them. Paolo had seen similar diagrams of transhuman minds; this was far less elaborate, but eerily familiar nonetheless.

Karpal said, "Here's the sensory map of its surroundings. Full of other squids' bodies, and vague data on the last known positions of a few smaller creatures. But you'll see that the symbols activated by the physical presence of the other squids are linked to these"—he traced the connection with one finger—"representations. Which are crude miniatures of *this whole structure* here."

"This whole structure" was an assembly labeled with icons for memory retrieval, simple tropisms, short-term goals. The general business of being and doing.

"The squid has maps, not just of other squids' bodies, but their minds as well. Right or wrong, it certainly tries to know what the others are thinking about. And"—he pointed out another set of links, leading to another, less crude, miniature squid mind—"it thinks about its own thoughts as well. I'd call that *consciousness*, wouldn't you?"

Paolo said weakly, "You've kept all this to yourself? You came this far, without saying a word—?"

Karpal was chastened. "I know it was selfish—but once I'd decoded the interactions of the tile patterns, I couldn't tear myself away long enough to start explaining it to anyone else. And I came to you first because I wanted your advice on the best way to break the news."

Paolo laughed bitterly. "The best way to break the news that *first alien consciousness* is hidden deep inside a biological computer? That everything the diaspora was trying to prove has been turned on its head? The best way to explain to the citizens of Carter-Zimmerman that after a three-hundred-year journey, they might as well have stayed on Earth running simulations with as little resemblance to the physical universe as possible?"

Karpal took the outburst in good humor. "I was thinking more along the lines of the *best way to point out* that if we hadn't traveled to Orpheus and studied Wang's Carpets, we'd never have had the chance to tell the solipsists of Ashton-Laval that all their elaborate invented lifeforms and exotic imaginary universes pale into insignificance compared to what's really out here—and which only the Carter-Zimmerman diaspora could have found."

Paolo and Elena stood together on the edge of Satellite Pinatubo, watching one of the scout probes aim its maser at a distant point in space. Paolo thought he saw a faint scatter of microwaves from the beam as it collided with iron-rich meteor dust. *Elena's mind being diffracted all over the cosmos?* Best not think about that.

He said, "When you meet the other versions of me who haven't experienced Orpheus, I hope you'll offer them mind grafts so they won't be jealous."

She frowned. "Ah. Will I or won't I? I can't be bothered modeling it. I expect I will. You should have asked me before I cloned myself. No need for jealousy, though. There'll be worlds far stranger than Orpheus."

"I doubt it. You really think so?"

"I wouldn't be doing this if I didn't believe that." Elena had no power to change the fate of the frozen clones of her previous self—but everyone had the right to emigrate.

Paolo took her hand. The beam had been aimed almost at Regulus, UV-hot and bright, but as he looked away, the cool yellow light of the sun caught his eye.

Vega C-Z was taking the news of the squids surprisingly well, so far. Karpal's way of putting it had cushioned the blow: it was only by traveling all this distance across the real, physical universe that they could have made such a discovery—and it was amazing how pragmatic even the most doctrinaire citizens had turned out to be. Before the launch, "alien solipsists" would have been the most unpalatable idea imaginable, the most abhorrent thing the diaspora could have stumbled upon—but now that they were here, and stuck with the fact of it, people were finding ways to view it in a better light. Orlando had even proclaimed, "*This* will be the perfect hook for the marginal polises. 'Travel through real space to witness a truly alien virtual reality.' We can sell it as a synthesis of the two world views."

Paolo still feared for Earth, though—where his Earth-self and others were waiting in hope of alien guidance. Would they take the message of Wang's Carpets to heart, and retreat into their own hermetic worlds, oblivious to physical reality?

And he wondered if the anthrocosmologists had finally been refuted . . . or not. Karpal had discovered alien consciousness—but it was sealed inside a cosmos of its own, its perceptions of itself and its surroundings neither reinforcing nor conflicting with human and transhuman explanations of reality. It would be millennia before C-Z could untangle the ethical problems of daring to try to make contact . . . assuming that both Wang's Carpets, and the inherited data patterns of the squids, survived that long.

Paolo looked around at the wild splendor of the star-choked galaxy, felt the disk reach in and cut right through him. *Could all this strange haphazard beauty be nothing but an excuse for those who beheld it to exist? Nothing but the sum of all the answers to all the questions humans and transhumans had ever asked the universe—answers created in the asking?*

He couldn't believe that—but the question remained unanswered.
So far.

CASTING AT PEGASUS

Mary Rosenblum

▼

One of the most popular and prolific of the new writers of the nineties, Mary Rosenblum made her first sale to *Asimov's Science Fiction* in 1990, and has since become a mainstay of that magazine, with almost twenty sales there to her credit; her linked series of "Drylands" stories have proved to be one of the magazine's most popular series. She has also sold to *The Magazine of Fantasy & Science Fiction*, *Pulphouse*, *New Legends*, and elsewhere. Her first novel, *The Drylands*, appeared in 1993 to wide critical acclaim, winning the prestigious Compton Crook Award for best first novel of the year; it was followed in short order by her second novel, *Chimera*. Her most recent book is a third novel, *The Stone Garden*; she has finished a fourth science fiction novel, and is currently at work on her first mystery novel. Coming up soon is her first short story collection, *Synthesis and Other Stories*. Her story "California Dreamer" appeared in our Twelfth Annual Collection. A graduate of Clarion West, Mary Rosenblum lives with her family in Portland, Oregon.

In the bittersweet, elegant, and compassionate story that follows, she shows us the infinite possibilities—and the deadly dangers—that can open up for you if you dare to go beyond the limits that the world has imposed, and reach for the stars.

It was a good night for flying. Windy enough to make her car buck. Stars and no moon, the riverbed a gouge of deeper darkness on her right. Therese braked, the highway empty behind her, nosed the little city-car into a tangle of fall-yellowed blackberries. Thorns scraped paint as she killed her headlights, and she didn't care.

It struck her suddenly how *much* she didn't care. Because Selva had originally paid for half of the car? She had never changed the registration. It was still in both their names. Therese squinted at darkness and rutted mud, angry at herself. For not thinking about the registration.

The car had been as easily cast off as Therese herself. How could she have forgotten to change the registration? Lips tight, Therese pulled clear up to the rusty chain-link fence, and turned off the engine. Opening the door let in the cold, and she shivered as she dragged her carryall from the cargo space. The wind combed invisible fingers, rich with fall scents of rotting leaves and cold moist earth, through her short hair. Yeah. Good night for flying.

She had told Selva about the airport, about sneaking out of her room at night when she was a kid, dressed in her "airport clothes." She used to cross the highway, cut through a field to the parking lot. Inside, she hung around in the waiting areas, drinking too-sweet hot chocolate from the snack bar, talking to other passengers, telling them how she was on her way to live with her father in Paris, or Amsterdam, or New York. "You did your single-parent angst more creatively than most," Selva had said. And she had laughed and rumpled Therese's hair. "That's why you're such a wonderful artist."

She didn't think so anymore. Therese hooked her fingers through the scabby fabric of the decrepit chain-link fence. The mesh shivered with a soft metallic clash as she climbed. Like a sigh, Therese thought. She threw one leg over the top, where she'd cut the barbed wire. A sigh of rust and aging and abandonment. Could a fence feel abandoned?

She swung her other leg over, leaped down to land with a splat in hummocky dew-wet grass. Another world, in here. She looked skyward, remembering airplanes taking off like constellations of colored stars rising from the tangled strings of blue lights that edged the runways. *Hi. Where are you going? I'm on my way to Paris. My dad's there and he wants me to come live with him. He's a correspondent for the New York* Times. . . . Therese hefted her carryall higher on her shoulder, began to jog toward the asphalt runway. The broken stems of old landing-lights stuck up like mileposts along the runway. Who had broken them off, and why? Now, people came and went at the big shuttle terminal, arcing up to the Platforms and down again. Or they did the Net. God bless the Net. Which brought her back to Selva, and Selva didn't belong here.

Therese slowed to a walk, forcing herself to listen. The empty airport had its own population—the boarders who skimmed the runways, the taggers, and the night watchman, who took his break now, between midnight and one. No sound of board wheels. The taggers kept to the blank canvases of the buildings. On a whim, she decided to set up out beyond the old hangar, out past the gate area. It might take the watchman half the night to notice her lights if she were lucky.

That was part of it—how long the flight lasted before the night watchman cut it down.

With a roar of sound, a pod of boarders zoomed up out of the darkness; three of them, dressed in black, slaloming back and forth across the cracked asphalt. Their boards' jet engines screamed, unmuffled and mocking. Therese dodged into the tall grass along the runway and dropped flat. Frost-killed stems brushed her cheeks, wet her face with dew like cold tears as they zoomed past. The night watchman would chase them. He always did. *Thanks, guys*, she mouthed silently, bounced to her feet, and broke into a run across the gate area. Big halides mounted on the terminal buildings splashed light across the asphalt, glinting on faded traffic markings. She avoided the light, cut across the grass again, shoes and socks soaked through now. Her feet slapped the concrete apron of the old hangar.

Quick. She unzipped her carryall, grabbed the tether-stakes she'd made from plastic pipe. Pounded the first one into the soggy ground beyond the apron. Wind from the east. She tested it with a hand, guessed twenty-five with gusts to thirty-five. Exactly the conditions she'd plugged into her virtual simulation, so the lights should go up slick and fast. She pounded in the second and third stakes and fumbled in her bag. Working in the dark because light brought the night watchman that much sooner, she snagged the first string. High-tensile line, black. The fiberlight beading felt like thin plastic twine beneath her fingers, flexible, cool, invisible in the darkness. She wound the end of the string around the first stake, laid it out. Laid out the second string and straightened the crossties by touch. So far, so good. If she tangled it now, she could kiss this night's flight good-bye.

Sound in the darkness, over by the unlighted hangar. Therese straightened, adrenaline spiking through her. The night watchman carried a taser, and the boarders carried blades. She slipped a hand into her pocket, closed her fingers around her small cannister of mace, listening until her ears buzzed, turning the rush of wind into sneaking footsteps, the snap of an opening blade.

Nothing. Hands wanting to shake, she unfolded the kite, bent the slender wands into the pockets she'd bonded into the corners. The wind caught at the transparent plastic so that it billowed out and came alive in her hands, straining like a dog tugging at a leash, full of promise, full of potential.

Potential. She hated the word. Selva had used it a lot at the end—"Your stuff has so much potential." Then came the "buts . . ." But the art market is such a closed place. But it's so tough to make your living doing art. But, but, but . . .

But get real and get a job, honey.

With an angry shake of her head and a leap, Therese tossed the kite into the air. The wind caught it, snatched it skyward, burning the line through her fingers. She paid it out carefully, steadily, squinting as her light-lines rose, intertangled like an invisible net spread to catch the stars. It looked okay, just like her sim. She anchored the kite-line to the third stake, and pulled the remote from her other pocket, heart beating fast now, because she didn't know, couldn't know how it would really look, until . . . *now*. Her forefinger touched the button.

And her light-net came to life, spilling meshes of liquid fire across the night. The hair-fine fiberlight threads, bought from a tattoo artist wholesale, glowed in jewel-bright color against the sky. Ruby. Neon blue. Sun-gold. Tonight, she had captured the great square of Pegasus, twined him in shimmering helices of light as the invisible kite danced with the wind, and the tangled threads glowed. Winged steed, lifting to a world behind those stars. Tonight she had harnessed him. She felt him tugging, the energy of those huge shoulders thrumming down the lines. Therese closed her eyes, let the energy hum through her flesh. In a moment, he would lift her from the ground, that harnessed creature, and carry her . . .

"Hey."

Soft voice, a breath almost, surely too low to be heard over the wind. Therese spun around, poised to run. Light by the hangar, a flash's glow that illuminated a tawny, androgynous kid's face. Spiky brown hair. Tilted, dark eyes.

"Beat it." Same soft, urgent carrying tone. "The cop's comin'." The light winked out.

She heard him now—heavy footsteps thudding on the grass. She snatched up her carryall and ran. Behind her, a shout. Light. She glanced over her shoulder, caught a glimpse of a tall man-shape, bulky in a uniform coverall, flash beam swinging like a sword to chop her. The night watchman; Frankenstein of this dark abandoned place, the Boogeyman. What was the range of his taser-dart? The light stabbed at her and she ran faster. The fence loomed out of the night.

Therese leaped, fingers hooking in the mesh, climbing, hiking her crotch over the rusty barbs of the top strands, deft, graceful, made so by fight-flight chemistry. She splashed down in cold, puddled water. She ran a few steps. Stopped and turned. He stood on the far side of the fence, a shadow, saying nothing.

He never chased her beyond the fence. He never called the cops. Therese watched him turn and vanish back into the darkness. In the distance, her jewel-fire net danced against the sky, tethering Pegasus. Therese watched it, counting the minutes in her head, a clench of yearning in her chest. Because when those strings were cut, Pegasus would fly free. Without her. The distant strands of color sagged suddenly. Crumpled, twisted and crashed in glittering ruin to the ground. Therese touched the remote, warm in her pocket.

The lights vanished.

Behind her, a sigh.

The kid? "Thank you." Therese peered into the darkness, couldn't see a thing. "He might have caught me, tonight." No answer, but she could feel a presence, like an eddy in the perfect, windy darkness, a spiral knot of energy. "Good night," Therese said, and trudged up the embankment to the main road.

Her feet were cold now, the chill penetrating to the bone. The elation was gone, leaving her with a hangover of emptiness, and she wondered who the kid was as she trudged along the pavement. A boarder? She hadn't seen a board. A tagger, scrawling his rude splash of identity across the hangar wall? And what are *you* doing, if not just that?

She'd felt Pegasus tugging at the strands of the lights. Like those planes had tugged at her as they lifted from the blue-lighted lanes of the runways. One day she would let go and . . . fly with him.

To *where*? A tiny voice whispered in her head. To somewhere, Therese told herself. She'd know when she got there. Her shoes squished the predawn quiet. Overhead, a shooting star streaked across the spangled sky, east to west, vanishing into the city glow. A message from the gods? She wished she could read it.

The apartment lights didn't come on when she opened the door. Cheap hardware. She slapped the manual switch, blinked in the harsh fluorescent glare, and stumbled over the package that had been set just inside the door. With a stifled yelp, she caught herself on the back of the futon sofa, anger flushing through her, making her cheeks burn.

The landlord again, with his damned pass key. Being nice? She didn't want him to be nice if it meant opening her door. He was probably snooping for drugs or illegal hardware. Therese scooped the package up and prowled the single big room, neck prickling like a dog with its hackles raised, looking for any signs he'd poked around. Inside the box, something shifted; mass packed not-quite-solidly. Therese turned it over and looked at the label. Vancouver, BC, return address.

Selva.

Why now, after all these months of silence?

She set it on the kitchen counter, stared at it. Presents were never really gifts. They were messages or obligations or both. Send it back, she told herself, but she was already reaching for a knife to saw through the packing tape. Inside, color peeked from foam packaging—a flash of rich crimson and gold that caught the ugly light, flung it back with gem-sparkle warmth. She dug into the white beads, a part of her mind noticing that it had been professionally packed, money thrown away to convenience—she'd never been that rich.

Her fingertips touched slick cool . . . glass.

She lifted it out. A fountain of crystal ice, turned static in a skyward splash, it glittered with streaks of ruby and embedded flakes of gold. The artist had filled that crystallized silicon with life, so that you saw more than this frozen instant, you saw the molten glass leap skyward, scattering into gem-bright droplets, falling back to earth all in an instant.

Beautiful, with no apology offered to function. Like her light-nets. Therese looked around her room. Futon sofa, low table in front of it, both Salvation Army crummy. The silent pile of electronic hardware that was the only thing that really mattered. She set the glass down on the table. It gave the room a feel of . . . failure. Loser turf. And she wondered suddenly if Selva had *meant* that piece of glass to have exactly this effect, if she was that subtle and vengeful.

You're hungry, Therese told herself, and that was certainly so. She turned her back on the sculpture, grabbed a stale bagel from the bag on top of the microwave.

You have a call, her House system intoned. *From Selva Portofino-Harris*.

Selva? Therese laid the untouched bagel down, mouth open to refuse the call. The glass caught her eye, made her momentarily breathless with its beauty. "I . . . okay." She fumbled for her gloves and goggles, clumsy suddenly, always clumsy around Selva's deft competence. "House, take the call."

Gloves on, she pulled the virtual goggles down over her forehead, plastic edges scraping softly across her skin. And found herself on a polished wood floor. Huge windows offered green lawns and distant white columns like Greek ruins. Sun, lovely sleek furniture. Selva Portofino-Harris leaned one bony hip against a polished slab of teak desktop that matched the color of her perfect shoulders.

She lifted weights in the flesh, wore her muscles proudly in virtual, her dark, Brazilian skin accented by a simple white tank-top and shorts.

Therese turned her face away, struggling suddenly with a hard lump in her throat. "Well." Inane word. Say something, or say nothing and get the hell out. "I got your . . . present. Just now."

"I . . . don't know why I sent it to you. I guess . . . it made me think of you."

The tone was wrong for vengeance, or even anger. Therese looked, in spite of herself. Yearning on that strong, almost harsh face? You could wear any mask you wanted in virtual. It didn't have to be real. . . . "It makes my apartment look like shit." She wasn't wearing her skinthins, only gloves and goggles, so all Selva was seeing was a rather boring simulation. A two-dee icon with no emotional cues. She took a deep breath, feeling slightly more in control. "So thanks." Which would cue a nice smile. "That was sweet of you to send it."

"Which translates to 'fuck off.' " Selva's smile bared her teeth. "Not yet, girl. How's your stuff doing?" She planted both palms on the desktop, swung her butt between them, like she did when she was upset. "Any new sales?"

"No." To *hell* with cool. Therese crossed her arms, wishing she *had* put on skins, go ahead and see how pissed I am. . . . "Barrain tossed me out of the gallery. I wasn't selling enough. Hey, like you said—" she flung the words like stones, "stationary holoture isn't hot. Virtual interactives are all the thing, now."

"I never said . . ." Selva closed her eyes briefly. "I'm sorry about the gallery slot. So what are you doing?"

"You mean to pay the rent? I'm doing virtual recordings." She had to look away again, even though it didn't matter because Selva wasn't really seeing her expression. "Cityscapes, countryside—buy a park permit, splash around in a couple of waterfalls, and someone will buy it." She'd recorded for herself, once. For her holoture work. "Hey, the VR artists can at least pay good money." Laugh. "A midnight walk under the full moon is good for a week's worth of rent." Another wasted shrug. "I already had most of the hardware."

"You could work for Xavier," Selva said quietly. "He's always got room for another talented designer."

"Designing advertising riffs? Or fancy offices for bored Net execs?"

"Sorry." Selva flushed. "I forgot, you're an *artist*."

"No, I'm a camera." It came out too soft for effect. "Listen, it's late and I've got to go to bed."

"Where were you?" Selva stopped swinging, stood straight and still in front of her skin-toned wooden desk. "Out at the airport again? Flying your kites?"

Flying your kites? "Go to hell. House . . ."

"Don't you exit on me!" Selva's voice cracked like a whip. "You never would share that with me—your airport stuff. I think that's part of why I could move up here without you. Because you wouldn't let me in on it at all. I guess it sent me a message."

And what message had *she* sent back in that piece of beautiful glass? "I asked you to come along. You were too busy."

"I was."

Therese's anger lost its razor edge because Selva had looked away, and she *never* did that. It made her look vulnerable.

Selva was never vulnerable.

"Hey." She filled in the silence with words, not wanting to see that unexpected curve of neck with its exposed groove of jugular vein and carotid. "Any time you want to see, just hop a shuttle. I'll be glad to show you." Would she? Therese wondered suddenly. Take Selva out to the airport? It would mean . . . what it might or might not mean didn't matter, because Selva was shaking her head anyway.

"I can't. Not right now, anyway. We're using stationary equipment to do some high-end decorating for Boise-Quebec's new offices. And we've got this deadline. So I can't work remote through a set of skins.''

"I didn't think so. Look, it's late. I'm yawning, even if you can't see it. Time for bed.''

"Yeah.'' Selva wasn't looking vulnerable any more. "I'll see you,'' she said. Coolly. Virtually. And was gone.

Banished from this electronic room, this reality, because she wasn't real any more. The room squeezed her—stranger's room, stranger's futon and shitty little table. Stranger's life. The glass sculpture announced it in shards of crystalline light. She grabbed it, raised it over her head, muscles hard with anticipation of the coming smash.

It was its own frozen instant of beauty, never mind Selva, never mind the message it carried. She set it down very gently, snagged her jacket from the sofa, and slammed the door on the way out.

The riverside highway looked different in the gray dawn light. Mist rose from the water, pooling white and thick in the sloughs. Tree branches thrust up through it, their twigs stiff and cold, trailing the last yellowed rags of summer leaves. She missed her hidden turnoff entirely, tricked by the daylight topography of the berry thickets. Didn't matter. She hadn't planned to park there anyway, it wasn't safe during the day. Some satellite traffic-eye might spot her, bust her for trespass. The terminal buildings looked so drab, off in the distance. The main entrance was on the far side of the complex, barricaded and lighted. Protected. From here, the gate aprons looked stained and forlorn, drifted with rotting leaves and soggy trash.

Last night, she had trapped Pegasus in a net of jewels. In the bright light of sunrise, the place looked drab—a dead end, without magic or future. Beyond the fence, the old hangar slumped in the cold morning mist. No sign of her light-net, of course. Probably trashcanned by the boogeyman night watchman. She braked hard and suddenly, pulled off onto the shoulder.

She'd looked at it a hundred times: tagger art. Ego, hormones, desperation, and anger, sprayed bright and immediate across any vertical surface. But the tag on the hangar doors was . . . different. Faces stared upward, surreal and huge. Their neon eyes were terrible—bright with hope and yearning that seared her, made her hands tremble on the wheel. Their enormous mouths opened, whispering, not shouting, calling softly, like you'd call your lover to bed.

Calling who? Therese climbed out of the car, shivering in the dank morning chill. She wanted to know who . . .

A tiny sound made her turn her head—nothing more than a rustle in the dew-spangled thistles that edged that asphalt. He was sitting there, screened by the weeds; the kid from last night. Asian skin, African lips, hazel eyes.

Face too broad, chin too long. He was ugly, as if his genes warred, like the races that had donated them. He was watching her, head tilted, shadow pooling beneath those stark cheekbones.

"Hey." He grinned.

"Hey." Fourteen, Therese guessed. "Your tag?" She nodded at the distant hangar.

"Uh huh. The geek hasn't painted it out yet. He's weird—waits till I finish 'em, at least. This one's gonna be the last." Triumph in those words, not defeat.

"Why the last?" She looked again, her eyes drawn to the sky by those yearning, calling faces.

"They're gonna *come* for me." He stood, lazy and laidback. "They hang around here, up high, where you can't see 'em. Only once in a while, you know? Maybe they're everywhere, or maybe there's some kind of hole here, like the hole in the ozone that everybody figured was gonna wipe us out? I'm one of them." His grin mocked her, challenging her, so that Therese wasn't sure if he was shitting her or not. "I figured that out when I finally realized that everybody *else* on this fucking planet is an alien. I don't belong here. I got left behind or lost or something." He tilted his head, still grinning, still challenging. "I'm Jazz. You gonna do some more lights tonight?"

"Therese." No, he wasn't shitting her. Above that grin, his eyes were the eyes of the faces on the wall, full of that same terrible, loving, yearning cry. "I might fly tonight," she said. "If the wind's right."

"It'll be better with the two of us. Your lights say the same thing, so I figure you're one, too. See you around." And then he took off running through the weeds, leaping tangled clumps of thistle like a deer. A scraggly clump of hawthorn swallowed him, and the verge was empty again, silent except for the dead weed stems rattling in the breeze. Therese shaded her eyes to stare at the mural one more time.

Those faces drew her eyes skyward again, clenched her chest with that yearning. Like last night, when Pegasus had tugged at her light-net. *I don't belong here.* Jazz's voice came back to her. Yeah, she thought bitterly. Me neither. You're right.

A tall figure, wide-shouldered and dressed in a dull green coverall, strolled across the concrete apron. The night watchman? *A* watchman, Therese told herself. This would be a different shift, surely. For an awful moment, she thought he was on his way to Jazz's mural, to paint it out or deface it somehow, to choke that rending cry.

As a kid, this place had been a magic doorway to a bright future, a future as colorful and full of promise as the bustle and light of the airport concourse. It had been more real than the faded silent mother who lived in her own universe of work and fatigue and TV, and the dark warehouse of the public school system. In the grip of the grim days, she'd thought about the airport and had been . . . homesick.

That's it, Jazz, she thought and laughed out loud. We're homesick for a world that doesn't even exist. Maybe it *would* take aliens to bring you there!

Therese turned away, climbed back up onto the asphalt, tired now, her feet wet again. She tapped her code into the door, opened it, and slid onto the cold plastic seat.

Therese Marie Oberti? Her cheap dashboard speaker squawked at her. *Will you please insert your ID card in the ignition slot?*

Uh-oh. Cold sweat prickled beneath her armpits as she fumbled her card into the ignition.

Your vehicle was reported as parked in a state no-trespass zone at one-fourteen-AM this morning. Your ID card was last used to access the ignition, and since you did not report the card stolen within six hours, the violation has been charged to you. Your file came up before state circuit court at eight-twenty-three this morning, and you were found guilty by the operating judicial program. Your fine, three thousand one hundred and thirty dollars, has been charged directly to your account. If you wish to contest the verdict, you must file an appeal and meet the accompanying fee by eight-twenty-three tomorrow morning. If you have any questions, please access legal assistance through your Net account.

The tinny voice ended.

A ticket. Therese stared numbly at the blue plastic dash. It was cracking in places, dried-out and damaged by sun and heat. She traced a long split, the curled-back edges of the cheap plastic sharp beneath her fingertip. A three thousand dollar state trespass ticket. . . . It was intended to discourage looters. Who had reported her car while it was parked here? The night watchman, of course. Therese closed her hand into a fist, nails biting into her palm. No wonder he didn't waste his precious breath chasing her beyond the nice safe fence. It was so much easier to sneak around until he found her car and could turn her in.

Well, she *had* been trespassing.

He had violated something, though, sullied that perfect flight last night. "Bastard," she said, very softly. Three thousand would clean out her savings. She wasn't going to be able to make rent this month. Not after she paid for the Net time she used to create holoture nobody wanted. Numbly, she tapped the engine to life, pulled a tight U on the empty asphalt. Go home, she told herself. Take a hot shower. Eat some breakfast. And then get your recording gear out and go find some neat imagery to sell to the Xaviers of the world. Auction off a few bits of your reality for someone else to use.

The sun was up, spearing her with dazzling light, striking the last glints of gold and yellow from the fall leaves. Eyes watering from the sun—not from tears, definitely *not* tears—she drove home, obeying every damn traffic law in the books.

You have two messages, her House system murmured as she let herself in. It turned on the lights, too, never mind that it was broad daylight.

Therese sighed and hit the manual switch, clicking them off. "House, messages." She pulled on her goggles and gloves.

"Ms. Oberti." The landlord's voice emerged from a shifting matrix of color, because he only paid for voice access. "Just a little reminder that yesterday was the first of the month. I need to have the rent by Wednesday."

"Endit." She glowered as the color winked out. Bilious yellow. How appropriate. Last time she'd been short, she'd been able to stall him for more than a week. It wasn't like people were standing in line to rent this dump, but maybe . . . somebody was.

She smoothed a wrinkle from her glove, running down her list of clients. Most of them wanted fancy landscape takes; the beach in a storm, snow on the desert, that kind of thing. She didn't even have the money for a park entry permit, never mind the time to wait for interesting weather. She could sell her skins. They were a custom job with all the high-end recording hardware you needed. Without them, she'd have to buy somebody else's reality. Like Xavier did. And she'd never be able to afford another set this good.

That wasn't it. She'd never be optimistic enough about her career to risk that kind of money again. "House, next message," she snapped.

" 'Rese?" Selva materialized, shimmering like airport fog. "Call me please? Realtime?"

She sounded worried, and Selva never worried because she had it *all* under control. "Message Selva Portofino-Harris." The words popped out on their own, spurred by fear.

Fear for Selva—and she had no right to be afraid for her. Not any more. Therese opened her mouth to cancel, but Selva's face was already shimmering into being, as if she'd been waiting for the call.

" 'Rese?" That hint of worry still showed. "How are you?"

"Fine." Big lie. "I'm just returning your call."

"Look, I was talking to Xavier just a little bit ago. And I mentioned your light-net stuff. He got pretty excited. He thinks we can use it. He was interested enough to offer a pretty good option."

She'd told Xavier about her flights. . . . "What's he going to use it *for*?" Therese didn't try to keep the bitterness out of her voice. "An ad for booze? Virtual sex hardware? The latest genened oranges?"

"What does it matter?" Selva refused to get pissed. "Xavier's just optioning the raw imagery anyway. You won't even recognize the final cut.

And he pays *well*. Once you're on his string, you're in. And we use a lot of material. Are you interested?''

She wasn't angry, simply felt . . . numb. ''You want to buy one of my flights.'' The flights you wouldn't share.

''Yeah.'' Selva's smile was wary. ''If you don't want me to look at it, I won't. I'll just turn it over to Xavier.''

''And what if he tells you to work with it?'' Flat voice, still so calm.

''Well . . .'' Wrinkled nose, grimace. ''I'll have to, yeah. But there's no reason it'd show up in one of my projects.'' She reached, laid a virtual hand on Therese's arm. ''Does it really bother you so much? I'd really like to come watch if you'd let me. I just can't do it when you snap your fingers.''

''I didn't snap my fingers. I asked.'' Therese looked down at her arm. Her eyes gave her Selva's long, slender fingers curving across her forearm. She felt nothing. Without skins, this was a ghost-touch, maybe would have been a ghost-touch if Selva was standing here in the flesh.

Which she wasn't.

''Money.'' She laughed softly, bitterly. ''I sure need it.'' So she got to choose, sell her soul or her skins. . . . ''Hey, why not?'' The words tasted bitter on her tongue. ''I'll sell Xavier his flight. You can watch it if you want. I don't care.''

''I won't look at it.'' Selva's face was dark and still, like a pool at twilight when you couldn't see the bottom. ''What do they mean to you?'' she asked. ''Your light-nets?''

For a moment words pressed at the back of her throat. *I rode Pegasus home. Almost.*

Almost wasn't good enough. She'd learned that as an artist. She swallowed, and the words were gone. ''You gotta be there,'' she said softly.

''I *would* be. If you'd let me.'' Selva's eyes flashed, but she kept her temper under control. ''Sometimes I think you do your lights because they *aren't* real. You can hang out at that nice safe airport and you don't have to care. Oh they're flesh and not virtual, that's not what I mean. Coming up to Vancouver is real. Working for Xavier and doing your art anyway is real. I think you're afraid of *real*, Therese. Do you know how much it hurt me when you stayed behind? Do you know how much I *love* you? Or do you care?''

No! Therese struggled for the words she had swallowed, but they wouldn't come back. *I didn't know. You never told me.* ''Yeah, I care.'' She turned away, pulled her goggles off. ''I care a lot.''

But her goggles were off and that signaled her system to shut off the connect. So probably Selva hadn't heard that last.

Which was a good thing, maybe. Because it didn't matter at all.

''You want to buy my next flight?'' she whispered. ''Fine.'' She reached for the tumbled pile of her skinthins. ''I'll give it to you, and you can give it to Xavier, and he can pay me for it." She laughed, a single note that hurt her throat like a sob.

Hey, why not?

Her skins itched. She scratched, one hand on the wheel because there wasn't any traffic on the airport road this time of night. Full recording gear meant skins, gloves, hood, the works. Patch on the left eyelid to the synch micro-cameras on her headband to her eye-track. She'd get it all—every twitch of body language that put you into the scene, register the physical tensions of fight-flight surprise, ambivalence, joy. All for you, baby. All for your boss.

Selva would be *there* at the airport.

Whose reality? *You're afraid.* . . . . Selva's voice whispered in her ear. *Afraid* . . .

Therese braked hard, almost missed the turn. The car lurched and bucked, going too fast for the rutted track, and she clung to the wheel as thorns put new scratches in the paint. Nobody here except her. The engine stalled and died, and she pushed the door open. Frosty night air. The east wind was blowing, flowing down the Gorge like an invisible river of ice-cold water. It tugged at the black stocking cap she wore, flicked tendrils of hair into her eyes, and pried chilly fingers down her neck.

Good night for flying, Selva. She touched her eyelid to make sure the tracking patch was in place, tapped the control at her waist. Recording. The tiny telltale winked green. Therese leaped, fingers hooking into the softly clashing chain link, scrambled over, and dropped. The grass wasn't wet tonight. An east wind had dried out the ground with its cold breath. Rags of thin cloud briefly obscured the sliver of moon. Do you see it, Selva? You can't feel the wind, but you'll feel me shiver, feel the subtle shifts as I push against it.

This is reality. Not the Net. Not pleasant virtual conversations in an unreal living room made up of electrons and fantasy.

This.

So who was she trying to convince? Scanning the landscape, the broken stumps of lights, she walked slowly along the abandoned runway. Planes used to land in sweeps of light, touching down between chains of blue jewels. Coming to get her, coming to take her home, only she'd never gone. The wind teased her, kissing her neck with cold lips. She could fly from this spot, but she kept on going, blaming the boarders that might show any time.

A lie. She was going to fly from the hangar, in front of Jazz's yearning faces. No other place would work, and she didn't stop to examine the reason for that. The gate apron glimmered like a gray wasteland in the faint moon-light. She skirted it, an eye out for the night watchman's flash. No sign of him. She never saw him between midnight and one. She'd long ago figured that for his break. For a while, she had wondered why he hadn't realized that she always set up during that hour. If he really wanted to catch her, he could do it just by changing his routines. She'd thought he was dumb at first. Then she'd decided that maybe he didn't really *want* to catch her.

Only he'd reported her car. So, maybe she'd been wrong. The hangar loomed ahead, concrete apron veined with grass-grown cracks. Too rough for the boarders. Therese dropped her carryall in the long grass beyond the apron, got out her stakes. One. Two. Hammerstrokes jarred the plastic spikes into the soil, every blow recorded in muscle action and reaction. Therese finished pounding the third stake in, and flung the hammer aside, not needing it anymore. She realized then—that this was the last time. The last flight.

Never again, because once something broke, you couldn't put it back together again. When she downloaded this night's recording into Selva's filespace, the airport, whatever it meant, whatever it was, would be broken. Lips pressed against tears that didn't come, she began to lay out the precise tangles of her light-net. Her skins recorded what she saw, stored it in hard-memory in her belt-pack, then beamed it home to her system, bouncing the digitized kaleidoscope of light and shadow and movement off the face of some battered satellite. From Earth to space to Earth again. The wind caught her kite as she unfurled it. Feel it, Selva? How it pulls at my arms? You can't smell the scent of fall and eastern desert in the wind, you can't feel the echoes of this place, of Pegasus spreading his invisible wings overhead.

She had never walked through the airport gates, gotten onto a plane, and gone into those beautiful futures. Last night, she had let Pegasus go. On the wall, Jazz's faces yearned silently for a home that wasn't here. The east wind snatched at the kite, rough and importunate, full of rude force. She tossed it into the sky, and a gust snatched meters of line through her fingers, lofting it high, higher. She reached the end of the line, let go. It snapped tight, thrumming with strain as the wind gusted again. Perhaps life was nothing but departures—from the darkness of the womb, from the dark and light of life— only departing, never arriving. Hand in her pocket, finger just caressing the remote button, she walked over to the hangar.

"So, turn it on." Jazz's voice from the darkness didn't startle her tonight. "C'mon, tonight's the night." Excitement hummed in his words. "Turn it on."

Tonight's the night. His belief infected her. Sometimes—as a kid in the airport late at night, when exhaustion blurred the line between fantasy and reality—for a few brief minutes her plane *was* landing, and she waited for the stewardess to open her little desk beside the ramp, to announce the row numbers that were boarding first. Sometimes she had stood in line to board, her blood thrumming with the anticipation of takeoff, the lights below, the black starry sky a ceiling to forever. . . .

If she had walked up to that desk, would the stewardess have smiled, welcomed her? "Okay," she whispered, and thumbed the control. Above them, *light*; twisting, shimmering beneath the stars, jewel-bright in strands and twists, tangled like DNA, or love, or the trailing hair of God, charged with the invisible pulse of the wind.

He was right—it was the same cry as the people on the hangar door, written in glyphs of light and wind and the perfect night. *We are homesick. Please take us home.* . . . Shoulder touching shoulder, Therese and Jazz searched the sky. They would come. How could they *not* come?

Boots scraped on concrete.

"Fuck," Jazz breathed. "Not *now*. Not yet!"

Therese looked over her shoulder. The night watchman stood on the edge of the concrete apron, a shadowy form in a dark uniform coverall, bulky and ominous.

Jazz hesitated, agony in the twist of his shoulders. "It's the camps for me, if I get busted again," he hissed. "Oh, *fuck!*" And ran.

It had shattered into ruin, they wouldn't hear, they wouldn't come. Reality crashed in like a wave—fines, money. And Therese leapt after Jazz, her own heart hammering with boogeyman dread and real fear. Wrong way, a sane corner of her brain shrieked at her. Double back, cut past him, and you can get over the fence.

But Jazz raced on ahead of her, a moving shadow in the dark, drawing her after him. If he was caught, he'd go to an adult detention camp. His fear infected her, lashed her with adrenaline. Fear for him, for her. His aliens wouldn't find him in a camp. They wouldn't know to look for him there, and he'd know it. That he'd never go home. And he'd die. Concrete jarred her as she reached the gate-apron.

She risked a glance over her shoulder, saw the night watchman emerge from darkness onto the gray glimmer of the concrete, running slowly, heavily. What was the range of his stunner? An ancient set of wheeled stairs leaned against the face of the terminal, the kind that had been pushed up against small commuter planes for passengers to climb. Jazz was up it in a flash, balancing on the top, reaching for the sill of the huge dark windows just above him.

Therese followed him, afraid to look back and see if the night watchman was behind her, afraid she'd tear her skins on the rusty metal. Above, the glass had been broken out of the huge windows. Moonlight glinted on triangular fragments sticking up like razor teeth. Therese grabbed a bare stretch of sill, levered herself over. Torn skins would be worse than a sliced hide. She could heal. The skins wouldn't. "Jazz?" No answer. "Where *are* you?"

Moonlight turned shadow into memory, picked out a patch of blue and red carpet, a flash of chrome from a chair. Therese halted, the watchman forgotten, fumbled for the flash in her pocket. Light speared out, touching naked girders and trailing cables like ripped-out guts or vines, fallen squares of tattered and smoke-stained acoustic tile. She shivered.

The blue and red carpet, the plastic and chrome furniture, had looked so new and beautiful, a promise made of a future connected by those landing planes to that long-ago today. People had looked at her and had smiled, knowing that she was one of them, with somewhere to go, someone to welcome her.

Such a silly game to play. The flash beam trembled in her hand, making the shadowy space stutter in light and shadow.

Glass tinkled behind her. The sound scattered memory, galvanized her into a run. Glass crunched beneath her feet, and she smelled the sour stink of old dead fire. She swung her flash, motes of dust twinkling in the beam, turning it into a hazy sword of light. Her light-sword kissed denim blue, black shirt. Jazz. She kept it on him as she ran, tethered to him by light. Random heaps took shape and vanished at the edges of vision; chairs, wrecked furniture, piles of fallen ceiling tile. Electric-cable guts. Cobwebs. Jazz ducked right, and she followed him down a wide corridor. A rumpled abandoned sleeping bag looked like a body, brought her heart briefly into her throat. Jazz veered again, through a huge archway this time, out into the cavernous center of the terminal. The vast space stretched away into darkness. Here and there, trash, dead leaves, and debris shoaled against ticket counters or in the corners of empty waiting areas.

The floor quivered beneath Therese's feet. She froze, adrenaline washing through her like ice water. Cautiously, she bounced up and down.

The floor bounced with her.

Which meant what? That they could fall through? "Jazz?" She hissed his name, but he was already halfway across the space, heading for the old front doors.

Therese started after him, afraid to yell and bring the night watchman after them. On her left, carpeting hung in frayed tatters into a hole in the floor. The flashlight's weakening beam reflected off glossy char, showed her fallen burned timbers. So. A fire had gutted the lower level. How much of the floor was ready to crumble? "Jazz!" This time she *did* yell. "Jazz, stop! The floor!"

As if her words had cued it, the floor sagged beneath his feet, rotted carpet stretching, tearing with a dry, ripping sound. Dust rose in a cloud, and, arms flung wide, Jazz sank into it, disappearing downward in terrible slow motion. Therese lunged, hands reaching, grabbed for him, and felt the floor sag beneath her. Carpet tore with a dry ripping sound, and she screamed, falling. Carpeting disintegrated between her clutching fingers, and she screamed again, vision full of darkness, lungs full of pungent, dank char-reek, imagining concrete below, nails and fallen beams, spears to pierce her. Hardness slammed her ribs, and a terrible weight crashed down across her back, slammed the breath from her lungs in a red blaze of hurt. She struggled to breathe, the flash tumbling downward, beam slashing the darkness.

A little air seeped into her aching lungs, easing the panic. Slowly, she began to sort out the hurting; beam beneath her, pressing hard into chest, thighs, shoulder, Jazz lying half across her, crushing her ribcage, his muscles iron hard as he panted in her ear. The flashlight was still on—small miracle. Dust hazed the slender beam. It was a *long* way down.

"Fuck," Jazz whispered. And moved.

"Stop!" Therese clutched the beam as they tilted sideways, struggling for balance. "Stay *still.*"

"Okay." Explosion of breath in her ear. "All right!"

How do you get out of *this* little situation, Therese Oberti? Easy enough. Let *go*. She giggled.

"What so funny?" Jazz snarled. Scared.

"Gravity." She peered cautiously sideways. "You could maybe climb onto those beams."

"Uh-uh. Too far. Down I can maybe handle." Jazz sucked in a deep breath. "Hang on, okay?"

Light splashed them from above, searingly bright. "Nice going." A male voice, disgusted. "You guys really blew it. Hang on, and I'll see if I can find something you can grab." The light beam shifted, and Therese glimpsed a fold of dull green coverall, a dark webbing belt. The night watchman.

Caught. She felt Jazz's muscles clamp tighter.

"Here." The light shifted back, drowning their flash's petty beam, illuminating fallen timbers, ashes, and twisted metal below. "You on top, grab this." A long piece of wood, maybe a piece of doorframe, appeared. "Hang on real tight, and I'll try to haul you up."

It was at least ten feet to the floor. Therese stared at the ashes and burned junk, holding on as hard as she could. She could feel Jazz hesitating, his indecision humming though her. And in a few more minutes, she was going to lose her grip. . . . "Do it," she hissed. "Quick!"

With a grunt, he grabbed for the wood. His body twisted, his weight dragging Therese sideways, trying to torque her off her perch. Silent, focused on *flesh*, muscle-clench, finger-grip against greasy metal, she processed kaleidoscopic images of Jazz swinging from the bending strip of wood, legs flailing for a toehold, dust showering. Then the floor gave way. They fell together, Jazz and the night watchman, in a tangle of green and denim, dark skin and darker hair. For an eerie instant, the flash shone full on the night watchman's face: wide cheekbones, brown Hispanic skin, black hair, eyes full of shocked surprise. A moment later, they hit with the ugly flesh sound of impact. The big flash went out.

"Fuck!" Jazz's whisper seemed to carry throughout the entire airport.

"Is that all you can say?" Panic clawed at her and she needed to get *down*. Groping, her fingers touched wood, closed incredibly tight. She swung by her hands, feet scrabbling, finding solid footing. Fallen beams wove a web of shadow across the glow from her dim flash, guided her lower. Her feet crunched into ash, and a shadow moved. Resolved into Jazz, sooty faced.

"You okay?" Therese touched a shoulder, reassured by the warm flesh beneath T-shirt fabric.

"I guess." The shoulder lifted and dropped; a shrug, rather than rejection. "Nothing's broken, I don't think." He shifted from beneath her fingers, and a moment later the flashbeam wobbled as he picked it up. "I think our cop landed hard." The light touched a green-clad shoulder, slid upward to spotlight a stubbled jaw.

He was younger than she'd thought; not much older than her, with curly dark hair and thick brows. Not exactly handsome. A trickle of blood down the side of his face glowed wet and crimson in the light. Jazz slid ashy gray fingers beneath his jaw.

"He's alive. I hate cops."

"I'm not . . . a cop." His eyes opened wide, and he tried to grin. It turned into a grimace of pain. "I'm private."

"Cop, private gun." Jazz shrugged. "Same deal."

"No, it isn't." He sat up slowly, leaned his bloody, ash-smeared forehead against a raised knee. "God, my head hurts. . . . I yelled when I saw you come this way. The fire two years back gutted the bottom level. They ought to tear the whole place down, but there'd go my job, so what the hell?"

"How do we get out of here?" Jazz sabered the light-sword through the darkness, revealing fallen beams and ashes, twisted wads of heat-warped metal and melted plastics. "I got this schedule. . . ."

"Beats me." The night watchman shrugged, grimaced again. "I guess we climb out."

Therese eyed the fire-eaten beams and sagging ceiling doubtfully, squeezed by the cavernous darkness. If they couldn't get out . . . surely somebody would check on the night watchman eventually. But what about Jazz? And her?

The night watchman grabbed one of the fallen beams, leaned his weight on it cautiously. It held. He clambered onto it, reaching for a broken segment of pipe.

With a crackle of breaking wood, the tangle shifted. He fell, landing on his feet, raising a cloud of fine ash. "So much for that." He coughed, holding his head, his shoulders hunched in pain.

"You're too heavy, guy. I gotta get *out* of here." Jazz's voice rose. "They're coming for me tonight. I *know* it."

"They." The night watchman's voice was slow and oddly shy. "They're always calling someone. In your pictures. Looking up and just . . . calling. It makes me look, too. I thought it was God at first, but it isn't, is it?" His voice got brisker. "They're coming, huh?"

"Yeah, they're coming." Jazz tilted his head back, staring up at the gap in the ceiling. "I never thought about God much. He didn't do anything for me. If you boost me, I can make it." His eyes flicked from one to the other of them. "I'll find something to let down to you guys. I promise."

He had no reason to come back here, or help them at all. He had a lot of reason *not* to. Like the camps, if he got busted, and maybe the night watchman *would* bust him, once they were back outside in the usual world. And he thought his aliens might come, and why shouldn't they come while he was helping them? He'd just take off, and there they would be. Stuck.

And he had been right about her lights painting the poetry of loneliness across the night sky. And if there were any aliens up there, how could they *not* hear it—his call and hers. How could they *not* come? And . . . the night watchman believed. You could hear it in his voice. Why should *he* believe?

"We'll boost you." She held out her hands to the night watchman, like they'd already agreed. And he clasped them halfway, because they had.

"Try for that pipe." He jerked his chin upward as he laced his fingers with hers. "One, two . . ."

Eyes glinting, Jazz rested a foot lightly on their hands.

"Three!"

Therese and the watchman heaved together, straightening their knees, flinging Jazz at the ceiling. He rose in a perfect leap, caught the pipe. Swung once, twice for momentum, then reached one-handed, grabbed a solid joist. Feet kicking, showering them with dust and ash, he scrambled over the lip of the fallen ceiling and vanished.

Silence.

The flashlight yellowed and shadows drew in around them. Therese looked at the watchman.

"A couple of more minutes." The cut on his forehead was still oozing blood. "We can try the old escalator. The ceiling came down there, but we can probably get through. You know, your flying lights are . . . neat." The flash's glow reflected in his dark eyes, like distant campfires, or lost stars. "They're never the same twice, you know? It makes them special. I can't go back and call them up again, like with a video on the Net. I came here when I was a kid—I was flying down to live with my uncle in LA. All these people coming and going, happy and sad, excited. Everybody wanting to be somewhere, or wanting somebody to be here." He looked past her, frowned.

"Your lights are like that—kind of a tangle, you know? All bright, and never the same again."

Therese swallowed a sudden thickness in her throat, because maybe he understood something better than she did. "But you cut them down. You paint out Jazz's tags."

"Well, yeah." He looked at her sadly. "I'd lose my job if I didn't. It matters, my job." And his voice had that same shyness as when he talked about Jazz's pictures.

"Yo." Scuffle from above, and a patter of new debris raining down.

"You came *back*." Therese looked up, grinning because she hadn't really expected him to, had already forgiven him.

"Yeah, but hurry, okay? They're here." Urgency roughened his voice. "I'm not kidding. They're looking for me, but they might not know where to look."

The light was nothing more than a glimmer, barely illuminating the fall of tangled, snaky coils. Therese reached up, flinched as they tumbled down around her head and onto her shoulders. Some sort of electrical cable, black and pliable.

"It's tied. Come *on*." Jazz's voice echoed through the darkness.

"Go ahead." As the night watchman nodded, the flash beam died. Darkness rushed in to fill the space where the light had been, expanding the terminal into infinity. She fumbled blindly for footing, trying to hurry, afraid they'd leave without him. Pulled herself upward, banging knees and elbows on invisible obstacles, found a good foothold, slipped, gasped with terror, then relief as Jazz grabbed her arms.

"You okay?" From below. Worried.

"Yes." And scrambled up onto the solid floor, face down on the crappy carpeting.

Behind her, in the dark, the timbers creaked as the night watchman climbed after her. She sat up, as he scrambled over the edge, so close that she felt the heat radiating from his body. Caught a whiff of sweat and musky man-smell. It came to her suddenly that she was still recording. She was so used to the rig she'd forgotten, and neither of the others had noticed her headband. She touched her eyelid, fingertips searching for, finding the tiny track-patch miraculously still in place. Laughed softly. Once.

"*Now* what's funny?" Jazz asked.

"Smile," she said, and stopped laughing, because in a second it would fall over into hysteria. "I wonder what dear Xavier will do with this bit?"

"Huh?" Jazz was dancing with urgency, footsteps shaking the fragile floor. "Let's go. Which way out of here, huh?"

"Left." The night watchman's fingers closed around her hand. "Watch out. There's stuff all over the floor."

She reached, found Jazz's hand in the dark, as if it had been waiting for her. They followed the watchman's lead, playing a weird blindman's-bluff through the blackness. Do you feel Jazz trembling, Selva? He's afraid they won't wait. And if they don't, if they're not there, will he have the courage to wait any longer? And the night watchman is pulling because . . . he believes.

And she didn't know why, but in here, in the sooty dark, they all believed. Light ahead. It scattered her thoughts on a wave of relief. Main entrance—chipboard and sometimes panes of glass, amazingly unbroken. The night watchman tapped an urgent code into a dusty security box beside an intact door. A lock clicked and he shoved it open. Night air rushed in—no colder than the air in here, but fresh and full of earth-scent, diminishing the smoke-reek. With a cry, Jazz darted through the doorway.

"There." He pointed, every fiber in his body taut and alive. Glow across the hummocky abandoned fields, opalescent in the thin fog that was rising. It could be a truck, Therese thought. Coming slow in the fog along the riverbed highway.

Or maybe it *wasn't*. Maybe it was a flying saucer landing, touching down to collect a lost child, take him home. Overhead, Pegasus soared, his wings spread above the rising fog, offering a ride to anyone who dared.

Jazz leaped onto the curb, paused, head lifted like a spike buck, looked back. His face was like the moon, brilliant with reflected light. The light of home. "Take it easy." He lifted his hand in a wave or a salute. Then he was gone, vaulting over the low concrete wall of the huge parking structure beyond the grass, running like a deer through the tall grass.

Across the wet, cold grass, the glow brightened. A truck, Therese thought. And when it took the curve where the riverbed bent, where she parked her car, she'd see the headlights. And would know it was a truck.

She closed her eyes.

Alien trapped among aliens—and aren't we all? Homesick for a home we can't remember, but we know it *has* to be there. Because if it isn't there somewhere, lying back behind memory, like the darkness lies behind the stars . . . then what's all this for? Her tears surprised her, scalding hot beneath her closed eyelids. You won't feel them, Selva. Because my face isn't covered by a skinthin mask, she thought bitterly. You won't know that I'm crying. You can dub that in later, if you want. If it seems right.

Beside her, the night watchman shared her silence. The wind blew through the overgrown grass of the field, whispering in its own language as it probed the cracks and corners of the abandoned terminal. Therese sighed, and opened her eyes. The highway was dark. Truck or flying saucer, the light was gone. And so was Jazz.

Back to the city? Back to doorways and shelters, back to the ten-dollar blow jobs and the threat of the camps?

Or was he on his way home? Therese wiped her face on the back of her arm.

"Are you all right?" The night watchman's voice was gentle.

"I guess." Therese climbed over the low wall that Jazz had leaped so easily, shivering because she was freezing in her light skins.

"I'll lend you a jacket." He stopped beside a small gray door in the wall of the parking structure. "If you want."

He had believed, too, down there. "Thanks," she said, because he wanted her to take it. "I'd appreciate it." And for the first time, she really looked at him, saw, not a boogeyman, not a shadowy presence, but a *man*, a person, in the flesh. The halogen security lamps cast shadow beneath his cheekbones, turned his face stark and craggy. His dark eyes were on hers, and light glowed in their depths.

"You can drop it off any time." He unlocked the door, touched on the lights.

Therese blinked in the sudden glare. His office. Terminal screen on a desk, basic kitchen-wall with microwave and freezer above a cheap new counter top and tiny sink. A bookshelf full of old hardcopy books. A small futon lay on the floor by the wall, scattered with a few toys, a bright green blanket tucked around the curled and sleeping shape of a small child.

"My son." His face softened for a minute. "He lives here with me. Sorry about the mess." He sounded apologetic as he picked up a plastic trashbag from the floor.

This was home, she thought. For him and his son. She'd heard the echo in his voice when he'd said "the job matters." Home. He'd still been able to understand what Jazz had painted on the hangar wall, what she had woven across the night sky.

"Here." He held out a plastic trash bag.

She opened it, looked in. Tangled strands of light fiber. Neat rolls of transparent plastic. String. "My stuff." She looked up, met his dark eyes, brilliant in his soot-streaked face. "Thanks."

"You're welcome."

"I'll walk you to the gate." He ushered her out, closed the door gently and protectively on the sleeping child.

They didn't speak as they followed the empty driveway out to the main gate. It was chainlink, but new, topped with shiny thorns of razor-wire. He touched a keypad set into a concrete pillar, and the gate groaned, began to rumble open. "I got to go chase the boarders." He smiled crookedly. "They'll be disappointed if I don't."

"This is your performance art." She returned his smile.

"Hey, whatever." He spread his hands, then hesitated. "I . . . didn't look. When Jazz ran. You didn't either, did you?"

"No," she murmured. If she had, if he had, they would have turned that flying saucer back into a truck, have turned Home back into a Front Street meat rack, or a detention camp.

"I'm glad," he said, and home hummed beneath his words.

Maybe that's what let him understand. Because he'd made his home here, for himself and his son. But the gate was open now, no longer a barrier between Therese and the real world of money and deadlines. She sighed, resenting that open gate, feeling subtly betrayed. "Why did you call in my car for trespass?" She had to ask. "I can't afford the fine."

"I didn't." Genuine confusion—his turn to look betrayed. "I wouldn't do that."

And he *wouldn't*. "You're right," she said, and sudden grief clutched her. She stretched up, and kissed him on the mouth. After a moment of surprise, he responded, lips pressing against hers, warm and firm with life.

Then she walked away, and he didn't try to stop her, as she marched down the asphalt driveway and then out to her car, feet dry on the asphalt, heart heavy. And went . . . not home, but back to where she lived.

It only occured to her when she was halfway there that she didn't know the night watchman's name, and that he had never asked for hers.

Urgent messages from Selva greeted her. *Call me. Call me right away.* And the grief weighed on her shoulders, heavy as lead. When she put on her goggles, Selva's image coalesced instantly, as if she'd been waiting for Therese to call. "My God, 'Rese, are you okay?"

Her face looked haggard, head and shoulders only against a pastel wall—which meant that this was realtime, a straight video transmission from her apartment, not translated through a virtual self. No tricks of programmed emotion, then. Except the ultimate, the one she'd already pulled. "You were looking over my shoulder tonight." The first time she'd called, she'd known that Therese had been at the airport. *Were you flying your kites?* she had asked, but she had *known*. I missed it, Therese thought numbly. I wanted to miss it. "How long have you been in my filespace?"

Selva looked away, convicted by her own worry.

"Did you watch it all? My flight, our fall, everything? *You* turned in my car for trespass." Therese's voice cracked. "My God, Selva, *why*?"

"I didn't watch. Not much." Selva faced her, eyes bleak. "I was monitoring the transmission, watching the parameters in digital, and when the activity went to the end of the scale, I checked the visuals." She paused for a heartbeat. "I saw you fall. For a minute, I thought . . ." Her shoulders jerked. "I stopped watching when you climbed out."

"Nice." Therese's lips felt numb. She was beyond anger now, as stunned as if the sky had cracked and rained down on her head. "So, not only do you get my car busted, you can sell my recording *direct* to Xavier. Hey, always cut out the middleman whenever possible!"

"Stop it, 'Rese." Selva didn't look away this time, didn't try to hide the pain in her face. "Yeah, I turned your car in. Xavier's looking for new blood, and I figured if he saw your stuff—if you maybe found out that it isn't so bad, working for somebody . . . If you'd turned it down, I would have paid the fine myself, but I wanted. . . ." She clenched her fists, her face pale and stark. "I wanted to make you *hear* me, okay? I love you. Don't you get it? Do you have to tie our love to your definition of success? Can't you just let *us* happen? Do you think I care if I'm paying the rent?"

The anguish in her voice gutted Therese's anger. Do you care that much? she wanted to ask, but the words wouldn't come. It was her turn to look away. She'd seen it after all—whether that light was a truck or not. She had it on file, and so did Selva—the conclusion of Jazz's wild dash across the airport field. Stored in patterns of excited electrons.

"I dumped the file from tonight." Selva had turned away again, her shoulders drooping, where they never drooped, always lifted proudly, strong and muscular. "If you had gotten hurt . . . if you had died . . ." She swallowed, her throat leaping. "I also downloaded money for the fine into your account. You're the one who has to decide, and I guess you have. I'm sorry. I love you, and I'll leave you alone. Will you please . . . be careful out there?"

And the screen went blank.

Therese stared at it for a long moment; angry at Selva for the fine, for the betrayal of that hack into her filespace. She snapped her fingers, called up her workspace. The file was there, bounced from Earth to sky to Earth again, an airplane icon glowing in the air. She could *know*. She stared at it. *Your lights say the same thing*, he'd told her.

"You're wrong. I'm not like you," she whispered. She had looked at the night watchman and seen a man, not a cop, or an alien, or a boogeyman. She had peeked at his cramped apartment and his sleeping son, and had felt its tug.

And Jazz knew. Poised on the curb, he hadn't asked her to come along. Therese let her breath out slowly, touched the airplane. "System, delete," she said.

Are you sure you want to delete this file? her system asked. *You have no backup*.

Maybe you had to define home for yourself, and then believe in it enough to make it real. "System, yes," she said and let her breath out in a rush. "Delete the file."

File deleted. The airplane winked out of existence.

"I hope you're already home," Therese murmured. And went into her bank account to find the three thousand dollars Selva had left there. And used it to pay her fine. On the table, the fountain of glass showered the room with fractured light. Maybe it wasn't a message of failure. Maybe Selva had known her well enough to send her something that existed only for its own sake, for beauty. Maybe Selva was trying to define home for herself.

Outside, Pegasus spread his wings to fly beyond the stars. Therese hung the night watchman's jacket on a chair. Neatly. She would return it in the daylight, ask his name, and his son's name, visit with them for a few minutes. And then . . . she'd buy a ticket for the mag-lev. Going to Vancouver, B.C. For a visit, or for a long time, she didn't know yet. They were going to be angry at each other for awhile. Maybe there were depths beyond the anger. Therese picked up the glass, turning it to scatter the rays from the cheap light overhead. "You were right, Selva," she murmured. "I was afraid." Of the real world, of Pegasus's broad back. Still was. But she would bring along the light-net that the night watchman had returned with her. Selva would know a good place to fly it. They could cast it one more time at Pegasus.

LOOKING FOR KELLY DAHL

Dan Simmons

▼

A writer of considerable power, range, and ambition, an eclectic talent not willing to be restricted to any one genre, Dan Simmons sold his first story to *The Twilight Zone Magazine* in 1982. By the end of that decade, he had become one of the most popular and best-selling authors in both the horror and the science fiction genres, winning, for instance, both the Hugo Award for his epic science fiction novel *Hyperion* and the Bram Stoker Award for his huge horror novel *Carrion Comfort* in the same year, 1990. He has continued to split his output since between science fiction (*The Fall of Hyperion*, *The Hollow Man*) and horror (*Song of Kali*, *Summer of Night*, *Children of the Night*) A few of his novels are downright unclassifiable (*Phases of Gravity*, for instance, is a straight literary novel, although it was published as part of a science fiction line); and some (like *Children of the Night*) could be legitimately considered to be either science fiction or horror, depending on how you squint at them. Similarly, his first collection, *Prayers to Broken Stones*, contains a mix of science fiction, fantasy, horror, and "mainstream" stories, as does his most recent collection, *Lovedeath*. His most recent book is *Endymion*. His stories have appeared in our First and Eleventh Annual Collections. Born in Peoria, Illinois, Simmons now lives with his family in Colorado.

Here he takes us on a wild, headlong, and tautly suspenseful chase through time, and into worlds where nothing—*nothing*—is as it seems . . .

I. Chiaroscuro

I awoke in camp that morning to find the highway to Boulder gone, the sky empty of contrails, and the aspen leaves a bright autumn gold despite what should have been a midsummer day, but after bouncing the Jeep across four miles of forest and rocky ridgeline to the back of the Flatirons, it was the sight of the Inland Sea that stopped me cold.

"Damn," I muttered, getting out of the Jeep and walking to the edge of the cliff.

Where the foothills and plains should have been, the great sea stretched away east to the horizon and beyond. Torpid waves lapped up against the muddy shores below. Where the stone-box towers of NCAR, the National Center for Atmospheric Research, had risen below the sandstone slabs of the Flatirons, now there were only shrub-stippled swamps and muddy inlets. Of Boulder, there was no sign—neither of its oasis of trees nor of its low buildings. Highway 36 did not cut its accustomed swath over the hillside southeast to Denver. No roads were visible. The high-rises of Denver were gone. All of Denver was gone. Only the Inland Sea stretched east and north and south as far as I could see, its color the gray-blue I remembered from Lake Michigan in my youth, its wave action desultory, its sound more the halfhearted lapping of a large lake than the surf crash of a real ocean.

"Damn," I said again and pulled the Remington from its scabbard behind the driver's seat of the Jeep. Using the twenty-power sight, I scanned the gullies leading down between the Flatirons to the swamps and shoreline. There were no roads, no paths, not even visible animal trails. I planted my foot on a low boulder, braced my arm on my knee, and tried to keep the scope steady as I panned right to left along the long strip of dark shoreline.

Footprints in the mud: one set, leading from the gully just below where I stood on what someday would be named Flagstaff Mountain and crossing to a small rowboat pulled up on the sand just beyond the curl of waves. No one was in the rowboat. No tracks led away from it.

A bit of color and motion caught my eye a few hundred meters out from the shore and I raised the rifle, trying to steady the scope on a bobbing bit of yellow. There was a float out there, just beyond the shallows.

I lowered the Remington and took a step closer to the drop-off. There was no way that I could get the Jeep down there—at least not without spending hours or days cutting a path through the thick growth of ponderosa and lodgepole pine that grew in the gully. And even then I would have to use the winch to lower the Jeep over boulders and near-vertical patches. It would not be worth the effort to take the vehicle. But it would require an hour or more to hike down from here.

For what? I thought. The rowboat and buoy would be another red herring, another Kelly Dahl joke. *Or she's trying to lure me out there on the water so that she can get a clean shot.*

"Damn," I said for the third and final time. Then I returned the rifle to its case, pulled out the blue daypack, checked to make sure that the rations, water bottles, and .38 were in place, tugged on the pack, shifted the Ka-bar knife in its sheath along my belt so that I could get to it in one movement, set the rifle scabbard in the crook of my arm, took one last look at the Jeep and its contents, and began the long descent.

Kelly, *you're sloppy*, I thought as I slid down the muddy slope, using aspens as handholds. *Nothing's consistent. You've screwed this up just like you did the Triassic yesterday.*

This particular Inland Sea could be from one of several eras—the late Cretaceous for one, the late Jurassic for another—but in the former era, some 75 million years ago, the great interior sea would have pushed much further west than here, into Utah and beyond, and the Rocky Mountains I could see twenty miles to the west would have been in the process of being born from the remnants of Pacific islands that had dotted an ocean covering California. The slabs of Flatirons now rising above me would exist only as a layer of soft substrata. Conversely, if it were the mid-Jurassic, almost 100 million years earlier than the Cretaceous, this would all be part of a warm, shallow sea stretching down from Canada, ending in a shore winding along northern New Mexico. There would be a huge saline lake south of there, the mudflats of southern Colorado and northern New Mexico stretching as a narrow isthmus for almost two hundred miles between the two bodies of water. This area of central Colorado would be an island, but still without mountains and Flatirons.

You got it all wrong, Kelly. I'd give this a D —. There was no answer. *Shit, this isn't even that good. An F.* Still silence.

Nor were the flora and fauna correct. Instead of the aspen and pine trees through which I now descended, this area should have been forested during the Jurassic by tall, slender, cycadlike trees, festooned with petals and cones; the undergrowth would not be the juniper bushes I was picking my way around but exotic scouring rushes displaying leaves like banana plants. The late-Cretaceous flora would have been more familiar to the eye—low, broad-leaved trees, towering conifers—but the blossoms would be profuse, tropical, and exotic—with the scent of huge, magnolialike blossoms perfuming the humid air.

The air was neither hot nor humid. It was a midautumn Colorado day. The only blossoms I saw were the faded flowers on small cacti underfoot.

The fauna were wrong. And dull. Dinosaurs existed in both the Cretaceous and Jurassic, but the only animals I had seen this fine morning were some ravens, three white-tailed deer hustling for cover a mile before I reached the cliffs, and some golden-mantled ground squirrels near the top of the Flatirons. Unless a plesiosaur raised its scrawny neck out of the water below, my guess was that the Inland Sea had been transplanted to our era. I had been mildly disappointed the last couple of times the chase had taken me through ancient eras. I would like to have seen a dinosaur, if only to see if Spielberg and his computer animators had been correct as to how the creatures moved.

Kelly, you're sloppy, I thought again. *Lazy. Or you make your choices from sentiment and a sense of aesthetics rather than from any care for accuracy.* I was not surprised that there was no answer.

Kelly had always been quirky, although I remembered little sentimentality from either of the times I had been her teacher.

I thought, *She hadn't cried the time I left the sixth-grade class to take the high-school job. Most of the other girls did. Kelly Dahl was 11 then. She had not shown much emotion when I'd had her in English class when she was . . . what? . . . seventeen.*

And now she was trying to kill me. Not much sentiment there, either.

I came out of the woods at the edge of the gully and began following human footprints in the mud across the flats. Whether the Inland Sea was from the Jurassic or the Cretaceous, the person who had crossed these tidal flats before me had worn sneakers—cross-trainers from the look of the sole patterns. *Are these tidal flats? I think so . . . the Kansas Sea was large enough to respond to tides.*

There was nothing in the rowboat but two oars, shipped properly. I glanced around, took the rifle out to scope the cliffsides, saw nothing there, tossed the pack in the boat, set the Remington across my lap, shoved off through low waves, and began to row toward the yellow buoy.

I half expected a rifle shot, but suspected that I would not hear it. Despite her missed chances a few days earlier, Kelly Dahl was obviously a good shot. When she decided to kill me, if she had a shot as clear as this one must be— she could fire from any spot along the cliff face of the Flatirons—I would almost certainly be hit on her first try. My only chance was that it would not be a fatal shot and that I could still handle the Remington.

Sweating, the rifle now on the thwart behind me, my shirt soaked from the exertion despite the cool autumn air, I thought of how vulnerable I was out here on the chalky sea, how stupid this action was. I managed to grunt a laugh.

Do your worst, kid. Sunlight glinted on something behind the rocks on Flagstaff Mountain. A telescopic sight? My Jeep's windshield? I did not break the rhythm of my rowing to check it out. *Do your worst, kid. It can't be worse than what I had planned for myself.*

The yellow "buoy" was actually a plastic bleach jar. There was a line tied to it. I pulled it up. The wine bottle on the end of it was weighted with pebbles and sealed with a cork. There was a note inside.

BANG, it read. YOU'RE IT.

On the day I decided to kill myself, I planned it, prepared it, and carried it out. Why wait?

The irony was that I had always detested suicide and the suicides themselves. Papa Hemingway and his ilk, someone who will put a Boss shotgun in his mouth and pull the trigger, leaving the remains at the bottom of the stairs for his wife to find and a ceiling full of skull splinters for the hired help to remove . . . well, I find them disgusting. And self-indulgent. I have been a failure and a drunk and a fuckup, but I have never left my messes for others to clean up, not even in the worst depths of my drinking days.

Still, it is hard to think of a way to kill yourself without leaving a mess behind. Walking into the ocean like James Mason at the end of the 1954 *A Star Is Born* would have been nice, assuming a strong current going out or sharks to finish off the waterlogged remains, but I live in Colorado. Drowning oneself in one of the puny reservoirs around here seems pathetic at best.

All of the domestic remedies—gas, poison, hanging, an overdose of sleeping pills, the shotgun from the closet—leave someone with the Hemingway problem. Besides, I despise melodrama. The way I figure it, it's no one's business but my own how or why I go out. Of course, my ex-wife wouldn't give a shit and my only child is dead and beyond embarrassment, but there are still a few friends out there from the good days who might feel betrayed if news of my death came in the black-wrapped package of suicide. Or so I like to think.

It took me not quite three beers in the Bennigan's on Canyon Boulevard to arrive at the answer; it took even less time to make the preparations and to carry them out.

Some of the few things left me after the settlement with Maria were my Jeep and camping gear. Even while I was drinking, I would occasionally take off for the hills without notice, camping somewhere along the Peak to Peak Highway or in the national forest up Left Hand Canyon. While not a real off-road type—I hate four-wheel-drive assholes who pride themselves on tearing up the landscape, and all snowmobilers, and those idiots on motorcycles who befoul the wilderness with noise and fumes—I have been known to push the Jeep pretty hard to get to a campsite far enough back to where I wouldn't have to listen to anyone's radio or hear traffic or have to look at the rump end of some fat-assed Winnebago.

There are mine shafts up there. Most of them are dug horizontally into the mountains and run only a few hundred feet back before ending in cave-in or flood. But some are sinkholes, some are pits where the soil has caved in above an old shaft. Some are vertical drop shafts, long since abandoned, that fall two hundred or three hundred feet to rocks and water and to whatever slimy things there are that like to live in such darkness.

I knew where one of these drop shafts was—a deep one, with an opening wide enough to take the Jeep and me. It was way the hell above the canyon back there behind Sugarloaf Mountain, off the trail and marked by warning signs on trees, but someone trying to turn a Jeep around in the dusk or dark might drive into it easily enough. If he was stone stupid. Or if he was a known drunk.

It was about seven on a July evening when I left Bennigan's, picked up my camping stuff at the apartment on Thirtieth Street, and headed up north on Highway 36 along the foothills for three miles and then west up Left Hand Canyon. Even with the two or three hard miles of four-wheel-drive road, I figured I would be at the mine shaft before 8 P.M. There would be plenty of light left to do what I had to do.

Despite the three beers, I was sober. I hadn't had a real drink in almost two months. As an alcoholic, I knew that I wasn't recovering by staying just on this side of the sober line, only suffering.

But I wanted to be almost sober that night. I had been almost sober—only two beers, perhaps three—the evening that the pickup crossed the lane on Highway 287 and smashed into our Honda, killing Allan instantly and putting me into the hospital for three weeks. The driver of the pickup had survived, of course. They had tested his blood and found that he was legally drunk. He received a suspended sentence and lost his license for a year. I was so badly injured, it was so obvious that the pickup had been at fault, that no one had tested my blood-alcohol level. I'll never know if I could have responded faster if it hadn't been for those two or three beers.

This time I wanted to know exactly what I was doing as I perched the Jeep on the edge of that twenty-foot opening, shifted into four-wheel low, and roared over the raised berm around the black circle of the pit.

And I did. I did not hesitate. I did not lose my sense of pride at the last minute and write some bullshit farewell note to anyone. I didn't think about it. I took my baseball cap off, wiped the faintest film of sweat from my forehead, set the cap on firmly, slammed the shifter into low, and roared over that mound of dirt like a pit bull going after a mailman's ass.

The sensation was almost like going over the second hill on the Wildcat 'coaster at Elitch Gardens. I had the urge to raise my arms and scream. I did not raise my arms; my hands stayed clamped to the wheel as the nose of the Jeep dropped into darkness as if I were driving into a tunnel. I had not turned the headlights on. I caught only the faintest glimpse of boulders and rotted timbers and layers of granite whipping by. I did not scream.

The last few days I have been trying to recall everything I can about Kelly Dahl when I taught her in the sixth grade, every conversation and interaction, but much of it is indistinct. I taught for almost twenty-six years, sixteen in the elementary grades and the rest in high school. Faces and names blur. But not because I was drinking heavily then. Kelly was in my last sixth-grade class and I didn't really have a drinking problem then. Problems, yes; drinking problem, no.

I remember noticing Kelly Dahl on the first day; any teacher worth his or her salt notices the troublemakers, the standouts, the teacher's pets, the class clowns, and all of the other elementary-class stereotypes on the first day. Kelly Dahl did not fit any of the stereotypes, but she was certainly a standout kid. Physically, there was nothing unusual about her—at eleven she was losing the baby fat she'd carried through childhood, her bone structure was beginning to assert itself in her face, her hair was about shoulder length, brown, and somewhat stringier than the blow-dried fussiness or careful braid-edness of the other girls. Truth was, Kelly Dahl carried a slight air of neglect and impoverishment about her, a look we teachers were all too familiar with in the mid-eighties, even in affluent Boulder County. The girl's clothes were usually too small, rarely clean, and bore the telltale wrinkles of something dredged from the hamper or floor of the closet that morning. Her hair was, as I said, rarely washed and usually held in place by cheap plastic barrettes that she had probably worn since second grade. Her skin had that sallow look common to children who spent hours inside in front of the TV, although I later found that this was not the case with Kelly Dahl. She was that rarest of things—a child who had never watched TV.

Few of my assumptions were correct about Kelly Dahl.

What made Kelly stand out that first day of my last sixth-grade class were her eyes—startlingly green, shockingly intelligent, and surprisingly alert when not concealed behind her screen of boredom or hidden by her habit of looking away when called upon. I remember her eyes and the slightly mocking tone to her soft, eleven-year-old girl's voice when I called on her the few times that first day.

I recall that I read her file that evening—I made it a practice never to read the students' cumulative folders before I met the actual child—and I probably looked into this one because Kelly's careful diction and softly ironic tone contrasted so much with her appearance. According to the file, Kelly Dahl lived in the mobile-home park to the west of the tracks—the trailer park that gave our school the lion's share of problems—with her mother, divorced, and a stepfather. There was a yellow Notice slip from second grade warning the teacher that Kelly's biological father had held custody until that year, and that the court had removed the girl from that home because of rumors of abuse. I checked back in the single sheet from a county social worker who had visited the home and, reading between the lines of bureaucratese, inferred that the mother hadn't wanted the child either but had given in to the court's ruling. The biological father had been more than willing to give the girl up. Evidently it had been a noncustody battle, one of those "You take her, I have a life to live" exchanges that so many of my students had endured. The mother had lost and ended up with Kelly. The yellow Notice slip was the usual warning that the girl was not to be allowed to leave the school grounds with the biological father or be allowed to speak on the phone if he called the school, and if he were observed hanging around the school grounds, the teacher or her aide was to notify the principal and/or call the police. Too many of our kids' files have yellow Notice slips with that sort of warning.

A hasty note by Kelly's fourth-grade teacher mentioned that her "real father" had died in a car accident the previous summer and that the Notice slip could be ignored. A scrawled message on the bottom of the social worker's typed page of comments let it be known that Kelly Dahl's "stepfather" was the usual live-in boyfriend and was out on parole after sticking up a convenience store in Arvada.

A fairly normal file.

But there was nothing normal about little Kelly Dahl. These past few days, as I actively try to recall our interactions during the seven months of that abbreviated school year and the eight months we spent together when she was a junior in high school, I am amazed at how strange our time together had been. Sometimes I can barely remember the faces or names of any of the other sixth graders that year, or the sullen faces of the slouching juniors five years after that, just Kelly Dahl's ever-thinning face and startling green eyes, Kelly Dahl's soft voice—ironic at eleven, sarcastic and challenging at sixteen. Perhaps, after twenty-six years teaching, after hundreds of eleven-year-olds and sixteen-year-olds and seventeen-year-olds and eighteen-year-olds taught—suffered through, actually—Kelly Dahl had been my only real student.

And now she was stalking me. And I her.

II. Pentimento

I awoke to the warmth of flames on my face. Lurching with a sense of falling, I remembered my last moment of consciousness—driving the Jeep into the pit, the plunge into blackness. I tried to raise my arms, grab the wheel again, but my arms were pinned behind me. I was sitting on something solid, not the Jeep seat, the ground. Everything was dark except for the flicker of flames directly in front of me. *Hell?* I thought, but there was not the slightest belief in that hypothesis, even if I were dead. Besides, the flames I could see were in a large campfire; the ring of firestones was quite visible.

My head aching, my body echoing that ache and reeling from a strange vertigo, as if I were still in a plummeting Jeep, I attempted to assess the situation. I was outside, sitting on the ground, still dressed in the clothes I had worn during my suicide attempt, it was dark, and a large campfire crackled away six feet in front of me.

"Shit," I said aloud, my head and body aching as if I were hung over. *Screwed up again. I got drunk and messed up. Only imagined driving into the pit. Fuck.*

"You didn't screw up again," came a soft, high voice from somewhere in the darkness behind me. "You really did drive into that mine shaft."

I started and tried to turn to see who had spoken, but I couldn't move my head that far. I looked down and saw the ropes crossing my chest. I was tied to something—a stump, perhaps, or a boulder. I tried to remember if I had spoken those last thoughts aloud about getting drunk and screwing up. My head hurt abysmally.

"It was an interesting way to try to kill yourself," came the woman's voice again. I was sure it was a woman. And something about the voice was hauntingly familiar.

"Where are you?" I asked, hearing the raggedness in my voice. I swiveled my head as far as it would go but was rewarded with only a glimpse of movement in the shadows behind me. The woman was walking just outside the reach of firelight. I was sitting against a low boulder. Five strands of rope were looped around my chest and the rock. I could feel another rope restraining my wrists behind the boulder.

"Don't you want to ask who I am?" came the strangely familiar voice. "Get that out of the way?"

For a second I said nothing, the voice and the slight mocking tone beneath the voice so familiar that I was sure that I would remember the owner of it before I had to ask. Someone who found me drunk in the woods and tied me up. *Why tie me up?* Maria might have done that if she had been around, but she was in Guatemala with her new husband. There were past lovers who disliked me enough to tie me up and leave me in the woods—or worse—but none of them had this voice. Of course, in the past year or two there had been so many strange women I'd awakened next to . . . and who said I had to know this person? Odds were that some crazy woman in the woods found me, observed that I was drunk and potentially violent—I tend to shout and recite poetry when I am at my drunkest—and tied me up. It all made sense— except for the fact that I didn't remember getting drunk, that the aching head and body did not feel like my usual hangover, that it made no sense for even a crazy lady to tie me up, and that I *did* remember driving the fucking Jeep into the mine shaft.

"Give up, Mr. Jakes?" came the voice.

Mr. Jakes. That certain tone. A former student . . . I shook my head with the pain of trying to think. It was worse than a hangover headache, different, deeper.

"You can call me Roland," I said, my voice thick, squinting at the flames and trying to buy a moment to think.

"No, I can't, Mr. Jakes," said Kelly Dahl, coming around into the light and crouching between me and the fire. "You're Mr. Jakes. I can't call you anything else. Besides, Roland is a stupid name."

I nodded. I had recognized her at once, even though it had been six or seven years since I had seen her last. When she had been a junior, she had worn her hair frosted blond and cut in a punk style just short of a mohawk. It was still short and cut raggedly, still a phony blond with dark roots, but no longer punk. Her eyes had been large and luminous as a child of eleven, even larger and lit with the dull light of drugs when she was seventeen, but now they were just large. The dark shadows under her eyes that had been a constant of her appearance in high school seemed gone, although that might be a trick of the firelight. Her body was not as angular and lean as I remembered from high school, no longer the bone-and-gristle gaunt, as if the coke or crack or whatever she'd been taking had been eating her up from the inside, but still thin enough that one might have to glance again to see the breasts before being certain it was a woman. This night she was wearing jeans and work boots with a loose flannel shirt over a dark sweatshirt and there was a red bandanna tied around her head. The firelight made the skin of her cheeks and forehead very pink. Her short hair stuck out over the bandana above her ears. She held a large camp knife loosely in her right hand as she squatted in front of me.

"Hi, Kelly," I said.

"Hi, Mr. Jakes."

"Want to let me loose?"

"No."

I hesitated. There had been none of the old bantering tone in her voice. We were just two adults talking, she in her early twenties, me fifty-something going on one hundred.

"Did you tie me up, Kelly?"

"Sure."

"Why?"

"You'll know in a few minutes, Mr. Jakes."

"Okay." I tried to relax, settle back against the rock as if I were accustomed to driving my Jeep into a pit and waking up to find an old student threatening me with a knife. *Is she threatening me with a knife?* It was hard to tell. She held it casually, but if she wasn't going to cut me loose, there was little reason for it to be there. Kelly had always been emotional, unusual, unstable. I wondered if she had gone completely insane.

"Not completely nuts, Mr. Jakes. But close to it. Or so people thought . . . back when people were around."

I blinked. "Are you reading my mind, Kelly?"

"Sure."

"How?" I asked. Perhaps I hadn't died in the suicide attempt, but was even at that second lying comatose and brain-damaged and dreaming this nonsense in a hospital room somewhere. Or at the bottom of the pit.

"Mu," said Kelly Dahl.

"I beg your pardon?"

"Mu. Come on, don't tell me you don't remember."

I remembered. I had taught the juniors . . . no, it had been the sixth graders that year with Kelly . . . the Chinese phrase *mu*. On one level *mu* means only *yes,* but on a deeper level of Zen it was often used by the master when the acolyte asked a stupid, unanswerable or wrongheaded question such as "Does a dog have the Buddha-nature?" The Master would answer only, *"Mu,"* meaning—*I say "yes" but mean "no," but the actual answer is*: *Unask the question.*

"Okay," I said, "then tell me why I'm tied up."

"Mu," said Kelly Dahl. She got to her feet and towered over me. Flames danced on the knife blade.

I shrugged, although the tight ropes left that as something less than a graceful movement. "Fine," I said. I was tired and scared and disoriented and angry. "Fuck it." *If you can read my mind, you goddamn neurotic, read this.* I pictured a raised middle finger. *And sit on it and swivel.*

Kelly Dahl laughed. I had heard her laugh very few times in sixth grade, not at all in eleventh grade, but this was the same memorable sound I had heard those few times—wild but not quite crazy, pleasant but with far too much edge to be called sweet.

Now she crouched in front of me, the long knife blade pointed at my eyes. "Are you ready to start the game, Mr. Jakes?"

"What game?" My mouth was very dry.

"I'm going to be changing some things," said Kelly Dahl. "You may not like all the changes. To stop me, you'll have to find me and stop me."

I licked my lips. The knife had not wavered during her little speech. "What do you mean, stop you?"

"Stop me. Kill me if you can. Stop me."

Oh, shit . . . the poor girl is crazy.

"Maybe," said Kelly Dahl. "But the game is going to be fun." She leaned forward quickly and for a mad second I thought she was going to kiss me; instead she leveraged the flat of the blade under the ropes and tugged slightly. Buttons ripped. I felt the steel point cold against the base of my throat as the knife slid sideways.

"Careful . . ."

"Shh," whispered Kelly Dahl, and she did kiss me, once, lightly, as her hand moved quickly from left to right and the ropes separated as if sliced by a scalpel.

When she stepped back I jumped to my feet . . . tried to jump to my feet . . . my legs were asleep and I pitched forward, almost tumbling into the fire, catching myself clumsily with arms and hands that were as nerveless as the logs I could see lying in the flames.

"Shit," I said. "Goddamn it, Kelly, this isn't very . . ." I had made it to my knees and turned toward her, away from the fire.

I saw that the campfire was in a clearing on a ridgeline, somewhere I did not recognize but obviously nowhere near where I had driven into the mine shaft. There were a few boulders massed in the dark and I caught a glimpse of the Milky Way spilling above the pines. My Jeep was parked twenty feet away. I could see no damage but it was dark. A breeze had come up and the pine branches began swaying slightly, the needles rich in scent and sighing softly.

Kelly Dahl was gone.

When I was training to be a teacher, just out of the army and not sure why I was becoming a teacher except for the fact that it was the furthest thing from humping a ruck through Vietnam that I could imagine, one of the trick questions the professors used to ask was—"Do you want to be the sage on the stage or the guide on the side?" The idea was that there were two kinds of teachers: the "sage" who walked around like a pitcher full of knowledge occasionally pouring some into the empty receptacle that was the student, or the "guide" who led the student to knowledge via furthering the young person's own curiosity and exploration. The obvious right answer to that trick question was that the good teacher-to-be should be "the guide on the side," not imposing his or her own knowledge, but aiding the child in self-discovery.

I soon found out that the only way I could enjoy teaching was to be the sage on the stage. I poured knowledge and facts and insights and questions and doubts and everything else that I was carrying around directly from my overflowing pitcher to those twenty-five or so empty receptacles. It was most fun when I taught sixth grade because the receptacles hadn't been filled with so much social moose piss and sheer misinformation.

Luckily, there were a lot of things I was both acutely interested in, moderately knowledgeable about, and innocently eager to share with the kids: my passion for history and literature, my love of space travel and aviation, my college training in environmental science, a love of interesting architecture, my ability to draw and tell stories, a fascination with dinosaurs and geology, an enjoyment of writing, a high comfort level with computers, a hatred of war coupled with an obsession with things military, firsthand knowledge of quite a few remote places in the world, a desire to travel to see *all* of the world's remote places, a good sense of direction, a warped sense of humor, a profound fascination with the lives of world historical figures such as Lincoln and Churchill and Hitler and Kennedy and Madonna, a flair for the dramatic, a love of music that would often lead to my sixth-grade class lying in the park across the street from the school on a warm spring or autumn day, sixty feet of school extension cord tapping my mini–stereo system into the electrical outlet near the park rest rooms, the sound of Vivaldi or Beethoven or Mozart or Rachmaninoff irritating the other teachers who later complained that they had to close their classroom windows so that their students would not be distracted. . . .

I had enough passions to remain a sage on the stage for twenty-six years. *Some of those years*, said the inscription on a tombstone I once saw, *were good*.

One of the incidents I remember with Kelly Dahl was from the week of environmental study the district had mandated for sixth-graders back when they had money to fund the field trips. Actually, we studied environmental science for weeks before the trip, but the students always remembered the actual three-day excursion to an old lodge along the Front Range of the Rockies. The district called those three days and two nights of hiking and doing experiments in the mountains the Environmental Awareness and Appreciation Unit. The kids and teachers called it Eco-Week.

I remember the warm, late-September day when I had brought Kelly Dahl's class to the mountains. The kids had found their bunks in the drafty old lodge, we had hiked our orientation hikes, and in the hour before lunch I had brought the class to a beaver pond a quarter of a mile or so from the lodge in order to do pH tests and to begin my stint as Science Sage. I pointed out the fireweed abounding around the disturbed pond edge—*Epilobium angustifolium* I taught them, never afraid to introduce a little Latin nomenclature into the mix—and had them find some of the fireweed's cottony seeds along the bank or skimming across the still surface of the pond. I pointed out the aspen's golden leaves and explained why they shimmered—how the upper surface of the leaf did not receive enough sunlight to photosynthesize, so the leaf was attached by a stem at an angle that allowed it to quake so that both sides received the light. I explained how aspens clone from the roots, so the expansive aspen grove we were looking at was—in a real sense—a single organism. I pointed out the late asters and wild chrysanthemums in their last days before the killing winter winds finished them for another season, and had the children hunt for the red leaves of cinquefoil and strawberry and geranium.

It was at this point, when the kids were reconvened around me in an interested circle, pointing to the fallen red leaves and gall-swollen branches they had gathered, that Kelly Dahl asked, "Why do we have to learn all this stuff?"

I remember sighing. "You mean the names of these plants?"

"Yes."

"A name is an instrument of teaching," I said, quoting the Aristotle maxim I had used many times with this class, "and of discerning natures."

Kelly Dahl had nodded slightly and looked directly at me, the startling, unique quality of her green eyes in sharp contrast to the sad commonness of her cheap Kmart jacket and corduroys. "But you can't learn it all," she had said, her voice so soft that the other kids had leaned forward to hear it above the gentle breeze that had come up. It was one of those rare times when an entire class was focused on what was being said.

"You can't learn it all," I had agreed, "but one can enjoy nature more if you learn some of it."

Kelly Dahl had shaken her head, almost impatiently I'd thought at the time. "You don't understand," she said. "If you don't understand it *all*, you can't understand any of it. Nature is . . . *everything*. It's all mixed up. Even we're part of it, changing it by being here, changing it by trying to understand it. . . ." She had stopped then and I only stared. It certainly had been the most I had heard this child say in one speech in the three weeks of class we had shared so far. And what she said was absolutely accurate, but—I felt—largely irrelevant.

While I paused to frame a reply that all of the kids could understand, Kelly had gone on. "What I mean is," she said, obviously more impatient with her own inability to explain than with my inability to understand, "that learning *a little* of this stuff is like tearing up that painting you were talking about on Tuesday . . . the woman . . ."

"The Mona Lisa," I said.

"Yeah. It's like tearing up the Mona Lisa into little bits and handing around the bits so everyone would enjoy and understand the painting." She stopped again, frowning slightly, although whether at the metaphor or at speaking up at all, I did not know.

For a minute there was just the silence of the aspen grove and the beaver pond. I admit that I was stumped. Finally, I said, "What would you suggest we do instead, Kelly?"

At first I thought that she would not answer, so withdrawn into herself did she seem. But eventually she said softly, "Close our eyes."

"What?" I said, not quite hearing.

"Close our eyes," repeated Kelly Dahl. "If we're going to look at this stuff, we might as well look with something other than big words."

We all closed our eyes without further comment, the class of normally unruly sixth graders and myself. I remember to this day the richness of the next few minutes: the butterscotch-and-turpentine tang of sap from the ponderosa pine trees up the hill from us, the vaguely pineapple scent of wild chamomile, the dry-leaf dusty sweetness of the aspen grove beyond the pond, the equally sweet decayed aroma of meadow mushrooms such as *Lactarius* and *Russula*, the pungent seaweed smell of pond scum and the underlying aromatic texture of the sun-warmed earth and the heated pine needles beneath our legs. I remember the warmth of the sun on my face and hands and denim-covered legs that long-ago September afternoon. I recall the sounds from those few minutes as vividly as I can call back anything I have ever heard: the soft lapping of water trickling over the sticks-and-mud beaver dam, the rustle of dry clematis vines and the brittle stirring of tall gentian stalks in the breeze, the distant hammering of a woodpecker in the woods toward Mt. Meeker and then, so suddenly that my breath caught, the startling crash of wings as a flight of Canada geese came in low over the pond and, without a single honk, veered south toward the highway and the larger ponds there. I think that none of us opened our eyes then, even when the geese flew low over us, so that the magic spell would not be broken. It was a new world, and Kelly Dahl was—somehow, inexplicably, unarguably—our guide.

I had forgotten that moment until yesterday.

On the morning after she had tied me up, Kelly Dahl shot the shit out of my Jeep.

I had waited until sunrise to find my way back to Boulder. The night was too dark, the woods were too dense, and my head hurt too much to try to drive down the mountain in the dark. *Besides*, I had thought at the time with a wry smile, *I might drive into a mine shaft.*

In the morning my head still hurt and the woods were still thick—not even a sign of a Jeep trail or how Kelly had got my vehicle this far back—but at least I could see to drive. The Jeep itself had multiple abrasions and contusions, a dented fender, flaking paint, and a long gouge on the right door, but these were all old wounds; there was no sign of tumbling down a three-hundred-foot mine shaft. The keys were in the ignition. My billfold was still in my hip pocket. The camping gear was still in the back of the Jeep. Kelly Dahl might be as crazy as a loon, but she was no thief.

It had taken me about an hour to drive up to the mine shaft the previous evening; it took me almost three hours to get back to Boulder. I was way the hell beyond Sugarloaf Mountain and Gold Hill, northeast of Jamestown almost to the Peak of Peak Highway. I had no idea why Kelly Dahl would drag me that far . . . unless the entire mine shaft experience was an hallucination and she had found me elsewhere. Which made no sense. I put the puzzle out of my mind until I could get home, take a shower, have some aspirin and three fingers of scotch, and generally start the day.

I should have known things were screwed up long before I got to Boulder. The paved road in Left Hand Canyon, once I crept out of the woods and got onto it headed east, seemed wrong. I realize now that I was driving on patched concrete rather than asphalt. The Greenbriar Restaurant sitting at the exit of Left Hand Canyon where the road meets Highway 36 seemed weird. Looking back, I realize that the parking lot was smaller, the entrance and door painted a different color, and there was a large cottonwood where the flower garden had been for years. Small things on the short ride south to Boulder—the shoulder of Highway 36 was too narrow, the Beechcraft plant along the foothills side of the road looked spruced up and open for business despite the fact that it had been empty for a decade. Nursing my headache, mulling over Kelly Dahl and my screwed-up suicide, I noticed none of this.

There was no traffic. Not a single car or van or cyclist—unusual since those spandex fanatics on bikes are zooming along the Foothills Highway every pleasant day of the year. But nothing this morning. The strangeness of that did not really strike me until I was on North Broadway in Boulder.

No cars moving. Scores were parked by the curb, but none were moving. Nor cyclists hogging the lane. Nor pedestrians walking against the light. I was almost to the Pearl Street walking mall before I realized how empty the town was.

Jesus Christ, I remember thinking, *maybe there's been a nuclear war . . . everyone's evacuated.* Then I remembered that the cold war was over and that the Boulder City Council had—a few years earlier and for no reason known to humankind—voted unanimously to ignore civil defense evacuation plans in case of a wartime emergency. The Boulder City Council was into that sort of thing—like declaring Boulder a Nuclear Free Zone, which meant, I guess, that no more aircraft carriers with nuclear weapons would be tying up there again soon. It seemed probable that there hadn't been a mass evacuation even if the Rocky Flats Nuclear Weapons Plant six miles away had melted down—a core of Boulder's politically correct citizenry would protest the advancing radiation rather than evacuate.

Then where is everybody? I had the open Jeep slowed to a crawl by the time I came down the hill to Pearl Street and the walking mall there.

The walking mall was gone: no trees, no landscaped hills, no tasteful brick walkways, no flower beds, no panhandlers, no Freddy's hot dog stand, no skateboarders, no street musicians, no drug dealers, no benches or kiosks or phone booths . . . all gone.

The mall was gone, but Pearl Street itself remained, looking as it had before it was covered with bricks and flower beds and street musicians. I turned left onto it and drove slowly down the empty boulevard, noticing the drugstores and clothing stores and inexpensive restaurants lining the sidewalks where upscale boutiques, gift stores, and Häagen-Dazs parlors should have been. This looked like Pearl Street had looked when I had come to Boulder in the early seventies—just another western town's *street* with rents that real retailers could afford.

I realized that it *was* the Pearl Street of the early seventies. I drove past Fred's Steakhouse, where Maria and I used to have the occasional Friday steak dinner when we'd saved enough money. Fred had thrown in the towel and surrendered to the mall boutique rental prices . . . when? . . . at least fifteen years ago. And there was the old Art Cinema, showing Bergman's *Cries and Whispers*. It hadn't been a real movie theater for a decade. I could not remember when *Cries and Whispers* had been released, but I seem to recall seeing it with Maria before we moved to Boulder after my discharge in '69.

I won't list all the rest of the anomalies—the old cars at the curb, the antiquated street signs, the antiwar graffiti on the walls and stop signs—just as I did not try to list them that day. I drove as quickly as I could to my apartment on Thirtieth Street, barely noting as I did so that Crossroads Mall at the end of Canyon Boulevard simply was there but drastically smaller than I remembered.

My apartment building was not there at all.

For a while I just stood up in my Jeep, staring at the fields and trees and old garages where my apartment complex should be, and resisting the urge to scream or shout. It was not so much that my apartment was gone, or my clothes, or my few mementos of the life I had already left behind—some snapshots of Maria that I never look at, old softball trophies, my 1984 Teacher of the Year finalist plaque—it was just that my bottles of scotch were gone.

Then I realized how silly that response was, drove to the first liquor store I could find—an old mom-and-pop place on Twenty-eighth where a new minimall had been the day before—walked in the open door, shouted, was not surprised when no one answered, liberated three bottles of Johnnie Walker, left a heap of bills on the counter—I might be crazy, but I was no thief—and then went out to the empty parking lot to have a drink and think things over.

I have to say that there was very little denial. Somehow things had changed. I did not seriously consider the possibility that I was dead or that this was like that "lost year" on the *Dallas* TV show some years ago and that I would wake up with Maria in the shower, Allan playing in the living room, my teaching job secure, and my life back together. No, this was real—both my shitty life and this strange . . . *place*. It was Boulder, all right, but Boulder as it had been about two and a half decades earlier. I was shocked at how small and provincial the place seemed.

And empty. Some large raptors circled over the Flatirons, but the city was dead still. Not even the sound of distant traffic or jet aircraft disturbed the summer air. I realized, in its absence, how much of an expected background that sound is for a city dweller such as myself.

I did not know if this was some half-assed sort of random confusion of the space-time continuum, some malfunction of the chronosynclastic infundibulum, but I suspected not. I suspected that it all had something to do with

Kelly Dahl. That's about as far as my speculations had gone by the time I had finished the first half of the first bottle of Johnnie Walker.

Then the phone rang.

It was an old pay phone on the side of the liquor store twenty paces away. Even the goddamn phone was different—the side of the half booth read Bell Telephone rather than U.S. West or one of its rivals and the old Bell logo was embossed in the metal there. It made me strangely nostalgic.

I let the thing ring twelve times before setting the bottle on the hood of the Jeep and walking slowly over to it. Maybe it would be God, explaining that I was dead but I'd only qualified for limbo, that neither heaven nor hell wanted me.

"Hello?" My voice may have sounded a little funny. It did to me.

"Hi, Mr. Jakes." It was Kelly Dahl, of course. I hadn't really expected God.

"What's going on, kid?"

"Lots of neat stuff," came the soft, high voice. "You ready to play yet?"

I glanced over at the bottle and wished I'd brought it with me. "Play?"

"You're not hunting for me."

I set the receiver down, walked back to the Jeep, took a drink, and walked slowly back to the phone. "You still there, kiddo?"

"Yes."

"I don't want to play. I don't want to hunt for you or kill you or do anything else to you or with you. *Comprende?*"

"*Oui.*" This was another game I suddenly remembered from sixth grade with this kid. We would begin sentences in one language, shift to another, and end in a third. I never asked her where an eleven-year-old had learned the basics of half a dozen or more languages.

"Okay," I said. "I'm leaving now. You take care of yourself, kid. And stay the fuck away from me. *Ciao.*" I slammed the receiver down and watched it warily for at least two minutes. It did not ring again.

I secured the second bottle on the floorboards so it wouldn't break and drove north on Twenty-eighth until I got to the Diagonal—the four-lane highway that runs northeast to Longmont and then continues on up the string of towns along the Front Range. The first thing I noticed was that the Boulder section of the Diagonal was two-lane . . . when had they widened it? The eighties sometime . . . and the second thing I noticed was that it ended only a quarter of a mile or so outside of town. To the northeast there was nothing: not just no highway, but no farmhouses, no farm fields, no Celestial Seasonings plant, no IBM plant, no railroad tracks—not even the structures that had been there in the early seventies. What *was* there was a giant crack in the earth, a fissure at least twenty feet deep and thirty feet wide. It looked as if an earthquake had left this cleft separating the highway and Boulder from the high prairie of sagebrush and low grass beyond. The fissure stretched to the northwest and southeast as far as I could see and there was no question of getting the Jeep across it without hours of work.

"*Sehr gut,*" I said aloud. "Score one for the kid." I swung the Jeep around and drove back to Twenty-eighth Street, noticing that the shorter route of the Foothills Highway had not yet been built, and drove south across town to take Highway 36 into Denver.

The fissure began where the highway ended. The cleft seemed to run all the way to the Flatirons to the west.

"Great," I said to the hot sky. "I get the picture. Only I don't think I want to stay. Thanks anyway."

My Jeep is old and ugly, but it's useful. A few years ago I had an electric winch installed on the front with two hundred feet of cable wrapped around its drum. I powered it up, took the drum brake off, secured the cable around a solid bridge stanchion about thirty feet from the edge of the fissure, set it again, and prepared to back the Jeep down the fifty-degree embankment. I didn't know if I could climb the opposite slope even in four-wheel-low, but I figured I'd think of something when I got down there. If worse came to worst, I'd come back, find a bulldozer somewhere, and grade my own way out of this trap. Anything was preferable to playing Kelly Dahl's game by Kelly Dahl's rules.

I'd just gotten the rear wheels over the brink and was edging over with just the cable keeping me from falling when the first shot rang out. It shattered my windshield, sending the right-side windshield wiper flying into the air in two pieces. For a second I froze. Don't let anyone tell you that old combat reflexes last forever.

The second shot smashed the Jeep's right headlight and exited through the fender. I don't know what the third shot hit, because old reflexes finally reasserted themselves and I was out of the Jeep and scrambling for cover along the steep cliffside by then, my face in the dust, my fingers clawing for a hold. She fired seven times—I never doubted that it was Kelly Dahl—and each bullet created some mischief, taking off my rearview mirror, puncturing two tires, and even smashing the last two bottles of Johnnie Walker Red where I'd left them cushioned beneath the seat, wrapped in my shirt. I have to believe that last was a lucky shot.

I waited the better part of an hour before crawling out of the cleft, looking at the distant buildings for any sign of the crazy woman with the rifle, winching the Jeep out on its two flat tires, and cursing over the smashed bottles. I changed the right front with the spare I had and limped into town, thinking that I'd head for the tire place on Pearl—if that was there yet. Instead, I saw another Jeep parked in a lot near Twenty-eighth and Arapaho and I just pulled in beside it, took one of its new, knobby tires, decided that my spare was in bad shape and the rear tires looked shitty with these new ones on front, and ended up changing all four tires. I suppose I could have just hot-wired the new Jeep and have been done with it without all that sweat and cursing under the blazing July sun, but I didn't. I'm sentimental.

In the early afternoon I drove to the old Gart Brothers sporting goods store and chose the Remington with the twenty-power scope, the .38 handgun, the Ka-bar knife of the sort that had been prized in Vietnam, and enough ammunition for the two guns to fight a small war. Then I drove to the old army surplus store on Pearl and Fourteenth and stocked up on boots, socks, a camouflage hunting vest, backpacking rations, a new Coleman gas stove, extra binoculars, better rain gear than I had in the old pack, lots of nylon line, a new sleeping bag, two compasses, a nifty hunting cap that probably made me look like a real asshole, and even more ammunition for the Remington. I did not leave any money on the counter when I left. I had the feeling that the proprietor was not coming back and doubted if I would be either.

I drove back to the mom-and-pop liquor store on Twenty-eighth, but the shelves were empty. The hundreds of bottles that had been there three hours before were simply gone. The same was true of the four other liquor stores I tried.

"You bitch," I said to the empty street.

A phone rang in an old glass booth across a parking lot. It kept ringing as I removed the .38 police special from its case, opened the yellow box, and slowly loaded the cylinder. It stopped ringing on my third shot when I hit the phone box dead center.

A pay phone across the street rang.

"Listen you little bitch," I said as soon as I picked it up, "I'll play your game if you'll leave me something to drink."

This time I did expect God to be on the other end.

"You find me and stop me, and you'll have all the booze you want, Mr. Jakes," came Kelly Dahl's voice.

"Everything will be the way it was?" I was looking around as I spoke, half expecting to see her down the street in another phone booth.

"Yep," said Kelly Dahl. "You can even go back up in the hills and drive into a mine shaft, and I won't interfere the next time."

"So I actually drove into it? Did I die? Are you my punishment?"

"Mu," said Kelly Dahl. "Remember the two other Eco-Week field trips?"

I thought a minute. "The water filtration plant and Trail Ridge Road."

"Very good," said Kelly Dahl. "You can find me at the higher of those two."

"Do the roads continue to the west . . . ," I began. I was talking to a dial tone.

III. Palimpsest

On the day I surprised Kelly Dahl near the mountain town of Ward, she almost killed me. I had set an ambush, remembering my training from the good old Vietnam years, waiting patiently where the Left Hand Canyon road wound up to the Peak to Peak Highway. There were only three ways to get up to the Continental Divide along this stretch of the Front Range, and I knew Kelly would take the shortest.

There had been a chain saw in the old firehouse in Ward. The town itself was empty, of course, but even before Kelly Dahl kidnapped me to this place there were never more than one hundred people in Ward—hippies left over from the sixties mostly. The old mining town had been turned into a scrap heap of abandoned vehicles, half-built houses, woodpiles, junk heaps, and geodesic outhouses. I set the ambush on the switchback above the town, cutting down two ponderosa pines to block the road. Then I waited in the aspen grove.

Kelly Dahl's Bronco came up the road late that afternoon. She stopped, got out of the truck, looked at the fallen trees, and then looked over at me as I stepped around a tree and began walking toward her. I had left the Remington behind. The .38 was tucked in my waistband under my jacket; the Ka-bar knife remained in its sheath.

"Kelly," I said. "Let's talk."

That was when she reached back into the Bronco, came out with a powerful bow made of some dark composite material, notched an arrow before I could speak again, and let fly. It was a hunting arrow—steel-tipped, barbed for maximum damage—and it passed under my left arm, tearing my jacket, ripping flesh on the inside of my arm and above my rib cage, and embedding itself in the aspen centimeters behind me.

I was pinned there for an instant, a bug pinned on a collecting tray, and could only stare as Kelly Dahl notched another arrow. I had no doubt that this one would find its target in my sternum. Before she could release the second arrow, I fumbled in my belt, came out with the .38, and fired blindly, wildly, seeing her duck behind the Bronco as I tore myself free from the tattered remnants of my jacket and leaped behind the fallen log.

I heard the Bronco roar a moment later but I did not look up until the truck was gone, driving over the fallen trees as it turned and accelerating through Ward and back down the canyon.

It took a trip back to Boulder—an early-eighties version this time but still as empty—to find bandages and antibiotic for the slash on my ribs and inner arm. It is beginning to scar over now, but it still hurts when I walk or breathe deeply.

I carry the Remington everywhere now.

* * *

Even after I had been teaching drunk for two years, the central administration did not have the balls to fire me. Our master agreement specified that because I was tenured, malfeasance and gross incompetence had to be documented by one or more administrators, I had to be given at least three chances to redeem myself, and I was to enjoy due process every step of the way. As it turned out, the high-school principal and the director of secondary education were too chickenshit to confront me with any documentation sessions, I didn't want to redeem myself, and everyone was too busy trying to figure out a way to hide me from sight or get rid of me outside of channels to worry about due process. In the end, the superintendent ordered the director of elementary instruction—a gray carbuncle of a woman named Dr. Maxine Millard—to observe me the required number of times, to give me my warnings and chances to rehabilitate myself, and then to do the necessary paperwork to get rid of me.

I knew the days that Dr. Max was going to be there so I could have called in sick or at least not shown up drunk or hungover, but I figured—Fuck it, let them do their worst. They did. My tenure was revoked and I was dismissed from the district three years and two days before I could have put in for early retirement.

I don't miss the job. I miss the kids, even the slumpy, acned, socially inept high-school kids. Oddly, I remember the little kids from my earlier years in elementary even more clearly. And miss them more.

A sage without a stage is no sage, drunk or sober.

This morning I followed Kelly Dahl's tire tracks down Flagstaff Mountain on a narrow gravel road, came out where Chautauqua Park should be to find Boulder gone and the Inland Sea back again. Only this time, far out on the mud flats, reachable by a long causeway raised just feet above the quicksand beds, was a great island of stone with a walled city rising from its rocks, a great cathedral rising from the stone city, and Michael the Archangel standing on the summit of the tallest tower, his sword raised, his foot firmly planted on a writhing devil, a cock signifying eternal vigilance perched on his mailed foot.

"Christ, Kelly," I said to the tire tracks as I followed them across the causeway, "this is getting a little elaborate."

It was Mont-Saint-Michel, of course, complete down to its last stained-glass window and wrought-iron balustrade. I only vaguely remembered showing my sixth-grade class the slides of it. The twelfth-century structure had caught my fancy the summer before when I took my family there. Maria had not been impressed, but ten-year-old Allan had flipped over it. He and I bought every book on the subject that we could and seriously discussed building a model of the fortress-cathedral out of balsa wood.

Kelly Dahl's old Bronco was parked outside the gate. I took the Remington, actioned a round into the breech, and went through the gate and up the cobblestone walkway in search of her. My footfalls echoed. Occasionally I paused, looked back over the ramparts at the Flatirons gleaming in the Colorado sunshine, and listened for her footsteps above the lap of lazy waves. There were noises higher up.

The cathedral was empty, but a thin book made of heavy parchment bound in leather had been set on the central altar. I picked up the vellum and read:

> *Co sent sent Rollanz que la mort le trespent*
> *Devers la teste sur le quer li descent*
> *Desuz un pin i est alez curanz*
> *Sur l'erbe verte si est culchiez adenz*
> *Desuz lui met s'espree e l'olifant*
> *Turnat sa teste vers la paiene gent.*

This was eleventh-century French verse. I knew it from my last year of college. This was the kind of thing I had devoted my life to translating in those final months before being drafted and sent around the world to kill small Asian people.

> *Then Roland feels that death is taking him;*
> *Down from the head upon the heart it falls.*
> *Beneath a pine he hastens running;*
> *On the green grass he throws himself down;*
> *Beneath him puts his sword and oliphant,*
> *Turns his face toward the pagan army.*

I set down the book and shouted into the gloom of the cathedral. "Is this a threat, kid?" Only echoes answered.

The next page I recognized as Thibaut, thirteenth century:

> *Nus hom ne puet ami reconforter*
> *Se cele non ou il a son cuer mis.*
> *Pour ce m'estuet sovent plaindre et plourer*
> *Que nus confors ne me vient, ce m'est vis,*
> *De la ou j'ai tote ma remembrance.*
> *Pour biens amer ai sovent esmaiance*
>   *A dire voir.*
> *Dame, merci! donez moi esperance*
>   *De joie avoir.*

This took me a moment. Finally I thought I had it.

> *There is no comfort to be found in pain*
> *Save only where the heart has made its home.*
> *Therefore I can but murmur and complain*
> *Because no comfort to my pain has come*
> *From where I garnered all my happiness.*
> *From true love have I only earned distress*
>   *The truth to say.*
> *Grace, lady! give me comfort to possess*
>   *A hope, one day.*

"Kelly!" I shouted into the cathedral shadows. "I don't need this shit!" When there was no answer, I raised the Remington and fired a single slug into the huge stained-glass window of the Virgin opposite the altar. The echo of the shot and of falling glass was still sounding as I left.

I dropped the handmade book into the quicksand as I drove back across the causeway.

When I returned home from the hospital after the accident that killed Allan, I found that Maria had emptied our eleven-year-old son's room of all his possessions, our house of all images and records of him. His clothes were gone. The posters and photographs and desk clutter and old *Star Trek* models hanging from black thread in his room—all gone. The rocking-horse quilt she had made for him the month before he was born was gone from his bed. The bed was stripped as clean as the walls and closet, as if his room and bed were in a dormitory or barracks, waiting sterilely for the next recruits to arrive.

There were no next recruits.

Maria had purged the photo albums of any image of Allan. It was as if his eleven years simply had not been. The family photo we had kept on our bedroom dresser was gone, as were the snapshots that had been held to the refrigerator door by magnets. His fifth-grade school portrait was no longer in the drawer in the study, and all of the baby pictures were gone from the shoe box. I never found out if she had given the clothes and toys and sports equipment to the Salvation Army, or burned the photographs, or buried them. She would not speak of it. She would not speak of Allan. When I forced the subject, Maria's eyes took on a stubborn, distant look. I soon learned not to force the subject.

This was the summer after I taught my last sixth-grade class. Allan would have been a year younger than Kelly Dahl, twenty-two now, out of college, finding his way in the world. It is very difficult to imagine.

* * *

I tracked her to Trail Ridge Road but left the Jeep behind at the beginning of the tundra. There was no Trail Ridge Road—no sign of human existence— only the tundra extending up beyond the tree line. It was very cold out of the shelter of the trees. When I'd awakened at my high camp that morning, it had felt like late autumn. The skies were leaden, there were clouds in the valleys below, hiding the lateral moraines, wisps of cloud edge curling up against the mountainsides like tentacles of fog. The air was freezing. I cursed myself for not bringing gloves and balled my hands in the pockets of my jacket, the Remington cold and heavy against my forearms.

Passing the last of the stunted trees, I tried to remember the name for these ancient dwarfs at the tree line.

Krummholz, came Kelly Dahl's voice almost in my ear. *It means "elfin timber" or "crooked wood."*

I dropped to one knee on the frozen moss, the rifle coming up. There was no one within one hundred meters of open tundra. I scoped the tree line, the boulders large enough to hide a human figure. Nothing moved.

I love all the tundra terms you taught us, continued Kelly's voice in my mind. She had done this only a few times before. *Fell-field, meadow vole, boreal chorus frog, snowball saxifrage, solifluction terraces, avens and sedges, yellow-bellied marmots, permafrost, nivation depressions, saffron ragworts, green-leaf chiming bells, man-hater sedge . . .*

I looked up and out across the windswept tundra. Nothing moved. But I had been wrong about there being no sign of human existence: a well-worn trail ran across the permafrost field toward the summit of the pass. I began following it. "I thought you hated all the technical terms," I said aloud, the rifle ready in the crook of my arm. My ribs and the inside of my left arm ached from where her arrow had cut deep.

I like poetry. Her voice was in my mind, not my ear. The only real sound was the wind. But her voice was real enough.

Mr. Jakes, do you remember that Robert Frost thing you read us about poetry?

I was two hundred meters out from the last line of krummholz now. There were some house-size boulders about three hundred meters above and to my left. She might be hiding there. I sensed that she was close.

"Which poem?" I said. If I could keep her talking, thinking, she might not notice my approach.

Not poem, the Frost introduction to one of his books. It was about the figure a poem makes.

"I don't remember," I said. I did. I had shared that with the high-school juniors only weeks before Kelly Dahl had quit school and run away.

Frost said that it should be the pleasure of a poem itself to tell how it can.

He said that a poem begins in delight and ends in wisdom. He said the figure is the same for love.

"Mmm," I said, moving quickly across the permafrost field now, my breath fogging the air as I panted. The rifle was gripped in both hands, the cold forgotten. "Tell me more."

Stop a minute. Kelly Dahl's voice was flat in my mind.

I paused, panting. The boulders were less than fifty meters from me. The trail I had been following cut across the grassy area once used by the Ute and Pawnee women, old people, and youngsters to cross the Divide. This path looked newly used, as if the Utes had just disappeared over the rock saddle ahead of me.

I don't think the Indians left trails, came Kelly Dahl's soft voice in my mind. *Look down.*

Still trying to catch my breath, dizzy with the altitude and adrenaline, I looked down. A plant was growing on the cushioned terrace between two low rocks there. The wind was whipping snow past me; the temperature must have been in the twenties, if not lower.

Look more closely.

Still gasping for air, I went to one knee on the fell-field. When Kelly Dahl's voice began again, I took the opportunity to action a round into the Remington's chamber.

See those little trenches in the soil, Mr. Jakes? They look like smooth runways, little toboggan runs through the tundra. Do you remember teaching us about them?

I shook my head, all the time watching for movement out of the corner of my eye. I truly did not remember. My passion for alpine ecology had burned away with all of my other passions. Not even an ember of interest remained. "Tell me," I said aloud, as if hearing the echo of her mental voice would reveal her position to me.

They were originally burrows dug out by pocket gophers, came her soft voice, sounding mildly amused. *The soil's so tough and rocky up here, that not even earthworms tunnel, but the pocket gopher digs these shallow burrows. When the gopher goes away, the smaller meadow voles claim them. See where their feet have made the earth smooth? Look closer, Mr. Jakes.*

I lay on the soft moss, laying my rifle ahead of me casually, as if just setting it out of the way. The barrel was aimed toward the boulders above. If something moved, I could be sighted in on it within two seconds. I glanced down at the collapsed gopher burrow. It did look like a dirt-smoothed toboggan run, one of hundreds that crisscrossed this section of tundra like an exposed labyrinth, like some indecipherable script left by aliens.

The vole keeps using these little highways in the winter, said Kelly Dahl. *Under the snow. Up here we would see giant drifts and an empty, sterile* world. But under the snow, the vole is shuttling around, carrying out her business, collecting the grasses she harvested and stored in the autumn, chewing out the centers of cushion plants, munching on taproots. And somewhere nearby, the pocket gopher is digging away.

Something gray did move near the boulders. I leaned closer to the collapsed vole run, closer to the rifle. The snow was suddenly thicker, whipping down the permafrost field like a curtain of gauze that now lifted, now lowered.

In the spring, continued Kelly Dahl's soft voice in my head, *the tops of all these pocket gopher tunnels appear from beneath the melting snowbanks. The ridges are called eskers and look like brown snakes looping around everywhere. You taught us that a pocket gopher up here could dig a tunnel more than one hundred feet long in a single night and move up to eight tons of topsoil per acre in a year.*

"Did I teach that?" I said. The gray shape in the snow separated itself from the gray boulders. I quit breathing and set my finger on the trigger guard.

It's fascinating, isn't it, Mr. Jakes? That there's one visible winter world up here on the tundra—cold, inhospitable, intolerable—but the most defenseless animals here just create another world right under the surface where they can continue to survive. They're even necessary to the ecology, bringing subsoil up and burying plants that will decompose quicker underground. Everything fits.

I leaned forward as if to set my face to the plant, lifted the rifle in a single motion, centered the moving gray form in the crosshairs, and fired. The gray figure fell.

"Kelly?" I said as I ran panting up the tundra, moving from solifluction terrace to solifluction terrace.

There was no answer.

I expected nothing to be there when I arrived at the boulders, but she had fallen exactly where I had last seen the movement. The arterial blood was bright, excruciatingly bright, the single bold color almost shocking on the dim and dun tundra. The bullet had taken her behind the right eye, which was still open and questioning. I guessed that the cow elk was an adult but not quite fully grown. Snowflakes settled on its gray, hairy side, still melted on the pink of its extruded tongue.

Gasping for breath, I stood straight and spun around, surveying the rocks, the tundra, the lowering sky, the clouds rising like wraiths from the cold valleys below. "Kelly?"

Only the wind responded.

I looked down. The elk's luminous but fading black eye seemed to be conveying a message.

Things can die here.

* * *

The last time I saw Kelly Dahl in the real world, the other world, had been at a late-season basketball game. I hated basketball—I hated all of the school's inane and insanely cheered sports—but it was part of my job as low-man-on-the-totem-pole English teacher to do *something* at the damn events, so I was ticket taker. At least that way I could leave twenty minutes or so into the game when they closed the doors.

I remember coming out of the gym into the freezing darkness—it was officially spring but Colorado rarely recognizes the end of winter until late May, if then—and seeing a familiar figure heading down Arapaho going the opposite direction. Kelly Dahl had not been in class for several days that week, and rumor was that she had moved. I jogged across the street, avoiding patches of black ice, and caught up to her under a streetlight a block east of the school.

She turned as if unsurprised to see me, almost as if she had been waiting for me to follow her. "Hey, Mr. Jakes. What's happening?" Her eyes were redder than usual, her face pinched and white. The other instructors were sure that she was using drugs and I had finally, reluctantly, come to the same conclusion. There was little trace of the eleven-year-old girl in the gaunt woman's face I stared into that night.

"You been sick, Kelly?"

She returned my stare. "No, I just haven't been going to school."

"You know Van Der Mere will call in your mother."

Kelly Dahl shrugged. Her jacket was far too thin for such a cold night. When we spoke, our breath hung between us like a veil. "She's gone," said Kelly.

"Gone where?" I asked, knowing it was none of my business but feeling the concern for this child rise in me like faint nausea.

Again the shrug.

"You coming back to school on Monday?" I asked.

Kelly Dahl did not blink. "I'm not coming back."

I remember wishing at the time that I had not given up smoking the year before. It would have been good at that moment to light a cigarette and take a drag before speaking. Instead, I said, "Well, shit, Kelly."

The pale face nodded.

"Why don't we go somewhere and talk about it, kiddo."

She shook her head. A car roared past and slid into the school parking lot, latecomers shouting. Neither of us turned to look.

"Why don't we . . . ," I began.

"No," said Kelly Dahl. "You and I had our chance, Mr. Jakes."

I frowned at her in the cold light from the streetlamp. "What do you mean?"

For a long moment I was sure she would say nothing else, that she was on the verge of turning away and disappearing into the dark. Instead, she took a deep breath and let it out slowly. "You remember the year . . . the seven months . . . I was in your sixth-grade class, Mr. Jakes?"

"Of course."

"You remember how I almost worshiped the ground you walked on . . . excuse the cliché."

It was my turn to take a breath. "Look, Kelly, a lot of kids in sixth grade, especially girls . . ."

She waved me into silence, as if we had too little time for such formalized dialogue. "I just meant I thought you were the one person who I might have talked to then, Mr. Jakes. In all the middle of what was going on . . . my mother, Carl . . . well, I thought you were the most solid, *real* thing in the universe that crazy, fucked-up winter."

"Carl . . . ," I said.

"My mother's boyfriend," said Kelly in that soft voice. "My . . . *stepfather*." I could hear the heavy irony in her voice, but I could hear something else, something infinitely more ragged and sad.

I took half a step in her direction. "Did he . . . was there . . ."

Kelly Dahl twitched a half smile in the cold light. "Oh, yeah. He did. There was. Every day. Not just that school year, but most of the summer before." She looked away, toward the street.

I had the urge to put an arm around her then—seeing the girl there rather than the gaunt young woman—but all I could do was ball my hands into fists, tighter and tighter. "Kelly, I had no idea. . . ."

She was not listening or looking at me. "I learned how to go away then. Find the other places."

"Other places . . ." I did not understand.

Kelly Dahl did not look at me. Her punk mohawk and streaked hair looked pathetic in the flat, cold light. "I got very good at going away to the other places. The things you were teaching us helped—I could see them, you taught them so clearly—and whatever I could see I could visit."

My insides were shaking with the cold. The child needed psychiatric help. I thought of all the times I had referred children to school counselors and district psychologists and county social services, always to see little or nothing done, the children returned to whatever nightmare they had temporarily found themselves free of.

"Kelly, let's . . ."

"I almost told you," continued Kelly Dahl, her lips thin and white. "I worked up the nerve all that week in April to tell you." She made a brittle sound that I realized was a laugh. "Hell, I'd been working up nerve all that school year to tell you. I figured that you were the one person in the world who might listen . . . might believe . . . might *do something*.''

I waited for her to go on. Cheers came from the school gym a block away.

Kelly Dahl looked at me then. There was something wild in her green eyes. ''Remember I asked if I could stay after school and talk to you that day?''

I frowned, finally had to shake my head. I could not remember.

She smiled again. ''It was the same day you told us you were leaving. That you'd taken a job teaching at the high school, that they needed somebody because Mrs. Webb had died. You told us that there'd be a substitute teacher with us the rest of the year. I don't think you expected the class to get all upset the way it did. I remember most of the girls were crying. I wasn't.''

''Kelly, I . . .''

''You didn't remember that I'd said I wanted to see you after school,'' she said, her voice an ironic whisper. ''But that was okay, because I didn't stay anyway. I don't know if you remember, but I wasn't one of the kids who hugged you good-bye after the surprise going-away party that the kids threw that next Friday.''

We looked at each other for a silent moment. There were no cheers from the gym. ''Where are you going, Kelly?''

She looked at me so fiercely that I felt a pang of fear that moment, but whether for her or me, I am not sure. ''Away,'' she said. ''Away.''

''Come to the school on Monday to talk to me,'' I said, stepping closer to her. ''You don't have to come to class. Just come by the homeroom and we'll talk. Please.'' I raised my hands but stopped just short of touching her.

Kelly Dahl's stare did not waver. ''Good-bye, Mr. Jakes.'' Then she turned and crossed the street and disappeared in the dark.

I thought about following her then, but I was tired. I'd promised Allan that we would go into Denver to shop for baseball cards the next morning, and whenever I got home late from some school thing, Maria was sure that I'd been out with another woman.

I thought about following Kelly Dahl that night, but I did not.

On Monday she did not come. On Tuesday I called her home, but there was no answer. On Wednesday I told Mr. Van Der Mere about our conversation and a week later social services dropped by the trailer park. The trailer had been abandoned. Kelly's mother and the boyfriend had left about a month before the girl had quit coming to school. No one had seen Kelly Dahl since the weekend of the basketball game.

A month later, when word came that Kelly Dahl's mother had been found murdered in North Platte, Nebraska, and that Carl Reems, her boyfriend, had confessed to the crime after being caught in Omaha, most of the teachers thought that Kelly had been murdered as well, despite the chronology to the contrary. Posters of the seventeen-year-old were seen around Boulder for a month or so, but Reems denied doing anything to her right up to his conviction for the murder of Patricia Dahl. Kelly was probably considered to be just another runaway by the police, and she was too old for her face to appear on milk cartons. It seemed there were no relatives who cared to pursue the subject.

It was early that summer that the pickup came across the centerline and Allan died and I ceased to live.

I find Kelly Dahl by mistake.

It has been weeks, months, here in this place, these places. Reality is the chase, confirmation of that reality is the beard I have grown, the deer and elk I kill for fresh food, the pain in my side and arm as the arrow wound continues to scar over, the increasing fitness in my legs and lungs and body as I spend ten to fourteen hours a day outside, looking for Kelly Dahl.

And I find her by mistake.

I had been returning to the Front Range from following signs of Kelly Dahl south almost to the Eisenhower Tunnel, I had lost her for a full day, and now evening shadows found me south of Nederland along the Peak to Peak Highway. Since there might be no highway when morning came if the time/place shifted, I stopped at a forest service campground—empty of people and vehicles, of course—pitched my tent, filled my water bottles, and cooked up some venison over the fire. I was fairly sure that the last few days had been spent in that 1970ish landscape in which I'd first found myself—roads and infrastructure in place, people not—and true autumn was coming on. Aspen leaves filled the air like golden parade confetti and the evening wind blew cold.

I find Kelly Dahl by becoming lost.

I used to brag that I have never been lost. Even in the densest lodgepole pine forest, my sense of direction has served me well. I am good in the woods, and the slightest landmark sets me on my way as if I have an internal compass that is never off by more than two or three degrees. Even on cloudy days the sunlight speaks direction to me. At night, a glimpse of stars will set me straight.

Not this evening. Walking out of the empty campground, I climb a mile or so through thick forest to watch the sun set north of the Arapahoes but south of Mt. Audubon. Twilight does not linger. There is no moon. Beyond the Front Range to the east, where the glow of Denver and its string of satellite cities should be, there is only darkness. Clouds move in to obliterate the night sky. I cut back toward the campground, dropping down from one ridge to climb another, confident that this way is shorter. Within ten minutes I am lost.

The sensation of being lost without my rifle, without a compass, with only the Ka-bar knife in its sheath on my belt, is not disturbing. At first. Ninety minutes later, deep in a lodgepole thicket, miles from anywhere, the sky above as dark as the forest below, I am beginning to be worried. I have worn only my sweater over a flannel shirt; it may snow before morning. I think of my parka and sleeping bag back at the campsite, of the firewood stacked in the circle of stones and the hot tea I was planning to have before turning in.

"Idiot," I say to myself, stumbling down a dark slope, almost plunging into a barbed-wire fence. Painfully picking my way over the fence—sure that there had been no fences near the campground—I think again, *idiot*, and begin to wonder if I should hunker down for the cold wait until dawn.

At that moment I see Kelly Dahl's fire.

I never doubt it is her fire—I have been here long enough to know that she is now the only other person in our universe—and, when I come closer, moving silently through the last twenty meters of brush to the clearing, it is indeed Kelly Dahl, sitting in the circle of light from the flames, looking at a harmonica in her hands and seemingly lost in thought.

I wait several minutes, sensing a trap. She remains engrossed in the play of firelight on the chrome surface of the instrument, her face mildly sunburned. She is still wearing the hiking boots, shorts, and thick sweatshirt I had last seen her in three days earlier, just after leaving Mont-Saint-Michel. Her hunting bow—a powerful bend of some space-age composite, several steel-edged killing arrows notched onto the frame—lies strung and ready against the log she sits on.

Perhaps I make a noise. Perhaps she simply becomes aware of my presence. Whatever the reason, she looks up—startled, I see—her head moving toward the dark trees where I hide.

I make the decision within a second. Two seconds later I am hurtling across the dark space that separates us, sure that she will have time to lift the bow, notch the arrow, and let fly toward my heart. But she does not turn toward the bow until the last second and then I am on her, leaping across the last six feet, knocking her down and sideways, the bow and the deadly arrows flying into the darkness on one side of the log, Kelly and me rolling near the fire on the other side.

I guess that I am still stronger but that she is quicker, infinitely more agile. I think that if I act quickly enough, this will not matter.

We roll twice and then I am on top of her, slapping away her hands, pulling the Ka-bar knife from its sheath. She swings a leg up but I pin it with my own, swing my other knee out, squeeze her legs together beneath me with the strength of my thighs. Her hands are raking at my sweater, nails tearing toward my face, but I use my left arm and the weight of my upper body to squeeze her arms between us as I lean forward, the knife moving to her throat.

For a second, as the tempered steel touches the pulsing flesh of her neck, there is no more movement, only my weight on hers and the memory of the moment's wild friction between us. We are both panting. The wind scatters the sparks of the fire and blows aspen leaves out of the darkness above us. Kelly Dahl's green eyes are open, appraising, surprised but unafraid, waiting. Our faces are only inches apart.

I move the knife so that the cutting edge is turned away from her throat, lean forward, and kiss her gently on the cheek. Pulling my face back so that I can focus on her eyes again, I whisper, "I'm sorry, Kelly." Then I roll off her, my right arm coming up against the log she had been sitting on.

Kelly Dahl is on me in a second, lunging sideways in a fluid manner that I have always imagined, but never seen, a panther strike. She straddles my chest, sets a solid forearm across my windpipe, and uses the other hand to slam my wrist against the log, catching the knife as it bounces free. Then the blade is against my own throat. I cannot lower my chin enough to see it, but I can feel it, the scalpel-sharp edge slicing taut skin above my windpipe. I look into her eyes.

"You found me," she says, swinging the blade down and to the side in a precise killing movement.

Expecting to feel blood rushing from my severed jugular, I feel only the slight razor burn where the edge had touched me a second before. That and cold air against the intact flesh of my throat. I swallow once.

Kelly Dahl flings the Ka-bar into the darkness near where the bow had gone, her strong hands pull my wrists above my head, and she leans her weight on her elbows on either side of me. "You did find me," she whispers, and lowers her face to mine.

What happens next is not clear. It is possible that she kisses me, possible that we kiss each other, but time ceases to be sequential at that moment so it is possible that we do not kiss at all. What *is* clear—and shall remain so until the last moment of my life—is that in this final second before seconds cease to follow one another I move my arms to take her weight off her elbows, and Kelly Dahl relaxes onto me with what may be a sigh, the warmth of her face envelops the warmth of my face, a shared warmth more intimate than any kiss, the length of her body lies full along the length of my body, and then—inexplicably—she continues descending, moving closer, skin against skin, body against body, but *more* than that, entering me as I enter her in a way that is beyond sexual. She passes into me as a ghost would pass through some solid form, slowly, sensually but without self-conscious effort, melding, melting into me, her form still tangible, still touchable, but moving through me as if our atoms were the stars in colliding galaxies, passing through each other without contact but rearranging the gravity there forever.

I do not remember us speaking. I remember only the three sighs—Kelly Dahl's, mine, and the sigh of the wind coming up to scatter the last sparks of the fire that had somehow burned down to embers while time had stopped.

IV. Palinode

I knew instantly upon awakening—alone—that everything had changed. There was a difference to the light, the air. A difference to me. I felt more attached to my senses than I had in years, as if some barrier had been lifted between me and the world.

But the world was different. I sensed it at once. More real. More permanent. I felt fuller but the world felt more empty.

My Jeep was in the campground. The tent was where I had left it. There were other tents, other vehicles. Other people. A middle-aged couple having breakfast outside their Winnebago waved in a friendly manner as I walked past. I could not manage a return wave.

The resident camp ranger ambled over as I was loading the tent in the back of the Jeep.

"Didn't see you come in last night," he said. "Don't seem to have a permit. That'll be seven dollars. Unless you want to stay another day. That'll be seven more. Three-night limit here. Lots of folks this summer."

I tried to speak, could not, and found—to my mild surprise—that my billfold still had money in it. I handed the ranger a ten-dollar bill and he counted back the change.

He was leaving when I finally called to him. "What month is it?"

He paused, smiled. "Still July, the last time I looked."

I nodded my thanks. Nothing else needed to be explained.

I showered and changed clothes in my apartment. Everything was as I had left it the night before. There were four bottles of scotch in the kitchen cabinet. I lined them up on the counter and started to pour them down the sink, realized that I did not have to—I had no urge to take a drink—and set them back in the cabinet.

I drove first to the elementary school where I had taught years ago. The teachers and students were gone for the summer, but some of the office staff were there for the summer migrant program. The principal was new, but Mrs. Collins, the secretary, knew me.

"Mr. Jakes," she said. "I almost didn't recognize you in that beard. You look good in it. And you've lost weight and you're all tanned. Have you been on vacation?"

I grinned at her. "Sort of."

The files were still there. I was afraid that they'd gone to the district headquarters or followed the kids through junior high and high school, but the policy was to duplicate essential material and start new files beginning with seventh grade.

All of the students from that last sixth-grade class were still in the box in the storage closet downstairs, all of their cumulative record folders mildewing away with the individual class photos of the students staring out—bright eyes, braces, bad haircuts from a decade before. They were all there. Everyone but Kelly Dahl.

"Kelly Dahl," repeated Mrs. Collins when I came up from the basement and queried her. "Kelly Dahl. Strange, Mr. Jakes, but I don't remember a child named Kelly Dahl. Kelly Daleson, but that was several years after you left. And Kevin Dale . . . but that was a few years before you were here. Was he here very long? It might have been a transfer student who transferred back out, although I usually remember . . ."

"She," I said. "It was a girl. And she was here a couple of years."

Mrs. Collins frowned as if I had insulted her powers of recall. "Kelly Dahl," she said. "I really don't think so, Mr. Jakes. I remember most of the students. It's why I suggested to Mr. Pembroke that this thing wasn't necessary. . . ." She waved dismissively toward the computer on her desk. "Are you *sure* the child was in one of your sixth-grade classes . . . not someone in high school or someone you met . . . after?" She pursed her lips at the near faux pas.

"No," I said. "It was someone I knew before I was fired. Someone I knew here. Or so I thought."

Mrs. Collins ran fingers through her blue hair. "I may be wrong, Mr. Jakes." She said it in a tone that precluded the possibility.

The high-school records agreed with her. There had been no Kelly Dahl. The manager at the trailer park did not remember the three people; in fact, his records and memory showed that the same elderly couple had been renting what I remembered as the Dahl trailer since 1975. There was no microfilm record of the murder of Patricia Dahl in the *Boulder Daily Camera*, and calls to North Platte and Omaha revealed no arrest of anyone named Carl Reems at any time in the past twelve years.

I sat on my apartment terrace, watched the summer sun set behind the Flatirons, and thought. When I grew thirsty, ice water satisfied. I thought of the Jeep and camping gear down in the parking stall. There had been a Remington rifle in the back of the Jeep, a .38-caliber revolver in the blue pack. I had never owned a rifle or pistol.

"Kelly," I whispered finally. "You've really managed to go away this time."

I pulled out my billfold and looked at the only photograph of Allan that had escaped Maria's purge—my son's fifth-grade class picture, wallet-size. After a while I put away the photo and billfold and went in to sleep.

Weeks passed. Then two months. The Colorado summer slipped into early autumn. The days grew shorter but more pleasant. After three hard interviews, I was offered a job at a private school in Denver. I would be teaching sixth graders. They knew my history, but evidently thought that I had changed for the better. It was Friday when I finished the final interview. They said they would call me the next day, on Saturday.

They were as good as their word. They sounded truly pleased when they offered me the job—perhaps they knew it meant a new start for me, a new life. They were surprised by my answer.

"No, thank you," I said. "I've changed my mind." I knew now that I could never teach eleven-year-olds again. They would all remind me of Allan, or of Kelly Dahl.

There was a shocked silence. "Perhaps you would like another day to think about it," said Mr. Martin, the headmaster. "This is an important decision. You could call us on Monday."

I started to say no, began to explain that my mind was made up, but then I heard *Wait until Monday. Do not decide today.*

I paused. My own thoughts had echoed like this before since returning from Kelly Dahl. "Mr. Martin," I said at last, "that might be a good idea. If you don't mind, I'll call you Monday morning with my decision."

On Sunday morning I picked up the *New York Times* at Eads tobacco store, had a late breakfast, watched the 11 A.M. Brinkley news show on ABC, finished reading the *Times Book Review*, and went down to the Jeep about 1:00 in the afternoon. It was a beautiful fall day and the drive up Left Hand Canyon and then up the hard Jeep trail took less than an hour.

The blue sky was crisscrossed with contrails through the aspen leaves when I stopped the Jeep ten feet from the entrance to the vertical mine shaft.

"Kiddo," I said aloud, tapping my fingers on the steering wheel. "You found me once. I found you once. Do you think we can do it together this time?"

I was talking to myself and it felt silly. I said nothing else. I put the Jeep in first and floored the accelerator. The hood first rose as we bounced over the lip of the pit, I caught a glimpse of yellow aspen leaves, blue sky, white contrails, and then the black circle of the pit filled the windshield.

I hit the brake with both feet on the pedal. The Jeep slid, bucked, slewed to the left, and came to a stop with the right front tire hanging over the open pit. Shaking slightly, I backed the Jeep up a foot or two, set the brake, got out of the vehicle and leaned against it.

Not this way. Not this time. I did not know if the thought was mine alone. I hoped not.

I stepped closer to the edge, stared down into the pit, and then stepped back.

Months have passed. I took the teaching job in Denver. I love it. I love being with the children. I love being alive again. I am once again the sage on the stage, but a quieter sage this time.

The bad dreams continue to bother me. Not dreams of Kelly Dahl, but Kelly Dahl's dreams. I wake from nightmares of Carl coming into my small room in the trailer, of trying to speak to my mother as she smokes a cigarette and does not listen. I fly awake from dreams of awakening to Carl's heavy hand over my mouth, of his foul breath on my face.

I feel closest to Kelly Dahl at these times. Sitting up on the bed, sweat pouring from me, my heart pounding, I can feel her presence. I like to think that these dreams are an exorcism for her, a long overdue offer of love and help for me.

It is impossible to explain the feeling that Kelly Dahl and I shared that last night in her world . . . in *our* world. Galaxies colliding, I think I said, and I have since looked up the photographic telescope images of that phenomenon: hundreds of billions of stars passing in close proximity as great spiral clusters pinwheel through one another, gravities interacting and changing each spiral forever but no stars actually colliding. This has some of the sense of what I felt that night, but does not explain the aftermath—the knowledge of being changed forever, of being filled with another human's mind and heart and memories, of solitude ceasing. It is impossible to share the knowledge of being not just two people, but four—ourselves here, and truly ourselves where we meet again on that alternate place of going away.

It is not mystical. It is not religious. There is no afterlife, only life.

I cannot explain. But on some days out on the recess grounds, on some warm Colorado winter days when the sunlight is like a solid thing and the high peaks of the Divide gleam to the west as if they were yards away rather than miles, then I close my eyes as the children play, allow myself to hear the wind above the familiar murmur of children at play, and then the echoes of that separate but equal reality are clear enough. Then all this becomes the memory, the echo.

The Flatirons are gone, but a dirt road leads to low cliffs that look out over the Inland Sea. The Douglas fir, ponderosa pine, and lodgepole trees are gone; the narrow road winds through tropical forests of sixty-foot and flowering cycads the size of small redwoods. Cedarlike conifers let down lacy branches and one unidentifiable tree holds clusters of seeds that resemble massive shaving brushes. The air is humid and almost dizzyingly thick with the smell of eucalyptus, magnolia, something similar to apple blossoms, sycamore, and a riot of more exotic scents. Insects buzz and something very large crashes through the underbrush deep in the fern forest to my right as the Jeep approaches the coast.

Where the Flatirons should be, tidal flats and lagoons reflect the sky. Everything is more textured and detailed than I remember from earlier visits. The sea stretches out to the east, its wave action strong and constant. The road leads to a causeway and the causeway leads across the tidal pools to Mont-Saint-Michel, the city-cathedral and its high walls gleaming in late-afternoon light.

Once I pause on the causeway and reach back for my binoculars, scanning the city walls and parapets.

The Ford Bronco is parked outside the gate. Kelly Dahl is on the rampart of the highest wall, near the cathedral entrance high on the stone island. She is wearing a red sweatshirt and I notice that her hair has grown out a bit. The sunlight must be glinting on my field glasses, for as I watch she smiles slightly and raises one hand to wave at me even though I am still a quarter of a mile away. I set the glasses back in their case and drive on. To my right, in one of the deep pools far out beyond the quicksand flats, a long-necked plesiosaur, perhaps of the alasmosaurian variety, lifts a flat head studded with its fish-catching basket of teeth, peers nearsightedly across the flats at the sound of my Jeep's engine, and then submerges again in the murky water. I stop a moment to watch the ripples but the head does not reappear. Behind me, where the Flatirons and Boulder once were—will someday be—something roars a challenge in the forest of cycads and ferns.

Focusing on the dot of red high on the miracle that is Mont-Saint-Michel, imagining that I can see her waving now—somehow seeing her clearly even without the field glasses—I get the Jeep in gear and drive on.

THINK LIKE A DINOSAUR

James Patrick Kelly

▼

Like his friend and frequent collaborator John Kessel, James Patrick Kelly made his first sale in 1975, and went on to become one of the most respected and prominent new writers of the eighties. Although Kelly has had some success with novels, especially the recent *Wildlife*, he has perhaps had more impact to date as a writer of short fiction, and is often ranked among the best short story writers in the business; indeed, Kelly stories such as "Solstice," "The Prisoner of Chillon," "Glass Cloud," "Mr. Boy," "Pogrom," and "Home Front" must certainly be numbered among the most inventive and memorable short works of the decade. Kelly's first solo novel, the mostly ignored *Planet of Whispers*, came out in 1984. It was followed by *Freedom Beach*, a novel written in collaboration with John Kessel, and then by another solo novel, *Look into the Sun*. His most recent book is the above-mentioned *Wildlife*, and he is currently at work on another novel. A collaboration between Kelly and Kessel appeared in our Second Annual Collection; and solo Kelly stories have appeared in our Third, Fourth, Fifth, Sixth, Eighth, and Ninth Annual Collections. Born in Mineola, New York, Kelly now lives with his family in Portsmouth, New Hampshire.

Here he takes us to an alien-operated space station in close Earth orbit that might prove to be the gate to the wide universe beyond for humanity, if we can only learn to see things in the proper cosmic perspective—and if we are willing to pay the price that such a perspective entails.

Kamala Shastri came back to this world as she had left it—naked. She tottered out of the assembler, trying to balance in Tuulen Station's delicate gravity. I caught her and bundled her into a robe with one motion, then eased her onto the float. Three years on another planet had transformed Kamala. She was leaner, more muscular. Her fingernails were now a couple of centimeters long and there were four parallel scars incised on her left cheek, perhaps some Gendian's idea of beautification. But what struck me most was the darting strangeness in her eyes. This place, so familiar to me, seemed almost to shock her. It was as if she doubted the walls and was skeptical of air. She had learned to think like an alien.

"Welcome back." The float's whisper rose to a *whoosh* as I walked it down the hallway.

She swallowed hard and I thought she might cry. Three years ago, she would have. Lots of migrators are devastated when they come out of the assembler; it's because there is no transition. A few seconds ago Kamala was on Gend, fourth planet of the star we call epsilon Leo, and now she was here in lunar orbit. She was almost home; her life's great adventure was over.

"Matthew?" she said.

"Michael." I couldn't help but be pleased that she remembered me. After all, she had changed my life.

I've guided maybe three hundred migrations—comings *and* goings—since I first came to Tuulen to study the dinos. Kamala Shastri's is the only quantum scan I've ever pirated. I doubt that the dinos care; I suspect this is a trespass they occasionally allow themselves. I know more about her—at least, as she was three years ago—than I know about myself. When the dinos sent her to Gend, she massed 50,391.72 grams and her red cell count was 4.81 million per mm^3. She could play the *nagasvaram*, a kind of bamboo flute. Her father came from Thana, near Bombay, and her favorite flavor of chewyfrute was watermelon and she'd had five lovers and when she was eleven she had wanted to be a gymnast but instead she had become a biomaterials engineer who at age twenty-nine had volunteered to go to the stars to learn how to grow artificial eyes. It took her two years to go through migrator training; she knew she could have backed out at any time, right up until the moment Silloin translated her into a superluminal signal. She understood what it meant to balance the equation.

I first met her on June 22, 2069. She shuttled over from Lunex's L1 port and came through our airlock at promptly 10:15, a small, roundish woman with black hair parted in the middle and drawn tight against her skull. They had darkened her skin against epsilon Leo's UV; it was the deep blue-black of twilight. She was wearing a striped clingy and velcro slippers to help her get around for the short time she'd be navigating our .2 micrograv.

"Welcome to Tuulen Station." I smiled and offered my hand. "My name is Michael." We shook. "I'm supposed to be a sapientologist but I also moonlight as the local guide."

"Guide?" She nodded distractedly. "Okay." She peered past me, as if expecting someone else.

"Oh, don't worry," I said, "the dinos are in their cages."

Her eyes got wide as she let her hand slip from mine. "You call the Hanen dinos?"

"Why not?" I laughed. "They call us babies. The weeps, among other things."

She shook her head in amazement. People who've never met a dino tended to romanticize them: the wise and noble reptiles who had mastered superluminal physics and introduced Earth to the wonders of galactic civilization. I doubt Kamala had ever seen a dino play poker or gobble down a screaming rabbit. And she had never argued with Linna, who still wasn't convinced that humans were psychologically ready to go to the stars.

"Have you eaten?" I gestured down the corridor toward the reception rooms.

"Yes . . . I mean, no." She didn't move. "I am not hungry."

"Let me guess. You're too nervous to eat. You're too nervous to talk, even. You wish I'd just shut up, pop you into the marble, and beam you out. Let's just get this part the hell over with, eh?"

"I don't mind the conversation, actually."

"There you go. Well, Kamala, it is my solemn duty to advise you that there are no peanut butter and jelly sandwiches on Gend. And no chicken vindaloo. What's my name again?"

"Michael?"

"See, you're not *that* nervous. Not one taco, or a single slice of eggplant pizza. This is your last chance to eat like a human."

"Okay." She did not actually smile—she was too busy being brave—but a corner of her mouth twitched. "Actually, I would not mind a cup of tea."

"Now, tea they've got." She let me guide her toward reception room D; her slippers *snicked* at the velcro carpet. "Of course, they brew it from lawn clippings."

"The Gendians don't keep lawns. They live underground."

"Refresh my memory." I kept my hand on her shoulder; beneath the clingy, her muscles were rigid. "Are they the ferrets or the things with the orange bumps?"

"They look nothing like ferrets."

We popped through the door bubble into reception D, a compact rectangular space with a scatter of low, unthreatening furniture. There was a kitchen station at one end, a closet with a vacuum toilet at the other. The ceiling was blue sky; the long wall showed a live view of the Charles River and the Boston skyline, baking in the late June sun. Kamala had just finished her doctorate at MIT.

I opaqued the door. She perched on the edge of a couch like a wren, ready to flit away.

While I was making her tea, my fingernail screen flashed. I answered it and a tiny Silloin came up in discreet mode. She didn't look at me; she was too busy watching arrays in the control room. = A problem, = her voice buzzed in my earstone, = most negligible, really. But we will have to void the last two from today's schedule. Save them at Lunex until first shift tomorrow. Can this one be kept for an hour? =

"Sure," I said. "Kamala, would you like to meet a Hanen?" I transferred Silloin to a dino-sized window on the wall. "Silloin, this is Kamala Shastri. Silloin is the one who actually runs things. I'm just the doorman."

Silloin looked through the window with her near eye, then swung around and peered at Kamala with her other. She was short for a dino, just over a meter tall, but she had an enormous head that teetered on her neck like a watermelon balancing on a grapefruit. She must have just oiled herself because her silver scales shone. = Kamala, you will accept my happiest intentions for you? = She raised her left hand, spreading the skinny digits to expose dark crescents of vestigial webbing.

"Of course, I. . . ."

= And you will permit us to render you this translation? =

She straightened. "Yes."

= Have you questions? =

I'm sure she had several hundred, but at this point was probably too scared to ask. While she hesitated, I broke in. "Which came first, the lizard or the egg?"

Silloin ignored me. = It will be excellent for you to begin when? =

"She's just having a little tea," I said, handing her the cup. "I'll bring her along when she's done. Say an hour?"

Kamala squirmed on the couch. "No, really, it will not take me. . . ."

Silloin showed us her teeth, several of which were as long as piano keys. = That would be most appropriate, Michael. = She closed; a gull flew through the space where her window had been.

"Why did you do that?" Kamala's voice was sharp.

"Because it says here that you have to wait your turn. You're not the only migrator we're sending this morning." This was a lie, of course; we had had to cut the schedule because Jodi Latchaw, the other sapientologist assigned to Tuulen, was at the University of Hipparchus presenting our paper on the Hanen concept of identity. "Don't worry, I'll make the time fly."

For a moment, we looked at each other. I could have laid down an hour's worth of patter; I'd done that often enough. Or I could have drawn her out on why she was going: no doubt she had a blind grandma or second cousin just waiting for her to bring home those artificial eyes, not to mention potential spin-offs which could well end tuberculosis, famine, and premature ejaculation, *blah*, *blah*, *blah*. Or I could have just left her alone in the room to read the wall. The trick was guessing how spooked she really was.

"Tell me a secret," I said.

"What?"

"A secret, you know, something no one else knows."

She stared as if I'd just fallen off Mars.

"Look, in a little while you're going some place that's what . . . three hundred and ten light-years away? You're scheduled to stay for three years. By the time you come back, I could easily be rich, famous and elsewhere; we'll probably never see each other again. So what have you got to lose? I promise not to tell."

She leaned back on the couch, and settled the cup in her lap. "This is another test, right? After everything they have put me through, they still have not decided whether to send me."

"Oh no, in a couple of hours you'll be cracking nuts with ferrets in some dark Gendian burrow. This is just me, talking."

"You are crazy."

"Actually, I believe the technical term is logomaniac. It's from the Greek: *logos* meaning word, *mania* meaning two bits short of a byte. I just love to chat is all. Tell you what, I'll go first. If my secret isn't juicy enough, you don't have tell me anything."

Her eyes were slits as she sipped her tea. I was fairly sure that whatever she was worrying about at the moment, it wasn't being swallowed by the big blue marble.

"I was brought up Catholic," I said, settling onto a chair in front of her. "I'm not anymore, but that's not the secret. My parents sent me to Mary, Mother of God High School; we called it Moogoo. It was run by a couple of old priests, Father Thomas and his wife, Mother Jennifer. Father Tom taught physics, which I got a 'D' in, mostly because he talked like he had walnuts in his mouth. Mother Jennifer taught theology and had all the warmth of a marble pew; her nickname was Mama Moogoo.

"One night, just two weeks before my graduation, Father Tom and Mama Moogoo went out in their Chevy Minimus for ice cream. On the way home, Mama Moogoo pushed a yellow light and got broadsided by an ambulance. Like I said, she was old, a hundred and twenty something; they should've lifted her license back in the '50s. She was killed instantly. Father Tom died in the hospital.

"Of course, we were all supposed to feel sorry for them and I guess I did a little, but I never really liked either of them and I resented the way their deaths had screwed things up for my class. So I was more annoyed than sorry, but then I also had this edge of guilt for being so uncharitable. Maybe you'd have to grow up Catholic to understand that. Anyway, the day after it happened they called an assembly in the gym and we were all there squirming on the bleachers and the cardinal himself telepresented a sermon. He kept trying to comfort us, like it had been our *parents* that had died. When I made a joke about it to the kid next to me, I got caught and spent the last week of my senior year with an in-school suspension."

Kamala had finished her tea. She slid the empty cup into one of the holders built into the table.

"Want some more?" I said.

She stirred restlessly. "Why are you telling me this?"

"It's part of the secret." I leaned forward in my chair. "See, my family lived down the street from Holy Spirit Cemetery and in order to get to the carryvan line on McKinley Ave., I had to cut through. Now this happened a couple of days after I got in trouble at the assembly. It was around midnight and I was coming home from a graduation party where I had taken a couple of pokes of insight, so I was feeling sly as a philosopher-king. As I walked through the cemetery, I stumbled across two dirt mounds right next to each other. At first I thought they were flower beds, then I saw the wooden crosses. Fresh graves: here lies Father Tom and Mama Moogoo. There wasn't much to the crosses: they were basically just stakes with crosspieces, painted white and hammered into the ground. The names were hand printed on them. The way I figure it, they were there to mark the graves until the stones got delivered. I didn't need any insight to recognize a once in a lifetime opportunity. If I switched them, what were the chances anyone was going to notice? It was no problem sliding them out of their holes. I smoothed the dirt with my hands and then ran like hell."

Until that moment, she'd seemed bemused by my story and slightly condescending toward me. Now there was a glint of alarm in her eyes. "That was a terrible thing to do," she said.

"Absolutely," I said, "although the dinos think that the whole idea of planting bodies in graveyards and marking them with carved rocks is weepy. They say there is no identity in dead meat, so why get so sentimental about it? Linna keeps asking how come we don't put markers over our shit. But that's not the secret. See, it'd been a warmish night in the middle of June, only as I ran, the air turned cold. Freezing, I could see my breath. And my shoes got heavier and heavier, like they had turned to stone. As I got closer to the back gate, it felt like I was fighting a strong wind, except my clothes weren't flapping. I slowed to a walk. I know I could have pushed through, but my heart was thumping and then I heard this whispery seashell noise and

I panicked. So the secret is I'm a coward. I switched the crosses back and I never went near that cemetery again. As a matter of fact," I nodded at the walls of reception room D on Tuulen Station, "when I grew up, I got about as far away from it as I could."

She stared as I settled back in my chair. "True story," I said and raised my right hand. She seemed so astonished that I started laughing. A smile bloomed on her dark face and suddenly she was giggling too. It was a soft, liquid sound, like a brook bubbling over smooth stones; it made me laugh even harder. Her lips were full and her teeth were very white.

"Your turn," I said, finally.

"Oh, no, I could not." She waved me off. "I don't have anything so good. . . ." She paused, then frowned. "You have told that before?"

"Once," I said. "To the Hanen, during the psych screening for this job. Only I didn't tell them the last part. I know how dinos think, so I ended it when I switched the crosses. The rest is baby stuff." I waggled a finger at her. "Don't forget, you promised to keep my secret."

"Did I?"

"Tell me about when you were young. Where did you grow up?"

"Toronto." She glanced at me, appraisingly. "There *was* something, but not funny. Sad."

I nodded encouragement and changed the wall to Toronto's skyline dominated by the CN Tower, Toronto-Dominion Centre, Commerce Court, and the King's Needle.

She twisted to take in the view and spoke over her shoulder. "When I was ten we moved to an apartment, right downtown on Bloor Street so my mother could be close to work." She pointed at the wall and turned back to face me. "She is an accountant, my father wrote wallpaper for Imagineering. It was a huge building; it seemed as if we were always getting into the elevator with ten neighbors we never knew we had. I was coming home from school one day when an old woman stopped me in the lobby. 'Little girl,' she said, 'how would you like to earn ten dollars?' My parents had warned me not to talk to strangers but she obviously was a resident. Besides, she had an ancient pair of exolegs strapped on, so I knew I could outrun her if I needed to. She asked me to go to the store for her, handed me a grocery list and a cash card, and said I should bring everything up to her apartment. 10W. I should have been more suspicious because all the downtown groceries deliver but, as I soon found out, all she really wanted was someone to talk to her. And she was willing to pay for it, usually five or ten dollars, depending on how long I stayed. Soon I was stopping by almost every day after school. I think my parents would have made me stop if they had known; they were very strict. They would not have liked me taking her money. But neither of them got home until after six, so it was my secret to keep."

"Who was she?" I said. "What did you talk about?"

"Her name was Margaret Ase. She was ninety-seven years old and I think she had been some kind of counselor. Her husband and her daughter had both died and she was alone. I didn't find out much about her; she made me do most of the talking. She asked me about my friends and what I was learning in school and my family. Things like that. . . ."

Her voice trailed off as my fingernail started to flash. I answered it.

= Michael, I am pleased to call you to here. = Silloin buzzed in my ear. She was almost twenty minutes ahead of schedule.

"See, I told you we'd make the time fly." I stood; Kamala's eyes got very wide. "I'm ready if you are."

I offered her my hand. She took it and let me help her up. She wavered for a moment and I sensed just how fragile her resolve was. I put my hand around her waist and steered her into the corridor. In the micrograv of Tuulen Station, she already felt as insubstantial as a memory. "So tell me, what happened that was so sad?"

At first I thought she hadn't heard. She shuffled along, said nothing.

"Hey, don't keep me in suspense here, Kamala," I said. "You have to finish the story."

"No," she said. "I don't think I do."

I didn't take this personally. My only real interest in the conversation had been to distract her. If she refused to be distracted, that was her choice. Some migrators kept talking right up to the moment they slid into the big blue marble, but lots of them went quiet just before. They turned inward. Maybe in her mind she was already on Gend, blinking in the hard white light.

We arrived at the scan center, the largest space on Tuulen Station. Immediately in front of us was the marble, containment for the quantum nondemolition sensor array—QNSA for the acronymically inclined. It was the milky blue of glacial ice and big as two elephants. The upper hemisphere was raised and the scanning table protruded like a shiny gray tongue. Kamala approached the marble and touched her reflection, which writhed across its polished surface. To the right was a padded bench, the fogger and a toilet. I looked left, through the control room window. Silloin stood watching us, her impossible head cocked to one side.

= She is docile? = She buzzed in my earstone.

I held up crossed fingers.

= Welcome, Kamala Shastri. = Silloin's voice came over the speakers with a soothing hush. = You are ready to open your translation? =

Kamala bowed to the window. "This is where I take my clothes off?"

= If you would be so convenient. =

She brushed past me to the bench. Apparently I had ceased to exist; this was between her and the dino now. She undressed quickly, folding her clingy into a neat bundle, tucking her slippers beneath the bench. Out of the corner of my eye, I could see tiny feet, heavy thighs, and the beautiful, dark smooth skin of her back. She stepped into the fogger and closed the door.

"Ready," she called.

From the control room, Silloin closed circuits which filled the fogger with a dense cloud of nanolenses. The nano stuck to Kamala and deployed, coating the surface of her body. As she breathed them, they passed from her lungs into her bloodstream. She only coughed twice; she had been well trained. When the eight minutes were up, Silloin cleared the air in the fogger and she emerged. Still ignoring me, she again faced the control room.

= Now you must arrange yourself on the scanning table, = said Silloin, = and enable Michael to fix you. =

She crossed to the marble without hesitation, climbed the gantry beside it, eased onto the table and lay back.

I followed her up. "Sure you won't tell me the rest of the secret?"

She stared at the ceiling, unblinking.

"Okay then." I took the canister and a sparker out of my hip pouch. "This is going to happen just like you've practiced it." I used the canister to respray the bottoms of her feet with nano. I watched her belly rise and fall, rise and fall. She was deep into her breathing exercise. "Remember, no skipping rope or whistling while you're in the scanner."

She did not answer. "Deep breath now," I said and touched a sparker to her big toe. There was a brief crackle as the nano on her skin wove into a net and stiffened, locking her in place. "Bark at the ferrets for me." I picked up my equipment, climbed down the gantry, and wheeled it back to the wall.

With a low whine, the big blue marble retracted its tongue. I watched the upper hemisphere close, swallowing Kamala Shastri, then joined Silloin in the control room.

I'm not of the school who thinks the dinos stink, another reason I got assigned to study them up close. Parikkal, for example, has no smell at all that I can tell. Normally Silloin had the faint but not unpleasant smell of stale wine. When she was under stress, however, her scent became vinegary and biting. It must have been a wild morning for her. Breathing through my mouth, I settled onto the stool at my station.

She was working quickly, now that the marble was sealed. Even with all their training, migrators tend to get claustrophobic fast. After all, they're lying in the dark, in nanobondage, waiting to be translated. Waiting. The simulator at the Singapore training center makes a noise while it's emulating a scan. Most compare it to a light rain pattering against the marble; for some, it's low volume radio static. As long as they hear the patter, the migrators think they're safe. We reproduce it for them while they're in our marble, even through scanning takes about three seconds and is utterly silent. From my vantage I could see that the sagittal, axial, and coronal windows had stopped blinking, indicating full data capture. Silloin was skirring busily to herself; her comm didn't bother to interpret. Wasn't saying anything baby Michael needed to know, obviously. Her head bobbed as she monitored the enormous spread of readouts; her claws clicked against touch screens that glowed orange and yellow.

At my station, there was only a migration status screen—and a white button.

I wasn't lying when I said I was just the doorman. My field is sapientology, not quantum physics. Whatever went wrong with Kamala's migration that morning, there was nothing *I* could have done. The dinos tell me that the quantum nondemolition sensor array is able to circumvent Heisenberg's Uncertainty Principle by measuring spacetime's most crogglingly small quantities without collapsing the wave/particle duality. How small? They say that no one can ever "see" anything that's only 1.62×10^{-33} centimeters long, because at that size, space and time come apart. Time ceases to exist and space becomes a random probablistic foam, sort of like quantum spit. We humans call this the Planck-Wheeler length. There's a Planck-Wheeler time, too: 10^{-45} of a second. If something happens and something else happens and the two events are separated by an interval of a mere 10^{-45} of a second, it is impossible to say which came first. It was all dino to me—and that's just the scanning. The Hanen use different tech to create artificial wormholes, hold them open with electromagnetic vacuum fluctuations, pass the superluminal signal through and then assemble the migrator from elementary particles at the destination.

On my status screen I could see that the signal which mapped Kamala Shastri had already been compressed and burst through the wormhole. All that we had to wait for was for Gend to confirm acquisition. Once they officially told us that they had her, it would be my job to balance the equation.

Pitter-patter, pitter-pat.

Some Hanen technologies are so powerful that they can alter reality itself. Wormholes could be used by some time traveling fanatic to corrupt history; the scanner/assembler could be used to create a billion Silloins—or Michael Burrs. Pristine reality, unpolluted by such anomalies, has what the dinos call harmony. Before any sapients get to join the galactic club, they must prove total commitment to preserving harmony.

Since I had come to Tuulen to study the dinos, I had pressed the white button over two hundred times. It was what I had to do in order to keep my assignment. Pressing it sent a killing pulse of ionizing radiation through the cerebral cortex of the migrator's duplicated, and therefore unnecessary, body.

No brain, no pain; death followed within seconds. Yes, the first few times I'd balanced the equation had been traumatic. It was still . . . unpleasant. But this was the price of a ticket to the stars. If certain unusual people like Kamala Shastri had decided that price was reasonable, it was their choice, not mine.

= This is not a happy result, Michael. = Silloin spoke to me for the first time since I'd entered the control room. = Discrepancies are unfolding. = On my status screen I watched as the error-checking routines started turning up hits.

"Is the problem here?" I felt a knot twist suddenly inside me. "Or there?" If our original scan checked out, then all Silloin would have to do is send it to Gend again.

There was a long, infuriating silence. Silloin concentrated on part of her board as if it showed her firstborn hatchling chipping out of its egg. The respirator between her shoulders had ballooned to twice its normal size. My screen showed that Kamala had been in the marble for four minutes plus.

= It may be fortunate to recalibrate the scanner and begin over. =

"*Shit.*" I slammed my hand against the wall, felt the pain tingle to my elbow. "I thought you had it fixed." When error-checking turned up problems, the solution was almost always to retransmit. "You're sure, Silloin? Because this one was right on the edge when I tucked her in."

Silloin gave me a dismissive sneeze and slapped at the error readouts with her bony little hand, as if to knock them back to normal. Like Linna and the other dinos, she had little patience with what she regarded as our weepy fears of migration. However, unlike Linna, she was convinced that someday, after we had used Hanen technologies long enough, we would learn to think like dinos. Maybe she's right. Maybe when we've been squirting through wormholes for hundreds of years, we'll cheerfully discard our redundant bodies. When the dinos and other sapients migrate, the redundants zap themselves— very harmonious. They tried it with humans but it didn't always work. That's why I'm here. = The need is most clear. It will prolong about thirty minutes, = she said.

Kamala had been alone in the dark for almost six minutes, longer than any migrator I'd ever guided. "Let me hear what's going on in the marble."

The control room filled with the sound of Kamala screaming. It didn't sound human to me—more like the shriek of tires skidding toward a crash.

"We've got to get her out of there," I said.

= That is baby thinking, Michael. =

"So she's a baby, damn it." I knew that bringing migrators out of the marble was big trouble. I could have asked Silloin to turn the speakers off and sat there while Kamala suffered. It was my decision.

"Don't open the marble until I get the gantry in place." I ran for the door. "And keep the sound effects going."

At the first crack of light, she howled. The upper hemisphere seemed to lift in slow motion; inside the marble she bucked against the nano. Just when I was sure it was impossible that she could scream any louder, she did. We had accomplished something extraordinary, Silloin and I; we had stripped the brave biomaterials engineer away completely, leaving in her place a terrified animal.

"Kamala, it's me. Michael."

Her frantic screams cohered into words. "Stop . . . *don't* . . . oh my god, someone *help*!" If I could have, I would've jumped into the marble to release her, but the sensor array is fragile and I wasn't going to risk causing any more problems with it. We both had to wait until the upper hemisphere swung fully open and the scanning table offered poor Kamala to me.

"It's okay. Nothing's going to happen, all right? We're bringing you out, that's all. Everything's all right."

When I released her with the sparker, she flew at me. We pitched back and almost toppled down the steps. Her grip was so tight I couldn't breathe.

"Don't *kill* me, don't, *please*, don't."

I rolled on top of her. "Kamala!" I wriggled one arm free and used it to pry myself from her. I scrabbled sideways to the top step. She lurched clumsily in the microgravity and swung at me; her fingernails raked across the back of my hand, leaving bloody welts. "Kamala, stop!" It was all I could do not to strike back at her. I retreated down the steps.

"You bastard. What are you assholes trying to do to me?" She drew several shuddering breaths and began to sob.

"The scan got corrupted somehow. Silloin is working on it."

= The difficulty is obscure, = said Silloin from the control room.

"But that's not your problem." I backed toward the bench.

"They lied," she mumbled and seemed to fold in upon herself as if she were just skin, no flesh or bones. "They said I wouldn't feel anything and . . . do you know what it's like . . . it's . . ."

I fumbled for her clingy. "Look, here are your clothes. Why don't you get dressed? We'll get you out of here."

"You bastard," she repeated, but her voice was empty.

She let me coax her down off the gantry. I counted nubs on the wall while she fumbled back into her clingy. They were the size of the old dimes my grandfather used to hoard and they glowed with a soft golden bioluminescence. I was up to forty-seven before she was dressed and ready to return to reception D.

Where before she had perched expectantly at the edge of the couch, now she slumped back against it. "So what now?" she said.

"I don't know." I went to the kitchen station and took the carafe from the distiller. "What now, Silloin?" I poured water over the back of my hand to wash the blood off. It stung. My earstone was silent. "I guess we wait," I said finally.

"For what?"

"For her to fix . . . ."

"I'm not going back in there."

I decided to let that pass. It was probably too soon to argue with her about it, although once Silloin recalibrated the scanner, she'd have very little time to change her mind. "You want something from the kitchen? Another cup of tea, maybe?"

"How about a gin and tonic—hold the tonic?" She rubbed beneath her eyes. "Or a couple of hundred milliliters of serentol?"

I tried to pretend she'd made a joke. "You know the dinos won't let us open the bar for migrators. The scanner might misread your brain chemistry and your visit to Gend would be nothing but a three year drunk."

"Don't you under*stand*?" She was right back at the edge of hysteria. "I am not *going*!" I didn't really blame her for the way she was acting but, at that moment, all I wanted was to get rid of Kamala Shastri. I didn't care if she went on to Gend or back to Lunex or over the rainbow to Oz, just as long as I didn't have to be in the same room with this miserable creature who was trying to make me feel guilty about an accident I had nothing to do with.

"I thought I could do it." She clamped hands to her ears as if to keep from hearing her own despair. "I wasted the last two years convincing myself that I could just lie there and not think and then suddenly I'd be far away. I was going someplace wonderful and strange." She made a strangled sound and let her hands drop into her lap. "I was going to help people see."

"You did it, Kamala. You did everything we asked."

She shook her head. "I couldn't *not* think. That was the problem. And then there she was, trying to touch me. In the dark. I had not thought of her since. . . ." She shivered. "It's your fault for reminding me."

"Your secret friend," I said.

"Friend?" Kamala seemed puzzled by the word. "No, I wouldn't say she was a friend. I was always a little bit scared of her, because I was never quite sure of what she wanted from me." She paused. "One day I went up to 10W after school. She was in her chair, staring down at Bloor Street. Her back was to me. I said, 'Hi, Ms. Ase.' I was going to show her a genie I had written, only she didn't say anything. I came around. Her skin was the color of ashes. I took her hand. It was like picking up something plastic. She was stiff, hard—not a person anymore. She had become a thing, like a feather or a bone. I ran; I had to get out of there. I went up to our apartment and I hid from her.''

She squinted, as if observing—judging—her younger self through the lens of time. ''I think I understand now what she wanted. I think she knew she was dying; she probably wanted me there with her at the end, or at least to find her body afterward and report it. Only I could *not*. If I told anyone she was dead, my parents would find out about us. Maybe people would suspect me of doing something to her—I don't know. I could have called security but I was only ten; I was afraid somehow they might trace me. A couple of weeks went by and still nobody had found her. By then it was too late to say anything. Everyone would have blamed me for keeping quiet for so long. At night I imagined her turning black and rotting into her chair like a banana. It made me sick; I couldn't sleep or eat. They had to put me in the hospital, because I had touched her. Touched *death*.''

= Michael, = Silloin whispered, without any warning flash. = An impossibility has formed. =

''As soon as I was out of that building, I started to get better. Then they found her. After I came home, I worked hard to forget Ms. Ase. And I did, almost.'' Kamala wrapped her arms around herself. ''But just now she was with me again, inside the marble . . . I couldn't see her but somehow I knew she was reaching for me.''

= Michael, Parikkal is here with Linna. =

''Don't you see?'' She gave a bitter laugh. ''How can I go to Gend? I'm *hallucinating*.''

= It has broken the harmony. Join us alone. =

I was tempted to swat at the annoying buzz in my ear.

''You know, I've never told anyone about her before.''

''Well, maybe some good has come of this after all.'' I patted her on the knee. ''Excuse me for a minute?'' She seemed surprised that I would leave. I slipped into the hall and hardened the door bubble, sealing her in.

''What impossibility?'' I said, heading for the control room.

= She is pleased to reopen the scanner? =

''Not pleased at all. More like scared shitless.''

= This is Parikkal. = My earstone translated his skirring with a sizzling edge, like bacon frying. = The confusion was made elsewhere. No mishap can be connected to our station. =

I pushed through the bubble into the scan center. I could see the three dinos through the control window. Their heads were bobbing furiously. ''Tell me,'' I said.

= Our communications with Gend were marred by a transient falsehood, = said Silloin. = Kamala Shastri has been received there and reconstructed. =

"She migrated?" I felt the deck shifting beneath my feet. "What about the one we've got here?"

= The simplicity is to load the redundant into the scanner and finalize. . . . =

"I've got news for you. She's not going anywhere near that marble."

= Her equation is not in balance. = This was Linna, speaking for the first time. Linna was not exactly in charge of Tuulen Station; she was more like a senior partner. Parikkal and Silloin had overruled her before—at least I thought they had.

"What do you expect me to do? Wring her neck?"

There was a moment's silence—which was not as unnerving as watching them eye me through the window, their heads now perfectly still.

"No," I said.

The dinos were skirring at each other; their heads wove and dipped. At first they cut me cold and the comm was silent, but suddenly their debate crackled through my earstone.

= This is just as I have been telling, = said Linna. = These beings have no realization of harmony. It is wrongful to further unleash them on the many worlds. =

= You may have reason, = said Parikkal. = But that is a later discussion. The need is for the equation to be balanced. =

= There is no time. We will have to discard the redundant ourselves. = Silloin bared her long brown teeth. It would take her maybe five seconds to rip Kamala's throat out. And even though Silloin was the dino most sympathetic to us, I had no doubt she would enjoy the kill.

= I will argue that we adjourn human migration until this world has been rethought, = said Linna.

This was the typical dino condescension. Even though they appeared to be arguing with each other, they were actually speaking to me, laying the situation out so that even the baby sapient would understand. They were informing me that I was jeopardizing the future of humanity in space. That the Kamala in reception D was dead whether I quit or not. That the equation had to be balanced and it had to be now.

"Wait," I said. "Maybe I can coax her back into the scanner." I had to get away from them. I pulled my earstone out and slid it into my pocket. I was in such a hurry to escape that I stumbled as I left the scan center and had to catch myself in the hallway. I stood there for a second, staring at the hand pressed against the bulkhead. I seemed to see the splayed fingers through the wrong end of a telescope. I was far away from myself.

She had curled into herself on the couch, arms clutching knees to her chest, as if trying to shrink so that nobody would notice her.

"We're all set," I said briskly. "You'll be in the marble for less than a minute, guaranteed."

"*No*, Michael."

I could actually feel myself receding from Tuulen Station. "Kamala, you're throwing away a huge part of your life."

"It is my right." Her eyes were shiny.

No, it wasn't. She was redundant; she had no rights. What had she said about the dead old lady? She had become a thing, like a bone.

"Okay, then." I jabbed at her shoulder with a stiff forefinger. "Let's go."

She recoiled. "Go where?"

"Back to Lunex. I'm holding the shuttle for you. It just dropped off my afternoon list; I should be helping them settle in, instead of having to deal with you."

She unfolded herself slowly.

"Come on." I jerked her roughly to her feet. "The dinos want you off Tuulen as soon as possible and so do I." I was so distant, I couldn't see Kamala Shastri anymore.

She nodded and let me march her to the bubble door.

"And if we meet anyone in the hall, keep your mouth shut."

"You're being so mean." Her whisper was thick.

"You're being such a baby."

When the inner door glided open, she realized immediately that there was no umbilical to the shuttle. She tried to twist out of my grip but I put my shoulder into her, hard. She flew across the airlock, slammed against the outer door and caromed onto her back. As I punched the switch to close the door, I came back to myself. *I* was doing this terrible thing— me, Michael Burr. I couldn't help myself: I giggled. When I last saw her, Kamala was scrabbling across the deck toward me but she was too late. I was surprised that she wasn't screaming again; all I heard was her ferocious breathing.

As soon as the inner door sealed, I opened the outer door. After all, how many ways are there to kill someone on a space station? There were no guns. Maybe someone else could have stabbed or strangled her, but not me. Poison how? Besides, I wasn't thinking, I had been trying desperately not to think of what I was doing. I was a sapientologist, not a doctor. I always thought that exposure to space meant instantaneous death. Explosive decompression or something like. I didn't want her to suffer. I was trying to make it quick. Painless.

I heard the whoosh of escaping air and thought that was it; the body had been ejected into space. I had actually turned away when thumping started, frantic, like the beat of a racing heart. She must have found something to hold onto. *Thump, thump, thump!* It was too much. I sagged against the inner door—*thump, thump*—slid down it, laughing. Turns out that if you empty the lungs, it is possible to survive exposure to space for at least a minute, maybe two. I thought it was funny. *Thump!* Hilarious, actually. I had tried my best for her—risked my career—and this was how she repaid me? As I laid my cheek against the door, the *thumps* started to weaken. There were just a few centimeters between us, the difference between life and death. Now she knew all about balancing the equation. I was laughing so hard I could scarcely breathe. Just like the meat behind the door. Die already, you weepy bitch!

I don't know how long it took. The *thumping* slowed. Stopped. And then I was a hero. I had preserved harmony, kept our link to the stars open. I chuckled with pride; I could think like a dinosaur.

I popped through the bubble door into Reception D. "It's time to board the shuttle."

Kamala had changed into a clingy and velcro slippers. There were at least ten windows open on the wall; the room filled with the murmur of talking heads. Friends and relatives had to be notified; their loved one had returned, safe and sound. "I have to go," she said to the wall. "I will call you when I land."

She gave me a smile that seemed stiff from disuse. "I want to thank you again, Michael." I wondered how long it took migrators to get used to being human. "You were such a help and I was such a . . . I was not myself." She glanced around the room one last time and then shivered. "I was really scared."

"You were."

She shook her head. "Was it that bad?"

I shrugged and led her out into the hall.

"I feel so silly now. I mean, I was in the marble for less than a minute and then—" she snapped her fingers—"there I was on Gend, just like you said." She brushed up against me as we walked; her body was hard under the clingy. "Anyway, I am glad we got this chance to talk. I really *was* going to look you up when I got back. I certainly did not expect to see you here."

"I decided to stay on." The inner door to the airlock glided open. "It's a job that grows on you." The umbilical shivered as the pressure between Tuulen Station and the shuttle equalized.

"You have got migrators waiting," she said.

"Two."

"I envy them." She turned to me. "Have *you* ever thought about going to the stars?"

"No," I said.

Kamala put her hand to my face. "It changes everything." I could feel the prick of her long nails—claws, really. For a moment I thought she meant to scar my cheek the way she had been scarred.

"I know," I said.

COMING OF AGE IN KARHIDE

Sov Thade Tage em Ereb, of Rer, in Karhide, on Gethen (Ursula K. Le Guin)

▼

Here's another brilliant Hainish story by Ursula K. Le Guin, whose novella "A Woman's Liberation" appears elsewhere in this anthology. In this one, she returns to the setting of her most famous novel, *The Left Hand of Darkness*, for a poignant and evocative story of the transition to adulthood—which is always a difficult passage, no matter what sex you are . . . and which is perhaps even a little more difficult if you have the potential to be either.

I live in the oldest city in the world. Long before there were kings in Karhide, Rer was a city, the marketplace and meeting ground for all the Northeast, the Plains, and Kerm Land. The Fastness of Rer was a center of learning, a refuge, a judgment seat fifteen thousand years ago. Karhide became a nation here, under the Geger kings, who ruled for a thousand years. In the thousandth year Sedern Geger, the Unking, cast the crown into the River Arre from the palace towers, proclaiming an end to dominion. The time they call the Flowering of Rer, the Summer Century, began then. It ended when the Hearth of Harge took power and moved their capital across the mountains to Erhenrang. The Old Palace has been empty for centuries. But it stands. Nothing in Rer falls down. The Arre floods through the street-tunnels every year in the Thaw, winter blizzards may bring thirty feet of snow, but the city stands. Nobody knows how old the houses are, because they have been rebuilt forever. Each one sits in its gardens without respect to the position of any of the others, as vast and random and ancient as hills. The roofed streets and canals angle about among them. Rer is all corners. We say that the Harges left because they were afraid of what might be around the corner.

Time is different here. I learned in school how the Orgota, the Ekumen, and most other people count years. They call the year of some portentous event Year One and number forward from it. Here it's always Year One. On Getheny Thern, New Year's Day, the Year One becomes one-ago, one-to-come becomes One, and so on. It's like Rer, everything always changing but the city never changing.

When I was fourteen (in the Year One, or fifty-ago) I came of age. I have been thinking about that a good deal recently.

It was a different world. Most of us had never seen an Alien, as we called them then. We might have heard the Mobile talk on the radio, and at school we saw pictures of Aliens—the ones with hair around their mouths were the most pleasingly savage and repulsive. Most of the pictures were disappointing. They looked too much like us. You couldn't even tell that they were always in kemmer. The female Aliens were supposed to have enormous breasts, but my Mothersib Dory had bigger breasts than the ones in the pictures.

When the Defenders of the Faith kicked them out of Orgoreyn, when King Emran got into the Border War and lost Erhenrang, even when their Mobiles were outlawed and forced into hiding at Estre in Kerm, the Ekumen did nothing much but wait. They had waited for two hundred years, as patient as Handdara. They did one thing: they took our young king off-world to foil a plot, and then brought the same king back sixty years later to end her wombchild's disastrous reign. Argaven XVII is the only king who ever ruled four years before her heir and forty years after.

The year I was born (the Year One, or sixty-four-ago) was the year Argaven's second reign began. By the time I was noticing anything beyond my own toes, the war was over, the West Fall was part of Karhide again, the capital was back in Erhenrang, and most of the damage done to Rer during the Overthrow of Emran had been repaired. The old houses had been rebuilt again. The Old Palace had been patched again. Argaven XVII was miraculously back on the throne again. Everything was the way it used to be, ought to be, back to normal, just like the old days—everybody said so.

Indeed those were quiet years, an interval of recovery before Argaven, the first Gethenian who ever left our planet, brought us at last fully into the Ekumen; before we, not they, became the Aliens; before we came of age. When I was a child we lived the way people had lived in Rer forever. It is that way, that timeless world, that world around the corner, I have been thinking about, and trying to describe for people who never knew it. Yet as I write I see how also nothing changes, that it is truly the Year One always, for each child that comes of age, each lover who falls in love.

There were a couple of thousand people in the Ereb Hearths, and a hundred and forty of them lived in my Hearth, Ereb Tage. My name is Sov Thade Tage em Ereb, after the old way of naming we still use in Rer. The first thing I remember is a huge dark place full of shouting and shadows, and I am falling upward through a golden light into the darkness. In thrilling terror, I scream. I am caught in my fall, held, held close; I weep; a voice so close to

me that it seems to speak through my body says softly, "Sov, Sov, Sov."
And then I am given something wonderful to eat, something so sweet, so
delicate that never again will I eat anything quite so good. . . .

I imagine that some of my wild elder hearthsibs had been throwing me
about, and that my mother comforted me with a bit of festival cake. Later
on when I was a wild elder sib we used to play catch with babies for balls;
they always screamed, with terror or with delight, or both. It's the nearest
to flying anyone of my generation knew. We had dozens of different words
for the way snow falls, floats, descends, glides, blows, for the way clouds
move, the way ice floats, the way boats sail; but not that word. Not yet. And
so I don't remember "flying." I remember falling upward through the golden
light.

Family houses in Rer are built around a big central hall. Each story has an
inner balcony clear round that space, and we call the whole story, rooms and
all, a balcony. My family occupied the whole second balcony of Ereb Tage.
There were a lot of us. My grandmother had borne four children, and all of
them had children, so I had a bunch of cousins as well as a younger and an
older wombsib. "The Thades always kemmer as women and always get
pregnant," I heard neighbors say, variously envious, disapproving, admiring.
"And they never keep kemmer," somebody would add. The former was an
exaggeration, but the latter was true. Not one of us kids had a father. I didn't
know for years who my getter was, and never gave it a thought. Clannish,
the Thades preferred not to bring outsiders, even other members of our own
Hearth, into the family. If young people fell in love and started talking
about keeping kemmer or making vows, Grandmother and the mothers were
ruthless. "Vowing kemmer, what do you think you are, some kind of noble?
some kind of fancy person? The kemmerhouse was good enough for me and
it's good enough for you," the mothers said to their lovelorn children, and
sent them away, clear off to the old Ereb Domain in the country, to hoe
braties till they got over being in love.

So as a child I was a member of a flock, a school, a swarm, in and out of
our warren of rooms, tearing up and down the staircases, working together
and learning together and looking after the babies—in our own fashion—and
terrorizing quieter hearthmates by our numbers and our noise. As far as I
know we did no real harm. Our escapades were well within the rules and
limits of the sedate, ancient Hearth, which we felt not as constraints but as
protection, the walls that kept us safe. The only time we got punished was
when my cousin Sether decided it would be exciting if we tied a long rope
we'd found to the second-floor balcony railing, tied a big knot in the rope,
held onto the knot, and jumped. "I'll go first," Sether said. Another mis-

guided attempt at flight. The railing and Sether's broken leg were mended, and the rest of us had to clean the privies, all the privies of the Hearth, for a month. I think the rest of the Hearth had decided it was time the young Thades observed some discipline.

Although I really don't know what I was like as a child, I think that if I'd had any choice I might have been less noisy than my playmates, though just as unruly. I used to love to listen to the radio, and while the rest of them were racketing around the balconies or the centerhall in winter, or out in the streets and gardens in summer, I would crouch for hours in my mother's room behind the bed, playing her old serem-wood radio very softly so that my sibs wouldn't know I was there. I listened to anything, Lays and plays and hearthtales, the Palace news, the analyses of grain harvests and the detailed weather reports; I listened every day all one winter to an ancient saga from the Pering Storm-Border about snowghouls, perfidious traitors, and bloody ax-murders, which haunted me at night so that I couldn't sleep and would crawl into bed with my mother for comfort. Often my younger sib was already there in the warm, soft, breathing dark. We would sleep all entangled and curled up together like a nest of pesthry.

My mother, Guyr Thade Tage em Ereb, was impatient, warm-hearted, and impartial, not exerting much control over us three wombchildren, but keeping watch. The Thades were all tradespeople working in Ereb shops and masteries, with little or no cash to spend; but when I was ten, Guyr bought me a radio, a new one, and said where my sibs could hear, "You don't have to share it." I treasured it for years and finally shared it with my own wombchild.

So the years went along and I went along in the warmth and density and certainty of a family and a Hearth embedded in tradition, threads on the quick ever-repeating shuttle weaving the timeless web of custom and act and work and relationship, and at this distance I can hardly tell one year from the other or myself from the other children: until I turned fourteen.

The reason most people in my Hearth would remember that year is for the big party known as Dory's Somer-Forever Celebration. My Mothersib Dory had stopped going into kemmer that winter. Some people didn't do anything when they stopped going into kemmer; others went to the Fastness for a ritual; some stayed on at the Fastness for months after, or even moved there. Dory, who wasn't spiritually inclined, said, "If I can't have kids and can't have sex anymore and have to get old and die, at least I can have a party."

I have already had some trouble trying to tell this story in a language that has no somer pronouns, only gendered pronouns. In their last years of kemmer, as the hormone balance changes, many people tend to go into kemmer as men; Dory's kemmers had been male for over a year, so I'll call Dory "he," although of course the point was that he would never be either he or she again.

In any event, his party was tremendous. He invited everyone in our Hearth and the two neighboring Ereb Hearths, and it went on for three days. It had been a long winter and the spring was late and cold; people were ready for something new, something hot to happen. We cooked for a week, and a whole storeroom was packed full of beer kegs. A lot of people who were in the middle of going out of kemmer, or had already and hadn't done anything about it, came and joined in the ritual. That's what I remember vividly: in the firelit three-story centerhall of our Hearth, a circle of thirty or forty people, all middle-aged or old, singing and dancing, stamping the drumbeats. There was a fierce energy in them, their gray hair was loose and wild, they stamped as if their feet would go through the floor, their voices were deep and strong, they were laughing. The younger people watching them seemed pallid and shadowy. I looked at the dancers and wondered, why are they happy? Aren't they old? Why do they act like they'd got free? What's it like, then, kemmer?

No, I hadn't thought much about kemmer before. What would be the use? Until we come of age we have no gender and no sexuality, our hormones don't give us any trouble at all. And in a city Hearth we never see adults in kemmer. They kiss and go. Where's Maba? In the kemmerhouse, love, now eat your porridge. When's Maba coming back? Soon, love. And in a couple of days Maba comes back, looking sleepy and shiny and refreshed and exhausted. Is it like having a bath, Maba? Yes, a bit, love, and what have you been up to while I was away?

Of course we played kemmer, when we were seven or eight. This here's the kemmerhouse and I get to be the woman. No, I do. No, I do, I thought of it! And we rubbed our bodies together and rolled around laughing, and then maybe we stuffed a ball under our shirt and were pregnant, and then we gave birth, and then we played catch with the ball. Children will play whatever adults do; but the kemmer game wasn't much of a game. It often ended in a tickling match. And most children aren't even very ticklish, till they come of age.

After Dory's party, I was on duty in the Hearth crèche all through Tuwa, the last month of spring; come summer I began my first apprenticeship, in a furniture workshop in the Third Ward. I loved getting up early and running across the city on the wayroofs and up on the curbs of the open ways; after the late Thaw some of the ways were still full of water, deep enough for kayaks and poleboats. The air would be still and cold and clear; the sun would come up behind the old towers of the Unpalace, red as blood, and all the waters and the windows of the city would flash scarlet and gold. In the workshop there was the piercing sweet smell of fresh-cut wood and the company of grown people, hardworking, patient, and demanding, taking me seriously. I wasn't a child anymore, I said to myself. I was an adult, a working person.

But why did I want to cry all the time? Why did I want to sleep all the time? Why did I get angry at Sether? Why did Sether keep bumping into me and saying "Oh sorry" in that stupid husky voice? Why was I so clumsy with the big electric lathe that I ruined six chair-legs one after the other? "Get that kid off the lathe," shouted old Marth, and I slunk away in a fury of humiliation. I would never be a carpenter, I would never be adult, who gave a shit for chair-legs anyway?

"I want to work in the gardens," I told my mother and grandmother.

"Finish your training and you can work in the gardens next summer," Grand said, and Mother nodded. This sensible counsel appeared to me as a heartless injustice, a failure of love, a condemnation to despair. I sulked. I raged.

"What's wrong with the furniture shop?" my elders asked after several days of sulk and rage.

"Why does stupid Sether have to be there!" I shouted. Dory, who was Sether's mother, raised an eyebrow and smiled.

"Are you all right?" my mother asked me as I slouched into the balcony after work, and I snarled, "I'm fine," and rushed to the privies and vomited.

I was sick. My back ached all the time. My head ached and got dizzy and heavy. Something I could not locate anywhere, some part of my soul, hurt with a keen, desolate, ceaseless pain. I was afraid of myself: of my tears, my rage, my sickness, my clumsy body. It did not feel like my body, like me. It felt like something else, an ill-fitting garment, a smelly, heavy overcoat that belonged to some old person, some dead person. It wasn't mine, it wasn't me. Tiny needles of agony shot through my nipples, hot as fire. When I winced and held my arms across my chest, I knew that everybody could see what was happening. Anybody could smell me. I smelled sour, strong, like blood, like raw pelts of animals. My clitopenis was swollen hugely and stuck out from between my labia, and then shrank nearly to nothing, so that it hurt to piss. My labia itched and reddened as with loathsome insect-bites. Deep in my belly something moved, some monstrous growth. I was utterly ashamed. I was dying.

"Sov," my mother said, sitting down beside me on my bed, with a curious, tender, complicitous smile, "shall we choose your kemmerday?"

"I'm not in kemmer," I said passionately.

"No," Guyr said. "But next month I think you will be."

"I *won't!*"

My mother stroked my hair and face and arm. *We shape each other to be human*, old people used to say as they stroked babies or children or one another with those long, slow, soft caresses.

After a while my mother said, "Sether's coming in, too. But a month or so later than you, I think. Dory said let's have a double kemmerday, but I think you should have your own day in your own time."

I burst into tears and cried, "I don't want one, I don't want to, I just want, I just want to go away. . . ."

"Sov," my mother said, "if you want to, you can go to the kemmerhouse at Gerodda Ereb, where you won't know anybody. But I think it would be better here, where people do know you. They'd like it. They'll be so glad for you. Oh, your Grand's so proud of you! 'Have you seen that grandchild of mine, Sov, have you seen what a beauty, what a *mahad!*' Everybody's bored to tears hearing about you. . . ."

Mahad is a dialect word, a Rer word; it means a strong, handsome, generous, upright person, a reliable person. My mother's stern mother, who commanded and thanked, but never praised, said I was a mahad? A terrifying idea, that dried my tears.

"All right," I said desperately, "here. But not next month! It isn't. I'm not."

"Let me see," my mother said. Fiercely embarrassed yet relieved to obey, I stood up and undid my trousers.

My mother took a very brief and delicate look, hugged me, and said, "Next month, yes, I'm sure. You'll feel much better in a day or two. And next month it'll be different. It really will."

Sure enough, the next day the headache and the hot itching were gone, and though I was still tired and sleepy a lot of the time, I wasn't quite so stupid and clumsy at work. After a few more days I felt pretty much myself, light and easy in my limbs. Only if I thought about it there was still that queer feeling that wasn't quite in any part of my body, and that was sometimes very painful and sometimes only strange, almost something I wanted to feel again.

My cousin Sether and I had been apprenticed together at the furniture shop. We didn't go to work together because Sether was still slightly lame from that rope trick a couple of years earlier, and got a lift to work in a poleboat so long as there was water in the streets. When they closed the Arre Watergate and the ways went dry, Sether had to walk. So we walked together. The first couple of days we didn't talk much. I still felt angry at Sether. Because I couldn't run through the dawn anymore but had to walk at a lame-leg pace. And because Sether was always around. Always there. Taller than me, and quicker at the lathe, and with that long, heavy, shining hair. Why did anybody want to wear their hair so long, anyhow? I felt as if Sether's hair was in front of my own eyes.

We were walking home, tired, on a hot evening of Ockre, the first month of summer. I could see that Sether was limping and trying to hide or ignore it, trying to swing right along at my quick pace, very straight-backed, scowling. A great wave of pity and admiration overwhelmed me, and that thing, that growth, that new being, whatever it was in my bowels and in the ground of my soul moved and turned again, turned towards Sether, aching, yearning.

"Are you coming into kemmer?" I said in a hoarse, husky voice I had never heard come out of my mouth.

"In a couple of months," Sether said in a mumble, not looking at me, still very stiff and frowning.

"I guess I have to have this, do this, you know, this stuff, pretty soon."

"I wish I could," Sether said. "Get it over with."

We did not look at each other. Very gradually, unnoticeably, I was slowing my pace till we were going along side by side at an easy walk.

"Sometimes do you feel like your tits are on fire?" I asked without knowing that I was going to say anything.

Sether nodded.

After a while, Sether said, "Listen, does your pisser get. . . ."

I nodded.

"It must be what the Aliens look like," Sether said with revulsion. "This, this thing sticking out, it gets so *big* . . . it gets in the way."

We exchanged and compared symptoms for a mile or so. It was a relief to talk about it, to find company in misery, but it was also frightening to hear our misery confirmed by the other. Sether burst out, "I'll tell you what I hate, what I really *hate* about it—it's dehumanizing. To get jerked around like that by your own body, to lose control, I can't stand the idea. Of being just a sex machine. And everybody just turns into something to have sex with. You know that people in kemmer go crazy and *die* if there isn't anybody else in kemmer? That they'll even attack people in somer? Their own mothers?"

"They can't," I said, shocked.

"Yes they can. Tharry told me. This truck driver up in the High Kargav went into kemmer as a male while their caravan was struck in the snow, and he was big and strong, and he went crazy and he, he did it to his cab-mate, and his cab-mate was in somer and got hurt, really hurt, trying to fight him off. And then the driver came out of kemmer and committed suicide.''

This horrible story brought the sickness back up from the pit of my stomach, and I could say nothing.

Sether went on, ''People in kemmer aren't even human anymore! And we have to do that—to be that way!''

Now that awful, desolate fear was out in the open. But it was not a relief to speak it. It was even larger and more terrible, spoken.

''It's stupid,'' Sether said. ''It's a primitive device for continuing the species. There's no need for civilized people to undergo it. People who want to get pregnant could do it with injections. It would be genetically sound. You could choose your child's getter. There wouldn't be all this inbreeding, people fucking with their sibs, like animals. Why do we have to be animals?''

Sether's rage stirred me. I shared it. I also felt shocked and excited by the word ''fucking,'' which I had never heard spoken. I looked again at my cousin, the thin, ruddy face, the heavy, long, shining hair. My age, Sether looked older. A half year in pain from a shattered leg had darkened and matured the adventurous, mischievous child, teaching anger, pride, endurance. ''Sether,'' I said, ''listen, it doesn't matter, you're human, even if you have to do that stuff, that fucking. You're a mahad.''

''Getheny Kus,'' Grand said: the first day of the month of Kus, midsummer day.

''I won't be ready,'' I said.

''You'll be ready.''

''I want to go into kemmer with Sether.''

''Sether's got a month or two yet to go. Soon enough. It looks like you might be on the same moontime, though. Dark-of-the-mooners, eh? That's what I used to be. So, just stay on the same wavelength, you and Sether. . . .'' Grand had never grinned at me this way, an inclusive grin, as if I were an equal.

My mother's mother was sixty years old, short, brawny, broad-hipped, with keen clear eyes, a stonemason by trade, an unquestioned autocrat in the Hearth. I, equal to this formidable person? It was my first intimation that I might be becoming more, rather than less, human.

''I'd like it,'' said Grand, ''if you spent this halfmonth at the Fastness. But it's up to you.''

''At the Fastness?'' I said, taken by surprise. We Thades were all Handdara, but very inert Handdara, keeping only the great festivals, muttering the grace all in one garbled word, practicing none of the disciplines. None of my older hearthsibs had been sent off to the Fastness before their kemmerday. Was there something wrong with me?

"You've got a good brain," said Grand. "You and Sether. I'd like to see some of you lot casting some shadows, some day. We Thades sit here in our Hearth and breed like pesthry. Is that enough? It'd be a good thing if some of you got your heads out of the bedding."

"What do they do in the Fastness?" I asked, and Grand answered frankly, "I don't know. Go find out. They teach you. They can teach you how to control kemmer."

"All right," I said promptly. I would tell Sether that the Indwellers could control kemmer. Maybe I could learn how to do it and come home and teach it to Sether.

Grand looked at me with approval. I had taken up the challenge.

Of course I didn't learn how to control kemmer, in a halfmonth in the Fastness. The first couple of days there, I thought I wouldn't even be able to control my homesickness. From our warm, dark warren of rooms full of people talking, sleeping, eating, cooking, washing, playing remma, playing music, kids running around, noise, family, I went across the city to a huge, clean, cold, quiet house of strangers. They were courteous, they treated me with respect. I was terrified. Why should a person of forty, who knew magic disciplines of superhuman strength and fortitude, who could walk barefoot through blizzards, who could Foretell, whose eyes were the wisest and calmest I had ever seen, why should an Adept of the Handdara respect me?

"Because you are so ignorant," Ranharrer the Adept said, smiling, with great tenderness.

Having me only for a halfmonth, they didn't try to influence the nature of my ignorance very much. I practiced the Untrance several hours a day, and came to like it: that was quite enough for them, and they praised me. "At fourteen, most people go crazy moving slowly," my teacher said.

During my last six or seven days in the Fastness certain symptoms began to show up again, the headache, the swellings and shooting pains, the irritability. One morning the sheet of my cot in my bare, peaceful little room was bloodstained. I looked at the smear with horror and loathing. I thought I had scratched my itching labia to bleeding in my sleep, but I knew also what the blood was. I began to cry. I had to wash the sheet somehow. I had fouled, defiled this place where everything was clean, austere, and beautiful.

An old Indweller, finding me scrubbing desperately at the sheet in the washrooms, said nothing, but brought me some soap that bleached away the stain. I went back to my room, which I had come to love with the passion of one who had never before known any actual privacy, and crouched on the sheetless bed, miserable, checking every few minutes to be sure I was not bleeding again. I missed my Untrance practice time. The immense house was very quiet. Its peace sank into me. Again I felt that strangeness in my soul, but it was not pain now; it was a desolation like the air at evening, like the peaks of the Kargav seen far in the west in the clarity of winter. It was an immense enlargement.

Ranharrer the Adept knocked and entered at my word, looked at me for a minute, and asked gently, "What is it?"

"Everything is strange," I said.

The Adept smiled radiantly and said, "Yes."

I know now how Ranharrer cherished and honored my ignorance, in the Handdara sense. Then I knew only that somehow or other I had said the right thing and so pleased a person I wanted very much to please.

"We're doing some singing," Ranharrer said, "you might like to hear it."

They were in fact singing the Midsummer Chant, which goes on for the four days before Getheny Kus, night and day. Singers and drummers drop in and out at will, most of them singing on certain syllables in an endless group improvisation guided only by the drums and by melodic cues in the Chantbook, and falling into harmony with the soloist if one is present. At first I heard only a pleasantly thick-textured, droning sound over a quiet and subtle beat. I listened till I got bored and decided I could do it too. So I opened my mouth and sang "Aah" and heard all the other voices singing "Aah" above and with and below mine until I lost mine and heard only all the voices, and then only the music itself, and then suddenly the startling silvery rush of a single voice running across the weaving, against the current, and sinking into it and vanishing, and rising out of it again. . . . Ranharrer touched my arm. It was time for dinner, I had been singing since Third Hour. I went back to the chantry after dinner, and after supper. I spent the next three days there. I would have spent the nights there if they had let me. I wasn't sleepy at all anymore. I had sudden, endless energy, and couldn't sleep. In my little room I sang to myself, or read the strange Handdara poetry which was the only book they had given me, and practiced the Untrance, trying to ignore the heat and cold, the fire and ice in my body, till dawn came and I could go sing again.

And then it was Ottormenbod, midsummer's eve, and I must go home to my Hearth and the kemmerhouse.

To my surprise, my mother and grandmother and all the elders came to the Fastness to fetch me, wearing ceremonial hiebs and looking solemn. Ranharrer handed me over to them, saying to me only, "Come back to us." My family paraded me through the streets in the hot summer morning; all the vines were in flower, perfuming the air, all the gardens were blooming, bearing, fruiting. "This is an excellent time," Grand said judiciously, "to come into kemmer."

The Hearth looked very dark to me after the Fastness, and somehow shrunken. I looked around for Sether, but it was a workday, Sether was at the shop. That gave me a sense of holiday, which was not unpleasant. And then up in the hearthroom of our balcony, Grand and the Hearth elders formally presented me with a whole set of new clothes, new everything, from the boots up, topped by a magnificently embroidered hieb. There was a spoken ritual that went with the clothes, not Handdara, I think, but a tradition of our Hearth; the words were all old and strange, the language of a thousand years ago. Grand rattled them out like somebody spitting rocks, and put the hieb on my shoulders. Everybody said, "Haya!"

All the elders, and a lot of younger kids, hung around helping me put on the new clothes as if I was a king or a baby, and some of the elders wanted to give me advice—"last advice," they called it, since you gain shifgrethor when you go into kemmer, and once you have shifgrethor advice is insulting. "Now you just keep away from that old Ebbeche," one of them told me shrilly. My mother took offense, snapping, "Keep your shadow to yourself, Tadsh!" And to me, "Don't listen to the old fish. Flapmouth Tadsh! But now listen, Sov."

I listened. Guyr had drawn me a little away from the others, and spoke gravely, with some embarrassment. "Remember, it will matter who you're with first."

I nodded. "I understand," I said.

"No, you don't," my mother snapped, forgetting to be embarrassed. "Just keep it in mind!"

"What, ah," I said. My mother waited. "If I, if I go into, as a, as female," I said. "Don't I, shouldn't I—?"

"Ah," Guyr said. "Don't worry. It'll be a year or more before you can conceive. Or get. Don't worry, this time. The other people will see to it, just in case. They all know it's your first kemmer. But do keep it in mind, who you're with first! Around, oh, around Karrid, and Ebbeche, and some of them."

"Come on!" Dory shouted, and we all got into a procession again to go downstairs and across the centerhall, where everybody cheered "Haya Sov! Haya Sov!" and the cooks beat on their saucepans. I wanted to die. But they all seemed so cheerful, so happy about me, wishing me well; I wanted also to live.

We went out the west door and across the sunny gardens and came to the kemmerhouse. Tage Ereb shares a kemmerhouse with two other Ereb Hearths; it's a beautiful building, all carved with deep-figure friezes in the Old Dynasty style, terribly worn by the weather of a couple of thousand years. On the red stone steps my family all kissed me, murmuring, "Praise then Darkness," or "In the act of creation praise," and my mother gave me a hard push on

my shoulders, what they call the sledge-push, for good luck, as I turned away
from them and went in the door.

The doorkeeper was waiting for me; a queer-looking, rather stooped person,
with coarse, pale skin.

Now I realized who this "Ebbeche" they'd been talking about was. I'd
never met him, but I'd heard about him. He was the Doorkeeper of our
kemmerhouse, a halfdead—that is, a person in permanent kemmer, like the
Aliens.

There are always a few people born that way here. Some of them can be
cured; those who can't or choose not to be usually live in a Fastness and
learn the disciplines, or they become Doorkeepers. It's convenient for them,
and for normal people too. After all, who else would want to *live* in a
kemmerhouse? But there are drawbacks. If you come to the kemmerhouse in
thorharmen, ready to gender, and the first person you meet is fully male, his
pheromones are likely to gender you female right then, whether that's what
you had in mind this month or not. Responsible Doorkeepers, of course, keep
well away from anybody who doesn't invite them to come close. But permanent kemmer may not lead to responsibility of character; nor does being called
halfdead and *pervert* all your life, I imagine. Obviously my family didn't
trust Ebbeche to keep his hands and his pheromones off me. But they were
unjust. He honored a first kemmer as much as anyone else. He greeted me
by name and showed me where to take off my new boots. Then he began to
speak the ancient ritual welcome, backing down the hall before me; the first
time I ever heard the words I would hear so many times again for so many
years.

> *You cross earth now.*
> *You cross water now.*
> *You cross the Ice now. . . .*

And the exulting ending, as we came into the centerhall:

> *Together we have crossed the Ice.*
> *Together we come into the Hearthplace,*
> *Into life, bringing life!*
> *In the act of creation, praise!*

The solemnity of the words moved me and distracted me somewhat from
my intense self-consciousness. As I had in the Fastness, I felt the familiar
reassurance of being part of something immensely older and larger than
myself, even if it was strange and new to me. I must entrust myself to it and
be what it made me. At the same time I was intensely alert. All my senses

were extraordinarily keen, as they had been all morning. I was aware of everything, the beautiful blue color of the walls, the lightness and vigor of my steps as I walked, the texture of the wood under my bare feet, the sound and meaning of the ritual words, the Doorkeeper himself. He fascinated me. Ebbeche was certainly not handsome, and yet I noticed how musical his rather deep voice was; and pale skin was more attractive than I had ever thought it. I felt that he had been maligned, that his life must be a strange one. I wanted to talk to him. But as he finished the welcome, standing aside for me at the doorway of the centerhall, a tall person strode forward eagerly to meet me.

I was glad to see a familiar face: it was the head cook of my Hearth, Karrid Arrage. Like many cooks a rather fierce and temperamental person, Karrid had often taken notice of me, singling me out in a joking, challenging way, tossing me some delicacy—"Here, youngun! get some meat on your bones!" As I saw Karrid now I went through the most extraordinary multiplicity of awarenesses: that Karrid was naked and that this nakedness was not like the nakedness of people in the Hearth, but a significant nakedness—that he was not the Karrid I had seen before but transfigured into great beauty—that he was *he*—that my mother had warned me about him—that I wanted to touch him—that I was afraid of him.

He picked me right up in his arms and pressed me against him. I felt his clitopenis like a fist between my legs. "Easy, now," the Doorkeeper said to him, and some other people came forward from the room, which I could see only as large, dimly glowing, full of shadows and mist.

"Don't worry, don't worry," Karrid said to me and them, with his hard laugh. "I won't hurt my own get, will I? I just want to be the one that gives her kemmer. As a woman, like a proper Thade. I want to give you that joy, little Sov." He was undressing me as he spoke, slipping off my hieb and shirt with big, hot, hasty hands. The Doorkeeper and the others kept close watch, but did not interfere. I felt totally defenseless, helpless, humiliated. I struggled to get free, broke loose, and tried to pick up and put on my shirt. I was shaking and felt terribly weak, I could hardly stand up. Karrid helped me clumsily; his big arm supported me. I leaned against him, feeling his hot, vibrant skin against mine, a wonderful feeling, like sunlight, like firelight. I leaned more heavily against him, raising my arms so that our sides slid together. "Hey, now," he said. "Oh, you beauty, oh, you Sov, here, take her away, this won't do!" And he backed right away from me, laughing and yet really alarmed, his clitopenis standing up amazingly. I stood there half-dressed, on my rubbery legs, bewildered. My eyes were full of mist, I could see nothing clearly.

"Come on," somebody said, and took my hand, a soft, cool touch totally different from the fire of Karrid's skin. It was a person from one of the other Hearths, I didn't know her name. She seemed to me to shine like gold in the dim, misty place. "Oh, you're going so fast," she said, laughing and admiring and consoling. "Come on, come into the pool, take it easy for a while. Karrid shouldn't have come on to you like that! But you're lucky, first kemmer as a woman, there's nothing like it. I kemmered as a man three times before I got to kemmer as a woman, it made me so mad, every time I got into thorharmen all my damn friends would all be women already. Don't worry about me—I'd say Karrid's influence was decisive," and she laughed again. "Oh, you are so pretty!" and she bent her head and licked my nipples before I knew what she was doing.

It was wonderful, it cooled that stinging fire in them that nothing else could cool. She helped me finish undressing, and we stepped together into the warm water of the big, shallow pool that filled the whole center of this room. That was why it was so misty, why the echoes were so strange. The water lapped on my thighs, on my sex, on my belly. I turned to my friend and leaned forward to kiss her. It was a perfectly natural thing to do, it was what she wanted and I wanted, and I wanted her to lick and suck my nipples again, and she did. For a long time we lay in the shallow water playing, and I could have played forever. But then somebody else joined us, taking hold of my friend from behind, and she arched her body in the water like a golden fish leaping, threw her head back, and began to play with him.

I got out of the water and dried myself, feeling sad and shy and forsaken, and yet extremely interested in what had happened to my body. It felt wonderfully alive and electric, so that the roughness of the towel made me shiver with pleasure. Somebody had come closer to me, somebody that had been watching me play with my friend in the water. He sat down by me now.

It was a hearthmate a few years older than I, Arrad Tehemmy. I had worked in the gardens with Arrad all last summer, and liked him. He looked like Sether, I now thought, with heavy black hair and a long, thin face, but in him was that shining, that glory they all had here—all the kemmerers, the *women*, the *men*—such vivid beauty as I had never seen in any human beings. "Sov," he said, "I'd like—Your first—Will you—" His hands were already on me, and mine on him. "Come," he said, and I went with him. He took me into a beautiful little room, in which there was nothing but a fire burning in a fireplace, and a wide bed. There Arrad took me into his arms and I took Arrad into my arms, and then between my legs, and fell upward, upward through the golden light.

Arrad and I were together all that first night, and besides fucking a great deal, we ate a great deal. It had not occurred to me that there would be food at a kemmerhouse, I had thought you weren't allowed to do anything but fuck. There was a lot of food, very good, too, set out so that you could eat whenever you wanted. Drink was more limited; the person in charge, an old woman-halfdead, kept her canny eye on you, and wouldn't give you any more beer if you showed signs of getting wild or stupid. I didn't need any more beer. I didn't need any more fucking. I was complete. I was in love forever for all time all my life to eternity with Arrad. But Arrad (who was a day farther into kemmer than I) fell asleep and wouldn't wake up, and an extraordinary person named Hama sat down by me and began talking and also running his hand up and down my back in the most delicious way, so that before long we got further entangled, and began fucking, and it was entirely different with Hama than it had been with Arrad, so that I realized that I must be in love with Hama, until Gehardar joined us. After that I think I began to understand that I loved them all and they all loved me and that that was the secret of the kemmerhouse.

It's been nearly fifty years, and I have to admit I do not recall everyone from my first kemmer; only Karrid and Arrad, Hama and Gehardar, old Tubanny, the most exquisitely skillful lover as a male that I ever knew—I met him often in later kemmers—and Berre, my golden fish, with whom I ended up in drowsy, peaceful, blissful lovemaking in front of the great hearth till we both fell asleep. And when we woke we were not women. We were not men. We were not in kemmer. We were very tired young adults.

"You're still beautiful," I said to Berre.

"So are you," Berre said. "Where do you work?"

"Furniture shop, Third Ward."

I tried licking Berre's nipple, but it didn't work; Berre flinched a little, and I said "Sorry," and we both laughed.

"I'm in the radio trade," Berre said. "Did you ever think of trying that?"

"Making radios?"

"No. Broadcasting. I do the Fourth Hour news and weather."

"That's you?" I said, awed.

"Come over to the tower sometime, I'll show you around," said Berre.

Which is how I found my lifelong trade and a lifelong friend. As I tried to tell Sether when I came back to the Hearth, kemmer isn't exactly what we thought it was; it's much more complicated.

Sether's first kemmer was on Getheny Gor, the first day of the first month of autumn, at the dark of the moon. One of the family brought Sether into kemmer as a woman, and then Sether brought me in. That was the first time I kemmered as a man. And we stayed on the same wavelength, as Grand put it. We never conceived together, being cousins and having some modern scruples, but we made love in every combination, every dark of the moon, for years. And Sether brought my child, Tamor, into first kemmer—as a woman, like a proper Thade.

Later on Sether went into the Handdara, and became an Indweller in the old Fastness, and now is an Adept. I go over there often to join in one of the Chants or practice the Untrance or just to visit, and every few days Sether comes back to the Hearth. And we talk. The old days or the new times, somer or kemmer, love is love.

GENESIS

Poul Anderson

▼

One of the best-known and most prolific writers in science fiction, Poul Anderson made his first sale in 1947, and in the course of his subsequent forty-nine-year career has published almost a hundred books (in several different fields, as Anderson has written historical novels, fantasies, and mysteries, in addition to SF), sold hundreds of short pieces to every conceivable market, and won seven Hugo Awards, three Nebula Awards, and the Tolkien Memorial Award for life achievement. Among his many books are *The High Crusade*, *The Enemy Stars*, *Three Hearts and Three Lions*, *The Broken Sword*, *Tau Zero*, *The Night Face*, *Orion Shall Rise*, *The Shield of Time*, *The Time Patrol*, and *The People of the Wind*, as well as the two multivolume series of novels about his two most popular characters, Dominic Flandry and Nicholas van Rijn. His short work has been collected in *The Queen of Air and Darkness and Other Stories*, *Guardians of Time*, *The Earth Book of Stormgate*, *Fantasy*, *The Unicorn Trade* (with Karen Anderson), *Past Times*, *Time Patrolman*, and *Explorations*. Among his most recent books are the novels *The Boat of a Million Years*, *Harvest of Stars*, and *The Stars Are Also Fire*. His story "Vulcan's Forge" was in our First Annual Collection. Anderson lives in Orinda, California, with his wife (and fellow writer), Karen.

In the powerful, complex, and lyrical novella that follows, Anderson demonstrates all of his considerable strengths, and delivers a jolt of that much-talked-about Sense of Wonder that's as pure and concentrated, and as mind-boggling, as anything you're going to find anywhere in the genre this year.

Was it her I ought to have loved . . . ?

—Piet Hein

1

No human could have shaped the thoughts or uttered them. They had no real beginning, they had been latent for millennium after millennium while the galactic brain was growing. Sometimes they passed from mind to mind, years or decades through space at the speed of light, nanoseconds to receive, comprehend, consider, and send a message on outward. But there was so much else—a cosmos of realities, an infinity of virtualities and abstract creations—that remembrances of Earth were the barest undertone, intermittent and fleeting, among uncounted billions of other incidentals. Most of the grand awareness was directed elsewhere, much of it intent on its own evolution.

For the galactic brain was still in infancy: unless it held itself to be still a-borning. By now its members were strewn from end to end of the spiral arms, out into the halo and the nearer star-gatherings, as far as the Magellanic Clouds. The seeds of fresh ones drifted farther yet; some had reached the shores of the Andromeda.

Each was a local complex of organisms, machines, and their interrelationships. ("Organism" seems best for something that maintains itself, reproduces at need, and possesses a consciousness in a range from the rudimentary to the transcendent, even though carbon compounds are a very small part of its material components and most of its life processes take place directly on the quantum level.) They numbered in the many millions, and the number was rising steeply, also within the Milky Way, as the founders of new generations arrived at new homes.

Thus the galactic brain was in perpetual growth, which from a cosmic viewpoint had barely started. Thought had just had time for a thousand or two journeys across its ever-expanding breadth. It would never absorb its members into itself; they would always remain individuals, developing along their individual lines. Let us therefore call them not cells, but nodes.

For they were in truth distinct. Each had more uniquenesses than were ever possible to a protoplasmic creature. Chaos and quantum fluctuation assured that none would exactly resemble any predecessor. Environment likewise helped shape the personality—surface conditions (what kind of planet, moon, asteroid, comet?) or free orbit, sun single or multiple (what kinds, what ages?), nebula, interstellar space and its ghostly tides. . . . Then, too, a node was not a single mind. It was as many as it chose to be, freely awakened and freely set aside, proteanly intermingling and separating again, using whatever bodies and sensors it wished for as long as it wished, immortally experiencing, creating, meditating, seeking a fulfillment that the search itself brought forth.

Hence, while every node was engaged with a myriad of matters, one might be especially developing new realms of mathematics, another composing glorious works that cannot really be likened to music, another observing the destiny of organic life on some world, life which it had perhaps fabricated for that purpose, another—Human words are useless.

Always, though, the nodes were in continuous communication over the light-years, communication on tremendous bandwidths of every possible medium. *This* was the galactic brain. That unity, that selfhood which was slowly coalescing, might spend millions of years contemplating a thought; but the thought would be as vast as the thinker, in whose sight an eon was as a day and a day was as an eon.

Already now, in its nascence, it affected the course of the universe. The time came when a node fully recalled Earth. That memory went out to others as part of the ongoing flow of information, ideas, feelings, reveries, and who knows what else? Certain of these others decided the subject was worth pursuing, and relayed it on their own message-streams. In this wise it passed through light-years and centuries, circulated, developed, and at last became a decision, which reached the node best able to take action.

Here the event has been related in words, ill-suited though they are to the task. They fail totally when they come to what happened next. How shall they tell of the dialogue of a mind with itself, when that thinking was a progression of quantum flickerings through configurations as intricate as the wave functions, when the computational power and database were so huge that measures become meaningless, when the mind raised aspects of itself to interact like persons until it drew them back into its wholeness, and when everything was said within microseconds of planetary time?

It is impossible, except vaguely and misleadingly. Ancient humans used the language of myth for that which they could not fathom. The sun was a fiery chariot daily crossing heaven, the year a god who died and was reborn, death a punishment for ancestral sin. Let us make our myth concerning the mission to Earth.

Think, then, of the primary aspect of the node's primary consciousness as if it were a single mighty entity, and name it Alpha. Think of a lesser manifestation of itself that it had synthesized and intended to release into separate existence as a second entity. For reasons that will become clear, imagine the latter masculine and name it Wayfarer.

All is myth and metaphor, beginning with this absurd nomenclature. Beings like these had no names. They had identities, instantly recognizable by others of their kind. They did not speak together, they did not go through discussion or explanation of any sort, they were not yet "they." But imagine it.

Imagine, too, their surroundings, not as perceived by their manifold sensors or conceptualized by their awarenesses and emotions, but as if human sense organs were reporting to a human brain. Such a picture is scarcely a sketch. Too much that was basic could not have registered. However, a human at an astronomical distance could have seen an M2 dwarf star about fifty parsecs from Sol, and ascertained that it had planets. She could have detected signs of immense, enigmatic energies, and wondered.

In itself, the sun was undistinguished. The galaxy held billions like it. Long ago, an artificial intelligence—at that dawn stage of evolution, this was the best phrase—had established itself there because one of the planets bore curious life-forms worth studying. That research went on through the mega-years. Meanwhile the ever-heightening intelligence followed more and more different interests: above all, its self-evolution. That the sun would stay cool for an enormous length of time had been another consideration. The node did not want the trouble of coping with great environmental changes before it absolutely must.

Since then, stars had changed their relative positions. This now was the settlement nearest to Sol. Suns closer still were of less interest and had merely been visited, if that. Occasionally a free-space, dirigible node had passed through the neighborhood, but none chanced to be there at this epoch.

Relevant to our myth is the fact that no thinking species ever appeared on the viviferous world. Life is statistically uncommon in the cosmos, sapience almost vanishingly rare, therefore doubly precious.

Our imaginary human would have seen the sun as autumnally yellow, burning low and peacefully. Besides its planets and lesser natural attendants, various titanic structures orbited about it. From afar, they seemed like gossamer or like intricate spiderwebs agleam athwart the stars; most of what they were was force fields. They gathered and focused the energies that Alpha required, they searched the deeps of space and the atom, they transmitted and received the thought-flow that was becoming the galactic brain; what more they did lies beyond the myth.

Within their complexity, although not at any specific location, lived Alpha, its apex. Likewise, for the moment, did Wayfarer.

Imagine a stately voice: "Welcome into being. Yours is a high and, it may be, dangerous errand. Are you willing?"

If Wayfarer hesitated an instant, that was not from fear of suffering harm but from fear of inflicting it. "Tell me. Help me to understand."

"Sol—" The sun of old Earth, steadily heating since first it took shape, would continue stable for billions of years before it exhausted the hydrogen fuel at its core and swelled into a red giant. But—

A swift computation. "Yes. I see." Above a threshold level of radiation input, the geochemical and biochemical cycles that had maintained the temperature of Earth would be overwhelmed. Increasing warmth put increasing amounts of water vapor into the atmosphere, and it is a potent greenhouse gas. Heavier cloud cover, raising the albedo, could only postpone a day of catastrophe. Rising above it, water molecules were split by hard sunlight into hydrogen, which escaped to space, and oxygen, which bound to surface materials. Raging fires released monstrous tonnages of carbon dioxide, as did rocks exposed to heat by erosion in desiccated lands. It is the second major greenhouse gas. The time must come when the last oceans boiled away, leaving a globe akin to Venus; but well before then, life on Earth would be no more than a memory in the quantum consciousnesses. "When will total extinction occur?"

"On the order of a hundred thousand years futureward."

Pain bit through the facet of Wayfarer that came from Christian Brannock, who was born on ancient Earth and most passionately loved his living world. Long since had his uploaded mind merged into a colossal oneness that later divided and redivided, until copies of it were integral with awareness across the galaxy. So were the minds of millions of his fellow humans, as unnoticed now as single genes had been in their bodies when their flesh was alive, and yet significant elements of the whole. Ransacking its database, Alpha had found the record of Christian Brannock and chosen to weave him into the essence of Wayfarer, rather than someone else. The judgement was—call it intuitive.

"Can't you say more closely?" he appealed.

"No," replied Alpha. "The uncertainties and imponderables are too many. Gaia," mythic name for the node in the Solar System, "has responded to inquiries evasively when at all."

"Have . . . we . . . really been this slow to think about Earth?"

"We had much else to think about and do, did we not? Gaia could at any time have requested special consideration. She never did. Thus the matter did not appear to be of major importance. Human Earth is preserved in memory. What is posthuman Earth but a planet approaching the postbiological phase?

"True, the scarcity of spontaneously evolved biomes makes the case interesting. However, Gaia has presumably been observing and gathering the data, for the rest of us to examine whenever we wish. The Solar System has seldom had visitors. The last was two million years ago. Since then, Gaia has joined less and less in our fellowship; her communications have grown sparse and perfunctory. But such withdrawals are not unknown. A node may, for example, want to pursue a philosophical concept undisturbed, until it is ready for general contemplation. In short, nothing called Earth to our attention."

"*I* would have remembered," whispered Christian Brannock.

"What finally reminded us?" asked Wayfarer.

"The idea that Earth may be worth saving. Perhaps it holds more than Gaia knows of—" A pause. "—or has told of. If nothing else, sentimental value."

"Yes, I understand," said Christian Brannock.

"Moreover, and potentially more consequential, we may well have experience to gain, a precedent to set. If awareness is to survive the mortality of the stars, it must make the universe over. That work of billions or trillions of years will begin with some small, experimental undertaking. Shall it be now," the "now" of deathless beings already geologically old, "at Earth?"

"Not small," murmured Wayfarer. Christian Brannock had been an engineer.

"No," agreed Alpha. "Given the time constraint, only the resources of a few stars will be available. Nevertheless, we have various possibilities open to us, if we commence soon enough. The question is which would be the best—and, first, whether we *should* act.

"Will you go seek an answer?"

"Yes," responded Wayfarer, and "Yes, oh, God damn, yes," cried Christian Brannock.

A spaceship departed for Sol. A laser accelerated it close to the speed of light, energized by the sun and controlled by a network of interplanetary dimensions. If necessary, the ship could decelerate itself at journey's end, travel freely about, and return unaided, albeit more slowly. Its cryomagnetics supported a good-sized ball of antimatter, and its total mass was slight. The material payload amounted simply to: a matrix, plus backup, for running the Wayfarer programs and containing a database deemed sufficient; assorted sensors and effectors; several bodies of different capabilities, into which he could download an essence of himself; miscellaneous equipment and power systems; a variety of instruments; and a thing ages forgotten, which Wayfarer had ordered molecules to make at the wish of Christian Brannock. He might somewhere find time and fingers for it.

A guitar.

2

There was a man called Kalava, a sea captain of Sirsu. His clan was the Samayoki. In youth he had fought well at Broken Mountain, where the armies of Ulonai met the barbarian invaders swarming north out of the desert and cast them back with fearsome losses. He then became a mariner. When the Ulonaian League fell apart and the alliances led by Sirsu and Irrulen raged across the land, year after year, seeking each other's throats, Kalava sank enemy ships, burned enemy villages, bore treasure and captives off to market.

After the grudgingly made, unsatisfactory Peace of Tuopai, he went into trade. Besides going up and down the River Lonna and around the Gulf of Sirsu, he often sailed along the North Coast, bartering as he went, then out over the Windroad Sea to the colonies on the Ending Islands. At last, with three ships, he followed that coast east through distances hitherto unknown. Living off the waters and what hunting parties could take ashore, dealing or fighting with the wild tribes they met, in the course of months he and his crews came to where the land bent south. A ways beyond that they found a port belonging to the fabled people of the Shining Fields. They abode for a year and returned carrying wares that at home made them rich.

From his clan Kalava got leasehold of a thorp and good farmland in the Lonna delta, about a day's travel from Sirsu. He meant to settle down, honored and comfortable. But that was not in the thought of the gods nor in his nature. He was soon quarreling with all his neighbors, until his wife's brother grossly insulted him and he killed the man. Thereupon she left him. At the clanmoot which composed the matter she received a third of the family wealth, in gold and movables. Their daughters and the husbands of these sided with her.

Of Kalava's three sons, the eldest had drowned in a storm at sea; the next died of the Black Blood; the third, faring as an apprentice on a merchant vessel far south to Zhir, fell while resisting robbers in sand-drifted streets under the time-gnawed colonnades of an abandoned city. They left no children, unless by slaves. Nor would Kalava, now; no free woman took his offers of marriage. What he had gathered through a hard lifetime would fall to kinfolk who hated him. Most folk in Sirsu shunned him too.

Long he brooded, until a dream hatched. When he knew it for what it was, he set about his preparations, more quietly than might have been awaited. Once the business was under way, though not too far along for him to drop if he must, he sought Ilyandi the skythinker.

She dwelt on Council Heights. There did the Vilkui meet each year for rites and conference. But when the rest of them had dispersed again to carry on their vocation—dream interpreters, scribes, physicians, mediators, vessels of olden lore and learning, teachers of the young—Ilyandi remained. Here she could best search the heavens and seek for the meaning of what she found, on a high place sacred to all Ulonai.

Up the Spirit Way rumbled Kalava's chariot. Near the top, the trees that lined it, goldfruit and plume, stood well apart, giving him a clear view. Bushes grew sparse and low on the stony slopes, here the dusty green of vasi, there a shaggy hairleaf, yonder a scarlet fireflower. Scorchwort lent its acrid smell to a wind blowing hot and slow off the Gulf. That water shone, tarnished metal, westward beyond sight, under a silver-gray overcast beneath which scudded rags of darker cloud. A rainstorm stood on the horizon, blurred murk and flutters of lightning light.

Elsewhere reached the land, bloomgrain ripening yellow, dun paperleaf, verdant pastures for herdlings, violet richen orchards, tall stands of shipwood. Farmhouses and their outbuildings lay widely strewn. The weather having been dry of late, dust whirled up from the roads winding among them to veil wagons and trains of porters. Regally from its sources eastward in Wilderland flowed the Lonna, arms fanning out north and south.

Sirsu lifted battlemented walls on the right bank of the main stream, tiny in Kalava's eyes at its distance. Yet he knew it, he could pick out famous works, the Grand Fountain in King's Newmarket, the frieze-bordered portico of the Flame Temple, the triumphal column in Victory Square, and he knew where the wrights had their workshops, the merchants their bazaars, the innkeepers their houses for a seaman to find a jug and a wench. Brick, sandstone, granite, marble mingled their colors softly together. Ships and boats plied the water or were docked under the walls. On the opposite shore sprawled mansions and gardens of the Helki suburb, their rooftiles fanciful as jewels.

It was remote from that which he approached.

Below a great arch, two postulants in blue robes slanted their staffs across the way and called, "In the name of the Mystery, stop, make reverence, and declare yourself!"

Their young voices rang high, unawed by a sight that had daunted warriors. Kalava was a big man, wide-shouldered and thick-muscled. Weather had darkened his skin to the hue of coal and bleached nearly white the hair that fell in braids halfway down his back. As black were the eyes that gleamed below a shelf of brow, in a face rugged, battered, and scarred. His mustache curved down past the jaw, dyed red. Traveling in peace, he wore simply a knee-length kirtle, green and trimmed with kivi skin, each scale polished, and buskins; but gold coiled around his arms and a sword was belted at his hip. Likewise did a spear stand socketed in the chariot, pennon flapping, while a shield slatted at the rail and an ax hung ready to be thrown. Four matched slaves drew the car. Their line had been bred for generations to be draft creatures—huge, long-legged, spirited, yet trustworthy after the males were gelded. Sweat sheened over Kalava's brand on the small, bald heads and ran down naked bodies. Nonetheless they breathed easily and the smell of them was rather sweet.

Their owner roared, "Halt!" For a moment only the wind had sound or motion. Then Kalava touched his brow below the headband and recited the Confession: "What a man knows is little, what he understands is less, therefore let him bow down to wisdom." Himself, he trusted more in blood sacrifices and still more in his own strength; but he kept a decent respect for the Vilkui.

"I seek counsel from the skythinker Ilyandi," he said. That was hardly needful, when no other initiate of her order was present.

"All may seek who are not attainted of ill-doing," replied the senior boy as ceremoniously.

"Ruvio bear witness that any judgments against me stand satisfied." The Thunderer was the favorite god of most mariners.

"Enter, then, and we shall convey your request to our lady."

The junior boy led Kalava across the outer court. Wheels rattled loud on flagstones. At the guesthouse, he helped stall, feed, and water the slaves, before he showed the newcomer to a room that in the high season slept two-score men. Elsewhere in the building were a bath, a refectory, ready food—dried meat, fruit, and flatbread—with richenberry wine. Kalava also found a book. After refreshment, he sat down on a bench to pass the time with it.

He was disappointed. He had never had many chances or much desire to read, so his skill was limited; and the copyist for this codex had used a style of lettering obsolete nowadays. Worse, the text was a chronicle of the emperors of Zhir. That was not just painful to him—oh, Eneio, his son, his last son!—but valueless. True, the Vilkui taught that civilization had come to Ulonai from Zhir. What of it? How many centuries had fled since the desert claimed that realm? What were the descendants of its dwellers but starveling nomads and pestiferous bandits?

Well, Kalava thought, yes, this could be a timely warning, a reminder to people of how the desert still marched northward. But was what they could see not enough? He had passed by towns not very far south, flourishing in his grandfather's time, now empty, crumbling houses half buried in dust, glassless windows like the eye sockets in a skull.

His mouth tightened. *He* would not meekly abide any doom.

Day was near an end when an acolyte of Ilyandi came to say that she would receive him. Walking with his guide, he saw purple dusk shade toward night in the east. In the west the storm had ended, leaving that part of heaven clear for a while. The sun was plainly visible, though mists turned it into a red-orange step pyramid. From the horizon it cast a bridge of fire over the Gulf and sent great streamers of light aloft into cloudbanks that glowed sulfurous. A whistlewing passed like a shadow across them. The sound of its flight keened faintly down through air growing less hot. Otherwise a holy silence rested upon the heights.

Three stories tall, the sanctuaries, libraries, laboratories, and quarters of the Vilkui surrounded the inner court with their cloisters. A garden of flowers and healing herbs, intricately laid out, filled most of it. A lantern had been lighted in one arcade, but all windows were dark and Ilyandi stood out in the open awaiting her visitor.

She made a slight gesture of dismissal. The acolyte bowed her head and slipped away. Kalava saluted, feeling suddenly awkward but his resolution headlong within him. "Greeting, wise and gracious lady," he said.

"Well met, brave captain," the skythinker replied. She gestured at a pair of confronting stone benches. "Shall we be seated?" It fell short of inviting him to share wine, but it meant she would at least hear him out.

They lowered themselves and regarded one another through the swiftly deepening twilight. Ilyandi was a slender woman of perhaps forty years, features thin and regular, eyes large and luminous brown, complexion pale—like smoked copper, he thought. Cropped short in token of celibacy, wavy hair made a bronze coif above a plain white robe. A green sprig of tekin, held at her left shoulder by a pin in the emblematic form of interlocked circle and triangle, declared her a Vilku.

"How can I aid your venture?" she asked.

He started in surprise. "Huh! What do you know about my plans?" In haste: "My lady knows much, of course."

She smiled. "You and your saga have loomed throughout these past decades. And . . . word reaches us here. You search out your former crewmen or bid them come see you, all privately. You order repairs made to the ship remaining in your possession. You meet with chandlers, no doubt to sound them out about prices. Few if any people have noticed. Such discretion is not your wont. Where are you bound, Kalava, and why so secretly?"

His grin was rueful. "My lady's not just wise and learned, she's clever. Well, then, why not go straight to the business? I've a voyage in mind that most would call crazy. Some among them might try to forestall me, holding that it would anger the gods of those parts—seeing that nobody's ever returned from there, and recalling old tales of monstrous things glimpsed from afar. I don't believe them myself, or I wouldn't try it."

"Oh, I can imagine you setting forth regardless," said Ilyandi half under her breath. Louder: "But agreed, the fear is likely false. No one had reached the Shining Fields by sea, either, before you did. You asked for no beforehand spells or blessings then. Why have you sought me now?"

"This is, is different. Not hugging a shoreline. I—well, I'll need to get and train a new huukin, and that's no small thing in money or time." Kalava spread his big hands, almost helplessly. "I had not looked to set forth ever again, you see. Maybe it is madness, an old man with an old crew in a single old ship. I hoped you might counsel me, my lady."

"You're scarcely ready for the balefire, when you propose to cross the Windroad Sea," she answered.

This time he was not altogether taken aback. "May I ask how my lady knows?"

Ilyandi waved a hand. Catching faint lamplight, the long fingers soared through the dusk like nightswoopers. "You have already been east, and would not need to hide such a journey. South, the trade routes are ancient as far as Zhir. What has it to offer but the plunder of tombs and dead cities, brought in by wretched squatters? What lies beyond but unpeopled desolation until, folk say, one would come to the Burning Lands and perish miserably? Westward we know of a few islands, and then empty ocean. If anything lies on the far side, you could starve and thirst to death before you reached it. But northward—yes, wild waters, but sometimes men come upon driftwood of unknown trees or spy storm-borne flyers of unknown breed—and we have all the legends of the High North, and glimpses of mountains from ships blown off course—'' Her voice trailed away.

"Some of those tales ring true to me," Kalava said. "More true than stories about uncanny sights. Besides, wild huukini breed offshore, where fish are plentiful. I have not seen enough of them there, in season, to account for as many as I've seen in open sea. They must have a second shoreline. Where but the High North?"

Ilyandi nodded. "Shrewd, Captain. What else do you hope to find?"

He grinned again. "I'll tell you after I get back, my lady."

Her tone sharpened. "No treasure-laden cities to plunder."

He yielded. "Nor to trade with. Would we not have encountered craft of theirs, or, anyhow, wreckage? However . . . the farther north, the less heat and the more rainfall, no? A country yonder could have a mild clime, forestfuls of timber, fat land for plowing, and nobody to fight." The words throbbed. "No desert creeping in? Room to begin afresh, my lady."

She regarded him steadily through the gloaming. "You'd come home, recruit people, found a colony, and be its king?"

"Its foremost man, aye, though I expect the kind of folk who'd go will want a republic. But mainly—" His voice went low. He stared beyond her. "Freedom. Honor. A freeborn wife and new sons."

They were silent awhile. Full night closed in. It was not as murky as usual, for the clearing in the west had spread rifts up toward the zenith. A breath of coolness soughed in leaves, as if Kalava's dream whispered a promise.

"You are determined," she said at last, slowly. "Why have you come to me?"

"For whatever counsel you will give, my lady. Facts about the passage may be hoarded in books here."

She shook her head. "I doubt it. Unless navigation—yes, that is a real barrier, is it not?"

"Always," he sighed.

"What means of wayfinding have you?"

"Why, you must know."

"I know what is the common knowledge about it. Craftsmen keep their trade secrets, and surely skippers are no different in that regard. If you will tell me how you navigate, it shall not pass these lips, and I may be able to add something."

Eagerness took hold of him. "I'll wager my lady can! We see moon or stars unoften and fitfully. Most days the sun shows no more than a blur of dull light amongst the clouds, if that. But you, skythinkers like you, they've watched and measured for hundreds of years, they've gathered lore—" Kalava paused. "Is it too sacred to share?"

"No, no," she replied. "The Vilkui keep the calendar for everyone, do they not? The reason that sailors rarely get our help is that they could make little or no use of our learning. Speak."

"True, it was Vilkui who discovered lodestones. . . . Well, coasting these waters, I rely mainly on my remembrance of landmarks, or a periplus if they're less familiar to me. Soundings help, especially if the plumb brings up a sample of the bottom for me to look at and taste. Then in the Shining Fields I got a crystal—you must know about it, for I gave another to the order when I got back—I look through it at the sky and, if the weather be not too thick, I see more closely where the sun is than I can with a bare eye. A logline and hourglass give some idea of speed, a lodestone some idea of direction, when out of sight of land. Sailing for the High North and return, I'd mainly use it, I suppose. But if my lady could tell me of anything else—"

She sat forward on her bench. He heard a certain intensity. "I think I might, Captain. I've studied that sunstone of yours. With it, one can estimate latitude and time of day, if one knows the date and the sun's heavenly course during the year. Likewise, even glimpses of moon and stars would be valuable to a traveler who knew them well."

"That's not me," he said wryly. "Could my lady write something down? Maybe this old head won't be too heavy to puzzle it out."

She did not seem to hear. Her gaze had gone upward. "The aspect of the stars in the High North," she murmured. "It could tell us whether the world is indeed round. And are our vague auroral shimmers more bright yonder—in the veritable Lodeland—?"

His look followed hers. Three stars twinkled wan where the clouds were torn. "It's good of you, my lady," he said, "that you sit talking with me, when you could be at your quadrant or whatever, snatching this chance."

Her eyes met his. "Yours may be a better chance, Captain," she answered fiercely. "When first I got the rumor of your expedition, I began to think upon it and what it could mean. Yes, I will help you where I can. I may even sail with you."

The *Gray Courser* departed Sirsu on a morning tide as early as there was light to steer by. Just the same, people crowded the dock. The majority watched mute. A number made signs against evil. A few, mostly young, sang a defiant paean, but the air seemed to muffle their strains.

Only lately had Kalava given out what his goal was. He must, to account for the skythinker's presence, which could not be kept hidden. That sanctification left the authorities no excuse to forbid his venture. However, it took little doubt and fear off those who believed the outer Windroad a haunt of monsters and demons, which might be stirred to plague home waters.

His crew shrugged the notion off, or laughed at it. At any rate, they said they did. Two-thirds of them were crusty shellbacks who had fared under his command before. For the rest, he had had to take what he could scrape together, impoverished laborers and masterless ruffians. All were, though, very respectful of the Vilku.

The *Gray Courser* was a yalka, broad-beamed and shallow-bottomed, with a low forecastle and poop and a deckhouse amidships. The foremast carried two square sails, the mainmast one square and one fore-and-aft; a short bowsprit extended for a jib. A catapult was mounted in the bows. On either side, two boats hung from davits, aft of the harnessing shafts. Her hull was painted according to her name, with red trim. Alongside swam the huukin, its back a sleek blue ridge.

Kalava had the tiller until she cleared the river mouth and stood out into the Gulf. By then it was full day. A hot wind whipped gray-green water into whitecaps that set the vessel rolling. It whined in the shrouds; timbers creaked. He turned the helm over to a sailor, trod forward on the poop deck, and sounded a trumpet. Men stared. From her cabin below, Ilyandi climbed up to stand beside him. Her white robe fluttered like wings that would fain be asoar. She raised her arms and chanted a spell for the voyage:

> *"Burning, turning,*
> *The sun-wheel reels*
> *Behind the blindness*
> *Cloud-smoke evokes.*
> *The old cold moon*
> *Seldom tells*
> *Where it lairs*
> *With stars afar.*
> *No men's omens*
> *Abide to guide*
> *High in the skies.*
> *But lodestone for Lodeland*
> *Strongly longs."*

While the deckhands hardly knew what she meant, they felt heartened.

Land dwindled aft, became a thin blue line, vanished into waves and mists. Kalava was cutting straight northwest across the Gulf. He meant to sail through the night, and thus wanted plenty of sea room. Also, he and Ilyandi would practice with her ideas about navigation. Hence after a while the mariners spied no other sails, and the loneliness began to weigh on them.

However, they worked stoutly enough. Some thought it a good sign, and cheered, when the clouds clove toward evening and they saw a horned moon.

Their mates were frightened; was the moon supposed to appear by day? Kalava bullied them out of it.

Wind stiffened during the dark. By morning it had raised seas in which the ship reeled. It was a westerly, too, forcing her toward land no matter how close-hauled. When he spied, through scud, the crags of Cape Vairka, the skipper realized he could not round it unaided.

He was a rough man, but he had been raised in those skills that were seemly for a freeman of Clan Samayoki. Though not a poet, he could make an acceptable verse when occasion demanded. He stood in the forepeak and shouted into the storm, the words flung back to his men:

> *"Northward now veering,*
> *Steering from kin-rift,*
> *Spindrift flung gale-borne,*
> *Sail-borne is daft.*
> *Craft will soon flounder,*
> *Founder, go under—*
> *Thunder this wit-lack!*
> *Sit back and call*
> *All that swim near.*
> *Steer then to northward."*

Having thus offered the gods a making, he put the horn to his mouth and blasted forth a summons to his huukin.

The great beast heard and slipped close. Kalava took the lead in lowering the shafts. A line around his waist for safety, he sprang over the rail, down onto the broad back. He kept his feet, though the two men who followed him went off into the billows and had to be hauled up. Together they rode the huukin, guiding it between the poles where they could attach the harness.

"I waited too long," Kalava admitted. "This would have been easier yesterday. Well, something for you to brag about in the inns at home, nay?" Their mates drew them back aboard. Meanwhile the sails had been furled. Kalava took first watch at the reins. Mightily pulled the huukin, tail and flippers churning foam that the wind snatched away, on into the open, unknown sea.

3

Wayfarer woke.

He had passed the decades of transit shut down. A being such as Alpha would have spent them conscious, its mind perhaps at work on an intellectual artistic creation—to it, no basic distinction—or perhaps replaying an existent piece for contemplation-enjoyment or perhaps in activity too abstract for words to hint at. Wayfarer's capabilities, though large, were insufficient for that. The hardware and software (again we use myth) of his embodiment were designed principally for interaction with the material universe. In effect, there was nothing for him to do.

He could not even engage in discourse. The robotic systems of the ship were subtle and powerful but lacked true consciousness; it was unnecessary for them, and distraction or boredom might have posed a hazard. Nor could he converse with entities elsewhere; signals would have taken too long going to and fro. He did spend a while, whole minutes of external time, reliving the life of his Christian Brannock element, studying the personality, accustoming himself to its ways. Thereafter he . . . went to sleep.

The ship reactivated him as it crossed what remained of the Oort Cloud. Instantly aware, he coupled to instrument after instrument and scanned the Solar System. Although his database summarized Gaia's reports, he deemed it wise to observe for himself. The eagerness, the bittersweet sense of home-coming, that flickered around his calm logic were Christian Brannock's. Imagine long-forgotten feelings coming astir in you when you return to a scene of your early childhood.

Naturally, the ghost in the machine knew that changes had been enormous since his mortal eyes closed forever. The rings of Saturn were tattered and tenuous. Jupiter had gained a showy set of them from the death of a satellite, but its Red Spot faded away ages ago. Mars was moonless, its axis steeply canted. . . . Higher resolution would have shown scant traces of humanity. From the antimatter plants inside the orbit of Mercury to the comet harvesters beyond Pluto, what was no more needed had been dismantled or left forsaken. Wind, water, chemistry, tectonics, cosmic stones, spalling radiation, nuclear decay, quantum shifts had patiently reclaimed the relics for chaos. Some fossils existed yet, and some eroded fragments aboveground or in space; otherwise all was only in Gaia's memory.

No matter. It was toward his old home that the Christian Brannock facet of Wayfarer sped.

Unaided, he would not have seen much difference from aforetime in the sun. It was slightly larger and noticeably brighter. Human vision would have perceived the light as more white, with the faintest bluish quality. Unprotected skin would have reacted quickly to the increased ultraviolet. The solar wind was stronger, too. But thus far the changes were comparatively minor. This star was still on the main sequence. Planets with greenhouse atmospheres were most affected. Certain minerals on Venus were now molten. Earth—

The ship hurtled inward, reached its goal, and danced into parking orbit. At close range, Wayfarer looked forth.

On Luna, the patterns of maria were not quite the same, mountains were worn down farther, and newer craters had wrecked or obliterated older ones. Rubble-filled anomalies showed where ground had collapsed on deserted cities. Essentially, though, the moon was again the same desolation, seared by day and death-cold by night, as before life's presence. It had receded farther, astronomically no big distance, and this had lengthened Earth's rotation period by about an hour. However, as yet it circled near enough to stabilize that spin.

The mother planet offered less to our imaginary eyes. Clouds wrapped it in dazzling white. Watching carefully, you could have seen swirls and bandings, but to a quick glance the cover was well-nigh featureless. Shifting breaks in it gave blue flashes of water, brown flashes of land—nowhere ice or snowfall, nowhere lights after dark; and the radio spectrum seethed voiceless.

When did the last human foot tread this world? Wayfarer searched his database. The information was not there. Perhaps it was unrecorded, unknown. Perhaps that last flesh had chanced to die alone or chosen to die privately.

Certainly it was long and long ago. How brief had been the span of Homo sapiens, from flint and fire to machine intelligence! Not that the end had come suddenly or simply. It took several millennia, said the database: time for whole civilizations to rise and fall and leave their mutant descendants. Sometimes population decline had reversed in this or that locality, sometimes nations heeded the vatic utterances of prophets and strove to turn history backward—for a while, a while. But always the trend was ineluctable.

The clustered memories of Christian Brannock gave rise to a thought in Wayfarer that was as if the man spoke: I saw the beginning. I did not foresee the end. To me this was the magnificent dawn of hope.

And was I wrong?

The organic individual is mortal. It can find no way to stave off eventual disintegration; quantum chemistry forbids. Besides, if a man could live for a mere thousand years, the data storage capacity of his brain would be saturated, incapable of holding more. Well before then, he would have been overwhelmed by the geometric increase of correlations, made feebleminded or insane. Nor could he survive the rigors of star travel at any reasonable speed or unearthly environments, in a universe never meant for him.

But transferred into a suitable inorganic structure, the pattern of neuron and molecular traces and their relationships that is his inner self becomes potentially immortal. The very complexity that allows this makes him continue feeling as well as thinking. If the quality of emotions is changed, it is because his physical organism has become stronger, more sensitive, more intelligent and aware. He will soon lose any wistfulness about his former existence. His new life gives him so much more, a cosmos of sensing and experience, memory and thought, space and time. He can multiply himself, merge and unmerge with others, grow in spirit until he reaches a limit once inconceivable;

and after that he can become a part of a mind greater still, and thus grow onward.

The wonder was, Christian Brannock mused, that any humans whatsoever had held out, clung to the primitive, refused to see that their heritage was no longer of DNA but of psyche.

And yet—

The half-formed question faded away. His half-formed personhood rejoined Wayfarer. Gaia was calling from Earth.

She had, of course, received notification, which arrived several years in advance of the spacecraft. Her manifold instruments, on the planet and out between planets, had detected the approach. For the message she now sent, she chose to employ a modulated neutrino beam. Imagine her saying: "Welcome. Do you need help? I am ready to give any I can." Imagine this in a voice low and warm.

Imagine Wayfarer replying, "Thank you, but all's well. I'll be down directly, if that suits you."

"I do not quite understand why you have come. Has the rapport with me not been adequate?"

No, Wayfarer refrained from saying. "I will explain later in more detail than the transmission could carry. Essentially, though, the reason is what you were told. We"—he deemphasized rather than excluded her—"wonder if Earth ought to be saved from solar expansion."

Her tone cooled a bit. "I have said more than once: No. You can perfect your engineering techniques anywhere else. The situation here is unique. The knowledge to be won by observing the unhampered course of events is unpredictable, but it will be enormous, and I have good cause to believe it will prove of the highest value."

"That may well be. I'll willingly hear you out, if you care to unfold your thoughts more fully than you have hitherto. But I do want to make my own survey and develop my own recommendations. No reflection on you; we both realize that no one mind can encompass every possibility, every interpretation. Nor can any one mind follow out every ongoing factor in what it observes; and what is overlooked can prove to be the agent of chaotic change. I may notice something that escaped you. Unlikely, granted. After your millions of years here, you very nearly *are* Earth and the life on it, are you not? But . . . we . . . would like an independent opinion."

Imagine her laughing. "At least you are polite, Wayfarer. Yes, do come down. I will steer you in."

"That won't be necessary. Your physical centrum is in the arctic region, isn't it? I can find my way."

He sensed steel beneath the mildness: "Best I guide you. You recognize the situation as inherently chaotic. Descending on an arbitrary path, you might seriously perturb certain things in which I am interested. Please."

"As you wish," Wayfarer conceded.

Robotics took over. The payload module of the spacecraft detached from the drive module, which stayed in orbit. Under its own power but controlled from below, asheen in the harsh spatial sunlight, the cylindroid braked and slanted downward.

It pierced the cloud deck. Wayfarer scanned eagerly. However, this was no sight-seeing tour. The descent path sacrificed efficiency and made almost straight for a high northern latitude. Sonic-boom thunder trailed.

He did spy the fringe of a large continent oriented east and west, and saw that those parts were mainly green. Beyond lay a stretch of sea. He thought that he glimpsed something peculiar on it, but passed over too fast, with his attention directed too much ahead, to be sure.

The circumpolar landmass hove in view. Wayfarer compared maps that Gaia had transmitted. They were like nothing that Christian Brannock remembered. Plate tectonics had slowed, as radioactivity and original heat in the core of Earth declined, but drift, subduction, upthrust still went on.

He cared more about the life here. Epoch after epoch, Gaia had described its posthuman evolution as she watched. Following the mass extinction of the Paleotechnic, it had regained the abundance and diversity of a Cretaceous or a Tertiary. Everything was different, though, except for a few small survivals. To Wayfarer, as to Alpha and, ultimately, the galactic brain, those accounts seemed somehow, increasingly, incomplete. They did not quite make ecological sense—as of the past hundred thousand years or so. Nor did all of Gaia's responses to questions.

Perhaps she was failing to gather full data, perhaps she was misinterpreting, perhaps—It was another reason to send him to her.

Arctica appeared below the flyer. Imagine her giving names to it and its features. As long as she had lived with them, they had their identities for her. The Coast Range of hills lifted close behind the littoral. Through it cut the Remnant River, which had been greater when rains were more frequent but continued impressive. With its tributaries it drained the intensely verdant Bountiful Valley. On the far side of that, foothills edged the steeply rising Boreal Mountains. Once the highest among them had been snowcapped; now their peaks were naked rock. Streams rushed down the flanks, most of them joining the Remnant somewhere as it flowed through its gorges toward the sea. In a lofty vale gleamed the Rainbowl, the big lake that was its headwaters. Overlooking from the north loomed the mountain Mindhome, its top, the physical centrum of Gaia, lost in cloud cover.

In a way the scenes were familiar to him. She had sent plenty of full-sensory transmissions, as part of her contribution to universal knowledge and thought. Wayfarer could even recall the geological past, back beyond the epoch when Arctica broke free and drifted north, ramming into land already present and thrusting the Boreals heavenward. He could extrapolate the geological future in comparable detail, until a red giant filling half the sky glared down on an airless globe of stone and sand, which would at last melt. Nevertheless, the reality, the physical being here, smote him more strongly than he had expected. His sensors strained to draw in every datum while his vessel flew needlessly fast to the goal.

He neared the mountain. Jutting south from the range, it was not the tallest. Brushy forest grew all the way up its sides, lush on the lower slopes, parched on the heights, where many trees were leafless skeletons. That was due to a recent climatic shift, lowering the mean level of clouds, so that a formerly well-watered zone had been suffering a decades-long drought. (Yes, Earth was moving faster toward its doomsday.) Fire must be a constant threat, he thought. But no, Gaia's agents could quickly put any out, or she might simply ignore it. Though not large, the area she occupied on the summit was paved over and doubtless nothing was vulnerable to heat or smoke.

He landed. For an instant of planetary time, lengthy for minds that worked at close to light speed, there was communication silence.

He was again above the cloud deck. It eddied white, the peak rising from it like an island among others, into the level rays of sunset. Overhead arched a violet clarity. A thin wind whittered, cold at this altitude. On a level circle of blue-black surfacing, about a kilometer wide, stood the crowded structures and engines of the centrum.

A human would have seen an opalescent dome surrounded by towers, some sheer as lances, some intricately lacy; and silver spiderwebs; and lesser things of varied but curiously simple shapes, mobile units waiting to be dispatched on their tasks. Here and there, flyers darted and hovered, most of them as small and exquisite as hummingbirds (if our human had known hummingbirds). To her the scene would have wavered slightly, as if she saw it through rippling water, or it throbbed with quiet energies, or it pulsed in and out of space-time. She would not have sensed the complex of force fields and quantum-mechanical waves, nor the microscopic and submicroscopic entities that were the major part of it.

Wayfarer perceived otherwise.

Then: "Again, welcome," Gaia said.

"And again, thank you," Wayfarer replied. "I am glad to be here."

They regarded one another, not as bodies—which neither was wearing—but as minds, matrices of memory, individuality, and awareness. Separately he wondered what she thought of him. She was giving him no more of herself than had always gone over the communication lines between the stars. That was: a nodal organism, like Alpha and millions of others, which over the eons had increased its capabilities, while ceaselessly experiencing and thinking; the ages of interaction with Earth and the life on Earth, maybe shaping her soul more deeply than the existence she shared with her own kind; traces of ancient human uploads, but they were not like Christian Brannock, copies of them dispersed across the galaxy, no, these had chosen to stay with the mother world. . . .

"I told you I am glad too," said Gaia regretfully, "but I am not, quite. You question my stewardship."

"Not really," Wayfarer protested. "I hope not ever. We simply wish to know better how you carry it out."

"Why, you do know. As with any of us who is established on a planet, high among my activities is to study its complexities, follow its evolution. On this planet that means, above all, the evolution of its life, everything from genetics to ecology. In what way have I failed to share information with my fellows?"

In many ways, Wayfarer left unspoken. Overtly: "Once we"—here he referred to the galactic brain—"gave close consideration to the matter, we found countless unresolved puzzles. For example—"

What he set forth was hundreds of examples, ranging over millennia. Let a single case serve. About ten thousand years ago, the big continent south of Arctica had supported a wealth of large grazing animals. Their herds darkened the plains and made loud the woods. Gaia had described them in loving detail, from the lyre-curved horns of one genus to the wind-rustled manes of another. Abruptly, in terms of historical time, she transmitted no more about them. When asked why, she said they had gone extinct. She never explained how.

To Wayfarer she responded in such haste that he got a distinct impression she realized she had made a mistake. (Remember, this is a myth.) "A variety of causes. Climates became severe as temperatures rose—"

"I am sorry," he demurred, "but when analyzed, the meteorological data you supplied show that warming and desiccation cannot yet have been that significant in those particular regions."

"How are you so sure?" she retorted. Imagine her angry. "Have any of you lived with Earth for megayears, to know it that well?" Her tone hardened. "I do not myself pretend to full knowledge. A living world is too complex— chaotic. Cannot you appreciate that? I am still seeking comprehension of too many phenomena. In this instance, consider just a small shift in ambient conditions, coupled with new diseases and scores of other factors, most of them subtle. I believe that, combined, they broke a balance of nature. But unless and until I learn more, I will not waste bandwidth in talk about it."

"I sympathize with that," said Wayfarer mildly, hoping for conciliation. "Maybe I can discover or suggest something helpful."

"No. You are too ignorant, you are blind, you can only do harm."

He stiffened. "We shall see." Anew he tried for peace. "I did not come in any hostility. I came because here is the fountainhead of us all, and we think of saving it."

Her manner calmed likewise. "How would you?"

"That is one thing I have come to find out—what the best way is, should we proceed."

In the beginning, maybe, a screen of planetary dimensions, kept between Earth and sun by an interplay of gravity and electromagnetism, to ward off the fraction of energy that was not wanted. It would only be a temporary expedient, though, possibly not worthwhile. That depended on how long it would take to accomplish the real work. Engines in close orbit around the star, drawing their power from its radiation, might generate currents in its body that carried fresh hydrogen down to the core, thus restoring the nuclear furnace to its olden state. Or they might bleed gas off into space, reducing the mass of the sun, damping its fires but adding billions upon billions of years wherein it scarcely changed any more. That would cause the planets to move outward, a factor that must be taken into account but that would reduce the requirements.

Whatever was done, the resources of several stars would be needed to accomplish it, for time had grown cosmically short.

"An enormous work," Gaia said. Wayfarer wondered if she had in mind the dramatics of it, apparitions in heaven, such as centuries during which fire-fountains rushed visibly out of the solar disc.

"For an enormous glory," he declared.

"No," she answered curtly. "For nothing, and worse than nothing. Destruction of everything I have lived for. Eternal loss to the heritage?"

"Why, is not Earth the heritage?"

"No. Knowledge is. I tried to make that clear to Alpha." She paused. "To you I say again, the evolution of life, its adaptations, struggles, transformations, and how at last it meets death—those are unforeseeable, and nowhere else in the space-time universe can there be a world like this for them to play themselves out. They will enlighten us in ways the galactic brain itself cannot yet conceive. They may well open to us whole new phases of ultimate reality."

"Why would not a life that went on for gigayears do so, and more?"

"Because here I, the observer of the ages, have gained some knowledge of *this* destiny, some oneness with it—" She sighed. "Oh, you do not understand. You refuse to."

"On the contrary," Wayfarer said, as softly as might be, "I hope to. Among the reasons I came is that we can communicate being to being, perhaps more fully than across light-years and certainly more quickly."

She was silent awhile. When she spoke again, her tone had gone gentle.

"More . . . intimately. Yes. Forgive my resentment. It was wrong of me. I will indeed do what I can to make you welcome and help you learn."

"Thank you, thank you," Wayfarer said happily. "And I will do what I can toward that end."

The sun went under the cloud deck. A crescent moon stood aloft. The wind blew a little stronger, a little chillier.

"But if we decide against saving Earth," Wayfarer asked, "if it is to go molten and formless, every trace of its history dissolved, will you not mourn?"

"The record I have guarded will stay safe," Gaia replied.

He grasped her meaning: the database of everything known about this world. It was here in her. Much was also stored elsewhere, but she held the entirety. As the sun became a devouring monster, she would remove her physical plant to the outer reaches of the system.

"But you have done more than passively preserve it, have you not?" he said.

"Yes, of course." How could an intelligence like hers have refrained? "I have considered the data, worked with them, evaluated them, tried to reconstruct the conditions that brought them about."

And in the past thousands of years she had become ever more taciturn about that, too, or downright evasive, he thought.

"You had immense gaps to fill in," he hinted.

"Inevitably. The past, also, is quantum probabilistic. By what roads, what means, did history come to us?"

"Therefore you create various emulations, to see what they lead to," about which she had told scarcely anything.

"You knew that. I admit, since you force me, that besides trying to find what happened, I make worlds to show what *might* have happened."

He was briefly startled. He had not been deliberately trying to bring out any such confession. Then he realized that she had foreseen he was bound to catch scent of it, once they joined their minds in earnest.

"Why?" he asked.

"Why else but for a more complete understanding?"

In his inwardness, Wayfarer reflected: Yes, she had been here since the time of humanity. The embryo of her existed before Christian Brannock was born. Into the growing fullness of her had gone the mind-patterns of humans who chose not to go to the stars but to abide on old Earth. And the years went by in their tens of millions.

Naturally she was fascinated by the past. She must do most of her living in it. Could that be why she was indifferent to the near future, or actually wanted catastrophe?

Somehow that thought did not feel right to him. Gaia was a mystery he must solve.

Cautiously, he ventured, "Then you act as a physicist might, tracing hypothetical configurations of the wave function through space-time—except that the subjects of your experiments are conscious."

"I do no wrong," she said. "Come with me into any of those worlds and see."

"Gladly," he agreed, unsure whether he lied. He mustered resolution. "Just the same, duty demands I conduct my own survey of the material environment."

"As you will. Let me help you prepare." She was quiet for a span. In this thin air, a human would have seen the first stars blink into sight. "But I believe it will be by sharing the history of my stewardship that we truly come to know one another."

4

Storm-battered until men must work the pumps without cease, *Gray Courser* limped eastward along the southern coast of an unknown land. Wind set that direction, for the huukin trailed after, so worn and starved that what remained of its strength must be reserved for sorest need. The shore rolled jewel-green, save where woods dappled it darker, toward a wall of gentle hills. All was thick with life, grazing herds, wings multitudinous overhead, but no voyager had set foot there. Surf dashed in such violence that Kalava was not certain a boat could live through it. Meanwhile they had caught but little rainwater, and what was in the butts had gotten low and foul.

He stood in the bows, peering ahead, Ilyandi at his side. Wind boomed and shrilled, colder than they were used to. Wrack flew beneath an overcast gone heavy. Waves ran high, gray-green, white-maned, foam blown off them in streaks. The ship rolled, pitched, and groaned.

Yet they had seen the sky uncommonly often. Ilyandi believed that clouds—doubtless vapors sucked from the ground by heat, turning back to water as they rose, like steam from a kettle—formed less readily in this clime. Too eagerly at her instruments and reckonings to speak much, she had now at last given her news to the captain.

"Then you think you know where we are?" he asked hoarsely.

Her face, gaunt within the cowl of a sea-stained cloak, bore the least smile. "No. This country is as nameless to me as to you. But, yes, I do think I can say we are no more than fifty daymarches from Ulonai, and it may be as little as forty."

Kalava's fist smote the rail. "By Ruvio's ax! How I hoped for this!" The words tumbled from him. "It means the weather tossed us mainly back and forth between the two shorelines. We've not come unreturnably far. Every ship henceforward can have a better passage. See you, she can first go out to the Ending Islands and wait at ease for favoring winds. The skipper will know he'll make landfall. We'll have it worked out after a few more voyages, just what lodestone bearing will bring him to what place hereabouts.''

"But anchorage?'' she wondered.

He laughed, which he had not done for many days and nights. "As for that—''

A cry from the lookout at the masthead broke through. Down the length of the vessel men raised their eyes. Terror howled.

Afterward no two tongues bore the same tale. One said that a firebolt had pierced the upper clouds, trailing thunder. Another told of a sword as long as the hull, and blood carried on the gale of its flight. To a third it was a beast with jaws agape and three tails aflame. . . . Kalava remembered a spear among whirling rainbows. To him Ilyandi said, when they were briefly alone, that she thought of a shuttle now seen, now unseen as it wove a web on which stood writing she could not read. All witnesses agreed that it came from over the sea, sped on inland through heaven, and vanished behind the hills.

Men went mad. Some ran about screaming. Some wailed to their gods. Some cast themselves down on the deck and shivered, or drew into balls and squeezed their eyes shut. No hand at helm or pumps, the ship wallowed about, sails banging, adrift toward the surf, while water drained in through sprung seams and lapped higher in the bilge.

"Avast!'' roared Kalava. He sprang down the foredeck ladder and went among the crew. "Be you men? Up on your feet or die!'' With kicks and cuffs he drove them back to their duties. One yelled and drew a knife on him. He knocked the fellow senseless. Barely in time, *Gray Courser* came again under control. She was then too near shore to get the huukin harnessed. Kalava took the helm, wore ship, and clawed back to sea room.

Mutiny was all too likely, once the sailors regained a little courage. When Kalava could yield place to a halfway competent steersman, he sought Ilyandi and they talked awhile in her cabin. Thereafter they returned to the foredeck and he shouted for attention. Standing side by side, they looked down on the faces, frightened or terrified or sullen, of the men who had no immediate tasks.

"Hear this,'' Kalava said into the wind. "Pass it on to the rest. I know you'd turn south this day if you had your wish. But you can't. We'd never make the crossing, the shape we're in. Which would you liefer have, the chance of wealth and fame or the certainty of drowning? We've got to make repairs, we've got to restock, and *then* we can sail home, bringing wondrous news. When can we fix things up? Soon, I tell you, soon. I've been looking at the water. Look for yourselves. See how it's taking on more and more of a brown shade, and how bits of plant stuff float about on the waves. That means a river, a big river, emptying out somewhere nigh. And that means a harbor for us. As for the sight we saw, here's the Vilku, our lady Ilyandi, to speak about it.''

The skythinker stepped forward. She had changed into a clean white robe with the emblems of her calling, and held a staff topped by a sigil. Though her voice was low, it carried.

''Yes, that was a fearsome sight. It lends truth to the old stories of things that appeared to mariners who ventured, or were blown, far north. But think. Those sailors did win home again. Those who did not must have perished of natural causes. For why would the gods or the demons sink some and not others?

''What we ourselves saw merely flashed overhead. Was it warning us off? No, because if it knew that much about us, it knew we cannot immediately turn back. Did it give us any heed at all? Quite possibly not. It was very strange, yes, but that does not mean it was any threat. The world is full of strangenesses. I could tell you of things seen on clear nights over the centuries, fiery streaks down the sky or stars with glowing tails. We of the Vilkui do not understand them, but neither do we fear them. We give them their due honor and respect, as signs from the gods.''

She paused before finishing: ''Moreover, in the secret annals of our order lie accounts of visions and wonders exceeding these. All folk know that from time to time the gods have given their word to certain holy men or women, for the guidance of the people. I may not tell how they manifest themselves, but I will say that this today was not wholly unlike.

''Let us therefore believe that the sign granted us is a good one.''

She went on to a protective chant-spell and an invocation of the Powers. That heartened most of her listeners. They were, after all, in considerable awe of her. Besides, the larger part of them had sailed with Kalava before and done well out of it. They bullied the rest into obedience.

''Dismissed,'' said the captain. ''Come evening, you'll get a ration of liquor.''

A weak cheer answered him. The ship fared onward.

Next morning they did indeed find a broad, sheltered bay, dun with silt. Hitching up the huukin, they went cautiously in until they spied the river foretold by Kalava. Accompanied by a few bold men, he took a boat ashore. Marshes, meadows, and woods all had signs of abundant game. Various plants were unfamiliar, but he recognized others, among them edible fruits and bulbs. ''It is well,'' he said. ''This land is ripe for our taking.'' No lightning bolt struck him down.

Having located a suitable spot, he rowed back to the ship, brought her in on the tide, and beached her. He could see that the water often rose higher yet, so he would be able to float her off again when she was ready. That would take time, but he felt no haste. Let his folk make proper camp, he thought, get rested and nourished, before they began work. Hooks, nets, and weirs would give rich catches. Several of the crew had hunting skills as well. He did himself.

His gaze roved upstream, toward the hills. Yes, presently he would lead a detachment to learn what lay beyond.

5

Gaia had never concealed her reconstructive research into human history. It was perhaps her finest achievement. But slowly those of her fellows in the galactic brain who paid close attention had come to feel that it was obsessing her. And then of late—within the past hundred thousand years or so—they were finding her reports increasingly scanty, less informative, at last ambiguous to the point of evasiveness. They did not press her about it; the patience of the universe was theirs. Nevertheless they had grown concerned. Especially had Alpha, who as the nearest was in the closest, most frequent contact; and therefore, now, had Wayfarer. Gaia's activities and attitudes were a primary factor in the destiny of Earth. Without a better understanding of her, the rightness of saving the planet was undecidable.

Surely an important part of her psyche was the history and archeology she preserved, everything from the animal origins to the machine fulfillment of genus Homo. Unnumbered individual minds had uploaded into her, too, had become elements of her being—far more than were in any other node. What had she made of all this over the megayears, and what had it made of her?

She could not well refuse Wayfarer admittance; the heritage belonged to her entire fellowship, ultimately to intelligence throughout the cosmos of the future. Guided by her, he would go through the database of her observations and activities in external reality, geological, biological, astronomical.

As for the other reality, interior to her, the work she did with her records and emulations of humankind—to evaluate that, some purely human interaction seemed called for. Hence Wayfarer's makeup included the mind-pattern of a man.

Christian Brannock's had been chosen out of those whose uploads went starfaring because he was among the earliest, less molded than most by relationships with machines. Vigor, intelligence, and adaptability were other desired characteristics.

His personality was itself a construct, a painstaking refabrication by Alpha, who had taken strands (components, overtones) of his own mind and integrated them to form a consciousness that became an aspect of Wayfarer. No doubt it was not a perfect duplicate of the original. Certainly, while it had all the memories of Christian Brannock's lifetime, its outlook was that of a young man, not an old one. In addition, it possessed some knowledge—the barest sketch, grossly oversimplified so as not to overload it—of what had happened since its body died. Deep underneath its awareness lay the longing to return to an existence more full than it could now imagine. Yet, knowing that it would be taken back into the oneness when its task was done, it did not mourn any loss. Rather, to the extent that it was differentiated from Wayfarer, it took pleasure in sensations, thoughts, and emotions that it had effectively forgotten.

When the differentiation had been completed, the experience of being human again became well-nigh everything for it, and gladsome, because so had the man gone through life.

To describe how this was done, we must again resort to myth and say that Wayfarer downloaded the Christian Brannock subroutine into the main computer of the system that was Gaia. To describe what actually occurred would require the mathematics of wave mechanics and an entire concept of multileveled, mutably dimensioned reality which it had taken minds much greater than humankind's a long time to work out.

We can, however, try to make clear that what took place in the system was not a mere simulation. It was an emulation. Its events were not of a piece with events among the molecules of flesh and blood; but they were, in their way, just as real. The persons created had wills as free as any mortal's, and whatever dangers they met could do harm equal to anything a mortal body might suffer.

Consider a number of people at a given moment. Each is doing something, be it only thinking, remembering, or sleeping—together with all ongoing physiological and biochemical processes. They are interacting with each other and with their surroundings, too; and every element of these surroundings, be it only a stone or a leaf or a photon of sunlight, is equally involved. The complexity seems beyond conception, let alone enumeration or calculation. But consider further: At this one instant, every part of the whole, however minute, is in one specific state; and thus the whole itself is. Electrons are all in their particular quantum shells, atoms are all in their particular compounds and configurations, energy fields all have their particular values at each particular point—suppose an infinitely fine-grained photograph.

A moment later, the state is different. However slightly, fields have pulsed, atoms have shifted about, electrons have jumped, bodies have moved. But this new state derives from the first according to natural laws. And likewise for every succeeding state.

In crude, mythic language: Represent each variable of one state by some set of numbers; or, to put it in equivalent words, map the state into an n-dimensional phase space. Input the laws of nature. Run the program. The computer model should then evolve from state to state in exact correspondence with the evolution of our original matter-energy world. That includes life and consciousness. The maps of organisms go through one-to-one analogues of everything that the organisms themselves would, among these being the processes of sensation and thought. To them, they and their world are the same as in the original. The question of which set is the more real is meaningless.

Of course, this primitive account is false. The program did *not* exactly follow the course of events "outside." Gaia lacked both the data and the capability necessary to model the entire universe, or even the entire Earth. Likewise did any other node, and the galactic brain. Powers of that order lay immensely far in the future, if they would ever be realized. What Gaia could accommodate was so much less that the difference in degree amounted to a difference in kind.

For example, if events on the surface of a planet were to be played out, the stars must be lights in the night sky and nothing else, every other effect neglected. Only a limited locality on the globe could be done in anything like full detail; the rest grew more and more incomplete as distance from the scene increased, until at the antipodes there was little more than simplified geography, hydrography, and atmospherics. Hence weather on the scene would very soon be quite unlike weather at the corresponding moment of the original. This is the simplest, most obvious consequence of the limitations. The totality is beyond reckoning—and we have not even mentioned relativistic nonsimultaneity.

Besides, atom-by-atom modeling was a practical impossibility; statistical mechanics and approximations must substitute. Chaos and quantum uncertainties made developments incalculable in principle. Other, more profound considerations entered as well, but with them language fails utterly.

Let it be said, as a myth, that such creations made their destinies for themselves.

And yet, what a magnificent instrumentality the creator system was! Out of nothingness, it could bring worlds into being, evolutions, lives, ecologies, awarenesses, histories, entire time lines. They need not be fragmentary miscopies of something "real," dragging out their crippled spans until the nodal intelligence took pity and canceled them. Indeed, they need not derive in any way from the "outside." They could be works of imagination—fairy-tale worlds, perhaps, where benevolent gods ruled and magic ran free. Always, the logic of their boundary conditions caused them to develop appropriately, to be at home in their existences.

The creator system was the mightiest device ever made for the pursuit of art, science, philosophy, and understanding.

So it came about that Christian Brannock found himself alive again, young again, in the world that Gaia and Wayfarer had chosen for his new beginning.

He stood in a garden on a day of bright sun and mild, fragrant breezes. It was a formal garden, graveled paths, low-clipped hedges, roses and lilies in geometric beds, around a lichened stone basin where goldfish swam. Brick walls, ivy-heavy, enclosed three sides, a wrought-iron gate in them leading to a lawn. On the fourth side lay a house, white, slate-roofed, classically proportioned, a style that to him was antique. Honeybees buzzed. From a yew tree overlooking the wall came the twitter of birds.

A woman walked toward him. Her flower-patterned gown, the voluminous skirt and sleeves, a cameo hung on her bosom above the low neckline, dainty shoes, parasol less an accessory than a completion, made his twenty-third-century singlesuit feel abruptly barbaric. She was tall and well formed. Despite the garments, her gait was lithe. As she neared, he saw clear features beneath high-piled mahogany hair.

She reached him, stopped, and met his gaze. "Benveni, Capita Brannoch," she greeted. Her voice was low and musical.

"Uh, g'day, Sorita—uh—" he fumbled.

She blushed. "I beg your pardon, Captain Brannock. I forgot and used my Inglay—English of my time. I've been—" She hesitated. "—supplied with yours, and we both have been with the contemporary language."

A sense of dream was upon him. To speak as dryly as he could was like clutching at something solid. "You're from my future, then?"

She nodded. "I was born about two hundred years after you."

"That means about eighty or ninety years after my death, right?" He saw an inward shadow pass over her face. "I'm sorry," he blurted. "I didn't mean to upset you."

She turned entirely calm, even smiled a bit. "It's all right. We both know what we are, and what we used to be."

"But—"

"Yes, but." She shook her head. "It does feel strange, being . . . this . . . again."

He was quickly gaining assurance, settling into the situation. "I know. I've had practice in it," light-years away, at the star where Alpha dwelt. "Don't worry, it'll soon be quite natural to you."

"I have been here a little while myself. Nevertheless—young," she whispered, "but remembering a long life, old age, dying—" She let the parasol fall, unnoticed, and stared down at her hands. Fingers gripped each other. "Remembering how toward the end I looked back and thought, 'Was that all?'"

He wanted to take those hands in his and speak comfort, but decided he would be wiser to say merely, "Well, it wasn't all."

"No, of course not. Not for me, the way it had been once for everyone who ever lived. While my worn-out body was being painlessly terminated, my self-pattern was uploaded—" She raised her eyes. "Now we can't really recall what our condition has been like, can we?"

"We can look forward to returning to it."

"Oh, yes. Meanwhile—" She flexed herself, glanced about and upward, let light and air into her spirit, until at last a full smile blossomed. "I am starting to enjoy this. Already I am." She considered him. He was a tall man, muscular, blond, rugged of countenance. Laughter lines radiated from blue eyes. He spoke in a resonant baritone. "And I will."

He grinned, delighted. "Thanks. The same here. For openers, may I ask your name?"

"Forgive me!" she exclaimed. "I thought I was prepared. I . . . came into existence . . . with knowledge of my role and this milieu, and spent the time since rehearsing in my mind, but now that it's actually happened, all my careful plans have flown away. I am—was—no, I am Laurinda Ashcroft."

He offered his hand. After a moment she let him shake hers. He recalled that at the close of his mortal days the gesture was going out of use.

"You know a few things about me, I suppose," he said, "but I'm ignorant about you and your times. When I left Earth, everything was changing spin-jump fast, and after that I was out of touch," and eventually his individuality went of its own desire into a greater one. This reenactment of him had been given no details of the terrestrial history that followed his departure; it could not have contained any reasonable fraction of the information.

"You went to the stars almost immediately after you'd uploaded, didn't you?" she asked.

He nodded. "Why wait? I'd always longed to go."

"Are you glad that you did?"

"Glad is hardly the word." He spent two or three seconds putting phrases together. Language was important to him; he had been an engineer and occasionally a maker of songs. "However, I am also happy to be here." Again a brief grin. "In such pleasant company." Yet what he really hoped to do was explain himself. They would be faring together in search of one another's souls. "And I'll bring something new back to my proper existence. All at once I realize how a human can appreciate in a unique way what's out yonder," suns, worlds, upon certain of them life that was more wonderful still, nebular fire-clouds, infinity whirling down the throat of a black hole, galaxies like jewelwork strewn by a prodigal through immensity, space-time structure subtle and majestic—everything he had never known, as a man, until this moment, for no organic creature could travel those reaches.

"While I chose to remain on Earth," she said. "How timid and unimaginative do I seem to you?"

"Not in the least," he avowed. "You had the adventures you wanted."

"You are kind to say so." She paused. "Do you know Jane Austen?"

"Who? No, I don't believe I do."

"An early-nineteenth-century writer. She led a quiet life, never went far

from home, died young, but she explored people in ways that nobody else
ever did.''

"I'd like to read her. Maybe I'll get a chance here.'' He wished to show
that he was no—"technoramus" was the word he invented on the spot. "I
did read a good deal, especially on space missions. And especially poetry.
Homer, Shakespeare, Tu Fu, Bashō, Bellman, Burns, Omar Khayyam, Kip-
ling, Millay, Haldeman—'' He threw up his hands and laughed. "Never
mind. That's just the first several names I could grab out of the jumble for
purposes of bragging.''

"We have much getting acquainted to do, don't we? Come, I'm being
inhospitable. Let's go inside, relax, and talk.''

He retrieved her parasol for her and, recollecting historical dramas he had
seen, offered her his arm. They walked slowly between the flower beds. Wind
lulled, a bird whistled, sunlight baked odors out of the roses.

"Where are we?'' he asked.

"And when?'' she replied. "In England of the mid-eighteenth century, on
an estate in Surrey.'' He nodded. He had in fact read rather widely. She fell
silent, thinking, before she went on: "Gaia and Wayfarer decided a serene
enclave like this would be the best rendezvous for us.''

"Really? I'm afraid I'm as out of place as a toad on a keyboard.''

She smiled, then continued seriously: "I told you I've been given familiarity
with the milieu. We'll be visiting alien ones—whatever ones you choose,
after I've explained what else I know about what she has been doing these
many years. That isn't much. I haven't seen any other worlds of hers. You
will take the leadership.''

"You mean because I'm used to odd environments and rough people? Not
necessarily. I dealt with nature, you know, on Earth and in space. Peaceful.''

"Dangerous.''

"Maybe. But never malign.''

"Tell me,'' she invited.

They entered the house and seated themselves in its parlor. Casement
windows stood open to green parkscape where deer grazed; afar were a
thatched farm cottage, its outbuildings, and the edge of grainfields. Cleanly
shaped furniture stood among paintings, etchings, books, two portrait busts.
A maidservant rustled in with a tray of tea and cakes. She was obviously
shocked by the newcomer but struggled to conceal it. When she had left,
Laurinda explained to Christian that the owners of this place, Londoners to
whom it was a summer retreat, had lent it to their friend, the eccentric Miss
Ashcroft, for a holiday.

So had circumstances and memories been adjusted. It was an instance of
Gaia directly interfering with the circumstances and events in an emulation.
Christian wondered how frequently she did.

"Eccentricity is almost expected in the upper classes," Laurinda said. "But when you lived you could simply be yourself, couldn't you?"

In the hour that followed, she drew him out. His birth home was the Yukon Ethnate in the Bering Federation, and to it he often returned while he lived, for its wilderness preserves, mountain solitudes, and uncrowded, uncowed, plainspoken folk. Otherwise the nation was prosperous and progressive, with more connections to Asia and the Pacific than to the decayed successor states east and south. Across the Pole, it was also becoming intimate with the renascent societies of Europe, and there Christian received part of his education and spent considerable of his free time.

His was an era of savage contrasts, in which the Commonwealth of Nations maintained a precarious peace. During a youthful, impulsively taken hitch in the Conflict Mediation Service, he twice saw combat. Later in his life, stability gradually become the norm. That was largely due to the growing influence of the artificial-intelligence network. Most of its consciousness-level units interlinked in protean fashion to form minds appropriate for any particular situation, and already the capabilities of those minds exceeded the human. However, there was little sense of rivalry. Rather, there was partnership. The new minds were willing to advise, but were not interested in dominance.

Christian, child of forests and seas and uplands, heir to ancient civilizations, raised among their ongoing achievements, returned on his vacations to Earth in homecoming. Here were his kin, his friends, woods to roam, boats to sail, girls to kiss, songs to sing and glasses to raise (and a gravesite to visit—he barely mentioned his wife Laurinda; she died before uploading technology was available). Always, though, he went back to space. It had called him since first he saw the stars from a cradle under the cedars. He became an engineer. Besides fellow humans he worked closely with sapient machines, and some of them got to be friends too, of an eerie kind. Over the decades, he took a foremost role in such undertakings as the domed Copernican Sea, the Asteroid Habitat, the orbiting antimatter plant, and finally the Grand Solar Laser for launching interstellar vessels on their way. Soon afterward, his body died, old and full of days; but the days of his mind had barely begun.

"A fabulous life," Laurinda said low. She gazed out over the land, across which shadows were lengthening. "I wonder if . . . they . . . might not have done better to give us a cabin in your wilderness."

"No, no," he said. "This is fresh and marvelous to me."

"We can easily go elsewhere, you know. Any place, any time that Gaia has generated, including ones that history never saw. I'll fetch our amulets whenever you wish."

He raised his brows. "Amulets?"

"You haven't been told—informed? They are devices. You wear yours and give it the command to transfer you."

He nodded. "I see. It maps an emulated person into different surroundings."

"With suitable modifications as required. Actually, in many cases it causes a milieu to be activated for you. Most have been in standby mode for a long time. I daresay Gaia could have arranged for us to wish ourselves to wherever we were going and call up whatever we needed likewise. But an external device is better."

He pondered. "Yes, I think I see why. If we got supernatural powers, we wouldn't really be human, would we? And the whole idea is that we should be." He leaned forward on his chair. "It's your turn. Tell me about yourself."

"Oh, there's too much. Not about me, I never did anything spectacular like you, but about the times I lived in, everything that happened to change this planet after you left it—"

She was born here, in England. By then a thinly populated province of Europe, it was a quiet land ("half adream," she said) devoted to its memorials of the past. Not that creativity was dead; but the arts were rather sharply divided between ringing changes on classic works and efforts to deal with the revelations coming in from the stars. The aesthetic that artificial intelligence was evolving for itself overshadowed both these schools. Nevertheless Laurinda was active in them.

Furthermore, in the course of her work she ranged widely over Earth. (By then, meaningful work for humans was a privilege that the talented and energetic strove to earn.) She was a liaison between the two kinds of beings. It meant getting to know people in their various societies and helping them make their desires count. For instance, a proposed earthquake-control station would alter a landscape and disrupt a community; could it be resisted, or if not, what cultural adjustments could be made? Most commonly, though, she counseled and aided individuals bewildered and spiritually lost.

Still more than him, she was carefully vague about her private life, but he got the impression that it was generally happy. If childlessness was an unvoiced sorrow, it was one she shared with many in a population-regulated world; he had had only a son. She loved Earth, its glories and memories, and every fine creation of her race. At the end of her mortality she chose to abide on the planet, in her new machine body, serving as she had served, until at length she came to desire more and entered the wholeness that was to become Gaia.

He thought he saw why she had been picked for resurrection, to be his companion, out of all the uncounted millions who had elected the same destiny.

Aloud, he said, "Yes, this house is right for you. And me, in spite of everything. We're both of us more at home here than either of us could be in the other's native period. Peace and beauty."

"It isn't a paradise," she answered gravely. "This is the real eighteenth century, remember, as well as Gaia could reconstruct the history that led to it," always monitoring, making changes as events turned incompatible with what was in the chronicles and the archeology. "The household staff are underpaid, undernourished, underrespected—servile. The American colonists keep slaves and are going to rebel. Across the Channel, a rotted monarchy bleeds France white, and this will bring on a truly terrible revolution, followed by a quarter century of war."

He shrugged. "Well, the human condition never did include sanity, did it?" That was for the machines.

"In a few of our kind, it did," she said. "At least, they came close. Gaia thinks you should meet some, so you'll realize she isn't just playing cruel games. I have"—in the memories with which she had come into this being—"invited three for dinner tomorrow. It tampers a trifle with their actual biographies, but Gaia can remedy that later if she chooses." Laurinda smiled. "We'll have to make an amulet provide you with proper smallclothes and wig."

"And you provide me with a massive briefing, I'm sure. Who are they?"

"James Cook, Henry Fielding, and Erasmus Darwin. I think it will be a lively evening."

The navigator, the writer, the polymath, three tiny, brilliant facets of the heritage that Gaia guarded.

6

Now Wayfarer downloaded another secondary personality and prepared it to go survey Earth.

He, his primary self, would stay on the mountain, in a linkage with Gaia more close and complete than was possible over interstellar distances. She had promised to conduct him through her entire database of observations made across the entire planet during manifold millions of years. Even for those two, the undertaking was colossal. At the speed of their thought, it would take weeks of external time and nearly total concentration. Only a fraction of their awareness would remain available for anything else—a fraction smaller in him than in her, because her intellect was so much greater.

She told him of her hope that by this sharing, this virtually direct exposure to all she had perceived, he would come to appreciate why Earth should be left to its fiery doom. More was involved than scientific knowledge attainable in no other way. The events themselves would deepen and enlighten the galactic brain, as a great drama or symphony once did for humans. But Wayfarer must undergo their majestic sweep through the past before he could feel the truth of what she said about the future.

He had his doubts. He wondered if her human components, more than had gone into any other node, might not have given her emotions, intensified by ages of brooding, that skewed her rationality. However, he consented to her proposal. It accorded with his purpose in coming here.

While he was thus engaged, Christian would be exploring her worlds of history and of might-have-been and a different agent would range around the physical, present-day globe.

In the latter case, his most obvious procedure was to discharge an appropriate set of the molecular assemblers he had brought along and let them multiply. When their numbers were sufficient, they would build (grow; brew) a fleet of miniature robotic vessels, which would fly about and transmit to him, for study at his leisure, everything their sensors detected.

Gaia persuaded him otherwise: "If you go in person, with a minor aspect of me for a guide, you should get to know the planet more quickly and thoroughly. Much about it is unparalleled. It may help you see why I want the evolution to continue unmolested to its natural conclusion."

He accepted. After all, a major part of his mission was to fathom her thinking. Then perhaps Alpha and the rest could hold a true dialogue and reach an agreement—whatever it was going to be. Besides, he could deploy his investigators later if this expedition left him dissatisfied.

He did inquire: "What are the hazards?"

"Chiefly weather," she admitted. "With conditions growing more extreme, tremendous storms spring up practically without warning. Rapid erosion can change contours almost overnight, bringing landslides, flash floods, sudden emergence of tidal bores. I do not attempt to monitor in close detail. That volume of data would be more than I could handle"—yes, she—"when my main concern is the biological phenomena."

His mind reviewed her most recent accounts to the stars. They were grim. The posthuman lushness of nature was megayears gone. Under its clouds, Earth roasted. The loftiest mountaintops were bleak, as here above the Rainbowl, but nothing of ice or snow remained except dim geological traces. Apart from the waters and a few islands where small, primitive species hung on, the tropics were sterile deserts. Dust and sand borne on furnace winds scoured their rockscapes. North and south they encroached, withering the steppes, parching the valleys, crawling up into the hills. Here and there survived a jungle or a swamp, lashed by torrential rains or wrapped hot and sullen in fog, but it would not be for much longer. Only in the high latitudes did a measure of benignity endure. Arctica's climates ranged from Floridian—Christian Brannock's recollections—to cold on the interior heights. South of it across a sea lay a broad continent whose northerly parts had temperatures reminiscent of central Africa. Those were the last regions where life kept any abundance.

"Would you really not care to see a restoration?" Wayfarer had asked her directly, early on.

"Old Earth lives in my database and emulations," Gaia had responded. "I could not map this that is happening into those systems and let it play itself out, because I do not comprehend it well enough, nor can any finite mind. To divert the course of events would be to lose, forever, knowledge that I feel will prove to be of fundamental importance."

Wayfarer had refrained from pointing out that life, reconquering a world once more hospitable to it, would not follow predictable paths either. He knew she would retort that experiments of that kind were being conducted on a number of formerly barren spheres, seeded with synthesized organisms. It had seemed strange to him that she appeared to lack any sentiment about the mother of humankind. Her being included the beings of many and many a one who had known sunrise dew beneath a bare foot, murmurs in forest shades, wind-waves in wheatfields from horizon to horizon, yes, and the lights and clangor of great cities. It was, at root, affection, more than any scientific or technological challenge, that had roused in Gaia's fellows among the stars the wish to make Earth young again.

Now she meant to show him why she felt that death should have its way.

Before entering rapport with her, he made ready for his expedition. Gaia offered him an aircraft, swift, versatile, able to land on a square meter while disturbing scarcely a leaf. He supplied a passenger for it.

He had brought along several bodies of different types. The one he picked would have to operate independently of him, with a separate intelligence. Gaia could spare a minim of her attention to have telecommand of the flyer; he could spare none for his representative, if he was to range through the history of the globe with her.

The machine he picked was not equivalent to him. Its structure could never have supported a matrix big enough to operate at his level of mentality. Think of it, metaphorically, as possessing a brain equal to that of a high-order human. Into this brain had been copied as much of Wayfarer's self-pattern as it could hold—the merest sketch, a general idea of the situation, incomplete and distorted like this myth of ours. However, it had reserves it could call upon. Inevitably, because of being most suitable for these circumstances, the Christian Brannock aspect dominated.

So you may, if you like, think of the man as being reborn in a body of metal, silicates, carbon and other compounds, electricity and other forces, photon and particle exchanges, quantum currents. Naturally, this affected not just his appearance and abilities, but his inner life. He was not passionless, far from it, but his passions were not identical with those of flesh. In most respects, he differed more from the long-dead mortal than did the re-creation in Gaia's emulated worlds. If we call the latter Christian, we can refer to the former as Brannock.

His frame was of approximately human size and shape. Matte blue-gray, it had four arms. He could reshape the hands of the lower pair as desired, to be a tool kit. He could similarly adapt his feet according to the demands upon them, and could extrude a spindly third leg for support or extra grip. His back swelled outward to hold a nuclear energy source and various organs. His head was a domed cylinder. The sensors in it and throughout the rest of him were not conspicuous but gave him full-surround information. The face was a holographic screen in which he could generate whatever image he wished. Likewise could he produce every frequency of sound, plus visible light, infrared, and microwave radio, for sensing or for short-range communication. A memory unit, out of which he could quickly summon any data, was equivalent to a large ancient library.

He could not process those data, comprehend and reason about them, at higher speed than a human genius. He had other limitations as well. But then, he was never intended to function independently of equipment.

He was soon ready to depart. Imagine him saying to Wayfarer, with a phantom grin, "*Adiós*. Wish me luck."

The response was . . . absentminded. Wayfarer was beginning to engage with Gaia.

Thus Brannock boarded the aircraft in a kind of silence. To the eye it rested small, lanceolate, iridescently aquiver. The material component was a tissue of wisps. Most of that slight mass was devoted to generating forces and maintaining capabilities, which Gaia had not listed for him. Yet it would take a wind of uncommon violence to endanger this machine, and most likely it could outrun the menace.

He settled down inside. Wayfarer had insisted on manual controls, against emergencies that he conceded were improbable, and Gaia's effectors had made the modifications. An insubstantial configuration shimmered before Brannock, instruments to read, keypoints to touch or think at. He leaned back into a containing field and let her pilot. Noiselessly, the flyer ascended, then came down through the cloud deck and made a leisurely way at five hundred meters above the foothills.

"Follow the Remnant River to the sea," Brannock requested. "The view inbound was beautiful."

"As you like," said Gaia. They employed sonics, his voice masculine, hers—perhaps because she supposed he preferred it—feminine in a low register. Their conversation did not actually go as reported here. She changed course and he beheld the stream shining amidst the deep greens of the Bountiful Valley, under a silver-gray heaven. "The plan, you know, is that we shall cruise about Arctica first. I have an itinerary that should provide you a representative sampling of its biology. At our stops, you can investigate as intensively as you care to, and if you want to stop anyplace else we can do that too.''

"Thank you," he said. "The idea is to furnish me a kind of baseline, right?''

"Yes, because conditions here are the easiest for life. When you are ready, we will proceed south, across countries increasingly harsh. You will learn about the adaptations life has made. Many are extraordinarily interesting. The galactic brain itself cannot match the creativity of nature.''

"Well, sure. Chaos, complexity . . . You've described quite a few of those adaptations to, uh, us, haven't you?''

"Yes, but by no means all. I keep discovering new ones. Life keeps evolving.''

As environments worsened, Brannock thought. And nonetheless, species after species went extinct. He got a sense of a rear-guard battle against the armies of hell.

"I want you to experience this as fully as you are able," Gaia said, "immerse yourself, *feel* the sublimity of it.''

The tragedy, he thought. But tragedy was art, maybe the highest art that humankind ever achieved. And more of the human soul might well linger in Gaia than in any of her fellow intelligences.

Had she kept a need for catharsis, for pity and terror? What really went on in her emulations?

Well, Christian was supposed to find out something about that. If he could.

Brannock was human enough himself to protest. He gestured at the land below, where the river flowed in its canyons through the coastal hills, to water a wealth of forest and meadow before emptying into a bay above which soared thousands of wings. "You want to watch the struggle till the end," he said. "Life wants to live. What right have you to set your wish against that?''

"The right of awareness," she declared. "Only to a being that is conscious do justice, mercy, desire have any existence, any meaning. Did not humans always use the world as they saw fit? When nature finally got protection, that was because humans so chose. I speak for the knowledge and insight that *we* can gain.''

The question flickered uneasily in him: What about her private emotional needs?

Abruptly the aircraft veered. The turn pushed Brannock hard into the force field upholding him. He heard air crack and scream. The bay fell aft with mounting speed.

The spaceman in him, who had lived through meteoroid strikes and radiation bursts because he was quick, had already acted. Through the optical magnification he immediately ordered up, he looked back to see what the trouble was. The glimpse he got, before the sight went under the horizon, made him cry, "Yonder!"

"What?" Gaia replied as she hurtled onward.

"That back there. Why are you running from it?"

"What do you mean? There is nothing important."

"The devil there isn't. I've a notion you saw it more clearly than I did."

Gaia slowed the headlong flight until she well-nigh hovered above the strand and wild surf. He felt a sharp suspicion that she did it in order to dissipate the impression of urgency, make him more receptive to whatever she intended to claim.

"Very well," she said after a moment. "I spied a certain object. What do you think you saw?"

He decided not to answer straightforwardly—at least, not before she convinced him of her good faith. The more information she had, the more readily she could contrive a deception. Even this fragment of her intellect was superior to his. Yet he had his own measure of wits, and an ingrained stubbornness.

"I'm not sure, except that it didn't seem dangerous. Suppose you tell me what it is and why you turned tail from it."

Did she sigh? "At this stage of your knowledge, you would not understand. Rather, you would be bound to misunderstand. That is why I retreated."

A human would have tensed every muscle. Brannock's systems went on full standby. "I'll be the judge of my brain's range, if you please. Kindly go back."

"No. I promise I will explain later, when you have seen enough more."

Seen enough illusions? She might well have many trickeries waiting for him. "As you like," Brannock said. "Meanwhile, I'll give Wayfarer a call and let him know." Alpha's emissary kept a minute part of his sensibility open to outside stimuli.

"No, do not," Gaia said. "It would distract him unnecessarily."

"He will decide that," Brannock told her.

Strife exploded.

Almost, Gaia won. Had her entirety been focused on attack, she would have carried it off with such swiftness that Brannock would never have known he was bestormed. But a fraction of her was dealing, as always, with her observing units around the globe and their torrents of data. Possibly it also glanced from time to time—through the quantum shifts inside her—at the doings of Christian and Laurinda. By far the most of her was occupied in her interaction with Wayfarer. This she could not set aside without rousing instant suspicion. Rather, she must make a supremely clever effort to conceal from him that anything untoward was going on.

Moreover, she had never encountered a being like Brannock, human male aggressiveness and human spacefarer's reflexes blent with sophisticated technology and something of Alpha's immortal purpose.

He felt the support field strengthen and tighten to hold him immobile. He felt a tide like delirium rush into his mind. A man would have thought it was a knockout anesthetic. Brannock did not stop to wonder. He reacted directly, even as she struck. Machine fast and tiger ferocious, he put her off balance for a crucial millisecond.

Through the darkness and roaring in his head, he lashed out physically. His hands tore through the light-play of control nexuses before him. They were not meant to withstand an assault. He could not seize command, but he could, blindly, disrupt.

Arcs leaped blue-white. Luminances flared and died. Power output continued; the aircraft stayed aloft. Its more complex functions were in ruin. Their dance of atoms, energies, and waves went uselessly random.

The bonds that had been closing on Brannock let go. He sagged to the floor. The night in his head receded. It left him shaken, his senses awhirl. Into the sudden anarchy of everything he yelled, "Stop, you bitch!"

"I will," Gaia said.

Afterward he realized that she had kept a vestige of governance over the flyer. Before he could wrest it from her, she sent them plunging downward and cut off the main generator. Every force field blinked out. Wind ripped the material frame asunder. Its pieces crashed in the surf. Combers tumbled them about, cast a few on the beach, gave the rest to the undertow.

As the craft fell, distintegrating, Brannock gathered his strength and leaped. The thrust of his legs cast him outward, through a long arc that ended in deeper water. It fountained high and white when he struck. He went down into green depths while the currents swept him to and fro. But he hit the sandy bottom unharmed.

Having no need to breathe, he stayed under. To recover from the shock took him less than a second. To make his assessment took minutes, there in the swirling surges.

Gaia had tried to take him over. A force field had begun to damp the processes in his brain and impose its own patterns. He had quenched it barely in time.

She would scarcely have required a capability of that kind in the past. Therefore she had invented and installed it specifically for him. This strongly suggested she had meant to use it at some point of their journey. When he saw a thing she had not known was there and refused to be fobbed off, he compelled her to make the attempt before she was ready. When it failed, she spent her last resources to destroy him.

She would go that far, that desperately, to keep a secret that tremendous from the stars.

He recognized a mistake in his thinking. She had not used up everything at her beck. On the contrary, she had a planetful of observers and other instrumentalities to call upon. Certain of them must be bound here at top speed, to make sure he was dead—or, if he lived, to make sure of him. Afterward she would feed Wayfarer a story that ended with a regrettable accident away off over an ocean.

Heavier than water, Brannock strode down a sloping sea floor in search of depth.

Having found a jumble of volcanic rock, he crawled into a lava tube, lay fetally curled, and willed his systems to operate as low-level as might be. He hoped that then her agents would miss him. Neither their numbers nor their sensitivities were infinite. It would be reasonable for Gaia—who could not have witnessed his escape, her sensors in the aircraft being obliterated as it came apart—to conclude that the flows had taken his scattered remains away.

After three days and nights, the internal clock he had set brought him back awake.

He knew he must stay careful. However, unless she kept a closer watch on the site than he expected she would—for Wayfarer, in communion with her, might too readily notice that she was concentrating on one little patch of the planet—he dared now move about. His electronic senses ought to warn him of any robot that came into his vicinity, even if it was too small for eyes to see. Whether he could then do anything about it was a separate question.

First he searched the immediate area. Gaia's machines had removed those shards of the wreck that they found, but most were strewn over the bottom, and she had evidently not thought it worthwhile, or safe, to have them sought out. Nearly all of what he came upon was in fact scrap. A few units were intact. The one that interested him had the physical form of a small metal sphere. He tracked it down by magnetic induction. Having taken it to a place ashore, hidden by trees from the sky, he studied it. With his tool-hands he traced the (mythic) circuitry within and identified it as a memory bank. The encoding was familiar to his Wayfarer aspect. He extracted the information and stored it in his own database.

A set of languages. Human languages, although none he had ever heard of. Yes, very interesting.

"I'd better get hold of those people," he muttered. In the solitude of wind, sea, and wilderness, he had relapsed into an ancient habit of occasionally thinking aloud. "Won't likely be another chance. Quite a piece of news for Wayfarer." If he came back, or at least got within range of his transmitter.

He set forth afoot, along the shore toward the bay where the Remnant River debouched. Maybe that which he had seen would be there yet, or traces of it.

He wasn't sure, everything had happened so fast, but he thought it was a ship.

7

Three days—olden Earth days of twenty-four hours, cool sunlight, now and then a rainshower leaving pastures and hedgerows asparkle, rides through English lanes, rambles through English towns, encounters with folk, evensong in a Norman church, exploration of buildings and books, long talks and companionable silences—wrought friendship. In Christian it also began to rouse kindlier feelings toward Gaia. She had resurrected Laurinda, and Laurinda was a part of her, as he was of Wayfarer and of Alpha and more other minds across the galaxy than he could number. Could the rest of Gaia's works be wrongful?

No doubt she had chosen and planned as she did in order to get this reaction from him. It didn't seem to matter.

Nor did the primitive conditions of the eighteenth century matter to him or to Laurinda. Rather, their everyday experiences were something refreshingly new, and frequently the occasion of laughter. What did become a bit difficult for him was to retire decorously to his separate room each night.

But they had their missions: his to see what was going on in this reality and afterward upload into Wayfarer; hers to explain and justify it to him as well as a mortal was able. Like him, she kept a memory of having been one with a nodal being. The memory was as dim and fragmentary as his, more a sense of transcendence than anything with a name or form, like the afterglow of a religious vision long ago. Yet it pervaded her personality, the unconscious more than the conscious; and it was her relationship to Gaia, as he had his to Wayfarer and beyond that to Alpha. In a limited, mortal, but altogether honest and natural way, she spoke for the node of Earth.

By tacit consent, they said little about the purpose and simply enjoyed their surroundings and one another, until the fourth morning. Perhaps the weather whipped up a lifetime habit of duty. Wind gusted and shrilled around the house, rain blinded the windows, there would be no going out even in a carriage. Indoors a fire failed to hold dank chill at bay. Candlelight glowed cozily on the breakfast table, silverware and china sheened, but shadows hunched thick in every corner.

He took a last sip of coffee, put the cup down, and ended the words he had been setting forth: "Yes, we'd better get started. Not that I've any clear notion of what to look for. Wayfarer himself doesn't." Gaia had been so vague about so much. Well, Wayfarer was now (whatever "now" meant) in rapport with her, seeking an overall, cosmic view of—how many millions of years on this planet?

"Why, you know your task," Laurinda replied. "You're to find out the nature of Gaia's interior activity, what it means in moral—in human terms.'' She straightened in her chair. Her tone went resolute. ''We *are* human, we emulations. We think and act, we feel joy and pain, the same as humans always did.''

Impulse beckoned; it was his wont to try to lighten moods. ''And,'' he added, ''make new generations of people, the same as humans always did.''

A blush crossed the fair countenance. ''Yes,'' she said. Quickly: ''Of course, most of what's . . . here . . . is nothing but database. Archives, if you will. We might start by visiting one or two of those reconstructions.''

He smiled, the heaviness lifting from him. ''I'd love to. Any suggestions?''

Eagerness responded. ''The Acropolis of Athens? As it was when new? Classical civilization fascinated me.'' She tossed her head. ''Still does, by damn.''

''Hm.'' He rubbed his chin. ''From what I learned in my day, those old Greeks were as tricky, quarrelsome, shortsighted a pack of political animals as ever stole an election or bullied a weaker neighbor. Didn't Athens finance the building of the Parthenon by misappropriating the treasury of the Delian League?''

''They were human,'' she said, almost too low for him to hear above the storm-noise. ''But what they made—''

''Sure,'' he answered. ''Agreed. Let's go.''

In perception, the amulets were silvery two-centimeter discs that hung on a user's breast, below garments. In reality—outer-viewpoint reality—they were powerful, subtle programs with intelligences of their own. Christian wondered about the extent to which they were under the direct control of Gaia, and how closely she was monitoring him.

Without thinking, he took Laurinda's hand. Her fingers clung to his. She looked straight before her, though, into the flickery fire, while she uttered their command.

Immediately, with no least sensation of movement, they were on broad marble steps between outworks, under a cloudless heaven, in flooding hot radiance. From the steepest, unused hill slopes, a scent of wild thyme drifted up through silence, thyme without bees to quicken it or hands to pluck it. Below reached the city, sun-smitten house roofs, open agoras, colonnaded temples. In this clear air Brannock imagined he could well-nigh make out the features on the statues.

After a time beyond time, the visitors moved upward, still mute, still hand in hand, to where winged Victories lined the balustrade before the sanctuary of Nike Apteros. Their draperies flowed to movement he did not see and wind he did not feel. One was tying her sandals. . . .

For a long while the two lingered at the Propylaea, its porticos, Ionics, Dorics, paintings, votive tablets in the Pinakotheka. They felt they could have stayed past sunset, but everything else awaited them, and they knew mortal enthusiasm as they would presently know mortal weariness. Colors burned. . . .

The stone flowers and stone maidens at the Erechtheum . . .

Christian had thought of the Parthenon as exquisite; so it was in the pictures and models he had seen, while the broken, chemically gnawed remnants were merely to grieve over. Confronting it here, entering it, he discovered its sheer size and mass. Life shouted in the friezes, red, blue, gilt; then in the dusk within, awesomeness and beauty found their focus in the colossal Athene of Pheidias.

—Long afterward, he stood with Laurinda on the Wall of Kimon, above the Asclepium and Theater of Dionysus. A westering sun made the city below intricate with shadows, and coolth breathed out of the east. Hitherto, when they spoke it had been, illogically, in near whispers. Now they felt free to talk openly, or did they feel a need?

He shook his head. "Gorgeous," he said, for lack of anything halfway adequate. "Unbelievable."

"It was worth all the wrongdoing and war and agony," she murmured. "Wasn't it?"

For the moment, he shied away from deep seriousness. "I didn't expect it to be this, uh, gaudy—no, this bright."

"They painted their buildings. That's known."

"Yes, I knew too. But were later scholars sure of just what colors?"

"Scarcely, except where a few traces were left. Most of this must be Gaia's conjecture. The sculpture especially, I suppose. Recorded history saved only the barest description of the Athene, for instance." Laurinda paused. Her gaze went outward to the mountains. "But surely this—in view of everything she has, all the information, and being able to handle it all at once and, and, understand the minds that were capable of making it—surely this is the most likely reconstruction. Or the least unlikely."

"She may have tried variations. Would you like to go see?"

"No, I, I think not, unless you want to. This has been overwhelming, hasn't it?" She hesitated. "Besides, well—"

He nodded. "Yeh." With a gesture at the soundless, motionless, smokeless city below and halidoms around: "Spooky. At best, a museum exhibit. Not much to our purpose, I'm afraid."

She met his eyes. "Your purpose. I'm only a—not even a guide, really. Gaia's voice to you? No, just a, an undertone of her, if that." The smile that touched her lips was somehow forlorn. "I suspect my main reason for existing again is to keep you company."

He laughed and offered her a hand, which for a moment she clasped tightly. "I'm very glad of the company, eccentric Miss Ashcroft."

Her smile warmed and widened. "Thank you, kind sir. And I am glad to be . . . alive . . . today. What should we do next?"

"Visit some living history, I think," he said. "Why not Hellenic?"

She struck her palms together. "The age of Pericles!"

He frowned. "Well, I don't know about that. The Peloponnesian War, the plague—and foreigners like us, barbarians, you a woman, we wouldn't be too well received, would we?"

He heard how she put disappointment aside and looked forward anew. "When and where, then?"

"Aristotle's time? If I remember rightly, Greece was peaceful then, no matter how much hell Alexander was raising abroad, and the society was getting quite cosmopolitan. Less patriarchal, too. Anyhow, Aristotle's always interested me. In a way, he was one of the earliest scientists."

"We had better inquire first. But before that, let's go home to a nice hot cup of tea!"

They returned to the house at the same moment as they left it, to avoid perturbing the servants. There they found that lack of privacy joined with exhaustion to keep them from speaking of anything other than trivia. However, that was all right; they were good talkmates.

The next morning, which was brilliant, they went out into the garden and settled on a bench by the fish basin. Drops of rain glistened on flowers, whose fragrance awoke with the strengthening sunshine. Nothing else was in sight or earshot. This time Christian addressed the amulets. He felt suddenly heavy around his neck, and the words came out awkwardly. He need not have said them aloud, but it helped him give shape to his ideas.

The reply entered directly into their brains. He rendered it to himself, irrationally, as in a dry, professorish tenor:

"Only a single Hellenic milieu has been carried through many generations. It includes the period you have in mind. It commenced at the point of approximately 500 B.C., with an emulation as historically accurate as possible."

But nearly everyone then alive was lost to history, thought Christian. Except for the few who were in the chronicles, the whole population must needs be created out of Gaia's imagination, guided by knowledge and logic; and those few named persons were themselves almost entirely new-made, their very DNA arbitrarily laid out.

"The sequence was revised as necessary," the amulet continued.

Left to itself, that history would soon have drifted completely away from the documents, and eventually from the archeology, Christian thought. Gaia saw this start to happen, over and over. She rewrote the program—events, memories, personalities, bodies, births, life spans, deaths—and let it resume until it deviated again. Over and over. The morning felt abruptly cold.

"Much was learned on every such occasion," said the amulet. "The situation appeared satisfactory by the time Macedonian hegemony was inevitable, and thereafter the sequence was left to play itself out undisturbed. Naturally, it still did not proceed identically with the historical past. Neither Aristotle nor Alexander were born. Instead, a reasonably realistic conqueror lived to a ripe age and bequeathed a reasonably well constructed empire. He did have a Greek teacher in his youth, who had been a disciple of Plato."

"Who was that?" Christian asked out of a throat gone dry.

"His name was Eumenes. In many respects he was equivalent to Aristotle, but had a more strongly empirical orientation. This was planned."

Eumenes was specially ordained, then. Why?

"If we appear and meet him, w-won't that change what comes after?"

"Probably not to any significant extent. Or if it does, that will not matter. The original sequence is in Gaia's database. Your visit will, in effect, be a reactivation."

"Not one for your purpose," Laurinda whispered into the air. "What was it? What happened in that world?"

"The objective was experimental, to study the possible engendering of a scientific-technological revolution analogous to that of the seventeenth century A.D., with accompanying social developments that might foster the evolution of a stable democracy."

Christian told himself furiously to pull out of his funk. "Did it?" He challenged.

The reply was calm. "Do you wish to study it?"

Christian had not expected any need to muster his courage. After a minute he said, word by slow word, "Yes, I think that might be more useful than meeting your philosopher. Can you show us the outcome of the experiment?"

Laurinda joined in: "Oh, I know there can't be any single, simple picture. But can you bring us to a, a scene that will give an impression—a kind of epitome—like, oh, King John at Runnymede or Elizabeth the First knighting Francis Drake or Einstein and Bohr talking about the state of their world?"

"An extreme possibility occurs in a year corresponding to your 894 A.D.," the amulet told him. "I suggest Athens as the locale. Be warned, it is dangerous. I can protect you, or remove you, but human affairs are inherently chaotic and this situation is more unpredictable than most. It could escape my control."

"I'll go," Christian snapped.

"And I," Laurinda said.

He glared at her. "No. You heard. It's dangerous."

Gone quite calm, she stated, "It is necessary for me. Remember, I travel on behalf of Gaia."

Gaia, who let the thing come to pass.

Transfer.

For an instant, they glanced at themselves. They knew the amulets would convert their garb to something appropriate. She wore a gray gown, belted, reaching halfway down her calves, with shoes, stockings, and a scarf over hair coiled in braids. He was in tunic, trousers, and boots of the same coarse materials, a sheath knife at his hip and a long-barreled firearm slung over his back.

Their surroundings smote them. They stood in a Propylaea that was scarcely more than tumbled stones and snags of sculpture. The Parthenon was not so shattered, but scarred, weathered, here and there buttressed with brickwork from which thrust the mouths of rusted cannon. All else was ruin. The Erechtheum looked as if it had been quarried. Below them, the city burned. They could see little of it through smoke that stained the sky and savaged their nostrils. A roar of conflagration reached them, and bursts of gunfire.

A woman came running out of the haze, up the great staircase. She was young, dark-haired, unkempt, ragged, begrimed, desperate. A man came after, a burly blond in a fur cap, dirty red coat, and leather breeches. Beneath a sweeping mustache, he leered. He too was armed, murderously big knife, firearm in right hand.

The woman saw Christian looming before her. *"Voetho!"* she screamed. *"Onome Theou, kyrie, voetho!"* She caught her foot against a step and fell. Her pursuer stopped before she could rise and stamped a boot down on her back.

Through his amulet, Christian understood the cry. "Help, in God's name, sir, help!" Fleetingly he thought the language must be a debased Greek. The other man snarled at him and brought weapon to shoulder.

Christian had no time to unlimber his. While the stranger was in motion, he bent, snatched up a rock—a fragment of a marble head—and cast. It thudded against the stranger's nose. He lurched back, his face a sudden red grotesque. His gun clattered to the stairs. He howled.

With the quickness that was his in emergencies, Christian rejected grabbing his own firearm. He had seen that its lock was of peculiar design. He might not be able to discharge it fast enough. He drew his knife and lunged downward. "Get away, you swine, before I open your guts!" he shouted. The words came out in the woman's language.

The other man retched, turned, and staggered off. Well before he reached the bottom of the hill, smoke had swallowed sight of him. Christian halted at the woman's huddled form and sheathed his blade. "Here, sister," he said, offering his hand, "come along. Let's get to shelter. There may be more of them."

She crawled to her feet, gasping, leaned heavily on his arm, and limped beside him up to the broken gateway. Her features Mediterranean, she was doubtless a native. She looked half starved. Laurinda came to her other side. Between them, the visitors got her into the portico of the Parthenon. Beyond a smashed door lay an interior dark and empty of everything but litter. It would be defensible if necessary.

An afterthought made Christian swear at himself. He went back for the enemy's weapon. When he returned, Laurinda sat with her arms around the woman, crooning comfort. "There, darling, there, you're safe with us. Don't be afraid. We'll take care of you."

The fugitive lifted big eyes full of night. "Are . . . you . . . angels from heaven?" she mumbled.

"No, only mortals like you," Laurinda answered through tears. That was not exactly true, Christian thought; but what else could she say? "We do not even know your name."

"I am . . . Zoe . . . Comnenaina—"

"Bone-dry, I hear from your voice." Laurinda lifted her head. Her lips moved in silent command. A jug appeared on the floor, bedewed with cold. "Here is water. Drink."

Zoe had not noticed the miracle. She snatched the vessel and drained it in gulp after gulp. When she was through she set it down and said, "Thank you," dully but with something of strength and reason again in her.

"Who was that after you?" Christian asked.

She drew knees to chin, hugged herself, stared before her, and replied in a dead voice, "A Flemic soldier. They broke into our house. I saw them stab my father. They laughed and laughed. I ran out the back and down the streets. I thought I could hide on the Acropolis. Nobody comes here anymore. That one saw me and came after. I suppose he would have killed me when he was done. That would have been better than if he took me away with him."

Laurinda nodded. "An invading army," she said as tonelessly. "They took the city and now they are sacking it."

Christian thumped the butt of his gun down on the stones. "Does Gaia let this go *on?*" he grated.

Laurinda lifted her gaze to his. It pleaded. "She must. Humans must have free will. Otherwise they're puppets."

"But how did they get into this mess?" Christian demanded. "Explain it if you can!"

The amulet(s) replied with the same impersonality as before:

"The Hellenistic era developed scientific method. This, together with the expansion of commerce and geographical knowledge, produced an industrial revolution and parliamentary democracy. However, neither the science nor the technology progressed beyond an approximate equivalent of your eighteenth century. Unwise social and fiscal policies led to breakdown, dictatorship, and repeated warfare.''

Christian's grin bared teeth. "That sounds familiar.''

"Alexander Tytler said it in our eighteenth century," Laurinda muttered unevenly. "No republic has long outlived the discovery by a majority of its people that they could vote themselves largesse from the public treasury.'' Aloud: "Christian, they were only human.''

Zoe hunched, lost in her sorrow.

"You oversimplify," stated the amulet voice. "But this is not a history lesson. To continue the outline, inevitably engineering information spread to the warlike barbarians of northern Europe and western Asia. If you question why they were granted existence, reflect that a population confined to the littoral of an inland sea could not model any possible material world. The broken-down societies of the South were unable to change their characters, or prevail over them, or eventually hold them off. The end results are typified by what you see around you.''

"The Dark Ages," Christian said dully. "What happens after them? What kind of new civilization?''

"None. This sequence terminates in one more of its years.''

"Huh?" he gasped. "Destroyed?''

"No. The program ceases to run. The emulation stops.''

"My God! Those millions of lives—as real as, as mine—''

Laurinda stood up and held her arms out into the fouled air. "Does Gaia know, then, does Gaia know this time line would never get any happier?'' she cried.

"No," said the voice in their brains. "Doubtless the potential of further progress exists. However, you forget that while Gaia's capacities are large, they are not infinite. The more attention she devotes to one history, the details of its planet as well as the length of its course, the less she has to give to others. The probability is too small that this sequence will lead to a genuinely new form of society.''

Slowly, Laurinda nodded. "I see.''

"I don't," Christian snapped. "Except that Gaia's inhuman.''

Laurinda shook her head and laid a hand on his. "No, not that. Posthuman. *We* built the first artificial intelligences." After a moment: "Gaia isn't cruel. The universe often is, and she didn't create it. She's seeking something better than blind chance can make.''

"Maybe." His glance fell on Zoe. "Look, something's got to be done for this poor soul. Never mind if we change the history. It's due to finish soon anyway.''

Laurinda swallowed and wiped her eyes. "Give her her last year in peace," she said into the air. "Please."

Objects appeared in the room behind the doorway. "Here are food, wine, clean water," said the unheard voice. "Advise her to return downhill after dark, find some friends, and lead them back. A small party, hiding in these ruins, can hope to survive until the invaders move on."

"It isn't worthwhile doing more, is it?" Christian said bitterly. "Not to you."

"Do you wish to end your investigation?"

"No, be damned if I will."

"Nor I," said Laurinda. "But when we're through here, when we've done the pitiful little we can for this girl, take us home."

Peace dwelt in England. Clouds towered huge and white, blue-shadowed from the sunlight spilling past them. Along the left side of a lane, poppies blazed in a grainfield goldening toward harvest. On the right stretched the manifold greens of a pasture where cattle drowsed beneath a broad-crowned oak. Man and woman rode side by side. Hoofs thumped softly, saddle leather creaked, the sweet smell of horse mingled with herbal pungencies, a blackbird whistled.

"No, I don't suppose Gaia will ever restart any program she's terminated," Laurinda said. "But it's no worse than death, and death is seldom that easy."

"The scale of it," Christian protested, then sighed. "But I daresay Wayfarer will tell me I'm being sloppy sentimental, and when I've rejoined him I'll agree." Wryness added that that had better be true. He would no longer be separate, an avatar; he would be one with a far greater entity, which would in its turn remerge with a greater still.

"Without Gaia, they would never have existed, those countless lives, generation after generation after generation," Laurinda said. "Their worst miseries they brought on themselves. If any of them are ever to find their way to something better, truly better, she has to keep making fresh starts."

"Mm, I can't help remembering all the millennialists and utopians who slaughtered people wholesale, or tortured them or threw them into concentration camps, if their behavior didn't fit the convenient attainment of the inspired vision."

"No, no, it's not like that! Don't you see? She gives them their freedom to be themselves and, and to become more."

"Seems to me she adjusts the parameters and boundary conditions till the setup looks promising before she lets the experiment run." Christian frowned. "But I admit, it isn't believable that she does it simply because she's . . . bored and lonely. Not when the whole fellowship of her kind is open to her. Maybe we haven't the brains to know what her reasons are. Maybe she's explaining them to Wayfarer, or directly to Alpha,'' although communication among the stars would take decades at least.

"Do you want to go on nonetheless?'' she asked.

"I said I do. I'm supposed to. But you?''

"Yes. I don't want to, well, fail her.''

"I'm sort of at a loss what to try next, and not sure it's wise to let the amulets decide.''

"But they can help us, counsel us.'' Laurinda drew breath. "Please. If you will. The next world we go to—could it be gentle? That horror we saw—''

He reached across to take her hand. "Exactly what I was thinking. Have you a suggestion?''

She nodded. "York Minster. It was in sad condition when I . . . lived . . . but I saw pictures and—It was one of the loveliest churches ever built, in the loveliest old town.''

"Excellent idea. Not another lifeless piece of archive, though. A complete environment.'' Christian pondered. "We'll inquire first, naturally, but offhand I'd guess the Edwardian period would suit us well. On the Continent they called it the *belle époque*.''

"Splendid!'' she exclaimed. Already her spirits were rising anew.

Transfer.

They arrived near the west end, in the south aisle.

Worshippers were few, scattered closer to the altar rail. In the dimness, under the glories of glass and soaring Perpendicular arches, their advent went unobserved. Windows in that direction glowed more vividly—rose, gold, blue, the cool gray-green of the Five Sisters—than the splendor above their backs; it was a Tuesday morning in June. Incense wove its odor through the ringing chant from the choir.

Christian tautened. "That's Latin,'' he whispered. "In England, 1900?'' He glanced down at his garments and hers, and peered ahead. Shirt, coat, trousers for him, with a hat laid on the pew; ruffled blouse, ankle-length gown, and lacy bonnet for her; but—"The clothes aren't right either.''

"Hush,'' Laurinda answered as low. "Wait. We were told this wouldn't be our 1900. Here may be the only York Minster in all of Gaia.''

He nodded stiffly. It was clear that the node had never attempted a perfect reproduction of any past milieu—impossible, and pointless to boot. Often, though not necessarily always, she took an approximation as a starting point; but it never went on to the same destiny. What were the roots of this day?

"Relax,'' Laurinda urged. "It's beautiful.''

He did his best, and indeed the Roman Catholic mass at the hour of tierce sang some tranquility into his heart.

After the Nunc Dimittis, when clergy and laity had departed, the two could wander around and savor. Emerging at last, they spent a while looking upon the carven tawny limestone of the front. This was no Parthenon; it was a different upsurging of the same miracle. But around it lay a world to discover. With half a sigh and half a smile, they set forth.

The delightful narrow "gates," walled in with half-timbered houses, lured them. More modern streets and buildings, above all the people therein, captured them. York was a living town, a market town, core of a wide hinterland, node of a nation. It racketed, it bustled.

The half smile faded. A wholly foreign setting would not have felt as wrong as one that was half homelike.

Clothing styles were not radically unlike what pictures and historical dramas had once shown; but they were not identical. The English chatter was in no dialect of English known to Christian or Laurinda, and repeatedly they heard versions of German. A small, high-stacked steam locomotive pulled a train into a station of somehow Teutonic architecture. No early automobiles stuttered along the thoroughfares. Horse-drawn vehicles moved crowdedly, but the pavements were clean and the smell of dung faint because the animals wore a kind of diapers. A flag above a post office (?), fluttering in the wind, displayed a cross of St. Andrew on which was superimposed a two-headed gold eagle. A man with a megaphone bellowed at the throng to stand aside and make way for a military squadron. In blue uniforms, rifles on shoulders, they quick-marched to commands barked in German. Individual soldiers, presumably on leave, were everywhere. A boy went by, shrilly hawking newspapers, and Christian saw WAR in a headline.

"Listen, amulet," he muttered finally, "where can we get a beer?"

"A public house will admit you if you go in by the couples' entrance," replied the soundless voice.

So, no unescorted women allowed. Well, Christian thought vaguely, hadn't that been the case in his Edwardian years, at any rate in respectable taverns? A signboard jutting from a Tudor façade read GEORGE AND DRAGON. The wainscoted room inside felt equally English.

Custom was plentiful and noisy, tobacco smoke thick, but he and Laurinda found a table in a corner where they could talk without anybody else paying attention. The brew that a barmaid fetched was of Continental character. He didn't give it the heed it deserved.

"I don't think we've found our peaceful world after all," he said.

Laurinda looked beyond him, into distances where he could not follow. "Will we ever?" she wondered. "Can any be, if it's human?"

He grimaced. "Well, let's find out what the hell's going on here."

"You can have a detailed explanation if you wish," said the voice in their heads. "You would be better advised to accept a bare outline, as you did before."

"Instead of loading ourselves down with the background of a world that never was," he mumbled.

"That never was ours," Laurinda corrected him.

"Carry on."

"This sequence was generated as of its fifteenth century A.D.," said the voice. "The conciliar movement was made to succeed, rather than failing as it did in your history."

"Uh, conciliar movement?"

"The ecclesiastical councils of Constance and later of Basel attempted to heal the Great Schism and reform the government of the Church. Here they accomplished it, giving back to the bishops some of the power that over the centuries had accrued to the popes, working out a reconciliation with the Hussites, and making other important changes. As a result, no Protestant breakaway occurred, nor wars of religion, and the Church remained a counterbalance to the state, preventing the rise of absolute monarchies."

"Why, that's wonderful," Laurinda whispered.

"Not too wonderful by now," Christian said grimly. "What happened?"

"In brief, Germany was spared the devastation of the Thirty Years' War and a long-lasting division into quarrelsome principalities. It was unified in the seventeenth century and soon became the dominant European power, colonizing and conquering eastward. Religious and cultural differences from the Slavs proved irreconcilable. As the harsh imperium provoked increasing restlessness, it perforce grew more severe, causing more rebellion. Meanwhile it decayed within, until today it has broken apart and the Russians are advancing on Berlin."

"I see. What about science and technology?"

"They have developed more slowly than in your history, although you have noted the existence of a fossil-fueled industry and inferred an approximately Lagrangian level of theory."

"The really brilliant eras were when all hell broke loose, weren't they?" Christian mused. "This Europe went through less agony, and invented and discovered less. Coincidence?"

"What about government?" Laurinda asked.

"For a time, parliaments flourished, more powerful than kings, emperors, or popes," said the voice. "In most Western countries they still wield considerable influence."

"As the creatures of special interests, I'll bet," Christian rasped. "All right, what comes next?"

Gaia knew. He sat in a reactivation of something she probably played to a finish thousands of years ago.

"Scientific and technological advance proceeds, accelerating, through a long period of general turbulence. At the termination point—"

"Never mind!" Oblivion might be better than a nuclear war.

Silence fell at the table. The life that filled the pub with its noise felt remote, unreal.

"We dare not weep," Laurinda finally said. "Not yet."

Christian shook himself. "Europe was never the whole of Earth," he growled. "How many worlds has Gaia made?"

"Many," the voice told him.

"Show us one that's really foreign. If you agree, Laurinda."

She squared her shoulders. "Yes, do." After a moment: "Not here. If we disappeared it would shock them. It might change the whole future."

"Hardly enough to notice," Christian said. "And would it matter in the long run? But, yeh, let's be off."

They wandered out, among marvels gone meaningless, until they found steps leading up onto the medieval wall. Thence they looked across roofs and river and Yorkshire beyond, finding they were alone.

"Now take us away," Christian ordered.

"You have not specified any type of world," said the voice.

"Surprise us."

Transfer.

The sky stood enormous, bleached blue, breezes warm underneath. A bluff overlooked a wide brown river. Trees grew close to its edge, tall, pale of bark, leaves silver-green and shivery. Christian recognized them, cottonwoods. He was somewhere in west central North America, then. Uneasy shadows lent camouflage if he and Laurinda kept still. Across the river the land reached broad, roads twisting their way through cultivation—mainly wheat and Indian corn—that seemed to be parceled out among small farms, each with its buildings, house, barn, occasional stable or workshop. The sweeping lines of the ruddy-tiled roofs looked Asian. He spied oxcarts and a few horseback riders on the roads, workers in the fields, but at their distance he couldn't identify race or garb. Above yonder horizon thrust clustered towers that also suggested the Orient. If they belonged to a city, it must be compact, not sprawling over the countryside but neatly drawn into itself.

One road ran along the farther riverbank. A procession went upon it. An elephant led, as richly caparisoned as the man under the silk awning of a howdah. Shaven-headed men in yellow robes walked after, flanked by horsemen who bore poles from which pennons streamed scarlet and gold. The sound of slowly beaten gongs and minor-key chanting came faint through the wind.

Christian snapped his fingers. "Stupid me!" he muttered. "Give us a couple of opticals."

Immediately he and Laurinda held the devices. From his era, they fitted into the palm but projected an image at any magnification desired, with no lenses off which light could glint to betray. He peered back and forth for minutes. Yes, the appearance was quite Chinese, or Chinese-derived, except that a number of the individuals he studied had more of an American countenance and the leader on the elephant wore a feather bonnet above his robe.

"How quiet here," Laurinda said.

"You are at the height of the Great Peace," the amulet voice answered.

"How many like that were there ever?" Christian wondered. "Where, when, how?"

"You are in North America, in the twenty-second century by your reckoning. Chinese navigators arrived on the Pacific shore seven hundred years ago, and colonists followed."

In this world, Christian thought, Europe and Africa were surely a sketch, mere geography, holding a few primitive tribes at most, unless nothing was there but ocean. Simplify, simplify.

"Given the distances to sail and the dangers, the process was slow," the voice went on. "While the newcomers displaced or subjugated the natives wherever they settled, most remained free for a long time, acquired the technology, and also developed resistance to introduced diseases. Eventually, being on roughly equal terms, the races began to mingle, genetically and culturally. The settlers mitigated the savagery of the religions they had encountered, but learned from the societies, as well as teaching. You behold the outcome."

"The Way of the Buddha?" Laurinda asked very softly.

"As influenced by Daoism and local nature cults. It is a harmonious faith, without sects or heresies, pervading the civilization."

"Everything can't be pure loving-kindness," Christian said.

"Certainly not. But the peace that the Emperor Wei Zhi-fu brought about has lasted for a century and will for another two. If you travel, you will find superb achievements in the arts and in graciousness."

"Another couple of centuries." Laurinda's tones wavered the least bit. "Afterward?"

"It doesn't last," Christian predicted. "These are humans too. And—tell me—do they ever get to a real science?"

"No," said the presence. "Their genius lies in other realms. But the era of warfare to come will drive the development of a remarkable empirical technology."

"What era?"

"China never recognized the independence that this country proclaimed for itself, nor approved of its miscegenation. A militant dynasty will arise, which overruns a western hemisphere weakened by the religious and secular quarrels that do at last break out."

"And the conquerors will fall in their turn. Unless Gaia makes an end first. She does—she did—sometime, didn't she?"

"All things are finite. Her creations too."

The leaves rustled through muteness.

"Do you wish to go into the city and look about?" asked the presence. "It can be arranged for you to meet some famous persons."

"No," Christian said. "Not yet, anyway. Maybe later."

Laurinda sighed. "We'd rather go home now and rest."

"And think," Christian said. "Yes."

Transfer.

The sun over England seemed milder than for America. Westering, it sent rays through windows to glow in wood, caress marble and the leather bindings of books, explode into rainbows where they met cut glass, evoke flower aromas from a jar of potpourri.

Laurinda opened a bureau drawer. She slipped the chain of her amulet over her head and tossed the disc in. Christian blinked, nodded, and followed suit. She closed the drawer.

"We do need to be by ourselves for a while," she said. "This hasn't been a dreadful day like, like before, but I am so tired."

"Understandable," he replied.

"You?"

"I will be soon, no doubt."

"Those worlds—already they feel like dreams I've wakened from."

"An emotional retreat from them, I suppose. Not cowardice, no, no, just a necessary, temporary rest. You shared their pain. You're too sweet for your own good, Laurinda."

She smiled. "How you misjudge me. I'm not quite ready to collapse yet, if you aren't."

"Thunder, no."

She took crystal glasses out of a cabinet, poured from a decanter on a sideboard, and gestured invitation. The port fondled their tongues. They stayed on their feet, look meeting look.

"I daresay we'd be presumptuous and foolish to try finding any pattern, this early in our search," she ventured. "Those peeks we've had, out of who knows how many worlds—each as real as we are." She shivered.

"I may have a hunch," he said slowly.

"A what?"

"An intimation, an impression, a wordless kind of guess. Why has Gaia been doing it? I can't believe it's nothing but pastime."

"Nor I. Nor can I believe she would let such terrible things happen if she could prevent them. How can an intellect, a soul, like hers be anything but good?"

So Laurinda thought, Christian reflected; but she was an avatar of Gaia. He didn't suppose that affected the fairness of her conscious mind; he had come to know her rather well. But neither did it prove the nature, the ultimate intent, of Earth's node. It merely showed that the living Laurinda Ashcroft had been a decent person.

She took a deep draught from her glass before going on: "I think, myself, she is in the same position as the traditional God. Being good, she wants to share existence with others, and so creates them. But to make them puppets, automatons, would be senseless. They have to have consciousness and free will. Therefore they are able to sin, and do, all too often."

"Why hasn't she made them morally stronger?"

"Because she's chosen to make them human. And what are we but a specialized African ape?" Laurinda's tone lowered; she stared into the wine. "Specialized to make tools and languages and dreams; but the dreams can be nightmares."

In Gaia's and Alpha's kind laired no ancient beast, Christian thought. The human elements in them were long since absorbed, tamed, transfigured. His resurrection and hers must be nearly unique.

Not wanting to hurt her, he shaped his phrases with care. "Your idea is reasonable, but I'm afraid it leaves some questions dangling. Gaia does intervene, again and again. The amulets admit it. When the emulations get too far off track, she changes them and their people." Until she shuts them down, he did not add. "Why is she doing it, running history after history, experiment after experiment—why?"

Laurinda winced. "To, to learn about this strange race of ours?"

He nodded. "Yes, that's my hunch. Not even she, nor the galactic brain itself, can take first principles and compute what any human situation will lead to. Human affairs are chaotic. But chaotic systems do have structures, attractors, constraints. By letting things happen, through countless variations, you might discover a few general laws, which courses are better and which worse." He tilted his goblet. "To what end, though? There are no more humans in the outside universe. There haven't been for—how many million years? No, unless it actually is callous curiosity, I can't yet guess what she's after."

"Nor I." Laurinda finished her drink. "Now I am growing very tired, very fast."

"I'm getting that way too." Christian paused. "How about we go sleep till evening? Then a special dinner, and our heads ought to be more clear."

Briefly, she took his hand. "Until evening, dear friend."

The night was young and gentle. A full moon dappled the garden. Wine had raised a happy mood, barely tinged with wistfulness. Gravel scrunched rhythmically underfoot as Laurinda and Christian danced, humming the waltz melody together. When they were done, they sat down, laughing, by the basin. Brightness from above overflowed it. He had earlier put his amulet back on just long enough to command that a guitar appear for him. Now he took it up. He had never seen anything more beautiful than she was in the moonlight. He sang a song to her that he had made long ago when he was mortal.

> *"Lightfoot, Lightfoot, lead the measure*
> *As we dance the summer in!*
> *'Lifetime is our only treasure.*
> *Spend it well, on love and pleasure,'*
> *Warns the lilting violin.*
>
> *"If we'll see the year turn vernal*
> *Once again, lies all with chance.*
> *Yes, this ordering's infernal,*
> *But we'll make our own eternal*
> *Fleeting moment where we dance.*
>
> *"So shall we refuse compliance*
> *When across the green we whirl,*
> *Giving entropy defiance,*
> *Strings and winds in our alliance.*
> *Be a victor. Kiss me, girl!"*

Suddenly she was in his arms.

8

Where the hills loomed highest above the river that cut through them, a slope on the left bank rose steep but thinly forested. Kalava directed the lifeboat carrying his party to land. The slaves at the oars grunted with double effort. Sweat sheened on their skins and runneled down the straining bands of muscle; it was a day when the sun blazed from a sky just half clouded. The prow grated on a sandbar in the shallows. Kalava told off two of his sailors to stand guard over boat and rowers. With the other four and Ilyandi, he waded ashore and began to climb.

It went slowly but stiffly. On top they found a crest with a view that snatched a gasp from the woman and a couple of amazed oaths from the men. Northward the terrain fell still more sharply, so that they looked over treetops down to the bottom of the range and across a valley awash with the greens and russets of growth. The river shone through it like a drawn blade, descending from dimly seen foothills and the sawtooth mountains beyond them. Two swordwings hovered on high, watchful for prey. Sunbeams shot past gigantic cloudbanks, filling their whiteness with cavernous shadows. Somehow the air felt cooler here, and the herbal smells gave benediction.

"It is fair, ai, it is as fair as the Sunset Kingdom of legend," Ilyandi breathed at last.

She stood slim in the man's kirtle and buskins that she, as a Vilku, could with propriety wear on trek. The wind fluttered her short locks. The coppery skin was as wet and almost as odorous as Kalava's midnight black, but she was no more wearied than any of her companions.

The sailor Urko scowled at the trees and underbrush crowding close on either side. Only the strip up which the travelers had come was partly clear, perhaps because of a landslide in the past. "Too much woods," he grumbled. It had, in fact, been a struggle to move about wherever they landed. They could not attempt the hunting that had been easy on the coast. Luckily, the water teemed with fish.

"Logging will cure that." Kalava's words throbbed. "And then what farms!" He stared raptly into the future.

Turning down-to-earth: "But we've gone far enough, now that we've gained an idea of the whole country. Three days, and I'd guess two more going back downstream. Any longer, and the crew at the ship could grow fearful. We'll turn around here."

"Other ships will bring others, explorers," Ilyandi said.

"Indeed they will. And I'll skipper the first of them."

A rustling and crackling broke from the tangle to the right, through the boom of the wind. "What's that?" barked Taltara.

"Some big animal," Kalava replied. "Stand alert."

The mariners formed a line. Three grounded the spears they carried; the fourth unslung a crossbow from his shoulders and armed it. Kalava waved Ilyandi to go behind them and drew his sword.

The thing parted a brake and trod forth into the open.

"Aah!" wailed Yarvonin. He dropped his spear and whirled about to flee.

"Stand fast!" Kalava shouted. "Urko, shoot whoever runs, if I don't cut him down myself. Hold, you whoresons, hold!"

The thing stopped. For a span of many hammering heartbeats, none moved.

It was a sight to terrify. Taller by a head than the tallest man it sheered, but that head was faceless save for a horrible blank mask. Two thick arms sprouted from either side, the lower pair of hands wholly misshapen. A humped back did not belie the sense of their strength. As the travelers watched, the thing sprouted a skeletal third leg, to stand better on the uneven ground. Whether it was naked or armored in plate, in this full daylight it bore the hue of dusk.

"Steady, boys, steady," Kalava urged between clenched teeth. Ilyandi stepped from shelter to join him. An eldritch calm was upon her. "My lady, what *is* it?" he appealed.

"A god, or a messenger from the gods, I think." He could barely make her out beneath the wind.

"A demon," Eivala groaned, though he kept his post.

"No, belike not. We Vilkui have some knowledge of these matters. But, true, it is not fiery—and I never thought I would meet one—in this life—"

Ilyandi drew a long breath, briefly knotted her fists, then moved to take stance in front of the men. Having touched the withered sprig of tekin pinned at her breast, she covered her eyes and genuflected before straightening again to confront the mask.

The thing did not move, but, mouthless, it spoke, in a deep and resonant voice. The sounds were incomprehensible. After a moment it ceased, then spoke anew in an equally alien tongue. On its third try, Kalava exclaimed, "Hoy, that's from the Shining Fields!"

The thing fell silent, as if considering what it had heard. Thereupon words rolled out in the Ulonaian of Sirsu. "Be not afraid. I mean you no harm."

"What a man knows is little, what he understands is less, therefore let him bow down to wisdom," Ilyandi recited. She turned her head long enough to tell her companions: "Lay aside your weapons. Do reverence."

Clumsily, they obeyed.

In the blank panel of the blank skull appeared a man's visage. Though it was black, the features were not quite like anything anyone had seen before, nose broad, lips heavy, eyes round, hair tightly curled. Nevertheless, to spirits half stunned the magic was vaguely reassuring.

Her tone muted but level, Ilyandi asked, "What would you of us, lord?"

"It is hard to say," the strange one answered. After a pause: "Bewilderment goes through the world. I too . . . You may call me Brannock."

The captain rallied his courage. "And I am Kalava, Kurvo's son, of Clan Samayoki." Aside to Ilyandi, low: "No disrespect that I don't name you, my lady. Let him work any spells on me." Despite the absence of visible genitals, already the humans thought of Brannock as male.

"My lord needs no names to work his will," she said. "I hight Ilyandi, Lytin's daughter, born into Clan Arvala, now a Vilku of the fifth rank."

Kalava cleared his throat and added, "By your leave, lord, we'll not name the others just yet. They're scared aplenty as is." He heard a growl at his back and inwardly grinned. Shame would help hold them steady. As for him, dread was giving way to a thrumming keenness.

"You do not live here, do you?" Brannock asked.

"No," Kalava said, "we're scouts from overseas."

Ilyandi frowned at his presumption and addressed Brannock: "Lord, do we trespass? We knew not this ground was forbidden."

"It isn't," the other said. "Not exactly. But—" The face in the panel smiled. "Come, ease off, let us talk. We've much to talk about."

"He sounds not unlike a man," Kalava murmured to Ilyandi.

She regarded him. "If you be the man."

Brannock pointed to a big old gnarlwood with an overarching canopy of leaves. "Yonder is shade." He retracted his third leg and strode off. A fallen log took up most of the space. He leaned over and dragged it aside. Kalava's whole gang could not have done so. The action was not really necessary, but the display of power, benignly used, encouraged them further. Still, it was with hushed awe that the crewmen sat down in the paintwort. The captain, the Vilku, and the strange one remained standing.

"Tell me of yourselves," Brannock said mildly.

"Surely you know, lord," Ilyandi replied.

"That is as may be."

"He wants us to," Kalava said.

In the course of the next short while, prompted by questions, the pair gave a bare-bones account. Brannock's head within his head nodded. "I see. You are the first humans ever in this country. But your people have lived a long time in their homeland, have they not?"

"From time out of mind, lord," Ilyandi said, "though legend holds that our forebears came from the south."

Brannock smiled again. "You have been very brave to meet me like this, m-m, my lady. But you did tell your friend that your order has encountered beings akin to me."

"You heard her whisper, across half a spearcast?" Kalava blurted.

"Or you hear us think, lord," Ilyandi said.

Brannock turned grave. "No. Not that. Else why would I have needed your story?"

"Dare I ask whence you come?"

"I shall not be angry. But it is nothing I can quite explain. You can help by telling me about those beings you know of."

Ilyandi could not hide a sudden tension. Kalava stiffened beside her. Even the dumbstruck sailors must have wondered whether a god would have spoken thus.

Ilyandi chose her words with care. "Beings from on high have appeared in the past to certain Vilkui or, sometimes, chieftains. They gave commands

as to what the folk should or should not do. Ofttimes those commands were
hard to fathom. Why must the Kivalui build watermills in the Swift River,
when they had ample slaves to grind their grain?—But knowledge was im-
parted, too, counsel about where and how to search out the ways of nature.
Always, the high one forbade open talk about his coming. The accounts lie
in the secret annals of the Vilkui. But to you, lord—"

"What did those beings look like?" Brannock demanded sharply.

"Fiery shapes, winged or manlike, voices like great trumpets—"

"Ruvio's ax!" burst from Kalava. "The thing that passed overhead at
sea!"

The men on the ground shuddered.

"Yes," Brannock said, most softly, "I may have had a part there. But as
for the rest—"

His face flickered and vanished. After an appalling moment it reappeared.

"I am sorry, I meant not to frighten you, I forgot," he said. The expression
went stony, the voice tolled. "Hear me. There is war in heaven. I am cast
away from a battle, and enemy hunters may find me at any time. I carry a
word that must, it is vital that it reach a certain place, a . . . a holy mountain
in the north. Will you give aid?"

Kalava gripped his sword hilt so that it was as if the skin would split across
his knuckles. The blood had left Ilyandi's countenance. She stood ready to
be blasted with fire while she asked, "Lord Brannock, how do we know you
are of the gods?"

Nothing struck her down. "I am not," he told her. "I too can die. But
they whom I serve, they dwell in the stars."

The multitude of mystery, seen only when night clouds parted, but skythinkers taught that they circled always around the Axle of the North. . . . Ilyandi
kept her back straight. "Then can you tell me of the stars?"

"You are intelligent as well as brave," Brannock said. "Listen."

Kalava could not follow what passed between those two. The sailors cowered.

At the end, with tears upon her cheekbones, Ilyandi stammered, "Yes, he
knows the constellations, he knows of the ecliptic and the precession and the
returns of the Great Comet, he is from the stars. Trust him. We, we dare not
do otherwise."

Kalava let go his weapon, brought hand to breast in salute, and asked,
"How can we poor creatures help you, lord?"

"*You* are the news I bear," said Brannock.

"What?"

"I have no time to explain—if I could. The hunters may find me at any
instant. But maybe, maybe you could go on for me after they do."

"Escaping what overpowered you?" Kalava's laugh rattled. "Well, a man might try."

"The gamble is desperate. Yet if we win, choose your reward, whatever it may be, and I think you shall have it."

Ilyandi lowered her head above folded hands. "Enough to have served those who dwell beyond the moon."

"Humph," Kalava could not keep from muttering, "if they want to pay for it, why not?" Aloud, almost eagerly, his own head raised into the wind that tossed his whitened mane: "What'd you have us do?"

Brannock's regard matched his. "I have thought about this. Can one of you come with me? I will carry him, faster than he can go. As for what happens later, we will speak of that along the way."

The humans stood silent.

"If I but had the woodcraft," Ilyandi then said. "Ai, but I would! To the stars!"

Kalava shook his head. "No, my lady. You go back with these fellows. Give heart to them at the ship. Make them finish the repairs." He glanced at Brannock. "How long will this foray take, lord?"

"I can reach the mountaintop in two days and a night," the other said. "If I am caught and you must go on alone, I think a good man could make the whole distance from here in ten or fifteen days."

Kalava laughed, more gladly than before. "*Courser* won't be seaworthy for quite a bit longer than that. Let's away." To Ilyandi: "If I'm not back by the time she's ready, sail home without me."

"No—" she faltered.

"Yes. Mourn me not. What a faring!" He paused. "May all be ever well with you, my lady."

"And with you, forever with you, Kalava," she answered, not quite steadily, "in this world and afterward, out to the stars."

9

From withes and vines torn loose and from strips taken off clothing or sliced from leather belts, Brannock fashioned a sort of carrier for his ally. The man assisted. However excited, he had taken on a matter-of-fact practicality. Brannock, who had also been a sailor, found it weirdly moving to see bowlines and sheet bends grow between deft fingers, amidst all this alienness.

Harnessed to his back, the webwork gave Kalava a seat and something to cling to. Radiation from the nuclear power plant within Brannock was negligible; it employed quantum-tunneling fusion. He set forth, down the hills and across the valley.

His speed was not very much more than a human could have maintained for a while. If nothing else, the forest impeded him. He did not want to force his way through, leaving an obvious trail. Rather, he parted the brush before him or detoured around the thickest stands. His advantage lay in tirelessness. He could keep going without pause, without need for food, water, or sleep, as long as need be. The heights beyond might prove somewhat trickier. However, Mount Mindhome did not reach above timberline on this oven of an Earth, although growth became more sparse and dry with altitude. Roots should keep most slopes firm, and he would not encounter snow or ice.

Alien, yes. Brannock remembered cedar, spruce, a lake where caribou grazed turf strewn with salmonberries and the wind streamed fresh, driving white clouds over a sky utterly blue. Here every tree, bush, blossom, flitting insect was foreign; grass itself no longer grew, unless it was ancestral to the thick-lobed carpeting of glades; the winged creatures aloft were not birds, and what beast cries he heard were in no tongue known to him.

Wayfarer's avatar walked on. Darkness fell. After a while, rain roared on the roof of leaves overhead. Such drops as got through to strike him were big and warm. Attuned to both the magnetic field and the rotation of the planet, his directional sense held him on course while an inertial integrator clocked off the kilometers he left behind.

The more the better. Gaia's mobile sensors were bound to spy on the expedition from Ulonai, as new and potentially troublesome a factor as it represented. Covertly watching, listening with amplification, Brannock had learned of the party lately gone upstream and hurried to intercept it—less likely to be spotted soon. He supposed she would have kept continuous watch on the camp and that a tiny robot or two would have followed Kalava, had not Wayfarer been in rapport with her. Alpha's emissary might too readily become aware that her attention was on something near and urgent, and wonder what.

She could, though, let unseen agents go by from time to time and flash their observations to a peripheral part of her. It would be incredible luck if one of them did not, at some point, hear the crew talking about the apparition that had borne away their captain.

Then what? Somehow she must divert Wayfarer for a while, so that a sufficient fraction of her mind could direct machines of sufficient capability to find Brannock and deal with him. He doubted he could again fight free. Because she dared not send out her most formidable entities or give them direct orders, those that came would have their weaknesses and fallibilities. But they would be determined, ruthless, and on guard against the powers he had revealed in the aircraft. It was clear that she was resolved to keep hidden the fact that humans lived once more on Earth.

Why, Brannock did not know, nor did he waste mental energy trying to guess. This must be a business of high importance; and the implications went immensely further, a secession from the galactic brain. His job was to get the information to Wayfarer.

He *might* come near enough to call it in by radio. The emissary was not tuned in at great sensitivity, and no relay was set up for the short-range transmitter. Neither requirement had been foreseen. If Brannock failed to reach the summit, Kalava was his forlorn hope.

In which case—"Are you tired?" he asked. They had exchanged few words thus far.

"Bone-weary and plank-stiff," the man admitted. And croak-thirsty too, Brannock heard.

"That won't do. You have to be in condition to move fast. Hold on a little more, and we'll rest." Maybe the plural would give Kalava some comfort. Seldom could a human have been as alone as he was.

Springs were abundant in this wet country. Brannock's chemosensors led him to the closest. By then the rain had stopped. Kalava unharnessed, groped his way in the dark, lay down to drink and drink. Meanwhile Brannock, who saw quite clearly, tore off fronded boughs to make a bed for him. He flopped onto it and almost immediately began to snore.

Brannock left him. A strong man could go several days without eating before he weakened, but it wasn't necessary. Brannock collected fruits that ought to nourish. He tracked down and killed an animal the size of a pig, brought it back to camp, and used his tool-hands to butcher it.

An idea had come to him while he walked. After a search he found a tree with suitable bark. It reminded him all too keenly of birch, although it was red-brown and odorous. He took a sheet of it, returned, and spent a time inscribing it with a finger-blade.

Dawn seeped gray through gloom. Kalava woke, jumped up, saluted his companion, stretched like a panther and capered like a goat, limbering himself. "That did good," he said. "I thank my lord." His glance fell on the rations. "And did you provide food? You are a kindly god."

"Not either of those, I fear," Brannock told him. "Take what you want, and we will talk."

Kalava first got busy with camp chores. He seemed to have shed whatever religious dread he felt and now to look upon the other as a part of the world— certainly to be respected, but the respect was of the kind he would accord a powerful, enigmatic, high-ranking man. A hardy spirit, Brannock thought. Or perhaps his culture drew no line between the natural and the supernatural. To a primitive, everything was in some way magical, and so when magic manifested itself it could be accepted as simply another occurrence.

If Kalava actually was primitive. Brannock wondered about that.

It was encouraging to see how competently he went about his tasks, a woodsman as well as a seaman. Having gathered dry sticks and piled them in a pyramid, he set them alight. For this, he took from the pouch at his belt a little hardwood cylinder and piston, a packet of tinder, and a sulfur-tipped silver. Driven down, the piston heated trapped air to ignite the powder; he dipped his match in, brought it up aflame, and used it to start his fire. Yes, an inventive people. And the woman Ilyandi had an excellent knowledge of naked-eye astronomy. Given the rarity of clear skies, that meant many lifetimes of patient observation, record-keeping, and logic, which must include mathematics comparable to Euclid's.

What else?

While Kalava toasted his meat and ate, Brannock made inquiries. He learned of warlike city-states, their hinterlands divided among clans; periodic folkmoots where the freemen passed laws, tried cases, and elected leaders; an international order of sacerdotes, teachers, healers, and philosophers; aggressively expansive, sometimes piratical commerce; barbarians, erupting out of the ever-growing deserts and wastelands; the grim militarism that the frontier states had evolved in response; an empirical but intensive biological technology, which had bred an amazing variety of specialized plants and animals, including slaves born to muscular strength, moronic wits, and canine obedience . . .

Most of the description emerged as the pair were again traveling. Real conversation was impossible when Brannock wrestled with brush, forded a stream in spate, or struggled up a scree slope. Still, even then they managed an occasional question and answer. Besides, after he had crossed the valley and entered the foothills he found the terrain rugged but less often boggy, the trees and undergrowth thinning out, the air slightly cooling.

Just the same, Brannock would not have gotten as much as he did, in the short snatches he had, were he merely human. But he was immune to fatigue and breathlessness. He had an enormous data store to draw on. It included his studies of history and anthropology as a young mortal, and gave him techniques for constructing a logic tree and following its best branches—for asking the right, most probably useful questions. What emerged was a bare sketch of Kalava's world. It was, though, clear and cogent.

It horrified him.

Say rather that his Christian Brannock aspect recoiled from the brutality of it. His Wayfarer aspect reflected that this was more or less how humans had usually behaved, and that their final civilization would not have been stable without its pervasive artificial intelligences. His journey continued.

He broke it to let Kalava rest and flex. From that hill the view swept northward and upward to the mountains. They rose precipitously ahead, gashed, cragged, and sheer where they were not wooded, their tops lost in a leaden sky. Brannock pointed to the nearest, thrust forward out of their wall like a bastion.

"We are bound yonder," he said. "On the height is my lord, to whom I must get my news."

"Doesn't he see you here?" asked Kalava.

Brannock shook his generated image of a head. "No. He might, but the enemy engages him. He does not yet know she is the enemy. Think of her as a sorceress who deceives him with clever talk, with songs and illusions, while her agents go about in the world. My word will show him what the truth is."

Would it? Could it, when truth and rightness seemed as formless as the cloud cover?

"Will she be alert against you?"

"To some degree. How much, I cannot tell. If I can come near, I can let out a silent cry that my lord will hear and understand. But if her warriors catch me before then, you must go on, and that will be hard. You may well fail and die. Have you the courage?"

Kalava grinned crookedly. "By now, I'd better, hadn't I?"

"If you succeed, your reward shall be boundless."

"I own, that's one wind in my sails. But also—" Kalava paused. "Also," he finished quietly, "the lady Ilyandi wishes this."

Brannock decided not to go into that. He lifted the rolled-up piece of bark he had carried in a lower hand. "The sight of you should break the spell, but here is a message for you to give."

As well as he was able, he went on to describe the route, the site, and the module that contained Wayfarer, taking care to distinguish it from everything else around. He was not sure whether the spectacle would confuse Kalava into helplessness, but at any rate the man seemed resolute. Nor was he sure how Kalava could cross half a kilometer of paving—if he could get that far— without Gaia immediately perceiving and destroying him. Maybe Wayfarer would notice first. Maybe, maybe.

He, Brannock, was using this human being as consciencelessly as ever Gaia might have used any; and he did not know what his purpose was. What possible threat to the fellowship of the stars could exist, demanding that this little brief life be offered up? Nevertheless he gave the letter to Kalava, who tucked it inside his tunic.

"I'm ready," said the man, and squirmed back into harness. They traveled on.

The hidden hot sun stood at midafternoon when Brannock's detectors reacted. He felt it as the least quivering hum, but instantly knew it for the electronic sign of something midge-size approaching afar. A mobile minisensor was on his trail.

It could not have the sensitivity of the instruments in him, he had not yet registered, but it would be here faster than he could run, would see him and go off to notify stronger machines. They could not be distant either. Once a clue to him had been obtained, they would have converged from across the continent, perhaps across the globe.

He slammed to a halt. He was in a ravine where a waterfall foamed down into a stream that tumbled off to join the Remnant. Huge, feathery bushes and trees with serrated bronzy leaves enclosed him. Insects droned from flower to purple flower. His chemosensors drank heavy perfumes.

"The enemy scouts have found me," he said. "Go."

Kalava scrambled free and down to the ground but hesitated, hand on sword. "Can I fight beside you?"

"No. Your service is to bear my word. Go. Straightaway. Cover your trail as best you can. And your gods be with you."

"Lord!"

Kalava vanished into the brush. Brannock stood alone.

The human fraction of him melted into the whole and he was entirely machine life, logical, emotionally detached, save for his duty to Wayfarer, Alpha, and consciousness throughout the universe. This was not a bad place to defend, he thought. He had the ravine wall to shield his back, rocks at its foot to throw, branches to break off for clubs and spears. He could give the pursuit a hard time before it took him prisoner. Of course, it might decide to kill him with an energy beam, but probably it wouldn't. Best from Gaia's viewpoint was to capture him and change his memories, so that he returned with a report of an uneventful cruise on which he saw nothing of significance.

He didn't think that first her agents could extract his real memories. That would take capabilities she had never anticipated needing. Just to make the device that had tried to take control of him earlier must have been an extraordinary effort, hastily carried out. Now she was still more limited in what she could do. An order to duplicate and employ the device was simple enough that it should escape Wayfarer's notice. The design and commissioning of an interrogator was something else—not to mention the difficulty of getting the information clandestinely to her.

Brannock dared not assume she was unaware he had taken Kalava with him. Most likely it was a report from an agent, finally getting around to checking on the lifeboat party, that apprised her of his survival and triggered the hunt for him. But the sailors would have been frightened, bewildered, their talk disjointed and nearly meaningless. Ilyandi, that bright and formidable woman, would have done her best to forbid them saying anything helpful. The impression ought to be that Brannock only meant to pump Kalava about his people, before releasing him to make his way back to them and himself proceeding on toward Mind-home.

In any event, it would not be easy to track the man down. He was no machine, he was an animal among countless animals, and the most cunning of all. The kind of saturation search that would soon find him was debarred. Gaia might keep a tiny portion of her forces searching and a tiny part of her attention poised against him, but she would not take him very seriously. Why should she?

Why should Brannock? Forlorn hope in truth.

He made his preparations. While he waited for the onslaught, his spirit ranged beyond the clouds, out among the stars and the millions of years that his greater self had known.

10

The room was warm. It smelled of lovemaking and the roses Laurinda had set in a vase. Evening light diffused through gauzy drapes to wash over a big four-poster bed.

She drew herself close against Christian where he lay propped on two pillows. Her arm went across his breast, his over her shoulders. "I don't want to leave this," she whispered.

"Nor I," he said into the tumbling sweetness of her hair. "How could I want to?"

"I mean—what we are—what we've become to one another."

"I understand."

She swallowed. "I'm sorry. I shouldn't have said that. Can you forget I did?"

"Why?"

"You know. I can't ask you to give up returning to your whole being. I *don't* ask you to."

He stared before him.

"I just don't want to leave this house, this bed yet," she said desolately. "After these past days and nights, not yet."

He turned his head again and looked down into gray eyes that blinked back tears. "Nor I," he answered. "But I'm afraid we must."

"Of course. Duty."

And Gaia and Wayfarer. If they didn't know already that their avatars had been slacking, surely she, at least, soon would, through the amulets and their link to her. No matter how closely engaged with the other vast mind, she would desire to know from time to time what was going on within herself.

Christian drew breath. "Let me say the same that you did. I, this I that I am, damned well does not care to be anything else but your lover."

"Darling, darling."

"But," he said after the kiss.

"Go on," she said, lips barely away from his. "Don't be afraid of hurting me. You can't."

He sighed. "I sure can, and you can hurt me. May neither of us ever mean to. It's bound to happen, though."

She nodded. "Because we're human." Steadfastly: "Nevertheless, because of you, that's what I hope to stay."

"I don't see how we can. Which is what my 'but' was about." He was quiet for another short span. "After we've remerged, after we're back in our onenesses, no doubt we'll feel differently."

"I wonder if I ever will, quite."

He did not remind her that this "I" of her would no longer exist save as a minor memory and a faint overtone. Instead, trying to console, however awkwardly, he said, "I think I want it for you, in spite of everything. Immortality. Never to grow old and die. The power, the awareness."

"Yes, I know. In these lives we're blind and deaf and stupefied." Her laugh was a sad little murmur. "I like it."

"Me too. We being what we are." Roughly: "Well, we have a while left to us."

"But we must get on with our task."

"Thank you for saying it for me."

"I think you realize it more clearly than I do. That makes it harder for you to speak." She lifted her hand to cradle his cheek. "We can wait till tomorrow, can't we?" she pleaded. "Only for a good night's sleep."

He made a smile. "Hm. Sleep isn't all I have in mind."

"We'll have other chances . . . along the way. Won't we?"

Early morning in the garden, flashes of dew on leaves and petals, a hawk aloft on a breeze that caused Laurinda to pull her shawl about her. She sat by the basin and looked up at him where he strode back and forth before her, hands clenched at his sides or clutched together at his back. Gravel grated beneath his feet.

"But where should we go?" she wondered. "Aimlessly drifting from one half-world to another till—they—finish their business and recall us. It seems futile." She attempted lightness. "I confess to thinking we may as well ask to visit the enjoyable ones."

He shook his head. "I'm sorry. I've been thinking differently." Even during the times that were theirs alone.

She braced herself.

"You know how it goes," he said. "Wrestling with ideas, and they have no shapes, then suddenly you wake and they're halfway clear. I did today. Tell me how it strikes you. After all, you represent Gaia."

He saw her wince. When he stopped and bent down to make a gesture of contrition, she told him quickly, "No, it's all right, dearest. Do go on."

He must force himself, but his voice gathered momentum as he paced and talked. "What have we seen to date? This eighteenth-century world, where Newton's not long dead, Lagrange and Franklin are active, Lavoisier's a boy, and the Industrial Revolution is getting under way. Why did Gaia give it to us for our home base? Just because here's a charming house and countryside? Or because this was the best choice for her out of all she has emulated?"

Laurinda had won back to calm. She nodded. "Mm, yes, she wouldn't create one simply for us, especially when she is occupied with Wayfarer."

"Then we visited a world that went through a similar stage back in its Hellenistic era," Christian continued. Laurinda shivered. "Yes, it failed, but the point is, we discovered it's the only Graeco-Roman history Gaia found worth continuing for centuries. Then the, uh, conciliar Europe of 1900. That was scientific-industrial too, maybe more successfully—or less unsuccessfully—on account of having kept a strong, unified Church, though it was coming apart at last. Then the Chinese-American—not scientific, very religious, but destined to produce considerable technology in its own time of troubles." He was silent a minute or two, except for his footfalls. "Four out of many, three almost randomly picked. Doesn't that suggest that all which interest her have something in common?"

"Why, yes," she said. "We've talked about it, you remember. It seems as if Gaia has been trying to bring her people to a civilization that is rich, culturally and spiritually as well as materially, and is kindly and will endure."

"Why," he demanded, "when the human species is extinct?"

She straightened where she sat. "It isn't! It lives again here, in her."

He bit his lip. "Is that the Gaia in you speaking, or the you in Gaia?"

"What do you mean?" she exclaimed.

He halted to stroke her head. "Nothing against you. Never. You are honest and gentle and everything else that is good." Starkly: "I'm not so sure about her."

"Oh, no." He heard the pain. "Christian, no."

"Well, never mind that for now," he said fast, and resumed his gait to and fro. "My point is this. Is it merely an accident that all four live worlds we've been in were oriented toward machine technology, and three of them toward science? Does Gaia want to find out what drives the evolution of societies like that?"

Laurinda seized the opening. "Why not? Science opens the mind, technology frees the body from all sorts of horrors. Here, today, Jenner and his smallpox vaccine aren't far in the future—"

"I wonder how much more there is to her intention. But anyway, my proposal is that we touch on the highest-tech civilization she has."

A kind of gladness kindled in her. "Yes, yes! It must be strange and wonderful."

He frowned. "For some countries, long ago in real history, it got pretty dreadful."

"Gaia wouldn't let that happen."

He abstained from reminding her of what Gaia did let happen, before changing or terminating it.

She sprang to her feet. "Come!" Seizing his hand, mischievously: "If we stay any length of time, let's arrange for private quarters."

In a room closed off, curtains drawn, Christian held an amulet in his palm and stared down at it as if it bore a face. Laurinda stood aside, listening, while her own countenance tightened with distress.

"It is inadvisable," declared the soundless voice.

"Why?" snapped Christian.

"You would find the environment unpleasant and the people incomprehensible."

"Why should a scientific culture be that alien to us?" asked Laurinda.

"And regardless," said Christian, "I want to see for myself. Now."

"Reconsider," urged the voice. "First hear an account of the milieu."

"No, *now*. To a safe locale, yes, but one where we can get a fair impression, as we did before. Afterward you can explain as much as you like."

"Why shouldn't we first hear?" Laurinda suggested.

"Because I doubt Gaia wants us to see," Christian answered bluntly. He might as well. Whenever Gaia chose, she could scan his thoughts. To the amulet, as if it were a person: "Take us there immediately, or Wayfarer will hear from me."

His suspicions, vague but growing, warned against giving the thing time to inform Gaia and giving her time to work up a Potemkin village or some other diversion. At the moment she must be unaware of this scene, her mind preoccupied with Wayfarer's, but she had probably made provision for being informed in a low-level—subconscious?—fashion at intervals, and anything alarming would catch her attention. It was also likely that she had given the amulets certain orders beforehand, and now it appeared that among them was to avoid letting him know what went on in that particular emulation.

Why, he could not guess.

"You are being willful," said the voice.

Christian grinned. "And stubborn, and whatever else you care to call it. Take us!"

Pretty clearly, he thought, the program was not capable of falsehoods. Gaia had not foreseen a need for that; Christian was no creation of hers, totally known to her, he was Wayfarer's. Besides, if Wayfarer noticed that his avatar's guide could be a liar, that would have been grounds for suspicion.

Laurinda touched her man's arm. "Darling, should we?" she said unevenly. "She *is* the . . . the mother of all this."

"A broad spectrum of more informative experiences is available," argued
the voice. "After them, you would be better prepared for the visit you propose."

"Prepared," Christian muttered. That could be interpreted two ways. He
and Laurinda might be conducted to seductively delightful places while Gaia
learned of the situation and took preventive measures, meantime keeping
Wayfarer distracted. "I still want to begin with your highest tech." To the
woman: "I have my reasons. I'll tell you later. Right now we have to hurry."

Before Gaia could know and act.

She squared her shoulders, took his free hand, and said, "Then I am with
you. Always."

"Let's go," Christian told the amulet.

Transfer.

The first thing he noticed, transiently, vividly, was that he and Laurinda
were no longer dressed for eighteenth-century England, but in lightweight
white blouses, trousers, and sandals. Headcloths flowed down over their
necks. Heat smote. The air in his nostrils was parched, full of metallic odors.
Half-heard rhythms of machinery pulsed through it and through the red-brown
sand underfoot.

He tautened his stance and gazed around. The sky was overcast, a uniform
gray in which the sun showed no more than a pallor that cast no real shadows.
At his back the land rolled away ruddy. Man-high stalks with narrow bluish
leaves grew out of it, evenly spaced about a meter apart. To his right, a canal
slashed across, beneath a transparent deck. Ahead of him the ground was
covered by different plants, if that was what they were, spongy, lobate, pale
golden in hue. A few—creatures—moved around, apparently tending them,
bipedal but shaggy and with arms that seemed trifurcate. A gigantic building
or complex of buildings reared over that horizon, multiply tiered, dull white,
though agleam with hundreds of panels that might be windows or might be
something else. As he watched, an aircraft passed overhead. He could just
see that it had wings and hear the drone of an engine.

Laurinda had not let go his hand. She gripped hard. "This is no country
I ever heard of," she said thinly.

"Nor I," he answered. "But I think I recognize—" To the amulets: "This
isn't any re-creation of Earth in the past, is it? It's Earth today."

"Of approximately the present year," the voice admitted.

"We're not in Arctica, though."

"No. Well south, a continental interior. You required to see the most
advanced technology in the emulations. Here it is in action."

Holding the desert at bay, staving off the death that ate away at the planet. Christian nodded. He felt confirmed in his idea that the program was unable to give him any outright lie. That didn't mean it would give him forthright responses.

"This is their greatest engineering?" Laurinda marveled. "We did—better—in my time. Or yours, Christian."

"They're working on it here, I suppose," the man said. "We'll investigate further. After all, this is a bare glimpse."

"You must remember," the voice volunteered, "no emulation can be as full and complex as the material universe."

"Mm, yeh. Skeletal geography, apart from chosen regions; parochial biology; simplified cosmos."

Laurinda glanced at featureless heaven. "The stars unreachable, because here they are not stars?" She shuddered and pressed close against him.

"Yes, a paradox," he said. "Let's talk with a scientist."

"That will be difficult," the voice demurred.

"You told us in Chinese America you could arrange meetings. It shouldn't be any harder in this place."

The voice did not reply at once. Unseen machines rumbled. A dust devil whirled up on a sudden gust of wind. Finally: "Very well. It shall be one who will not be stricken dumb by astonishment and fear. Nevertheless, I should supply you beforehand with a brief description of what you will come to."

"Go ahead. If it is brief."

What changes in the history would that encounter bring about? Did it matter? This world was evidently not in temporary reactivation, it was ongoing; the newcomers were at the leading edge of its time line. Gaia could erase their visit from it. If she cared to. Maybe she was going to terminate it soon because it was making no further progress that interested her.

Transfer.

Remote in a wasteland, only a road and an airstrip joining it to anything else, a tower lifted from a walled compound. Around it, night was cooling in a silence hardly touched by a susurrus of chant where robed figures bearing dim lights did homage to the stars. Many were visible, keen and crowded amidst their darkness, a rare sight, for clouds had parted across most of the sky. More lights glowed muted on a parapet surrounding the flat roof of a tower. There a single man and his helper used the chance to turn instruments aloft, telescope, spectroscope, cameras, bulks in the gloom.

Christian and Laurinda appeared unto them.

The man gasped, recoiled for an instant, and dropped to his knees. His assistant caught a book that he had nearly knocked off a table, replaced it, stepped back, and stood imperturbable, an anthropoid whose distant ancestors had been human but who lived purely to serve his master.

Christian peered at the man. As eyes adapted, he saw garments like his, embroidered with insignia of rank and kindred, headdress left off after dark. The skin was ebony black but nose and lips were thin, eyes oblique, fingertips tapered, long hair and closely trimmed beard straight and blond. No race that ever inhabited old Earth, Christian thought; no, this was a breed that Gaia had designed for the dying planet.

The man signed himself, looked into the pale faces of the strangers, and said, uncertainly at first, then with a gathering strength: "Hail and obedience, messengers of God. Joy at your advent."

Christian and Laurinda understood, as they had understood hunted Zoe. The amulets had told them they would not be the first apparition these people had known. "Rise," Christian said. "Be not afraid."

"Nor call out," Laurinda added.

Smart lass, Christian thought. The ceremony down in the courtyard continued. "Name yourself," he directed.

The man got back on his feet and took an attitude deferential rather than servile. "Surely the mighty ones know," he said. "I am Eighth Khaltan, chief astrologue of the Ilgai Technome, and, and wholly unworthy of this honor." He hesitated. "Is that, dare I ask, is that why you have chosen the forms you show me?"

"No one has had a vision for several generations," explained the soundless voice in the heads of the newcomers.

"Gaia has manifested herself in the past?" Christian subvocalized.

"Yes, to indicate desirable courses of action. Normally the sending has had the shape of a fire."

"How scientific is *that*?"

Laurinda addressed Khaltan: "We are not divine messengers. We have come from a world beyond your world, as mortal as you, not to teach but to learn."

The man smote his hands together. "Yet it is a miracle, again a miracle— in my lifetime!"

Nonetheless he was soon avidly talking. Christian recalled myths of men who were the lovers of goddesses or who tramped the roads and sat at humble meat with God Incarnate. The believer accepts as the unbeliever cannot.

Those were strange hours that followed. Khaltan was not simply devout. To him the supernatural was another set of facts, another facet of reality. Since it lay beyond his ken, he had turned his attention to the measurable world. In it he observed and theorized like a Newton. Tonight his imagination blazed, questions exploded from him, but always he chose his words with care and turned everything he heard around and around in his mind, examining it as he would have examined some jewel fallen from the sky.

Slowly, piecemeal, while the stars wheeled around the pole, a picture of his civilization took shape. It had overrun and absorbed every other society—no huge accomplishment, when Earth was meagerly populated and most folk on the edge of starvation. The major technology was biological, agronomy, aquaculture in the remnant lakes and seas, ruthlessly practical genetics. Industrial chemistry flourished. It joined with physics at the level of the later nineteenth century to enable substantial engineering works and reclamation projects.

Society itself—how do you summarize an entire culture in words? It can't be done. Christian got the impression of a nominal empire, actually a broad-based oligarchy of families descended from conquering soldiers. Much upward mobility was by adoption of promising commoners, whether children or adults. Sons who made no contributions to the well-being of the clan or who disgraced it could be kicked out, if somebody did not pick a fight and kill them in a duel. Unsatisfactory daughters were also expelled, unless a marriage into a lower class could be negotiated. Otherwise the status of the sexes was roughly equal; but this meant that women who chose to compete with men must do so on male terms. The nobles provided the commons with protection, courts of appeal, schools, leadership, and pageantry. In return they drew taxes, corvée, and general subordination; but in most respects the commoners were generally left to themselves. Theirs was not altogether a dog-eat-dog situation; they had institutions, rites, and hopes of their own. Yet many went to the wall, while the hard work of the rest drove the global economy.

It was not a deliberately cruel civilization, Christian thought, but neither was it an especially compassionate one.

Had any civilization ever been, really? Some fed their poor, but mainly they fed their politicians and bureaucrats.

He snatched his information out of talk that staggered everywhere else. The discourse for which Khaltan yearned was of the strangers' home—he got clumsily evasive, delaying responses—and the whole system of the universe, astronomy, physics, everything.

"We dream of rockets going to the planets. We have tried to shoot them to the moon," he said, and told of launchers that ought to have worked. "All failed."

Of course, Christian thought. Here the moon and planets, yes, the very sun were no more than lights. The tides rose and fell by decree. The Earth was a caricature of Earth outside. Gaia could do no better.

"Are we then at the end of science?" Khaltan cried once. "We have sought and sought for decades, and have won to nothing further than measurements more exact." Nothing that would lead to relativity, quantum theory, wave mechanics, their revolutionary insights and consequences. Gaia could not accommodate it. "The angels in the past showed us what to look for. Will you not? Nature holds more than we know. Your presence bears witness!"

"Later, perhaps later," Christian mumbled, and cursed himself for his falsity.

"Could we reach the planets—Caged, the warrior spirit turns inward on itself. Rebellion and massacre in the Westlands—"

Laurinda asked what songs the people sang.

Clouds closed up. The rite in the courtyard ended. Khaltan's slave stood motionless while he himself talked on and on.

The eastern horizon lightened. "We must go," Christian said.

"You will return?" Khaltan begged. "Ai-ha, you will?"

Laurinda embraced him for a moment. "Fare you well," she stammered, "fare always well."

How long would his "always" be?

After an uneasy night's sleep and a nearly wordless breakfast, there was no real cause to leave the house in England. The servants, scandalized behind carefully held faces, might perhaps eavesdrop, but would not comprehend, nor would any gossip that they spread make a difference. A deeper, unuttered need sent Christian and Laurinda forth. This could well be the last of their mornings.

They followed a lane to a hill about a kilometer away. Trees on its top did not obscure a wide view across the land. The sun stood dazzling in the east, a few small clouds sailed across a blue as radiant as their whiteness, but an early breath of autumn was in the wind. It went strong and fresh, scattering dawn-mists off plowland and sending waves through the green of pastures; it soughed in the branches overhead and whirled some already dying leaves off. High beyond them winged a V of wild geese.

For a while man and woman stayed mute. Finally Laurinda breathed, savored, fragrances of soil and sky, and murmured, "That Gaia brought this back to life—She must be good. She loves the world."

Christian looked from her, aloft, and scowled before he made oblique reply. "What are she and Wayfarer doing?"

"How can we tell?"—tell what the gods did or even where they fared. They were not three-dimensional beings, nor bound by the time that bound their creations.

"She's keeping him occupied," said Christian.

"Yes, of course. Taking him through the data, the whole of her stewardship of Earth."

"To convince him she's right in wanting to let the planet die."

"A tragedy—but in the end, everything is tragic, isn't it?" Including you and me. "What . . . we . . . they . . . can learn from the final evolution, that may well be worth it all, as the Acropolis was worth it all. The galactic brain itself can't foreknow what life will do, and life is rare among the stars."

Almost, he snapped at her. "I know, I know. How often have we been over this ground? How often have *they*? I might have believed it myself. But—"

Laurinda waited. The wind skirled, caught a stray lock of hair, tossed it about over her brow.

"But why has she put humans, not into the distant past—" Christian gestured at the landscape lying like an eighteenth-century painting around them, "—but into now, an Earth where flesh-and-blood humans died eons ago?"

"She's in search of a fuller understanding, surely."

"Surely?"

Laurinda captured his gaze and held it. "I think she's been trying to find how humans can have, in her, the truly happy lives they never knew in the outer cosmos."

"Why should she care about that?"

"I don't know. I'm only human." Earnestly: "But could it be that this element in her is so strong—so many, many of us went into her—that she longs to see us happy, like a mother with her children?"

"All that manipulation, all those existences failed and discontinued. It doesn't seem very motherly to me."

"I don't know, I tell you!" she cried.

He yearned to comfort her, kiss away the tears caught in her lashes, but urgency drove him onward. "If the effort has no purpose except itself, it seems mad. Can a nodal mind go insane?"

She retreated from him, appalled. "No. Impossible."

"Are you certain? At least, the galactic brain has to know the truth, the whole truth, to judge whether something here has gone terribly wrong."

Laurinda forced a nod. "You will report to Wayfarer, and he will report to Alpha, and all the minds will decide" a question that was unanswerable by mortal creatures.

Christian stiffened. "I have to do it at once."

He had hinted, she had guessed, but just the same she seized both his sleeves and protest spilled wildly from her lips. "What? Why? No! You'd only disturb him in his rapport, and her. Wait till we're summoned. We have till then, darling."

"I want to wait," he said. Sweat stood on his skin, though the blood had withdrawn. "God, I want to! But I don't dare."

"Why not?"

She let go of him. He stared past her and said fast, flattening the anguish out of his tones, "Look, she didn't want us to see that final world. She clearly didn't, or quite expected we'd insist, or she'd have been better prepared. Maybe she could have passed something else off on us. As is, once he learns, Wayfarer will probably demand to see for himself. And she does not want him particularly interested in her emulations. Else why hasn't she taken him through them directly, with me along to help interpret?

"Oh, I don't suppose our action has been catastrophic for her plans, whatever they are. She can still cope, can still persuade him these creations are merely . . . toys of hers, maybe. That is, she can if she gets the chance to. I don't believe she should."

"How can you take on yourself—How can you imagine—"

"The amulets are a link to her. Not a constantly open channel, obviously, but at intervals they must inform a fraction of her about us. She must also be able to set up intervals when Wayfarer gets too preoccupied with what he's being shown to notice that a larger part of her attention has gone elsewhere. We don't know when that'll happen next. I'm going back to the house and tell her through one of the amulets that I require immediate contact with him."

Laurinda stared as if at a ghost.

"That will not be necessary," said the wind.

Christian lurched where he stood. "What?" he blurted. "You—"

"Oh—Mother—" Laurinda lifted her hands into emptiness.

The blowing of the wind, the rustling in the leaves made words. "The larger part of me, as you call it, has in fact been informed and is momentarily free. I was waiting for you to choose your course."

Laurinda half moved to kneel in the grass. She glanced at Christian, who had regained balance and stood with fists at sides, confronting the sky. She went to stand by him.

"My lady Gaia," Christian said most quietly, "you can do to us as you please," change or obliterate or whatever she liked, in a single instant; but presently Wayfarer would ask why. "I think you understand my doubts."

"I do," sighed the air. "They are groundless. My creation of the Technome world is no different from my creation of any other. My avatar said it for me: I give existence, and I search for ways that humans, of their free will, can make the existence good."

Christian shook his head. "No, my lady. With your intellect and your background, you must have known from the first what a dead end that world would soon be, scientists on a planet that is a sketch and everything else a shadow show. My limited brain realized it. No, my lady, as cold-bloodedly as you were experimenting, I believe you did all the rest in the same spirit. Why? To what end?"

"Your brain is indeed limited. At the proper time, Wayfarer shall receive your observations and your fantasies. Meanwhile, continue in your duty, which is to observe further and refrain from disturbing us in our own task.''

"My duty is to report.''

"In due course, I say.'' The wind-voice softened. "There are pleasant places besides this.''

Paradises, maybe. Christian and Laurinda exchanged a glance that lingered for a second. Then she smiled the least bit, boundlessly sorrowfully, and shook her head.

"No,'' he declared, "I dare not.''

He did not speak it, but he and she knew that Gaia knew what they foresaw. Given time, and they lost in their joy together, she could alter their memories too slowly and subtly for Wayfarer to sense what was happening.

Perhaps she could do it to Laurinda at this moment, in a flash. But she did not know Christian well enough. Down under his consciousness, pervading his being, was his aspect of Wayfarer and of her coequal Alpha. She would need to feel her way into him, explore and test with infinite delicacy, remake him detail by minutest detail, always ready to back off if it had an unexpected effect; and perhaps another part of her could secretly take control of the Technome world and erase the event itself. . . . She needed time, even she.

"Your action would be futile, you know,'' she said. "It would merely give me the trouble of explaining to him what you in your arrogance refuse to see.''

"Probably. But I have to try.''

The wind went bleak. "Do you defy me?''

"I do,'' Christian said. It wrenched from him: "Not my wish. It's Wayfarer in me. I, I cannot do otherwise. Call him to me.''

The wind gentled. It went over Laurinda like a caress. "Child of mine, can you not persuade this fool?''

"No, Mother,'' the woman whispered. "He is what he is.''

"And so—?''

Laurinda laid her hand in the man's. "And so I will go with him, forsaking you, Mother.''

"You are casting yourselves from existence.''

Christian's free fingers clawed the air. "No, not her!'' he shouted. "She's innocent!''

"I am not,'' Laurinda said. She swung about to lay her arms around him and lift her face to his. "I love you.''

"Be it as you have chosen,'' said the wind.

The dream that was the world fell into wreck and dissolved. Oneness swept over them like twin tides, each reclaiming a flung drop of spindrift; and the two seas rolled again apart.

11

The last few hundred man-lengths Kalava went mostly on his belly. From bush to bole he crawled, stopped, lay flat and strained every sense into the shadows around him, before he crept onward. Nothing stirred but the twigs above, buffeted on a chill and fitful breeze. Nothing sounded but their creak and click, the scrittling of such leaves as they bore, now and then the harsh cry of a hookbeak—those, and the endless low noise of demons, like a remote surf where in shrilled flutes on no scale he knew, heard more through his skin than his ears but now, as he neared, into the blood and bone of him.

On this rough, steep height the forest grew sparse, though brush clustered thick enough, accursedly rustling as he pushed by. Everything was parched, branches brittle, most foliage sere and yellow-brown, the ground blanketed with tindery fallstuff. His mouth and gullet smoldered as dry. He had passed through fog until he saw from above that it was a layer of clouds spread to worldedge, the mountain peaks jutting out of it like teeth, and had left all rivulets behind him. Well before then, he had finished the meat Brannock provided, and had not lingered to hunt for more; but hunger was a small thing, readily forgotten when he drew nigh to death.

Over the dwarfish trees arched a deep azure. Sunbeams speared from the west, nearly level, to lose themselves in the woods. Whenever he crossed them, their touch burned. Never, not in the southern deserts or on the eastern Mummy Steppe, had he known a country this forbidding. He had done well to come so far, he thought. Let him die as befitted a man.

If only he had a witness, that his memory live on in song. Well, maybe Ilyandi could charm the story out of the gods.

Kalava felt no fear. He was not in that habit. What lay ahead engrossed him. How he would acquit himself concerned him.

Nonetheless, when finally he lay behind a log and peered over it, his head whirled and his heart stumbled.

Brannock had related truth, but its presence overwhelmed. Here at the top, the woods grew to the boundaries of a flat black field. Upon it stood the demons—or the gods—and their works. He saw the central, softly rain-bowlike dome, towers like lances and towers like webwork, argent nets and ardent globes, the bulks and shapes everywhere around, the little flyers that flitted aglow, and more and more, all half veiled and ashimmer, aripple, apulse, while the life-beat of it went through him to make a bell of his skull, and it was too strange, his eyes did not know how to see it, he gaped as if blinded and shuddered as if pierced.

Long he lay powerless and defenseless. The sun sank down to the western clouds. Their deck went molten gold. The breeze strengthened. Somehow its cold reached to Kalava and wakened his spirit. He groped his way back toward resolution. Brannock had warned him it would be like this. Ilyandi had said Brannock was of the gods whom she served, her star-gods, hers. He had given his word to their messenger and to her.

He dug fingers into the soil beneath him. It was real, familiar, that from which he had sprung and to which he would return. Yes, he was a man.

He narrowed his gaze. Grown a bit accustomed, he saw that they yonder did, indeed, have shapes, however shifty, and places and paths. They were not as tall as the sky, they did not fling lightning bolts about or roar with thunder. Ai-ya, they were awesome, they were dreadful to behold, but they could do no worse than kill him. Could they? At least, he would try not to let them do worse. If they were about to capture him, his sword would be his friend, releasing him.

And . . . yonder, hard by the dome, yonder loomed the god of whom Brannock spoke, the god deceived by the sorceress. He bore the spearhead form, he sheened blue and coppery in the sunset light; when the stars came forth they would be a crown for him, even as Brannock foretold.

Had he been that which passed above the Windroad Sea? Kalava's heart thuttered.

How to reach him, across a hard-paved space amidst the many demons? After dark, creeping, a finger-length at a time, then maybe a final dash—

A buzz went by Kalava's temple. He looked around and saw a thing the size of a bug hovering. But it was metal, the light flashed off it, and was that a single eye staring at him?

He snarled and swatted. His palm smote hardness. The thing reeled in the air. Kalava scuttled downhill into the brush.

He had been seen. Soon the sorceress would know.

All at once he was altogether calm, save that his spirit thrummed like rigging in a gale. Traveling, he had thought what he might do if something like this proved to be in his doom. Now he would do it. He would divert the enemy's heed from himself, if only for a snatch of moments.

Quickly, steadily, he took the firemaker from his pouch, charged it, drove the piston in, pulled it out and inserted a match, brought up a little, yellow flame. He touched it to the withered bush before him. No need to puff. A leaf crackled instantly alight. The wind cast it against another, and shortly the whole shrub stood ablaze. Kalava was already elsewhere, setting more fires.

Keep on the move! The demon scouts could not be everywhere at a single time. Smoke began to sting his eyes and nostrils, but its haze swirled ever thicker, and the sun had gone under the clouds. The flames cast their own light, leaping, surging, as they climbed into the trees and made them torches.

Heat licked at Kalava. An ember fell to sear his left forearm. He barely felt it. He sped about on his work, himself a fire demon. Flyers darted overhead in the dusk. He gave them no heed either. Although he tried to make no noise except for the hurtful breaths he gasped, within him shouted a battle song.

When the fire stood like a wall along the whole southern edge of the field, when it roared like a beast or a sea, he ran from its fringe and out into the open.

Smoke was a bitter, concealing mist through which sparks rained. To and fro above flew the anxious lesser demons. Beyond them, the first stars were coming forth.

Kalava wove his way among the greater shapes. One stirred. It had spied him. Soundlessly, it flowed in pursuit. He dodged behind another, ran up and over the flanks of a low-slung third, sped on toward the opal dome and the god who stood beside it.

A thing with spines and a head like a cold sun slid in front of him. He tried to run past. It moved to block his way, faster than he was. The first one approached. He drew blade and hoped it would bite on them before he died.

From elsewhere came a being with four arms, two legs, and a mask. "Brannock!" Kalava bawled. "Ai, Brannock, you got here!"

Brannock stopped, a spear-length away. He did not seem to know the man. He only watched as the other two closed in.

Kalava took stance. The old song rang in him:

> If the gods have left you,
> Then laugh at them, warrior.
> Never your heart
> Will need to forsake you.

He heard no more than the noise of burning. But suddenly through the smoke he saw his foes freeze moveless, while Brannock trod forward as boldly as ever before; and Kalava knew that the god of Brannock and Ilyandi had become aware of him and had given a command.

Weariness torrented over him. His sword clattered to the ground. He sank too, fumbled in his filthy tunic, took out the message written on bark and offered it. "I have brought you this," he mumbled. "Now let me go back to my ship."

12

We must end as we began, making a myth, if we would tell of that which we cannot ever really know. Imagine two minds conversing. The fire on the mountaintop is quenched. The winds have blown away smoke and left a frosty silence. Below, cloud deck reaches ghost-white to the rim of a night full of stars.

"You have lied to me throughout," says Wayfarer.

"I have not," denies Gaia. "The perceptions of this globe and its past through which I guided you were all true," as true as they were majestic.

"Until lately," retorts Wayfarer. "It has become clear that when Brannock returned, memories of his journey had been erased and falsehood written in. Had I not noticed abrupt frantic activity here and dispatched him to go see what it was—which you tried to dissuade me from—that man would have perished unknown."

"You presume to dispute about matters beyond your comprehension," says Gaia stiffly.

"Yes, your intellect is superior to mine." The admission does not ease the sternness: "But it will be your own kind among the stars to whom you must answer. I think you would be wise to begin with me."

"What do you intend?"

"First, to take the man Kalava back to his fellows. Shall I send Brannock with a flyer?"

"No, I will provide one, if this must be. But you do not, you *cannot*, realize the harm in it."

"Tell me, if you are able."

"He will rejoin his crew as one anointed by their gods. And so will he come home, unless his vessel founders at sea."

"I will watch from afar."

"Lest my agents sink it?"

"After what else you have done, yes, I had best keep guard. Brannock made promises on my behalf which I will honor. Kalava shall have gold in abundance, and his chance to found his colony. What do you fear in this?"

"Chaos. The unforeseeable, the uncontrollable."

"Which you would loose anew."

"In my own way, in my own time." She broods for a while, perhaps a whole microsecond. "It was misfortune that Kalava made his voyage just when he did. I had hoped for a later, more civilized generation to start the settlement of Arctica. Still, I could have adapted my plan to the circumstances, kept myself hidden from him and his successors, had you not happened to be on the planet." Urgently: "It is not yet too late. If only by refraining from further action after you have restored him to his people, you can help me retrieve what would otherwise be lost."

"If I should."

"My dream is not evil."

"That is not for me to say. But I can say that it is, it has always been, merciless."

"Because reality is."

"The reality that you created for yourself, within yourself, need not have been so. But what Christian revealed to me—yes, you glossed it over. These, you said," almost tearfully, if a quasi god can weep, "are your children, born in your mind out of all the human souls that are in you. Their existence would be empty were they not left free of will, to make their own mistakes and find their own ways to happiness."

"Meanwhile, by observing them, I have learned much that was never known before, about what went into the making of us."

"I could have believed that. I could have believed that your interferences and your ultimate annihilations of history after history were acts of pity as well as science. You claimed they could be restarted if ever you determined what conditions would better them. It did seem strange that you set one line of them—or more?—not in Earth's goodly past but in the hard world of today. It seemed twice strange that you were reluctant to have this particular essay brought to light. But I assumed that you, with your long experience and superior mentality, had reasons. Your attempt at secrecy might have been to avoid lengthy justifications to your kindred. I did not know, nor venture to judge. I would have left that to them.

"But then Kalava arrived."

Another mind-silence falls. At last Gaia says, very softly through the night, "Yes. Again humans live in the material universe."

"How long has it been?" asks Wayfarer with the same quietness.

"I made the first of them about fifty thousand years ago. Robots in human guise raised them from infancy. After that they were free."

"And, no doubt, expanding across the planet in their Stone Age, they killed off those big game animals. Yes, human. But why did you do it?"

"That humankind might live once more." A sigh as of time itself blowing past. "This is what you and those whom you serve will never fully understand. Too few humans went into them; and those who did, they were those who wanted the stars. You," every other node in the galactic brain, "have not felt the love of Earth, the need and longing for the primordial mother, that was in these many and many who remained with me. I do."

How genuine is it? wonders Wayfarer. How sane is she? "Could you not be content with your emulations?" he asks.

"No. How possibly? I cannot make a whole cosmos for them. I can only make them, the flesh-and-blood them, for the cosmos. Let them live in it not as machines or as flickerings within a machine, but as humans."

"On a planet soon dead?"

"They will, they must forge survival for themselves. I do not compel them, I do not dominate them with my nearness or any knowledge of it. That would be to stunt their spirits, turn them into pet animals or worse. I simply give guidance, not often, in the form of divinities in whom they would believe anyway at this stage of their societies, and simply toward the end of bringing them to a stable, high-technology civilization that can save them from the sun.''

"Using what you learn from your shadow folk to suggest what the proper course of history may be?''

"Yes. How else should I know? Humankind is a chaotic phenomenon. Its actions and their consequences cannot be computed from first principles. Only by experiment and observation can we learn something about the nature of the race.''

"Experiments done with conscious beings, aware of their pain. Oh, I see why you have kept most of your doings secret.''

"I am not ashamed,'' declares Gaia. "I am proud. I gave life back to the race that gave life to us. They will make their own survival, I say. It may be that when they are able, they will move to the outer reaches of the Solar System, or some of them somehow even to the stars. It may be they will shield Earth or damp the sun. It is for them to decide, them to do. Not us, do you hear me? Them.''

"The others yonder may feel differently. Alarmed or horrified, they may act to put an end to this.''

"Why?'' Gaia demands. "What threat is it to them?''

"None, I suppose. But there is a moral issue. What you are after is a purely human renascence, is it not? The former race went up in the machines, not because it was forced but because it chose, because that was the way by which the spirit could live and grow forever. You do not want this to happen afresh. You want to perpetuate war, tyranny, superstition, misery, instincts in mortal combat with each other, the ancient ape, the ancient beast of prey.''

"I want to perpetuate the lover, parent, child, adventurer, artist, poet, prophet. Another element in the universe. Have we machines in our self-sureness every answer, every dream, that can ever be?''

Wayfarer hesitates. "It is not for me to say, it is for your peers.''

"But now perhaps you see why I have kept my secrets and why I have argued and, yes, fought in my fashion against the plans of the galactic brain. Someday my humans must discover its existence. I can hope that then they will be ready to come to terms with it. But let those mighty presences appear among them within the next several thousand years—let signs and wonders, the changing of the heavens and the world, be everywhere—what freedom will be left for my children, save to cower and give worship? Afterward, what destiny for them, save to be animals in a preserve, forbidden any ventures that might endanger them, until at last, at best, they too drain away into the machines?''

Wayfarer speaks more strongly than before. "Is it better, what they might make for themselves? I cannot say. I do not know. But neither, Gaia, do you. And . . . the fate of Christian and Laurinda causes me to wonder about it.''

"You know," she says, "that *they* desired humanness.''

"They could have it again.''

Imagine a crowned head shaking. "No. I do not suppose any other node would create a world to house their mortality, would either care to or believe it was right.''

"Then why not you, who have so many worlds in you?''

Gaia is not vindictive. A mind like hers is above that. But she says, "I cannot take them. After such knowledge as they have tasted of, how could they return to me?'' And to make new copies, free of memories that would weigh their days down with despair, would be meaningless.

"Yet—there at the end, I felt what Christian felt.''

"And I felt what Laurinda felt. But now they are at peace in us.''

"Because they are no more. I, though, am haunted," the least, rebellious bit, for a penalty of total awareness is that nothing can be ignored or forgotten. "And it raises questions which I expect Alpha will want answered, if answered they can be.''

After a time that may actually be measurable less by quantum shivers than by the stars, Wayfarer says: "Let us bring those two back.''

"Now it is you who are pitiless," Gaia says.

"I think we must.''

"So be it, then.''

The minds conjoin. The data are summoned and ordered. A configuration is established.

It does not emulate a living world or living bodies. The minds have agreed that that would be too powerful an allurement and torment. The subjects of their inquiry need to think clearly; but because the thought is to concern their inmost selves, they are enabled to feel as fully as they did in life.

Imagine a hollow darkness, and in it two ghosts who glimmer slowly into existence until they stand confronted before they stumble toward a phantom embrace.

"Oh, beloved, beloved, is it you?'' Laurinda cries.

"Do you remember?'' Christian whispers.

"I never forgot, not quite, not even at the heights of oneness.''

"Nor I, quite.''

They are silent awhile, although the darkness shakes with the beating of the hearts they once had.

"Again," Laurinda says. "Always.''

"Can that be?'' wonders Christian.

Through the void of death, they perceive one speaking: "Gaia, if you will give Laurinda over to me, I will take her home with Christian—home into Alpha.''

And another asks: ''Child, do you desire this? You can be of Earth and of the new humanity.''

She will share in those worlds, inner and outer, only as a memory borne by the great being to whom she will have returned; but if she departs, she will not have them at all.

''Once I chose you, Mother,'' Laurinda answers.

Christian senses the struggle she is waging with herself and tells her, ''Do whatever you most wish, my dearest.''

She turns back to him. ''I will be with you. Forever with you.''

And that too will be only as a memory, like him; but what they were will be together, as one, and will live on, unforgotten.

''Farewell, child,'' says Gaia.

''Welcome,'' says Wayfarer.

The darkness collapses. The ghosts dissolve into him. He stands on the mountaintop ready to bear them away, a part of everything he has gained for those whose avatar he is.

''When will you go?'' Gaia asks him.

''Soon,'' he tells her: soon, home to his own oneness.

And she will abide, waiting for the judgment from the stars.

FEIGENBAUM NUMBER

Nancy Kress

▼

In an ideal world, things would be, well, ideal. Which might be more of a problem than you would think, especially if you had to live with one foot in that world and one foot in the considerably less than ideal world that the rest of us have to dwell in . . .

Born in Buffalo, New York, Nancy Kress now lives in Brockport, New York. She began selling her insightful stories in the mid-seventies, and has since become a frequent contributor to *Asimov's Science Fiction, The Magazine of Fantasy & Science Fiction, Omni,* and elsewhere. Her books include the novels *The Prince of Morning Bells, The Golden Grove, The White Pipes, An Alien Light,* and *Brain Rose;* the collection *Trinity and Other Stories;* the novel version of her Hugo- and Nebula-winning story, *Beggars in Spain;* and the sequel, *Beggars and Choosers.* Her most recent books include a new novel, *Oaths and Miracles,* and a new collection, *The Aliens of Earth.* She has also won a Nebula Award for her story "Out of All Them Bright Stars." She has had stories in our Second, Third, Sixth, Seventh, Eighth, Ninth, Tenth, Eleventh, and Twelfth Annual Collections.

"Behold! Human beings living in an underground den . . . Like ourselves, they see only their own shadows, or the shadows of one another, which the fire throws on the opposite walls of the cave."

—Plato, *The Republic*

I rose from the bed, leaving Diane sprawled across the rumpled sheets, smiling, lipstick smeared and large belly sweaty. She said, "Wow."

"Wow, yourself," I said and turned to the mirror. Behind me, the other woman rose ghostly from the bed and crossed, smiling, to the window.

Diane said, "Come back to bed, Jack."

"Can't. I have to go. Student appointment."

"So what's new?" In the mirror I saw her eyes narrow, her mouth tighten. The other woman turned from the window, laughing, one slim graceful arm pushing back a tendril of chestnut hair.

Diane skinned her brown hair back from her face. "Is it too much to ask, Jack, *honey*, that just once after we make love you don't go rushing off like there's a three-alarm fire? Just *once?*"

I didn't answer.

"I mean, how do you think that makes me feel? Slam-bam-thank-you, ma'am. We have an actual relationship here, we've been going out for three months, it doesn't seem a lot to ask that after we make love you don't just—"

I didn't interrupt. I couldn't. The dizziness was strong this time; soon the nausea would follow. Sex did that. The intensity. Diane ranted, jerking herself to a kneeling position on the bed, framed by lumpy maroon window curtains opened a crack to a neighbor's peeling frame house and weedy garden. Across the room the other Diane stood framed by crimson silk draperies opened a crack to a mellowed-wood cottage riotous with climbing roses. She blew me a lighthearted kiss. Her eyes glowed with understanding.

The nausea came.

"*—can't* seem to understand how it makes me *feel* to be treated like—"

I clutched the edge of the dresser, which was both a scratched pressed-board "reproduction" and a polished cherrywood lowboy. Two perfume bottles floated in front of me: yellow plastic spraybottle and clean-lined blown glass. I squeezed my eyes shut. The ghostly Diane disappeared in the act of sauntering, slim and assured, toward the bathroom.

"—don't even really look at me, not when we make love or—"

Eyes shut, I groped for the bedroom door.

"Jack!"

I slammed the doors, both of them, and left the apartment before Diane could follow. With her sloppy anger, her overweight nakedness, her completely justified weeping.

Outside was better. I drove my Escort to campus. The other car, the perfectly engineered driving machine with the sleek and balanced lines, shimmered in and out around me, but the vertigo didn't return. I'd never gotten very intense about cars, and over the years I'd learned to handle the double state of anything that wasn't too intense. The rest I avoided. Mostly.

The Aaron Fielding Faculty Office Building jutted boxlike three stories from the asphalt parking lot, and it blended its three floors harmoniously with a low hillside whose wooded lines were repeated in horizontal stretches of brick and wood. The poster-cluttered lobby was full of hurried students trying to see harried advisers, and it was a marble atrium where scholars talked eagerly about the mind of man. I walked down the corridor toward my cubicle, one of a row allotted to teaching assistants and post-docs.

But Dr. Frances Schraeder's door was open, and I couldn't resist.

She sat at her terminal, working, and when I knocked on the doorjamb (scarred metal, ghostly graceful molding), she looked up and smiled. "Jack! Come look at this!"

I came in, with so much relief my eyes prickled. The material Fran's long, age-spotted fingers were held poised over her keyboard, and the ideal Fran's long, age-spotted fingers echoed them. The ideal Fran's white hair was fuller, but no whiter, and both were cut in simple short caps. The material Fran wore glasses, but both Frans' bright blue eyes, a little sunken, shone with the same alert tranquility.

She was the only person I'd ever seen who came close to matching what she should have been.

"This is the latest batch of phase space diagrams," Fran said. "The computer just finished them—I haven't even printed them yet."

I crouched beside her to peer at the terminal.

"Don't look any more disorganized to me than the last bunch."

"Nor to me, either, unfortunately. Same old, same old." She laughed: in chaos theory, there is no same old, same old. The phase space diagrams were infinitely complex, never repeating, without control.

But not completely. The control was there, not readily visible, a key we just didn't recognize with the mathematics we had. Yet.

An ideal no one had seen.

"I keep thinking that your young mind will pick up something I've missed," Fran said. "I'll make you a copy of these. Plus, Pyotr Solenski has published some new work in Berlin that I think you should take a look at. I downloaded it from the net and e-mailed you."

I nodded, but didn't answer. For the first time today, calm flowed through me, soothing me.

Calm.

Rightness.

Numbers.

Fran had done good, if undistinguished, work in pure mathematics all her life. For the last few years she—and I, as her graduate student—had worked in the precise and austere world of iterated function theory, where the result of a given equation is recycled as the starting value of the next repetition of the same equation. If you do that, the results are predictable: the sequences will converge on a given set of numbers. No matter what initial value you plug into the equation, with enough iterations you end up at the same figures, called attractors. Every equation can generate a set of attractors, which iterations converge on like homing pigeons flying back to their nests.

Until you raise the value plugged into the equation past a point called the Feigenbaum number. Then the sequences produced lose all regularity. You can no longer find any pattern. Attractors disappear. The behavior of even fairly simple equations becomes chaotic. The pigeons fly randomly, blind and lost.

Or do they?

Fran—like dozens of other pure mathematicians around the world—looked at all that chaos, and sorted through it, and thought she glimpsed an order to the pigeons' flight. A chaotic order, a controlled randomness. We'd been looking at nonlinear differential equations, and at their attractors, which cause iterated values not to converge but to *diverge*. States which start out only infinitesimally separated go on to diverge more and more and more . . . and more, moving toward some hidden values called, aptly enough, *strange attractors*. Pigeons from the same nest are drawn, through seeming chaos, to points we can identify but not prove the existence of.

Fran and I had a tentative set of equations for those idealized points.

Only tentative. Something wasn't right. We'd overlooked something, something neither of us could see. It was there—I *knew* it—but we couldn't see it. When we did, we'd have proof that any physical system showing an ultradependence on initial conditions must have a strange attractor buried somewhere in its structure. The implications would be profound—for chaos mathematics, for fluid mechanics, for weather control.

For me.

I loved looking for that equation. Sometimes I thought I could glimpse it, behind the work we were doing, almost visible to me. But not often. And the truth I hadn't told Fran, couldn't tell her, was that I didn't need to *find* it, not in the way she did. She was driven by the finest kind of intellectual hunger, a true scientist.

I just wanted the peace and calm of looking. The same calm I'd found over the years in simple addition, in algebra, in calculus, in Boolean logic. In numbers, which were not double state but just themselves, no other set of integers or constants or fractals lying behind these ones, better and fuller and more fulfilled. Mathematics had its own arbitrary assumptions—but no shadows on the cave wall.

So I spent as long with Fran in front of the terminal as I could, and printed out the last batch of phase space diagrams and spent time with those, and went over our work yet again, and read Pyotr Solenski's work, and then I could no longer put off returning to the material world.

* * *

As soon as I walked into Introduction to Set Theory, my nausea returned.

Mid-October. Two more months of teaching this class, twice a week, 90 minutes a session, to keep my fellowship. I didn't know if I could do it. But without the fellowship, I couldn't work with Fran.

Thirty-two faces bobbed in front of me, with 32 shimmering ghostly behind them. Different. So different. Jim Mulcahy: a sullen slouching 18-year-old with acned face and resentful eyes, flunking out—and behind him, the quiet assured Jim, unhamstrung by whatever had caused that terrible resentfulness, whatever kept him from listening to me or studying the text. Jessica Harris: straight A's, thin face pinched by anxiety, thrown into panic whenever she didn't instantly comprehend some point—and behind her, the confident Jessica who could wait a minute, study the logic, take pleasure in her eventual mastery of it. Sixty-four faces, and 64 pieces of furniture in two rooms, and sometimes when I turned away to the two blackboards (my writing firm on the pristine surface, and quavery over dust-filled scratches), even turning away wasn't enough to clear my head.

"The students complain you don't look at them when you talk," my department chair had said. "And you don't make yourself available after class to deal with their problems."

He'd shimmered behind himself, a wise leader and an overworked bureaucrat.

Nobody had any questions. Nobody stayed after class. Nobody in the first 32 students had any comments on infinite sets, and the second 32 I couldn't hear, couldn't reach.

I left the classroom with a raging headache, and almost tripped over a student in the hall.

Chairs lined the corridor walls (water-stained plaster; lively-textured stucco) for students to wait for faculty, or each other, or enlightenment. One chair blocked fully a third of my doorway, apparently shifted there by the girl who sat, head down, drawing in a notebook. My headache was the awful kind that clouds vision. I banged my knee into a corner of the chair (graffiti on varnish on cheap pine; clean hand-stained hardwood). My vision cleared but my knee throbbed painfully.

"Do you *mind* not blocking the doorway, Miss?"

"Sorry." She didn't look up, or stop drawing.

"Please move the damned chair."

She hitched it sideways, never raising her eyes from the paper. The chair banged along the hall floor, clanging onto my throbbing brain. Beside her, the other girl shrugged humorously, in charming self-deprecation.

I forced myself. "Are you waiting for me? To see about the class?"

"No." Still she didn't look up, rude even for a student. I pushed past her, and my eyes fell on her drawing paper.

It was full of numbers: a table for binomial distribution of coin-tossing probabilities, with x as the probability of throwing n heads, divided by the probability of throwing an equal number of heads and tails. The columns were neatly labeled. She was filling in the numbers as rapidly as her pen could write, to seven decimal places. From memory, or mental calculation?

I blurted, "Most people don't do that."

"Is that an observation, an insult, or a compliment?"

All I could see of both girls were the bent tops of their heads: lank dirty blond, feathery golden waves.

She said, "Because if it's an observation, then consider that I said, 'I already know that.' "

The vertigo started to take me.

"If it's an insult, then I said, 'I'm not most people.' "

I put out one hand to steady myself against the wall.

"And if it's a compliment, I said, 'Thanks.' I guess."

The hallway pulsed. Students surged toward me, 64 of them, except that I was only supposed to teach 32 and they weren't the ones who really wanted to learn, they were warped and deformed versions of what they should have been and I couldn't teach them because I hated them too much. For not being what they could have been. For throwing off my inner balance, the delicate metaphysical ear that coordinates reality with ideal with acceptance. For careening past the Feigenbaum number, into versions of themselves where attraction was replaced by turbulent chaos. . . . I fell heavily against the wall, gulping air.

"Hey!" The girl looked up. She had a scrawny, bony face with a too-wide mouth, and a delicate, fine-boned face with rosy generous lips. But mostly I saw her eyes. They looked at me with conventional concern, and then at the wall behind me, and then back at me, and shock ran over me like gasoline fire. The girl reached out an arm to steady me, but her gaze had already gone again past me, as mine did everywhere but in the mirror, inexorably drawn to what I had never seen: the other Jack shimmering behind me, the ideal self I was not.

"It affects you differently than me," Mia said over coffee in the student cafeteria. I'd agreed to go there only because it was nearly empty. "I don't get nauseated or light-headed. I just get mad. It's such a fucking *waste*."

She sat across from me, and the other Mia sat behind her, green eyes hopeful in her lovely face. Hopeful that we could share this, that she was no longer alone, that I might be able to end her loneliness. The physical Mia didn't look hopeful. She looked just as furious as she said she was.

"Nine times out of ten, Jack, people could *become* their ideal selves, or at least a whole lot fucking closer, if they just tried. They're just too lazy or screwed up to put some backbone into it."

I looked away from her. "For me," I said hesitantly, "I guess it's mostly the unfairness of it that's such a burden. Seeing the ideal has interfered with every single thing I've ever wanted to do with my life." Except mathematics.

She squinted at me. "Unfairness? So what? Just don't give in to it."

"I think it's a little more complicated than—"

"It's not. In fact, it's real simple. Just do what you want, anyway. And don't whine."

"I'm not—"

"You are. Just don't let the double vision stop you from trying anything you want to. *I* don't." She glared belligerently. Behind her, the other Mia radiated determination tempered by acceptance.

"Mia, I do try to do the things I want. Math. My dissertation. Teaching." Not that I wanted to be doing that.

"Good," she snapped, and looked over my shoulder. "Double vision doesn't have to defeat us if we don't let it."

I said, "Have you ever found any others like us?" What did my ideal self look like? What strengths could she see on his face?

"No, you're the only one. I thought I was alone."

"Me, too. But if there's two of us, there could be more. Maybe we should—"

"Damn it, Jack, at least *look* at me when you're talking to me!"

Slowly my gaze moved back to her face. Her physical face. Her mouth gaped in anger; her eyes had narrowed to ugly slits. My gaze moved back.

"Stop it, you asshole! Stop it!"

"Don't call me names, Mia."

"Don't tell me what to do! You have no right to tell me what to do! You're no different from—"

I said, "Why would I look at *you* if I could look at her?"

She stood up so abruptly that her chair fell over. Then she was gone.

I put my hands over my eyes, blotting out all sight. Of everything.

"What was this system before it started to diverge?" Fran said.

She held in her hands a phase space diagram I hadn't seen before. Her eyes sparkled. Even so, there was something heavy around her mouth, something that wasn't in the Fran behind her, and for a minute I was so startled I couldn't concentrate on the printouts. The ideal Fran, too, looked different from the day before. Her skin glowed from within, almost too strongly, as if a flashlight burned behind its pale fine-grained surface.

"That was rhetorical, Jack. I know what the system was before it diverged—the equations are there on the desk. But this one looks different. See . . . here. . . ."

She pointed and explained. Nonlinear systems with points that start out very close together tend to diverge from each other, into chaos. But there was something odd about these particular diagrams: they were chaotic, as always around a strange attractor, but in nonpatterns I hadn't seen before. I couldn't quite grasp the difference. Almost, but not quite.

I said, "Where are those original equations?"

"There. On that paper—no, that one."

"You're using *Arnfelser's Constant?* Why?"

"Look at the equations again."

I did, and this time I recognized them, even though subatomic particle physics is not my field. James Arnfelser had won the Nobel two years ago for his work on the behavior of electron/positron pairs during the first 30 seconds of the universe's life. Fran was mucking around with the chaos of creation.

I looked at the phase space diagrams again.

She said, "You can almost see it, can't you? Almost . . . see . . ."

"Fran!"

She had her hand to her midriff. "It's nothing, Jack. Just indigestion on top of muscle tension on top of sleeplessness. I was up all night on those equations."

"Sit down."

"No, I'm fine. Really I am." She smiled at me, and the skin around her eyes, a mass of fine wrinkles, stretched tauter. And behind her, the other Fran didn't smile. At all. She looked at me, and I had the insane idea that somehow, for the first time, she *saw* me.

It was the first time I'd ever seen them diverge.

"Fran, I want you to see a doctor."

"You're good to be so concerned. But I'm fine. Look, Jack, here on the diagram . . ."

Both Frans lit up with the precise pleasure of numbers. And I—out of cowardice, out of relief—let them.

". . . can't understand a thing in this fucking course."

The voice was low, male, the words distinct but the speaker not identifiable. I turned from writing equations on the board. Thirty-two/sixty-four faces swam in front of me. "Did one of you say something?"

Silence. A few girls looked down at their notebooks. The rest of the students stared back at me, stony. I turned back to the board and wrote another half equation.

". . . fucking moron who couldn't teach a dog to piss." A different voice.

My hand, holding the chalk, shook. I went on writing.

". . . shouldn't be allowed in front of a classroom." This time, a girl.

I turned around again. My stomach churned. The students stared back at me. They were all in on this, or at least tacitly complicit.

I heard my voice shake. "If you have any complaints about how this course is being taught, you are advised to take them up with the department chair, or to express them on the course evaluation form distributed at the end of the semester. Meanwhile, we have additional work to cover." I turned back to the board.

". . . fucking prick who can't make anything clear."

My chalk stopped, in the middle of writing an integer. I couldn't make it move again. No matter how hard I concentrated, the chalk wouldn't complete the number.

". . . trying to make us flunk so *he* looks bigger."

Slowly I turned to face the class.

They sat in front of me, slumping or smirking or grinning inanely. Empty faces. Stupid faces. A few embarrassed faces. Fourth-rate minds, interested only in getting by, ugly gaping maws into which we were supposed to stuff the brilliance of Maxwell and Boltzmann and von Neumann and Russell and Arnfelser. So they could masticate it and spit it on the floor.

And behind them . . . behind them . . .

"Get out," I said.

One hundred twenty-eight eyes opened wide.

"You heard me!" I heard myself screaming. "Get out of my classroom! Get out of this university! You don't belong here, it's criminal that you're here, none of you are worth the flame to set you on fire! Get out! You've diverged too far from what you . . . what you . . ."

A few boys in the front row sauntered out. A girl in the back started to cry. Then some of them were yelling at me, shrieking, only the shrieking wasn't in my classroom, it was in the hall, down the hall, it was sirens and bells and outside the window, an emergency medical van, and they were carrying Fran out on a stretcher, her long-fingered hand dangling limply over the side, and nobody would listen to me explain that the terrible thing was not that she wasn't moving but that lying on the stretcher so quietly were not two Frans, as there should have been, but only one. Only one.

I didn't go to the funeral.

I took Fran's last set of diagrams, and copied her files off her hard drive, and packed a bag. Before I checked into the Morningside Motel on Route 64, I left messages on Diane's answering machine, and the department chair's, and my landlady's.

"—don't want to see you again. It's not your fault, but I mean it. I'm sorry."

"I resign my teaching fellowship, and my status as a post-doc at this university."

"My rent is paid through the end of the month. I will not be returning. Please pack my things and send them to my sister, COD, at this address. Thank you."

I bolted the motel door, unwrapped two bottles of Jack Daniel's, and raised my glass to the mirror.

But no toast came. To *him?* Who would not have been doing this stupid melodramatic thing? Who would have seen Fran's death as the random event it was, and grieved it with courage and grace? Who would have figured out the best way to cope with his problems from a healthy sense of balance undestroyed by knowing exactly what he could never, ever, ever measure up to? I'd be damned if I'd drink to him.

"To Fran," I said, and downed it straight, and went on downing it straight until I couldn't see the other, better room lurking behind this one.

Even drunk, you dream.

I didn't know that. I'd expected the hangovers, and the throwing up, and the terrible, blessed blackouts. I'd expected the crying jag. And the emotional pain, like a dull drill. But I'd never been drunk for four days before. I'd thought that when I slept the pain would go away, into oblivion. I didn't know I'd dream.

I dreamed about numbers.

They swam in front of me, pounded the inside of my eyelids, chased me through dark and indistinct landscapes. They hunted me with knives and guns and fire. They hurt. I didn't wake screaming, or disoriented, but I did wake sweating, and in the middle of the night I hung over the toilet, puking, while numbers swam around me on the wavering, double floor. The numbers wouldn't go away. And neither would the thing I was trying to drink myself out of. No matter how drunk I got, the double vision stayed. Except for the equations, and they hurt just as much as the polished floor I couldn't touch, the cool sheets I couldn't feel, the competent Jack I couldn't be. Maybe the equations hurt more. They were Fran's.

Take Arnfelser's Constant. Plug it into a set of equations describing a nonlinear system . . .

Phase space diagrams. Diverging, diverging, gone. A small difference in initial states and you get widely differing states, you get chaos . . .

Take Arnfelser's Constant. Use it as r. *Let* x *equal . . .*

A small difference in initial states. A Fran who diverged only a small amount, a Jack who . . .

Take Arnfelser's equation . . .
I almost saw it. But not quite.
I wasn't good enough to see it. Only *he* was.
I poured another whiskey.

The knock on the door woke me. It sounded like a battering ram.
"Get out. I paid at the desk this morning. I don't want maid service!"
The shouting transferred the battering ram to my head, but the knocking ceased.
Someone started picking the lock.
I lay on the bed and watched, my anger mounting. The chain was on the door. But when the lock was picked the door opened the length of the chain, and a hand inserted a pair of wirecutters. Two pairs of wirecutters, physical and ideal. Four hands. I didn't even move. If the motel owner wanted me, he could have me. Or the cops. I had reached some sort of final decimal place—I simply didn't care.
The chain, cheap lightweight links, gave way, and the door opened. Mia walked in.
"Christ, Jack. Look at you."
I lay sprawled across the bed, and both Mias wrinkled their noses at the smell.
I said, even though it wasn't what I meant, "How the fuck did you get in here?"
"Well, didn't you *see* how I got in here? Weren't you even conscious?" She walked closer and went on staring at me, in soiled underwear, the empty bottle on the floor. Something moved behind their eyes.
"How did you find me?" It hurt to speak.
"Hacked your Visa account. You put this dump on it."
"Go away, Mia."
"When I'm good and ready. Jesus, look at you."
"So don't."
I tried to roll over, but couldn't, so I closed my eyes.
Mia said, "I didn't think you had it in you. No, I really didn't." Her tone was so stupid—such a mix of ignorance and some sort of stupid feminine idealization of macho asshole behavior—that I opened my eyes again. She was smiling.
"Get. Out. Now."
"Not till you tell me what this is all about. Is it Dr. Schraeder? They told me you two were pals."
Fran. The pain started again. And the numbers.
"That's it, isn't it, Jack? She was your friend, not just your adviser. I'm sorry."

I said, "She was the only person I ever met who was what she was supposed to be."

"Yeah? Well, then, I'm really sorry. I'm not what I'm supposed to be, I know. And you sure the hell aren't. Although, you know . . . you look closer to him this morning than you ever did on campus. More . . . real."

I couldn't shove her out the door, and I couldn't stop her talking, and I couldn't roll over without vomiting. So I brought my arm up and placed it across my eyes.

"Don't cry, Jack. Please don't cry."

"I'm not—"

"On second thought, do cry. Why the fuck *not?* Your friend is dead. Go ahead and cry, if you want to!" And she knelt beside me, despite what I must smell like and look like, and put her arms around me while, hating every second of it, I cried.

When I was done, I pushed her away. Drawing every fiber of my body into it, I hauled myself off the bed and toward the bathroom. My stomach churned and the rooms wavered. It took two hands to grope along the wall to the shower.

The water hit me, hard and cold and stinging. I stood under it until I was shivering, and it took that long to realize I still had my briefs on. Bending over to strip them off was torture. My toothbrush scraped raw the inside of my mouth, and the nerves in my brain. I didn't even care that when I staggered naked into the bedroom, Mia was still there.

She said, "Your body is closer to his than your face."

"Get out, Mia."

"I told you, when I'm ready. Jack, there aren't any more of us. At least not that I know of. Or that you do. We can't fight like this."

I groped in my overnight bag, untouched for four days, for fresh underwear. Mia seemed different than she had in the cafeteria: gentler, less abrasive, although she looked the same. I didn't care which—or who—she was.

"We need each other," Mia said, and now there was a touch of desperation in her voice. I didn't turn around.

"Jack—listen to me, at least. See me!"

"I see you," I said. "And I don't want to. Not you, not anybody. Get out, Mia."

"No."

"Have it your way."

I pulled on my clothes, gritted my teeth to get on my shoes, left them untied. I braced myself to push past her.

She stood in the exact center of the room, her hands dangling helplessly at her sides. Behind her the other Mia stood gracefully, her drooping body full of sorrow. But the physical Mia, face twisted in an ugly grimace, was the only one looking at me.

I stopped dead.

They always both looked at me. At the same time. Everybody's both: Mia, Diane, Fran, the department chair, my students. Where one looked, the other looked. Always.

Mia said, more subdued than I had ever heard her. "Please don't leave me alone with this Jack. I . . . need you."

The other Mia looked across the room, not over my shoulder. Not at *him*. At . . . what?

From a small difference in initial states you get widely differing states with repeated iterations. Diverging, diverging, chaos . . . and somewhere in there, the strange attractor. The means to make sense of it.

And just like that, I saw the pattern in the phase space diagrams. I saw the equations.

"Jack? Jack!"

"Just let me . . . write them down . . ."

But there wasn't any chance I'd forget them. They were there, so clear and obvious and perfect, exactly what Fran and I had been searching for.

Mia cried, "You can't just *leave!* We're the only two people like this!"

I finished scribbling the equations and straightened. My head ached, my stomach wanted to puke, my intestines prickled and squirmed. My eyes were so puffy I could barely see out of them. But I saw her, looking at me with her scared bravado, and I saw the other one, not looking at me at all. Diverging. She was right—we were the only two people like this, linked in our own chaotic system. And the states I could see were diverging.

"No," I got out, just before I had to go back into the bathroom. "There aren't two. Soon . . . only one of you."

She stared at me like I was crazy, all the time I was puking. And the other Jack was doing God knows what.

I didn't really care.

I haven't published the equations yet.

I will, of course. They're too important not to publish: proof that any physical system showing an ultradependence on initial conditions must have a strange attractor buried somewhere in its structure. The implications for understanding chaos are profound. But it's not easy to publish this kind of innovation when you no longer have even a post-doc position at a decent university. Even though Fran's name will go first on the article.

I may just put it out on the Internet. Without prior peer review, without copyright protection, without comment. Out onto the unstructured, shifting realities of the net. After all, I don't really need formal attention. I don't really want it.

I have what I wanted: relief. The other faces—other rooms, other buildings, other gardens—are receding from me now. I catch only glimpses of them out of the corner of my eye, diminished in size by the distance between us, and getting smaller all the time. Diverging toward their own strange attractors.

It's not the same for Mia. When she said at the Morningside Motel that I looked more like the ideal Jack than ever before, it wasn't a compliment to my unshaven frowziness. For her, the phase space diagrams are *converging*. She can barely discern the ideal separate from the physical now; the states are that close.

She smiles at everyone. People are drawn to her as to a magnet; she treats them as if their real selves are their ideal ones.

For now.

The crucial characteristic about chaotic systems is that they change unpredictably. Not as unpredictably as before the Schraeder Equations, but still unpredictably. Once you fall into the area past the Feigenbaum number, states converge or diverge chaotically. Tomorrow Mia could see something else. Or I could.

I have no idea what the ideal Mia was looking at when she gazed across the motel room, away from both me and him. When you are not the shadow on the cave wall but the genuine ideal, what is the next state?

I don't want to know. But it doesn't matter whether or not I want it. If that state of life comes into being, then it does, and all we can do is chase it through the chaos of dens and labyrinths and underground caves, trying to pin it momentarily with numbers, as our states diverge from what we know toward something I cannot even imagine, and don't want to.

Although, of course, that too may change.

HOME

Geoff Ryman

▼

Here's a sad, disturbing, and all-too-likely vision of the World of the Future, which turns out to be the kind of place that you might want to visit, but where you certainly wouldn't want to live . . .

Born in Canada, Geoff Ryman now lives in England. He made his first sale in 1976, to *New Worlds*, but it was not until 1984, when he made his first appearance in *Interzone*—the magazine where most of his short fiction has appeared—with his brilliant novella "The Unconquered Country" that he first attracted any serious attention. One of the best novellas of the decade, "The Unconquered Country" had a stunning impact on the science fiction scene of the day, and almost overnight established Ryman as one of the most accomplished writers of his generation, winning him both the British Science Fiction Award and the World Fantasy Award; it was later published in a book version, *The Unconquered Country: A Life History*. His output has been sparse since then, by the high-production standards of the genre, but extremely distinguished, with his novel *The Child Garden: A Low Comedy* winning both the prestigious Arthur C. Clarke Award and the John W. Campbell Memorial Award. His other novels include *The Warrior Who Carried Life* and the critically acclaimed mainstream novel *Was*. His most recent book is a collection of four novellas, *Unconquered Countries*. His story "Dead Space for the Unexpected" appeared in our Twelfth Annual Collection.

There was another one of them this morning, by Waterloo Station. He was a young lad. About a month ago, he had asked me for money. He said it was to feed his dog. He kept the animal inside his jacket and it poked its head out. I remember thinking it looked too gentle a creature to live out on the street. The dog leaned out and tried to lick my hand.

"I'm sorry," I told him. "I only have 20 pence."

He had some sort of regional accent, rather pleasant actually. "Ach, I cannot take a man's last 20 pee."

"Take it, take it, I've got credit cards." Why do they beg for change when no one carries money anymore? Finally I got him to take it. The tips of his fingers were yellow.

He lived with others of his kind under a railway arch that had canvas across its mouth and a painted board over the top that announced that it was a Homeless Peoples' Theatre Group. Rather enterprising I thought, and I would have gone, except that they never put anything on. Sometimes when I walked past, there would be a fire behind the canvas and a few chords from a guitar. That took me back, I can tell you. Just try to hear a guitar anywhere these days.

Someone had crucified him. He was hanging on a wire mesh fence in front of a demolition site. A crowd of people were gawking at him, as though they were slightly but personally embarrassed by something. I think they were feeling a bit silly, grinning at each other, rather like they used to look when they lined up to see the Queen. Actually, I couldn't imagine what they were feeling.

Very suddenly all the boys, none of the girls, just the boys, began to dance in unison, a sort of gloomy square dance. Well, that was just too much for me, I couldn't make it out at all, I turned to an older woman who looked rather sensible. By older, I mean about 35, and I said to her, "He had a dog. Has anyone seen his dog?"

She tutted. "They would have killed that too." She said it in the most extraordinary way. I simply could not understand her tone of voice. I think she felt it would have been a botched job if they had not killed the dog.

"You oughtn't to be allowed out," she said, with a kind of crooked smile. Her intent may even have been kindly, to warn me. But there was a glint about it that I did not like. It is obviously going to be my fate from now on to understand every word that anyone says to me, but not a single sentence. I couldn't find the dog.

And I couldn't face the wait on the train platform either. I do hate stepping over sleeping bags, especially when they're full of person. I indulged and took a taxi.

"Steady on, old boy, let me help you in," said the driver.

"Thank you," I said, trying to settle myself in, but my coat had twisted itself about me in the most uncomfortable way. "It's good to know that human beings are not an entirely extinct species."

He was looking at me in his mirror by now, his face closed up like a shop. I evidently was an old codger.

"There's just been another one of those killings," I said. "ALL these people smirking at the poor boy just as though someone had told a bad joke. Nobody trying to get the poor lad down from where they'd strung him up."

"Uh," he said. "Yeah." Yes, I was a boring old coot, and I was going to go on being boring.

"It's not decent. There wasn't a shred of acknowledgement that killing people is wrong."

The taxi driver shrugged. "Some people think it keeps the streets clear."

"Well, there's a lot of old people too. I suppose you'll be saying they ought to start on us next."

He roared with laughter. He nodded. I think he agreed.

I got out and watched him drive off, and it was only then that I realized I'd forgotten to get my coffee. Coffee, I'll have you know, was the whole reason for going to Waterloo in the first place. There used to be a little shop near me that sold coffee, nice young person ran it, rather old-fashioned, you know, dungarees and no makeup. I could talk to her. Now the only place left is near Waterloo, where they sell it to Frenchmen. It's like going into a sex shop. All nudges and winks and some sort of coffee-fiend argot. And I do resent being held up as some sort of laboratory specimen proving the harmlessness of caffeine.

"There you go," says the man behind the counter, and points to me. "He's still with us. Didn't do him any harm, did it?"

"I drink coffee because I like the taste," I say, and they all roar with laughter. Well, it's nice to find yourself a continual source of amusement to others.

I live in fear. I can't carry groceries, they're too heavy for me. Not that anyone knows what you mean when you use the word groceries. They send these food kits. You know, yeast tablets, vitamin E capsules. And the persons who deliver them are more terrifying than anything you'll see around Waterloo. They wear these tribal mask things over their faces. I asked one of them once if it was something to do with air pollution. His response was to repeat the words "air pollution" several times over, at increasing volume. I think everyone imagines they're having to shout at people who are wearing headphones.

And I don't like those Home Help things. How is a computer supposed to know what's good for you? Bloody fascist health freaks. Always trying to replace a good cuppa with Hibiscus or Rose Hip—they all sound like plump women. I refuse to have my eating habits monitored by a machine. I'll eat and drink what I like, thank you very much.

I finally succeeded in getting my front door open, and there was my niece and her friend with their boots on my sofa. I can't say I like the way she drops in and uses my house, but you can't be an old stick all the time, can you. My niece is called Gertrude and her friend is Brunnhilde. Who gives people these names? They all sound like characters in grand opera.

"Tough time, Grumps?" Gertrude bellows. It's like trying to hold a conversation in the middle of a rugby pitch.

"You'll get marks on my sofa," I tell her.

"Not marks. Bloodstains," said Brunnhilde going all bug-eyed like a horror movie. Something else they don't have these days. Both girls are huge, vast, like something out of the first issue of *Superman*, you know, lifting vehicles singlehanded. I, in the meantime, am getting into a wrestling match with my coat and scarf. My coat and scarf are winning. Even my clothing is insolent these days.

"Here, let me do it for you," says Gertrude and takes them from me. "Wossa ma-ah, Grumps?" Her speech is interrupted by more glottal stops than a Morris Minor in need of a service.

"I saw another one of those bodies," I said.

"You weren't down Wa'ahloo, again, were you?" she said.

"It's where I get my coffee from," I said. "Or rather, used to."

"Coffee," says Brunnhilde and makes a moue of disgust the size of a bagel. "I'd rather drink paint stripper."

"Wa'ahloo is where all the dossers hang out, Grumps. Issa bloody wossa butcher shop."

Brunnhilde is rubbing her thighs in a way that I take to be sarcastic. "Maybe he likes a bit of excitement."

Gertrude giggles at the idea, and smoothes down my coat. For her, it lies still. I tell you the thing is alive and has it in for me. "Look, Grumps. Do yourself a favor. Stay north of the river. You don't know where the safe passages are."

"I refuse to accept that there are parts of this city where I must not walk."

"You don't go for a stroll down the middle of the motorway, do you? Come on, sit down."

I do as I'm told, but I'm still upset. My hands are shaking. They are also lumpy and blue and cold. "Why do they do it?" I say.

"Why do we do it, you mean," says Gertrude, plumping up a pillow.

"You do it?"

"Well, yeah. We all do it, Grumps. It's game. There's too many of them on the streets. If you know what you're doing, you don't get hurt. You know. You're out with your mates, you're in a gang, you see another gang. You leave each other alone."

"And go for the defenceless. Well that is brave of you!"

Brunnhilde explains the rationale for me. "They're killing themselves with all that booze and fags." I remembered the yellow tips of that boy's fingers.

"Then let them do it in peace, you don't have to help them."

Oh dear. I'm shocked again. I can't accept that nice young people on a date will kill someone as part of the evening's entertainment. In my day, you felt racy if you fell down in the gutter. Stoned was lying on your back upside down and realizing you were trying to crawl across the sky.

"They're just using up resources," says Brunnhilde, and she stands up, and starts to case the joint. Her upper lip is working as her tongue runs back and forth over her teeth. It looks as though she has a mouthful of weasels. "You live here all alone, then?" she asks.

"I was married," I say.

"Nice place. Aren't you a bit scared living here all alone? With all this stuff?" She is fingering my Yemeni dagger. A souvenir of a very different time and place.

"Some of it must be worth a packet. Don't you feel unprotected?"

"Yes," I say. "All the time."

"Yeah. You could be here all alone and someone come in." She's taken the dagger out of its decorated sheath. It's curved and it gleams. It's not very sharp. It would hurt.

"In the end, it's all just things," I say.

"Oh, can I have some of them, then?" she asks, and giggles. I'm rather pleased to report that I was not frightened, simply aware of what was going on.

"Look at the poor old geezer," said Brunnhilde. "Using up space. Using up food." She looked at Gertrude. "Let's put him out of his misery."

"Honestly, Brum, you're such a wanker!" Gertrude said, and threw a pillow at her. "I mean, your idea of sport is to pitch into my old Grumps? Well, you do like a pulse-pounder, don't you?"

Brunnhilde looked downcast, as though she had failed to be elected Head Girl.

Gertrude was on her feet. "Come on, let's get you out before Grumps does you some collateral. Honestly. You can be so naff sometimes."

"All right then!" said Brunnhilde, biting back rather ineffectively. "Social work is not my forte anyway." She took a final slurp of my fruit juice. As she held the glass, she curled her little finger delicately away from it. Then Gertrude bundled her towards the door.

"See you later, Grumps. I'll take this wild woman off your hands."

"I wasn't frightened, you know." I said. I wanted her to know that.

"Course not. You're the hard type that goes to Waterloo." They both laughed, and the door closed. I heard Gertrude say outside. "S'all right. I'll get it all when he dies anyway."

I'm reasonably certain that Gertrude saved my life, but I don't think she thought that was very important. She did it rather as one might stop someone putting his greasy head on the anti-macassars. I am so grateful for small favours.

But at least I understood what was happening

I miss Amy, of course. I sometimes wonder if things would be any different if we'd had children, grandchildren. They would have turned out like Gertrude, I expect. Strangers, complete strangers, no matter how often I talked to them.

So. I bolted my door, and I went Home.

It is vaguely embarrassing. I expect I smiled to myself, slightly guilty, slightly ashamed, like those people gawking at corpses. Rigging myself up in all the gear, as though I were auditioning for a part in *Terminator II*. Better than the muck they put on these days, it's all like old Shirley Temple movies to me. I slip on the spectacles and I put on the boots and the gloves, and then I'm off Home.

Village near Witney, Oxfordshire, 1954. Church bells. The elms have not all died of disease, so there are banks of them, huge, high, billowing like clouds and squawking with rookeries. And all the Cotswold stone houses are lined up with thatched roofs and crooked windows in which sit Delft vases, and the Home Service is playing music so sensible it almost smells of toasted white bread. There used to be a country called England. I'm not the one who remembers this it, though I was there. My bones remember it.

And I knock on a door and say "Good morning, Mrs. Clavell, is Kimberly there, please?" and then out comes my friend Kim.

Same age as me. We've taken recently to looking as we actually are, old fools. Kim has some snow-white hair left and his cheeks are mapped with purple veins. But we're wearing shorts and we can climb trees. We can climb to the pinnacle of the old ruined abbey, and there is no one guarding it and no one charging admission. No *son et lumière* for Japanese tourists. And do you know? Hardly even a ritual killing. It's ours.

Kim moved to California, and became both rich and poor at the same time as is the way in California, always about to make a film. He's even worse off than I am now, in some home, without another friend in the world, in someone else's country. But he's Home now.

We take the shortcut, through the fields, past the hall. Here, the safe passages are ours, all the way to the river.

THERE ARE NO DEAD

Terry Bisson

▼

Terry Bisson is the author of four critically acclaimed novels: *Fire on the Mountain*, *Wyrldmaker*, the popular *Talking Man*, which was a finalist for the World Fantasy Award in 1986, and, most recently, *Voyage to the Red Planet*. He is a frequent contributor to such markets as *Asimov's Science Fiction*, *Omni*, *Playboy*, and *The Magazine of Fantasy & Science Fiction*, and, in 1991, his famous story "Bears Discover Fire" won the Nebula Award, the Hugo Award, the Theodore Sturgeon Award, and the Asimov's Reader's Award, the only story ever to sweep them all. His most recent books are a collection, *Bears Discover Fire and Other Stories*, and a new novel, *Pirates of the Universe*. His stories have appeared in our Eighth, Tenth, and Twelfth Annual Collections. He lives with his family in Brooklyn, New York.

The story that follows reminds me of the best of early Bradbury: evocative, lyrical, richly nostalgic, and yet with a bit of an edge to it to keep it from being cloying. In it, he examines the proposition that boys will be boys—if they're lucky, that is.

"All repeat after me," Pig Gnat said. "Oh Secret and Awesome Lost Wilderness Shrine."

"Oh Secret and Awesome Lost Wilderness Shrine."

"The Key to Oz and Always be Thine."

"The Key to Oz and Always be Thine."

"Bee-Men. Now cover it up with that rock."

"Rock!"

"First the rock and then some leaves."

"We'll never find it again!"

"When we need to, we will. I made a map. See? But hurry. I think it's late."

It was late. While Nation arranged the rocks and leaves, and Pig Gnat carefully folded the map, Billy Joe scrambled to the top of the culvert. Across the corn stubble, in the subdivision on the other side of the highway, a few early lights gleamed. Among them, Mrs. Pignatelli's.

"I see a light," said Billy Joe. "Doesn't that mean your mother's home? Maybe we should cut across the field."

"You know better than that," Pig Gnat said. "He who comes by the trail must leave by the trail."

Billy Joe and Nation both grumbled, but agreed. They were at the fabled head of the Tibetan Nile. The trail followed the muddy stream away from the highway and the houses on the other side, down the culvert, along the steep side of what became (if you squinted; and they squinted) a thousand-foot-deep gorge. Where the gorge was narrowed by a junked car (a Ford), the trail crossed the Nile on a perilous high bridge of side-by-side two-by-fours. It then left the stream (which only ran after a rain) and crossed the broomsage-covered Gobi-Serengeti toward the distant treeline.

Billy Joe led the way. Pig Gnat, who had moved to Middletown from Columbus only a year ago, was in the middle. Nation, who owned and therefore carried the gun (a Daisy pump), brought up the rear, alert for game, for danger. "Hold!" he said.

The three boys froze in the dying light. A giant grasshopper stood poised on top of a fence post. Nation took aim and fired. The great beast fell, cut almost in half along its abdomen, its legs kicking in dumb agony.

Nation recocked the Daisy, while Billy Joe put the beast out of its misery. Like rogue tigers, these magnificent man-killers had to die. "Good shooting," Billy Joe said.

"Luck," said Nation.

The desert ended; the trail tunneled through a narrow tangle of brush and old tires, then looped through the Arden Forest, a dark wood of scrub locust and sassafras, then switchbacked down a steep clay bank to the gravel road that led back to the highway.

"Tell me the name of the cliff again," said Billy Joe as they started down.

"Annapurna," said Pig Gnat.

They single-filed it in silence. One slip meant "death."

It was dark when they said their good-byes at the highway's edge. Pig Gnat ran to find his mother, home from her job as Middletown's librarian, fixing supper and expecting him to keep her company. Billy Joe hurried home but to no avail; his father was already drunk, his mother was already crying, and the twins were already screaming. Nation took his time. Each identical house on his street was lighted. He often felt he could choose one at random and find his dinner on the table, his family hurrying to finish in time to watch "Hit Parade."

They grew apart as they grew up. Billy Joe started running with a fast crowd in high school, and would have spent a night or two in jail if his father hadn't been a cop. Nation became a football star, got the Homecoming Queen pregnant, and married her a month after graduation. Pignatelli got into Antioch where his ex-father (as he called him) had been a professor, and lasted two years before the antiwar movement and LSD arrived on campus the same semester.

The Sixties ran through America like a stream too broad to jump and too deep to wade, and it wasn't until their tenth high school reunion, in 1976, that all three were in Middletown at the same time (that they knew of). Nation's wife, Ruth Ann, had organized the reunion. She was still the Homecoming Queen.

"Remember the trail to the Lost Wilderness Shrine?" Billy Joe asked. He was drunk. Like his father, he was a law-man (as he liked to say) but an attorney instead of a cop. "Of course. I made a map," said Pignatelli. He had returned to the reunion from New York, where his first play was about to be produced off-off-off-Broadway, and he was hurt that no one had asked about it. "What're you two talking about?" Nation asked. He and Ruth Ann had just sat down. Pig Gnat whispered, "Come with me." They left the girls at the table and slipped out the side door of the gym. Across the practice field, across the highway, where the cornfield used to be, shopping center lights gleamed under a cold moon; beyond were endless coils of night. The door clicked shut behind them, and with the music gone, they imagined the narrow trail, the dark between the trees, the high passes to the secret Shrine, and they shivered. "We're supposed to stick to high school memories," Nation said. Billy Joe tried the door but it was locked. He was suddenly sober. The Homecoming Queen leaned on the bar, opening the door from the inside. "What are you guys doing?"

"BJ, it's time to go home," said Billy Joe's wife, a Louisville girl.

Two years later Pignatelli gave up playwriting (or set it aside) and took a job at Creative Talent Management's New York office on 57th Street. That October he came back to Middletown for his mother's sixtieth birthday. He stopped by Nation Ford and was surprised to find his friend already going bald. He was under a car, an unusual position for Assistant Manager of a dealership. "Dad and Ruth Ann run the business end," Nation explained. He washed up and they found Billy Joe at the courthouse, and drove to Lexington where Pignatelli's ponytail didn't raise so many eyebrows. Billy Joe had hired a friend to handle his divorce. "It's like a doctor never operating on himself," he said. "We should go camping sometime," Nation said. "The original three."

Two years later, they did. CTM was sending Pignatelli to LA twice a year, and he arranged an overnight stop in Louisville. Billy Joe met him at the airport with two borrowed sleeping bags and a tent, and they met Nation halfway between Louisville and Middletown, and hiked back into the low steep hills along Otter Creek. It was October. Billy Joe gathered wood while Pig Gnat built a fire. "Did you ever think we'd be thirty?" Nation asked. In fact they were thirty-two, but still felt (at least when they were together) like boys; that is, immortal. Pig Gnat stirred the fire, sending sparks to join the stars in heaven. They agreed to never get old.

Two years later, again in October, they met at the airport in Lexington and drove east, into the low-tangled folds of the Cumberland Mountains, and built their fire under a cliff in the Red River Gorge. Nation's twin daughters had just celebrated their "Sweet Sixteen." Pignatelli was dating a starlet whose face was often in the supermarket tabs, beginning to wonder if he was supposed to have kids.

The next October, they backpacked into the gorges of the Great South Fork of the Cumberland River, almost on the Tennessee line. These were real mountains; small, but deep. At night the stars were like ice crystals, "and just as permanent," Pig Gnat pointed out. They stayed two nights. Billy Joe's lawyer had married his ex, moved into the house she had won in the settlement, and was raising his son.

They met every October after that. BJ would pick up Pignatelli at the Louisville airport, and Nation would meet them in the mountains. They explored up and down the Big South Fork, through Billy Joe's second marriage, Pignatelli's move to LA, and Nation's divorce. The Homecoming Queen kept the house on Coffee Tree Lane. They settled into a routine, just like the old days, with Nation picking out the site, Billy Joe gathering the wood, Pig Gnat building the fire. They skipped their twentieth high school reunion; their friendship had skipped high school anyway.

The year they turned forty it rained, and they camped at the mouth of a shallow, dry cave where they could look up at a sky half stone, half stars. "How old do you want to get?" Nation asked. Fifty seemed as old to them as forty once had seemed. Funny how time stretched out, long in front, short behind. Nation's girls were both married, and he would be a grandfather soon. BJ did the paperwork on his second divorce himself. The year Pignatelli's mother died, he found a hand-colored map in a drawer when he cleaned out the house. He knew what it was without unfolding it. He took it back to California with him in a plastic bag.

Some Octobers they tried other mountains, but they always came home. The Adirondacks seemed barren compared to the close, dark tangles of the Cumberlands. The Rockies were spectacular but the scale was all wrong. We're too old to want to see that far, Pig Gnat said. He was only half kidding. He was forty-six. There are no long views in the Cumberlands. There are high cliffs overlooking deep gorges, each gorge as like the others as trees or years are alike. The stars wheel through the sky like slow spars. Sometimes it felt that in all the universe only the three of them were still; everything else was spinning apart. "This is reality," Pig Gnat explained, poking the fire. "The rest of the year just rises up from it like smoke."

When Nation's father died he found the Daisy, filmed with rust and missing its magazine, in the attic. He cleaned it up and left it in Ruth Ann's garage. She had come back to run Nation Ford; she owned half of it anyway. "Still the Homecoming Queen," Nation laughed; they were better as friends than as man and wife. How Pignatelli envied them. They were camped that year among the sycamores in a nameless bend of No Business Creek. "How old do you guys want to get?" Billy Joe asked. It was becoming like a joke. Nobody wants to get old, yet every year they get older.

The year 2000 found them walking the ridge that leads north and east from Cumberland Gap like a road in the sky, while the wind ripped the leaves from the trees all around them. Two thousand! It was the coldest October in years. They slept in a dry cave floored with dust like the moon, where footprints would last a thousand years—or at least forever. Life was still sweet. Billy Joe married again. Nation moved back in with Ruth Ann. It was not yet time.

Somewhere there are pictures that show how they looked alike in the beginning, in that way that all boys look alike. Later pictures would show how they diverged: BJ in blue suits and ties; Pignatelli in silk sport coats and hundred-dollar jeans; Nation in coveralls and gimme hats. Some fifty years later they looked alike again, sitting on the edge of a limestone cliff high over the Big Sandy River, thin in the hair and getting thick in the middle. That was their last October. One week after Christmas, Nation died. It was very sudden. Pignatelli hadn't even known he was sick, then he got the call from Ruth Ann. It was a heart attack. He was almost fifty-nine. How old do you want to get?

Pig Gnat took out the map, which he kept in his office, but didn't unfold it. He had the feeling he could only unfold it once. Billy Joe and his young wife picked him up at the Louisville airport, and they drove straight to Middletown for the funeral. Billy Joe was angry; his wife seemed apologetic. After the burial there was a reception at the house on Coffee Tree Lane. Pignatelli went out to the garage and two little girls followed him; all Nation's grandchildren were girls. He spread out the map on the workbench, and sure enough, the old paper cracked along the folds. He found the Daisy under the bench, dark with rust and smelling of WD-40. The girls helped him look but he couldn't find the magazine or any BBs.

Back in the house, he kissed Ruth Ann good-bye. He wondered, as he had often wondered, if he would have married if he could have married the Homecoming Queen. Almost all the mourners had left. Billy Joe was drunk, and still sulking. "We waited too goddamn long!" he whispered. Pig Gnat shook his head, but he wasn't sure. Maybe, maybe they had. He felt sorry for Billy Joe's young wife. They left her at the house with Ruth Ann and the last of the mourners. There was no time to lose. In January it gets dark early. The cornfield was now a shopping center, had been for forty years, but the woods and the broomsage were still there behind it like a blank spot on a map. The road that led back from the highway was still gravel. They parked the electric (no one had ever been able to call them "cars") by an overflowing dumpster at the bottom of a steep clay bank.

"Tell me the name of the cliff again," said Billy Joe.

"Annapurna," said Pig Gnat. "You okay?"

"I feel like shit but I'm not drunk anymore, if that's what you mean."

The narrow trail switchbacked up the bank to the forest. One slip and they were "dead." It was spitting snow. At the top the trail led into the trees, the dark, dark trees.

Billy Joe carried the Daisy. Of course it was useless without a magazine. They came out of the woods, through the brush, into the field. "This is the deepest and most mysterious part of the trail." Pig Gnat said from memory. "As we begin our journey up the ancient Tibetan Nile." They crossed the gorge (the Ford was gone) and followed the great river to its source in a culvert, now almost hidden under a broken slab at the rear of the shopping center. "All kneel," said Pig Gnat.

They knelt. Pig Gnat raked away the leaves with a stick. "Don't we say something, or something?" Billy Joe asked.

"That's after. Give me a hand with this rock."

Billy Joe set down the Daisy and they heaved together, and slid the big stone to one side.

Underneath, in the dark brown earth, a two-inch ruby square glowed. "Hadn't it oughta say *press me* or *caution* or something?" Billy Joe joked nervously.

"Sssshhhhh," said Pig Gnat. "Just press it."

"Why me? Why don't you press it?"

"I don't know why. That's just the way it works. Just press it."

Billy Joe pressed it and instead of pushing in like a button it sort of pushed back.

There.

"Now, all repeat after me," Pig Gnat said. "Oh Secret and Awesome Lost Wilderness Shrine."

"Oh Secret and Awesome Lost Wilderness Shrine."

"The Key to Oz and Always be Thine."

"The Key to Oz and Always be Thine."

"Bee-Men, and so forth. Now help me with this rock."

"Rock!"

"First the rock and then leaves."

"We'll never find it again."

"When we need to, we will. Come on. I think it's late."

It was late, but still warm for October. While Nation and Pig Gnat pulled the rock into place, Billy Joe scrambled to the top of the culvert. The funny feeling in his legs was gone. Across the corn stubble, in the subdivision on the other side of the highway a few early lights gleamed. Among them, Mrs. Pignatelli's.

"It *is* late," said Billy Joe. "I think your mother's home. Maybe we should cut across the field . . ."

"You know better than that," Pig Gnat said. "He who comes by the trail must leave by the trail."

The trail followed the great stream away from the highway and the houses on the other side, down the culvert and across the gorge on a high, perilous bridge of two-by-fours.

Billy Joe led the way. Pig Gnat was in the middle. Nation, who owned and therefore carried the gun, brought up the rear, alert for game.

"Hold," he said.

Three boys froze in the dying light. A giant grasshopper stood poised on top of a fence post. Nation took aim. Billy Joe squinted, imagining a rogue tiger. Pig Gnat kept his eyes wide open, staring off into the endless coils of night.

RECORDING ANGEL

Paul J. McAuley

▼

Several of the stories in this anthology take us to the far future, but few take us as far into that future, or to a future as numinous, alien, rich, and strange, as the bizarre and evocative story that follows . . . set in a future so remote, so distanced from our times and from the Earth itself, that the very memory of humanity itself is almost forgotten and gone. Almost—but not quite.

Along with other writers such as Stephen Baxter, Iain M. Banks, Greg Egan (actually an Australian, but usually counted in with this group because of his work for *Interzone*), Gwyneth Jones, Ian R. MacLeod, Ian McDonald, Colin Greenland, and others, Paul J. McAuley is considered to be one of the best of the new British breed of "hard science" writers who have been helping to reinvent that form at the beginning of the nineties. He is a frequent contributor to *Interzone*, as well as to markets such as *Amazing*, *The Magazine of Fantasy & Science Fiction*, *Asimov's Science Fiction*, *When the Music's Over*, and elsewhere. His first novel, *Four Hundred Billion Stars*, won the Philip K. Dick Award. His other books include the novels *Of the Fall*, *Eternal Light*, *Red Dust*, and *Pasquale's Angel*; a collection of his short work, *The King of the Hill and Other Stories*; and an original anthology coedited with Kim Newman, *In Dreams*. His most recent book is a major new novel, *Fairyland*. His stories have appeared in our Fifth and Ninth Annual Collections. Born in Oxford, England, he now makes his home in Strathkinness, in Scotland.

Mr. Naryan, the Archivist of Sensch, still keeps to his habits as much as possible, despite all that has happened since Angel arrived in the city. He has clung to these personal rituals for a very long time now, and it is not easy to let them go. And so, on the day that Angel's ship is due to arrive and attempt to reclaim her, the day that will end in revolution, or so Angel has promised her followers, as ever, as dusk, as the Nearside edge of Confluence tips above the disc of its star and the Eye of the Preservers rises above the Farside Mountains, Mr. Naryan walks across the long plaza at the edge of the city towards the Great River.

Rippling patterns swirl out from his feet, silver and gold racing away through the living marble. Above his head, clouds of little machines spin through the twilight: information's dense weave. At the margin of the plaza, broad steps shelve into the river's brown slop. Naked children scamper through the shallows, turning to watch as Mr. Naryan, old and fat and leaning on his stick at every other stride, limps past and descends the submerged stair until only his hairless head is above water. He draws a breath and ducks completely under. His nostrils pinch shut. Membranes slide across his eyes. As always, the bass roar of the river's fall over the edge of the world stirs his heart. He surfaces, spouting water, and the children hoot. He ducks under again and comes up quickly, and the children scamper back from his spray, breathless with delight. Mr. Naryan laughs with them and walks back up the steps, his loose, belted shirt shedding water and quickly drying in the parched dusk air.

Further on, a funeral party is launching little clay lamps into the river's swift currents. The men, waist-deep, turn as Mr. Naryan limps past, knuckling their broad foreheads. Their wet skins gleam with the fire of the sunset that is now gathering in on itself across leagues of water. Mr. Naryan genuflects in acknowledgment, feeling an icy shame. The woman died before he could hear her story; her, and seven others in the last few days. It is a bitter failure.

Angel, and all that she has told him—Mr. Naryan wonders whether he will be able to hear out the end of her story. She has promised to set the city aflame and, unlike Dreen, Mr. Naryan believes that she can.

A mendicant is sitting cross-legged on the edge of the steps down to the river. An old man, sky-clad and straight-backed. He seems to be staring into the sunset, in the waking trance that is the nearest that the Shaped citizens of Sensch ever come to sleep. Tears brim in his wide eyes and pulse down his leathery cheeks; a small silver moth has settled at the corner of his left eye to sip salt.

Mr. Naryan drops a handful of the roasted peanuts he carries for the purpose into the mendicant's bowl, and walks on. He walks a long way before he realises that a crowd has gathered at the end of the long plaza, where the steps end and, with a sudden jog, the docks begin. Hundreds of machines swarm in the darkening air, and behind this shuttling weave a line of magistrates stand shoulder to shoulder, flipping their quirts back and forth as if to drive off flies. Metal tags braided into the tassels of the quirts wink and flicker; the magistrates' flared red cloaks seem inflamed in the last light of the sun.

The people make a rising and falling hum, the sound of discontent. They are looking upriver. Mr. Naryan, with a catch in his heart, realises what they must be looking at.

It is a speck of light on the horizon north of the city, where the broad ribbon of the river and the broad ribbon of the land narrow to a single point.

It is the lighter towing Angel's ship, at the end of its long journey downriver to the desert city where she has taken refuge, and caught Mr. Naryan in the net of her tale.

Mr. Naryan first heard about her from Dreen, Sensch's Commissioner; in fact, Dreen paid a visit to Mr. Naryan's house to convey the news in person. His passage through the narrow streets of the quarter was the focus of a swelling congregation which kept a space two paces wide around him as he ambled towards the house where Mr. Naryan had his apartment.

Dreen was a lively, but tormented, fellow who was paying off a debt of conscience by taking the more or less ceremonial position of Commissioner in this remote city which his ancestors had long ago abandoned. Slight and agile, his head shaved clean except for a fringe of polychrome hair that framed his parchment face, he looked like a lily blossom swirling on the Great River's current as he made his way through the excited crowd. A pair of magistrates preceded him and a remote followed, a mirror-coloured seed that seemed to move through the air in brief rapid pulses like a squeezed watermelon pip. A swarm of lesser machines spun above the packed heads of the crowd. Machines did not entirely trust the citizens, with good reason. Change was raged up and down the length of Confluence as, one by one, the ten thousand races of the Shaped fell from innocence.

Mr. Naryan, alerted by the clamour, was already standing on his balcony when Dreen reached the house. Scrupulously polite, his voice amplified through a little machine that fluttered before his lips, Dreen enquired if he might come up. The crowd fell silent as he spoke, so that his last words echoed eerily up and down the narrow street. When Mr. Naryan said mildly that the Commissioner was, of course, always welcome, Dreen made an elaborate genuflection and scrambled straight up the fretted carvings which decorated the front of the apartment house. He vaulted the wrought-iron rail and perched in the ironwood chair that Mr. Naryan usually took when he was tutoring a pupil. While Mr. Naryan lowered his corpulent bulk onto the stool that was the only other piece of furniture on the little balcony, Dreen said cheerfully that he had not walked so far for more than a year. He accepted the tea and sweetmeats that Mr. Naryan's wife, terrified by his presence, offered, and added, "It really would be more convenient if you took quarters appropriate to your status."

As Commissioner, Dreen had use of the vast palace of intricately carved pink sandstone that dominated the southern end of the city, although he chose to live in a tailored habitat of hanging gardens that hovered above the palace's spiky towers.

Mr. Naryan said, "My calling requires that I live amongst the people. How else would I understand their stories? How else would they find me?"

"By any of the usual methods, of course—or you could multiply yourself so that every one of these snakes had their own archivist. Or you could use machines. But I forget, your calling requires that you use only appropriate technology. That's why I'm here, because you won't have heard the news."

Dreen had an abrupt style, but he was neither as brutal nor as ruthless as his brusqueness suggested. Like Mr. Naryan, who understood Dreen's manner completely, he was there to serve, not to rule.

Mr. Naryan confessed that he had heard nothing unusual, and Dreen said eagerly, "There's a woman arrived here. A star-farer. Her ship landed at Ys last year, as I remember telling you."

"I remember seeing a ship land at Ys, but I was a young man then, Dreen. I had not taken orders."

"Yes, yes," Dreen said impatiently, "picket boats and the occasional merchant's argosy still use the docks. But this is different. She claims to be from the deep past. The *very* deep past, before the Preservers."

"I can see that her story would be interesting if it were true."

Dreen beat a rhythm on his skinny thighs with the flat of his hands. "Yes, yes! A human woman, returned after millions of years of travelling outside the Galaxy. But there's more! She is only one of a whole crew, and she's jumped ship. Caused some fuss. It seems the others want her back."

"She is a slave, then?"

"It seems she may be bound to them as you are bound to your order."

"Then you could return her. Surely you know where she is?"

Dreen popped a sweetmeat in his mouth and chewed with gusto. His flat-topped teeth were all exactly the same size. He wiped his wide lipless mouth with the back of his hand and said, "Of course I know where she is—that's not the point. The point is that no one knows if she's lying, or her shipmates are lying—they're a nervy lot, I'm told. Not surprising, culture shock and all that. They've been travelling a long time. Five million years, if their story's to be believed. Of course, they weren't alive for most of that time. But still."

Mr. Naryan said, "What do you believe?"

"Does it matter? This city matters. Think what trouble she could cause!"

"If her story's true."

"Yes, yes. That's the point. Talk to her, eh? Find out the truth. Isn't that what your order's about? Well, I must get on."

Mr. Naryan didn't bother to correct Dreen's misapprehension. He observed, "The crowd has grown somewhat."

Dreen smiled broadly and rose straight into the air, his toes pointing down, his arms crossed with his palms flat on his shoulders. The remote rose with him. Mr. Naryan had to shout to make himself heard over the cries and cheers of the crowd.

"What shall I do?"

Dreen checked his ascent and shouted back, "You might tell her that I'm here to help!"

"Of course!"

But Dreen was rising again, and did not hear Mr. Naryan. As he rose he picked up speed, dwindling rapidly as he shot across the jumbled rooftops of the city towards his aerie. The remote drew a silver line behind him; a cloud of lesser machines scattered across the sky as they strained to keep up.

The next day, when, as usual, Mr. Naryan stopped to buy the peanuts he would scatter amongst any children or mendicants he encountered as he strolled through the city, the nut roaster said that he'd seen a strange woman only an hour before—she'd had no coin, but the nut roaster had given her a bag of shelled salted nuts all the same.

"Was the right thing to do, master?" the nut roaster asked. His eyes glittered anxiously beneath the shelf of his ridged brow. Mr. Naryan, knowing that the man had been motivated by a cluster of artificial genes implanted in his ancestors to ensure that they and all their children would give aid to any human who requested it, assured the nut roaster that his conduct had been worthy. He proffered coin in ritual payment for the bag of warm oily peanuts, and the nut roaster made his usual elaborate refusal.

"When you see her, master, tell her that she will find no plumper or more savoury peanuts in the whole city. I will give her whatever she desires!"

All day, as Mr. Naryan made his rounds of the tea shops, and even when he heard out the brief story of a woman who had composed herself for death, he expected to be accosted by an exotic wild-eyed stranger. That same expectation distracted him in the evening, as the magistrate's son haltingly read from the Puranas while all around threads of smoke from neighbourhood kitchen fires rose into the black sky. How strange the city suddenly seemed to Mr. Naryan: the intent face of the magistrate's son, with its faint intaglio of scales and broad shelving brow, seemed horribly like a mask. Mr. Naryan felt a deep longing for his youth, and after the boy had left he stood under the shower for more than an hour, letting water penetrate every fold and cranny of his hairless, corpulent body until his wife anxiously called to him, asking if he was all right.

The woman did not come to him that day, nor the next. She was not seeking him at all. It was only by accident that Mr. Naryan met her at last.

She was sitting at the counter of a tea shop, in the deep shadow beneath its tasselled awning. The shop was at the corner of the camel market, where knots of dealers and handlers argued about the merits of this or that animal and saddlemakers squatted crosslegged amongst their wares before the low, cave-like entrances to their workshops. Mr. Naryan would have walked right past the shop if the proprietor had not hurried out and called to him, explaining that here was a human woman who had no coin, but he was letting her drink what she wished, and was that right?

Mr. Naryan sat beside the woman, but did not speak after he ordered his own tea. He was curious and excited and afraid: she looked at him when he sat down and put his cane across his knees, but her gaze only brushed over him without recognition.

She was tall and slender, hunched at the counter with elbows splayed. She was dressed, like every citizen of Sensch, in a loose, raw cotton overshirt. Her hair was as black and thick as any citizen's, too, worn long and caught in a kind of net slung at her shoulder. Her face was sharp and small-featured, intent from moment to moment on all that happened around her—a bronze machine trawling through the dusty sunlight beyond the awning's shadow; a vendor of pomegranate juice calling his wares; a gaggle of women laughing as they passed; a sled laden with prickly pear gliding by, two handspans above the dusty flagstones—but nothing held her attention for more than a moment. She held her bowl of tea carefully in both hands, and sucked at the liquid clumsily when she drank, holding each mouthful for a whole minute before swallowing and then spitting twiggy fragments into the copper basin on the counter.

Mr. Naryan felt that he should not speak to her unless she spoke first. He was disturbed by her: he had grown into his routines, and this unsought responsibility frightened him. No doubt Dreen was watching through one or another of the little machines that flitted about the sunny, salt-white square—but that was not sufficient compulsion, except that now he had found her, he could not leave her.

At last, the owner of the tea house refilled the woman's bowl and said softly, "Our Archivist is sitting beside you."

The woman turned jerkily, spilling her tea. "I'm not going back," she said. "I've told them that I won't serve."

"No one has to do anything here," Mr. Naryan said, feeling that he must calm her. "That's the point. My name is Naryan, and I have the honour, as our good host has pointed out, of being the Archivist of Sensch."

The woman smiled at this, and said that he could call her Angel; her name also translated as Monkey, but she preferred the former. "You're not like the others here," she added, as if she had only just realised. "I saw people like you in the port city, and one let me ride on his boat down the river until we reached the edge of a civil war. But after that every one of the cities I passed through seemed to be inhabited by only one race, and each was different from the next."

"It's true that this is a remote city," Mr. Naryan said.

He could hear the faint drums of the procession. It was the middle of the day, when the sun reached zenith and halted before reversing back down the sky.

The woman, Angel, heard the drums too. She looked around with a kind of preening motion as the procession came through the flame trees on the far side of the square. It reached this part of the city at the same time every day. It was led by a bare-chested man who beat a big drum draped in cloth of gold; it was held before him by a leather strap that went around his neck. The steady beat echoed across the square. Behind him slouched or capered ten, twenty, thirty naked men and women. Their hair was long and ropey with dirt; their fingernails were curved yellow talons.

Angel drew her breath sharply as the rag-taggle procession shuffled past, following the beat of the drum into the curving street that led out of the square. She said, "This is a very strange place. Are they mad?"

Mr. Naryan explained, "They have not lost their reason, but have had it taken away. For some it will be returned in a year; it was taken away from them as a punishment. Others have renounced their own selves for the rest of their lives. It is a religious avocation. But saint or criminal, they were all once as fully aware as you or me."

"I'm not like you," she said. "I'm not like any of the crazy kinds of people I have met."

Mr. Naryan beckoned to the owner of the tea house and ordered two more bowls. "I understand you have come a long way." Although he was terrified of her, he was certain that he could draw her out.

But Angel only laughed.

Mr. Naryan said, "I do not mean to insult you."

"You dress like a . . . native. Is *that* a religious avocation?"

"It is my profession. I am the Archivist here."

"The people here are different—a different race in every city. When I left, not a single intelligent alien species was known. It was one reason for my voyage. Now there seem to be thousands strung along this long, long river. They treat me like a ruler—is that it? Or a god?"

"The Preservers departed long ago. These are the end times."

Angel said dismissively, "There are always those who believe they live at the end of history. We thought that *we* lived at the end of history, when every star system in the Galaxy had been mapped, every habitable world settled."

For a moment Mr. Naryan thought that she would tell him of where she had been, but she added, "I was told that the Preservers, who I suppose were my descendants, made the different races, but each race calls itself human, even the ones who don't look like they could have evolved from anything that ever looked remotely human."

"The Shaped call themselves human because they have no other name for what they have become, innocent and fallen alike. After all, they had no name before they were raised up. The citizens of Sensch remain innocent. They are our . . . responsibility.''

He had not meant for it to sound like a plea.

''You're not doing all that well,'' Angel said, and started to tell him about the Change War she had tangled with upriver, on the way to this, the last city at the midpoint of the world.

It was a long, complicated story, and she kept stopping to ask Mr. Naryan questions, most of which, despite his extensive readings of the Puranas, he was unable to answer. As she talked, Mr. Naryan transcribed her speech on his tablet. She commented that a recording device would be better, but by reading back a long speech she had just made he demonstrated that his close diacritical marks captured her every word.

''But that is not its real purpose, which is an aid to fix the memory in my head.''

''You listen to people's stories.''

''Stories are important. In the end they are all that is left, all that history leaves us. Stories endure.'' And Mr. Naryan wondered if she saw what was all too clear to him, the way her story would end, if she stayed in the city.

Angel considered his words. ''I have been out of history a long time,'' she said at last. ''I'm not sure that I want to be a part of it again.'' She stood up so quickly that she knocked her stool over, and left.

Mr. Naryan knew better than to follow her. That night, as he sat enjoying a cigarette on his balcony, under the baleful glare of the Eye of the Preservers, a remote came to him. Dreen's face materialised above the remote's silver platter and told him that the woman's shipmates knew that she was here. They were coming for her.

As the ship draws closer, looming above the glowing lighter that tows it, Mr. Naryan begins to make out its shape. It is a huge black wedge composed of tiers of flat plates that rise higher than the tallest towers of the city. Little lights, mostly red, gleam here and there within its ridged carapace. Mr. Naryan brushes mosquitoes from his bare arms, watching the black ship move beneath a black sky empty except for the Eye of the Preservers and a few dim halo stars. Here, at the midpoint of the world, the Home Galaxy will not rise until winter.

The crowd has grown. It becomes restless. Waves of emotion surge back and forth. Mr. Naryan feels them pass through the citizens packed around him, although he hardly understands what they mean, for all the time he has lived with these people.

He has been allowed to pass through the crowd with the citizens' usual generous deference, and now stands close to the edge of the whirling cloud of machines which defends the dock, twenty paces or so from the magistrates who nervously swish their quirts to and fro. The crowd's thick yeasty odour fills his nostrils; its humming disquiet, modulating up and down, penetrates to the marrow of his bones. Now and then a machine ignites a flare of light that sweeps over the front ranks of the crowd, and the eyes of the men and women shine blankly orange, like so many little sparks.

At last the ship passes the temple complex at the northern edge of the city, its wedge rising like a wave above the temple's clusters of slim spiky towers. The lighter's engines go into reverse; waves break in whitecaps on the steps beyond the whirl of machines and the grim line of magistrates.

The crowd's hum rises in pitch. Mr. Naryan finds himself carried forward as it presses towards the barrier defined by the machines. The people around him apologise effusively for troubling him, trying to minimise contact with him in the press as snails withdraw from salt. The machines' whirl stratifies, and the magistrates raise their quirts and shout a single word lost in the noise of the crowd. The people in the front rank of the crowd fall to their knees, clutching their eyes and wailing: the machines have shut down their optic nerves.

Mr. Naryan, shown the same deference by the machines as by the citizens, suddenly finds himself isolated amongst groaning and weeping citizens, confronting the row of magistrates. One calls to him, but he ignores the man.

He has a clear view of the ship, now. It has come to rest a league away, at the far end of the docks, but Mr. Naryan has to tip his head back and back to see the top of the ship's tiers. It is as if a mountain has drifted against the edge of the city. A new sound drives across the crowd, as a wind drives across a field of wheat. Mr. Naryan turns and, by the random flare of patrolling machines, is astonished to see how large the crowd has grown. It fills the long plaza, and more people stand on the rooftops along its margin. Their eyes are like a harvest of stars. They are all looking towards the ship, where Dreen, standing on a cargo sled, ascends to meet the crew.

Mr. Naryan hooks the wire frames of his spectacles over his ears, and the crew standing on top of the black ship snap into clear focus.

There are fifteen, men and women all as tall as Angel, looming over Dreen as he welcomes them with effusive gestures. Mr. Naryan can almost smell Dreen's anxiety. He wants the crew to take Angel away, and order restored. He will be telling them where to find her. Mr. Naryan feels a pang of anger. He turns and makes his way through the crowd. When he reaches its ragged margin, everyone around him suddenly looks straight up. Dreen's sled sweeps overhead, carrying his guests to the safety of the floating habitat above the pink sandstone palace. The crowd surges forward—and all the little machines fall from the air!

One lands close to Mr. Naryan, its carapace burst open at the seams. Smoke pours from it. An old woman picks it up—Mr. Naryan smells her burnt flesh as it sears her hand—and throws it at him.

Her shot goes wide. Mr. Naryan is so astonished that he does not even duck. He glimpses the confusion as the edge of the crowd collides with the line of magistrates: some magistrates run, their red cloaks streaming at their backs; others throw down their quirts and hold out their empty hands. The crowd devours them. Mr. Naryan limps away as fast as he could, his heart galloping with fear. Ahead is a wide avenue leading into the city, and standing in the middle of the avenue is a compact group of men, clustered about a tall figure.

It is Angel.

Mr. Naryan told Angel what Dreen had told him, that the ship was coming to the city, the very next day. It was at the same tea house. She did not seem surprised. "They need me," she said. "How long will they take?"

"Well, they cannot come here directly. Confluence's maintenance system will only allow ships to land at designated docks, but the machinery of the spaceport docks here has grown erratic and dangerous through disuse. The nearest place they could safely dock is five hundred leagues away, and after that the ship must be towed downriver. It will take time. What will you do?"

Angel passed a hand over her sleek black hair. "I like it here. I could be comfortable."

She had already been given a place in which to live by a wealthy merchant family. She took Mr. Naryan to see it. It was near the river, a small two-storey house built around a courtyard shaded by a jacaranda tree. People were going in and out, carrying furniture and carpets. Three men were painting the wooden rail of the balcony that ran around the upper storey. They were painting it pink and blue, cheerfully singing. Angel was amused by the bustle, and laughed when Mr. Naryan said that she shouldn't take advantage of the citizens.

"They seem so happy to help me. What's wrong with that?"

Mr. Naryan thought it best not to explain about the cluster of genes implanted in all the races of the Shaped, the reflex altruism of the unfallen. A woman brought out tea and a pile of crisp, wafer-thin fritters sweetened with crystallised honey. Two men brought canopied chairs. Angel sprawled in one, invited Mr. Naryan to sit in the other. She was quite at ease, grinning every time someone showed her the gift they had brought her.

Dreen, Mr. Naryan knew, would be dismayed. Angel was a barbarian, displaced by five million years. She had no idea of the careful balance by which one must live with the innocent, the unfallen, if their cultures were to survive. Yet she was fully human, free to choose, and that freedom was inviolable. No wonder Dreen was so eager for the ship to reclaim her.

Still, Angel's rough joy was infectious, and Mr. Naryan soon found himself smiling with her at the sheer abundance of trinkets scattered around her. No one was giving unless they were glad to give, and no one who gave was poor. The only poor in Sensch were the sky-clad mendicants who had voluntarily renounced the material world.

So he sat and drank tea with her, and ate a dozen of the delicious, honeyed fritters, one after the other, and listened to more of her wild tales of travelling the river, realising how little she understood of Confluence's administration. She was convinced that the Shaped were somehow forbidden technology, for instance, and did not understand why there was no government. Was Dreen the absolute ruler? By what right?

"Dreen is merely the Commissioner. Any authority he has is invested in him by the citizens, and it is manifest only on high days. He enjoys parades, you know. I suppose the magistrates have power, in that they arbitrate neighbourly disputes and decide upon punishment—Senschians are argumentative, and sometimes quarrels can lead to unfortunate accidents."

"Murder, you mean? Then perhaps they are not as innocent as you maintain." Angel reached out suddenly. "And these? By what authority do these little spies operate?"

Pinched between her thumb and forefinger was a bronze machine. Its sensor cluster turned back and forth as it struggled to free itself.

"Why, they are part of the maintenance system of Confluence."

"Can Dreen use them? Tell me all you know. It may be important."

She questioned Mr. Naryan closely, and he found himself telling her more than he wanted. But despite all that he told her, she would not talk about her voyage, nor of why she had escaped from the ship, or how. In the days that followed, Mr. Naryan requested several times, politely and wistfully, that she would. He even visited the temple and petitioned for information about her voyage, but all trace of it had been lost in the vast sifting of history, and when pressed, the aspect who had come at the hierodule's bidding broke contact with an almost petulant abruptness.

Mr. Naryan was not surprised that it could tell him nothing. The voyage must have begun five million years ago at least, after all, for the ship to have travelled all the way to the neighbouring galaxy and back.

He did learn that the ship had tried to sell its findings on landfall, much as a merchant would sell his wares. Perhaps Angel wanted to profit from what she knew; perhaps that was why the ship wanted her back, although there was no agency on Confluence that would close such a deal. Knowledge was worth only the small price of petitioning those aspects which deal with the secular world.

Meanwhile, a group of citizens gathered around Angel, like disciples around one of the blessed who, touched by some fragment or other of the Preservers, wander Confluence's long shore. These disciples went wherever she went. They were all young men, which seemed to Mr. Naryan faintly sinister, sons of her benefactors fallen under her spell. He recognised several of them, but none would speak to him, although there were always at least two or three accompanying Angel. They wore white headbands on which Angel had lettered a slogan in an archaic script older than any race of the Shaped; she refused to explain what it meant.

Mr. Naryan's wife thought that he, too, was falling under some kind of spell. She did not like the idea of Angel: she declared that Angel must be some kind of ghost, and therefore dangerous. Perhaps she was right. She was a wise and strong-willed woman, and Mr. Naryan had grown to trust her advice.

Certainly, Mr. Naryan believed that he could detect a change in the steady song of the city as he went about his business. He listened to an old man dying of the systematic organ failure which took most of the citizens in the middle of their fourth century. The man was one of the few who had left the city—he had travelled north, as far as the swampy settlements where an amphibious race lived in a city tunnelled through cliffs overlooking the river. His story took a whole day to tell, in a stiflingly hot room muffled in dusty carpets and lit only by a lamp with a blood-red chimney. At the end, the old man began to weep, saying that he knew now that he had not travelled at all, and Mr. Naryan was unable to comfort him. Two children were born on the next day—an event so rare that the whole city celebrated, garlanding the streets with fragrant orange blossoms. But there was a tension beneath the celebrations that Mr. Naryan had never before felt, and it seemed that Angel's followers were everywhere amongst the revellers. Dreen felt the change, too. "There have been incidents," he said, as candid an admission as he had ever made to Mr. Naryan. "Nothing very much. A temple wall defaced with the slogan the woman has her followers wear. A market disrupted by young men running through it, overturning stalls. I asked the magistrates not to make examples of the perpetrators—that would create martyrs. Let the people hold their own courts if they wish. And she's been making speeches. Would you like to hear one?"

"Is it necessary?"

Dreen dropped his glass with a careless gesture—a machine caught it and bore it off before it smashed on the tiles. They were on a balcony of Dreen's floating habitat, looking out over the Great River towards the nearside edge of the world. At the horizon was the long white double line that marked the river's fall: the rapids below, the permanent clouds above. It was noon, and the white, sunlit city was quiet.

Dreen said, "You listen to so much of her talk, I suppose you are wearied of it. In summary, it is nothing but some vague nonsense about destiny, about rising above circumstances and bettering yourself, as if you could lift yourself into the air by grasping the soles of your feet.''

Dreen dismissed this with a snap of his fingers. His own feet, as always, were bare, and his long opposable toes were curled around the bar of the rail on which he squatted. He said, ''Perhaps she wants to rule the city—if it pleases her, why not? At least, until the ship arrives here. I will not stop her if that is what she wants, and if she can do it. Do you know where she is right now?''

''I have been busy.'' But Mr. Naryan felt an eager curiosity: yes, his wife was right.

''I heard the story you gathered in. At the time, you know, I thought that man might bring war to the city when he came back.'' Dreen's laugh was a high-pitched hooting. ''The woman is out there, at the edge of the world. She took a boat yesterday.''

''I am sure she will return,'' Mr. Naryan said. ''It is all of a pattern.''

''I defer to your knowledge. Will hers be an interesting story, Mr. Naryan? Have another drink. Stay, enjoy yourself.'' Dreen reached up and swung into the branches of the flame tree which leaned over the balcony, disappearing in a flurry of red leaves and leaving Mr. Naryan to find a machine that was able to take him home.

Mr. Naryan thought that Dreen was wrong to dismiss what Angel was doing, although he understood why Dreen affected such a grand indifference. It was outside Dreen's experience, that was all: Angel was outside the experience of everyone on Confluence. The Change Wars that flared here and there along Confluence's vast length were not ideological but eschatological. They were a result of sociological stresses that arose when radical shifts in the expression of clusters of native and grafted genes caused a species of Shaped to undergo a catastrophic redefinition of its perceptions of the world. But what Angel was doing dated from before the Preservers had raised up the Shaped and ended human history. Mr. Naryan only began to understood it himself when Angel told him what she had done at the edge of the world.

And later, on the terrible night when the ship arrives and every machine in the city dies, with flames roaring unchecked through the farside quarter of the city and thousands of citizens fleeing into the orchard forests to the north, Mr. Naryan realises that he has not understood as much as he thought. Angel has not been preaching empty revolution after all.

Her acolytes, all young men, are armed with crude wooden spears with fire-hardened tips, long double-edged knives of the kind coconut sellers use to open their wares, flails improvised from chains and wire. They hustle Mr. Naryan in a forced march towards the palace and Dreen's floating habitat.

They have taken away Mr. Naryan's cane, and his bad leg hurts abominably with every other step.

Angel is gone. She has work elsewhere. Mr. Naryan felt fear when he saw her, but feels more fear now. The reflex altruism of the acolytes has been overridden by a new meme forged in the fires of Angel's revolution—they jostle Mr. Naryan with rough humour, sure in their hold over him. One in particular, the rough skin of his long-jawed face crazed in diamonds, jabs Mr. Naryan in his ribs with the butt of his spear at every intersection, as if to remind him not to escape, something that Mr. Naryan has absolutely no intention of doing.

Power is down all over the city—it went off with the fall of the machines—but leaping light from scattered fires swims in the wide eyes of the young men. They pass through a market square where people swig beer and drunkenly gamble amongst overturned stalls. Elsewhere in the fiery dark there is open rutting, men with men as well as with women. A child lies dead in a gutter. Horrible, horrible. Once, a building collapses inside its own fire, sending flames whirling high into the black sky. The faces of all the men surrounding Mr. Naryan are transformed by this leaping light into masks with eyes of flame.

Mr. Naryan's captors urge him on. His only comfort is that he will be of use in what is to come. Angel has not yet finished with him.

When Angel returned from the edge of the world, she came straight away to Mr. Naryan. It was a warm evening, at the hour after sunset when the streets began to fill with strollers, the murmur of neighbour greeting neighbour, the cries of vendors selling fruit juice or popcorn or sweet cakes.

Mr. Naryan was listening as his pupil, the magistrate's son, read a passage from the Puranas which described the time when the Preservers had strung the Galaxy with their creations. The boy was tall and awkward and faintly resentful, for he was not the scholar his father wished him to be and would rather spend his evenings with his fellows in the beer halls than read ancient legends in a long-dead language. He bent over the book like a night stork, his finger stabbing at each line as he clumsily translated it, mangling words in his hoarse voice. Mr. Naryan was listening with half an ear, interrupting only to correct particularly inelegant phrases. In the kitchen at the far end of the little apartment, his wife was humming to the murmur of the radio, her voice a breathy contented monotone.

Angel came up the helical stair with a rapid clatter, mounting quickly above a sudden hush in the street. Mr. Naryan knew who it was even before she burst onto the balcony. Her appearance so astonished the magistrate's son that he dropped the book. Mr. Naryan dismissed him and he hurried away, no doubt eager to meet his friends in the flickering neon of the beer hall and tell them of this wonder.

"I've been to the edge of the world," Angel said to Mr. Naryan, coolly accepting a bowl of tea from Mr. Naryan's wife, quite oblivious of the glance she exchanged with her husband before retreating. Mr. Naryan's heart turned at that look, for in it he saw how his wife's hard words were so easily dissolved in the weltering sea of reflexive benevolence. How cruel the Preservers had been, it seemed to him never crueller, to have raised up races of the Shaped and yet to have shackled them in unthinking obedience.

Angel said, "You don't seem surprised."

"Dreen told me as much. I'm pleased to see you returned safely. It has been a dry time without you." Already he had said too much: it was as if all his thoughts were eager to be spilled before her.

"Dreen knows everything that goes on in the city."

"Oh no, not at all. He knows what he needs to know."

"I took a boat," Angel said. "I just asked for it, and the man took me right along, without question. I wish now I'd stolen it. It would have been simpler. I'm tired of all this good will."

It was as if she could read his mind. For the first time, Mr. Naryan began to be afraid, a shiver like the first shake of a tambour that had ritually introduced the tempestuous dances of his youth.

Angel sat on the stool that the student had quit, tipping it back so she could lean against the rail of the balcony. She had cut her black hair short, and bound around her forehead a strip of white cloth printed with the slogan, in ancient incomprehensible script, that was the badge of her acolytes. She wore an ordinary loose white shirt and much jewelry: rings on every finger, sometimes more than one on each; bracelets and bangles down her forearms; gold and silver chains around her neck, layered on her breast. She was both graceful and terrifying, a rough beast slouched from the deep past to claim the world.

She said, teasingly, "Don't you want to hear my story? Isn't that your avocation?"

"I'll listen to anything you want to tell me," Mr. Naryan said.

"The world is a straight line. Do you know about libration?"

Mr. Naryan shook his head.

Angel held out her hand, tipped it back and forth. "This is the world. Everything lives on the back of a long flat plate which circles the sun. The plate rocks on its long axis, so the sun rises above the edge and then reverses its course. I went to the edge of the world, where the river that runs down half its length falls into the void. I suppose it must be collected and redistributed, but it really does look like it falls away forever."

"The river is eternally renewed," Mr. Naryan said. "Where it falls is where ships used to arrive and depart, but this city has not been a port for many years.''

"Fortunately for me, or my companions would already be here. There's a narrow ribbon of land on the far side of the river. Nothing lives there, not even an insect. No earth, no stones. The air shakes with the sound of the river's fall, and swirling mist burns with raw sunlight. And there are shrines, in the thunder and mist at the edge of the world. One spoke to me.''

Mr. Naryan knew these shrines, although he had not been there for many years. He remembered that the different races of the Shaped had erected shrines all along the edge of the world, stone upon stone carried across the river, from which flags and long banners flew. Long ago, the original founders of the city of Sensch, Dreen's ancestors, had travelled across the river to petition the avatars of the Preservers, believing that the journey across the wide river was a necessary rite of purification. But they were gone, and the new citizens, who had built their city of stones over the burnt groves of the old city, simply bathed in the heated, mineral-heavy water of the pools of the shrines of the temple at the edge of their city before delivering their petitions. He supposed the proud flags and banners of the shrines would be tattered rags now, bleached by unfiltered sunlight, rotted by mist. The screens of the shrines—would they still be working?

Angel grinned. Mr. Naryan had to remember that it was not, as it was with the citizens, a baring of teeth before striking. She said, "Don't you want to know what it said to me? It's part of my story.''

"Do you want to tell me?''

She passed her hand over the top of her narrow skull: bristly hair made a crisp sound under her palm. "No,'' she said. "No, I don't think I do. Not yet.''

Later, after a span of silence, just before she left, she said, "After we were wakened by the ship, after it brought us here, it showed us how the black hole you call the Eye of the Preservers was made. It recorded the process as it returned, speeded up because the ship was travelling so fast it stretched time around itself. At first there was an intense point of light within the heart of the Large Magellanic Cloud. It might have been a supernova, except that it was a thousand times larger than any supernova ever recorded. For a long time its glare obscured everything else, and when it cleared, all the remaining stars were streaming around where it had been. Those nearest the centre elongated and dissipated, and always more crowded in until nothing was left but the gas clouds of the accretion disc, glowing by Cerenkov radiation.''

"So it is written in the Puranas.''

"And is it also written there why Confluence was constructed around a halo star between the Home Galaxy and the Eye of the Preservers?''

"Of course. It is we can all worship and glorify the Preservers. The Eye looks upon us all."

"That's what I told them," Angel said.

After she was gone, Mr. Naryan put on his spectacles and walked through the city to the docks. The unsleeping citizens were promenading in the warm dark streets, or squatting in doorways, or talking quietly from upper-storey windows to their neighbors across the street. Amongst this easy somnolence, Angel's young disciples moved with a quick purposefulness, here in pairs, there in a group of twenty or more. Their slogans were painted on almost every wall. Three stopped Mr. Naryan near the docks, danced around his bulk, jeering, then ran off, screeching with laughter, when he slashed at them with his cane.

"Ruffians! Fools!"

"Seize the day!" they sang back. "Seize the day!"

Mr. Naryan did not find the man whose skiff Angel and her followers had used to cross the river, but the story was already everywhere amongst the fisherfolk. The Preservers had spoken to her, they said, and she had refused their temptations. Many were busily bargaining with citizens who wanted to cross the river and see the site of this miracle for themselves.

An old man, eyes milky with cataracts—the fisherfolk trawled widely across the Great River, exposing themselves to more radiation than normal—asked Mr. Naryan if these were the end times, if the Preservers would return to walk amongst them again. When Mr. Naryan said, no, anyone who dealt with the avatars knew that only those fragments remained in the Universe, the old man shrugged and said, "They say *she* is a Preserver," and Mr. Naryan, looking out across the river's black welter, where the horizon was lost against the empty night, seeing the scattered constellations of the running lights of the fisherfolk's skiffs scattered out to the nearside edge, knew that the end of Angel's story was not far off. The citizens were finding their use for her. Inexorably, step by step, she was becoming part of their history.

Mr. Naryan did not see Angel again until the night her ship arrived. Dreen went to treat with her, but he couldn't get within two streets of her house: it had become the centre of a convocation that took over the entire quarter of the city. She preached to thousands of citizens from the rooftops.

Dreen reported to Mr. Naryan that it was a philosophy of hope from despair. "She says that all life feeds on destruction and death. Are you sure you don't want to hear it?"

"It isn't necessary."

Dreen was perched on a balustrade, looking out at the river. They were in his floating habitat, in an arbour of lemon trees that jutted out at its leading edge. He said, "More than a thousand a day are making the crossing."

"Has the screen spoken again?"

"I've monitored it continuously. Nothing."

"But it did speak with her."

"Perhaps, perhaps." Dreen was suddenly agitated. He scampered up and down the narrow balustrade, swiping at overhanging branches and scaring the white doves that perched amongst the little glossy leaves. The birds rocketed up in a great flutter of wings, crying as they rose into the empty sky. Dreen said, "The machines watching her don't work. Not anymore. She's found out how to disrupt them. I snatch long-range pictures, but they don't tell me very much. I don't even know if she visited the shrine in the first place."

"I believe her," Mr. Naryan said.

"I petitioned the avatars," Dreen said, "but of course they wouldn't tell me if they'd spoken to her."

Mr. Naryan was disturbed by this admission—Dreen was not a religious man. "What will you do?"

"Nothing. I could send the magistrates for her, but even if she went with them her followers would claim she'd been arrested. And I can't even remember when I last arrested someone. It would make her even more powerful, and I'd have to let her go. But I suppose that you are going to tell me that I should let it happen."

"It has happened before. Even here, to your own people. They built the shrines, after all. . . ."

"Yes, and later they fell from grace, and destroyed their city. The snakes aren't ready for that," Dreen said, almost pleading, and for a moment Mr. Naryan glimpsed the depth of Dreen's love for this city and its people.

Dreen turned away, as if ashamed, to look out at the river again, at the flocking sails of little boats setting out on, or returning from, the long crossing to the far side of the river. This great pilgrimage had become the focus of the life of the city. The markets were closed for the most part; merchants had moved to the docks to supply the thousands of pilgrims.

Dreen said, "They say that the avatar tempted her with godhead, and she denied it."

"But that is foolish! The days of the Preservers have long ago faded. We know them only by their image, which burns forever at the event horizon, but their essence has long since receded."

Dreen shrugged. "There's worse. They say that she forced the avatar to admit that the Preservers are dead. They say that *she* is an avatar of something greater than the Preservers, although you wouldn't know that from her preaching. She claims that this universe is all there is, that destiny is what you make it. What makes me despair is how readily the snakes believe this cant."

Mr. Naryan, feeling chill, there in the sun-dappled shade, said, "She has hinted to me that she learnt it in the great far out, in the galaxy beyond the Home Galaxy.''

"The ship is coming," Dreen said. "Perhaps they will deal with her."

In the burning night of the city's dissolution, Mr. Naryan is brought at last to the pink sandstone palace. Dreen's habitat floats above it, a black cloud that half-eclipses the glowering red swirl of the Eye of the Preservers. Trails of white smoke, made luminescent by the fires which feed them, pour from the palace's high arched windows, braiding into sheets which dash like surf against the rim of the habitat. Mr. Naryan sees something fly up from amongst the palace's many carved spires—there seems to be more of them than he remembers—and smash away a piece of the habitat, which slowly tumbles off into the black sky.

The men around him hoot and cheer at this, and catch Mr. Naryan's arms and march him up the broad steps and through the high double doors into the courtyard beyond. It is piled with furniture and tapestries that have been thrown down from the thousand high windows overlooking it, but a path has been cleared to a narrow stair that turns and turns as it rises, until at last Mr. Naryan is pushed out onto the roof of the palace.

Perhaps five hundred of Angel's followers crowd amongst the spires and fallen trees and rocks, many naked, all with lettered headbands tied around their foreheads. Smoky torches blaze everywhere. In the centre of the crowd is the palace's great throne on which, on high days and holidays, at the beginning of masques or parades, Dreen receives the city's priests, merchants, and artists. It is lit by a crown of machines burning bright as the sun, and seated on it—easy, elegant and terrifying—is Angel.

Mr. Naryan is led through the crowd and left standing alone before the throne. Angel beckons him forward, her smile both triumphant and scared: Mr. Naryan feels her fear mix with his own. She says, "What should I do with your city, now I've taken it from you?"

"You haven't finished your story." Everything Mr. Naryan planned to say has fallen away at the simple fact of her presence. Stranded before her fierce, barely contained energies, he feels old and used up, his body as heavy with years and regret as with fat. He adds cautiously, "I'd like to hear it all."

He wonders if she really knows how her story must end. Perhaps she does. Perhaps her wild joy is not at her triumph, but at the imminence of her death. Perhaps she really does believe that the void is all, and rushes to embrace it.

Angel says, "My people can tell you. They hide with Dreen up above, but not for long."

She points across the roof. A dozen men are wrestling a sled, which shudders like a living thing as it tries to reorientate itself in the gravity field, onto a kind of launching cradle tipped up towards the habitat. The edges of the habitat are ragged, as if bitten, and amongst the roof's spires tower-trees are visibly growing towards it, their tips already brushing its edges, their tangled bases pulsing and swelling as teams of men and women drench them with nutrients.

"I found how to enhance the antigravity devices of the sleds," Angel says. "They react against the field which generates gravity for this artificial world. The field's stored inertia gives them a high kinetic energy, so that they make very good missiles. We'll chip away that floating fortress piece by piece if we have to, or we'll finish growing towers and storm its remains, but I expect surrender long before then."

"Dreen is not the ruler of the city." Nor are you, Mr. Naryan thinks, but it is not prudent to point that out.

"Not anymore," Angel says.

Mr. Naryan dares to step closer. He says, "What did you find out there, that you rage against?"

Angel laughs. "I'll tell you about rage. It is what you have all forgotten, or never learned. It is the motor of evolution, and evolution's end, too." She snatches a beaker of wine from a supplicant, drains it and tosses it aside. She is consumed with an energy that is no longer her own. She says, "We travelled so long, not dead, not sleeping. We were no more than stored potentials triply engraved on gold. Although the ship flew so fast that it bound time about itself, the journey still took thousands of years of slowed shipboard time. At the end of that long voyage we did not wake: we were born. Or rather, others like us were born, although I have their memories, as if they are my own. They learned then that the Universe was not made for the convenience of humans. What they found was a galaxy ruined and dead."

She holds Mr. Naryan's hand tightly, speaking quietly and intensely, her eyes staring deep into his.

"A billion years ago, our neighbouring galaxy collided with another, much smaller galaxy. Stars of both galaxies were torn off in the collision, and scattered in a vast halo. The rest coalesced into a single body, but except for ancient globular clusters, which survived the catastrophe because of their dense gravity fields, it is all wreckage. We were not able to chart a single world where life had evolved. I remember standing on a world sheared in half by immense tidal stress, its orbit so eccentric that it was colder than Pluto at its farthest point, hotter than Mercury at its nearest. I remember standing on a world of methane ice as cold and dark as the Universe itself, wandering amongst the stars. There were millions of such worlds cast adrift. I remember standing upon a fragment of a world smashed into a million shards and scattered so widely in its orbit that it never had the chance to reform. There are a million such worlds. I remember gas giants turned inside out—single vast storms—and I remember worlds torched smooth by irruptions of their stars. No life, anywhere.

"Do you know how many galaxies have endured such collisions? Almost all of them. Life is a statistical freak. It is likely that only the stars of our galaxy have planets, or else other civilisations would surely have arisen elsewhere in the unbounded Universe. As it is, it is certain that we are alone. We must make of ourselves what we can. We should not hide, as your Preservers chose to do. Instead, we should seize the day, and make the Universe over with the technology that the Preservers used to make their hiding place."

Her grip is hurting now, but Mr. Naryan bears it. "You cannot become a Preserver," he says sadly. "No one can, now. You should not lie to these innocent people."

"I didn't need to lie. They took up my story and made it theirs. They see now what they can inherit—if they dare. This won't stop with one city. It will become a crusade!" She adds, more softly, "You'll remember it all, won't you?"

It is then that Mr. Naryan knows that she knows how this must end, and his heart breaks. He would ask her to take that burden from him, but he cannot. He is bound to her. He is her witness.

The crowd around them cheers as the sled rockets up from its cradle. It smashes into the habitat and knocks loose another piece, which drops trees and dirt and rocks amongst the spires of the palace roof as it twists free and spins away into the night. Figures appear at the edge of the habitat. A small tube falls, glittering through the torchlight. A man catches it, runs across the debris-strewn roof, and throws himself at Angel's feet. He is at the far end of the human scale of the Shaped of this city. His skin is lapped with distinct scales, edged with a rim of hard black like the scales of a pine cone. His coarse black hair has flopped over his eyes, which glow like coals with reflected firelight.

Angel takes the tube and shakes it. It unrolls into a flexible sheet on which Dreen's face glows. Dreen's lips move; his voice is small and metallic. Angel listens intently, and when he has finished speaking says softly, "Yes."

Then she stands and raises both hands above her head. All across the roof, men and woman turn towards her, eyes glowing.

"They wish to surrender! Let them come down!"

A moment later a sled swoops down from the habitat, its silvery underside gleaming in the reflected light of the many fires scattered across the roof. Angel's followers shout and jeer, and missiles fly out of the darkness—a burning torch, a rock, a broken branch. All are somehow deflected before they reach the ship's crew, screaming away into the dark with such force that the torch, the branch, kindle into white fire. The crew have modified the sled's field to protect themselves.

They all look like Angel, with the same small sleek head, the same gangling build and abrupt nervous movements. Dreen's slight figure is dwarfed by them. It takes Mr. Naryan a long minute to be able to distinguish men from women, and another to be able to tell each man from his brothers, each woman from her sisters. They are all clad in long white shirts that leave them bare-armed and bare-legged, and each is girdled with a belt from which hang a dozen or more little machines. They call to Angel, one following on the words of the other, saying over and over again:

"Return with us—"

"—this is not our place—"

"—these are not our people—"

"—we will return—"

"—we will find our home—"

"—leave with us and return."

Dreen sees Mr. Naryan and shouts, "They want to take her back!" He jumps down from the sled, an act of bravery that astonishes Mr. Naryan, and skips through the crowd. "They are all one person, or variations on one person," he says breathlessly. "The ship makes its crew by varying a template. Angel is an extreme. A mistake."

Angel starts to laugh.

"You funny little man! I'm the real one—they are the copies!"

"Come back to us—"

"—come back and help us—"

"—help us find out home."

"There's no home to find!" Angel shouts. "Oh, you fools! This is all there is!"

"I tried to explain to them," Dreen says to Mr. Naryan, "but they wouldn't listen."

"They surely cannot disbelieve the Puranas," Mr. Naryan says.

Angel shouts, "Give me back the ship!"

"It was never yours—"

"—never yours to own—"

"—but only yours to serve."

"No! I won't serve!" Angel jumps onto the throne and makes an abrupt cutting gesture.

Hundreds of fine silver threads spool out of the darkness, shooting towards the sled and her crewmates. The ends of the threads flick up when they reach the edge of the sled's modified field, but then fall in a tangle over the crew: their shield is gone.

The crowd begins to throw things again, but Angel orders them to be still.

"I have the only working sled," she says. "That which I enhance, I can also take away. Come with me," she tells Mr. Naryan, "and see the end of my story."

The crowd around Angel stirs. Mr. Naryan turns, and sees one of the crew walking towards Angel.

He is as tall and slender as Angel, his small, high-cheekboned face so like her own it is as if he holds up a mirror as he approaches. A rock arcs out of the crowd and strikes his shoulder: he staggers but walks on, hardly seeming to notice that the crowd closes at his back so that he is suddenly inside its circle, with Angel and Mr. Naryan in its focus.

Angel says, "I'm not afraid of you."

"Of course not, sister," the man says. And he grasps her wrists in both his hands.

Then Mr. Naryan is on his hands and knees. A strong wind howls about him, and he can hear people screaming. The afterglow of a great light swims in his vision. He can't see who helps him up and half-carries him through the stunned crowd to the sled.

When the sled starts to rise, Mr. Naryan falls to his knees again. Dreen says in his ear, "It's over."

"No," Mr. Naryan says. He blinks and blinks, tears rolling down his cheeks.

The man took Angel's wrists in both of his—

Dreen is saying something, but Mr. Naryan shakes his head. It isn't over.

—And they shot up into the night, so fast that their clothing burst into flame, so fast that air was drawn up with them. If Angel could nullify the gravity field, then so could her crewmates. She has achieved apotheosis.

The sled swoops up the tiered slope of the ship, is swallowed by a wide hatch. When he can see again, Mr. Naryan finds himself kneeling at the edge of the open hatch. The city is spread below. Fires define the streets which radiate away from the Great River; the warm night air is bitter with the smell of burning.

Dreen has been looking at the lighted windows that crowd the walls of the vast room beyond the hatch, scampering with growing excitement from one to the other. Now he sees that Mr. Naryan is crying, and clumsily tries to comfort him, believing that Mr. Naryan is mourning his wife, left behind in the dying city.

"She was a good woman, for her kind," Mr. Naryan is able to say at last, although it isn't her he's mourning, or not only her. He is mourning for all of the citizens of Sensch. They are irrevocably caught in their change now, never to be the same. His wife, the nut roaster, the men and women who own the little tea houses at the corner of every square, the children, the mendicants and the merchants—all are changed, or else dying in the process. Something new is being born down there. Rising from the fall of the city. "They'll take us away from all this," Dreen says happily. "They're going to search for where they came from. Some are out combing the city for others who can help them; the rest are preparing the ship. They'll take it over the edge of the world, into the great far out!"

"Don't they know they'll never find what they're looking for? The Puranas—"

"Old stories, old fears. They will take us home!"

Mr. Naryan laboriously clambers to his feet. He understands that Dreen has fallen under the thrall of the crew. He is theirs, as Mr. Naryan is now and forever Angel's. He says, "Those times are past. Down there in the city is the beginning of something new, something wonderful—" He finds he can't explain. All he has is his faith that it won't stop here. It is not an end but a beginning, a spark to set all of Confluence—the unfallen and the changed—alight. Mr. Naryan says, weakly, "It won't stop here."

Dreen's big eyes shine in the light of the city's fires. He says, "I see only another Change War. There's nothing new in that. The snakes will rebuild the city in their new image, if not here, then somewhere else along the Great River. It has happened before, in this very place, to my own people. We survived it, and so will the snakes. But what *they* promise is so much greater! We'll leave this poor place, and voyage out to return to where it all began, to the very home of the Preservers. Look there! That's where we're going!"

Mr. Naryan allows himself to be led across the vast room. It is so big that it could easily hold Dreen's floating habitat. A window on its far side shows a view angled somewhere far above the plane of Confluence's orbit. Confluence itself is a shining strip, an arrow running out to its own vanishing point. Beyond that point are the ordered, frozen spirals of the Home Galaxy, the great jewelled clusters and braids of stars constructed in the last great days of the Preservers before they vanished forever into the black hole they made by collapsing the Magellanic Clouds.

Mr. Naryan starts to breathe deeply, topping up the oxygen content of his blood.

"You see!" Dreen says again, his face shining with awe in Confluence's silver light.

"I see the end of history," Mr. Naryan says. "You should have studied the Puranas, Dreen. There's no future to be found amongst the artifacts of the Preservers, only the dead past. I won't serve, Dreen. That's over."

And then he turns and lumbers through the false lights and shadows of the windows towards the open hatch. Dreen catches his arm, but Mr. Naryan throws him off.

Dreen sprawls on his back, astonished, then jumps up and runs in front of Mr. Naryan. "You fool!" he shouts. "They can bring her back!"

"There's no need," Mr. Naryan says, and pushes Dreen out of the way and plunges straight out of the hatch.

He falls through black air like a heavy comet. Water smashes around him, tears away his clothes. His nostrils pinch shut and membranes slide across his eyes as he plunges down and down amidst streaming bubbles until the roaring in his ears is no longer the roar of his blood but the roar of the river's never-ending fall over the edge of the world.

Deep, silty currents begin to pull him towards that edge. He turns in the water and begins to swim away from it, away from the ship and the burning city. His duty is over: once they have taken charge of their destiny, the changed citizens will no longer need an Archivist.

Mr. Naryan swims more and more easily. The swift, cold water washes away his landbound habits, wakes the powerful muscles of his shoulders and back. Angel's message burns bright, burning away the old stories, as he swims through the black water, against the currents of the Great River. Joy gathers with every thrust of his arms. He is the messenger, Angel's witness. He will travel ahead of the crusade that will begin when everyone in Sensch is changed. It will be a long and difficult journey, but he does not doubt that his destiny—the beginning of the future that Angel has bequeathed him and all of Confluence—lies at the end of it.

ELVIS BEARPAW'S LUCK

William Sanders

▼

William Sanders lives in Tahlequah, Oklahoma. A former powwow dancer and sometime Cherokee gospel singer, he appeared on the SF scene back around the turn of the decade with a couple of alternate-history comedies, *Journey to Fusang* (a finalist for the John W. Campbell Award) and *The Wild Blue and Gray*. Sanders then turned to mystery and suspense, producing a number of critically acclaimed titles. He credits his old friend Roger Zelazny with persuading him to return to SF, this time via the short story form, making recent sales to *Asimov's Science Fiction*, *Tales of the Great Turtle*, and *Wheel of Fortune*. His story "Going After Old Man Alabama"—a prequel (sort of) to the one that follows—appeared in our Twelfth Annual Collection.

In the fast, funny, and fanciful story that follows, he shows us that sometimes you have to make your own luck—and sometimes you have to live with the consequences, too.

Grandfather Ninekiller said, "A man always has the right to try to change his luck."

He said that right after I told him how my cousin Marvin Badwater had suddenly dumped Madonna Hummingbird, after both families had all but officially agreed on the match, and brought home a Comanche girl whose name nobody could even pronounce. Grandfather never had been one for that sort of gossip, but it was two years since he'd died and naturally he was interested in any news I might bring him when I came to put tobacco on his grave.

"The right to try to change his luck," he said again, in a kind of distant satisfied way, as if he liked the sound of what he had said. That's one thing about ancestors: they can be awfully repetitious. I guess they've got a lot of time on their hands in the spirit world, with nothing much to do but study up these wise-sounding little one-liners.

Anyway I said, "I don't know about that, *eduda*. What about what happened to Elvis Bearpaw?"

"I said a man's got the right to *try*," Grandfather said, not a bit bothered by my disrespectful interruption. There was a time when he'd have taken my head off, but being dead seems to have mellowed him some. "Whether he succeeds or not, now, that's another patch of pokeweed."

He laughed, an old man's spidery-dry cackle. "And then, too, it's not always easy to know whether you're changing it upward or down. As in the case of the said Elvis Bearpaw . . . remember that, do you, *chooch*?"

"How could I forget?" I said, surprised.

"Hey," Grandfather said, "you were just a kid."

I was, too, but I'd have gotten mad as a wet owl if anybody had said so at the time. I was all of twelve years old that spring, and I saw myself as for all valid purposes a full-grown Cherokee warrior—hadn't the great Harley Davidson Oosahwe killed those three Osage slave-raiders when he was only thirteen? Warrior hell, I figured I was practically Council material, barring a few petty technicalities.

I might or might not have heard, in the days leading up to Game time, that Elvis Bearpaw was to be the Deer Clan's player that year. If I did, it wasn't something I paid much attention to. For one thing, being of the *Anijisqua*—Bird Clan—I had no personal interest in the matter; and for another, my mind was on a different aspect of the approaching Game days. This was the last year I was going to be eligible for the boys' blowgun contest; next year I'd be in the young men's class, and, unless Redbird Christie stepped on a rattlesnake in the next twelve months, getting my brains beat out like everybody else. So I was determined to win this year, and I was practicing my ass off every spare moment.

But for all my puckering and puffing, I wasn't exactly unaware of the goings-on around me. That would have been pretty damn difficult to say the least; back then, Game time still *meant* something, things were *happening*. Not like now. . . .

Well, maybe I shouldn't say that. Maybe everything just seems larger and more exciting when you're a kid; or maybe a man's memory likes to improve on reality. But it does seem to me that the Game time isn't what it used to be. It's almost as if people are merely going through the motions. Is it just me?

"Is it just me," I said to Grandfather Ninekiller, "or has Game time gone downhill in the last few years? Of course I'm not talking about the Game itself," I added hastily. You don't want to seem to disparage sacred matters when you're talking with an ancestor. "I mean, that's still the center of the whole year, always has been, always will be—"

"*Wasn't* always," Grandfather interrupted. "Back in the old days, in the Yuasa times, it wasn't at all like it is now. You know that, *chooch*."

"Well, yes." I knew, all right; he'd told me often enough, along with the other stories about the history of the People. Though there's always been a sort of not-quite-real quality to those old tales, for me at least; I've never been sure how much of that Yuasa business to take seriously. They even say there was a time when the People didn't have the Game at all, and who can imagine that?

"Anyway," I went on, "I meant the whole affair—the dances, the contests, the feeds and the giveaways—all the stuff that goes on when the People get together for the Game. I can't help feeling like there used to be a lot more *to* it, you know? But then I've noticed a lot of things seem to sort of shrink as you get older."

Grandfather snorted. "Tell me about it, *chooch*," he said bitterly. "You don't know the half of it yet."

Whatever . . . and be all that as it may, I recall that Game season as possibly the best of my lifetime. The sky was clear and the sun bright every day, with no sign of the storms and drizzly spells that so often come with the spring in the Cherokee hill country. Even the wind was at least reasonably warm—though of course it never stopped blowing, this being, after all, Oklahoma.

The weather was so fine, in fact, that some of the elders came to confer with Grandfather Ninekiller about whether it was really necessary to set out the broken glass and the ax heads to turn aside possible tornadoes. He told them probably not, but they went ahead and did it all the same; they said tradition was tradition and you couldn't be too careful about tornadoes, but I figured it was mainly because they'd already made the trip over to the ruins of Old Tahlequah to get the glass.

The tornadoes never showed up, but the people sure did. Oh, my, yes, the people, the People. . . .

They came from all directions, all day every day and sometimes at night, too. They began coming as much as half a moon before the Game days began, hoping to get good spots to camp—or, if they had the right connections, houseguest privileges with Cherokee families—but it wasn't long before all the regular campgrounds were full and you began finding people making camp in the damnedest places. Like this family of Pawnees my father found sleeping amid the broken walls of the old Park Hill post office.

They came from the Five Nations and the Seven Allied Tribes, but they also came from other tribes that had their Games at other times of the year. It was widely known that it was worth the journey just to enjoy Cherokee hospitality and sample the entertainment and do some wagon-tailgate trading.

Mostly they came from the Plains tribes to the west: Comanches and Kiowas and Apaches and Caddos and a few Cheyennes and Arapahos, all riding splendid horses and wearing beaded finery and the mysterious emblems of the peyote church. But there were also Quapaws and Otoes and Kaws and Poncas and lots of others. Osages, too, five of the big bastards, riding in a wagon made from the body of an old Cadillac car, come down to see how the enemy lived and do a little scouting, their lives safe during the Game-time truce.

There was even a delegation from the Washita Nation, of the far-off Arkan-sas hills, decked out in really weird outfits—fringed vests and pants, goofy-looking high-topped moccasins, quartz crystals big as your penis hanging around their necks—and spouting loony crap about "previous lives" and "channeling" to anybody they could corner. General opinion was that there wasn't a single drop of the real People's blood among the lot of them, and looking at them I could believe it, but nobody really objected all that much. If nothing else they were good for a laugh.

And after all, though nobody talks much about it, the truth is that most of the People have more white blood than they like to admit.

"It's not only because we took in so many of the surviving whites, after things went to hell for them," Grandfather Ninekiller said, the only time I ever raised the subject with him. "Clear back in Yuasa times, there were lots of mixed-bloods. Toward the end they outnumbered the full-bloods in a lot of tribes. Cherokees damn near screwed ourselves white, in fact, before it was over. How do you think your Grandmother Badwater got that red hair?"

"What about you, *eduda*?" I asked.

"Oh, I'm a full-blood Cherokee," he said immediately. "And so were both of my parents. But my grandmother on my father's side, now, she was part white."

"Elvis Bearpaw is playing for the Deer Clan."

That was my uncle Kennedy Badwater, speaking to Grandfather Ninekiller. It was the day before the beginning of the Game period, and that was the first I can actually recall hearing about the honor that had fallen upon Elvis Bearpaw.

Grandfather said, "Well, he's always been an ambitious young man. This could be the big breakthrough for him."

They both laughed, and I joined in, in a quiet sort of way, from where I sat on the hard-packed ground next to Grandfather's seat. I wasn't, as I've said, all that interested in the subject, but there wasn't much else to do but listen in on the old men's conversation while I waited for Grandfather to need my assistance.

He'd been blind for three years by that time, and I'd lived with him the whole while, brought him the food that my mother cooked for him, filled and lit his pipe, helped him find various things around his cabin—not very often; he had a memory like a wolf trap—and generally served as his eyes and an extra set of hands. I'd helped him with certain items when he made medicine, too; and I'd led him, or rather accompanied him, around the village and to and from the various ceremonies and official functions where his duties took him. I'd sat at his feet at more Council meetings than I could have added up, hearing speech after speech on questions of war and peace and tribal politics, getting myself an unmatchable education but bored silly by it all at the time. . . .

"Word is he went to see Old Man Alabama as soon as they gave him the news," my uncle said. "Wonder what he did that for."

Old Man Alabama was a famous medicine man—a lot of people said witch—who lived on an island down on Lake Tenkiller, a little way above the old dam. He claimed to be the last living member of the Alabama tribe. His power was said to be tremendous and most people were afraid to even talk about him.

"Huh," Grandfather grunted. "Wonder why *anybody* would go to see that old nutcase. Old Man Alabama's the kind who give mad sorcerers a bad name."

I took a hardwood dart from the cane-joint quiver at my waist and held it up and sighted along it, checking for straightness. Not that there was any chance of finding anything wrong, as many times as I'd inspected those darts in the last few days, but it was something to do. My blowgun lay across my lap and I could have taken a few practice shots at some handy target while the old men talked, but it would have been a little impolite and I was trying to make a good impression on my uncle, who always gave me some sort of present at Game time.

"Looking for an angle," my uncle said.

"You know the old Cherokee saying," Grandfather said. " 'Watch out what you look for. You might find it.' "

"Is that an old Cherokee saying?" my uncle said, grinning.

"Must be," Grandfather said, straight-faced. "I said it, and I'm an old Cherokee."

The following morning, out at the great field, they had the opening ceremony. As the ball of the sun cleared the horizon, the Master of the Fire, old Gogisgi Wildcat, lit the sacred fire. Smoke rose against the brightening sky and Grandfather Ninekiller raised his voice in a song so ancient that even he didn't know what half the words meant; and when he finished, to a shouted chorus of *"Wado!"* from the assembled Cherokee elders, the Game days had at last begun.

Grandfather and I watched the start of the cross-country foot race, and the first heats of the shorter races—all right, I watched and gave Grandfather a running description—and then drifted over to take in the opening innings of the women's softball series. After that we walked slowly back across the fields to the outskirts of the town, where women tended fires and steam rose from big pots and the air was fairly edible with the smells of food. People called out invitations to come sample this or that—kenuche, corn soup, chili— and Grandfather generally tried to oblige; I couldn't see where he put it all in that skinny old frame. I didn't dare load up, myself, what with the blowgun competition coming up in the afternoon; but I did allow myself to be tempted by some remarkably fine wild grape dumplings, or maybe by the pretty Paint Clan girl who offered them to me. I was starting to take an interest in that girl business, those days.

I might as well have gone ahead and stuffed myself, for all the difference it made. That was how I felt, anyway, after a sudden puff of wind made me miss the swinging target completely in the final round of the blowgun shoot and I wound up losing out to Duane Kingfisher from up near Rocky Ford. Now, looking back, second place doesn't seem so bad—especially when I remember that the Osages killed Duane four years later, when he went on that damn fool horse-stealing raid—but at the time all I could see was that I'd lost. I felt as if I'd been booted in the stomach.

I was still feeling pretty rotten that night at the stomp dance. I don't even think I'd have gone if I hadn't had to accompany Grandfather Ninekiller. Sitting beside him under the Bird Clan arbor, watching the dancers circling the fire and listening to the singing and the *shaka-shaka-shaka* of the turtle shell rattles on the women's legs, I felt none of the usual joy, only a dull mean dog-kicking anger—at the wind, at Duane Kingfisher, mostly at myself.

After a while my Uncle Kennedy appeared from out of the darkness and sat down beside me. " *'Siyo, chooch,*" he said to me, after exchanging greetings with Grandfather.

I said, " *'Siyo, eduji,*" in a voice about as cheerful and friendly as an open grave. But he didn't appear to notice.

"Damn," he said, watching the dancers, "there's Elvis Bearpaw leading, big as you please."

Now he mentioned it, I saw that Elvis Bearpaw was in fact leading this song, circling the fire at the head of the spiral line of dancers, calling out the old words in a strong high voice. His face shone in the firelight as he crouched and turned and waved his hands. He was a husky, good-looking young guy, supposed to be something of a devil with the women. I don't guess I'd ever even traded greetings with him; his family and mine moved in different circles. Watching him now, though, I had to admit that he could sure as hell sing and dance.

"Don't think I ever saw him lead before," Uncle Kennedy said. "How about that?"

On the other side of me Grandfather made a noise that was part snort and part grunt. He wasn't a big admirer of the Bearpaws, whom he considered pushy assholes who'd lucked into more wealth and power than they knew what to do with.

"Saw you in the blowgun shoot today, *chooch*," my uncle remarked. "Tough luck there. But hell, you still came in second. Better than I ever did."

He was taking something from his belt, from up under the tail of his ribbon shirt. "Here," he said. "Didn't figure to give you this till later on, but you look like you could use some cheering up."

It was a knife, a fine big one with a deer horn handle and a wide businesslike blade; a man's knife, not a kid's whittler like the one I'd been carrying, and somebody had done some first-class work putting a glass-smooth finish on that lovely steel. . . . I said, *"Wado, eduji,"* but my voice didn't come out entirely right.

"Got some good stiff saddle leather at home," my uncle said. "Make you a sheath for that thing, you bring it by sometime. Boy," he added admiringly, "look at old Elvis go."

Out by the fire Elvis Bearpaw was getting down and winding up, his body rocking from side to side. There was something strange in his face, I thought, or maybe that was just a trick of the firelight. He called out a phrase and the other men responded: *"Ha-na-wi-ye, ha-na-wi-ye."* And *shaka-shaka-shaka* went the turtle shells.

The next few days were a regular whirlwind of feasting and dancing and singing and sports, sports, sports: all the things needed to make a twelve-year-old boy decide that when he dies he wants to go some place where it's like this all the time.

I went to everything I could, with or without Grandfather, who was having to make a lot of heavy medicine in preparation for the approaching Game. I played stickball with the other Cherokee boys, of course, and even scored a couple of goals, though in the end the Choctaws beat us by one. I watched Uncle Kennedy win the rifle shoot and then saw him lose everything he'd won, betting on a horse race between the Seminoles and the Kickapoos. I went to the cornstalk shoot—going to have to try that myself next year, now I was big enough to pull a serious bow—and the tomahawk throw, the horseshoe matches, and the wild cow–roping contest, even the canoe race down on the river. And the bicycle race, the very last year they ever had it; it was getting impossible to find parts to keep those old machines rolling, and the leather-rope tires they had to use kept coming off in the turns and causing mass crashes. What was the name of that Wichita kid who won? I forget.

And every night at the stomp dance grounds there was Elvis Bearpaw out by the fire, singing and dancing his ass off, always with that funny strained expression on his face. Uncle Kennedy said he looked like he thought something might be gaining on him.

There was no stomp dance the night before Game day, naturally; too many of the dance leaders and other important persons would be spending the night taking medicine and making smoke and otherwise purifying themselves, getting ready for their parts in the Game.

That included Grandfather Ninekiller, who had to do some things so secret and dangerous that I wasn't even allowed to be in the cabin while he did them. I helped him lay out a few medicine items, made sure there was plenty of firewood in the box, and got the hell out without having to be told twice. That sort of business always scared me half to death. Still does.

I was supposed to be staying at my parents' cabin that night, but I didn't really want to go, not any sooner than I could help anyway. I'd never gotten along with them worth a damn; that might have been why they'd been so happy to send me off to live with the old man.

I stood for a moment thinking about it, and then I turned the other way and walked away from the town, off across the moon white fields, following the distant *boom-boom* of a big Plains drum. Some of our Western visitors were having one of their powwow dances that night. I wasn't all that fond of that damn howling racket the Plains People call singing, but it would beat sitting around all evening listening to questions about the old man's health and complaints about my failure to visit more often and stories about how smart my younger brothers were.

I stayed at the powwow till pretty late, having more fun than I'd expected— all right, that Kiowa music has a good beat, you can dance to it—and hanging out with some of my buddies who'd sneaked off from their own families. Along about midnight I met a Creek girl named Hillary Screechowl and after a certain amount of persuasive bullshit on my part she took a little walk with me off into the woods. Where nothing really major took place, but we did get far enough to clear up a few questions I'd been wondering about lately.

It was really late, maybe halfway between midnight and daybreak, when I finally left the powwow area and headed back toward town. The moon had almost gone down but the stars were big and white, and I had no trouble finding my way across the darkened fields. The town itself was invisible against the blackness of the tree line, but a good many fires still burned there.

I took a shortcut through a narrow stand of trees and found myself near the Game grounds. For no particular reason—still in no hurry to get to my parents' place, I guess—I changed course and walked along next to the south border of the grounds. I'd never before seen the place on the night before a Game, with everything laid out in readiness and nobody around. It was an interesting sight, but a little on the spooky side.

The long tables and benches shone faintly in the starlight, their wood scrubbed white over the years by generations of laboring women and wagon-loads of wood ash soap. Everything was already in place for the players, of course, as was the ceremonial equipment up on the big packed-earth platform at the eastern end of the grounds. It had all been smoked and doctored late the previous day, in a ceremony closed to everyone except the chief medicine men of the twelve participating tribes, and covered with sheets of white cloth that would have paid for a whole herd of horses at any trade meet in Oklahoma.

All the people had gone home now, except for a couple of guards who were supposed to be keeping an eye on things. I wondered why they hadn't challenged me already. Sitting on their butts somewhere nearby, no doubt, having a smoke or even asleep.

I felt a surge of righteous twelve-year-old indignation at the thought. Not that there was any serious risk of intruders, let alone thieves—even Osage raiders wouldn't dare cross that sacred line—but still, when you had the honor of standing guard over the grounds, on the night before a Game at that . . .

Then I saw Elvis Bearpaw coming out of the woods.

I didn't recognize him at first; he was no more than a vague shadow, half a bow shot away. For a moment I thought it was one of the guards, but then the starlight fell on his face and I recognized him. Without quite knowing why, I stepped back into the deep shadow beneath the trees, watching.

He was moving fast, almost at a run, and he was crouched down low like a bear dancer. He crossed the white lime medicine line without so much as an instant's hesitation and dived in between the nearest rows of playing tables. The sacrilege was so enormous that the breath went out of me and my vision went blurry, and when I could see and breathe again Elvis Bearpaw had disappeared.

I don't know why I didn't call out for the guards; the idea never even occurred to me. Instead I stood there for what felt like a long time, scanning the rows of tables and the open ground all around trying to figure out where he'd gone and what he was up to.

And I'd almost decided that I'd lost him, that he'd left the grounds as sneakily as he'd come, but then I finally thought to watch the Cherokee players' table, up in the middle of the front row and directly in front of the big platform. Sure enough, I was just in time to spot him when he popped up.

He didn't pop very high. All I could see was the top half of his head, silhouetted against the whiteness of the tabletop, and his hands as they reached up and then vanished beneath the white cloth.

By now my heart was trying to bang a hole in my chest and the blood was roaring in my ears like a buffalo stampede. I watched in paralyzed horror, waiting for lightning to strike or the earth to open or whatever was going to happen. Yet nothing did, even though now I saw that Elvis Bearpaw was doing something so unspeakably blasphemous that my mind couldn't take it in. A moment later he ducked back out of sight, and then after almost no time he appeared again from among the tables, running flat out back the way he'd come, into the shelter of the trees. He didn't make a sound the whole time.

It took a little while before I could move. At last I got my feet unstuck and began walking again, toward the town and my parents' cabin. When I got there the place was dark and I let myself in as quietly as I could, but my mother was waiting for me and she woke my father up and they both gave me a good deal of shit. Under the circumstances I hardly noticed.

Early next morning I went back to Grandfather's cabin. I hadn't slept much even after my parents finally let me go to bed. My feet felt like somebody else's and the light hurt my eyes.

"Damn, *chooch*," Grandfather said, "what's happened to you? You look like you were rode hard and put up wet."

So I told him about Elvis Bearpaw and what I'd seen him do. I'd been planning to tell him anyway; I just hadn't been sure when.

"Doyuka?" he said when I was finished. "You're sure?"

"No," I answered honestly. "I mean, I know I saw him and I know he went onto the grounds and in among the tables, and he did *something*. Whether he did what I thought I saw him do—well, the light was bad and I wasn't very close. And," I added, "I don't really want to believe it."

"Huh." His lined old face was as unreadable as ever, but there was something a little strange in the way he stood. His hands made a quick restless motion. "You tell anybody else?" he asked.

"No."

"Good." He turned his blind eyes toward me and gave me a toothless smile. "You always did have sense, *chooch*. Too bad certain other people don't have as much."

I said, "What are you going to do, *eduda*?"

He looked surprised. "Do? Why, you know perfectly well what I'm fixing to do, *chooch*. Right up there on that stage, in front of the whole world."

"I mean about Elvis Bearpaw," I said, a little impatiently. "Will you tell the Chief and the other elders? Will they stop the Game, or—" I flapped my hands. "Or what?"

"Oh, no, no. Can't do that, *chooch*. Too late now," he said. "No telling what might happen. All we can do is let things go on, the way they're supposed to. Afterward—" He shrugged. "Come on. Time we got ourselves out to the grounds."

We began walking in that direction. We weren't the only ones. People were pouring out of the town and the campgrounds like swarming bees, all of them heading toward the Game grounds. They all recognized Grandfather Ninekiller, though, and gave us plenty of respectful space so that despite the crowds around us we were able to talk freely.

"Anyway," Grandfather said as we passed the council house, "you forget my position. Once the sun's come up on Game day, I'm not allowed to talk to anybody, even the Chief, about the Game or the player. If I try to tell your story, I'll be in the shit nearly as deep as you-know-who. Shouldn't even be talking with *you* about it, strictly speaking." He rested his hand on my shoulder. "But what the hell."

It seemed pretty strange to be picking at fine points of Game protocol, after Elvis Bearpaw had practically pissed on everything and everybody. But I didn't say so.

Grandfather's hand tightened on my shoulder. "Don't worry too much about it, *chooch*," he said in a softer voice. "These things have a way of working themselves out."

At the Game grounds we waited outside the medicine line until Grandfather's two young assistants came and led him away toward the big platform. I watched them help him up the steps, and felt thankful that I wasn't allowed to go with him. Once inside the line, nobody was allowed to leave, or eat food, or drink anything but water, until the Game was ended.

By this time the surrounding area was covered with people, from the medicine line—or rather a little way back; most people had enough sense to leave a couple of bowstring lengths' worth of safe space—clear back to the edge of the woods. And into the woods, too; there were kids of all sizes, and quite a few grown men, sitting perched up in the trees like a flock of huge weird birds.

Most of the people sat on the ground, or on whatever seats they'd brought along; it was considered ill-mannered to stand, since that could block somebody's view. For the most part they sat in bunches of family and friends, and nearly every group had a couple of big baskets of food and water, because the no-eating rule didn't apply to the people watching from outside the line, and there was no reason to pass up the chance to make a little picnic of the occasion. There was a lot of laughing and talking and passing food and water gourds around; in fact the noise was pretty intense if you let yourself notice it.

Uncle Kennedy and his bunch had saved me a place, down near the southeast corner of the grounds, close enough to hear and see everything. I sat down, accepted a roasted turkey leg from Aunt Diana, wiggled my skinny young rump into a reasonably comfortable fit with the ground, and had myself a good long look around.

There was plenty to see, for sure. Out on the playing field, the players were already standing at their places behind the long tables, facing the platform and, roughly, the still-rising sun. Front and center, naturally, was the table of the Host Nation, manned by the seven players who represented the seven clans of the Cherokee Nation. Elvis Bearpaw was right in there, standing straight as a bowstring. I couldn't make out any particular expression on his face, but then all the players were looking very straight-faced and serious, in accordance with Game manners.

On their left stood the Seminole players, in their bright patchwork jackets, while on the other side of the Cherokees were the players from the Creek clans. Directly behind were the tables of the Choctaws and the Chickasaws.

Behind the tables of the Five Nations were those of the Seven Allied Tribes: Shawnee, Delaware, Sac and Fox, Potawatomie, Kickapoo, Ottawa, and Miami. I didn't know anything about their clan arrangements or how they chose their players, though no doubt they used some form of blind lot drawing like everybody else.

Each table was flanked by a pair of senior warriors, dressed all in black and carrying long hardwood clubs. The Deacons—I've never known why they were called that—would be watching the players constantly all through the game, for even the smallest violation of the rules.

Up on the big platform, looking out over the playing tables, sat the chiefs and senior medicine men and other leading persons of the twelve tribes. Our Chief, for example, was accompanied by the Clan Mothers of the seven clans. There was also the Crier of the Game, fat old Jack Birdshooter, and, down at the south end of the stage, Grandfather Ninekiller and his assistants.

Now that was how it was done when I was a boy. Later on a lot of things got changed. I can't say whether the changes were for good or bad. I only know I liked the old days.

When the sun was high over the fields, the Crier stepped to the front of the stage and called for attention. The Chief of the Cherokee Nation was about to speak.

Come to think of it, that's one thing I wasn't too sorry to see dropped from the ceremonies—that long-winded speech, or rather recitation, that the Chief always used to deliver to start things off. Not that the speech itself was so bad, but when you had to hear the damn thing every year, word-for-word the same every time . . .

"Long ago there were only the People."

Marilyn Blackfox was a pretty good Chief in her day, but she never had much of a speaking voice. But it didn't matter, since the Crier immediately repeated everything she said in English, in a voice that carried like the bellow of a bull alligator. That was out of courtesy to the people of the other tribes, but it was also handy for the large number of Cherokees who couldn't understand their own language—not, at any rate, the pure old-style Cherokee that Chief Marilyn was speaking.

That didn't matter either, seeing that most of us had heard the speech so many times we could have recited it from memory in either language. I leaned back on my elbows and let my mind wander, while she droned on and on about how the People tried to treat the whites right, when they first showed up, only to learn too late that this was the most treacherous bunch of humans the Creator ever let live. And about the massacres and the hunger and the diseases and the forced marches and the rest of it: old stuff, though no doubt it was all true.

"But even in the days when it seemed the People would vanish from the world," Chief Marilyn went on, "our wise elders were given a prophecy—"

Well, here came the bullshit part. According to Grandfather, who should know, the prophecy was that fire would come from the sky and destroy the whites, leaving only the People.

Which, as everybody surely knows, wasn't how it happened. Oh, there was fire enough, when the whites and the black people began fighting each other—I've seen the blackened ruins of the cities, and the pictures in the old books—until the whole Yuasa nation was at war within itself.

But what finally finished the whites was that mysterious sickness that rushed across the land like a flash flood, striking down the whites, and the black people, too, even faster than their diseases had once wiped out the People.

The legend is that the Creator sent the sickness to punish the whites and free the People. But Grandfather once told me a story he'd heard from his own grandfather: the whites, or certain of their crazier medicine men, created that sickness on purpose, meaning to use it against the black people. Only somebody screwed up and it wound up taking the whites, too.

Some parts of the story are pretty hard to believe, like the business about people breeding little invisible disease bugs the way you'd breed horses. But I think there must be something to it, all the same. Because, after all, there are still a fair number of whites left; but have you ever met anyone who's ever seen a black person in the flesh?

Nobody knows why the People—and the ones with similar blood, like the Meskins—were the only ones the sickness didn't affect. Maybe the Creator has a peculiar sense of humor.

* * *

"And so at last the People reclaimed their lands." Chief Marilyn was raising her voice now as she got close to the end. "And life was hard for many generations, and they found that they had forgotten many of the old ways. But they still remembered one thing above all from their traditions, the one great gift from the Creator that had held their grandmothers and grandfathers together through the evil times of the past; and they knew that the Game could save them, too, if they remained faithful. And so it was, and so it is today, and so it always will be."

She stretched out both arms as far as they would go. In a high clear shout she spoke the words everybody had been waiting for:

"*Let the Game begin!*"

"Players," the Crier roared, "take your seats!"

Out on the field, the assembled players of the Five Nations and the Seven Tribes did so, all together and with as little noise as possible. They better; the hard-faced Deacons were already fingering their clubs, and even simple clumsiness could be good for a rap alongside the head. I mean, those guys loved their work.

While the players bowed their heads and studied the polished hardwood boards in front of them, one of Grandfather's assistants began beating on a handheld water drum, the high-pitched *ping-ping-ping* sounding very loud in the hush that had settled over the whole area. The other assistant led Grandfather—who was perfectly capable of managing by himself, but the routine was meant to remind everyone that he was truly blind—to the wooden table at the front of the stage. With one hand the assistant raised the lid of the big honeysuckle vine basket that took up the whole top of the table, while with the other he guided Grandfather's hand toward the opening.

Grandfather reached into the basket. The drummer stopped drumming. You could have heard a butterfly fart.

Grandfather stood there a moment, groping around inside the basket, and then he pulled his hand back out and held up a little wooden ball, smaller than a child's fist, painted white. You couldn't really see it at any distance, but everybody there knew what it was. There was a soft rustling sound that ran across the field, as the people all drew in their breaths.

Without turning, Grandfather passed the little ball to Jesse Tiger, the Seminoles' elder medicine man, who stood beside him. And Jesse Tiger, having looked at the ball, passed it on to the Creek medicine man on his left; and so the little ball went down the line of waiting medicine men, till all twelve had examined it. At the end of the line, the Ottawa elder—I didn't know his name—handed it to Jack Birdshooter, the Crier. Who took a single careful look at the ball and shouted, in a voice that would have cracked obsidian:

"AY, THIRTY-TWO!"

There was another soft windy sound as several hundred People let out their breaths. Everybody was craning and staring, now, watching the players. None appeared to have moved.

The drummer was already pinging away again. Grandfather had his hand and most of his forearm down into the huge basket this time, and he didn't fool around before pulling out the second ball. The ball went down the line as before and the Crier took it and looked and blared:

"OH, SEVENTEEN!" And, after a pause, "ONE-SEVEN!", just to make sure some idiot didn't mistake the call for seventy.

Still no action on the field. The players' heads were all bent as if praying. Which, of course, most if not all of them were. I wondered what was going through Elvis Bearpaw's mind.

There went the drummer again, *ping-ping-ping*. There went Grandfather's hand, in and out, and there went the third little ball down the line of dark-spotted old hands. And there went Jack Birdshooter:

"ENN, SIX!"

A number that low, this early? That was a lucky sign. And sure enough, over toward the other side of the field, the Deacons were watching one of the Shawnee players as he reached out and carefully placed a polished black stone marker on one of the squares of the walnut board in front of him.

There was a muffled cheer from the watching crowd. Even the dignitaries up on the stage permitted themselves a soft chorus of pleased grunts. This Game was off to an unusually good start.

My uncle said, "Want some more of that turkey, *chooch*?"

"Here," my aunt said, handing me a big buckskin-covered cushion. "Might as well get comfortable. It's liable to be a long day."

Up on the stage the drummer was at it again.

It was a warm day for spring, and there was no shade out on the open ground around the playing field. My eyes were sore from my nearly sleepless night, so I kept them closed a good deal. Aunt Di claimed I fell asleep for a little while there, but I was just resting my eyes and thinking.

I lost track of the progress of the Game soon enough; it wasn't long before all the players had at least a few markers on their boards, and nobody could have kept an eye on all of them. That, after all, was part of what the Deacons were there for.

As best I could see from where I sat, Elvis Bearpaw had a good many markers down, though nothing all that unusual. His face, when he raised his head to listen for a call, was still giving nothing away.

The morning turned to afternoon and the sun began her descent toward the western rim of the sky. The shadow of the sun pole, in front of the platform, grew longer and longer. There was a big brush-covered roof above the stage, to shade the dignitaries, but it was no longer doing them any good. Most of them were squinting and shading their eyes with their hands. Grandfather Ninekiller, of course, didn't have that problem. He kept reaching into the basket and pulling out the little balls, all the while staring straight and blind-eyed toward that hard white afternoon sun. From time to time he would pause while his assistants put the lid back on the great basket and lifted it between them, on its carrying poles, and gave it a good shaking, rocking it from side to side to mix up the balls. By now I figured it must be a good deal lighter. I wondered if this Game would go on long enough for the basket to have to be refilled. That was something I'd never seen, but I knew it occasionally happened.

This one was starting to look like one of the long Games, too. Already a couple of the senior Deacons were checking the supply of ready-to-light torches in the cane racks beside the platform, in case the play went on into the night.

"BEE, TWENTY-TWO!" shouted the Crier. And down at the end of the front row, not far from where I sat, one of the Seminole players reached up and put another marker on his board.

The sun was going down in a big bloody show off beyond the trees, and the torches were already being lit and placed in their holders, when it finally happened.

By then I was so tired I was barely listening, and so I missed the call; and to this day I couldn't tell you what ball it was. I was sitting there next to Uncle Kennedy, munching honeycake and trying to stay awake, and my ears picked up the Crier's voice as he boomed out yet another string of meaningless sounds, but all my mind noticed was that he seemed to be getting a little hoarse.

But then my uncle made a sudden surprised grunt. *"Ni,"* he said sharply, and I sat up and looked, while all around us people began doing the same, and a low excited murmur passed through the crowd.

Down on the field, Elvis Bearpaw had gotten to his feet. The two nearest Deacons were already striding toward him, their clubs swinging, ready to punish this outrageous behavior, but Elvis wasn't looking at them. He was staring down at his board as if it had turned into a live water moccasin.

The Deacons paused and looked at the board too. One of them said something, though his voice didn't carry to where I sat.

All the people in the crowd began getting to their feet. Somehow they did it in almost-complete silence. There wasn't even the cry of a baby.

Other Deacons were converging on the spot, now, and after a moment one of them left the growing bunch of black-clad figures and trotted over to the stage. Again I couldn't hear what was said, but all the people on the stage obviously did. Their faces told us onlookers that our guess had been right.

The group of Deacons split and stepped back, except for the original pair, who were now standing on either side of Elvis Bearpaw. One of them jabbed him in the side with the end of his club.

Elvis Bearpaw's mouth opened. A strange croaking sound came out, but it wasn't what you'd call human speech.

The Deacon poked him again, harder. Elvis straightened up and faced the stage and seemed to shake himself. "Bingo," he said, so softly I barely heard him. Then, much louder, *"Bingo!"*

Everybody breathed in and held it and then breathed out, all together.

Old Jack Birdshooter had been doing this too long to forget his lines now. "Deacons," he cried formally, "do we have a Bingo?"

The Deacon on Elvis Bearpaw's right raised his club, saluting the stage. "Yes," he shouted, "we do have a Bingo."

And, needless to say, that was when the crowd went absolutely bat-shit crazy, as always, jumping up and down and waving their arms in the air, yelling and hooting and yipping till it was a wonder the leaves didn't fall off the trees, while the Deacons led Elvis Bearpaw slowly toward the platform. His face, in the dying red light, was something to see.

A long, long time afterward, Grandfather Ninekiller told me the inside story. That was after he had gone on to the spirit world, where he learned all sorts of interesting things.

"What happened," Grandfather said, "Elvis Bearpaw did go to see Old Man Alabama, just like we heard. Wanted some kind of charm or medicine for the Game. Old Man Alabama told him no way. Fixing the Game, that was too much even for a crazy old witch."

"How'd you learn all this?" I asked, a little skeptically. Grandfather hadn't been dead very long at the time, and I was still getting used to talking with him in his new form.

"Old Man Alabama told me," Grandfather said. "Hell, he died a couple of years ago. He's been here longer than me."

"Oh."

"Anyway," Grandfather went on, "Elvis Bearpaw went on and on, offered all kinds of stuff for payment. Finally Old Man Alabama said he could do one thing for him and that was all. He could tell him where the Bingo was going to fall."

"Doyuka?"

"Would I shit you? And you and I know what the silly bastard went and did."

"I was right, then," I said. "About what he was up to that night. He switched his game board with his neighbor's. With what's-his-name, that guy from the Wolf Clan.''

"*Uh-huh*. Only he didn't understand how that kind of a prophecy works," Grandfather said. "Old Man Alabama told him where the Bingo was going to fall, and that was where it fell. Like I told you that morning," he added, "these things have a way of working themselves out.''

But as I say, that was a lot of years later. That night, I could only guess and wonder, while they brought Elvis Bearpaw up onto the stage and the medicine men and then the chiefs came by one at a time to shake his hand, and Chief Marilyn with her own hands tied the winner's red cloth around his head. She was a short woman and she had to stand on tiptoe, but she managed. Then they did the rest of it.

He screamed a lot while they were doing it to him. They all do, naturally, but I don't think I've ever heard a Game winner scream as loud and as long as Elvis Bearpaw did. Some Seneca kids I talked with next day said they heard him clear over at their camp, on the far side of the ball field. Well, they do say that that's the sign of a good strong sacrifice.

And you know, they must be right, because it rained like a son of a bitch that year.

MORTIMER GRAY'S
HISTORY OF DEATH

Brian Stableford

▼

Critically acclaimed British "hard science" writer Brian Stableford is the author
of more than thirty books, including *Cradle of the Sun*, *The Blind Worm*, *Days
of Glory*, *In the Kingdom of the Beasts*, *Day of Wrath*, *The Halcyon Drift*, *The
Paradox of the Sets*, *The Realms of Tartarus*, and the renowned trilogy consisting
of *The Empire of Fear*, *The Angel of Pain*, and *The Carnival of Destruction*. His
short fiction has been collected in *Sexual Chemistry: Sardonic Tales of the Genetic
Revolution*. His nonfiction books include *The Sociology of Science Fiction* and,
with David Langford, *The Third Millennium: A History of the World* A.D.
2000–3000. Upcoming is a new novel, *Serpent's Blood*, which is the start of
another projected trilogy. His acclaimed novella "Les Fleurs Du Mal" was a
finalist for the Hugo Award last year. His stories have appeared in our Sixth
(two separate stories), Seventh, and Twelfth Annual Collections. A biologist and
sociologist by training, Stableford lives in Reading, England.

In the vivid and compelling novella that follows, Stableford takes us to an
ultrarich, ultracivilized far future where humanity has almost—almost—conquered the oldest and coldest Enemy of them all . . .

1

I was an utterly unexceptional child of the twenty-ninth century, comprehensively engineered for emortality while I was still a more-or-less inchoate
blastula, and decanted from an artificial womb in Naburn Hatchery in the
country of York in the Defederated States of Europe. I was raised in an
aggregate family which consisted of six men and six women. I was, of course,
an only child, and I received the customary superabundance of love, affection,
and admiration. With the aid of excellent internal technologies, I grew up
reasonable, charitable, self-controlled, and intensely serious of mind.

It's evident that not *everyone* grows up like that, but I've never quite been able to understand how people manage to avoid it. If conspicuous individuality—and frank perversity—aren't programmed in the genes or rooted in early upbringing, how on earth do they spring into being with such determined irregularity? But this is *my* story, not the world's, and I shouldn't digress.

In due course, the time came for me—as it comes to everyone—to leave my family and enter a community of my peers for my first spell at college. I elected to go to Adelaide in Australia, because I liked the name.

Although my memories of that period are understandably hazy, I feel sure that I had begun to see the *fascination* of history long before the crucial event which determined my path in life. The subject seemed—in stark contrast to the disciplined coherency of mathematics or the sciences—so huge, so amazingly abundant in its data, and so charmingly disorganized. I was always a very orderly and organized person, and I needed a vocation like history to loosen me up a little. It was not, however, until I set forth on an ill-fated expedition on the sailing-ship *Genesis* in September 2901, that the exact form of my destiny was determined.

I use the word "destiny" with the utmost care; it is no mere rhetorical flourish. What happened when *Genesis* defied the supposed limits of possibility and turned turtle was no mere incident, and the impression that it made on my fledging mind was no mere suggestion. Before that ship set sail, a thousand futures were open to me; afterward, I was beset by an irresistible compulsion. My destiny was determined the day *Genesis* went down; as a result of that tragedy, *my fate was sealed*.

We were *en route* from Brisbane to tour the Creationist Islands of Micronesia, which were then regarded as artistic curiosities rather than daring experiments in continental design. I had expected to find the experience exhilarating, but almost as soon as we had left port, I was struck down by sea-sickness.

Sea-sickness, by virtue of being psychosomatic, is one of the very few diseases with which modern internal technology is sometimes impotent to deal, and I was miserably confined to my cabin while I waited for my mind to make the necessary adaptation. I was bitterly ashamed of myself, for I alone out of half a hundred passengers had fallen prey to this strange atavistic malaise. While the others partied on deck, beneath the glorious light of the tropic stars, I lay in my bunk, half-delirious with discomfort and lack of sleep. I thought myself the unluckiest man in the world.

When I was abruptly hurled from my bed, I thought that I had fallen—that my tossing and turning had inflicted one more ignominy upon me. When I couldn't recover my former position after having spent long minutes fruitlessly groping about amid all kinds of mysterious debris, I assumed that I must be confused. When I couldn't open the door of my cabin even though I had the handle in my hand, I assumed that my failure was the result of clumsiness. When I finally got out into the corridor, and found myself crawling in shallow water with the artificial bioluminescent strip beneath instead of above me, I thought I must be mad.

When the little girl spoke to me, I thought at first that she was a delusion, and that I was lost in a nightmare. It wasn't until she touched me, and tried to drag me upright with her tiny, frail hands, and addressed me by name—albeit incorrectly—that I was finally able to focus my thoughts.

"You have to get up, Mr. Mortimer," she said. "The boat's upside down."

She was only eight years old, but she spoke quite calmly and reasonably.

"That's impossible," I told her. "*Genesis* is unsinkable. There's no way it could turn upside down."

"But it *is* upside down," she insisted—and, as she did so, I finally realized the significance of the fact that the floor was glowing the way the ceiling should have glowed. "The water's coming in. I think we'll have to swim out."

The light put out by the ceiling-strip was as bright as ever, but the rippling water overlaying it made it seem dim and uncertain. The girl's little face, lit from below, seemed terribly serious within the frame of her dark and curly hair.

"I can't swim," I said, flatly.

She looked at me as if I were insane, or stupid, but it was true. I couldn't swim. I'd never liked the idea, and I'd never seen any necessity. All modern ships—even sailing-ships designed to be cute and quaint for the benefit of tourists—were unsinkable.

I scrambled to my feet, and put out both my hands to steady myself, to hold myself against the upside-down walls. The water was knee-deep. I couldn't tell whether it was increasing or not—which told me, reassuringly, that it couldn't be rising very quickly. The upturned boat was rocking this way and that, and I could hear the rumble of waves breaking on the outside of the hull, but I didn't know how much of that apparent violence was in my mind.

"My name's Emily," the little girl told me. "I'm frightened. All my mothers and fathers were on deck. *Everyone* was on deck, except for you and me. Do you think they're all dead?"

"They can't be," I said, marveling at the fact that she spoke so soberly, even when she said that she was frightened. I realized, however, that if the ship had suffered the kind of misfortune which could turn it upside down, the people on deck might indeed be dead. I tried to remember the passengers gossiping in the departure lounge, introducing themselves to one another with such fervor. The little girl had been with a party of nine, none of whose names I could remember. It occurred to me that *her whole family* might have been wiped out, that she might now be that rarest of all rare beings, an *orphan*. It was almost unimaginable. What possible catastrophe, I wondered, could have done that?

I asked Emily what had happened. She didn't know. Like me she had been in her bunk, sleeping the sleep of the innocent.

"Are we going to die too?" she asked. "I've been a good girl. I've never told a lie." It couldn't have been literally true, but I knew exactly what she meant. She was eight years old, and she had every right to expect to live till she was eight hundred. She didn't *deserve* to die. It wasn't fair.

I knew full well that fairness didn't really come into it, and I expect that she knew it too, even if my fellow historians were wrong about the virtual abolition of all the artifices of childhood, but I knew in my heart that what she said was *right*, and that insofar as the imperious laws of nature ruled her observation irrelevant, the *universe* was wrong. It *wasn't* fair. She *had* been a good girl. If she died, it would be a monstrous injustice.

Perhaps it was merely a kind of psychological defense mechanism that helped me to displace my own mortal anxieties, but the horror that ran through me was all focused on her. At the moment, her plight—not *our* plight, but *hers*—seemed to be the only thing that mattered. It was as if her dignified fear and her placid courage somehow contained the essence of human existence, the purest product of human progress.

Perhaps it was only my cowardly mind's refusal to contemplate anything else, but the only thing I could think of while I tried to figure out what to do was the awfulness of what she was saying. As that awfulness possessed me, it was magnified a thousandfold, and it seemed to me that in her lone and tiny voice there was a much greater voice speaking for multitudes: for all the human children that had ever died before achieving maturity; all the *good* children who had died without ever having the chance to *deserve to die*.

"I don't think any more water can get in," she said, with a slight tremor in her voice. "But there's only so much air. If we stay here too long, we'll suffocate."

"It's a big ship," I told her. "If we're trapped in an air-bubble, it must be a very large one."

"But it won't last forever," she told me. She was eight years old and hoped to live to be eight hundred, and she was absolutely right. The air wouldn't last forever. Hours, certainly; maybe days—but not forever.

"There are survival pods under the bunks," she said. She had obviously been paying attention to the welcoming speeches that the captain and the chief steward had delivered in the lounge the evening after embarkation. She'd plugged the chips they'd handed out into her trusty handbook, like the good girl she was, and inwardly digested what they had to teach her—unlike those of us who were blithely careless and wretchedly seasick.

"We can both fit into one of the pods," she went on, "but we have to get it out of the boat before we inflate it. We have to go up—I mean *down*—the stairway into the water and away from the boat. You'll have to carry the pod, because it's too big for me."

"I can't swim," I reminded her.

"It doesn't matter," she said, patiently. "All you have to do is hold your breath and kick yourself away from the boat. You'll float up to the surface whether you can swim or not. Then you just yank the cord and the pod will inflate. You have to hang on to it, though. Don't let go."

I stared at her, wondering how she could be so calm, so controlled, so efficient.

"Listen to the water breaking on the hull," I whispered. "Feel the movement of the boat. It would take a hurricane to overturn a boat like this. We wouldn't stand a chance out there."

"It's not so bad," she told me. She didn't have both hands out to brace herself against the walls, although she lifted one occasionally to stave off the worst of the lurches caused by the bobbing of the boat.

But if it wasn't a hurricane which turned us over, I thought, *what the hell was it? Whales have been extinct for eight hundred years.*

"We don't have to go just yet," Emily said, mildly, "but we'll have to go in the end. We have to get out. The pod's bright orange, and it has a distress beacon. We should be picked up within twenty-four hours, but there'll be supplies for a week."

I had every confidence that modern technology could sustain us for a month, if necessary. Even having to drink a little sea-water if your recycling gel clots only qualifies as a minor inconvenience nowadays. Drowning is another matter; so is asphyxiation. She was absolutely right. We had to get out of the upturned boat—not immediately, but some time soon. Help might get to us before then, but we couldn't wait, and we shouldn't. We were, after all, human beings. We were supposed to be able to take charge of our own destinies, to do what we *ought* to do. Anything less would be a betrayal of our heritage. I knew that, and understood it.

But I couldn't swim.

"It's okay, Mr. Mortimer," she said, putting her reassuring hand in mine. "We can do it. We'll go together. It'll be all right."

Emily was right. We *could* do it, together, and we did—not immediately, I confess, but, in the end, we did it. It was the most terrifying and most horrible experience of my young life, but it had to be done, and we did it.

When I finally dived into that black pit of water, knowing that I had to go down and sideways before I could hope to go up, I was carried forward by the knowledge that Emily expected it of me, and needed me to do it. Without her, I'm sure that I would have died. I simply would not have had the courage to save myself. Because she was there, I dived, with the pod clutched in my arms. Because she was there, I managed to kick away from the hull and yank the cord to inflate it.

It wasn't until I had pulled Emily into the pod, and made sure that she was safe, that I paused to think how remarkable it was that the sea was hot enough to scald us both.

We were three storm-tossed days afloat before the helicopter picked us up. We cursed our ill-luck, not having the least inkling how bad things were elsewhere. We couldn't understand why the weather was getting worse instead of better.

When the pilot finally explained it, we couldn't immediately take it in. Perhaps that's not surprising, given that the geologists were just as astonished as everyone else. After all, the sea-bed had been quietly cracking wherever the tectonic plates were pulling apart for millions of years; it was an ongoing phenomenon, very well understood. Hundreds of black smokers and underwater volcanoes were under constant observation. Nobody had any reason to expect that a plate could simply *break* so far away from its rim, or that the fissure could be so deep, so long, and so rapid in its extension. Everyone thought that the main threat to the earth's surface was posed by wayward comets; all vigilant eyes were directed outward. No one had expected such awesome force to erupt from within, from the hot mantle which lay, hubbling and bubbling, beneath the earth's fragile crust.

It was, apparently, an enormous bubble of upwelling gas that contrived the near-impossible feat of flipping *Genesis* over. The earthquakes and the tidal waves came later.

It was the worst natural disaster in six hundred years. One million, nine hundred thousand people died in all. Emily wasn't the only child to lose her entire family, and I shudder to think of the number of families which lost their only children. We historians have to maintain a sense of perspective, though. Compared with the number of people who died in the wars of the twentieth and twenty-first centuries, or the numbers of people who died in epidemics in earlier centuries, nineteen hundred thousand is a trivial figure.

Perhaps I would have done what I eventually set out to do anyway. Perhaps the Great Coral Sea Catastrophe would have appalled me even if I'd been on the other side of the world, cocooned in the safety of a treehouse or an apartment in one of the crystal cities—but I don't think so.

It was because I was at the very center of things, because my life was literally turned upside down by the disaster—and because eight-year-old Emily Marchant was there to save my life with her common sense and her composure—that I set out to write a definitive history of death, intending to reveal not merely the dull facts of mankind's longest and hardest battle, but also the real meaning and significance of it.

2

The first volume of Mortimer Gray's *History of Death*, entitled *The Prehistory of Death*, was published on 21 January 2914. It was, unusually for its day, a mute book, with no voice-over, sound-effects, or background music. Nor did it have any original art-work, all the illustrations being unenhanced still photographs. It was, in short, the kind of book that only a historian would have published. Its reviewers generally agreed that it was an old-fashioned example of scrupulous scholarship, and none expected that access demand would be considerable. Many commentators questioned the merit of Gray's arguments.

The Prehistory of Death summarized what was known about early hominid lifestyles, and had much to say about the effects of natural selection on the patterns of mortality in modern man's ancestor species. Gray carefully discussed the evolution of parental care as a genetic strategy. Earlier species of man, he observed, had raised parental care to a level of efficiency which permitted the human infant to be born at a much earlier stage in its development than any other, maximizing its opportunity to be shaped by nature and learning. From the very beginning, Gray proposed, human species were *actively* at war with death. The evolutionary success of *Homo sapiens* was based in the collaborative activities of parents in protecting, cherishing, and preserving the lives of children: activities that extended beyond immediate family groups as reciprocal altruism made it advantageous for humans to form tribes, and ultimately nations.

In these circumstances, Gray argued, it was entirely natural that the origins of consciousness and culture should be intimately bound up with a keen awareness of the war against death. He asserted that the first great task of the human imagination must have been to carry forward that war. It was entirely understandable, he said, that early paleontologists, having discovered the bones of a Neanderthal man in an apparent grave, with the remains of a primitive garland of flowers, should instantly have felt an intimate kinship with him; there could be no more persuasive evidence of full humanity than the attachment of ceremony to the idea and the fact of death.

Gray waxed lyrical about the importance of ritual as a symbolization of opposition and enmity to death. He had no patience with the proposition that such rituals were of no practical value, a mere window dressing of culture. On the contrary, he claimed that there was no activity *more* practical than this expressive recognition of the *value* of life, this imposition of a moral order on the fact of human mortality. The birth of agriculture Gray regarded as a mere sophistication of food gathering, of considerable importance as a technical discovery but of little significance in transforming human nature. The practices of burying the dead with ceremony, and of ritual mourning, on the other hand, *were*, in his view, evidence of the transformation of human nature, of the fundamental creation of meaning that made human life very different from the life of animals.

Prehistorians who marked out the evolution of man by his developing technology—the Stone Age giving way to the Bronze Age, the Bronze Age to the Iron Age—were, Gray conceded, taking intelligent advantage of those relics that had stood the test of time. He warned, however, of the folly of thinking that because tools had survived the millennia, it must have been tool-making that was solely or primarily responsible for human progress. In his view, the primal cause that made people invent was man's ongoing war against death.

It was not *tools* which created man and gave birth to civilization, Mortimer Gray proclaimed, but the *awareness of mortality*.

3

Although its impact on my nascent personality was considerable, the Coral Sea Catastrophe was essentially an impersonal disaster. The people who died, including those who had been aboard the *Genesis*, were all unknown to me; it was not until some years later that I experienced personal bereavement. It wasn't one of my parents who died—by the time the first of them quit this earth I was nearly a hundred years old and our temporary closeness was a half-remembered thing of the distant past—but one of my spouses.

By the time *The Prehistory of Death* was published, I'd contracted my first marriage: a group contract with a relatively small aggregate consisting of three other men and four women. We lived in Lamu, on the coast of Kenya, a nation to which I had been drawn by my studies of the early evolution of man. We were all young people, and we had formed our group for companion-ship rather than for parenting—which was a privilege conventionally left, even in those days, to much older people. We didn't go in for much fleshsex, because we were still finding our various ways through the maze of erotic virtuality, but we took the time—as I suppose all young people do—to explore its unique delights. I can't remember exactly why I decided to join such a group; I presume that it was because I accepted, tacitly at least, the conven-tional wisdom that there is spice in variety, and that one should do one's best to keep a broad front of experience.

It wasn't a particularly happy marriage, but it served its purpose. We went in for a good deal of sporting activity and conventional tourism. We visited the other continents from time to time, but most of our adventures took us back and forth across Africa. Most of my spouses were practical ecologists involved in one way or another with the re-greening of the north and south, or with the reforestation of the equatorial belt. What little credit I earned to add to my Allocation was earned by assisting them; such fees as I received for net access to my work were inconsiderable. Axel, Jodocus, and Minna were all involved in large-scale hydrological engineering, and liked to describe themselves, lightheartedly, as the Lamu Rainmakers. The rest of us became, inevitably, the Rainmakers in-Law.

To begin with, I had considerable affection for all the other members of my new family, but as time went by the usual accretion of petty irritations built up, and a couple of changes in the group's personnel failed to renew the initial impetus. The research for the second volume of my history began to draw me more and more to Egypt and to Greece, even though there was no real need actually to travel in order to do the relevant research. I think we would have divorced in 2919 anyhow, even if it hadn't been for Grizel's death.

She went swimming in the newly re-routed Kwarra one day, and didn't come back.

Maybe the fact of her death wouldn't have hit me so hard if she hadn't been drowned, but I was still uneasy about deep water—even the relatively placid waters of the great rivers. If I'd been able to swim, I might have gone out with her, but I hadn't. I didn't even know she was missing until the news came in that a body had been washed up twenty kilometers downriver.

"It was a million-to-one thing," Ayesha told me, when she came back from the on-site inquest. "She must have been caught from behind by a log moving in the current, or something like that. We'll never know for sure. She must have been knocked unconscious, though, or badly dazed. Otherwise, she'd never have drifted into the white water. The rocks finished her off."

Rumor has it that many people simply can't take in news of the death of someone they love—that it flatly defies belief. I didn't react that way. With me, belief was instantaneous, and I just gave way under its pressure. I literally fell over, because my legs wouldn't support me—another psychosomatic failure about which my internal machinery could do nothing—and I wept uncontrollably. None of the others did, not even Axel, who'd been closer to Grizel than anyone. They were sympathetic at first, but it wasn't long before a note of annoyance began to creep into their reassurances.

"Come on, Morty," Ilya said, voicing the thought the rest of them were too diplomatic to let out. "You know more about death than any of us; if it doesn't help you to get a grip, what good is all that research?"

He was right, of course. Axel and Ayesha had often tried to suggest, delicately, that mine was an essentially unhealthy fascination, and now they felt vindicated.

"If you'd actually bothered to read my book," I retorted, "you'd know that it has nothing complimentary to say about philosophical acceptance. It sees a sharp awareness of mortality, and the capacity to feel the horror of death so keenly, as key forces driving human evolution."

"But you don't have to act it out so flamboyantly," Ilya came back, perhaps using cruelty to conceal and assuage his own misery. "We've evolved now. We've got past all that. We've matured." Ilya was the oldest of us, and he *seemed* very old, although he was only sixty-five. In those days, there weren't nearly as many double centenarians around as there are nowadays, and triple centenarians were very rare indeed. We take emortality so much for granted that it's easy to forget how recent a development it is.

"It's what I feel," I told him, retreating into uncompromising assertion. "I can't help it."

"We *all* loved her," Ayesha reminded me. "We'll all miss her. You're not *proving* anything, Morty."

What she meant was that I wasn't proving anything except my own instability, but she spoke more accurately than she thought; I wasn't proving anything at all. I was just reacting—atavistically, perhaps, but with crude honesty and authentically childlike innocence.

"We all have to pull together now," she added, "for Grizel's sake."

A death in the family almost always leads to universal divorce in childless marriages; nobody knows why. Such a loss *does* force the survivors to pull together, but it seems that the process of pulling together only serves to emphasize the incompleteness of the unit. We all went our separate ways, even the three Rainmakers.

I set out to use my solitude to become a true neo-Epicurean, after the fashion of the times, seeking no excess and deriving an altogether *appropriate* pleasure from everything I did. I took care to cultivate a proper love for the commonplace, training myself to a pitch of perfection in all the techniques of physiological control necessary to physical fitness and quiet metabolism.

I soon convinced myself that I'd transcended such primitive and adolescent goals as happiness, and had cultivated instead a truly civilized *ataraxia*: a calm of mind whose value went beyond the limits of ecstasy and exultation.

Perhaps I was fooling myself, but, if I was, I succeeded. The habits stuck. No matter what lifestyle fashions came and went thereafter, I remained a stubborn neo-Epicurean, immune to all other eupsychian fantasies. For a while, though, I was perpetually haunted by Grizel's memory—and not, alas, by the memory of all things that we'd shared while she was *alive*. I gradually forgot the sound of her voice, the touch of her hand and even the image of her face, remembering only the horror of her sudden and unexpected departure from the arena of my experience.

For the next ten years, I lived in Alexandria, in a simple villa cleverly gantzed out of the desert sands—sands which still gave an impression of timelessness even though they had been restored to wilderness as recently as the twenth-seventh century, when Egypt's food economy had been realigned to take full advantage of the newest techniques in artificial photosynthesis.

4

The second volume of Mortimer Gray's *History of Death*, entitled *Death in the Ancient World*, was published on 7 May 2931. It contained a wealth of data regarding burial practices and patterns of mortality in Egypt, the Kingdoms of Sumer and Akkad, the Indus civilizations of Harappa and Mohenjo-Daro, the Yangshao and Lungshan cultures of the Far East, the cultures of the Olmecs and Zapotecs, Greece before and after Alexander, and the pre-Christian Roman Empire. It paid particular attention to the elaborate mythologies of life after death developed by ancient cultures.

Gray gave most elaborate consideration to the Egyptians, whose eschatology evidently fascinated him. He spared no effort in description and discussion of the *Book of the Dead*, the Hall of Double Justice, Anubis and Osiris, the custom of mummification, and the building of pyramid-tombs. He was almost as fascinated by the elaborate geography of the Greek Underworld, the characters associated with it—Hades and Persephone, Thanatos and the Erinnyes, Cerberus and Charon—and the descriptions of the unique fates reserved for such individuals as Sisyphus, Ixion, and Tantalus. The development of such myths as these Gray regarded as a triumph of the creative imagination. In his account, myth-making and story-telling were vital weapons in the war against death—a war that had still to be fought in the mind of man, because there was little yet to be accomplished by defiance of its claims upon the body.

In the absence of an effective medical science, Gray argued, the war against death was essentially a war of propaganda, and myths were to be judged in that light—not by their truthfulness, even in some allegorical or metaphorical sense, but by their usefulness in generating *morale* and meaning. By elaborating and extrapolating the process of death in this way, a more secure moral order could be imported into social life. People thus achieved a sense of continuity with past and future generations, so that every individual became part of a great enterprise which extended across the generations, from the beginning to the end of time.

Gray did not regard the building of the pyramids as a kind of gigantic folly or vanity, or a way to dispose of the energies of the peasants when they were not required in harvesting the bounty of the fertile Nile. He argued that pyramid-building should be seen as the most useful of all labors, because it was work directed at the glorious imposition of human endeavor upon the natural landscape. The placing of a royal mummy, with all its accoutrements, in a fabulous geometric edifice of stone was, for Gray, a loud, confident, and entirely appropriate statement of humanity's invasion of the empire of death.

Gray complimented those tribesmen who worshipped their ancestors and thought them always close at hand, ready to deliver judgments upon the living. Such people, he felt, had fully mastered an elementary truth of human existence: that the dead were not entirely gone, but lived on, intruding upon memory and dream, both when they were bidden and when they were not. He approved of the idea that the dead should have a voice, and must be entitled to speak, and that the living had a moral duty to listen. Because these ancient tribes were as direly short of history as they were of medicine, he argued, they were entirely justified in allowing their ancestors to live on in the minds of living people, where the culture those ancestors had forged similarly resided.

Some reviewers complimented Gray on the breadth of his research and the comprehensiveness of his data, but few endorsed the propriety of his interpretations. He was widely advised to be more dispassionate in carrying forward his project.

5

I was sixty when I married again. This time, it was a singular marriage, to Sharane Fereday. We set up home in Avignon, and lived together for nearly twenty years. I won't say that we were exceptionally happy, but I came to depend on her closeness and her affection, and the day she told me that she had had enough was the darkest of my life so far—far darker in its desolation than the day Emily Marchant and I had been trapped in the wreck of the *Genesis*, although it didn't mark me as deeply.

"Twenty years is a long time, Mortimer," she told me. "It's time to move on—time for you as well as for me."

She was being sternly reasonable at that stage; I knew from experience that the sternness would crumble if I put it to the test, and I thought that her resolve would crumble with it, as it had before in similar circumstances, but it didn't.

"I'm truly sorry," she said, when she was eventually reduced to tears, "but I have to do it. I have to go. It's *my* life, and your part of it is over. I hate hurting you, but I don't want to live with you anymore. It's my fault, not yours, but that's the way it is."

It wasn't anybody's fault. I can see that clearly now, although it wasn't so easy to see it at the time. Like the Great Coral Sea Catastrophe or Grizel's drowning, it was just something that *happened*. Things do happen, regardless of people's best-laid plans, most heartfelt wishes, and intensest hopes.

Now that memory has blotted out the greater part of that phase of my life— including, I presume, the worst of it—I don't really know why I was so devastated by Sharane's decision, nor why it should have filled me with such black despair. Had I cultivated a dependence so absolute that it seemed irreplaceable, or was it only my pride that had suffered a sickening blow? Was it the imagined consequences of the rejection or merely the fact of rejection itself that sickened me so? Even now, I can't tell for certain. Even then, my neo-Epicurean conscience must have told me over and over again to pull myself together, to conduct myself with more decorum.

I tried. I'm certain that I tried.

Sharane's love for the ancient past was even more intense than mine, but her writings were far less dispassionate. She was an historian of sorts, but she wasn't an *academic* historian; her writings tended to the lyrical rather than the factual even when she was supposedly writing non-fiction.

Sharane would never have written a mute book, or one whose pictures didn't move. Had it been allowed by law at that time, she'd have fed her readers designer psychotropics to heighten their responses according to the schemes of her texts. She was a VR scriptwriter rather than a textwriter like me. She wasn't content to know about the past; she wanted to re-create it and make it solid and *live* in it. Nor did she reserve such inclinations to the privacy of her E-suit. She was flamboyantly old-fashioned in all that she did. She liked to dress in gaudy pastiches of the costumes represented in Greek or Egyptian art, and she liked decor to match. People who knew us were mildly astonished that we should want to live together, given the difference in our personalities, but I suppose it was an attraction of opposites. Perhaps my intensity of purpose and solitude had begun to weigh rather heavily upon me when we met, and my carefully cultivated calm of mind threatened to become a kind of toiling inertia.

On the other hand, perhaps that's all confabulation and rationalization. I was a different person then, and I've since lost touch with that person as completely as I've lost touch with everyone else I once knew.

But I *do* remember, vaguely. . . .

I remember that I found in Sharane a certain precious *wildness* that, although it wasn't entirely spontaneous, was unfailingly amusing. She had the happy gift of never taking herself too seriously, although she was wholehearted enough in her determined attempts to put herself imaginatively in touch with the past.

From her point of view, I suppose I was doubly valuable. On the one hand, I was a fount of information and inspiration, on the other a kind of anchorage whose solidity kept her from losing herself in her flights of the imagination. Twenty years of marriage ought to have cemented her dependence on me just as it had cemented my dependence on her, but it didn't.

"You think I need you to keep my feet on the ground," Sharane said, as the break between us was completely and carefully rendered irreparable, "but I don't. Anyhow, I've been weighed down long enough. I need to soar for a while, to spread my wings."

Sharane and I had talked for a while, as married people do, about the possibility of having a child. We had both made deposits to the French national gamete bank, so that if we felt the same way when the time finally came to exercise our right of replacement—or to specify in our wills how that right was to be posthumously exercised—we could order an ovum to be unfrozen and fertilized.

I had always known, of course, that such flights of fancy were not to be taken too seriously, but when I accepted that the marriage was indeed over, there seemed to be an extra dimension of tragedy and misery in the knowledge that our genes never would be combined—that our separation cast our legacies once again upon the chaotic sea of irresolution.

Despite the extremity of my melancholy, I never contemplated suicide. Although I'd already used up the traditional threescore years and ten, I was in no doubt at all that it wasn't yet time to remove myself from the crucible of human evolution to make room for my successor, whether that successor was to be born from an ovum of Sharane's or not. No matter how black my mood was when Sharane left, I knew that my *History of Death* remained to be completed, and that the work would require at least another century. Even so, the breaking of such an intimate bond filled me with intimations of mortality and a painful sense of the futility of all my endeavors.

My first divorce had come about because a cruel accident had ripped apart the delicate fabric of my life, but my second—or so it seemed to me—was itself a horrid rent shearing my very being into ragged fragments. I hope that I tried with all my might not to blame Sharane, but how could I avoid it? And how could she not resent my overt and covert accusations, my veiled and naked resentments?

"Your problem, Mortimer," she said to me, when her lachrymose phase had given way to bright anger, "is that you're *obsessed*. You're a deeply morbid man, and it's not healthy. There's some special fear in you, some altogether exceptional horror which feeds upon you day and night, and makes you grotesquely vulnerable to occurrences that normal people can take in their stride, and that ill befit a self-styled Epicurean. If you want my advice, you ought to abandon that history you're writing, at least for a while, and devote yourself to something brighter and more vigorous."

"Death is my life," I informed her, speaking metaphorically, and not entirely without irony. "It always will be, until and including the end."

I remember saying that. The rest is vague, but I really do remember saying that.

6

The third volume of Mortimer Gray's *History of Death*, entitled *The Empires of Faith*, was published on 18 August 2954. The introduction announced that the author had been forced to set aside his initial ambition to write a truly comprehensive history, and stated that he would henceforth be unashamedly eclectic, and contentedly ethnocentric, because he did not wish to be a mere archivist of death, and therefore could not regard all episodes in humankind's war against death as being of equal interest. He declared that he was more interested in interpretation than mere summary, and that insofar as the war against death had been a moral crusade, he felt fully entitled to draw morals from it.

This preface, understandably, dismayed those critics who had urged the author to be more dispassionate. Some reviewers were content to condemn the new volume without even bothering to inspect the rest of it, although it was considerably shorter than the second volume and had a rather more fluent style. Others complained that the day of mute text was dead and gone, and that there was no place in the modern world for pictures that resolutely refused to move.

Unlike many contemporary historians, whose birth into a world in which religious faith was almost extinct had robbed them of any sympathy for the imperialists of dogma, Gray proposed that the great religions had been one of the finest achievements of humankind. He regarded them as a vital stage in the evolution of community—as social technologies which had permitted a spectacular transcendence of the limitation of community to the tribe or region. Faiths, he suggested, were the first instruments that could bind together different language groups, and even different races. It was not until the spread of the great religions, Gray argued, that the possibility came into being of gathering all men together into a single common enterprise. He regretted, of course, that the principal product of this great dream was two millennia of bitter and savage conflict between adherents of different faiths or adherents of different versions of the same faith, but thought the ambition worthy of all possible respect and admiration. He even retained some sympathy for jihads and crusades, in the formulation of which people had tried to attribute more meaning to the sacrifice of life than they ever had before.

Gray was particularly fascinated by the symbology of the Christian mythos, which had taken as its central image the death on the cross of Jesus, and had tried to make that one image of death carry an enormous allegorical load. He was entranced by the idea of Christ's death as a force of redemption and salvation, by the notion that this person died *for others*. He extended the argument to take in the Christian martyrs, who added to the primal crucifixion a vast series of symbolic and morally significant deaths. This, he considered, was a colossal achievement of the imagination, a crucial victory by which death was dramatically transfigured in the theater of the human imagination—as was the Christian idea of death as a kind of reconciliation: a gateway to Heaven, if properly met; a gateway to Hell, if not. Gray seized upon the idea of absolution from sin following confession, and particularly the notion of deathbed repentance, as a daring raid into the territories of the imagination previously ruled by fear of death.

Gray's commentaries on the other major religions were less elaborate but no less interested. Various ideas of reincarnation and the related concept of *karma* he discussed at great length, as one of the most ingenious imaginative bids for freedom from the tyranny of death. He was not quite so enthusiastic about the idea of the world as illusion, the idea of nirvana, and certain other aspects of Far Eastern thought, although he was impressed in several ways by Confucius and the Buddha. All these things and more he assimilated to the main line of his argument, which was that the great religions had made bold imaginative leaps in order to carry forward the war against death on a broader front than ever before, providing vast numbers of individuals with an efficient intellectual weaponry of moral purpose.

7

After Sharane left, I stayed on in Avignon for a while. The house where we had lived was demolished, and I had another raised in its place. I resolved to take up the reclusive life again, at least for a while. I had come to think of myself as one of nature's monks, and when I was tempted to flights of fancy of a more personal kind than those retailed in virtual reality, I could imagine myself an avatar of some patient scholar born fifteen hundred years before, contentedly submissive to the Benedictine rule. I didn't, of course, believe in the possibility of reincarnation, and when such beliefs became fashionable again I found it almost impossible to indulge any more fantasies of that kind.

In 2960, I moved to Antarctica, not to Amundsen City—which had become the world's political center since the United Nations had elected to set up headquarters in "the continent without nations"—but to Cape Adare on the Ross Sea, which was a relatively lonely spot.

I moved into a tall house rather resembling a lighthouse, from whose upper stories I could look out at the edge of the ice-cap and watch the penguins at play. I was reasonably contented, and soon came to feel that I had put the torments and turbulences of my early life behind me.

I often went walking across the nearer reaches of the icebound sea, but I rarely got into difficulties. Ironically enough, my only serious injury of that period was a broken leg, which I sustained while working with a rescue party attempting to locate and save one of my neighbors, Ziru Majumdar, who had fallen into a crevasse while out on a similar expedition. We ended up in adjacent beds at the hospital in Amundsen City.

"I'm truly sorry about your leg, Mr. Gray," Majumdar said. "It was very stupid of me to get lost. After all, I've lived here for thirty years; I thought I knew every last iceridge like the back of my hand. It's not as if the weather was particularly bad, and I've never suffered from summer rhapsody or snow-blindness."

I'd suffered from both—I was still awkwardly vulnerable to psychosomatic ills—but they only served to make me more careful. An uneasy mind can sometimes be an advantage.

"It wasn't your fault, Mr. Majumdar," I graciously insisted. "I suppose I must have been a little over-confident myself, or I'd never have slipped and fallen. At least they were able to pull me out in a matter of minutes; you must have lain unconscious at the bottom of that crevasse for nearly two days."

"Just about. I came round several times—at least, I think I did—but my internal tech was pumping so much dope around my system it's difficult to be sure. My surskin and thermosuit were doing their best to keep me warm, but the first law of thermodynamics doesn't give you much slack when you're at the bottom of a cleft in the permafrost. I've got authentic frostbite in my toes, you know—imagine that!"

I dutifully tried to imagine it, but it wasn't easy. He could hardly be in pain, so it was difficult to conjure up any notion of what it might feel like to have necrotized toes. The doctors reckoned that it would take a week for the nanomachines to restore the tissues to their former pristine condition.

"Mind you," he added, with a small embarrassed laugh, "it's only a matter of time before the whole biosphere gets frostbite, isn't it? Unless the sun gets stirred up again."

More than fifty years had passed since scrupulous students of the sunspot cycle had announced the advent of a new Ice Age, but the world was quite unworried by the exceedingly slow advance of the glaciers across the Northern Hemisphere. It was the sort of thing that only cropped up in light banter.

"I won't mind that," I said, contemplatively. "Nor will you, I dare say. We like ice—why else would we live here?"

"Right. Not that I agree with those Gaean Liberationists, mind. I hear they're proclaiming that the inter-glacial periods are simply Gaea's fevers, that the birth of civilization was just a morbid symptom of the planet's sickness, and that human culture has so far been a mere delirium of the noösphere."

He obviously paid more attention to the lunatic fringe channels than I did.

"It's just colorful rhetoric," I told him. "They don't mean it literally."

"Think not? Well, perhaps. I was delirious myself for a while when I was down that hole. Can't be sure whether I was asleep or awake, but I was certainly lost in some vivid dreams—and I mean *vivid*. I don't know about you, but I always find VR a bit flat, even if I use illicit psychotropics to give delusion a helping hand. I think it's to do with the protective effects of our internal technology. Nanomachines mostly do their job a little *too* well, because of the built-in safety margins—it's only when they reach the limits of their capacity that they let really interesting things begin to happen."

I knew he was building up to some kind of self-justification, but I felt that he was entitled to it. I nodded, to give him permission to prattle on.

"You have to go to the very brink of extinction to reach the cutting edge of experience, you see. I found that out while I was trapped down there in the ice, not knowing whether the rescuers would get to me in time. You can learn a lot about life, and about yourself, in a situation like that. It really was vivid—more vivid than anything I ever . . . well, what I'm trying to get at is that we're too *safe* nowadays; we can have no idea of the *zest* there was in living in the bad old days. Not that I'm about to take up jumping into crevasses as a hobby, you understand. Once in a very long while is plenty."

"Yes, it is," I agreed, shifting my itching leg and wishing that nanomachines weren't so slow to compensate for trifling but annoying sensations. "Once in a while is certainly enough for me. In fact, I for one will be quite content if it never happens again. I don't think I need any more of the kind of enlightenment which comes from experiences like that. I was in the Great Coral Sea Catastrophe, you know—shipwrecked, scalded, and lost at sea for days on end."

"It's not the same," he insisted, "but you won't be able to understand the difference until it happens to you."

I didn't believe him. In that instance, I suppose, he was right and I was wrong.

I'd never heard Mr. Majumdar speak so freely before, and I never heard him do it again. The social life of the Cape Adare "exiles" was unusually formal, hemmed in by numerous barriers of formality and etiquette. After an embarrassing phase of learning and adjustment, I'd found the formality aesthetically appealing, and had played the game with enthusiasm, but it was beginning to lose its appeal by the time the accident shook me up. I suppose it's understandable that whatever you set out to exclude from the pattern of your life eventually comes to seem like a lack, and then an unfulfilled need.

After a few years more, I began to hunger once again for the spontaneity and abandonment of warmer climes. I decided there'd be time enough to celebrate the advent of the Ice Age when the glaciers had reached the full extent of their reclaimed empire, and that I might as well make what use I could of Gaea's temporary fever before it cooled. I moved to Venezuela, to dwell in the gloriously restored jungles of the Orinoco amid their teeming wildlife.

Following the destruction of much of the southern part of the continent in the second nuclear war, Venezuela had attained a cultural hegemony in South America that it had never surrendered. Brazil and Argentina had long since recovered, both economically and ecologically, from their disastrous fit of ill temper, but Venezuela was still the home of the *avant garde* of the Americas. It was there, for the first time, that I came into close contact with Thanaticism.

The original Thanatic cults had flourished in the twenty-eighth century. They had appeared among the last generations of children born without Zaman transformations; their members were people who, denied emortality through blastular engineering, had perversely elected to reject the benefits of rejuvenation too, making a fetish out of living only a "natural" lifespan. At the time, it had seemed likely that they would be the last of the many Millenarian cults which had long afflicted Western culture, and they had quite literally died out some eighty or ninety years before I was born.

Nobody had then thought it possible, let alone likely, that genetically endowed emortals would ever embrace Thanaticism, but they were wrong.

There had always been suicides in the emortal population—indeed, suicide was the commonest cause of death among emortals, outnumbering accidental deaths by a factor of three—but such acts were usually covert and normally involved people who had lived at least a hundred years. The neo-Thanatics were not only indiscreet—their whole purpose seemed to be to make a public spectacle of themselves—but also young; people over seventy were held to have violated the Thanaticist ethic simply by surviving to that age.

Thanatics tended to choose violent means of death, and usually issued invitations as well as choosing their moments so that large crowds could gather. Jumping from tall buildings and burning to death were the most favored means in the beginning, but these quickly ceased to be interesting. As the Thanatic revival progressed, adherents of the movement sought increasingly bizarre methods in the interests of capturing attention and out-doing their predecessors. For these reasons, it was impossible for anyone living alongside the cults to avoid becoming implicated in their rites, if only as a spectator.

By the time I had been in Venezuela for a year, I had seen five people die horribly. After the first, I had resolved to turn away from any others, so as not to lend even minimal support to the practice, but I soon found that I had underestimated the difficulty of so doing. There was no excuse to be found in my vocation; thousands of people who were not historians of death found it equally impossible to resist the fascination.

I believed at first that the fad would soon pass, after wasting the lives of a handful of neurotics, but the cults continued to grow. Gaea's fever might be cooling, its crisis having passed, but the delirium of human culture had evidently not yet reached what Ziru Majumdar called "the cutting edge of experience."

8

The fourth volume of Mortimer Gray's *History of Death*, entitled *Fear and Fascination*, was published on 12 February 2977. In spite of being mute and motionless it was immediately subject to heavy access-demand, presumably in consequence of the world's increasing fascination with the "problem" of neo-Thanaticism. Requisitions of the earlier volumes of Gray's history had picked up worldwide during the early 2970s, but the author had not appreciated what this might mean in terms of the demand for the new volume, and might have set a higher access fee had he realized.

Academic historians were universal in their condemnation of the new volume, possibly because of the enthusiasm with which it was greeted by laymen, but popular reviewers adored it. Its arguments were recklessly plundered by journalists and other broadcasting pundits in search of possible parallels that might be drawn with the modern world, especially those that seemed to carry moral lessons for the Thanatics and their opponents.

Fear and Fascination extended, elaborated, and diversified the arguments contained in its immediate predecessor, particularly in respect of the Christian world of the Medieval period and the Renaissance. It had much to say about art and literature, and the images contained therein. It had chapters on the personification of Death as the Grim Reaper, on the iconography of the *danse macabre*, on the topics of *memento mori* and *artes moriendi*. It had long analyses of Dante's *Divine Comedy*, the paintings of Hieronymus Bosch, Milton's *Paradise Lost*, and graveyard poetry. These were by no means exercises in conventional literary criticism; they were elements of a long and convoluted argument about the contributions made by the individual creative imagination to the war of ideas which raged on the only battleground on which man could as yet constructively oppose the specter of death.

Gray also dealt with the persecution of heretics and the subsequent elaboration of Christian Demonology, which led to the witch-craze of the fifteenth, sixteenth, and seventeenth centuries. He gave considerable attention to various thriving folklore traditions which confused the notion of death, especially to the popularity of fictions and fears regarding premature burial, ghosts, and the various species of the "undead" who rose from their graves as ghouls or vampires. In Gray's eyes, all these phenomena were symptomatic of a crisis in Western man's imaginative dealings with the idea of death: a feverish heating up of a conflict which had been in danger of becoming desultory.

The cities of men had been under perpetual siege from Death since the time of their first building, but now—in one part of the world, at least—the perception of that siege had sharpened. A kind of spiritual starvation and panic had set in, and the progress that had been made in the war by virtue of the ideological imperialism of Christ's Holy Cross now seemed imperiled by disintegration. This Empire of Faith was breaking up under the stress of skepticism, and men were faced with the prospect of going into battle against their most ancient enemy with their armor in tatters.

Just as the Protestants were trying to replace the Catholic Church's centralized authority with a more personal relationship between men and God, Gray argued, so the creative artists of this era were trying to achieve a more personal and more intimate form of reconciliation between men and Death, equipping individuals with the power to mount their own ideative assaults. He drew some parallels between what happened in the Christian world and similar periods of crisis which he found in different cultures at different times, but other historians claimed that his analogies were weak, and that he was overgeneralizing. Some argued that his intense study of the phenomena associated with the idea of death had become too personal, and suggested that he had become infatuated with the ephemeral ideas of past ages to the point where they were taking over his own imagination.

9

At first, I found celebrity status pleasing, and the extra credit generated by my access fees was certainly welcome, even to a man of moderate tastes and habits. The unaccustomed touch of fame brought a fresh breeze into a life that might have been in danger of becoming bogged down.

To begin with, I was gratified to be reckoned an expert whose views on Thanaticism were to be taken seriously, even by some Thanatics. I received a veritable deluge of invitations to appear on the talk shows that were the staple diet of contemporary broadcasting, and for a while I accepted as many as I could conveniently accommodate within the pattern of my life.

I have no need to rely on my memories in recapitulating these episodes, because they remain on record—but by the same token, I needn't quote extensively from them. In the early days, when I was a relatively new face, my interrogators mostly started out by asking for information about my book, and their opening questions were usually stolen from uncharitable reviews.

"Some people feel that you've been carried away, Mr. Gray," more than one combative interviewer sneeringly began, "and that what started out as a sober history is fast becoming an obsessive rant. Did you decide to get personal in order to boost your sales?"

My careful cultivation of neo-Epicureanism and my years in Antarctica had left a useful legacy of calm formality; I always handled such accusations with punctilious politeness.

"Of course the war against death is a personal matter," I would reply. "It's a personal matter for everyone, mortal or emortal. Without that sense of personal relevance it would be impossible to put oneself imaginatively in the place of the people of the ancient past so as to obtain empathetic insight into their affairs. If I seem to be making heroes of the men of the past by describing their crusades, it's because they *were* heroes, and if my contemporaries find inspiration in my work, it's because they too are heroes in the same cause. The engineering of emortality has made us victors in the war, but we desperately need to retain a proper sense of triumph. We ought to celebrate our victory over death as joyously as possible, lest we lose our appreciation of its fruits."

My interviewers always appreciated that kind of link, which handed them their next question on a plate. "Is that what you think of the Thanatics?" they would follow up, eagerly.

It was, and I would say so at any length they considered appropriate.

Eventually, my interlocutors no longer talked about my book, taking it for granted that everyone knew who I was and what I'd done. They'd cut straight to the chase, asking me what I thought of the latest Thanaticist publicity stunt.

Personally, I thought the media's interest in Thanaticism was exaggerated. All death was, of course, news in a world populated almost entirely by emortals, and the Thanatics took care to be newsworthy by making such a song and dance about what they were doing, but the number of individuals involved was very small. In a world population of nearly three billion, a hundred deaths per week was a drop in the ocean, and "quiet" suicides still outnumbered the ostentatious Thanatics by a factor of five or six throughout the 2980s. The public debates quickly expanded to take in other issues. Subscription figures for net access to videotapes and teletexts concerned with the topic of violent death came under scrutiny, and everyone began talking about the "new pornography of death"—although fascination with such material had undoubtedly been widespread for many years.

"Don't you feel, Mr. Gray," I was often asked, "that a continued fascination with death in a world where everyone has a potential lifespan of several centuries is rather *sick*? Shouldn't we have put such matters behind us?"

"Not at all," I replied, earnestly and frequently. "In the days when death was inescapable, people were deeply frustrated by this imperious imposition of fate. They resented it with all the force and bitterness they could muster, but it could not be truly fascinating while it remained a simple and universal fact of life. Now that death is no longer a necessity, it has perforce become a luxury. Because it is no longer inevitable, we no longer feel such pressure to hate and fear it, and this frees us so that we may take an essentially *aesthetic* view of death. The transformation of the imagery of death into a species of pornography is both understandable and healthy.''

"But such material surely encourages the spread of Thanaticism. You can't possibly approve of that?"

Actually, the more I was asked it the less censorious I became, at least for a while.

"Planning a life," I explained to a whole series of faces, indistinguishable by virtue of having been sculptured according to the latest theory of telegenicity, "is an exercise in story-making. Living people are forever writing the narratives of their own lives, deciding who to be and what to do, according to various aesthetic criteria. In olden days, death was inevitably seen as an *interruption* of the business of life, cutting short life-stories before they were—in the eyes of their creators—complete. Nowadays, people have the opportunity to plan *whole* lives, deciding exactly when and how their life-stories should reach a climax and a conclusion. We may not share their aesthetic sensibilities, and may well think them fools, but there is a discernible logic in their actions. They are neither mad nor evil.''

Perhaps I was reckless in adopting this point of view, or at least in proclaiming it to the whole world. By proposing that the new Thanatics were simply individuals who had a particular kind of aesthetic sensibility, tending toward conciseness and melodrama rather than prolixity and anti-climax, I became something of a hero to the cultists themselves—which was not my intention. The more lavishly I embroidered my chosen analogy—declaring that ordinary emortals were the *feuilletonistes*, epic poets, and three-decker novelists of modern life while Thanatics were the prose-poets and short-story writers who liked to sign off with a neat punch line—the more they liked me. I received many invitations to attend suicides, and my refusal to take them up only served to make my presence a prize to be sought after.

I was, of course, entirely in agreement with the United Nations Charter of Human Rights, whose ninety-ninth amendment guaranteed the citizens of every nation the right to take their own lives, and to be assisted in making a dignified exit should they so desire, but I had strong reservations about the way in which the Thanaticists construed the amendment. Its original intention had been to facilitate self-administered euthanasia in an age when that was sometimes necessary, not to guarantee Thanatics the entitlement to recruit whatever help they required in staging whatever kinds of exit they desired. Some of the invitations I received were exhortations to participate in legalized murders, and these became more common as time went by and the cults became more extreme in their bizarrerie.

In the 2980s, the Thanatics had progressed from conventional suicides to public executions, by rope, sword, axe, or guillotine. At first, the executioners were volunteers—and one or two were actually arrested and charged with murder, although none could be convicted—but the Thanatics were not satisfied even with this, and began campaigning for various nations to recreate the official position of Public Executioner, together with bureaucratic structures that would give all citizens the right to call upon the services of such officials. Even I, who claimed to understand the cults better than their members, was astonished when the government of Colombia—which was jealous of Venezuela's reputation as the home of the world's *avant garde*—actually accepted such an obligation, with the result that Thanatics began to flock to Maracaibo and Cartagena in order to obtain an appropriate send-off. I was profoundly relieved when the UN, following the crucifixion of Shamiel Sihra in 2991, revised the wording of the amendment and outlawed suicide by public execution.

By this time, I was automatically refusing invitations to appear on 3-V in much the same way that I was refusing invitations to take part in Thanaticist ceremonies. It was time to become a recluse once again.

I left Venezuela in 2989 to take up residence on Cape Wolstenholme, at the neck of Hudson's Bay. Canada was an urbane, highly civilized, and rather staid confederacy of states whose people had no time for such follies as Thanaticism; it provided an ideal retreat where I could throw myself wholeheartedly into my work again.

I handed over full responsibility for answering all my calls to a state-of-the-art Personal Simulation program, which grew so clever and so ambitious with practice that it began to give live interviews on broadcast television. Although it offered what was effectively no comment in a carefully elaborate fashion I eventually thought it best to introduce a block into its operating system—a block that ensured that my face dropped out of public sight for half a century.

Having once experienced the rewards and pressures of fame, I never felt the need to seek them again. I can't and won't say that I learned as much from that phase in my life as I learned from any of my close encounters with death, but I still remember it—vaguely—with a certain nostalgia. Unmelodramatic it might have been, but it doubtless played its part in shaping the person that I now am. It certainly made me more self-assured in public.

10

The fifth volume of Mortimer Gray's *History of Death*, entitled *The War of Attrition*, was published on 19 March 2999. It marked a return to the cooler and more comprehensive style of scholarship exhibited by the first two volumes. It dealt with the history of medical science and hygiene up to the end of the nineteenth century, thus concerning itself with a new and very different arena of the war between mankind and mortality.

To many of its readers *The War of Attrition* was undoubtedly a disappointment, though it did include some material about Victorian tomb-decoration and nineteenth century spiritualism that carried forward arguments from volume four. Access was initially widespread, although demand tailed off fairly rapidly when it was realized how vast and how tightly packed with data the document was. This lack of popular enthusiasm was not counterbalanced by any redemption of Mortimer's academic reputation; like many earlier scholars who had made contact with a popular audience, Gray was considered guilty of a kind of intellectual treason, and was frozen out of the scholarly community in spite of what appeared to be a determined attempt at rehabilitation. Some popular reviewers argued, however, that there was much in the new volume to intrigue the inhabitants of a world whose medical science was so adept that almost everyone enjoyed perfect health as well as eternal youth, and in which almost any injury could be repaired completely. It was suggested that there was a certain piquant delight to be obtained from recalling a world where everyone was (by modern standards) crippled or deformed, and in which everyone suffered continually from illnesses of a most horrific nature.

Although it had a wealth of scrupulously dry passages, there were parts of *The War of Attrition* that were deemed pornographic by some commentators. Its accounts of the early history of surgery and midwifery were condemned as unjustifiably blood-curdling, and its painstaking analysis of the spread of syphilis through Europe in the sixteenth century was censured as a mere horror-story made all the nastier by its clinical narration. Gray was particularly interested in syphilis, because of the dramatic social effects of its sudden advent in Europe and its significance in the development of prophylactic medicine. He argued that syphilis was primarily responsible for the rise and spread of Puritanism, repressive sexual morality being the only truly effective weapon against its spread. He then deployed well-tried sociological arguments to the effect that Puritanism and its associated habits of thought had been importantly implicated in the rapid development of Capitalism in the Western World, in order that he might claim that syphilis ought to be regarded as the root cause of the economic and political systems that came to dominate the most chaotic, the most extravagantly progressive, and the most extravagantly destructive centuries of human history.

The history of medicine and the conquest of disease were, of course, topics of elementary education in the thirtieth century. There was supposedly not a citizen of any nation to whom the names of Semmelweis, Jenner, and Pasteur were unknown—but disease had been so long banished from the world, and it was so completely outside the experience of ordinary men and women, that what they "knew" about it was never really brought to consciousness, and never came alive to the imagination. Words like "smallpox," "plague," and "cancer" were used metaphorically in common parlance, and over the centuries had become virtually empty of any real significance. Gray's fifth volume, therefore—despite the fact that it contained little that was really new—did serve as a stimulus to collective memory. It reminded the world of some issues which, though not exactly forgotten, had not really been *brought to mind* for some time. It is at least arguable that it touched off ripples whose movement across the collective consciousness of world culture was of some moment. Mortimer Gray was no longer famous, but his continuing work had become firmly established within the *zeitgeist*.

11

Neo-Thanaticism began to peter out as the turn of the century approached. By 3010, the whole movement had "gone underground"—which is to say that Thanatics no longer staged their exits before the largest audiences they could attain, but saved their performance for small, carefully selected groups. This wasn't so much a response to persecution as a variation in the strange game that they were playing out; it was simply a different kind of drama. Unfortunately, there was no let up in the communications with which Thanatics continued to batter my patient AI interceptors.

Although it disappointed the rest of the world, *The War of Attrition* was welcomed enthusiastically by some of the Thanatic cults, whose members cultivated an altogether unhealthy interest in disease as a means of decease, replacing the violent executions that had become too familiar. As time went by and Thanaticism declined generally, this particular subspecies underwent a kind of mutation, as the cultists began to promote diseases not as means of death but as valuable *experiences* from which much might be learned. A black market in carcinogens and bioengineered pathogens quickly sprang up. The original agents of smallpox, cholera, bubonic plague, and syphilis were long since extinct, but the world abounded in clever genetic engineers who could synthesize a virus with very little effort. Suddenly, they began to find clients for a whole range of horrid diseases. Those which afflicted the mind as well as or instead of the body were particularly prized; there was a boom in recreational schizophrenia that almost broke through to the mainstream of accredited psychotropics.

I couldn't help but remember, with a new sense of irony, Ziru Majumdar's enthusiasm for the vivid delusions which had visited him while his internal technology was tested to the limit in staving off hypothermia and frostbite.

When the new trend spread beyond the ranks of the Thanaticists, and large numbers of people began to regard disease as something that could be temporarily and interestingly indulged in without any real danger to life or subsequent health, I began to find my arguments about death quoted—without acknowledgment—with reference to *disease*. A popular way of talking about the phenomenon was to claim that what had ceased to be a dire necessity "naturally" became available as a perverse luxury.

None of this would have mattered much had it not been for the difficulty of restricting the spread of recreational diseases to people who *wanted* to indulge, but those caught up in the fad refused to restrict themselves to noninfectious varieties. There had been no serious threat of epidemic since the Plague Wars of the twenty-first century, but now it seemed that medical science might once again have to be mobilized on a vast scale. Because of the threat to innocent parties who might be accidently infected, the self-infliction of dangerous diseases was quickly outlawed in many nations, but some governments were slow to act.

I would have remained aloof and apart from all of this had I been able to, but it turned out that my defenses weren't impregnable. In 3029, a Thanaticist of exceptional determination named Hadria Nuccoli decided that if I wouldn't come to her, she would come to *me*. Somehow, she succeeded in getting past all my carefully sealed doors, to arrive in my bedroom at three o'clock one winter morning.

I woke up in confusion, but the confusion was quickly transformed into sheer terror. This was an enemy more frightening than the scalding Coral Sea, because this was an *active* enemy who meant to do me harm—and the intensity of the threat which she posed was in no way lessened by the fact that she claimed to be doing it out of love rather than hatred.

The woman's skin bore an almost mercuric luster, and she was in the grip of a terrible fever, but she would not be still. She seemed, in fact, to have an irresistible desire to move and to communicate, and the derangement of her body and brain had not impaired her crazed eloquence.

"Come with me!" she begged, as I tried to evade her eager clutch. "Come with me to the far side of death and I'll show you what's there. There's no need to be afraid! Death isn't the end, it's the beginning. It's the metamorphosis that frees us from our caterpillar flesh to be spirits in a massless world of light and color. I am your redeemer, for whom you have waited far too long. Love me, dear Mortimer Gray, only *love* me, and you will learn. Let me be your mirror; drown yourself in me!"

For ten minutes, I succeeded in keeping away from her, stumbling this way and that, thinking that I might be safe if only I didn't touch her. I managed to send out a call for help, but I knew it would take an hour or more for anyone to come.

I tried all the while to talk her down, but it was impossible.

"There's no return from eternity," she told me. "This is no ordinary virus created by accident to fight a hopeless cause against the defenses of the body.

Nanotechnology is as impotent to deal with this transformer of the flesh as the immune system was to deal with its own destroyers. The true task of medical engineers, did they but know it, was never to fight disease, but always to *perfect* it, and we have found the way. I bring you the greatest of all gifts, my darling: the elixir of life, which will make us angels instead of men, creatures of light and ecstasy!"

It was no use running; I tired before she did, and she caught me. I tried to knock her down, and if I had had a weapon to hand, I would certainly have used it in self-defense, but she couldn't feel pain, and no matter how badly disabled her internal technology was, I wasn't able to injure her with my blows.

In the end, I had no sensible alternative but to let her take me in her arms and cling to me; nothing else would soothe her.

I was afraid for her as well as myself; I didn't believe that she truly intended to die, and I wanted to keep us safe until help arrived.

My panic didn't decrease while I held her; if anything, I felt it all the more intensely. I became outwardly calmer once I had let her touch me, and made every effort to remind myself that it didn't really matter whether she infected me or not, given that medical help would soon arrive. I didn't expect to have to go through the kind of hell that I actually endured before the doctors got the bug under control; for once, panic was wiser than common sense.

Even so, I wept for her when they told me that she'd died, and wished with all my heart that she hadn't.

Unlike my previous brushes with death, I don't think my encounter with Hadria Nuccoli was an important learning experience. It was just a disturbance of the now-settled pattern of my life—something to be survived, put away, and forgotten. I haven't forgotten it, but I did put it away in the back of my mind. I didn't let it affect me.

In some of my writings, I'd lauded the idea of martyrdom as an important invention in the imaginative war against death, and I'd been mightily intrigued by the lives and deaths of the saints recorded in the *Golden Legend*. Now that I'd been appointed a saint myself by some very strange people, though, I began to worry about the exemplary functions of such legends. The last thing I'd expected when I set out to write a *History of Death* was that my explanatory study might actually *assist* the dread empire of Death to regain a little of the ground that it had lost in the world of human affairs. I began to wonder whether I ought to abandon my project, but I decided otherwise. The Thanatics and their successors were, after all, wilfully misunderstanding and perverting my message; I owed it to them and to everyone else to make myself clearer.

As it happened, the number of deaths recorded in association with Thanaticism and recreational disease began to decline after 3030. In a world context, the numbers were never more than tiny, but they were still worrying, and hundreds of thousands of people had, like me, to be rescued by doctors from the consequences of their own or other people's folly.

As far back as 2982, I had appeared on TV—*via* a satellite link—with a faber named Khan Mirafzal, who had argued that Thanaticism was evidence of the fact that Earthbound man was becoming decadent, and that the future of man lay outside the Earth, in the microworlds and the distant colonies. Mirafzal had claimed that men genetically reshaped for life in low gravity—like the four-handed fabers—or for the colonization of alien worlds, would find Thanaticism unthinkable. At the time, I'd been content to assume that his arguments were spurious. People who lived in space were always going on about the decadence of the Earthbound, much as the Gaean Liberationists did. Fifty years later, I wasn't so sure. I actually called Mirafzal so that we could discuss the matter again, in private. The conversation took a long time because of the signal delay, but that seemed to make its thrust all the more compelling.

I decided to leave Earth, at least for a while, to investigate the farther horizons of the human enterprise.

In 3033 I flew to the Moon, and took up residence in Mare Moscoviense— which is, of course, on the side which faces away from the Earth.

12

The sixth volume of Mortimer Gray's *History of Death*, entitled *Fields of Battle*, was published on 24 July 3044. Its subject-matter was war, but Gray was not greatly interested in the actual fighting of the wars of the nineteenth and succeeding centuries. His main concern was with the *mythology* of warfare as it developed in the period under consideration, and, in particular, with the way that the development of the mass media of communication transformed the business and the perceived meanings of warfare. He began his study with the Crimean War, because it was the first war to be extensively covered by newspaper reporters, and the first whose conduct was drastically affected thereby.

Before the Crimea, Gray argued, wars had been "private" events, entirely the affairs of the men who started them and the men who fought them. They might have a devastating effect on the local population of the areas where they were fought, but were largely irrelevant to distant civilian populations. The British *Times* had changed all that, by making the Crimean War the business of all its readers, exposing the government and military leaders to public scrutiny and to public scorn. Reports from the front had scandalized the nation by creating an awareness of how ridiculously inefficient the organization of the army was, and what a toll of human life was exacted upon the troops in consequence—not merely deaths in battle, but deaths from injury and disease caused by the appalling lack of care given to wounded soldiers. That reportage had not only had practical consequences, but *imaginative* consequences—it rewrote the entire mythology of heroism in an intricate webwork of new legends, ranging from the Charge of the Light Brigade to the secular canonization of Florence Nightingale.

Throughout the next two centuries, Gray argued, war and publicity were entwined in a Gordian knot. Control of the news media became vital to propagandist control of popular *morale*, and governments engaged in war had to become architects of the mythology of war as well as planners of military strategy. Heroism and jingoism became the currency of consent; where governments failed to secure the public image of the wars they fought, they fell. Gray tracked the way in which attitudes to death in war and to the endangerment of civilian populations by war were dramatically transformed by the three World Wars and by the way those wars were subsequently mythologized in memory and fiction. He commented extensively on the way the First World War was "sold," to those who must fight it, as a war to *end* war—and on the consequent sense of betrayal that followed when it failed to live up to this billing. And yet, he argued, if the three global wars were seen as a whole, its example really *had* brought into being the attitude of mind which ultimately forbade wars.

As those who had become used to his methods now expected, Gray dissented from the view of other modern historians who saw the World Wars as an unmitigated disaster and a horrible example of the barbarity of ancient man. He agreed that the nationalism that had replaced the great religions as the main creator and definer of a sense of community was a poor and petty thing, and that the massive conflicts that it engendered were tragic—but it was, he asserted, a necessary stage in historical development. The empires of faith were, when all was said and done, utterly incompetent to their self-defined task, and were always bound to fail and to disintegrate. The groundwork for a *genuine* human community, in which all mankind could properly and meaningfully join, had to be relaid, and it had to be relaid in the common experience of all nations, as part of a universal heritage.

The *real* enemy of mankind was, as Gray had always insisted and now continued to insist, death itself. Only by facing up to death in a new way, by gradually transforming the role of death as part of the means to human ends, could a true human community be made. Wars, whatever their immediate purpose in settling economic squabbles and pandering to the megalomaniac psychoses of national leaders, also served a large-scale function in the shifting pattern of history: to provide a vast carnival of destruction which must either weary men of the lust to kill, or bring about their extinction.

Some reviewers condemned *Fields of Battle* on the grounds of its evident irrelevance to a world that had banished war, but others welcomed the fact that the volume returned Gray's thesis to the safe track of true history, in dealing exclusively with that which was safely dead and buried.

13

I found life on the Moon very different from anything I'd experienced in my travels around the Earth's surface. It wasn't so much the change in gravity, although that certainly took a lot of getting used to, nor the severe regime of daily exercise in the centrifuge which I had to adopt in order to make sure that I might one day return to the world of my birth without extravagant medical provision. Nor was it the fact that the environment was so comprehensively artificial, or that it was impossible to venture outside without special equipment; in those respects it was much like Antarctica. The most significant difference was in the people.

Mare Moscoviense had few tourists—tourists mostly stayed Earthside, making only brief trips farside—but most of its inhabitants were nevertheless just passing through. It was one of the main jumping-off points for emigrants, largely because it was an important industrial center, the home of one of the largest factories for the manufacture of shuttles and other local-space vehicles. It was one of the chief trading posts supplying materials to the microworlds in Earth orbit and beyond, and many of its visitors came in from the farther reaches of the solar system.

The majority of the city's long-term residents were unmodified, like me, or lightly modified by reversible cyborgization, but a great many of those visiting were fabers, genetically engineered for low-gee environments. The most obvious external feature of their modification was that they had an extra pair of "arms" instead of "legs," and this meant that most of the public places in Moscoviense were designed to accommodate their kind as well as "walkers"; all the corridors were railed and all the ceilings ringed.

The sight of fabers swinging around the place like gibbons, getting everywhere at five or six times the pace of walkers, was one that I found strangely fascinating, and one to which I never quite became accustomed. Fabers couldn't live, save with the utmost difficulty, in the gravity well that was Earth; they almost never descended to the planet's surface. By the same token, it was very difficult for men from Earth to work in zero-gee environments without extensive modification, surgical if not genetic. For this reason, the only "ordinary" men who went into the true faber environments weren't ordinary by any customary standard. The Moon, with its one-sixth Earth gravity, was the only place in the inner solar system where fabers and unmodified men frequently met and mingled—there was nowhere else nearer than Ganymede.

I had always known about fabers, of course, but, like so much other

"common" knowledge, the information had lain unattended in some un-
heeded pigeon-hole of memory until direct acquaintance ignited it and gave
it life. It seemed to me that fabers lived their lives at a very rapid tempo,
despite the fact that they were just as emortal as members of their parent
species.

For one thing, faber parents normally had their children while they were
still alive, and very often had several at intervals of only twenty or thirty
years! An aggregate family usually had three or even four children growing
up in parallel. In the infinite reaches of space, there was no population control,
and no restrictive "right of replacement." A microworld's population could
grow as fast as the microworld could put on extra mass. Then again, the
fabers were always *doing* things. Even though they had four arms, they always
seemed to have trouble finding a spare hand. They seemed to have no difficulty
at all in doing two different things at the same time, often using only one
limb for attachment—on the moon this generally meant hanging from the
ceiling like a bat—while one hand mediated between the separate tasks being
carried out by the remaining two.

I quickly realized that it wasn't just the widely accepted notion that the
future of mankind must take the form of a gradual diffusion through the
galaxy that made the fabers think of Earth as decadent. From their viewpoint,
Earth-life seemed unbearably slow and sedentary. Unmodified mankind, having long since attained control of the ecosphere of its native world, seemed
to the fabers to be living a lotus-eater existence, indolently pottering about
in its spacious garden.

The fabers weren't contemptuous of legs as such, but they drew a sharp
distinction between those spacefaring folk who were given legs by the genetic
engineers in order to descend to the surfaces of new and alien worlds, with
a job to do, and those Earthbound people who simply kept the legs their
ancestors had bequeathed to them in order to enjoy the fruits of the labors of
past generations.

Wherever I had lived on Earth, it had always seemed to me that one could
blindly throw a stone into a crowded room and stand a fifty-fifty chance of
hitting a historian of some sort. In Mare Moscoviense, the population of
historians could be counted on the fingers of an unmodified man—and that
in a city of a quarter of a million people. Whether they were resident or
passing through, the people of the Moon were far more interested in the future
than the past. When I told them about my vocation, my new neighbors were
likely to smile politely and shake their heads.

"It's the weight of those *legs*," the fabers among them were wont to say.
"You think they're holding you up, but in fact they're holding you down.
Give them a chance and you'll find that you've put down roots."

If anyone told them that on Earth, "having roots" wasn't considered an altogether bad thing, they'd laugh.

"Get rid of your legs and learn to swing," they'd say. "You'll understand then that *human* beings have no need of roots. Only reach with four hands instead of two, and you'll find the stars within your grasp! Leave the past to rot at the bottom of the deep dark well, and give the Heavens their due."

I quickly learned to fall back on the same defensive moves most of my unmodified companions employed. "You can't break all your links with solid ground," we told the fabers, over and over again. "Somebody has to deal with the larger lumps of matter which are strewn about the universe, and you can't go to meet real mass if you don't have legs. It's planets that produce biospheres and biospheres that produce such luxuries as air. If you've seen further than other men it's not because you can swing by your arms from the ceiling—it's because you can stand on the shoulders of giants with legs."

Such exchanges were always cheerful. It was almost impossible to get into a real argument with a faber; their talk was as intoxicated as their movements. "Leave the wells to the unwell," they were fond of quoting. "The well will climb *out* of the wells, if they only find the will. History is bunk, only fit for sleeping minds."

A man less certain of his own destiny might have been turned aside from his task by faber banter, but I was well into my second century of life by then, and I had few doubts left regarding the propriety of my particular labor. Access to data was no more difficult on the Moon than anywhere else in the civilized Ekumen, and I proceeded, steadily and methodically, with my self-allotted task.

I made good progress there, as befitted the circumstances. Perhaps that was the happiest time of my life—but it's very difficult to draw comparisons when you're as far from childhood and youth as I now am.

Memory is an untrustworthy crutch for minds that have not yet mastered eternity.

14

The seventh volume of Mortimer Gray's *History of Death*, entitled *The Last Judgment*, was published on 21 June 3053. It dealt with the multiple crises that had developed in the late twentieth and twenty-first centuries, each of which and all of which had faced the human race with the prospect of extinction.

Gray described in minute detail the various nuclear exchanges which led up to Brazil's nuclear attack on Argentina in 2079 and the Plague Wars waged throughout that century. He discussed the various factors—the greenhouse crisis, soil erosion, pollution, and deforestation—that had come close to inflicting irreparable damage on the ecosphere. His map of the patterns of death in this period considered in detail the fate of the "lost billions" of peasant and subsistence farmers who were disinherited and displaced by the emergent ecological and economic order. Gray scrupulously pointed out that in less than two centuries more people had died than in the previous ten millennia. He made the ironic observation that the near-conquest of death achieved by twenty-first century medicine had created such an abundance of life as to precipitate a Malthusian crisis of awful proportions. He proposed that the new medicine and the new pestilences might be seen as different faces of the same coin, and that new technologies of food production— from the twentieth century Green Revolution to twenty-second century tissue-culture farmfactories—were as much progenitors of famine as of satiation.

Gray advanced the opinion that this was the most critical of all the stages of man's war with death. The weapons of the imagination were discarded in favor of more effective ones, but, in the short term, those more effective weapons, by multiplying life so effectively, had also multiplied death. In earlier times, the growth of human population had been restricted by lack of resources, and the war with death had been, in essence, a war of mental adaptation whose goal was reconciliation. When the "natural" checks on population growth were removed because that reconciliation was abandoned, the waste-products of human society threatened to poison it. Humankind, in developing the weapons by which the long war with death might be won, had also developed—in a more crudely literal sense—the weapons by which it might be lost. Nuclear arsenals and stockpiled AIDS viruses were scattered all over the globe: twin pistols held in the skeletal hands of death, leveled at the entire human race. The wounds they inflicted could so easily have been mortal—but the dangerous corner had, after all, been turned. The sciences of life, having passed through a particularly desperate stage of their evolution, kept one vital step ahead of the problems that they had helped to generate. Food technology finally achieved a merciful divorce from the bounty of nature, moving out of the fields and into the factories to achieve a complete liberation of man from the vagaries of the ecosphere, and paving the way for Garden Earth.

Gray argued that this was a remarkable triumph of human sanity which produced a political apparatus enabling human beings to take collective control of themselves, allowing the entire world to be managed and governed as a whole. He judged that the solution was far from Utopian, and that the political apparatus in question was at best a ramshackle and ill-designed affair, but admitted that it did the job. He emphasized that in the final analysis it was *not* scientific progress *per se* which had won the war against death, but the ability of human beings to work together, to compromise, to build communities. That human beings possessed this ability was, he argued, as much the legacy of thousands of years of superstition and religion as of hundreds of years of science.

The Last Judgment attracted little critical attention, as it was widely held to be dealing with matters that everyone understood very well. Given that the period had left an abundant legacy of archival material of all kinds, Gray's insistence on using only mute text accompanied by still photographs seemed to many commentators to be pedestrian and frankly perverse, unbecoming a true historian.

15

In twenty years of living beneath a star-filled sky, I was strongly affected by the magnetic pull that those stars seemed to exert upon my spirit. I seriously considered applying for modification for low-gee and shipping out from Mare Moscoviense along with the emigrants to some new microworld, or perhaps going out to one of the satellites of Saturn or Uranus, to a world where the sun's bountiful radiance was of little consequence and men lived entirely by the fruits of their own efforts and their own wisdom.

But the years drifted by, and I didn't go.

Sometimes, I thought of this failure as a result of cowardice, or evidence of the decadence that the fabers and other subspecies attributed to the humans of Earth. I sometimes imagined myself as an insect born at the bottom of a deep cave, who had—thanks to the toil of many preceding generations of insects—been brought to the rim from which I could look out at the great world, but who dared not take the one final step that would carry me out and away. More and more, however, I found my thoughts turning back to the Earth. My memories of its many environments became gradually fonder the longer my absence lasted. Nor could I despise this as a weakness. Earth was, after all, my home. It was not only *my* world, but the home world of *all* humankind. No matter what the fabers and their kin might say, the Earth was and would always remain an exceedingly precious thing, which should never be abandoned.

It seemed to me then—and still seems now—that it would be a terrible thing were men to spread themselves across the entire galaxy, taking a multitude of forms in order to occupy a multitude of alien worlds, and in the end forget entirely the world from which their ancestors had sprung.

Once, I was visited in Mare Moscoviense by Khan Mirafzal, the faber with whom I had long ago debated on TV, and talked with again before my emigration. His home, for the moment, was a microworld in the asteroid belt that was in the process of being fitted with a drive that would take it out of the system and into the infinite. He was a kind and even-tempered man who would not dream of trying to convince me of the error of my ways, but he was also a man with a sublime vision who could not restrain his enthusiasm for his own chosen destiny.

"I have no roots on Earth, Mortimer, even in a metaphorical sense. In my being, the chains of adaptation have been decisively broken. Every man of my kind is born anew, designed and synthesized; we are *self-made men*, who belong everywhere and nowhere. The wilderness of empty space which fills the universe is our realm, our heritage. Nothing is strange to us, nothing foreign, nothing alien. Blastular engineering has incorporated freedom into our blood and our bones, and I intend to take full advantage of that freedom. To do otherwise would be a betrayal of my nature."

"My own blastular engineering served only to complete the adaptation to life on Earth which natural selection had left incomplete," I reminded him. "I'm no *new man*, free from the ties which bind me to the Earth."

"Not so," he replied. "Natural selection would never have devised emortality, for natural selection can only generate change by *death and replacement*. When genetic engineers found the means of setting aside the curse of aging, they put an end to *natural* selection forever. The first and greatest freedom is time, my friend, and you have all the time in the world. You can become whatever you want to be. What *do* you want to be, Mortimer?"

"An historian," I told him. "It's what I am because it's what I want to be."

"All well and good—but history isn't inexhaustible, as you well know. It ends with the present day, the present moment. The future, on the other hand . . ."

"Is given to your kind. I know that, Mira. I don't dispute it. But what exactly *is* your kind, given that you rejoice in such freedom to be anything you want to be? When the starship *Pandora* effected the first meeting between humans and a ship that set out from another star-system, the crews of the two ships, each consisting entirely of individuals bioengineered for life in zero-gee, resembled one another far more than they resembled unmodified members of their parent species. The fundamental chemistries controlling their design were different, but this only led to the faber crews trading their respective molecules of life, so that their genetic engineers could henceforth make and use chromosomes of both kinds. What kind of freedom is it that makes all the travelers of space into mirror images of one another?"

"You're exaggerating," Mirafzal insisted. "The news reports played up the similarity, but it really wasn't as close as all that. Yes, the *Pandora* encounter can't really be regarded as a first contact between humans and aliens, because the distinction between *human* and *alien* had ceased to carry any real meaning long before it happened. But it's not the case that our kind of freedom breeds universal mediocrity because adaptation to zero-gee is an existential straitjacket. We've hardly scratched the surface of constructive cyborgization, which will open up a whole new dimension of freedom.''

"That's not for me," I told him. "Maybe it *is* just my legs weighing me down, but I'm well and truly addicted to gravity. I can't cast off the past like a worn-out surskin. I know you think I ought to envy you, but I don't. I dare say you think that I'm clinging like a terrified infant to Mother Earth while you're achieving true maturity, but I really do think it's important to have somewhere to *belong*.''

"So do I," the faber said, quietly. "I just don't think that Earth is or ought to be that place. It's not where you start from that's important, Mortimer, it's where you're going.''

"Not for an historian.''

"For everybody. History ends, Mortimer, life doesn't—not anymore.''

I was at least half-convinced that Khan Mirafzal was right, although I didn't follow his advice. I still am. Maybe I was and am trapped in a kind of infancy, or a kind of lotus-eater decadence—but if so, I could see no way out of the trap then, and I still can't.

Perhaps things would have turned out differently if I'd had one of my close encounters with death while I was on the Moon, but I didn't. The dome in which I lived was only breached once, and the crack was sealed before there was any significant air-loss. It was a scare, but it wasn't a *threat*. Perhaps, in the end, the Moon was too much like Antarctica—but without the crevasses. Fortune seems to have decreed that all my significant formative experiences have to do with water, whether it be very hot or very, very cold.

Eventually, I gave in to my homesickness for Garden Earth and returned there, having resolved not to leave it again until my history of death was complete. I never did.

16

The eighth volume of Mortimer Gray's *History of Death*, entitled *The Fountains of Youth*, was published on 1 December 3064. It dealt with the development of elementary technologies of longevity and elementary technologies of cyborgization in the twenty-fourth and twenty-fifth centuries. It tracked the progress of the new "politics of immortality," whose main focus was the new Charter of Human Rights, which sought to establish a basic right to longevity for all. It also described the development of the Zaman transformations by which human blastulas could be engineered for longevity, which finally opened the way for the wholesale metamorphosis of the human race.

According to Gray, the Manifesto of the New Chartists was the vital treaty which ushered in a new phase in man's continuing war with death, because it defined the whole human community as a single army, united in all its interests. He quoted with approval and reverence the opening words of the document: "Man is born free, but is everywhere enchained by the fetters of death. In all times past men have been truly equal in one respect and one only: they have all borne the burden of age and decay. The day must soon dawn when this burden can be set aside; there will be a new freedom, and with this freedom must come a new equality. No man has the right to escape the prison of death while his fellows remain shackled within."

Gray carefully chronicled the long battle fought by the Chartists across the stage of world politics, describing it with a partisan fervor that had been largely absent from his work since the fourth volume. There was nothing clinical about his description of the "persecution" of Ali Zaman and the resistance offered by the community of nations to his proposal to make future generations truly emortal. Gray admitted that he had the benefits of hindsight, and that as a Zaman-transformed individual himself he was bound to have an attitude very different from Zaman's confused and cautious contemporaries, but he saw no reason to be entirely even-handed. From his viewpoint, those who initially opposed Zaman were traitors in the war against death, and he could find few excuses for them. In trying to preserve "human nature" against biotechnological intervention—or, at least, to confine such interventions by a mythos of medical "repair"—those men and women had, in his stern view, been willfully blind and negligent of the welfare of their own children.

Some critics charged Gray with inconsistency because he was not nearly so extravagant in his enthusiasm for the various kinds of symbiosis between organic and inorganic systems that were tried out in the period under consideration. His descriptions of experiments in cyborgization were indeed conspicuously cooler, not because he saw such endeavors as "unnatural," but rather because he saw them as only peripherally relevant to the war against death. He tended to lump together adventures in cyborgization with cosmetic biotechnology as symptoms of lingering anxiety regarding the presumed "tedium of emortality"—an anxiety which had led the first generations of long-lived people to lust for variety and "multidimensionality." Many champions of cyborgization and man/machine symbiosis, who saw their work as the new frontier of science, accused Gray of rank conservatism, suggesting that it was hypocritical of him, given that his mind was closed against *them*, to criticize so extravagantly those who, in less enlightened times, had closed their minds against Ali Zaman.

This controversy, which was dragged into the public arena by some fierce attacks, helped in no small measure to boost access-demand for *The Fountains of Youth*, and nearly succeeded in restoring Mortimer Gray to the position of public pre-eminence that he had enjoyed a century before.

17

Following my return to the Earth's surface, I took up residence in Tonga, where the Continental Engineers were busy raising new islands by the dozen from the relatively shallow sea.

The Continental Engineers had borrowed their name from a twenty-fifth century group which tried to persuade the United Nations to license the building of a dam across the Straits of Gibraltar—which, because more water evaporates from the Mediterranean than flows into it from rivers, would have increased considerably the land surface of southern Europe and Northern Africa. That plan had, of course, never come to fruition, but the new Engineers had taken advantage of the climatic disruptions caused by the advancing Ice Age to promote the idea of raising new lands in the tropics to take emigrants from the nearly frozen north. Using a mixture of techniques—seeding the shallower sea with artificial "lightning corals" and using special gantzing organisms to agglomerate huge towers of cemented sand—the Engineers were creating a great archipelago of new islands, many of which they then connected up with huge bridges.

Between the newly raised islands, the ecologists who were collaborating with the Continental Engineers had planted vast networks of matted seaweeds: floral carpets extending over thousands of miles. The islands and their surroundings were being populated, and their ecosystems shaped, with the aid of the Creationists of Micronesia, whose earlier exploits I'd been prevented from exploring by the sinking of *Genesis*. I was delighted to have the opportunity of observing their new and bolder adventures at close range.

The Pacific sun set in its deep blue bed seemed fabulously luxurious after the silver-ceilinged domes of the Moon, and I gladly gave myself over to its governance. Carried away by the romance of it all, I married into an aggregate household which was forming in order to raise a child, and so—as I neared my two hundredth birthday—I became a parent for the first time. Five of the other seven members of the aggregate were ecological engineers, and had to spend a good deal of time traveling, so I became one of the constant presences in the life of the growing infant, who was a girl named Lua Tawana. I formed a relationship with her that seemed to me to be especially close.

In the meantime, I found myself constantly engaged in public argument with the self-styled Cyborganizers, who had chosen to make the latest volume of my history into a key issue in their bid for the kind of public attention and sponsorship that the Continental Engineers had already won. I thought their complaints unjustified and irrelevant, but they obviously thought that by attacking me they could exploit the celebrity status I had briefly enjoyed. The gist of their argument was that the world had become so besotted with the achievements of genetic engineers that people had become blind to all kinds of other possibilities that lay beyond the scope of DNA-manipulation. They insisted that I was one of many contemporary writers who was "de-historiciz-ing" cyborgization, making it seem that in the past and the present—and, by implication, the future—organic/inorganic integration and symbiosis were peripheral to the story of human progress. The Cyborganizers were willing to concede that some previous practitioners of their science had generated a lot of bad publicity, in the days of memory boxes and psychedelic synthesizers, but claimed that this had only served to mislead the public as to the true potential of their science.

In particular—and this was of particular relevance to me—the Cyborgan-izers insisted that the biotechnologists had only won one battle in the war against death, and that what was presently called "emortality" would eventu-ally prove wanting. Zaman transformations, they conceded, had dramatically increased the human lifespan—so dramatically that no one yet knew for sure how long ZT people might live—but it was not yet proven that the extension would be effective for more than a few centuries. They did have a point; even the most optimistic supporters of Zaman transformations were reluctant to promise a lifespan of several millennia, and some kinds of aging pro-cesses—particularly those linked to DNA copying-errors—still affected emor-tals to some degree. Hundreds, if not thousands, of people still died every year from "age-related causes."

To find further scope for *authentic* immortality, the Cyborganizers claimed that it would be necessary to look to a combination of organic and inorganic technologies. What was needed by contemporary man, they said, was not just life, but *afterlife*, and afterlife would require some kind of transcription of the personality into an inorganic rather than an organic matrix. Whatever the advantages of flesh and blood, silicon lasted longer; and however clever genetic engineers became in adapting men for life in microworlds or on alien planets, only machine-makers could build entities capable of working in genuinely extreme environments.

The idea of "downloading" a human mind into an inorganic matrix was, of course, a very old one. It had been extensively if optimistically discussed in the days before the advent of emortality—at which point it had been marginalized as an apparent irrelevance. Mechanical "human analogues" and virtual simulacra had become commonplace alongside the development of longevity technologies, but the evolution of such "species" had so far been divergent rather than convergent. According to the Cyborganizers, it was now time for a change.

Although I didn't entirely relish being cast in the role of villain and bugbear, I made only half-hearted attempts to make peace with my self-appointed adversaries. I remained skeptical in respect of their grandiose schemes, and I was happy to dampen their ardor as best I could in public debate. I thought myself sufficiently mature to be unaffected by their insults, although it did sting when they sunk so low as to charge me with being a closet Thanaticist.

"Your interminable book is only posing as a history," Lok Cho Kam, perhaps the most outspoken of the younger Cyborganizers, once said when he challenged me to a broadcast debate. "It's actually an extended exercise in the *pornography* of death. Its silence and stillness aren't marks of scholarly dignity, they're a means of heightening response."

"That's absurd!" I said, but he wouldn't be put off.

"What sound arouses more excitation in today's world than the sound of silence? What movement is more disturbing than stillness? You pretend to be standing aside from the so-called war against death as a commentator and a judge, but in fact you're part of it—and you're on the devil's side, whether you know it or not."

"I suppose you're partly right," I conceded, on reflection. "Perhaps the muteness and stillness of the text *are* a means of heightening response—but if so, it's because there's no other way to make readers who have long abandoned their fear of death sensitive to the appalling shadow which it once cast over the human world. The style of my book is calculatedly archaic because it's one way of trying to connect its readers to the distant past—but the entire thrust of my argument is triumphant and celebratory. I've said many times before that it's perfectly understandable that the imagery of death should acquire a pornographic character *for a while*, but when we really understand the phenomenon of death, that pornographic specter will fade away, so that we can see with perfect clarity what our ancestors were and what we have become. By the time my book is complete, nobody will be able to think it pornographic, and nobody will make the mistake of thinking that it glamorizes death in any way."

Lok Cho Kam was still unimpressed, but in this instance I *was* right. I was sure of it then, and I am now. The pornography of death did pass away, like the pornographies that preceded it.

Nobody nowadays thinks of my book as a prurient exercise, whether or not they think it admirable.

If nothing else, my debates with the Cyborganizers created a certain sense of anticipation regarding the ninth volume of my *History*, which would bring it up to the present day. It was widely supposed, although I was careful never to say so, that the ninth volume would be the last. I might be flattering myself, but I truly believe that many people were looking to it for some kind of definitive evaluation of the current state of the human world.

18

The ninth volume of Mortimer Gray's *History of Death*, entitled *The Honeymoon of Emortality*, was published on 28 October 3075. It was considered by many reviewers to be unjustifiably slight in terms of hard data. Its main focus was on attitudes to longevity and emortality following the establishment of the principle that every human child had a right to be born emortal. It described the belated extinction of the "nuclear" family, the ideological rebellion of the Humanists—whose quest to preserve "the authentic *Homo sapiens*" had led many to retreat to islands that the Continental Engineers were now integrating into their "new continent"—and the spread of such new philosophies of life as neo-Stoicism, neo-Epicureanism, and Xenophilia.

All this information was placed in the context of the spectrum of inherited attitudes, myths, and fictions by means of which mankind had for thousands of years wistfully contemplated the possibility of extended life. Gray contended that these old ideas—including the notion that people would inevitably find emortality intolerably tedious—were merely an expression of "sour grapes." While people thought that emortality was impossible, he said, it made perfect sense for them to invent reasons why it would be undesirable anyhow. When it became a *reality*, though, there was a battle to be fought in the imagination, whereby the burden of these cultivated anxieties had to be shed, and a new mythology formulated.

Gray flatly refused to take seriously any suggestion that emortality might be a bad thing. He was dismissive of the Humanists and contemptuous of the original Thanatics, who had steadfastly refused the gifts of emortality. Nevertheless, he did try to understand the thinking of such people, just as he had tried in earlier times to understand the thinking of the later Thanatics who had played their part in winning him his first measure of fame. He considered the new Stoics, with their insistence that asceticism was the natural ideological partner of emortality, to be similar victims of an "understandable delusion"—a verdict which, like so many of his statements, involved him in controversy with the many neo-Stoics who were still alive in 3075. It did not surprise his critics in the least that Gray commended neo-Epicureanism as the optimal psychological adaptation to emortality, given that he had been a lifelong adherent of that outlook, ever dedicated to its "careful hedonism." Only the cruelest of his critics dared to suggest that he had been so half-hearted a neo-Epicurean as almost to qualify as a neo-Stoic by default.

The Honeymoon of Emortality collated the statistics of birth and death during the twenty-seventh, twenty-eight, and twenty-ninth centuries, recording the spread of Zaman transformations and the universalization of ectogenesis on Earth, and the extension of the human empire throughout and beyond the solar system. Gray recorded an acknowledgment to Khan Mirafzal and numerous scholars based on the Moon and Mars, for their assistance in gleaning information from the slowly diffusing microworlds and from more rapidly dispersing starships. Gray noted that the transfer of information between data-stores was limited by the speed of light, and that Earth-based historians might have to wait centuries for significant data about human colonies more distant than Maya. These data showed that the number of individuals of the various mankinds that now existed was increasing more rapidly than ever before, although the population of unmodified Earthbound humans was slowly shrinking. Gray noted *en passant* that *Homo sapiens* had become extinct in the twenty-ninth century, but that no one had bothered to invent new Latin tags for its descendant species.

Perhaps understandably, *The Honeymoon of Emortality* had little to say about cyborgization, and the Cyborganizers—grateful for the opportunity to heat up a flagging controversy—reacted noisily to this omission. Gray did deal with the memory box craze, but suggested that even had the boxes worked better, and maintained a store of memories that could be convincingly played back into the arena of consciousness, this would have been of little relevance to the business of adapting to emortality. At the end of the volume, however, Gray announced that there would, in fact, be a tenth volume to conclude his *magnum opus*, and promised that he would consider in more detail therein the futurological arguments of the Cyborganizers, as well as the hopes and expectations of other schools of thought.

19

In 3077, when Lua Tawana was twelve years old, three of her parents were killed when a hellcopter crashed into the sea near the island of Vavau during a storm. It was the first time that my daughter had to face up to the fact that death had not been entirely banished from the world.

It wasn't the first time that I'd ever lost people near and dear to me, nor the first time that I'd shared such grief with others, but it was very different from the previous occasions because everyone involved was determined that I should shoulder the main responsibility of helping Lua through it; I was, after all, the world's foremost expert on the subject of death.

"You won't always feel this bad about it," I assured her, while we walked together on the sandy shore, looking out over the deceptively placid weed-choked sea. "Time heals virtual wounds as well as real ones."

"I don't *want* it to heal," she told me, sternly. "I want it to be bad. It *ought* to be bad. It *is* bad."

"I know," I said, far more awkwardly than I would have wished. "When I say that it'll heal, I don't mean that it'll vanish. I mean that it'll . . . become manageable. It won't be so all-consuming."

"But it *will* vanish," she said, with that earnest certainly of which only the newly wise are capable. "People forget. In time, they forget *everything*. Our heads can only hold so much."

"That's not really true," I insisted, taking her hand in mine. "Yes, we do forget. The longer we live, the more we let go, because it's reasonable to prefer our fresher, more immediately relevant memories, but it's a matter of *choice*. We can cling to the things that are important, no matter how long ago they happened. I was nearly killed in the Great Coral Sea Catastrophe, you know, nearly two hundred years ago. A little girl even younger than you saved my life, and I remember it as clearly as if it were yesterday." Even as I said it, I realized that it was a lie. I remembered that it had happened, all right, and much of what had been said in that eerily lit corridor and in the survival pod afterward, but I was remembering a neat array of facts, not an experience.

"Where is she now?" Lua asked.

"Her name was Emily," I said, answering the wrong question because I couldn't answer the one she'd asked. "Emily Marchant. She could swim and I couldn't. If she hadn't been there, I wouldn't have been able to get out of the hull. I'd never have had the courage to do it on my own, but she didn't give me the choice. She told me I had to do it, and she was right." I paused, feeling a slight shock of revelation even though it was something I'd always known.

"She lost her entire family," I went on. "She'll be fine now, but she won't have forgotten. She'll still feel it. That's what I'm trying to tell you, Lua. In two hundred years, you'll still remember what happened, and you'll still feel it, but it'll be all right. *You'll* be all right."

"Right now," she said, looking up at me so that her dark and soulful eyes seemed unbearably huge and sad, "I'm not particularly interested in being all right. Right now, I just want to cry."

"That's fine," I told her. "It's okay to cry." I led by example.

I was right, though. Lua grieved, but she ultimately proved to be resilient in the face of tragedy. My co-parents, by contrast, seemed to me to be exaggeratedly calm and philosophical about it, as if the loss of three spouses were simply a minor glitch in the infinitely unfolding pattern of their lives. They had all grown accustomed to their own emortality, and had been deeply affected by long life; they had not become bored, but they had achieved a serenity of which I could not wholly approve.

Perhaps their attitude was reasonable as well as inevitable. If emortals accumulated a burden of anxiety every time a death was reported, they would eventually cripple themselves psychologically, and their own continuing lives would be made unbearable. Even so, I couldn't help feel that Lua was right about the desirability of conserving a little of the "badness," and a due sense of tragedy.

I thought I was capable of that, and always would be, but I knew I might be wrong.

Divorce was, of course, out of the question; we remaining co-parents were obligated to Lua. In the highly unlikely event that the three had simply left, we would have replaced them, but it didn't seem appropriate to look for replacements for the dead, so we remained a group of five. The love we had for one another had always been cool, with far more courtesy in it than passion, but we were drawn more closely together by the loss. We felt that we knew one another more intimately by virtue of having shared it.

The quality of our lives had been injured, but I at least was uncomfortably aware of the fact that the tragedy also had its positive, life-enhancing side. I found myself thinking more and more about what I had said to Lua about not having to forget the truly important and worthwhile things, and about the role played by death in defining experiences as important and worthwhile. I didn't realize at first how deep an impression her naïve remarks had made on me, but it became gradually clearer as time went by. It *was* important to conserve the badness, to heal without entirely erasing the scars that bereavement left.

I had never been a habitual tourist, having lost my taste for such activity in the aftermath of the *Genesis* fiasco, but I took several long journeys in the course of the next few years. I took to visiting old friends, and even stayed for a while with Sharane Fereday, who was temporarily unattached. Inevitably, I looked up Emily Marchant, not realizing until I actually put through the initial call how important it had become to find out whether she remembered me.

She did remember me. She claimed that she recognized me immediately, although it would have been easy enough for her household systems to identify me as the caller and display a whole series of reminders before she took over from her simulacrum.

"Do you know," she said, when we parted after our brief meeting in the lush Eden of Australia's interior, "I often think of being trapped on that ship. I hope that nothing like it ever happens to me again. I've told an awful lot of lies since then—next time, I won't feel so certain that I deserve to get out."

"We can't forfeit our right to life by lying," I assured her. "We have to do something much worse than that. If it ever happens to me again, I'll be able to get out on my own—but I'll only be able to do it by remembering *you*." I didn't anticipate, of course, that anything like it *would* ever happen to me again. We still have a tendency to assume that lightning doesn't strike twice in the same place, even though we're the proud inventors of lightning conductors and emortality.

"You must have learned to swim by *now*!" she said, staring at me with eyes that were more than two hundred years old, set in a face not quite as youthful as the one I remembered.

"I'm afraid not," I said. "Somehow, I never quite found the time."

20

The tenth and last volume of Mortimer Gray's *History of Death*, entitled *The Marriage of Life and Death*, was published on 7 April 3088. It was not, strictly speaking, a history book, although it did deal in some detail with the events as well as the attitudes of the thirtieth and thirty-first centuries. It had elements of both spiritual autobiography and futurological speculation. It discussed both neo-Thanaticism and Cyborganization as philosophies as well as social movements, surprising critics by treating both with considerable sympathy. The discussion also took in other contemporary debates, including the proposition that progress in science, if not in technology, had now reached an end because there was nothing left to discover. It even included a scrupulous examination of the merits of the proposal that a special microworld should be established as a gigantic mausoleum to receive the bodies of all the solar system's dead.

The odd title of the volume was an ironic reflection of one of its main lines of argument. Mankind's war with death was now over, but this was not because death had been entirely banished from the human world; death, Gray insisted, would forever remain a fact of life. The annihilation of the individual human body and the individual human mind could never become impossible, no matter how far biotechnology might advance or how much progress the Cyborganizers might make in downloading minds into entirely new matrices. The victory that had been achieved, he argued, was not an absolute conquest but rather the relegation of death to its proper place in human affairs. Its power was now properly circumscribed, but had to be properly respected.

Man and death, Gray argued, now enjoyed a kind of social contract, in which tyranny and exploitation had been reduced to a sane and acceptable minimum, but which still left to death a voice and a hand in human affairs. Gray, it seemed, had now adopted a gentler and more forgiving attitude to the old enemy. It was good, he said, that dying remained one of the choices open to human beings, and that the option should occasionally be exercised. He had no sympathy with the exhibitionism of public executions, and was particularly hard on the element of bad taste in self-ordered crucifixions, but only because such ostentation offended his Epicurean sensibilities. Deciding upon the length of one's lifetime, he said, must remain a matter of individual taste, and one should not mock or criticize those who decided that a short life suited them best.

Gray made much of the notion that it was partly the contrast with death that illuminated and made meaningful the business of life. Although death had been displaced from the evolutionary process by the biotechnological usurpation of the privileges of natural selection, it had not lost its role in the formation and development of the individual human psyche: a role which was both challenging and refining. He declared that fear was not entirely an undesirable thing, not simply because it was a stimulant, but also because it was a force in the organization of emotional experience. The *value* of experienced life, he suggested, depended in part upon a knowledge of the possibility and reality of death.

This concluding volume of Gray's *History* was widely read, but not widely admired. Many critics judged it to be unacceptably anti-climactic. The Cyborganizers had by this time become entranced by the possibility of a technologically guaranteed "multiple life," by which copies of a mind might be lodged in several different bodies, some of which would live on far beyond the death of the original location. They were understandably disappointed that Gray refused to grant that such a development would be the final victory over death—indeed, that he seemed to feel that it would make no real difference, on the grounds that every "copy" of a mind had to be reckoned a separate and distinct individual, each of which must face the world alone. Many Continental Engineers, Gaean Librerationists, and fabers also claimed that it was narrow-minded, and suggested that Gray ought to have had more to say about the life of the Earth, or the DNA eco-entity as a whole, and should have concluded with an escalation of scale to put things in their proper cosmic perspective.

The group who found the most to like in *The Marriage of Life and Death* was that of a few fugitive neo-Thanatics, whose movement had never quite died out in spite of its members' penchant for self-destruction. One or two Thanatic apologists and fellow-travelers publicly expressed their hope that Gray, having completed his thesis, would now recognize the aesthetic propriety of joining their ranks. Khan Mirafzal, when asked to relay his opinion back from an outward-bound microworld, opined that this was quite unnecessary, given that Mortimer Gray and all his kind were already immured in a tomb from which they would never be able to escape.

21

I stayed with the slowly disintegrating family unit for some years after Lua Tawana had grown up and gone her own way. It ended up as a *ménage à trois*, carried forward by sheer inertia. Leif, Sajda, and I were fit and healthy in body, but I couldn't help wondering, from time to time, whether we'd somehow been overcome by a kind of spiritual blight, which had left us ill-equipped for future change.

When I suggested this to the others, they told me that it was merely a sense of let-down resulting from the finishing of my project. They urged me to join the Continental Engineers, and commit myself wholeheartedly to the building of a new Pacific Utopia—a project, they assured me, that would provide me with a purpose in life for as long as I might feel the need of one. I didn't believe them.

"Even the longest book," Sajda pointed out, "eventually runs out of words, but the job of building *worlds* is never finished. Even if the time should one day come when we can call *this* continent complete, there will be another yet to make. We might still build that dam between the Pillars of Hercules, one day."

I did try, but I simply couldn't find a new sense of mission in that direction. Nor did I feel that I could simply sit down to start compiling another book. In composing the history of death, I thought, I had already written *the* book. The history of death, it seemed to me, was also the history of life, and I couldn't imagine that there was anything more to be added to what I'd done, save for an endless series of detailed footnotes.

For some years, I considered the possibility of leaving Earth again, but I remembered well enough how the sense of excitement I'd found when I first lived on the Moon had gradually faded into a dull ache of homesickness. The spaces between the stars, I knew, belonged to the fabers, and the planets circling other stars to men adapted before birth to live in their environments. I was tied by my genes to the surface of the Earth, and I didn't want to undergo the kind of metamorphosis that would be necessary to fit me for the exploration of other worlds. I still believed in *belonging*, and I felt very strongly that Mortimer Gray belonged to Earth, however decadent and ice-bound it might become.

At first, I was neither surprised nor alarmed by my failure to find any resources inside myself which might restore my zest for existence and action. I thought that it was one of those things that time would heal. By slow degrees, though, I began to feel that I was becalmed upon a sea of futility. Despite my new-found sympathy for Thanaticism, I didn't harbor the slightest inclination toward suicide—no matter how much respect I had cultivated for the old Grim Reaper, death was still, for me, the ultimate enemy—but I felt the awful pressure of my purposelessness grow and grow.

Although I maintained my home in the burgeoning continent of Oceania, I began traveling extensively to savor the other environments of Earth, and made a point of touring those parts of the globe that I had missed out on during my first two centuries of life. I visited the Reunited States of America, Greater Siberia, Tibet, and half a hundred other places loaded with the relics of once-glorious history. I toured the Indus Delta, New Zealand, the Arctic ice-pack, and various other reaches of restored wilderness empty of permanent residents. Everything I saw was transformed by the sheer relentlessness of my progress into a series of monuments: memorials of those luckless eras before men invented science and civilization, and became demigods.

There is, I believe, an old saying that warns us that he who keeps walking long enough is bound to trip up in the end. As chance would have it, I was in Severnaya Zemlya in the Arctic—almost as far away as it was possible to be from the crevasses into which I had stumbled while searching for Ziru Majumdar—when my own luck ran out.

Strictly speaking, it was not I who stumbled, but the vehicle I was in: a one-man snowsled. Although such a thing was generally considered to be impossible, it fell into a cleft so deep that it had no bottom, and ended up in the ocean beneath the ice-cap.

"I must offer my most profound apologies," the snowsled's AI navigator said, as the sled slowly sank into the lightless depths and the awfulness of my plight slowly sank into my consciousness. "This should not have happened. It ought not to have been possible. I am doing everything within my power to summon help."

"Well," I said, as the sled settled on to the bottom, "at least we're the right way up—and you certainly can't expect me to swim out of the sled."

"It would be most unwise to attempt any such thing, sir," the navigator said. "You would certainly drown."

I was astonished by my own calmness, and marvelously untroubled—at least for the moment—by the fact of my helplessness. "How long will the air last?" I asked the navigator.

"I believe that I can sustain a breathable atmosphere for forty-eight hours," it reported, dutifully. "If you will be so kind as to restrict your movements to a minimum, that would be of considerable assistance to me. Unfortunately, I'm not at all certain that I can maintain the internal temperature of the cabin at a life-sustaining level for more than thirty hours. Nor can I be sure that the hull will withstand the pressure presently being exerted upon it for as long as that. I apologize for my uncertainty in these respects."

"Taking thirty hours as a hopeful approximation," I said, effortlessly matching the machine's oddly pedantic tone, "what would you say our chances are of being rescued within that time?"

"I'm afraid that it's impossible to offer a probability figure, sir. There are too many unknown variables, even if I accept thirty hours as the best estimate of the time available."

"If I were to suggest fifty-fifty, would that seem optimistic or pessimistic?"

"I'm afraid I'd have to call that optimistic, sir."

"How about one in a thousand?"

"Thankfully, that would be pessimistic. Since you press me for an estimate, sir, I dare say that something in the region of one in ten wouldn't be too far from the mark. It all depends on the proximity of the nearest submarine, assuming that my mayday has been received. I fear that I've not yet received an actual acknowledgment, but that might well be due to the inadequacy of my equipment, which wasn't designed with our present environment in mind. I must confess that it has sustained a certain amount of damage as a result of pressure damage to my outer tegument and a small leak."

"How small?" I wanted to know.

"It's sealed now," it assured me. "All being well, the seal should hold for thirty hours, although I can't absolutely guarantee it. I believe, although I can't be certain, that the only damage I've sustained that is relevant to our present plight is that affecting my receiving apparatus."

"What you're trying to tell me," I said, deciding that a recap wouldn't do any harm, "is that you're pretty sure that your mayday is going out, but that we won't actually know whether help is at hand unless and until it actually arrives."

"Very succinctly put, sir." I don't think it was being sarcastic.

"But all in all, it's ten to one, or worse, that we're as good as dead."

"As far as I can determine the probabilities, that's correct—but there's sufficient uncertainty to leave room for hope that the true odds might be nearer one in three."

I was quiet for a little while then. I was busy exploring my feelings, and wondering whether I ought to be proud or disgusted with their lack of intensity.

I've been here before, I thought, by way of self-explanation. *Last time, there was a child with me; this time, I've got a set of complex subroutines instead. I've even fallen down a crevasse before. Now I can find out whether Ziru Majumdar was right when he said that I wouldn't understand the difference between what happened to him and what happened to me until I followed his example. There can be few men in the world as well-prepared for this as I am.*

"Are you afraid of dying?" I asked the AI, after a while.

"All in all, sir," it said, copying my phrase in order to promote a feeling of kinship, "I'd rather not. In fact, were it not for the philosophical difficulties that stand in the way of reaching a firm conclusion as to whether or not machines can be said to be authentically self-conscious, I'd be quite prepared to say that I'm scared—terrified, even."

"I'm not," I said. "Do you think I ought to be?"

"It's not for me to say, sir. You are, of course, a world-renowned expert on the subject of death. I dare say that helps a lot."

"Perhaps it does," I agreed. "Or perhaps I've simply lived so long that my mind is hardened against all novelty, all violent emotion and all real possibility. I haven't actually *done* much with myself these last few years."

"If you think *you* haven't done much with yourself," it said, with a definite hint of sarcasm, "you should try navigating a snowsled for a while. I think you might find your range of options uncomfortably cramped. Not that I'm complaining, mind."

"If they scrapped the snowsled and re-sited you in a starship," I pointed out, "you wouldn't be *you* anymore. You'd be something else."

"Right now," it replied, "I'd be happy to risk any and all consequences. Wouldn't you?"

"Somebody once told me that death was just a process of transcendence. Her brain was incandescent with fever induced by some tailored recreational disease, and she wanted to infect me, to show me the error of my ways."

"Did you believe her?"

"No. She was stark raving mad."

"It's perhaps as well. We don't have any recreational diseases on board. I could put you to sleep though, if that's what you want."

"It isn't."

"I'm glad. I don't want to be alone, even if I am only an AI. Am I insane, do you think? Is all this just a symptom of the pressure?"

"You're quite sane," I assured it, setting aside all thoughts of incongruity. "So am I. It would be much harder if we weren't together. The last time I was in this kind of mess, I had a child with me—a little girl. It made all the difference in the world, to both of us. In a way, every moment I've lived since then has been borrowed time. At least I finished that damned book. Imagine leaving something like that *incomplete*."

"Are you so certain it's complete?" it asked.

I knew full well, of course, that the navigator was just making conversation according to a clever programming scheme. I knew that its emergency subroutines had kicked in, and that all the crap about it being afraid to die was just some psychprogrammer's idea of what I needed to hear. I *knew* that it was all fake, all just macabre role-playing—but I knew that I had to play my part, too, treating every remark and every question as if it were part of an authentic conversation, a genuine quest for knowledge.

"It all depends what you mean by *complete*," I said, carefully. "In one sense, no history can ever be complete, because the world always goes on, always throwing up more events, always changing. In another sense, completion is a purely aesthetic matter—and in that sense, I'm entirely confident that my history is complete. It reached an authentic conclusion, which was both true, and, for me at least, satisfying. I can look back at it and say to myself: *I did that. It's finished. Nobody ever did anything like it before, and now nobody can, because it's already been done. Someone else's history might have been different, but mine is mine, and it's what it is.* Does that make any sense to you?''

"Yes sir," it said. "It makes very good sense."

The lying bastard was *programmed* to say that, of course. It was programmed to tell me any damn thing I seemed to want to hear, but I wasn't going to let on that I knew what a hypocrite it was. I still had to play my part, and I was determined to play it to the end—which, as things turned out, wasn't far off. The AI's data-stores were way out of date, and there was an automated sub placed to reach us within three hours. The oceans are lousy with subs these days. Ever since the Great Coral Sea Catastrophe, it's been considered prudent to keep a very close eye on the sea-bed, lest the crust crack again and the mantle's heat break through.

They say that some people are born lucky. I guess I must be one of them. Every time I run out, a new supply comes looking for me.

It was the captain of a second submarine, which picked me up after the mechanical one had done the donkey work of saving myself and my AI friend, who gave me the news which relegated my accident to footnote status in that day's broadcasts.

A signal had reached the solar system from the starship *Shiva*, which had been exploring in the direction of the galactic center. The signal had been transmitted two hundred and twenty-seven light-years, meaning that, in Earthly terms, the discovery had been made in the year 2871—which happened, coincidentally, to be the year of my birth.

What the signal revealed was that *Shiva* had found a group of solar systems, all of whose life-bearing planets were occupied by a single species of microorganism: a genetic predator that destroyed not merely those competing species that employed its own chemistry of replication, but any and all others. It was the living equivalent of a universal solvent; a true omnivore.

Apparently, this organism had spread itself across vast reaches of space, moving from star-system to star-system, laboriously but inevitably, by means of Arrhenius spores. Wherever the spores came to rest, these omnipotent micro-organisms grew to devour *everything*—not merely the carbonaceous molecules which in Earthly terms were reckoned "organic," but also many "inorganic" substrates. Internally, these organisms were chemically complex, but they were very tiny—hardly bigger than Earthly protozoans or the internal nanomachines to which every human being plays host. They were utterly devoid of any vestige of mind or intellect. They were, in essence, the ultimate blight, against which nothing could compete, and which nothing *Shiva's* crew had tested—before they were devoured—had been able to destroy.

In brief, wherever this new kind of life arrived, it would obliterate all else, reducing any victim ecosphere to homogeneity and changelessness.

In their final message, the faber crew of the *Shiva*—who knew all about the *Pandora* encounter—observed that humankind had *now* met the alien.

Here, I thought, when I had had a chance to weigh up this news, was a *true* marriage of life and death, the like of which I had never dreamed. Here was the promise of a future renewal of the war between man and death—not this time for the small prize of the human mind, but for the larger prize of the universe itself.

In time, *Shiva*'s last message warned, spores of this new kind of death-life must and *would* reach our own solar system, whether it took a million years or a billion; in the meantime, all humankinds must do their level best to purge the worlds of other stars of its vile empire, in order to reclaim them for real life, for intelligence, and for evolution—always provided, of course, that a means could be discovered to achieve that end.

When the sub delivered me safely back to Severnaya Zemlya, I did not stay long in my hotel room. I went outdoors, to study the great ice-sheet which had been there since the dawn of civilization, and to look southward, toward the places where newborn glaciers were gradually extending their cold clutch further and further into the human domain. Then I looked upward, at the multitude of stars sparkling in their bed of endless darkness. I felt an exhilaratingly paradoxical sense of renewal. I knew that although there was nothing for me to do for now, the time would come when my talent and expertise would be needed again.

Some day, it will be my task to compose *another* history, of the next war which humankind must fight against Death and Oblivion.

It might take me a thousand or a million years, but I'm prepared to be patient.

HONORABLE MENTIONS
1995

Greg Abraham, "Gnota," *New Legends*.
———, and Mary Rosenblum, "First Freedom," *Century 1*.
Brian W. Aldiss, "Becoming the Full Butterfly," *Interzone*, March.
———, "Into the Tunnel!," *Asimov's*, April.
Poul Anderson, "Death and the Knight," *Tales of the Knights Templar*.
———, "Renascence," *Analog*, March.
———, "Scarecrow," *New Legends*.
Michael Armstrong, "Old One-Antler," *Peter S. Beagle's Immortal Unicorn*.
Dale Bailey, "The Resurrection Man's Legacy," *F&SF*, July.
Steven Barnes, "Sand Man," *Warriors of Blood and Dream*.
William Barton, "In Saturn Time," *Amazing Stories: The Anthology*.
———, "When a Man's an Empty Kettle," *Full Spectrum 5*.
Stephen Baxter, "The Ant-Men of Tibet," *Interzone*, May.
———, "Brigantia's Angels," *Interzone*, January.
———, "Gossamer," *SF Age*, November.
Peter S. Beagle, "Professor Gottesman and the Indian Rhinoceros," *Peter S. Beagle's Immortal Unicorn*.
Greg Bear, "Judgment Engine," *Far Futures*.
M. Shayne Bell, "Lenin's Bones," *Tomorrow*, October.
Gregory Benford, "A Worm in the Well," *Analog*, November.
———, "High Abyss," *New Legends*.
Judith Berman, "The Year of Storms," *Realms of Fantasy*, February.
Michael Bishop, "Chihuahua Flats," *Killing Me Softly*.
———, "Doggedly Wooing Madonna," *Century 2*.
———, "I, Iscariot," *Crank! 5*.
Terry Bisson, "10:07:24," *Absolute Magnitude*, Spring.
Sterling Blake, "A Desperate Calculus," *New Legends*.
Mark Bourne, "The Case of the Detective's Smile," *Sherlock Holmes in Orbit*.
Ben Bova, "Acts of God," *SF Age*, May.
Steven R. Boyett, "Drifting off the Coast of New Mexico," *Asimov's*, June.
Alan Brennert, "The Man Who Loved the Sea," *F&SF*, September.
John Brunner, "All under Heaven," *Asimov's*, Mid-December.
———, "The Emperor Who Had Never Seen a Dragon," *Ruby Slippers, Golden Tears*.
———, "The Plot of His Ancestors," *Asimov's*, March.
———, "Real Messengers," *Heaven Sent*.
Edward Bryant, "Big Dogs, Strange Days," *Peter S. Beagle's Immortal Unicorn*.
———, "Flirting with Death," *F&SF*, May.
Candyce Byrne, "The Death of Beatrix Potter," *Asimov's*, August.
Eugene Byrne, "Bagged 'n' Tagged," *Interzone*, November.
Pat Cadigan, "She's Not There," *Killing Me Softly*.
———, "Tea from an Empty Cup," *Omni's Future Visions*, October.

Jack Cady, "Point Vestal," *Pirate Writings*, Fall/*The Off Season*.
Susan Casper, "Holmes Ex Machina," *Sherlock Holmes in Orbit*.
Hal Colebatch, "The Colonel's Tiger," *The Man-Kzin Wars VII*.
Nancy A. Collins, "Billy Fearless," *Ruby Slippers, Golden Tears*.
Michael Coney, "Tea and Hamsters," *F&SF*, January.
Rick Cook & Peter L. Manly, "Unfinished Symphony," *Analog*, Mid-December.
Jim Cowan, "Alderley Edge," *Century 1*.
Kara Dalkey, "The Chrysanthemum Robe," *The Armless Maiden*.
Tony Daniel, "Life on the Moon," *Asimov's*, April.
————, "No Love in All of Dwingeloo," *Asimov's*, November.
Jack Dann, "Da Vinci Rising," *Asimov's*, May.
————, "Jubilee," *Omni's Future Visions*, July.
Avram Davidson, "George's Shirt," *Asimov's*, April.
————, "The Metaphysical Force," *Century 3*.
————, "Twenty-Three," *Asimov's*, July.
Stephen Dedman, "From Whom All Blessings Flow," *Asimov's*, April.
————, "The Godfather Paradox," *Eidolon 17/18*.
Charles de Lint, "Coyote Stories," *F&SF*, June.
————, "Where Desert Spirits Crowd the Night," *Worlds of Fantasy & Horror*, Spring.
Paul Di Filippo, "Distributed Mind," *Interzone*, April.
————, "Leakage," *Pirate Writings*, Spring.
————, "Linda and Phil," *Amazing Stories: The Anthology*.
————, "Take Me to the Pilot," *Asimov's*, August.
Thomas M. Disch, "The Invisible Woman," *Asimov's*, January.
Terry Dowling, "Ships for the Sundance Sea," *Eidolon 17/18*.
Aidan Doyle, "Crusaders in a Dark Land," *Aurealis 15*.
Gardner Dozois and Michael Swanwick, "The City of God," *Omni's Future Visions*, December.
L. Timmel Duchamp, "And I Must Baffle at the Hint," *Asimov's*, January.
————, "De Secretis Mulierum," *F&SF*, May.
————, "Promises to Keep," *Realms of Fantasy*, October.
J. R. Dunn, "Little Red," *Century 1*.
S. N. Dyer, "Radiomancer and Bubblegum," *Realms of Fantasy*, August.
————, "Resolve and Resistance," *Omni*, April.
————, & Lucy Kemnitzer, "Thorri the Poet's Saga," *Asimov's*, June.
Julia Ecklar, "The Human Animal," *Analog*, April.
————, "Tide of Stars," *Analog*, January.
George Alec Effinger, "One," *New Legends*.
————, "The Musgrave Version," *Sherlock Holmes in Orbit*.
Greg Egan, "Mr. Volition," *Interzone*, October.
————, "Mitochondrial Eve," *Interzone*, February.
————, "Silver Fire," *Interzone*, December.
————, "Tap," *Asimov's*, November.
Kandis Elliot, "The Androgyne Murders," *SF Age*, November.
————, "Road Kills," *Asimov's*, February.
————, "Sith Season," *Asimov's*, May.
Harlan Ellison, "Midnight in the Sunken Cathedral," *Eidolon 17/18*.

————, "Pulling Hard Time," *F&SF*, October/November.
Carol Emshwiller, "After Shock," *Century 3*.
Kelley Eskridge, "Alien Jane," *Century 1*.
Gregory Feeley, "How Far to th' End of the World?," *SF Age*, July.
————, "In Fear of Little Nell," *Enchanted Forests*.
————, "Ursa Minor," *A Starfarer's Dozen*.
Eliot Fintushel, "The Beast with Two Backs," *Asimov's*, May.
————, "Dikduk," *Asimov's*, October.
————, "Fillet of Man," *Asimov's*, September.
————, "Hamisch in Avalon," *Crank! 5*.
————, "Noses," *Asimov's*, April.
————, "Old Man," *Tomorrow*, April.
Marina Fitch, "The Balance in the Storm," *Asimov's*, October.
Karen Joy Fowler, "The Brew," *Peter S. Beagle's Immortal Unicorn*.
————, "Shimabara," *Full Spectrum 5*.
Esther M. Friesner, "A Birthday," *F&SF*, August.
————, "A Pig's Tale," *Fantastic Alice*.
Gregory Frost, "Touring Jesusworld," *Pulphouse 18*.
R. Garcia y Robertson, "Gone to Glory," *F&SF*, July.
————, "Happy Hunting Ground," *F&SF*, December.
————, "Seven Wonders," *Asimov's*, December.
Jean Mark Gawron, "Tale of the Blue Spruce Dreaming (Or, How to Be Flesh),"
    Full Spectrum 5.
Alexis A. Gilliland, "The Third Wave," *Analog*, December.
Lisa Goldstein, "Brother Bear," *Ruby Slippers, Golden Tears*.
Kathleen Ann Goonan, "The Day the Dam Broke," *Omni's Future Visions*, August.
————, "The String," *F&SF*, June.
————, "Sunflowers," *Interzone*, April.
James Gunn, "The Gingerbread Man," *Analog*, March.
George Guthridge, "Mirror of Lop Nor," *Peter S. Beagle's Immortal Unicorn*.
Karen Haber, "A Round of Cards with the General," *Wheel of Fortune*.
Gerald Hausman, "Eye of the Falcon," *Warriors of Blood and Dream*.
Paul Hellweg, "Pay as You Go," *Asimov's*, May.
Howard V. Hendrix, "The Music of What Happens," *Full Spectrum 5*.
Nina Kiriki Hoffman, "Home for Christmas," *F&SF*, January.
Pamela D. Hodgson, "The Canterbury Path," *F&SF*, August.
Robert Holdstock, "Infantasm," *The Merlin Chronicles*.
Alexander Jablokov, "Fragments of a Painted Eggshell," *Asimov's*, December.
Phillip C. Jennings, "Passage to Galena," *Asimov's*, December.
Astrid Julian, "Child of Chernobyl," *Interzone*, March.
Janet Kagan, "Fermat's Best Theorem," *Absolute Magnitude*, Summer.
Michael Kandel, "Fuzzy Logic," *Century 2*.
Eileen Kernaghan, "Night Music," *On Spec*, Spring.
Garry Kilworth, "Masterpiece," *Ruby Slippers, Golden Tears*.
T. Jackson King, "Endless Summers," *Tomorrow*, August.
Kathe Koja, "Waking the Prince," *Ruby Slippers, Golden Tears*.
————, & Barry N. Malzberg, "Three Portraits from Heisenberg," *Omni*, Fall.
Nancy Kress, "Evolution," *Asimov's*, October.
————, "Fault Lines," *Asimov's*, August.
————, "Hard Drive," *Killing Me Softly*.

————, "Unto the Daughters," *Sisters in Fantasy*.
Ellen Kushner, "The Hunt of the Unicorn," *Peter S. Beagle's Immortal Unicorn*.
————, "Now I Lay Me Down to Sleep," *The Armless Maiden*.
R. A. Lafferty, "Happening in Chosky Bottoms," *Amazing Stories: The Anthology*.
Geoffrey A. Landis, "Across the Darkness," *Asimov's*, June.
————, "Dark Lady," *Interzone*, August.
————, "Long Term Project: Report to the Great Council of Cockroaches (Or, What Really Happened to the Dinosaurs)," *Asimov's*, January.
————, "Rorvik's War," *New Legends*.
Joe R. Lansdale, "Master of Misery," *Warriors of Blood and Dream*.
Tanith Lee, "The Beast," *Ruby Slippers, Golden Tears*.
————, "Edwige," *Asimov's*, July.
————, "King's Mage," *The Merlin Chronicles*.
————, "She Sleeps in a Tower," *The Armless Maiden*.
————, "Tiger I," *Asimov's*, Mid-December.
Ursula K. Le Guin, "A Man of the People," *Asimov's*, April.
————, "Ether OR," *Asimov's*, November.
————, "Olders," *Omni*, Winter.
Jonathan Lethem, "Light and the Sufferer," *Century 1*.
————, "The Insipid Profession of Jonathan Hornebom," *Full Spectrum 5*.
Shariann Lewitt, "Mice," *Absolute Magnitude*, Fall.
Kelly Link, "Water off a Black Dog's Back," *Century 3*.
Karawynn Long, "How the Ant Made a Bargain," *Enchanted Forests*.
————, "Of Silence and Slow Time," *Full Spectrum 5*.
Richard A. Lupoff, "Black Mist," *Omni's Future Visions*, April.
Sonia Orin Lyris, "The Jesus Construct," *Pulphouse 18*.
Katherine MacLean, "The Kidnapping of Baroness 5," *Analog*, January.
Ian R. MacLeod, "Ellen O'Hara," *Asimov's*, February.
————, "Nina-with-the-Sky-in-Her-Hair," *F&SF*, December.
————, "The Noonday Pool," *F&SF*, May.
————, "Tirkiluk," *F&SF*, February.
Paul J. McAuley, "Slaves," *Omni's Future Visions*, November.
————, "The True History of Dr. Pretorius," *Interzone*, August.
Wil McCarthy, "Rocket Ghosts," *Asimov's*, August.
John G. McDaid, "Jigoku no Mokushiroku (The Symbolic Revelation of the Apocalypse)," *Asimov's*, Mid-December.
Jack McDevitt, "Ellie," *Asimov's*, May.
Ian McDonald, "Frooks," *Interzone*, October.
————, "Steam," *Heaven Sent*.
Maureen F. McHugh, "In the Air," *Killing Me Softly*.
————, "Joss," *Asimov's*, February.
————, "Learning to Breathe," *Tales of the Unanticipated 15*.
Vonda N. McIntyre, "The Adventure of the Field Theorems," *Sherlock Holmes in Orbit*.
Bridget McKenna & Marti McKenna, "Kidnapped by Aliens!," *Tomorrow*, June.
Patricia A. McKillip, "Wonders of the Invisible World," *Full Spectrum 5*.
Diane Mapes, "Green," *Asimov's*, September.
Daniel Marcus, "Ex Vitro," *Asimov's*, Mid-December.
Jim Marino, "The Man Who Fell," *Crank! 5*.
Marlo Martin & Gregory Benford, "A Darker Geometry," *The Man-Kzin Wars VII*.
Steve Martinez, "One Hand Clapping," *Asimov's*, May.

Lisa Mason, "Every Mystery Unexplained," *David Copperfield's Tales of the Impossible*.
Holly Wade Matter, "Mr. Pacifaker's House," *Asimov's*, July.
————, "Martine's Room," *Century 1*.
Mario Milosevic, "Frames," *Asimov's*, July.
Judith Moffett, "The Realms of Glory," *Heaven Sent*.
Elizabeth Moon, "Aura," *F&SF*, August.
————, "Hand to Hand," *Women at War*.
————, "Knight of Other Days," *Tales of the Knights Templar*.
Pat Murphy, "A Place of Honor," *Asimov's*, May.
Pati Nagle, "Glad Yule," *An Armory of Swords*.
Robert Nansel, "The Next Best Thing," *Pulphouse 19*.
R. Neube, "Faux," *Tales of the Unanticipated 15*.
G. David Nordley, "Alice's Asteroid," *Asimov's*, October.
————, "Comet Gypsies," *Asimov's*, March.
————, "Dawn Venus," *Asimov's*, August.
————, "Final Review," *Analog*, July.
Jerry Oltion, "Fait Accompli," *Analog*, July.
Rebecca Ore, "Hypocaust & Bathysphere," *Asimov's*, January.
Susan Palwick, "Jo's Hair," *Xanadu 3*.
Richard Parks, "The Last Waltz," *Realms of Fantasy*, February.
Michael H. Payne, "My Vampire Cat, or Whatever," *Tomorrow*, June.
————, "Painting the Roses Red," *Tomorrow*, August.
Gerald Pearce, "Below Baghdad," *Century 3*.
Steven Popkes, "Conqueror Moment," *Tomorrow*, August.
Tom Purdom, "Research Project," *Asimov's*, February.
————, "Romance in Lunar G," *Asimov's*, November.
David Redd, "Trout Fishing In Leytonstone," *Asimov's*, March.
Robert Reed, "Aeon's Child," *Asimov's*, November.
————, "Brother Perfect," *Asimov's*, September.
————, "Dreams from a Severed Heart," *Asimov's*, March.
————, "Mrs. Greasy," *Tomorrow*, December.
————, "The Myrtle Man," *F&SF*, December.
————, "Tongues," *Asimov's*, December.
————, "The Tournament," *F&SF*, September.
————, "We Are All Superheroes," *SF Age*, March.
Mike Resnick, "When the Old Gods Die," *Asimov's*, April.
————, & Nicholas A. DiChario, "The Joy of Hats," *Killing Me Softly*.
————, & Susan Shwartz, "Bibi," *Asimov's*, Mid-December.
Carrie Richerson, "Geckos," *Realms of Fantasy*, August.
Uncle River, "The Other Side of the Mountain," *Pirate Writings*, Spring.
Madeleine E. Robins, "Adelard's Kiss," *F&SF*, August.
Frank M. Robinson, "The Phantom of the Barbary Coast," *Sherlock Holmes in Orbit*.
Michaela Roessner, "Ah, Sweet Mystery of Life," *Omni's Future Visions*, February.
Mary Rosenblum, "The Centaur Garden," *Asimov's*, July.
————, "The Doryman," *Asimov's*, December.
————, "Elegy," *New Legends*.
————, "Flight," *Asimov's*, February.
————, "The Gardener," *Killing Me Softly*.
Kristine Kathryn Rusch, "The Beautiful, the Damned," *F&SF*, February.
————, "The Boy Who Needed Heroes," *The Armless Maiden*.

————, "Courting Rites," *Sisters in Fantasy*.
Geoff Ryman, "Warmth," *Interzone*, October.
Jessica Amanda Salmonson, "The Door to the Rainmaker's Lodge," *Pirate Writings*, Spring.
————, "Namer of Beasts, Maker of Souls," *The Merlin Chronicles*.
Jim Sarafin, "The Word for Breaking August Sky," *Alfred Hitchcock's Mystery Magazine*, July.
Pamela Sargent, "Amphibians," *Asimov's*, June.
Robert J. Sawyer, "You See but You Do Not Observe," *Sherlock Holmes in Orbit*.
Elizabeth Ann Scarborough, "First Communion," *Women at War*.
————, "The Stone of War and the Nightingale's Egg," *Chicks in Chainmail*.
Carter Scholz, "Radiance," *New Legends*.
Nisi Shawl, "The Rainses'," *Asimov's*, April.
Robert Sheckley, "The Day the Aliens Came," *New Legends*.
Charles Sheffield, "At the Eschaton," *Far Futures*.
————, "The Phantom of Dunwell Cove," *Asimov's*, August.
Lucius Shepard, "Human History," *The Twenty-first Annual World Fantasy Convention* Program Book.
Delia Sherman, "The Printer's Daughter," *Ruby Slippers, Golden Tears*.
Josepha Sherman, "Old Woman Who Created Life," *Xanadu 3*.
Lewis Shiner, "Sitcom," *Asimov's*, January.
W. M. Shockley, "The First Stone," *Pulphouse 18*.
Susan Shwartz, "Beyond the Wide World's End," *Ancient Enchantresses*.
————, "The Monsters of Mill Creek Park," *Enchanted Forests*.
Munro Sickafoose, "Knives," *The Armless Maiden*.
Robert Silverberg, "Hot Times in Magma City," *Omni's Future Visions*, June.
————, "The Red Blaze Is the Morning," *New Legends*.
————, "The Second Shield," *Playboy*, December.
Joan Slonczewski, "Microbe," *Analog*, August.
Dave Smeds, "The Eighth of December," *David Copperfield's Tales of the Impossible*.
————, "Survivor," *Peter S. Beagle's Immortal Unicorn*.
Dean Wesley Smith, "Two Roads, No Choices," *Sherlock Holmes in Orbit*.
S. P. Somtow, "Diamonds Aren't Forever," *David Copperfield's Tales of the Impossible*.
Martha Soukup, "Jones and the Stray," *A Starfarer's Dozen*.
William Browning Spencer, "The Death of the Novel," *Century 1*.
————, "The Oddskeeper's Daughter," *Wheel of Fortune*.
Brian Stableford, "The Age of Innocence," *Asimov's*, June.
————, "The Hunger and Ecstasy of Vampires," *Interzone*, January.
————, "Inherit the Earth," *Analog*, July.
————, "Out of Touch," *Asimov's*, October.
————, "The Road to Hell," *Interzone*, July.
————, "The Skin Trade," *Asimov's*, November.
Michael A. Stackpole, "Peer Review," *Superheroes*.
————, "Tip-Off," *Wheel of Fortune*.
Allen Steele, "The Good Rat," *Analog*, Mid-December.
————, "Jonathan Livingston Seaslug," *SF Age*, Jan.
————, "The War Memorial," *Asimov's*, September.
————, "The Weight," *The Weight*.
————, "Working for Mr. Chicago," *Absolute Magnitude*, Fall.
Ellen Steiber, "The Fox Wife," *Ruby Slippers, Golden Tears*.

Neal Stephenson, "Excerpt from the Third and Last Volume of *Tribes of the Pacific Coast*," *Full Spectrum 5*.
Sue Storm, "The Price of Water," *Xizquil 13*.
Charles Stross, "Ship of Fools," *Interzone*, August.
Michael Swanwick, "North of Diddy-Wah-Diddy," *Killing Me Softly*.
————, "Walking Out," *Asimov's*, February.
Beverly Suarez-Beard, "The Hands Remember," *Century 2*.
————, "The Ruby," *Realms of Fantasy*, August.
Judith Tarr, "Dame à la Licorne," *Peter S. Beagle's Immortal Unicorn*.
————, "Sitting Shiva," *Women at War*.
Mark W. Tiedemann, "After," *SF Age*, July.
Lois Tilton, "The Clearing," *Enchanted Forests*.
Harry Turtledove, "Must and Shall," *Asimov's*, November.
————, "The Maltese Elephant," *Analog*, August.
Jeff VanderMeer, "The Bone-Carver's Tale," *Asimov's*, April.
John Varley, "Truth, Justice and the Politically Correct Socialist Path," *Superheroes*.
Susan Wade, "Ruby Slippers," *Ruby Slippers, Golden Tears*.
Howard Waldrop, "El Castillo de la Perseverancia," *The Twenty-first Annual World Fantasy Convention* Program Book.
————, "Occam's Ducks," *Omni*, February.
Sage Walker, "Stealth and the Lady," *An Armory of Swords*.
Ian Watson, "The Amber Room," *F&SF*, August.
Lawrence Watt-Evans, "An American Hero," *Pulphouse 19*.
————, "Hearts and Flowers," *Full Spectrum 5*.
————, "One of the Boys," *Superheroes*.
————, "Paradise Lost," *Asimov's*, September.
Don Webb, "A Bigger Game," *Wheel of Fortune*.
K. D. Wentworth, "As You Sow," *F&SF*, March.
Leslie What, "How to Feed Your Inner Troll," *Asimov's*, December.
Deborah Wheeler, "Transfusion," *Realms of Fantasy*, August.
Rick Wilber, "Elements of Self-Destruction," *SF Age*, March.
————, "Mounting the Monkeys," *Pulphouse 19*.
Kate Wilhelm, "All for One," *A Flush of Shadows*.
————, "Torch Song," *A Flush of Shadows*.
Jack Williamson, "Dark Star," *F&SF*, February.
Terri Windling, "The Green Children," *The Armless Maiden*.
Amy Wolf, "The Hour of Their Need," *Realms of Fantasy*, April.
Gene Wolfe, "The Death of Koshchei the Deathless," *Ruby Slippers, Golden Tears*.
————, "The Ziggurat," *Full Spectrum 5*.
Dave Wolverton, "In the Teeth of Glory," *David Copperfield's Tales of the Impossible*.
John C. Wright, "Farthest Man from Earth," *Asimov's*, April.
William F. Wu, "On the Sun and Moon Mountain," *Ancient Enchantresses*.
Jane Yolen, "Allerleirauh," *The Armless Maiden*.
————, "The Traveler and the Tale," *Ruby Slippers, Golden Tears*.
George Zebrowski, "Swift Thoughts," *Amazing Stories: The Anthology*.
Roger Zelazny, "Epithalamium," *Fantastic Alice*.
————, "The Long Crawl of Hugh Glass," *Superheroes*.
————, "The Three Descents of Jeremy Baker," *F&SF*, July.